BIG NATE
DOUBLE OR NOTHING

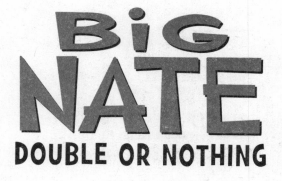

More

BiG NATE

adventures from

Lincoln Peirce

Novels:

BIG NATE: IN A CLASS BY HIMSELF

BIG NATE STRIKES AGAIN

BIG NATE: ON A ROLL

BIG NATE GOES FOR BROKE

BIG NATE FLIPS OUT

BIG NATE: IN THE ZONE

BIG NATE LIVES IT UP

BIG NATE BLASTS OFF

Activity Books:

BIG NATE BOREDOM BUSTER

BIG NATE FUN BLASTER

BIG NATE DOODLEPALOOZA

BIG NATE LAUGH-O-RAMA

BIG NATE SUPER SCRIBBLER

BIG NATE PUZZLEMANIA

Comic Compilations:

BIG NATE: GENIUS MODE

BIG NATE: MR. POPULARITY

Novel Bind-ups:

BIG NATE: DOUBLE TROUBLE

BIG NATE: BACK TO BACK HITS

BIG NATE: TWICE THE 'TUDE

Lincoln Peirce

BiG NATE
DOUBLE OR NOTHING

HARPER
An Imprint of HarperCollinsPublishers

BIG NATE is a registered trademark of Scripps Licensing Inc.

These comic strips first appeared in newspapers from
November 5, 2007, through June 8, 2008, and from
June 9, 2008, through January 10, 2009.

Big Nate: Double or Nothing

Big Nate: What Could Possibly Go Wrong?
Copyright © 2012 by Scripps Licensing Inc.

Big Nate: Here Goes Nothing
Copyright © 2012 by Scripps Licensing Inc.

www.harpercollinschildrens.com
www.bignatebooks.com

Go to www.bignate.com to read the *Big Nate* comic strip.

ISBN 978-0-06-311411-1

Typography by Andrea Vandergrift
21 22 23 24 25   PC/LSCH   10 9 8 7 6 5 4 3 2 1
❖
First Edition

BIG NATE
DOUBLE OR NOTHING

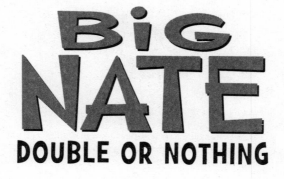

Lincoln Peirce

BiG NATE

WHAT COULD POSSIBLY GO WRONG?

MRS. GODFREY TO THE RESCUE

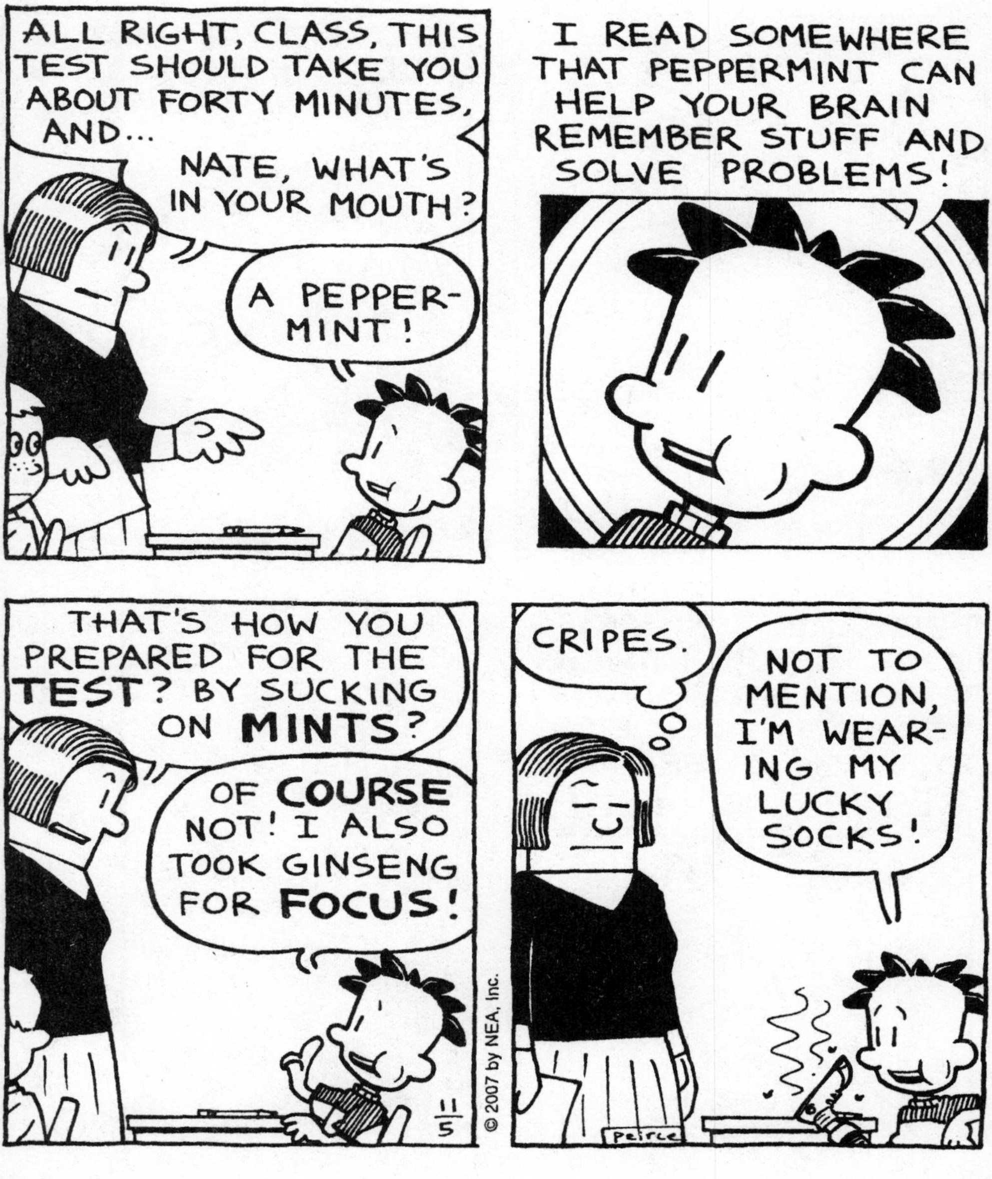
ALL RIGHT, CLASS, THIS TEST SHOULD TAKE YOU ABOUT FORTY MINUTES, AND...
NATE, WHAT'S IN YOUR MOUTH?
A PEPPER-MINT!
I READ SOMEWHERE THAT PEPPERMINT CAN HELP YOUR BRAIN REMEMBER STUFF AND SOLVE PROBLEMS!
THAT'S HOW YOU PREPARED FOR THE TEST? BY SUCKING ON MINTS?
OF COURSE NOT! I ALSO TOOK GINSENG FOR FOCUS!
11/5
© 2007 by NEA, Inc.
CRIPES.
NOT TO MENTION, I'M WEAR-ING MY LUCKY SOCKS!
Peirce

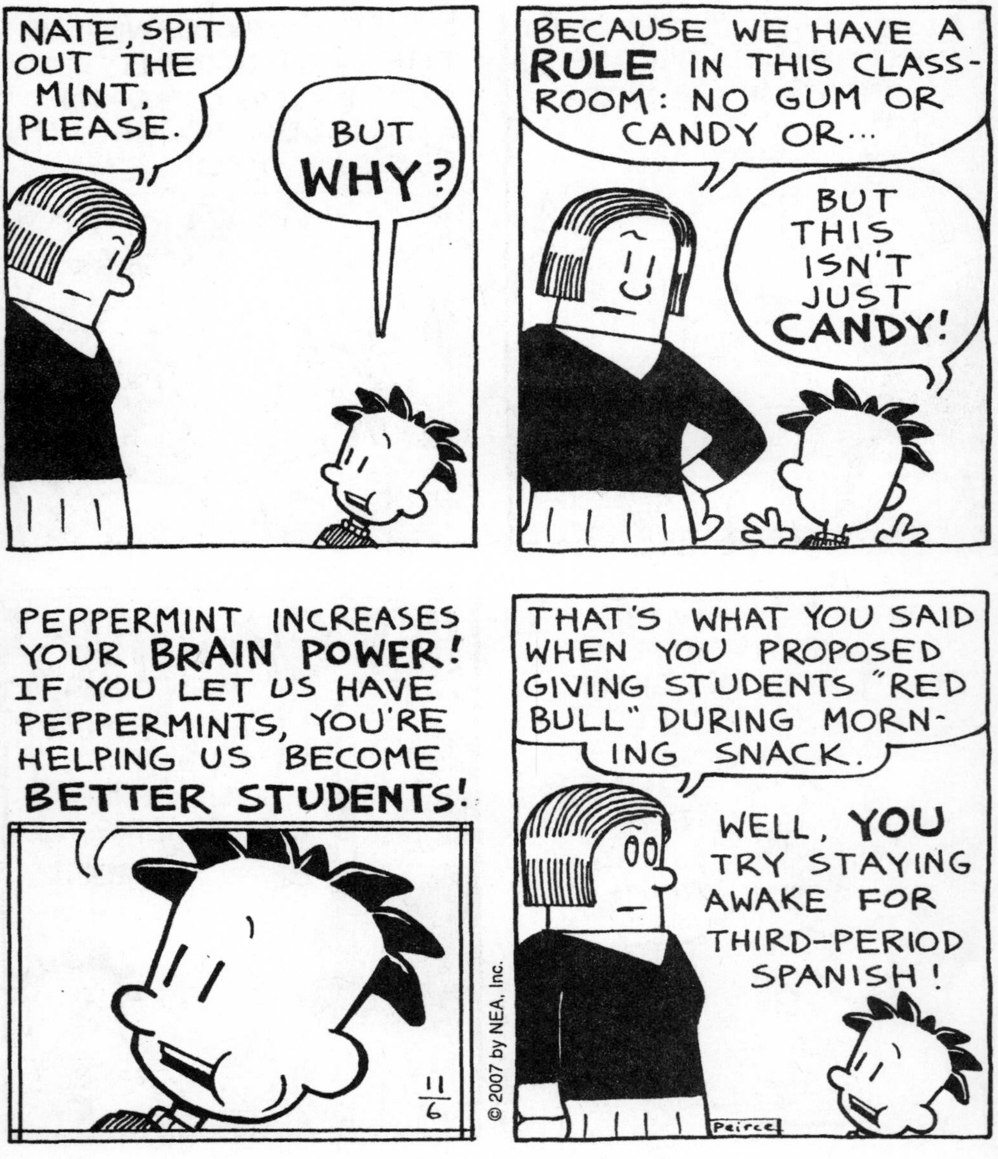
NATE, SPIT OUT THE MINT, PLEASE.
BUT WHY?
BECAUSE WE HAVE A RULE IN THIS CLASSROOM: NO GUM OR CANDY OR...
BUT THIS ISN'T JUST CANDY!
PEPPERMINT INCREASES YOUR BRAIN POWER! IF YOU LET US HAVE PEPPERMINTS, YOU'RE HELPING US BECOME BETTER STUDENTS!
11/6
THAT'S WHAT YOU SAID WHEN YOU PROPOSED GIVING STUDENTS "RED BULL" DURING MORNING SNACK.
WELL, YOU TRY STAYING AWAKE FOR THIRD-PERIOD SPANISH!
Peirce

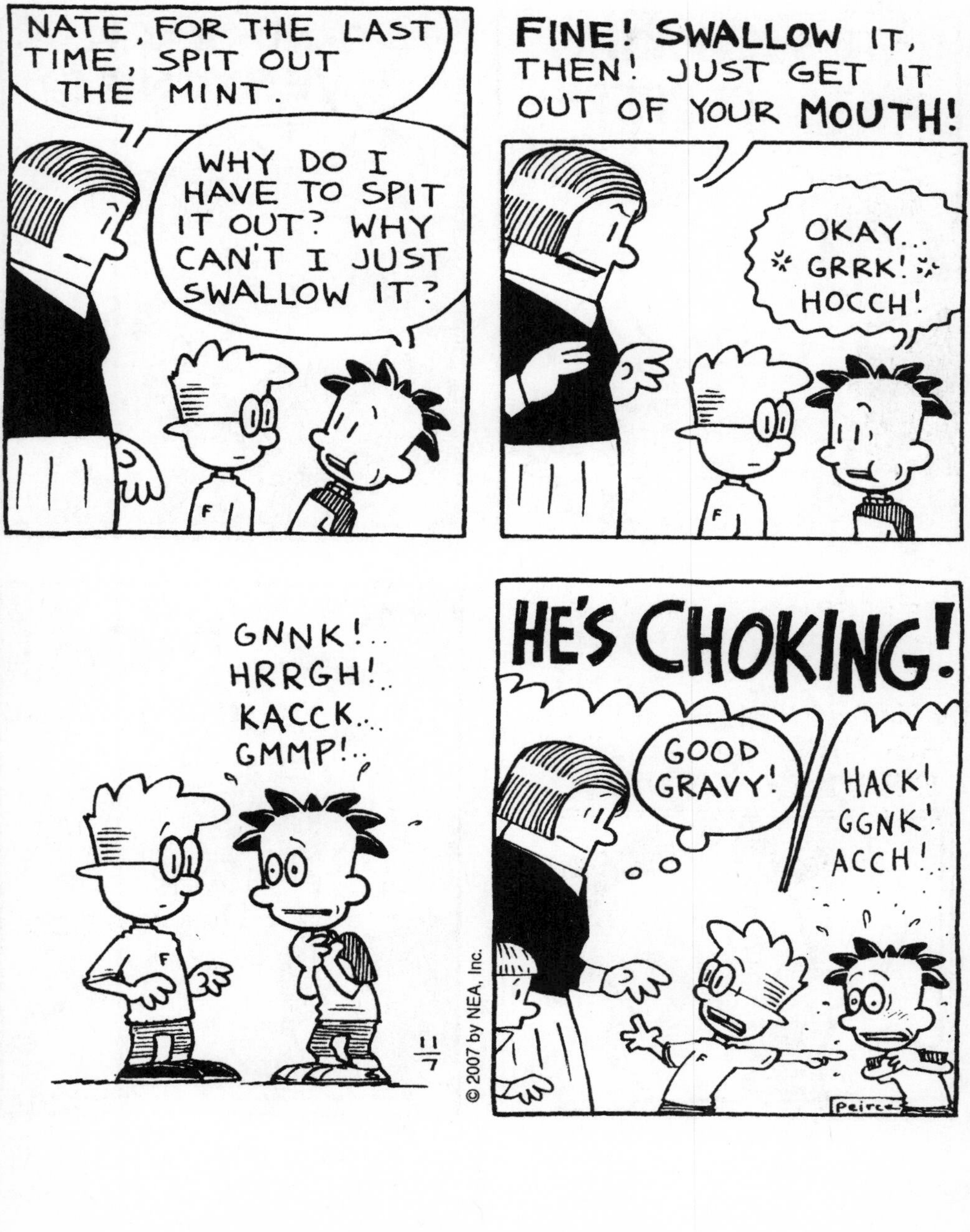
NATE, FOR THE LAST TIME, SPIT OUT THE MINT.
WHY DO I HAVE TO SPIT IT OUT? WHY CAN'T I JUST SWALLOW IT?
FINE! SWALLOW IT, THEN! JUST GET IT OUT OF YOUR MOUTH!
OKAY... GRRK! HOCCH!
GNNK!.. HRRGH!.. KACCK... GMMP!..
11/7
© 2007 by NEA, Inc.
HE'S CHOKING!
GOOD GRAVY!
HACK! GGNK! ACCH!..
Peirce

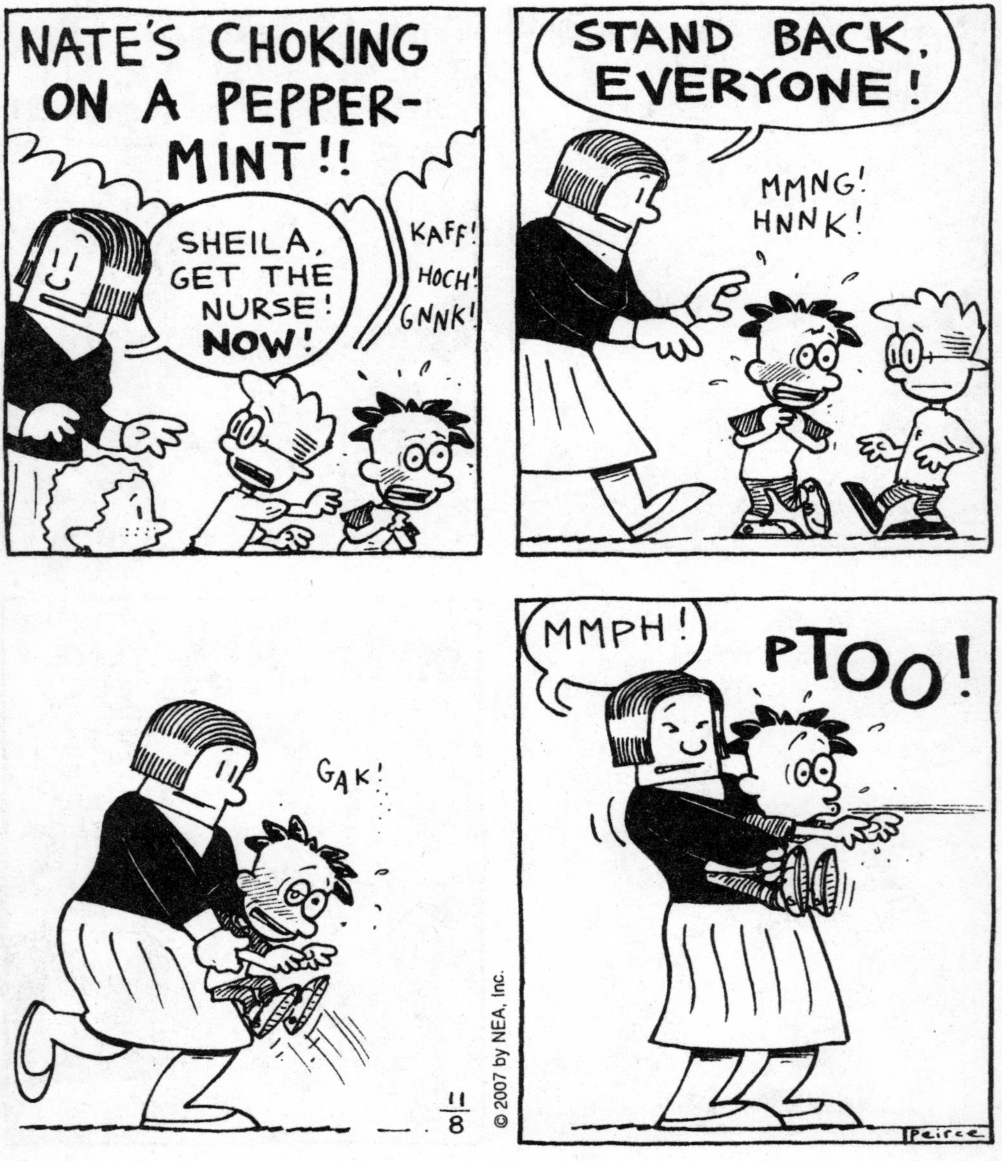
NATE'S CHOKING ON A PEPPER-MINT!!
SHEILA, GET THE NURSE! NOW!
KAFF! HOCH! GNNK!
STAND BACK, EVERYONE!
MMNG! HNNK!
GAK!
MMPH!
PTOO!
11/8
© 2007 by NEA, Inc.
Peirce

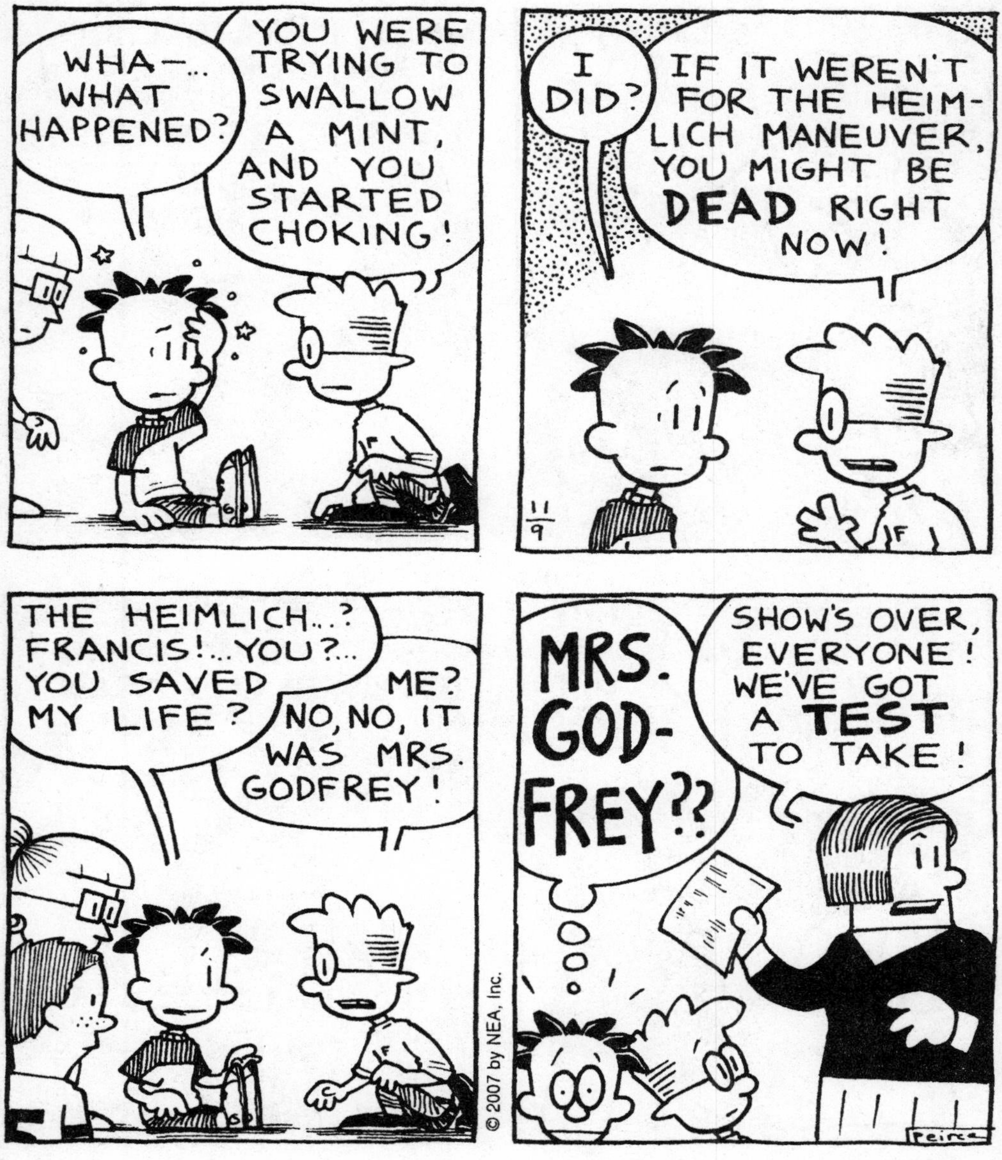
WHA-... WHAT HAPPENED?
YOU WERE TRYING TO SWALLOW A MINT, AND YOU STARTED CHOKING!
I DID?
IF IT WEREN'T FOR THE HEIMLICH MANEUVER, YOU MIGHT BE DEAD RIGHT NOW!
11/9
THE HEIMLICH...? FRANCIS!...YOU?... YOU SAVED ME? MY LIFE?
NO, NO, IT WAS MRS. GODFREY!
MRS. GOD-FREY??
SHOW'S OVER, EVERYONE! WE'VE GOT A TEST TO TAKE!
peirce

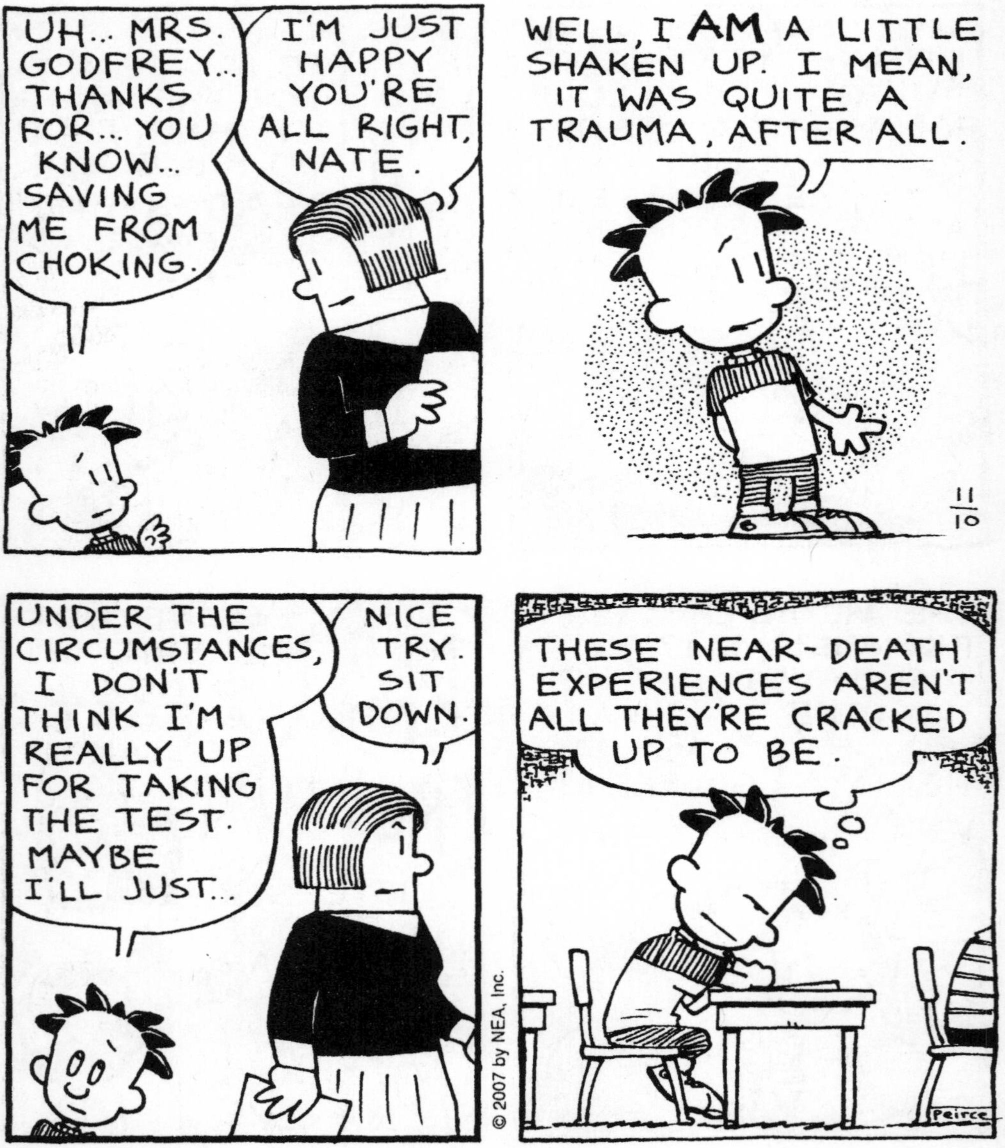
UH... MRS. GODFREY... THANKS FOR... YOU KNOW... SAVING ME FROM CHOKING.
I'M JUST HAPPY YOU'RE ALL RIGHT, NATE.
WELL, I AM A LITTLE SHAKEN UP. I MEAN, IT WAS QUITE A TRAUMA, AFTER ALL.
11/10
UNDER THE CIRCUMSTANCES, I DON'T THINK I'M REALLY UP FOR TAKING THE TEST. MAYBE I'LL JUST...
NICE TRY. SIT DOWN.
© 2007 by NEA, Inc.
THESE NEAR-DEATH EXPERIENCES AREN'T ALL THEY'RE CRACKED UP TO BE.
Peirce

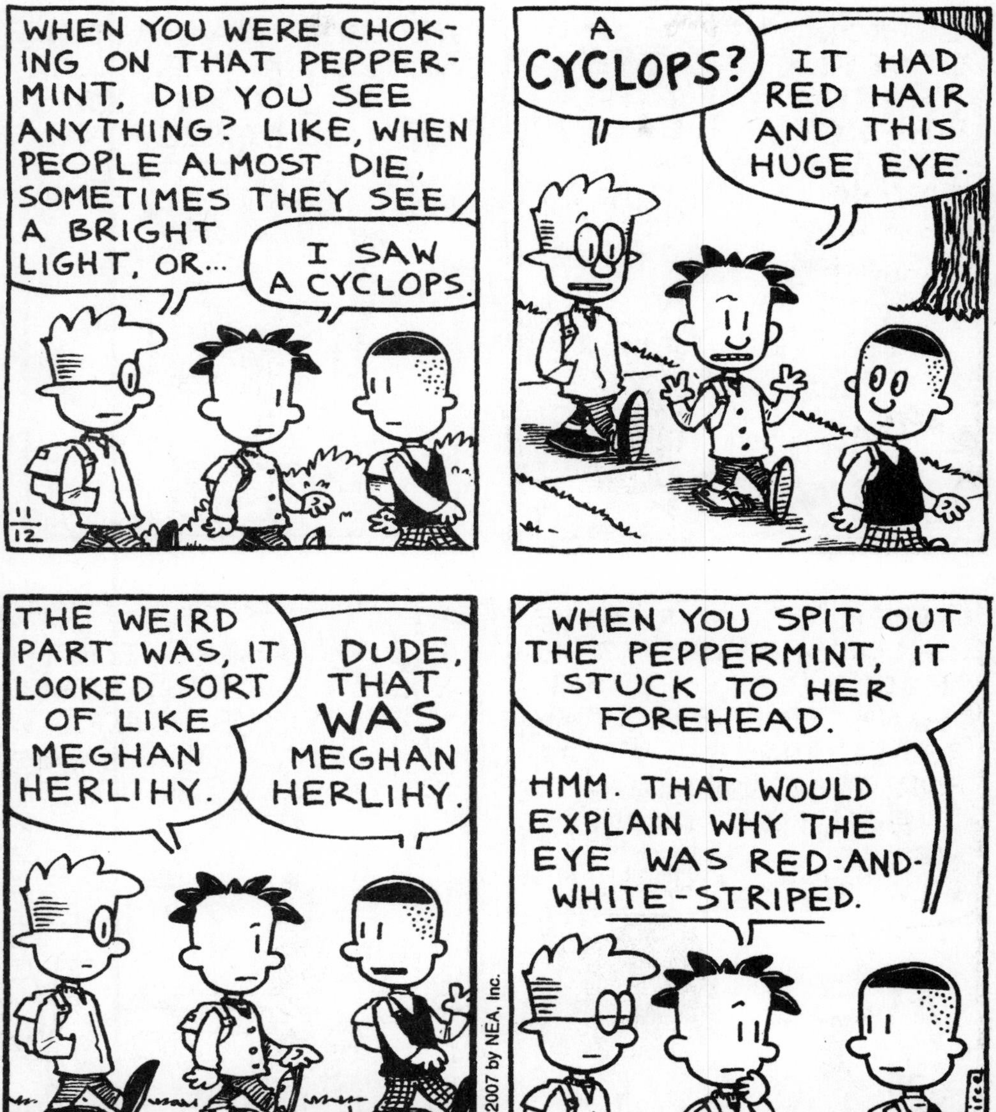
WHEN YOU WERE CHOKING ON THAT PEPPERMINT, DID YOU SEE ANYTHING? LIKE, WHEN PEOPLE ALMOST DIE, SOMETIMES THEY SEE A BRIGHT LIGHT, OR...
I SAW A CYCLOPS.
11/12
A CYCLOPS?
IT HAD RED HAIR AND THIS HUGE EYE.
THE WEIRD PART WAS, IT LOOKED SORT OF LIKE MEGHAN HERLIHY.
DUDE, THAT WAS MEGHAN HERLIHY.
© 2007 by NEA, Inc.
WHEN YOU SPIT OUT THE PEPPERMINT, IT STUCK TO HER FOREHEAD.
HMM. THAT WOULD EXPLAIN WHY THE EYE WAS RED-AND-WHITE-STRIPED.
Peirce

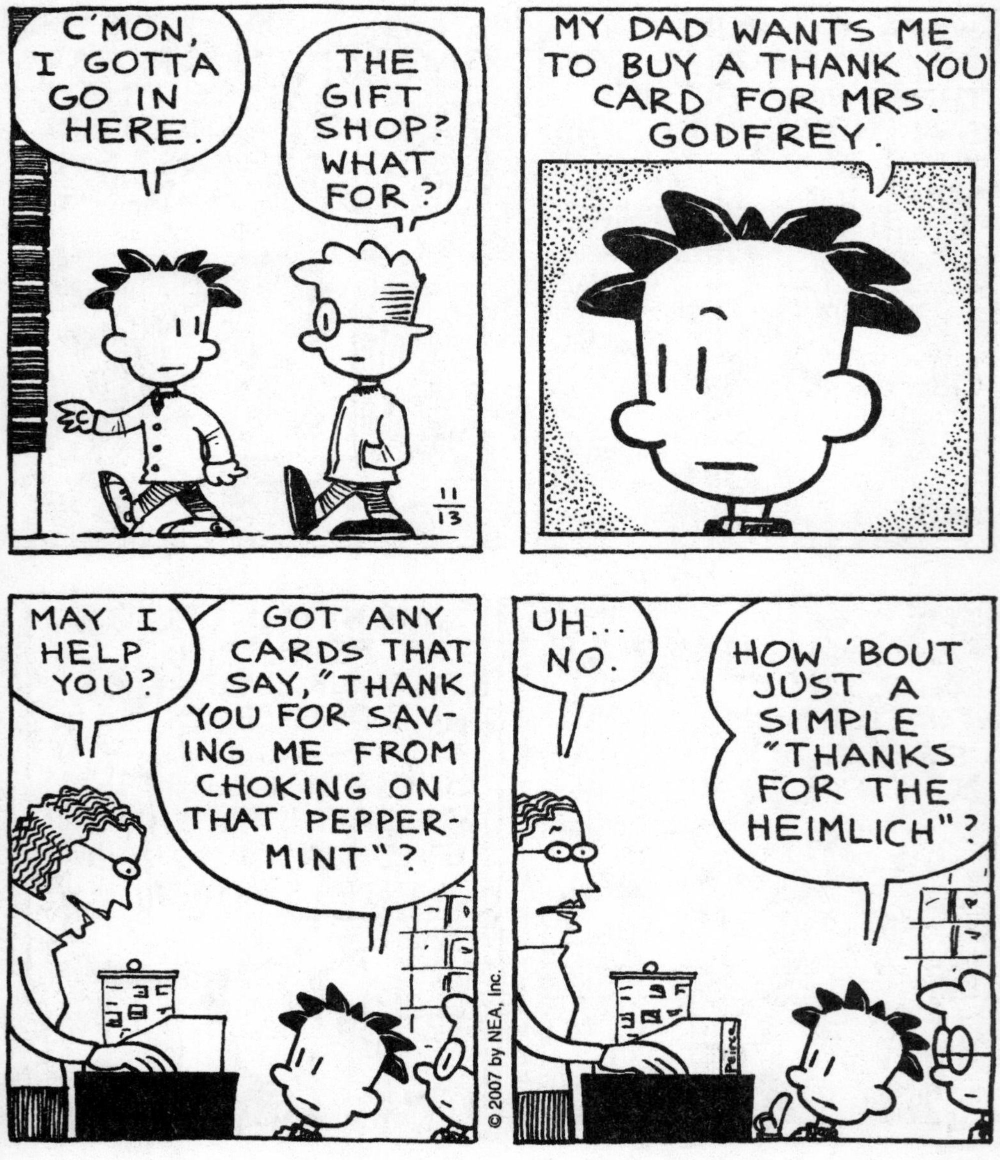
C'MON, I GOTTA GO IN HERE.
THE GIFT SHOP? WHAT FOR?
11/13
MY DAD WANTS ME TO BUY A THANK YOU CARD FOR MRS. GODFREY.
MAY I HELP YOU?
GOT ANY CARDS THAT SAY, "THANK YOU FOR SAVING ME FROM CHOKING ON THAT PEPPERMINT"?
© 2007 by NEA, Inc.
UH... NO.
HOW 'BOUT JUST A SIMPLE "THANKS FOR THE HEIMLICH"?

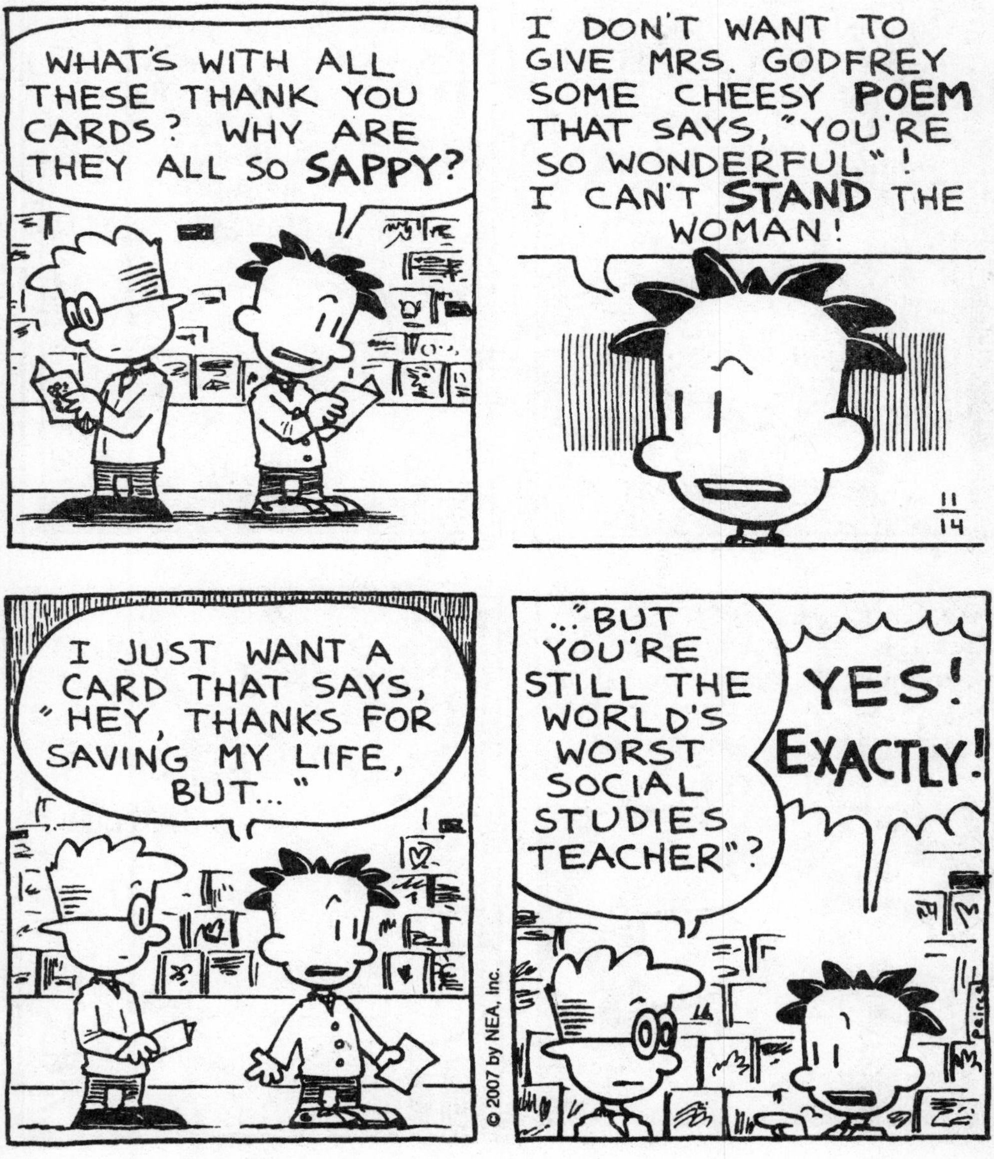
WHAT'S WITH ALL THESE THANK YOU CARDS? WHY ARE THEY ALL SO SAPPY?
I DON'T WANT TO GIVE MRS. GODFREY SOME CHEESY POEM THAT SAYS, "YOU'RE SO WONDERFUL"! I CAN'T STAND THE WOMAN!
11/14
I JUST WANT A CARD THAT SAYS, "HEY, THANKS FOR SAVING MY LIFE, BUT..."
©2007 by NEA, Inc.
..."BUT YOU'RE STILL THE WORLD'S WORST SOCIAL STUDIES TEACHER"?
YES! EXACTLY!
Peirce

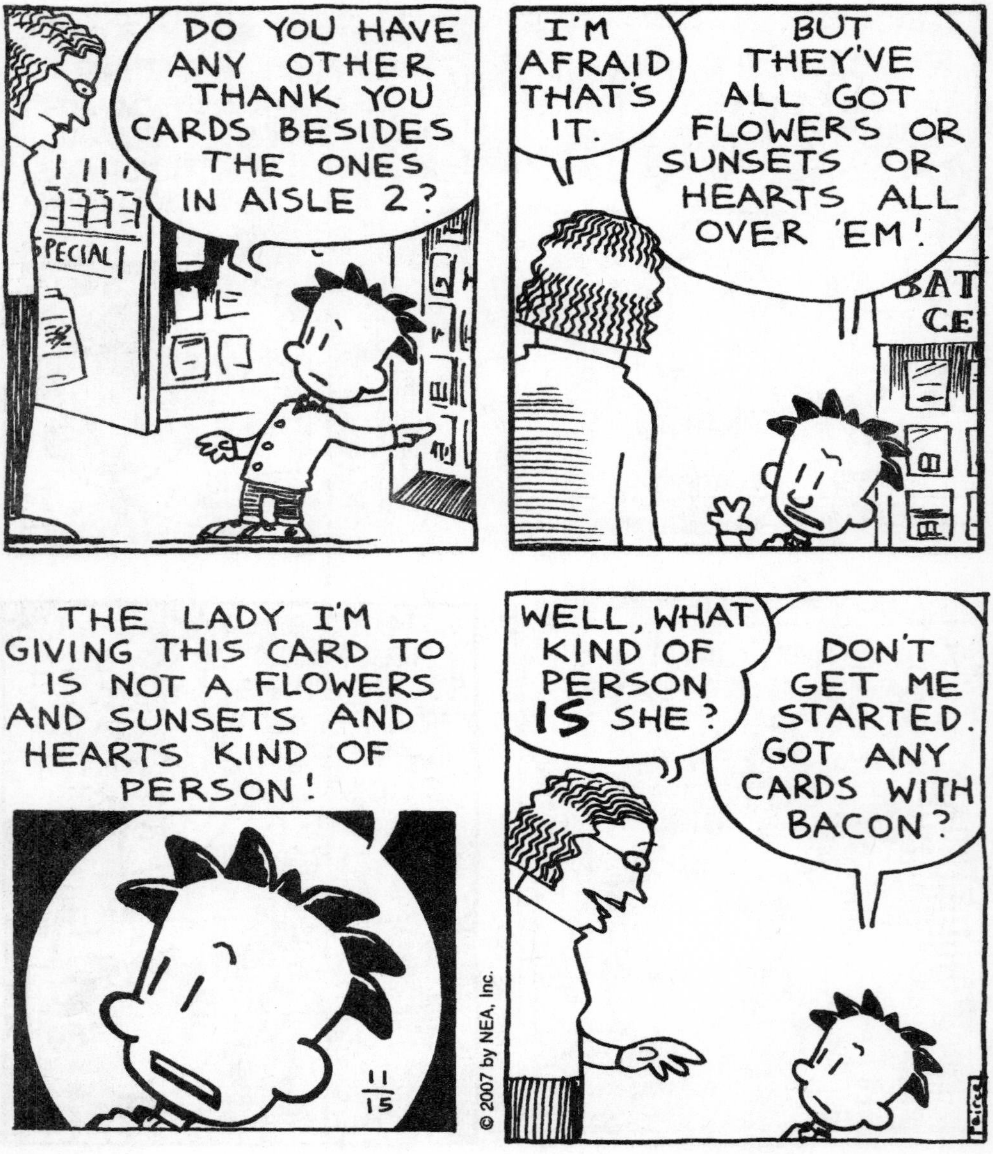
DO YOU HAVE ANY OTHER THANK YOU CARDS BESIDES THE ONES IN AISLE 2?
SPECIAL
I'M AFRAID THAT'S IT.
BUT THEY'VE ALL GOT FLOWERS OR SUNSETS OR HEARTS ALL OVER 'EM!
THE LADY I'M GIVING THIS CARD TO IS NOT A FLOWERS AND SUNSETS AND HEARTS KIND OF PERSON!
11/15
WELL, WHAT KIND OF PERSON **IS** SHE?
DON'T GET ME STARTED. GOT ANY CARDS WITH BACON?

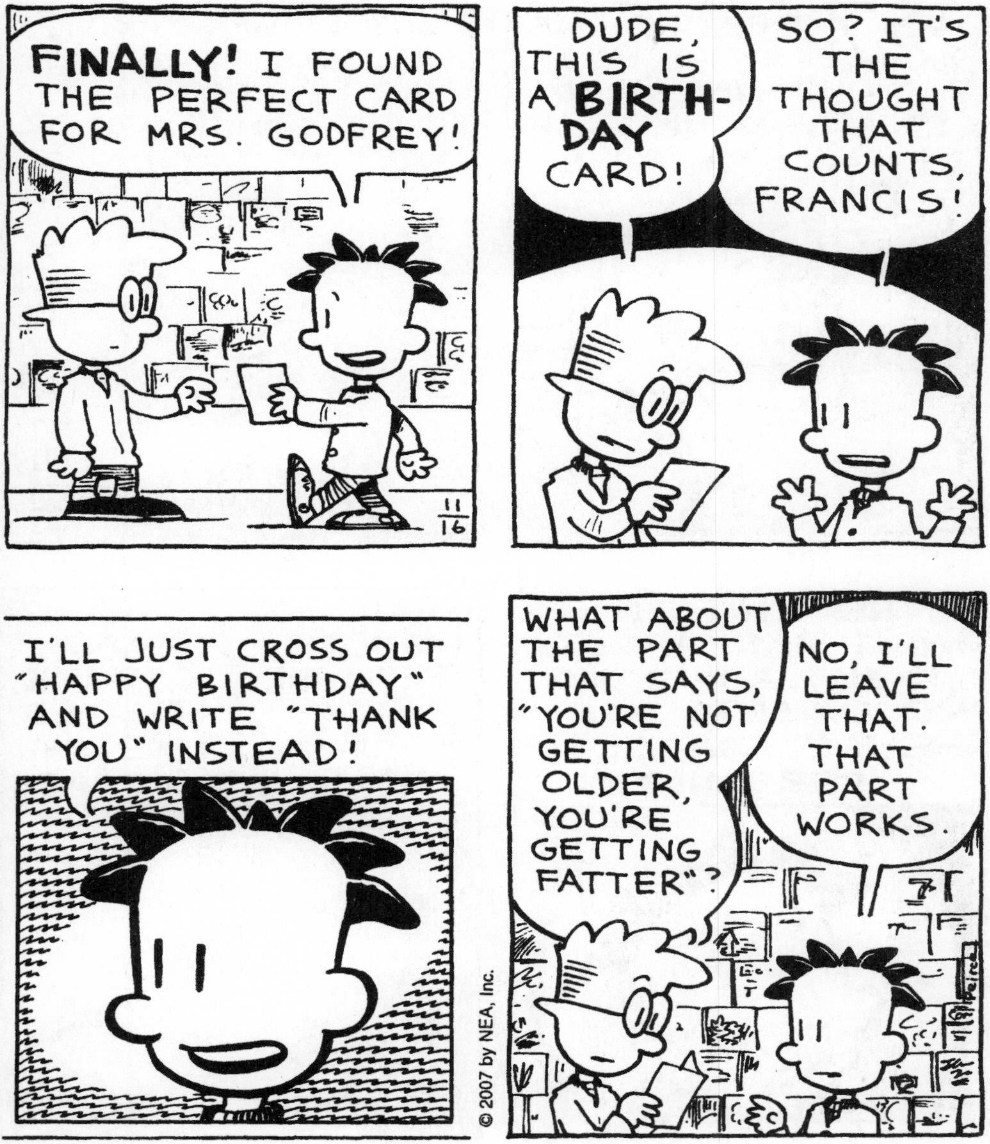
FINALLY! I FOUND THE PERFECT CARD FOR MRS. GODFREY!
11/16
DUDE, THIS IS A BIRTHDAY CARD!
SO? IT'S THE THOUGHT THAT COUNTS, FRANCIS!
I'LL JUST CROSS OUT "HAPPY BIRTHDAY" AND WRITE "THANK YOU" INSTEAD!
WHAT ABOUT THE PART THAT SAYS, "YOU'RE NOT GETTING OLDER, YOU'RE GETTING FATTER"?
NO, I'LL LEAVE THAT. THAT PART WORKS.
Peirce

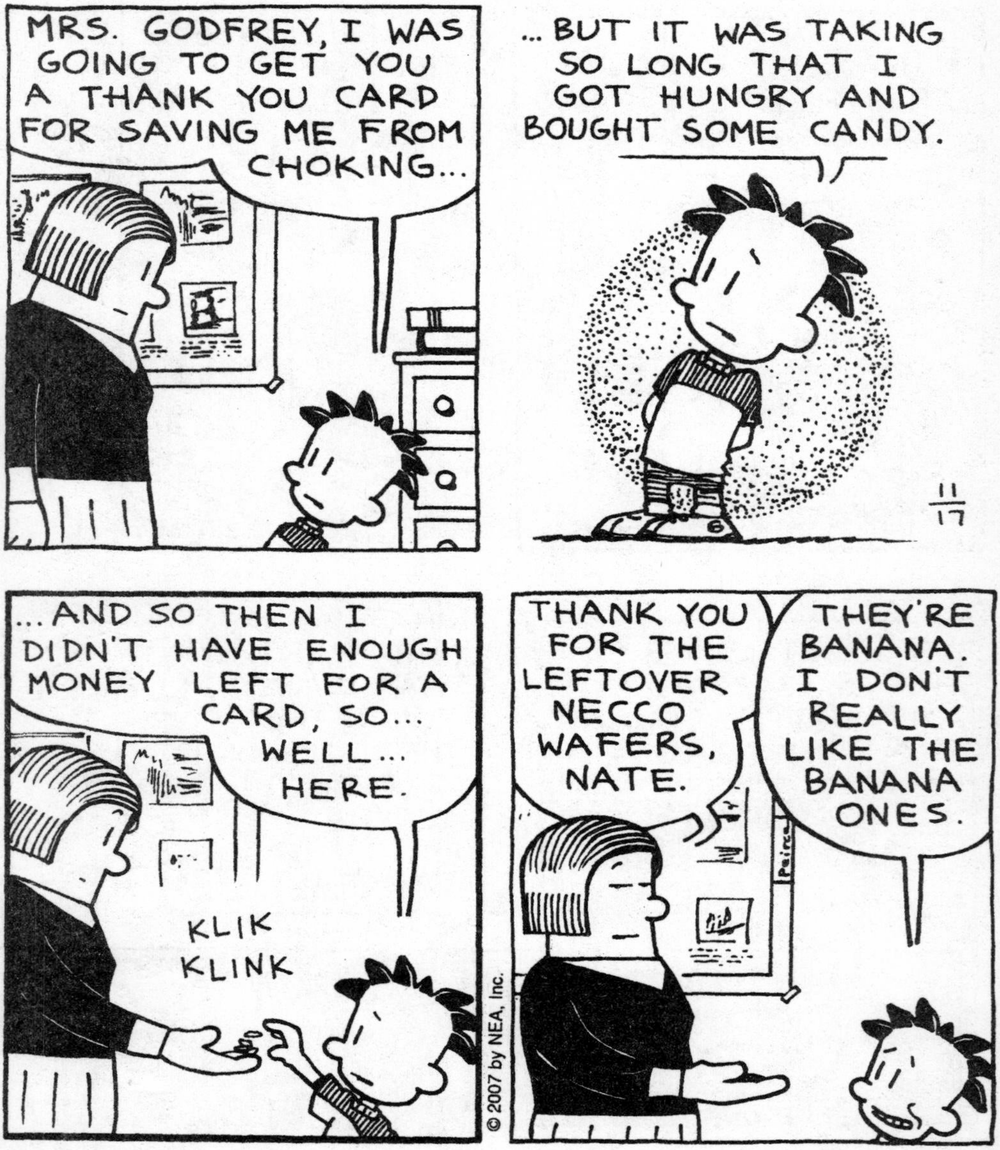
MRS. GODFREY, I WAS GOING TO GET YOU A THANK YOU CARD FOR SAVING ME FROM CHOKING...
... BUT IT WAS TAKING SO LONG THAT I GOT HUNGRY AND BOUGHT SOME CANDY.
11/17
... AND SO THEN I DIDN'T HAVE ENOUGH MONEY LEFT FOR A CARD, SO... WELL... HERE.
KLIK KLINK
© 2007 by NEA, Inc.
THANK YOU FOR THE LEFTOVER NECCO WAFERS, NATE.
THEY'RE BANANA. I DON'T REALLY LIKE THE BANANA ONES.

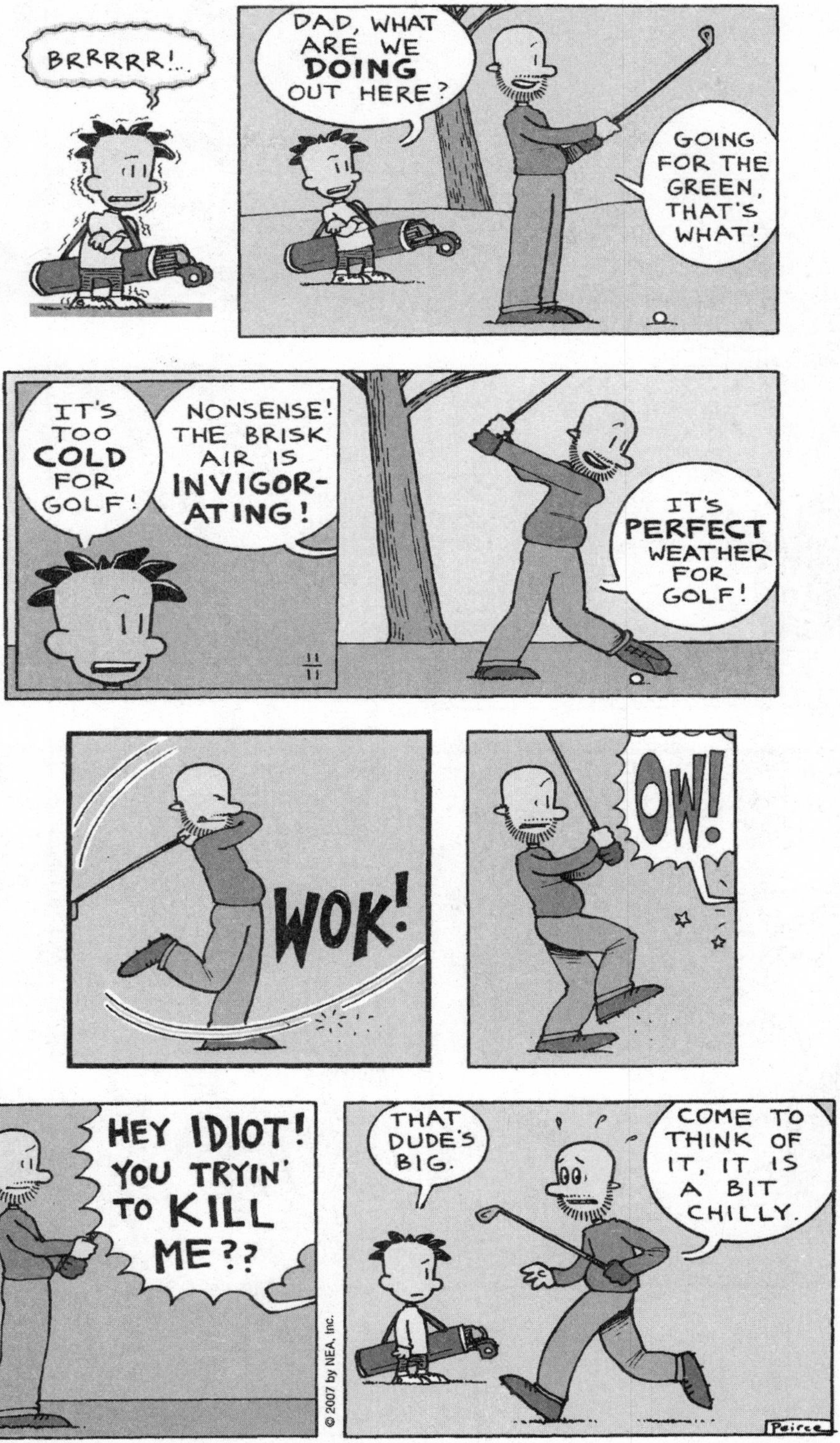
BRRRRR!...
DAD, WHAT ARE WE DOING OUT HERE?
GOING FOR THE GREEN, THAT'S WHAT!
IT'S TOO COLD FOR GOLF!
NONSENSE! THE BRISK AIR IS INVIGOR-ATING!
IT'S PERFECT WEATHER FOR GOLF!
WOK!
OW!
HEY IDIOT! YOU TRYIN' TO KILL ME??
© 2007 by NEA, Inc.
THAT DUDE'S BIG.
COME TO THINK OF IT, IT IS A BIT CHILLY.
Peirce

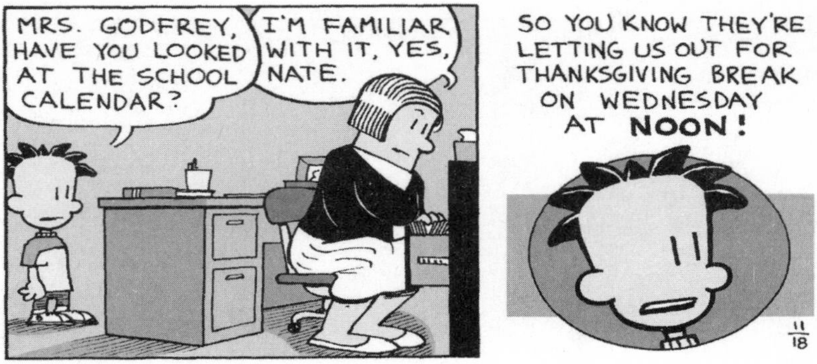
MRS. GODFREY, HAVE YOU LOOKED AT THE SCHOOL CALENDAR?
I'M FAMILIAR WITH IT, YES, NATE.
SO YOU KNOW THEY'RE LETTING US OUT FOR THANKSGIVING BREAK ON WEDNESDAY AT **NOON**!
11/18

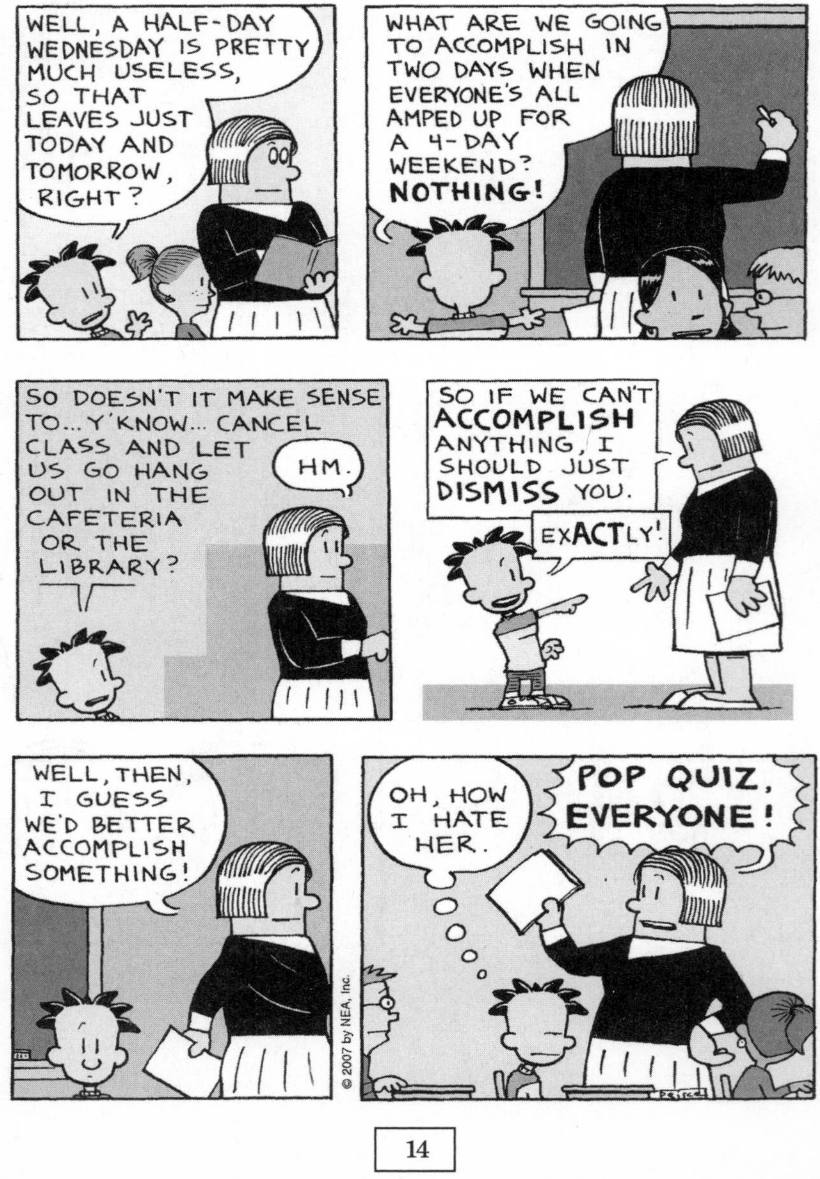
WELL, A HALF-DAY WEDNESDAY IS PRETTY MUCH USELESS, SO THAT LEAVES JUST TODAY AND TOMORROW, RIGHT?
WHAT ARE WE GOING TO ACCOMPLISH IN TWO DAYS WHEN EVERYONE'S ALL AMPED UP FOR A 4-DAY WEEKEND? **NOTHING!**
SO DOESN'T IT MAKE SENSE TO... Y'KNOW... CANCEL CLASS AND LET US GO HANG OUT IN THE CAFETERIA OR THE LIBRARY?
HM.
SO IF WE CAN'T **ACCOMPLISH** ANYTHING, I SHOULD JUST **DISMISS** YOU.
EX**ACT**LY!
WELL, THEN, I GUESS WE'D BETTER ACCOMPLISH SOMETHING!
OH, HOW I HATE HER.
POP QUIZ, EVERYONE!
© 2007 by NEA, Inc.

WHO WANTS TO PLAY SOCIAL STUDIES JEOPARDY?

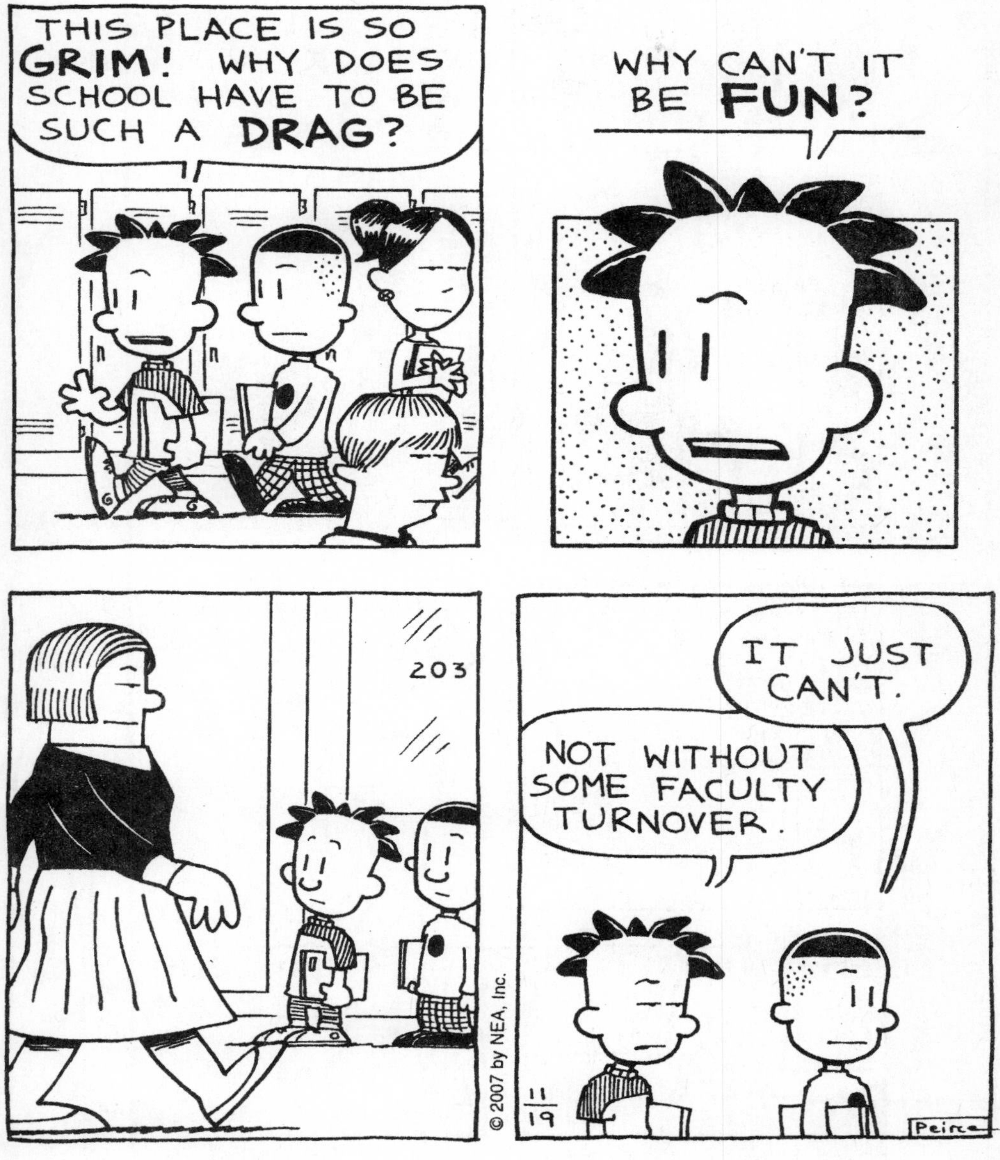
THIS PLACE IS SO **GRIM**! WHY DOES SCHOOL HAVE TO BE SUCH A **DRAG**?
WHY CAN'T IT BE **FUN**?
203
IT JUST CAN'T.
NOT WITHOUT SOME FACULTY TURNOVER.
11/19
Peirce

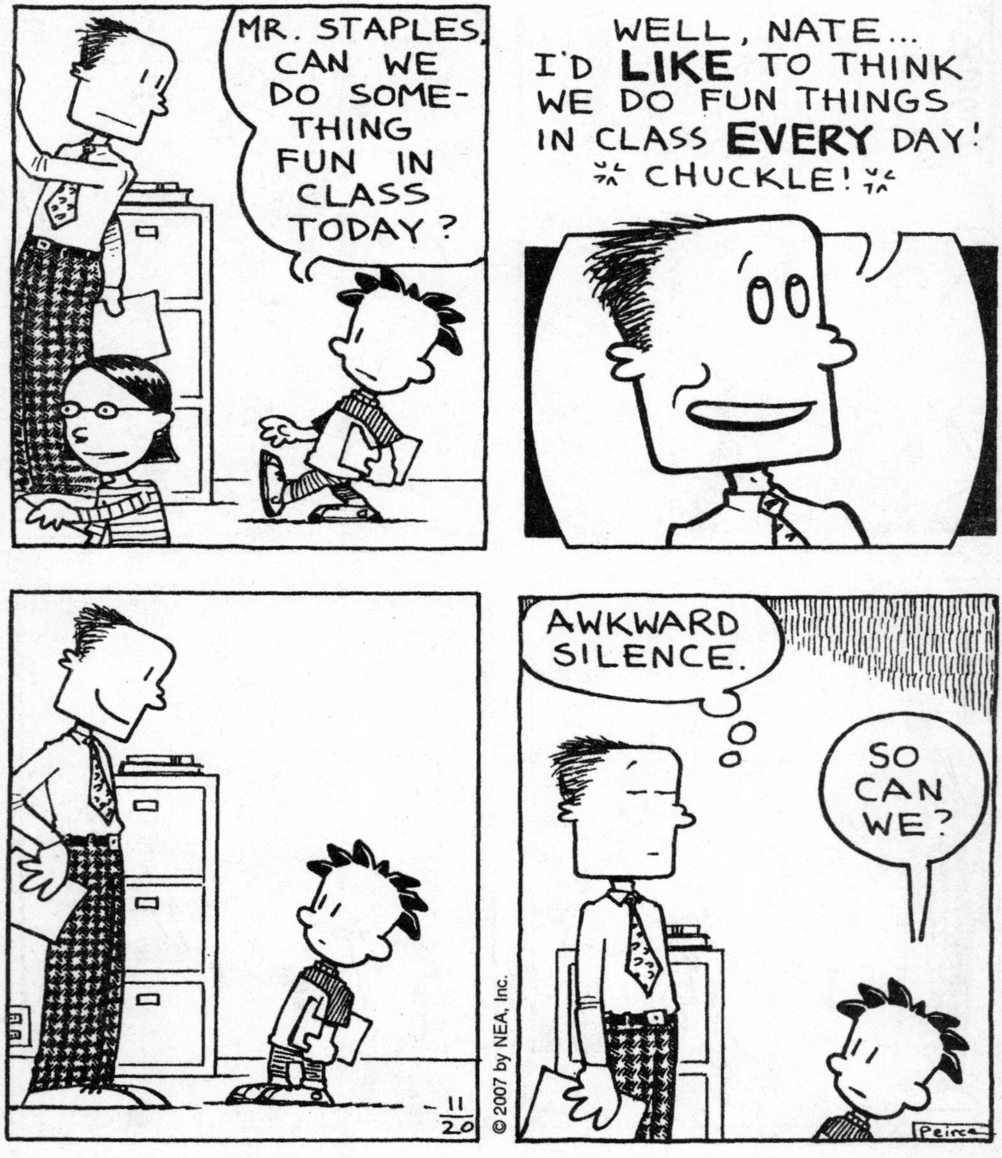
MR. STAPLES, CAN WE DO SOMETHING FUN IN CLASS TODAY?
WELL, NATE... I'D **LIKE** TO THINK WE DO FUN THINGS IN CLASS **EVERY** DAY! CHUCKLE!
11 20
© 2007 by NEA, Inc.
AWKWARD SILENCE.
SO CAN WE?
Peirce

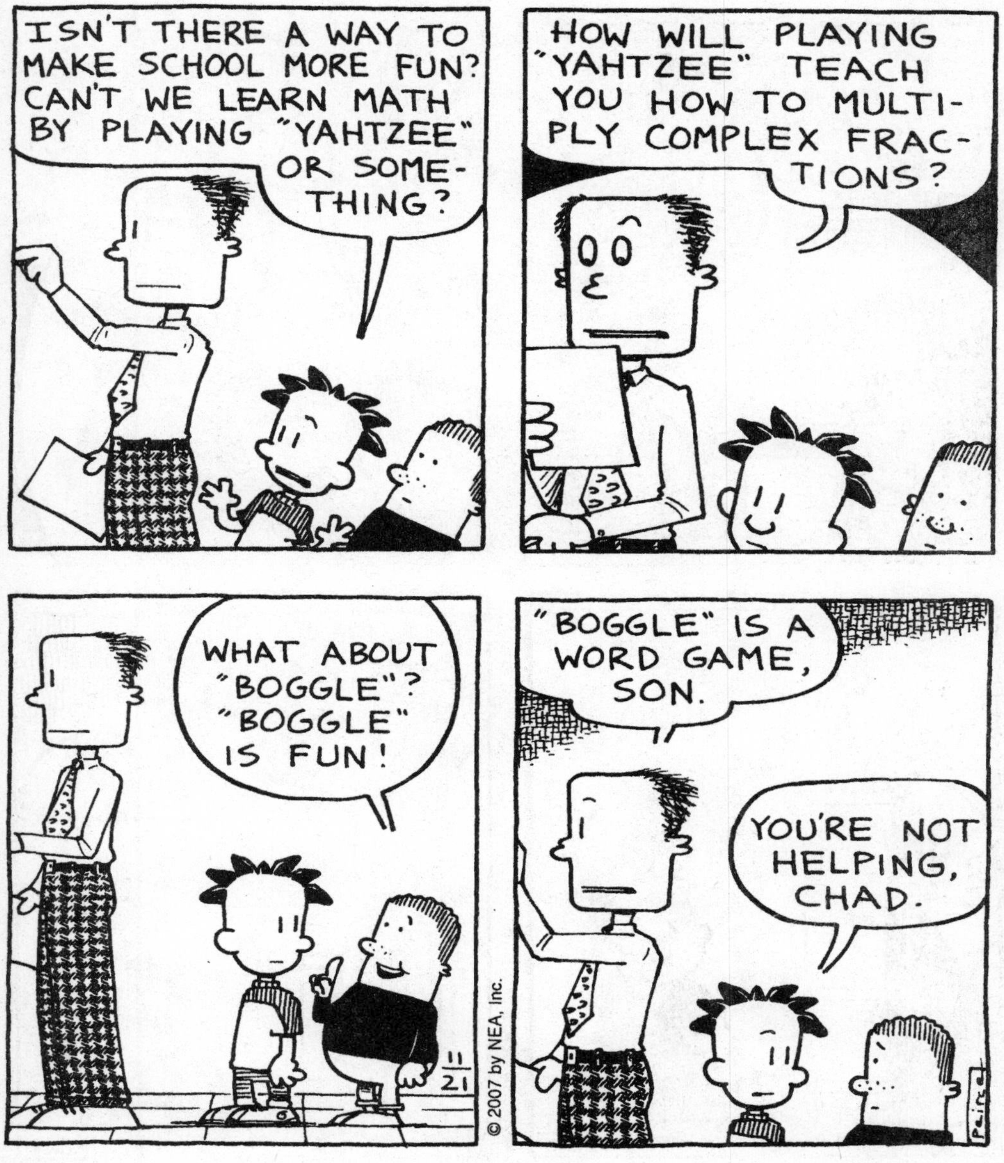
ISN'T THERE A WAY TO MAKE SCHOOL MORE FUN? CAN'T WE LEARN MATH BY PLAYING "YAHTZEE" OR SOME-THING?
HOW WILL PLAYING "YAHTZEE" TEACH YOU HOW TO MULTI-PLY COMPLEX FRAC-TIONS?
WHAT ABOUT "BOGGLE"? "BOGGLE" IS FUN!
11/21
© 2007 by NEA, Inc.
"BOGGLE" IS A WORD GAME, SON.
YOU'RE NOT HELPING, CHAD.
Peirce

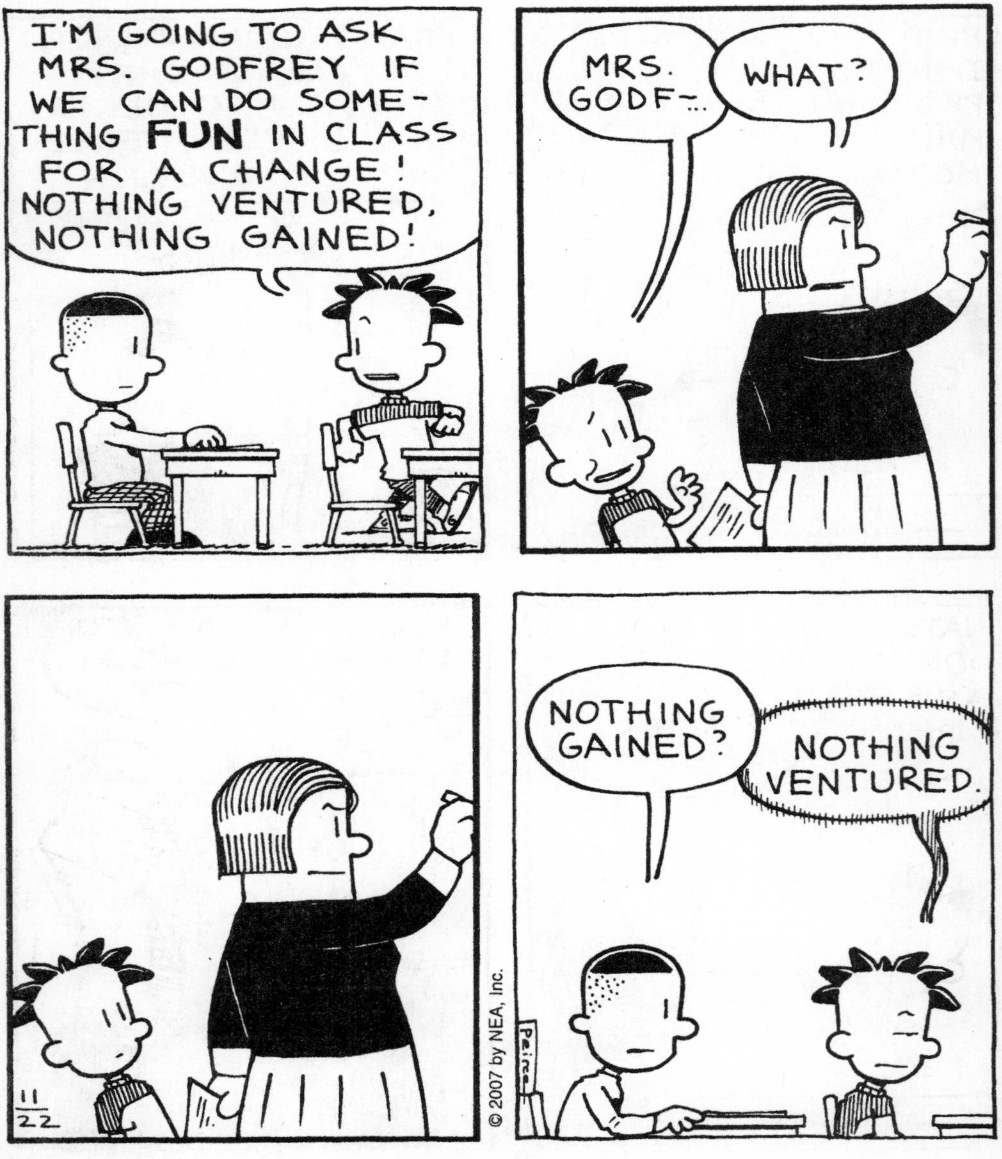
I'M GOING TO ASK MRS. GODFREY IF WE CAN DO SOMETHING FUN IN CLASS FOR A CHANGE! NOTHING VENTURED, NOTHING GAINED!
MRS. GODF-...
WHAT?
11/22
© 2007 by NEA, Inc.
NOTHING GAINED?
NOTHING VENTURED.
Peirce

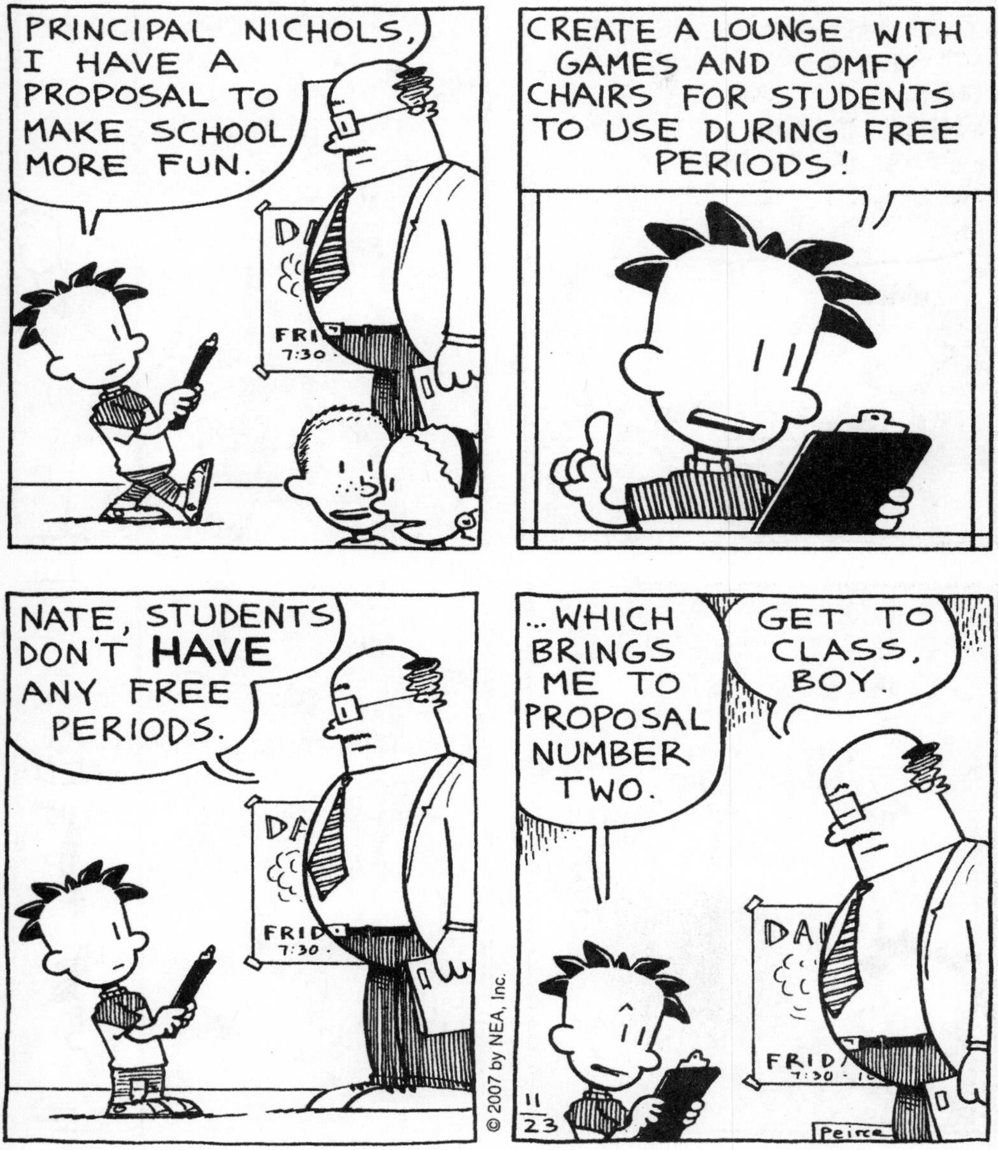
PRINCIPAL NICHOLS, I HAVE A PROPOSAL TO MAKE SCHOOL MORE FUN.
CREATE A LOUNGE WITH GAMES AND COMFY CHAIRS FOR STUDENTS TO USE DURING FREE PERIODS!
NATE, STUDENTS DON'T **HAVE** ANY FREE PERIODS.
...WHICH BRINGS ME TO PROPOSAL NUMBER TWO.
GET TO CLASS, BOY.
© 2007 by NEA, Inc.
11/23
Peirce

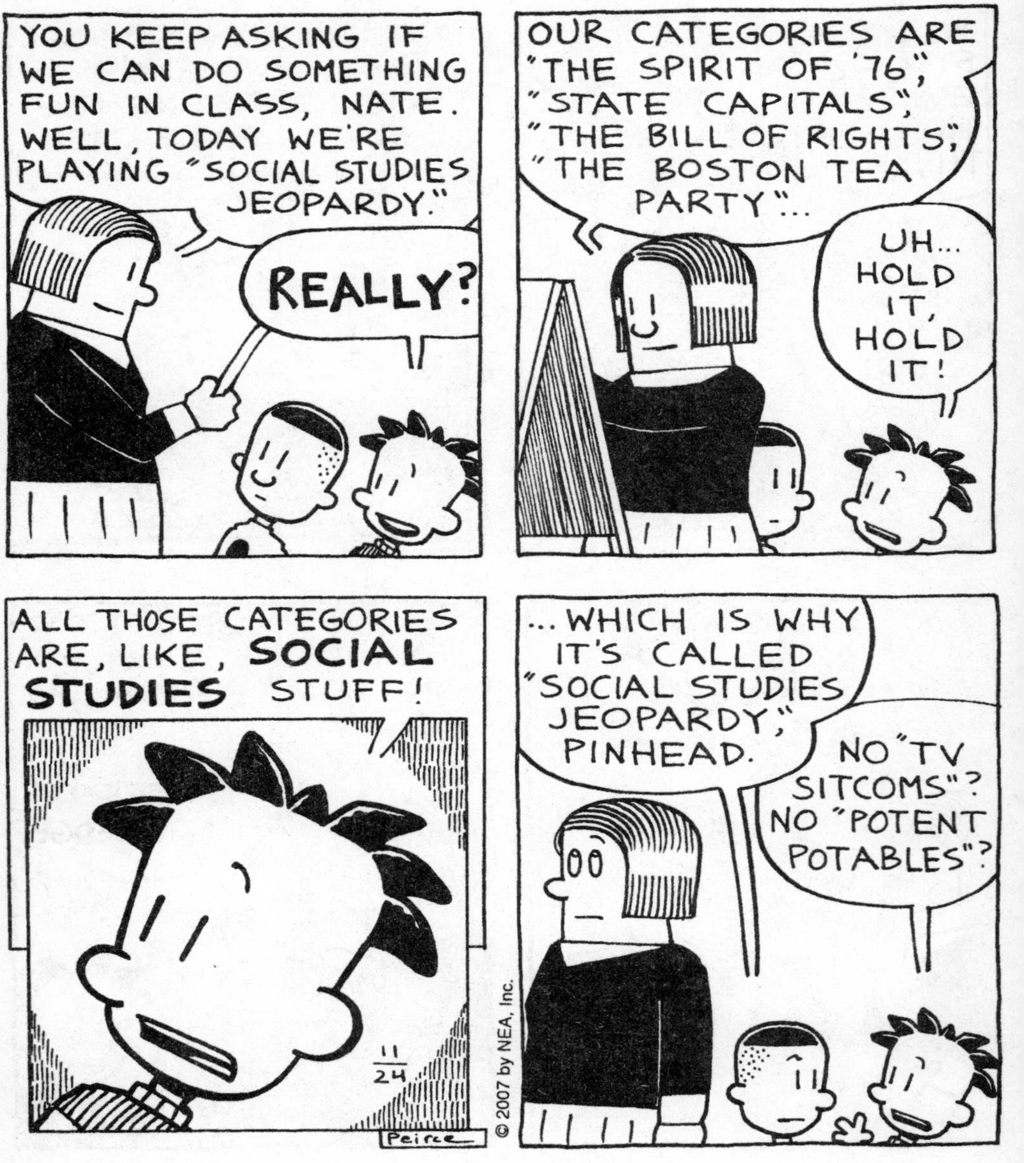
YOU KEEP ASKING IF WE CAN DO SOMETHING FUN IN CLASS, NATE. WELL, TODAY WE'RE PLAYING "SOCIAL STUDIES JEOPARDY."
REALLY?
OUR CATEGORIES ARE "THE SPIRIT OF '76," "STATE CAPITALS," "THE BILL OF RIGHTS," "THE BOSTON TEA PARTY"...
UH... HOLD IT, HOLD IT!
ALL THOSE CATEGORIES ARE, LIKE, SOCIAL STUDIES STUFF!
11
24
Peirce
...WHICH IS WHY IT'S CALLED "SOCIAL STUDIES JEOPARDY," PINHEAD.
NO "TV SITCOMS"? NO "POTENT POTABLES"?

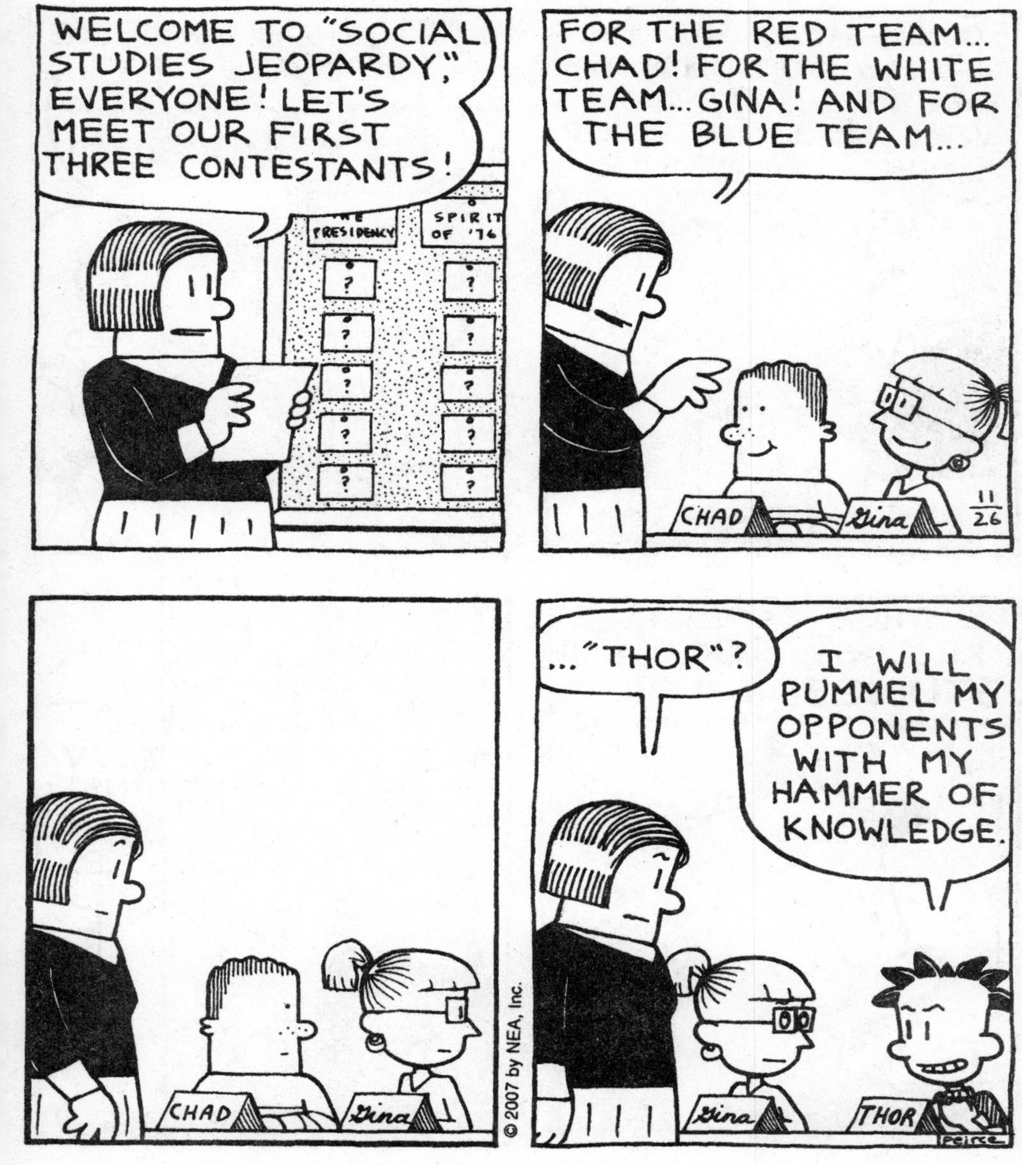
WELCOME TO "SOCIAL STUDIES JEOPARDY," EVERYONE! LET'S MEET OUR FIRST THREE CONTESTANTS!
PRESIDENCY
SPIRIT OF '76
FOR THE RED TEAM... CHAD! FOR THE WHITE TEAM... GINA! AND FOR THE BLUE TEAM...
CHAD
Gina
11
26
CHAD
Gina
..."THOR"?
I WILL PUMMEL MY OPPONENTS WITH MY HAMMER OF KNOWLEDGE.
Gina
THOR
peirce

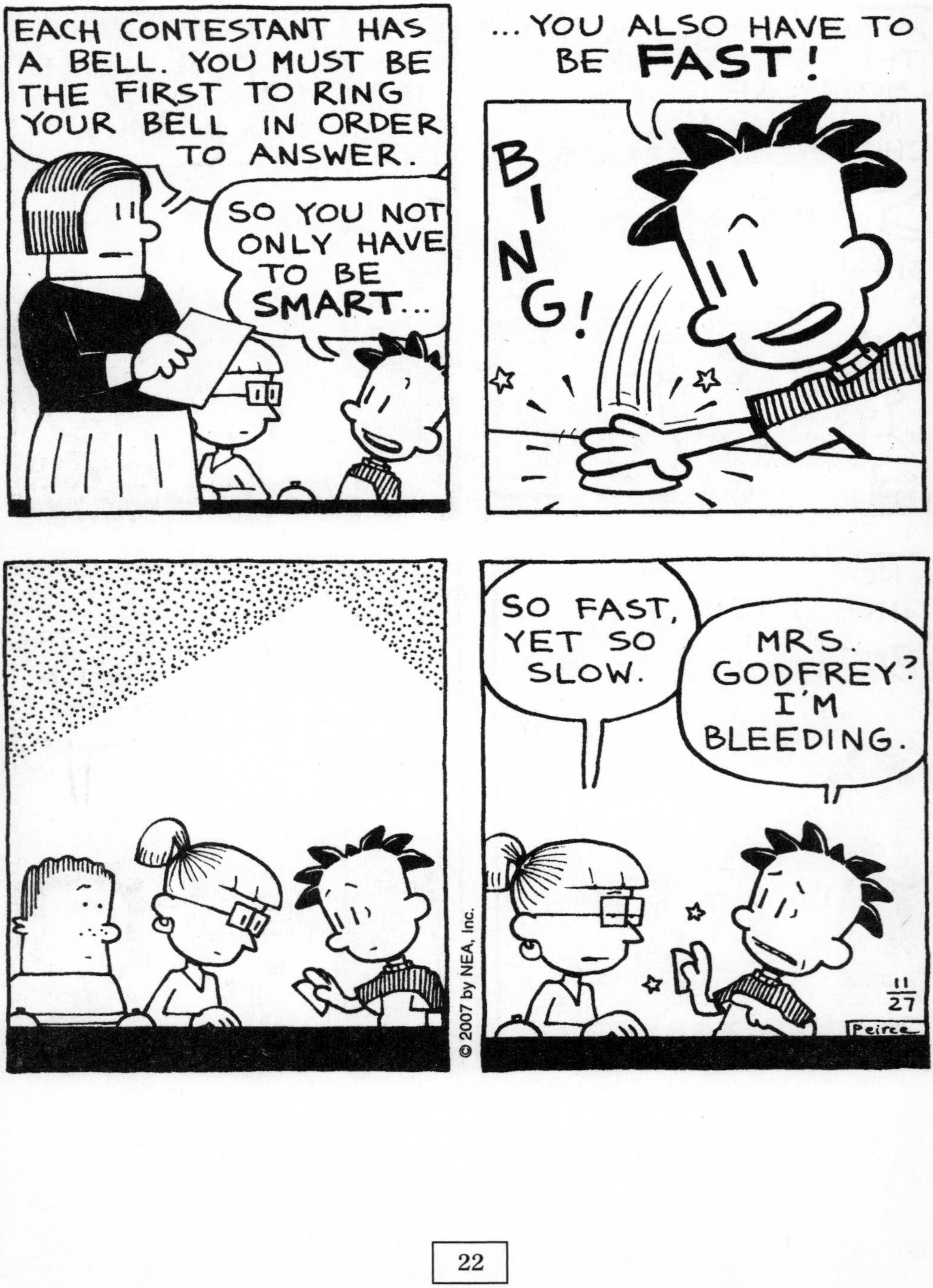
EACH CONTESTANT HAS A BELL. YOU MUST BE THE FIRST TO RING YOUR BELL IN ORDER TO ANSWER.
SO YOU NOT ONLY HAVE TO BE SMART...
...YOU ALSO HAVE TO BE FAST!
BING!
SO FAST, YET SO SLOW.
MRS. GODFREY? I'M BLEEDING.
11
27
Peirce
© 2007 by NEA, Inc.

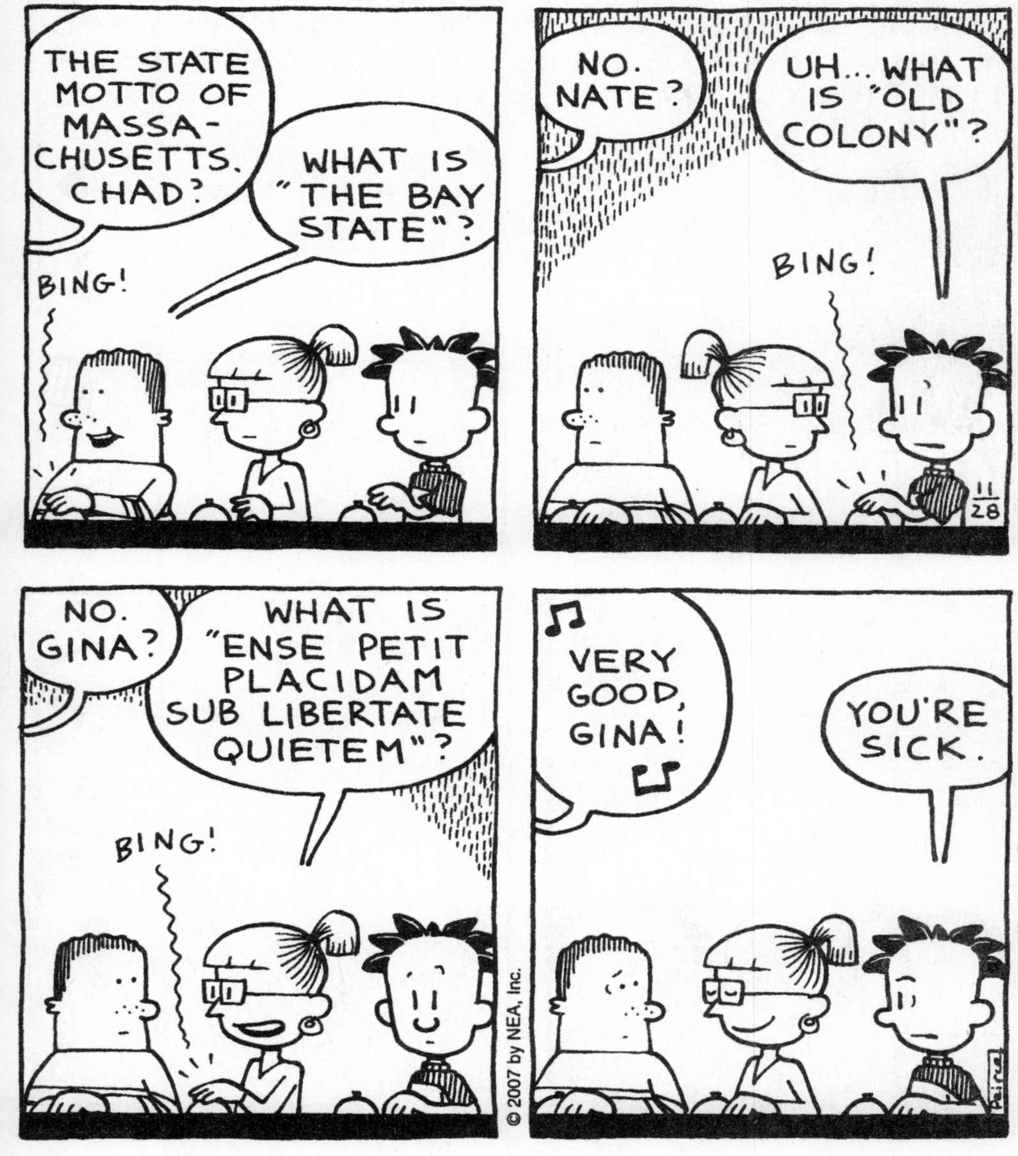
THE STATE MOTTO OF MASSA-CHUSETTS. CHAD?
WHAT IS "THE BAY STATE"?
BING!
NO. NATE?
UH... WHAT IS "OLD COLONY"?
BING!
11/28
NO. GINA?
WHAT IS "ENSE PETIT PLACIDAM SUB LIBERTATE QUIETEM"?
BING!
VERY GOOD, GINA!
YOU'RE SICK.
Peirce

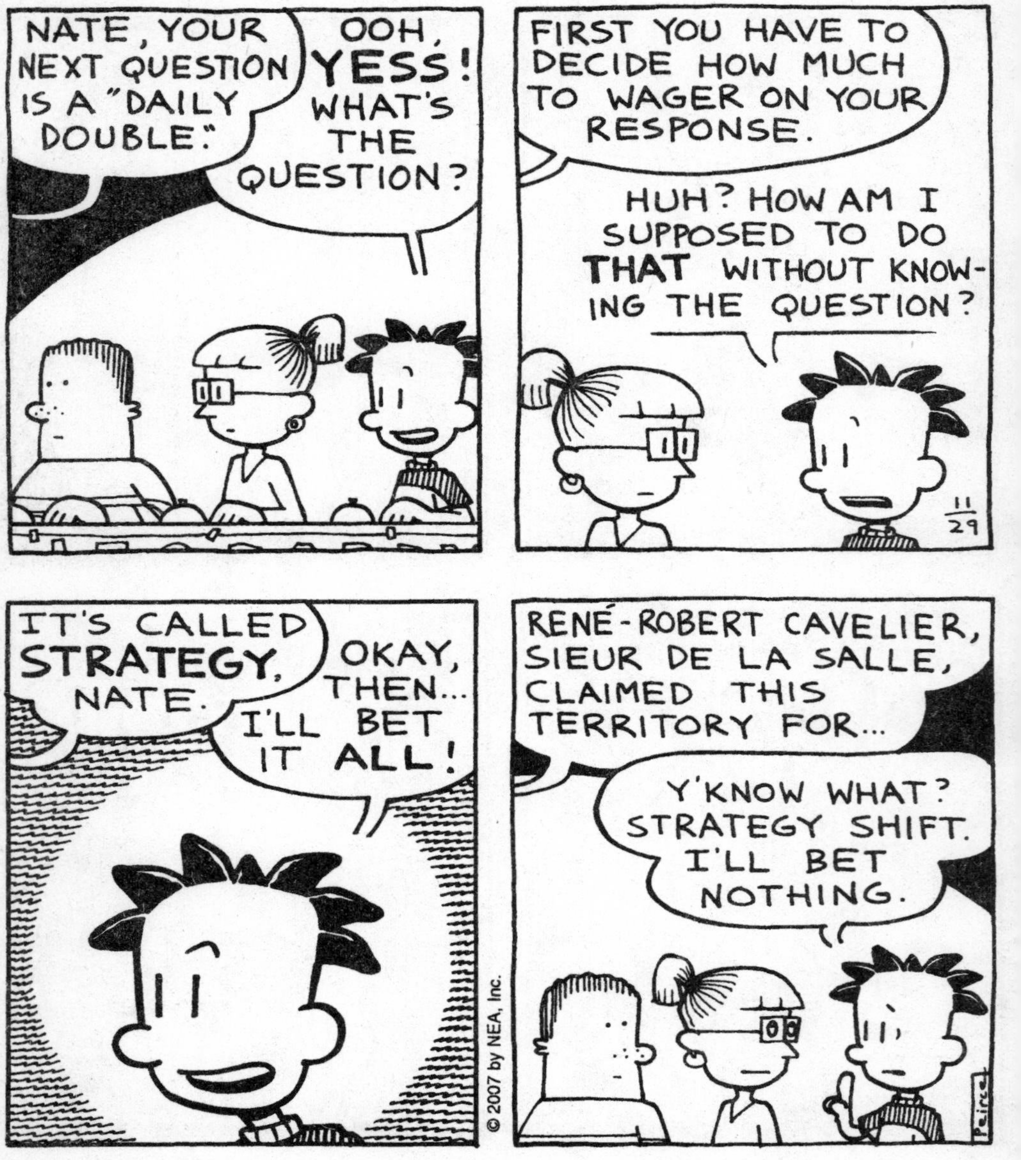
NATE, YOUR NEXT QUESTION IS A "DAILY DOUBLE."
OOH, YESS! WHAT'S THE QUESTION?
FIRST YOU HAVE TO DECIDE HOW MUCH TO WAGER ON YOUR RESPONSE.
HUH? HOW AM I SUPPOSED TO DO THAT WITHOUT KNOWING THE QUESTION?
11 29
IT'S CALLED STRATEGY, NATE.
OKAY, THEN... I'LL BET IT ALL!
© 2007 by NEA, Inc.
RENÉ-ROBERT CAVELIER, SIEUR DE LA SALLE, CLAIMED THIS TERRITORY FOR...
Y'KNOW WHAT? STRATEGY SHIFT. I'LL BET NOTHING.
Peirce

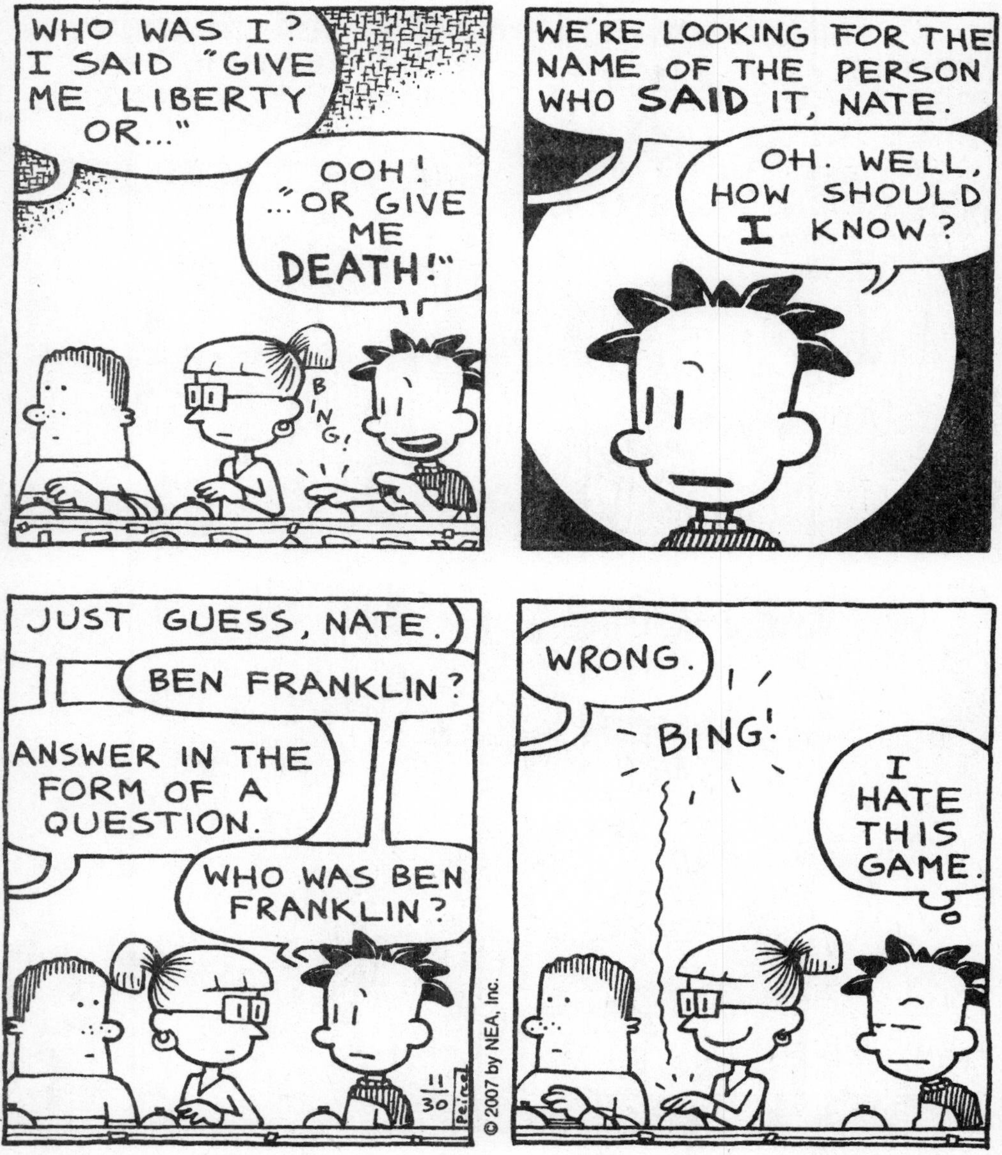
WHO WAS I? I SAID "GIVE ME LIBERTY OR..."
OOH! ..."OR GIVE ME DEATH!"
B I N G!
WE'RE LOOKING FOR THE NAME OF THE PERSON WHO SAID IT, NATE.
OH. WELL, HOW SHOULD I KNOW?
JUST GUESS, NATE.
BEN FRANKLIN?
ANSWER IN THE FORM OF A QUESTION.
WHO WAS BEN FRANKLIN?
11/30
Peirce
WRONG.
BING!
I HATE THIS GAME.

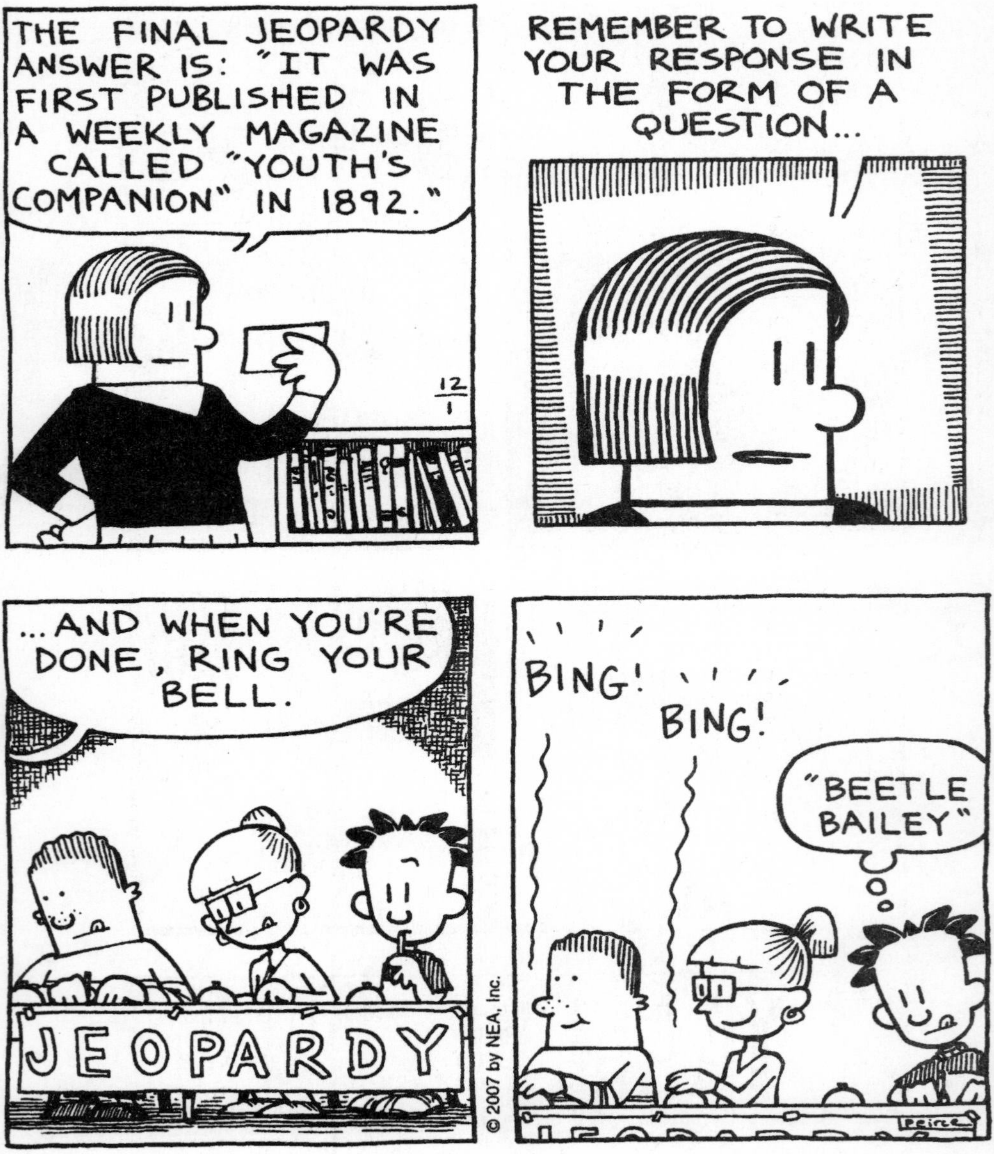
THE FINAL JEOPARDY ANSWER IS: "IT WAS FIRST PUBLISHED IN A WEEKLY MAGAZINE CALLED "YOUTH'S COMPANION" IN 1892."
12/1
REMEMBER TO WRITE YOUR RESPONSE IN THE FORM OF A QUESTION...
...AND WHEN YOU'RE DONE, RING YOUR BELL.
JEOPARDY
© 2007 by NEA, Inc.
BING!
BING!
"BEETLE BAILEY"
Peirce

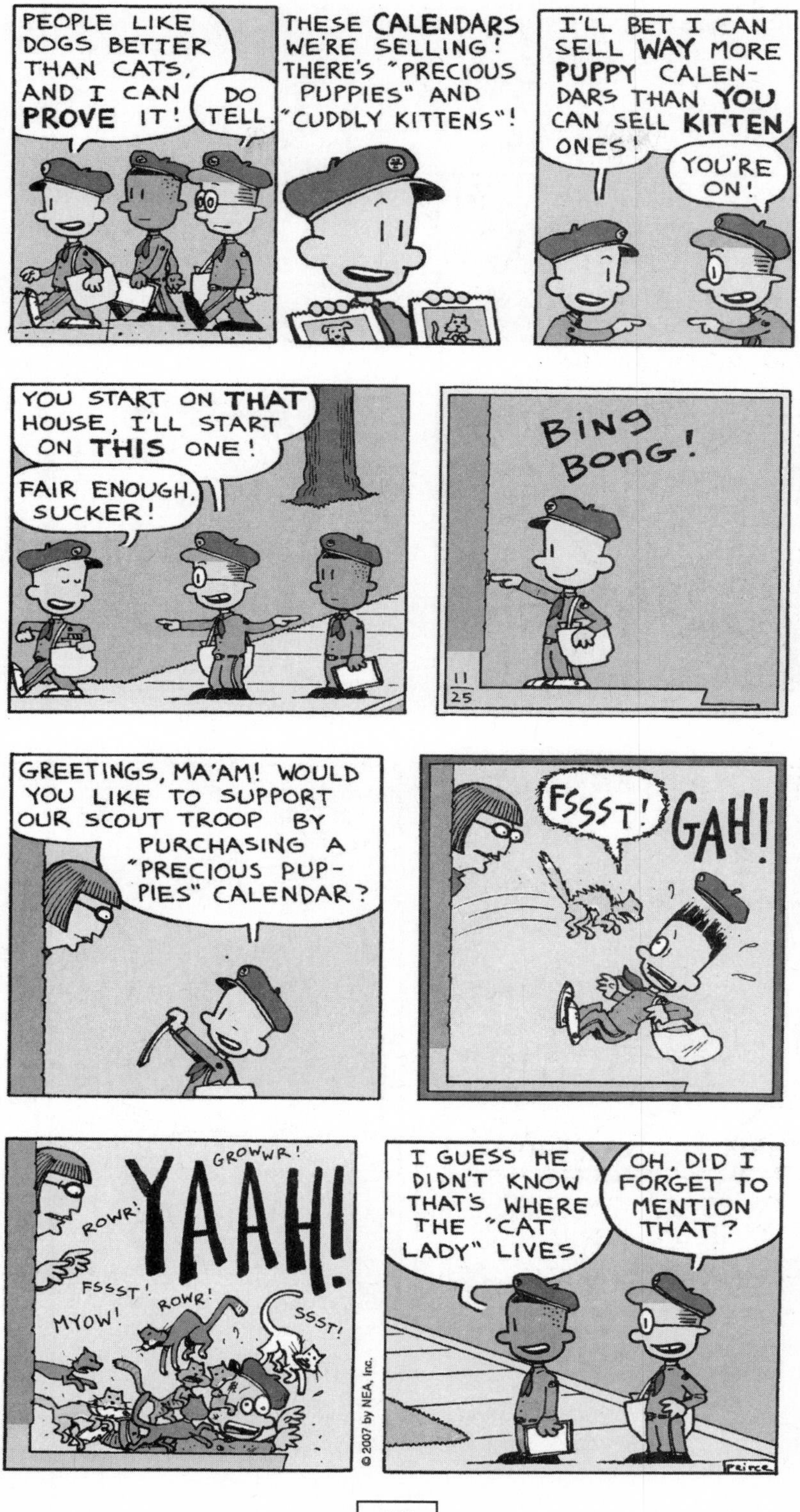
PEOPLE LIKE DOGS BETTER THAN CATS, AND I CAN **PROVE** IT!
DO TELL.
THESE **CALENDARS** WE'RE SELLING! THERE'S "PRECIOUS PUPPIES" AND "CUDDLY KITTENS"!
I'LL BET I CAN SELL **WAY** MORE **PUPPY** CALENDARS THAN **YOU** CAN SELL **KITTEN** ONES!
YOU'RE ON!
YOU START ON **THAT** HOUSE, I'LL START ON **THIS** ONE!
FAIR ENOUGH, SUCKER!
BING BONG!
11/25
GREETINGS, MA'AM! WOULD YOU LIKE TO SUPPORT OUR SCOUT TROOP BY PURCHASING A "PRECIOUS PUPPIES" CALENDAR?
FSSST!
GAH!
GROWWR!
ROWR!
YAAH!
FSSST!
ROWR!
MYOW!
SSST!
I GUESS HE DIDN'T KNOW THAT'S WHERE THE "CAT LADY" LIVES.
OH, DID I FORGET TO MENTION THAT?
Peirce

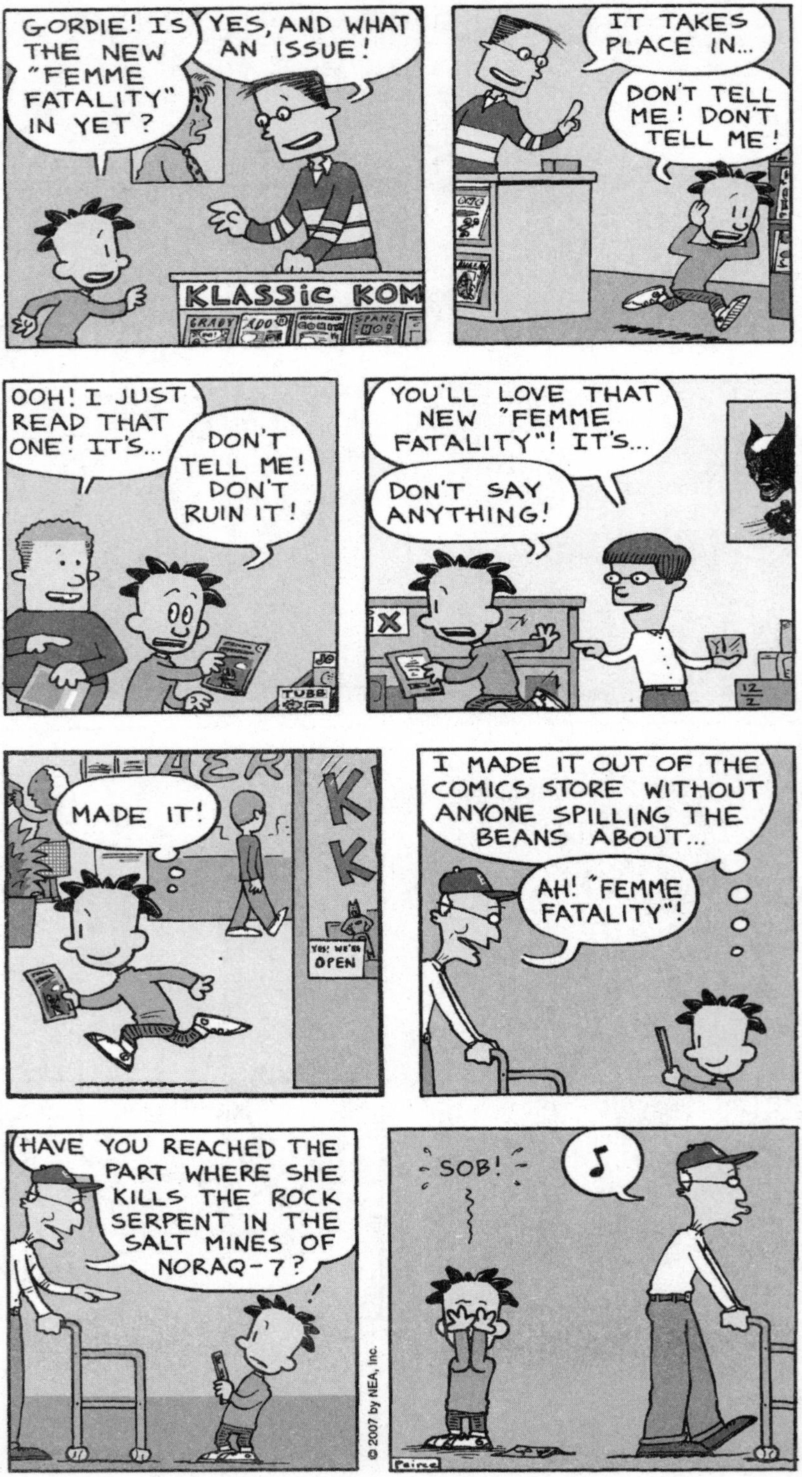
GORDIE! IS THE NEW "FEMME FATALITY" IN YET?
YES, AND WHAT AN ISSUE!
KLASSic KOM
IT TAKES PLACE IN...
DON'T TELL ME! DON'T TELL ME!
OOH! I JUST READ THAT ONE! IT'S...
DON'T TELL ME! DON'T RUIN IT!
YOU'LL LOVE THAT NEW "FEMME FATALITY"! IT'S...
DON'T SAY ANYTHING!
MADE IT!
OPEN
I MADE IT OUT OF THE COMICS STORE WITHOUT ANYONE SPILLING THE BEANS ABOUT...
AH! "FEMME FATALITY"!
HAVE YOU REACHED THE PART WHERE SHE KILLS THE ROCK SERPENT IN THE SALT MINES OF NORAQ-7?
!
SOB!
♪
© 2007 by NEA, Inc.

HERE COMES JENNY!

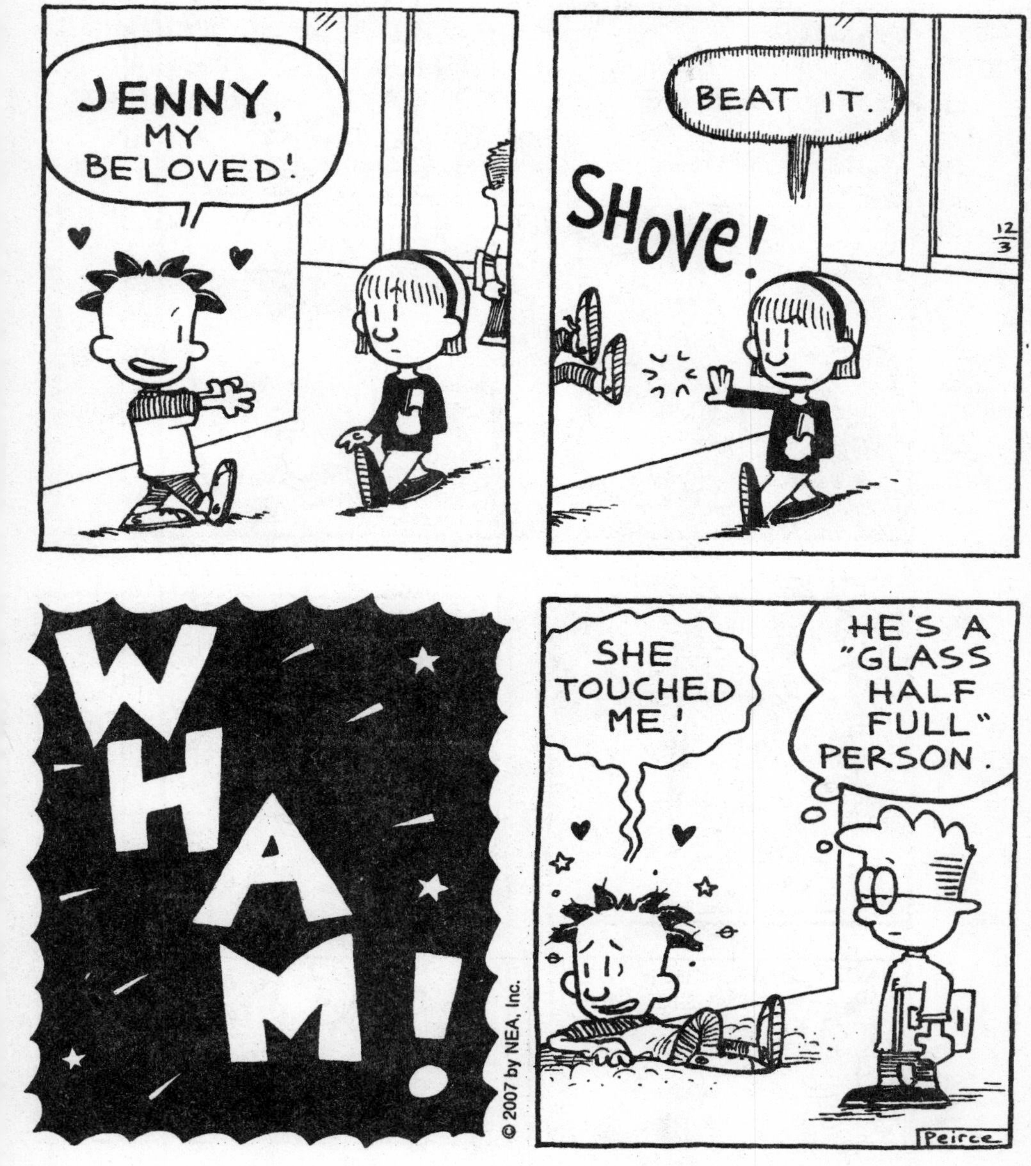
JENNY, MY BELOVED!
BEAT IT.
SHOVE!
12/3
WHAM!
SHE TOUCHED ME!
HE'S A "GLASS HALF FULL" PERSON.
Peirce

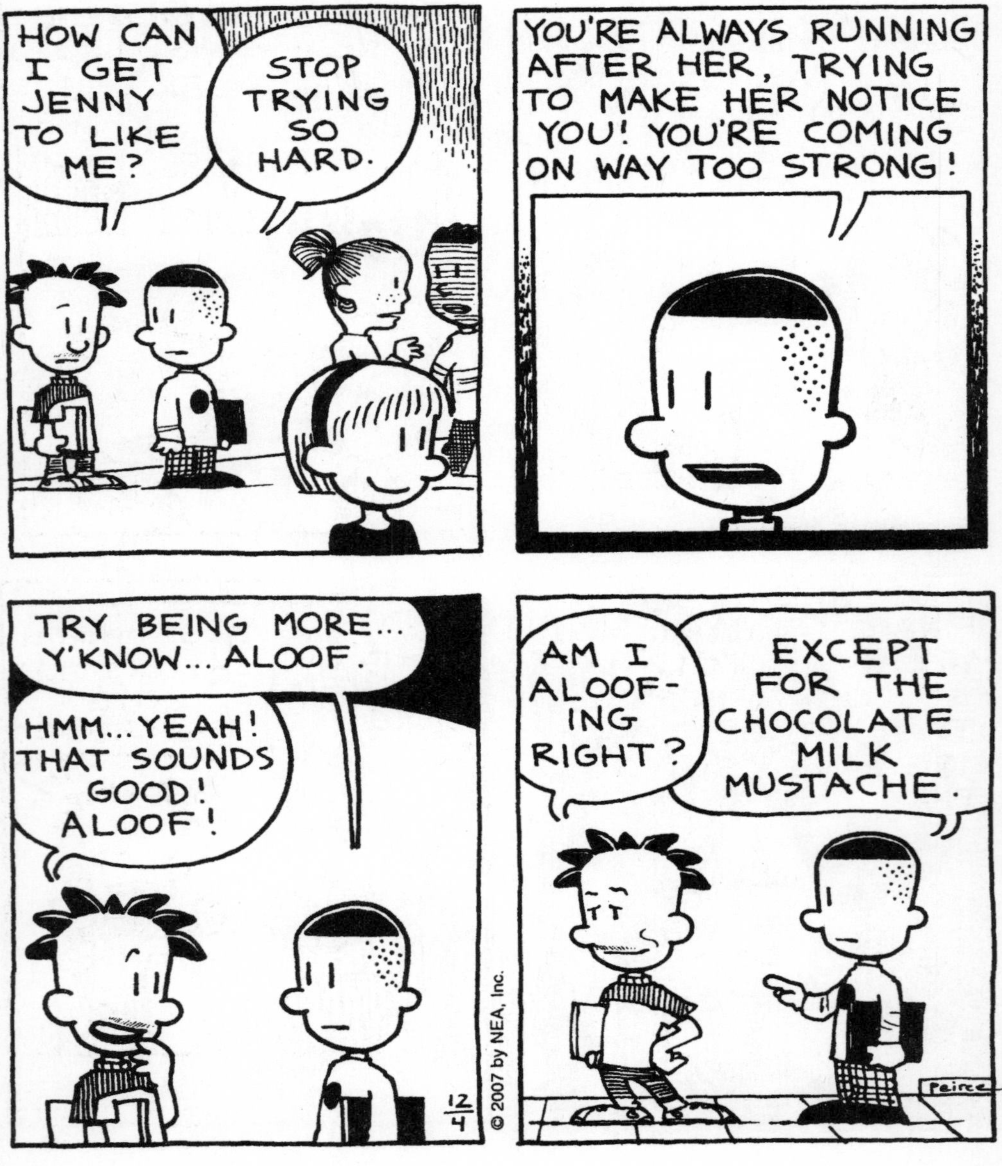
HOW CAN I GET JENNY TO LIKE ME?
STOP TRYING SO HARD.
YOU'RE ALWAYS RUNNING AFTER HER, TRYING TO MAKE HER NOTICE YOU! YOU'RE COMING ON WAY TOO STRONG!
TRY BEING MORE... Y'KNOW... ALOOF.
HMM... YEAH! THAT SOUNDS GOOD! ALOOF!
12/4
© 2007 by NEA, Inc.
AM I ALOOF-ING RIGHT?
EXCEPT FOR THE CHOCOLATE MILK MUSTACHE.
Peirce

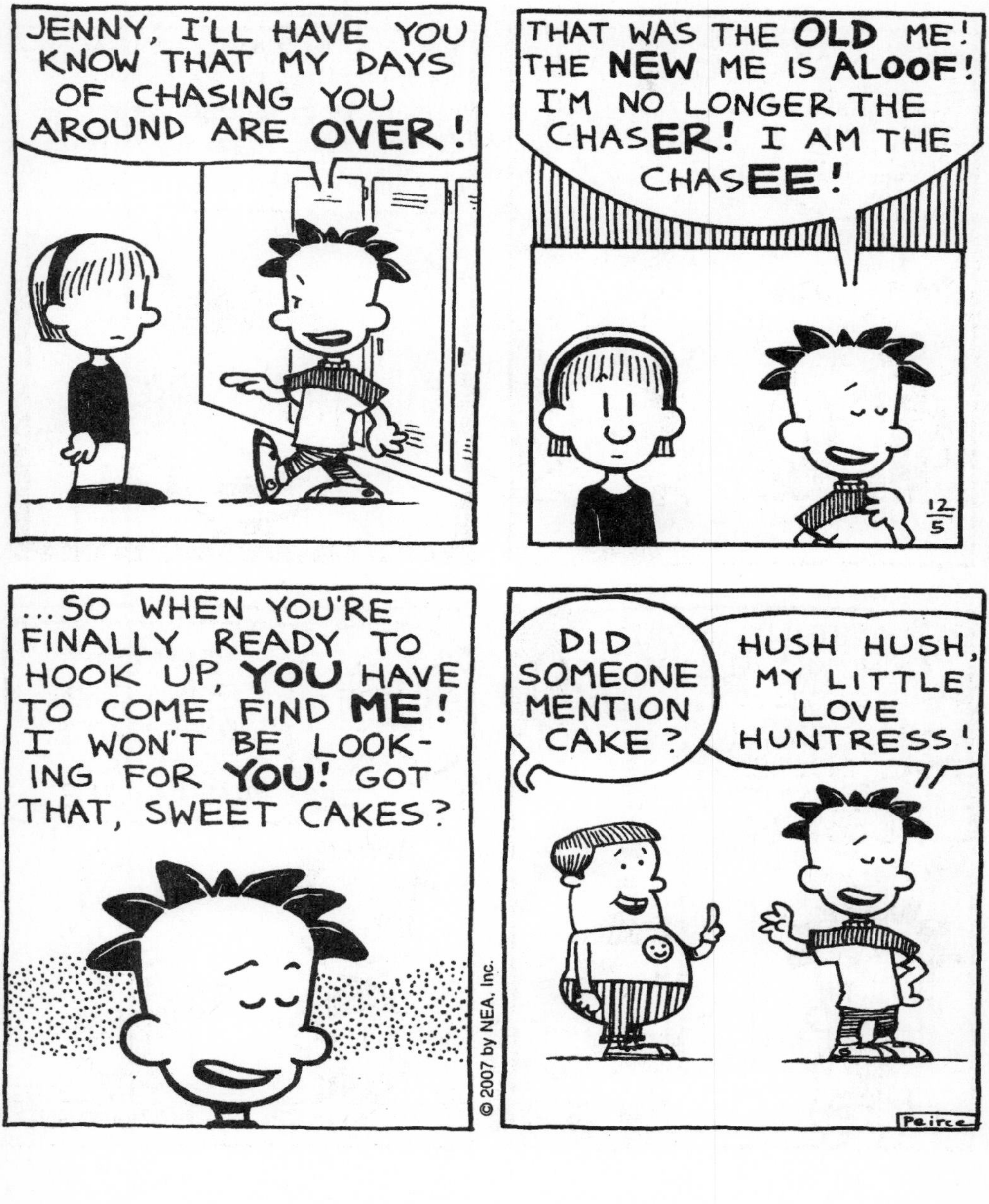
JENNY, I'LL HAVE YOU KNOW THAT MY DAYS OF CHASING YOU AROUND ARE OVER!
THAT WAS THE OLD ME! THE NEW ME IS ALOOF! I'M NO LONGER THE CHASER! I AM THE CHASEE!
12/5
...SO WHEN YOU'RE FINALLY READY TO HOOK UP, YOU HAVE TO COME FIND ME! I WON'T BE LOOK-ING FOR YOU! GOT THAT, SWEET CAKES?
© 2007 by NEA, Inc.
DID SOMEONE MENTION CAKE?
HUSH HUSH, MY LITTLE LOVE HUNTRESS!
Peirce

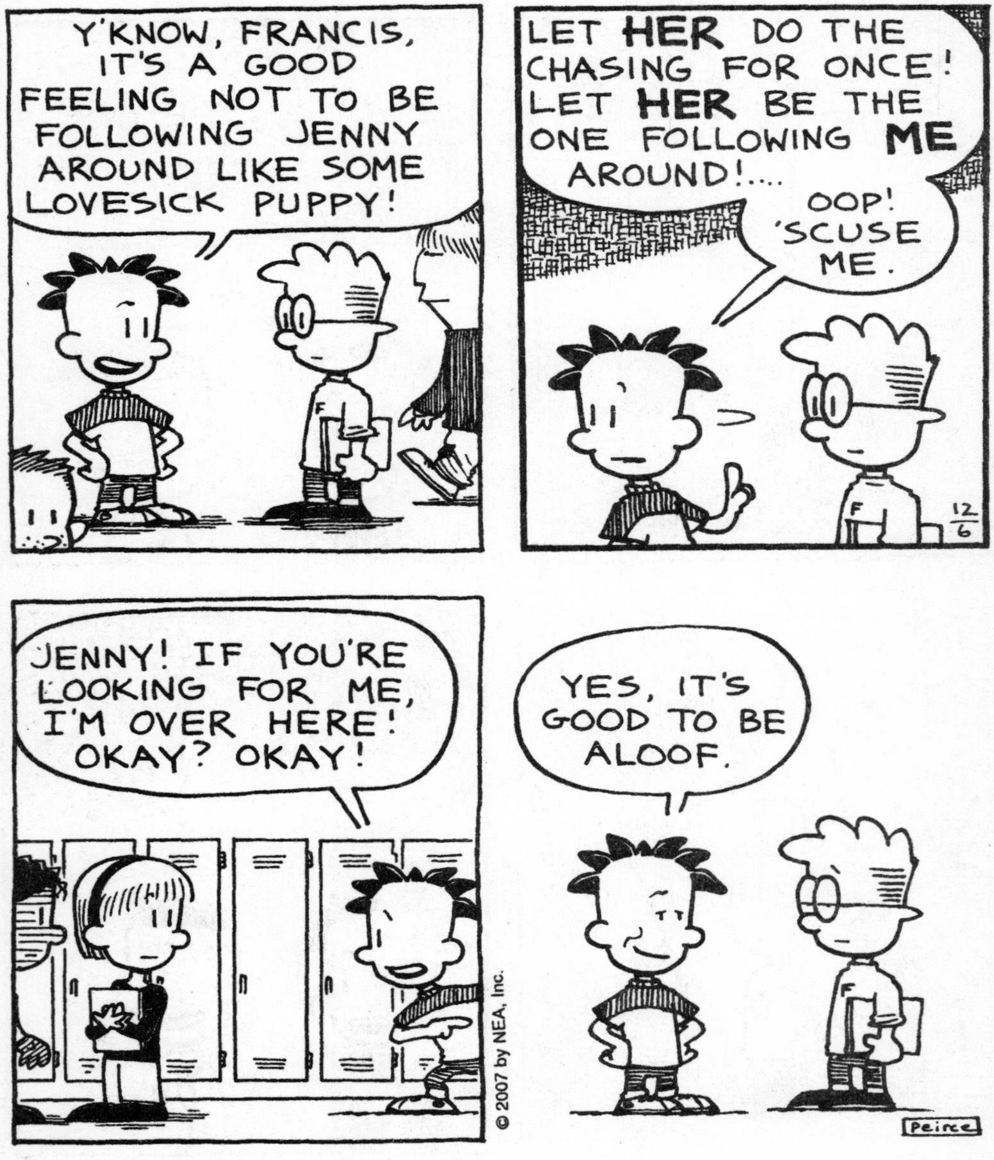

Y'KNOW, FRANCIS, IT'S A GOOD FEELING NOT TO BE FOLLOWING JENNY AROUND LIKE SOME LOVESICK PUPPY!
LET HER DO THE CHASING FOR ONCE! LET HER BE THE ONE FOLLOWING ME AROUND!....
OOP! 'SCUSE ME.
12/6
JENNY! IF YOU'RE LOOKING FOR ME, I'M OVER HERE! OKAY? OKAY!
YES, IT'S GOOD TO BE ALOOF.
Peirce

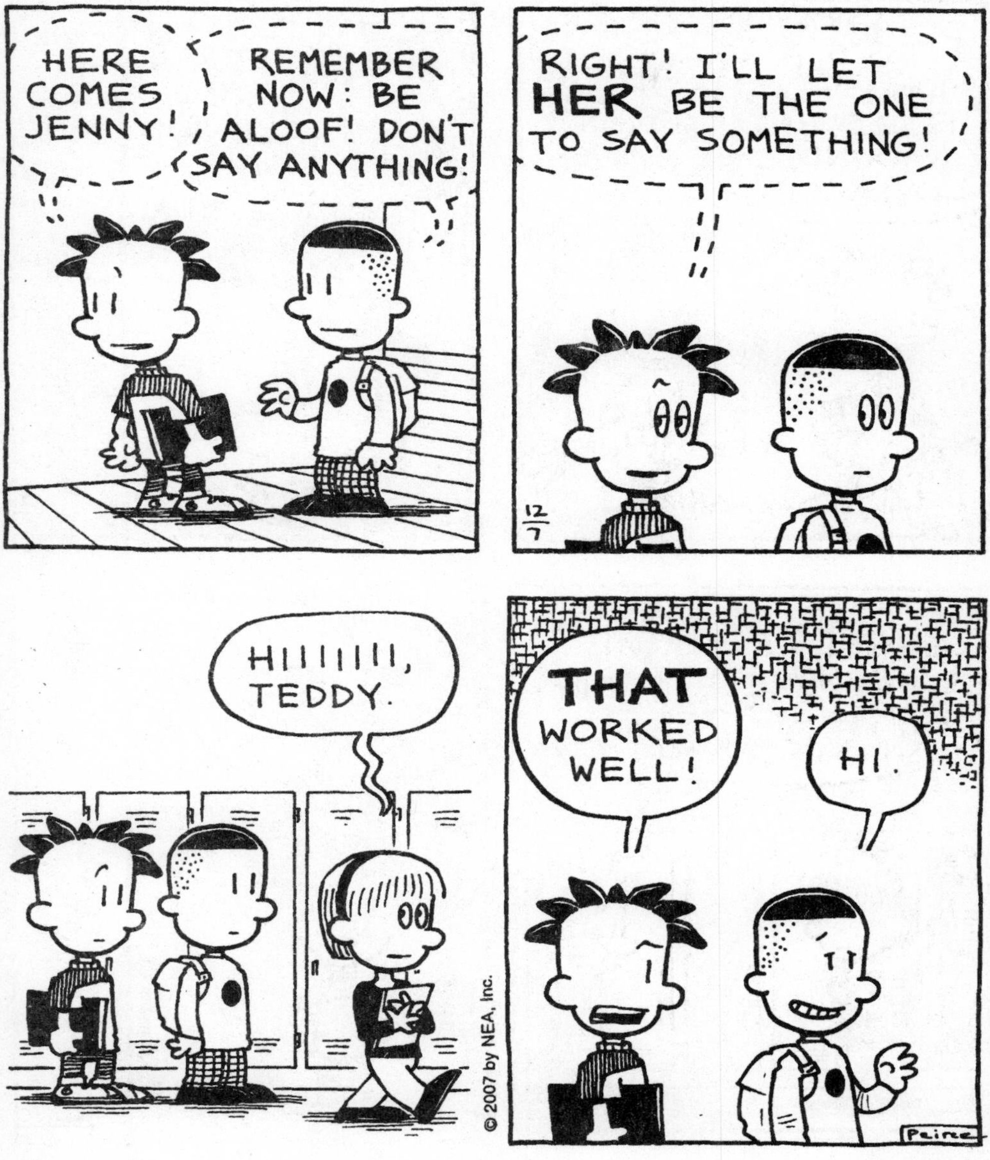
HERE COMES JENNY!
REMEMBER NOW: BE ALOOF! DON'T SAY ANYTHING!
RIGHT! I'LL LET **HER** BE THE ONE TO SAY SOMETHING!
12/7
HIIIIIII, TEDDY.
© 2007 by NEA, Inc.
THAT WORKED WELL!
HI.
Peirce

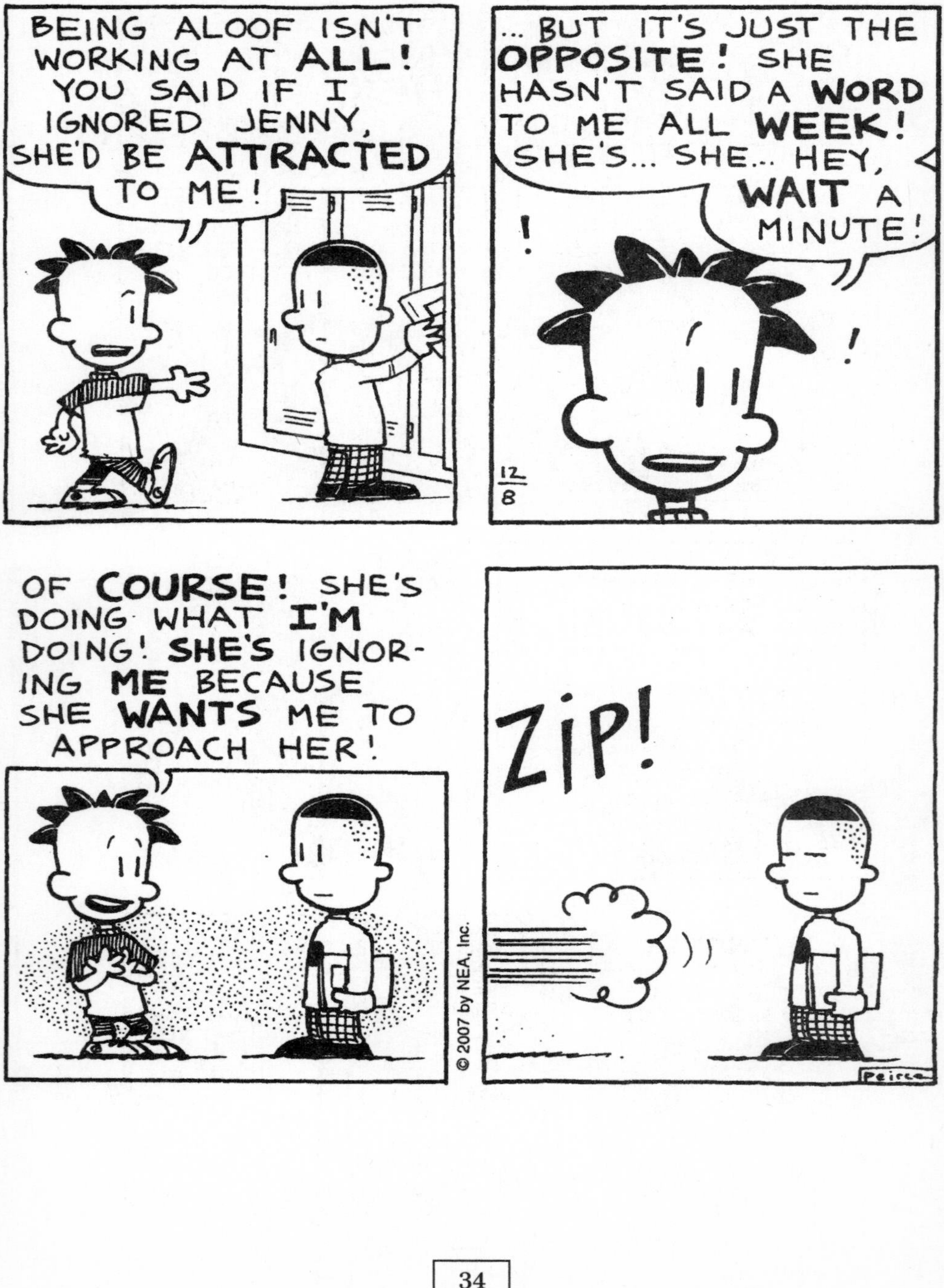
BEING ALOOF ISN'T WORKING AT ALL! YOU SAID IF I IGNORED JENNY, SHE'D BE ATTRACTED TO ME!
... BUT IT'S JUST THE OPPOSITE! SHE HASN'T SAID A WORD TO ME ALL WEEK! SHE'S... SHE... HEY, WAIT A MINUTE!
!
!
12
8
OF COURSE! SHE'S DOING WHAT I'M DOING! SHE'S IGNORING ME BECAUSE SHE WANTS ME TO APPROACH HER!
ZIP!
Peirce

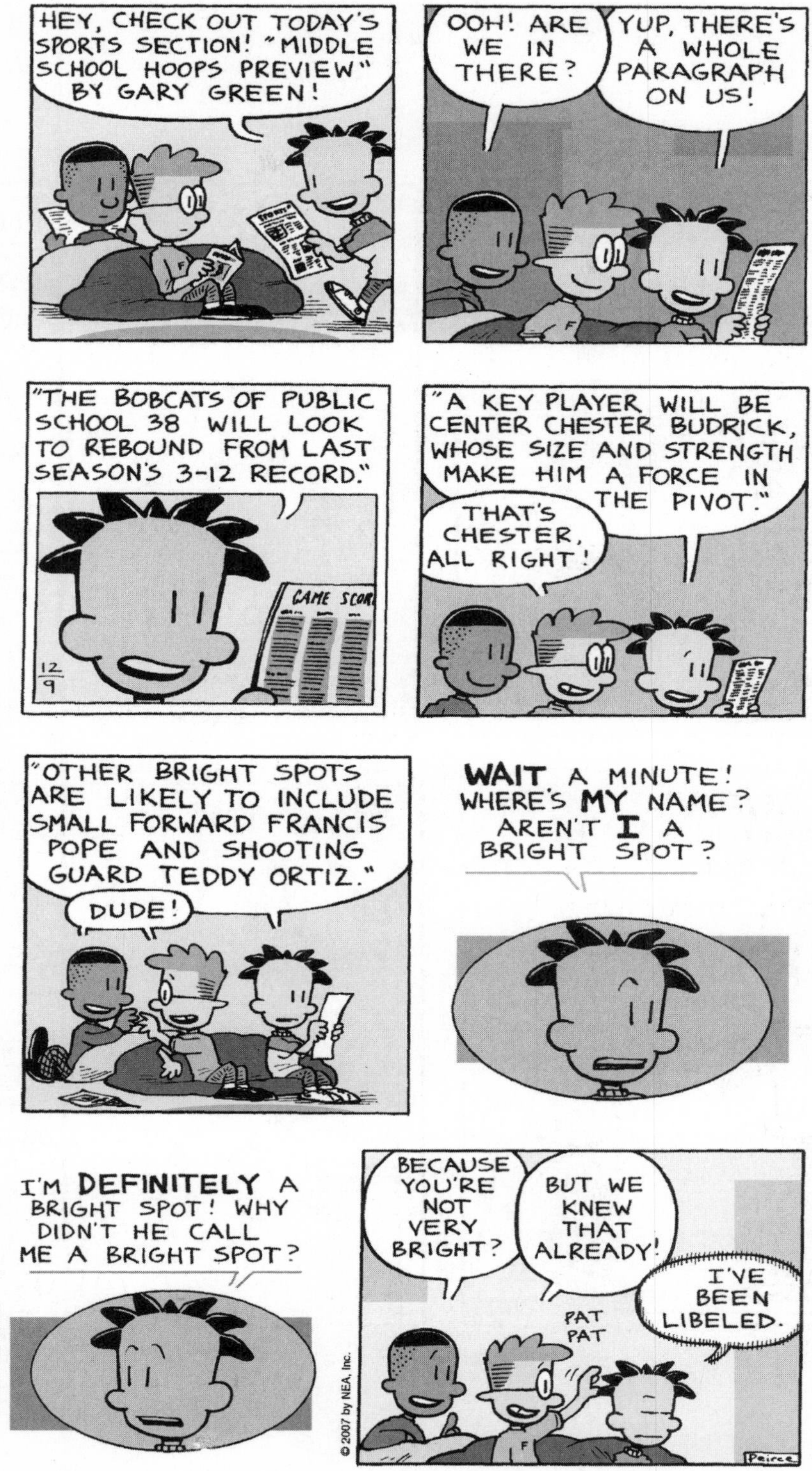

HEY, CHECK OUT TODAY'S SPORTS SECTION! "MIDDLE SCHOOL HOOPS PREVIEW" BY GARY GREEN!
OOH! ARE WE IN THERE?
YUP, THERE'S A WHOLE PARAGRAPH ON US!
"THE BOBCATS OF PUBLIC SCHOOL 38 WILL LOOK TO REBOUND FROM LAST SEASON'S 3-12 RECORD."
GAME SCOR
12/9
"A KEY PLAYER WILL BE CENTER CHESTER BUDRICK, WHOSE SIZE AND STRENGTH MAKE HIM A FORCE IN THE PIVOT."
THAT'S CHESTER, ALL RIGHT!
"OTHER BRIGHT SPOTS ARE LIKELY TO INCLUDE SMALL FORWARD FRANCIS POPE AND SHOOTING GUARD TEDDY ORTIZ."
DUDE!
WAIT A MINUTE! WHERE'S MY NAME? AREN'T I A BRIGHT SPOT?
I'M DEFINITELY A BRIGHT SPOT! WHY DIDN'T HE CALL ME A BRIGHT SPOT?
BECAUSE YOU'RE NOT VERY BRIGHT?
BUT WE KNEW THAT ALREADY!
PAT PAT
I'VE BEEN LIBELED.
Peirce
© 2007 by NEA, Inc.

CHAMPS, OR NOT?

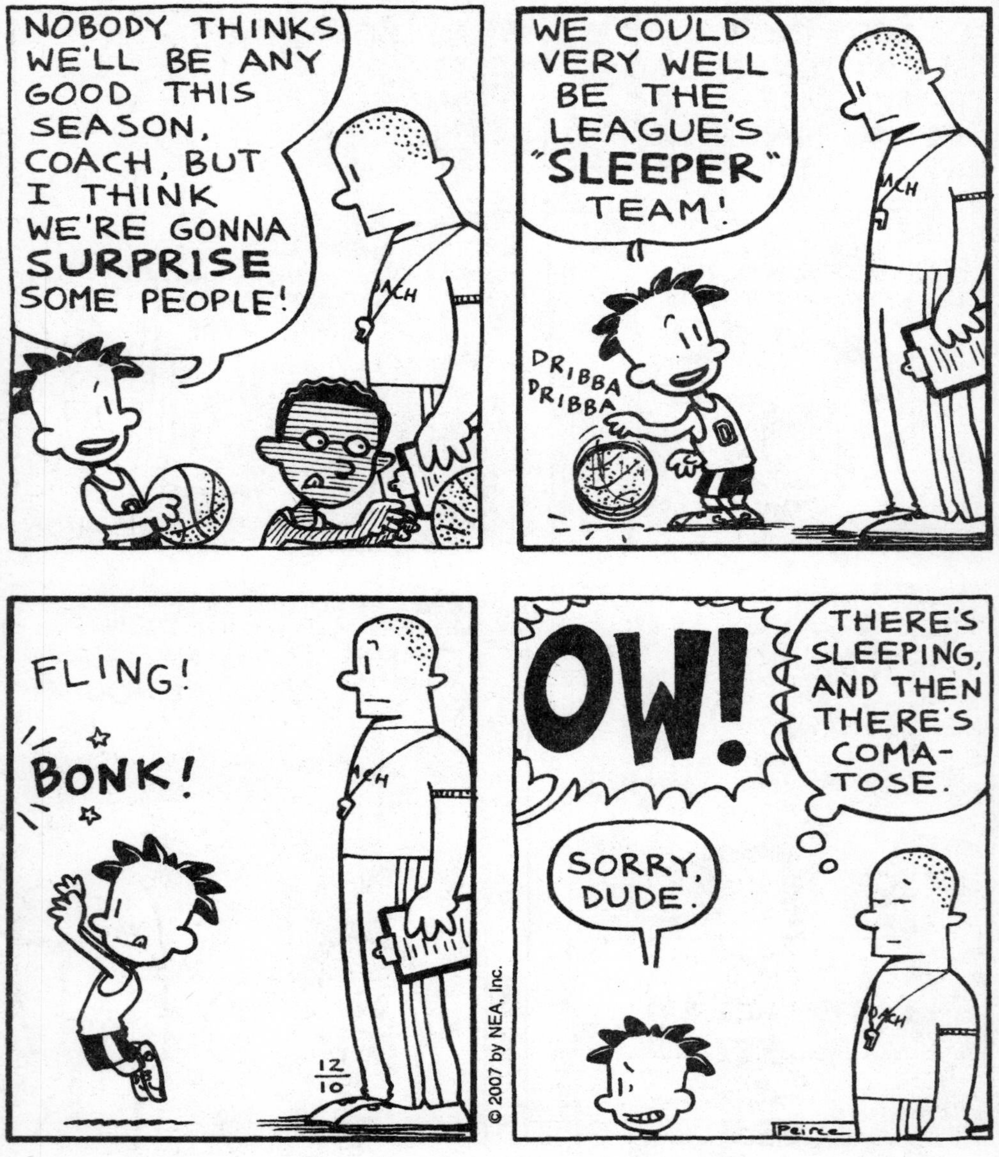
NOBODY THINKS WE'LL BE ANY GOOD THIS SEASON, COACH, BUT I THINK WE'RE GONNA **SURPRISE** SOME PEOPLE!
WE COULD VERY WELL BE THE LEAGUE'S "**SLEEPER**" TEAM!
DRIBBA DRIBBA
FLING!
BONK!
12/10
© 2007 by NEA, Inc.
OW!
THERE'S SLEEPING, AND THEN THERE'S COMA-TOSE.
SORRY, DUDE.
Peirce

COACH, YOU DON'T SEEM CONVINCED THAT OUR TEAM HAS WHAT IT TAKES TO BE A **POWER-HOUSE!**
DON'T YOU THINK WE HAVE THE TOOLS TO WIN?
HEY, DORKUS, YOUR SHORTS ARE ON BACKWARD.
THEY ARE?
I DON'T THINK HAVING ENOUGH TOOLS IS A PROBLEM.
12/11
Peirce

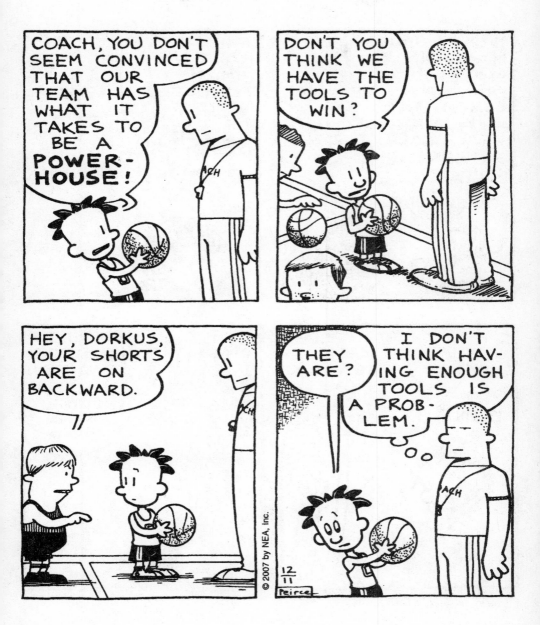

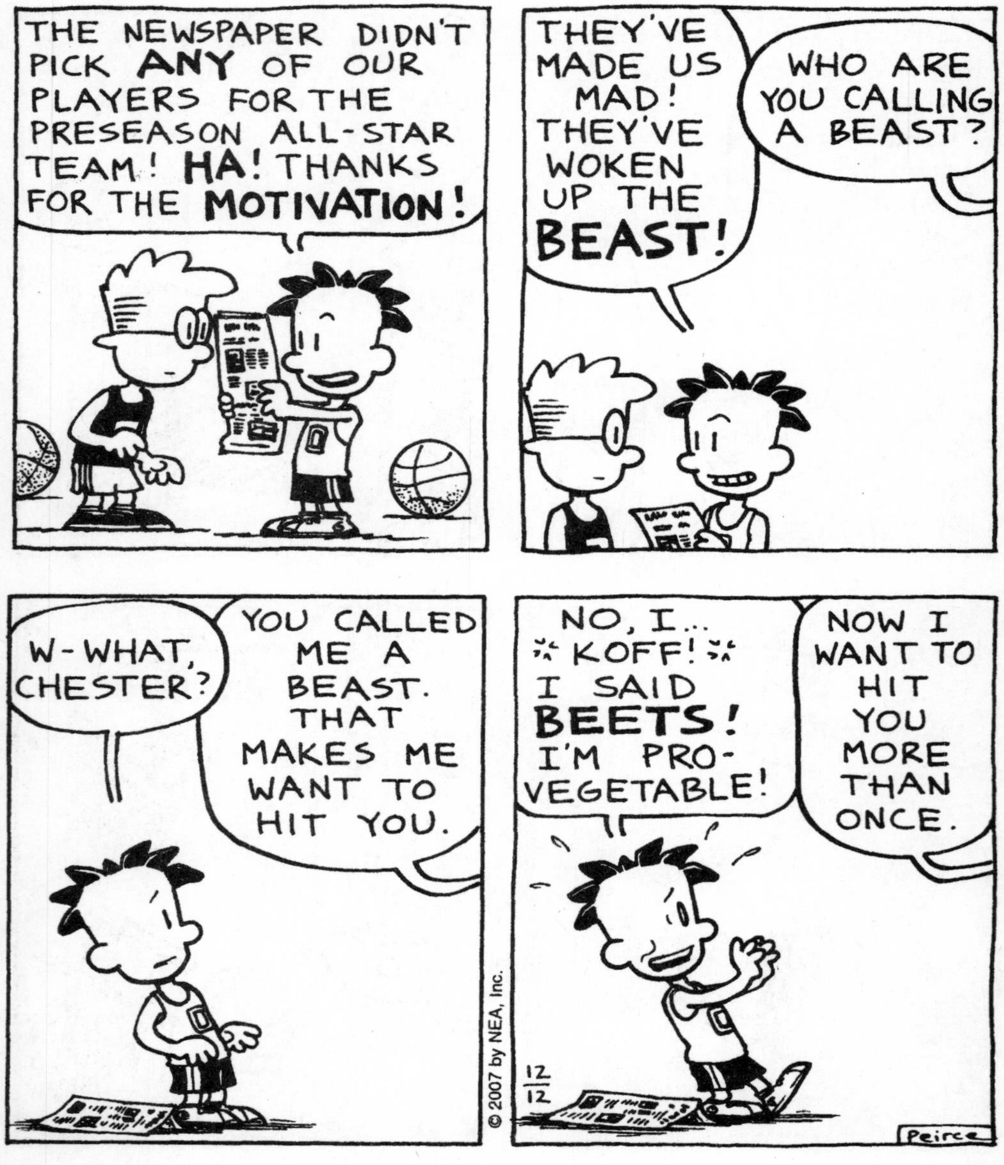
THE NEWSPAPER DIDN'T PICK **ANY** OF OUR PLAYERS FOR THE PRESEASON ALL-STAR TEAM! **HA!** THANKS FOR THE **MOTIVATION!**
THEY'VE MADE US MAD! THEY'VE WOKEN UP THE **BEAST!**
WHO ARE YOU CALLING A BEAST?
W-WHAT, CHESTER?
YOU CALLED ME A BEAST. THAT MAKES ME WANT TO HIT YOU.
NO, I... KOFF! I SAID **BEETS!** I'M PRO-VEGETABLE!
NOW I WANT TO HIT YOU MORE THAN ONCE.
© 2007 by NEA, Inc.
12/12
Peirce

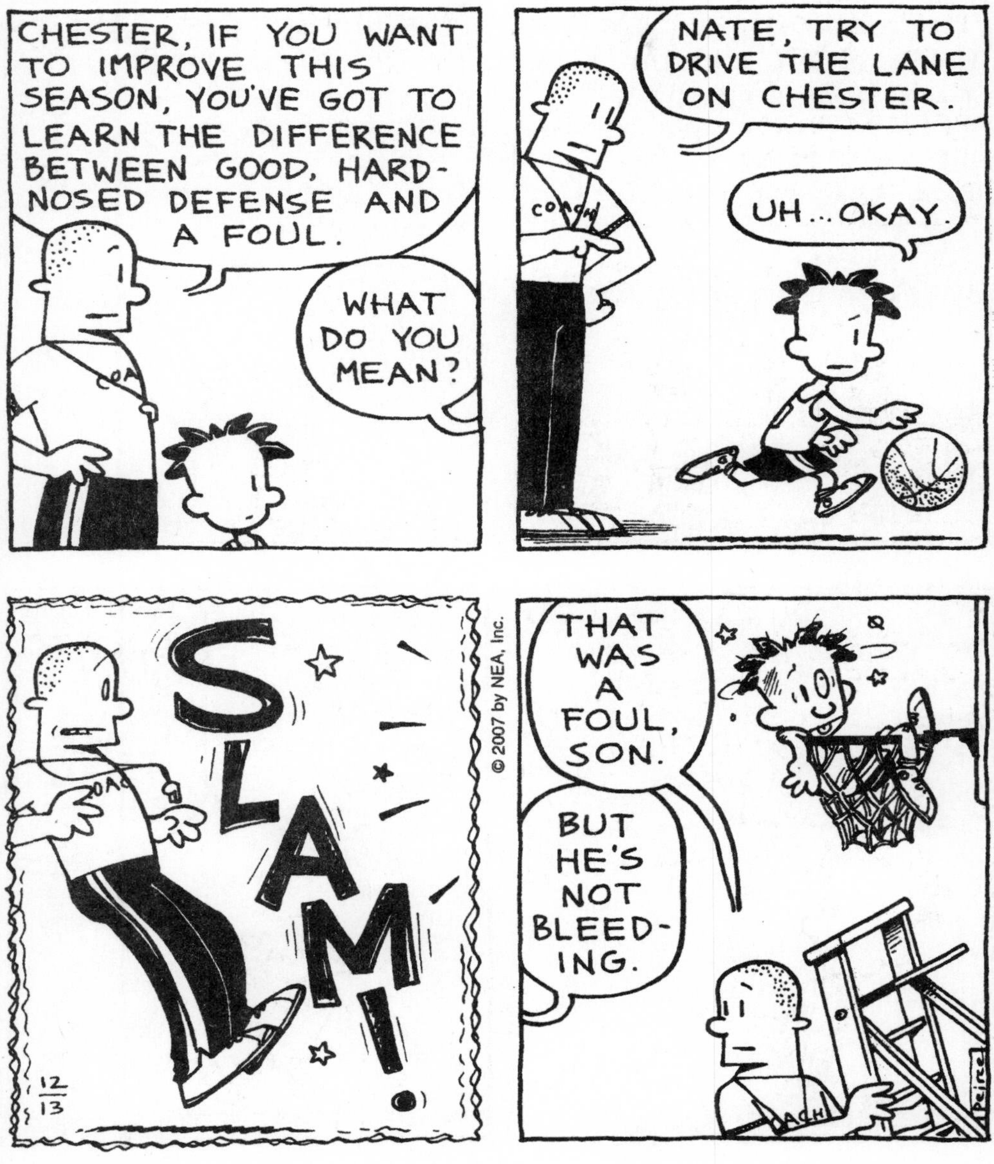
CHESTER, IF YOU WANT TO IMPROVE THIS SEASON, YOU'VE GOT TO LEARN THE DIFFERENCE BETWEEN GOOD, HARD-NOSED DEFENSE AND A FOUL.
WHAT DO YOU MEAN?
NATE, TRY TO DRIVE THE LANE ON CHESTER.
UH... OKAY.
SLAM!
THAT WAS A FOUL, SON.
BUT HE'S NOT BLEED-ING.
© 2007 by NEA, Inc.
12/13
Peirce

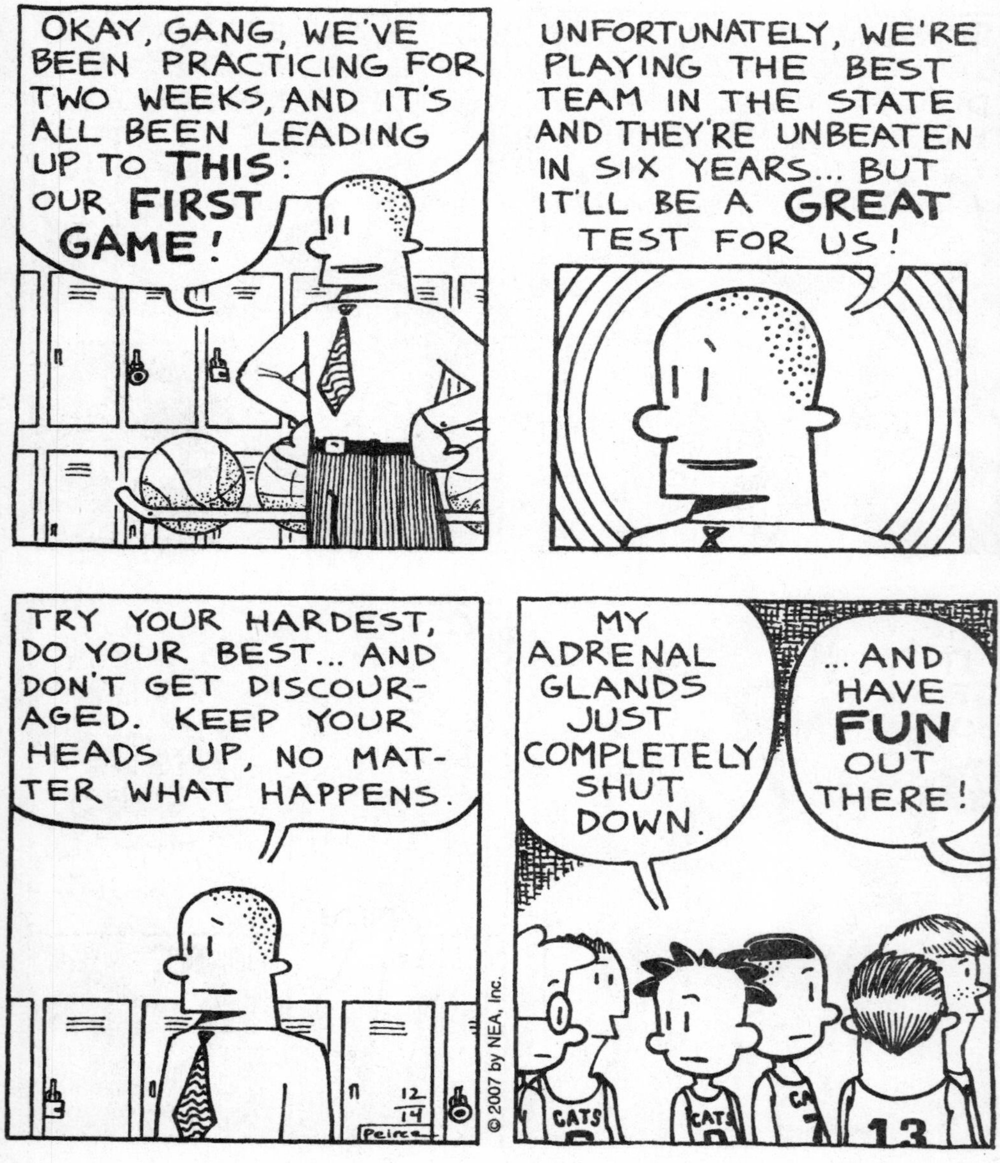
OKAY, GANG, WE'VE BEEN PRACTICING FOR TWO WEEKS, AND IT'S ALL BEEN LEADING UP TO THIS: OUR FIRST GAME!
UNFORTUNATELY, WE'RE PLAYING THE BEST TEAM IN THE STATE AND THEY'RE UNBEATEN IN SIX YEARS... BUT IT'LL BE A GREAT TEST FOR US!
TRY YOUR HARDEST, DO YOUR BEST... AND DON'T GET DISCOURAGED. KEEP YOUR HEADS UP, NO MATTER WHAT HAPPENS.
12/14
Peirce
MY ADRENAL GLANDS JUST COMPLETELY SHUT DOWN.
...AND HAVE FUN OUT THERE!
CATS
CATS
13

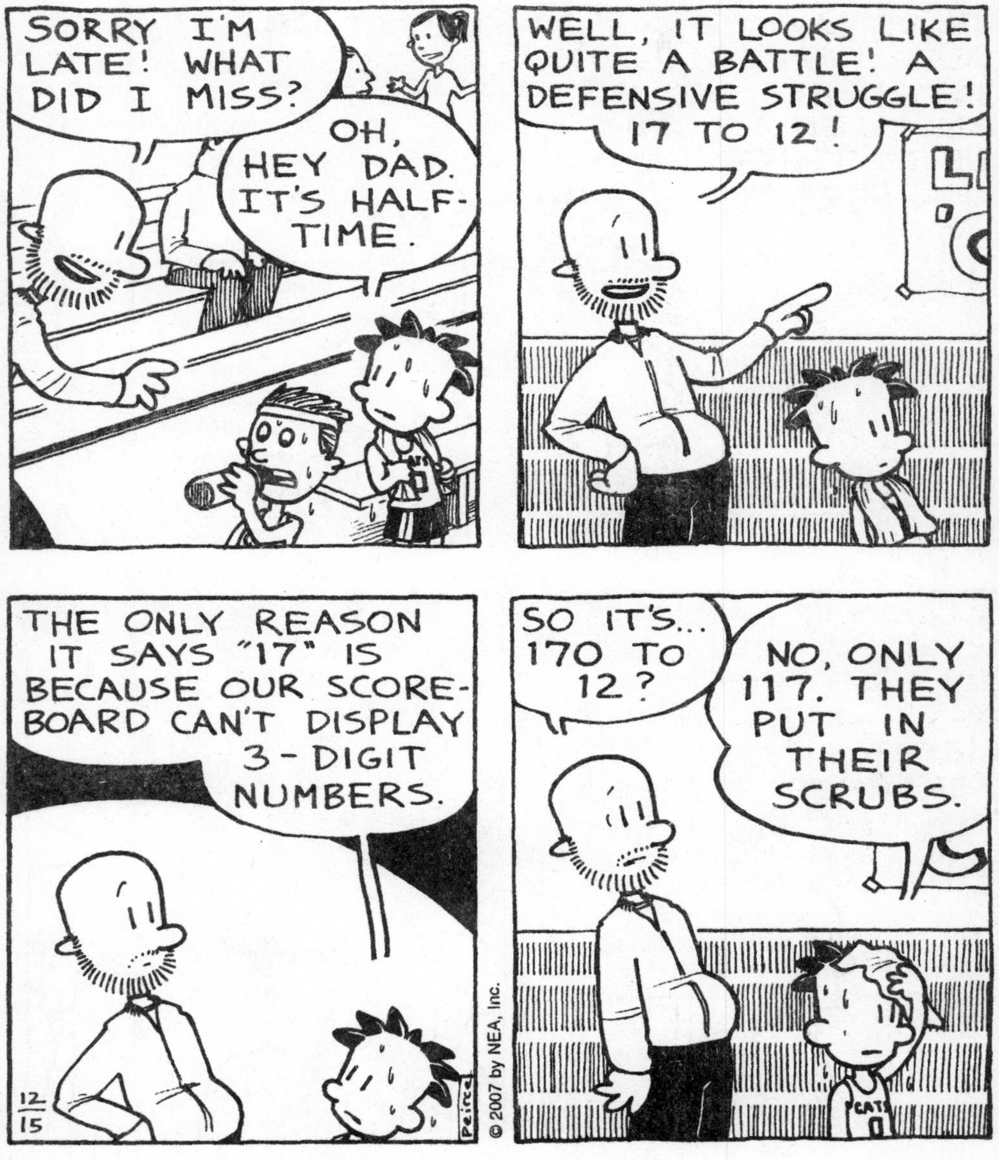
SORRY I'M LATE! WHAT DID I MISS?
OH, HEY DAD. IT'S HALF-TIME.
WELL, IT LOOKS LIKE QUITE A BATTLE! A DEFENSIVE STRUGGLE! 17 TO 12!
THE ONLY REASON IT SAYS "17" IS BECAUSE OUR SCORE-BOARD CAN'T DISPLAY 3-DIGIT NUMBERS.
12/15
Peirce
SO IT'S... 170 TO 12?
NO, ONLY 117. THEY PUT IN THEIR SCRUBS.

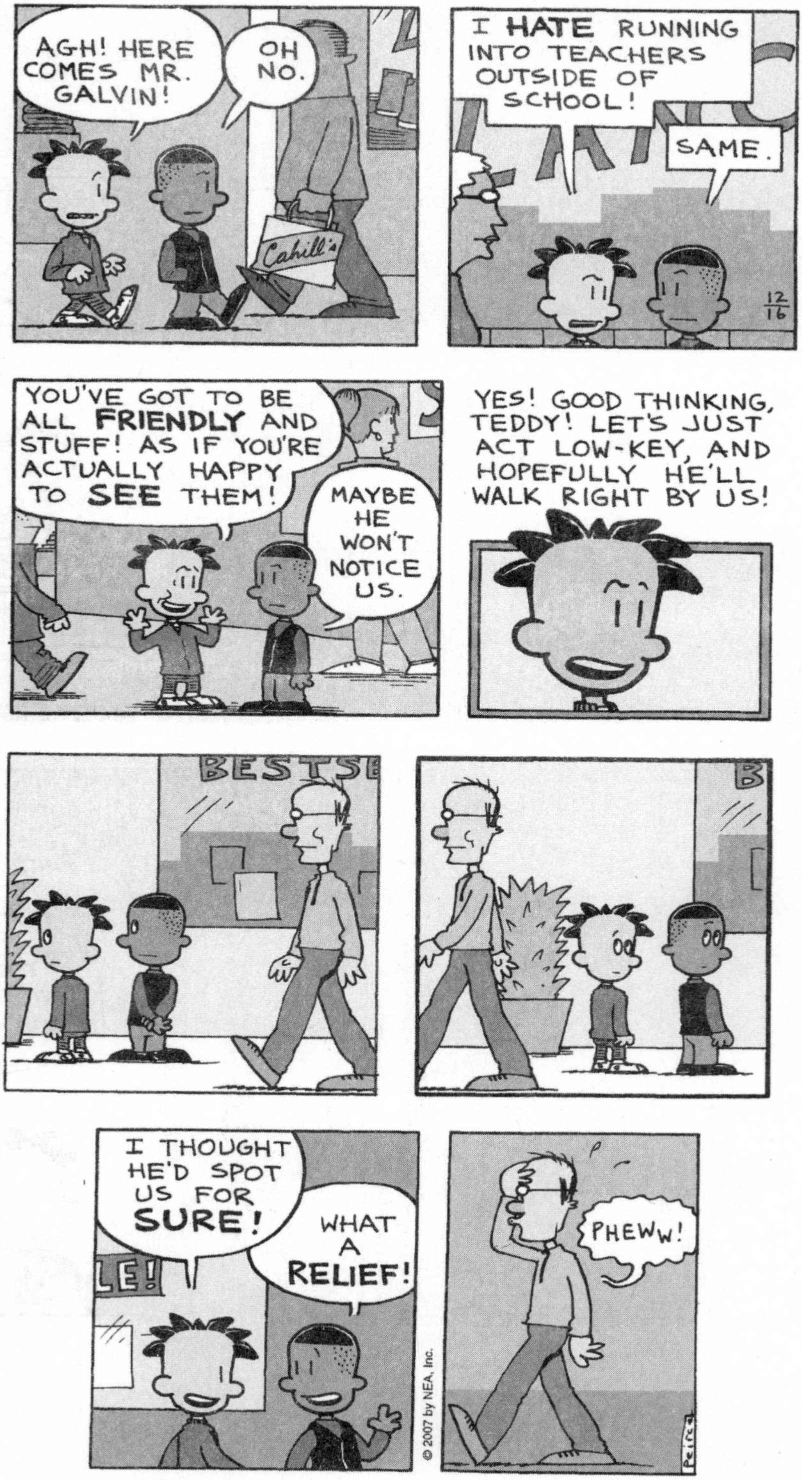
AGH! HERE COMES MR. GALVIN!
OH NO.
Cahill's
I HATE RUNNING INTO TEACHERS OUTSIDE OF SCHOOL!
SAME.
12/16
YOU'VE GOT TO BE ALL FRIENDLY AND STUFF! AS IF YOU'RE ACTUALLY HAPPY TO SEE THEM!
MAYBE HE WON'T NOTICE US.
YES! GOOD THINKING, TEDDY! LET'S JUST ACT LOW-KEY, AND HOPEFULLY HE'LL WALK RIGHT BY US!
BESTSE
B
I THOUGHT HE'D SPOT US FOR SURE!
WHAT A RELIEF!
LE!
PHEWW!
Peirce

DOGS VS. CATS

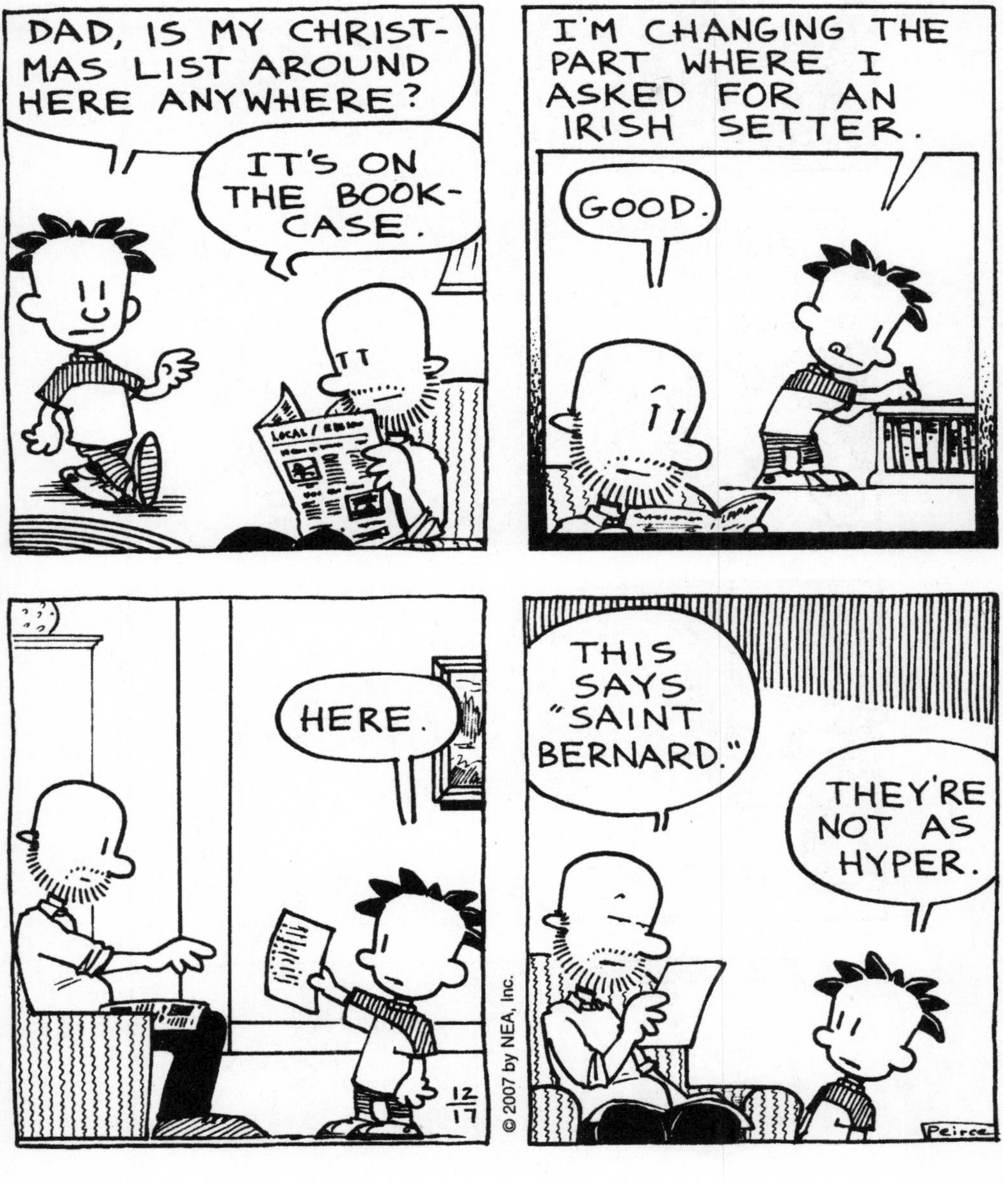

DAD, IS MY CHRISTMAS LIST AROUND HERE ANYWHERE?
IT'S ON THE BOOKCASE.
I'M CHANGING THE PART WHERE I ASKED FOR AN IRISH SETTER.
GOOD.
HERE.
© 2007 by NEA, Inc.
12/17
THIS SAYS "SAINT BERNARD."
THEY'RE NOT AS HYPER.
Peirce

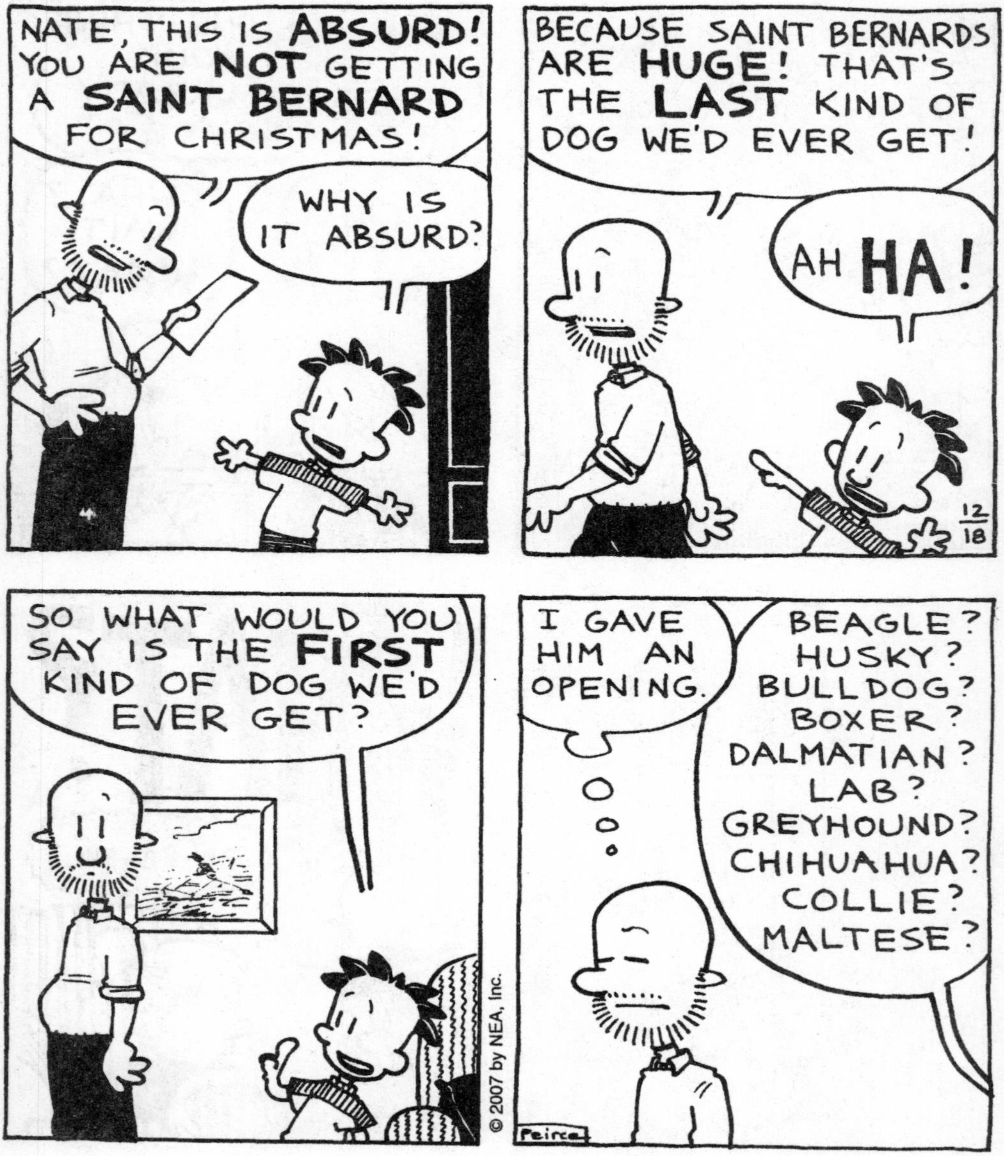
NATE, THIS IS **ABSURD**! YOU ARE **NOT** GETTING A **SAINT BERNARD** FOR CHRISTMAS!
WHY IS IT ABSURD?
BECAUSE SAINT BERNARDS ARE **HUGE**! THAT'S THE **LAST** KIND OF DOG WE'D EVER GET!
AH **HA**!
12/18
SO WHAT WOULD YOU SAY IS THE **FIRST** KIND OF DOG WE'D EVER GET?
I GAVE HIM AN OPENING.
BEAGLE? HUSKY? BULLDOG? BOXER? DALMATIAN? LAB? GREYHOUND? CHIHUAHUA? COLLIE? MALTESE?
© 2007 by NEA, Inc.
Peirce

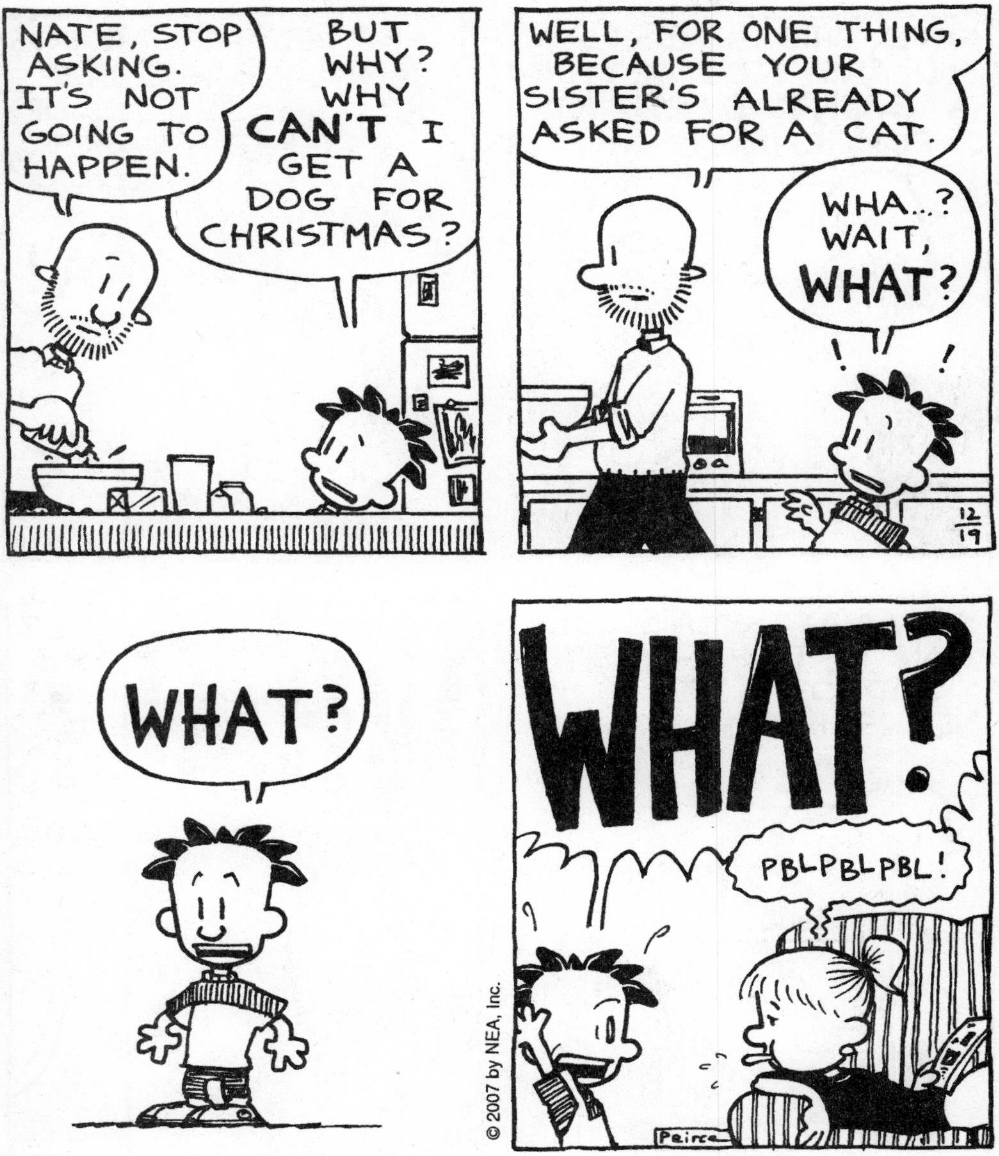
NATE, STOP ASKING. IT'S NOT GOING TO HAPPEN.
BUT WHY? WHY **CAN'T** I GET A DOG FOR CHRISTMAS?
WELL, FOR ONE THING, BECAUSE YOUR SISTER'S ALREADY ASKED FOR A CAT.
WHA...? WAIT, **WHAT?**
! !
12/19
WHAT?
WHAT?
PBLPBLPBL!
Peirce
© 2007 by NEA, Inc.

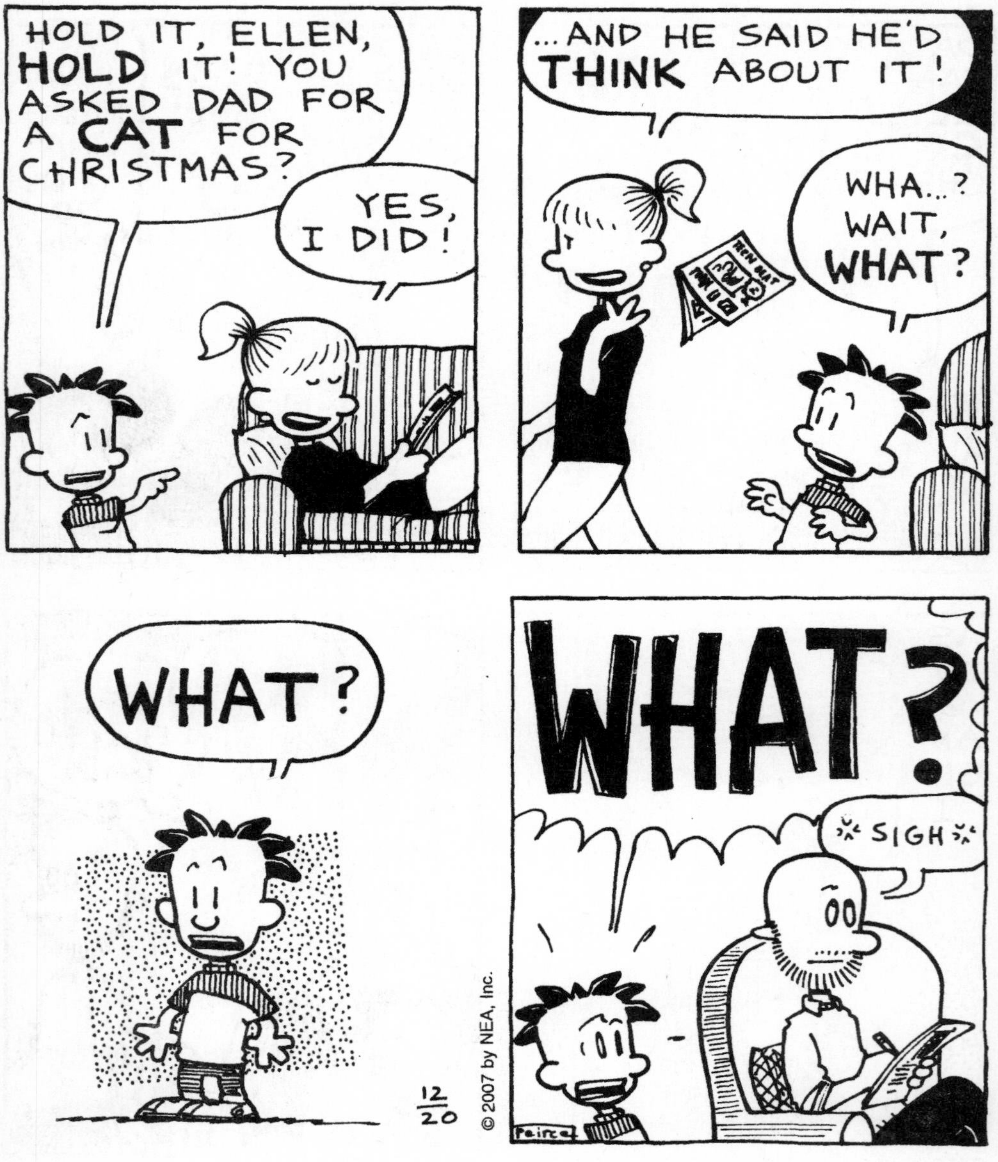
HOLD IT, ELLEN, HOLD IT! YOU ASKED DAD FOR A CAT FOR CHRISTMAS?
YES, I DID!
...AND HE SAID HE'D THINK ABOUT IT!
WHA...? WAIT, WHAT?
WHAT?
WHAT?
SIGH
12/20
Peirce

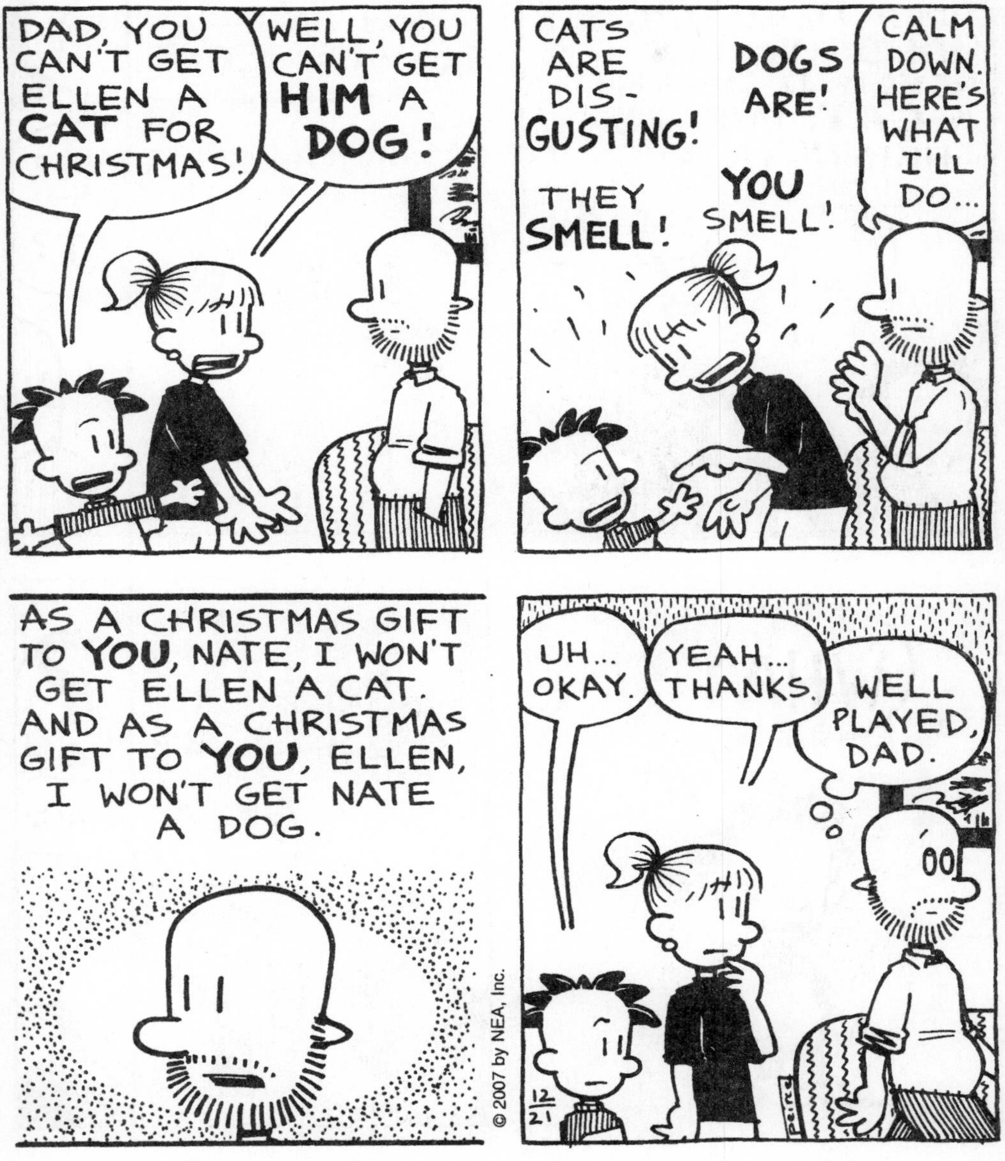
DAD, YOU CAN'T GET ELLEN A CAT FOR CHRISTMAS!
WELL, YOU CAN'T GET HIM A DOG!
CATS ARE DIS-GUSTING!
DOGS ARE!
THEY SMELL!
YOU SMELL!
CALM DOWN. HERE'S WHAT I'LL DO...
AS A CHRISTMAS GIFT TO YOU, NATE, I WON'T GET ELLEN A CAT. AND AS A CHRISTMAS GIFT TO YOU, ELLEN, I WON'T GET NATE A DOG.
© 2007 by NEA, Inc.
UH... OKAY.
YEAH... THANKS.
WELL PLAYED, DAD.
12/21
PEIRCE

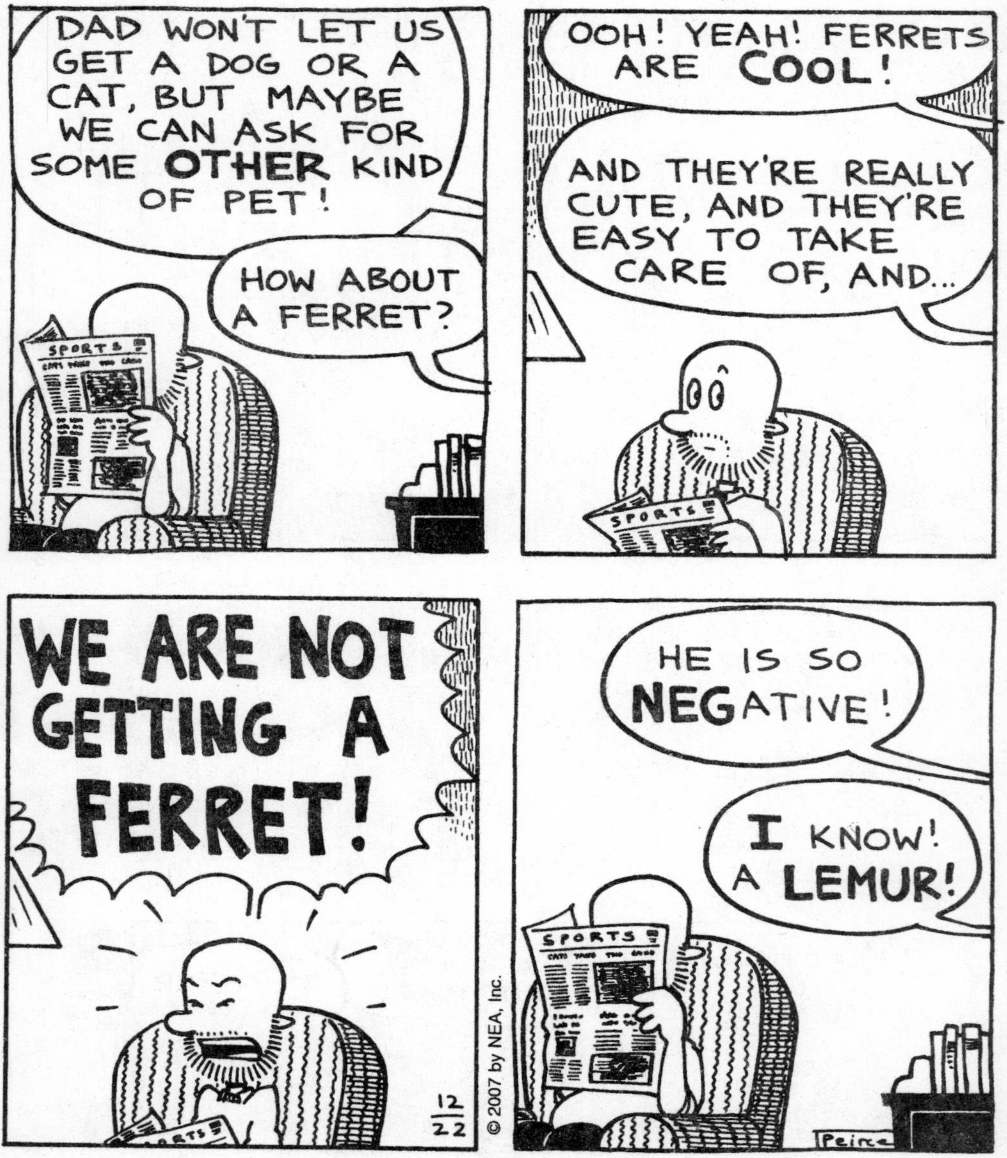
DAD WON'T LET US GET A DOG OR A CAT, BUT MAYBE WE CAN ASK FOR SOME OTHER KIND OF PET!
HOW ABOUT A FERRET?
SPORTS
OOH! YEAH! FERRETS ARE COOL!
AND THEY'RE REALLY CUTE, AND THEY'RE EASY TO TAKE CARE OF, AND...
SPORTS
WE ARE NOT GETTING A FERRET!
12/22
HE IS SO NEGATIVE!
I KNOW! A LEMUR!
SPORTS
Peirce

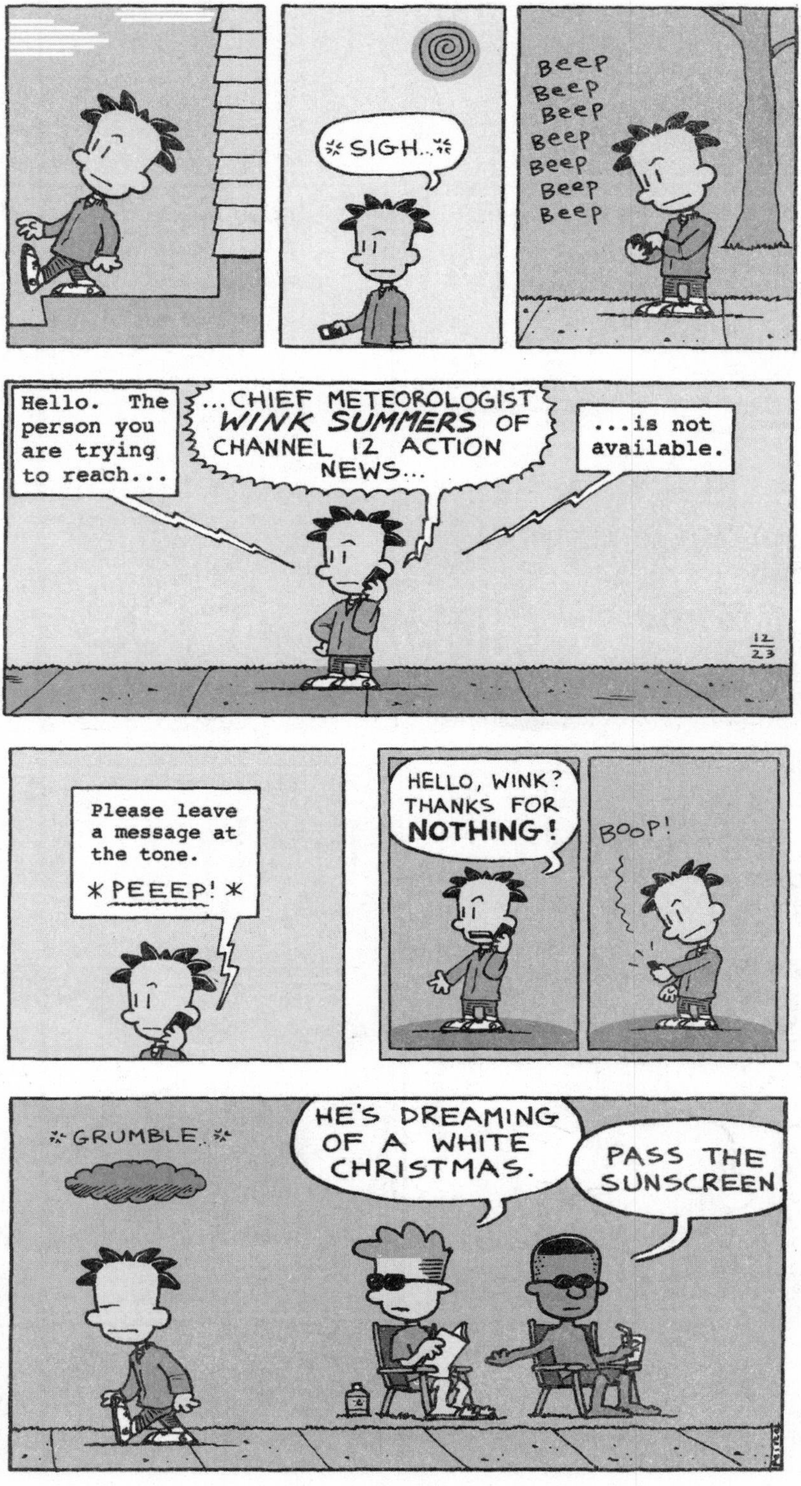

SIGH...
Beep Beep Beep Beep Beep Beep Beep
Hello. The person you are trying to reach...
...CHIEF METEOROLOGIST WINK SUMMERS OF CHANNEL 12 ACTION NEWS...
...is not available.
Please leave a message at the tone.
PEEEP!
HELLO, WINK? THANKS FOR NOTHING!
BOOP!
GRUMBLE...
HE'S DREAMING OF A WHITE CHRISTMAS.
PASS THE SUNSCREEN.

'TIS THE SEASON

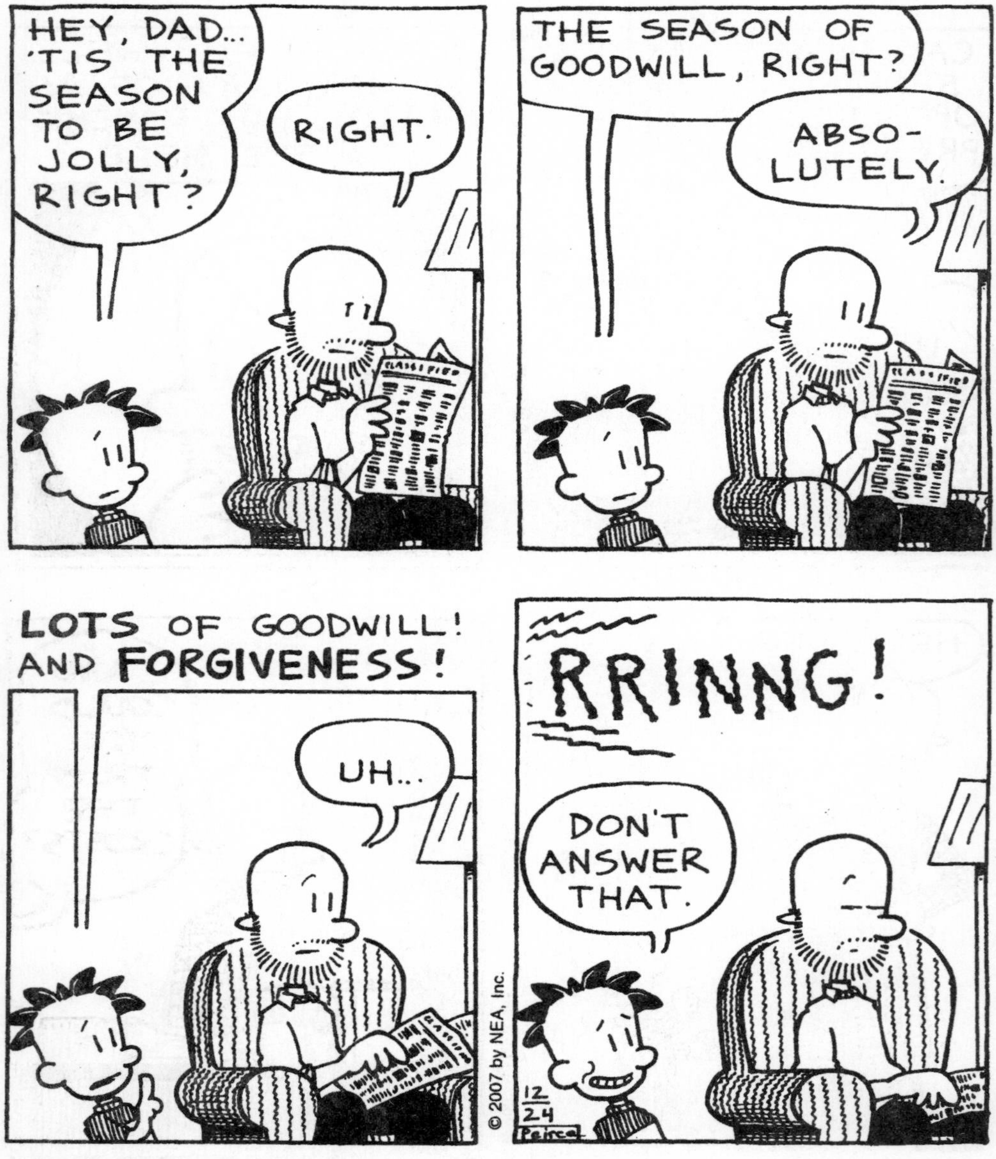
HEY, DAD... 'TIS THE SEASON TO BE JOLLY, RIGHT?
RIGHT.
THE SEASON OF GOODWILL, RIGHT?
ABSO-LUTELY.
LOTS OF GOODWILL! AND FORGIVENESS!
UH...
RRINNG!
DON'T ANSWER THAT.
© 2007 by NEA, Inc.
12 24
Peirce

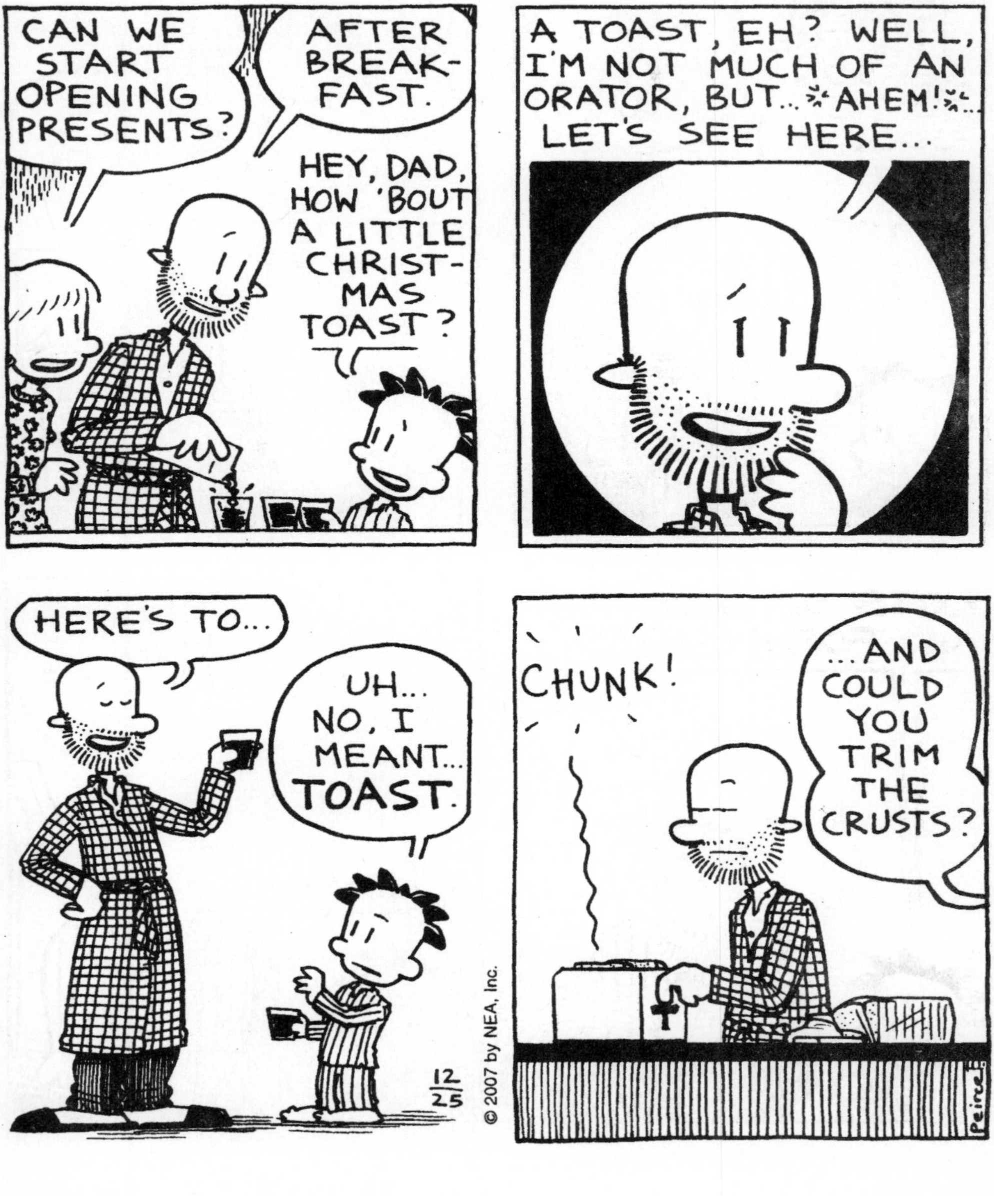
CAN WE START OPENING PRESENTS?
AFTER BREAK-FAST.
HEY, DAD, HOW 'BOUT A LITTLE CHRIST-MAS TOAST?
A TOAST, EH? WELL, I'M NOT MUCH OF AN ORATOR, BUT... AHEM!... LET'S SEE HERE...
HERE'S TO...
UH... NO, I MEANT... TOAST.
12/25
© 2007 by NEA, Inc.
CHUNK!
...AND COULD YOU TRIM THE CRUSTS?
Peirce

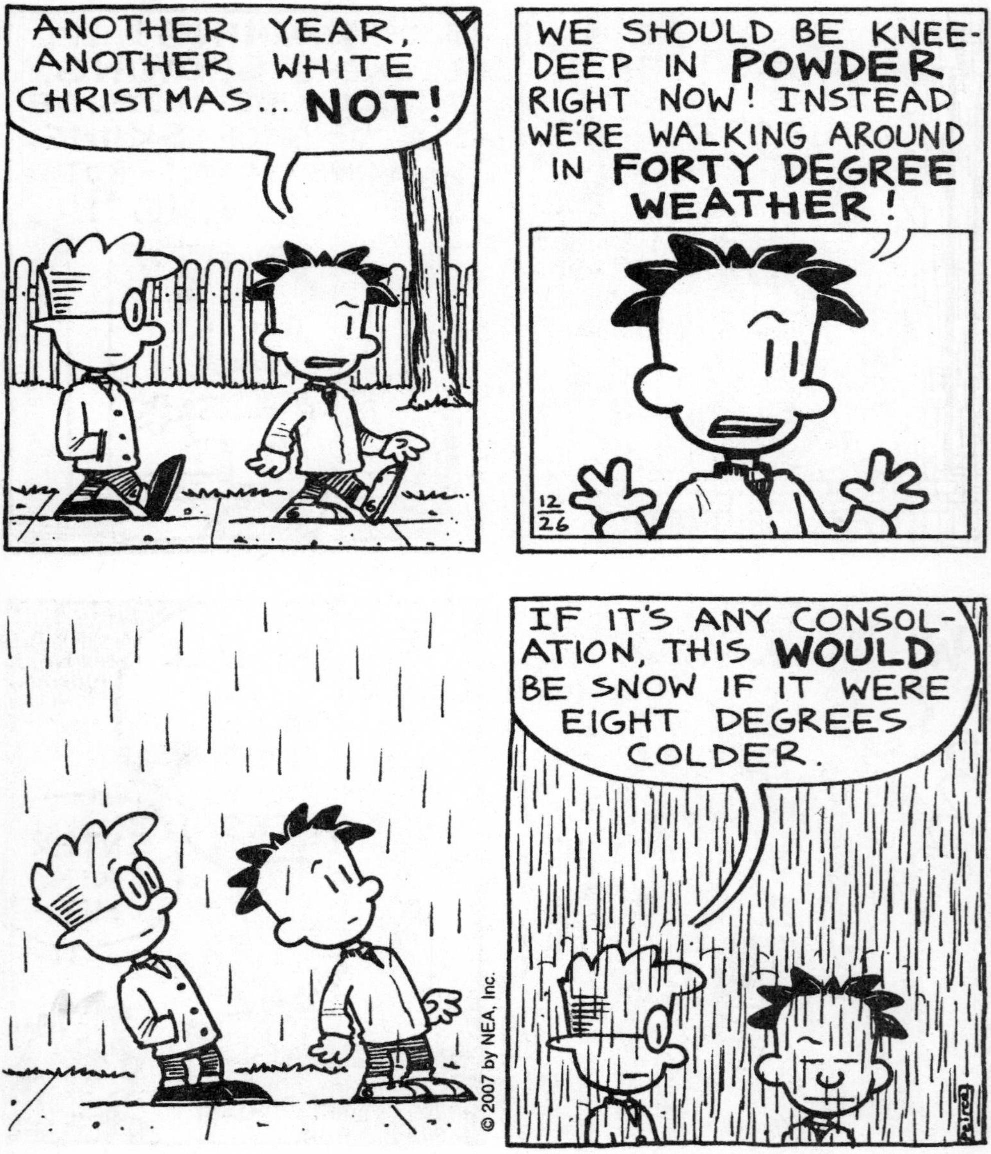
ANOTHER YEAR, ANOTHER WHITE CHRISTMAS... NOT!
WE SHOULD BE KNEE-DEEP IN POWDER RIGHT NOW! INSTEAD WE'RE WALKING AROUND IN FORTY DEGREE WEATHER!
12/26
IF IT'S ANY CONSOLATION, THIS WOULD BE SNOW IF IT WERE EIGHT DEGREES COLDER.
© 2007 by NEA, Inc.
Peirce

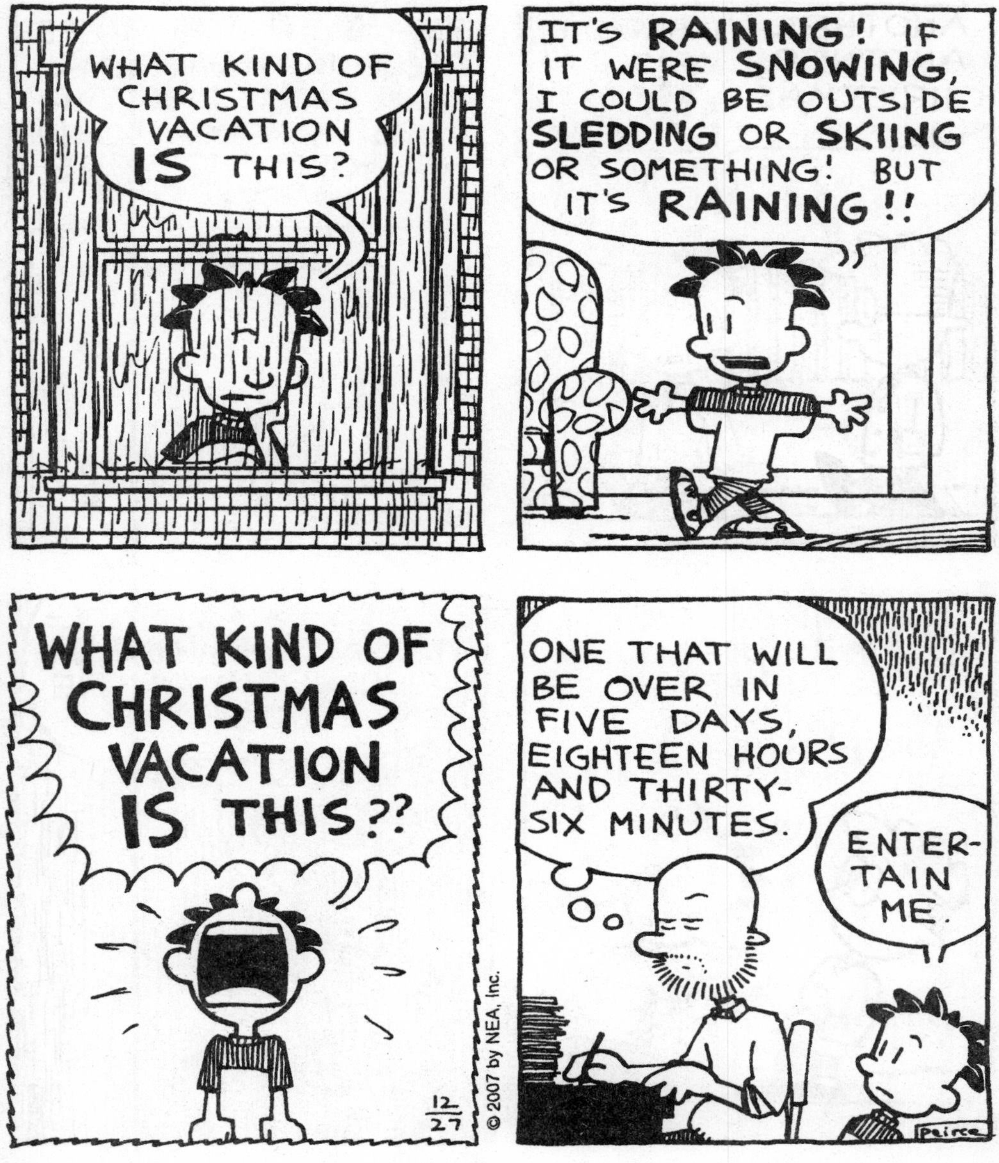
WHAT KIND OF CHRISTMAS VACATION IS THIS?
IT'S RAINING! IF IT WERE SNOWING, I COULD BE OUTSIDE SLEDDING OR SKIING OR SOMETHING! BUT IT'S RAINING!!
WHAT KIND OF CHRISTMAS VACATION IS THIS??
12/27
© 2007 by NEA, Inc.
ONE THAT WILL BE OVER IN FIVE DAYS, EIGHTEEN HOURS AND THIRTY-SIX MINUTES.
ENTER-TAIN ME.
PEIRCE

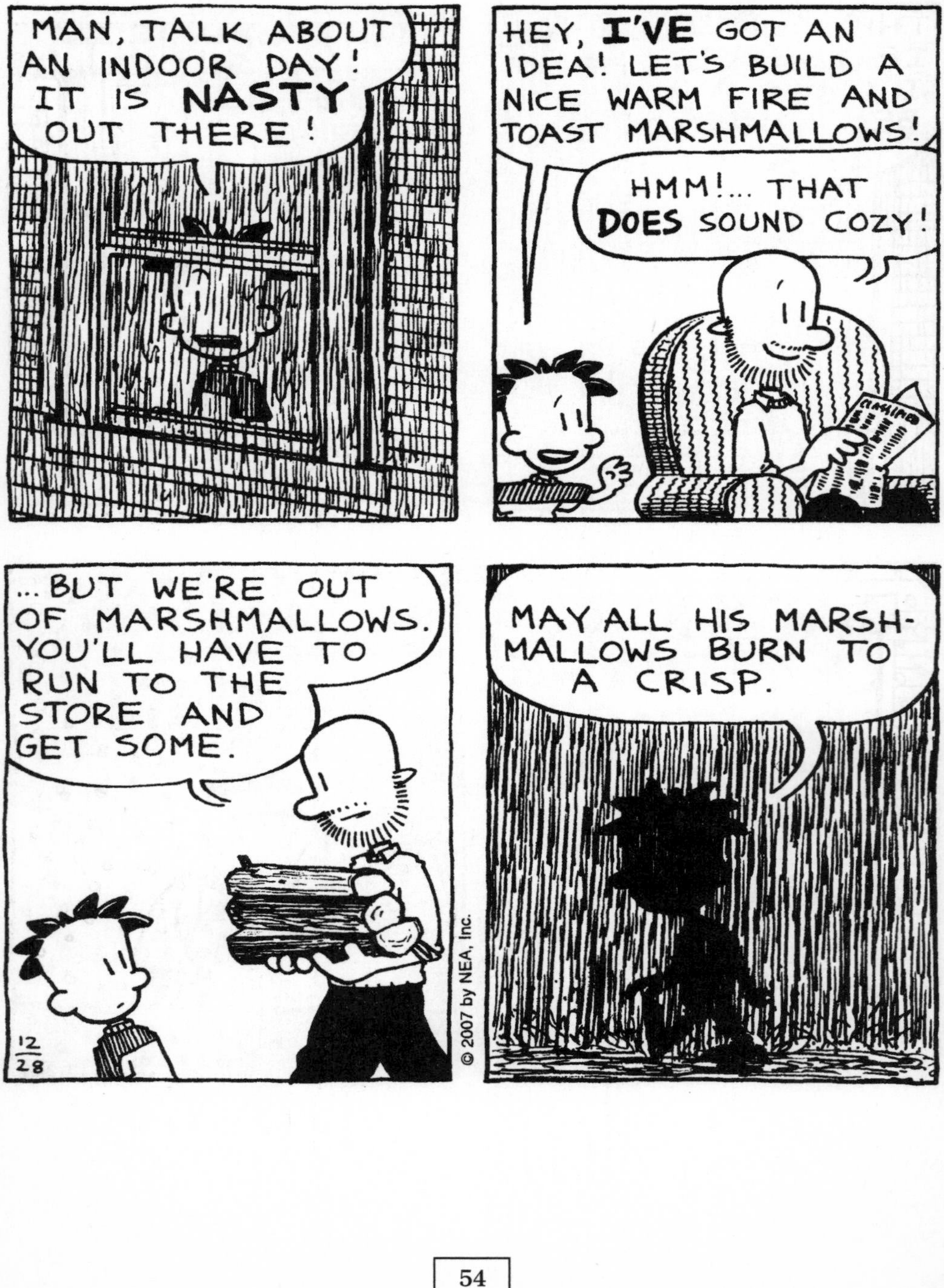
MAN, TALK ABOUT AN INDOOR DAY! IT IS **NASTY** OUT THERE!
HEY, **I'VE** GOT AN IDEA! LET'S BUILD A NICE WARM FIRE AND TOAST MARSHMALLOWS!
HMM!... THAT **DOES** SOUND COZY!
...BUT WE'RE OUT OF MARSHMALLOWS. YOU'LL HAVE TO RUN TO THE STORE AND GET SOME.
12/28
© 2007 by NEA, Inc.
MAY ALL HIS MARSH-MALLOWS BURN TO A CRISP.

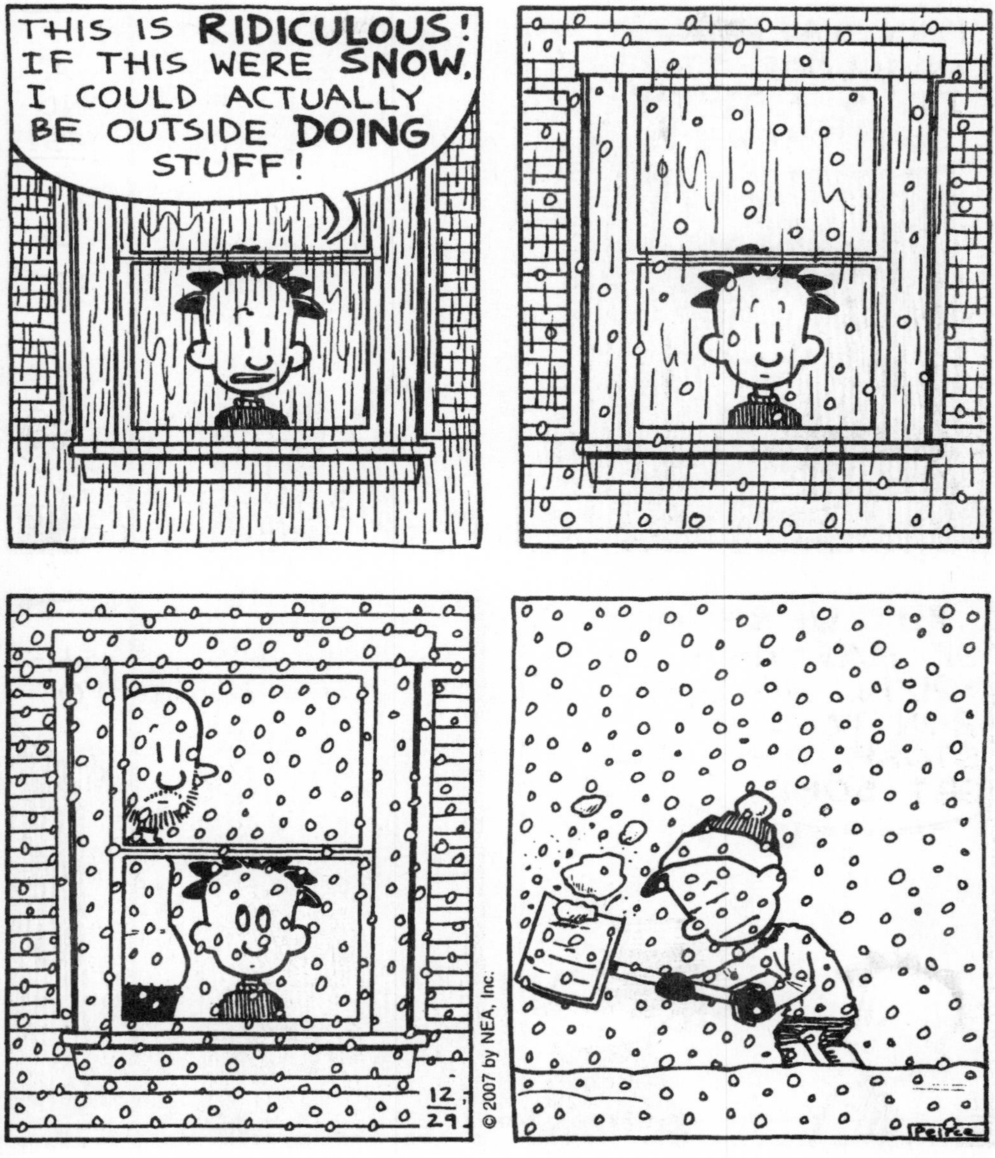
THIS IS RIDICULOUS! IF THIS WERE SNOW, I COULD ACTUALLY BE OUTSIDE DOING STUFF!
12, 29
Peirce

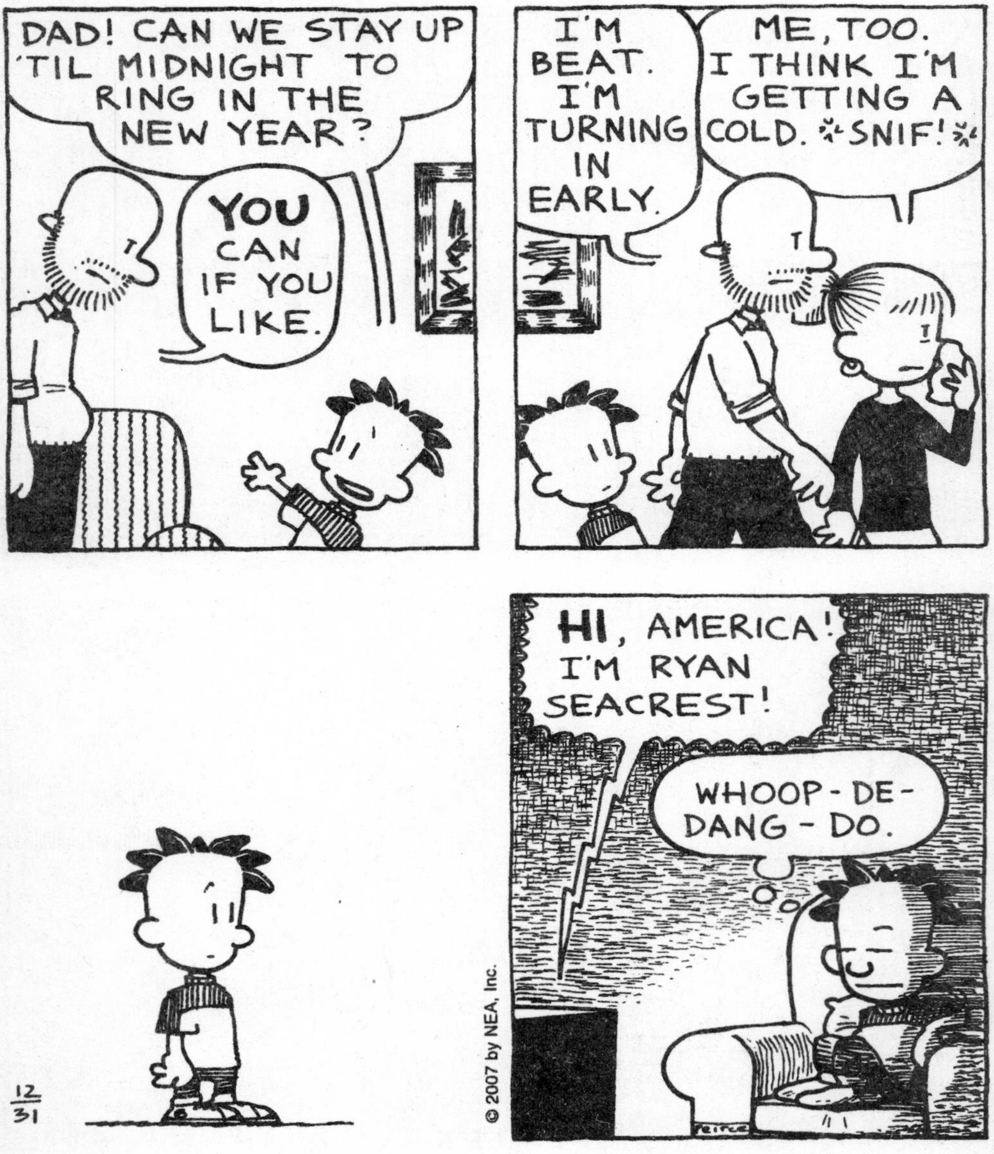
DAD! CAN WE STAY UP 'TIL MIDNIGHT TO RING IN THE NEW YEAR?
YOU CAN IF YOU LIKE.
I'M BEAT. I'M TURNING IN EARLY.
ME, TOO. I THINK I'M GETTING A COLD. SNIF!
HI, AMERICA! I'M RYAN SEACREST!
WHOOP-DE-DANG-DO.
12/31
© 2007 by NEA, Inc.

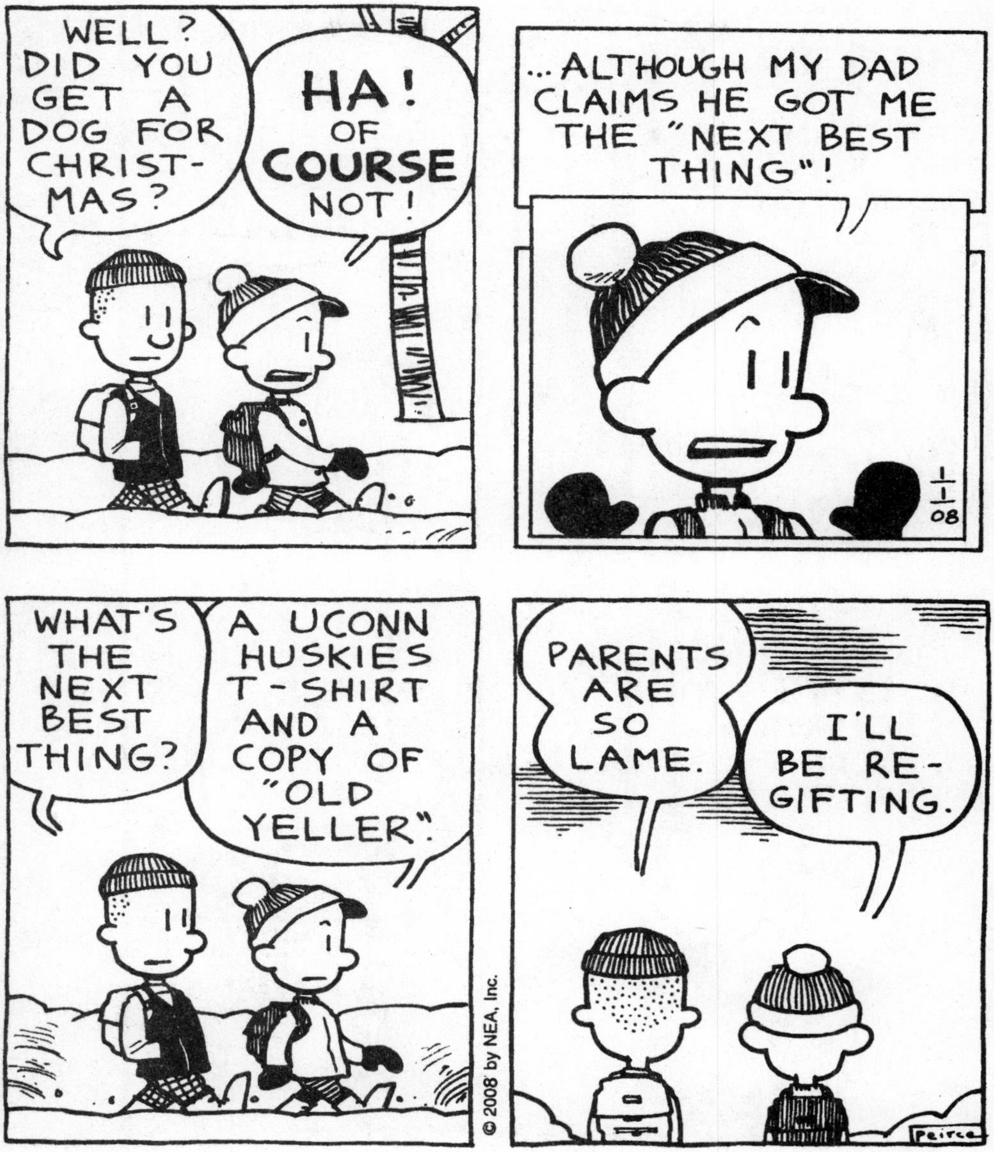
WELL? DID YOU GET A DOG FOR CHRIST-MAS?
HA! OF COURSE NOT!
...ALTHOUGH MY DAD CLAIMS HE GOT ME THE "NEXT BEST THING"!
1/1/08
WHAT'S THE NEXT BEST THING?
A UCONN HUSKIES T-SHIRT AND A COPY OF "OLD YELLER".
© 2008 by NEA, Inc.
PARENTS ARE SO LAME.
I'LL BE RE-GIFTING.
Peirce

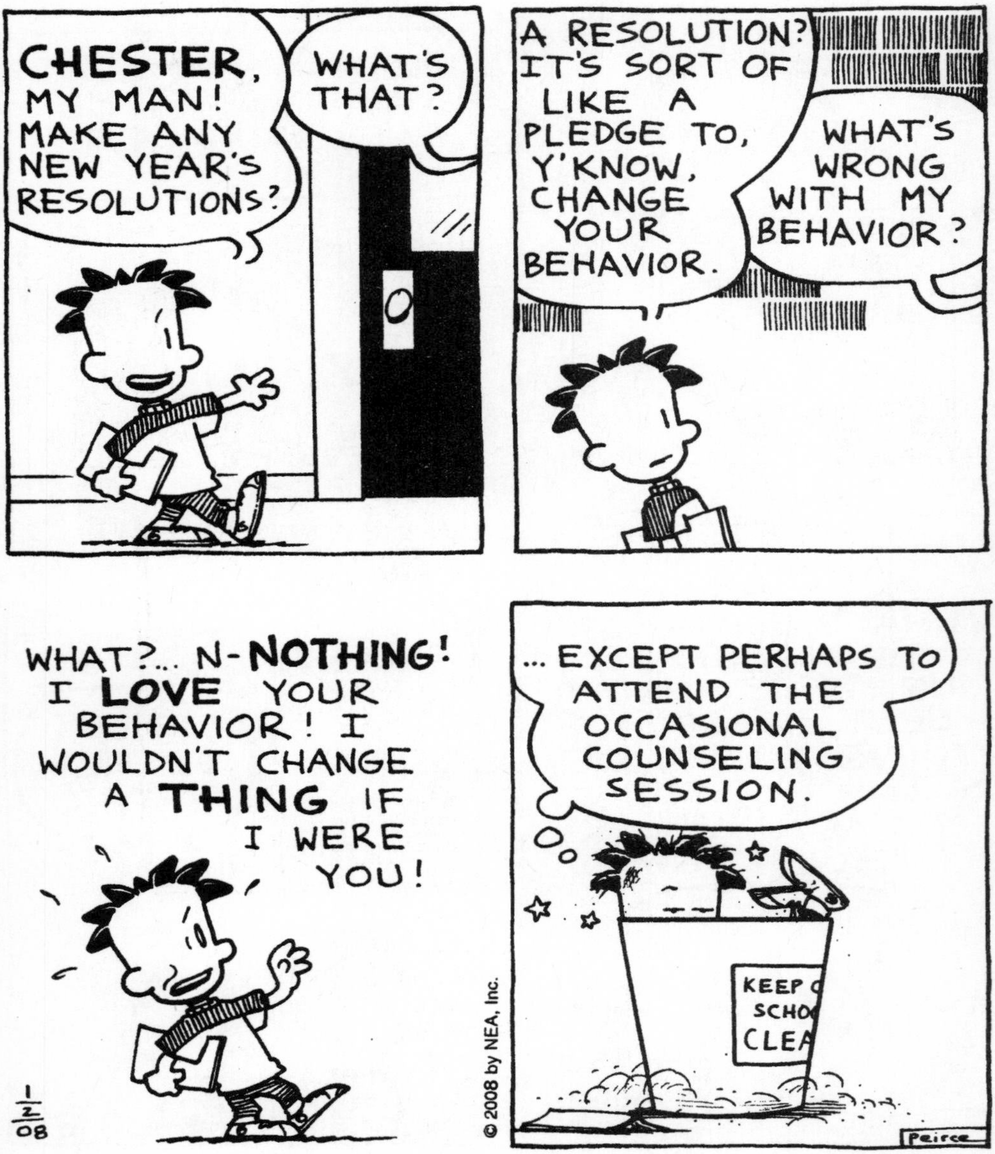
CHESTER, MY MAN! MAKE ANY NEW YEAR'S RESOLUTIONS?
WHAT'S THAT?
A RESOLUTION? IT'S SORT OF LIKE A PLEDGE TO, Y'KNOW, CHANGE YOUR BEHAVIOR.
WHAT'S WRONG WITH MY BEHAVIOR?
WHAT?... N-NOTHING! I LOVE YOUR BEHAVIOR! I WOULDN'T CHANGE A THING IF I WERE YOU!
1/2/08
© 2008 by NEA, Inc.
... EXCEPT PERHAPS TO ATTEND THE OCCASIONAL COUNSELING SESSION.
KEEP
SCHO
CLEA
Peirce

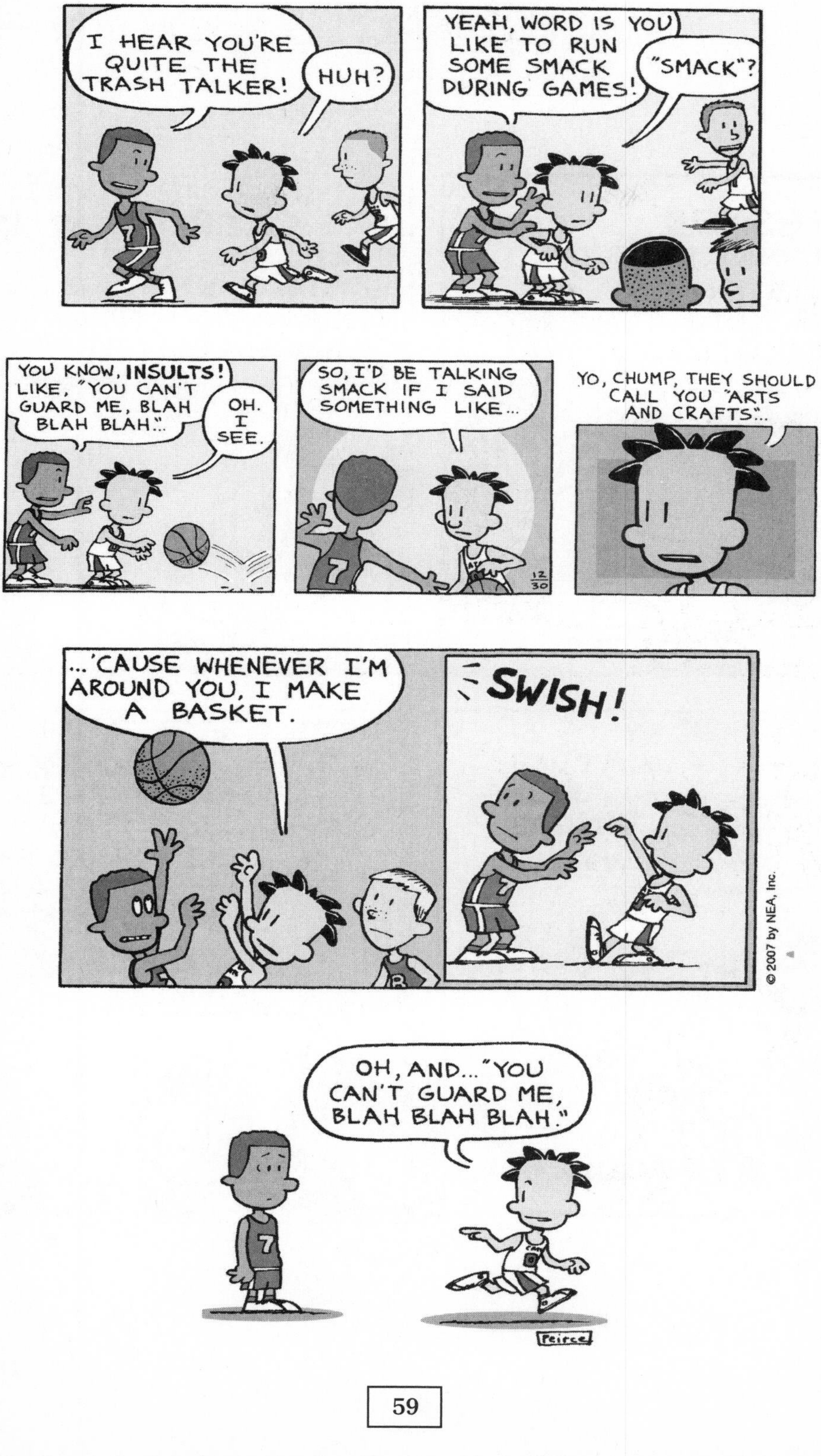
I HEAR YOU'RE QUITE THE TRASH TALKER!
HUH?
YEAH, WORD IS YOU LIKE TO RUN SOME SMACK DURING GAMES!
"SMACK"?
YOU KNOW, **INSULTS!** LIKE, "YOU CAN'T GUARD ME, BLAH BLAH BLAH."...
OH. I SEE.
SO, I'D BE TALKING SMACK IF I SAID SOMETHING LIKE...
12 30
YO, CHUMP, THEY SHOULD CALL YOU "ARTS AND CRAFTS"...
...'CAUSE WHENEVER I'M AROUND YOU, I MAKE A BASKET.
SWISH!
OH, AND... "YOU CAN'T GUARD ME, BLAH BLAH BLAH."
Peirce

THE BOOK OF FACTS = BOR-ING!

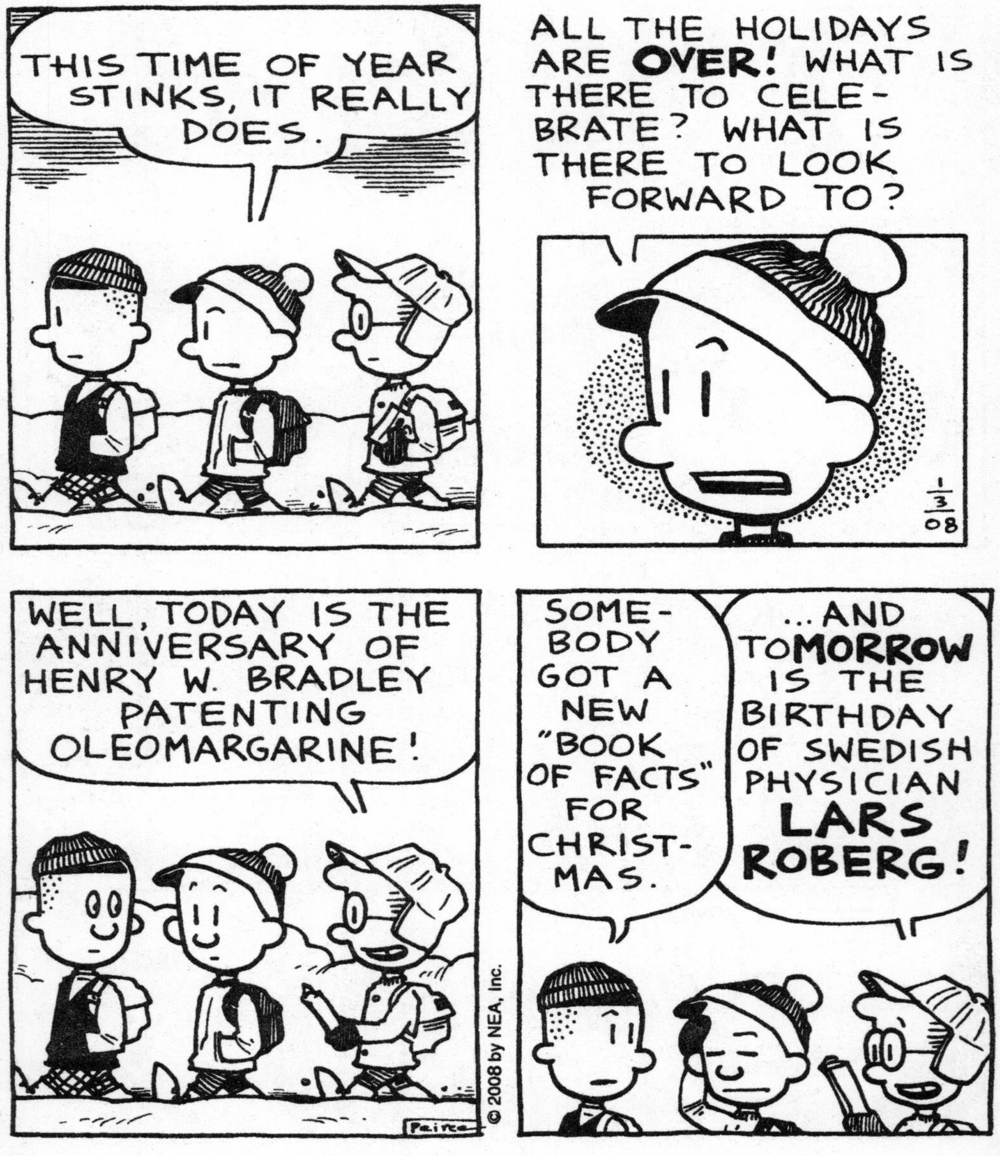
THIS TIME OF YEAR STINKS, IT REALLY DOES.
ALL THE HOLIDAYS ARE OVER! WHAT IS THERE TO CELE- BRATE? WHAT IS THERE TO LOOK FORWARD TO?
1/3/08
WELL, TODAY IS THE ANNIVERSARY OF HENRY W. BRADLEY PATENTING OLEOMARGARINE!
© 2008 by NEA, Inc.
Peirce
SOME- BODY GOT A NEW "BOOK OF FACTS" FOR CHRIST- MAS.
...AND TOMORROW IS THE BIRTHDAY OF SWEDISH PHYSICIAN LARS ROBERG!

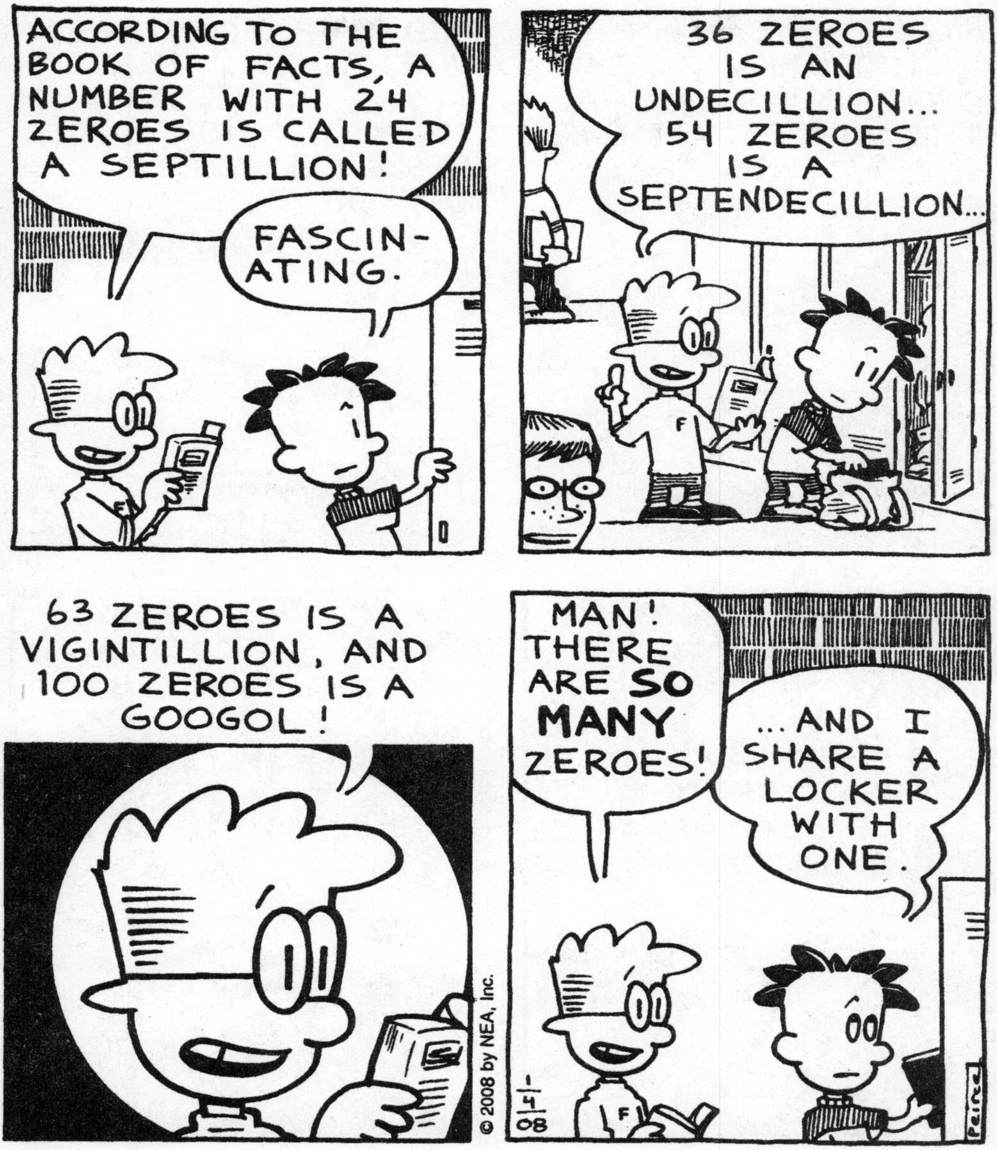
ACCORDING TO THE BOOK OF FACTS, A NUMBER WITH 24 ZEROES IS CALLED A SEPTILLION!
FASCIN-ATING.
36 ZEROES IS AN UNDECILLION... 54 ZEROES IS A SEPTENDECILLION...
63 ZEROES IS A VIGINTILLION, AND 100 ZEROES IS A GOOGOL!
MAN! THERE ARE **SO MANY** ZEROES!
...AND I SHARE A LOCKER WITH ONE.
© 2008 by NEA, Inc.
1/4/08
PEIRCE

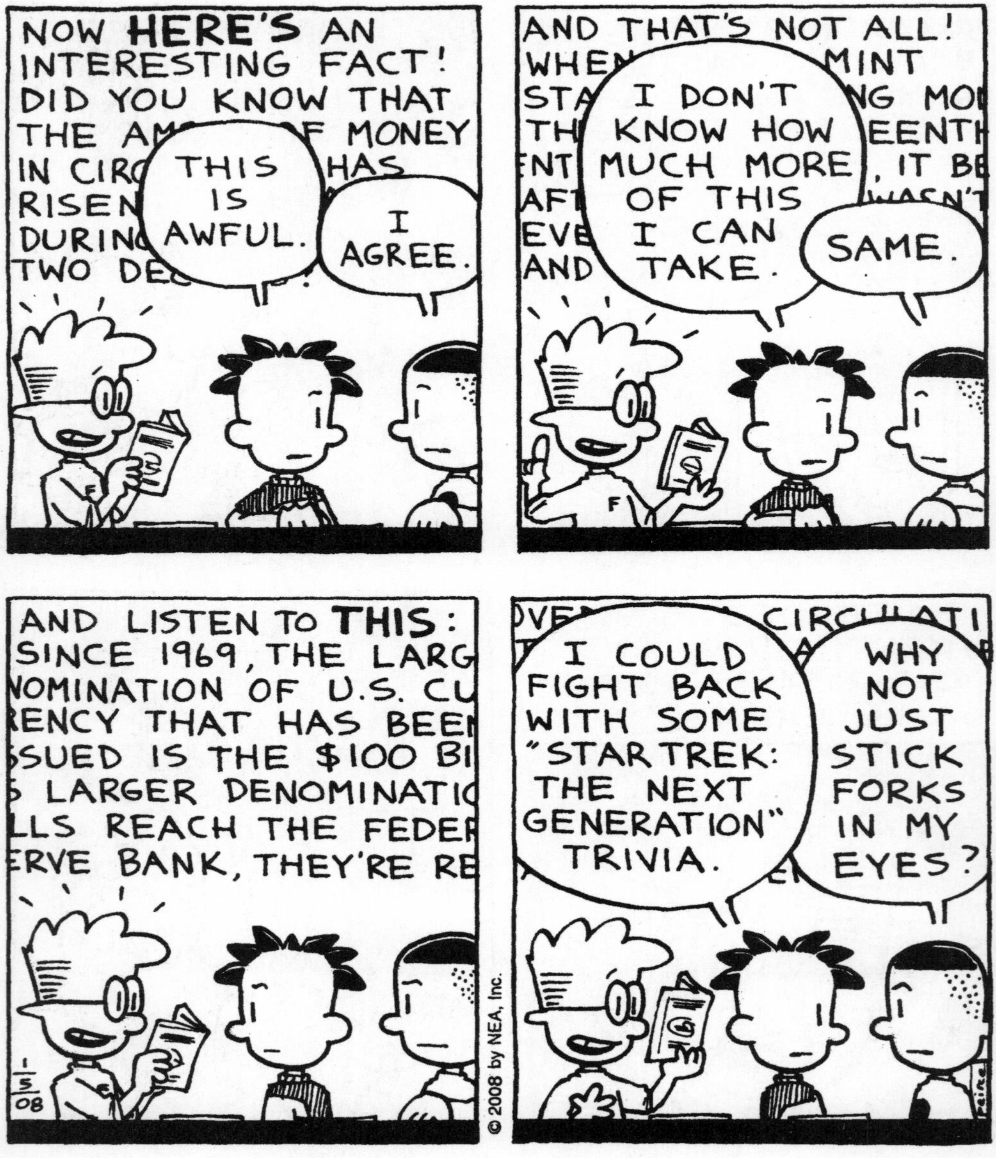
NOW HERE'S AN INTERESTING FACT! DID YOU KNOW THAT
THIS IS AWFUL.
I AGREE.
AND THAT'S NOT ALL!
I DON'T KNOW HOW MUCH MORE OF THIS I CAN TAKE.
SAME.
AND LISTEN TO THIS:
SINCE 1969, THE LARG
NOMINATION OF U.S. CU
RENCY THAT HAS BEEN
SSUED IS THE $100 BI
LARGER DENOMINATI
LLS REACH THE FEDER
ERVE BANK, THEY'RE RE
1/5/08
I COULD FIGHT BACK WITH SOME "STAR TREK: THE NEXT GENERATION" TRIVIA.
WHY NOT JUST STICK FORKS IN MY EYES?

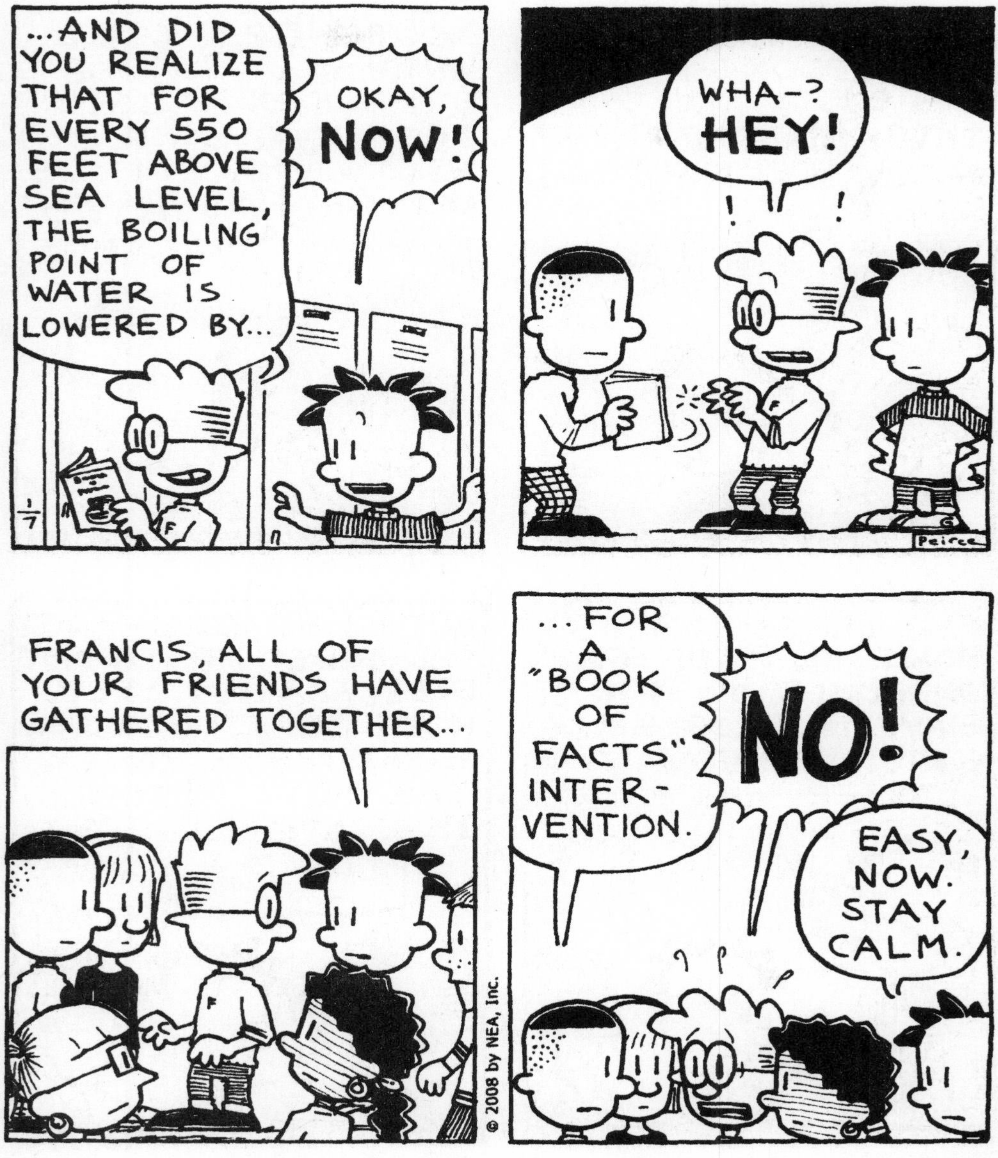
...AND DID YOU REALIZE THAT FOR EVERY 550 FEET ABOVE SEA LEVEL, THE BOILING POINT OF WATER IS LOWERED BY...
OKAY, NOW!
WHA-? HEY!
Peirce
FRANCIS, ALL OF YOUR FRIENDS HAVE GATHERED TOGETHER...
...FOR A "BOOK OF FACTS" INTER-VENTION.
NO!
EASY, NOW. STAY CALM.
© 2008 by NEA, Inc.

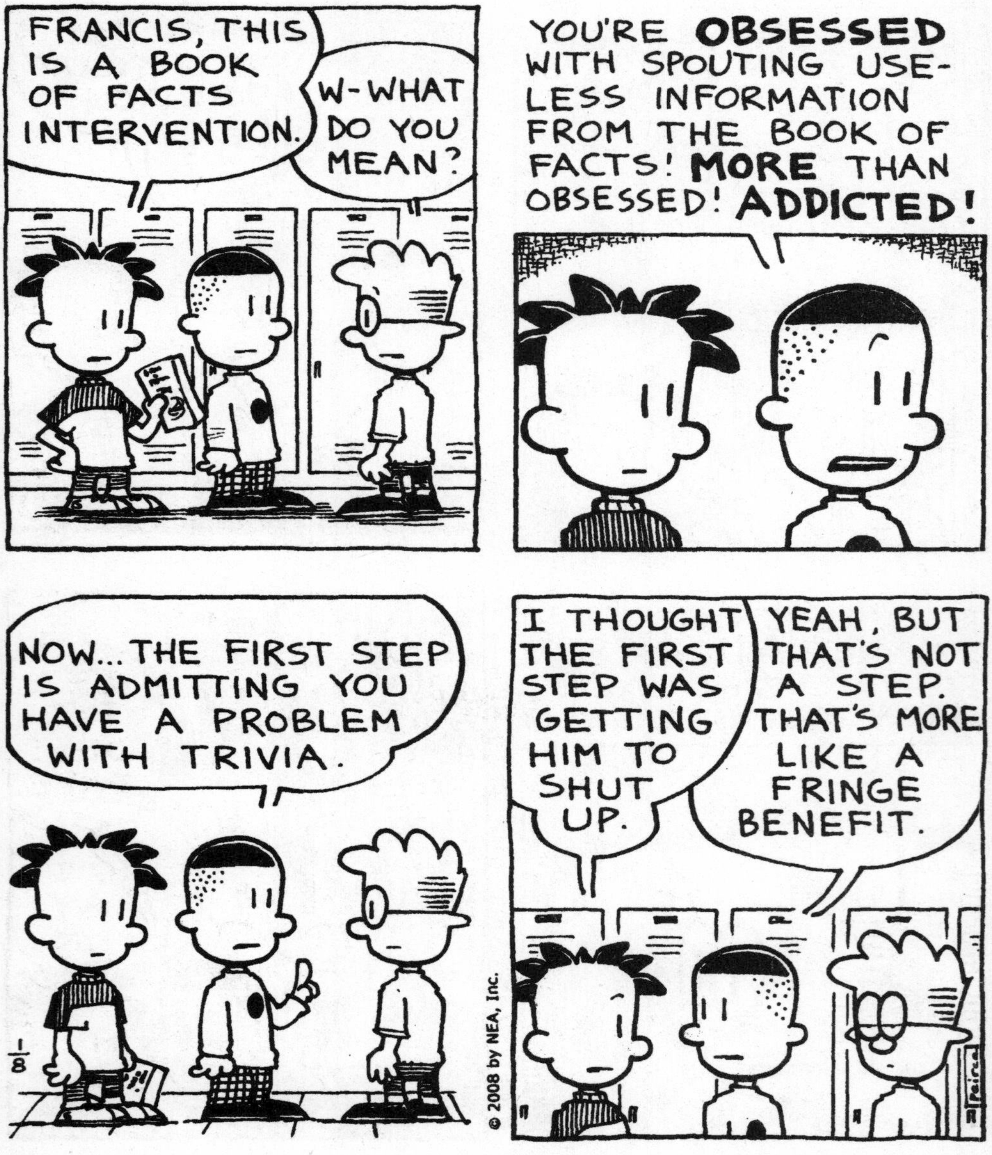
FRANCIS, THIS IS A BOOK OF FACTS INTERVENTION.
W-WHAT DO YOU MEAN?
YOU'RE **OBSESSED** WITH SPOUTING USE-LESS INFORMATION FROM THE BOOK OF FACTS! **MORE** THAN OBSESSED! **ADDICTED!**
NOW... THE FIRST STEP IS ADMITTING YOU HAVE A PROBLEM WITH TRIVIA.
I THOUGHT THE FIRST STEP WAS GETTING HIM TO SHUT UP.
YEAH, BUT THAT'S NOT A STEP. THAT'S MORE LIKE A FRINGE BENEFIT.
1/8
© 2008 by NEA, Inc.

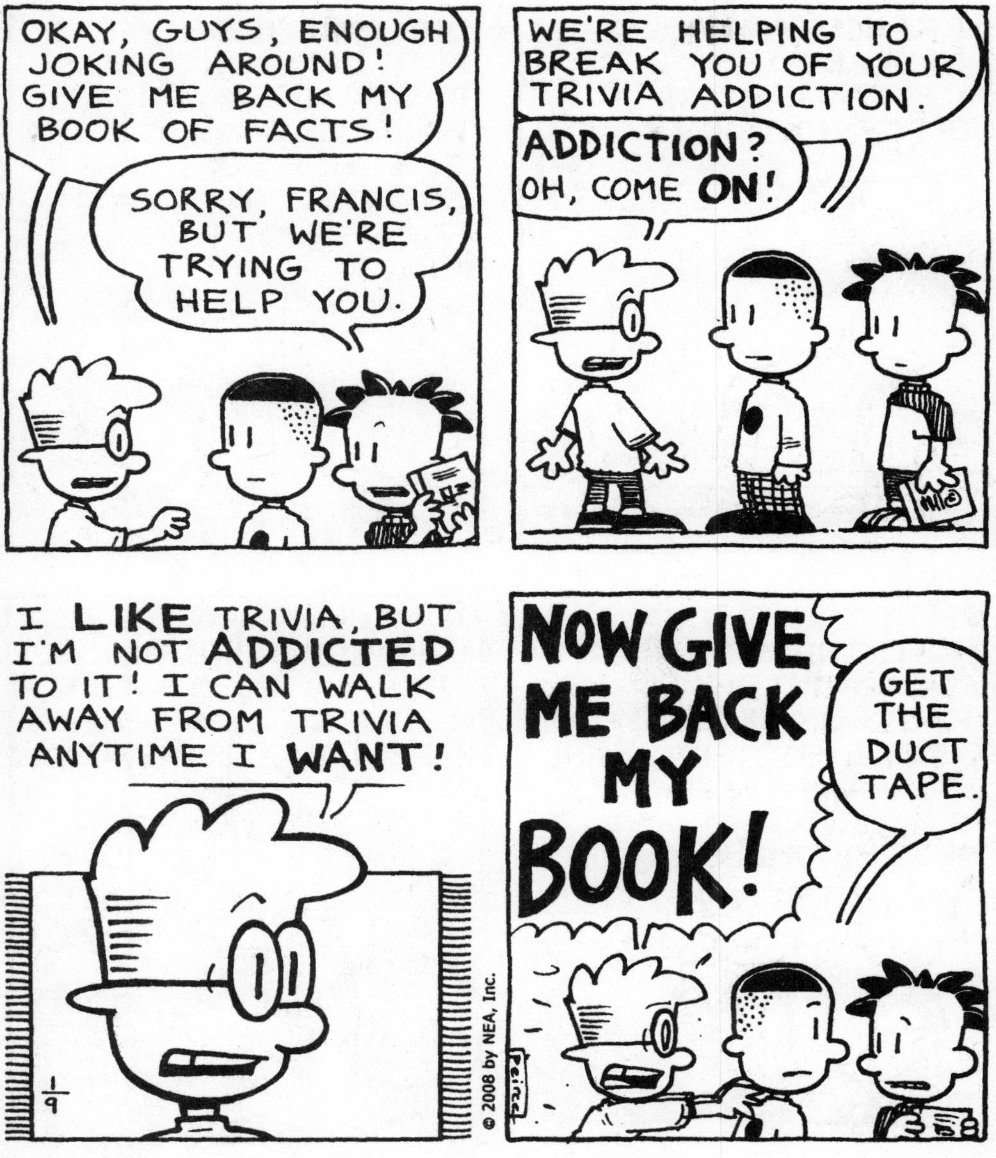
OKAY, GUYS, ENOUGH JOKING AROUND! GIVE ME BACK MY BOOK OF FACTS!
SORRY, FRANCIS, BUT WE'RE TRYING TO HELP YOU.
WE'RE HELPING TO BREAK YOU OF YOUR TRIVIA ADDICTION.
ADDICTION? OH, COME ON!
I LIKE TRIVIA, BUT I'M NOT ADDICTED TO IT! I CAN WALK AWAY FROM TRIVIA ANYTIME I WANT!
NOW GIVE ME BACK MY BOOK!
GET THE DUCT TAPE.
1/9
© 2008 by NEA, Inc.

HOW'S FRANCIS DOING WITHOUT HIS BOOK OF FACTS?
NOT GOOD.
DID YOU KNOW THAT THE CAPITAL OF DJIBOUTI IS ROSEAU? WAIT!... NO, THAT CAN'T BE RIGHT... UH... THE CAPITAL OF ROSEAU IS...
UH... HOLD IT, LET ME START OVER!... DID YOU KNOW THAT THE COMPOSER ARTURO "HOT LIPS" O'FARRILL WAS... UM... NO, WAIT, HIS NICKNAME WASN'T "HOT LIPS", IT WAS... DANG, WHAT **WAS** IT?...
1/10
© 2008 by NEA, Inc.
OKAY, LET'S TALK ABOU
AILROADS! THE NUMBER
S OF TRACK
30 WAS O
BRITNEY S
NO, DOES
SENSE! I'LL HAVE G
HE'S TRYING TO FREE-STYLE.
THIS IS UGLY.

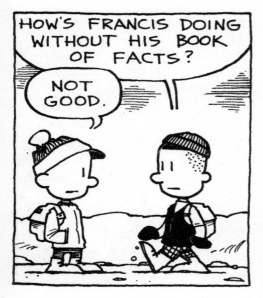

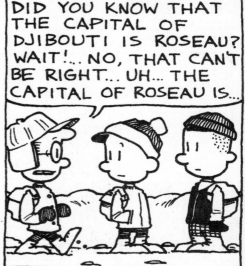

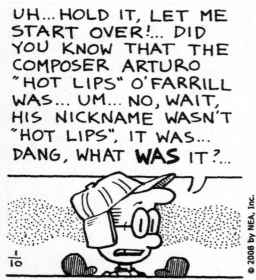

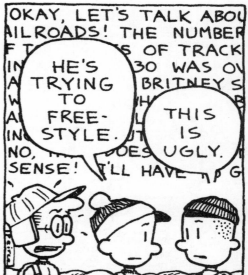

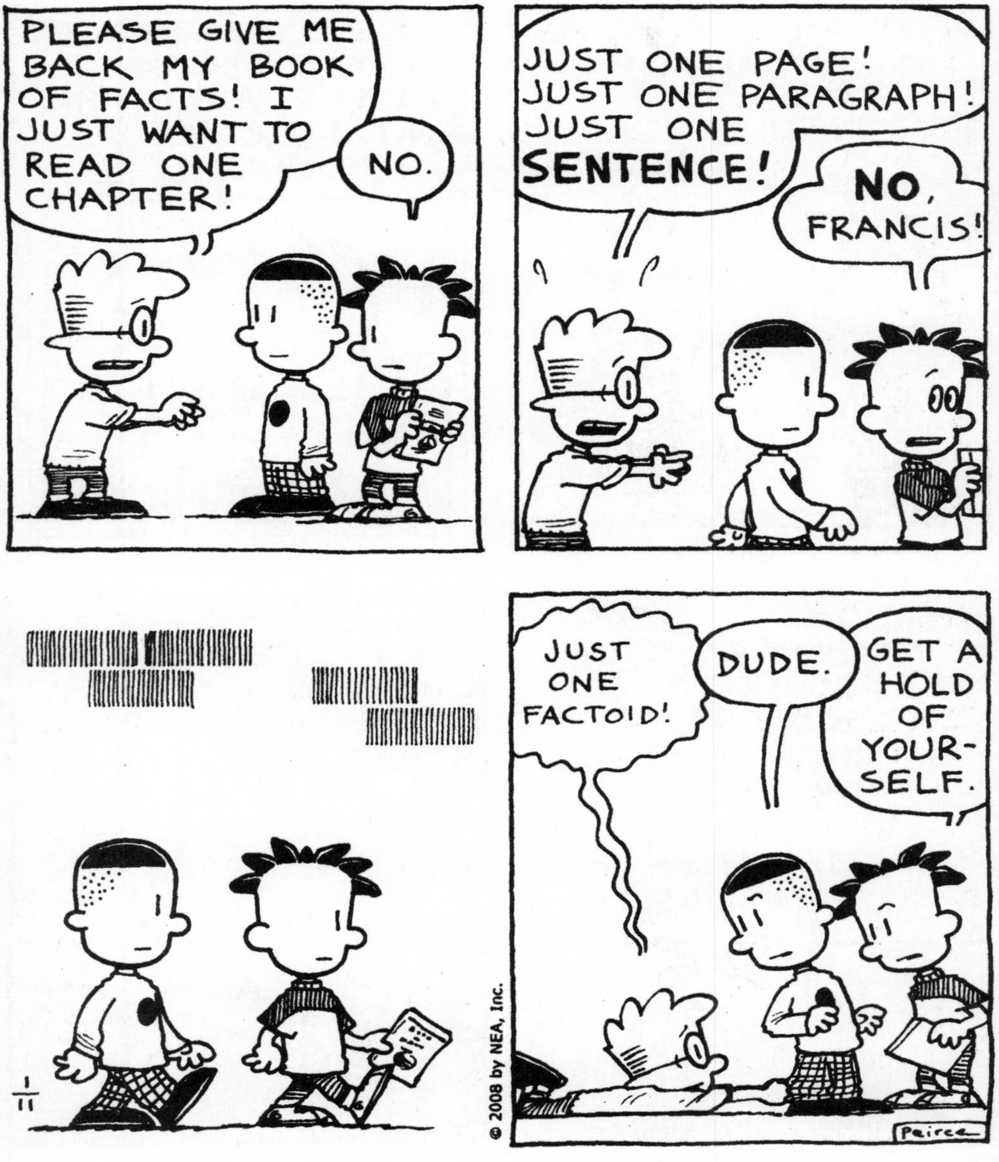
PLEASE GIVE ME BACK MY BOOK OF FACTS! I JUST WANT TO READ ONE CHAPTER!
NO.
JUST ONE PAGE! JUST ONE PARAGRAPH! JUST ONE **SENTENCE!**
NO, FRANCIS!
1/11
JUST ONE FACTOID!
DUDE.
GET A HOLD OF YOUR-SELF.
Peirce

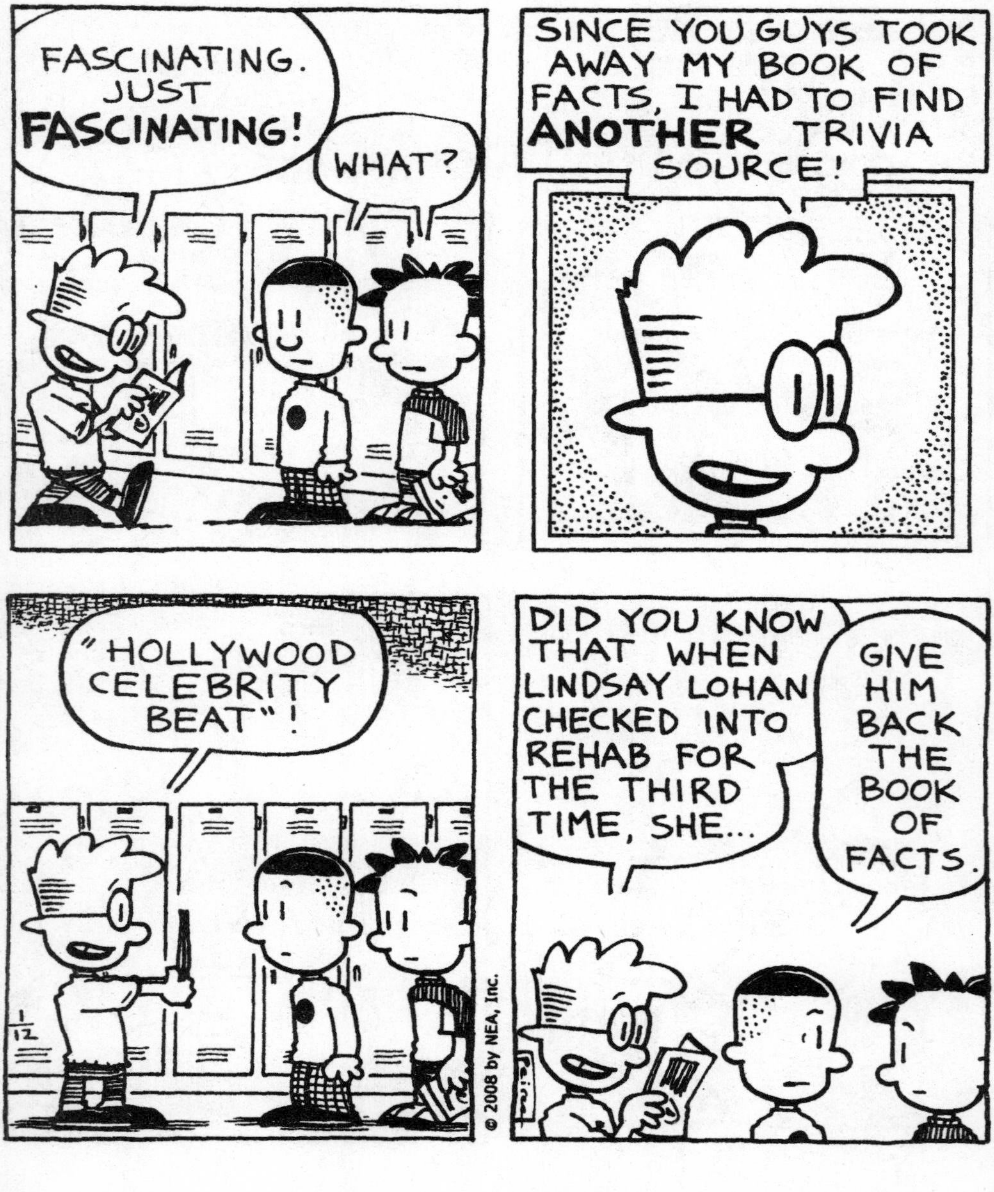
FASCINATING. JUST **FASCINATING!**
WHAT?
SINCE YOU GUYS TOOK AWAY MY BOOK OF FACTS, I HAD TO FIND **ANOTHER** TRIVIA SOURCE!
"HOLLYWOOD CELEBRITY BEAT"!
1/12
© 2008 by NEA, Inc.
DID YOU KNOW THAT WHEN LINDSAY LOHAN CHECKED INTO REHAB FOR THE THIRD TIME, SHE...
GIVE HIM BACK THE BOOK OF FACTS.

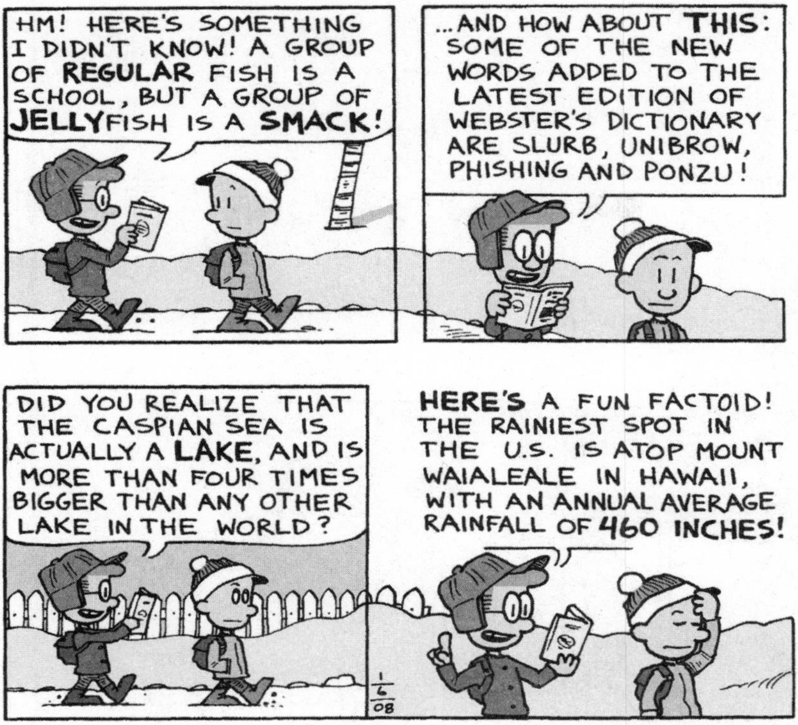

HM! HERE'S SOMETHING I DIDN'T KNOW! A GROUP OF REGULAR FISH IS A SCHOOL, BUT A GROUP OF JELLYFISH IS A SMACK!
...AND HOW ABOUT THIS: SOME OF THE NEW WORDS ADDED TO THE LATEST EDITION OF WEBSTER'S DICTIONARY ARE SLURB, UNIBROW, PHISHING AND PONZU!
DID YOU REALIZE THAT THE CASPIAN SEA IS ACTUALLY A LAKE, AND IS MORE THAN FOUR TIMES BIGGER THAN ANY OTHER LAKE IN THE WORLD?
1/6/08
HERE'S A FUN FACTOID! THE RAINIEST SPOT IN THE U.S. IS ATOP MOUNT WAIALEALE IN HAWAII, WITH AN ANNUAL AVERAGE RAINFALL OF 460 INCHES!

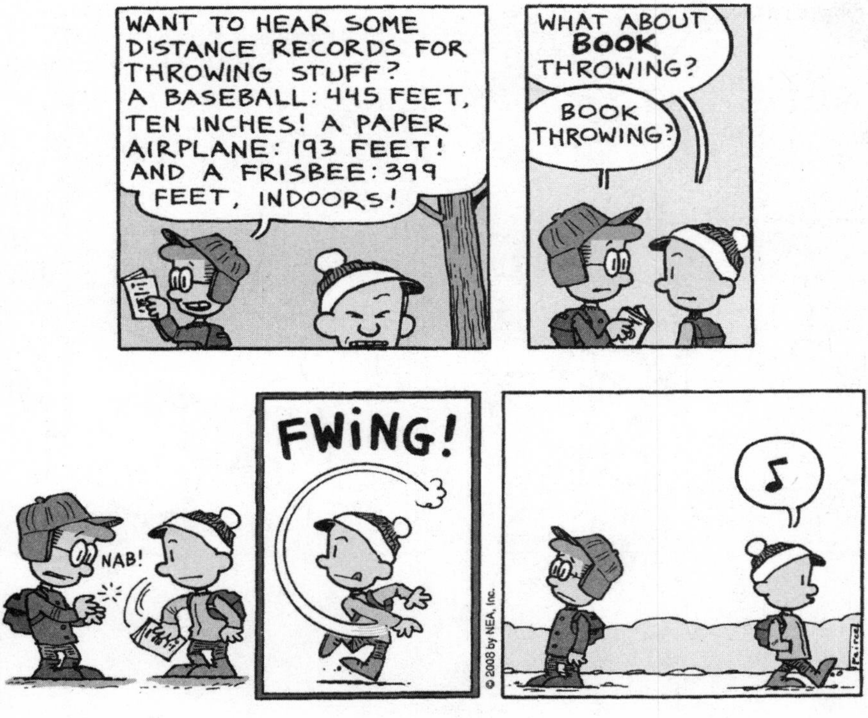

WANT TO HEAR SOME DISTANCE RECORDS FOR THROWING STUFF? A BASEBALL: 445 FEET, TEN INCHES! A PAPER AIRPLANE: 193 FEET! AND A FRISBEE: 399 FEET, INDOORS!
WHAT ABOUT BOOK THROWING?
BOOK THROWING?
NAB!
FWING!
© 2008 by NEA, Inc.
Peirce

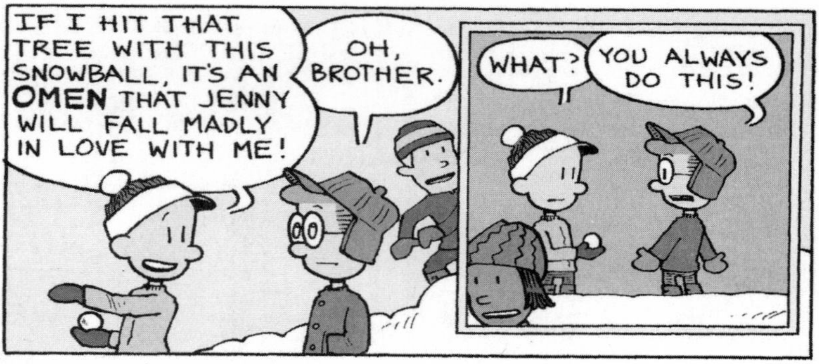
IF I HIT THAT TREE WITH THIS SNOWBALL, IT'S AN OMEN THAT JENNY WILL FALL MADLY IN LOVE WITH ME!
OH, BROTHER.
WHAT?
YOU ALWAYS DO THIS!

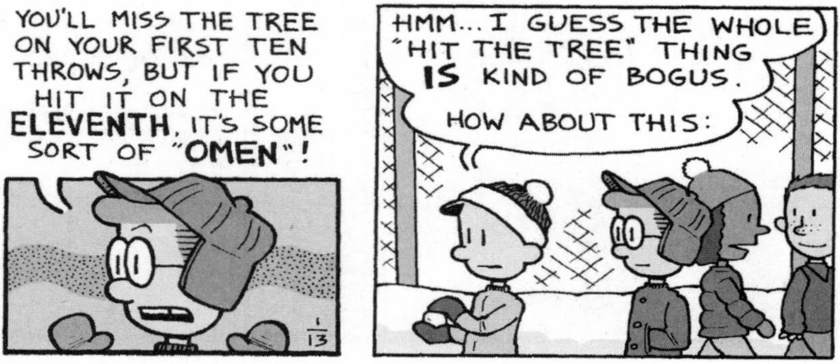
YOU'LL MISS THE TREE ON YOUR FIRST TEN THROWS, BUT IF YOU HIT IT ON THE ELEVENTH, IT'S SOME SORT OF "OMEN"!
HMM... I GUESS THE WHOLE "HIT THE TREE" THING IS KIND OF BOGUS.
HOW ABOUT THIS:

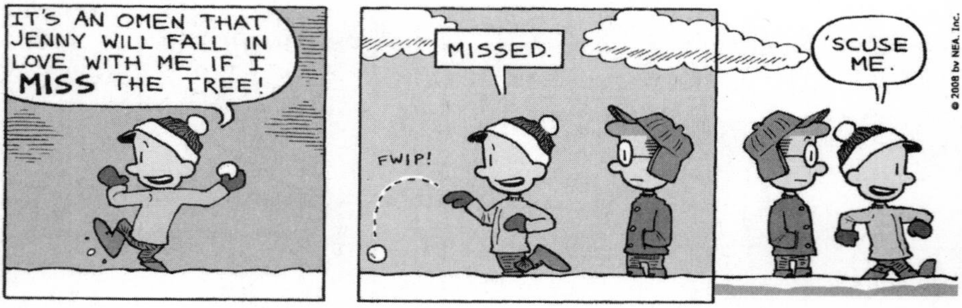
IT'S AN OMEN THAT JENNY WILL FALL IN LOVE WITH ME IF I MISS THE TREE!
MISSED.
FWIP!
'SCUSE ME.

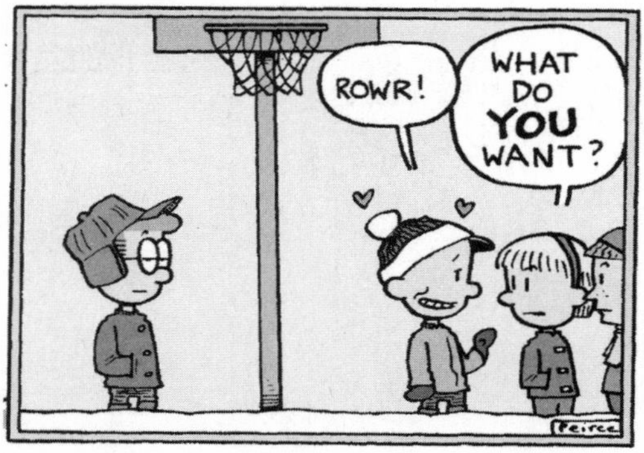
ROWR!
WHAT DO YOU WANT?
Peirce

RELAX...OR ELSE!

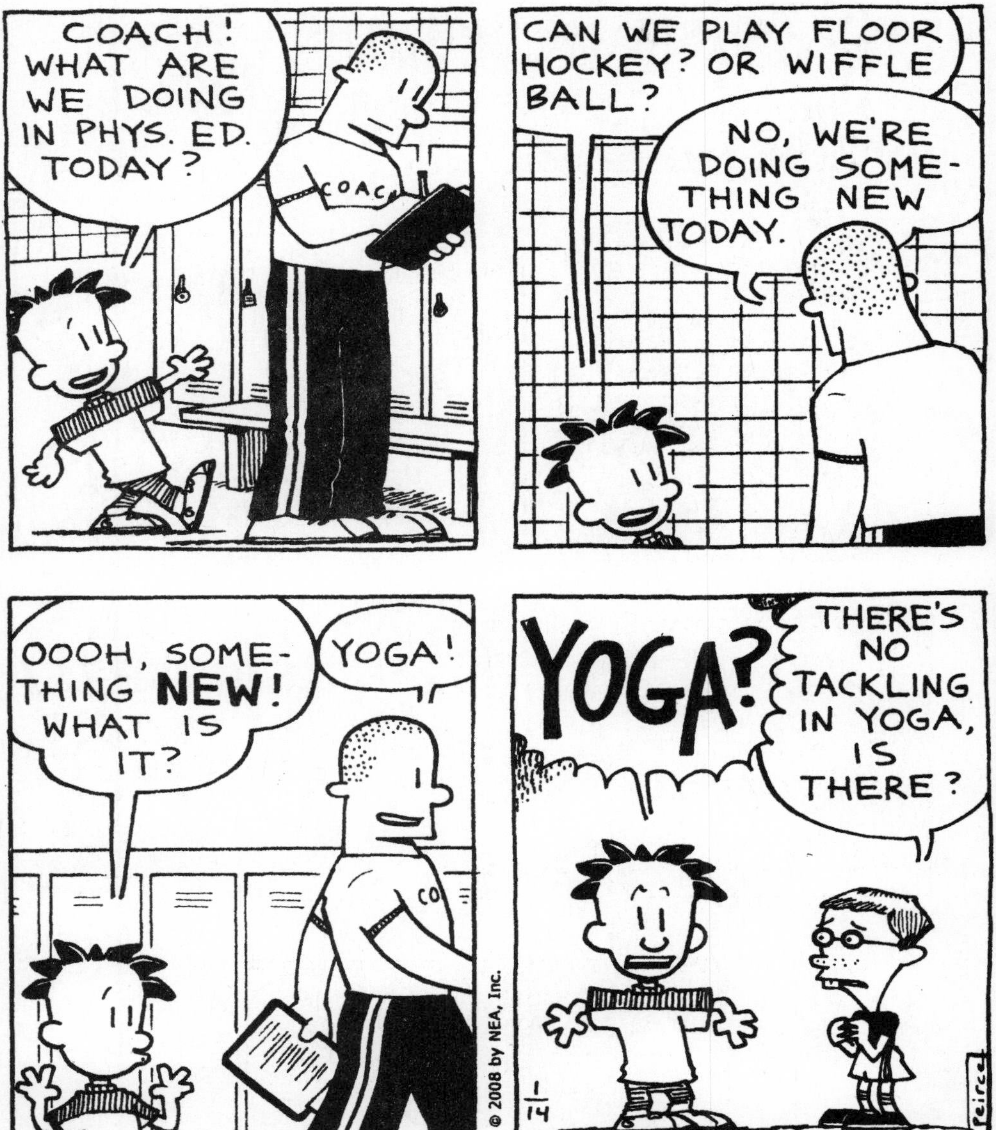

COACH! WHAT ARE WE DOING IN PHYS. ED. TODAY?
COAC
CAN WE PLAY FLOOR HOCKEY? OR WIFFLE BALL?
NO, WE'RE DOING SOMETHING NEW TODAY.
OOOH, SOMETHING **NEW**! WHAT IS IT?
YOGA!
CO
© 2008 by NEA, Inc.
YOGA?
THERE'S NO TACKLING IN YOGA, IS THERE?
1/14
peirce

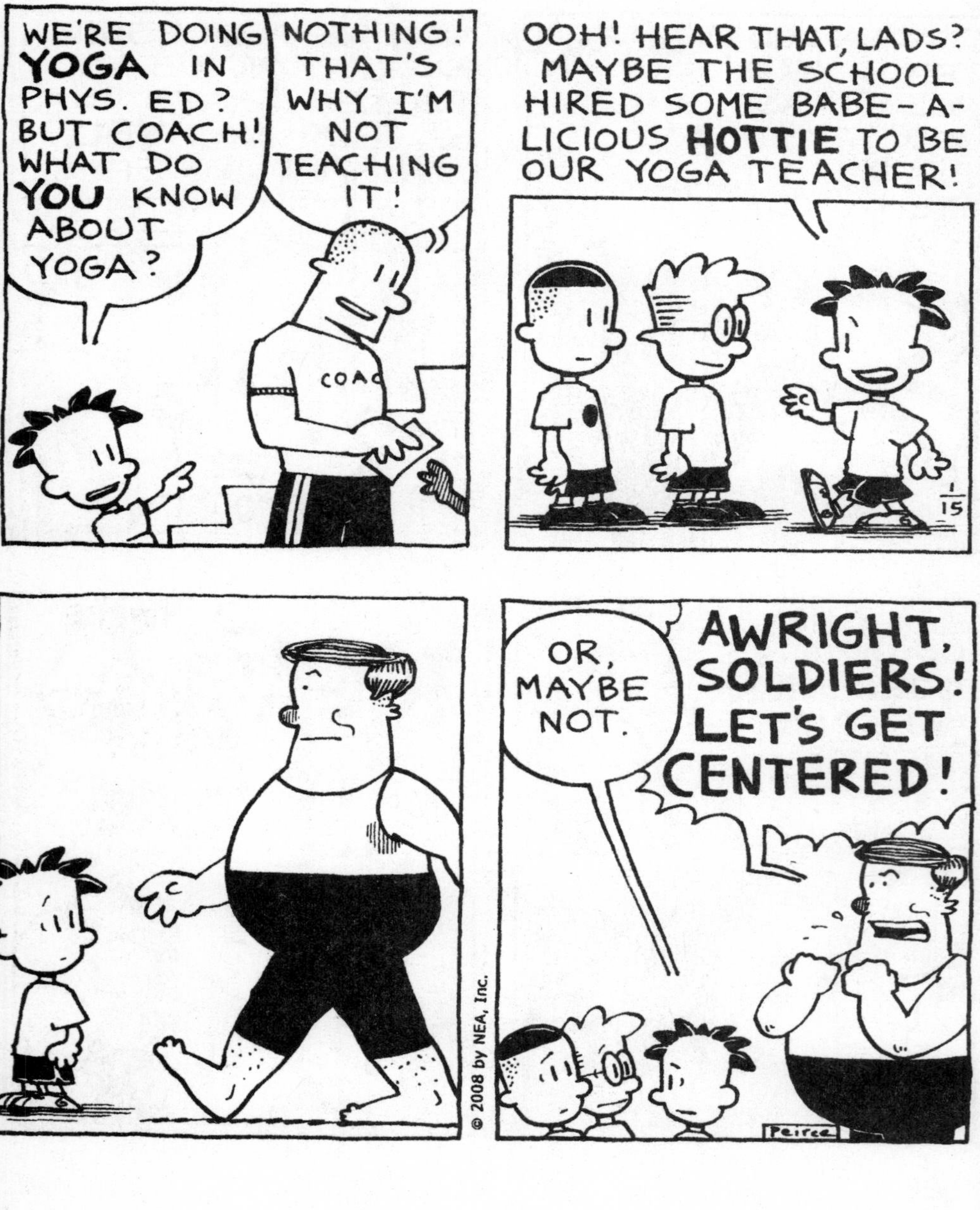
WE'RE DOING **YOGA** IN PHYS. ED? BUT COACH! WHAT DO **YOU** KNOW ABOUT YOGA?
NOTHING! THAT'S WHY I'M NOT TEACHING IT!
COAC
OOH! HEAR THAT, LADS? MAYBE THE SCHOOL HIRED SOME BABE-A-LICIOUS **HOTTIE** TO BE OUR YOGA TEACHER!
1/15
© 2008 by NEA, Inc.
OR, MAYBE NOT.
AWRIGHT, SOLDIERS! LET'S GET CENTERED!
Peirce

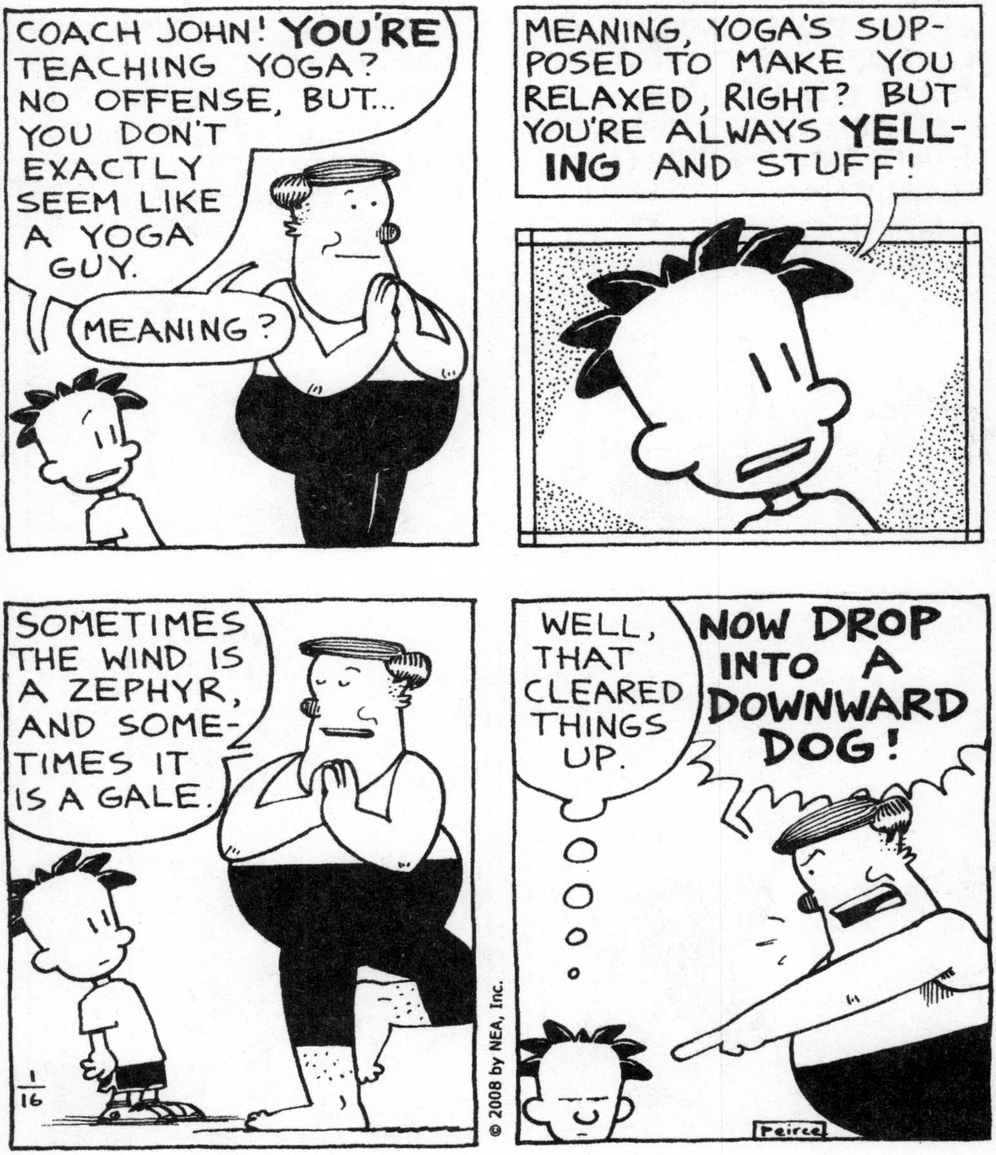
COACH JOHN! YOU'RE TEACHING YOGA? NO OFFENSE, BUT... YOU DON'T EXACTLY SEEM LIKE A YOGA GUY.
MEANING?
MEANING, YOGA'S SUPPOSED TO MAKE YOU RELAXED, RIGHT? BUT YOU'RE ALWAYS YELLING AND STUFF!
SOMETIMES THE WIND IS A ZEPHYR, AND SOMETIMES IT IS A GALE.
1/16
© 2008 by NEA, Inc.
WELL, THAT CLEARED THINGS UP.
NOW DROP INTO A DOWNWARD DOG!
Peirce

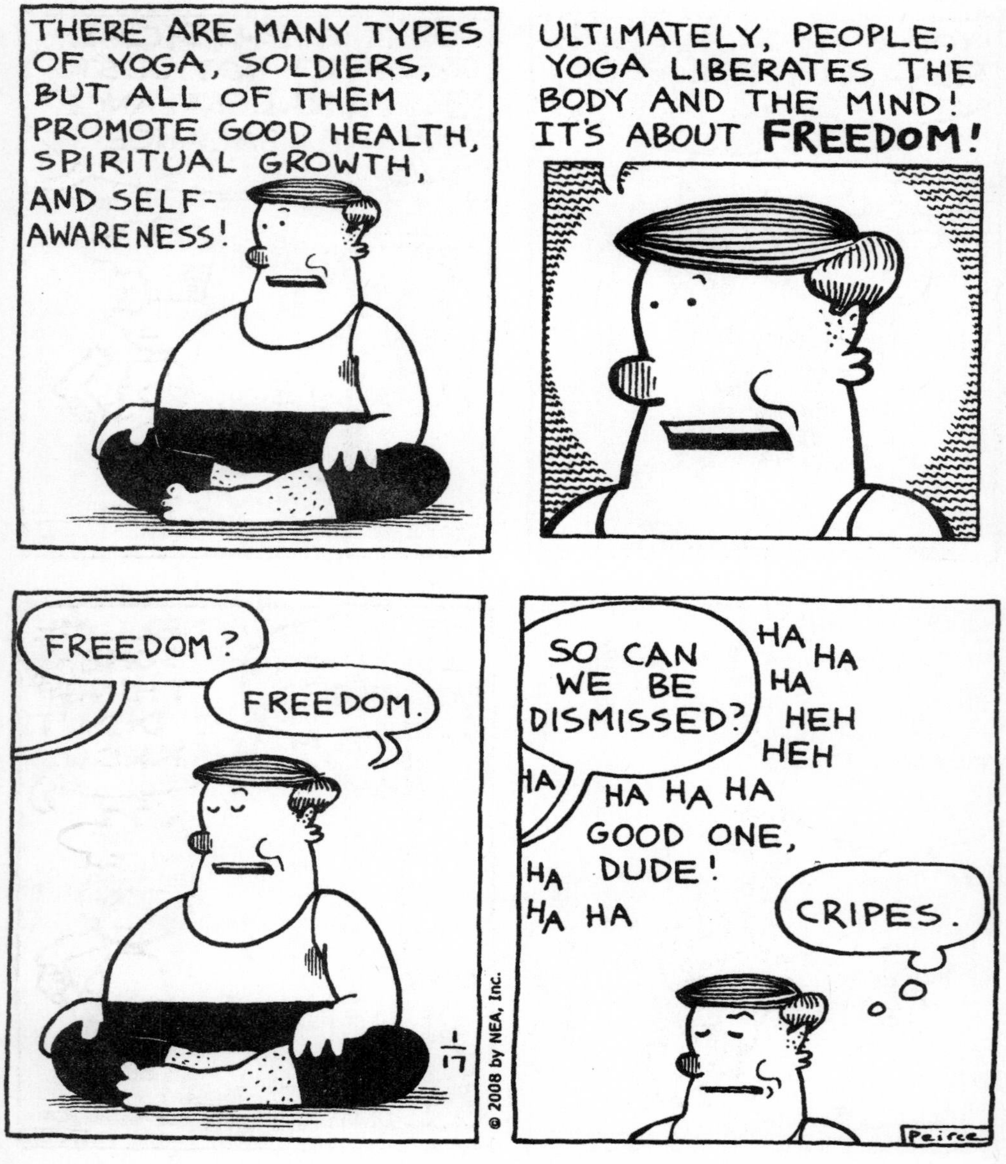
THERE ARE MANY TYPES OF YOGA, SOLDIERS, BUT ALL OF THEM PROMOTE GOOD HEALTH, SPIRITUAL GROWTH, AND SELF-AWARENESS!
ULTIMATELY, PEOPLE, YOGA LIBERATES THE BODY AND THE MIND! IT'S ABOUT **FREEDOM!**
FREEDOM?
FREEDOM.
1-17
SO CAN WE BE DISMISSED?
HA HA HA HEH HEH
HA
HA HA HA
GOOD ONE, DUDE!
HA HA HA
CRIPES.
Peirce

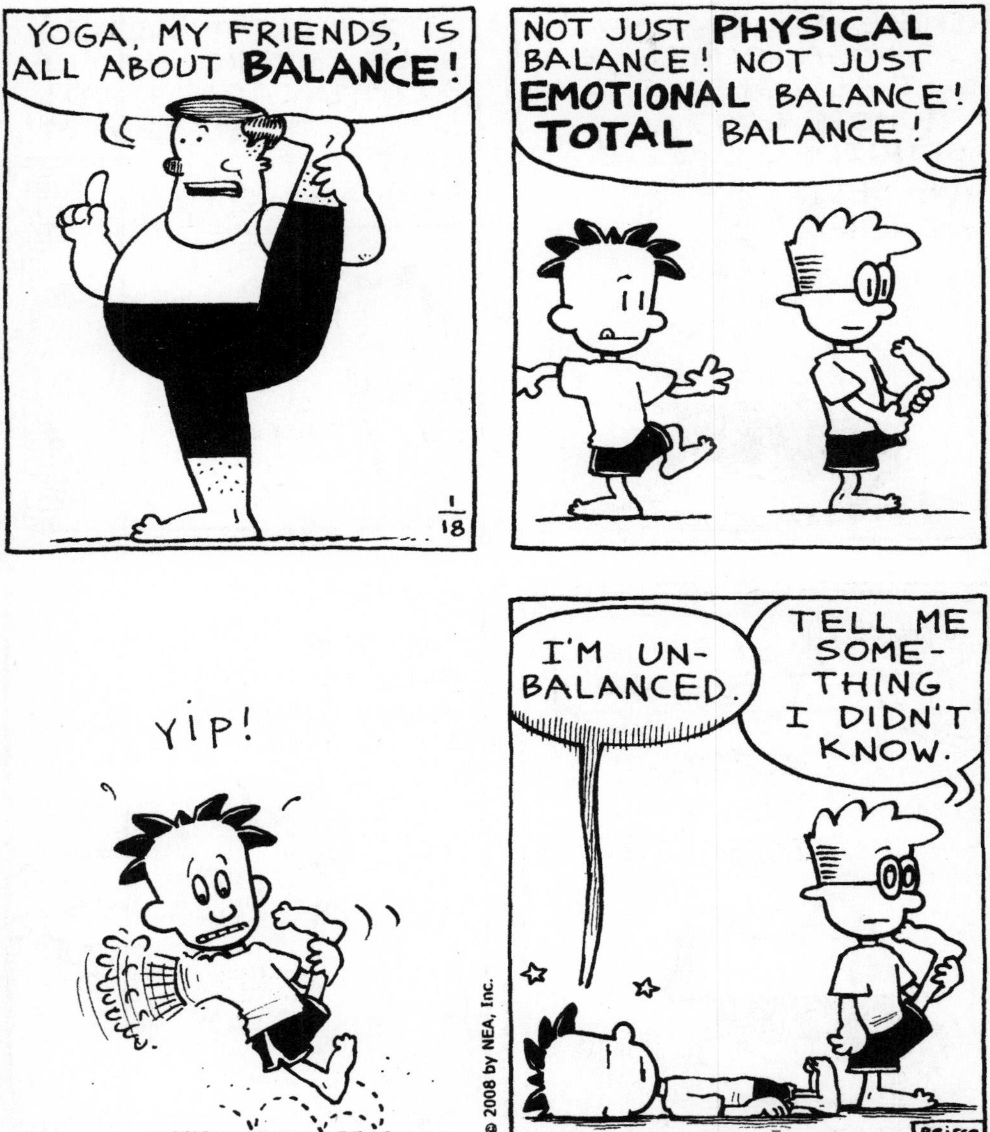
YOGA, MY FRIENDS, IS ALL ABOUT BALANCE!
1/18
NOT JUST PHYSICAL BALANCE! NOT JUST EMOTIONAL BALANCE! TOTAL BALANCE!
YIP!
I'M UN-BALANCED.
TELL ME SOME-THING I DIDN'T KNOW.
peirce

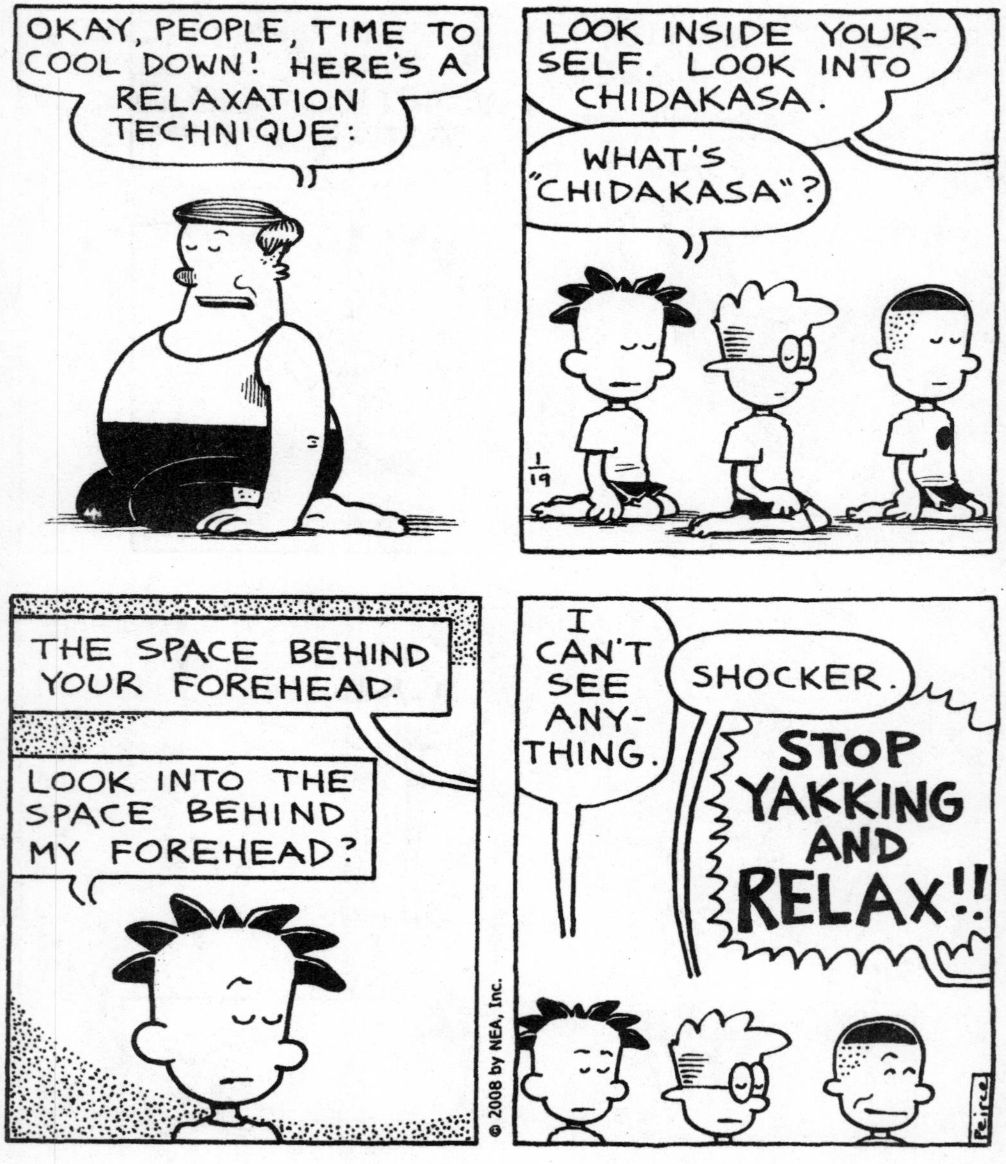

OKAY, PEOPLE, TIME TO COOL DOWN! HERE'S A RELAXATION TECHNIQUE:
LOOK INSIDE YOURSELF. LOOK INTO CHIDAKASA.
WHAT'S "CHIDAKASA"?
1/19
THE SPACE BEHIND YOUR FOREHEAD.
LOOK INTO THE SPACE BEHIND MY FOREHEAD?
© 2008 by NEA, Inc.
I CAN'T SEE ANYTHING.
SHOCKER.
STOP YAKKING AND RELAX!!
Peirce

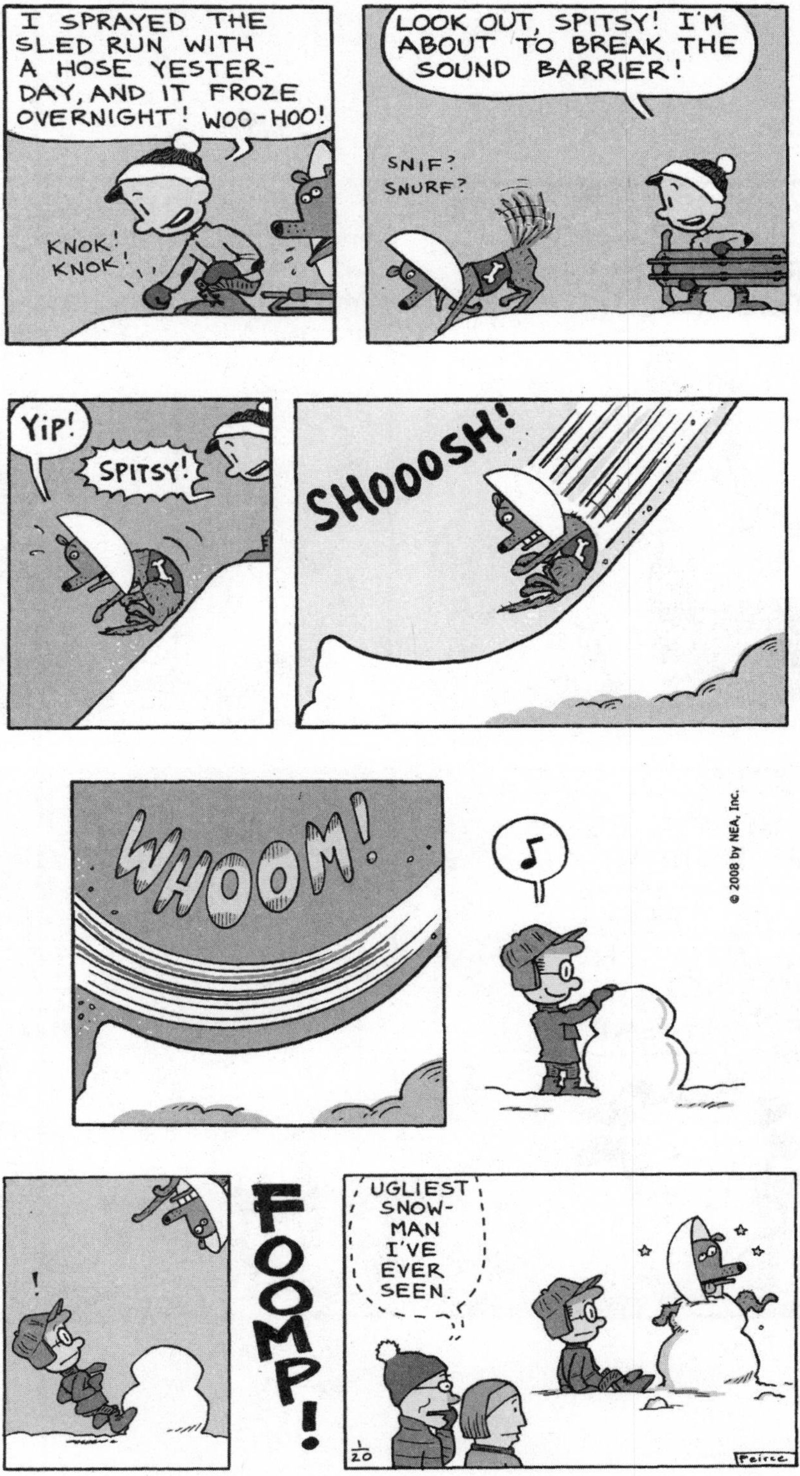
I SPRAYED THE SLED RUN WITH A HOSE YESTERDAY, AND IT FROZE OVERNIGHT! WOO-HOO!
KNOK! KNOK!
LOOK OUT, SPITSY! I'M ABOUT TO BREAK THE SOUND BARRIER!
SNIF? SNURF?
YIP!
SPITSY!
SHOOOSH!
WHOOM!
!
FOOMP!
UGLIEST SNOW-MAN I'VE EVER SEEN.
1 20
Peirce

ART À LA NATE

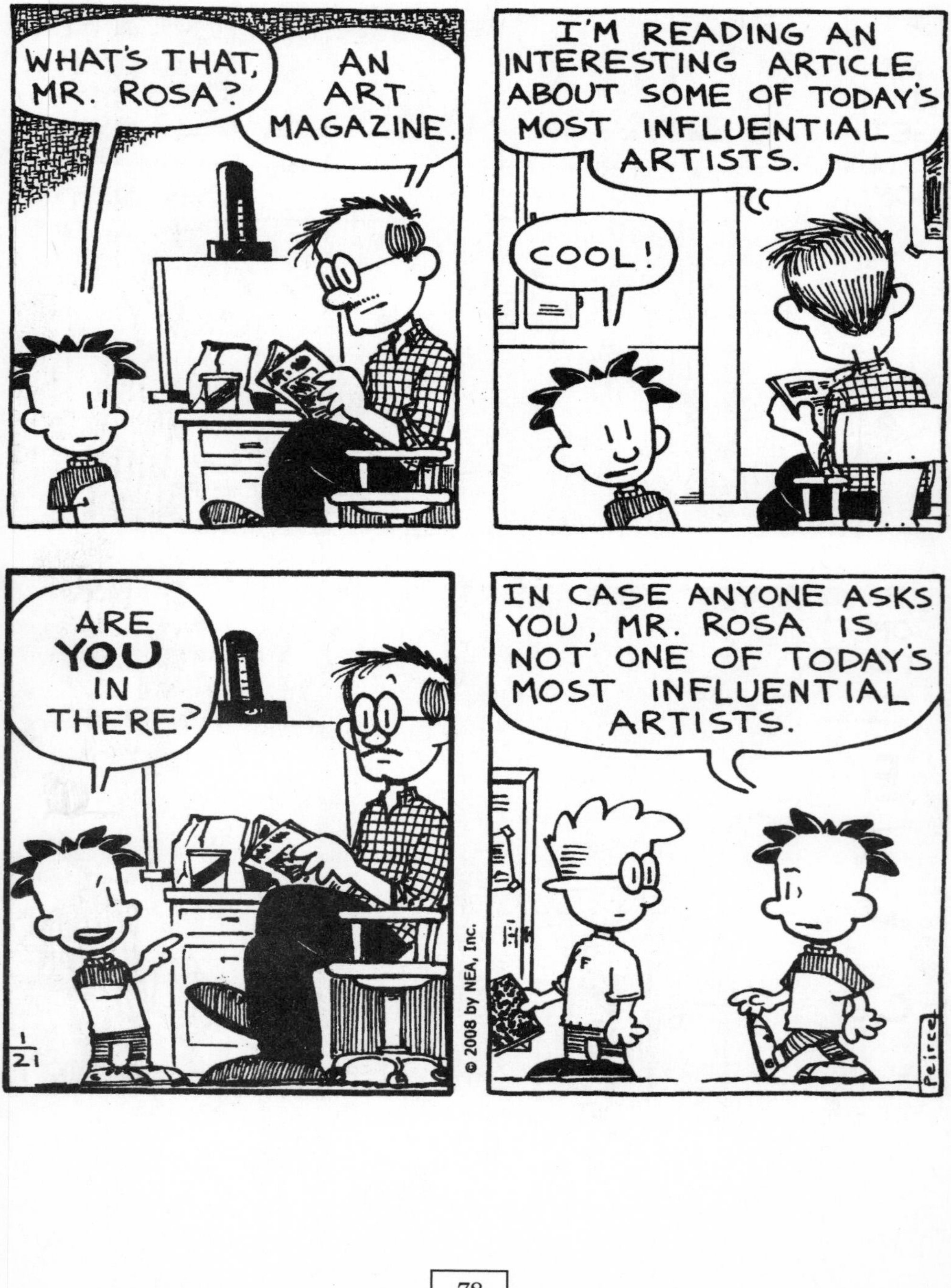
WHAT'S THAT, MR. ROSA?
AN ART MAGAZINE.
I'M READING AN INTERESTING ARTICLE ABOUT SOME OF TODAY'S MOST INFLUENTIAL ARTISTS.
COOL!
ARE YOU IN THERE?
IN CASE ANYONE ASKS YOU, MR. ROSA IS NOT ONE OF TODAY'S MOST INFLUENTIAL ARTISTS.
1/21
© 2008 by NEA, Inc.
Peirce

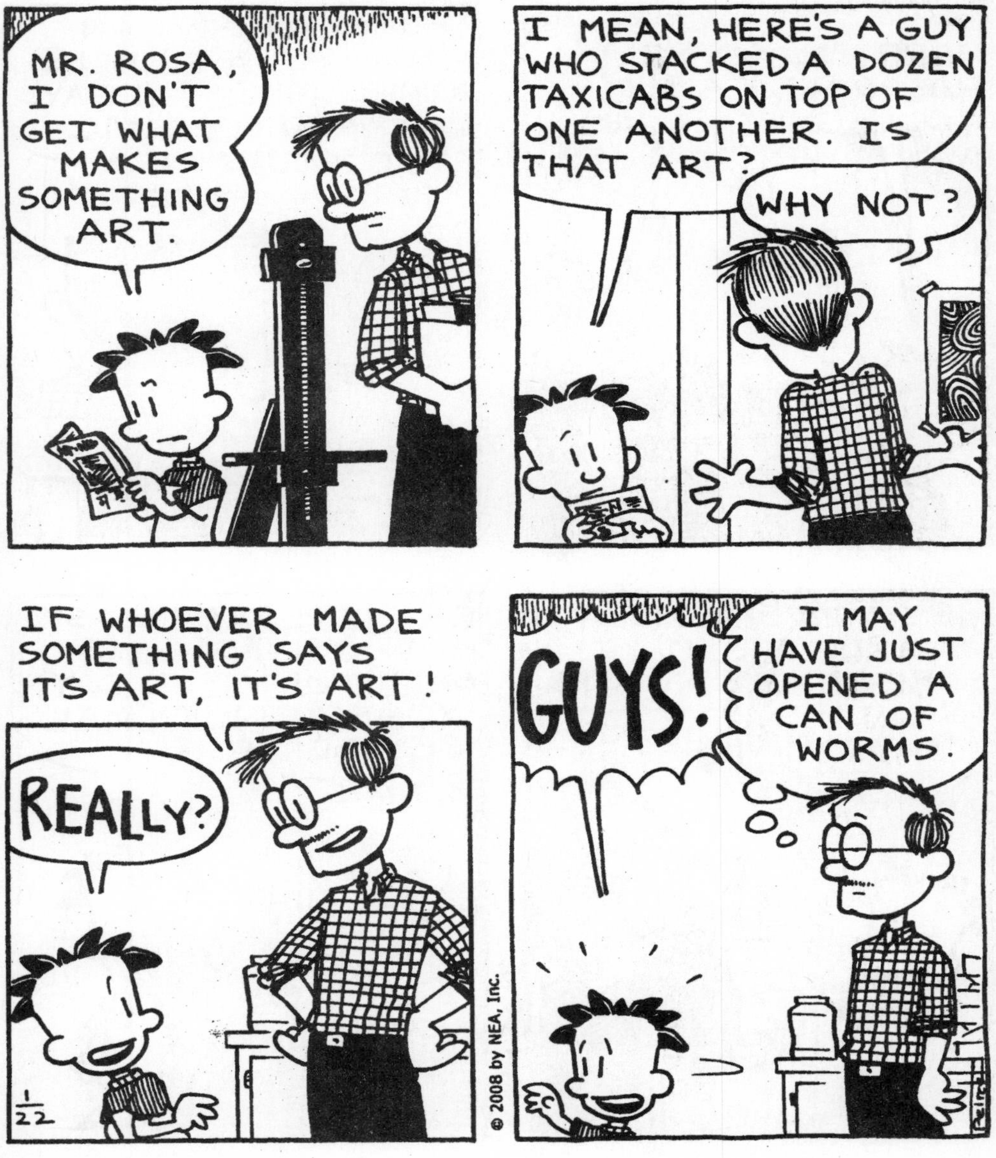
MR. ROSA, I DON'T GET WHAT MAKES SOMETHING ART.
I MEAN, HERE'S A GUY WHO STACKED A DOZEN TAXICABS ON TOP OF ONE ANOTHER. IS THAT ART?
WHY NOT?
IF WHOEVER MADE SOMETHING SAYS IT'S ART, IT'S ART!
REALLY?
1/22
GUYS!
I MAY HAVE JUST OPENED A CAN OF WORMS.

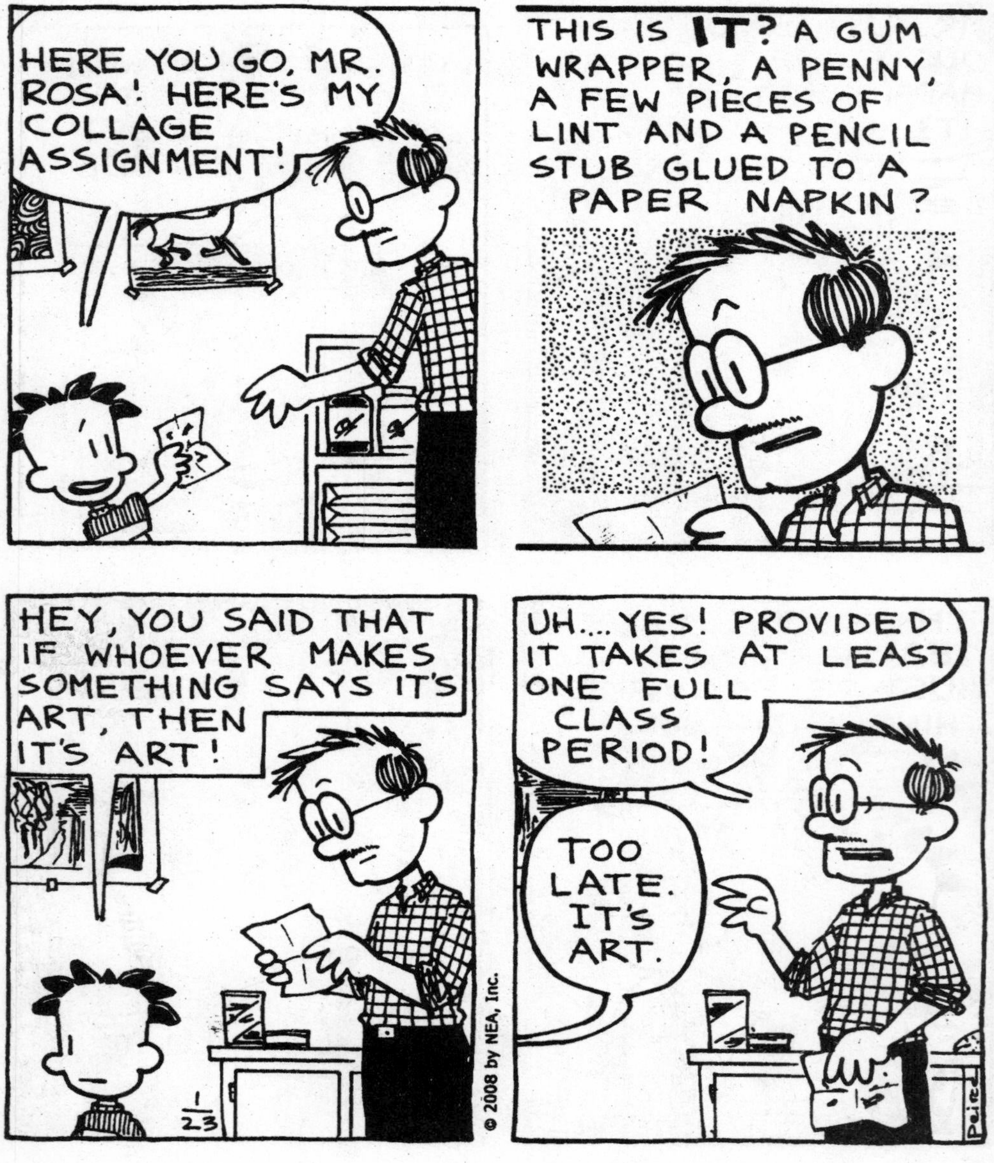
HERE YOU GO, MR. ROSA! HERE'S MY COLLAGE ASSIGNMENT!
THIS IS IT? A GUM WRAPPER, A PENNY, A FEW PIECES OF LINT AND A PENCIL STUB GLUED TO A PAPER NAPKIN?
HEY, YOU SAID THAT IF WHOEVER MAKES SOMETHING SAYS IT'S ART, THEN IT'S ART!
1/23
© 2008 by NEA, Inc.
UH... YES! PROVIDED IT TAKES AT LEAST ONE FULL CLASS PERIOD!
TOO LATE. IT'S ART.
Peirce

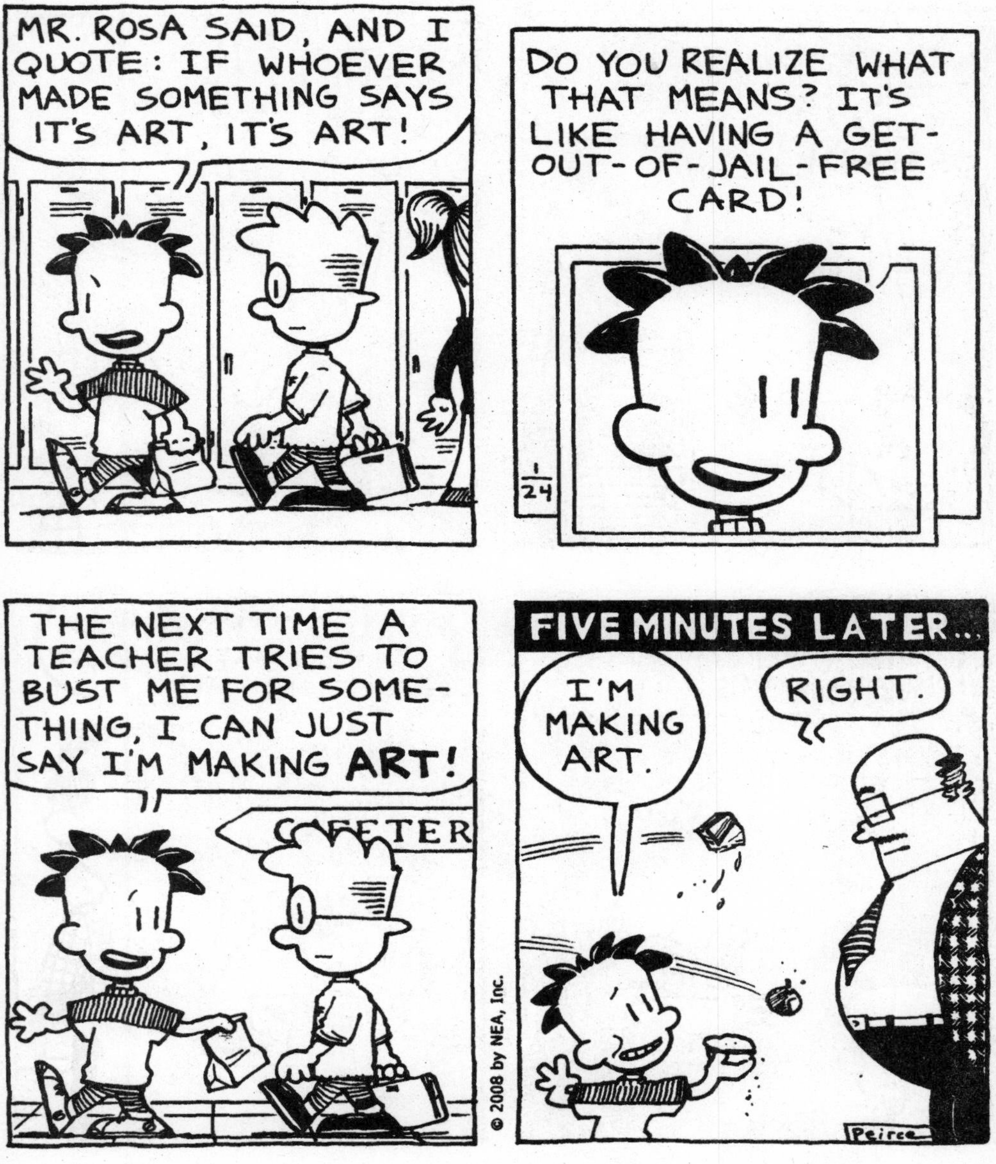

MR. ROSA SAID, AND I QUOTE: IF WHOEVER MADE SOMETHING SAYS IT'S ART, IT'S ART!
DO YOU REALIZE WHAT THAT MEANS? IT'S LIKE HAVING A GET-OUT-OF-JAIL-FREE CARD!
1/24
THE NEXT TIME A TEACHER TRIES TO BUST ME FOR SOME-THING, I CAN JUST SAY I'M MAKING **ART**!
FIVE MINUTES LATER...
I'M MAKING ART.
RIGHT.
Peirce
© 2008 by NEA, Inc.

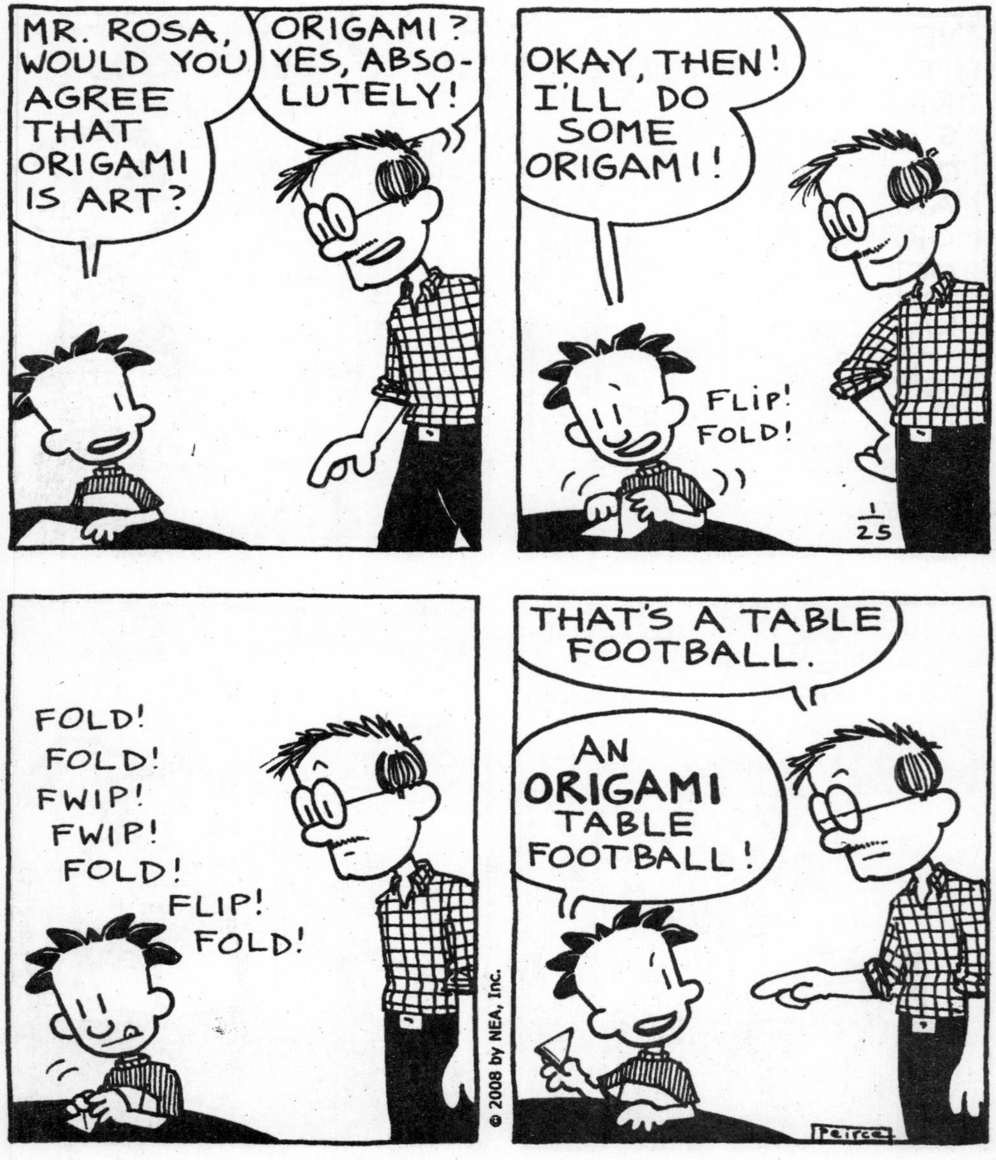
MR. ROSA, WOULD YOU AGREE THAT ORIGAMI IS ART?
ORIGAMI? YES, ABSO-LUTELY!
OKAY, THEN! I'LL DO SOME ORIGAMI!
FLIP! FOLD!
1/25
FOLD! FOLD! FWIP! FWIP! FOLD! FLIP! FOLD!
© 2008 by NEA, Inc.
THAT'S A TABLE FOOTBALL.
AN ORIGAMI TABLE FOOTBALL!
Peirce

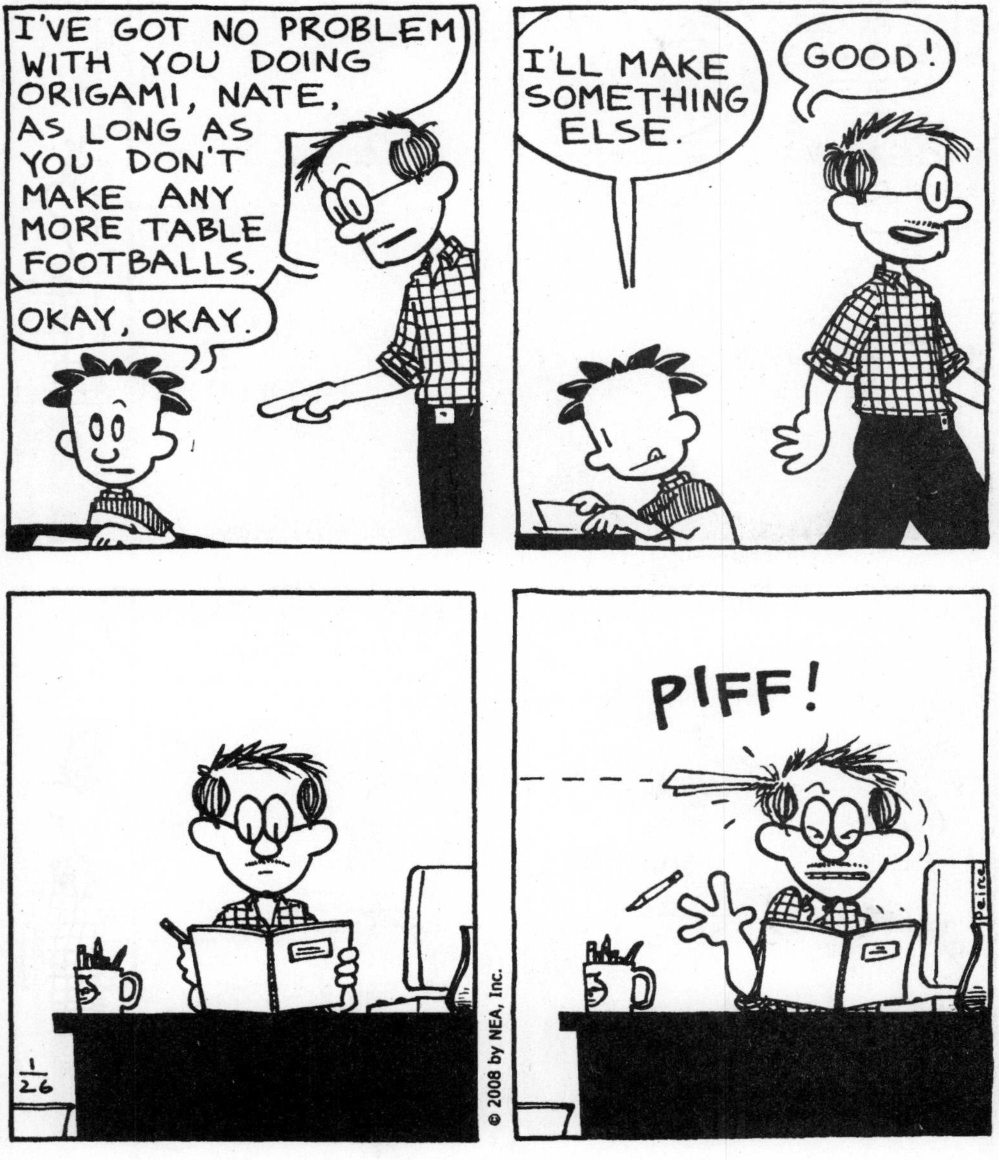
I'VE GOT NO PROBLEM WITH YOU DOING ORIGAMI, NATE, AS LONG AS YOU DON'T MAKE ANY MORE TABLE FOOTBALLS.
OKAY, OKAY.
I'LL MAKE SOMETHING ELSE.
GOOD!
1/26
© 2008 by NEA, Inc.
PIFF!

RRRINNNG!

1/27

HOO!
HOO!
GASP!
PUFF!

© 2008 by NEA, Inc.

WRIGHT

BEAT YOU TO IT.

WRIGHT

I HATE REPORT CARD DAY.

WHO GETS AN "UNSATISFACTORY" IN STUDY HALL?

Peirce

WHO'S THE PERFECT COUPLE?

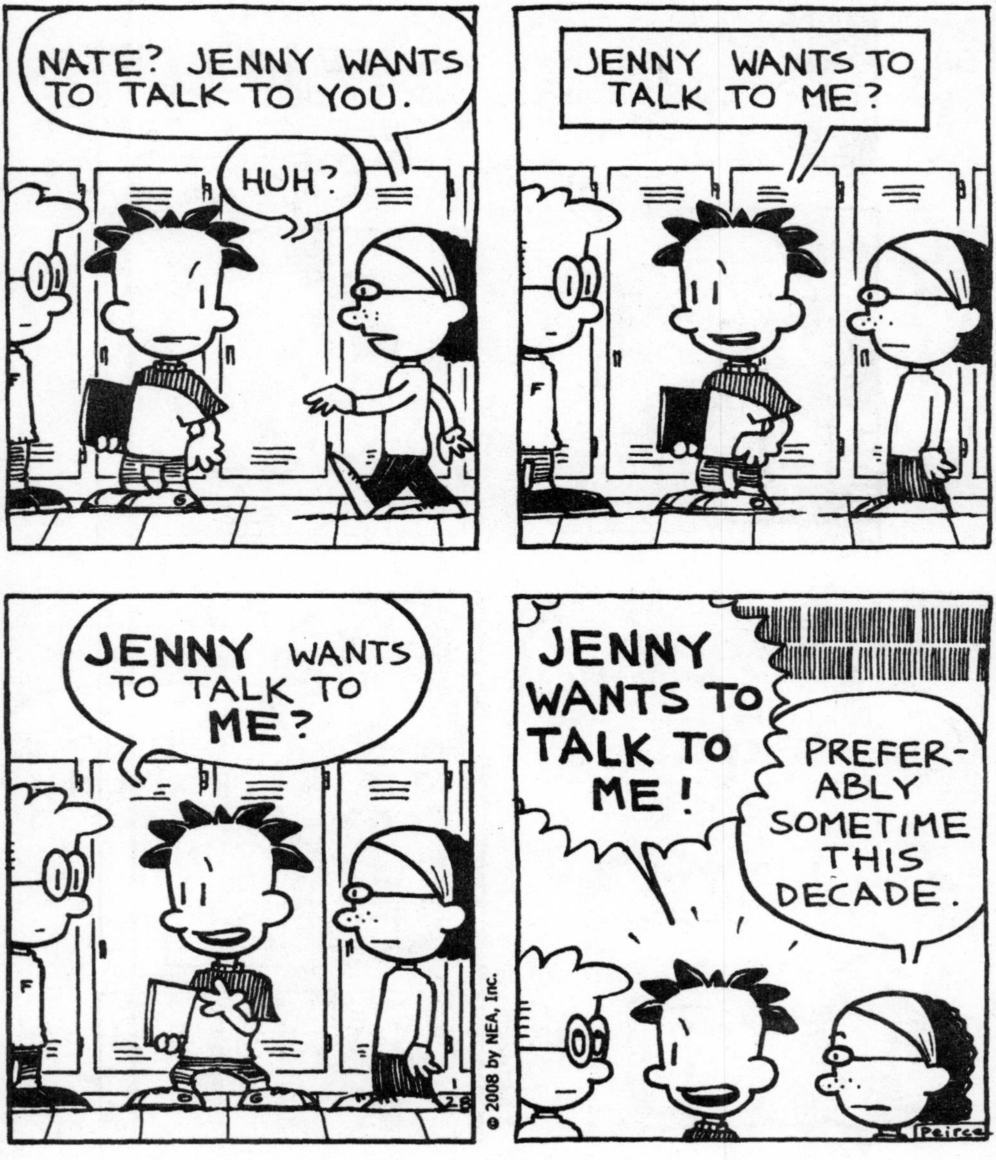
NATE? JENNY WANTS TO TALK TO YOU.
HUH?
JENNY WANTS TO TALK TO ME?
JENNY WANTS TO TALK TO ME?
JENNY WANTS TO TALK TO ME!
PREFER-ABLY SOMETIME THIS DECADE.
© 2008 by NEA, Inc.
Peirce

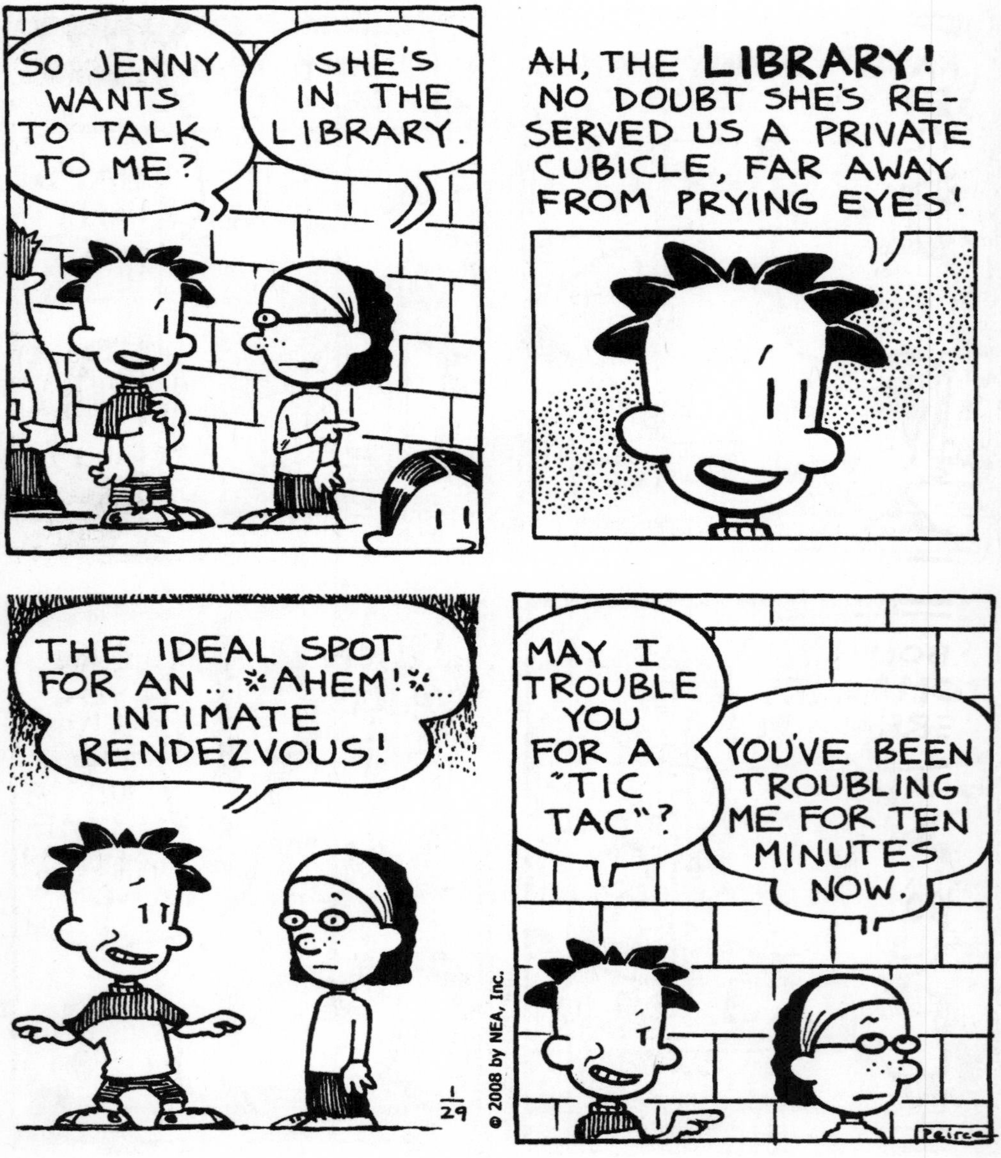
SO JENNY WANTS TO TALK TO ME?
SHE'S IN THE LIBRARY.
AH, THE LIBRARY! NO DOUBT SHE'S RESERVED US A PRIVATE CUBICLE, FAR AWAY FROM PRYING EYES!
THE IDEAL SPOT FOR AN... *AHEM!*... INTIMATE RENDEZVOUS!
MAY I TROUBLE YOU FOR A "TIC TAC"?
YOU'VE BEEN TROUBLING ME FOR TEN MINUTES NOW.
1/29
© 2008 by NEA, Inc.
Peirce

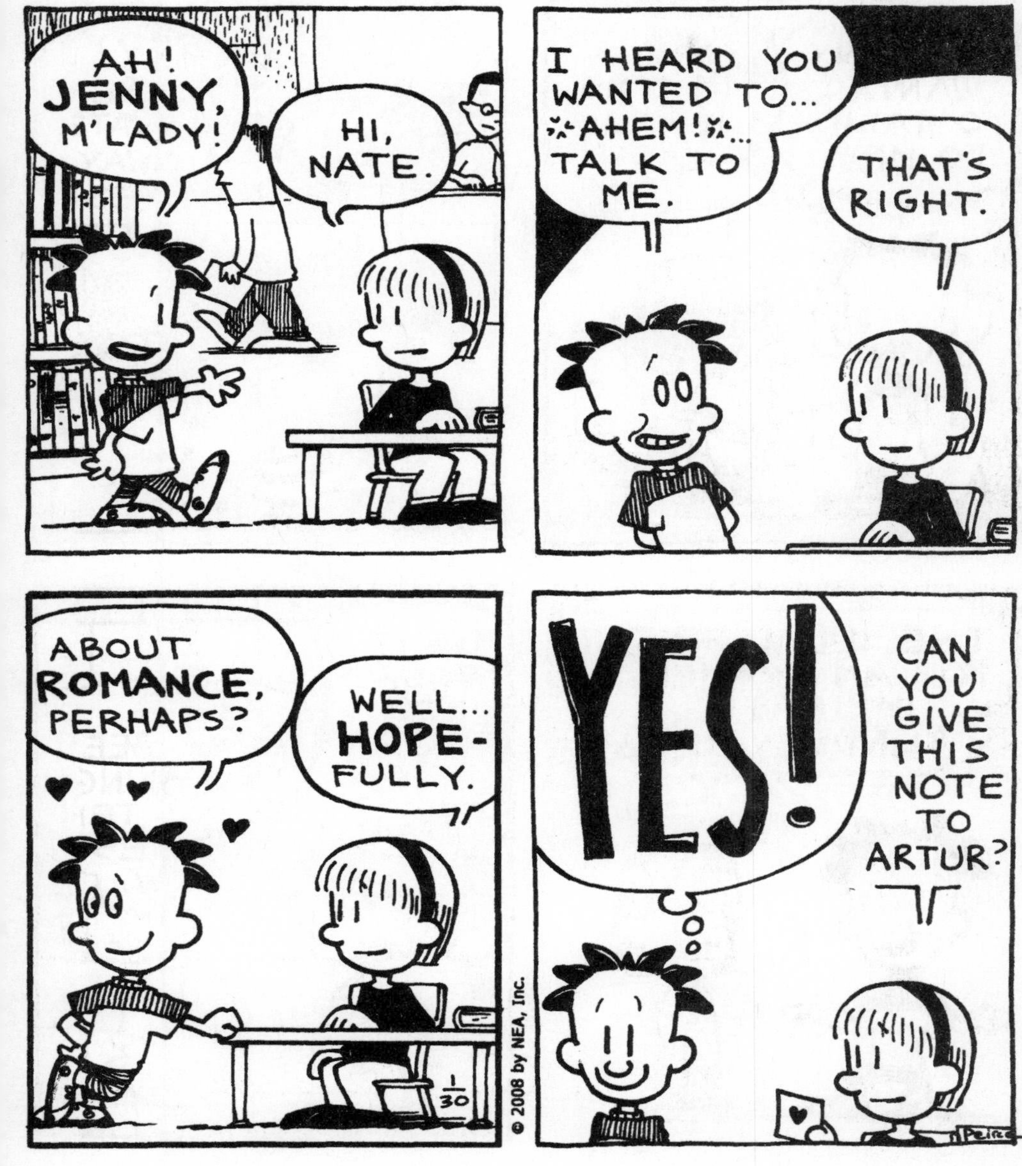
AH! JENNY, M'LADY!
HI, NATE.
I HEARD YOU WANTED TO... AHEM!... TALK TO ME.
THAT'S RIGHT.
ABOUT ROMANCE, PERHAPS?
WELL... HOPE-FULLY.
YES!
CAN YOU GIVE THIS NOTE TO ARTUR?
1/30
© 2008 by NEA, Inc.
Peirce

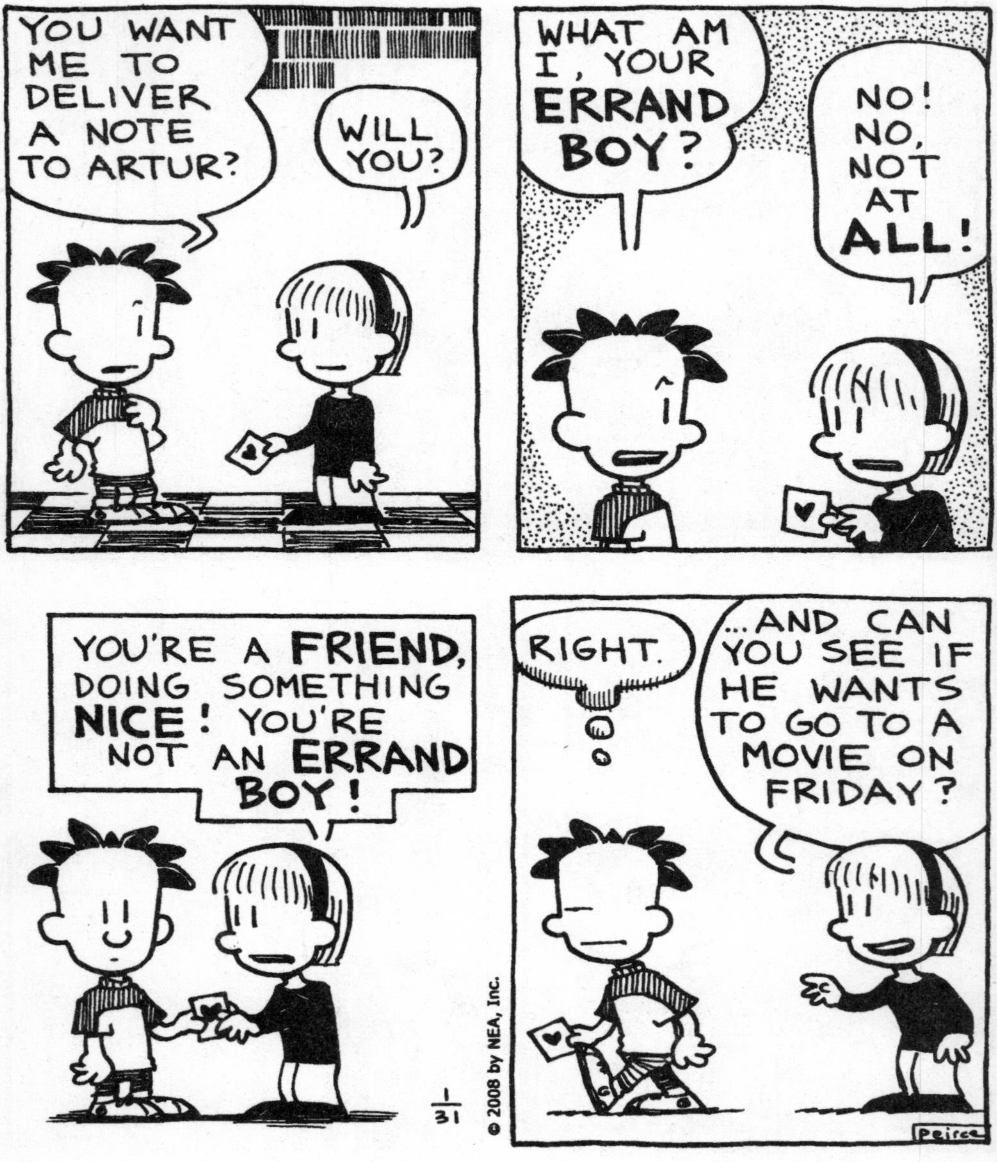
YOU WANT ME TO DELIVER A NOTE TO ARTUR?
WILL YOU?
WHAT AM I, YOUR ERRAND BOY?
NO! NO, NOT AT ALL!
YOU'RE A FRIEND, DOING SOMETHING NICE! YOU'RE NOT AN ERRAND BOY!
RIGHT.
...AND CAN YOU SEE IF HE WANTS TO GO TO A MOVIE ON FRIDAY?
1/31
© 2008 by NEA, Inc.
Peirce

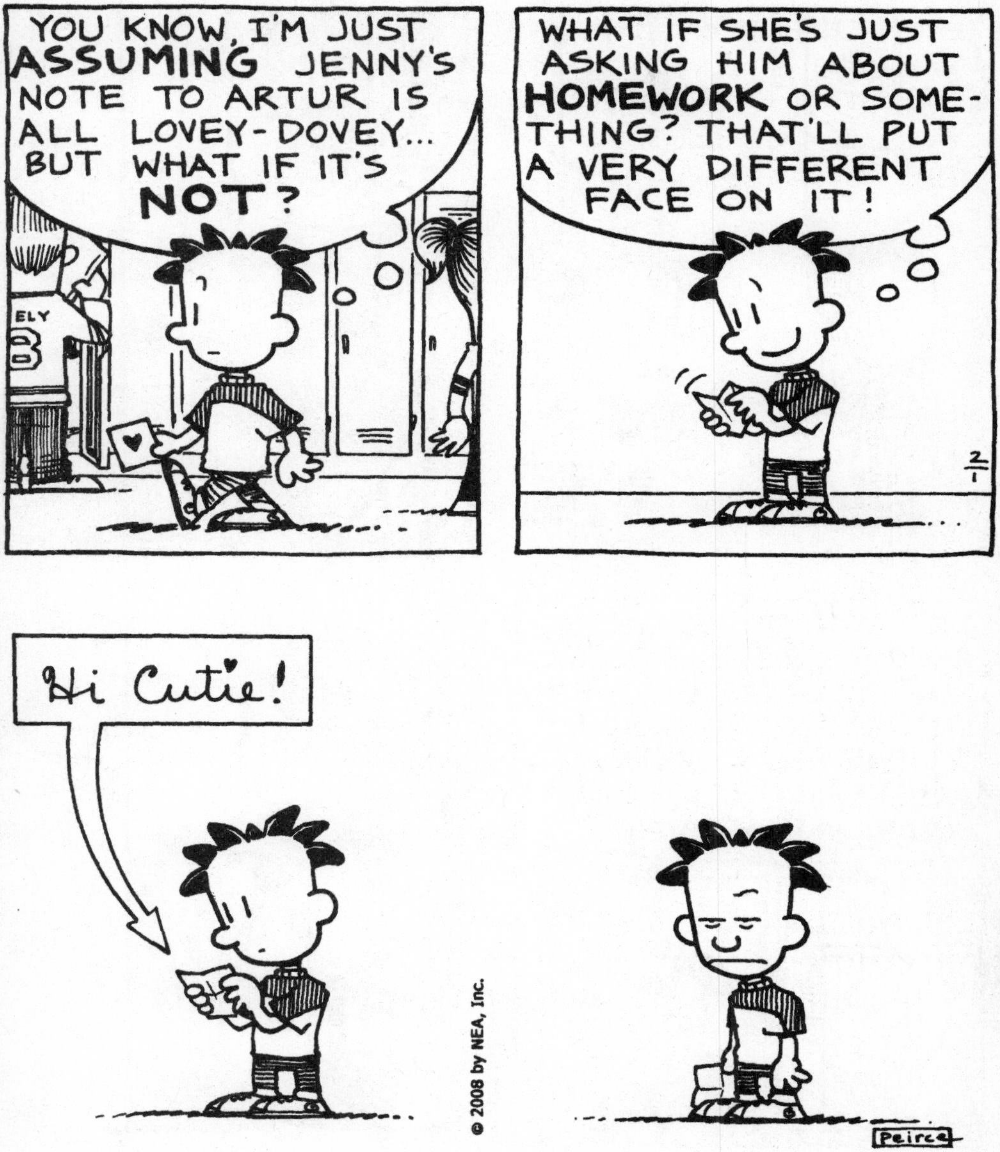
YOU KNOW, I'M JUST **ASSUMING** JENNY'S NOTE TO ARTUR IS ALL LOVEY-DOVEY... BUT WHAT IF IT'S **NOT**?
ELY
WHAT IF SHE'S JUST ASKING HIM ABOUT **HOMEWORK** OR SOMETHING? THAT'LL PUT A VERY DIFFERENT FACE ON IT!
2/1
Hi Cutie!
Peirce

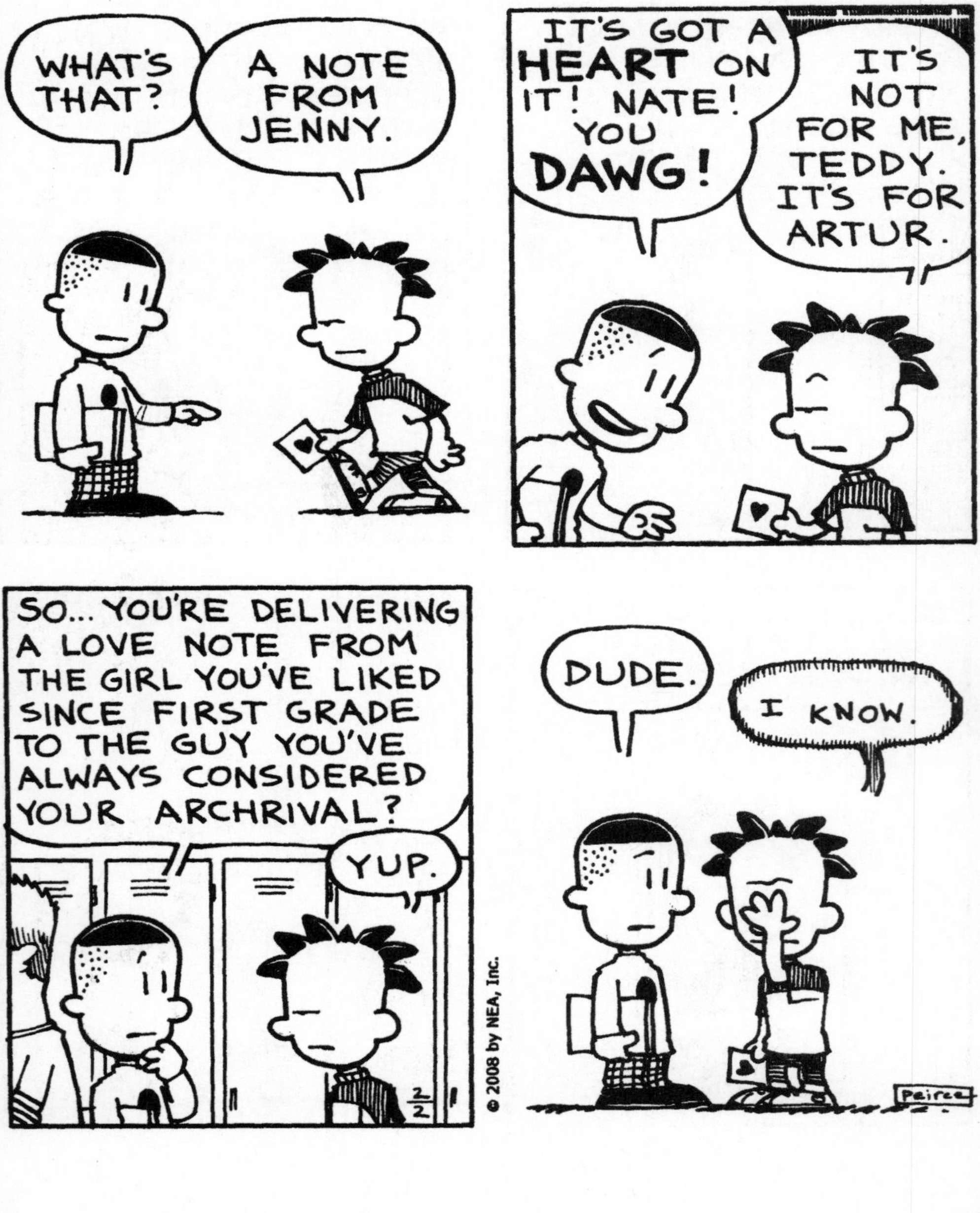
WHAT'S THAT?
A NOTE FROM JENNY.
IT'S GOT A HEART ON IT! NATE! YOU DAWG!
IT'S NOT FOR ME, TEDDY. IT'S FOR ARTUR.
SO... YOU'RE DELIVERING A LOVE NOTE FROM THE GIRL YOU'VE LIKED SINCE FIRST GRADE TO THE GUY YOU'VE ALWAYS CONSIDERED YOUR ARCHRIVAL?
YUP.
© 2008 by NEA, Inc.
2/2
DUDE.
I KNOW.
Peirce

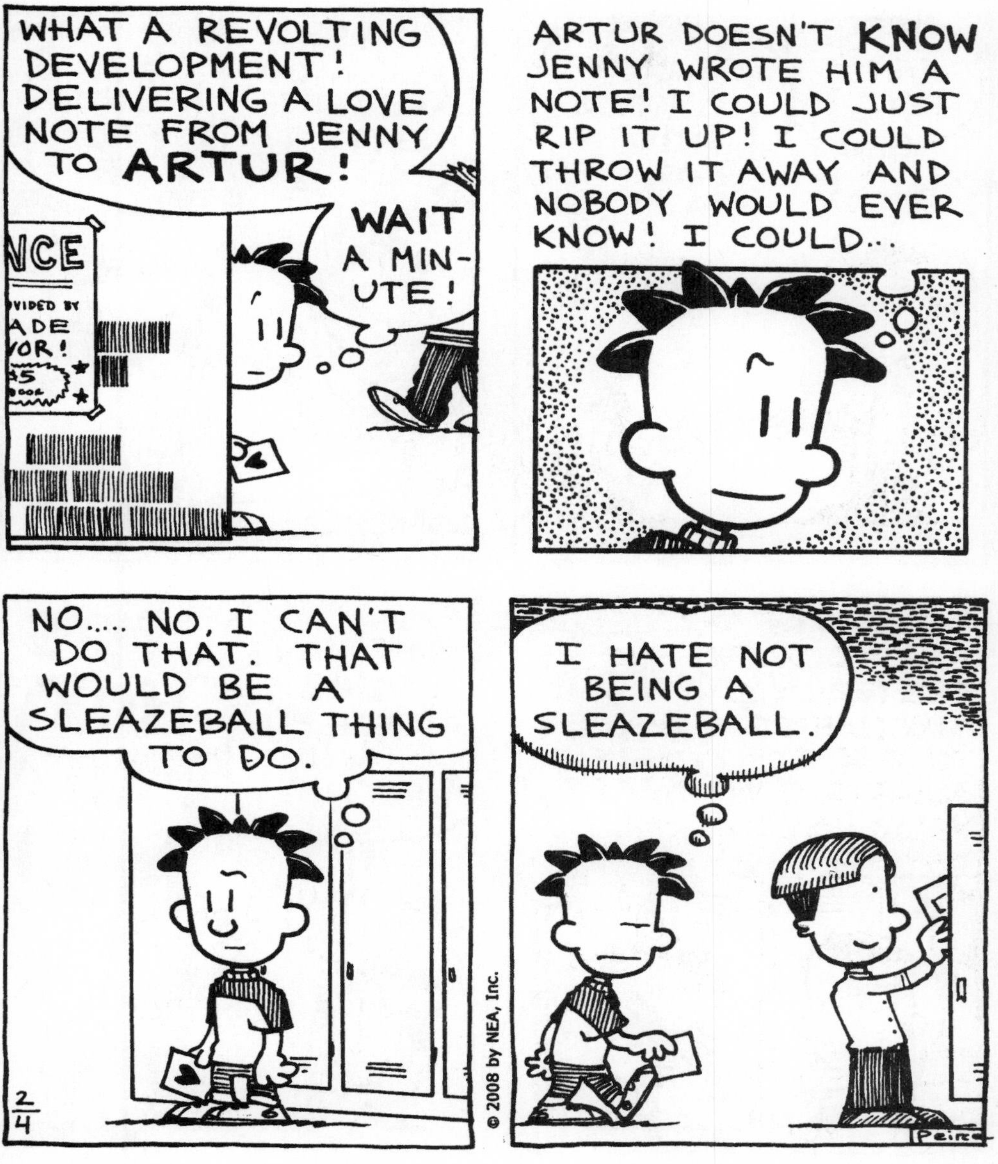
WHAT A REVOLTING DEVELOPMENT! DELIVERING A LOVE NOTE FROM JENNY TO **ARTUR**!
WAIT A MIN-UTE!
ARTUR DOESN'T **KNOW** JENNY WROTE HIM A NOTE! I COULD JUST RIP IT UP! I COULD THROW IT AWAY AND NOBODY WOULD EVER KNOW! I COULD...
NO.... NO, I CAN'T DO THAT. THAT WOULD BE A SLEAZEBALL THING TO DO.
© 2008 by NEA, Inc.
I HATE NOT BEING A SLEAZEBALL.

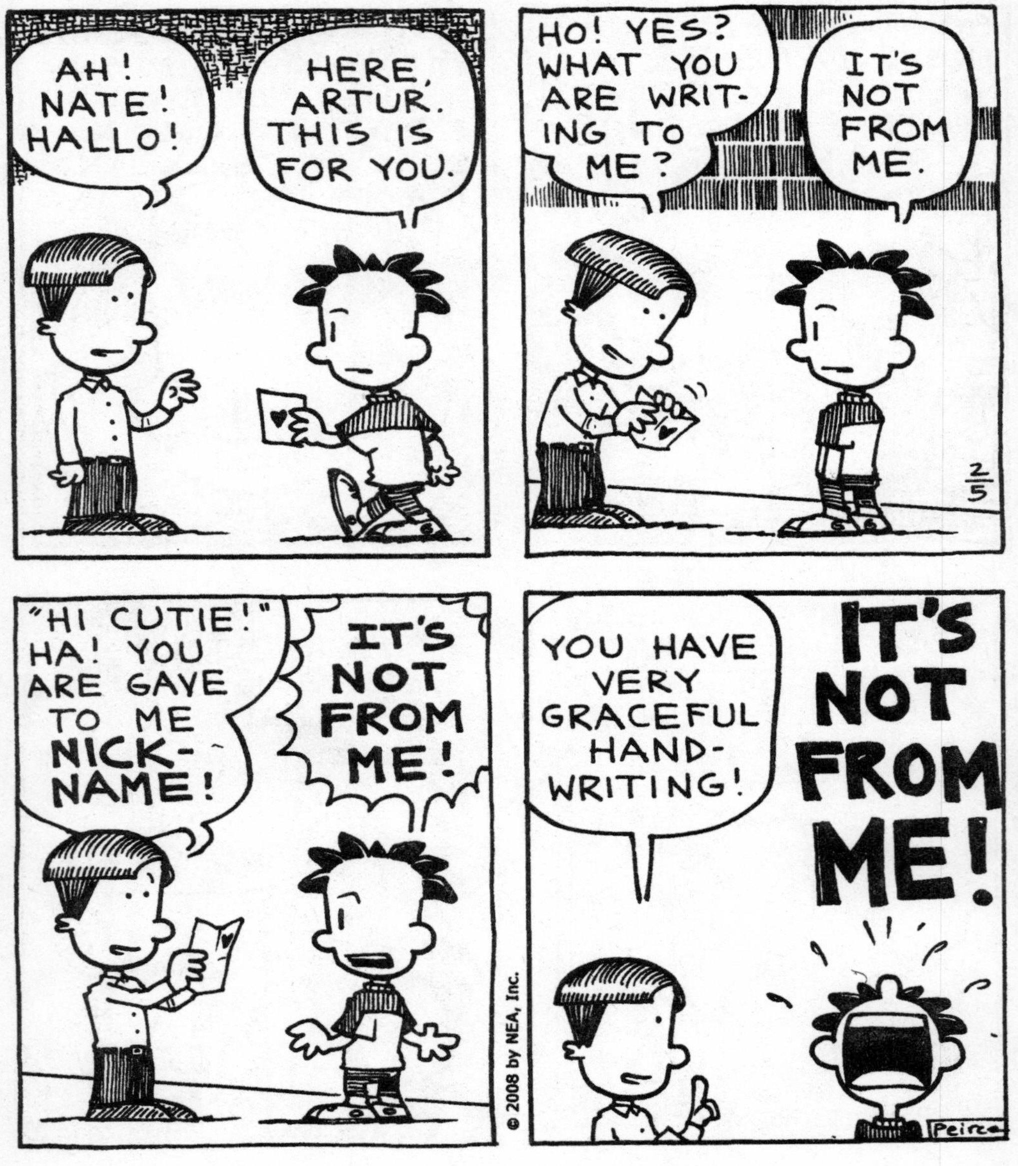
AH! NATE! HALLO!
HERE, ARTUR. THIS IS FOR YOU.
HO! YES? WHAT YOU ARE WRITING TO ME?
IT'S NOT FROM ME.
2/5
"HI CUTIE!" HA! YOU ARE GAVE TO ME NICKNAME!
IT'S NOT FROM ME!
© 2008 by NEA, Inc.
YOU HAVE VERY GRACEFUL HANDWRITING!
IT'S NOT FROM ME!
Peirce

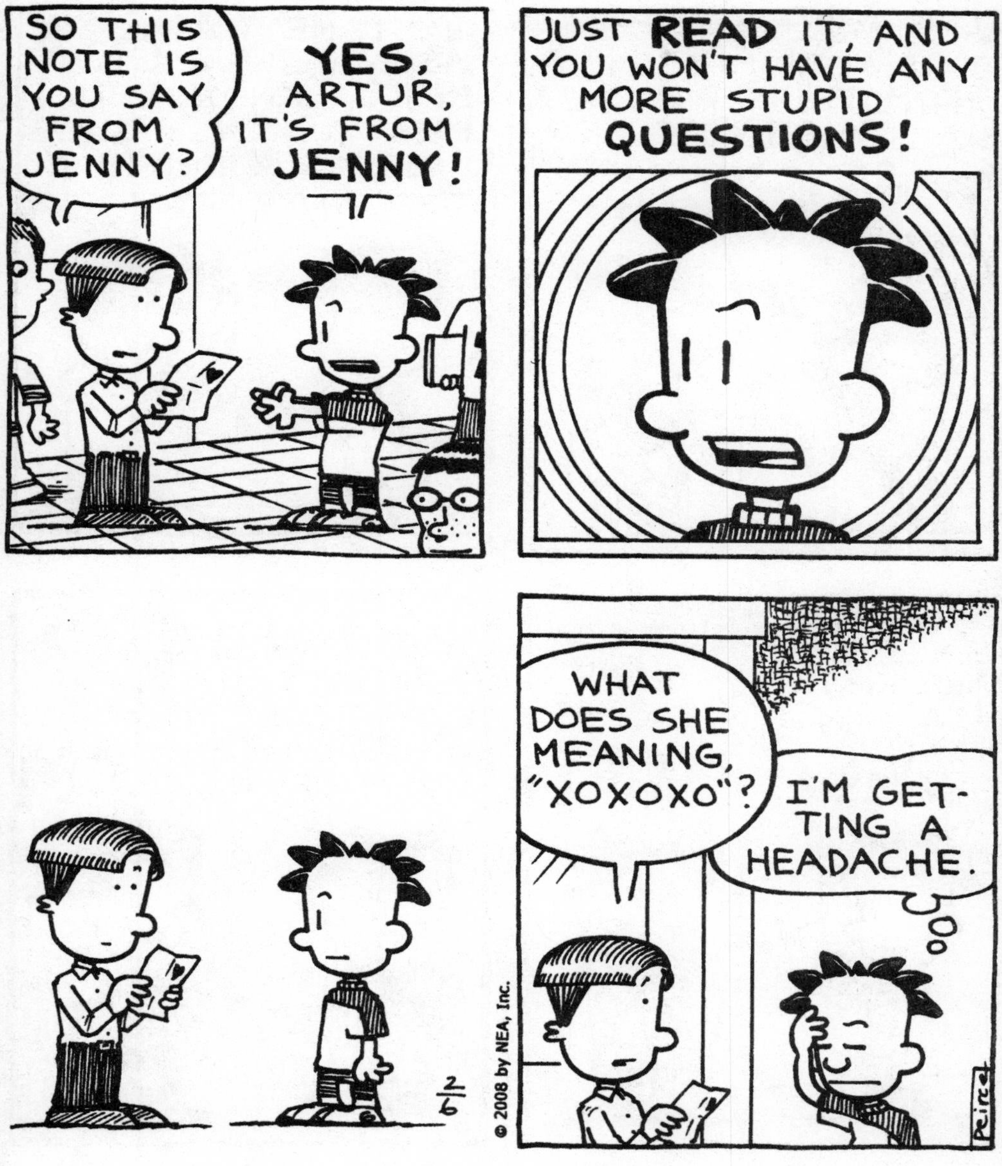
SO THIS NOTE IS YOU SAY FROM JENNY?
YES, ARTUR, IT'S FROM JENNY!
JUST READ IT, AND YOU WON'T HAVE ANY MORE STUPID QUESTIONS!
WHAT DOES SHE MEANING, "XOXOXO"?
I'M GETTING A HEADACHE.
6/2
© 2008 by NEA, Inc.
Peirce

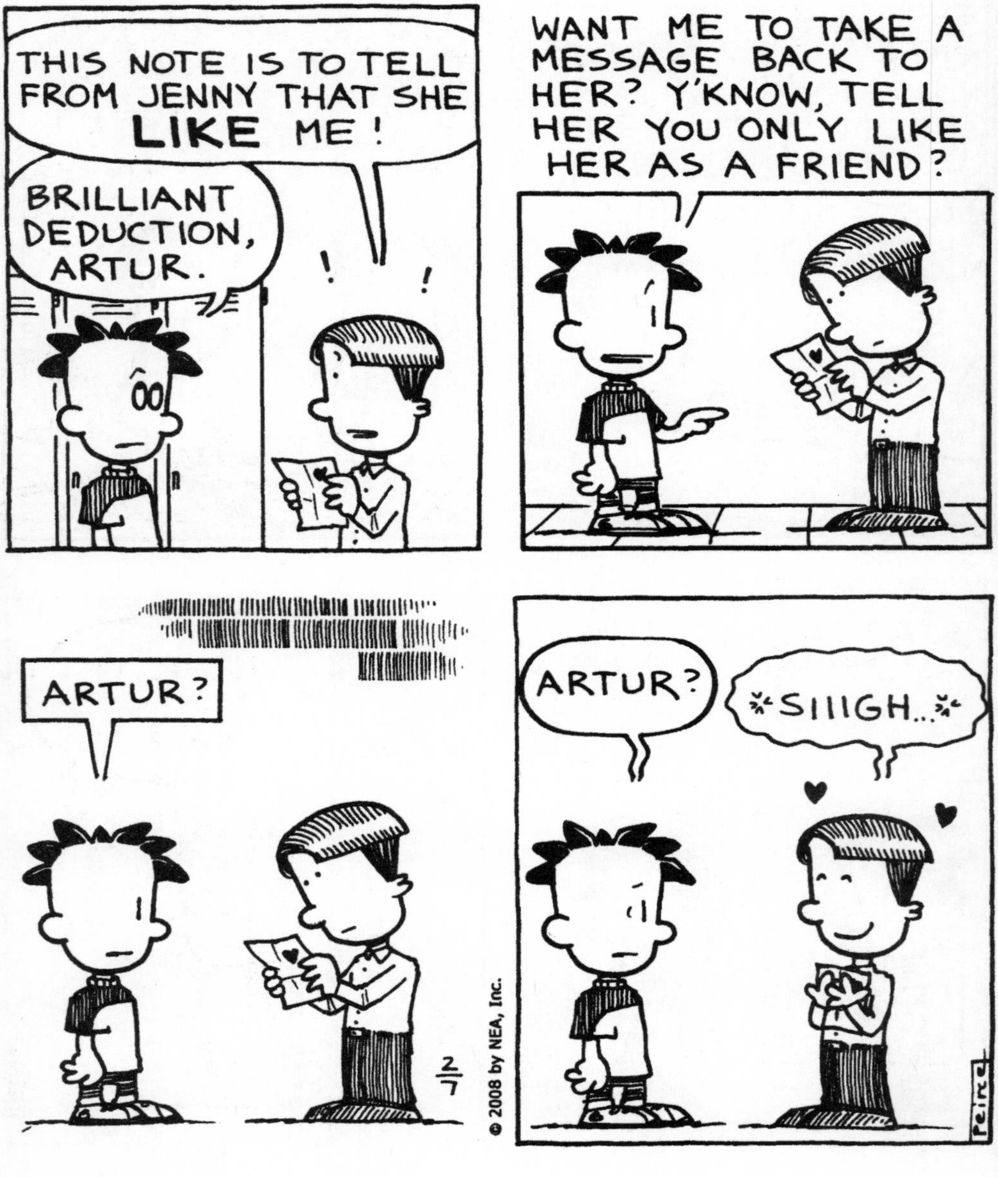
THIS NOTE IS TO TELL FROM JENNY THAT SHE LIKE ME!
BRILLIANT DEDUCTION, ARTUR.
!
!
WANT ME TO TAKE A MESSAGE BACK TO HER? Y'KNOW, TELL HER YOU ONLY LIKE HER AS A FRIEND?
ARTUR?
2/7
© 2008 by NEA, Inc.
ARTUR?
SIIIGH...
Peirce

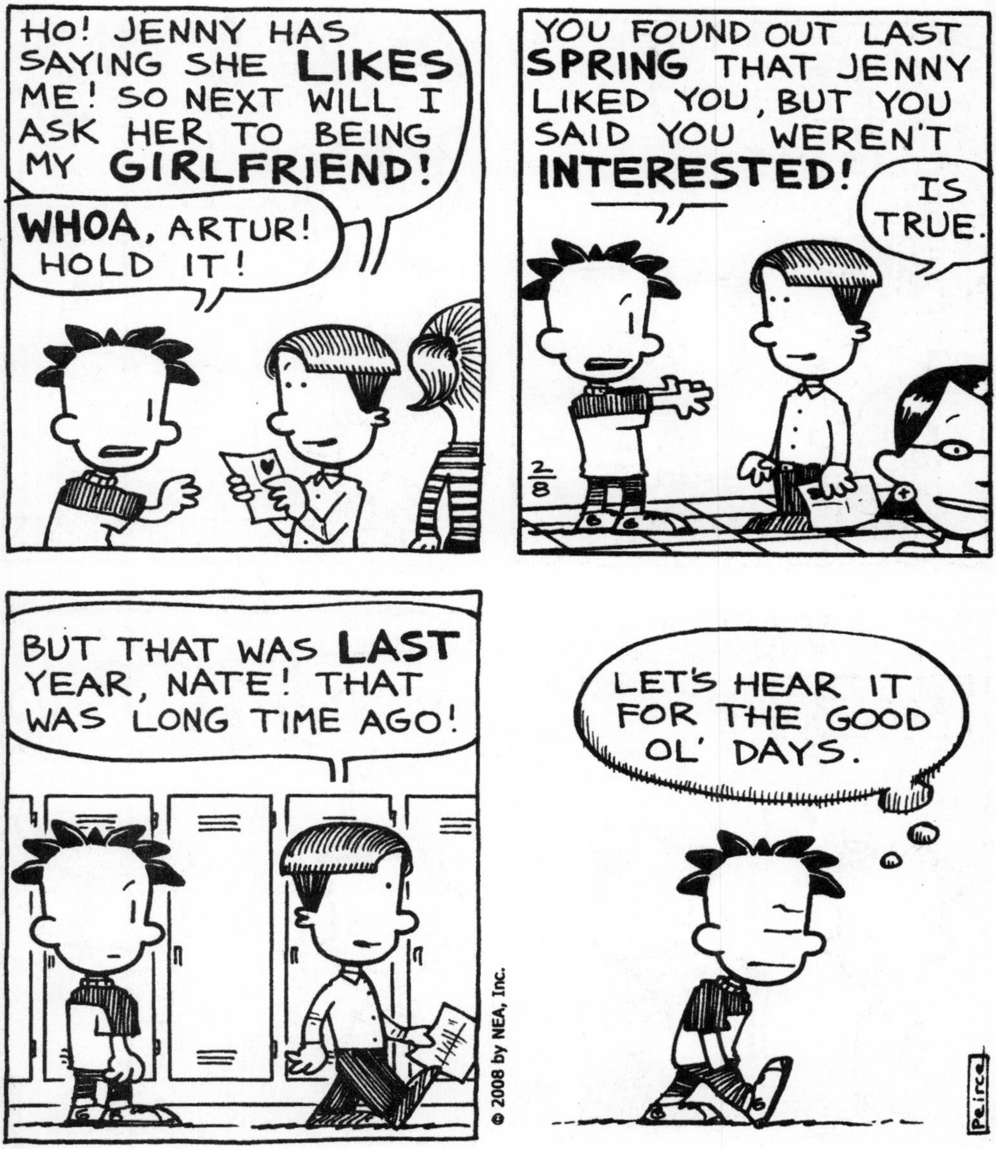
HO! JENNY HAS SAYING SHE LIKES ME! SO NEXT WILL I ASK HER TO BEING MY GIRLFRIEND!
WHOA, ARTUR! HOLD IT!
YOU FOUND OUT LAST SPRING THAT JENNY LIKED YOU, BUT YOU SAID YOU WEREN'T INTERESTED!
IS TRUE.
2/8
BUT THAT WAS LAST YEAR, NATE! THAT WAS LONG TIME AGO!
© 2008 by NEA, Inc.
LET'S HEAR IT FOR THE GOOD OL' DAYS.
Peirce

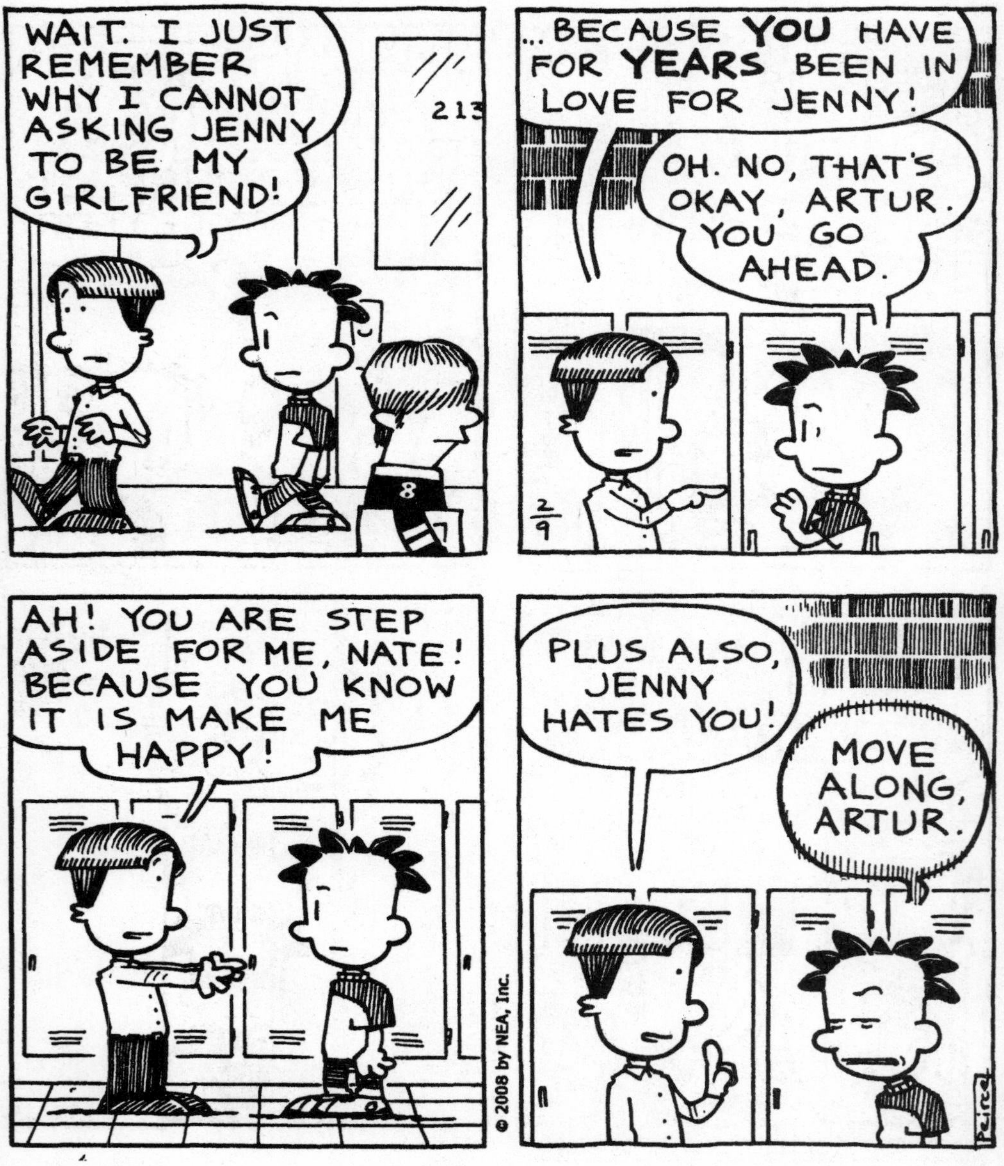
WAIT. I JUST REMEMBER WHY I CANNOT ASKING JENNY TO BE MY GIRLFRIEND!
213
8
...BECAUSE YOU HAVE FOR YEARS BEEN IN LOVE FOR JENNY!
OH. NO, THAT'S OKAY, ARTUR. YOU GO AHEAD.
2/9
AH! YOU ARE STEP ASIDE FOR ME, NATE! BECAUSE YOU KNOW IT IS MAKE ME HAPPY!
© 2008 by NEA, Inc.
PLUS ALSO, JENNY HATES YOU!
MOVE ALONG, ARTUR.
Peirce

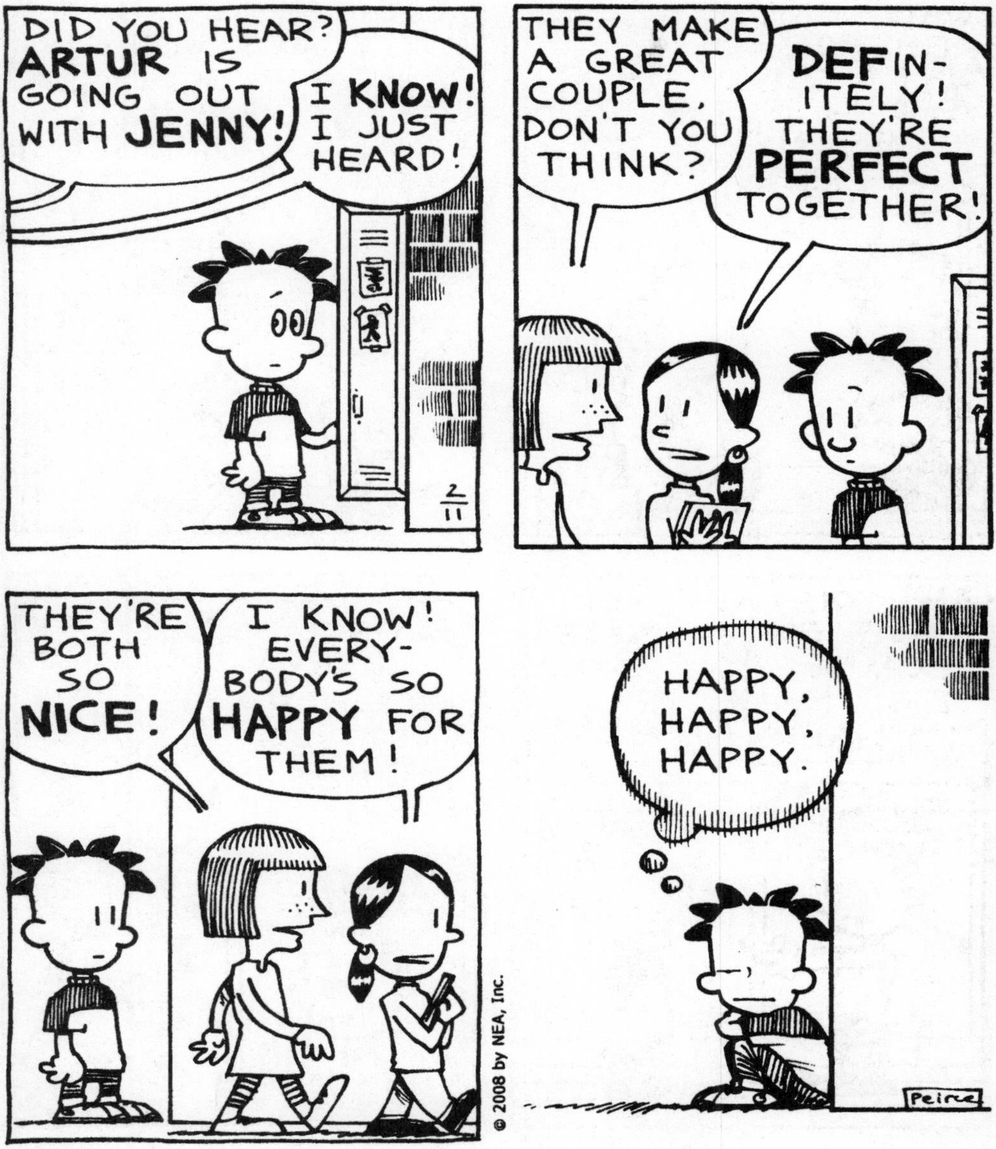
DID YOU HEAR? ARTUR IS GOING OUT WITH JENNY!
I KNOW! I JUST HEARD!
2/11
THEY MAKE A GREAT COUPLE, DON'T YOU THINK?
DEFIN-ITELY! THEY'RE PERFECT TOGETHER!
THEY'RE BOTH SO NICE!
I KNOW! EVERY-BODY'S SO HAPPY FOR THEM!
© 2008 by NEA, Inc.
HAPPY, HAPPY, HAPPY.
Peirce

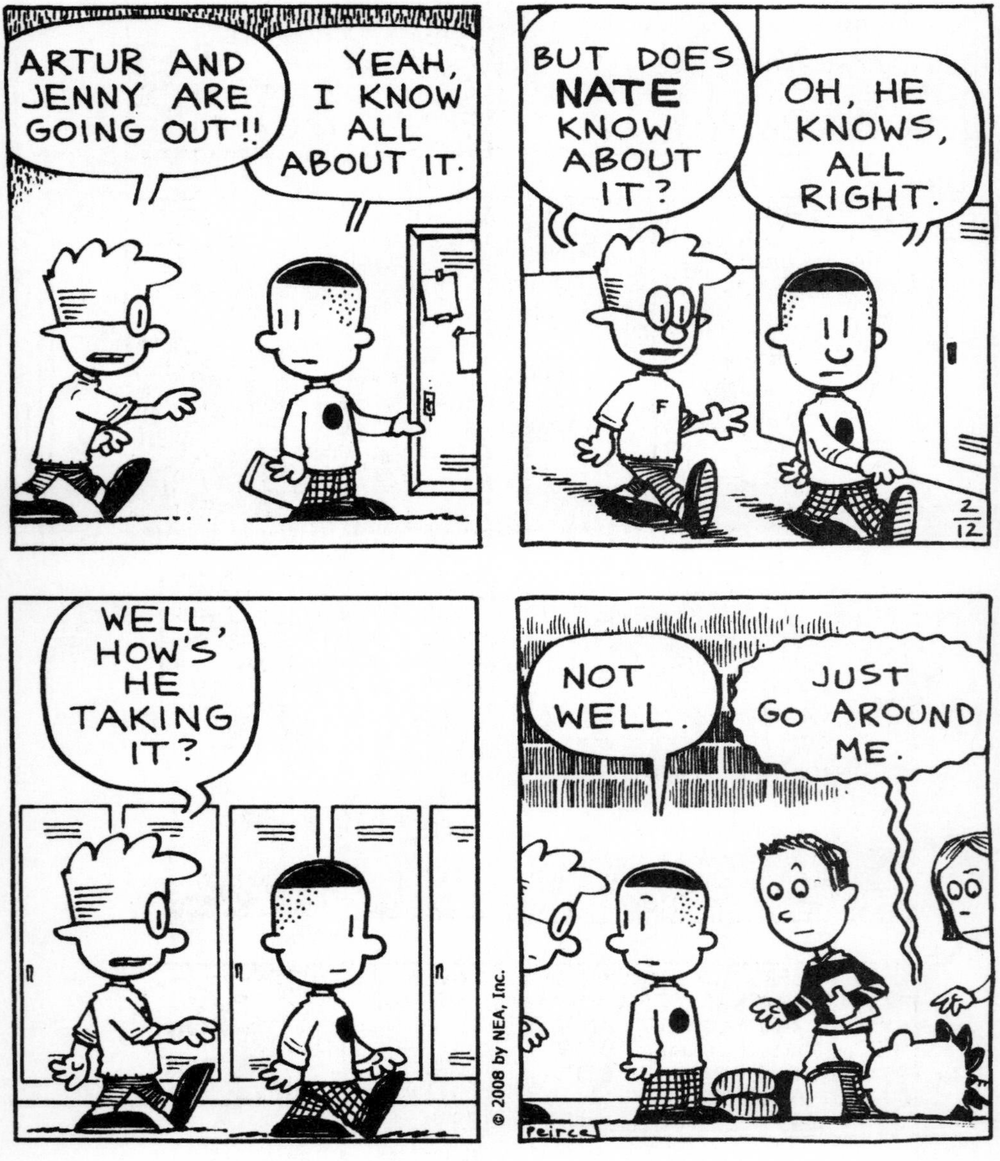
ARTUR AND JENNY ARE GOING OUT!!
YEAH, I KNOW ALL ABOUT IT.
BUT DOES NATE KNOW ABOUT IT?
OH, HE KNOWS, ALL RIGHT.
2/12
WELL, HOW'S HE TAKING IT?
NOT WELL.
JUST GO AROUND ME.
Peirce
© 2008 by NEA, Inc.

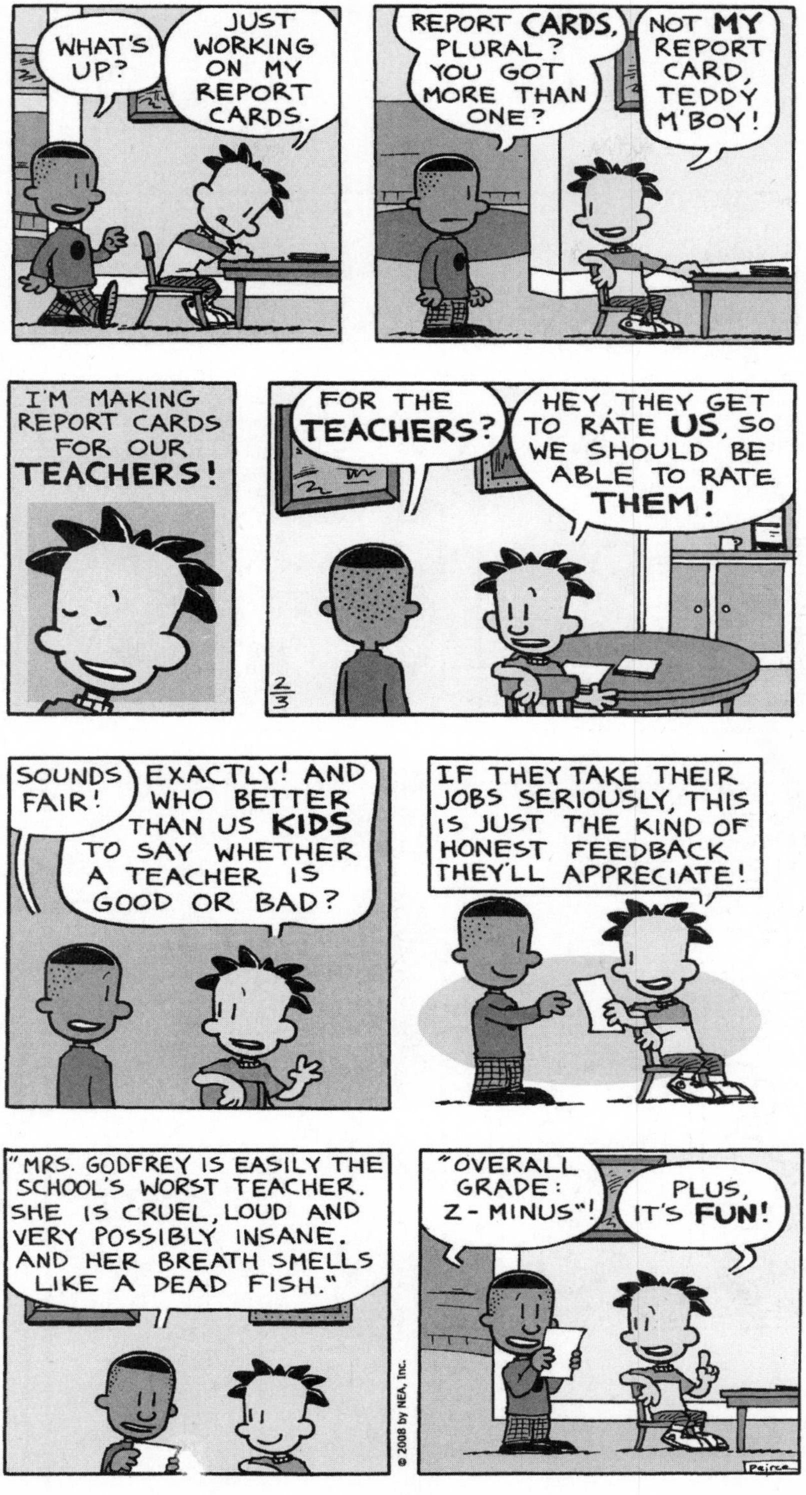
WHAT'S UP?
JUST WORKING ON MY REPORT CARDS.
REPORT CARDS, PLURAL? YOU GOT MORE THAN ONE?
NOT MY REPORT CARD, TEDDY M'BOY!
I'M MAKING REPORT CARDS FOR OUR TEACHERS!
FOR THE TEACHERS?
HEY, THEY GET TO RATE US, SO WE SHOULD BE ABLE TO RATE THEM!
2/3
SOUNDS FAIR!
EXACTLY! AND WHO BETTER THAN US KIDS TO SAY WHETHER A TEACHER IS GOOD OR BAD?
IF THEY TAKE THEIR JOBS SERIOUSLY, THIS IS JUST THE KIND OF HONEST FEEDBACK THEY'LL APPRECIATE!
"MRS. GODFREY IS EASILY THE SCHOOL'S WORST TEACHER. SHE IS CRUEL, LOUD AND VERY POSSIBLY INSANE. AND HER BREATH SMELLS LIKE A DEAD FISH."
"OVERALL GRADE: Z-MINUS"!
PLUS, IT'S FUN!
© 2008 by NEA, Inc.
Peirce

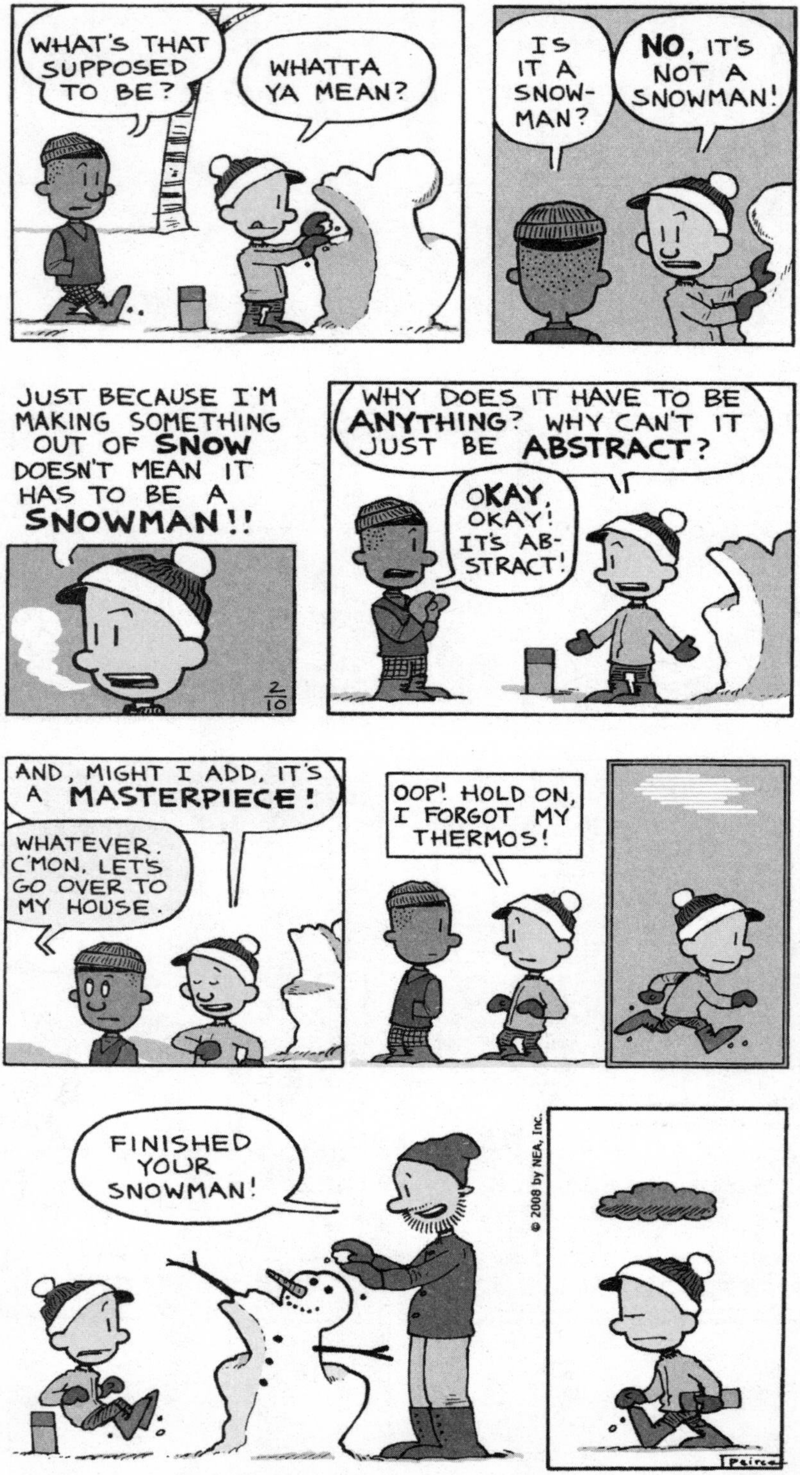
WHAT'S THAT SUPPOSED TO BE?
WHATTA YA MEAN?
IS IT A SNOW-MAN?
NO, IT'S NOT A SNOWMAN!
JUST BECAUSE I'M MAKING SOMETHING OUT OF SNOW DOESN'T MEAN IT HAS TO BE A SNOWMAN!!
2/10
WHY DOES IT HAVE TO BE ANYTHING? WHY CAN'T IT JUST BE ABSTRACT?
OKAY, OKAY! IT'S AB-STRACT!
AND, MIGHT I ADD, IT'S A MASTERPIECE!
WHATEVER. C'MON, LET'S GO OVER TO MY HOUSE.
OOP! HOLD ON, I FORGOT MY THERMOS!
FINISHED YOUR SNOWMAN!
© 2008 by NEA, Inc.
Peirce

LUNCH BLUES

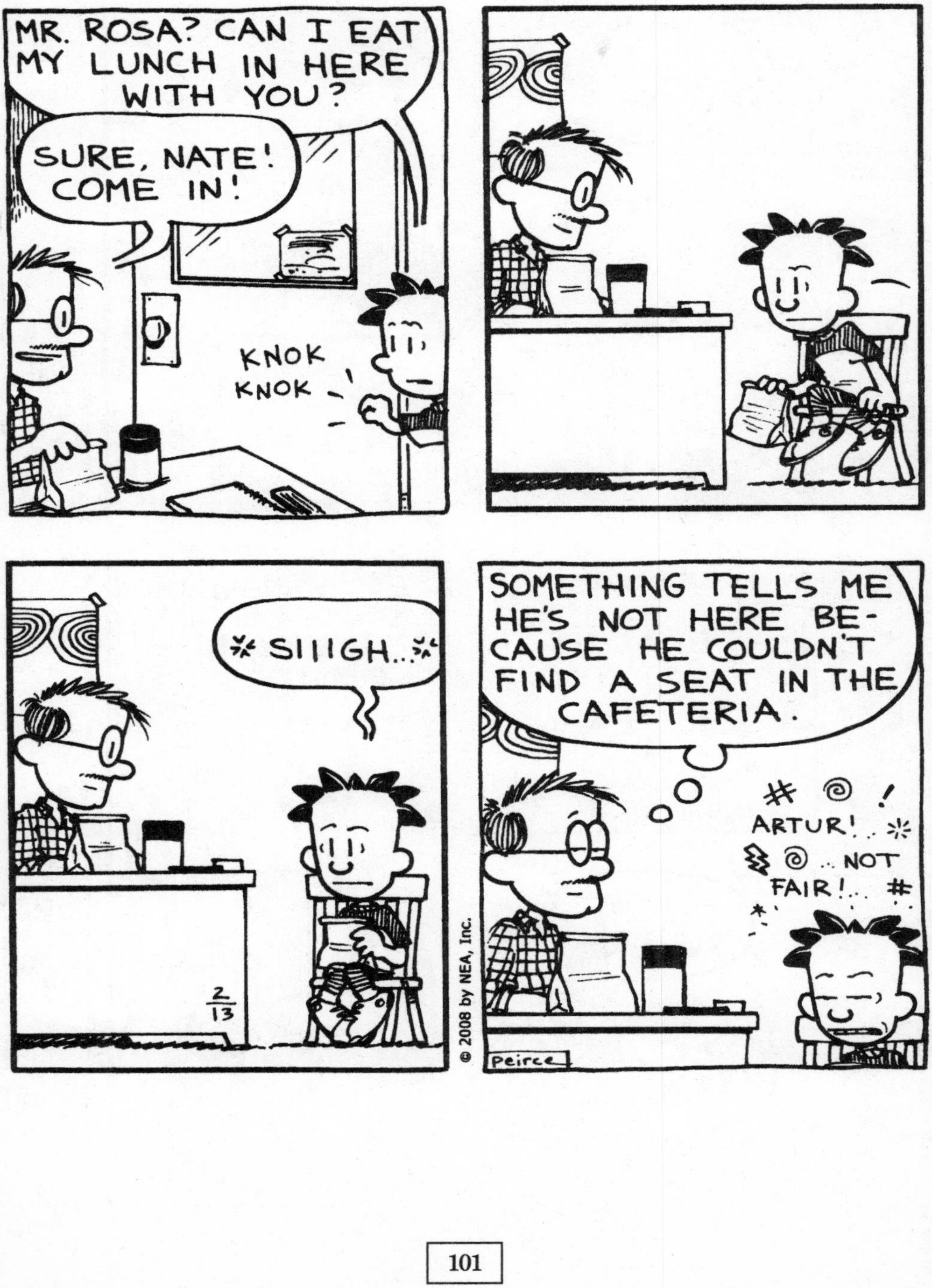
MR. ROSA? CAN I EAT MY LUNCH IN HERE WITH YOU?
SURE, NATE! COME IN!
KNOK KNOK
* SIIIGH... *
2/13
© 2008 by NEA, Inc.
SOMETHING TELLS ME HE'S NOT HERE BE-CAUSE HE COULDN'T FIND A SEAT IN THE CAFETERIA.
@ ! ARTUR! ... @ ... NOT FAIR! ...
Peirce

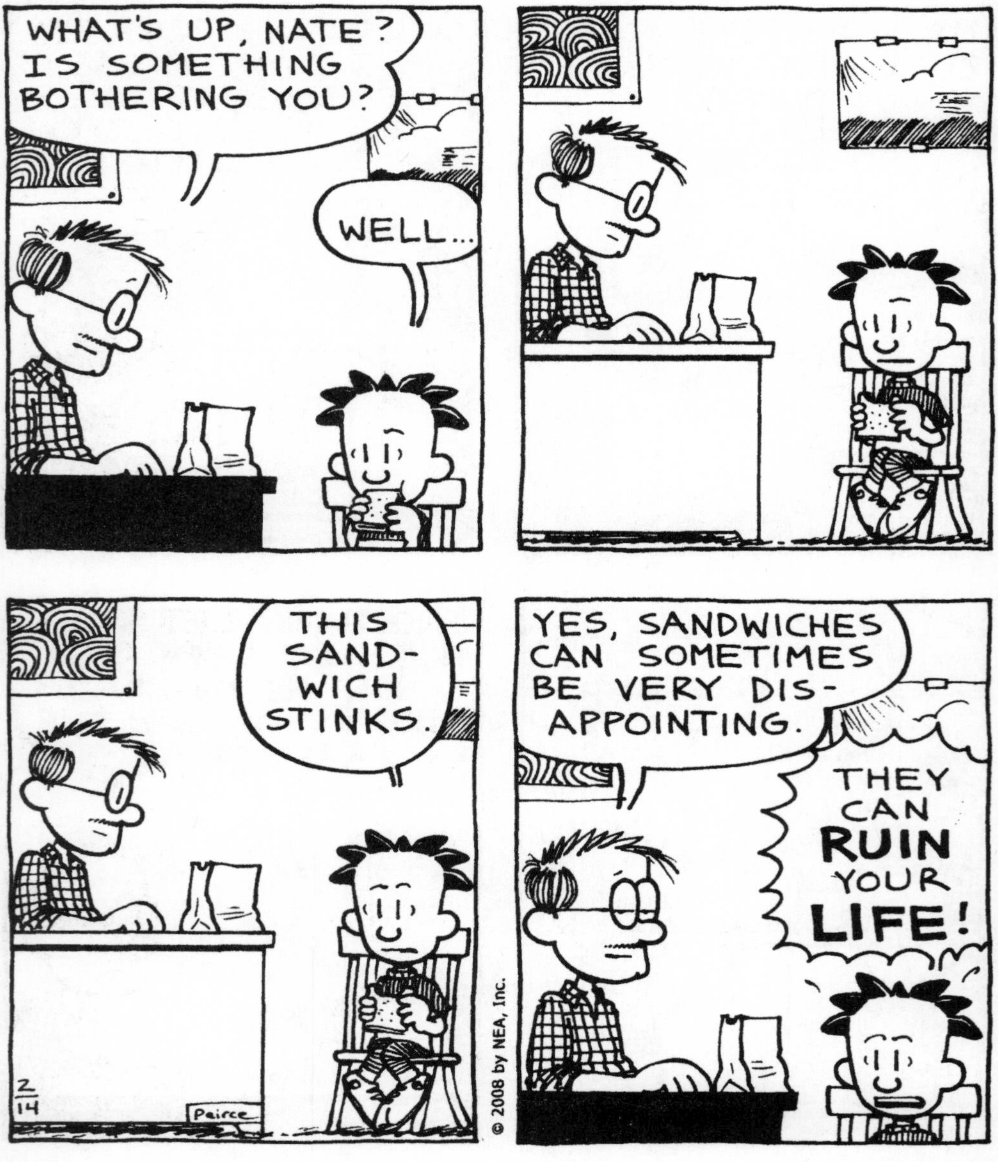
WHAT'S UP, NATE? IS SOMETHING BOTHERING YOU?
WELL...
THIS SAND- WICH STINKS.
2/14
Peirce
© 2008 by NEA, Inc.
YES, SANDWICHES CAN SOMETIMES BE VERY DIS- APPOINTING.
THEY CAN RUIN YOUR LIFE!

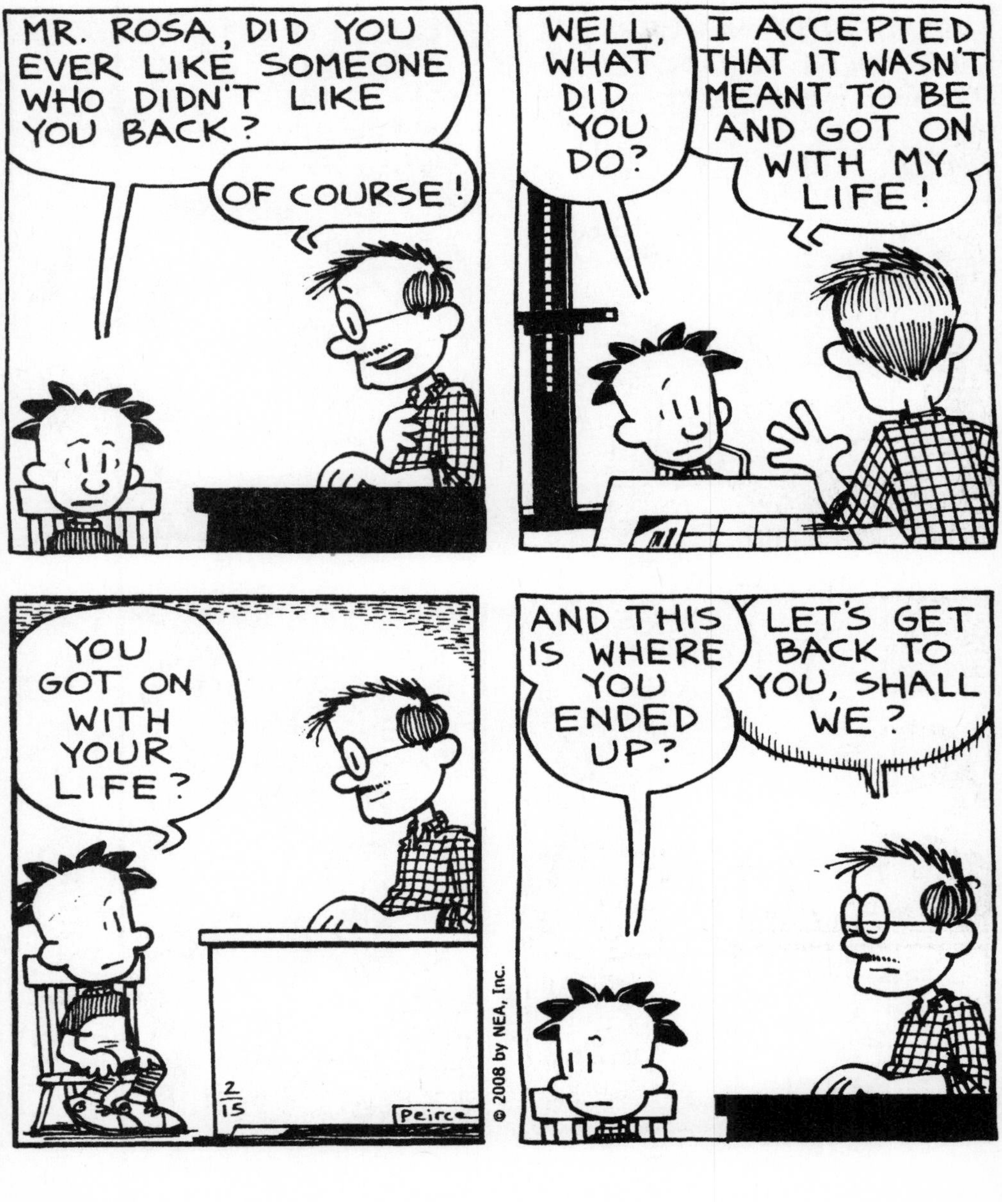
MR. ROSA, DID YOU EVER LIKE SOMEONE WHO DIDN'T LIKE YOU BACK?
OF COURSE!
WELL, WHAT DID YOU DO?
I ACCEPTED THAT IT WASN'T MEANT TO BE AND GOT ON WITH MY LIFE!
YOU GOT ON WITH YOUR LIFE?
2/15
Peirce
AND THIS IS WHERE YOU ENDED UP?
LET'S GET BACK TO YOU, SHALL WE?

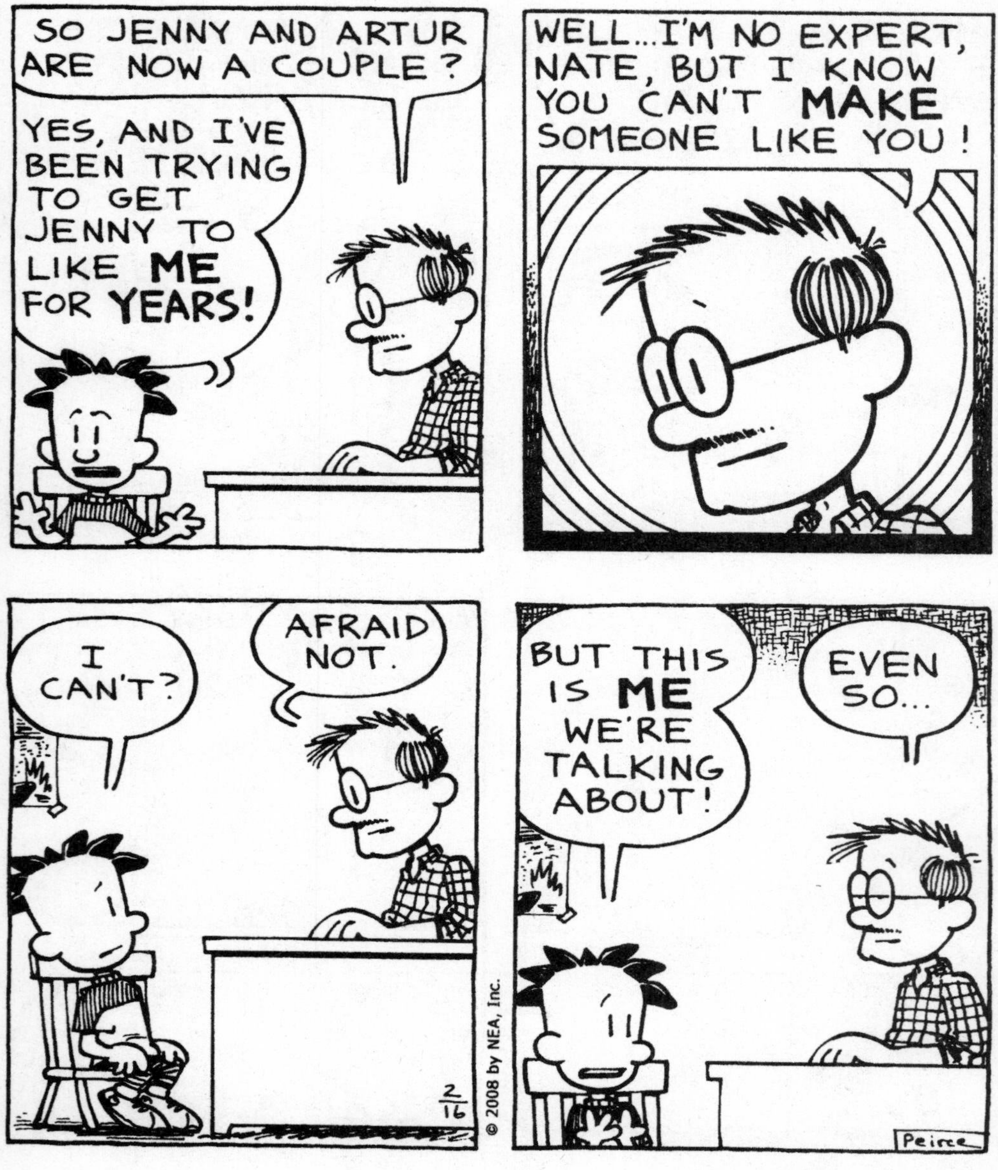
SO JENNY AND ARTUR ARE NOW A COUPLE?
YES, AND I'VE BEEN TRYING TO GET JENNY TO LIKE ME FOR YEARS!
WELL...I'M NO EXPERT, NATE, BUT I KNOW YOU CAN'T MAKE SOMEONE LIKE YOU!
I CAN'T?
AFRAID NOT.
2/16
BUT THIS IS ME WE'RE TALKING ABOUT!
EVEN SO...
Peirce

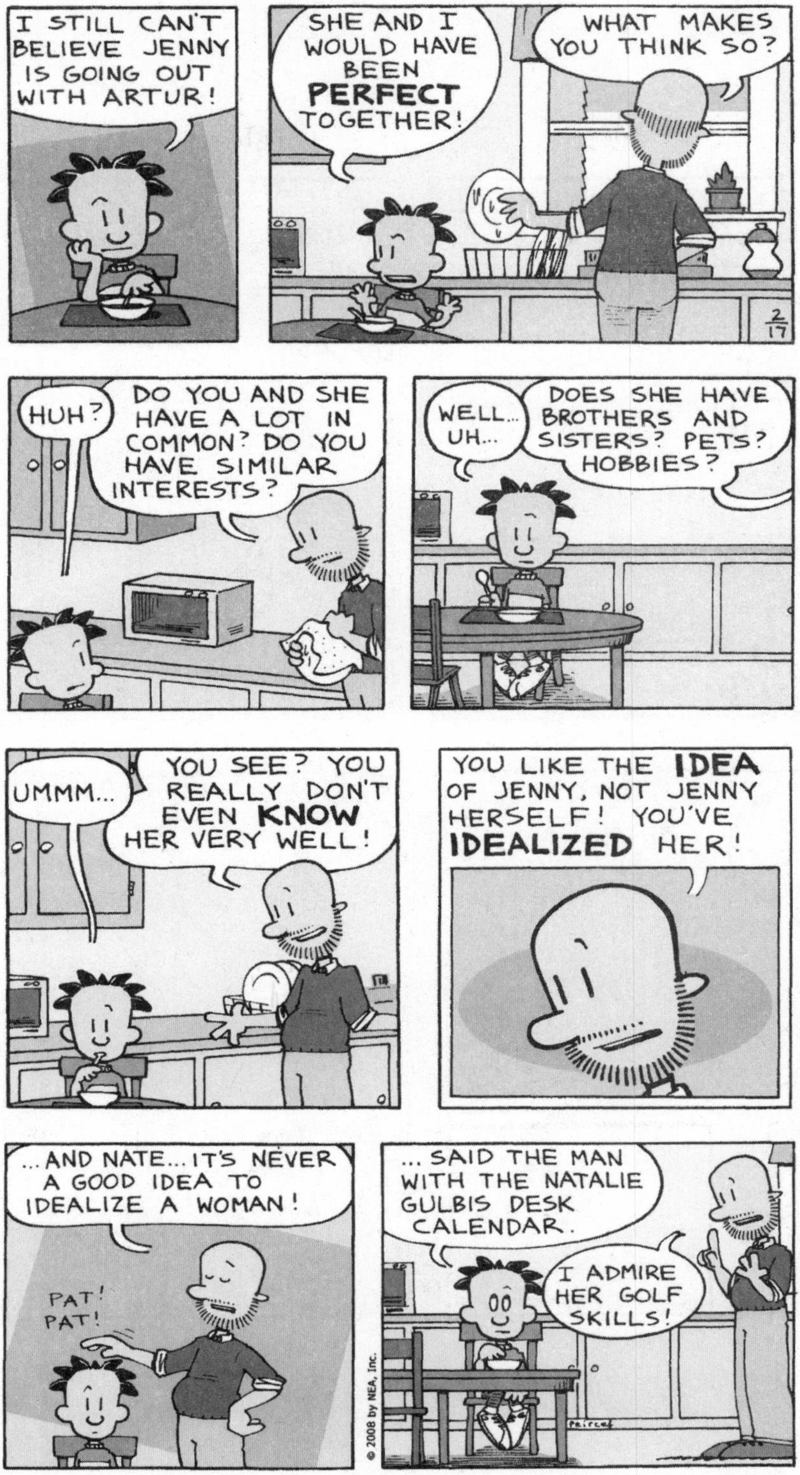
I STILL CAN'T BELIEVE JENNY IS GOING OUT WITH ARTUR!
SHE AND I WOULD HAVE BEEN PERFECT TOGETHER!
WHAT MAKES YOU THINK SO?
2/17
HUH?
DO YOU AND SHE HAVE A LOT IN COMMON? DO YOU HAVE SIMILAR INTERESTS?
WELL... UH...
DOES SHE HAVE BROTHERS AND SISTERS? PETS? HOBBIES?
UMMM...
YOU SEE? YOU REALLY DON'T EVEN KNOW HER VERY WELL!
YOU LIKE THE IDEA OF JENNY, NOT JENNY HERSELF! YOU'VE IDEALIZED HER!
...AND NATE... IT'S NEVER A GOOD IDEA TO IDEALIZE A WOMAN!
PAT! PAT!
...SAID THE MAN WITH THE NATALIE GULBIS DESK CALENDAR.
I ADMIRE HER GOLF SKILLS!
© 2008 by NEA, Inc.

NATE WRIGHT, FOOD CRITIC

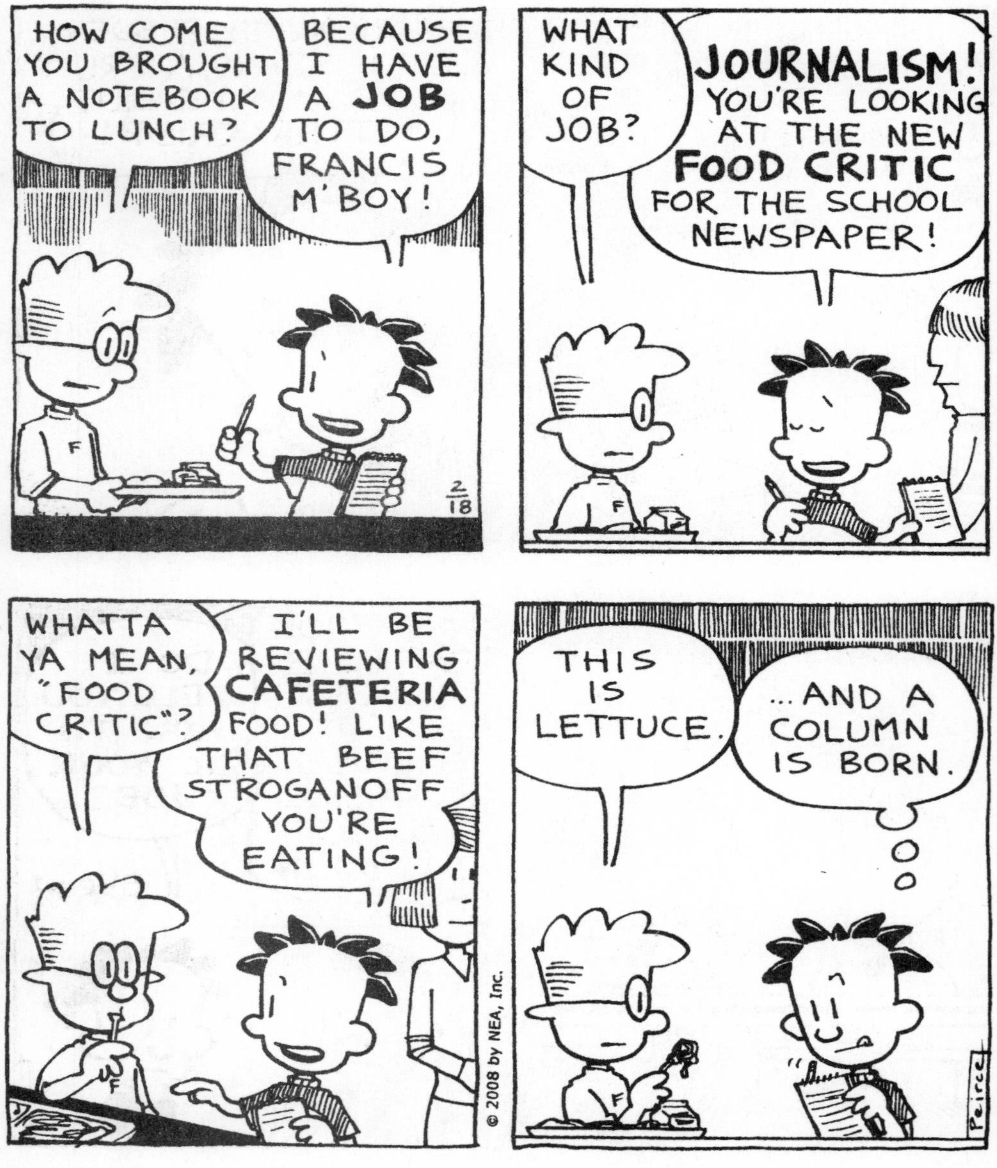

HOW COME YOU BROUGHT A NOTEBOOK TO LUNCH?
BECAUSE I HAVE A **JOB** TO DO, FRANCIS M'BOY!
2/18
WHAT KIND OF JOB?
JOURNALISM! YOU'RE LOOKING AT THE NEW **FOOD CRITIC** FOR THE SCHOOL NEWSPAPER!
WHATTA YA MEAN, "FOOD CRITIC"?
I'LL BE REVIEWING **CAFETERIA** FOOD! LIKE THAT BEEF STROGANOFF YOU'RE EATING!
© 2008 by NEA, Inc.
THIS IS LETTUCE.
...AND A COLUMN IS BORN.
Peirce

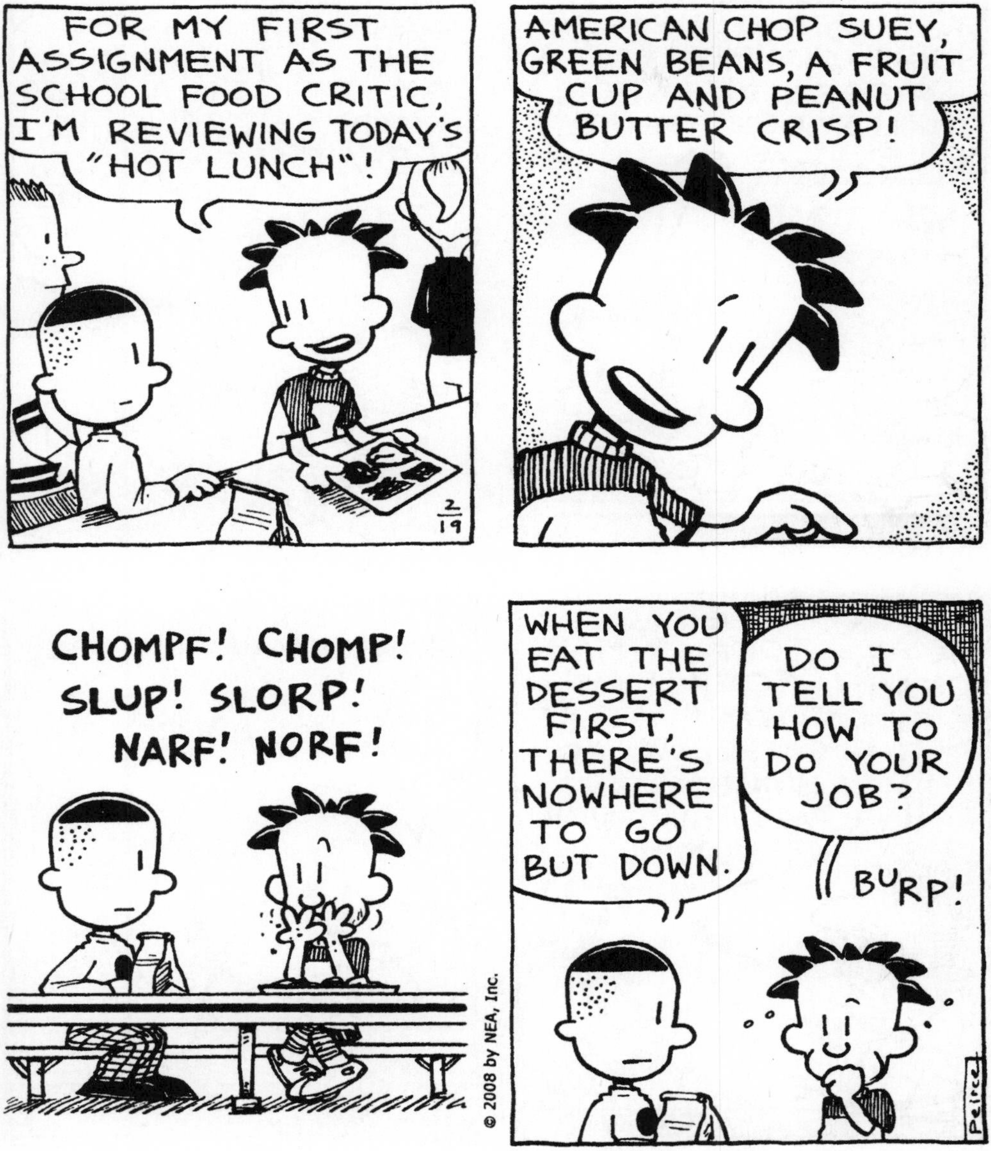
FOR MY FIRST ASSIGNMENT AS THE SCHOOL FOOD CRITIC, I'M REVIEWING TODAY'S "HOT LUNCH"!
2/19
AMERICAN CHOP SUEY, GREEN BEANS, A FRUIT CUP AND PEANUT BUTTER CRISP!
CHOMPF! CHOMP! SLUP! SLORP! NARF! NORF!
WHEN YOU EAT THE DESSERT FIRST, THERE'S NOWHERE TO GO BUT DOWN.
DO I TELL YOU HOW TO DO YOUR JOB?
BURP!
Peirce
© 2008 by NEA, Inc.

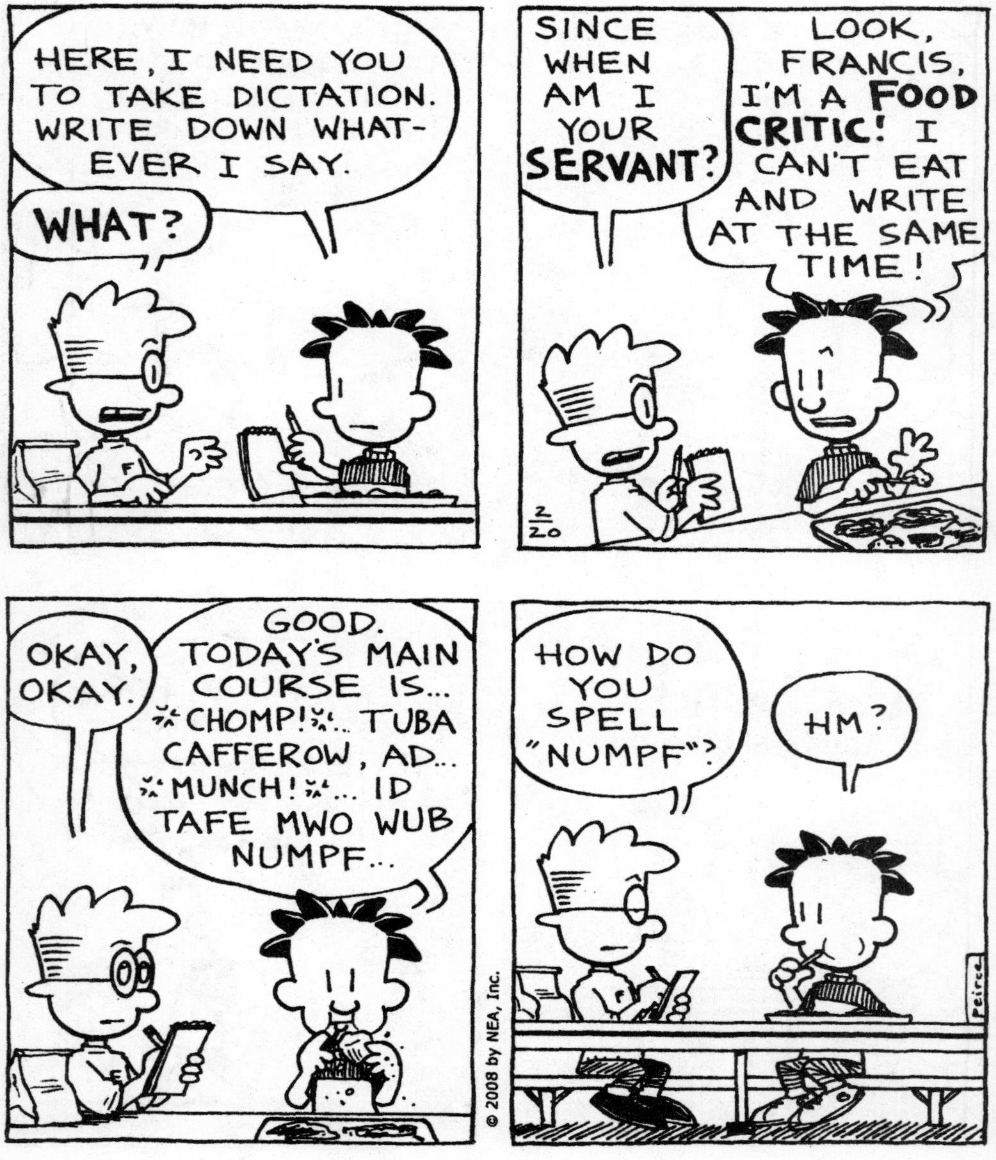
HERE, I NEED YOU TO TAKE DICTATION. WRITE DOWN WHATEVER I SAY.
WHAT?
SINCE WHEN AM I YOUR SERVANT?
LOOK, FRANCIS, I'M A FOOD CRITIC! I CAN'T EAT AND WRITE AT THE SAME TIME!
2/20
OKAY, OKAY.
GOOD. TODAY'S MAIN COURSE IS... CHOMP!... TUBA CAFFEROW, AD... MUNCH!... ID TAFE MWO WUB NUMPF...
© 2008 by NEA, Inc.
HOW DO YOU SPELL "NUMPF"?
HM?
Peirce

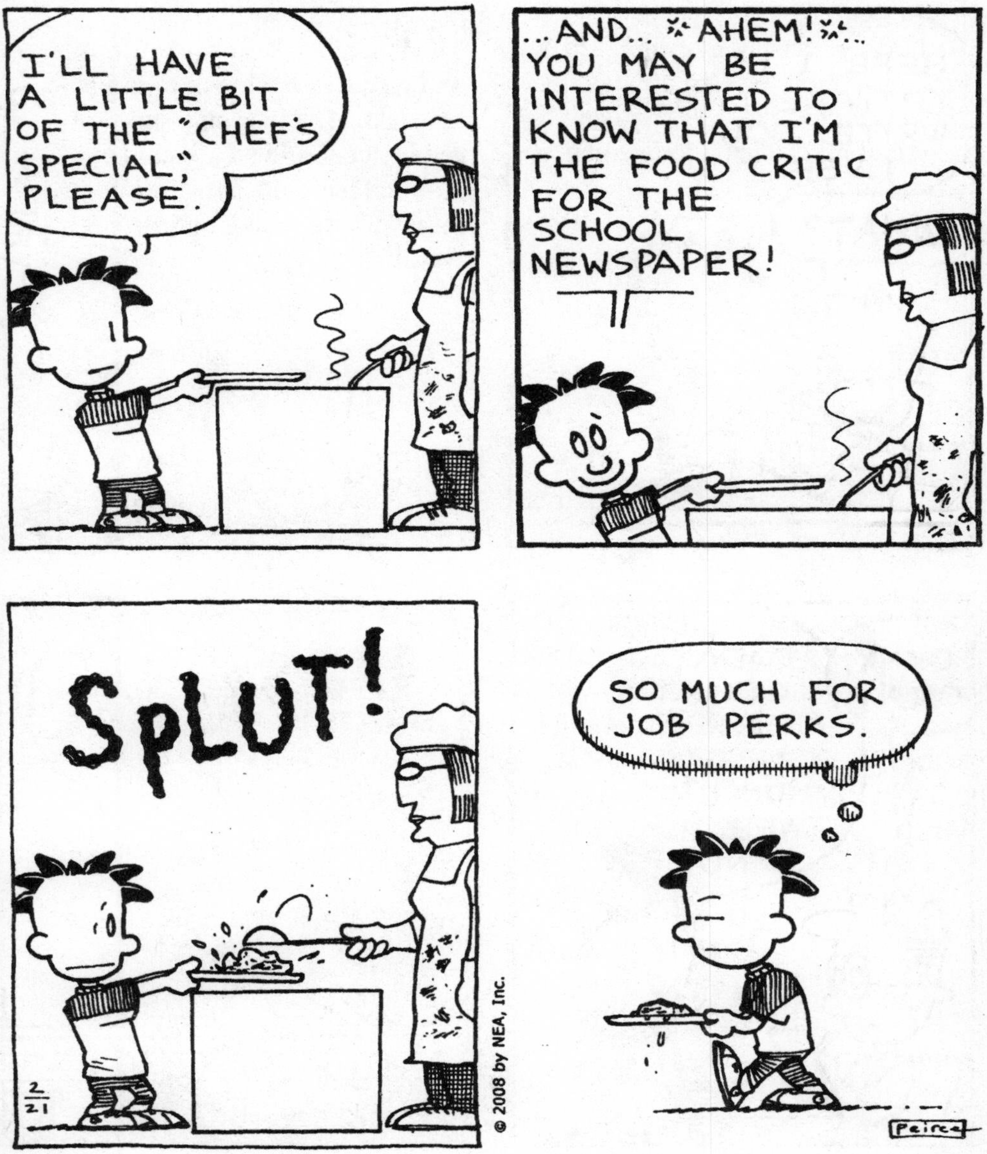
I'LL HAVE A LITTLE BIT OF THE "CHEF'S SPECIAL," PLEASE.
...AND... *AHEM!*... YOU MAY BE INTERESTED TO KNOW THAT I'M THE FOOD CRITIC FOR THE SCHOOL NEWSPAPER!
SPLUT!
SO MUCH FOR JOB PERKS.
2/21
© 2008 by NEA, Inc.
Peirce

At 11:35 yesterday morning, as I sat in the cafeteria looking down at the "lunch" before me, I immediately regretted my decision to become the school food critic.

The so-called "fish sticks" looked and tasted like a block of moist sawdust. The garden salad was reminiscent of a sickly chia pet. And the ice-cold Tater Tots appeared to have been cooked under a 60-watt light bulb.

Of the bread pudding I will say only two words: gag reflex. I spent most of the afternoon getting violently ill in the second-floor bathroom. TOMORROW: MEAT LOAF CONFIDENTIAL!

IN THE FOOD CRITIC BIZ, THAT'S WHAT IS KNOWN AS "DISHING IT OUT."

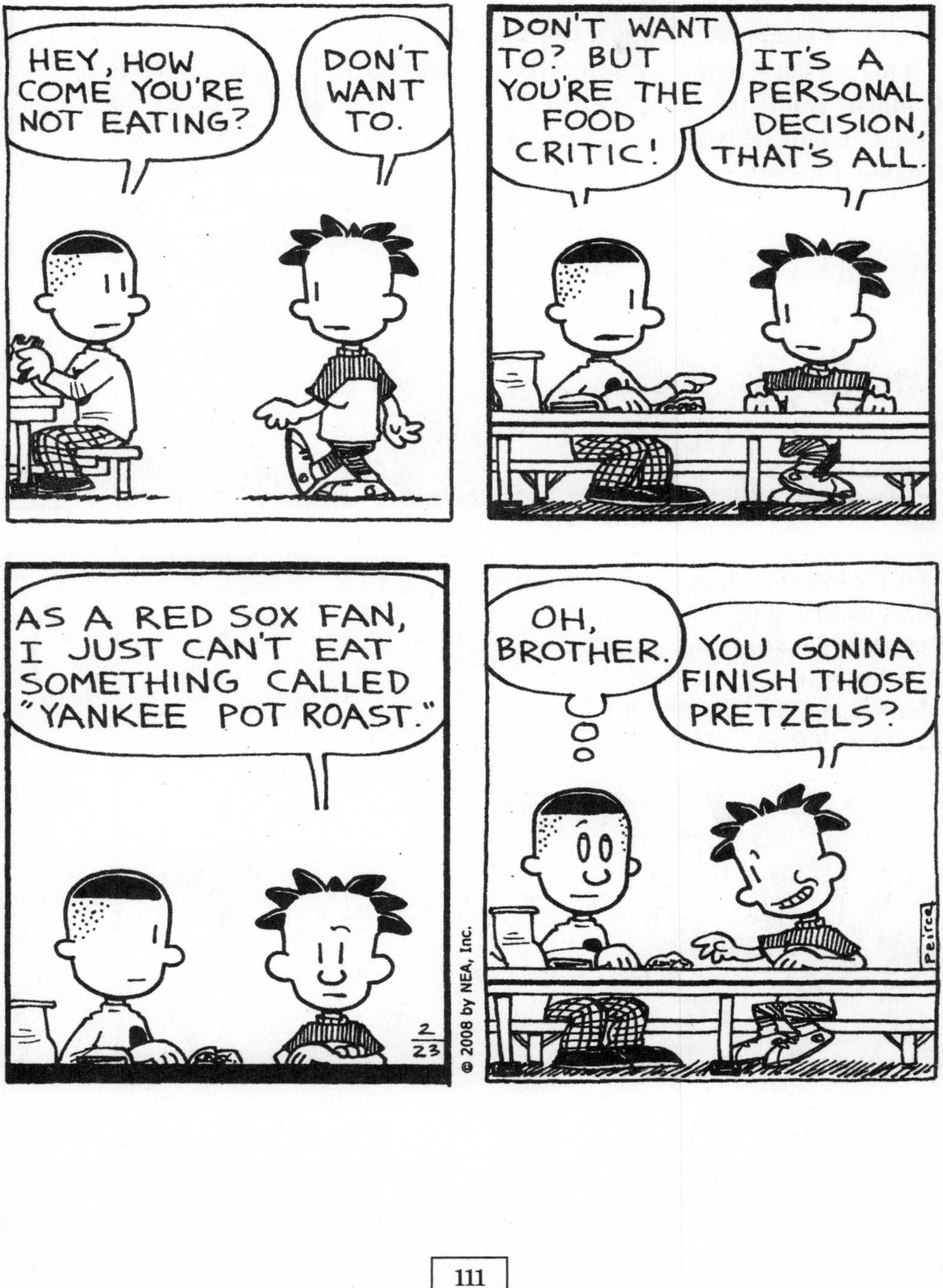
HEY, HOW COME YOU'RE NOT EATING?
DON'T WANT TO.
DON'T WANT TO? BUT YOU'RE THE FOOD CRITIC!
IT'S A PERSONAL DECISION, THAT'S ALL.
AS A RED SOX FAN, I JUST CAN'T EAT SOMETHING CALLED "YANKEE POT ROAST."
OH, BROTHER.
YOU GONNA FINISH THOSE PRETZELS?
2/23
PEIRCE
© 2008 by NEA, Inc.

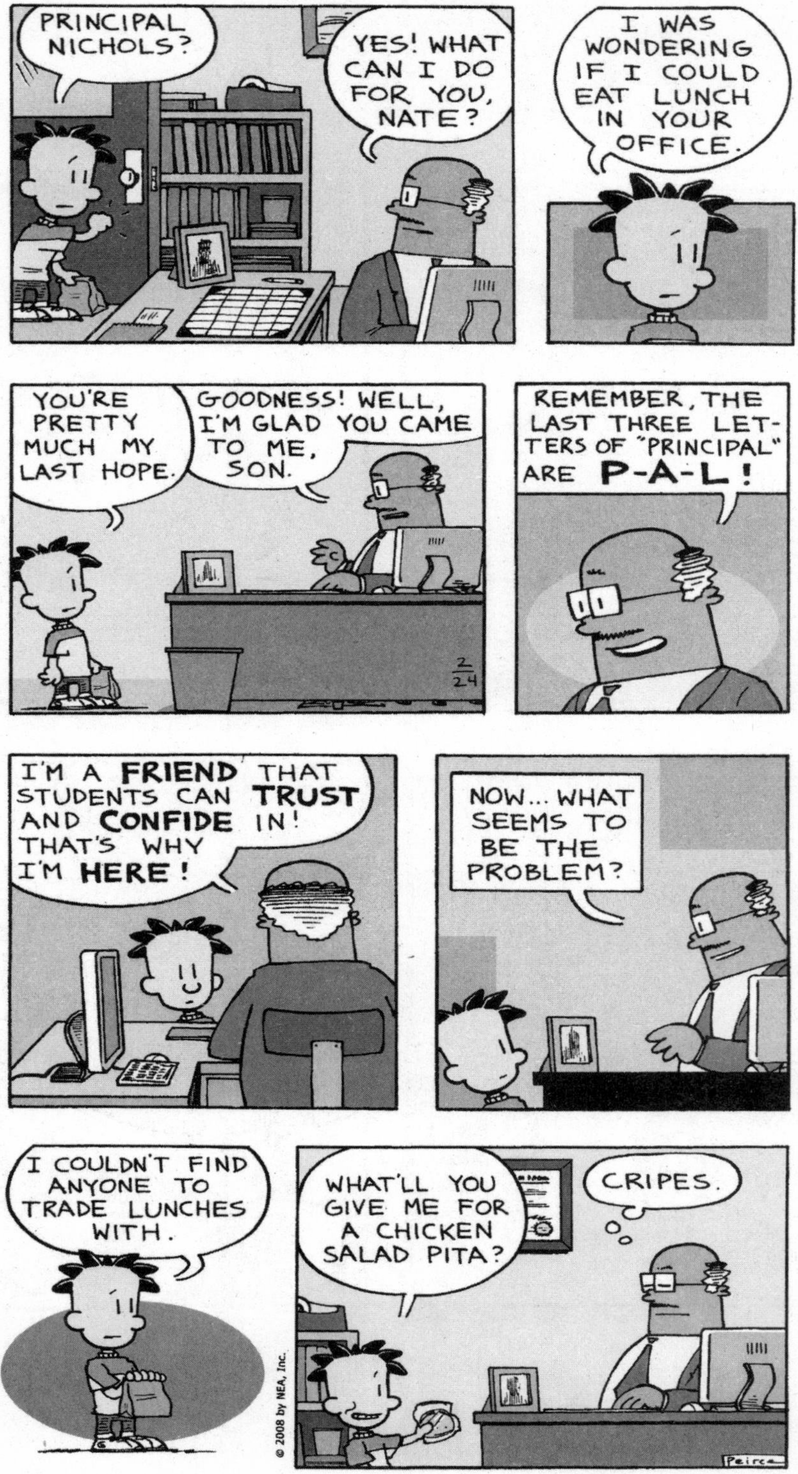
PRINCIPAL NICHOLS?
YES! WHAT CAN I DO FOR YOU, NATE?
I WAS WONDERING IF I COULD EAT LUNCH IN YOUR OFFICE.
YOU'RE PRETTY MUCH MY LAST HOPE.
GOODNESS! WELL, I'M GLAD YOU CAME TO ME, SON.
2
24
REMEMBER, THE LAST THREE LETTERS OF "PRINCIPAL" ARE P-A-L!
I'M A FRIEND THAT STUDENTS CAN TRUST AND CONFIDE IN! THAT'S WHY I'M HERE!
NOW... WHAT SEEMS TO BE THE PROBLEM?
I COULDN'T FIND ANYONE TO TRADE LUNCHES WITH.
WHAT'LL YOU GIVE ME FOR A CHICKEN SALAD PITA?
CRIPES.
Peirce

WHAT'S WITH BODY LANGUAGE?

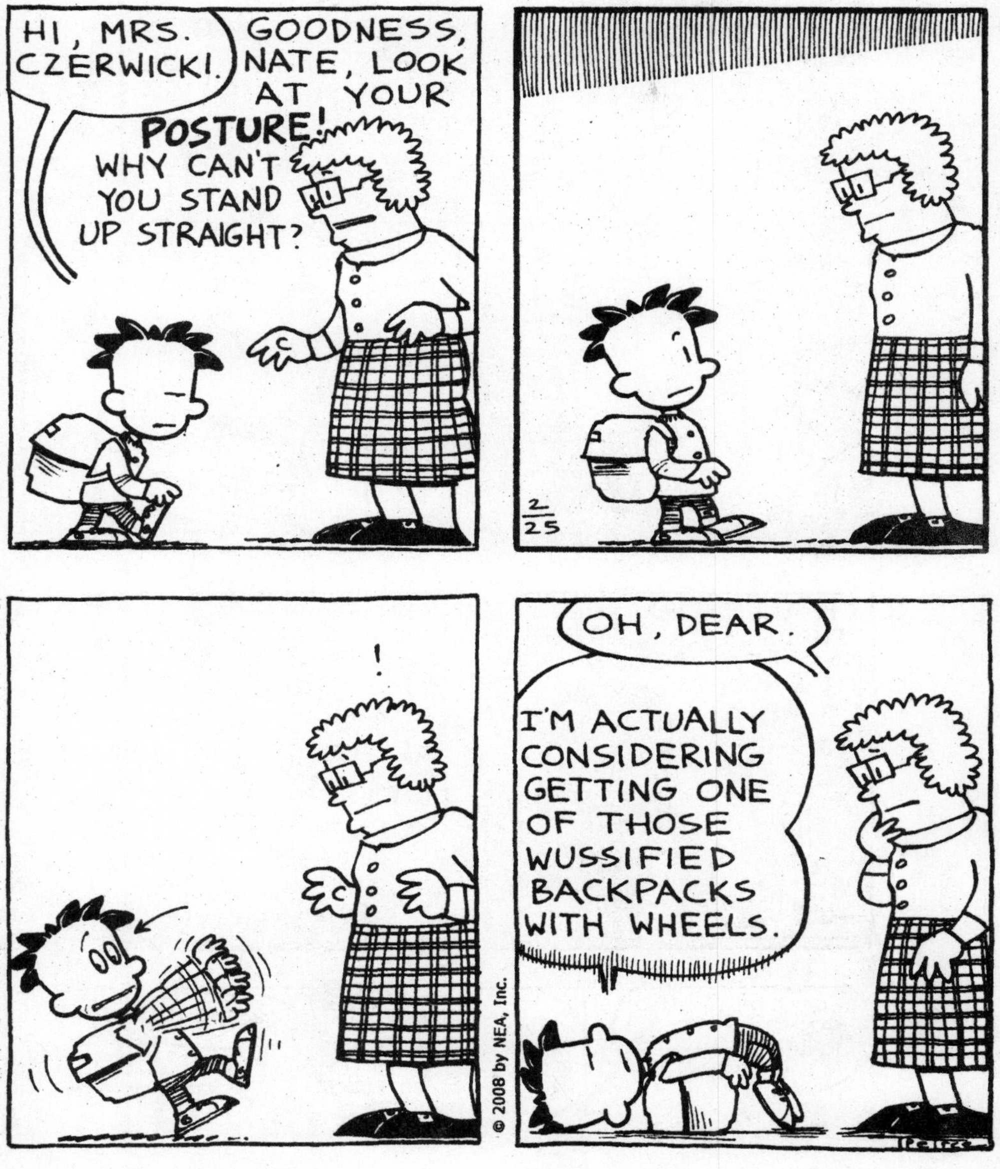
HI, MRS. CZERWICKI.
GOODNESS, NATE, LOOK AT YOUR POSTURE! WHY CAN'T YOU STAND UP STRAIGHT?
2/25
!
OH, DEAR.
I'M ACTUALLY CONSIDERING GETTING ONE OF THOSE WUSSIFIED BACKPACKS WITH WHEELS.
© 2008 by NEA, Inc.

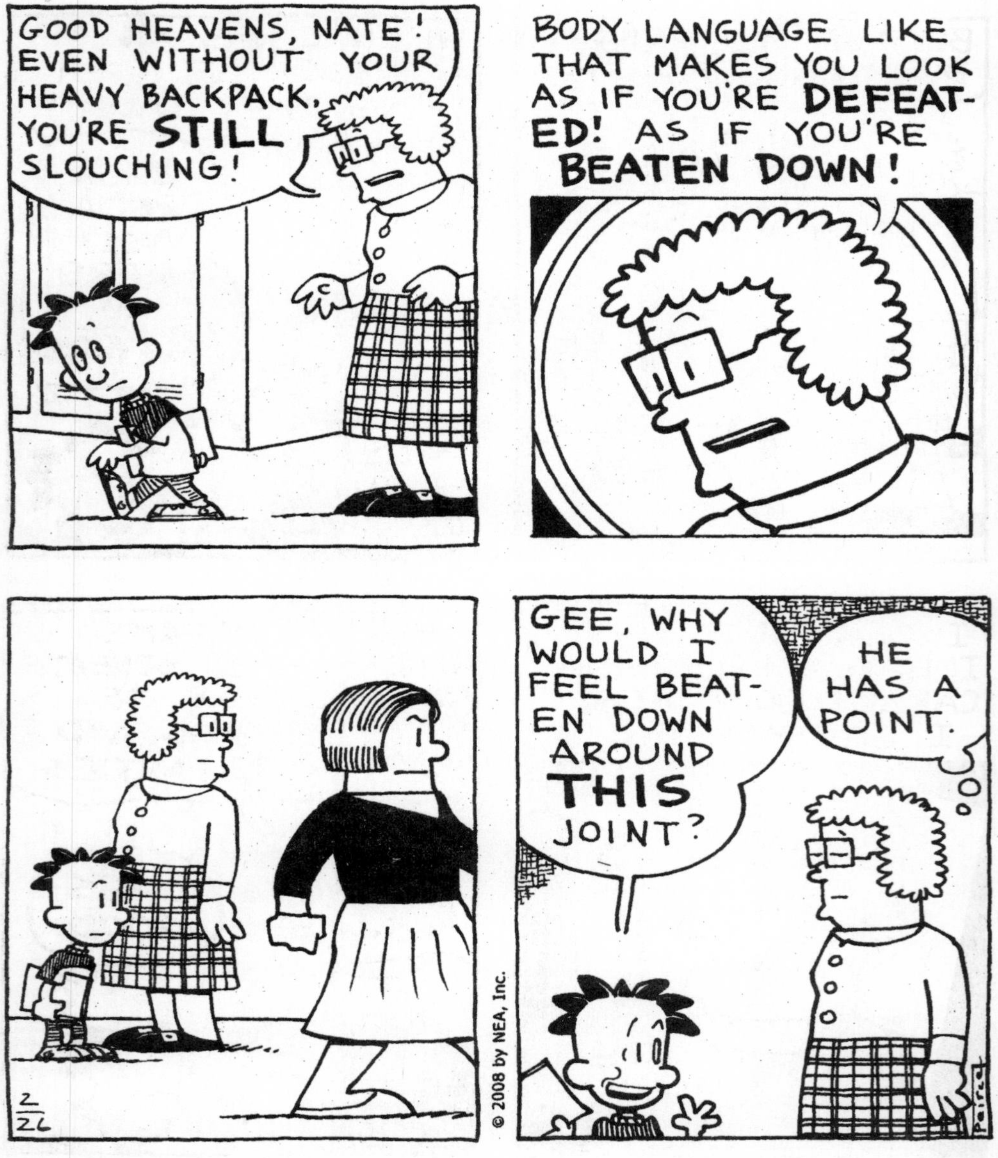
GOOD HEAVENS, NATE! EVEN WITHOUT YOUR HEAVY BACKPACK, YOU'RE STILL SLOUCHING!
BODY LANGUAGE LIKE THAT MAKES YOU LOOK AS IF YOU'RE DEFEATED! AS IF YOU'RE BEATEN DOWN!
2/26
© 2008 by NEA, Inc.
GEE, WHY WOULD I FEEL BEATEN DOWN AROUND THIS JOINT?
HE HAS A POINT.
Peirce

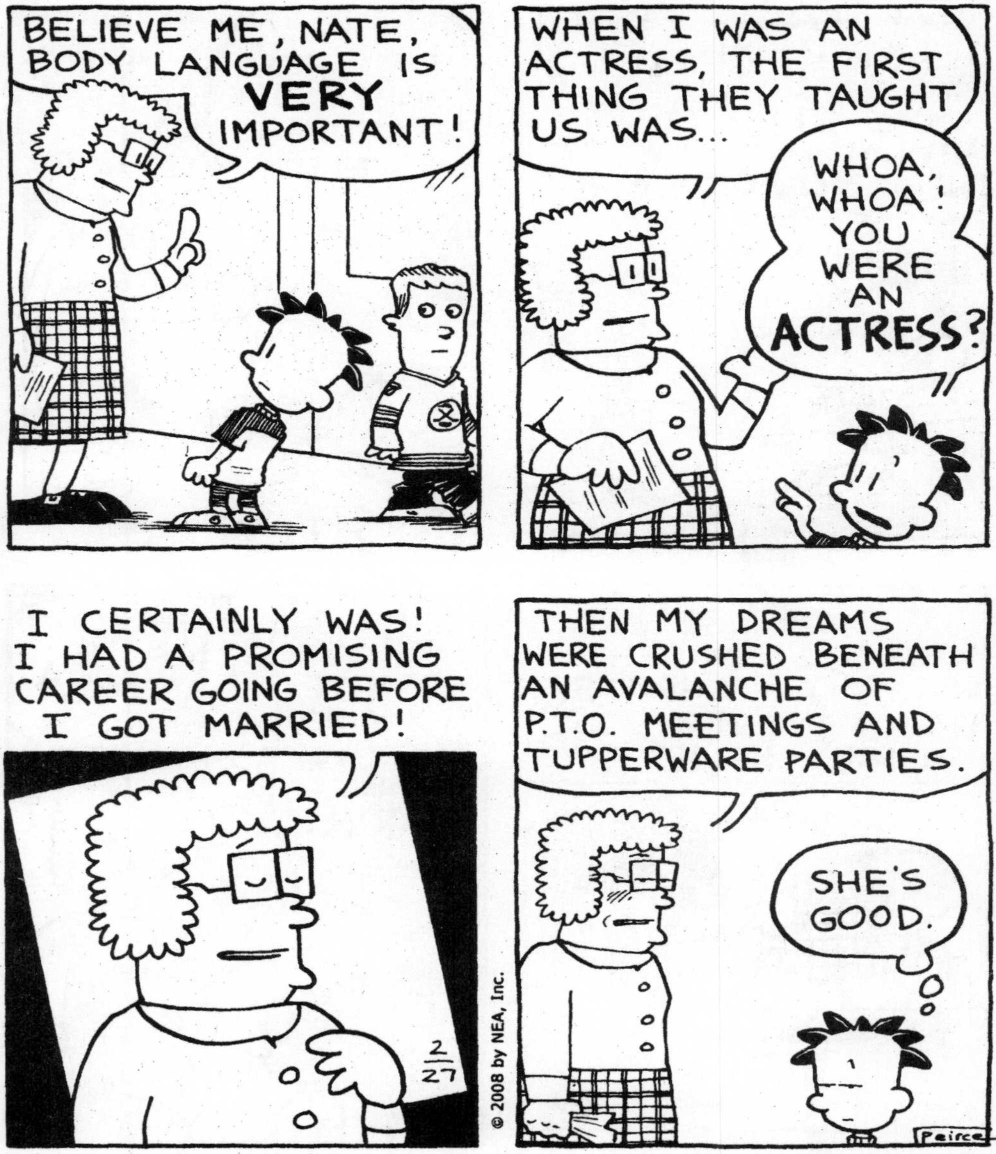
BELIEVE ME, NATE, BODY LANGUAGE IS VERY IMPORTANT!
WHEN I WAS AN ACTRESS, THE FIRST THING THEY TAUGHT US WAS...
WHOA, WHOA! YOU WERE AN ACTRESS?
I CERTAINLY WAS! I HAD A PROMISING CAREER GOING BEFORE I GOT MARRIED!
2/27
© 2008 by NEA, Inc.
THEN MY DREAMS WERE CRUSHED BENEATH AN AVALANCHE OF P.T.O. MEETINGS AND TUPPERWARE PARTIES.
SHE'S GOOD.
Peirce

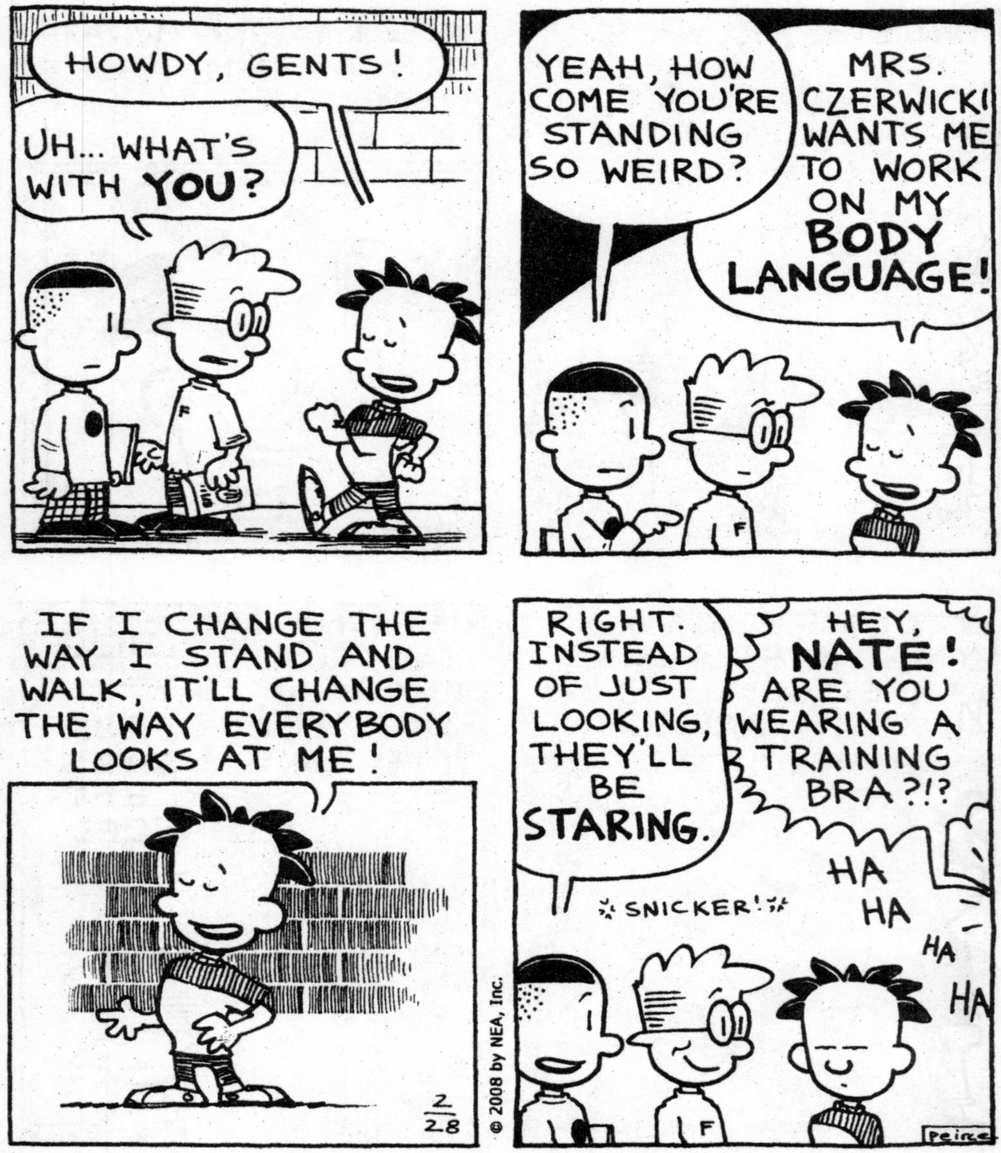
HOWDY, GENTS!
UH... WHAT'S WITH YOU?
YEAH, HOW COME YOU'RE STANDING SO WEIRD?
MRS. CZERWICKI WANTS ME TO WORK ON MY BODY LANGUAGE!
IF I CHANGE THE WAY I STAND AND WALK, IT'LL CHANGE THE WAY EVERYBODY LOOKS AT ME!
2 28
© 2008 by NEA, Inc.
RIGHT. INSTEAD OF JUST LOOKING, THEY'LL BE STARING.
HEY, NATE! ARE YOU WEARING A TRAINING BRA?!?
SNICKER!
HA HA HA HA
PEIRCE

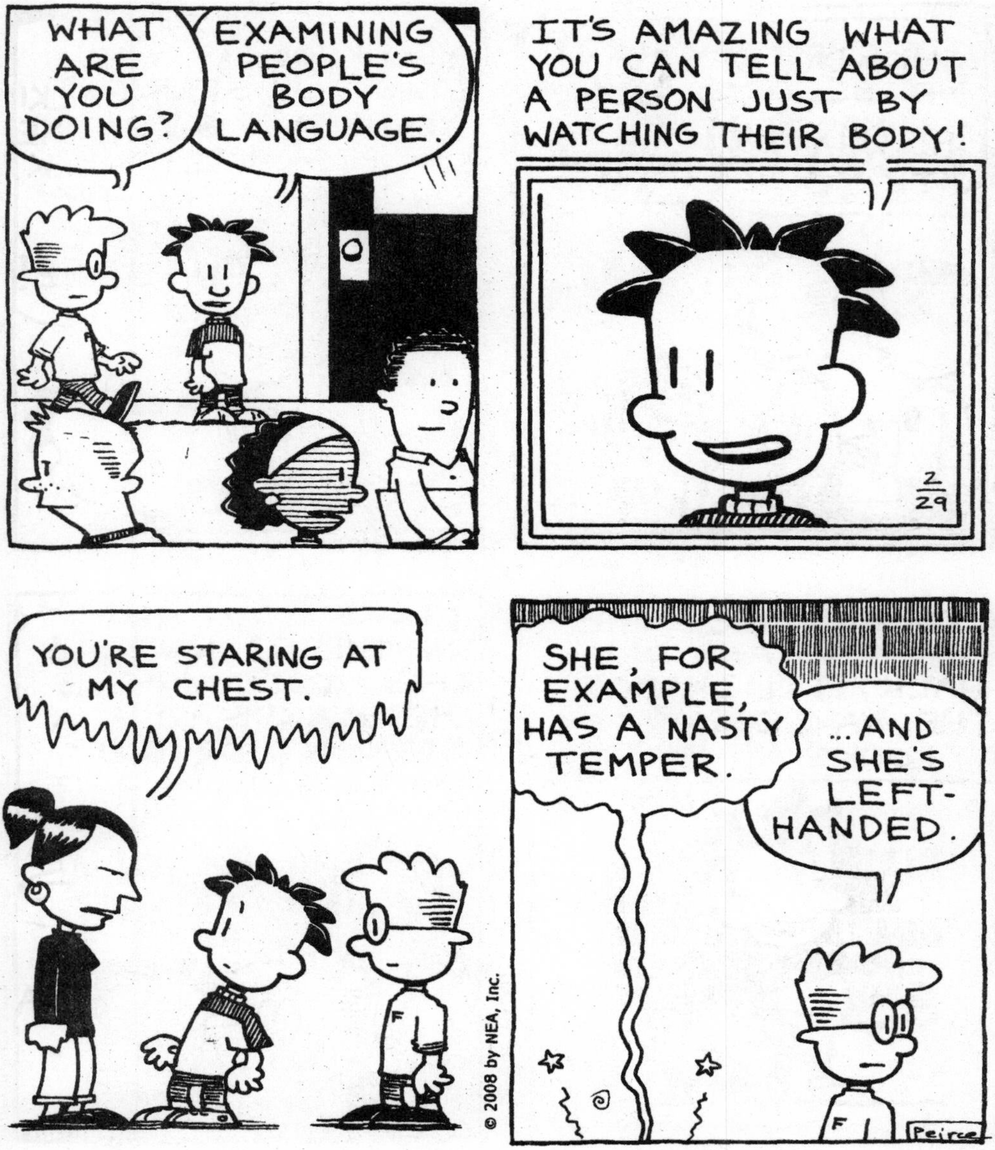
WHAT ARE YOU DOING?
EXAMINING PEOPLE'S BODY LANGUAGE.
IT'S AMAZING WHAT YOU CAN TELL ABOUT A PERSON JUST BY WATCHING THEIR BODY!
2
29
YOU'RE STARING AT MY CHEST.
SHE, FOR EXAMPLE, HAS A NASTY TEMPER.
...AND SHE'S LEFT-HANDED.
Peirce

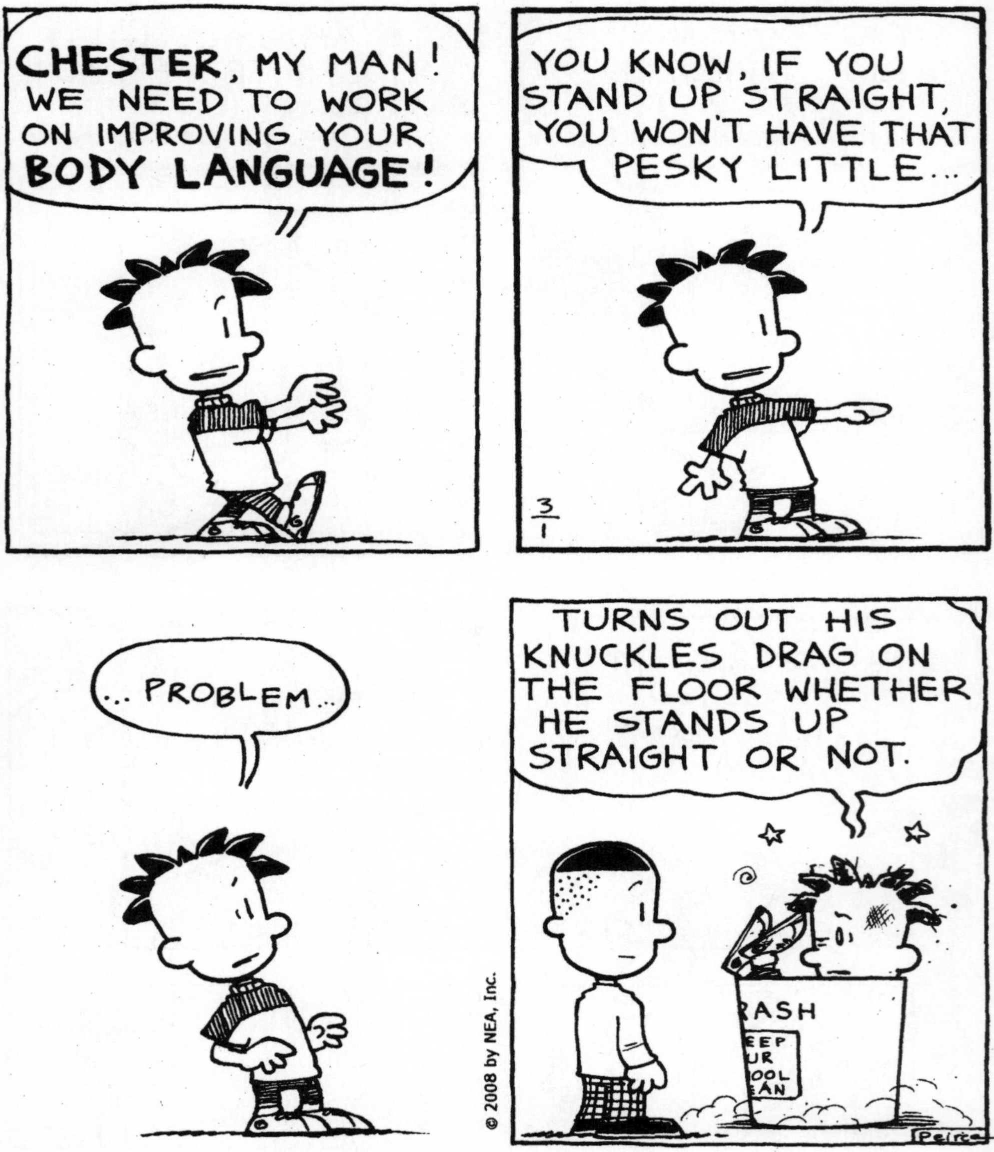
CHESTER, MY MAN! WE NEED TO WORK ON IMPROVING YOUR BODY LANGUAGE!
YOU KNOW, IF YOU STAND UP STRAIGHT, YOU WON'T HAVE THAT PESKY LITTLE...
3/1
... PROBLEM...
TURNS OUT HIS KNUCKLES DRAG ON THE FLOOR WHETHER HE STANDS UP STRAIGHT OR NOT.
RASH
EEP
UR
OOL
EAN

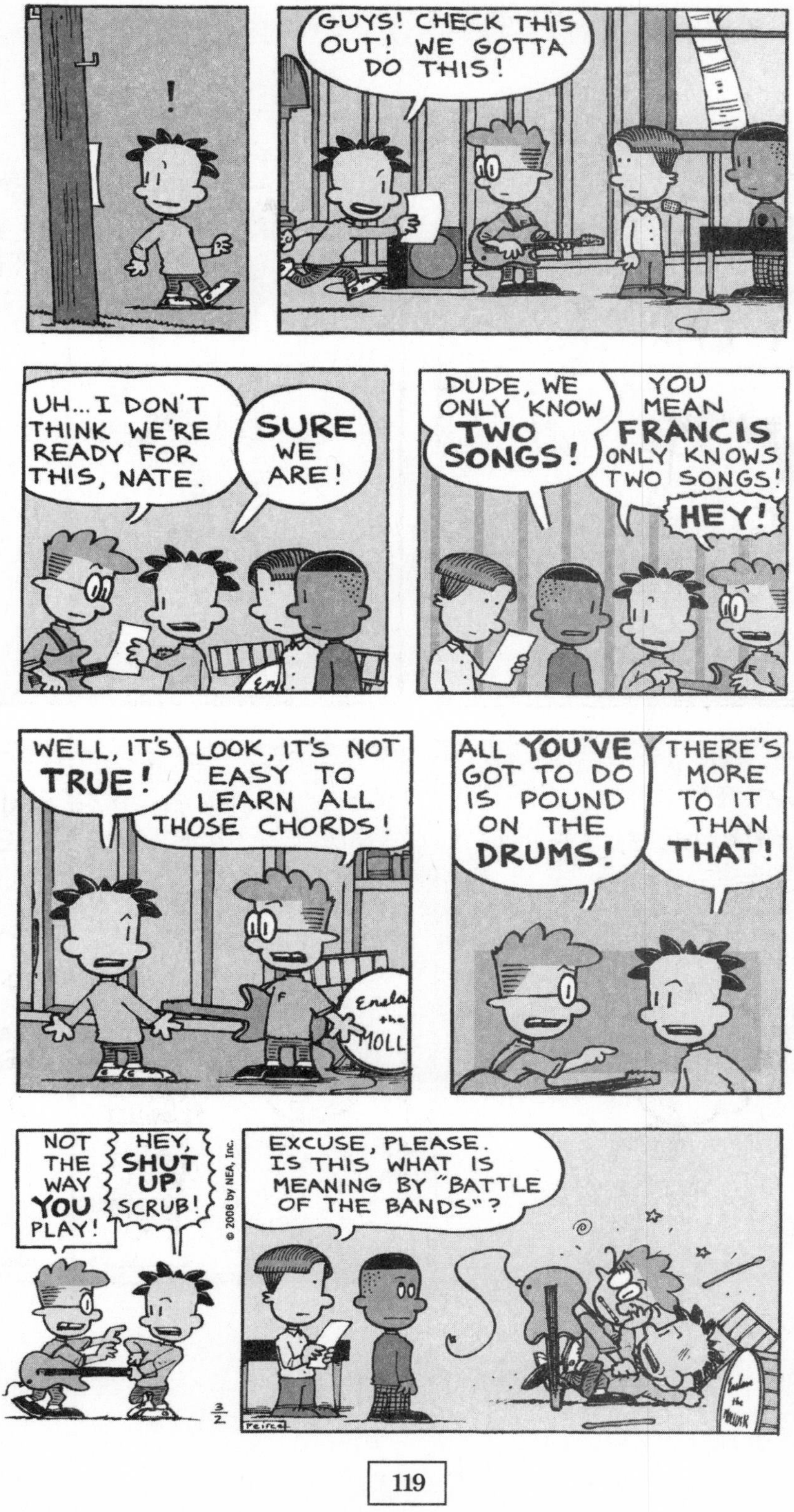
!
GUYS! CHECK THIS OUT! WE GOTTA DO THIS!
UH... I DON'T THINK WE'RE READY FOR THIS, NATE.
SURE WE ARE!
DUDE, WE ONLY KNOW TWO SONGS!
YOU MEAN FRANCIS ONLY KNOWS TWO SONGS!
HEY!
WELL, IT'S TRUE!
LOOK, IT'S NOT EASY TO LEARN ALL THOSE CHORDS!
ALL YOU'VE GOT TO DO IS POUND ON THE DRUMS!
THERE'S MORE TO IT THAN THAT!
NOT THE WAY YOU PLAY!
HEY, SHUT UP, SCRUB!
© 2008 by NEA, Inc.
EXCUSE, PLEASE. IS THIS WHAT IS MEANING BY "BATTLE OF THE BANDS"?
3/2
PEIRCE

RUBBER BANDS RULE!

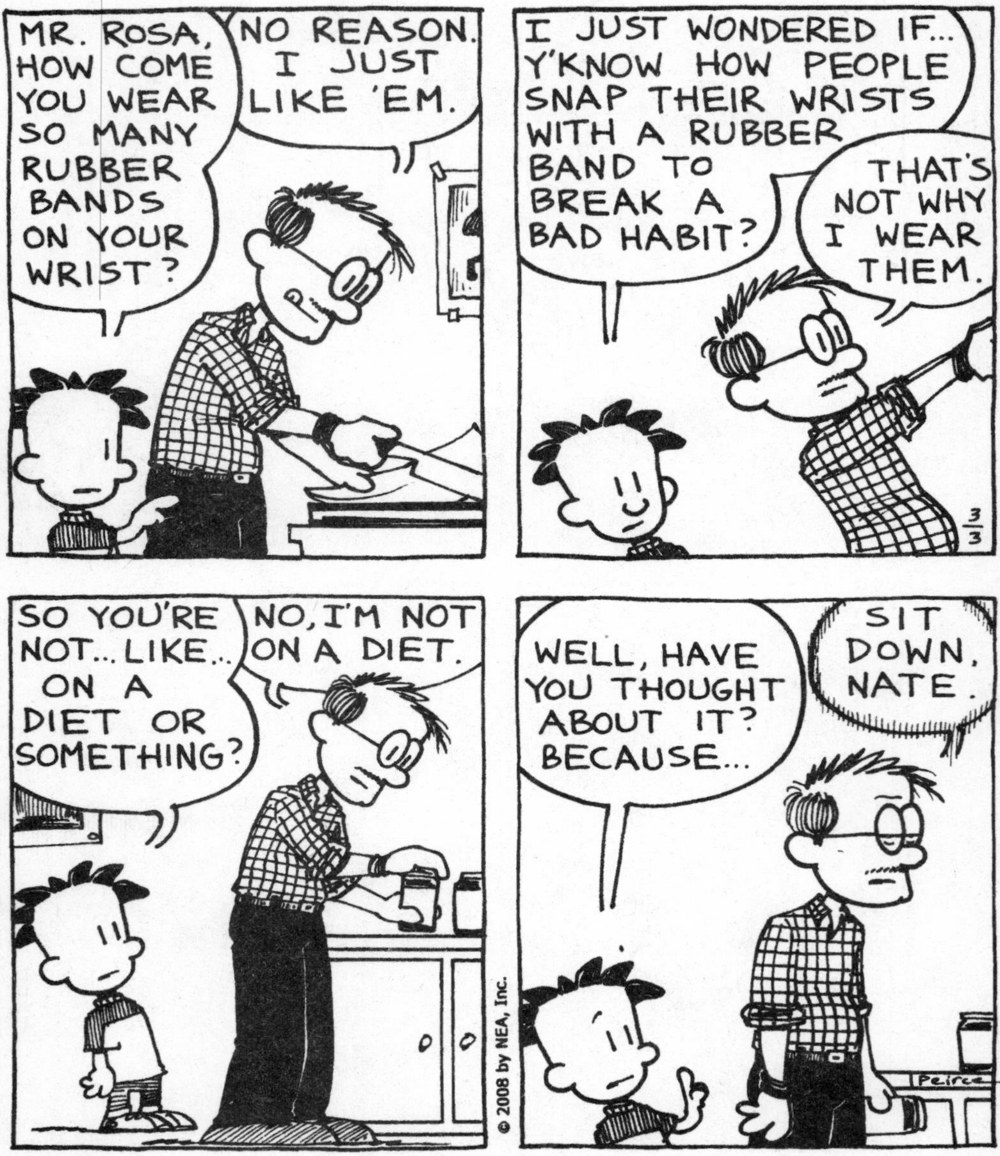
MR. ROSA, HOW COME YOU WEAR SO MANY RUBBER BANDS ON YOUR WRIST?
NO REASON. I JUST LIKE 'EM.
I JUST WONDERED IF... Y'KNOW HOW PEOPLE SNAP THEIR WRISTS WITH A RUBBER BAND TO BREAK A BAD HABIT?
THAT'S NOT WHY I WEAR THEM.
3/3
SO YOU'RE NOT... LIKE... ON A DIET OR SOMETHING?
NO, I'M NOT ON A DIET.
© 2008 by NEA, Inc.
WELL, HAVE YOU THOUGHT ABOUT IT? BECAUSE...
SIT DOWN, NATE.
Peirce

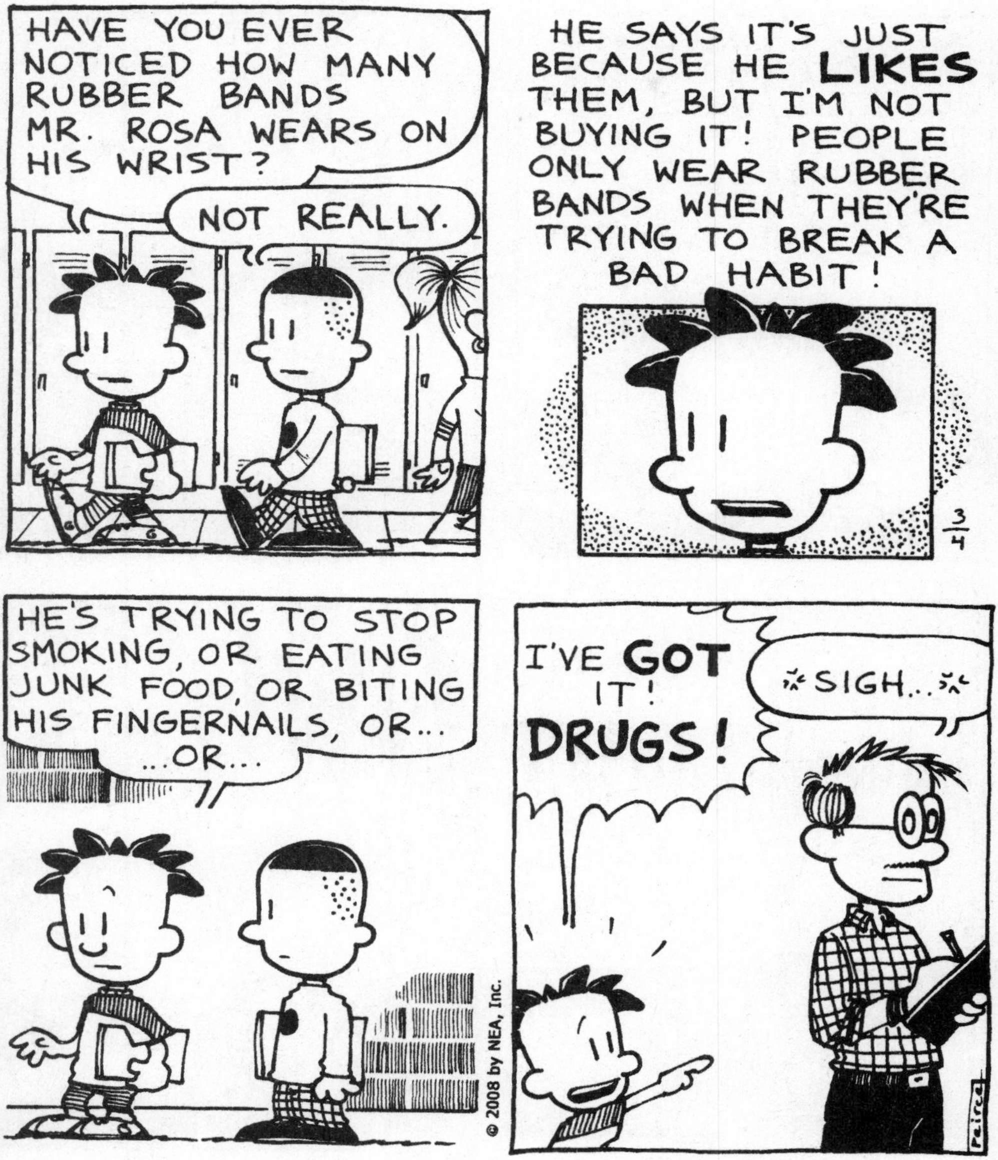
HAVE YOU EVER NOTICED HOW MANY RUBBER BANDS MR. ROSA WEARS ON HIS WRIST?
NOT REALLY.
HE SAYS IT'S JUST BECAUSE HE **LIKES** THEM, BUT I'M NOT BUYING IT! PEOPLE ONLY WEAR RUBBER BANDS WHEN THEY'RE TRYING TO BREAK A BAD HABIT!
3/4
HE'S TRYING TO STOP SMOKING, OR EATING JUNK FOOD, OR BITING HIS FINGERNAILS, OR... ...OR...
© 2008 by NEA, Inc.
I'VE **GOT** IT! **DRUGS!**
SIGH...
Peirce

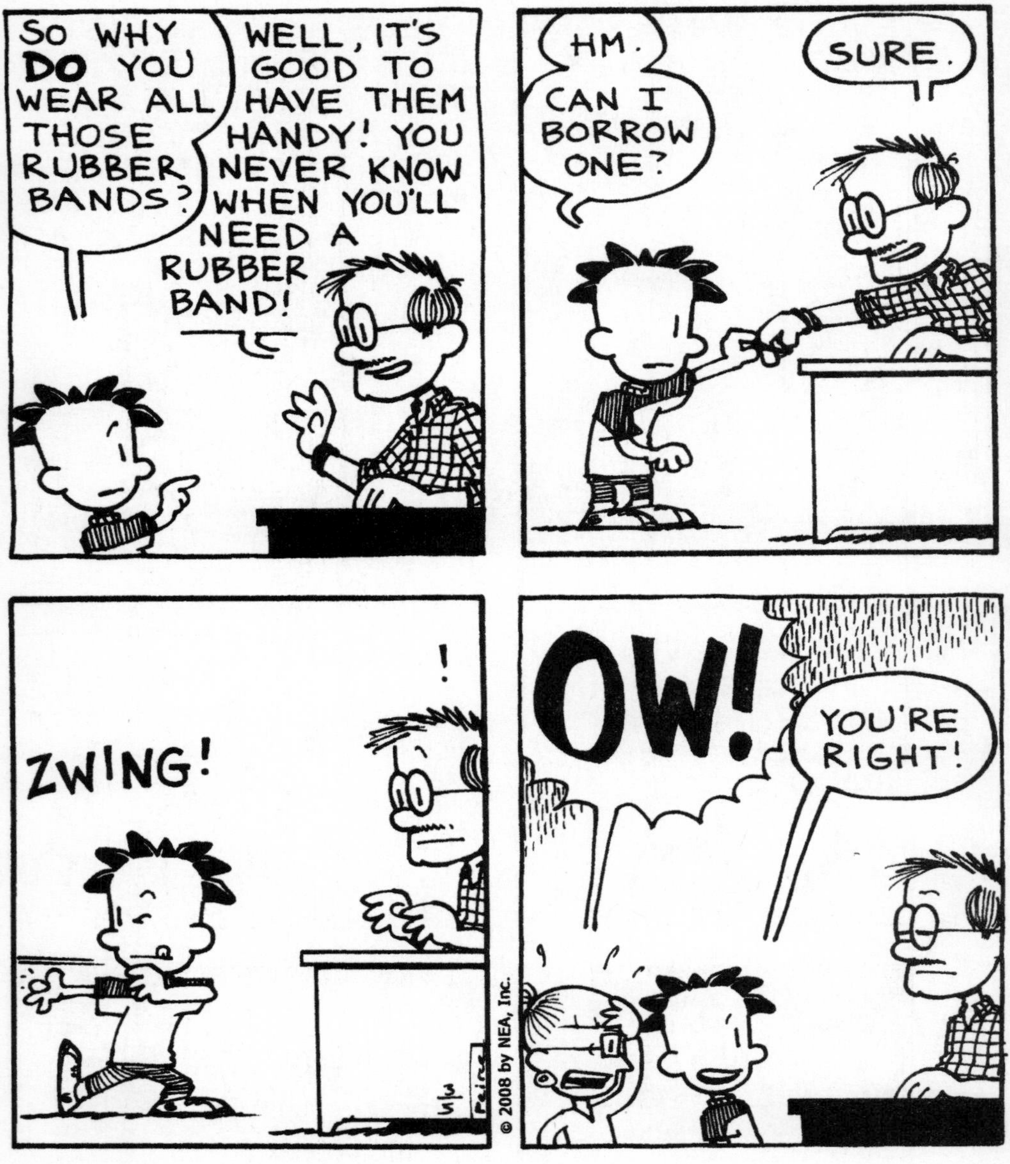
SO WHY DO YOU WEAR ALL THOSE RUBBER BANDS?
WELL, IT'S GOOD TO HAVE THEM HANDY! YOU NEVER KNOW WHEN YOU'LL NEED A RUBBER BAND!
HM.
CAN I BORROW ONE?
SURE.
!
ZWING!
© 2008 by NEA, Inc.
OW!
YOU'RE RIGHT!

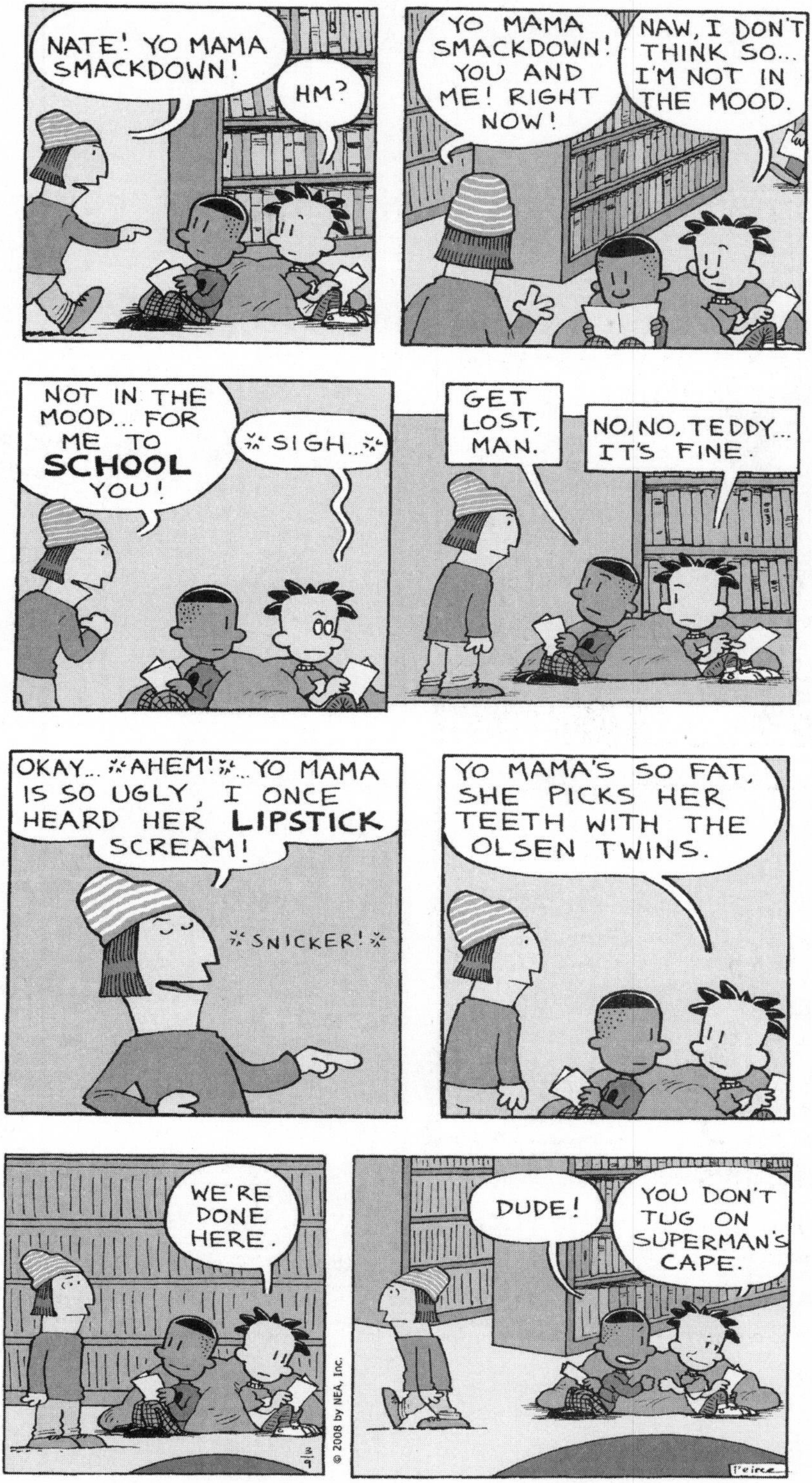
NATE! YO MAMA SMACKDOWN!
HM?
YO MAMA SMACKDOWN! YOU AND ME! RIGHT NOW!
NAW, I DON'T THINK SO... I'M NOT IN THE MOOD.
NOT IN THE MOOD... FOR ME TO **SCHOOL** YOU!
SIGH...
GET LOST, MAN.
NO, NO, TEDDY... IT'S FINE.
OKAY... *AHEM!*... YO MAMA IS SO UGLY, I ONCE HEARD HER **LIPSTICK** SCREAM!
SNICKER!
YO MAMA'S SO FAT, SHE PICKS HER TEETH WITH THE OLSEN TWINS.
WE'RE DONE HERE.
DUDE!
YOU DON'T TUG ON SUPERMAN'S CAPE.
© 2008 by NEA, Inc.
3/9
Peirce

ARE YOU COOL ENOUGH?

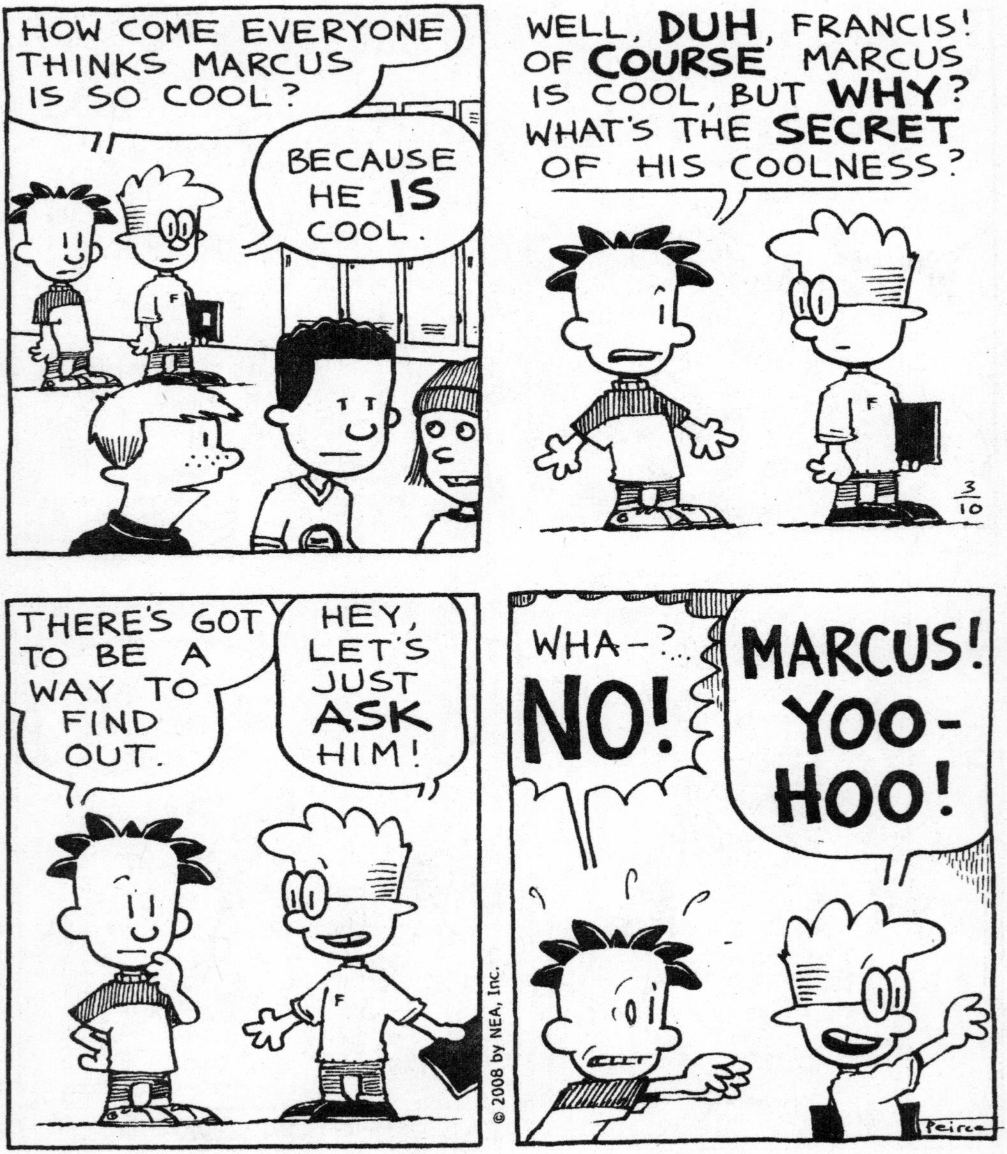

HOW COME EVERYONE THINKS MARCUS IS SO COOL?
BECAUSE HE **IS** COOL.
WELL, **DUH**, FRANCIS! OF **COURSE** MARCUS IS COOL, BUT **WHY**? WHAT'S THE **SECRET** OF HIS COOLNESS?
3/10
THERE'S GOT TO BE A WAY TO FIND OUT.
HEY, LET'S JUST **ASK** HIM!
© 2008 by NEA, Inc.
WHA-?...
NO!
MARCUS! YOO-HOO!
Peirce

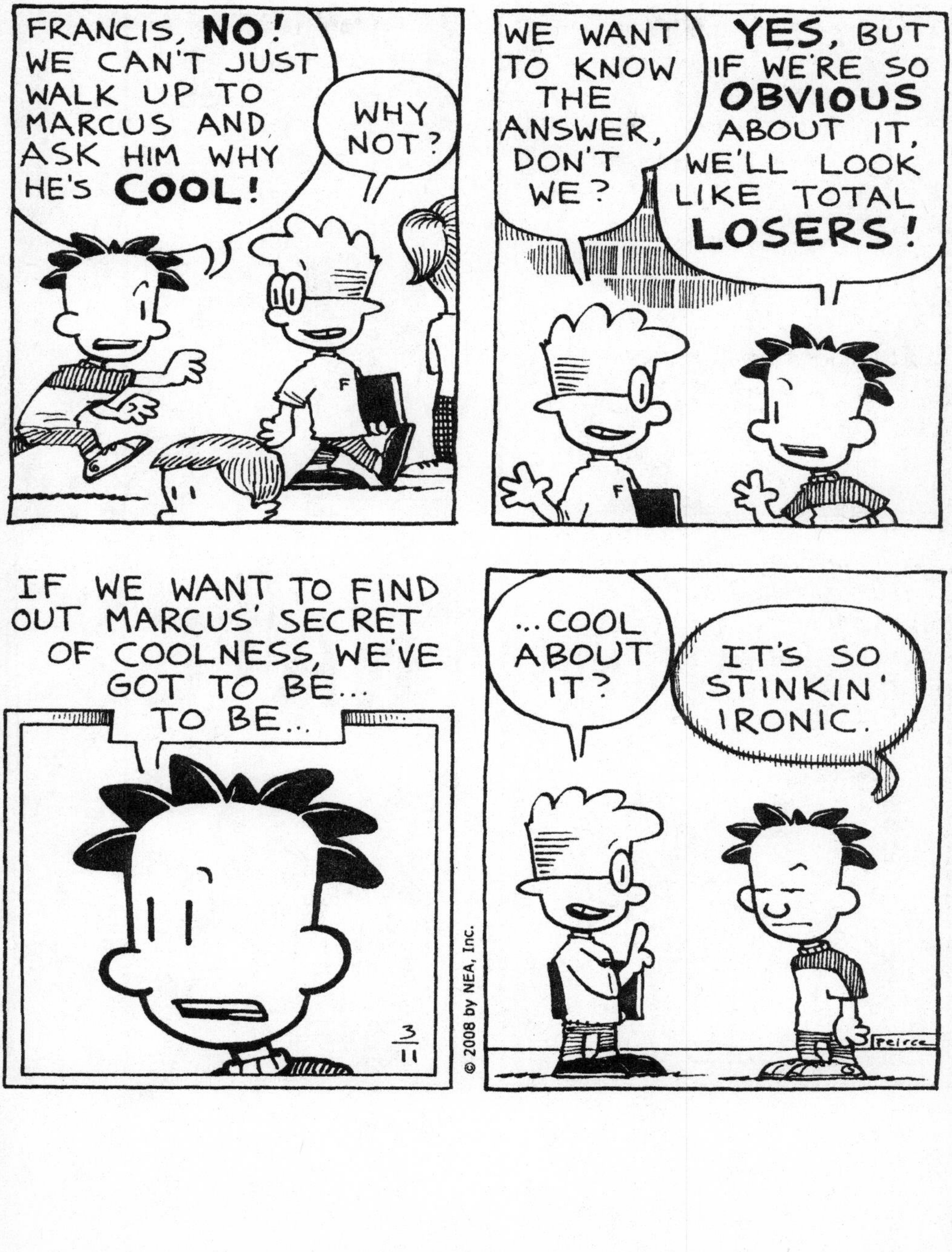
FRANCIS, NO! WE CAN'T JUST WALK UP TO MARCUS AND ASK HIM WHY HE'S COOL!
WHY NOT?
WE WANT TO KNOW THE ANSWER, DON'T WE?
YES, BUT IF WE'RE SO OBVIOUS ABOUT IT, WE'LL LOOK LIKE TOTAL LOSERS!
IF WE WANT TO FIND OUT MARCUS' SECRET OF COOLNESS, WE'VE GOT TO BE... TO BE...
...COOL ABOUT IT?
IT'S SO STINKIN' IRONIC.
3/11
© 2008 by NEA, Inc.
Peirce

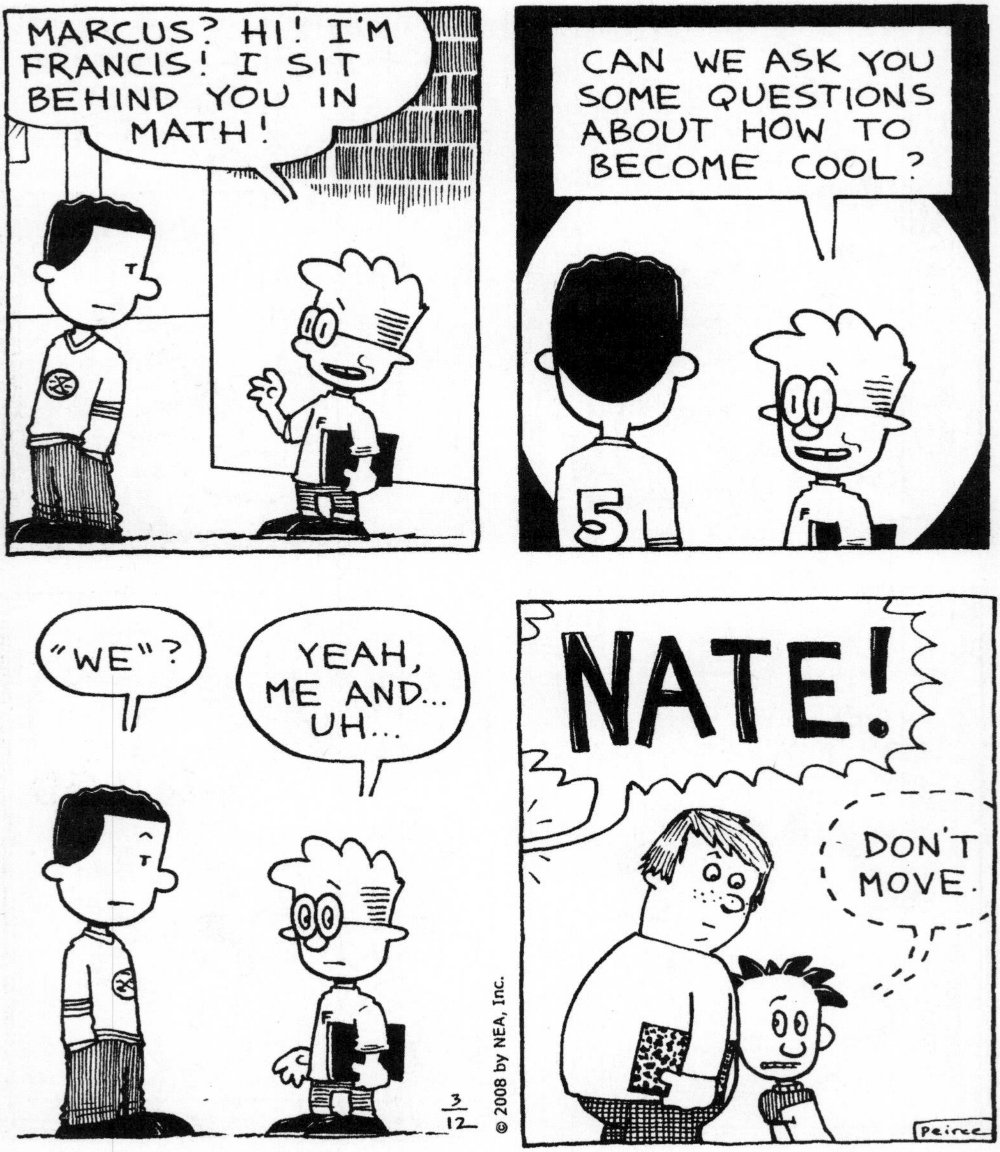
MARCUS? HI! I'M FRANCIS! I SIT BEHIND YOU IN MATH!
CAN WE ASK YOU SOME QUESTIONS ABOUT HOW TO BECOME COOL?
"WE"?
YEAH, ME AND... UH...
NATE!
DON'T MOVE.
3/12
© 2008 by NEA, Inc.
Peirce

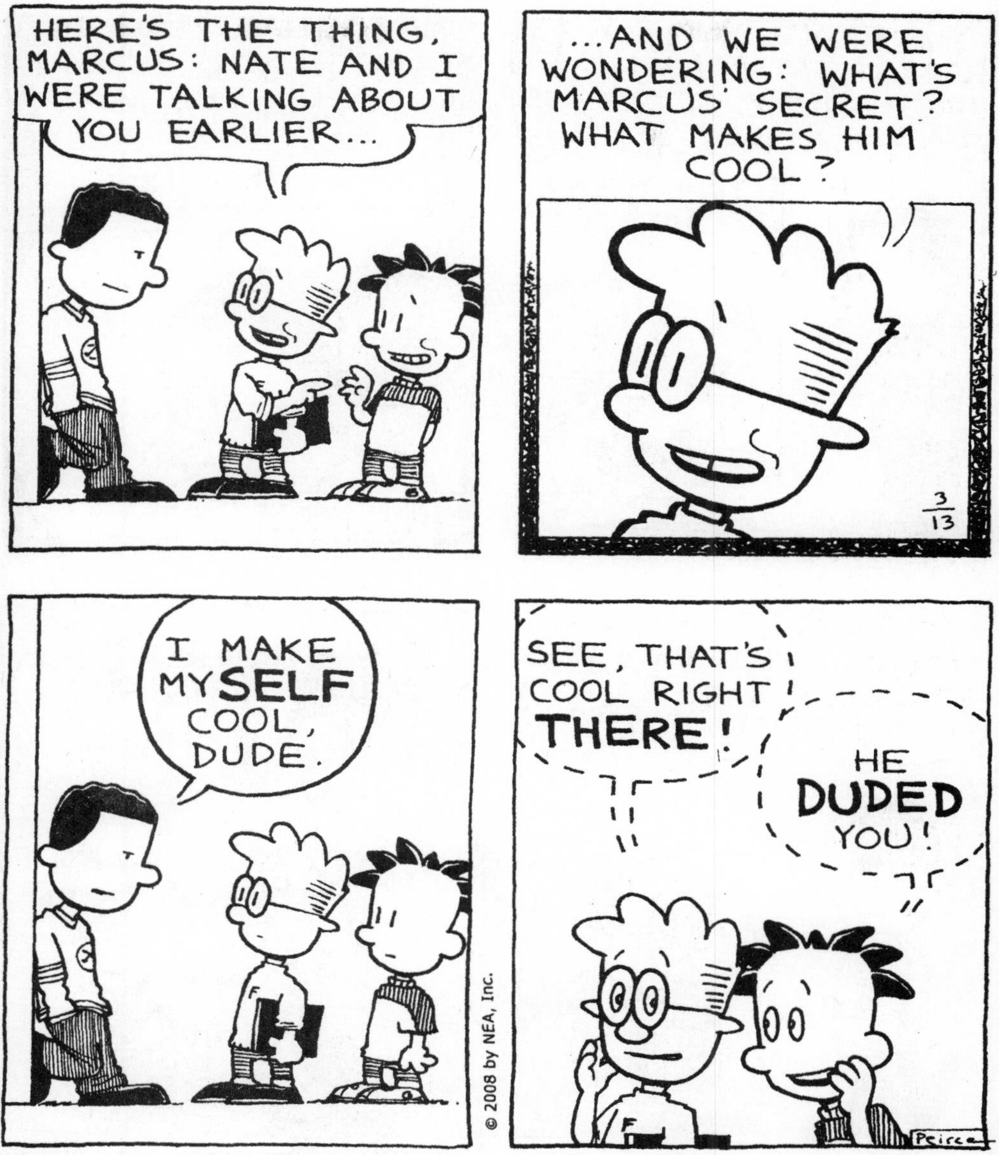
HERE'S THE THING, MARCUS: NATE AND I WERE TALKING ABOUT YOU EARLIER...
...AND WE WERE WONDERING: WHAT'S MARCUS' SECRET? WHAT MAKES HIM COOL?
3/13
I MAKE MY**SELF** COOL, DUDE.
© 2008 by NEA, Inc.
SEE, THAT'S COOL RIGHT **THERE**!
HE **DUDED** YOU!
Peirce

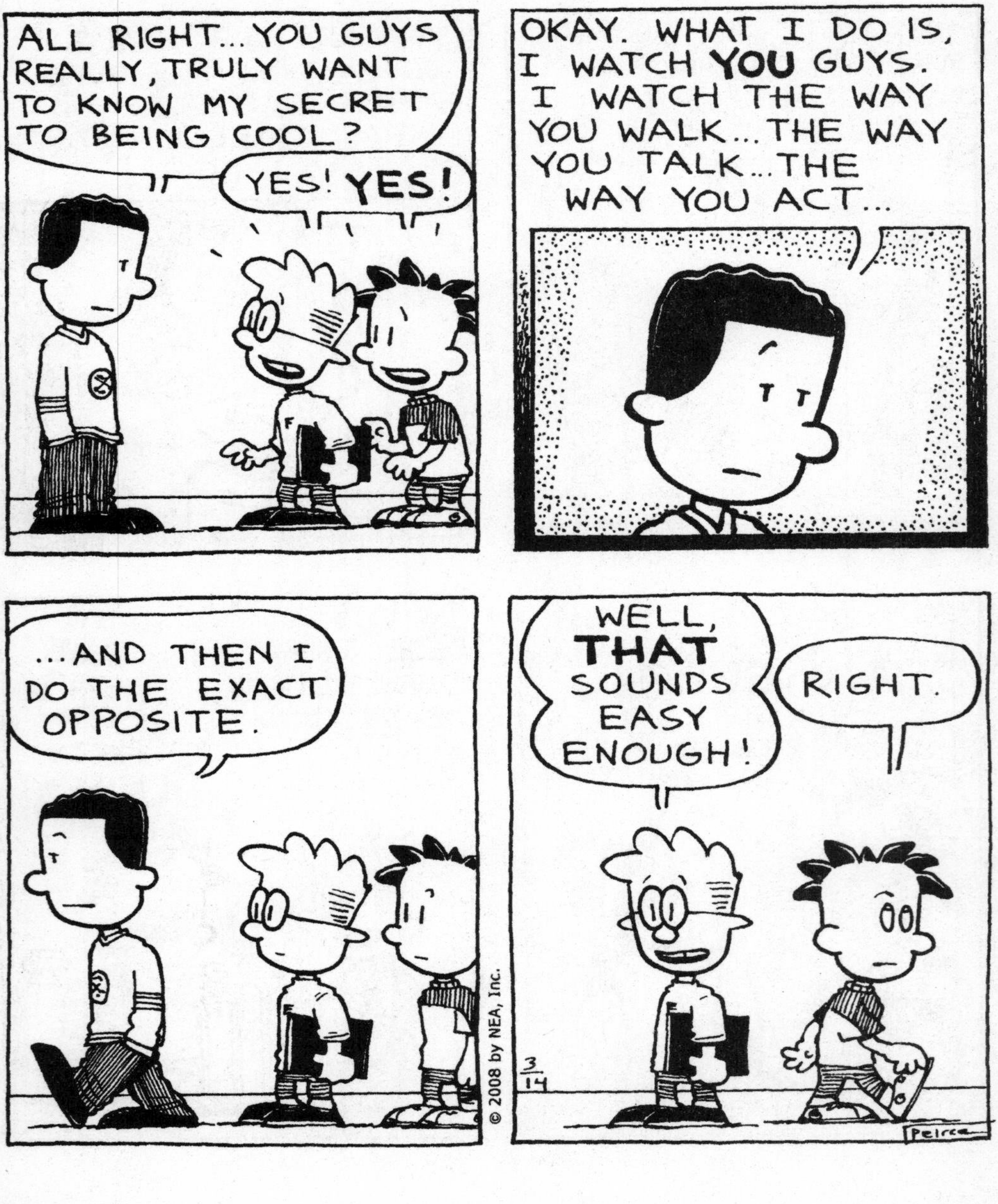
ALL RIGHT... YOU GUYS REALLY, TRULY WANT TO KNOW MY SECRET TO BEING COOL?
YES! YES!
OKAY. WHAT I DO IS, I WATCH YOU GUYS. I WATCH THE WAY YOU WALK... THE WAY YOU TALK... THE WAY YOU ACT...
...AND THEN I DO THE EXACT OPPOSITE.
WELL, THAT SOUNDS EASY ENOUGH!
RIGHT.
© 2008 by NEA, Inc.
3/14
Peirce

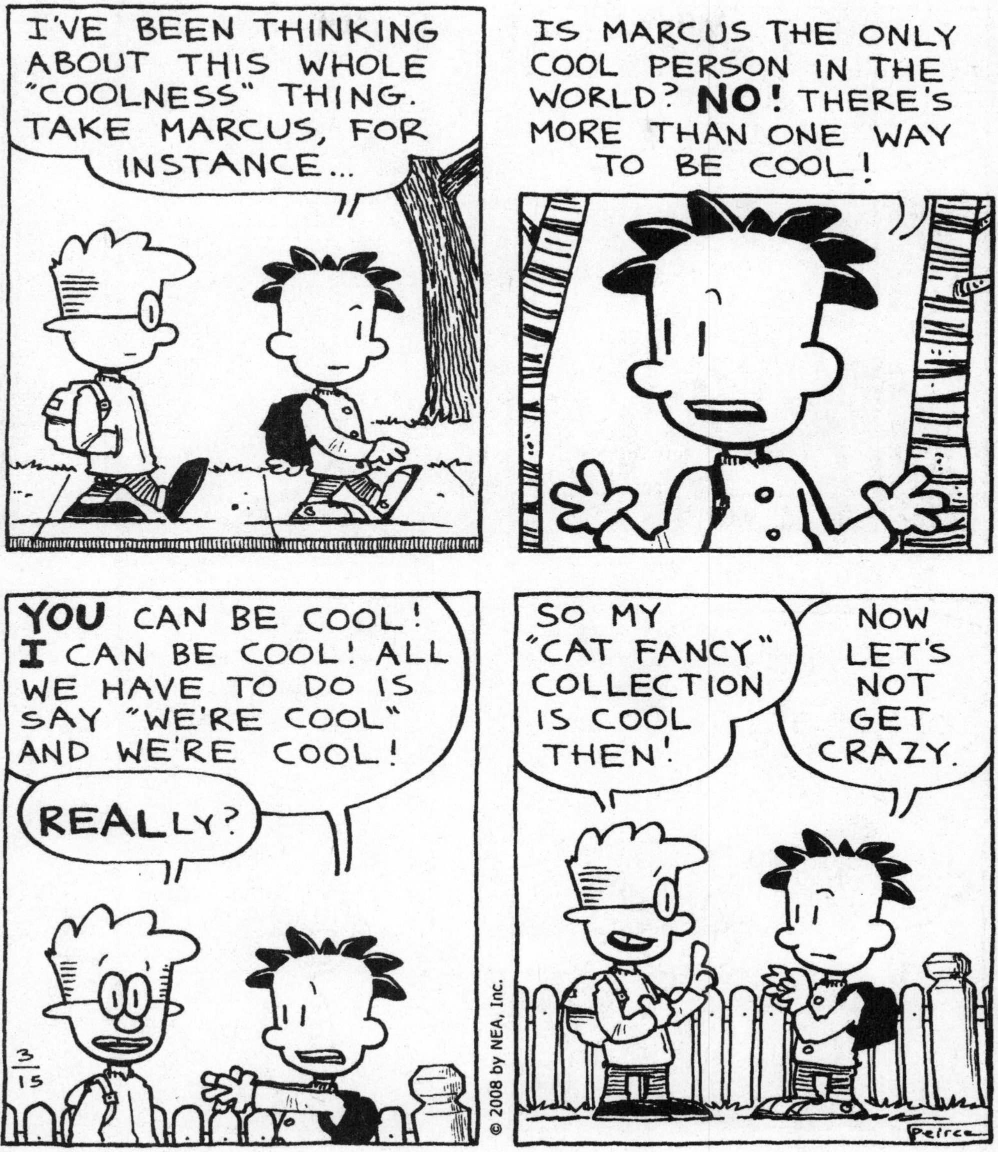
I'VE BEEN THINKING ABOUT THIS WHOLE "COOLNESS" THING. TAKE MARCUS, FOR INSTANCE...
IS MARCUS THE ONLY COOL PERSON IN THE WORLD? NO! THERE'S MORE THAN ONE WAY TO BE COOL!
YOU CAN BE COOL! I CAN BE COOL! ALL WE HAVE TO DO IS SAY "WE'RE COOL" AND WE'RE COOL!
REALLY?
3/15
© 2008 by NEA, Inc.
SO MY "CAT FANCY" COLLECTION IS COOL THEN!
NOW LET'S NOT GET CRAZY.
Peirce

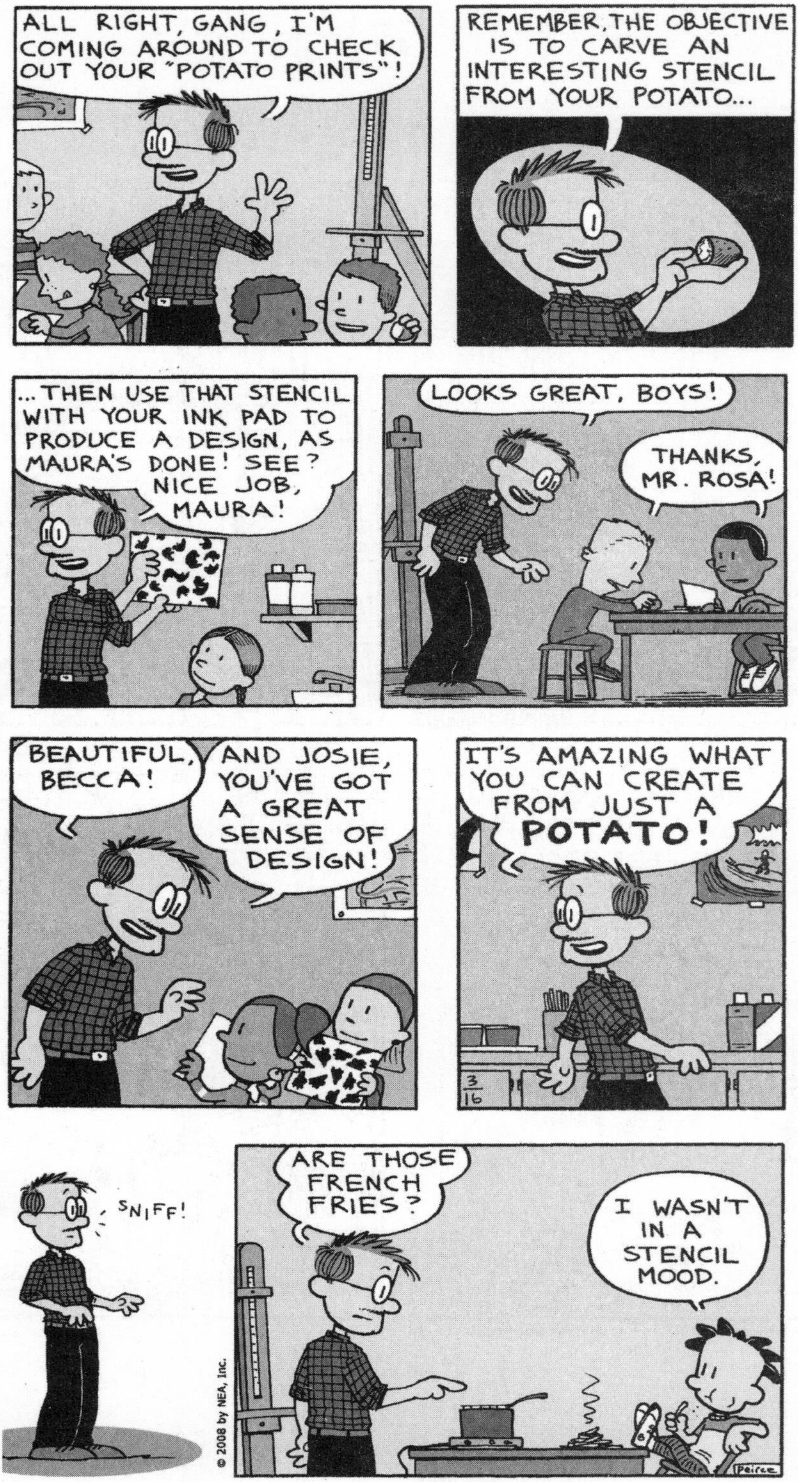
ALL RIGHT, GANG, I'M COMING AROUND TO CHECK OUT YOUR "POTATO PRINTS"!
REMEMBER, THE OBJECTIVE IS TO CARVE AN INTERESTING STENCIL FROM YOUR POTATO...
...THEN USE THAT STENCIL WITH YOUR INK PAD TO PRODUCE A DESIGN, AS MAURA'S DONE! SEE?
NICE JOB, MAURA!
LOOKS GREAT, BOYS!
THANKS, MR. ROSA!
BEAUTIFUL, BECCA!
AND JOSIE, YOU'VE GOT A GREAT SENSE OF DESIGN!
IT'S AMAZING WHAT YOU CAN CREATE FROM JUST A POTATO!
3/16
SNIFF!
ARE THOSE FRENCH FRIES?
I WASN'T IN A STENCIL MOOD.
© 2008 by NEA, Inc.
Peirce

THE PERFECT DATE

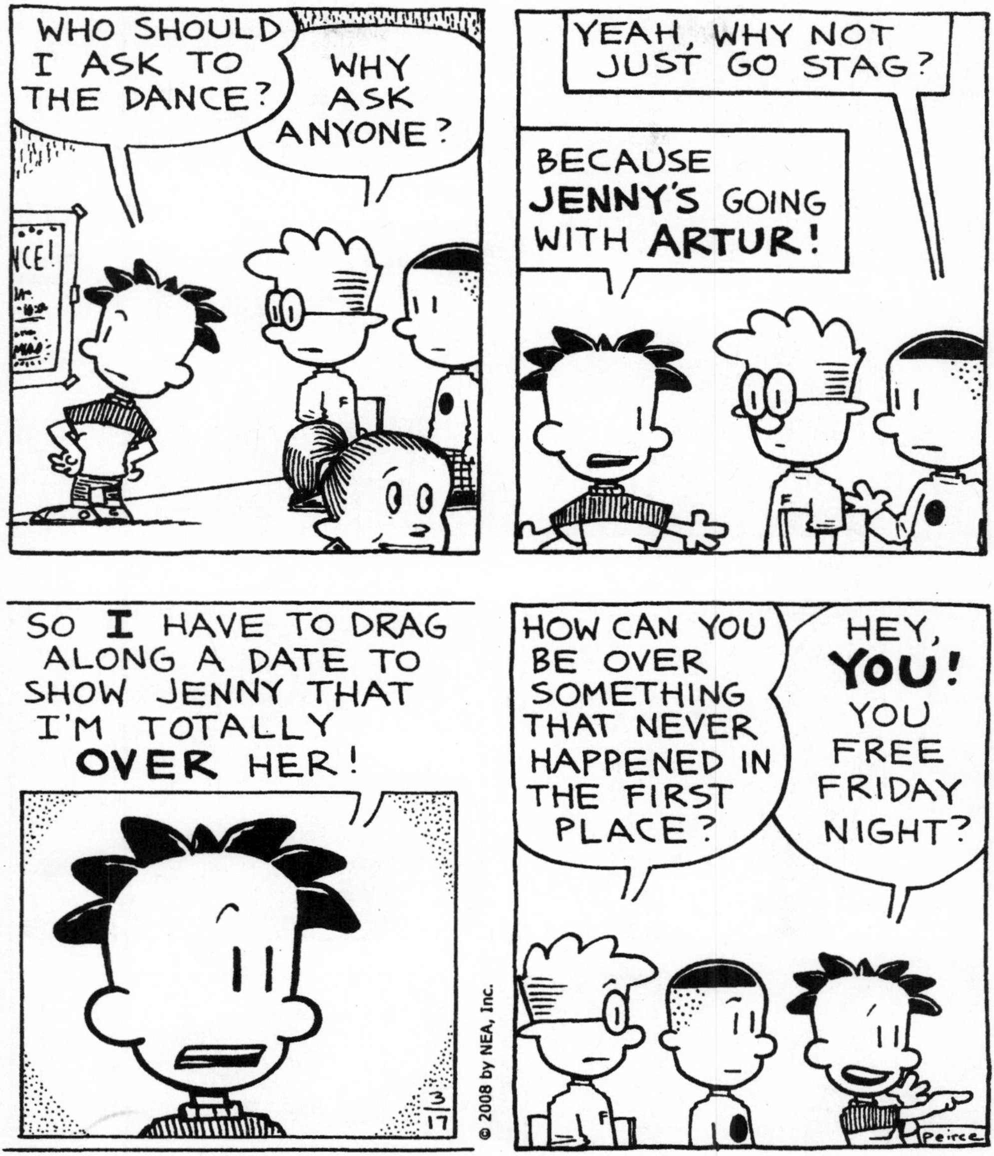

WHO SHOULD I ASK TO THE DANCE?
WHY ASK ANYONE?
YEAH, WHY NOT JUST GO STAG?
BECAUSE JENNY'S GOING WITH ARTUR!
SO I HAVE TO DRAG ALONG A DATE TO SHOW JENNY THAT I'M TOTALLY OVER HER!
3/17
© 2008 by NEA, Inc.
HOW CAN YOU BE OVER SOMETHING THAT NEVER HAPPENED IN THE FIRST PLACE?
HEY, YOU! YOU FREE FRIDAY NIGHT?
Peirce

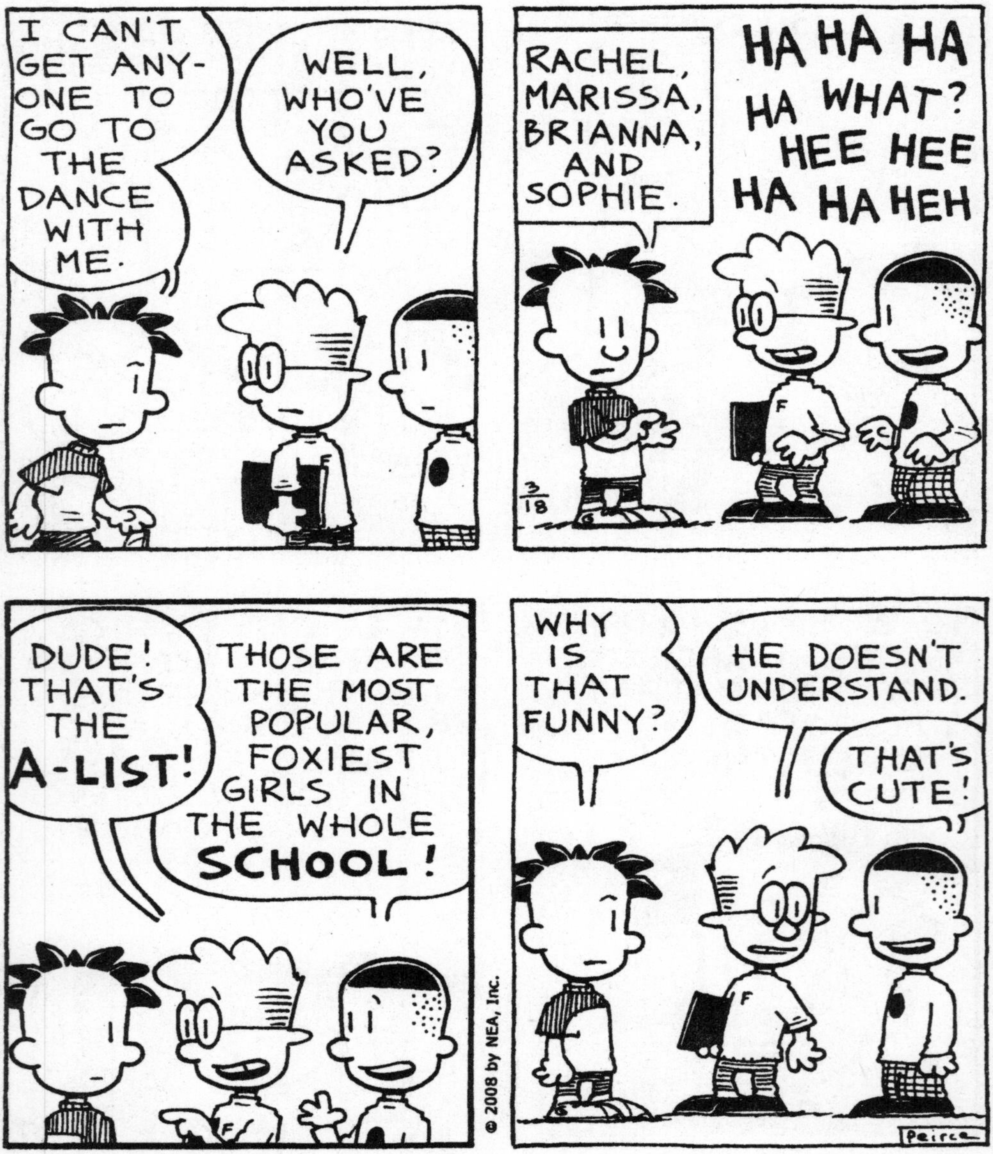
I CAN'T GET ANYONE TO GO TO THE DANCE WITH ME.
WELL, WHO'VE YOU ASKED?
RACHEL, MARISSA, BRIANNA, AND SOPHIE.
HA HA HA HA WHAT? HEE HEE HA HA HEH
3/18
DUDE! THAT'S THE A-LIST!
THOSE ARE THE MOST POPULAR, FOXIEST GIRLS IN THE WHOLE SCHOOL!
© 2008 by NEA, Inc.
WHY IS THAT FUNNY?
HE DOESN'T UNDERSTAND.
THAT'S CUTE!
Peirce

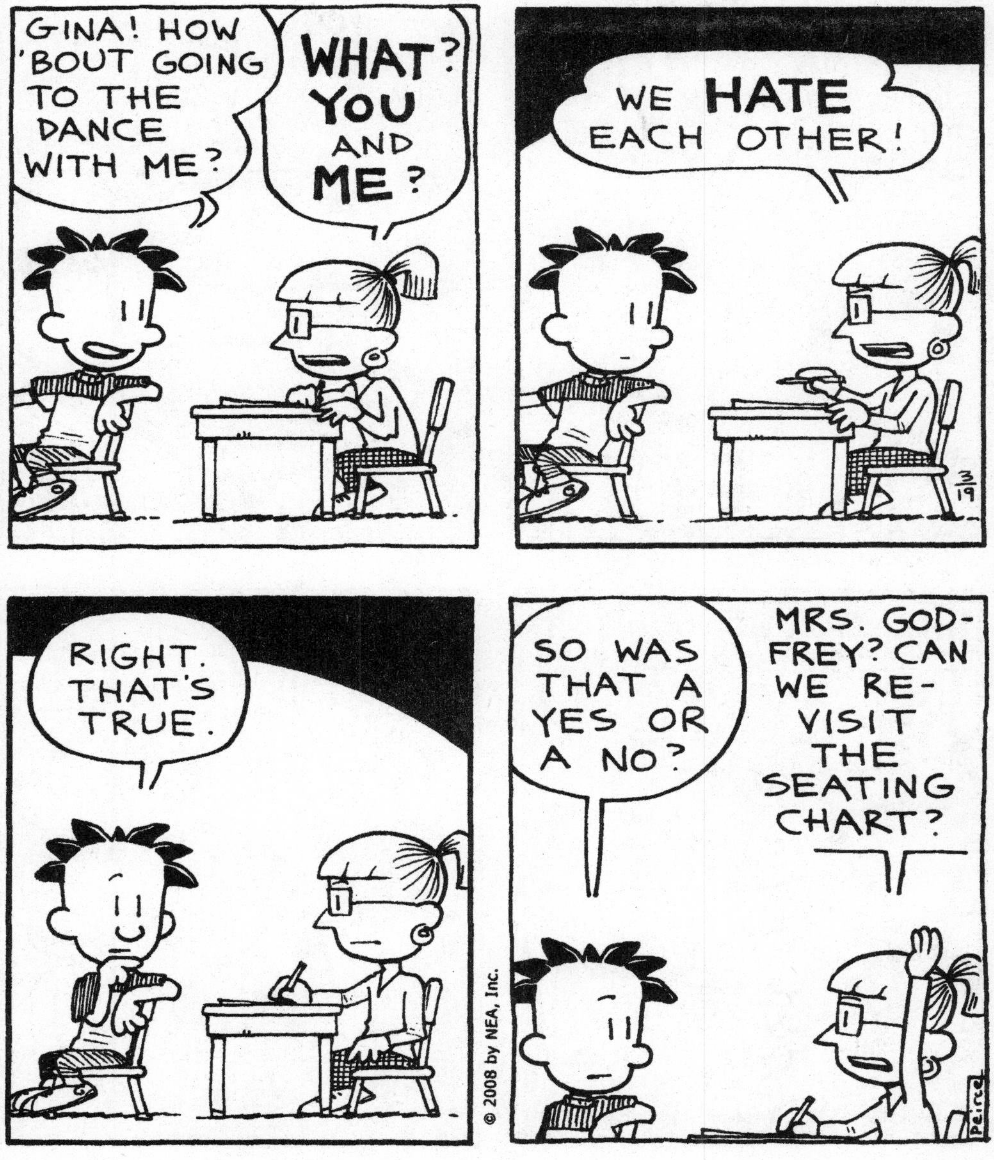
GINA! HOW 'BOUT GOING TO THE DANCE WITH ME?
WHAT? YOU AND ME?
WE HATE EACH OTHER!
RIGHT. THAT'S TRUE.
SO WAS THAT A YES OR A NO?
MRS. GOD-FREY? CAN WE RE-VISIT THE SEATING CHART?
3/19
PEIRCE

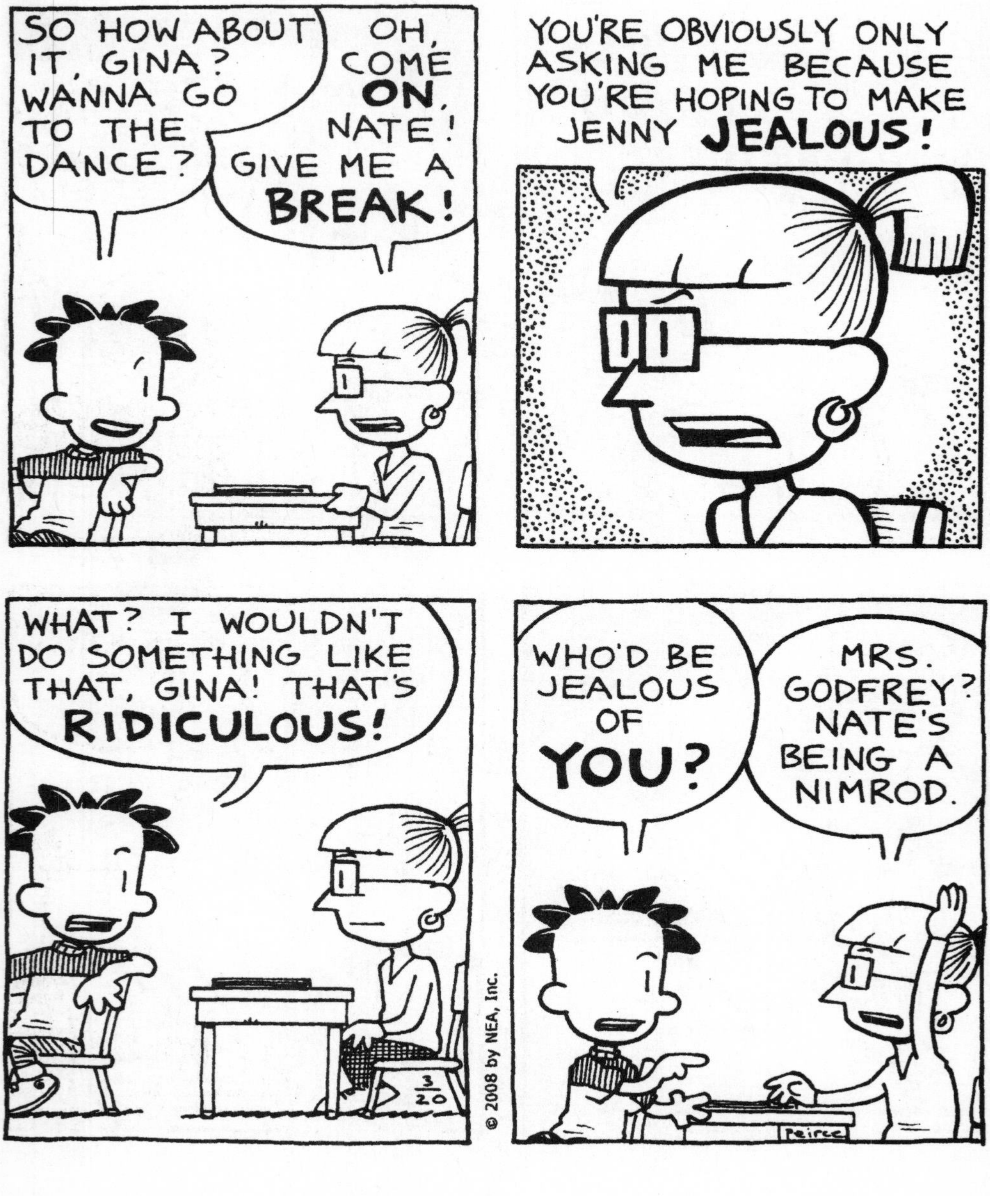
SO HOW ABOUT IT, GINA? WANNA GO TO THE DANCE?
OH, COME ON, NATE! GIVE ME A BREAK!
YOU'RE OBVIOUSLY ONLY ASKING ME BECAUSE YOU'RE HOPING TO MAKE JENNY JEALOUS!
WHAT? I WOULDN'T DO SOMETHING LIKE THAT, GINA! THAT'S RIDICULOUS!
3/20
WHO'D BE JEALOUS OF YOU?
MRS. GODFREY? NATE'S BEING A NIMROD.
Peirce

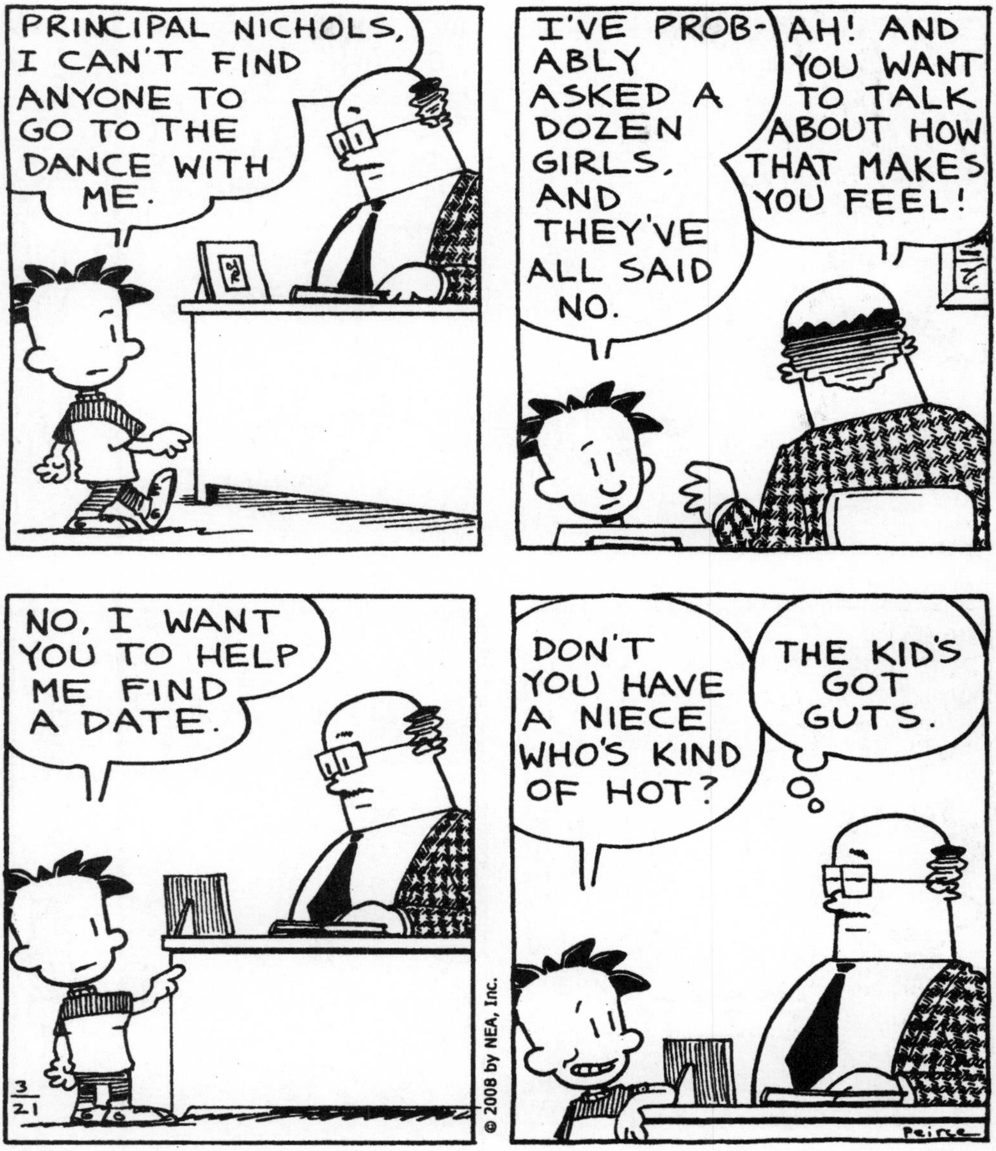
PRINCIPAL NICHOLS, I CAN'T FIND ANYONE TO GO TO THE DANCE WITH ME.
I'VE PROBABLY ASKED A DOZEN GIRLS. AND THEY'VE ALL SAID NO.
AH! AND YOU WANT TO TALK ABOUT HOW THAT MAKES YOU FEEL!
NO, I WANT YOU TO HELP ME FIND A DATE.
3/21
© 2008 by NEA, Inc.
DON'T YOU HAVE A NIECE WHO'S KIND OF HOT?
THE KID'S GOT GUTS.
Peirce

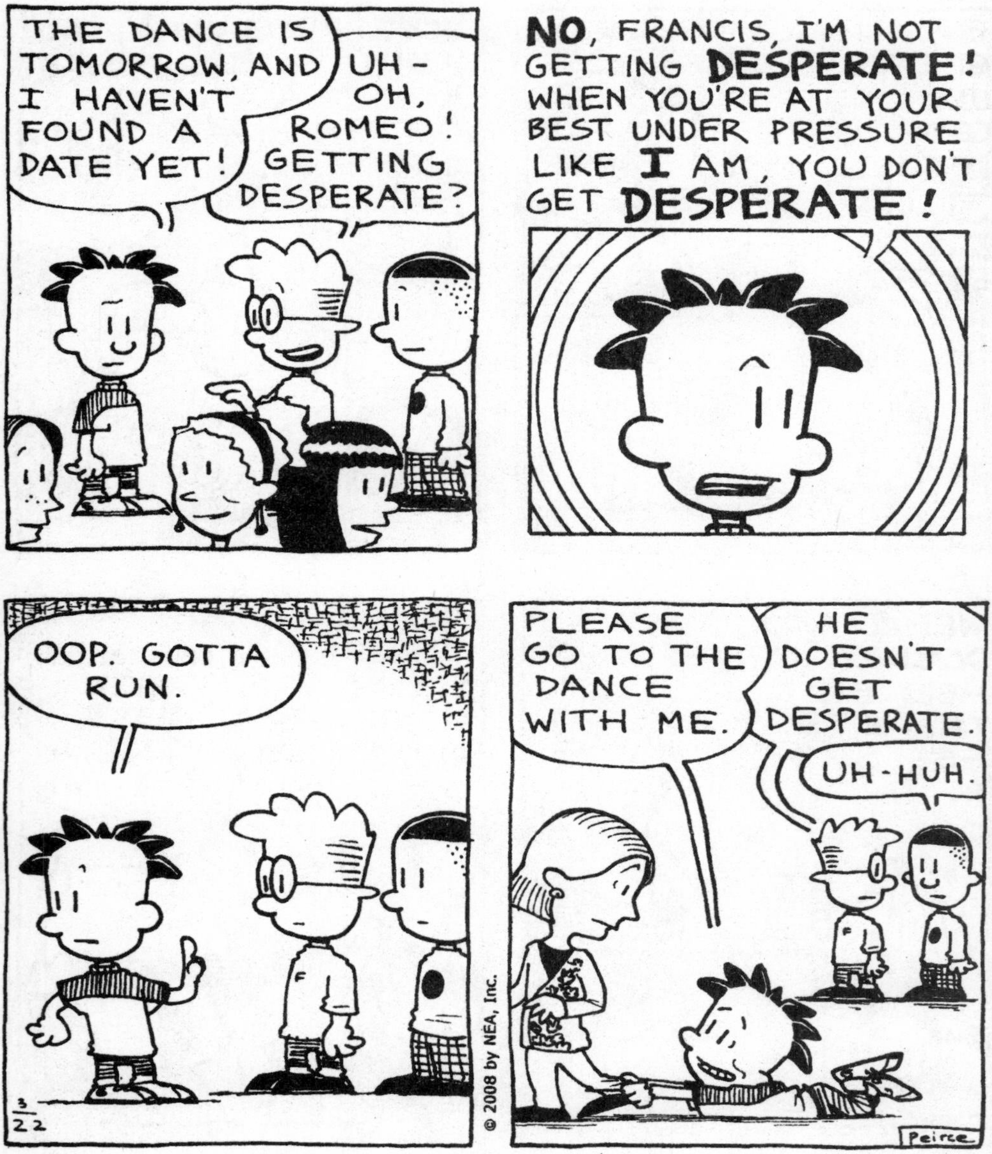
THE DANCE IS TOMORROW, AND I HAVEN'T FOUND A DATE YET!
UH-OH, ROMEO! GETTING DESPERATE?
NO, FRANCIS, I'M NOT GETTING DESPERATE! WHEN YOU'RE AT YOUR BEST UNDER PRESSURE LIKE I AM, YOU DON'T GET DESPERATE!
OOP. GOTTA RUN.
3/22
© 2008 by NEA, Inc.
PLEASE GO TO THE DANCE WITH ME.
HE DOESN'T GET DESPERATE.
UH-HUH.
Peirce

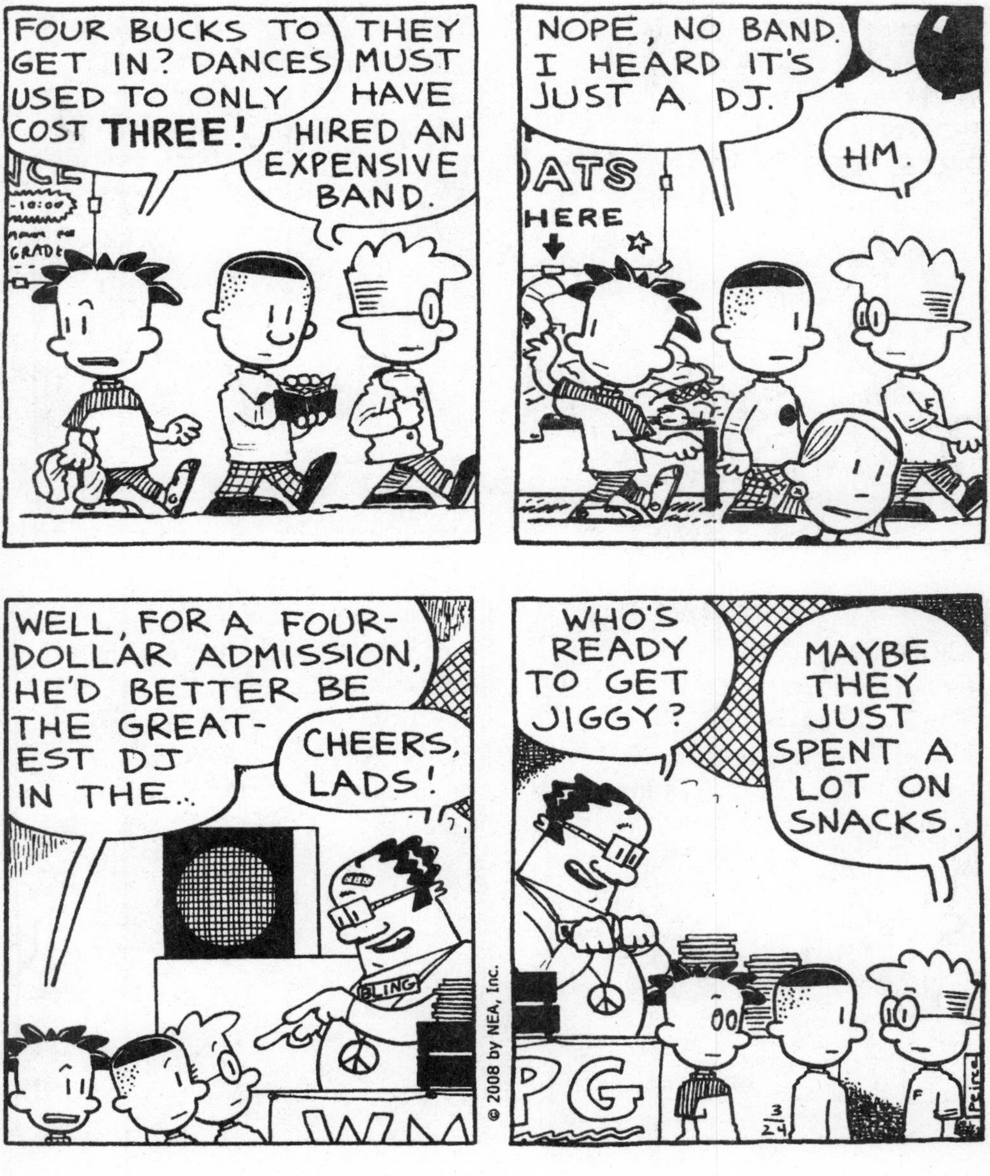
FOUR BUCKS TO GET IN? DANCES USED TO ONLY COST **THREE!**
THEY MUST HAVE HIRED AN EXPENSIVE BAND.
NOPE, NO BAND. I HEARD IT'S JUST A DJ.
HM.
HERE
WELL, FOR A FOUR-DOLLAR ADMISSION, HE'D BETTER BE THE GREAT-EST DJ IN THE...
CHEERS, LADS!
BLING
WHO'S READY TO GET JIGGY?
MAYBE THEY JUST SPENT A LOT ON SNACKS.
© 2008 by NEA, Inc.
3/24
Peirce

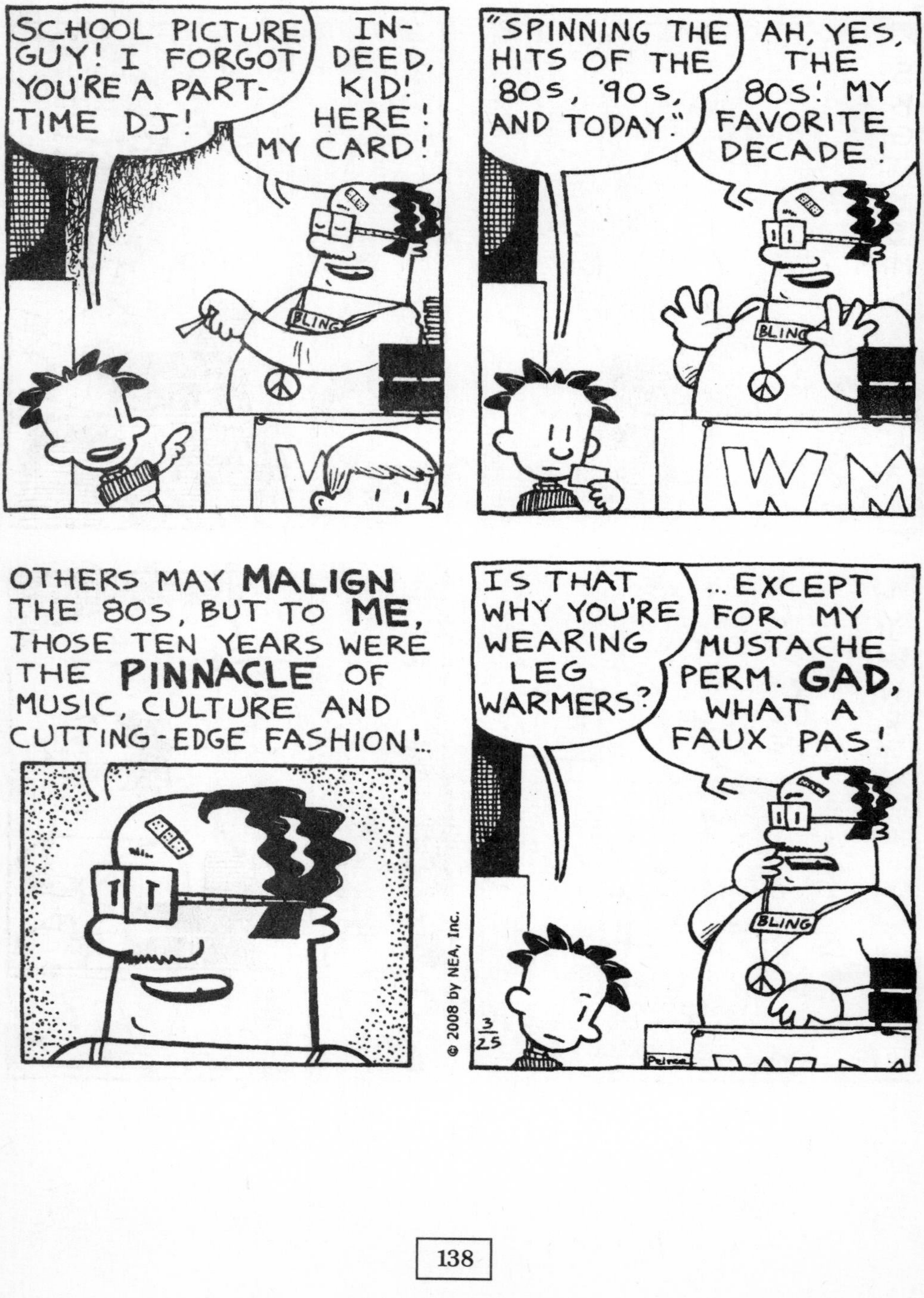
SCHOOL PICTURE GUY! I FORGOT YOU'RE A PART-TIME DJ!
INDEED, KID! HERE! MY CARD!
BLING
"SPINNING THE HITS OF THE '80s, '90s, AND TODAY."
AH, YES, THE 80s! MY FAVORITE DECADE!
BLING
OTHERS MAY **MALIGN** THE 80s, BUT TO **ME**, THOSE TEN YEARS WERE THE **PINNACLE** OF MUSIC, CULTURE AND CUTTING-EDGE FASHION!..
IS THAT WHY YOU'RE WEARING LEG WARMERS?
...EXCEPT FOR MY MUSTACHE PERM. **GAD**, WHAT A FAUX PAS!
BLING
3/25
Peirce

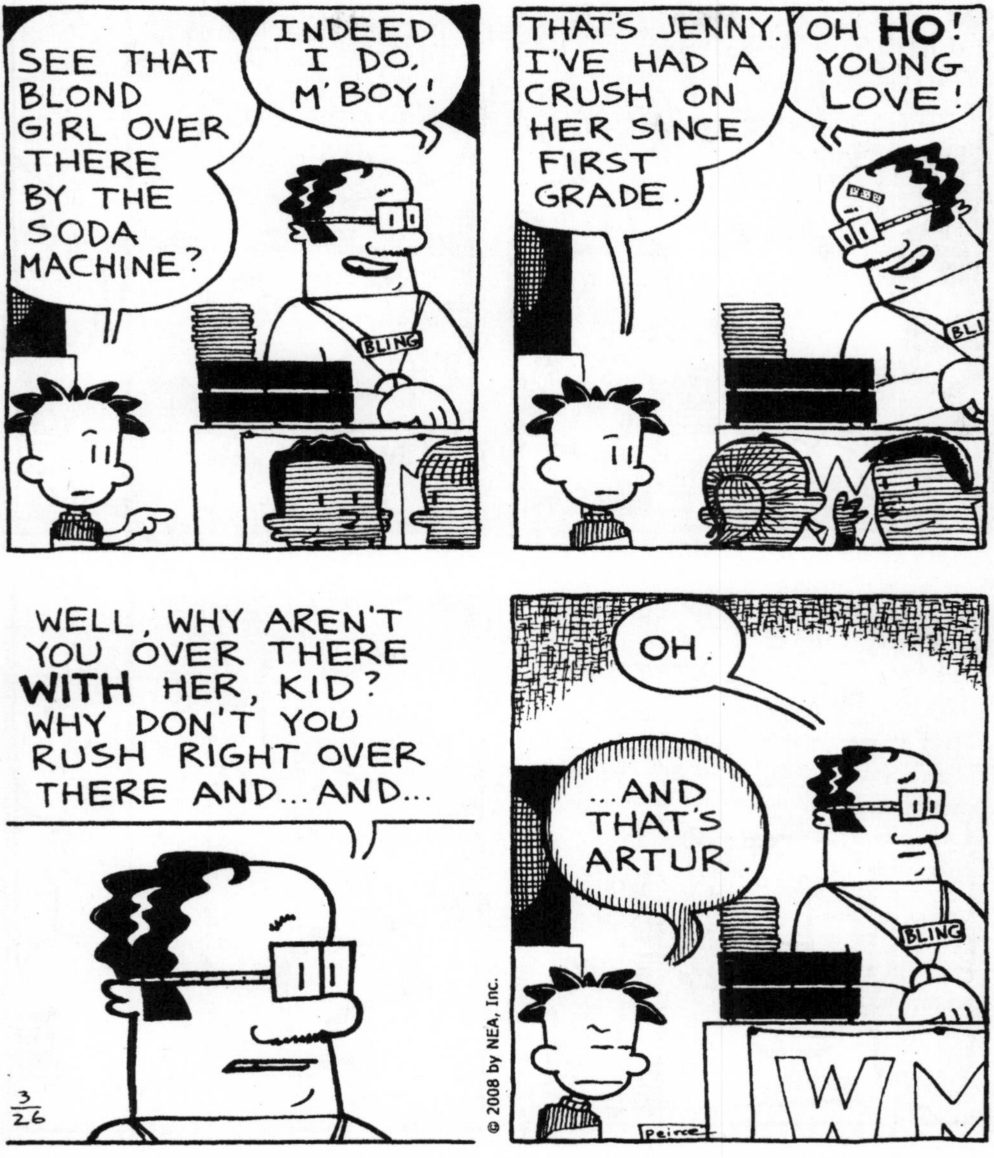
SEE THAT BLOND GIRL OVER THERE BY THE SODA MACHINE?
INDEED I DO, M'BOY!
BLING
THAT'S JENNY. I'VE HAD A CRUSH ON HER SINCE FIRST GRADE.
OH HO! YOUNG LOVE!
WELL, WHY AREN'T YOU OVER THERE WITH HER, KID? WHY DON'T YOU RUSH RIGHT OVER THERE AND... AND...
3/26
OH.
...AND THAT'S ARTUR.
BLING
© 2008 by NEA, Inc.
Peirce

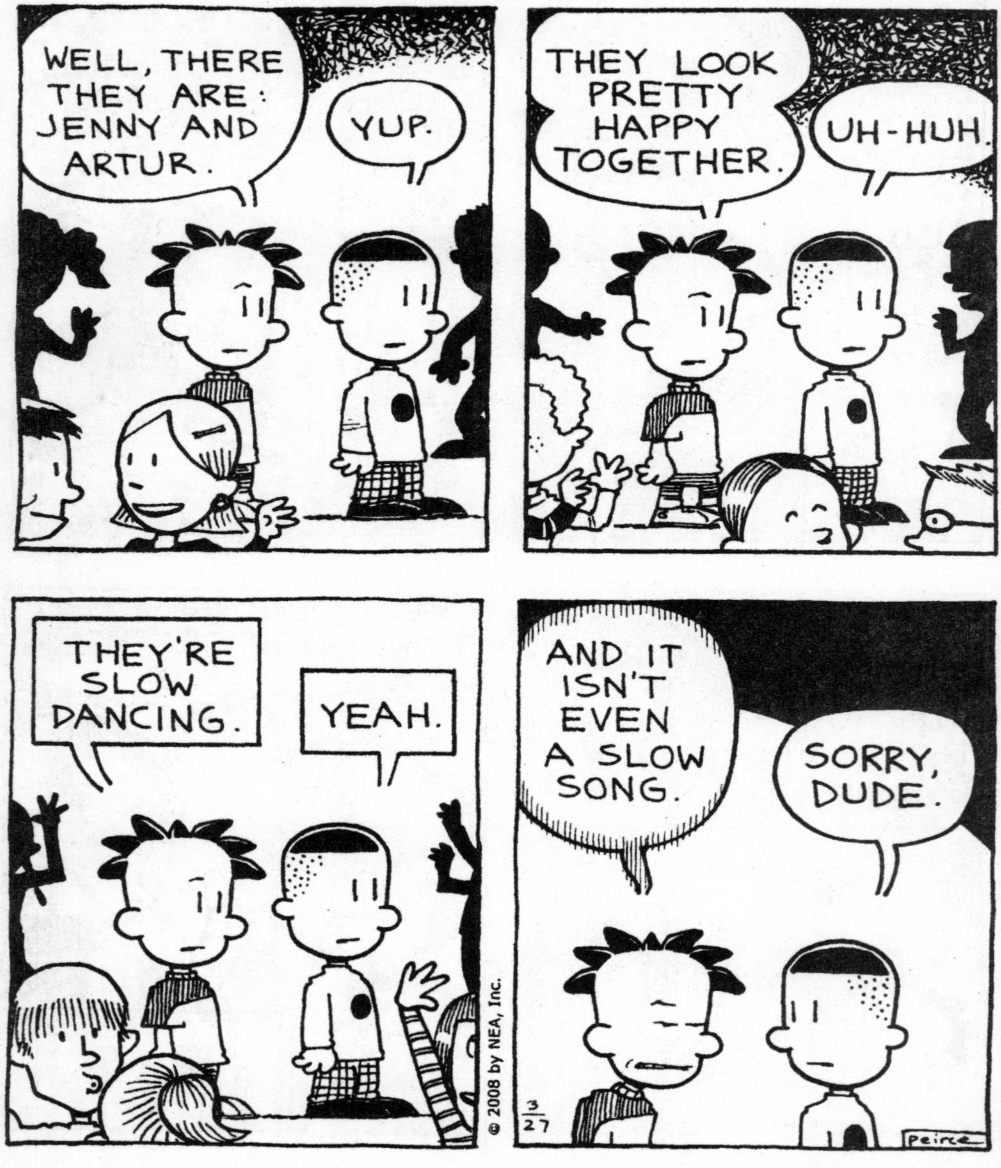

WELL, THERE THEY ARE: JENNY AND ARTUR.
YUP.
THEY LOOK PRETTY HAPPY TOGETHER.
UH-HUH.
THEY'RE SLOW DANCING.
YEAH.
AND IT ISN'T EVEN A SLOW SONG.
SORRY, DUDE.
3/27
Peirce

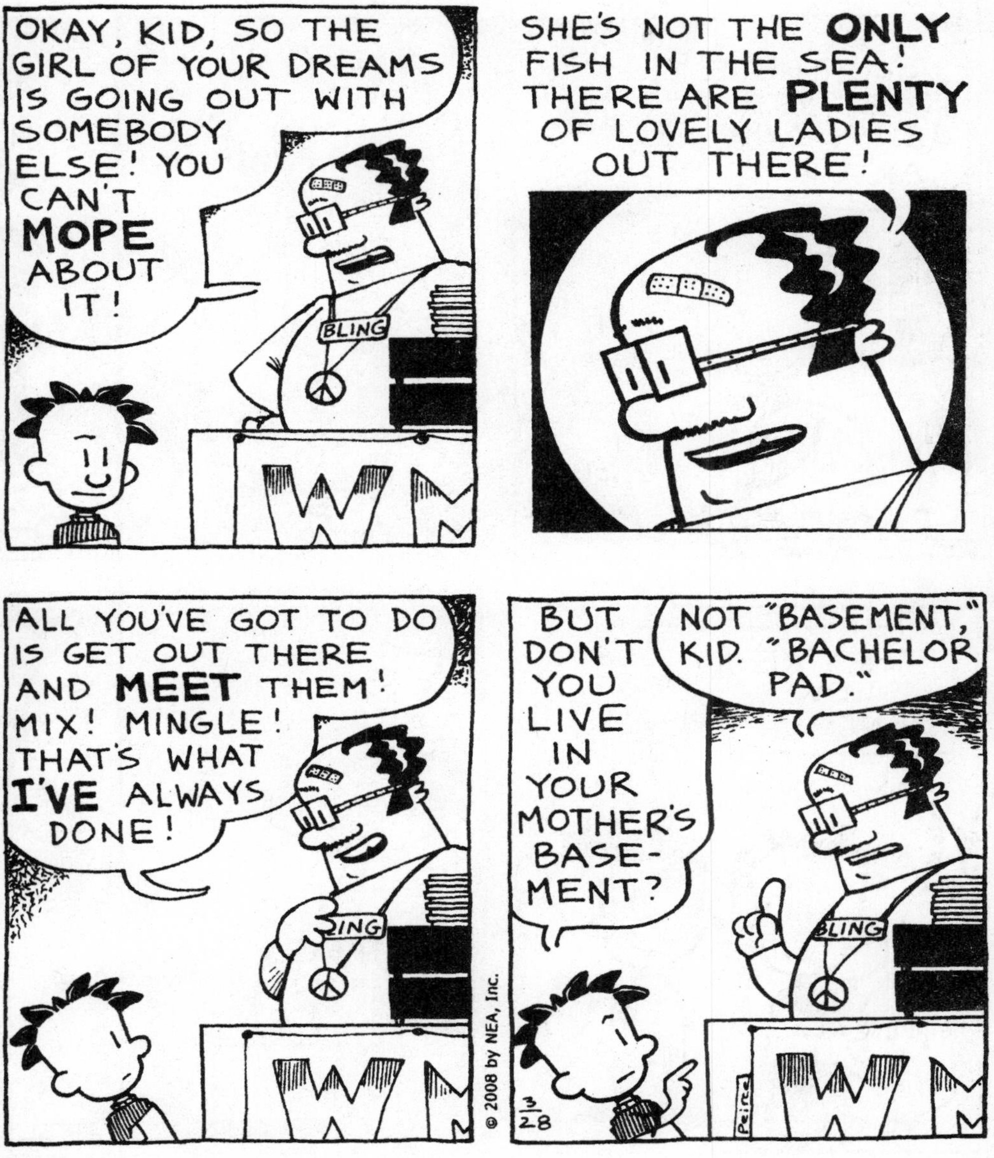

OKAY, KID, SO THE GIRL OF YOUR DREAMS IS GOING OUT WITH SOMEBODY ELSE! YOU CAN'T **MOPE** ABOUT IT!
BLING
SHE'S NOT THE **ONLY** FISH IN THE SEA! THERE ARE **PLENTY** OF LOVELY LADIES OUT THERE!
ALL YOU'VE GOT TO DO IS GET OUT THERE AND **MEET** THEM! MIX! MINGLE! THAT'S WHAT **I'VE** ALWAYS DONE!
BUT DON'T YOU LIVE IN YOUR MOTHER'S BASEMENT?
NOT "BASEMENT," KID. "BACHELOR PAD."
BLING
© 2008 by NEA, Inc.
3/28
Peirce

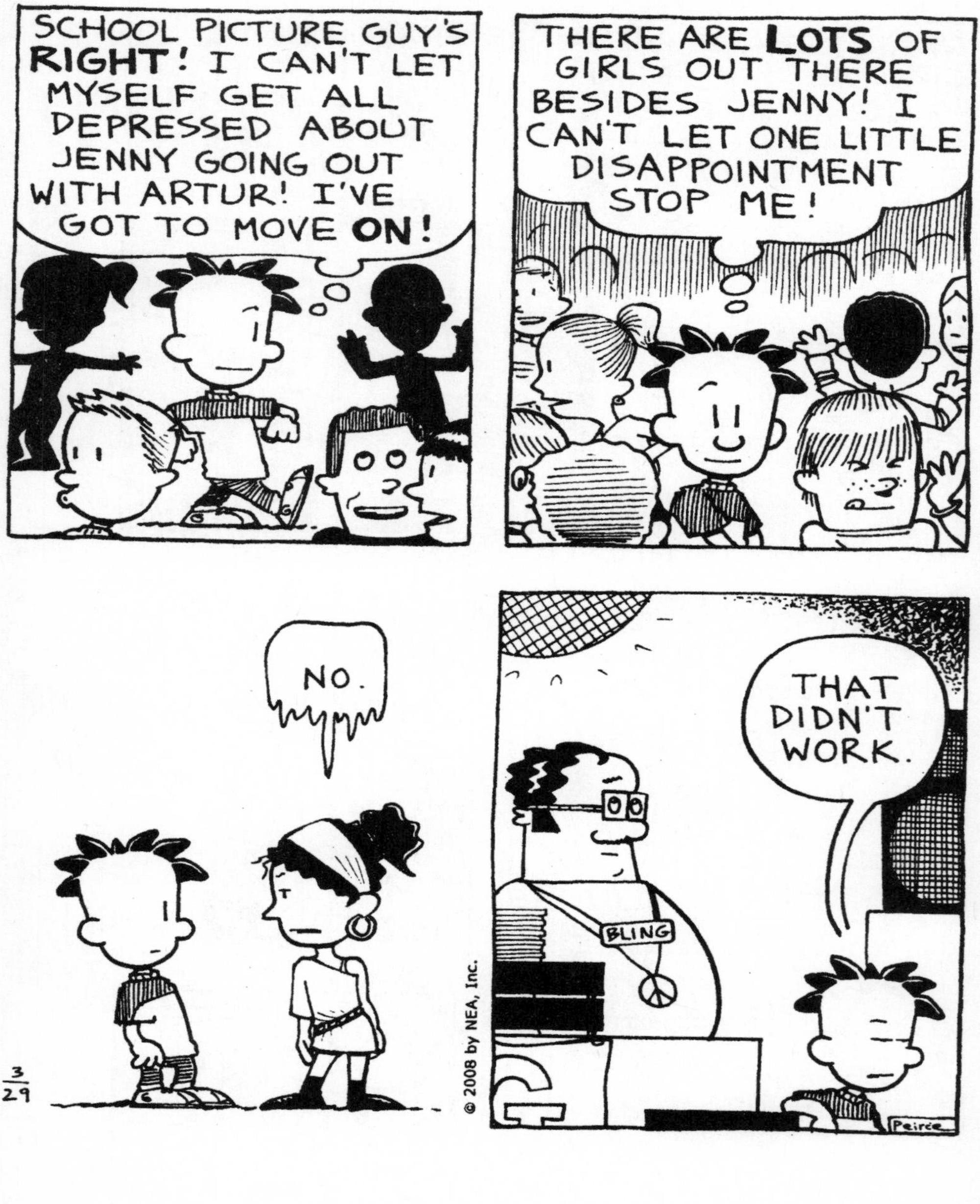
SCHOOL PICTURE GUY'S RIGHT! I CAN'T LET MYSELF GET ALL DEPRESSED ABOUT JENNY GOING OUT WITH ARTUR! I'VE GOT TO MOVE ON!
THERE ARE LOTS OF GIRLS OUT THERE BESIDES JENNY! I CAN'T LET ONE LITTLE DISAPPOINTMENT STOP ME!
NO.
THAT DIDN'T WORK.
BLING
3/29
© 2008 by NEA, Inc.
Peirce

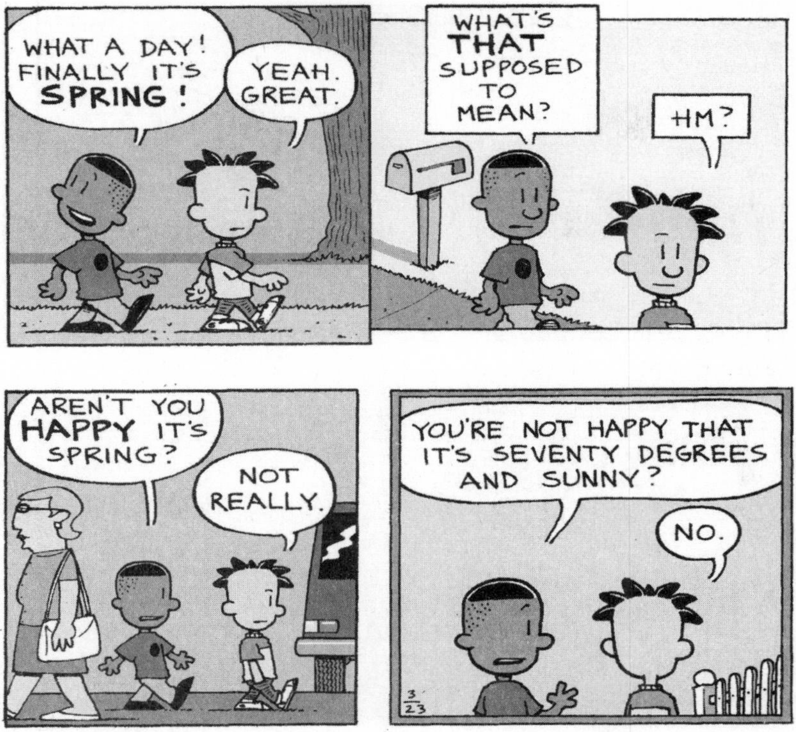
WHAT A DAY! FINALLY IT'S SPRING!
YEAH. GREAT.
WHAT'S THAT SUPPOSED TO MEAN?
HM?
AREN'T YOU HAPPY IT'S SPRING?
NOT REALLY.
YOU'RE NOT HAPPY THAT IT'S SEVENTY DEGREES AND SUNNY?
NO.
3 23

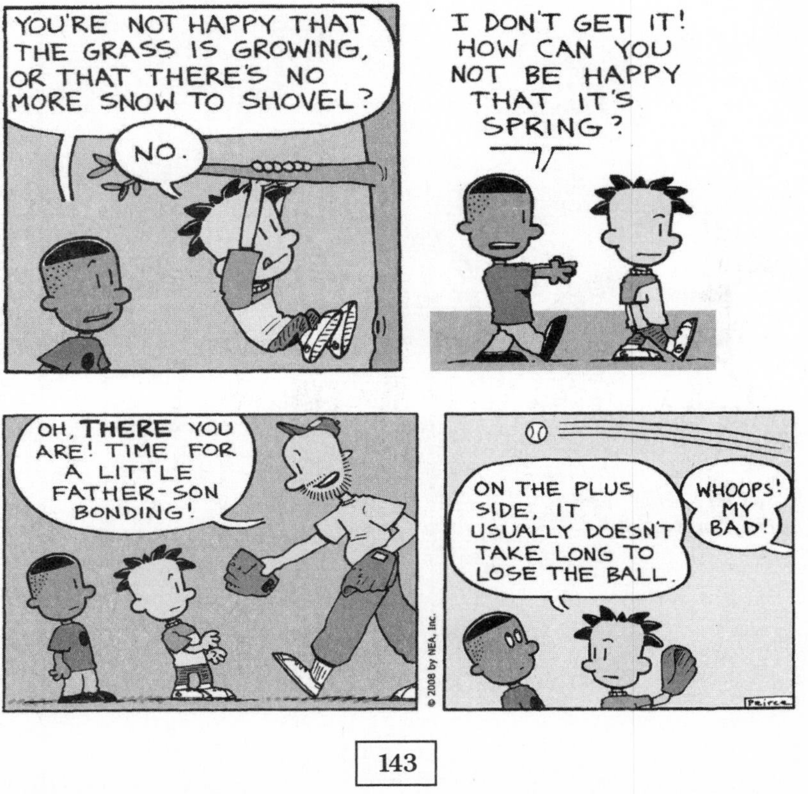
YOU'RE NOT HAPPY THAT THE GRASS IS GROWING, OR THAT THERE'S NO MORE SNOW TO SHOVEL?
NO.
I DON'T GET IT! HOW CAN YOU NOT BE HAPPY THAT IT'S SPRING?
OH, THERE YOU ARE! TIME FOR A LITTLE FATHER-SON BONDING!
ON THE PLUS SIDE, IT USUALLY DOESN'T TAKE LONG TO LOSE THE BALL.
WHOOPS! MY BAD!
© 2008 by NEA, Inc.

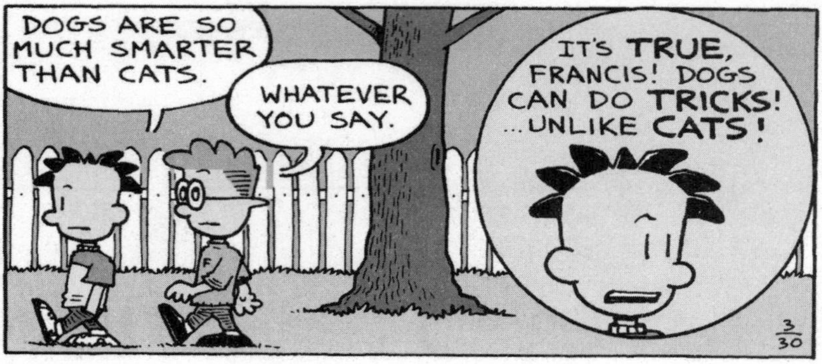
DOGS ARE SO MUCH SMARTER THAN CATS.
WHATEVER YOU SAY.
IT'S TRUE, FRANCIS! DOGS CAN DO TRICKS! ...UNLIKE CATS!
3/30

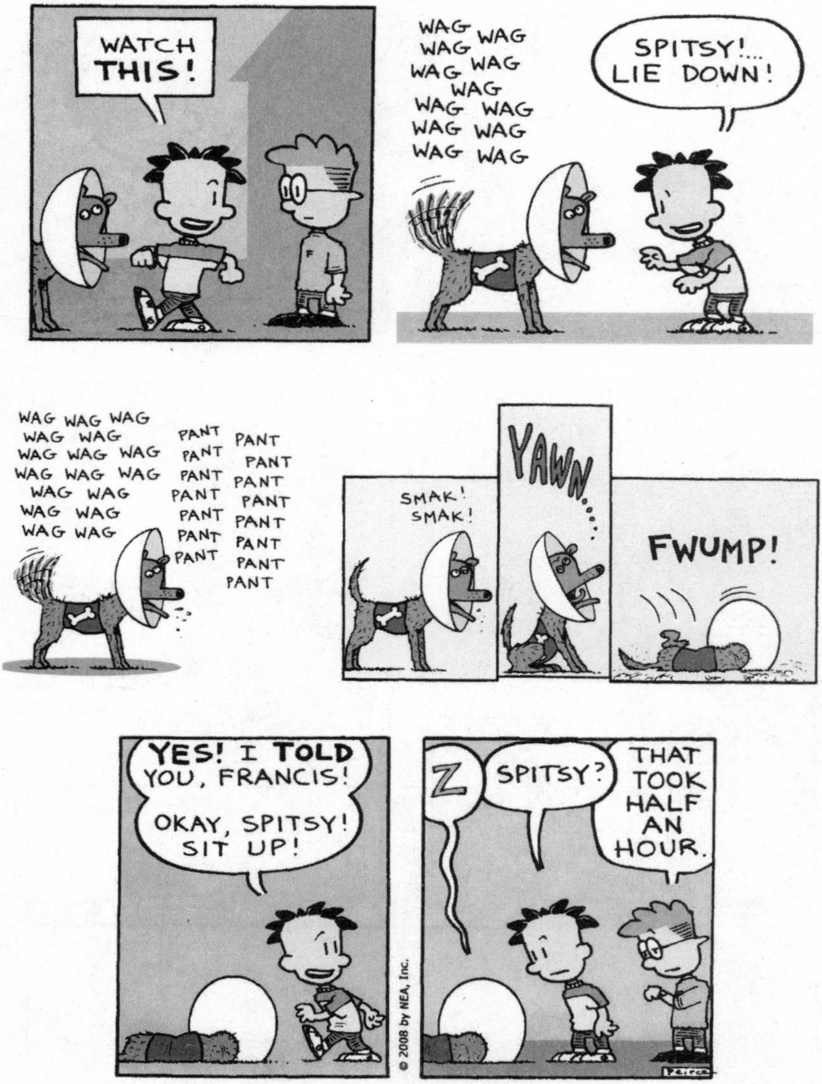
WATCH THIS!
WAG WAG WAG WAG WAG WAG WAG WAG WAG WAG WAG WAG WAG
SPITSY!... LIE DOWN!
WAG WAG WAG WAG WAG WAG WAG WAG WAG WAG WAG WAG WAG WAG WAG WAG WAG WAG
PANT PANT PANT PANT PANT PANT PANT PANT PANT PANT PANT PANT PANT PANT PANT PANT
SMAK! SMAK!
YAWN....
FWUMP!
YES! I TOLD YOU, FRANCIS!
OKAY, SPITSY! SIT UP!
Z
SPITSY?
THAT TOOK HALF AN HOUR.

DETENTION, AGAIN

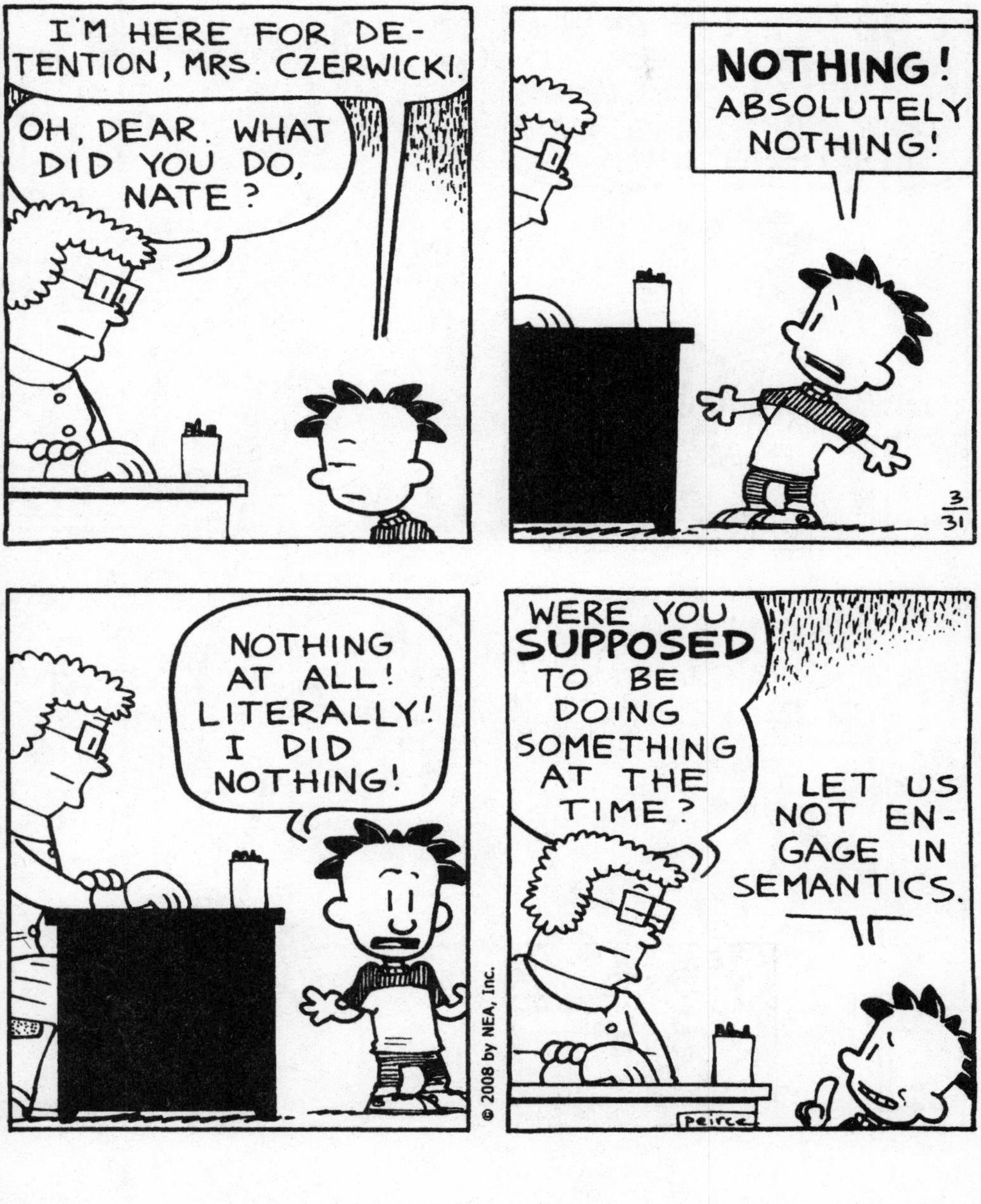
I'M HERE FOR DE-TENTION, MRS. CZERWICKI.
OH, DEAR. WHAT DID YOU DO, NATE?
NOTHING! ABSOLUTELY NOTHING!
3/31
NOTHING AT ALL! LITERALLY! I DID NOTHING!
WERE YOU SUPPOSED TO BE DOING SOMETHING AT THE TIME?
LET US NOT EN-GAGE IN SEMANTICS.
peirce

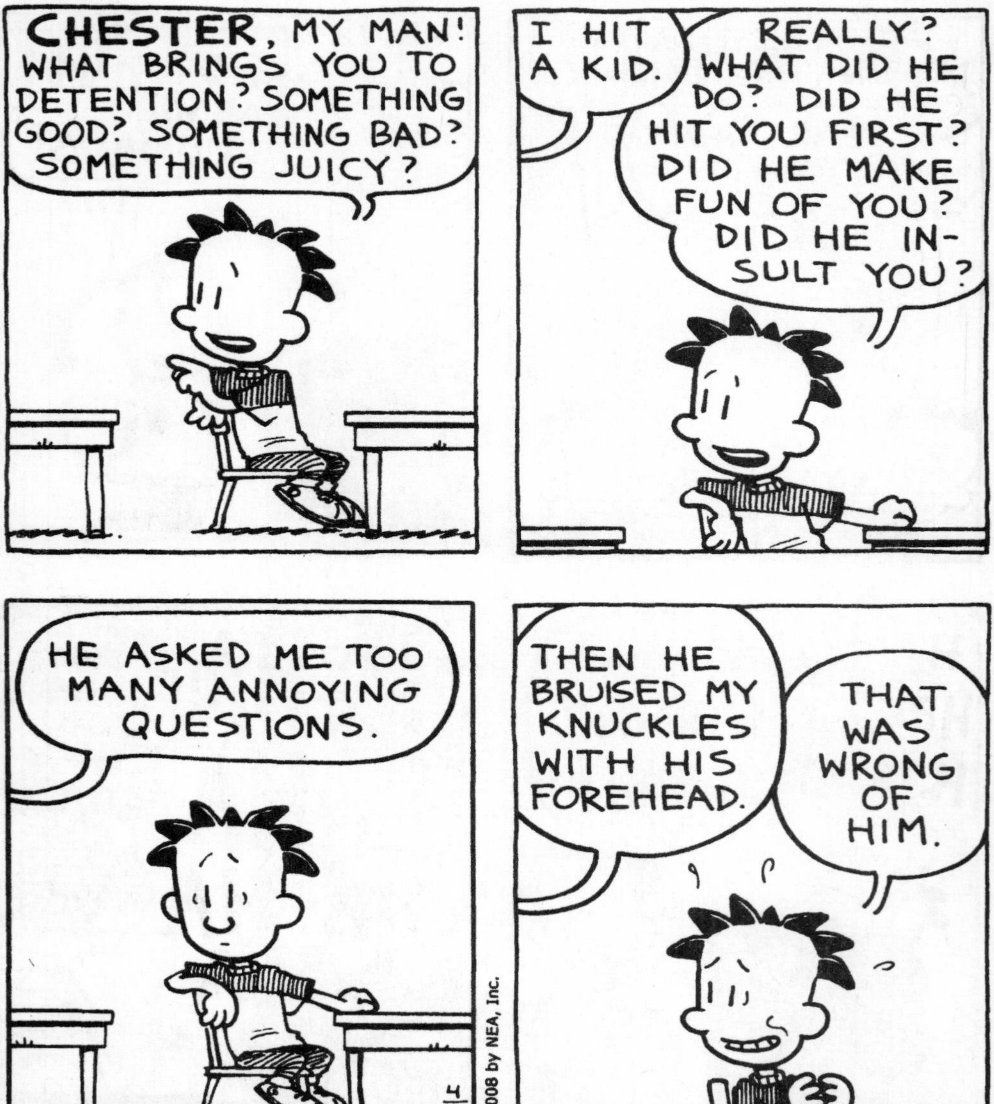
CHESTER, MY MAN! WHAT BRINGS YOU TO DETENTION? SOMETHING GOOD? SOMETHING BAD? SOMETHING JUICY?
I HIT A KID.
REALLY? WHAT DID HE DO? DID HE HIT YOU FIRST? DID HE MAKE FUN OF YOU? DID HE IN-SULT YOU?
HE ASKED ME TOO MANY ANNOYING QUESTIONS.
© 2008 by NEA, Inc.
THEN HE BRUISED MY KNUCKLES WITH HIS FOREHEAD.
THAT WAS WRONG OF HIM.

WE'RE HERE FOR DETENTION, MRS. CZERWICKI.
FOR DOING WHAT, BOYS?
ROOM
WELL, WE... HEH HEH!...
HA HA!
HA HA HA HO HO HEH HEH HA HA HA HA HA HA HEH HA
4/2
Peirce
© 2008 by NEA, Inc.
HA HA HA HA HA HA HA HA
I HATE THIS JOB.

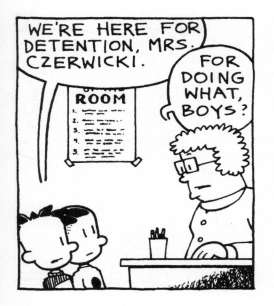

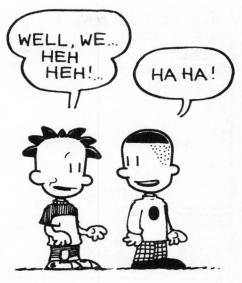

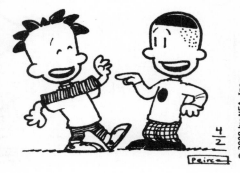

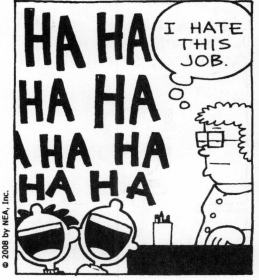

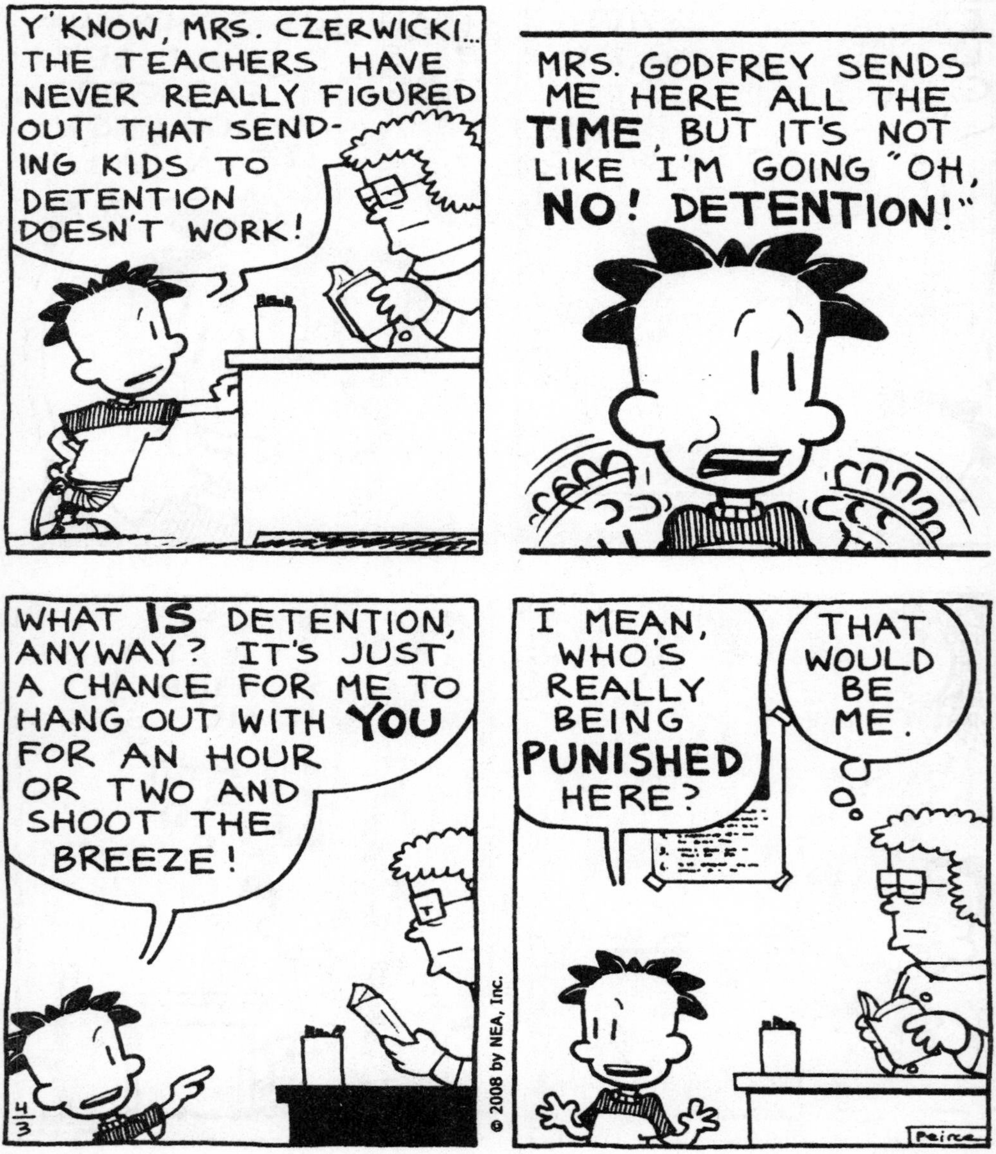
Y'KNOW, MRS. CZERWICKI... THE TEACHERS HAVE NEVER REALLY FIGURED OUT THAT SENDING KIDS TO DETENTION DOESN'T WORK!
MRS. GODFREY SENDS ME HERE ALL THE TIME, BUT IT'S NOT LIKE I'M GOING "OH, NO! DETENTION!"
WHAT IS DETENTION, ANYWAY? IT'S JUST A CHANCE FOR ME TO HANG OUT WITH YOU FOR AN HOUR OR TWO AND SHOOT THE BREEZE!
I MEAN, WHO'S REALLY BEING PUNISHED HERE?
THAT WOULD BE ME.
© 2008 by NEA, Inc.
Peirce

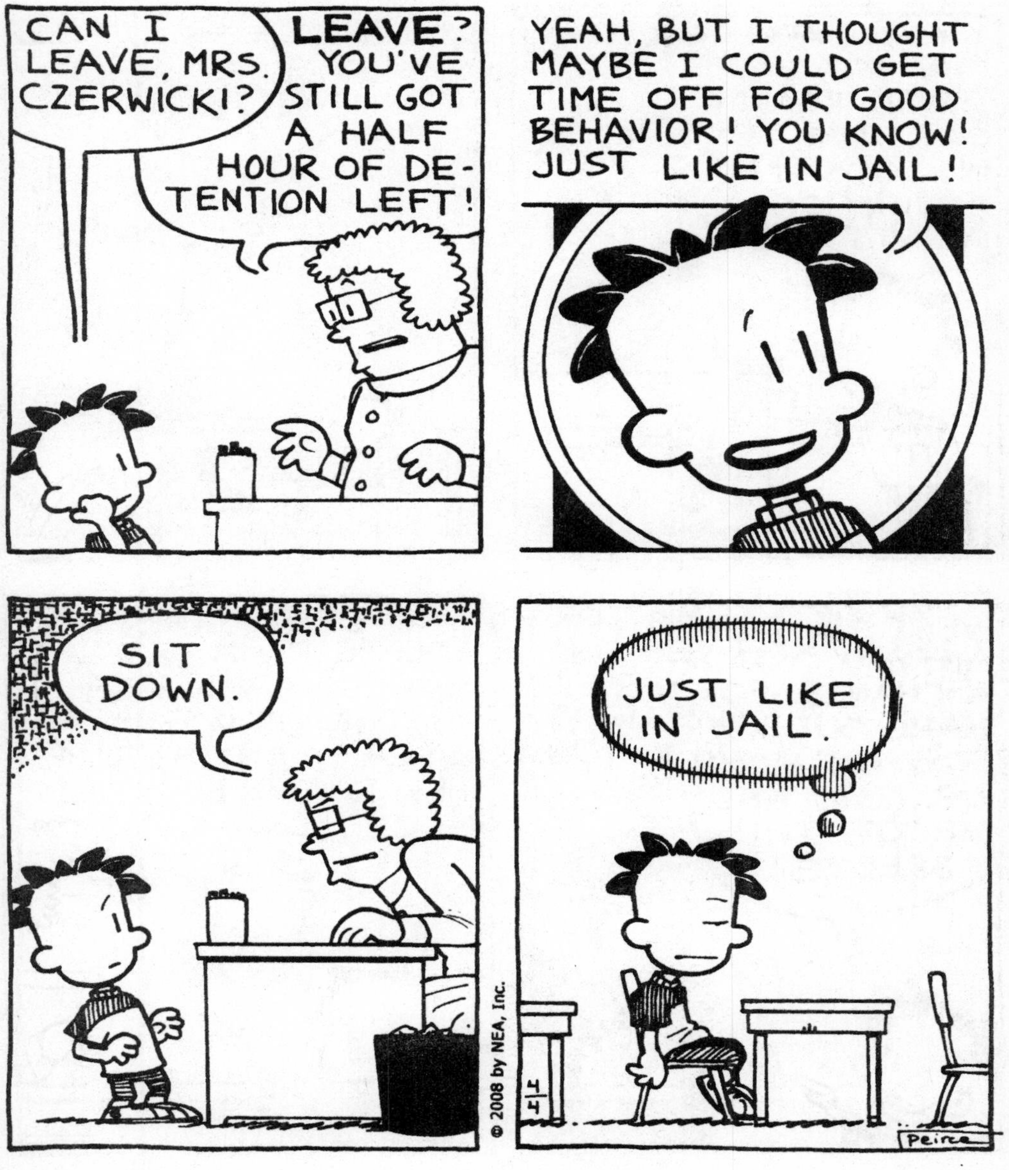
CAN I LEAVE, MRS. CZERWICKI?
LEAVE? YOU'VE STILL GOT A HALF HOUR OF DE-TENTION LEFT!
YEAH, BUT I THOUGHT MAYBE I COULD GET TIME OFF FOR GOOD BEHAVIOR! YOU KNOW! JUST LIKE IN JAIL!
SIT DOWN.
JUST LIKE IN JAIL.
© 2008 by NEA, Inc.
Peirce

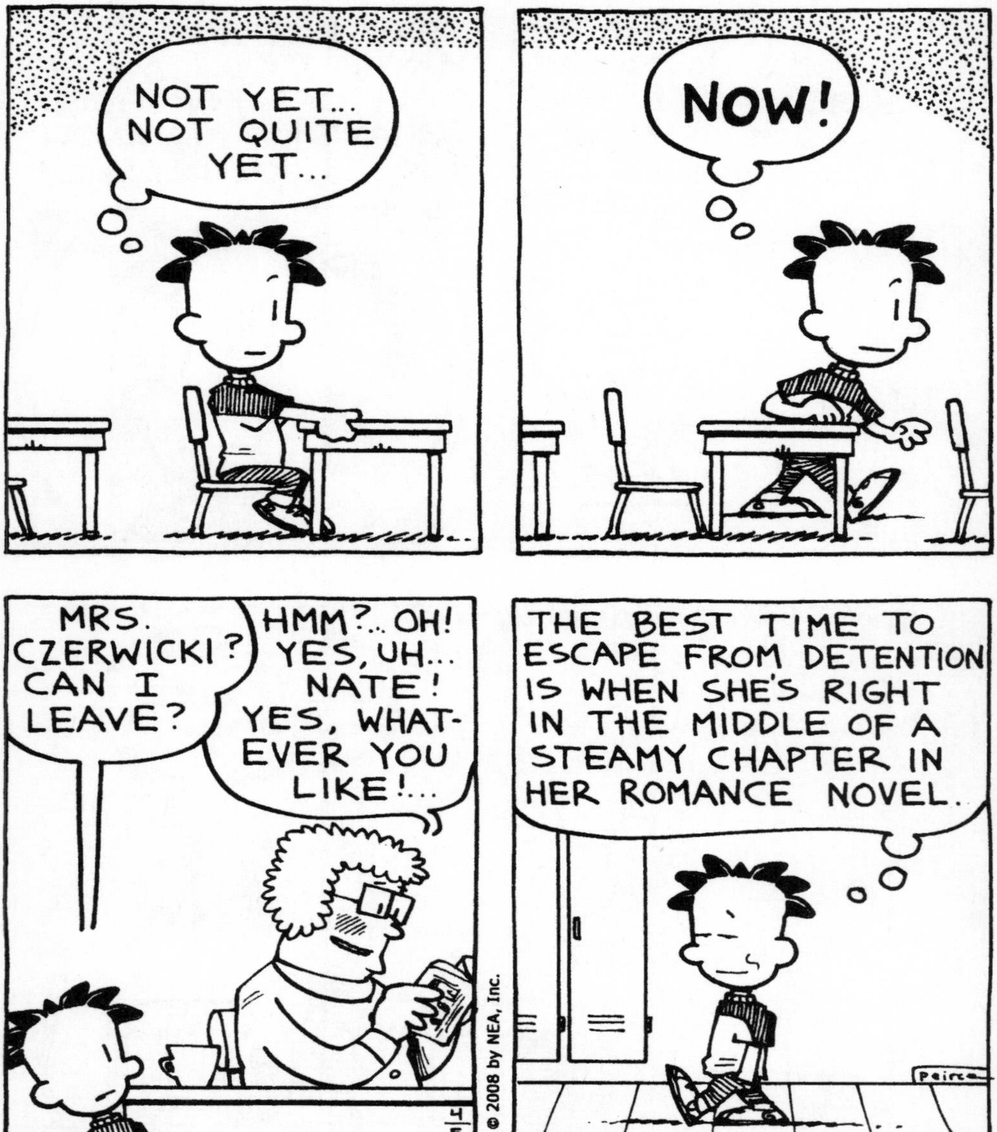
NOT YET... NOT QUITE YET...
NOW!
MRS. CZERWICKI? CAN I LEAVE?
HMM?... OH! YES, UH... NATE! YES, WHATEVER YOU LIKE!...
THE BEST TIME TO ESCAPE FROM DETENTION IS WHEN SHE'S RIGHT IN THE MIDDLE OF A STEAMY CHAPTER IN HER ROMANCE NOVEL.
© 2008 by NEA, Inc.
Peirce

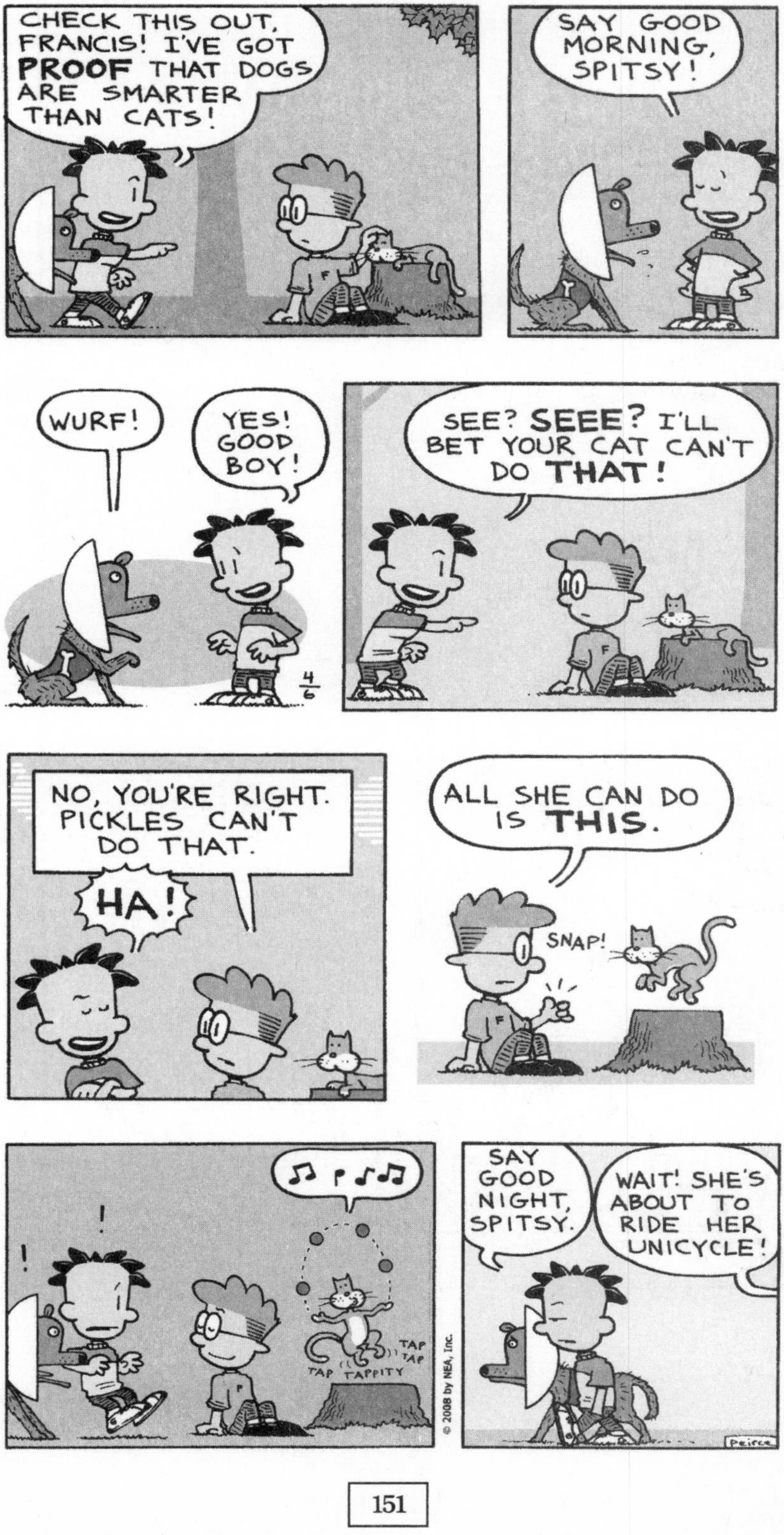
CHECK THIS OUT, FRANCIS! I'VE GOT PROOF THAT DOGS ARE SMARTER THAN CATS!
SAY GOOD MORNING, SPITSY!
WURF!
YES! GOOD BOY!
4/6
SEE? SEEE? I'LL BET YOUR CAT CAN'T DO THAT!
NO, YOU'RE RIGHT. PICKLES CAN'T DO THAT.
HA!
ALL SHE CAN DO IS THIS.
SNAP!
!
!
TAP TAPPITY
TAP TAP
© 2008 by NEA, Inc.
SAY GOOD NIGHT, SPITSY.
WAIT! SHE'S ABOUT TO RIDE HER UNICYCLE!
Peirce

BOOK BUDDIES, NATE'S WAY

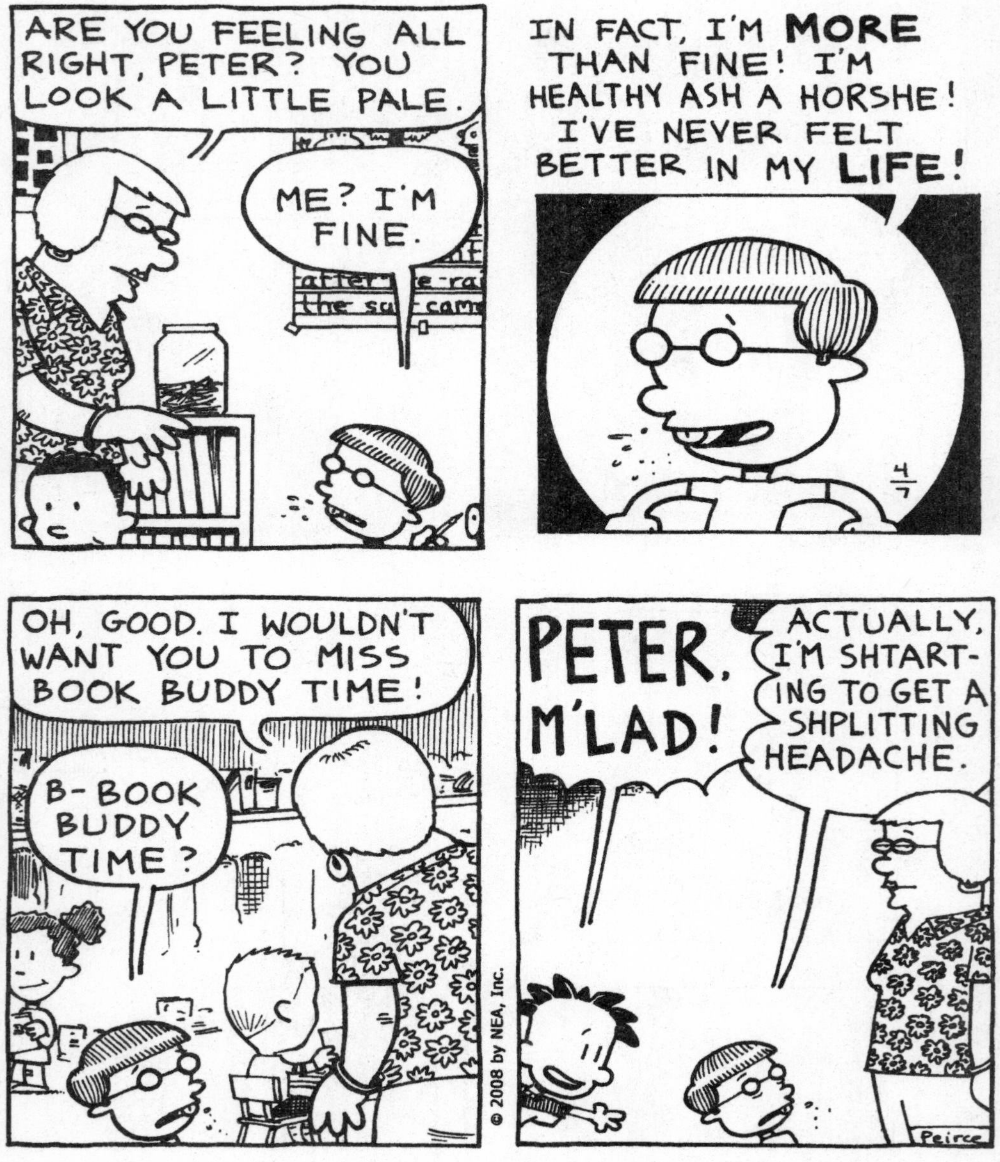
ARE YOU FEELING ALL RIGHT, PETER? YOU LOOK A LITTLE PALE.
ME? I'M FINE.
IN FACT, I'M **MORE** THAN FINE! I'M HEALTHY ASH A HORSHE! I'VE NEVER FELT BETTER IN MY **LIFE**!
OH, GOOD. I WOULDN'T WANT YOU TO MISS BOOK BUDDY TIME!
B-BOOK BUDDY TIME?
PETER, M'LAD!
ACTUALLY, I'M SHTARTING TO GET A SHPLITTING HEADACHE.
© 2008 by NEA, Inc.
Peirce

LOOK... NO OFFENSHE, BUT YOU DON'T NEED TO BE HERE.

PETER, I'M SUPPOSED TO HELP YOU WITH YOUR READING!

I DON'T **NEED** HELP! JUSHT GO HANG OUT IN THE COMPUTER LAB OR SHOMETHING!

THAT WOULD BE NEGLECTING MY ROLE AS YOUR BOOK BUDDY!

SEE? "BOOK BUDDIES MENTOR AND ENCOURAGE FIRST-GRADERS IN THEIR READING, FOSTERING A LOVE OF BOOKS AND PROMOTING..."

BOOK BUDDIES

© 2008 by NEA, Inc.

4/8

...WHAT'S THAT WORD?

"LITERACY."

Peirce

153

WHAT'S TODAY'S BOOK, PETER?
YOU WOULDN'T BE INTERESHTED.
WHAT? LOOK, PETER, HOW CAN I **TUTOR** YOU IF YOU WON'T TELL ME WHAT YOU'RE **READING**? HOW CAN I BE YOUR BOOK BUDDY WHEN YOU'VE GOT **THAT** ATTITUDE?
WELL, IF YOU MUSHT KNOW, I'M JUSHT SHTARTING GEORGE BERNARD SHAW'S PLAY, "MAN AND SHUPERMAN."
OOH, **SUPERMAN**! GOOD STUFF!
4/9
ANY WONDER WOMAN ACTION IN THERE?
GADZOOKSH.
Peirce
© 2008 by NEA, Inc.

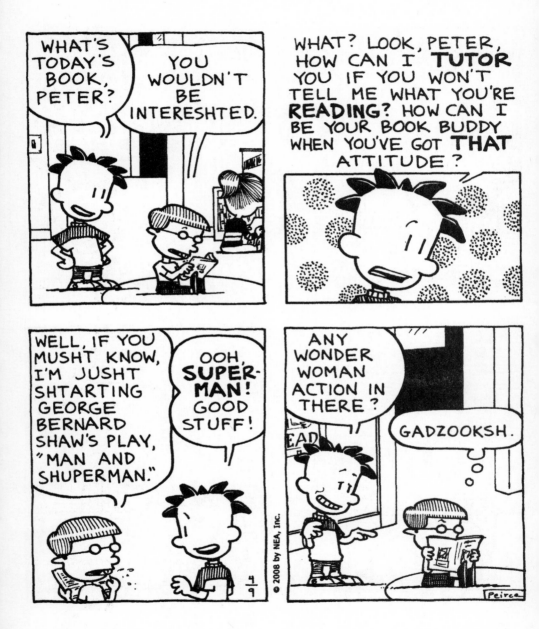

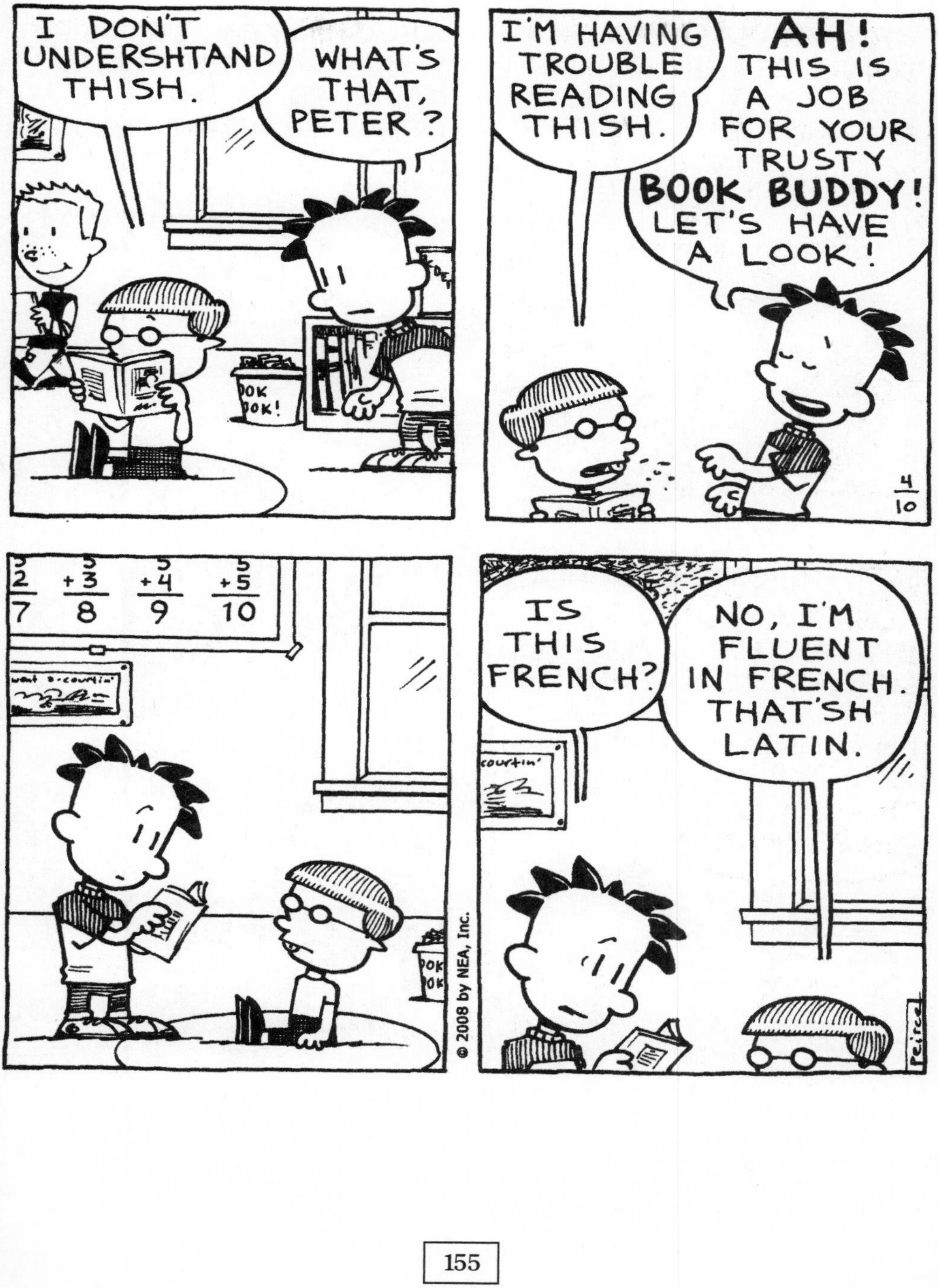
I DON'T UNDERSHTAND THISH.
WHAT'S THAT, PETER?
I'M HAVING TROUBLE READING THISH.
AH! THIS IS A JOB FOR YOUR TRUSTY **BOOK BUDDY!** LET'S HAVE A LOOK!
4/10
IS THIS FRENCH?
NO, I'M FLUENT IN FRENCH. THAT'SH LATIN.
© 2008 by NEA, Inc.
Peirce

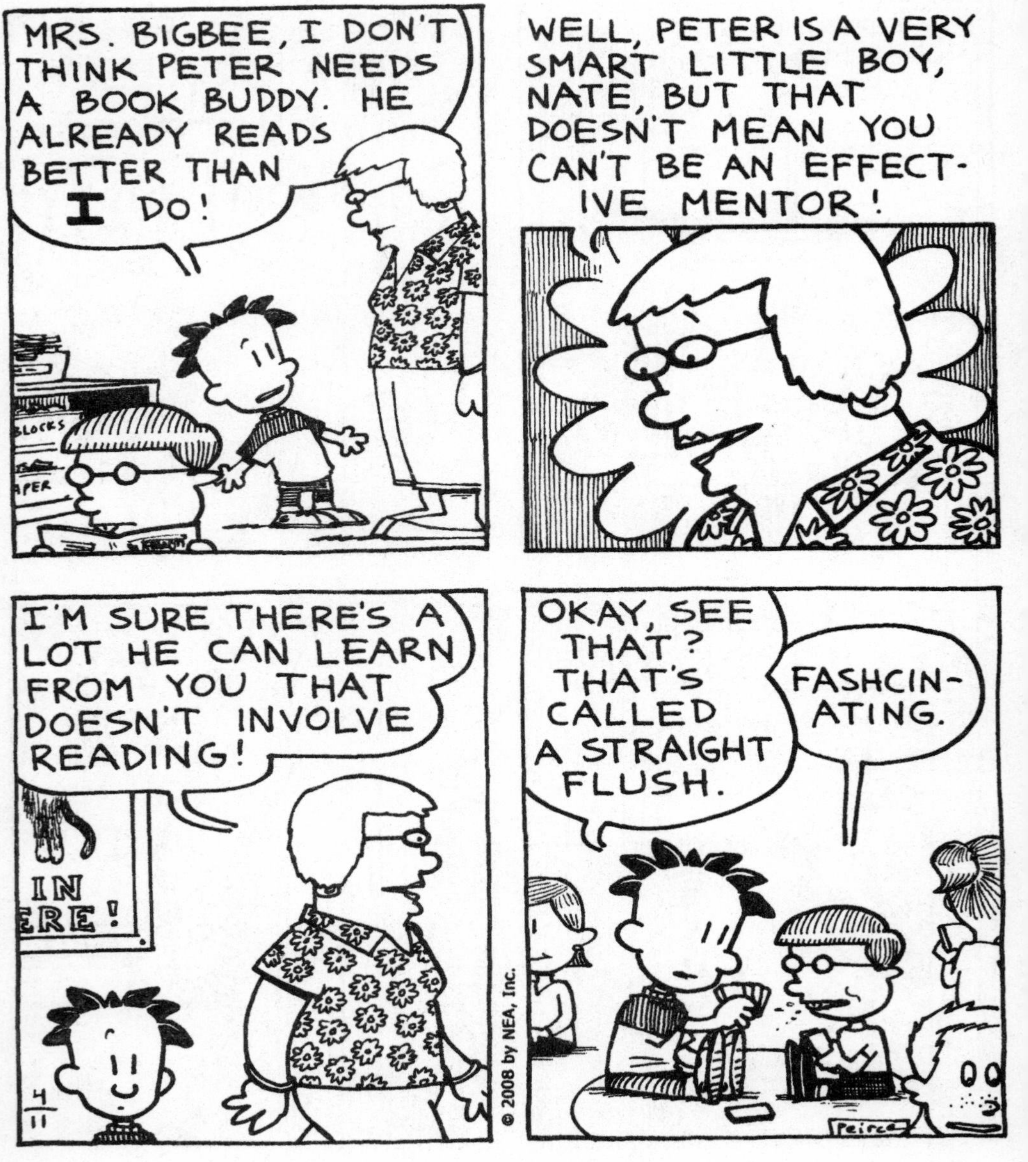

MRS. BIGBEE, I DON'T THINK PETER NEEDS A BOOK BUDDY. HE ALREADY READS BETTER THAN I DO!
BLOCKS
APER
WELL, PETER IS A VERY SMART LITTLE BOY, NATE, BUT THAT DOESN'T MEAN YOU CAN'T BE AN EFFECT-IVE MENTOR!
I'M SURE THERE'S A LOT HE CAN LEARN FROM YOU THAT DOESN'T INVOLVE READING!
IN
ERE!
4/11
© 2008 by NEA, Inc.
OKAY, SEE THAT? THAT'S CALLED A STRAIGHT FLUSH.
FASHCIN-ATING.
Peirce

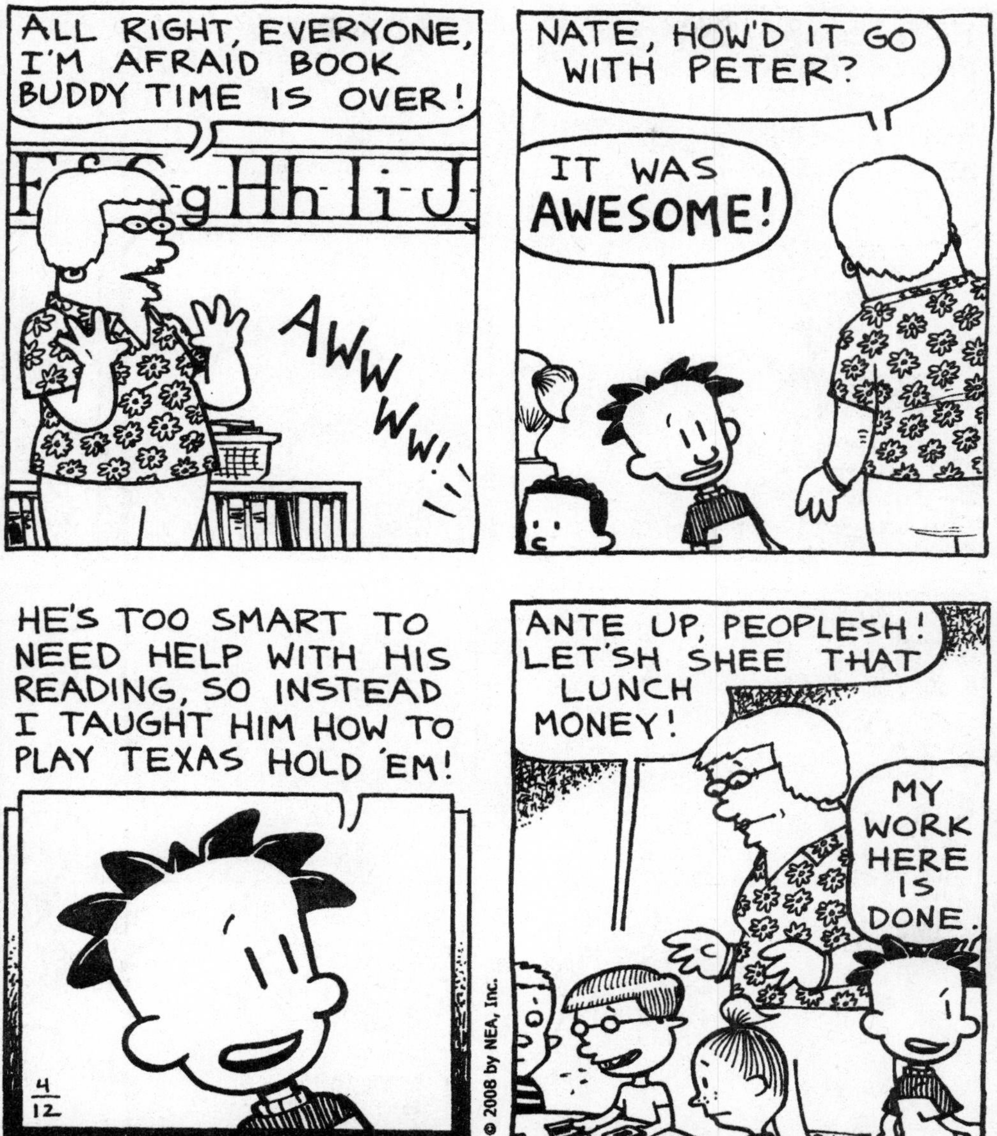
ALL RIGHT, EVERYONE, I'M AFRAID BOOK BUDDY TIME IS OVER!
Ff Gg Hh Ii J
AWWWWW!
NATE, HOW'D IT GO WITH PETER?
IT WAS AWESOME!
HE'S TOO SMART TO NEED HELP WITH HIS READING, SO INSTEAD I TAUGHT HIM HOW TO PLAY TEXAS HOLD 'EM!
4/12
ANTE UP, PEOPLESH! LET'SH SHEE THAT LUNCH MONEY!
MY WORK HERE IS DONE.
Peirce

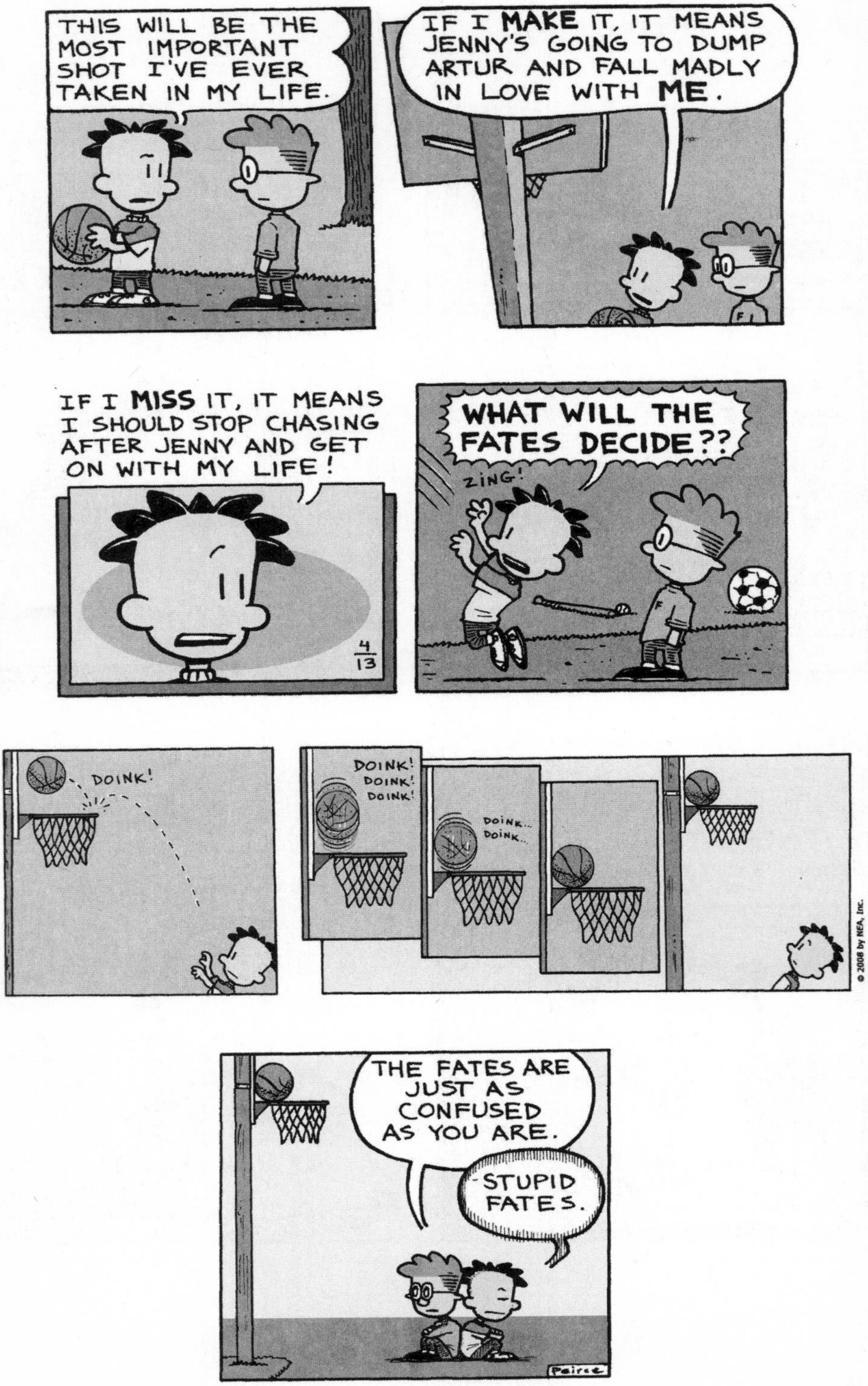
THIS WILL BE THE MOST IMPORTANT SHOT I'VE EVER TAKEN IN MY LIFE.
IF I MAKE IT, IT MEANS JENNY'S GOING TO DUMP ARTUR AND FALL MADLY IN LOVE WITH ME.
IF I MISS IT, IT MEANS I SHOULD STOP CHASING AFTER JENNY AND GET ON WITH MY LIFE!
4/13
WHAT WILL THE FATES DECIDE??
ZING!
DOINK!
DOINK! DOINK! DOINK!
DOINK... DOINK...
© 2008 by NEA, Inc.
THE FATES ARE JUST AS CONFUSED AS YOU ARE.
STUPID FATES.
Peirce

CRUSHED

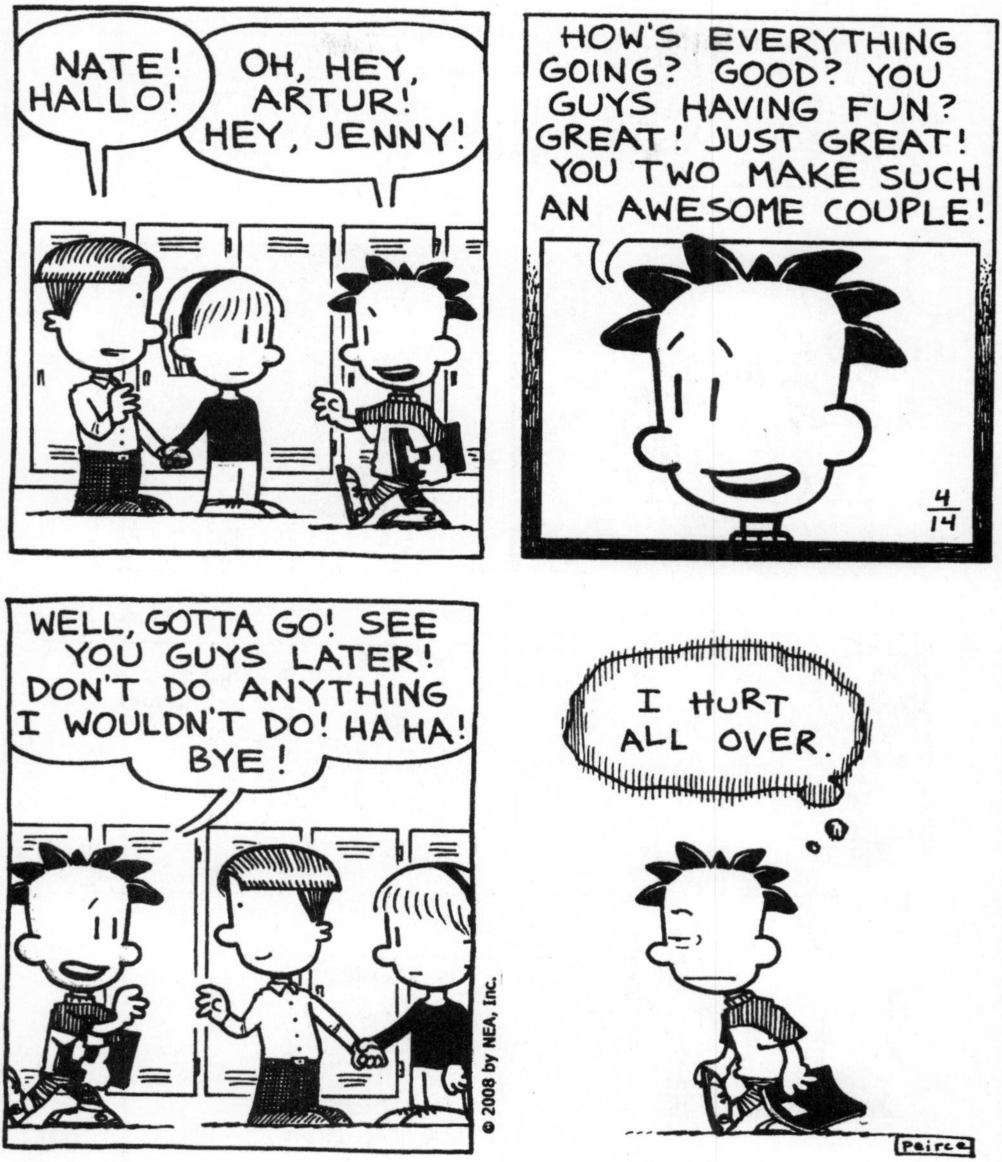
NATE! HALLO!
OH, HEY, ARTUR! HEY, JENNY!
HOW'S EVERYTHING GOING? GOOD? YOU GUYS HAVING FUN? GREAT! JUST GREAT! YOU TWO MAKE SUCH AN AWESOME COUPLE!
4/14
WELL, GOTTA GO! SEE YOU GUYS LATER! DON'T DO ANYTHING I WOULDN'T DO! HA HA! BYE!
© 2008 by NEA, Inc.
I HURT ALL OVER.
peirce

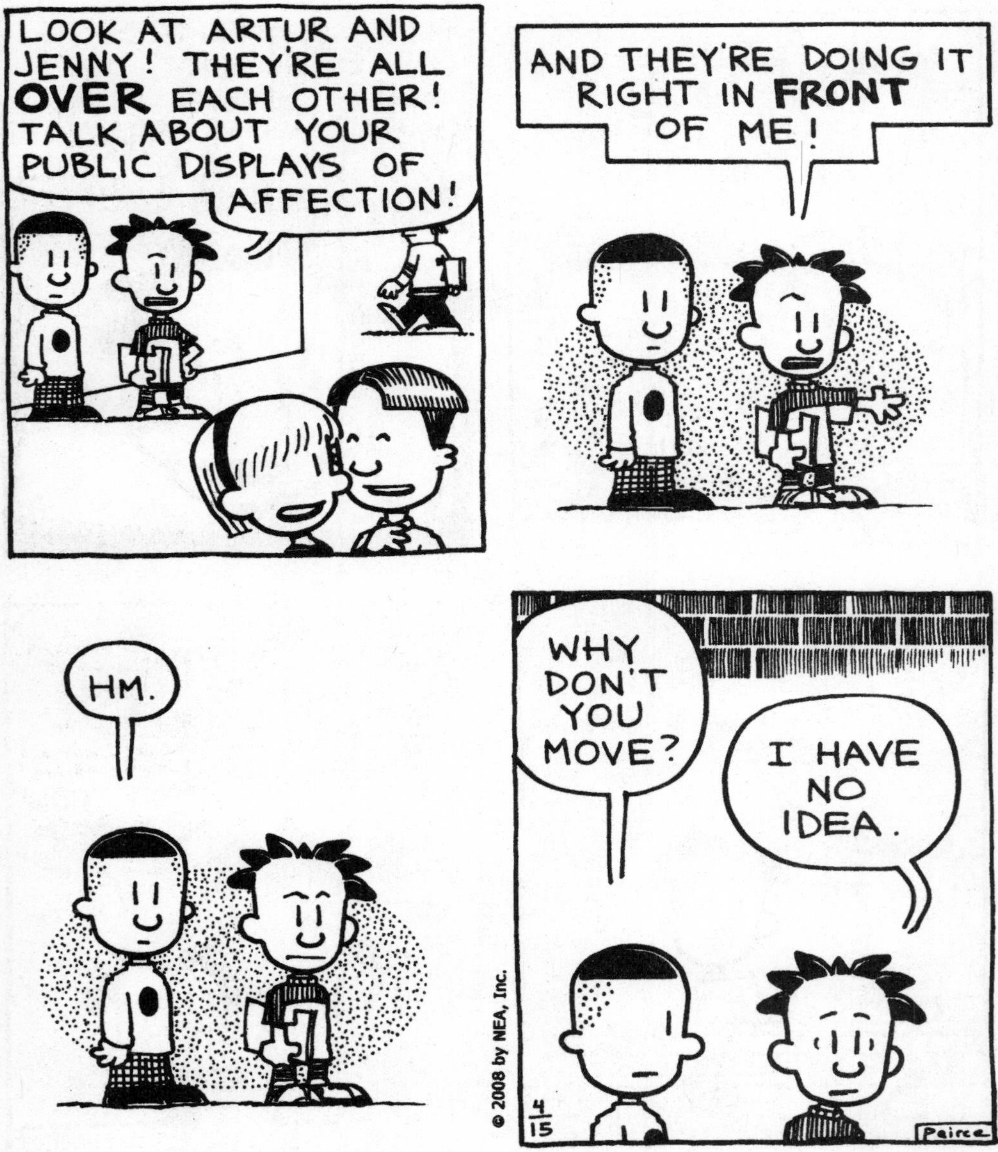
LOOK AT ARTUR AND JENNY! THEY'RE ALL **OVER** EACH OTHER! TALK ABOUT YOUR PUBLIC DISPLAYS OF AFFECTION!
AND THEY'RE DOING IT RIGHT IN **FRONT** OF ME!
HM.
WHY DON'T YOU MOVE?
I HAVE NO IDEA.
© 2008 by NEA, Inc.
4/15
Peirce

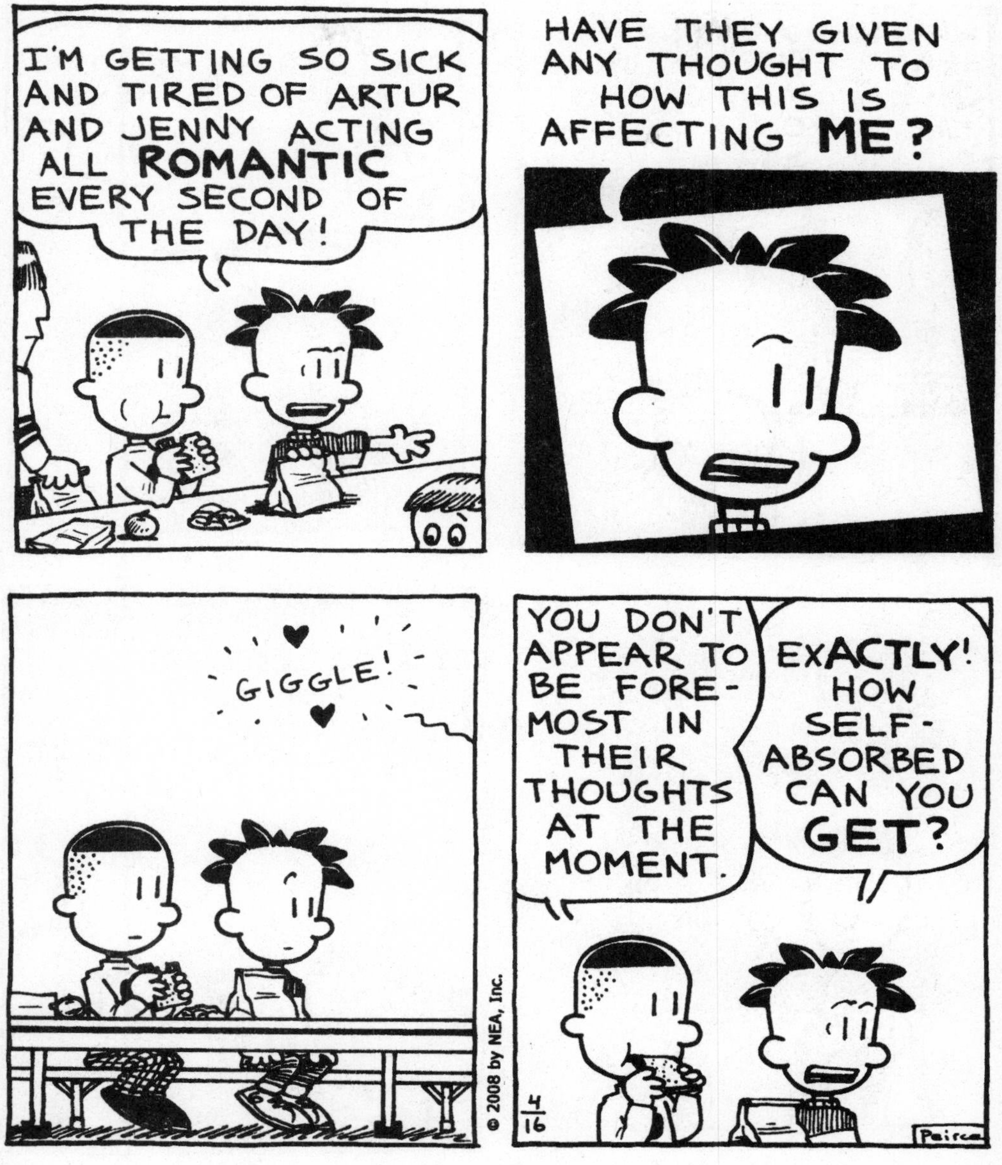
I'M GETTING SO SICK AND TIRED OF ARTUR AND JENNY ACTING ALL ROMANTIC EVERY SECOND OF THE DAY!
HAVE THEY GIVEN ANY THOUGHT TO HOW THIS IS AFFECTING ME?
GIGGLE!
YOU DON'T APPEAR TO BE FORE-MOST IN THEIR THOUGHTS AT THE MOMENT.
EXACTLY! HOW SELF-ABSORBED CAN YOU GET?
© 2008 by NEA, Inc.
4/16
Peirce

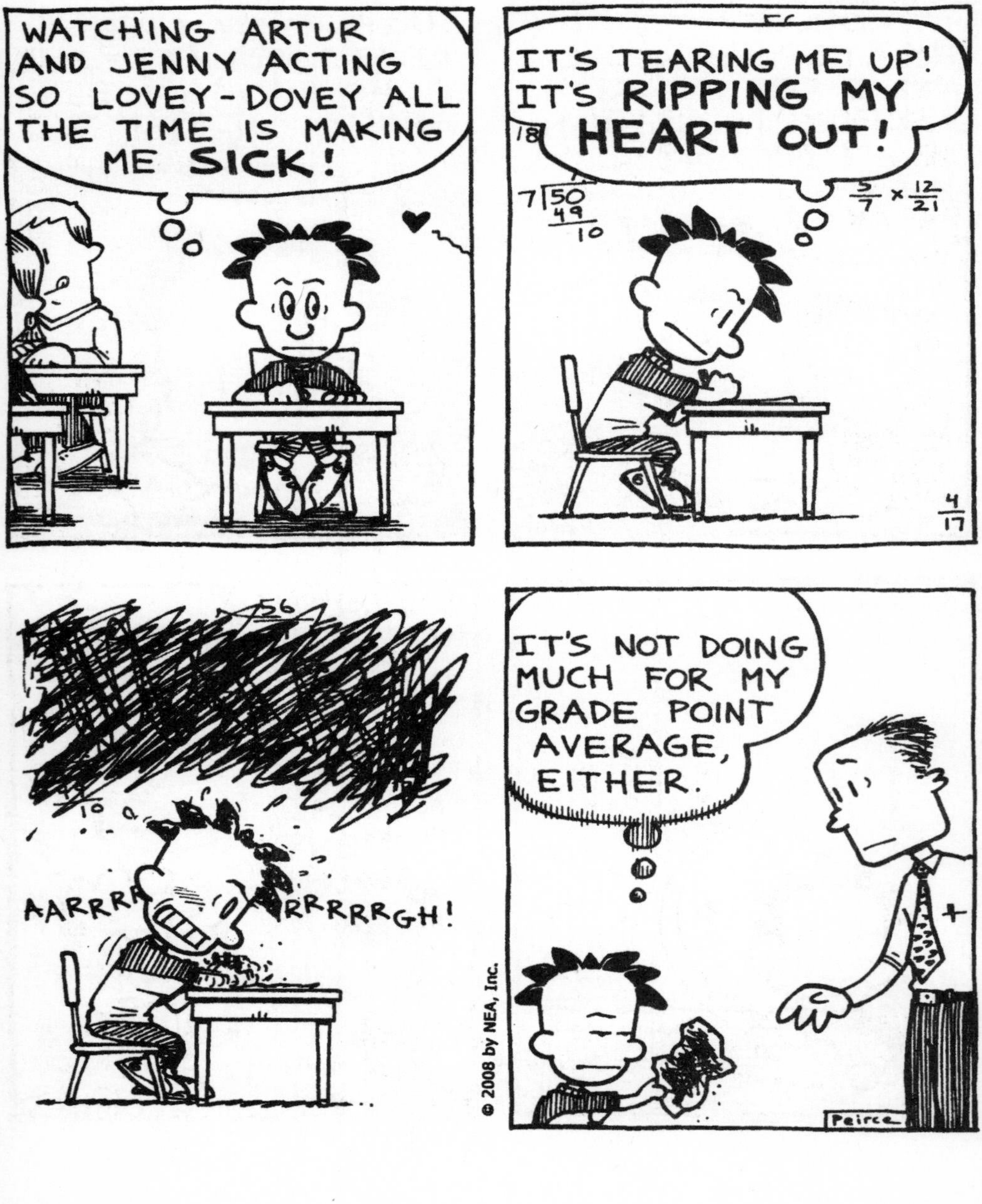
WATCHING ARTUR AND JENNY ACTING SO LOVEY-DOVEY ALL THE TIME IS MAKING ME SICK!
IT'S TEARING ME UP! IT'S RIPPING MY HEART OUT!
AARRRRRRRRRRGH!
IT'S NOT DOING MUCH FOR MY GRADE POINT AVERAGE, EITHER.
Peirce
© 2008 by NEA, Inc.

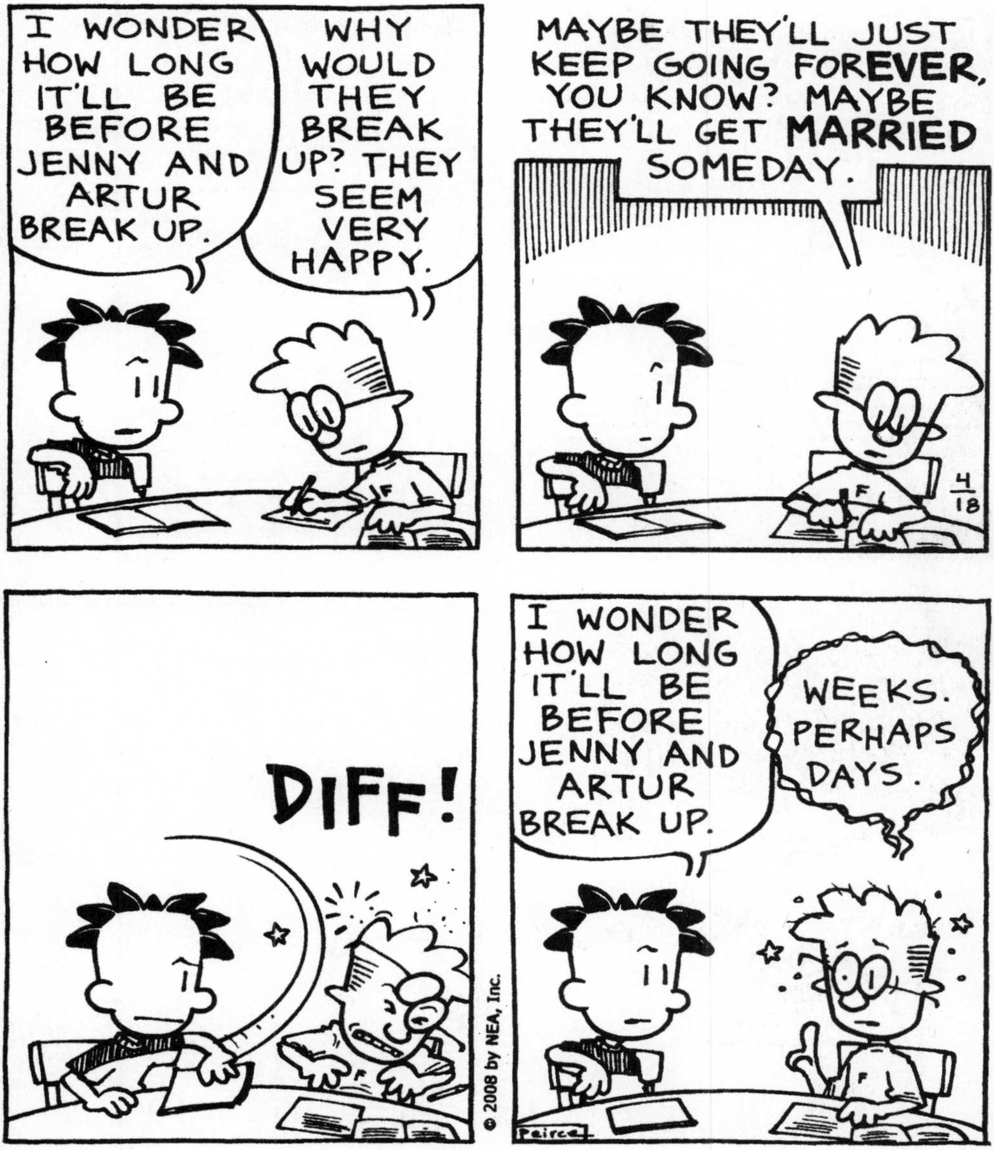
I WONDER HOW LONG IT'LL BE BEFORE JENNY AND ARTUR BREAK UP.
WHY WOULD THEY BREAK UP? THEY SEEM VERY HAPPY.
MAYBE THEY'LL JUST KEEP GOING FOR**EVER**, YOU KNOW? MAYBE THEY'LL GET **MARRIED** SOMEDAY.
4/18
DIFF!
I WONDER HOW LONG IT'LL BE BEFORE JENNY AND ARTUR BREAK UP.
WEEKS. PERHAPS DAYS.
Peirce
© 2008 by NEA, Inc.

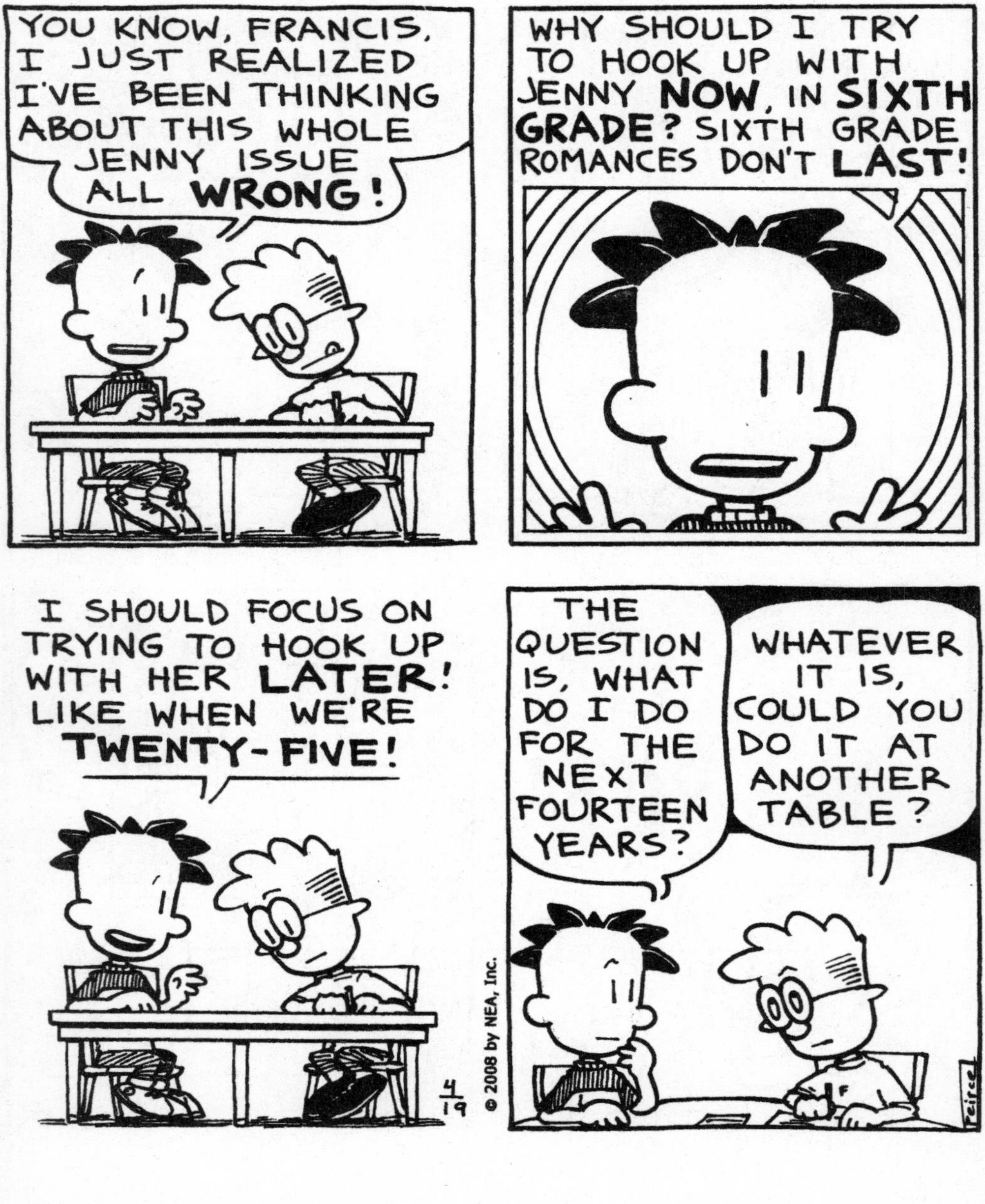
YOU KNOW, FRANCIS, I JUST REALIZED I'VE BEEN THINKING ABOUT THIS WHOLE JENNY ISSUE ALL **WRONG**!
WHY SHOULD I TRY TO HOOK UP WITH JENNY **NOW**, IN **SIXTH GRADE**? SIXTH GRADE ROMANCES DON'T **LAST**!
I SHOULD FOCUS ON TRYING TO HOOK UP WITH HER **LATER**! LIKE WHEN WE'RE **TWENTY-FIVE**!
THE QUESTION IS, WHAT DO I DO FOR THE NEXT FOURTEEN YEARS?
WHATEVER IT IS, COULD YOU DO IT AT ANOTHER TABLE?
4/19
© 2008 by NEA, Inc.
Peirce

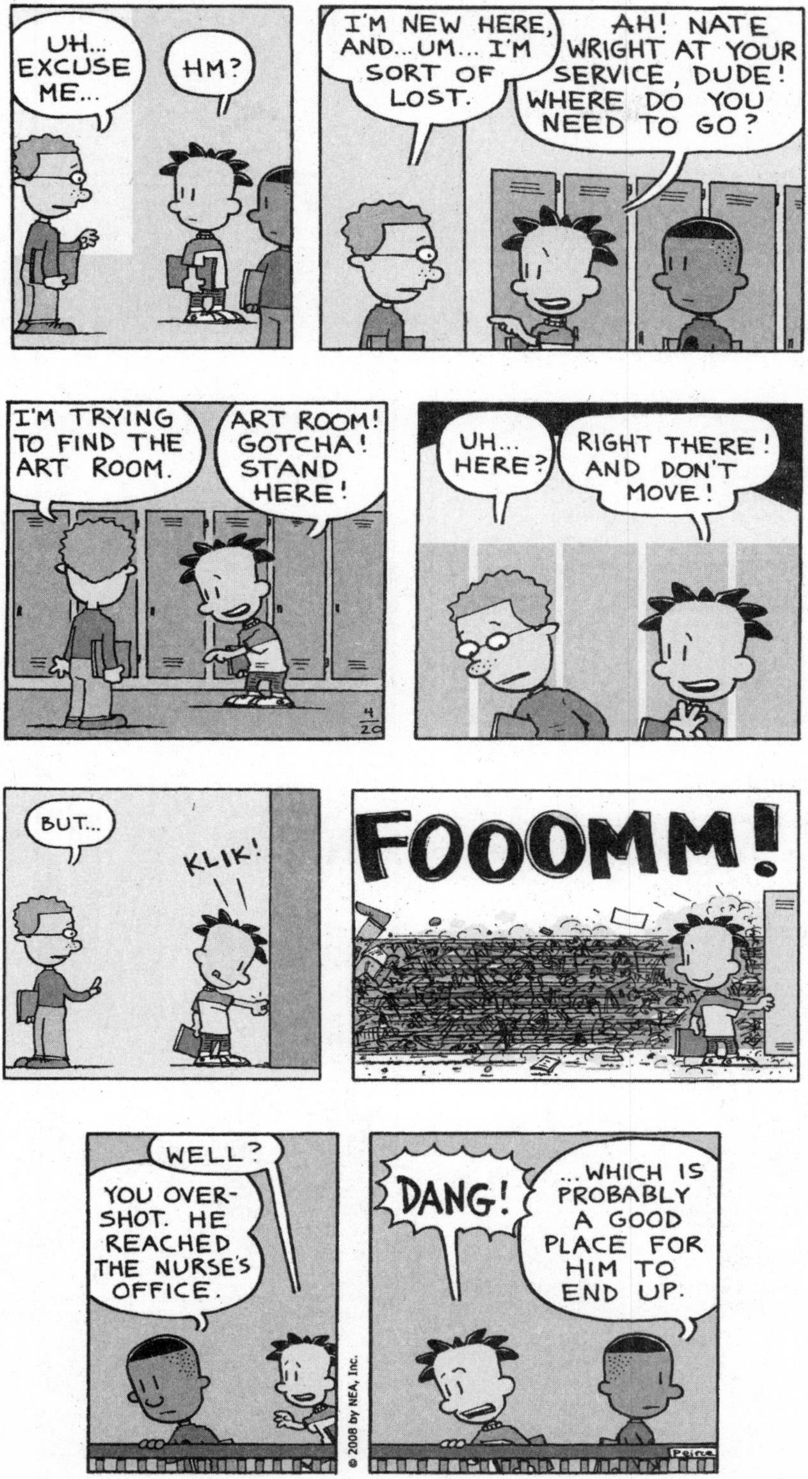
UH... EXCUSE ME...
HM?
I'M NEW HERE, AND... UM... I'M SORT OF LOST.
AH! NATE WRIGHT AT YOUR SERVICE, DUDE! WHERE DO YOU NEED TO GO?
I'M TRYING TO FIND THE ART ROOM.
ART ROOM! GOTCHA! STAND HERE!
UH... HERE?
RIGHT THERE! AND DON'T MOVE!
BUT...
KLIK!
FOOOMM!
WELL?
YOU OVER-SHOT. HE REACHED THE NURSE'S OFFICE.
DANG!
...WHICH IS PROBABLY A GOOD PLACE FOR HIM TO END UP.
© 2008 by NEA, Inc.
Peirce

SECRET FAN

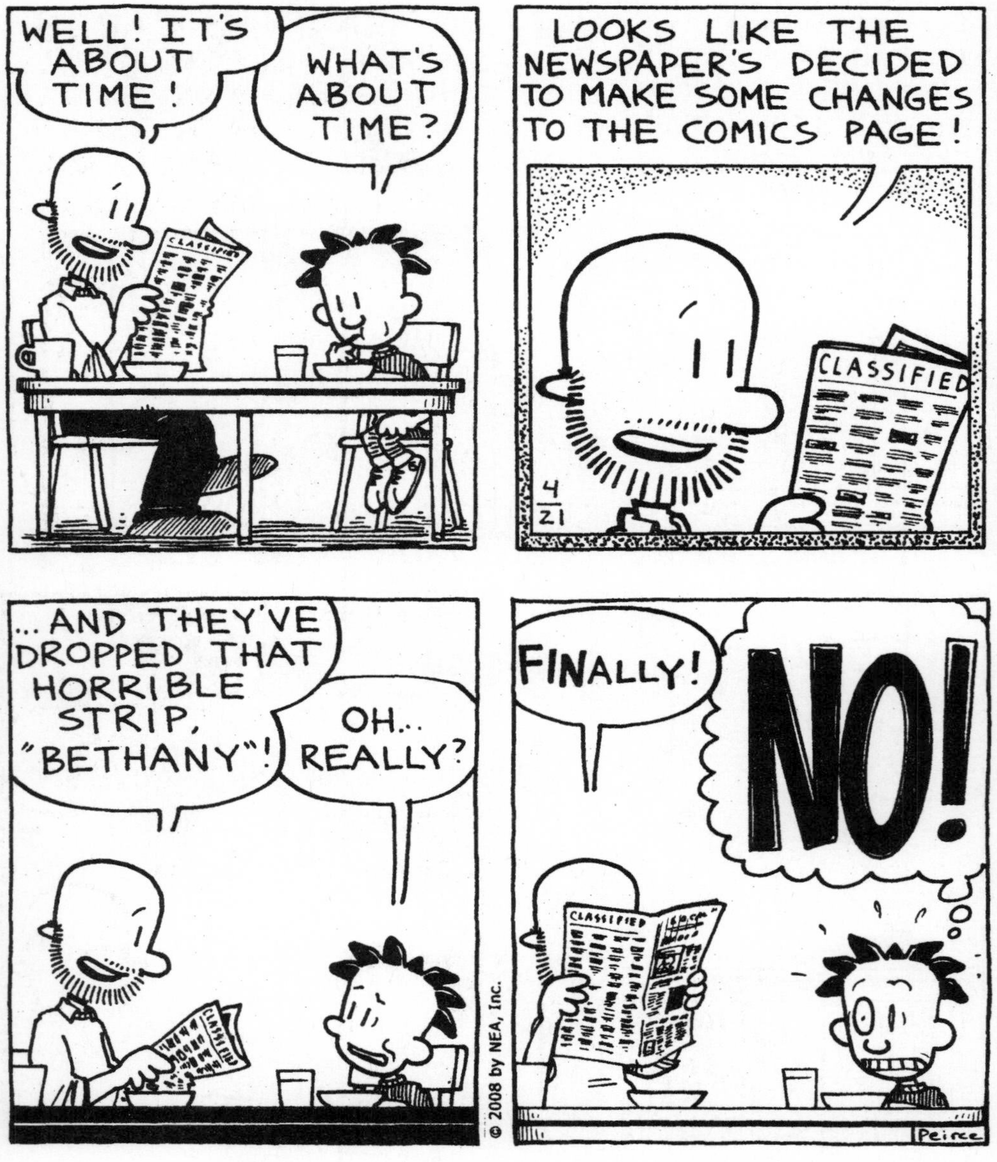

WELL! IT'S ABOUT TIME!
WHAT'S ABOUT TIME?
CLASSIFIED
LOOKS LIKE THE NEWSPAPER'S DECIDED TO MAKE SOME CHANGES TO THE COMICS PAGE!
CLASSIFIED
4/21
...AND THEY'VE DROPPED THAT HORRIBLE STRIP, "BETHANY"!
OH... REALLY?
© 2008 by NEA, Inc.
FINALLY!
NO!
CLASSIFIED
Peirce

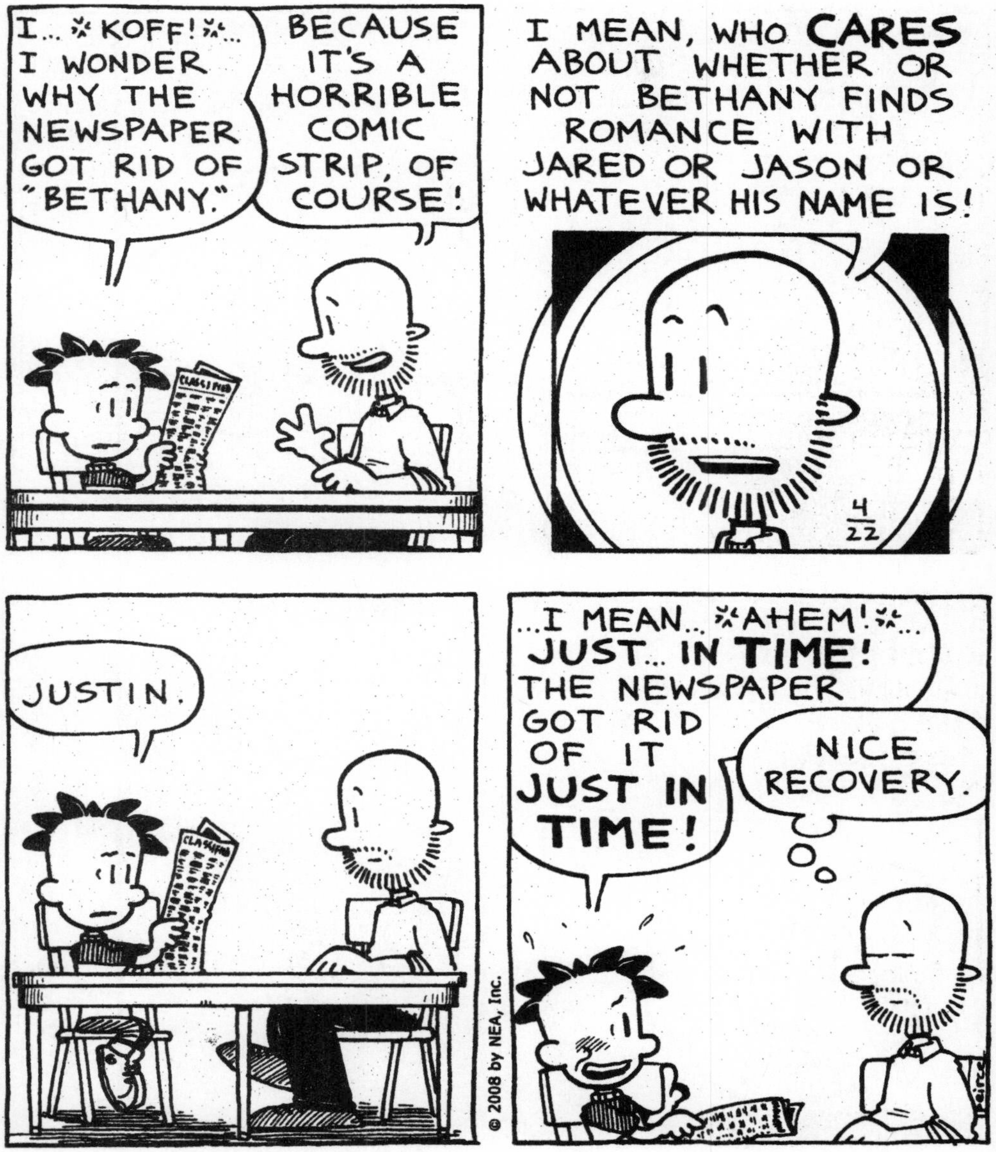
I... *KOFF!*... I WONDER WHY THE NEWSPAPER GOT RID OF "BETHANY."
BECAUSE IT'S A HORRIBLE COMIC STRIP, OF COURSE!
I MEAN, WHO CARES ABOUT WHETHER OR NOT BETHANY FINDS ROMANCE WITH JARED OR JASON OR WHATEVER HIS NAME IS!
4/22
JUSTIN.
...I MEAN... *AHEM!*... JUST... IN TIME! THE NEWSPAPER GOT RID OF IT JUST IN TIME!
NICE RECOVERY.
© 2008 by NEA, Inc.

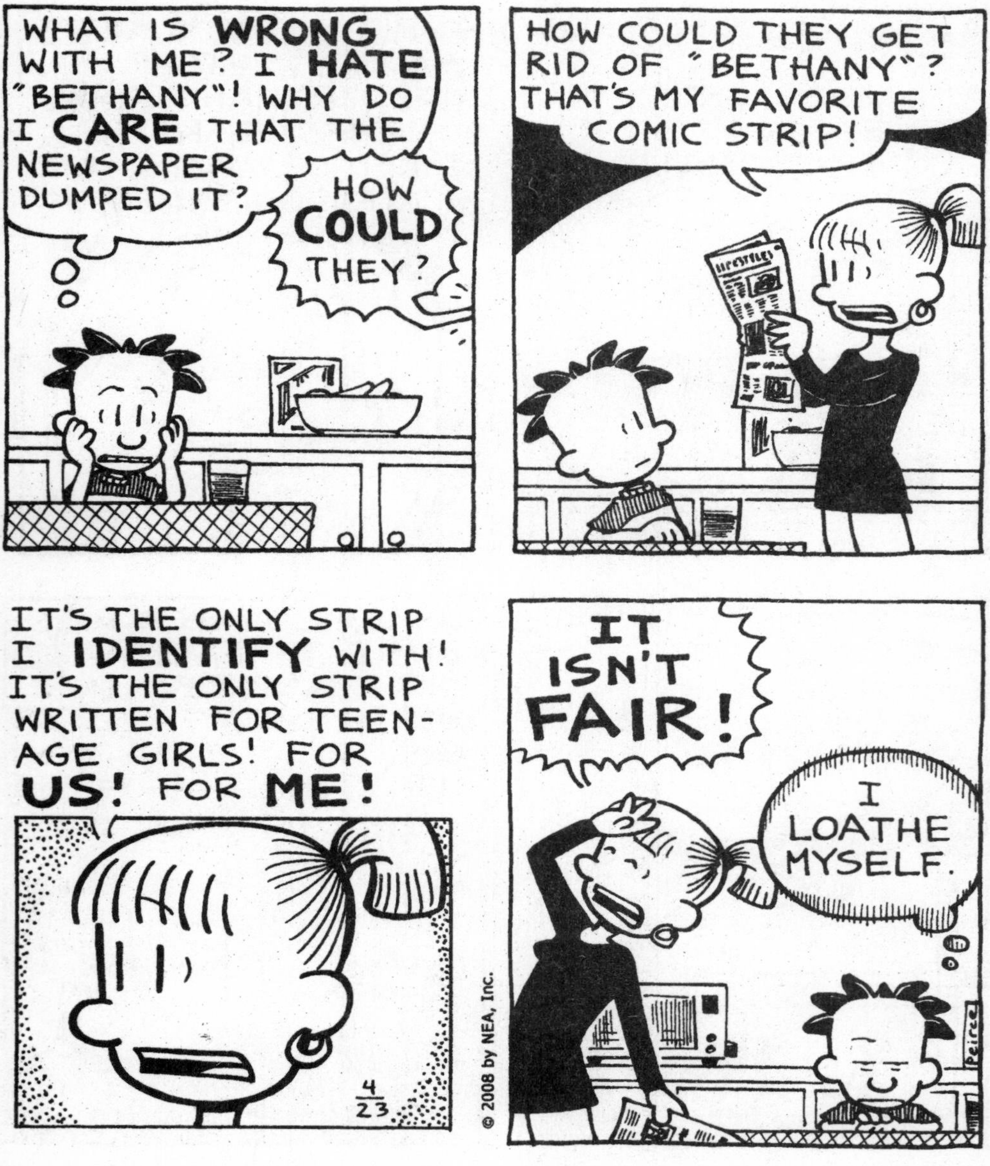
WHAT IS WRONG WITH ME? I HATE "BETHANY"! WHY DO I CARE THAT THE NEWSPAPER DUMPED IT?
HOW COULD THEY?
HOW COULD THEY GET RID OF "BETHANY"? THAT'S MY FAVORITE COMIC STRIP!
IT'S THE ONLY STRIP I IDENTIFY WITH! IT'S THE ONLY STRIP WRITTEN FOR TEEN-AGE GIRLS! FOR US! FOR ME!
4/23
IT ISN'T FAIR!
I LOATHE MYSELF.
Peirce

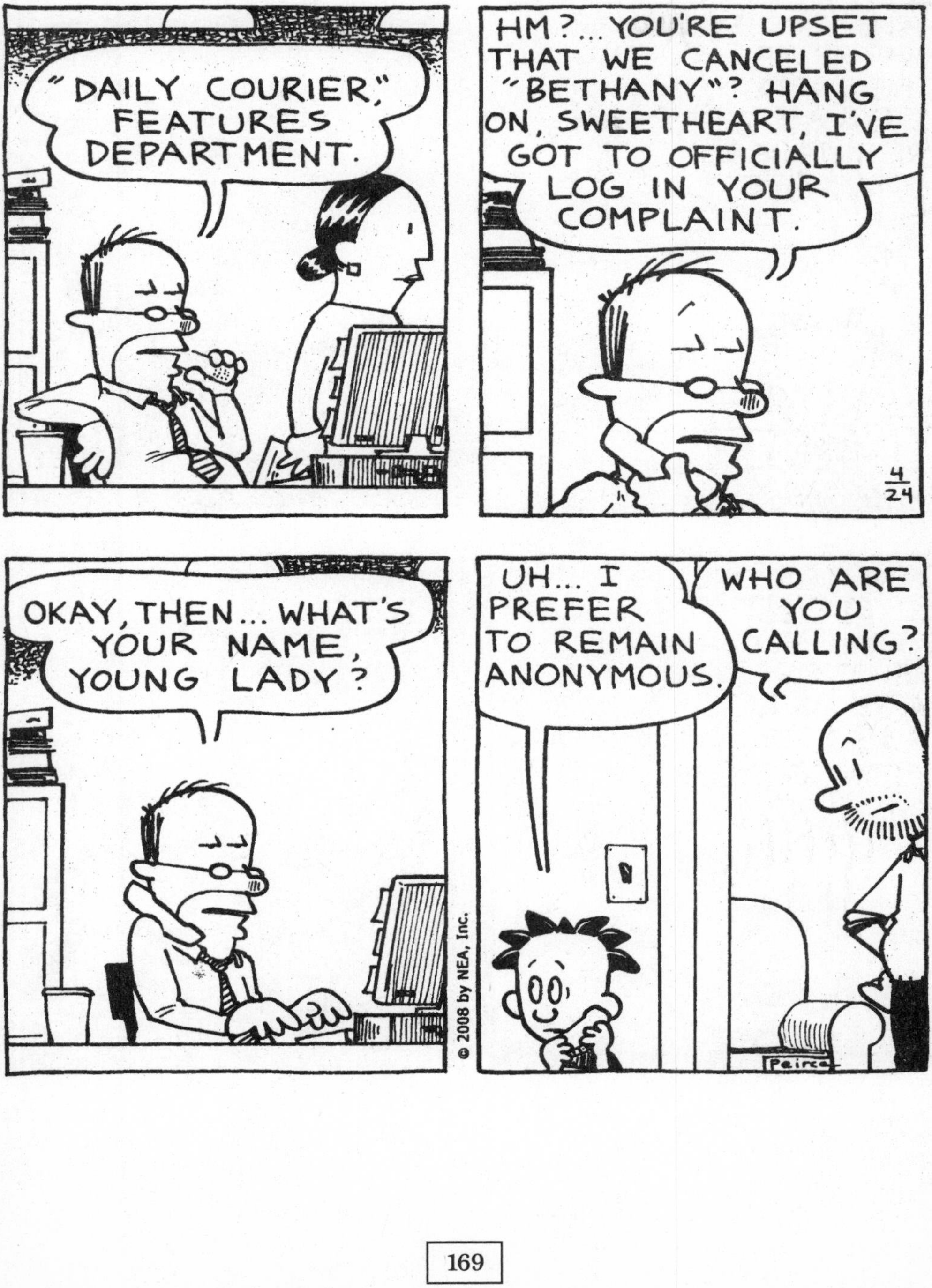
"DAILY COURIER," FEATURES DEPARTMENT.
HM?... YOU'RE UPSET THAT WE CANCELED "BETHANY"? HANG ON, SWEETHEART, I'VE GOT TO OFFICIALLY LOG IN YOUR COMPLAINT.
4/24
OKAY, THEN... WHAT'S YOUR NAME, YOUNG LADY?
UH... I PREFER TO REMAIN ANONYMOUS.
WHO ARE YOU CALLING?
Peirce

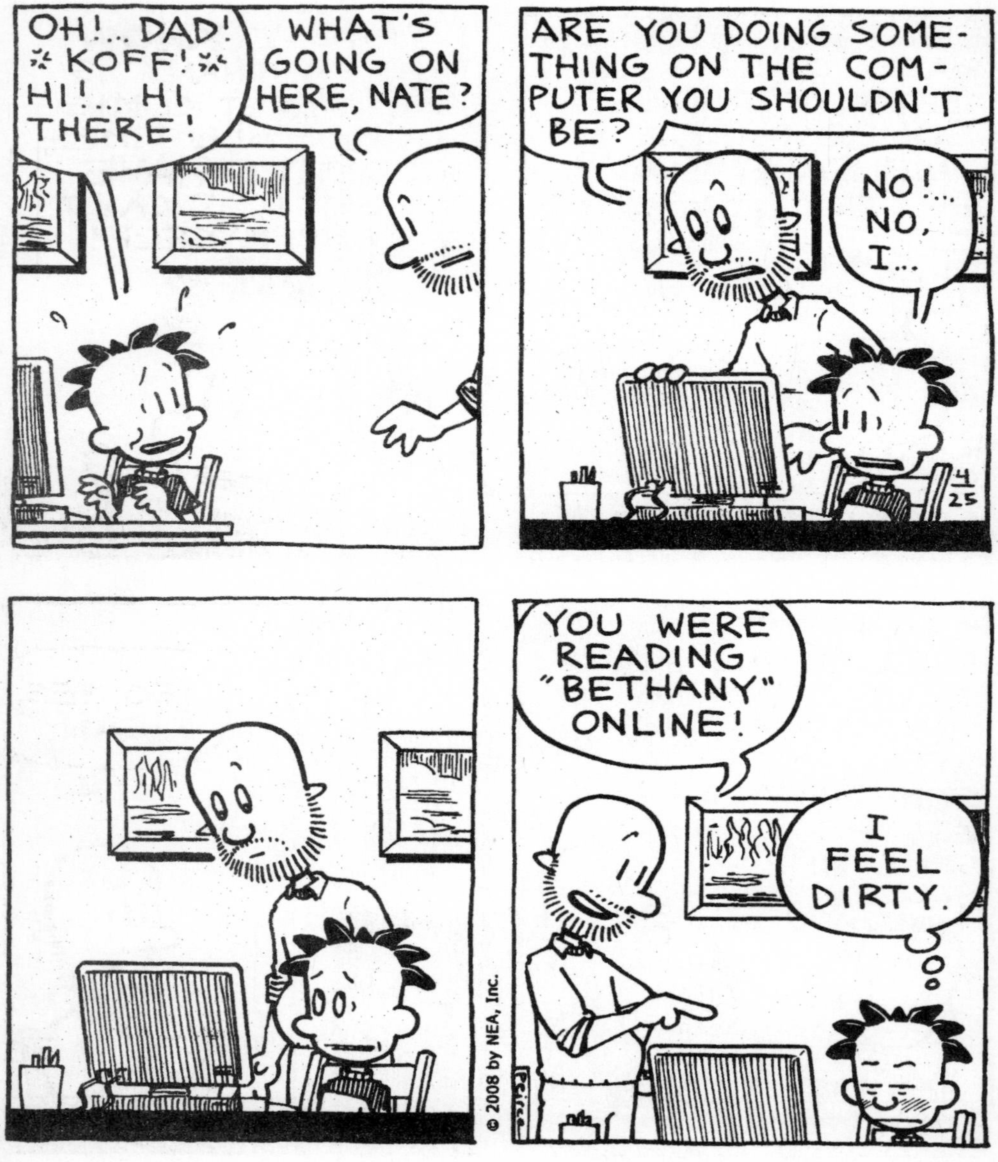
OH!... DAD! *KOFF!* HI!... HI THERE!
WHAT'S GOING ON HERE, NATE?
ARE YOU DOING SOMETHING ON THE COMPUTER YOU SHOULDN'T BE?
NO!... NO, I...
4/25
YOU WERE READING "BETHANY" ONLINE!
I FEEL DIRTY.
PEIRCE

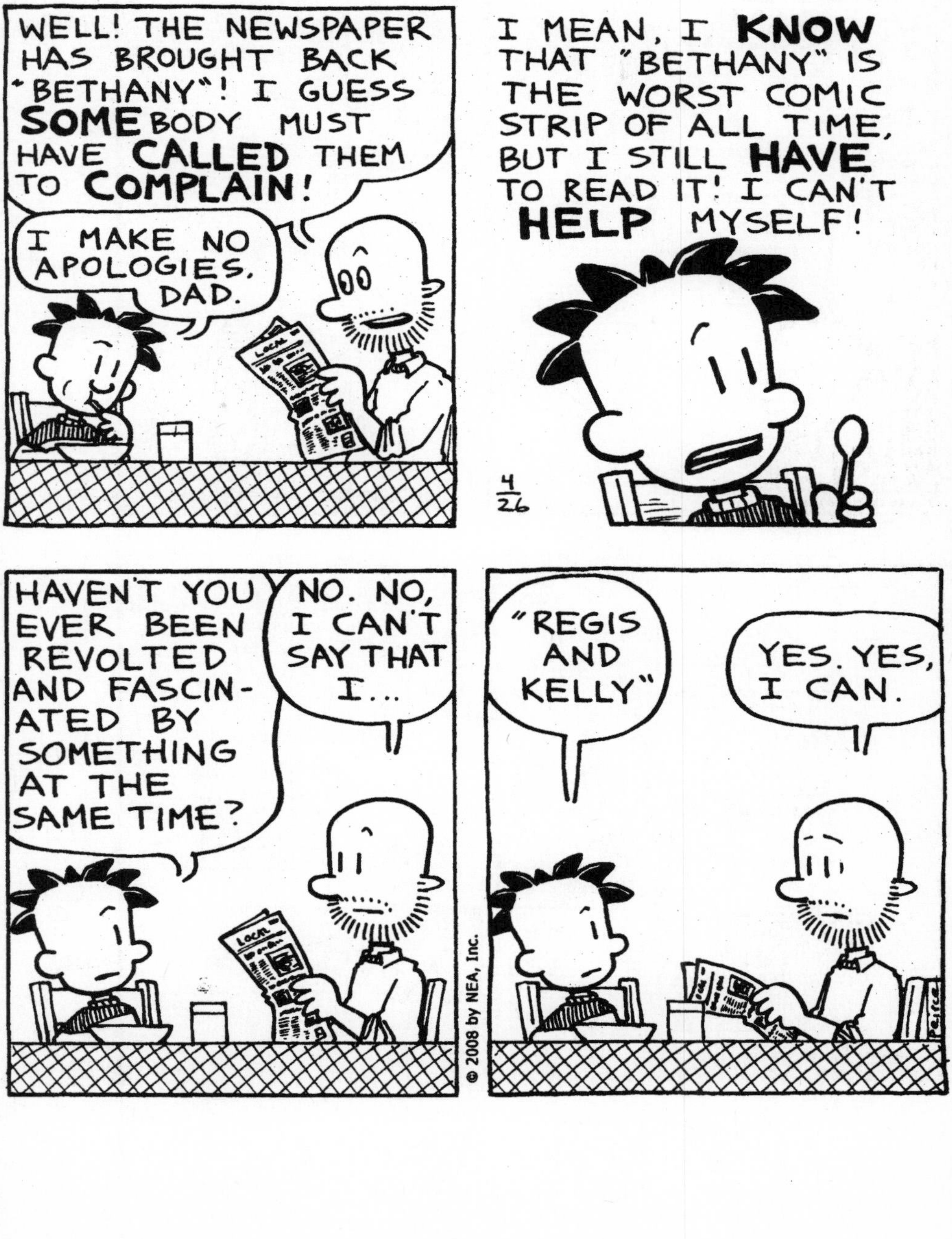
WELL! THE NEWSPAPER HAS BROUGHT BACK "BETHANY"! I GUESS SOMEBODY MUST HAVE CALLED THEM TO COMPLAIN!
I MAKE NO APOLOGIES, DAD.
LOCAL
I MEAN, I KNOW THAT "BETHANY" IS THE WORST COMIC STRIP OF ALL TIME, BUT I STILL HAVE TO READ IT! I CAN'T HELP MYSELF!
4/26
HAVEN'T YOU EVER BEEN REVOLTED AND FASCIN-ATED BY SOMETHING AT THE SAME TIME?
NO. NO, I CAN'T SAY THAT I...
LOCAL
"REGIS AND KELLY"
YES. YES, I CAN.
PEIRCE
© 2008 by NEA, Inc.

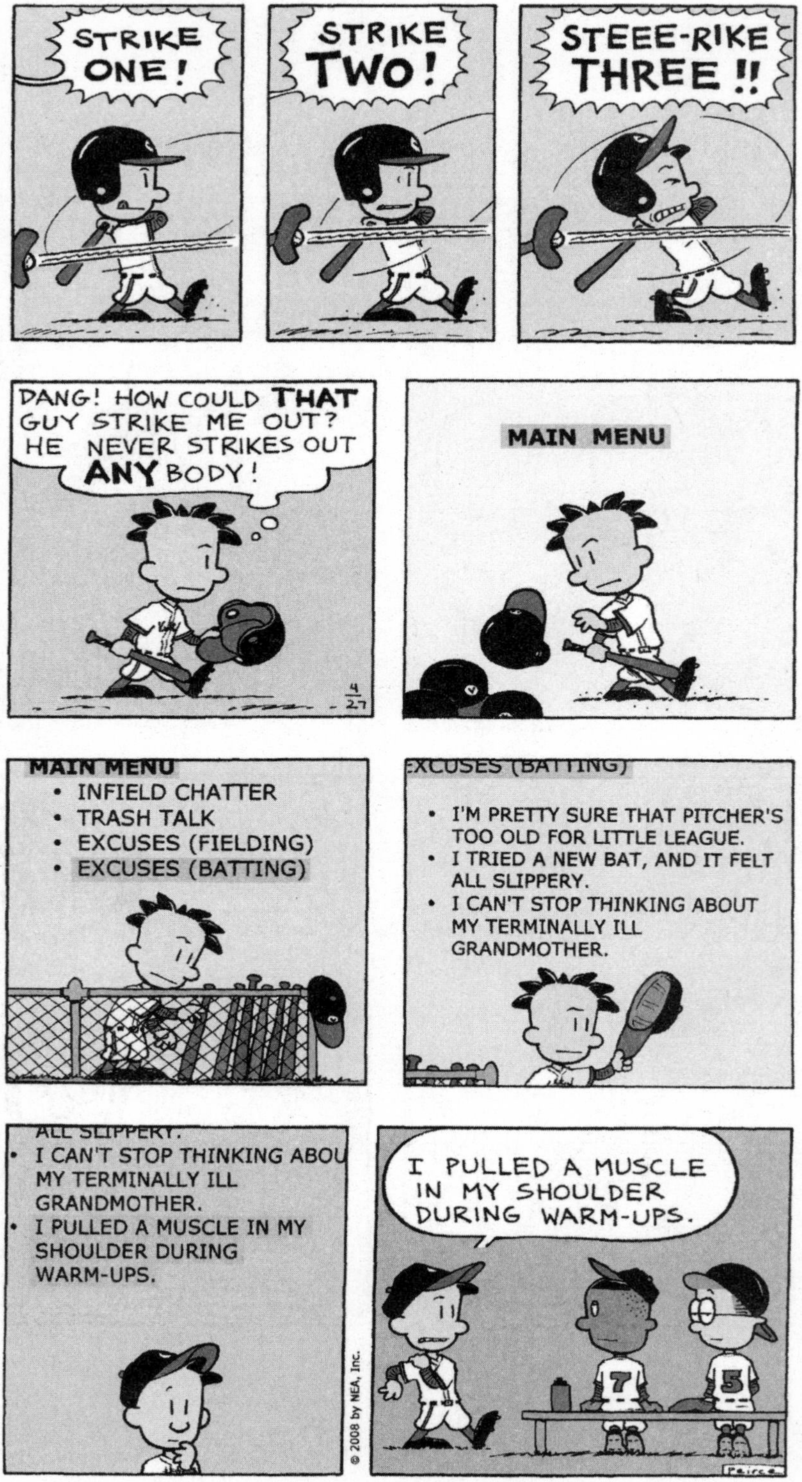
STRIKE ONE!
STRIKE TWO!
STEEE-RIKE THREE !!
DANG! HOW COULD THAT GUY STRIKE ME OUT? HE NEVER STRIKES OUT ANYBODY!
4 27
MAIN MENU
MAIN MENU
• INFIELD CHATTER
• TRASH TALK
• EXCUSES (FIELDING)
• EXCUSES (BATTING)
EXCUSES (BATTING)
• I'M PRETTY SURE THAT PITCHER'S TOO OLD FOR LITTLE LEAGUE.
• I TRIED A NEW BAT, AND IT FELT ALL SLIPPERY.
• I CAN'T STOP THINKING ABOUT MY TERMINALLY ILL GRANDMOTHER.
ALL SLIPPERY.
• I CAN'T STOP THINKING ABOU
MY TERMINALLY ILL GRANDMOTHER.
• I PULLED A MUSCLE IN MY SHOULDER DURING WARM-UPS.
© 2008 by NEA, Inc.
I PULLED A MUSCLE IN MY SHOULDER DURING WARM-UPS.
7
5
PEIRCE

BATTER UP!

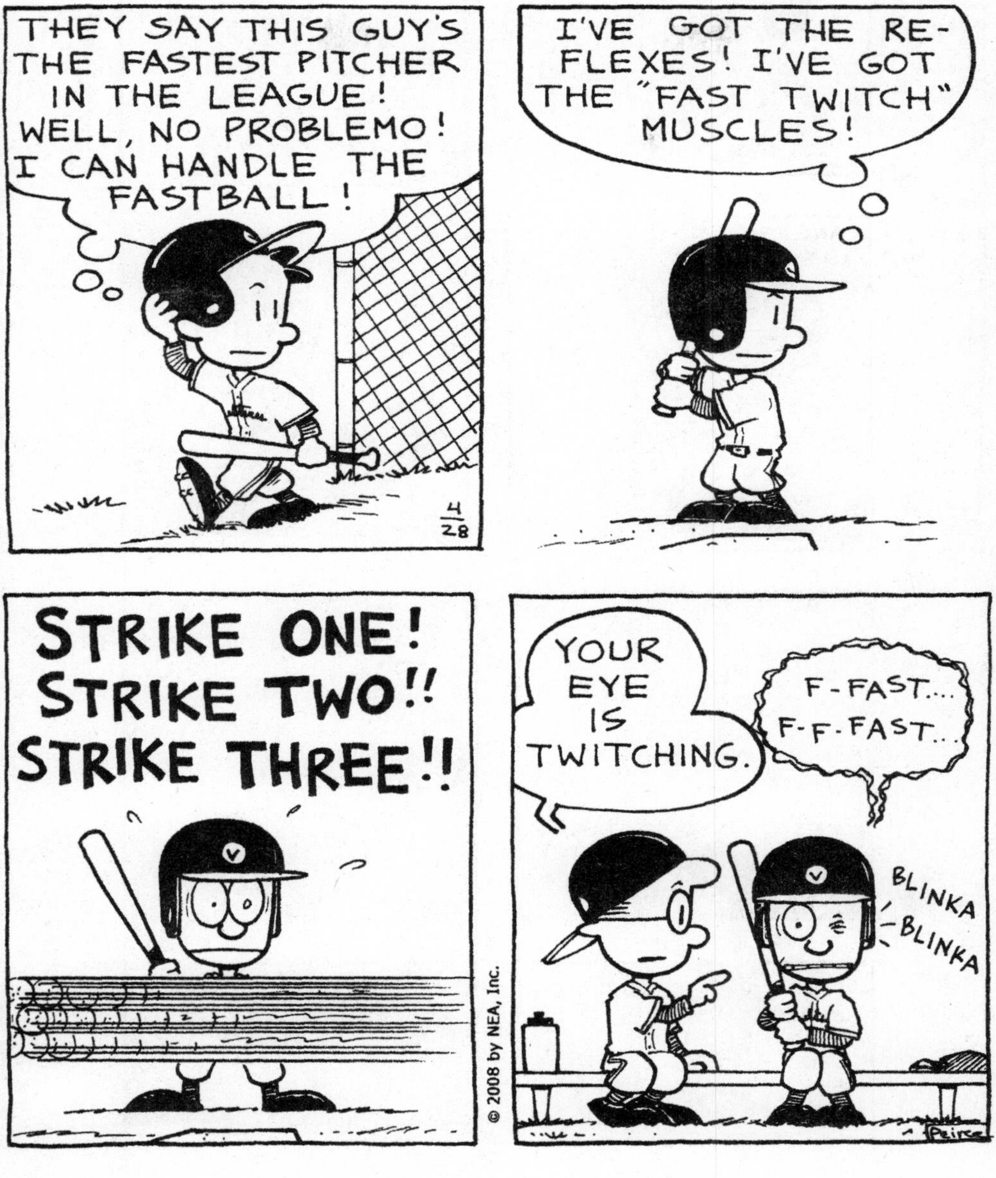
THEY SAY THIS GUY'S THE FASTEST PITCHER IN THE LEAGUE! WELL, NO PROBLEMO! I CAN HANDLE THE FASTBALL!
4/28
I'VE GOT THE RE-FLEXES! I'VE GOT THE "FAST TWITCH" MUSCLES!
STRIKE ONE! STRIKE TWO!! STRIKE THREE!!
© 2008 by NEA, Inc.
YOUR EYE IS TWITCHING.
F-FAST... F-F-FAST...
BLINKA
BLINKA
Peirce

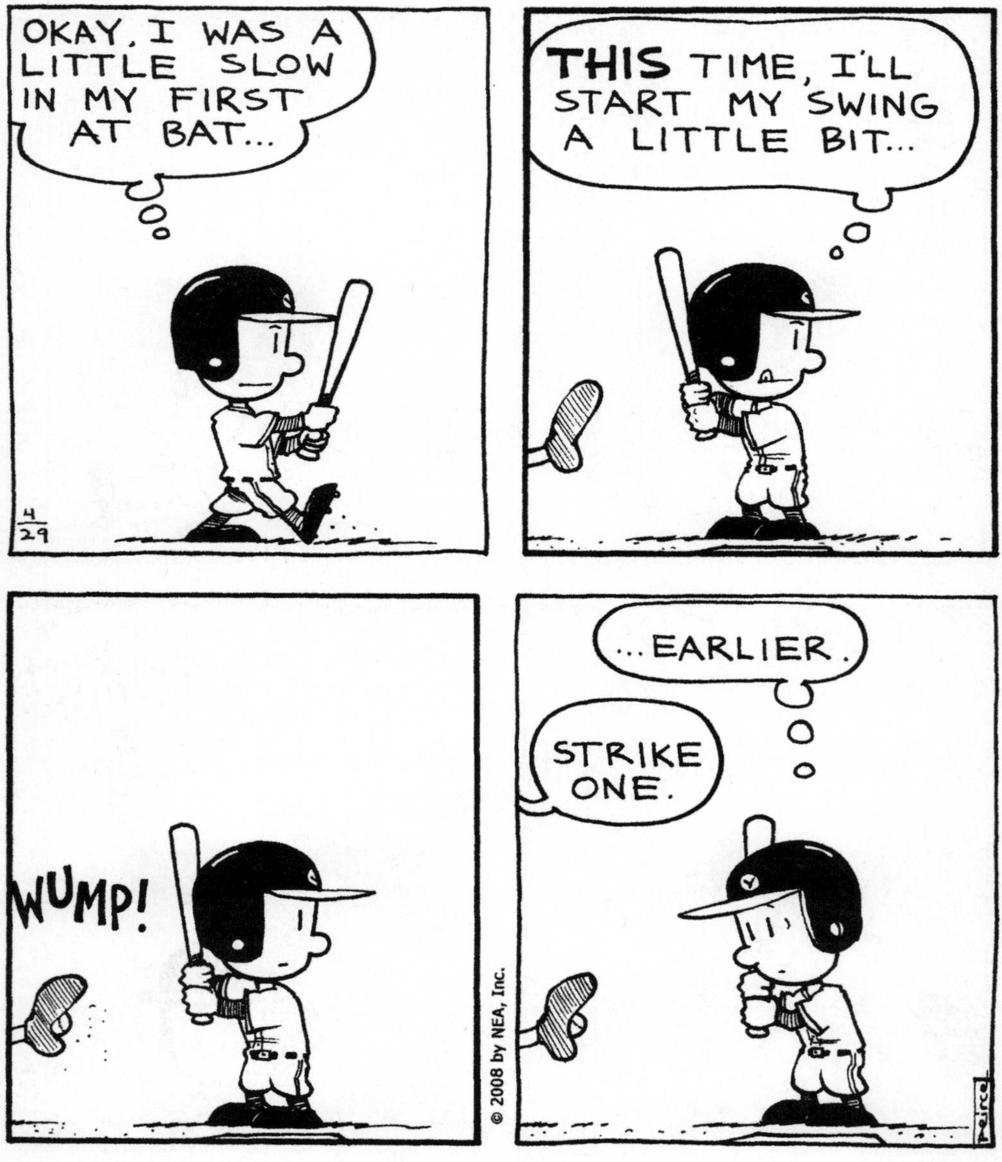
OKAY, I WAS A LITTLE SLOW IN MY FIRST AT BAT...
THIS TIME, I'LL START MY SWING A LITTLE BIT...
WUMP!
...EARLIER.
STRIKE ONE.

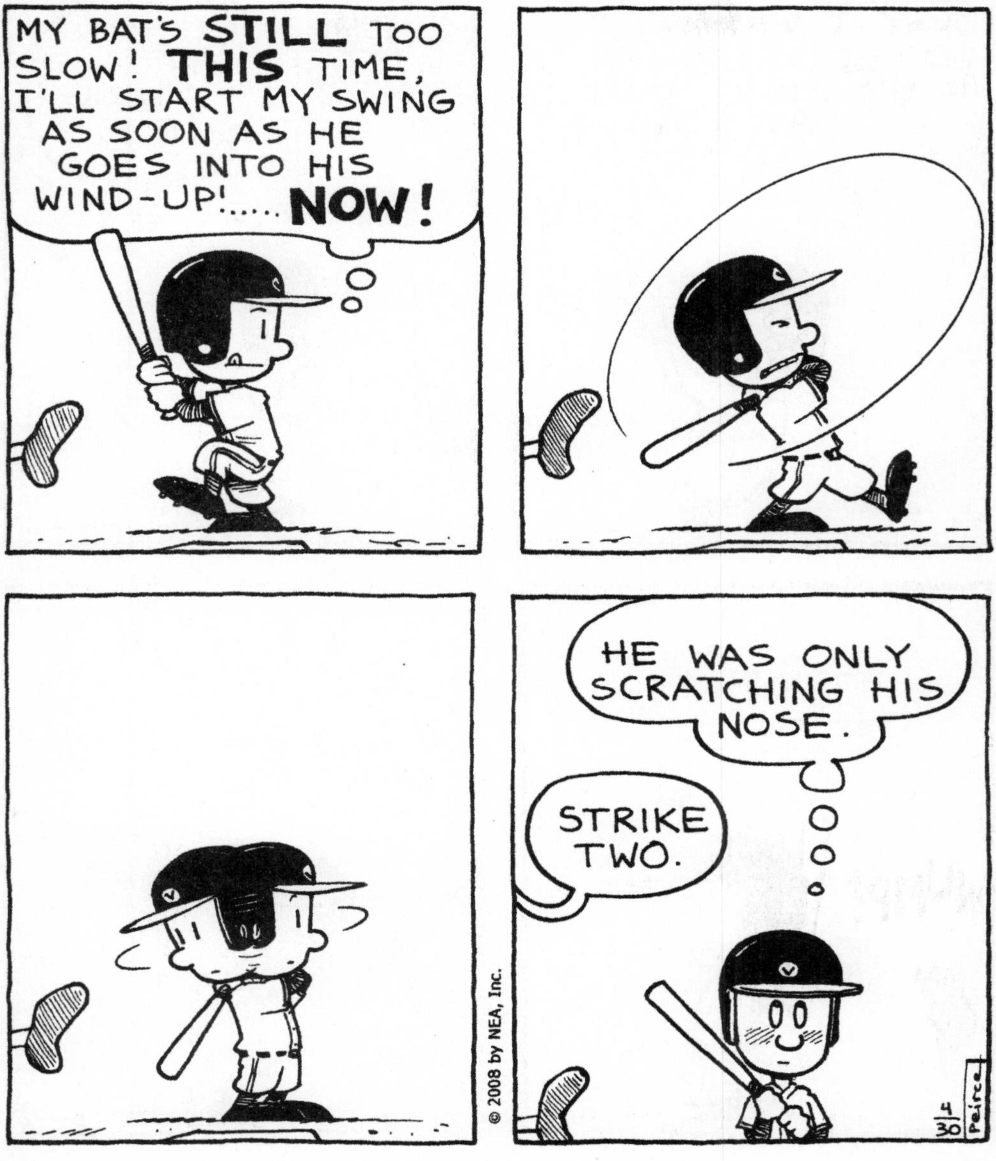
MY BAT'S STILL TOO SLOW! THIS TIME, I'LL START MY SWING AS SOON AS HE GOES INTO HIS WIND-UP!..... NOW!
HE WAS ONLY SCRATCHING HIS NOSE.
STRIKE TWO.
© 2008 by NEA, Inc.
3/4 30 Peirce

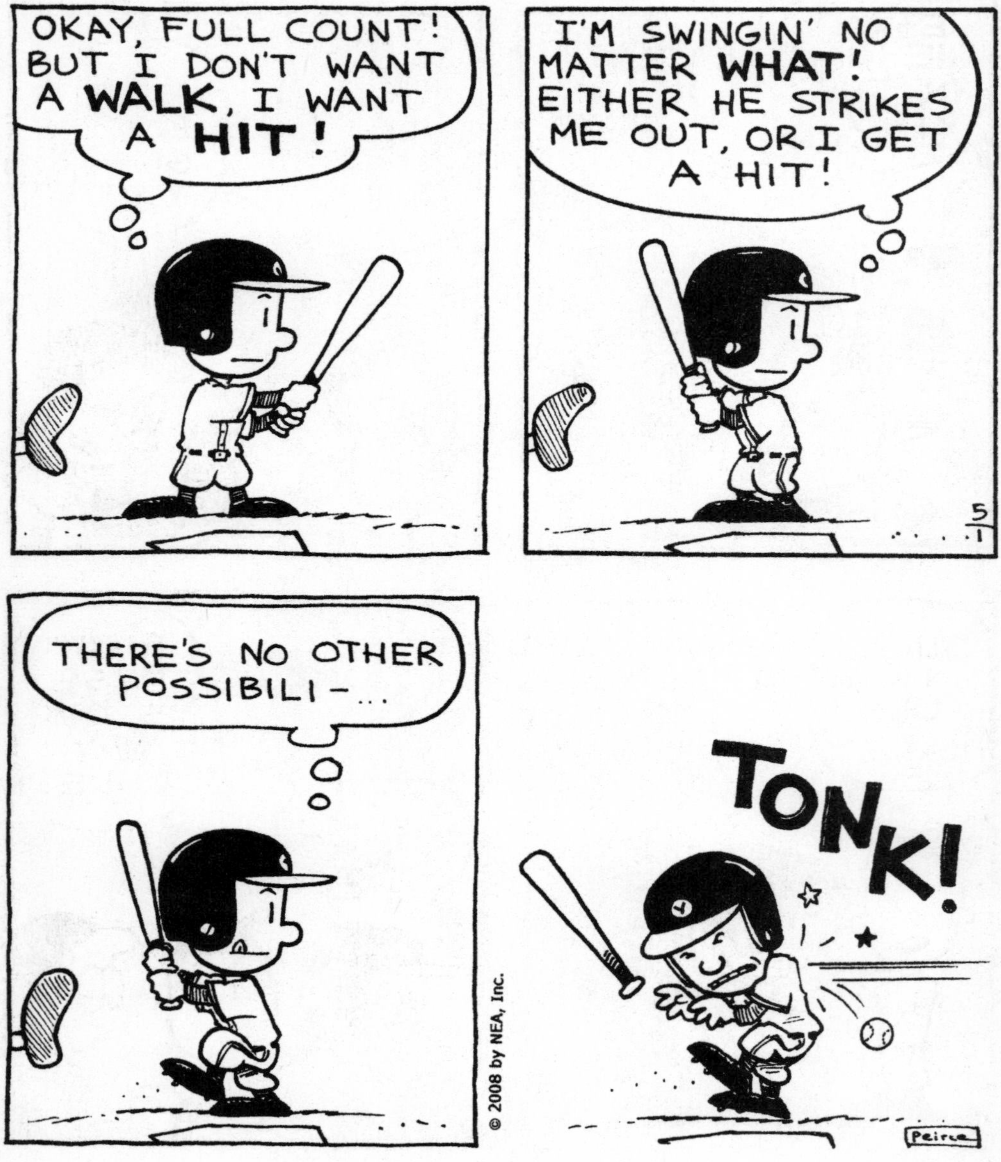
OKAY, FULL COUNT! BUT I DON'T WANT A **WALK**, I WANT A **HIT**!
I'M SWINGIN' NO MATTER **WHAT**! EITHER HE STRIKES ME OUT, OR I GET A HIT!
5/1
THERE'S NO OTHER POSSIBILI-...
TONK!
Peirce

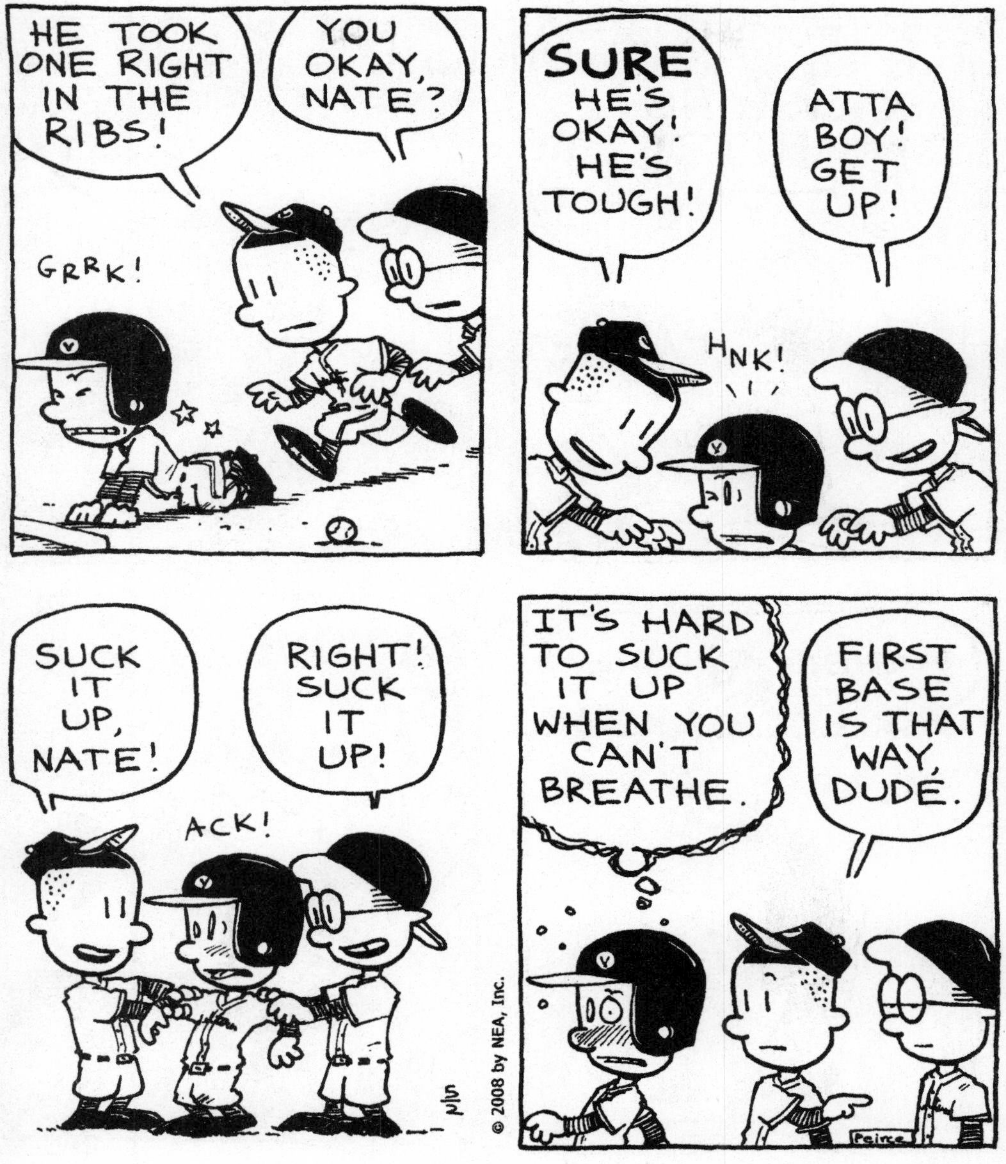
HE TOOK ONE RIGHT IN THE RIBS!
YOU OKAY, NATE?
GRRK!
SURE HE'S OKAY! HE'S TOUGH!
ATTA BOY! GET UP!
HNK!
SUCK IT UP, NATE!
RIGHT! SUCK IT UP!
ACK!
IT'S HARD TO SUCK IT UP WHEN YOU CAN'T BREATHE.
FIRST BASE IS THAT WAY, DUDE.
Peirce

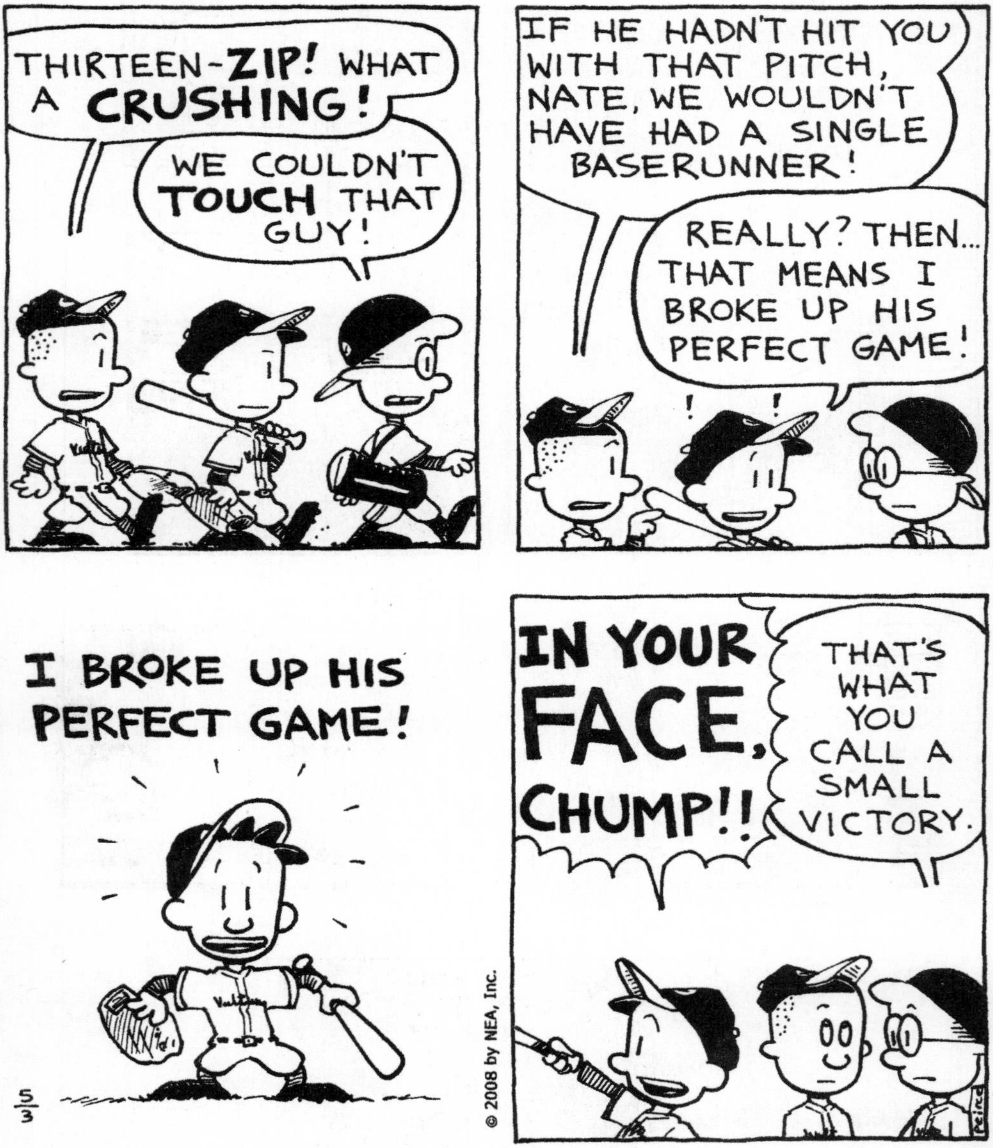
THIRTEEN-ZIP! WHAT A CRUSHING!
WE COULDN'T TOUCH THAT GUY!
IF HE HADN'T HIT YOU WITH THAT PITCH, NATE, WE WOULDN'T HAVE HAD A SINGLE BASERUNNER!
REALLY? THEN... THAT MEANS I BROKE UP HIS PERFECT GAME!
I BROKE UP HIS PERFECT GAME!
IN YOUR FACE, CHUMP!!
THAT'S WHAT YOU CALL A SMALL VICTORY.

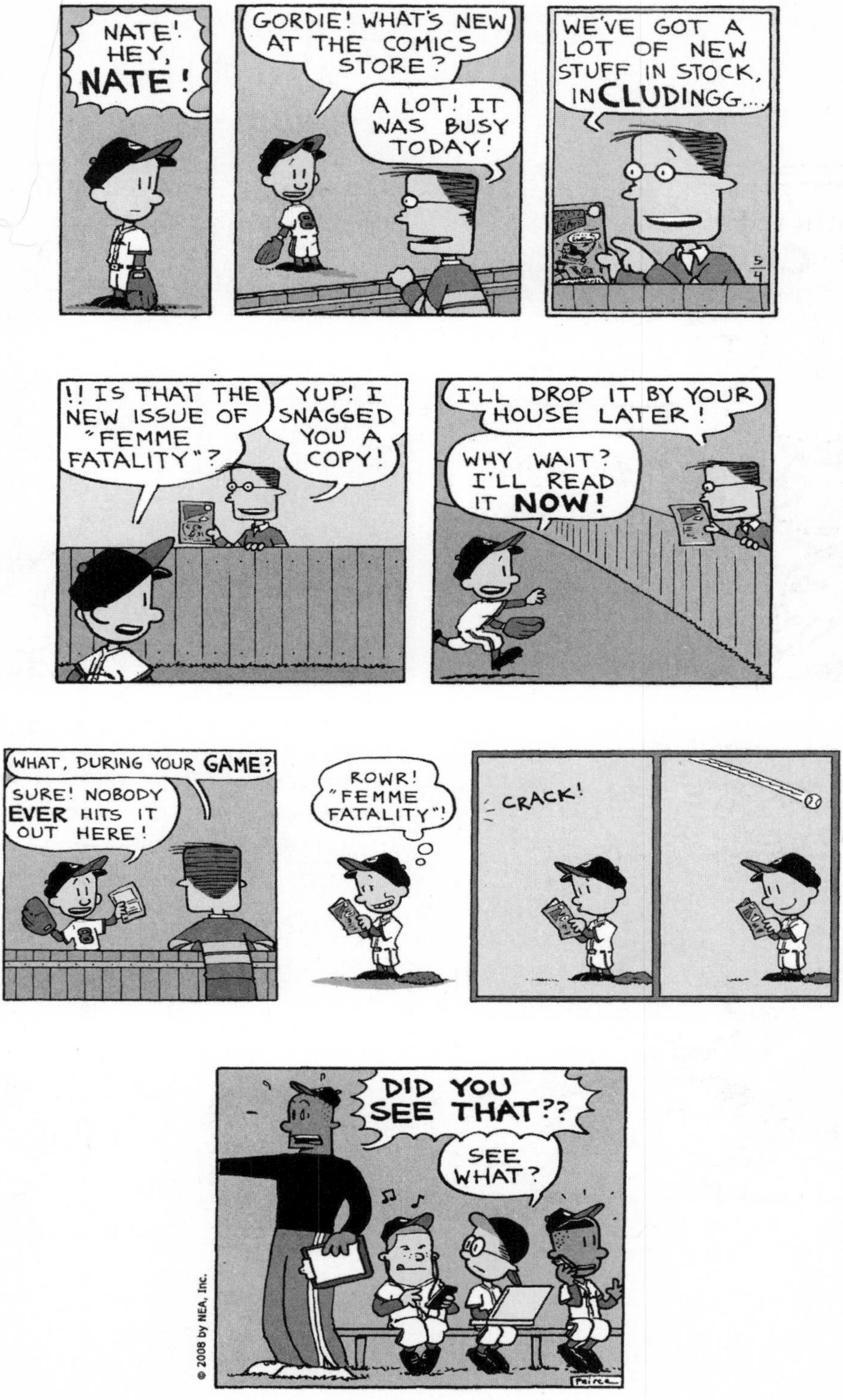
NATE! HEY, NATE!
GORDIE! WHAT'S NEW AT THE COMICS STORE?
A LOT! IT WAS BUSY TODAY!
WE'VE GOT A LOT OF NEW STUFF IN STOCK, INCLUDINGG....
5/4
!! IS THAT THE NEW ISSUE OF "FEMME FATALITY"?
YUP! I SNAGGED YOU A COPY!
I'LL DROP IT BY YOUR HOUSE LATER!
WHY WAIT? I'LL READ IT NOW!
WHAT, DURING YOUR GAME?
SURE! NOBODY EVER HITS IT OUT HERE!
ROWR! "FEMME FATALITY"!
CRACK!
DID YOU SEE THAT??
SEE WHAT?
© 2008 by NEA, Inc.
PEIRCE

WHAT COULD POSSIBLY GO WRONG?

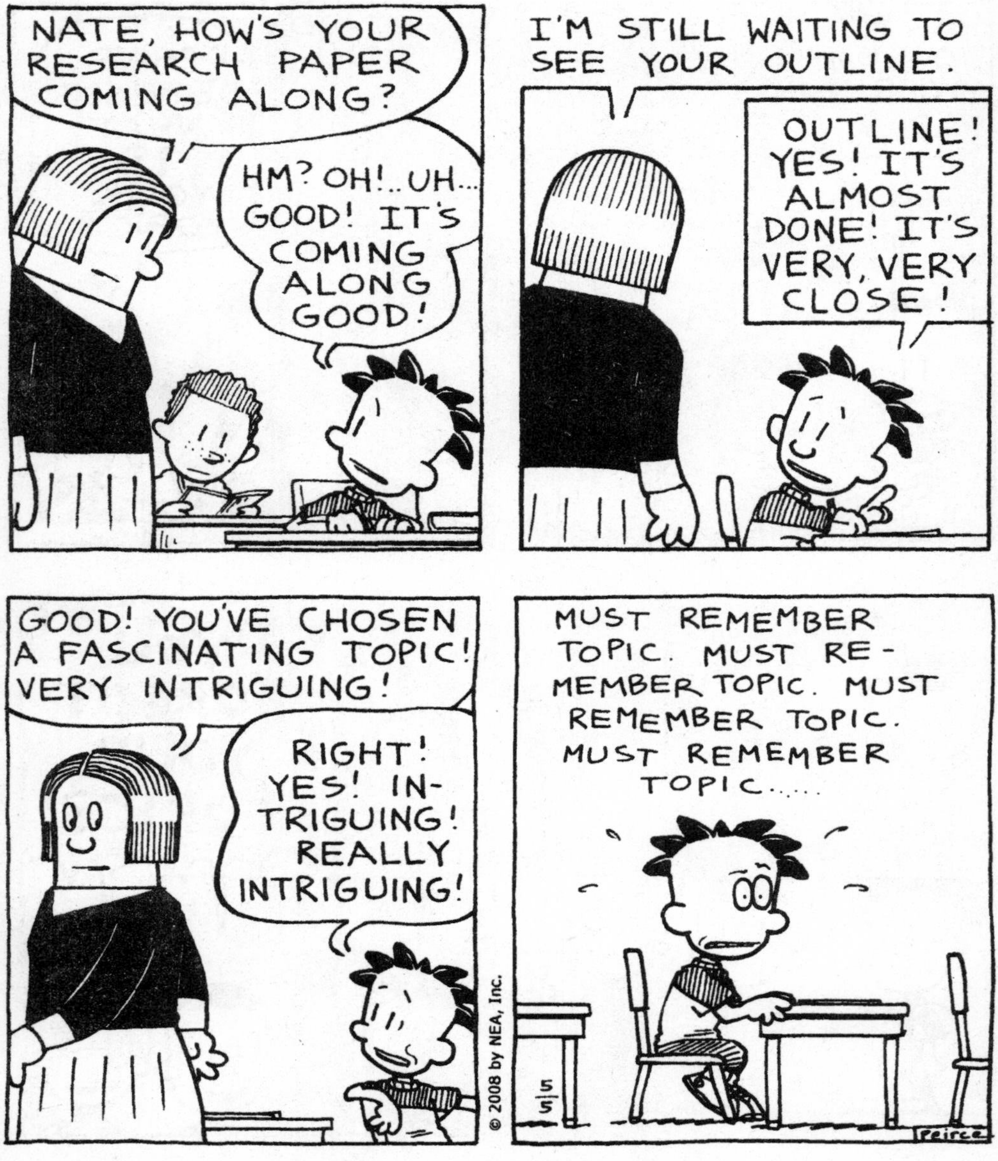
NATE, HOW'S YOUR RESEARCH PAPER COMING ALONG?
HM? OH!..UH... GOOD! IT'S COMING ALONG GOOD!
I'M STILL WAITING TO SEE YOUR OUTLINE.
OUTLINE! YES! IT'S ALMOST DONE! IT'S VERY, VERY CLOSE!
GOOD! YOU'VE CHOSEN A FASCINATING TOPIC! VERY INTRIGUING!
RIGHT! YES! IN-TRIGUING! REALLY INTRIGUING!
© 2008 by NEA, Inc.
MUST REMEMBER TOPIC. MUST RE-MEMBER TOPIC. MUST REMEMBER TOPIC. MUST REMEMBER TOPIC.....
5/5
Peirce

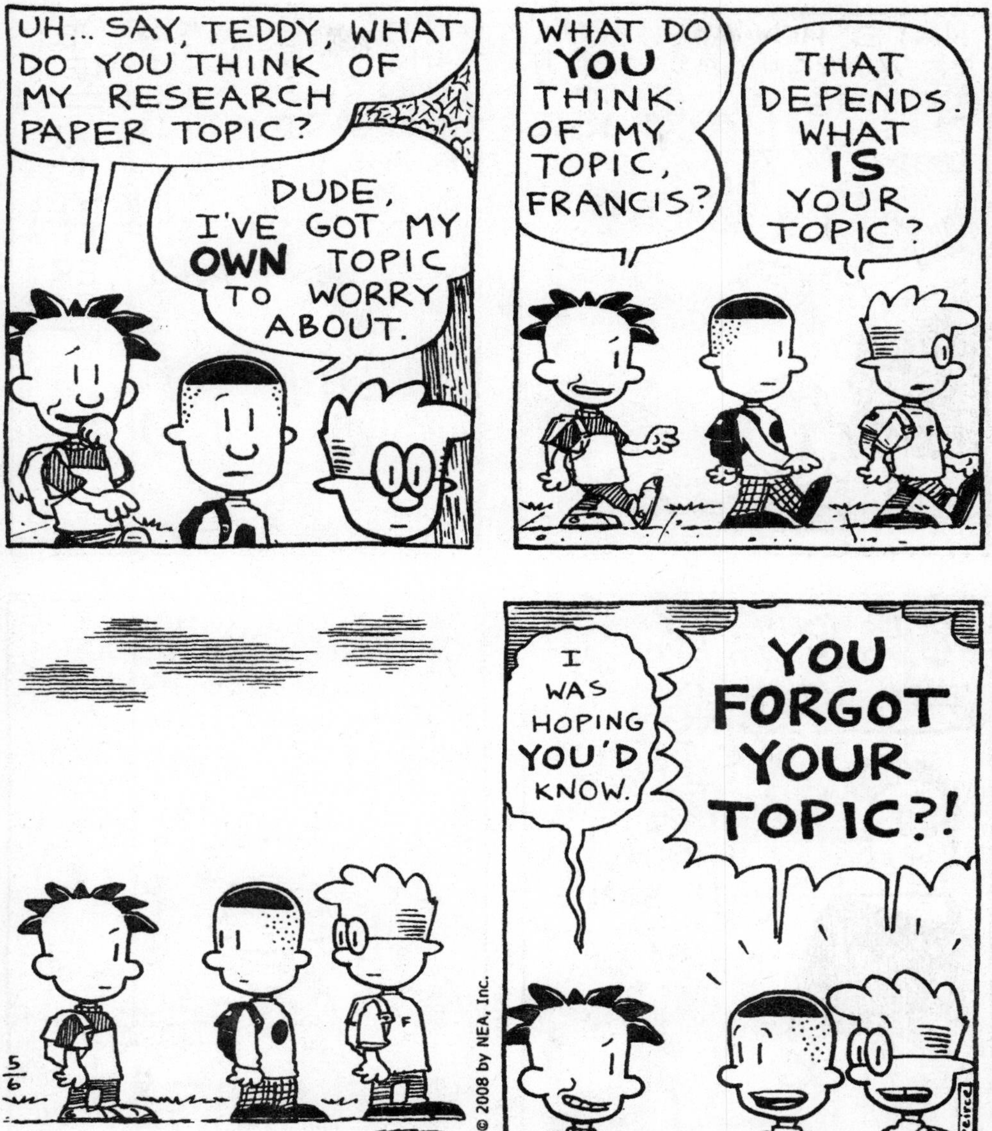
UH... SAY, TEDDY, WHAT DO YOU THINK OF MY RESEARCH PAPER TOPIC?
DUDE, I'VE GOT MY **OWN** TOPIC TO WORRY ABOUT.
WHAT DO **YOU** THINK OF MY TOPIC, FRANCIS?
THAT DEPENDS. WHAT **IS** YOUR TOPIC?
5/6
© 2008 by NEA, Inc.
I WAS HOPING **YOU'D** KNOW.
YOU FORGOT YOUR TOPIC?!
PEIRCE

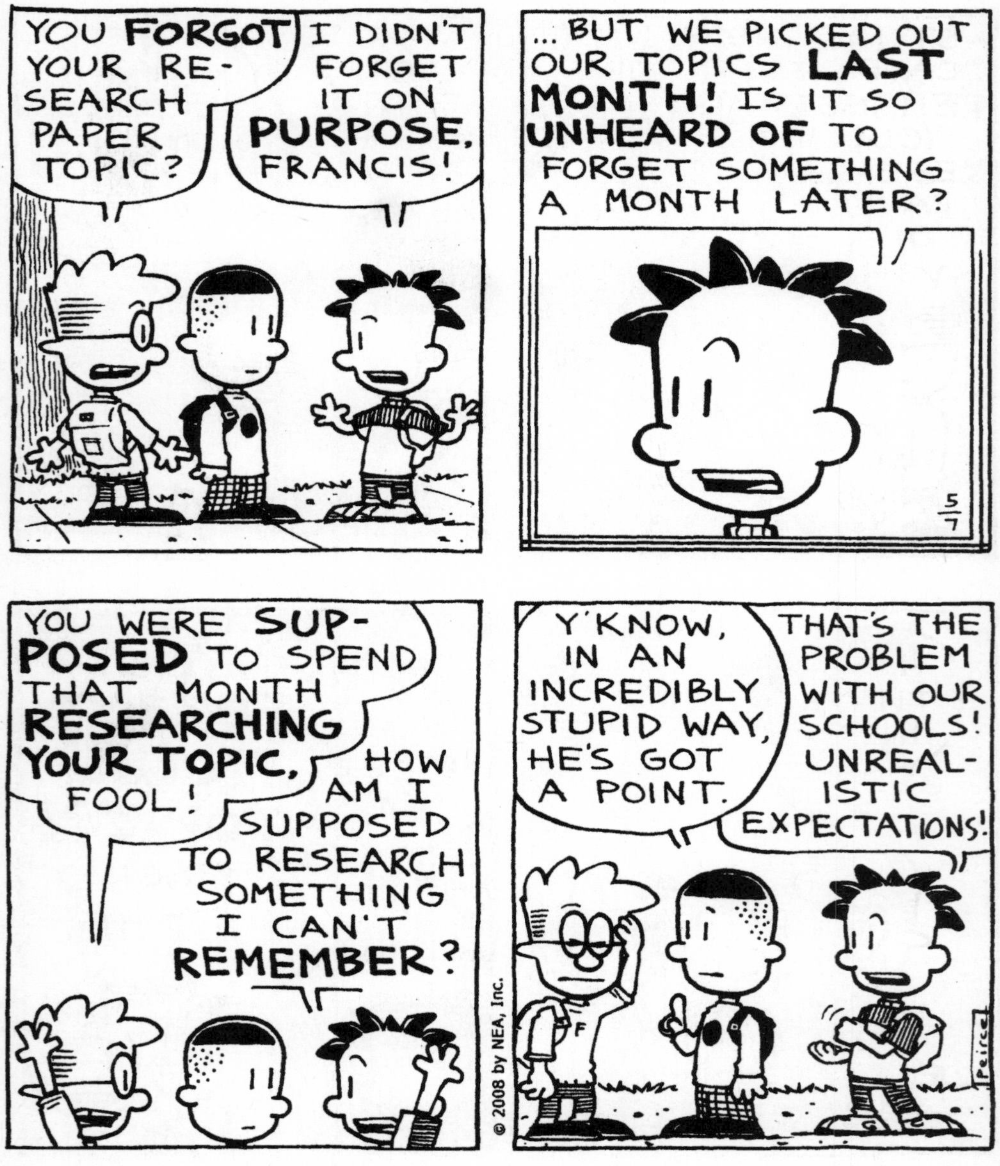

YOU FORGOT YOUR RESEARCH PAPER TOPIC?
I DIDN'T FORGET IT ON PURPOSE, FRANCIS!
... BUT WE PICKED OUT OUR TOPICS LAST MONTH! IS IT SO UNHEARD OF TO FORGET SOMETHING A MONTH LATER?
5/7
YOU WERE SUPPOSED TO SPEND THAT MONTH RESEARCHING YOUR TOPIC, FOOL!
HOW AM I SUPPOSED TO RESEARCH SOMETHING I CAN'T REMEMBER?
© 2008 by NEA, Inc.
Y'KNOW, IN AN INCREDIBLY STUPID WAY, HE'S GOT A POINT.
THAT'S THE PROBLEM WITH OUR SCHOOLS! UNREALISTIC EXPECTATIONS!
Peirce

STILL CAN'T REMEMBER YOUR RESEARCH PAPER TOPIC?
NO. MY MIND IS A BLANK.
ALL I REMEMBER FOR SURE IS THAT IT HAD SOMETHING TO DO WITH THE REVOLUTIONARY WAR!
HM... WELL, THAT'S VERY INTERESTING...
...CONSIDERING WE'RE STUDYING THE CIVIL WAR!
OKAY, WHATEVER. I KNEW IT WAS ONE OF THE BIGGIES.
5/8
© 2008 by NEA, Inc.
Peirce

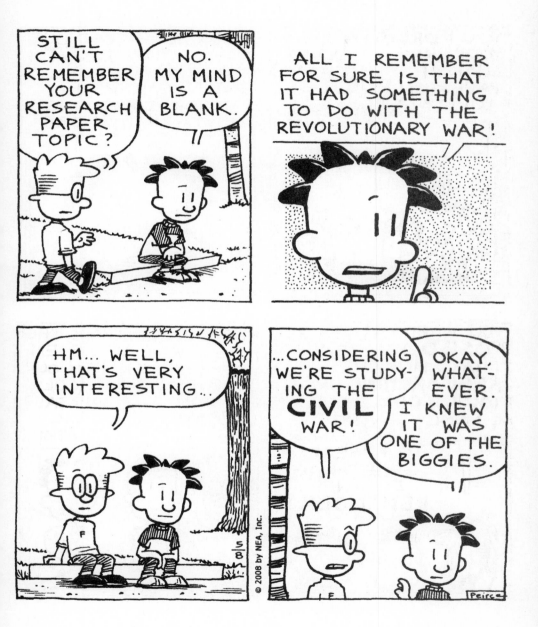

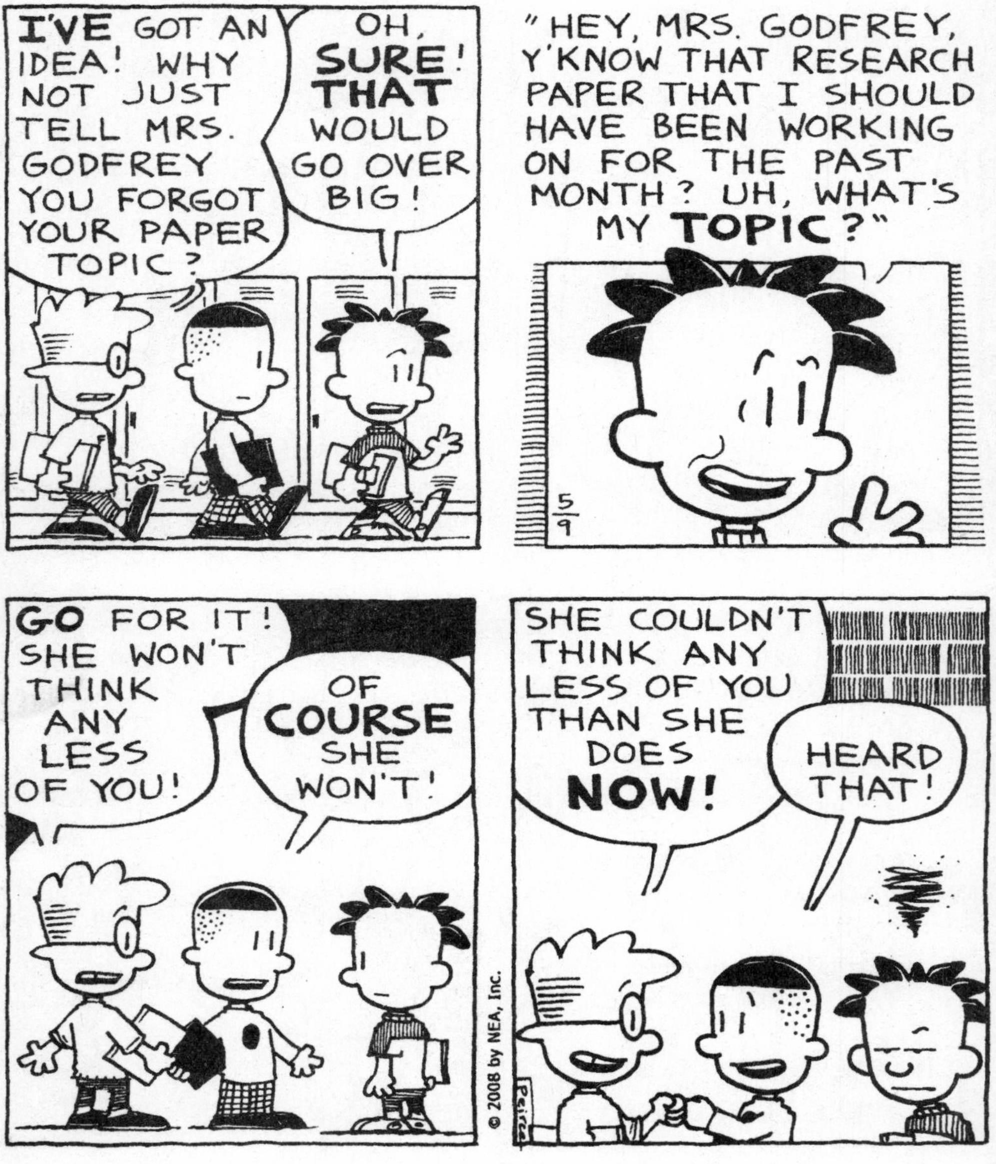
I'VE GOT AN IDEA! WHY NOT JUST TELL MRS. GODFREY YOU FORGOT YOUR PAPER TOPIC?
OH, SURE! THAT WOULD GO OVER BIG!
"HEY, MRS. GODFREY, Y'KNOW THAT RESEARCH PAPER THAT I SHOULD HAVE BEEN WORKING ON FOR THE PAST MONTH? UH, WHAT'S MY TOPIC?"
5/9
GO FOR IT! SHE WON'T THINK ANY LESS OF YOU!
OF COURSE SHE WON'T!
© 2008 by NEA, Inc.
SHE COULDN'T THINK ANY LESS OF YOU THAN SHE DOES NOW!
HEARD THAT!
Peirce

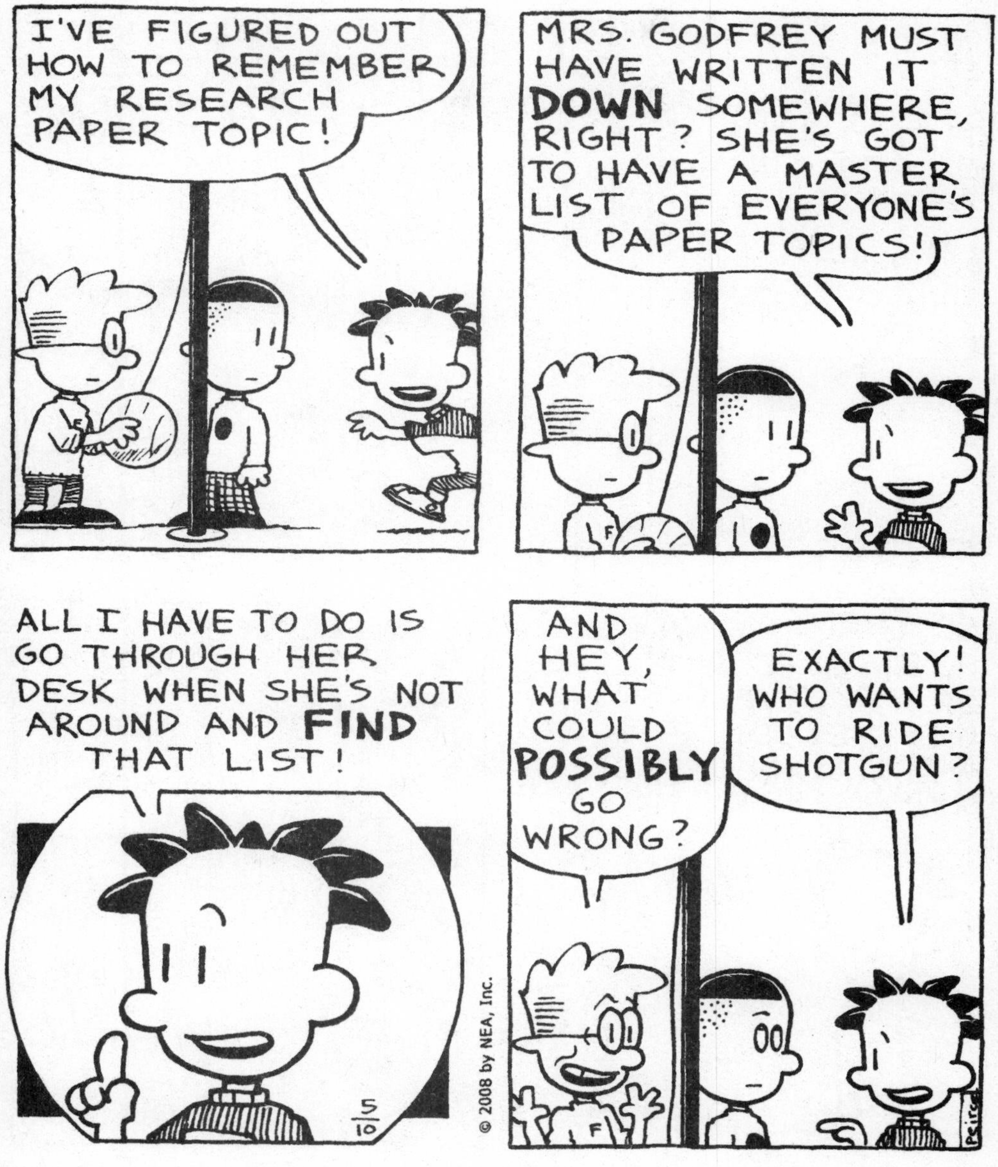
I'VE FIGURED OUT HOW TO REMEMBER MY RESEARCH PAPER TOPIC!
MRS. GODFREY MUST HAVE WRITTEN IT **DOWN** SOMEWHERE, RIGHT? SHE'S GOT TO HAVE A MASTER LIST OF EVERYONE'S PAPER TOPICS!
ALL I HAVE TO DO IS GO THROUGH HER DESK WHEN SHE'S NOT AROUND AND **FIND** THAT LIST!
5/10
AND HEY, WHAT COULD **POSSIBLY** GO WRONG?
EXACTLY! WHO WANTS TO RIDE SHOTGUN?
Peirce

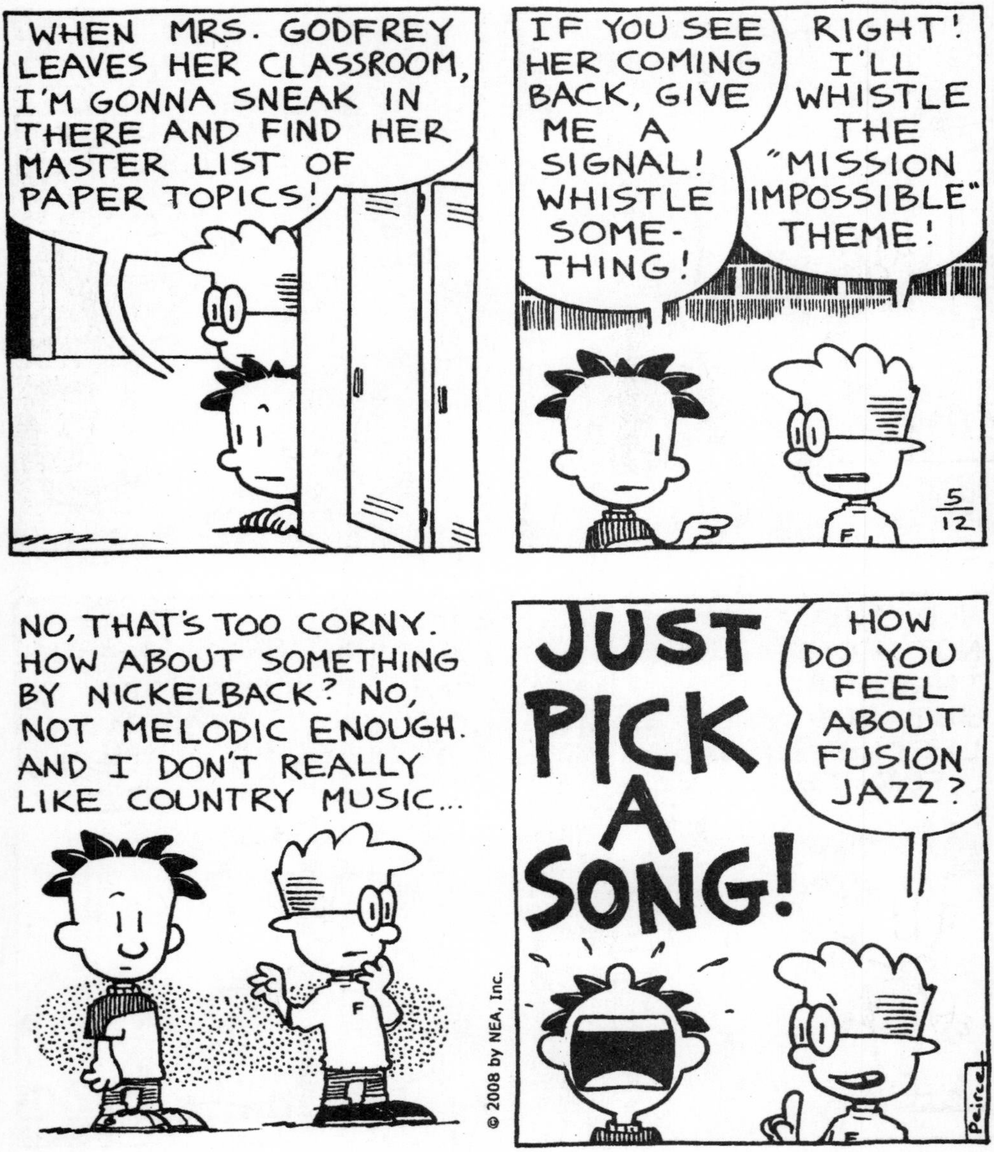
WHEN MRS. GODFREY LEAVES HER CLASSROOM, I'M GONNA SNEAK IN THERE AND FIND HER MASTER LIST OF PAPER TOPICS!
IF YOU SEE HER COMING BACK, GIVE ME A SIGNAL! WHISTLE SOMETHING!
RIGHT! I'LL WHISTLE THE "MISSION IMPOSSIBLE" THEME!
F
5/12
NO, THAT'S TOO CORNY. HOW ABOUT SOMETHING BY NICKELBACK? NO, NOT MELODIC ENOUGH. AND I DON'T REALLY LIKE COUNTRY MUSIC...
F
© 2008 by NEA, Inc.
JUST PICK A SONG!
HOW DO YOU FEEL ABOUT FUSION JAZZ?
Peirce

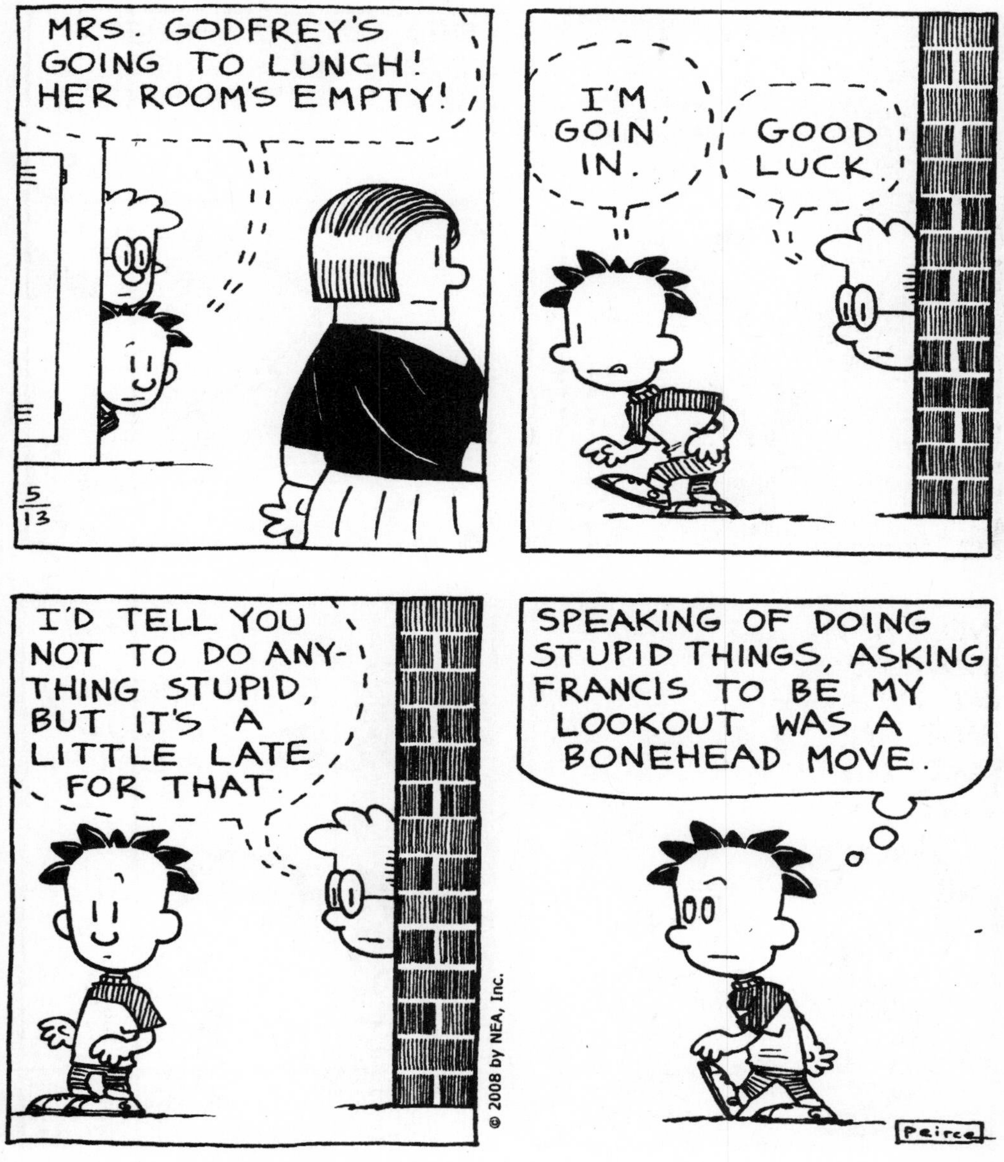
MRS. GODFREY'S GOING TO LUNCH! HER ROOM'S EMPTY!
5/13
I'M GOIN' IN.
GOOD LUCK.
I'D TELL YOU NOT TO DO ANY-THING STUPID, BUT IT'S A LITTLE LATE FOR THAT.
© 2008 by NEA, Inc.
SPEAKING OF DOING STUPID THINGS, ASKING FRANCIS TO BE MY LOOKOUT WAS A BONEHEAD MOVE.
Peirce

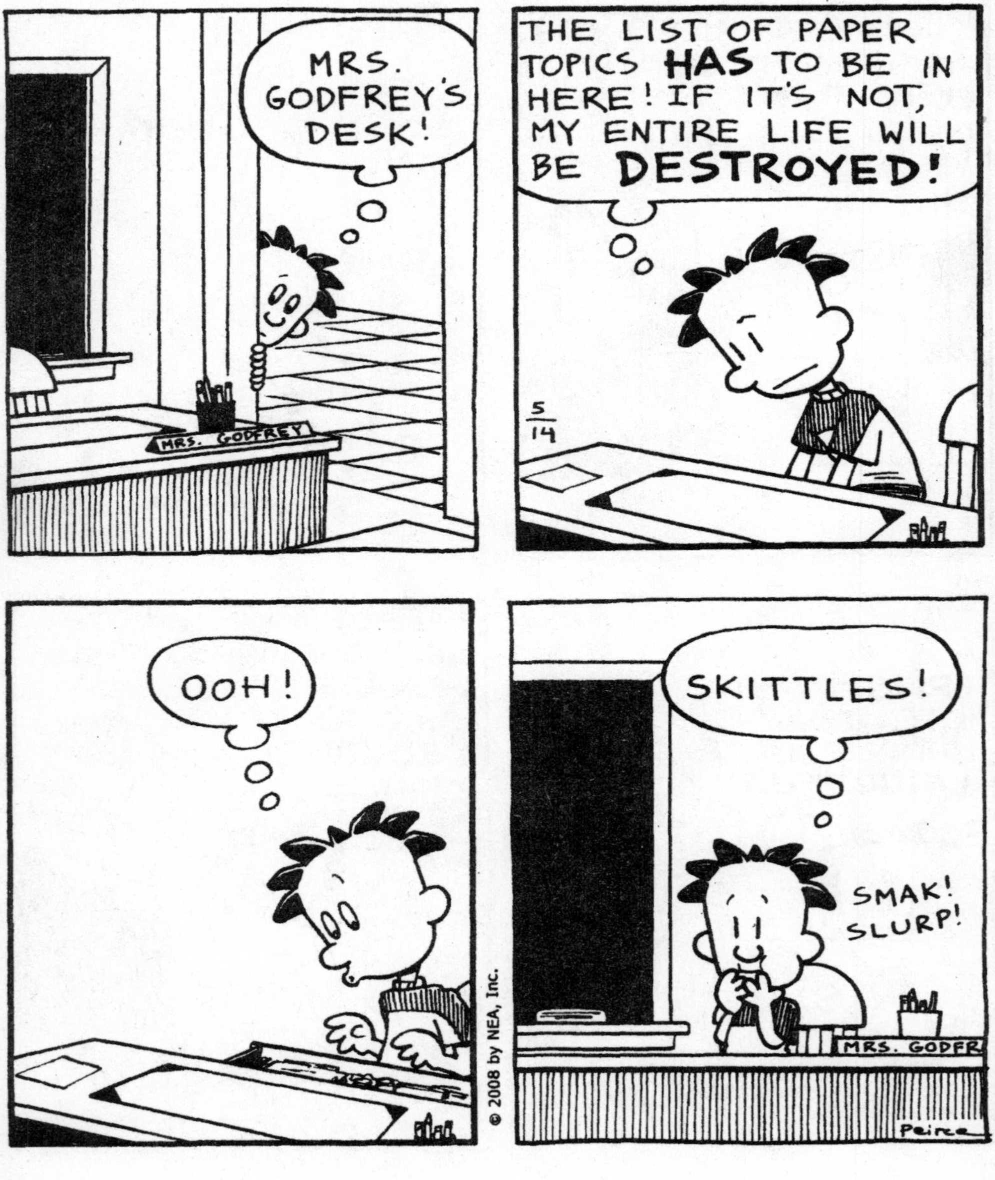
MRS. GODFREY'S DESK!
MRS. GODFREY
THE LIST OF PAPER TOPICS **HAS** TO BE IN HERE! IF IT'S NOT, MY ENTIRE LIFE WILL BE **DESTROYED!**
5/14
OOH!
SKITTLES!
SMAK! SLURP!
MRS. GODFR
Peirce

YIP!! HERE SHE COMES! GOTTA GIVE NATE THE WARNING SIGNAL!
PFF! FFT! FOOH! PFFH!
POOFF! PHFF! WHOOHF! FOO!
5/15
© 2008 by NEA, Inc.
WELL, HI THERE, MRS. GOD-FREY!
? ?
Peirce

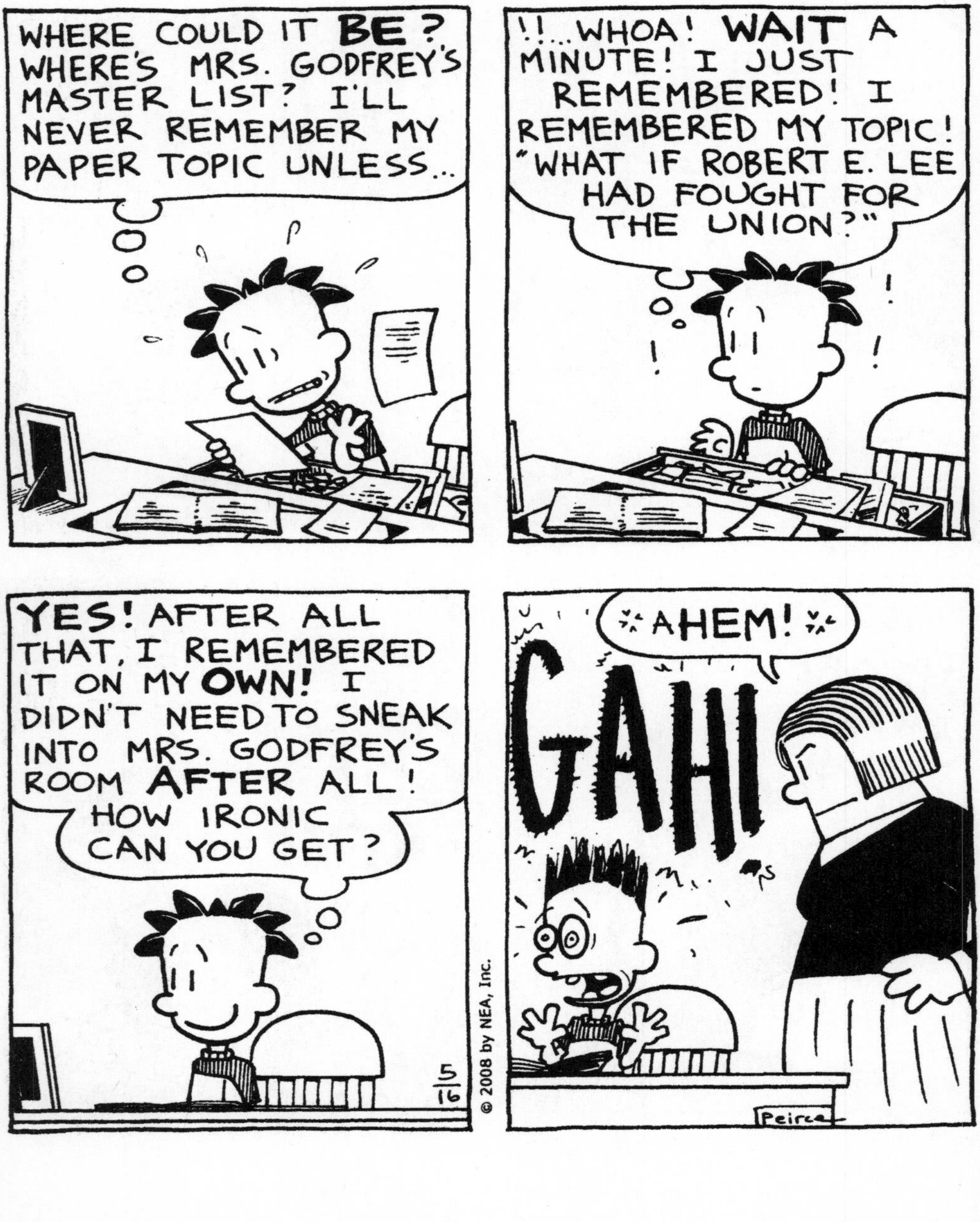

WHERE COULD IT BE? WHERE'S MRS. GODFREY'S MASTER LIST? I'LL NEVER REMEMBER MY PAPER TOPIC UNLESS...
!!...WHOA! WAIT A MINUTE! I JUST REMEMBERED! I REMEMBERED MY TOPIC! "WHAT IF ROBERT E. LEE HAD FOUGHT FOR THE UNION?"
YES! AFTER ALL THAT, I REMEMBERED IT ON MY OWN! I DIDN'T NEED TO SNEAK INTO MRS. GODFREY'S ROOM AFTER ALL! HOW IRONIC CAN YOU GET?
5/16
AHEM!
GAH!
Peirce

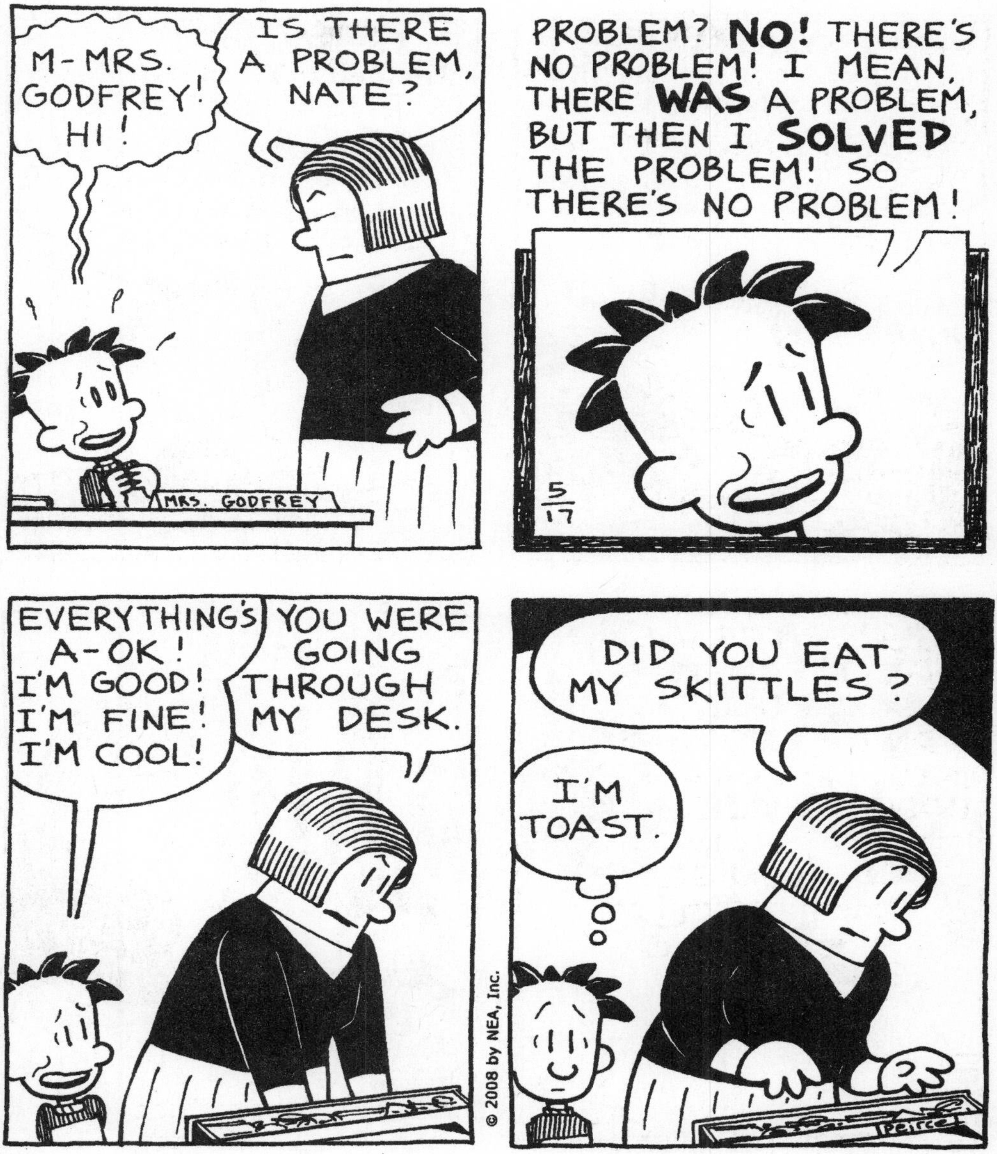
M-MRS. GODFREY! HI!
IS THERE A PROBLEM, NATE?
MRS. GODFREY
PROBLEM? NO! THERE'S NO PROBLEM! I MEAN, THERE WAS A PROBLEM, BUT THEN I SOLVED THE PROBLEM! SO THERE'S NO PROBLEM!
5/17
EVERYTHING'S A-OK! I'M GOOD! I'M FINE! I'M COOL!
YOU WERE GOING THROUGH MY DESK.
© 2008 by NEA, Inc.
DID YOU EAT MY SKITTLES?
I'M TOAST.
PEIRCE

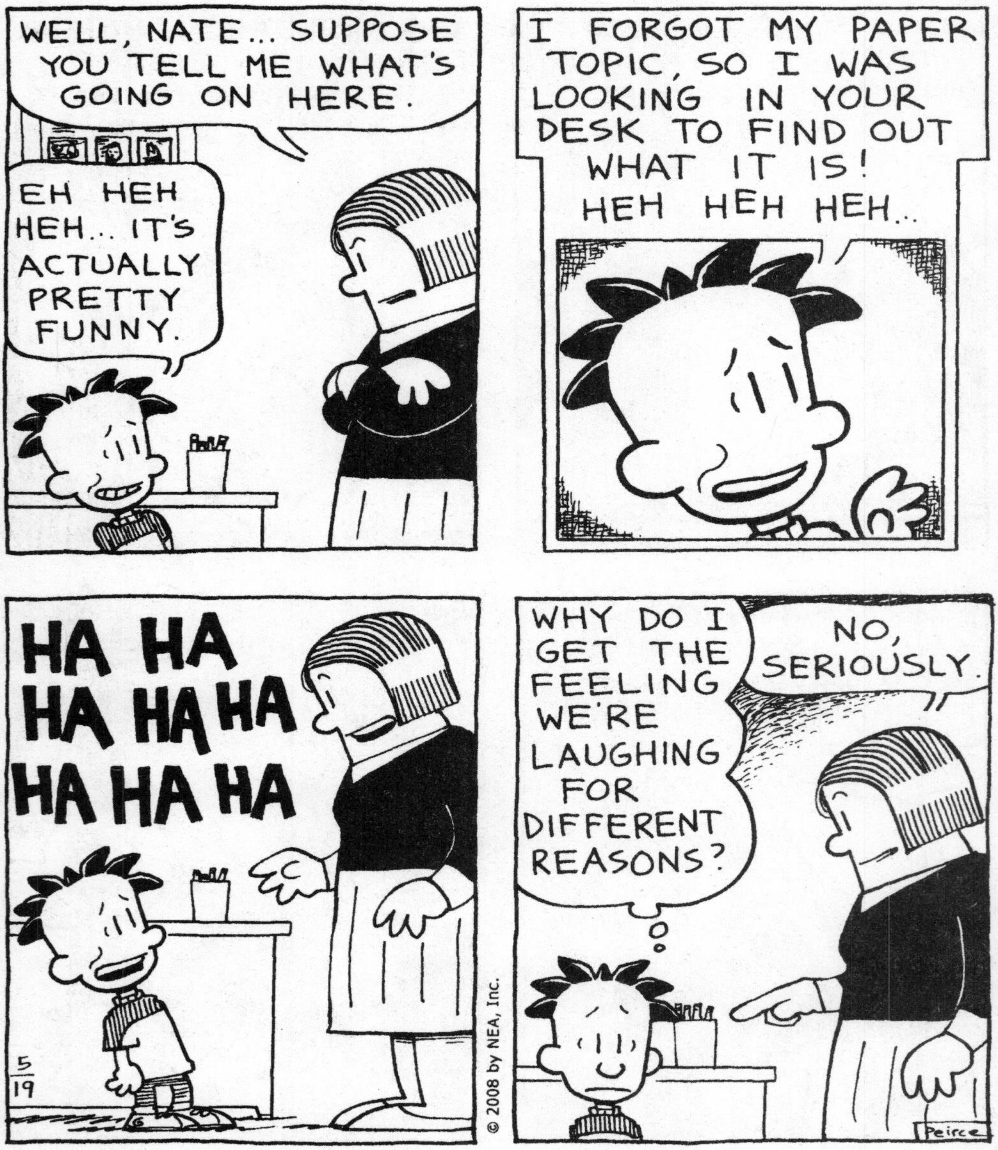
WELL, NATE... SUPPOSE YOU TELL ME WHAT'S GOING ON HERE.
EH HEH HEH... IT'S ACTUALLY PRETTY FUNNY.
I FORGOT MY PAPER TOPIC, SO I WAS LOOKING IN YOUR DESK TO FIND OUT WHAT IT IS! HEH HEH HEH...
HA HA HA HA HA HA HA HA
5/19
© 2008 by NEA, Inc.
WHY DO I GET THE FEELING WE'RE LAUGHING FOR DIFFERENT REASONS?
NO, SERIOUSLY.
Peirce

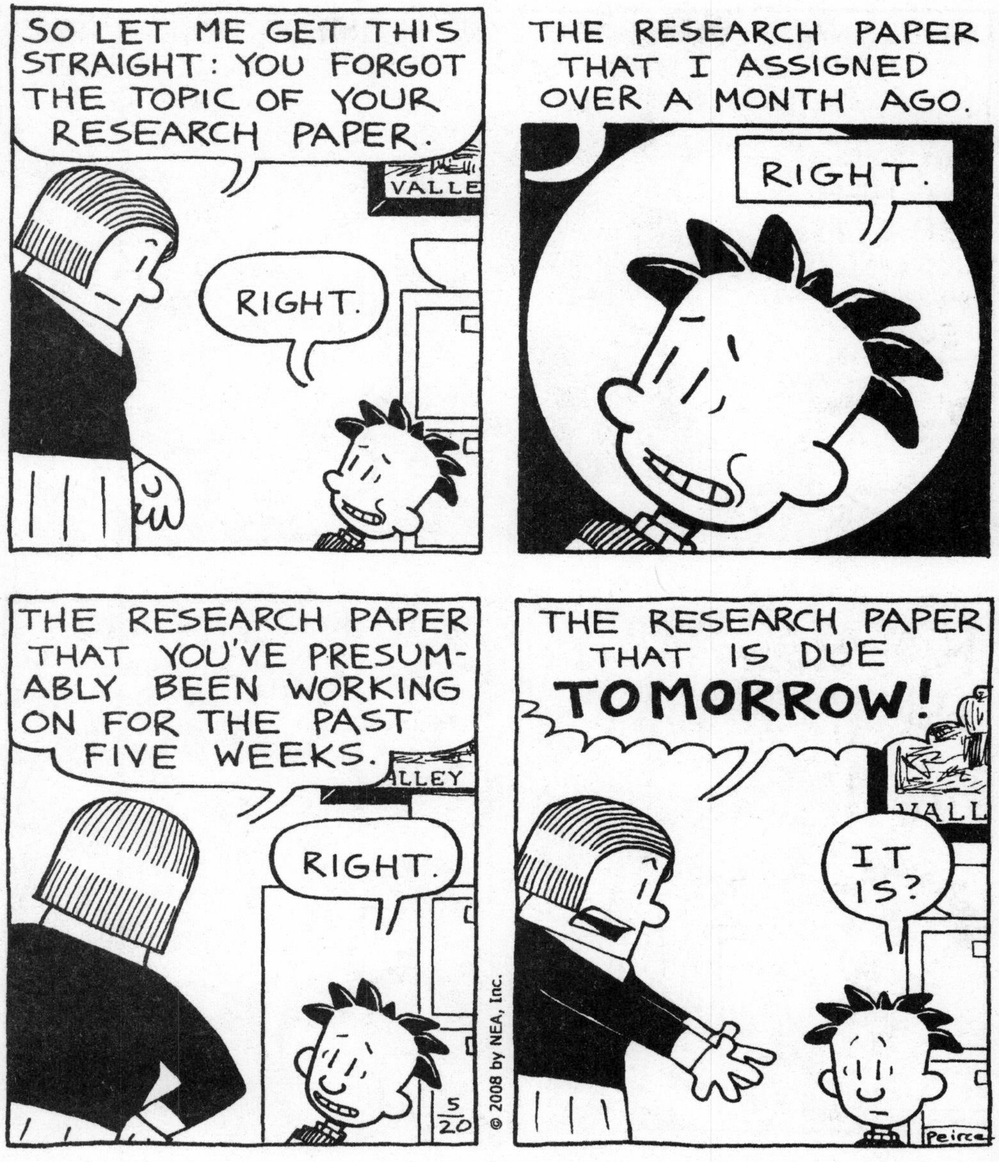
SO LET ME GET THIS STRAIGHT: YOU FORGOT THE TOPIC OF YOUR RESEARCH PAPER.
RIGHT.
THE RESEARCH PAPER THAT I ASSIGNED OVER A MONTH AGO.
RIGHT.
THE RESEARCH PAPER THAT YOU'VE PRESUMABLY BEEN WORKING ON FOR THE PAST FIVE WEEKS.
RIGHT.
5/20
THE RESEARCH PAPER THAT IS DUE **TOMORROW!**
IT IS?
Peirce

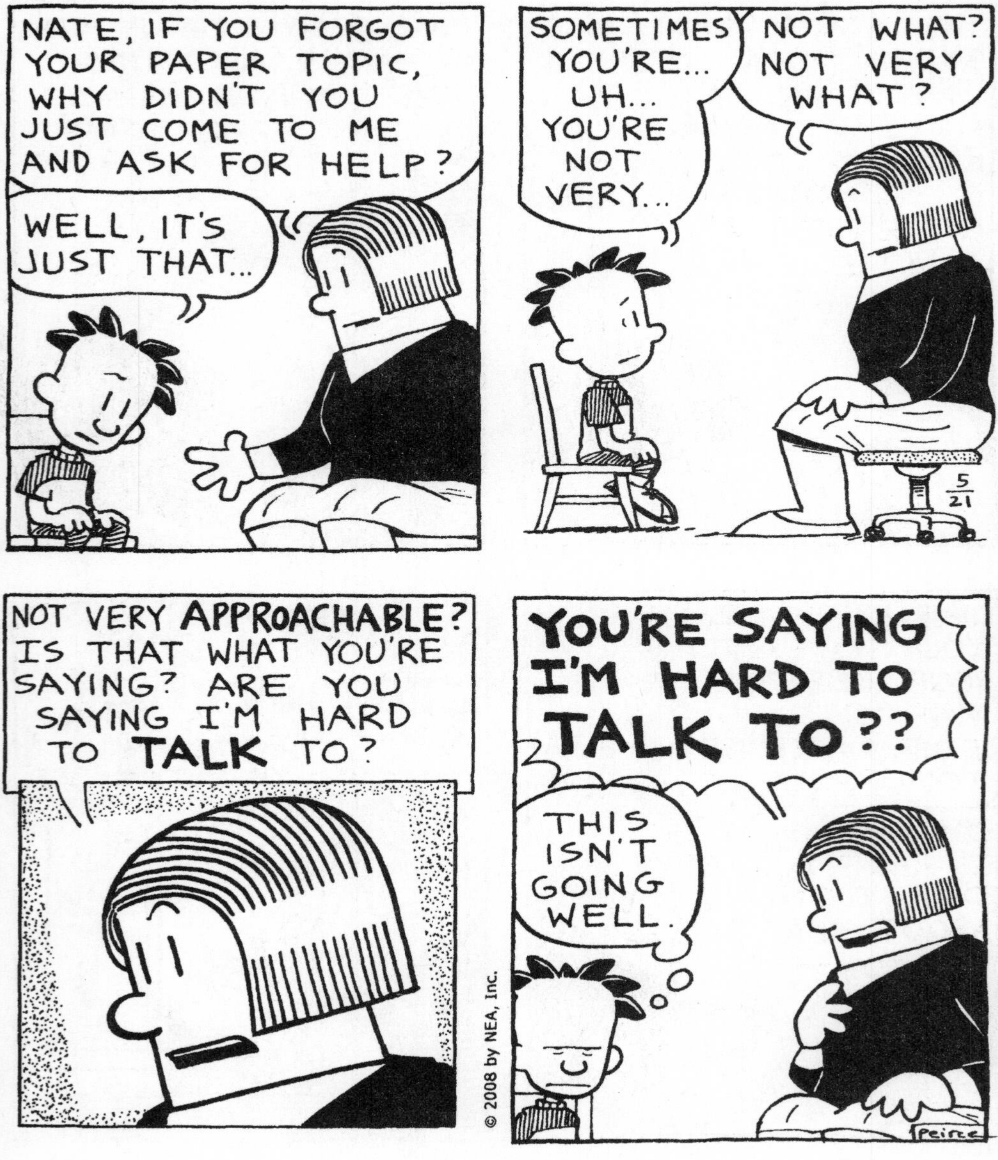
NATE, IF YOU FORGOT YOUR PAPER TOPIC, WHY DIDN'T YOU JUST COME TO ME AND ASK FOR HELP?
WELL, IT'S JUST THAT...
SOMETIMES YOU'RE... UH... YOU'RE NOT VERY...
NOT WHAT? NOT VERY WHAT?
5/21
NOT VERY **APPROACHABLE**? IS THAT WHAT YOU'RE SAYING? ARE YOU SAYING I'M HARD TO **TALK** TO?
YOU'RE SAYING I'M HARD TO TALK TO??
THIS ISN'T GOING WELL.
Peirce

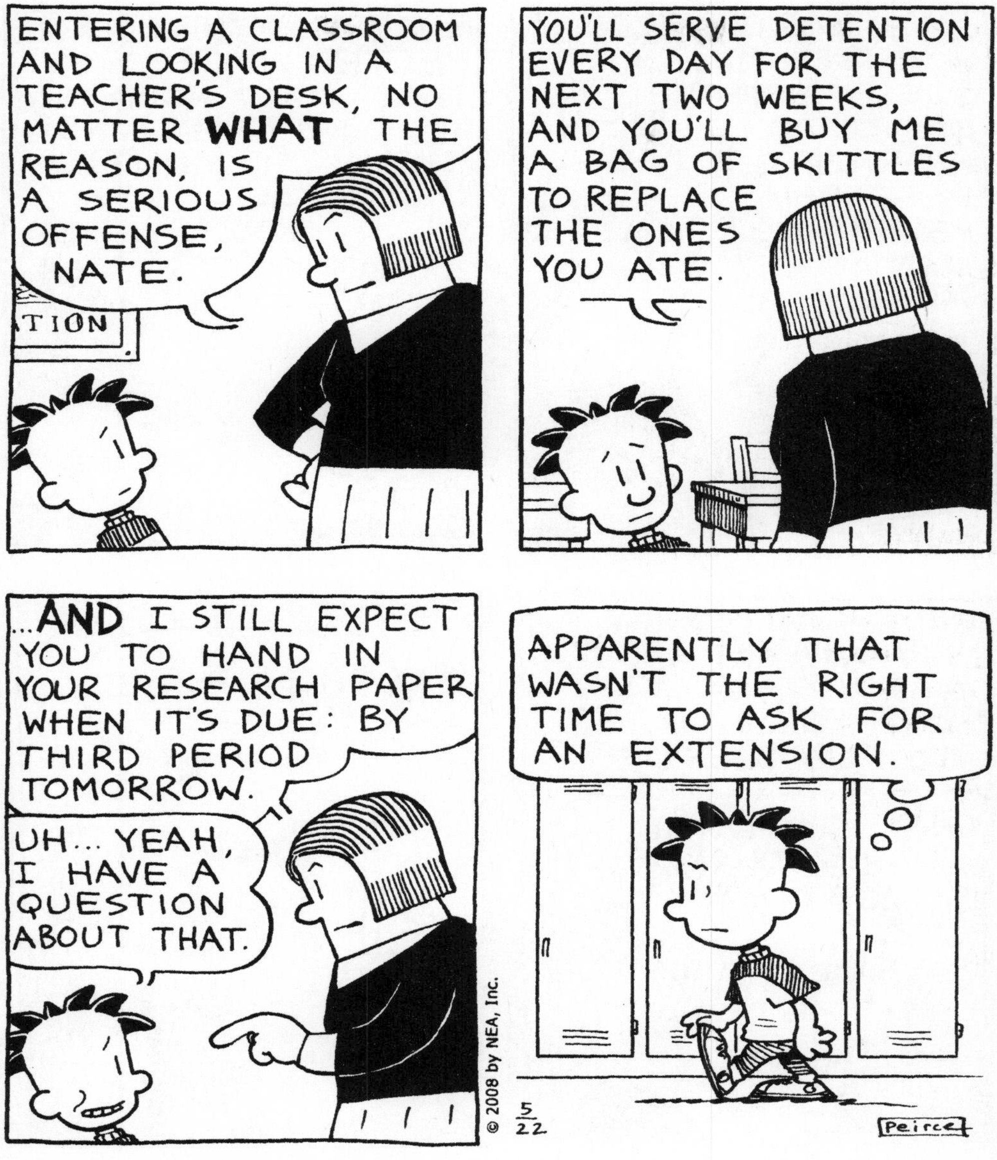
ENTERING A CLASSROOM AND LOOKING IN A TEACHER'S DESK, NO MATTER **WHAT** THE REASON, IS A SERIOUS OFFENSE, NATE.
YOU'LL SERVE DETENTION EVERY DAY FOR THE NEXT TWO WEEKS, AND YOU'LL BUY ME A BAG OF SKITTLES TO REPLACE THE ONES YOU ATE.
...**AND** I STILL EXPECT YOU TO HAND IN YOUR RESEARCH PAPER WHEN IT'S DUE: BY THIRD PERIOD TOMORROW.
UH... YEAH, I HAVE A QUESTION ABOUT THAT.
APPARENTLY THAT WASN'T THE RIGHT TIME TO ASK FOR AN EXTENSION.
© 2008 by NEA, Inc.
5/22
Peirce

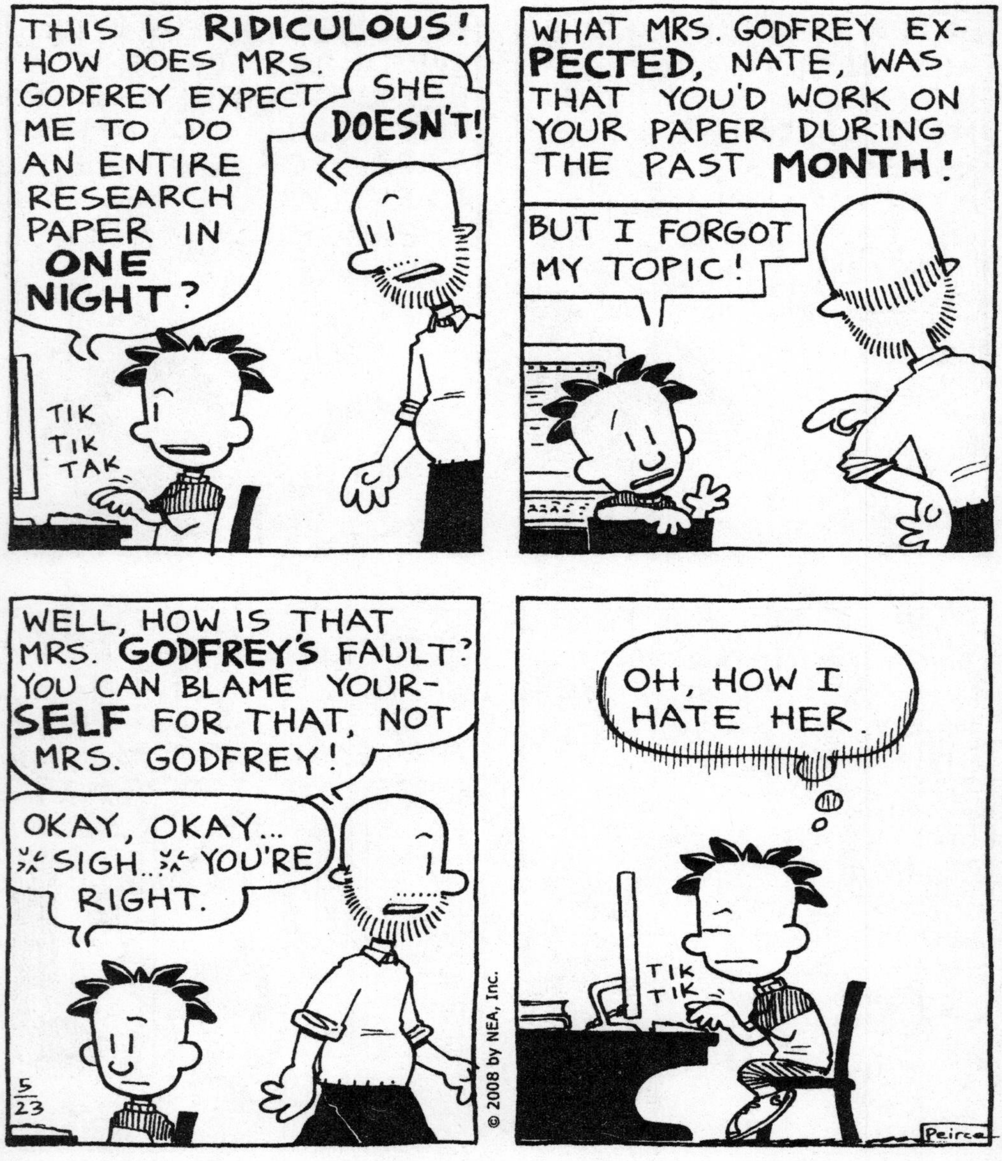
THIS IS RIDICULOUS! HOW DOES MRS. GODFREY EXPECT ME TO DO AN ENTIRE RESEARCH PAPER IN ONE NIGHT?
SHE DOESN'T!
TIK TIK TAK
WHAT MRS. GODFREY EXPECTED, NATE, WAS THAT YOU'D WORK ON YOUR PAPER DURING THE PAST MONTH!
BUT I FORGOT MY TOPIC!
WELL, HOW IS THAT MRS. GODFREY'S FAULT? YOU CAN BLAME YOURSELF FOR THAT, NOT MRS. GODFREY!
OKAY, OKAY... *SIGH..* YOU'RE RIGHT.
5/23
© 2008 by NEA, Inc.
OH, HOW I HATE HER.
TIK TIK
Peirce

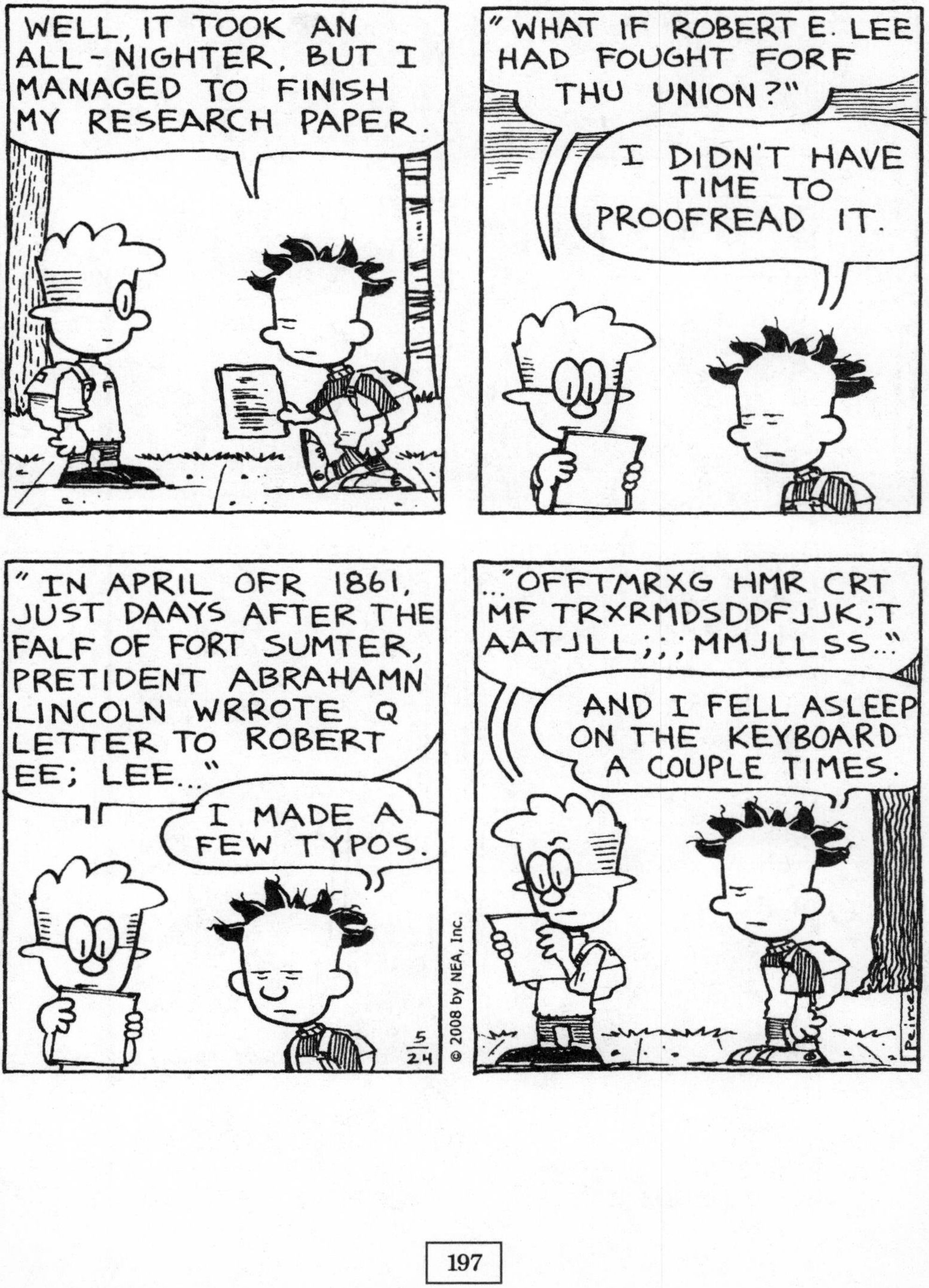
WELL, IT TOOK AN ALL-NIGHTER, BUT I MANAGED TO FINISH MY RESEARCH PAPER.
"WHAT IF ROBERT E. LEE HAD FOUGHT FORF THU UNION?"
I DIDN'T HAVE TIME TO PROOFREAD IT.
"IN APRIL OFR 1861, JUST DAAYS AFTER THE FALF OF FORT SUMTER, PRETIDENT ABRAHAMN LINCOLN WRROTE Q LETTER TO ROBERT EE; LEE..."
I MADE A FEW TYPOS.
5
24
© 2008 by NEA, Inc.
..."OFFTMRXG HMR CRT MF TRXRMDSDDFJJK;T AATJLL;;;MMJLLSS..."
AND I FELL ASLEEP ON THE KEYBOARD A COUPLE TIMES.
Peirce

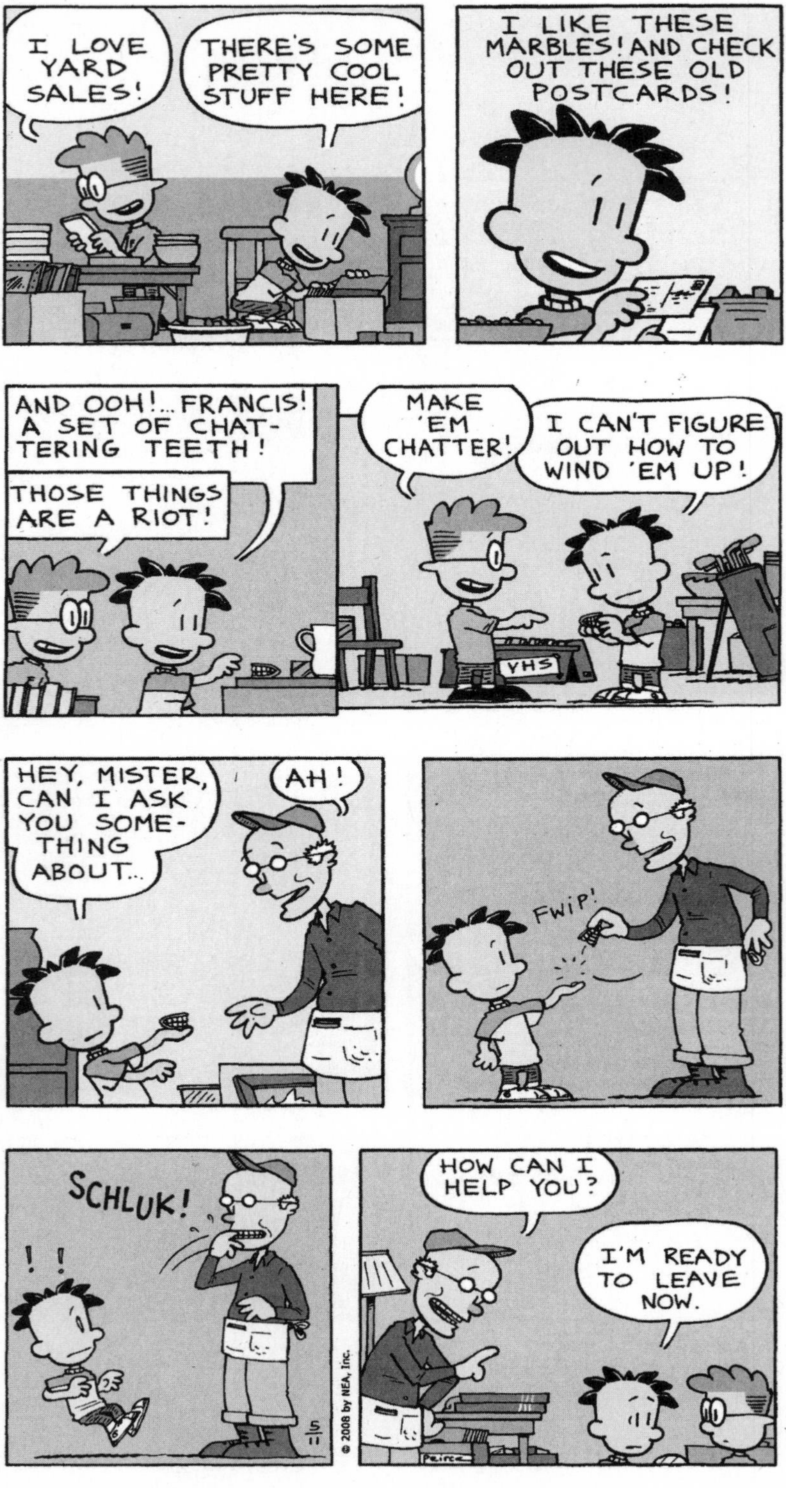

I LOVE YARD SALES!
THERE'S SOME PRETTY COOL STUFF HERE!
I LIKE THESE MARBLES! AND CHECK OUT THESE OLD POSTCARDS!
AND OOH!... FRANCIS! A SET OF CHAT-TERING TEETH!
THOSE THINGS ARE A RIOT!
MAKE 'EM CHATTER!
I CAN'T FIGURE OUT HOW TO WIND 'EM UP!
YHS
HEY, MISTER, CAN I ASK YOU SOME-THING ABOUT...
AH!
FWIP!
SCHLUK!
! !
© 2008 by NEA, Inc.
HOW CAN I HELP YOU?
I'M READY TO LEAVE NOW.
Peirce

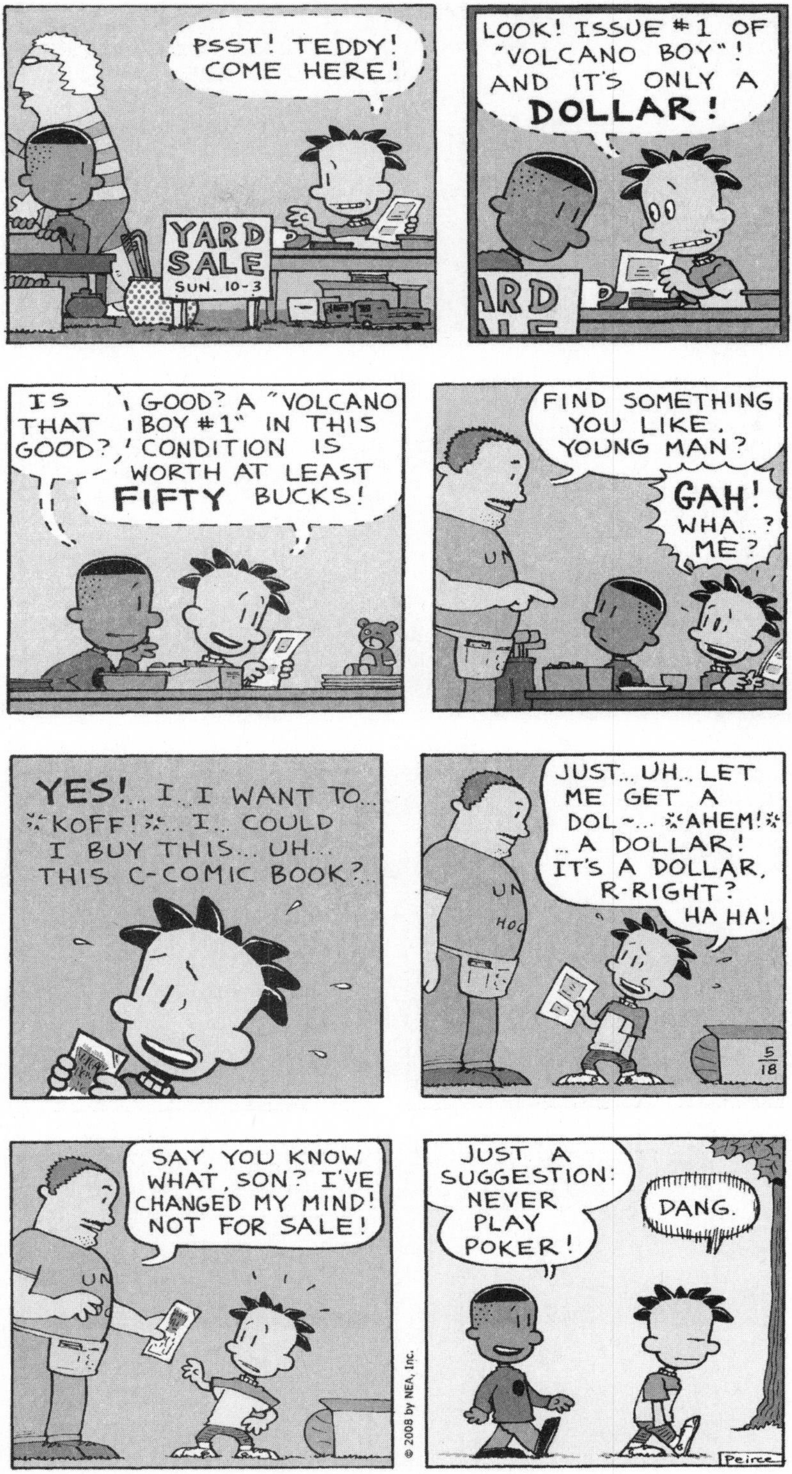
PSST! TEDDY! COME HERE!
YARD SALE SUN. 10-3
LOOK! ISSUE #1 OF "VOLCANO BOY"! AND IT'S ONLY A DOLLAR!
IS THAT GOOD?
GOOD? A "VOLCANO BOY #1" IN THIS CONDITION IS WORTH AT LEAST FIFTY BUCKS!
FIND SOMETHING YOU LIKE, YOUNG MAN?
GAH! WHA...? ME?
YES!... I...I WANT TO... *KOFF!*... I... COULD I BUY THIS... UH... THIS C-COMIC BOOK?...
JUST... UH... LET ME GET A DOL-... *AHEM!* ... A DOLLAR! IT'S A DOLLAR, R-RIGHT? HA HA!
5/18
SAY, YOU KNOW WHAT, SON? I'VE CHANGED MY MIND! NOT FOR SALE!
© 2008 by NEA, Inc.
JUST A SUGGESTION: NEVER PLAY POKER!
DANG.
Peirce

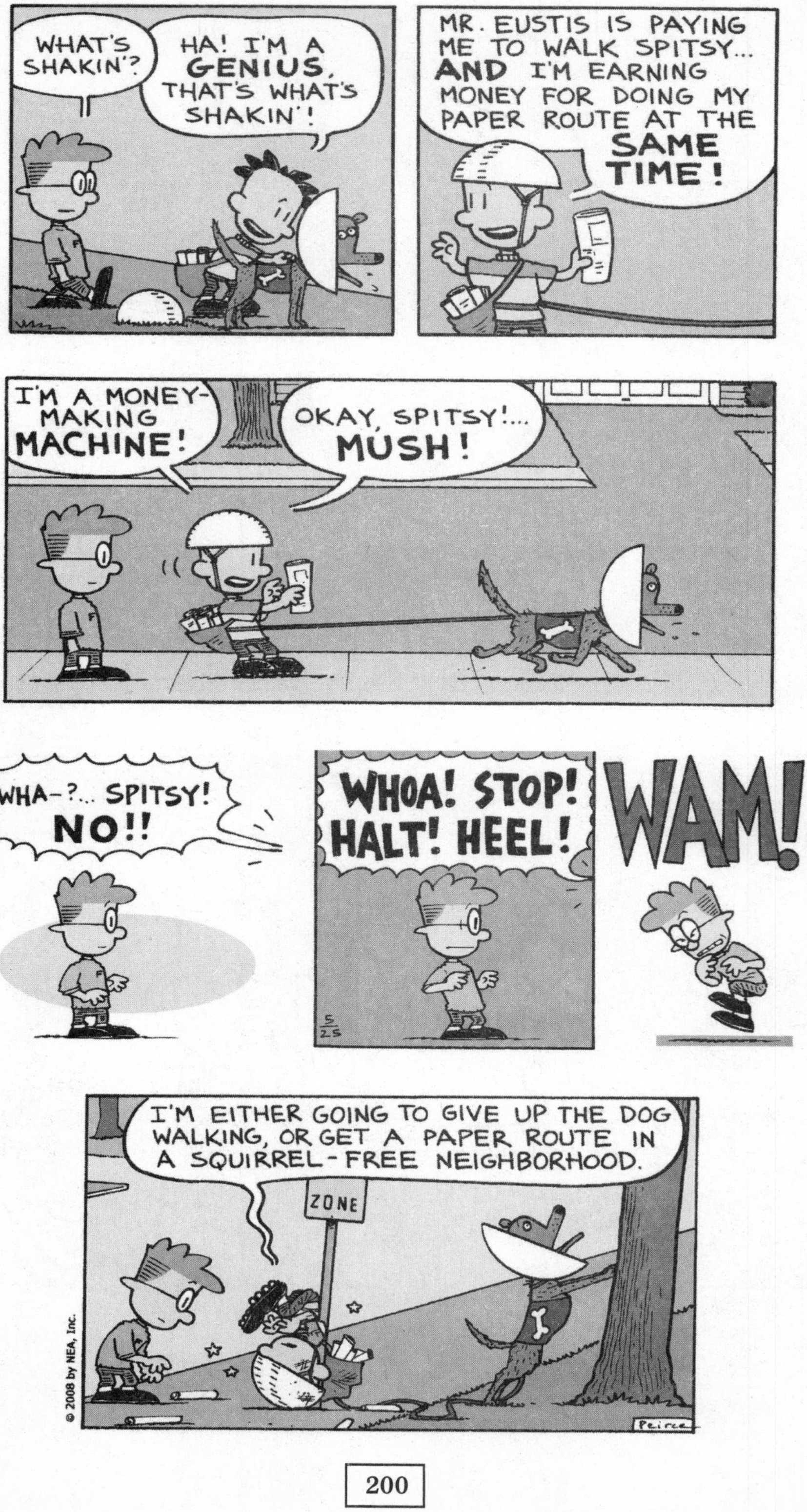
WHAT'S SHAKIN'?
HA! I'M A **GENIUS**, THAT'S WHAT'S SHAKIN'!
MR. EUSTIS IS PAYING ME TO WALK SPITSY... **AND** I'M EARNING MONEY FOR DOING MY PAPER ROUTE AT THE **SAME TIME!**
I'M A MONEY-MAKING **MACHINE!**
OKAY, SPITSY!... **MUSH!**
WHA-?... SPITSY! **NO!!**
WHOA! STOP! HALT! HEEL!
WAM!
I'M EITHER GOING TO GIVE UP THE DOG WALKING, OR GET A PAPER ROUTE IN A SQUIRREL-FREE NEIGHBORHOOD.
ZONE
© 2008 by NEA, Inc.
Peirce

THE LIST

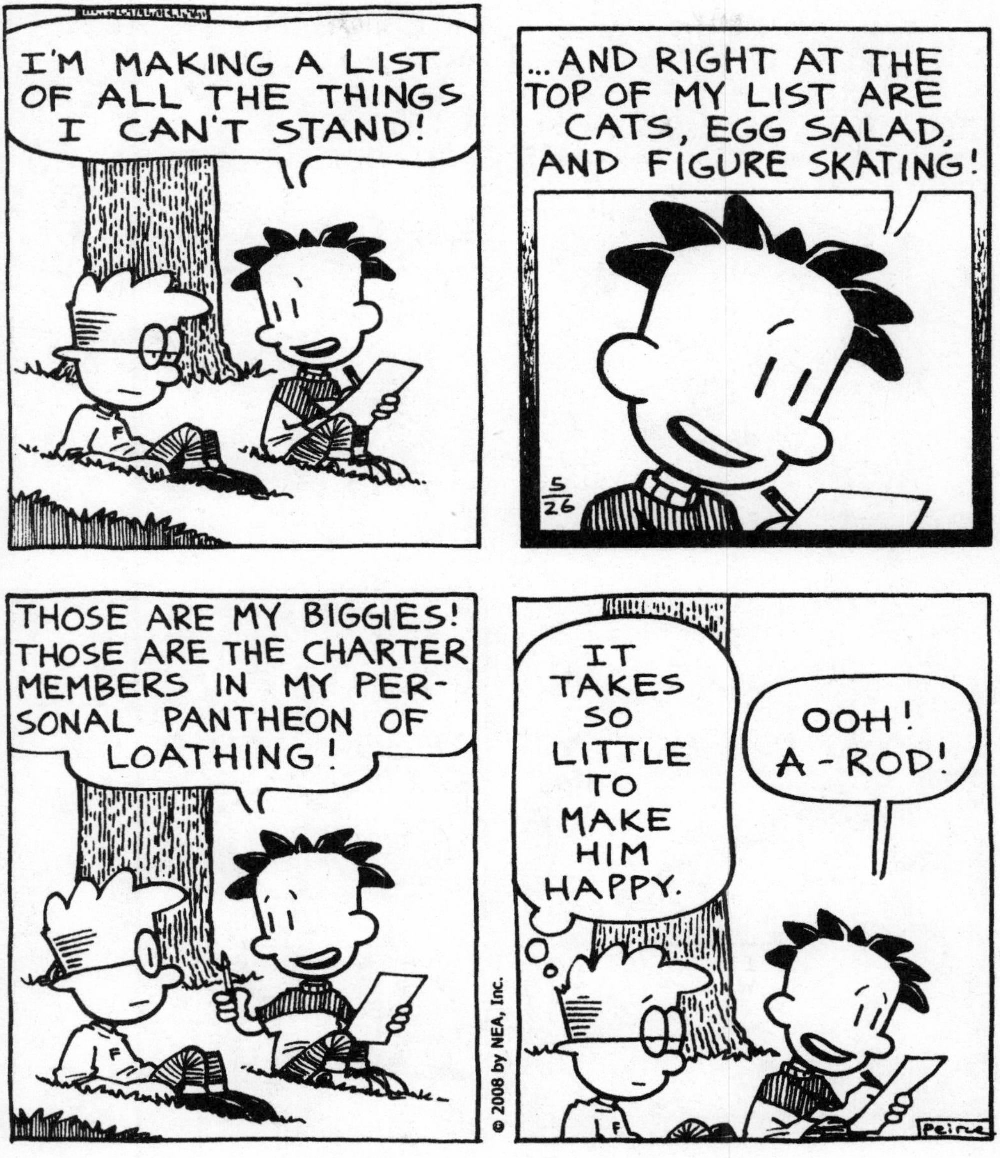

I'M MAKING A LIST OF ALL THE THINGS I CAN'T STAND!
...AND RIGHT AT THE TOP OF MY LIST ARE CATS, EGG SALAD, AND FIGURE SKATING!
5/26
THOSE ARE MY BIGGIES! THOSE ARE THE CHARTER MEMBERS IN MY PERSONAL PANTHEON OF LOATHING!
© 2008 by NEA, Inc.
IT TAKES SO LITTLE TO MAKE HIM HAPPY.
OOH! A-ROD!
Peirce

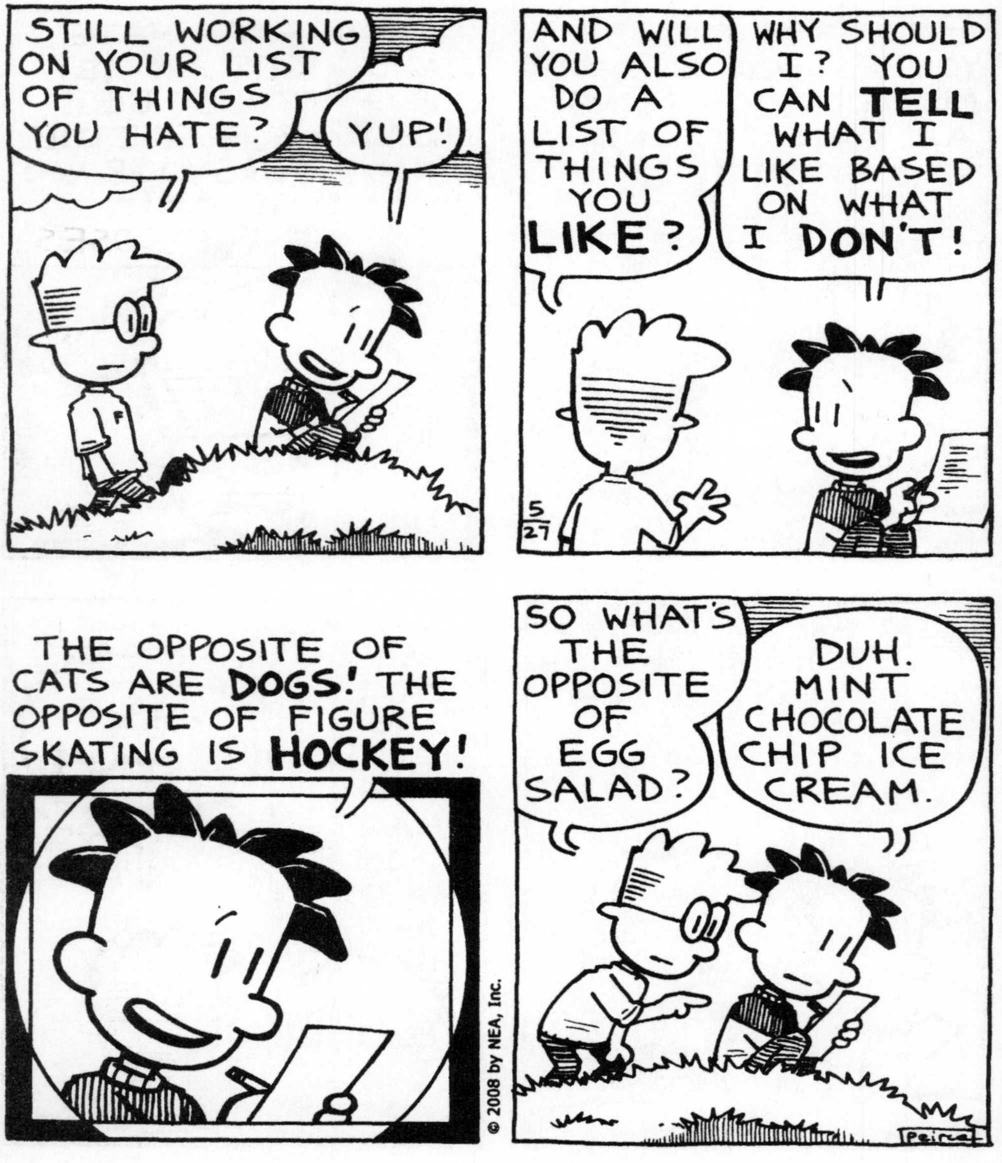
STILL WORKING ON YOUR LIST OF THINGS YOU HATE?
YUP!
5/27
AND WILL YOU ALSO DO A LIST OF THINGS YOU LIKE?
WHY SHOULD I? YOU CAN TELL WHAT I LIKE BASED ON WHAT I DON'T!
THE OPPOSITE OF CATS ARE DOGS! THE OPPOSITE OF FIGURE SKATING IS HOCKEY!
© 2008 by NEA, Inc.
SO WHAT'S THE OPPOSITE OF EGG SALAD?
DUH. MINT CHOCOLATE CHIP ICE CREAM.
PEIRCE

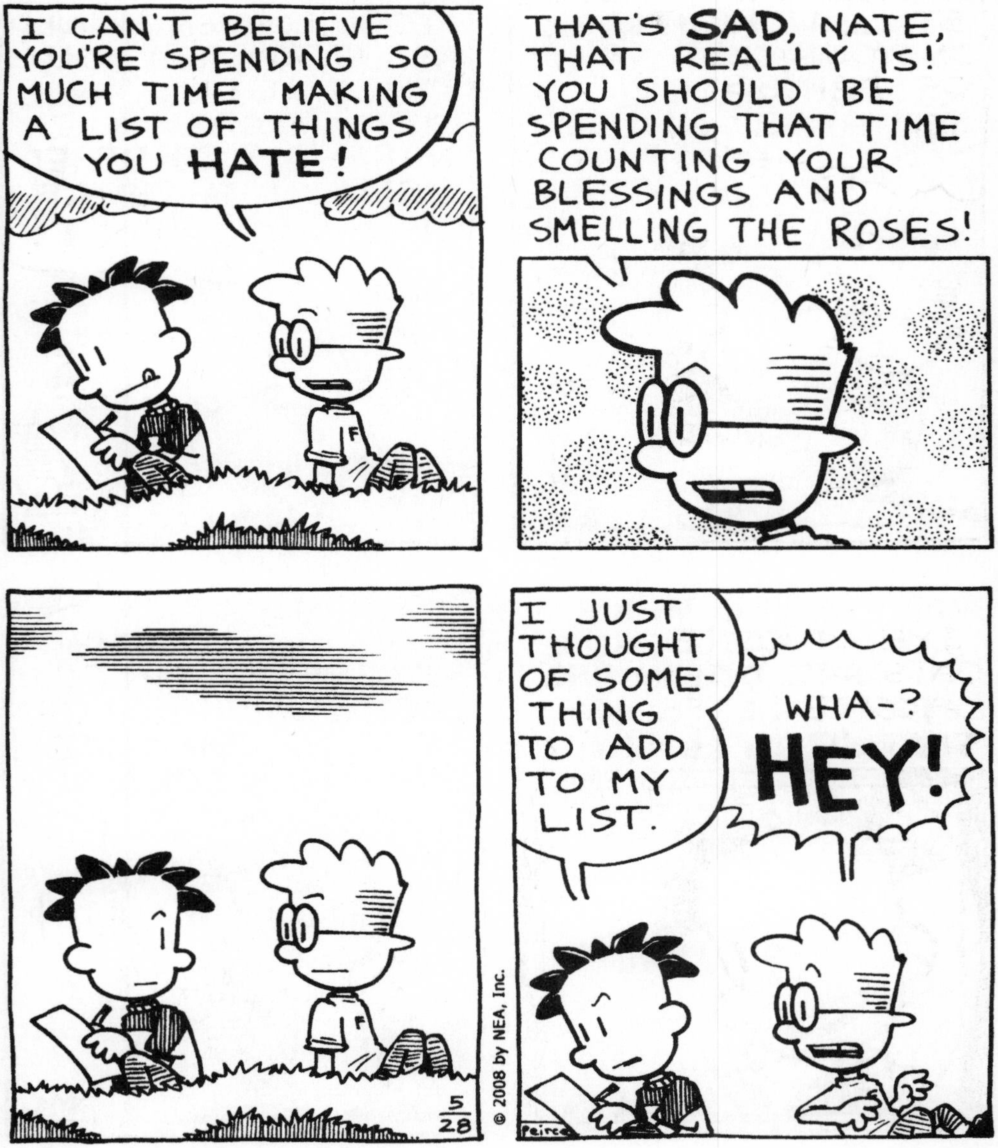
I CAN'T BELIEVE YOU'RE SPENDING SO MUCH TIME MAKING A LIST OF THINGS YOU HATE!
THAT'S SAD, NATE, THAT REALLY IS! YOU SHOULD BE SPENDING THAT TIME COUNTING YOUR BLESSINGS AND SMELLING THE ROSES!
5/28
© 2008 by NEA, Inc.
I JUST THOUGHT OF SOME-THING TO ADD TO MY LIST.
WHA-? HEY!
Peirce

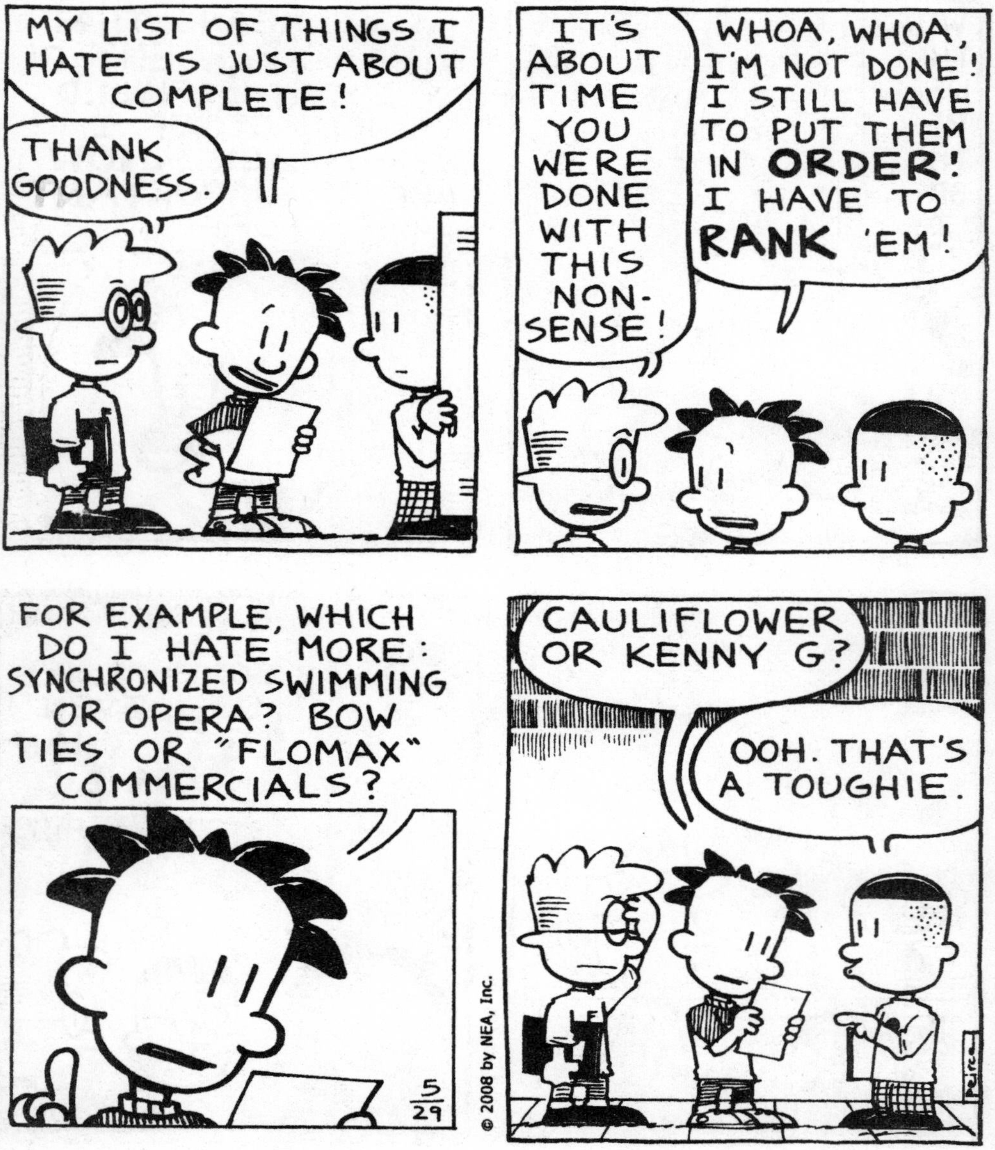
MY LIST OF THINGS I HATE IS JUST ABOUT COMPLETE!
THANK GOODNESS.
IT'S ABOUT TIME YOU WERE DONE WITH THIS NON-SENSE!
WHOA, WHOA, I'M NOT DONE! I STILL HAVE TO PUT THEM IN ORDER! I HAVE TO RANK 'EM!
FOR EXAMPLE, WHICH DO I HATE MORE: SYNCHRONIZED SWIMMING OR OPERA? BOW TIES OR "FLOMAX" COMMERCIALS?
5/29
© 2008 by NEA, Inc.
CAULIFLOWER OR KENNY G?
OOH. THAT'S A TOUGHIE.
Peirce

BRAINIAC

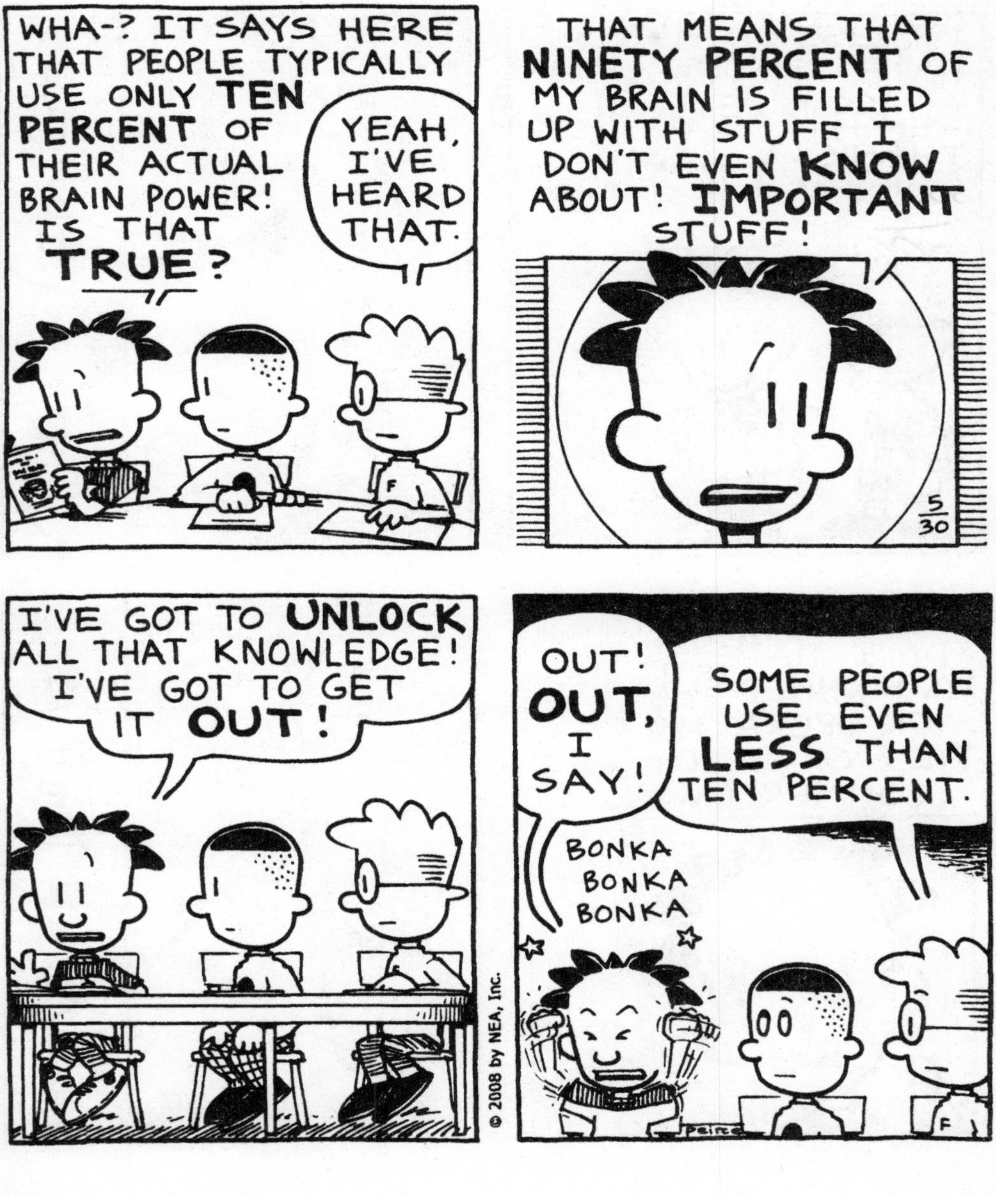

WHA-? IT SAYS HERE THAT PEOPLE TYPICALLY USE ONLY **TEN PERCENT** OF THEIR ACTUAL BRAIN POWER! IS THAT **TRUE**?
YEAH, I'VE HEARD THAT.
THAT MEANS THAT **NINETY PERCENT** OF MY BRAIN IS FILLED UP WITH STUFF I DON'T EVEN **KNOW** ABOUT! **IMPORTANT** STUFF!
5/30
I'VE GOT TO **UNLOCK** ALL THAT KNOWLEDGE! I'VE GOT TO GET IT **OUT**!
© 2008 by NEA, Inc.
OUT! **OUT**, I SAY!
SOME PEOPLE USE EVEN **LESS** THAN TEN PERCENT.
BONKA BONKA BONKA

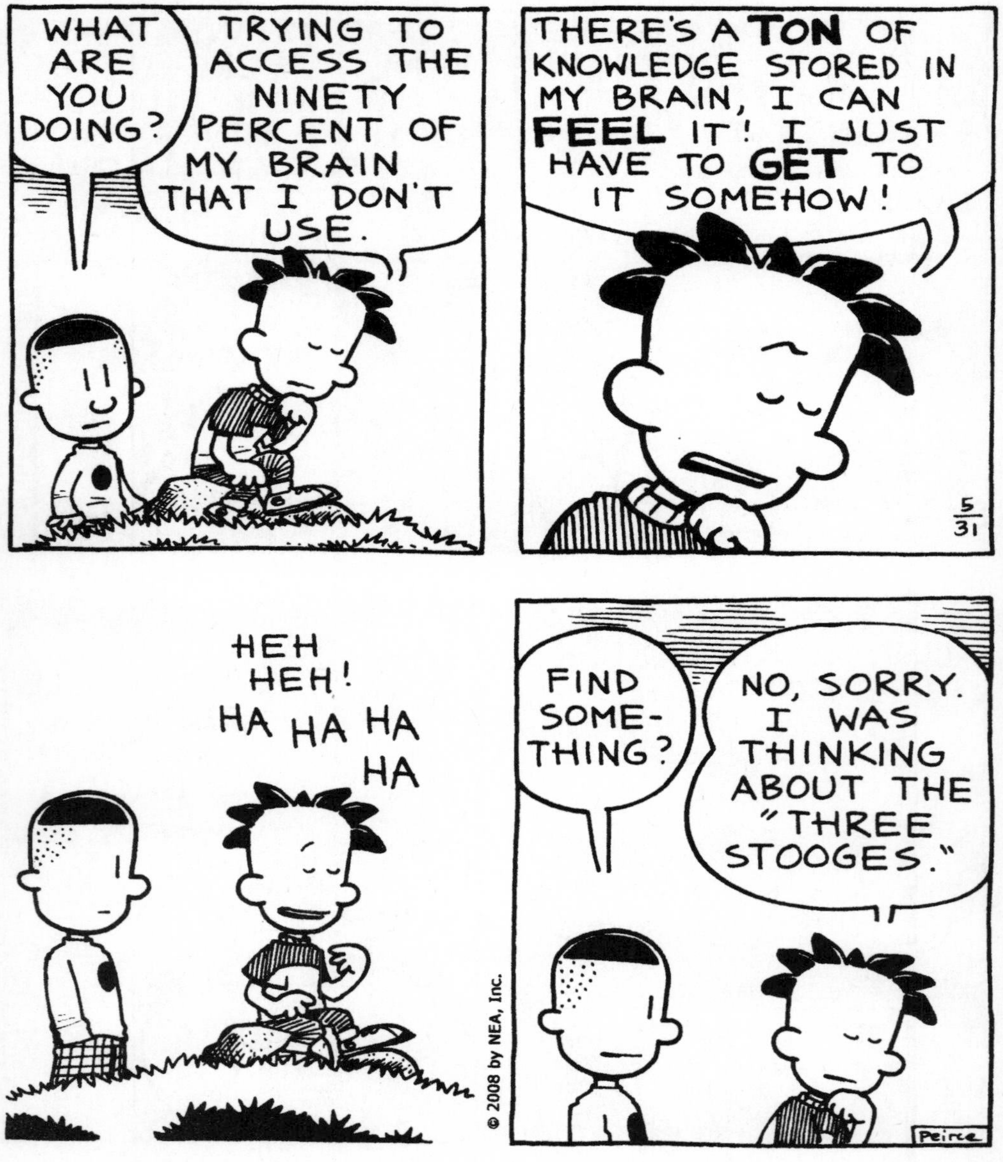
WHAT ARE YOU DOING?
TRYING TO ACCESS THE NINETY PERCENT OF MY BRAIN THAT I DON'T USE.
THERE'S A TON OF KNOWLEDGE STORED IN MY BRAIN, I CAN FEEL IT! I JUST HAVE TO GET TO IT SOMEHOW!
5/31
HEH HEH!
HA HA HA HA
FIND SOME-THING?
NO, SORRY. I WAS THINKING ABOUT THE "THREE STOOGES."
© 2008 by NEA, Inc.
Peirce

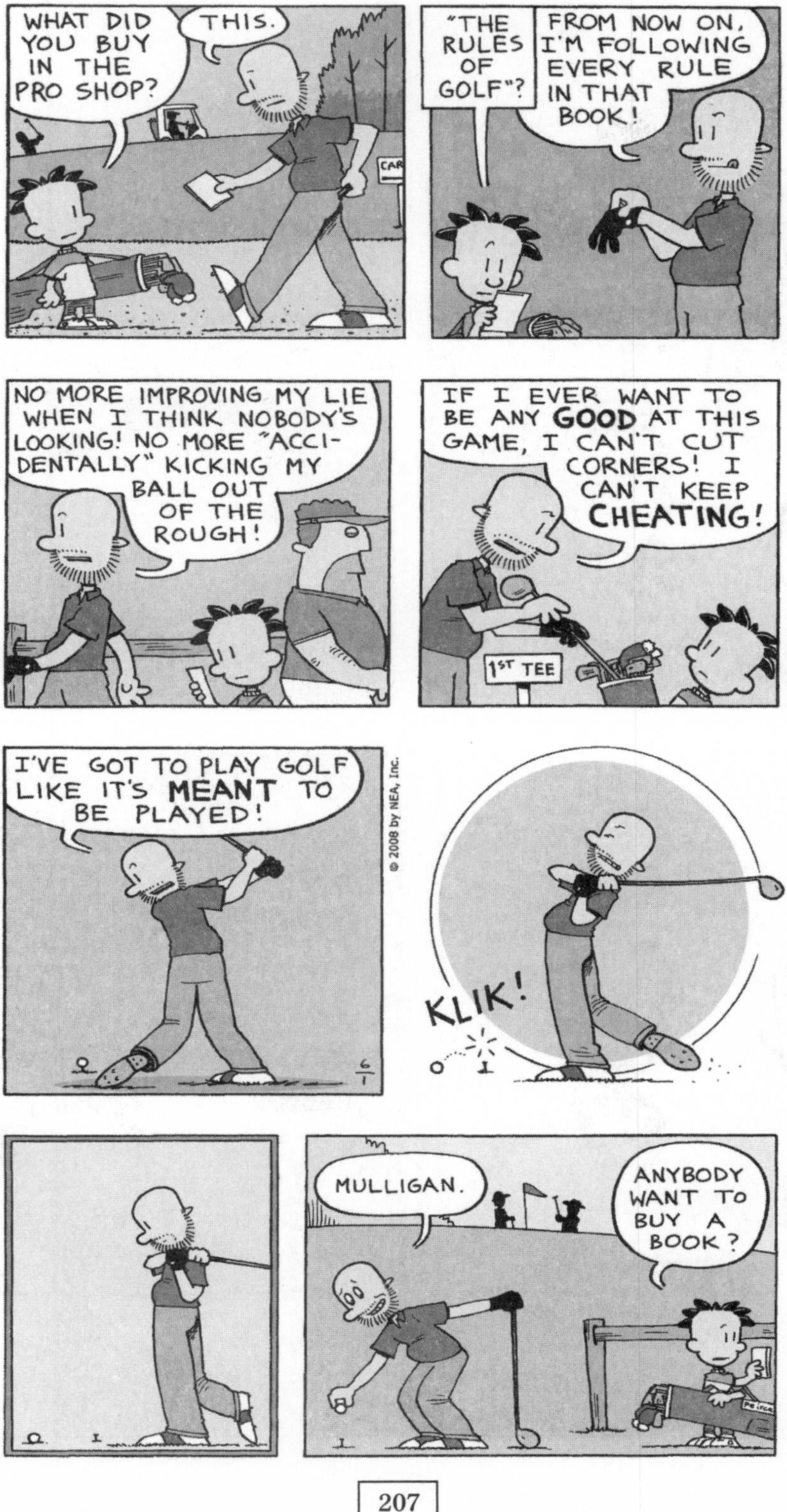
WHAT DID YOU BUY IN THE PRO SHOP?
THIS.
CAR
"THE RULES OF GOLF"?
FROM NOW ON, I'M FOLLOWING EVERY RULE IN THAT BOOK!
NO MORE IMPROVING MY LIE WHEN I THINK NOBODY'S LOOKING! NO MORE "ACCIDENTALLY" KICKING MY BALL OUT OF THE ROUGH!
IF I EVER WANT TO BE ANY GOOD AT THIS GAME, I CAN'T CUT CORNERS! I CAN'T KEEP CHEATING!
1ST TEE
I'VE GOT TO PLAY GOLF LIKE IT'S MEANT TO BE PLAYED!
© 2008 by NEA, Inc.
6/1
KLIK!
MULLIGAN.
ANYBODY WANT TO BUY A BOOK?

ROCKIN' OUT

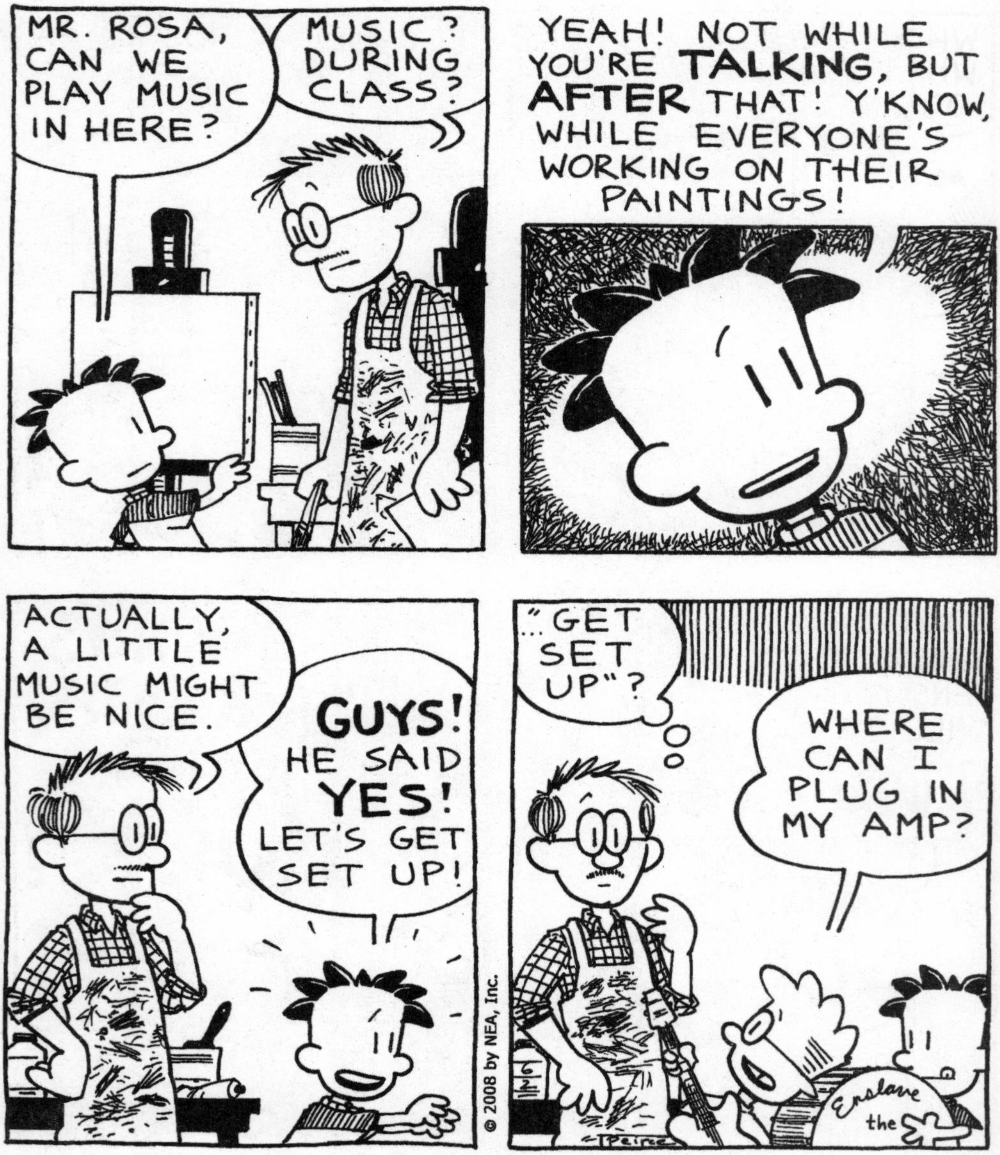
MR. ROSA, CAN WE PLAY MUSIC IN HERE?
MUSIC? DURING CLASS?
YEAH! NOT WHILE YOU'RE **TALKING**, BUT **AFTER** THAT! Y'KNOW, WHILE EVERYONE'S WORKING ON THEIR PAINTINGS!
ACTUALLY, A LITTLE MUSIC MIGHT BE NICE.
GUYS! HE SAID **YES!** LET'S GET SET UP!
..."GET SET UP"?
WHERE CAN I PLUG IN MY AMP?
© 2008 by NEA, Inc.
Enslave the

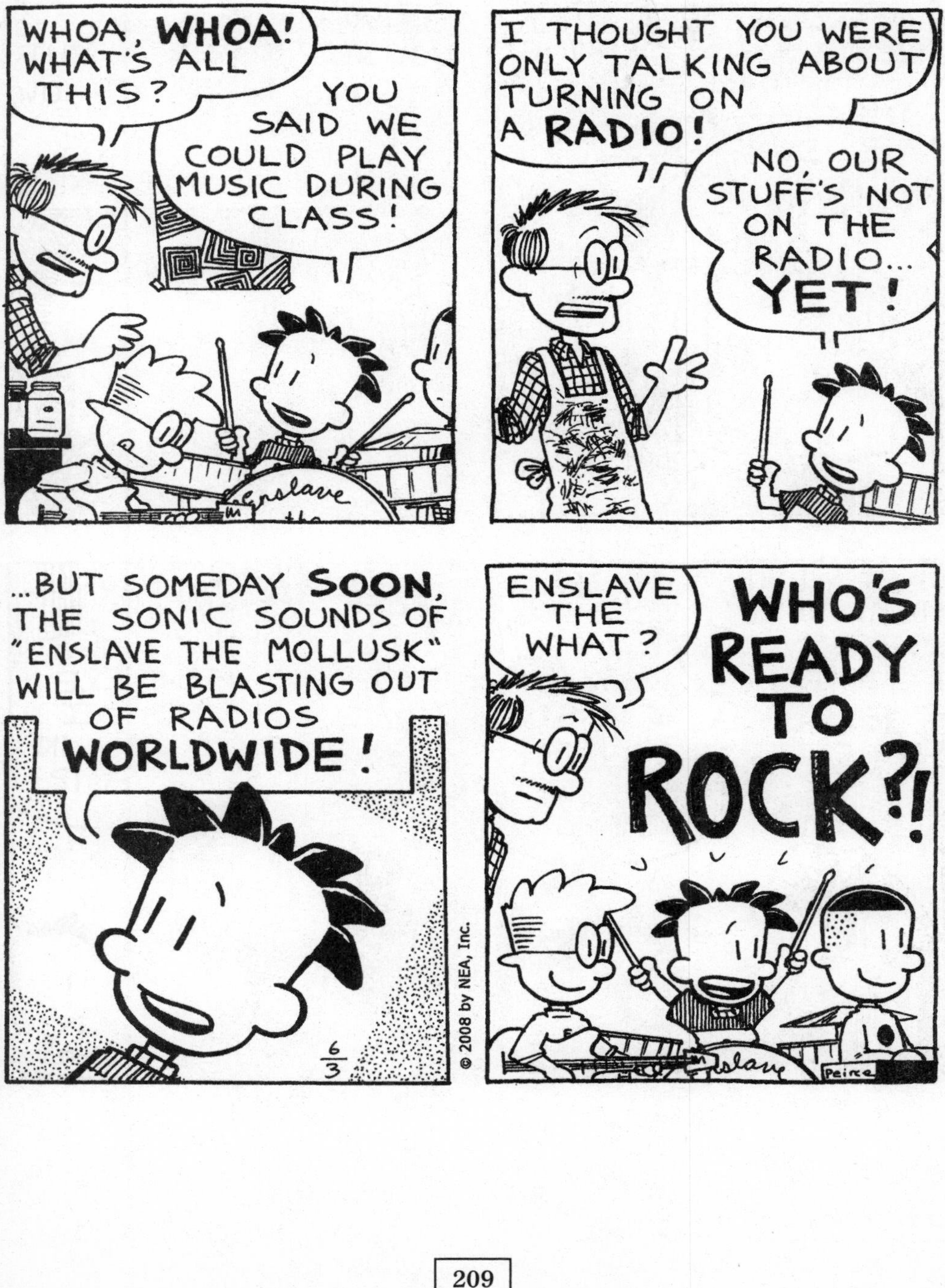
WHOA, WHOA! WHAT'S ALL THIS?
YOU SAID WE COULD PLAY MUSIC DURING CLASS!
Enslave
I THOUGHT YOU WERE ONLY TALKING ABOUT TURNING ON A RADIO!
NO, OUR STUFF'S NOT ON THE RADIO... YET!
...BUT SOMEDAY SOON, THE SONIC SOUNDS OF "ENSLAVE THE MOLLUSK" WILL BE BLASTING OUT OF RADIOS WORLDWIDE!
6/3
ENSLAVE THE WHAT?
WHO'S READY TO ROCK?!
Peirce

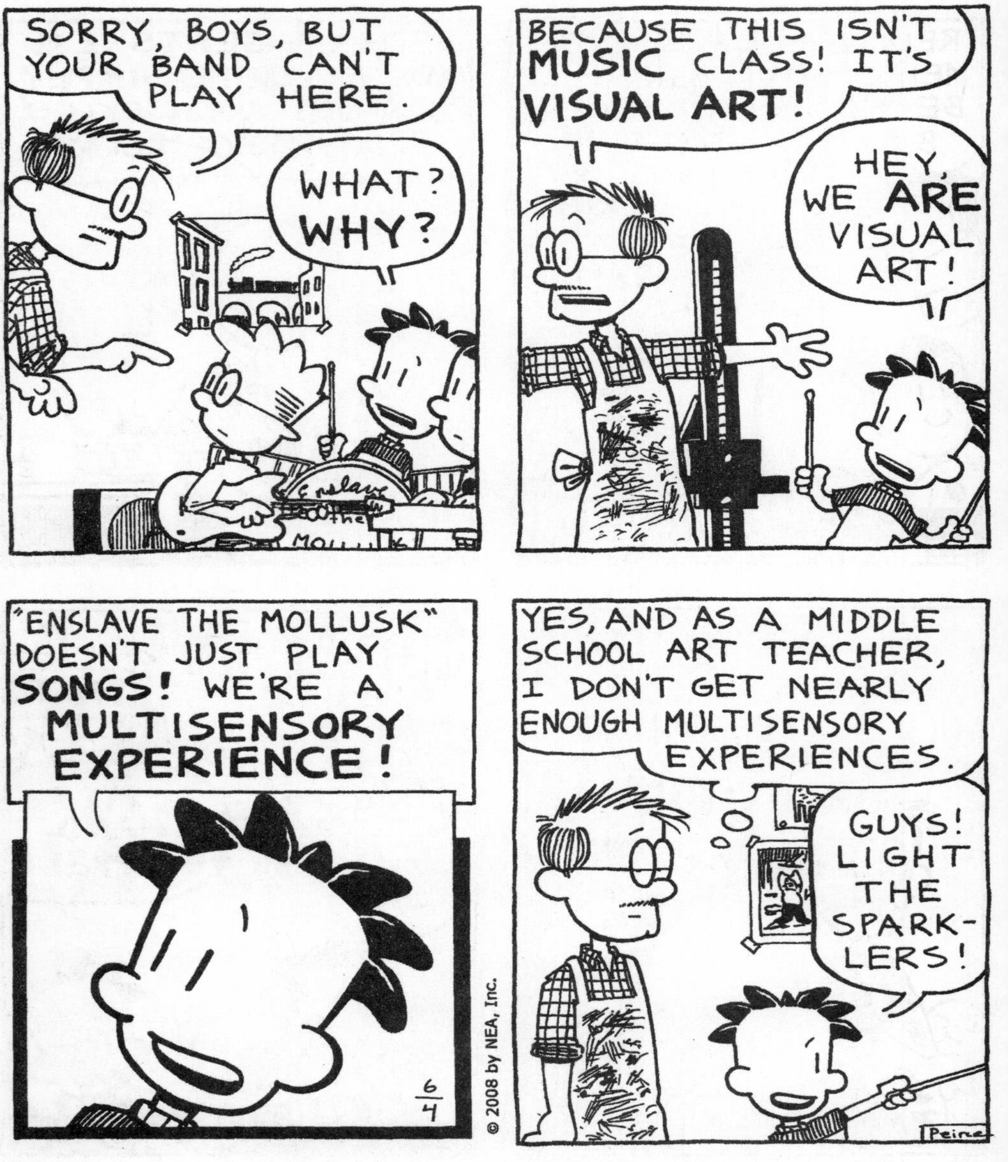
SORRY, BOYS, BUT YOUR BAND CAN'T PLAY HERE.
WHAT? WHY?
BECAUSE THIS ISN'T MUSIC CLASS! IT'S VISUAL ART!
HEY, WE ARE VISUAL ART!
"ENSLAVE THE MOLLUSK" DOESN'T JUST PLAY SONGS! WE'RE A MULTISENSORY EXPERIENCE!
6/4
YES, AND AS A MIDDLE SCHOOL ART TEACHER, I DON'T GET NEARLY ENOUGH MULTISENSORY EXPERIENCES.
GUYS! LIGHT THE SPARKLERS!
Peirce

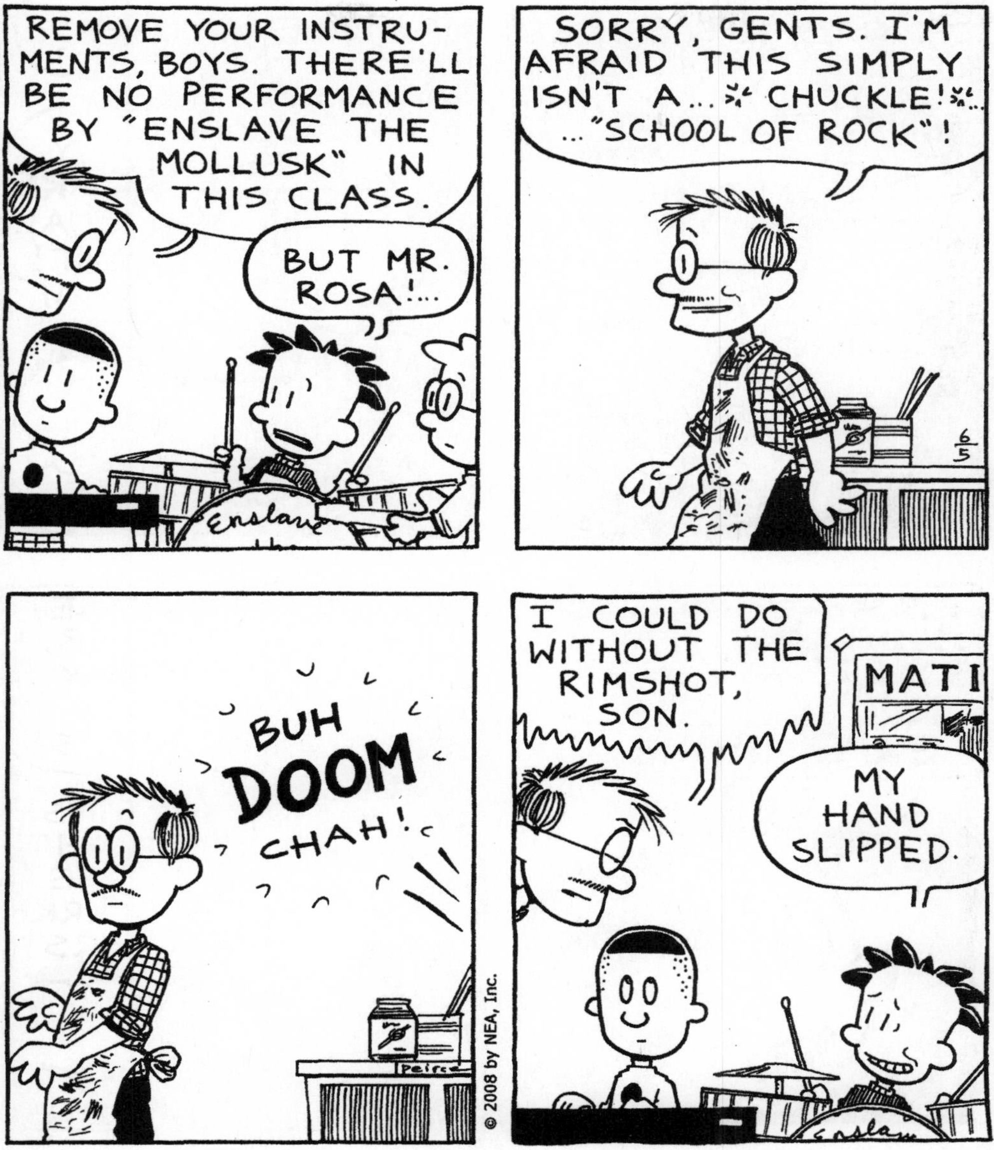
REMOVE YOUR INSTRUMENTS, BOYS. THERE'LL BE NO PERFORMANCE BY "ENSLAVE THE MOLLUSK" IN THIS CLASS.
BUT MR. ROSA!...
Enslave
SORRY, GENTS. I'M AFRAID THIS SIMPLY ISN'T A... CHUCKLE! ...."SCHOOL OF ROCK"!
6/5
BUH DOOM CHAH!
I COULD DO WITHOUT THE RIMSHOT, SON.
MATI
MY HAND SLIPPED.

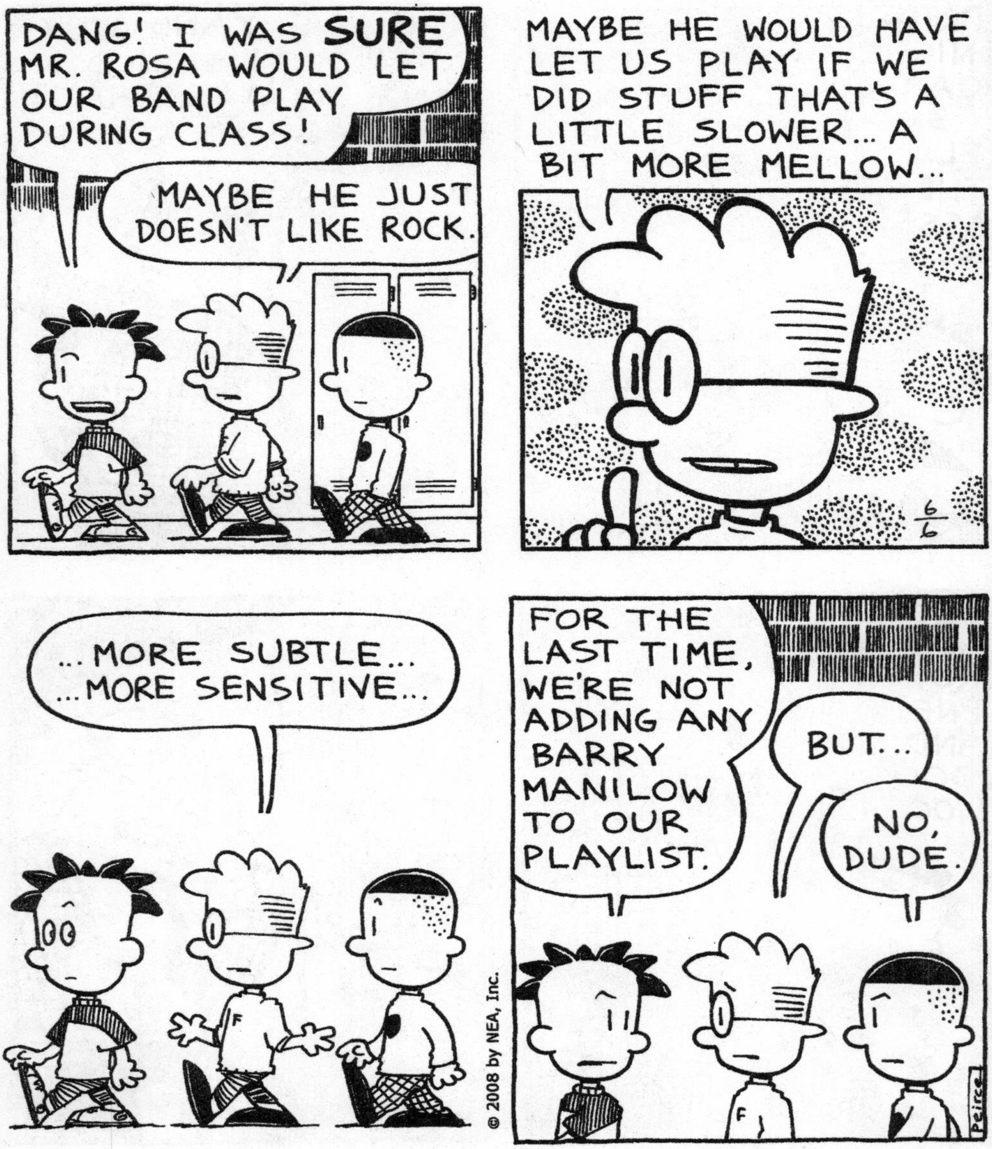
DANG! I WAS **SURE** MR. ROSA WOULD LET OUR BAND PLAY DURING CLASS!
MAYBE HE JUST DOESN'T LIKE ROCK.
MAYBE HE WOULD HAVE LET US PLAY IF WE DID STUFF THAT'S A LITTLE SLOWER... A BIT MORE MELLOW...
6/6
...MORE SUBTLE... ...MORE SENSITIVE...
© 2008 by NEA, Inc.
FOR THE LAST TIME, WE'RE NOT ADDING ANY BARRY MANILOW TO OUR PLAYLIST.
BUT...
NO, DUDE.
Peirce

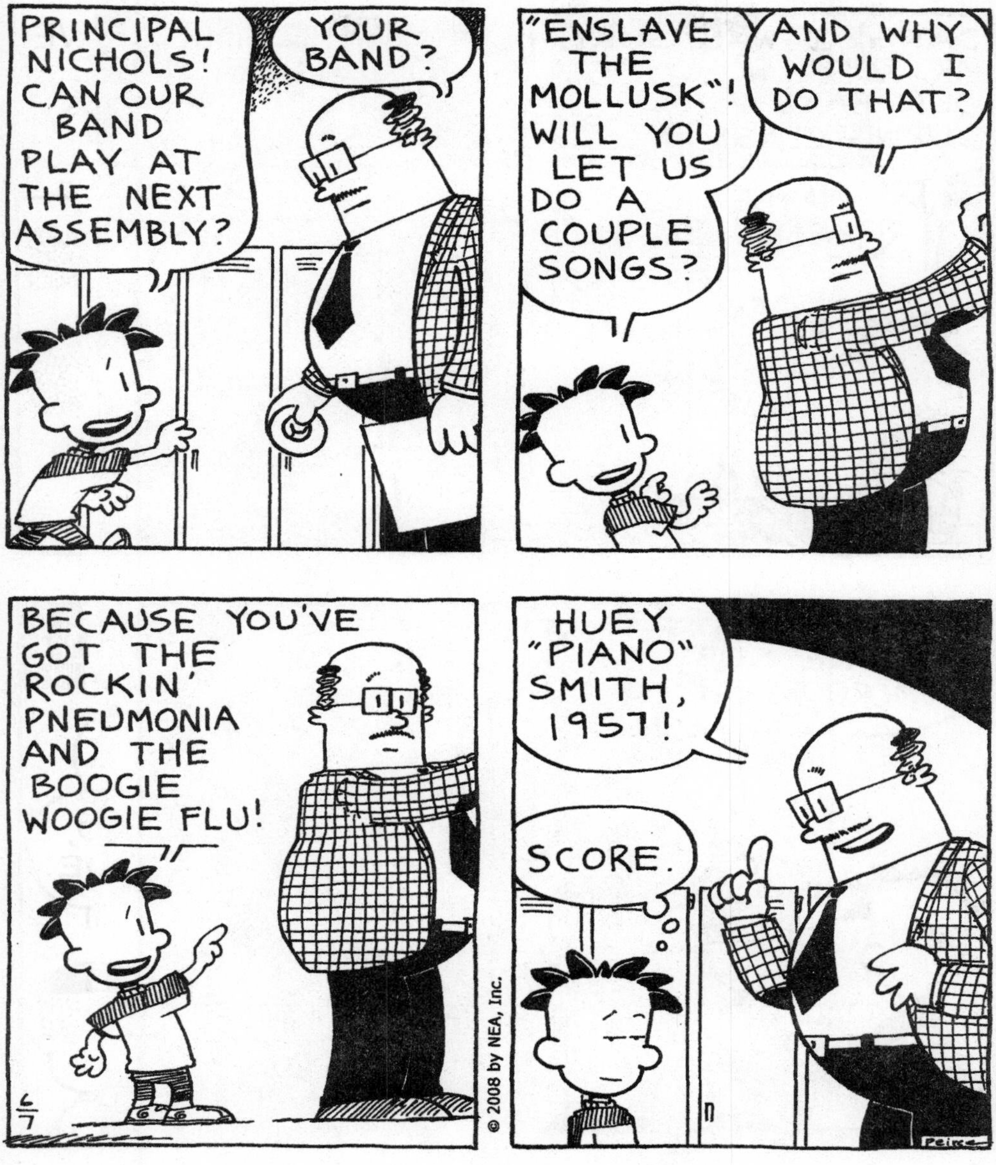
PRINCIPAL NICHOLS! CAN OUR BAND PLAY AT THE NEXT ASSEMBLY?
YOUR BAND?
"ENSLAVE THE MOLLUSK"! WILL YOU LET US DO A COUPLE SONGS?
AND WHY WOULD I DO THAT?
BECAUSE YOU'VE GOT THE ROCKIN' PNEUMONIA AND THE BOOGIE WOOGIE FLU!
6/7
© 2008 by NEA, Inc.
HUEY "PIANO" SMITH, 1957!
SCORE.
Peirce

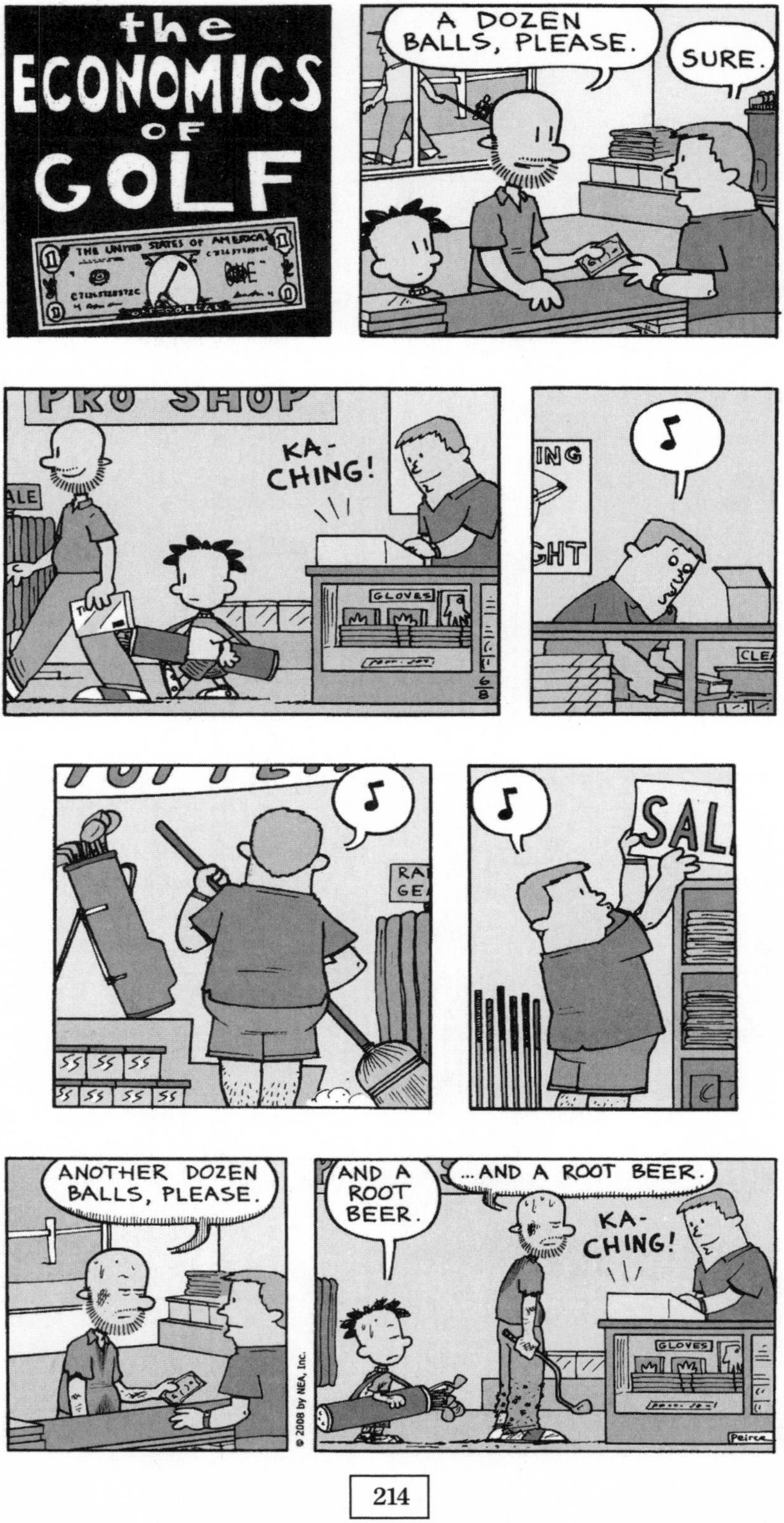
the ECONOMICS OF GOLF
THE UNITED STATES OF AMERICA
A DOZEN BALLS, PLEASE.
SURE.
PRO SHOP
KA-CHING!
GLOVES
ANOTHER DOZEN BALLS, PLEASE.
AND A ROOT BEER.
...AND A ROOT BEER.
KA-CHING!
GLOVES
© 2008 by NEA, Inc.
Peirce

Lincoln Peirce

BiG NATE

HERE GOES NOTHING

THE SHOW MUST GO ON

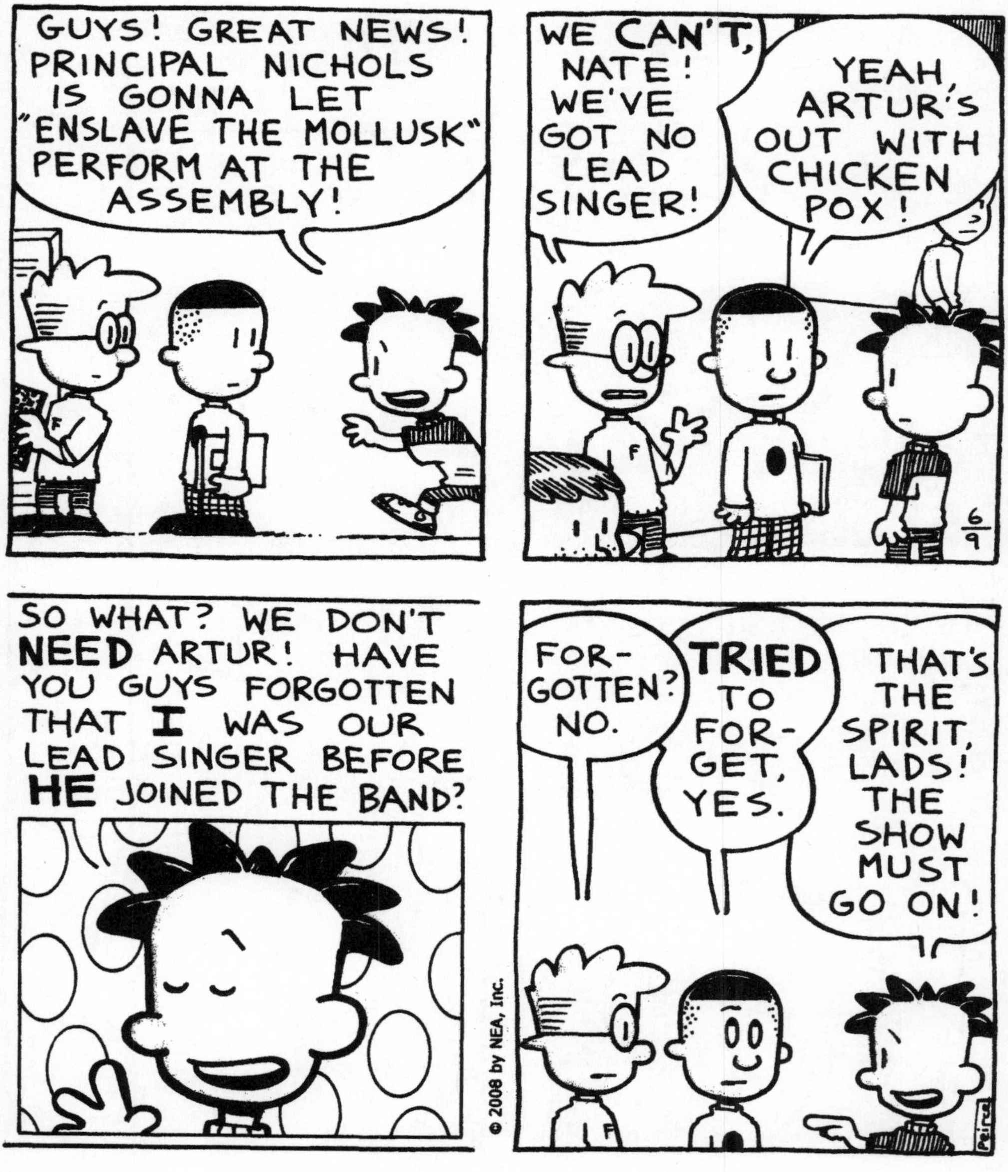
GUYS! GREAT NEWS! PRINCIPAL NICHOLS IS GONNA LET "ENSLAVE THE MOLLUSK" PERFORM AT THE ASSEMBLY!
WE **CAN'T**, NATE! WE'VE GOT NO LEAD SINGER!
YEAH, ARTUR'S OUT WITH CHICKEN POX!
6/9
SO WHAT? WE DON'T **NEED** ARTUR! HAVE YOU GUYS FORGOTTEN THAT **I** WAS OUR LEAD SINGER BEFORE **HE** JOINED THE BAND?
FORGOTTEN? NO.
TRIED TO FORGET, YES.
THAT'S THE SPIRIT, LADS! THE SHOW MUST GO ON!
© 2008 by NEA, Inc.
Peirce

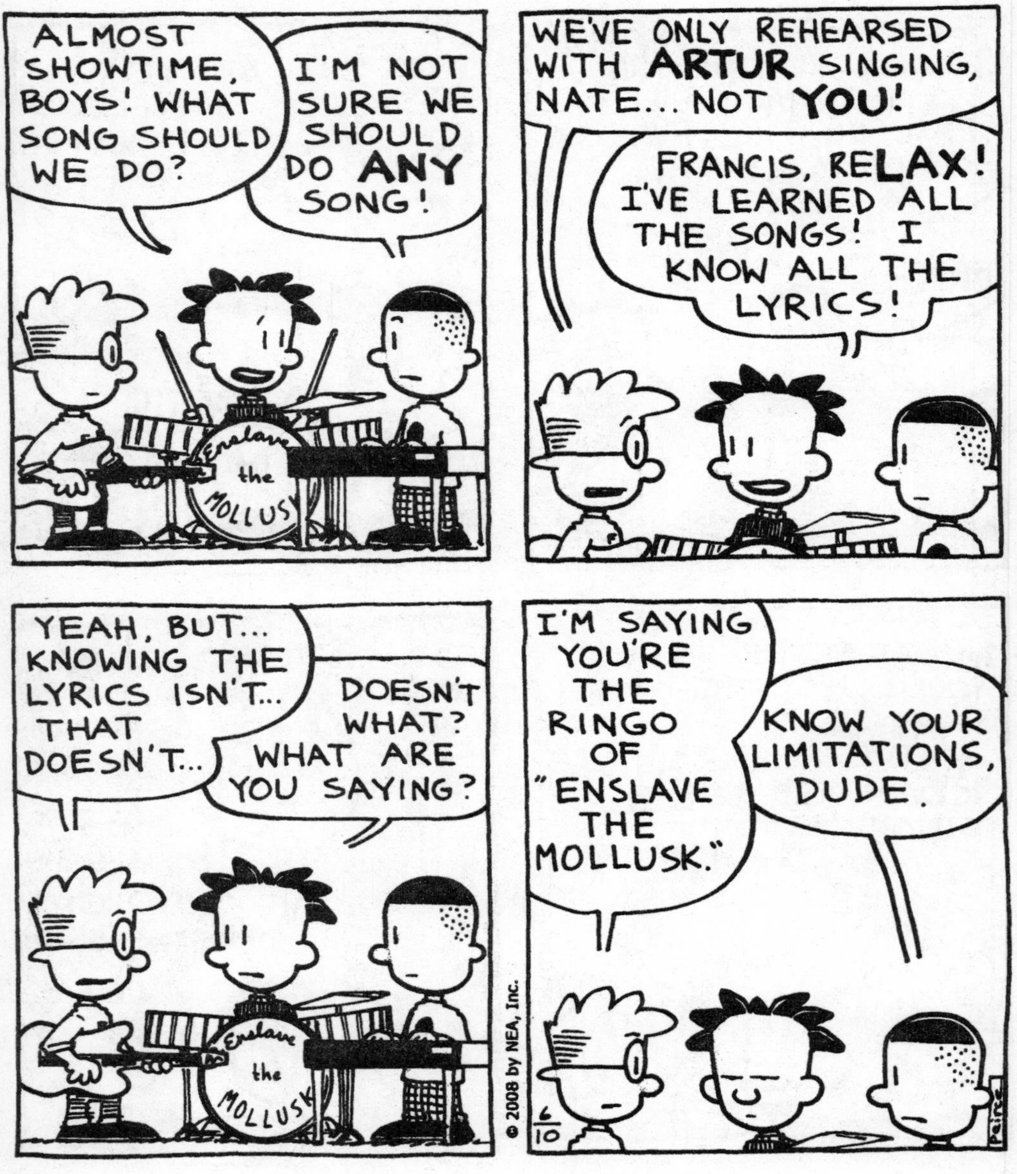
ALMOST SHOWTIME, BOYS! WHAT SONG SHOULD WE DO?
I'M NOT SURE WE SHOULD DO ANY SONG!
Enslave the MOLLUSK
WE'VE ONLY REHEARSED WITH ARTUR SINGING, NATE... NOT YOU!
FRANCIS, RELAX! I'VE LEARNED ALL THE SONGS! I KNOW ALL THE LYRICS!
YEAH, BUT... KNOWING THE LYRICS ISN'T... THAT DOESN'T...
DOESN'T WHAT? WHAT ARE YOU SAYING?
Enslave the MOLLUSK
I'M SAYING YOU'RE THE RINGO OF "ENSLAVE THE MOLLUSK."
KNOW YOUR LIMITATIONS, DUDE.
© 2008 by NEA, Inc.
6/10
Peirce

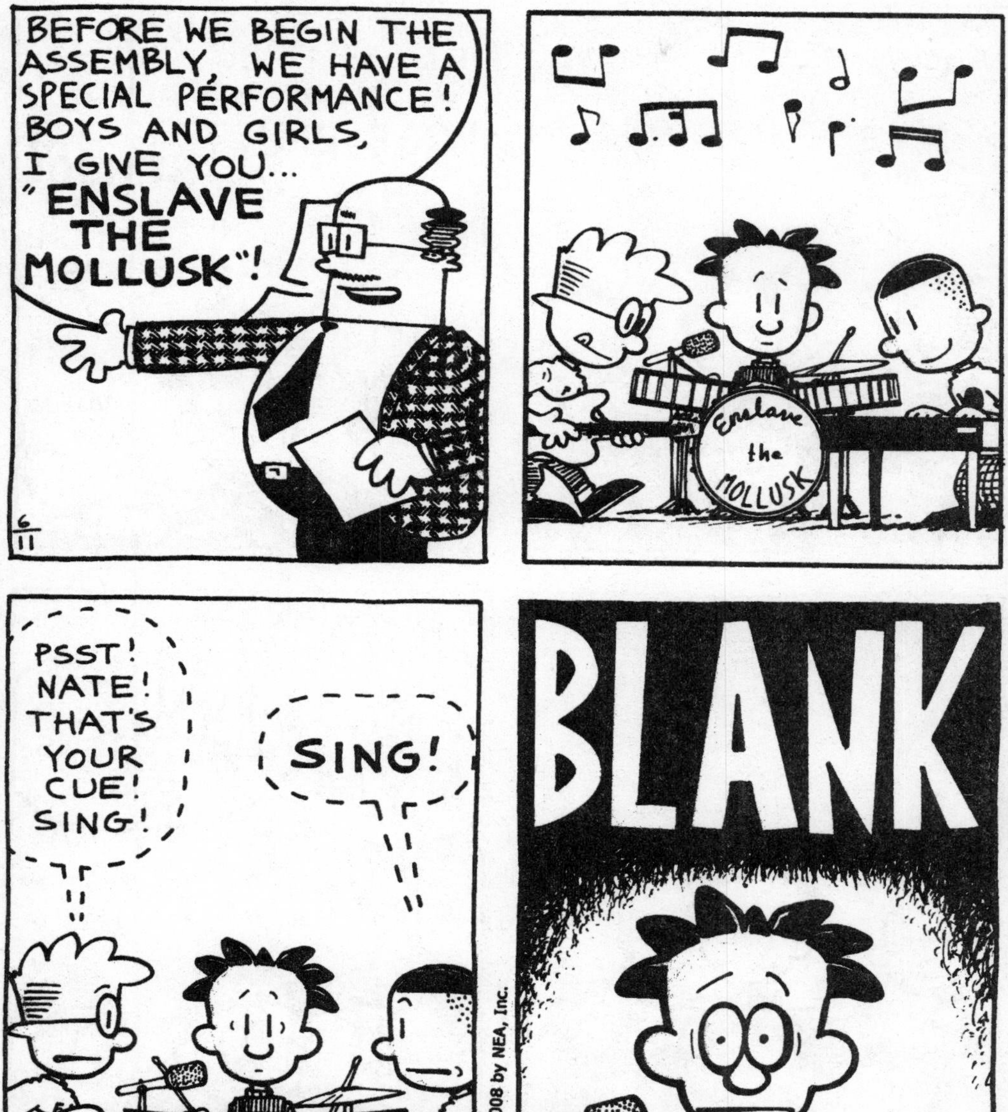
BEFORE WE BEGIN THE ASSEMBLY, WE HAVE A SPECIAL PERFORMANCE! BOYS AND GIRLS, I GIVE YOU... "ENSLAVE THE MOLLUSK"!
Enslave the MOLLUSK
PSST! NATE! THAT'S YOUR CUE! SING!
SING!
BLANK
© 2008 by NEA, Inc.
peirce

GO AHEAD, NATE! SING!
SING!
WHAT IS YOUR PROBLEM?
NATE, THE WHOLE SCHOOL IS WATCHING!
Enslave the MOLLUSK
WE'VE FINALLY FIGURED OUT HOW TO SHUT HIM UP.
LOOKS LIKE "HEART OF GOLD" IS NOW AN INSTRUMENTAL.
6/12

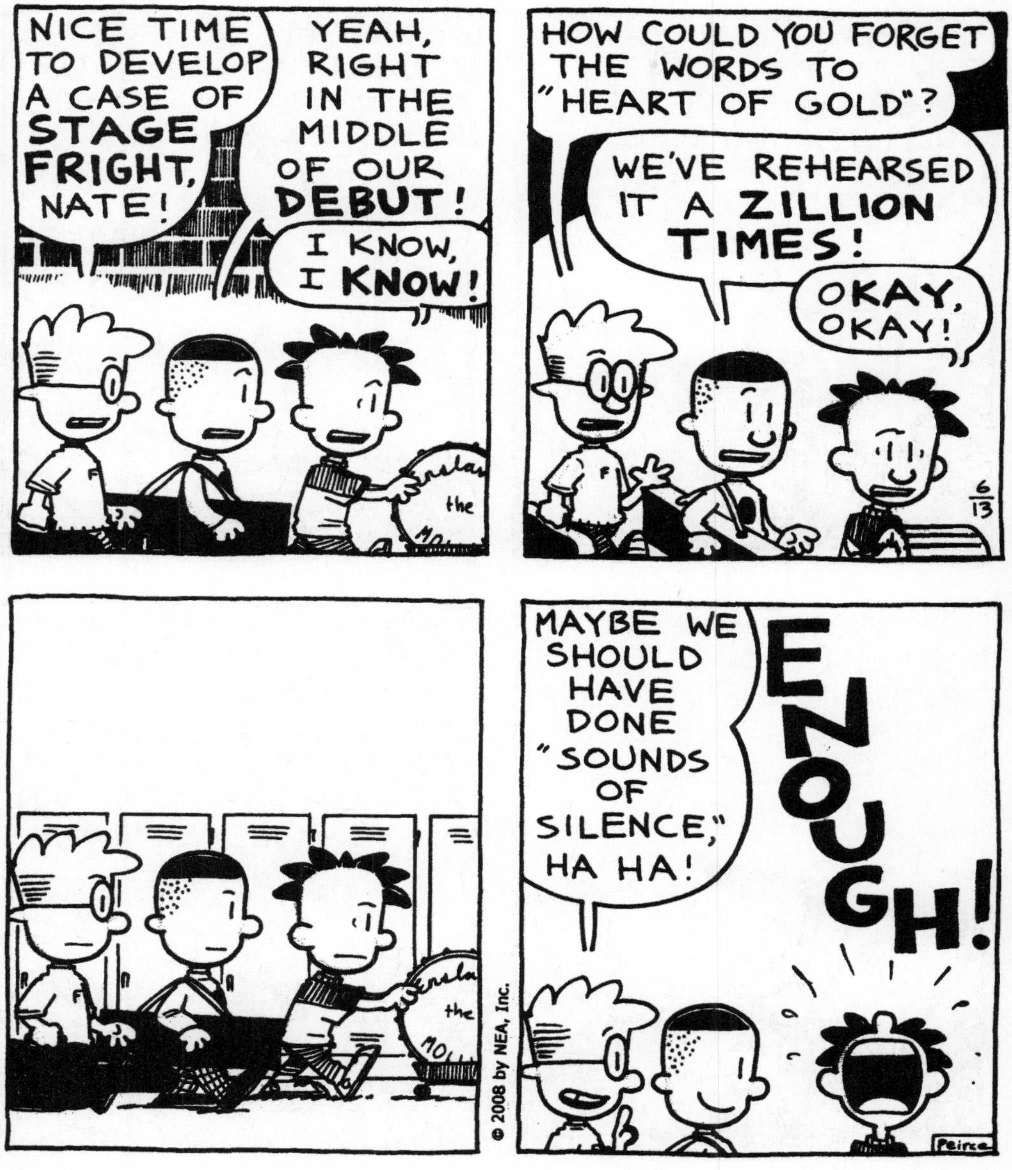
NICE TIME TO DEVELOP A CASE OF **STAGE FRIGHT**, NATE!
YEAH, RIGHT IN THE MIDDLE OF OUR **DEBUT**!
I KNOW, I **KNOW**!
HOW COULD YOU FORGET THE WORDS TO "HEART OF GOLD"?
WE'VE REHEARSED IT A **ZILLION TIMES**!
OKAY, OKAY!
6/13
MAYBE WE SHOULD HAVE DONE "SOUNDS OF SILENCE," HA HA!
ENOUGH!
Peirce

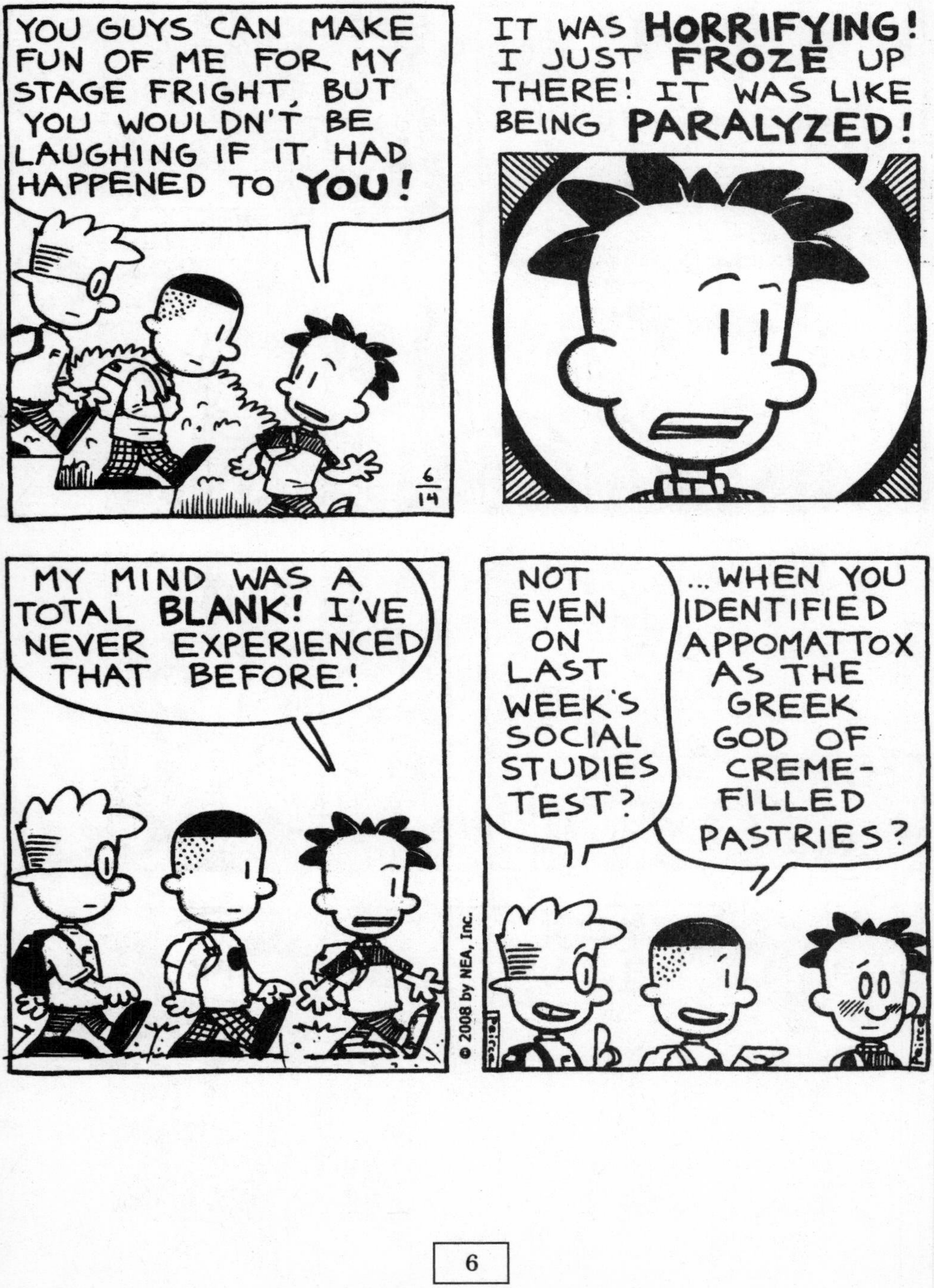
YOU GUYS CAN MAKE FUN OF ME FOR MY STAGE FRIGHT, BUT YOU WOULDN'T BE LAUGHING IF IT HAD HAPPENED TO **YOU**!
6/14
IT WAS **HORRIFYING**! I JUST **FROZE** UP THERE! IT WAS LIKE BEING **PARALYZED**!
MY MIND WAS A TOTAL **BLANK**! I'VE NEVER EXPERIENCED THAT BEFORE!
© 2008 by NEA, Inc.
NOT EVEN ON LAST WEEK'S SOCIAL STUDIES TEST?
...WHEN YOU IDENTIFIED APPOMATTOX AS THE GREEK GOD OF CREME-FILLED PASTRIES?
Peirce

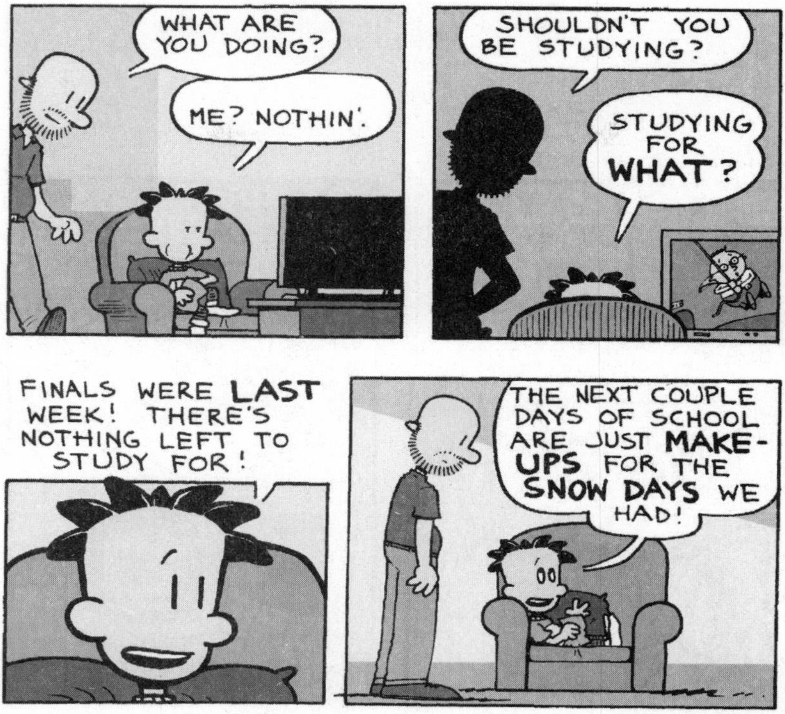

WHAT ARE YOU DOING?
ME? NOTHIN'.
SHOULDN'T YOU BE STUDYING?
STUDYING FOR **WHAT**?
FINALS WERE **LAST** WEEK! THERE'S NOTHING LEFT TO STUDY FOR!
THE NEXT COUPLE DAYS OF SCHOOL ARE JUST **MAKE-UPS** FOR THE **SNOW DAYS** WE HAD!

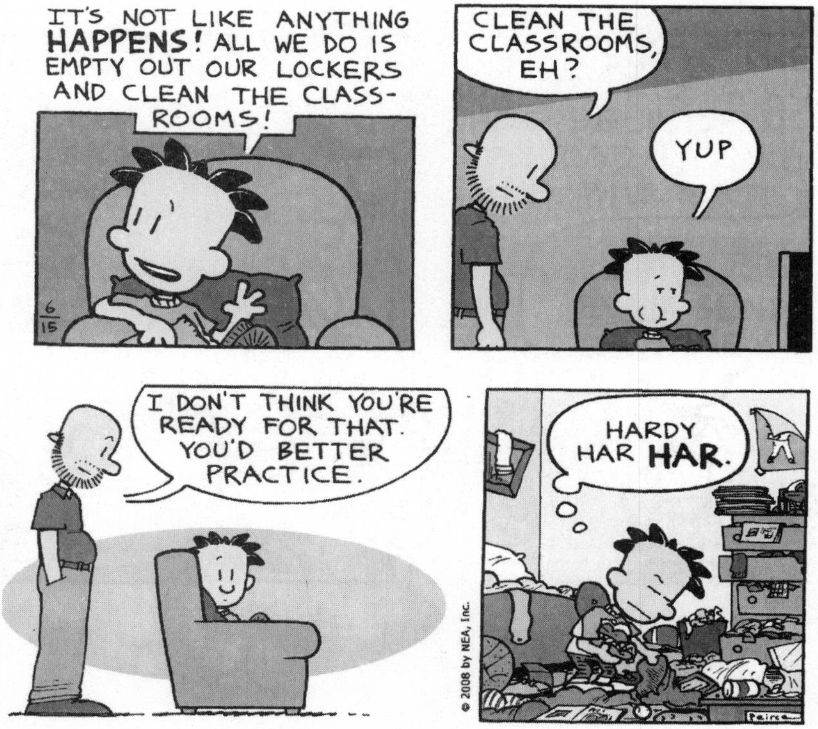

IT'S NOT LIKE ANYTHING **HAPPENS**! ALL WE DO IS EMPTY OUT OUR LOCKERS AND CLEAN THE CLASS-ROOMS!
6/15
CLEAN THE CLASSROOMS, EH?
YUP
I DON'T THINK YOU'RE READY FOR THAT. YOU'D BETTER PRACTICE.
HARDY HAR **HAR**.
© 2008 by NEA, Inc.
Peirce

PRANKED!

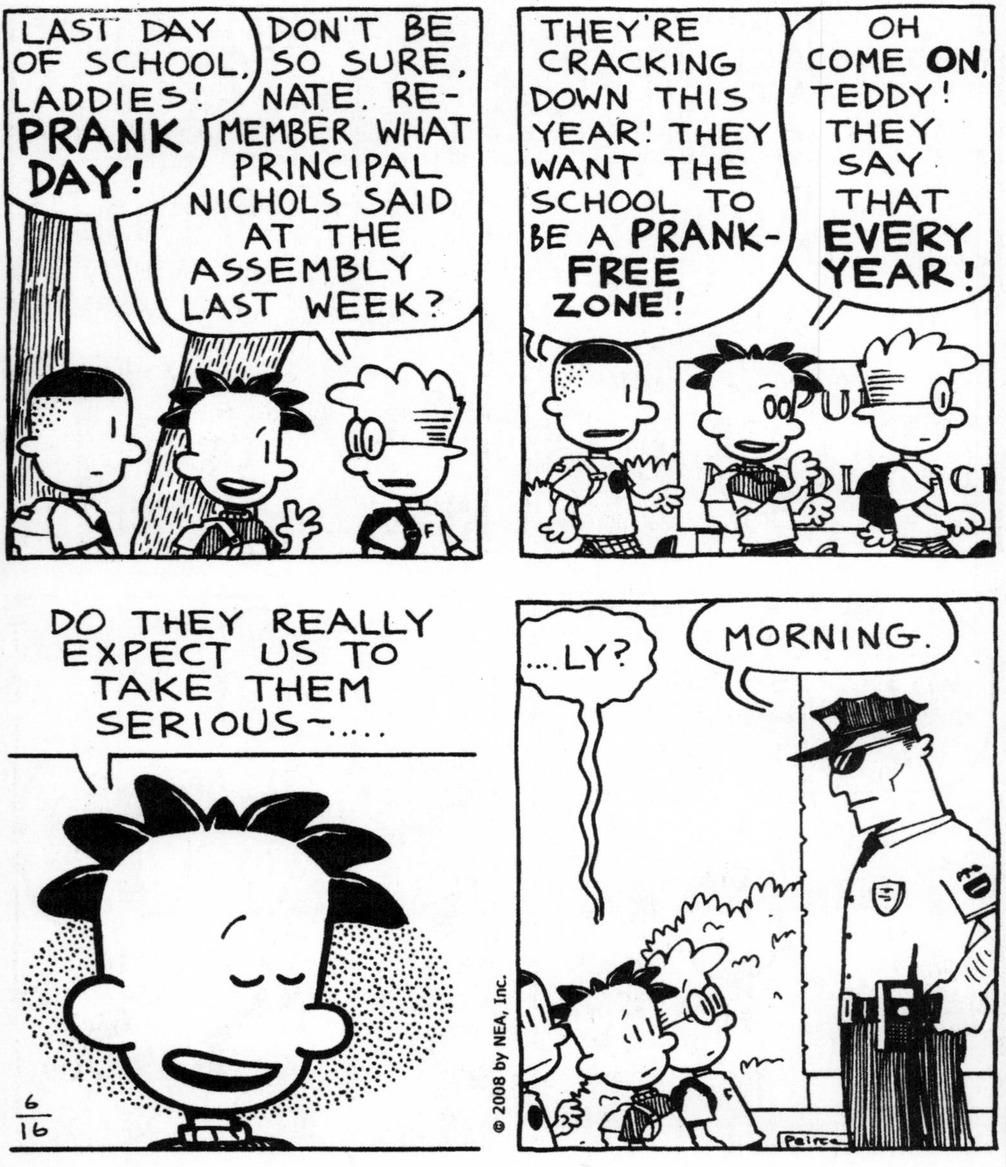

LAST DAY OF SCHOOL, LADDIES! **PRANK DAY!**
DON'T BE SO SURE, NATE. REMEMBER WHAT PRINCIPAL NICHOLS SAID AT THE ASSEMBLY LAST WEEK?
THEY'RE CRACKING DOWN THIS YEAR! THEY WANT THE SCHOOL TO BE A **PRANK-FREE ZONE!**
OH COME **ON**, TEDDY! THEY SAY THAT **EVERY YEAR!**
DO THEY REALLY EXPECT US TO TAKE THEM SERIOUS-.....
....LY?
MORNING.
6/16
© 2008 by NEA, Inc.
Peirce

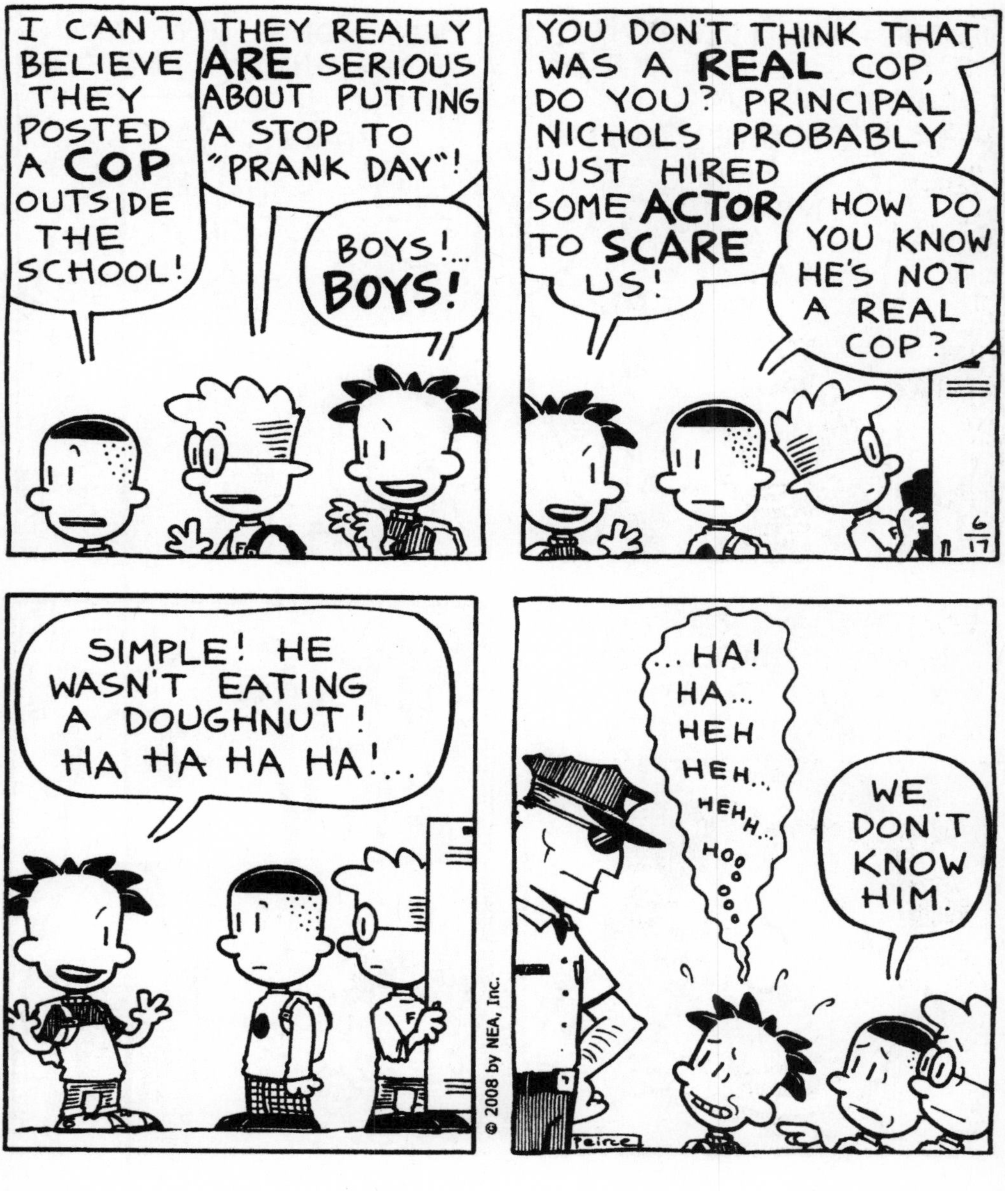
I CAN'T BELIEVE THEY POSTED A COP OUTSIDE THE SCHOOL!
THEY REALLY ARE SERIOUS ABOUT PUTTING A STOP TO "PRANK DAY"!
BOYS!... BOYS!
YOU DON'T THINK THAT WAS A REAL COP, DO YOU? PRINCIPAL NICHOLS PROBABLY JUST HIRED SOME ACTOR TO SCARE US!
HOW DO YOU KNOW HE'S NOT A REAL COP?
6/17
SIMPLE! HE WASN'T EATING A DOUGHNUT! HA HA HA HA!...
© 2008 by NEA, Inc.
...HA! HA... HEH HEH... HEHH... HOOOOOO
WE DON'T KNOW HIM.
peirce

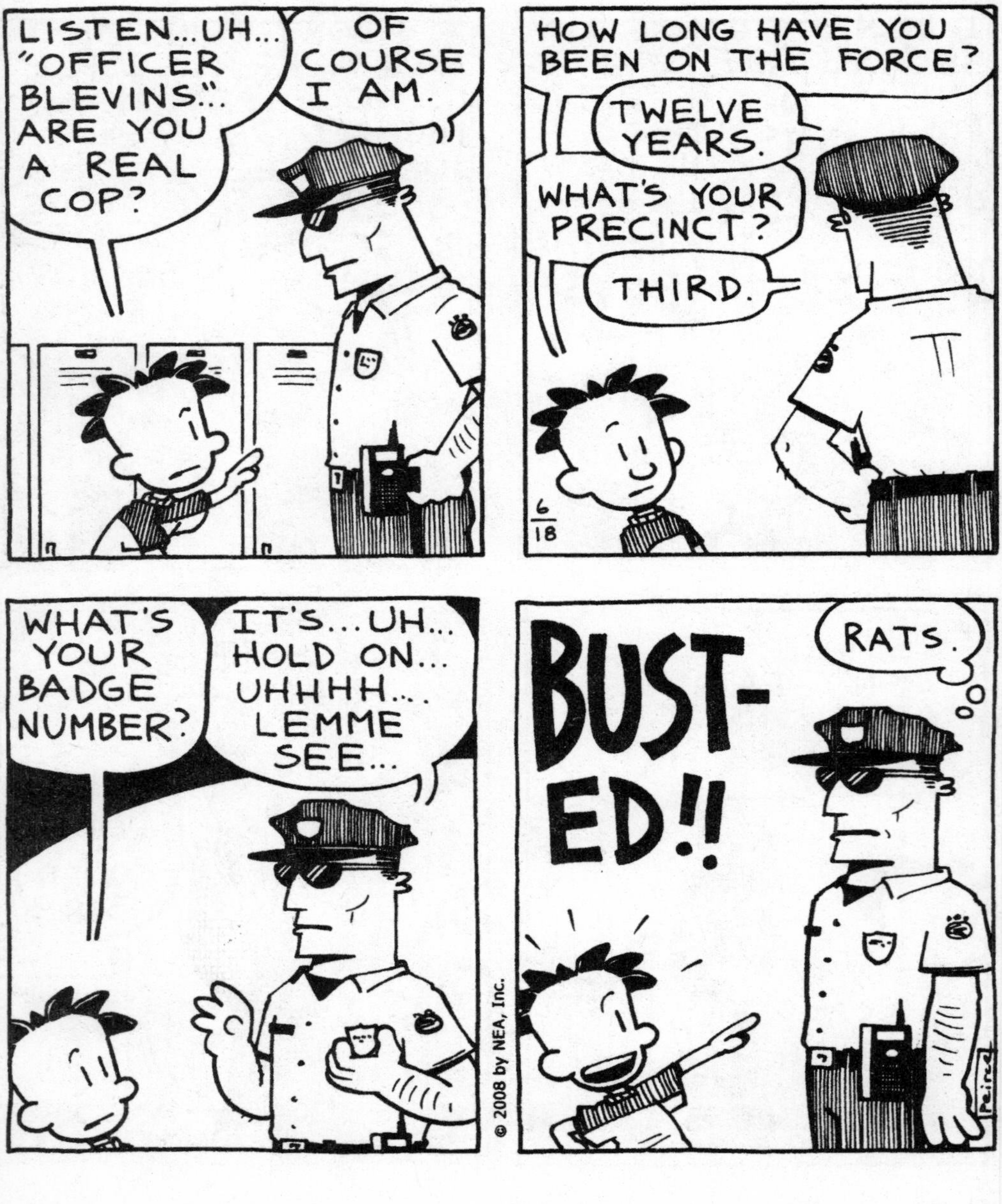
LISTEN...UH... "OFFICER BLEVINS"... ARE YOU A REAL COP?
OF COURSE I AM.
HOW LONG HAVE YOU BEEN ON THE FORCE?
TWELVE YEARS.
WHAT'S YOUR PRECINCT?
THIRD.
6/18
WHAT'S YOUR BADGE NUMBER?
IT'S...UH... HOLD ON... UHHHH.... LEMME SEE...
BUST-ED!!
RATS.
Peirce

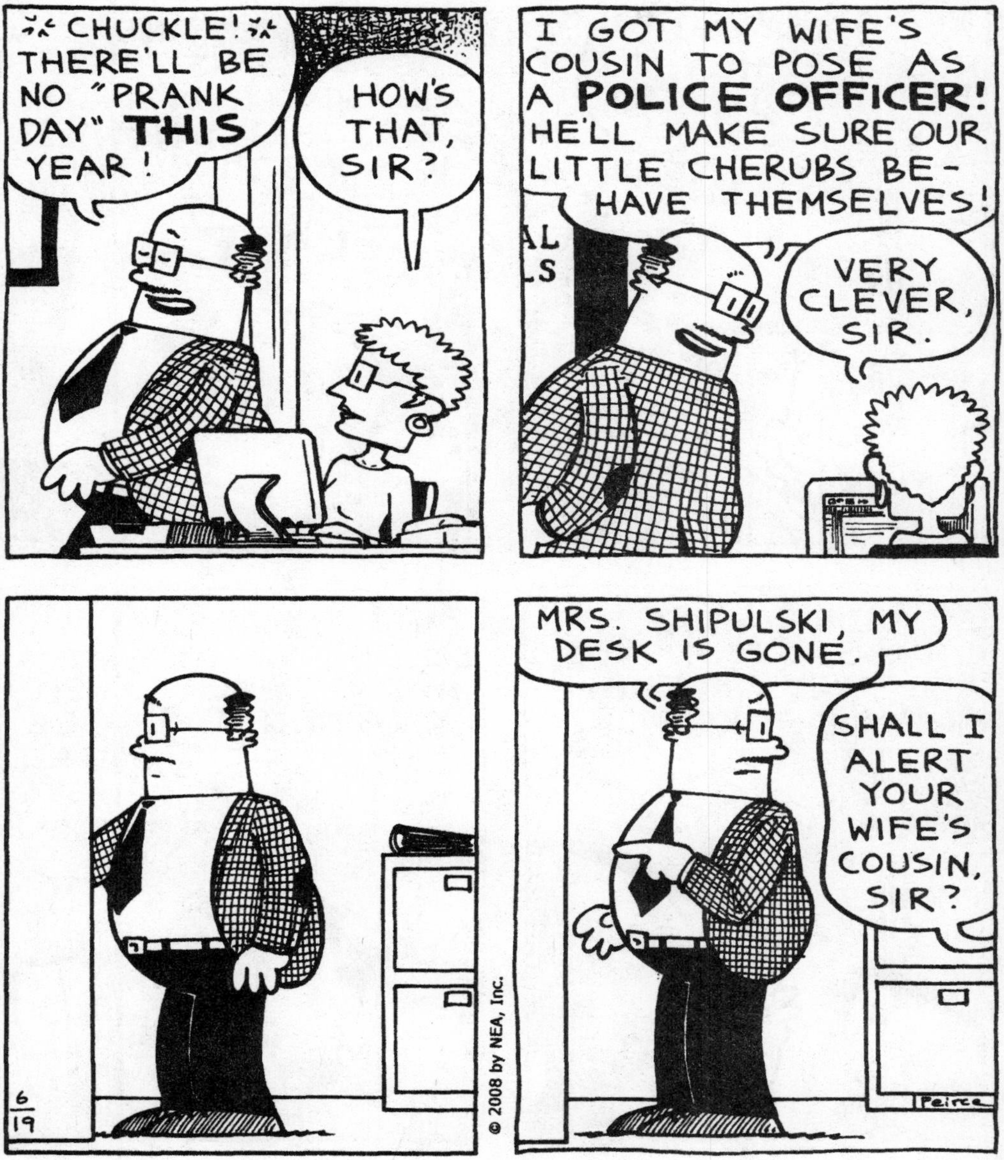

CHUCKLE! THERE'LL BE NO "PRANK DAY" **THIS** YEAR!
HOW'S THAT, SIR?
I GOT MY WIFE'S COUSIN TO POSE AS A **POLICE OFFICER!** HE'LL MAKE SURE OUR LITTLE CHERUBS BEHAVE THEMSELVES!
VERY CLEVER, SIR.
6/19
MRS. SHIPULSKI, MY DESK IS GONE.
SHALL I ALERT YOUR WIFE'S COUSIN, SIR?
Peirce

AH! PRINCIPAL NICHOLS! HEY, I JUST WANTED TO SAY: GOOD TRY!

I MEAN, POSTING A BOGUS COP OUTSIDE THE SCHOOL ON "PRANK DAY"? THAT **SHOWED** ME SOMETHING! THAT TOLD ME YOU'RE A **PLAYER!**

IT DIDN'T **WORK**, OF COURSE, BUT THAT'S ALL PART OF THE GIVE-AND-TAKE! YOU TRY TO PLAY PRANKS ON **US, WE** TRY TO PLAY PRANKS ON **YOU!**

SIR? THERE'S A LOCUST SWARM IN THE TEACHERS' LOUNGE.

WELL, I SEE YOU'RE BUSY! TOODLES!

© 2008 by NEA, Inc.

Peirce

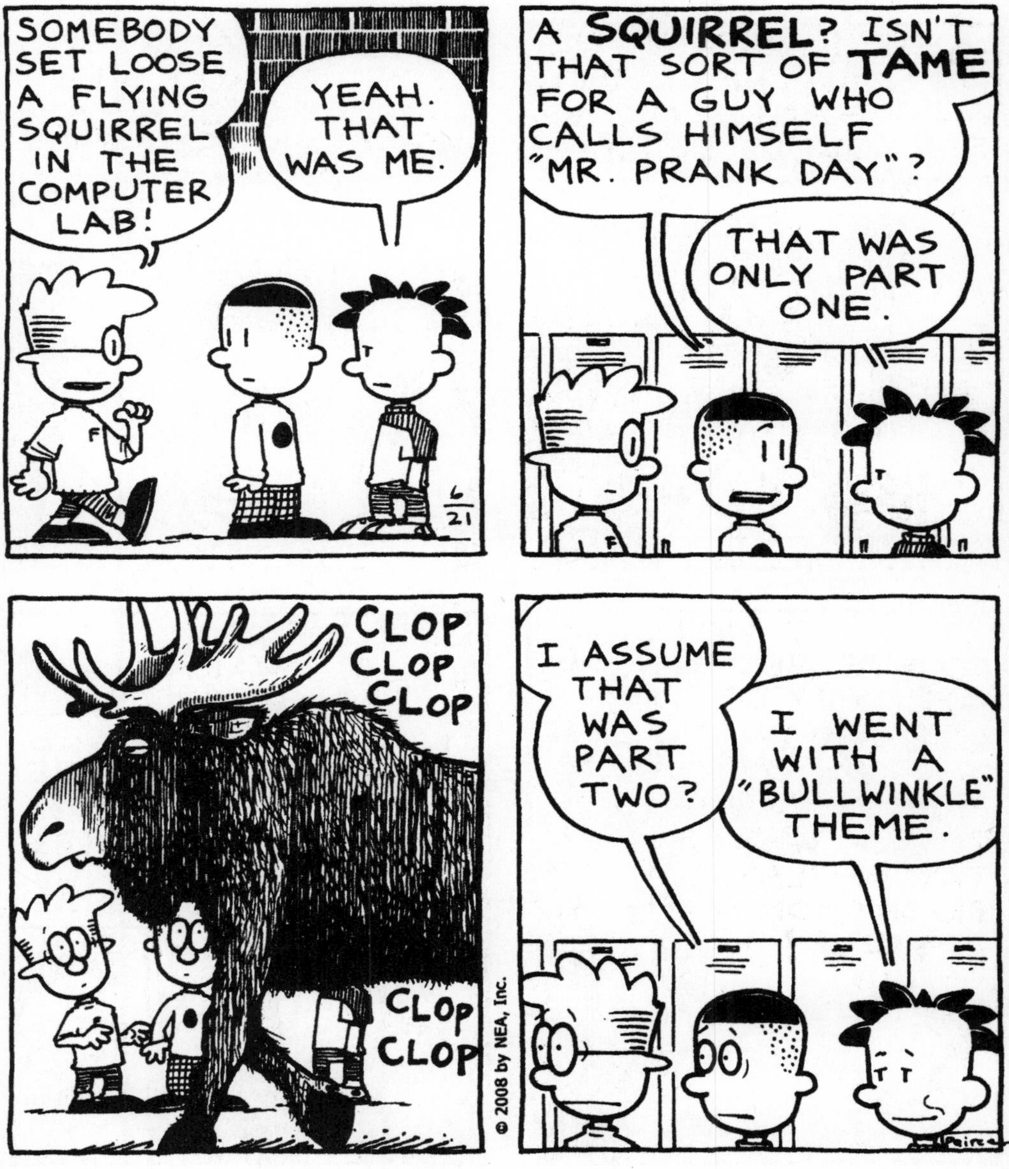
SOMEBODY SET LOOSE A FLYING SQUIRREL IN THE COMPUTER LAB!
YEAH. THAT WAS ME.
6/21
A SQUIRREL? ISN'T THAT SORT OF TAME FOR A GUY WHO CALLS HIMSELF "MR. PRANK DAY"?
THAT WAS ONLY PART ONE.
CLOP CLOP CLOP
CLOP CLOP
© 2008 by NEA, Inc.
I ASSUME THAT WAS PART TWO?
I WENT WITH A "BULLWINKLE" THEME.

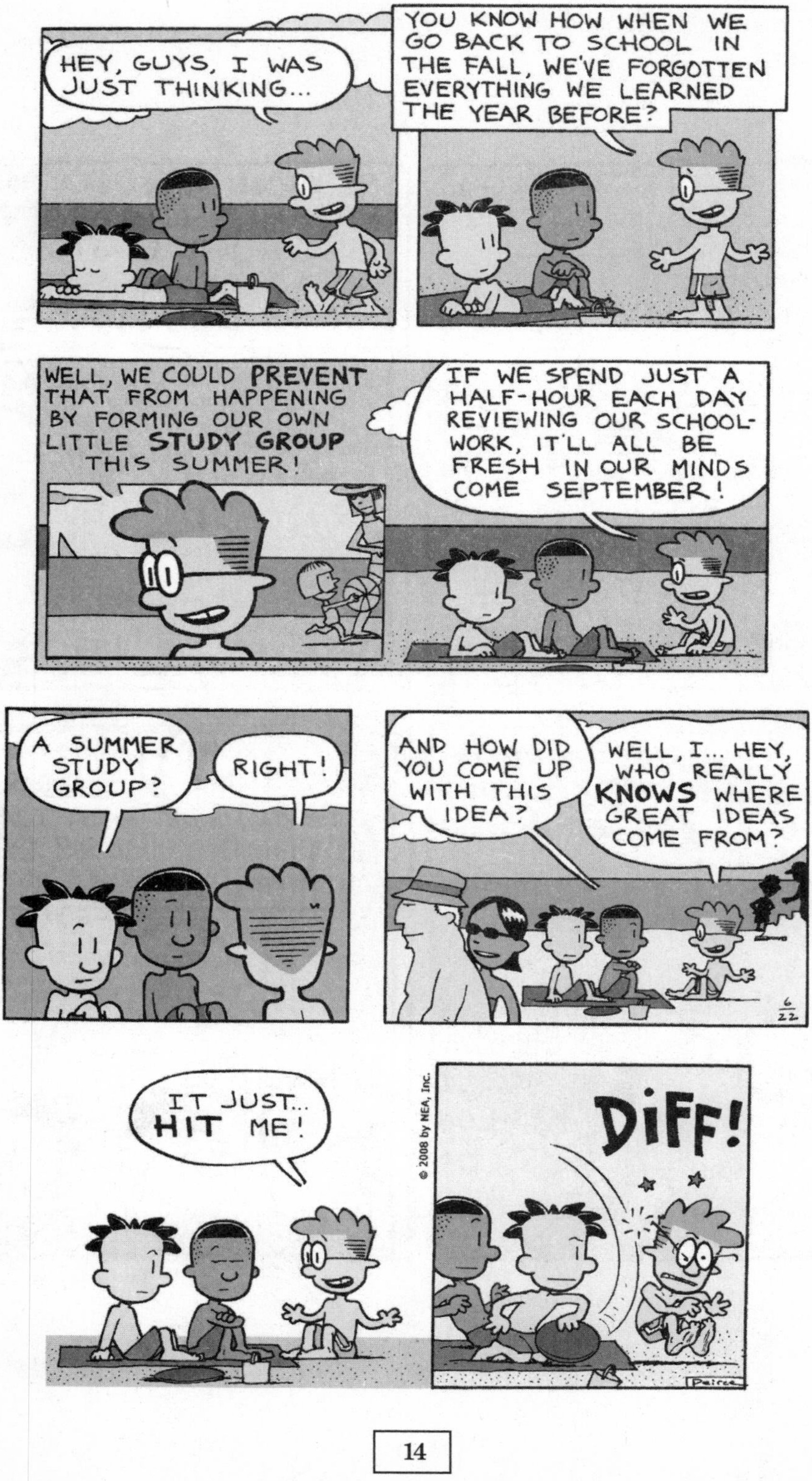
HEY, GUYS, I WAS JUST THINKING...
YOU KNOW HOW WHEN WE GO BACK TO SCHOOL IN THE FALL, WE'VE FORGOTTEN EVERYTHING WE LEARNED THE YEAR BEFORE?
WELL, WE COULD PREVENT THAT FROM HAPPENING BY FORMING OUR OWN LITTLE STUDY GROUP THIS SUMMER!
IF WE SPEND JUST A HALF-HOUR EACH DAY REVIEWING OUR SCHOOL-WORK, IT'LL ALL BE FRESH IN OUR MINDS COME SEPTEMBER!
A SUMMER STUDY GROUP?
RIGHT!
AND HOW DID YOU COME UP WITH THIS IDEA?
WELL, I... HEY, WHO REALLY KNOWS WHERE GREAT IDEAS COME FROM?
6/22
IT JUST... HIT ME!
© 2008 by NEA, Inc.
DiFF!
Peirce

THE SUMMER OF NATE

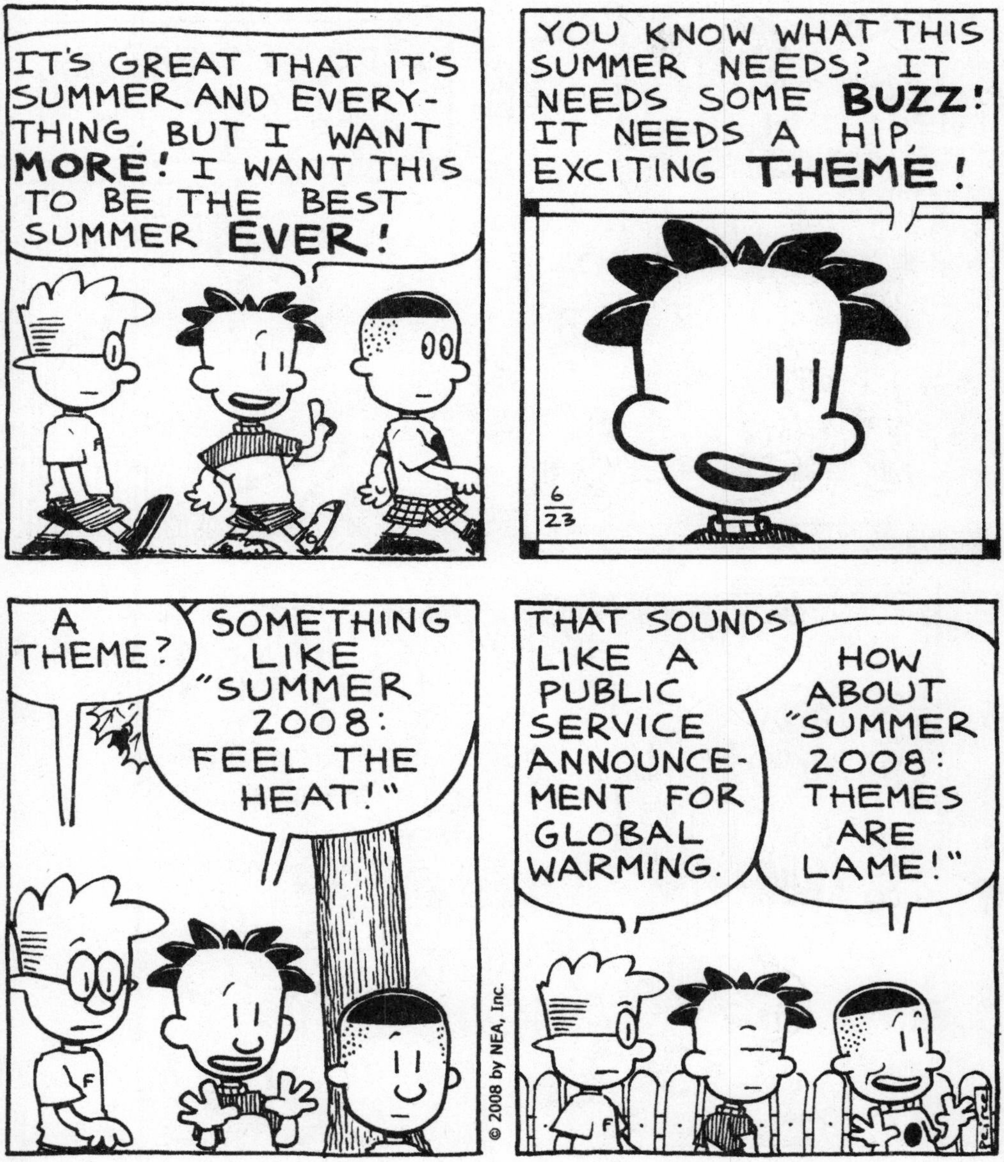

IT'S GREAT THAT IT'S SUMMER AND EVERYTHING, BUT I WANT MORE! I WANT THIS TO BE THE BEST SUMMER EVER!
YOU KNOW WHAT THIS SUMMER NEEDS? IT NEEDS SOME BUZZ! IT NEEDS A HIP, EXCITING THEME!
6/23
A THEME?
SOMETHING LIKE "SUMMER 2008: FEEL THE HEAT!"
© 2008 by NEA, Inc.
THAT SOUNDS LIKE A PUBLIC SERVICE ANNOUNCEMENT FOR GLOBAL WARMING.
HOW ABOUT "SUMMER 2008: THEMES ARE LAME!"

HERE'S A GOOD THEME: "2008: THE SUMMER OF NATE!"
...OR "SUMMER '08: GET READY FOR TEDDY!"
6/24
NOTHING RHYMES WITH FRANCIS.
Peirce

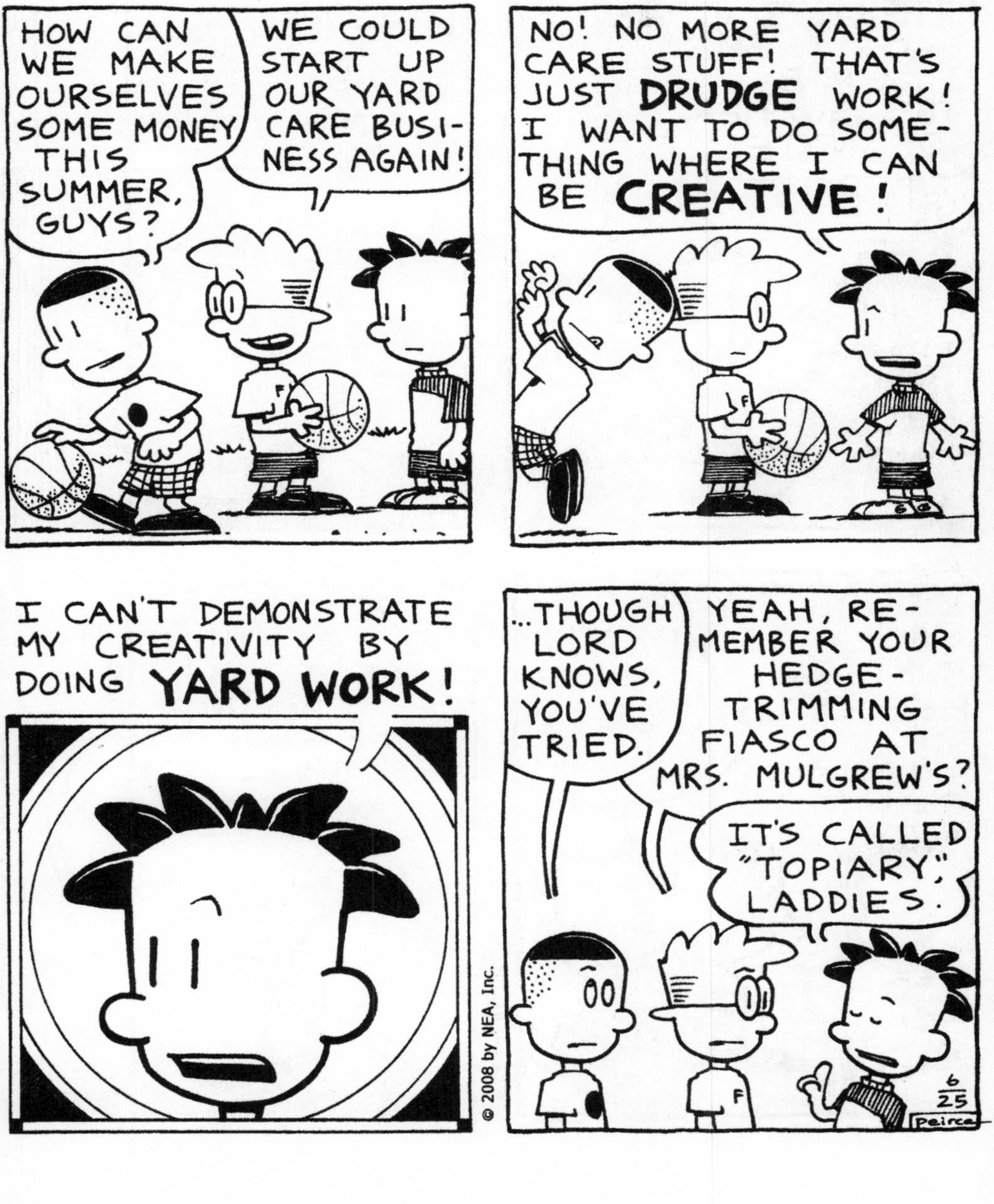
HOW CAN WE MAKE OURSELVES SOME MONEY THIS SUMMER, GUYS?
WE COULD START UP OUR YARD CARE BUSINESS AGAIN!
NO! NO MORE YARD CARE STUFF! THAT'S JUST DRUDGE WORK! I WANT TO DO SOMETHING WHERE I CAN BE CREATIVE!
I CAN'T DEMONSTRATE MY CREATIVITY BY DOING YARD WORK!
YEAH, REMEMBER YOUR HEDGE-TRIMMING FIASCO AT MRS. MULGREW'S?
...THOUGH LORD KNOWS, YOU'VE TRIED.
IT'S CALLED "TOPIARY," LADDIES.
6/25
Peirce

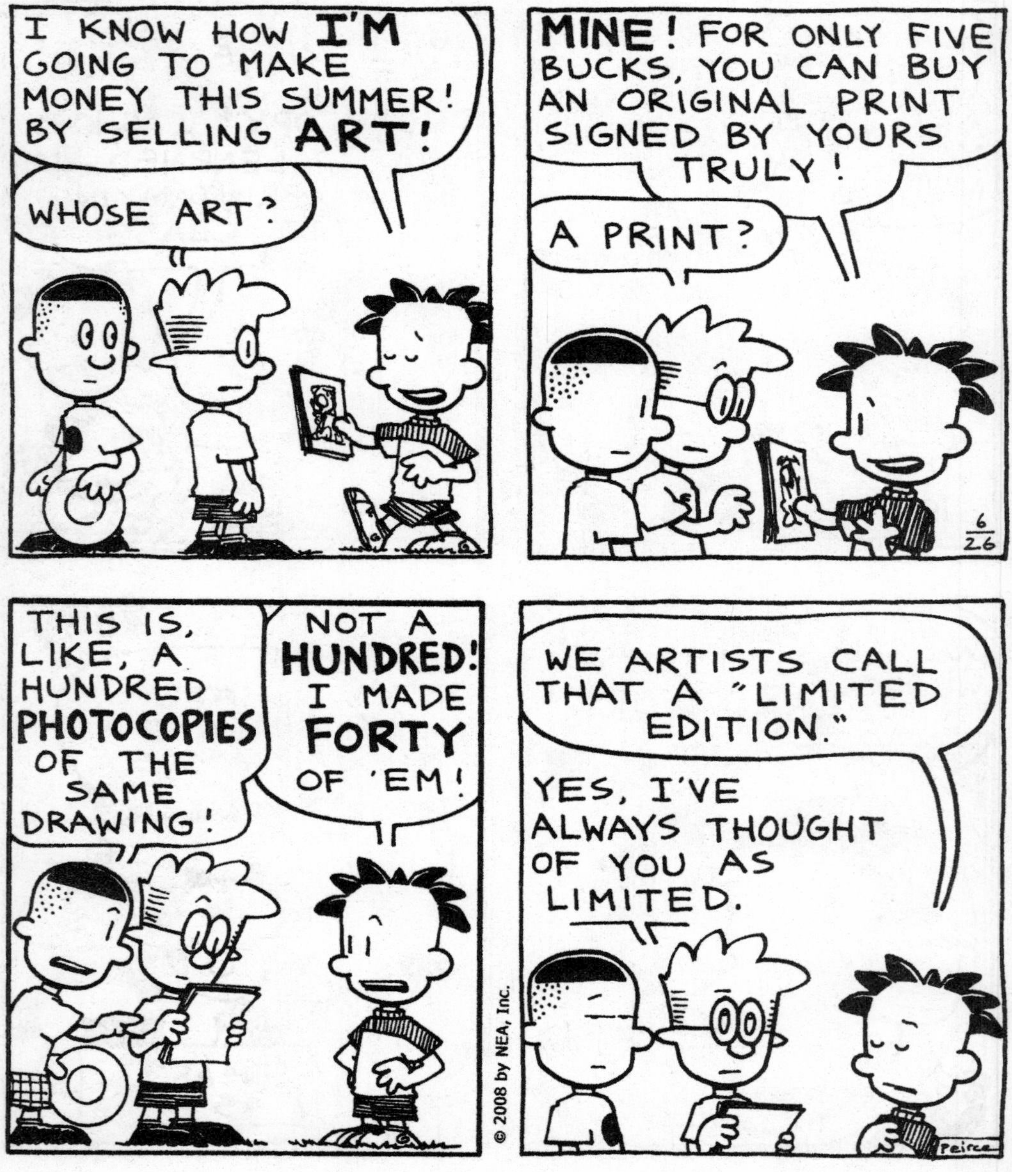

I KNOW HOW I'M GOING TO MAKE MONEY THIS SUMMER! BY SELLING ART!
WHOSE ART?
MINE! FOR ONLY FIVE BUCKS, YOU CAN BUY AN ORIGINAL PRINT SIGNED BY YOURS TRULY!
A PRINT?
6/26
THIS IS, LIKE, A HUNDRED PHOTOCOPIES OF THE SAME DRAWING!
NOT A HUNDRED! I MADE FORTY OF 'EM!
WE ARTISTS CALL THAT A "LIMITED EDITION."
YES, I'VE ALWAYS THOUGHT OF YOU AS LIMITED.
Peirce

HEY THERE, KID! WANNA BUY AN ART PRINT BY YOURS TRULY, NATE WRIGHT?
A PRINT?
FINE ART $5
THIS ISN'T A PRINT! THIS IS JUST A PHOTOCOPY! I SHOULD KNOW, I LEARNED ALL ABOUT PRINTMAKING IN ART CLASS!
6/27
WE DID LITHOGRAPHY, WOODCUTS, INTAGLIO, SILKSCREENING AND DRYPOINT.
FINE ART $5
I HATE PRIVATE SCHOOLS.
FINE ART $5
© 2008 by NEA, Inc.

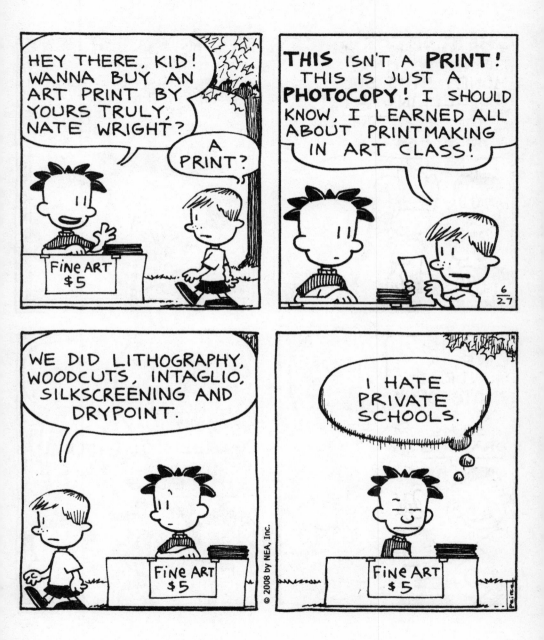

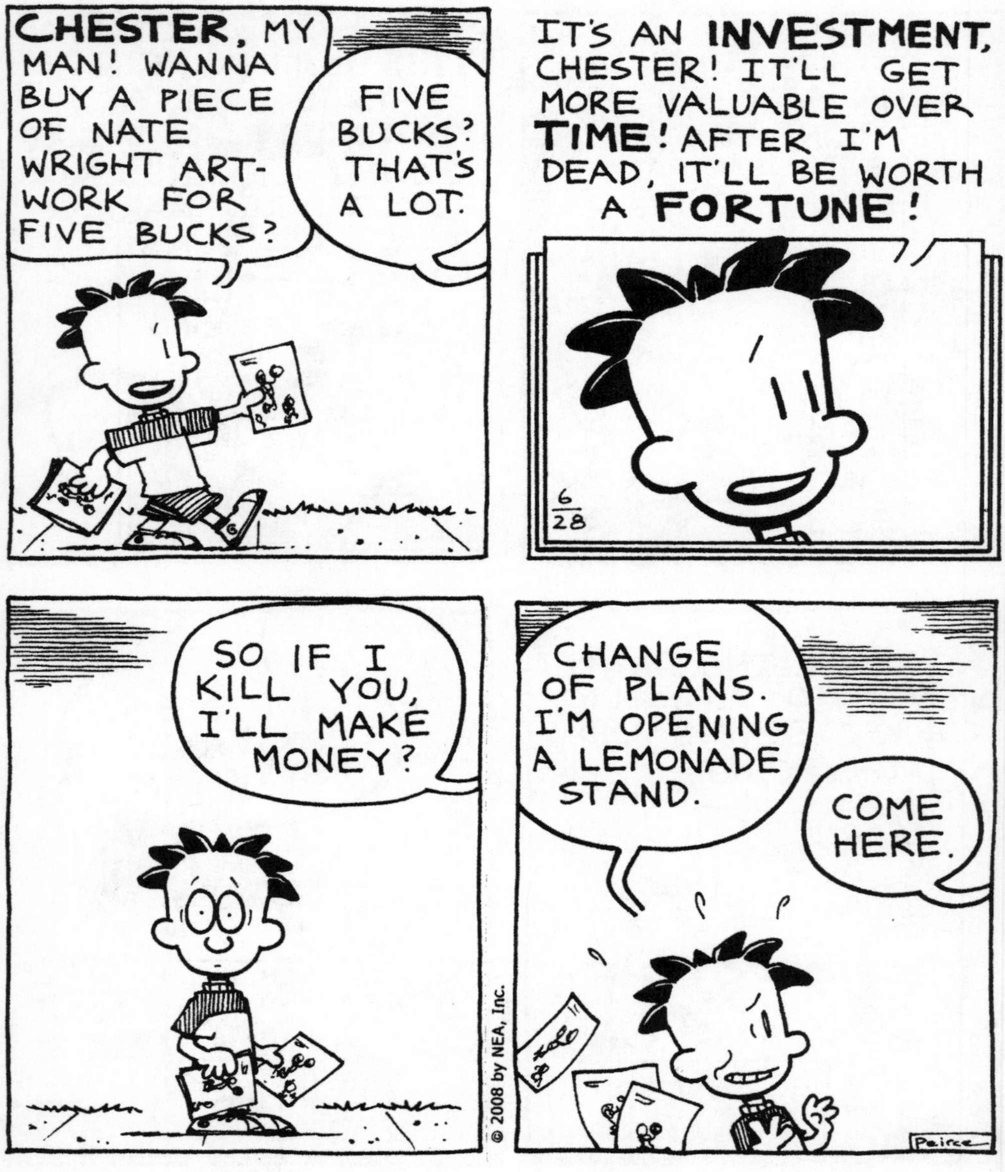
CHESTER, MY MAN! WANNA BUY A PIECE OF NATE WRIGHT ART-WORK FOR FIVE BUCKS?
FIVE BUCKS? THAT'S A LOT.
IT'S AN INVESTMENT, CHESTER! IT'LL GET MORE VALUABLE OVER TIME! AFTER I'M DEAD, IT'LL BE WORTH A FORTUNE!
6
28
SO IF I KILL YOU, I'LL MAKE MONEY?
© 2008 by NEA, Inc.
CHANGE OF PLANS. I'M OPENING A LEMONADE STAND.
COME HERE.
Peirce

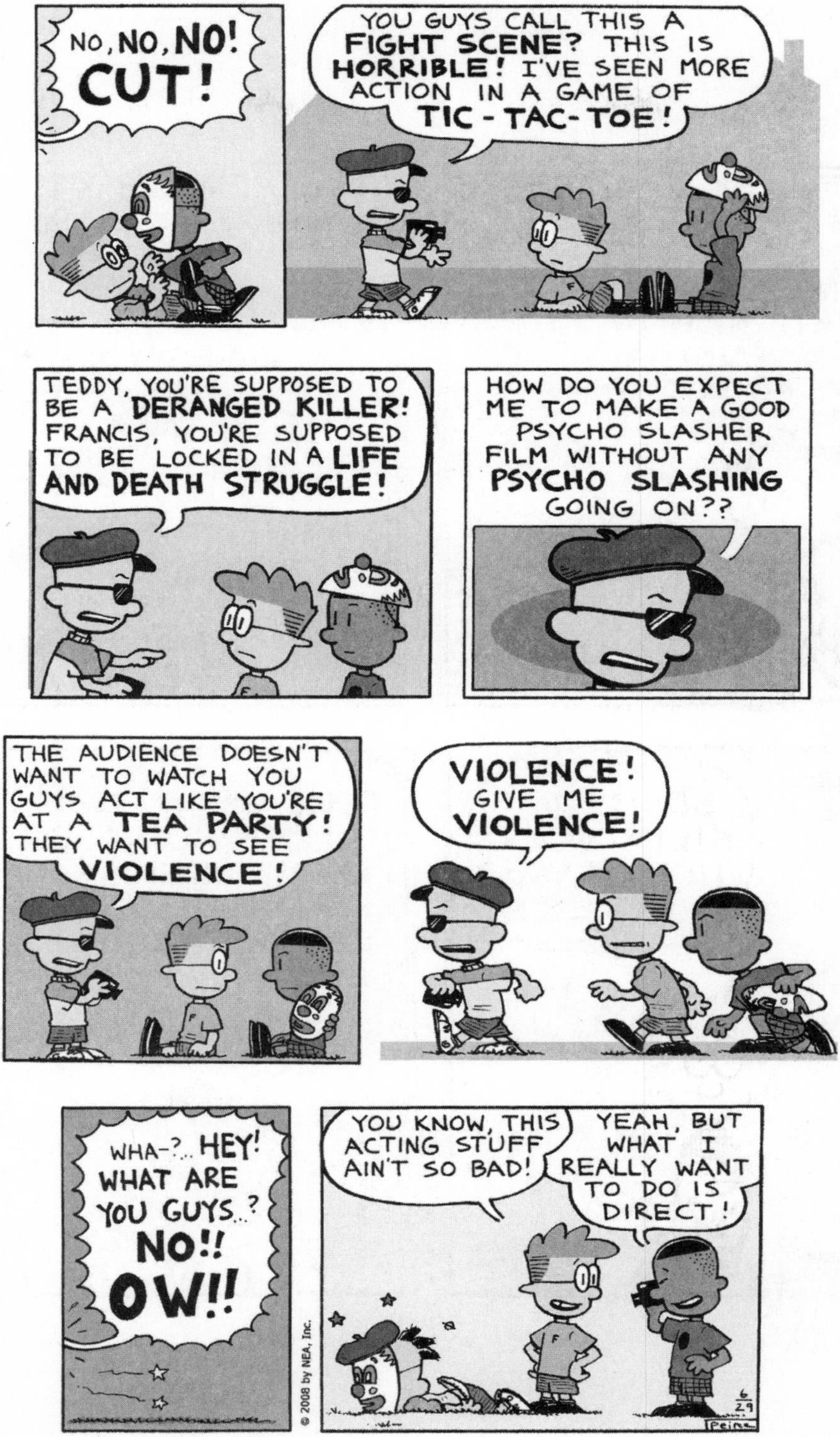
NO, NO, NO! CUT!
YOU GUYS CALL THIS A FIGHT SCENE? THIS IS HORRIBLE! I'VE SEEN MORE ACTION IN A GAME OF TIC-TAC-TOE!
TEDDY, YOU'RE SUPPOSED TO BE A DERANGED KILLER! FRANCIS, YOU'RE SUPPOSED TO BE LOCKED IN A LIFE AND DEATH STRUGGLE!
HOW DO YOU EXPECT ME TO MAKE A GOOD PSYCHO SLASHER FILM WITHOUT ANY PSYCHO SLASHING GOING ON??
THE AUDIENCE DOESN'T WANT TO WATCH YOU GUYS ACT LIKE YOU'RE AT A TEA PARTY! THEY WANT TO SEE VIOLENCE!
VIOLENCE! GIVE ME VIOLENCE!
WHA-?.. HEY! WHAT ARE YOU GUYS..? NO!! OW!!
YOU KNOW, THIS ACTING STUFF AIN'T SO BAD!
YEAH, BUT WHAT I REALLY WANT TO DO IS DIRECT!
6 29
Peirce

WILD RIDE

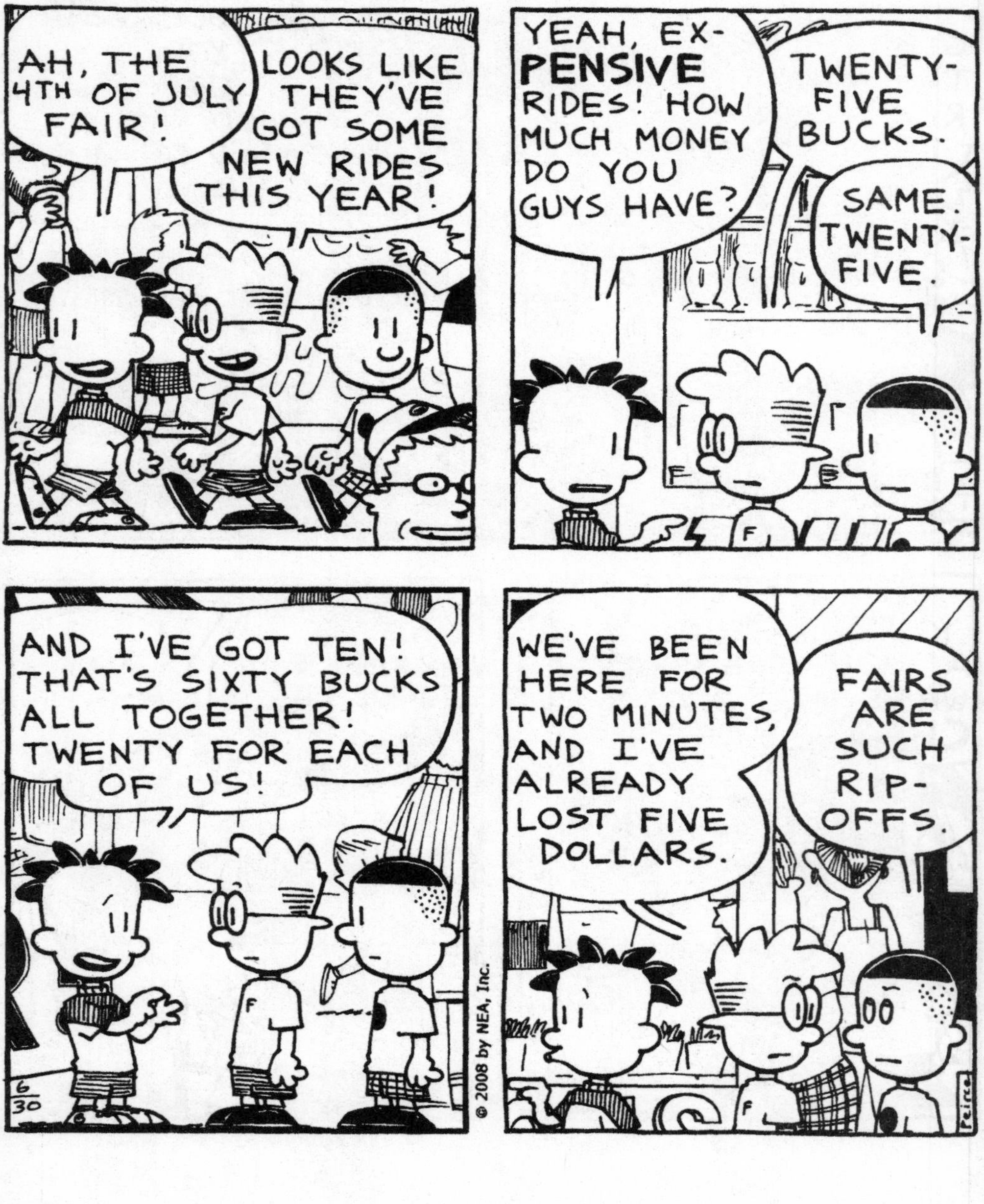

AH, THE 4TH OF JULY FAIR!
LOOKS LIKE THEY'VE GOT SOME NEW RIDES THIS YEAR!
YEAH, EX-**PENSIVE** RIDES! HOW MUCH MONEY DO YOU GUYS HAVE?
TWENTY-FIVE BUCKS.
SAME. TWENTY-FIVE.
AND I'VE GOT TEN! THAT'S SIXTY BUCKS ALL TOGETHER! TWENTY FOR EACH OF US!
6/30
© 2008 by NEA, Inc.
WE'VE BEEN HERE FOR TWO MINUTES, AND I'VE ALREADY LOST FIVE DOLLARS.
FAIRS ARE SUCH RIP-OFFS.
Peirce

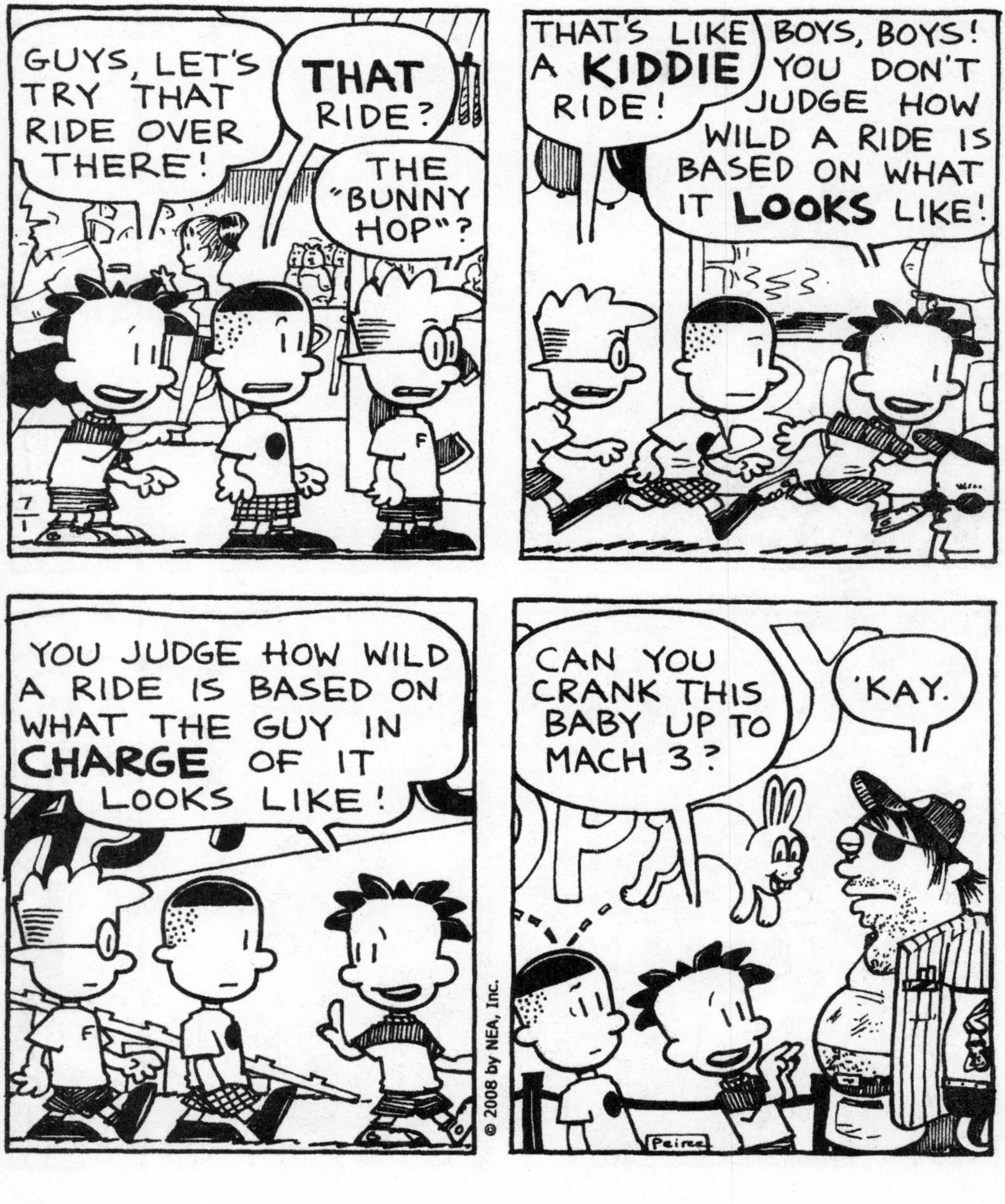
GUYS, LET'S TRY THAT RIDE OVER THERE!
THAT RIDE?
THE "BUNNY HOP"?
THAT'S LIKE A KIDDIE RIDE!
BOYS, BOYS! YOU DON'T JUDGE HOW WILD A RIDE IS BASED ON WHAT IT LOOKS LIKE!
YOU JUDGE HOW WILD A RIDE IS BASED ON WHAT THE GUY IN CHARGE OF IT LOOKS LIKE!
CAN YOU CRANK THIS BABY UP TO MACH 3?
'KAY.
© 2008 by NEA, Inc.
Peirce

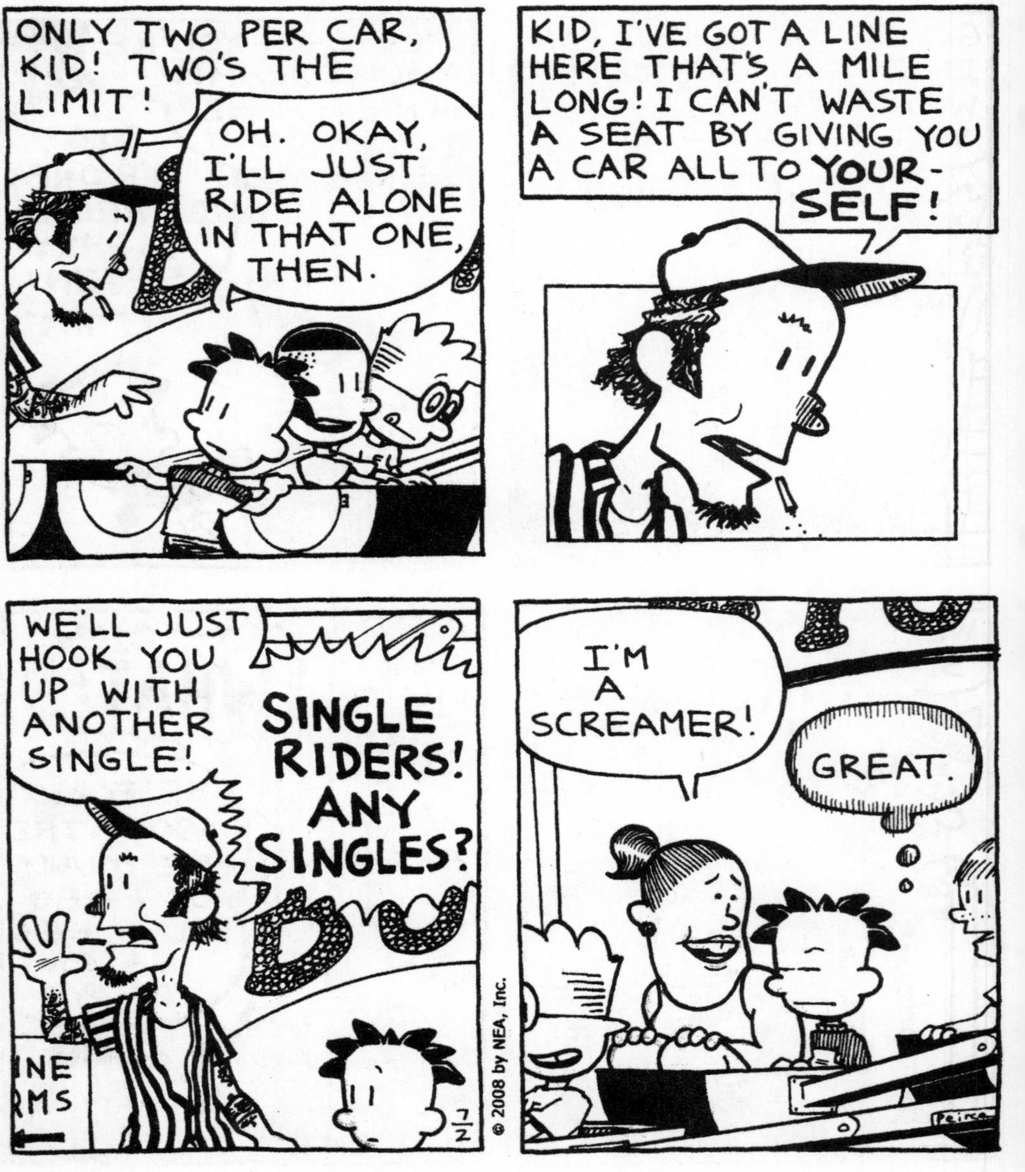
ONLY TWO PER CAR, KID! TWO'S THE LIMIT!
OH. OKAY, I'LL JUST RIDE ALONE IN THAT ONE, THEN.
KID, I'VE GOT A LINE HERE THAT'S A MILE LONG! I CAN'T WASTE A SEAT BY GIVING YOU A CAR ALL TO **YOUR-SELF**!
WE'LL JUST HOOK YOU UP WITH ANOTHER SINGLE!
SINGLE RIDERS! ANY SINGLES?
I'M A SCREAMER!
GREAT.
© 2008 by NEA, Inc.

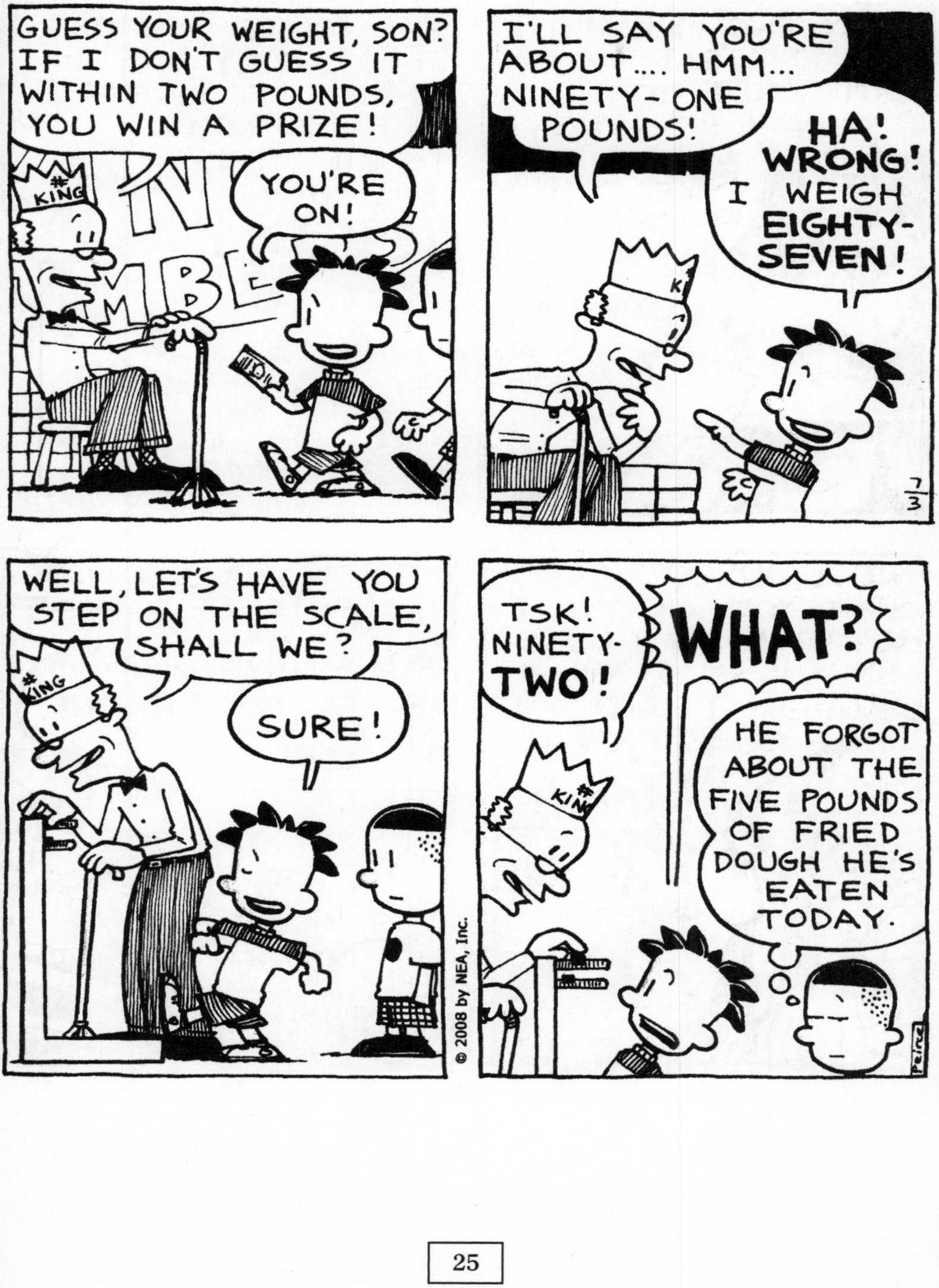
GUESS YOUR WEIGHT, SON? IF I DON'T GUESS IT WITHIN TWO POUNDS, YOU WIN A PRIZE!
YOU'RE ON!
I'LL SAY YOU'RE ABOUT.... HMM... NINETY-ONE POUNDS!
HA! WRONG! I WEIGH EIGHTY-SEVEN!
7/3
WELL, LET'S HAVE YOU STEP ON THE SCALE, SHALL WE?
SURE!
© 2008 by NEA, Inc.
TSK! NINETY-TWO!
WHAT?
HE FORGOT ABOUT THE FIVE POUNDS OF FRIED DOUGH HE'S EATEN TODAY.
Peirce

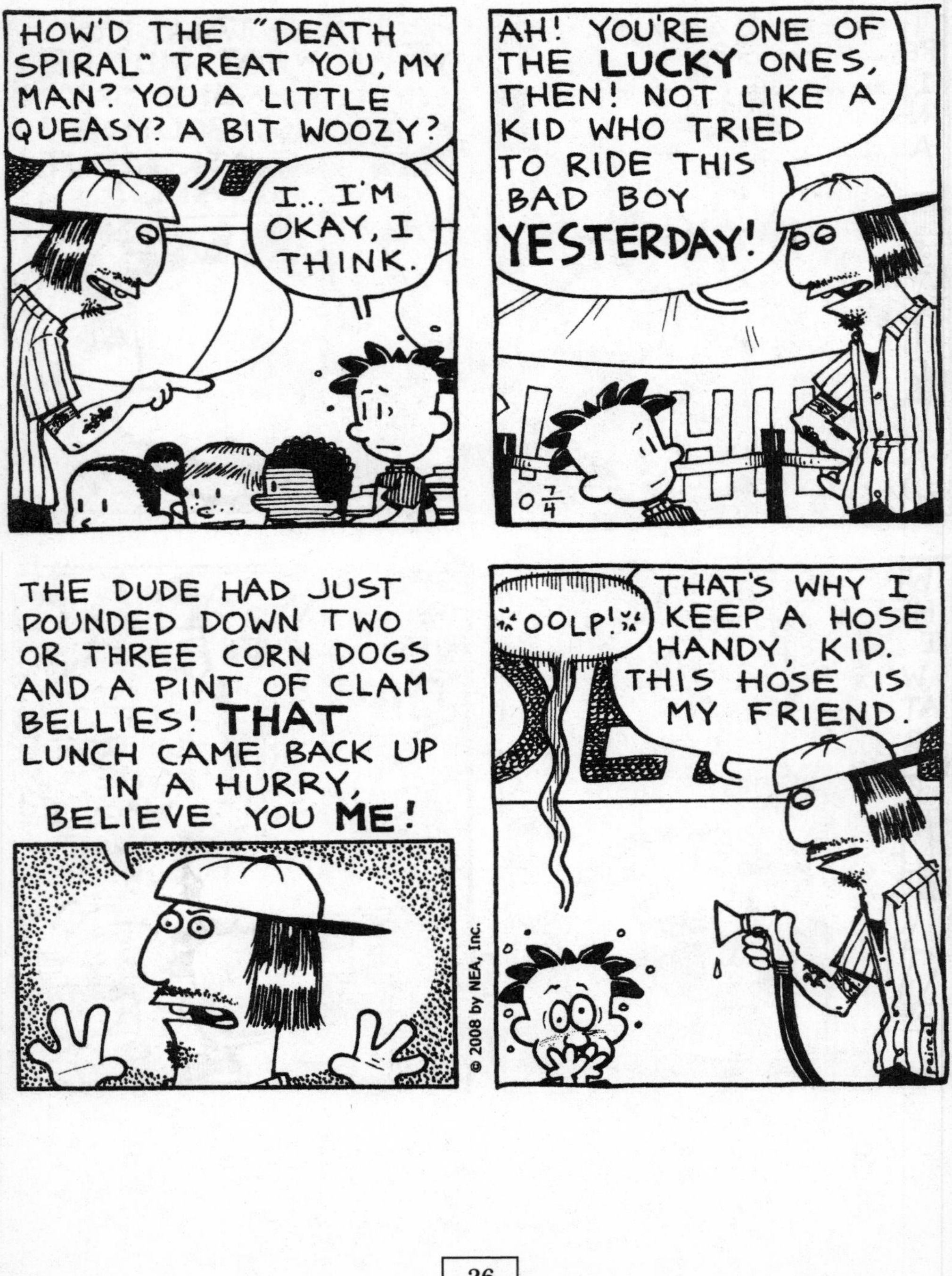

HOW'D THE "DEATH SPIRAL" TREAT YOU, MY MAN? YOU A LITTLE QUEASY? A BIT WOOZY?
I... I'M OKAY, I THINK.
AH! YOU'RE ONE OF THE LUCKY ONES, THEN! NOT LIKE A KID WHO TRIED TO RIDE THIS BAD BOY YESTERDAY!
THE DUDE HAD JUST POUNDED DOWN TWO OR THREE CORN DOGS AND A PINT OF CLAM BELLIES! THAT LUNCH CAME BACK UP IN A HURRY, BELIEVE YOU ME!
OOLP!
THAT'S WHY I KEEP A HOSE HANDY, KID. THIS HOSE IS MY FRIEND.

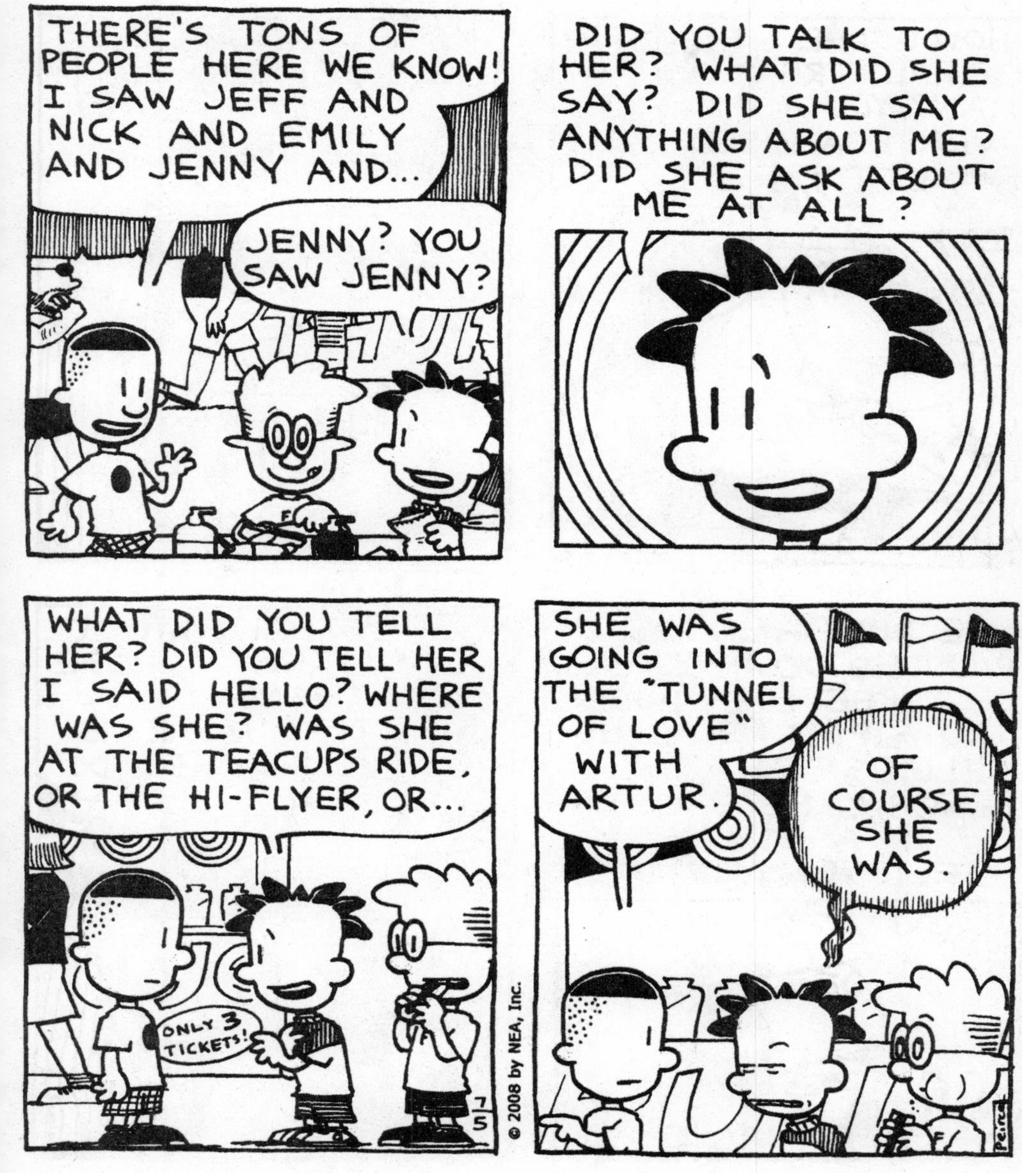
THERE'S TONS OF PEOPLE HERE WE KNOW! I SAW JEFF AND NICK AND EMILY AND JENNY AND...
JENNY? YOU SAW JENNY?
DID YOU TALK TO HER? WHAT DID SHE SAY? DID SHE SAY ANYTHING ABOUT ME? DID SHE ASK ABOUT ME AT ALL?
WHAT DID YOU TELL HER? DID YOU TELL HER I SAID HELLO? WHERE WAS SHE? WAS SHE AT THE TEACUPS RIDE, OR THE HI-FLYER, OR...
ONLY 3 TICKETS!
7/5
© 2008 by NEA, Inc.
SHE WAS GOING INTO THE "TUNNEL OF LOVE" WITH ARTUR.
OF COURSE SHE WAS.
Peirce

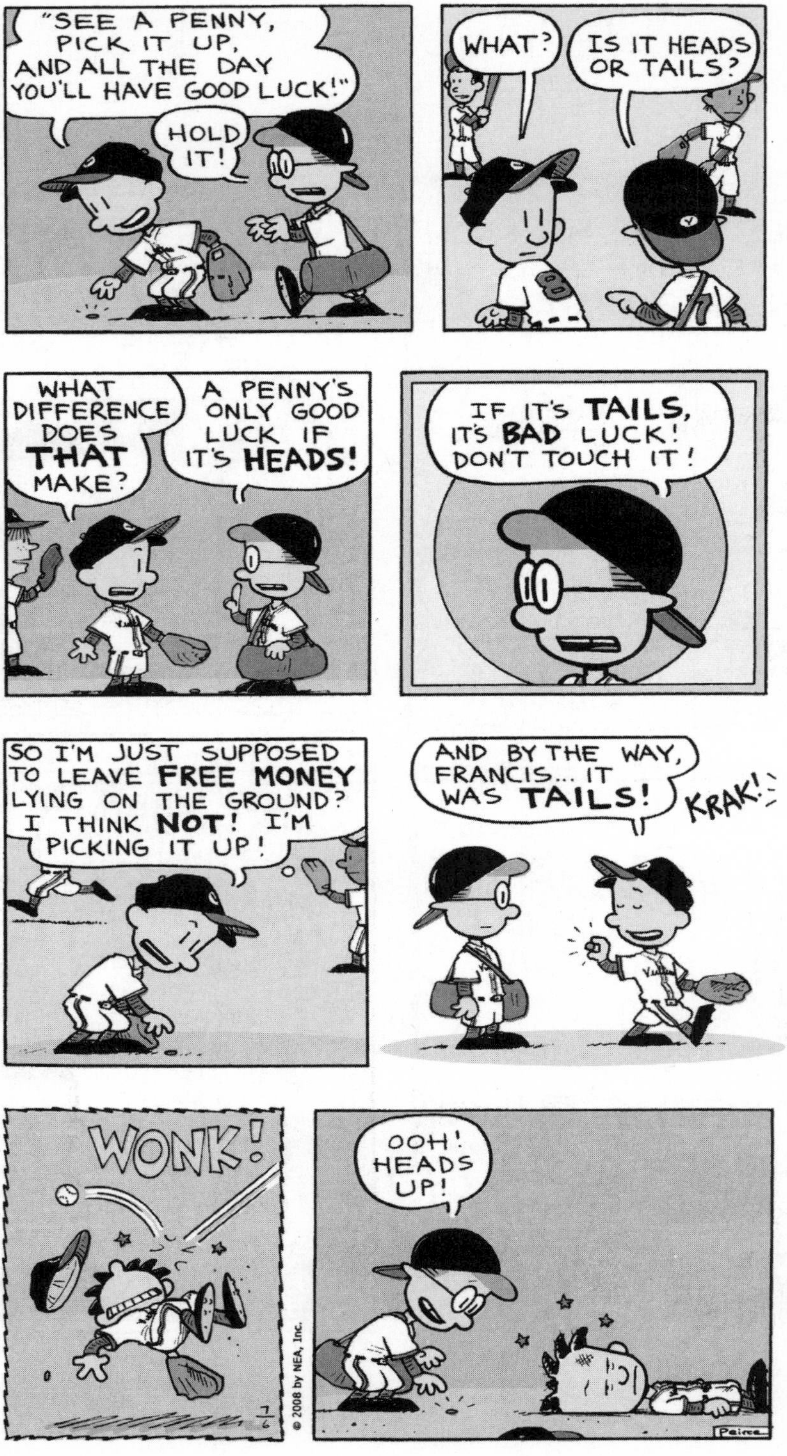
"SEE A PENNY, PICK IT UP, AND ALL THE DAY YOU'LL HAVE GOOD LUCK!"
HOLD IT!
WHAT?
IS IT HEADS OR TAILS?
WHAT DIFFERENCE DOES THAT MAKE?
A PENNY'S ONLY GOOD LUCK IF IT'S HEADS!
IF IT'S TAILS, IT'S BAD LUCK! DON'T TOUCH IT!
SO I'M JUST SUPPOSED TO LEAVE FREE MONEY LYING ON THE GROUND? I THINK NOT! I'M PICKING IT UP!
AND BY THE WAY, FRANCIS... IT WAS TAILS!
KRAK!
WONK!
7/6
© 2008 by NEA, Inc.
OOH! HEADS UP!
Peirce

WHAT BAD LUCK?

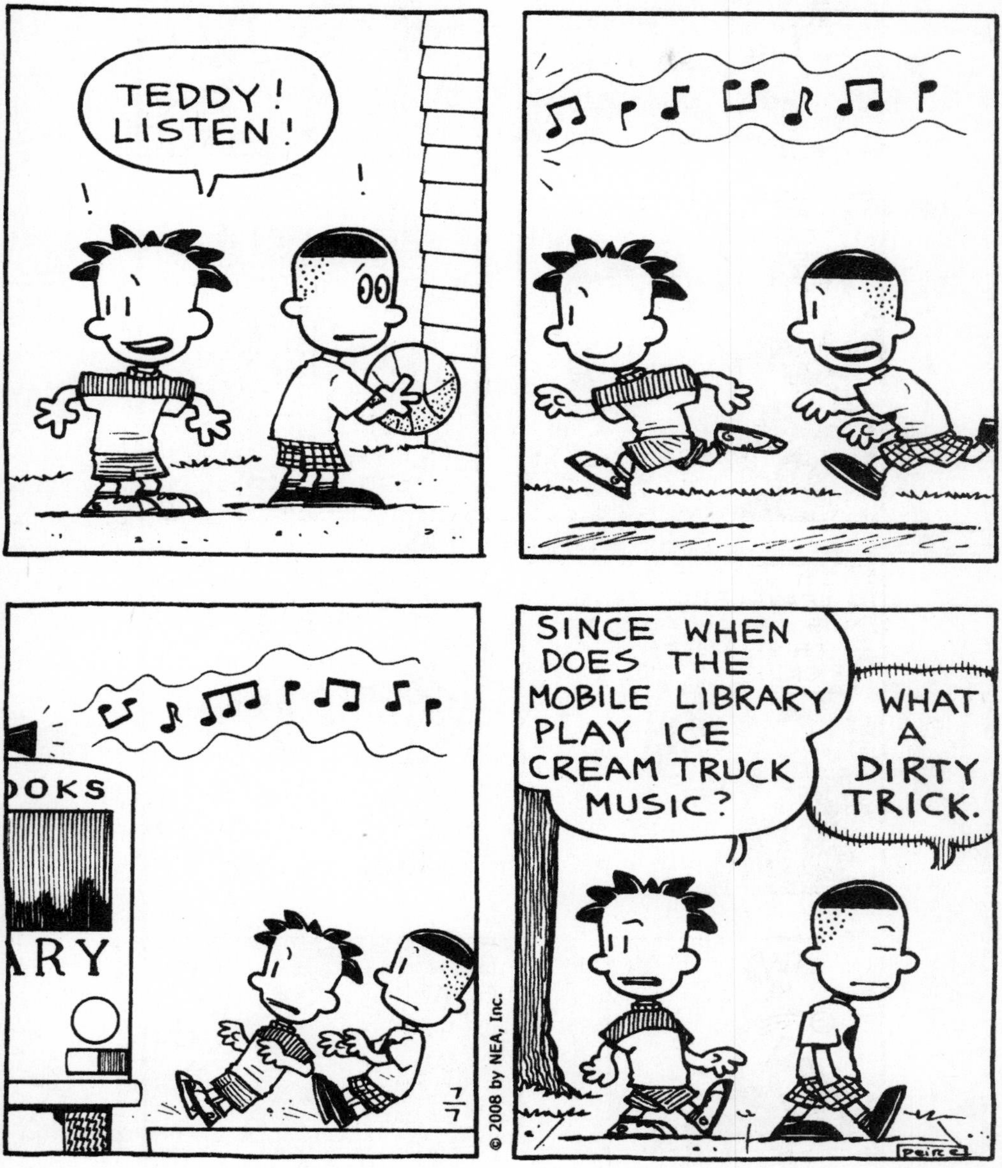

TEDDY! LISTEN!
!
!
SINCE WHEN DOES THE MOBILE LIBRARY PLAY ICE CREAM TRUCK MUSIC?
WHAT A DIRTY TRICK.

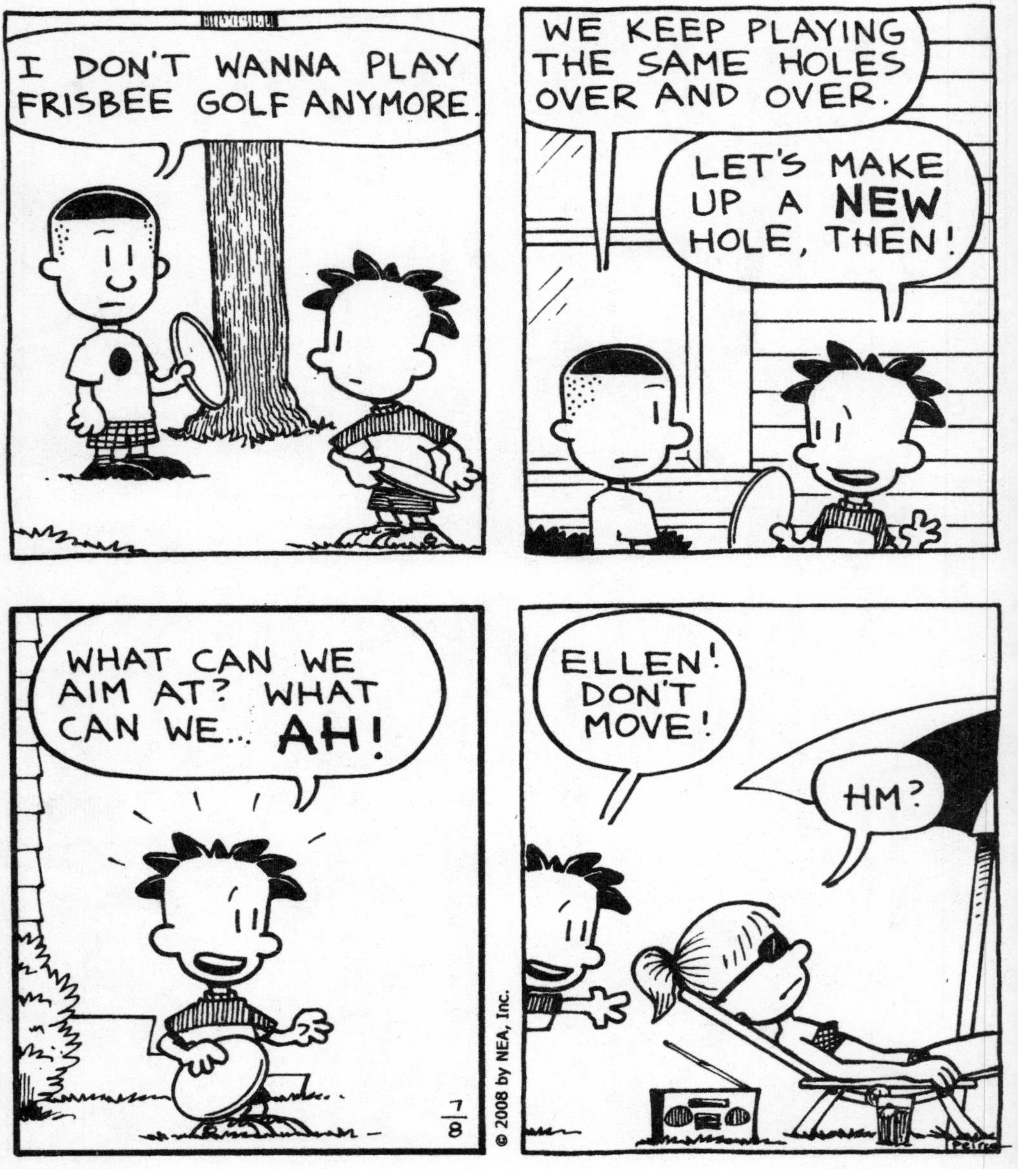
I DON'T WANNA PLAY FRISBEE GOLF ANYMORE.
WE KEEP PLAYING THE SAME HOLES OVER AND OVER.
LET'S MAKE UP A **NEW** HOLE, THEN!
WHAT CAN WE AIM AT? WHAT CAN WE... **AH!**
7/8
© 2008 by NEA, Inc.
ELLEN! DON'T MOVE!
HM?

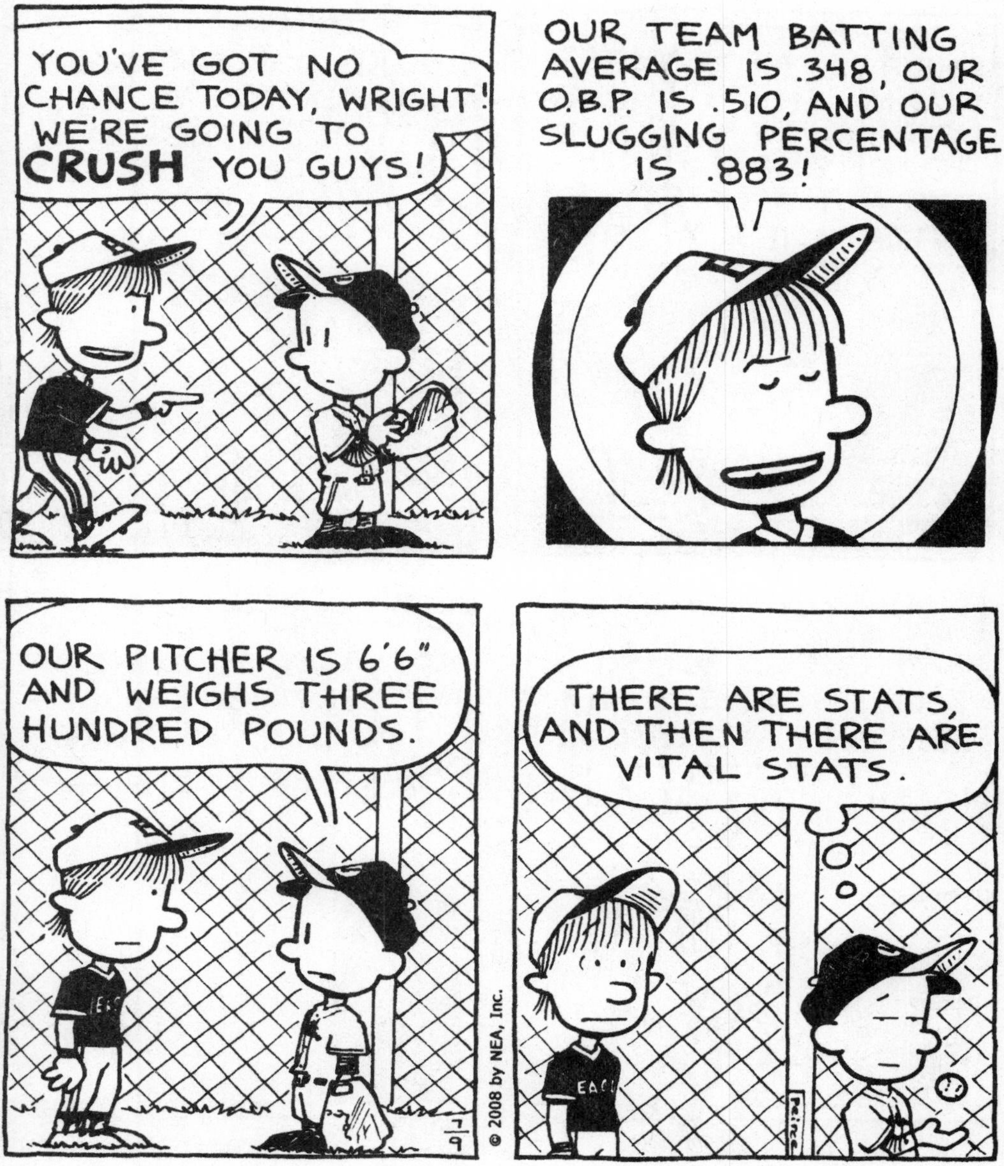
YOU'VE GOT NO CHANCE TODAY, WRIGHT! WE'RE GOING TO **CRUSH** YOU GUYS!
OUR TEAM BATTING AVERAGE IS .348, OUR O.B.P. IS .510, AND OUR SLUGGING PERCENTAGE IS .883!
OUR PITCHER IS 6'6" AND WEIGHS THREE HUNDRED POUNDS.
THERE ARE STATS, AND THEN THERE ARE VITAL STATS.
© 2008 by NEA, Inc.
7/9

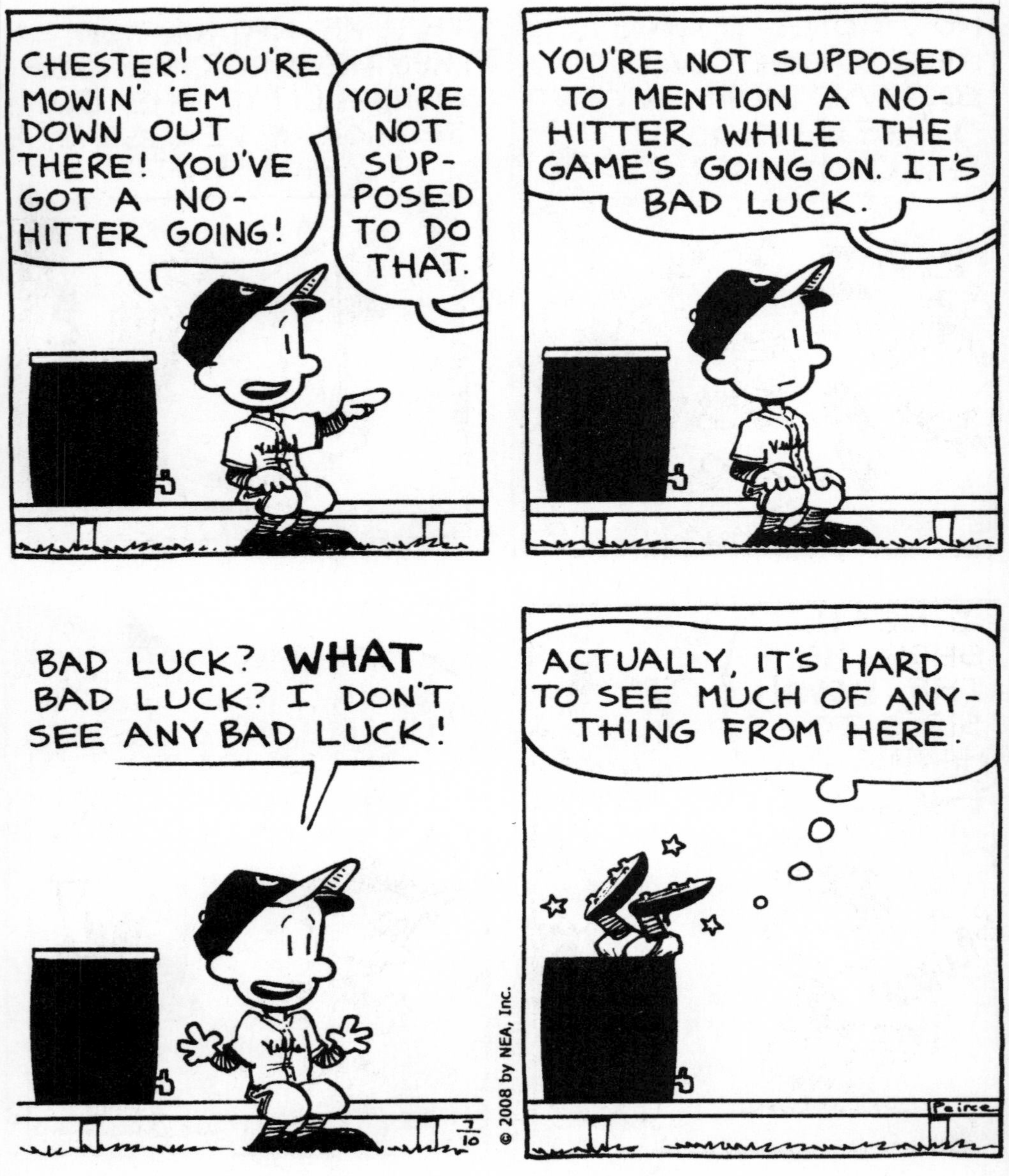
CHESTER! YOU'RE MOWIN' 'EM DOWN OUT THERE! YOU'VE GOT A NO-HITTER GOING!
YOU'RE NOT SUP-POSED TO DO THAT.
YOU'RE NOT SUPPOSED TO MENTION A NO-HITTER WHILE THE GAME'S GOING ON. IT'S BAD LUCK.
BAD LUCK? **WHAT** BAD LUCK? I DON'T SEE ANY BAD LUCK!
ACTUALLY, IT'S HARD TO SEE MUCH OF ANY-THING FROM HERE.

DOGS=AWESOME

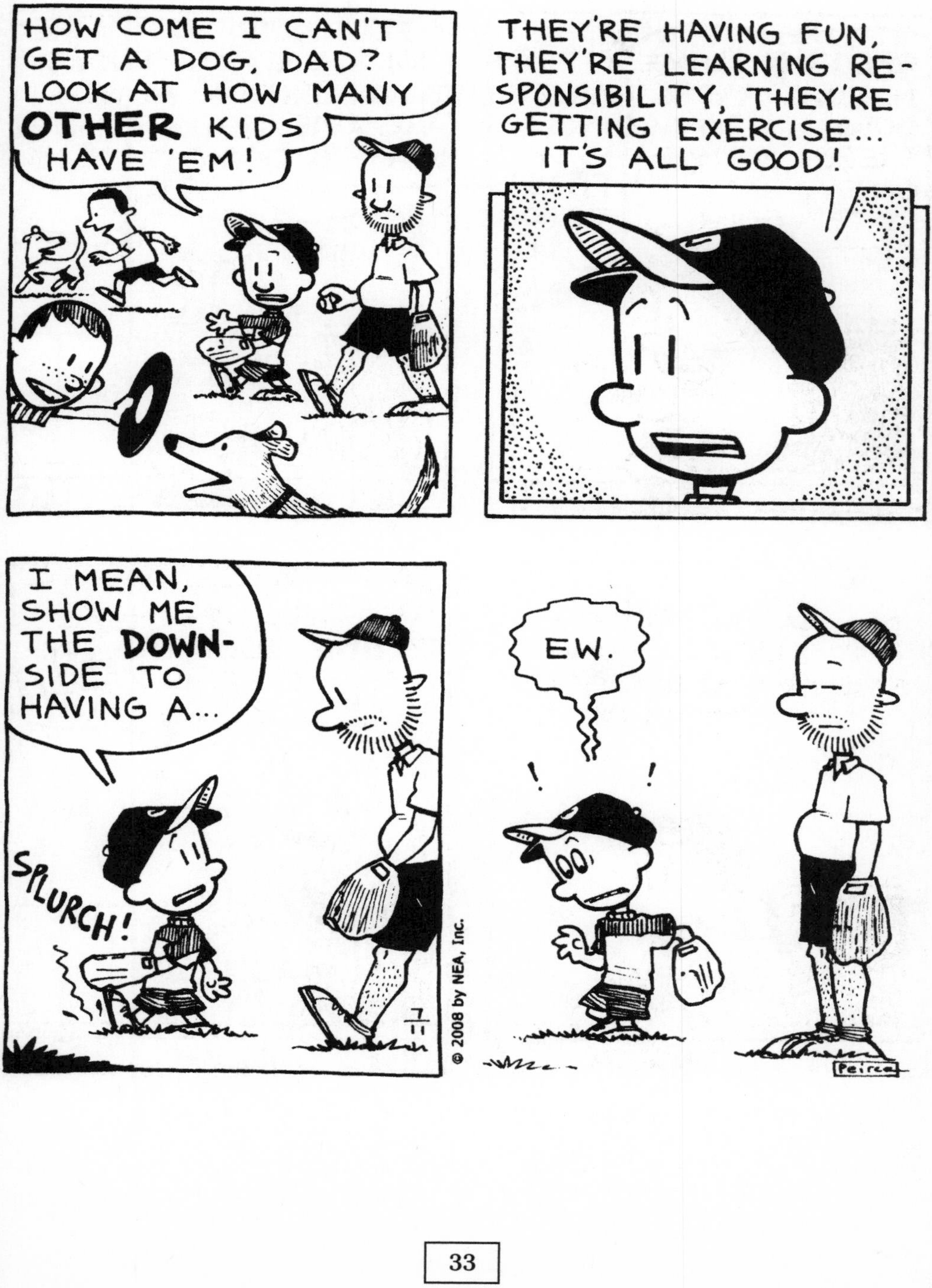

HOW COME I CAN'T GET A DOG, DAD? LOOK AT HOW MANY **OTHER** KIDS HAVE 'EM!
THEY'RE HAVING FUN, THEY'RE LEARNING RE-SPONSIBILITY, THEY'RE GETTING EXERCISE... IT'S ALL GOOD!
I MEAN, SHOW ME THE **DOWN**-SIDE TO HAVING A...
SPLURCH!
© 2008 by NEA, Inc.
7/11
EW.
! !
Peirce

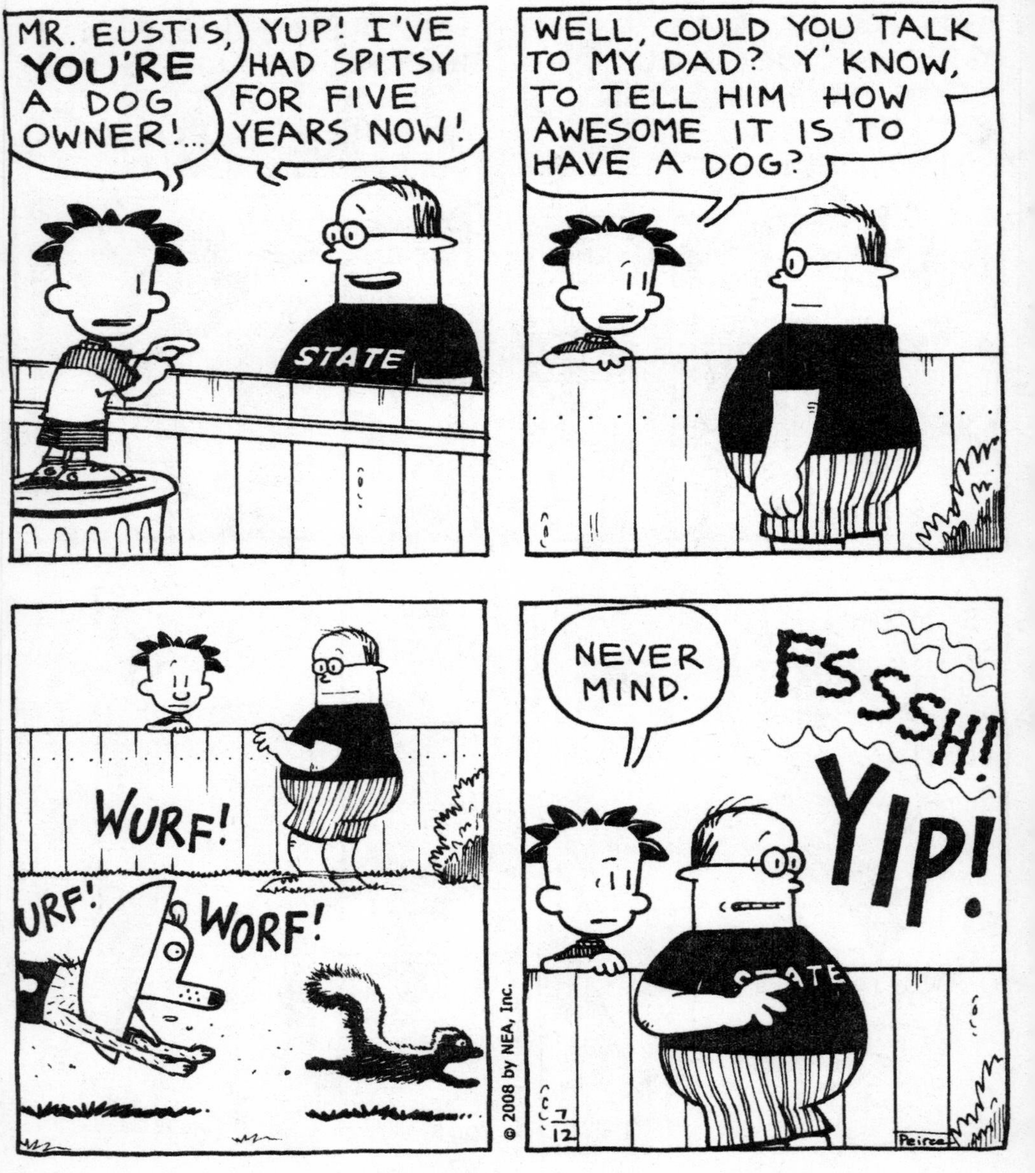
MR. EUSTIS, YOU'RE A DOG OWNER!...
YUP! I'VE HAD SPITSY FOR FIVE YEARS NOW!
STATE
WELL, COULD YOU TALK TO MY DAD? Y'KNOW, TO TELL HIM HOW AWESOME IT IS TO HAVE A DOG?
WURF!
URF!
WORF!
© 2008 by NEA, Inc.
NEVER MIND.
FSSSH!
YIP!
STATE
Peirce

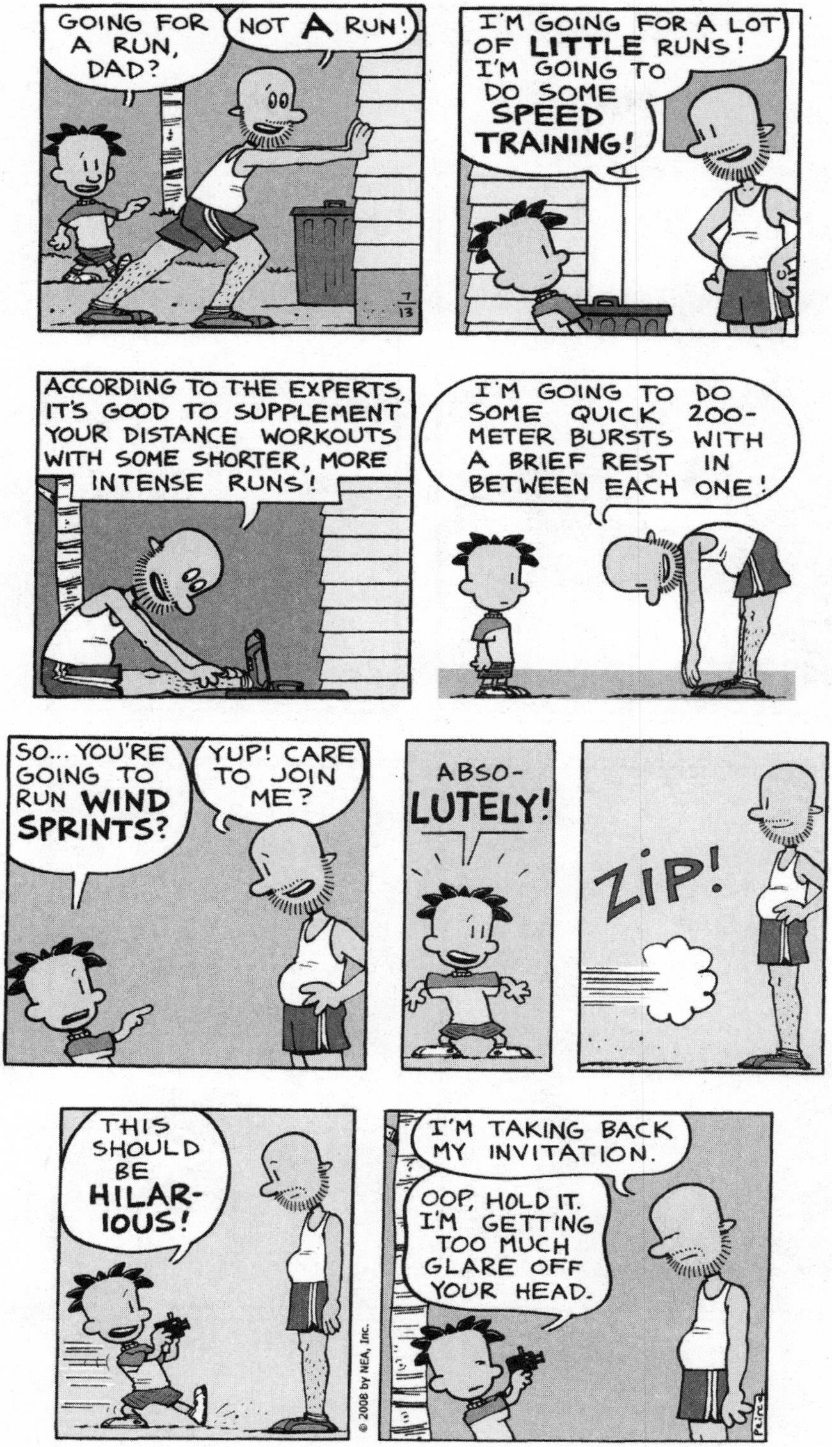
GOING FOR A RUN, DAD?
NOT A RUN!
I'M GOING FOR A LOT OF LITTLE RUNS! I'M GOING TO DO SOME SPEED TRAINING!
ACCORDING TO THE EXPERTS, IT'S GOOD TO SUPPLEMENT YOUR DISTANCE WORKOUTS WITH SOME SHORTER, MORE INTENSE RUNS!
I'M GOING TO DO SOME QUICK 200-METER BURSTS WITH A BRIEF REST IN BETWEEN EACH ONE!
SO... YOU'RE GOING TO RUN WIND SPRINTS?
YUP! CARE TO JOIN ME?
ABSO-LUTELY!
ZIP!
THIS SHOULD BE HILAR-IOUS!
© 2008 by NEA, Inc.
I'M TAKING BACK MY INVITATION.
OOP, HOLD IT. I'M GETTING TOO MUCH GLARE OFF YOUR HEAD.

HUNGRY FOR VICTORY

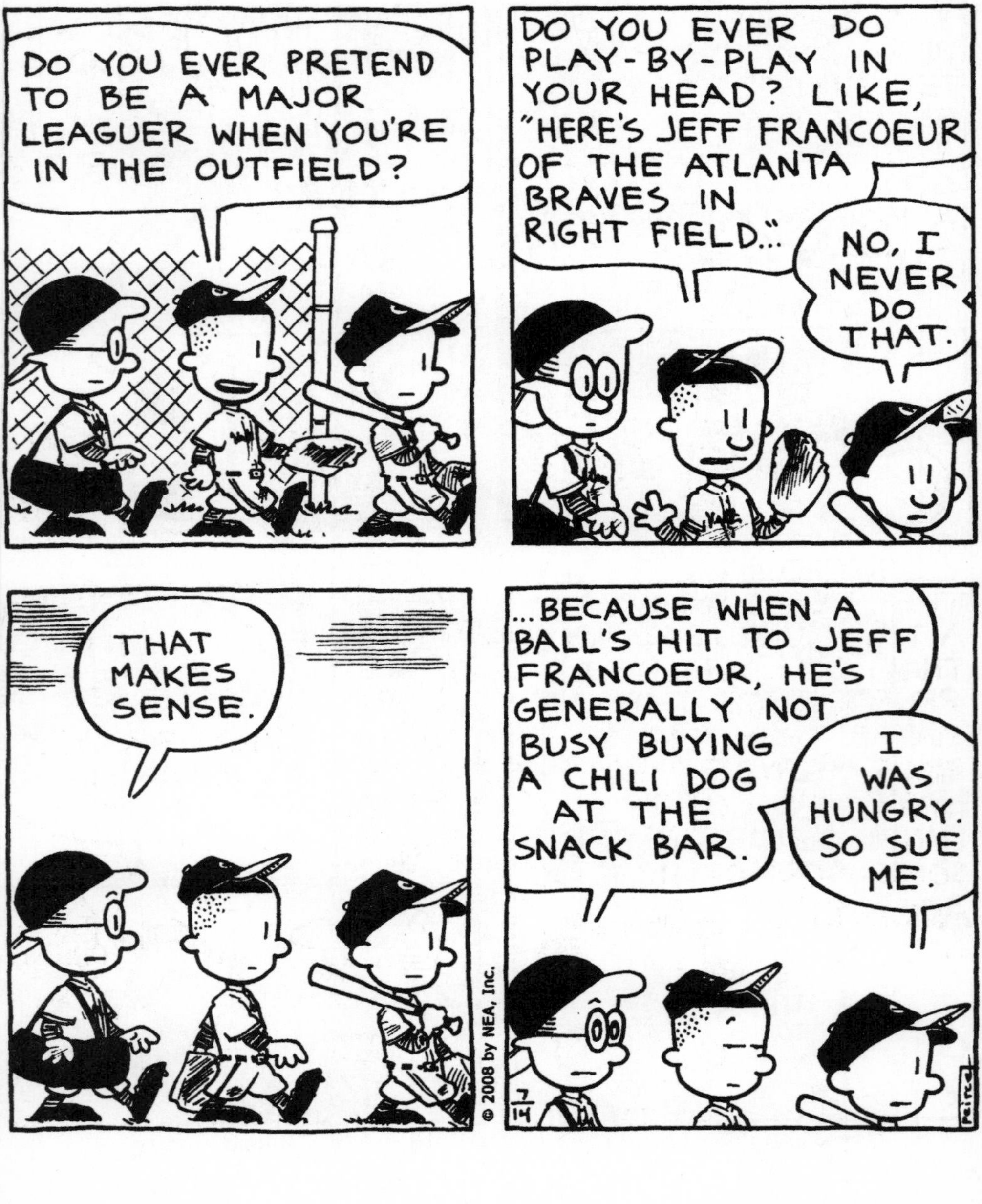

DO YOU EVER PRETEND TO BE A MAJOR LEAGUER WHEN YOU'RE IN THE OUTFIELD?
DO YOU EVER DO PLAY-BY-PLAY IN YOUR HEAD? LIKE, "HERE'S JEFF FRANCOEUR OF THE ATLANTA BRAVES IN RIGHT FIELD..."
NO, I NEVER DO THAT.
THAT MAKES SENSE.
...BECAUSE WHEN A BALL'S HIT TO JEFF FRANCOEUR, HE'S GENERALLY NOT BUSY BUYING A CHILI DOG AT THE SNACK BAR.
I WAS HUNGRY. SO SUE ME.
© 2008 by NEA, Inc.
7/14
Peirce

DOUBLE DATE

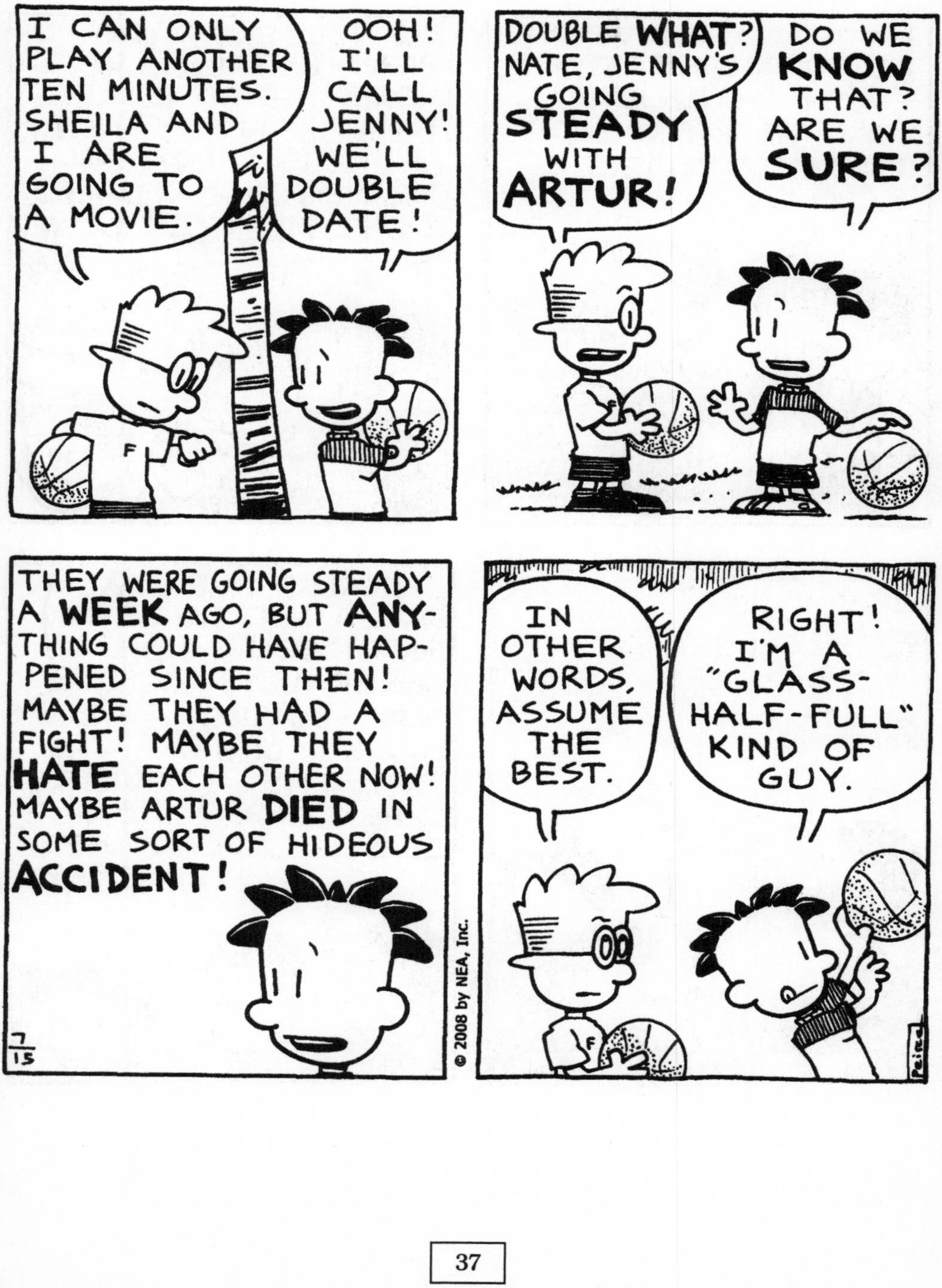
I CAN ONLY PLAY ANOTHER TEN MINUTES. SHEILA AND I ARE GOING TO A MOVIE.
OOH! I'LL CALL JENNY! WE'LL DOUBLE DATE!
DOUBLE WHAT? NATE, JENNY'S GOING STEADY WITH ARTUR!
DO WE KNOW THAT? ARE WE SURE?
THEY WERE GOING STEADY A WEEK AGO, BUT ANYTHING COULD HAVE HAPPENED SINCE THEN! MAYBE THEY HAD A FIGHT! MAYBE THEY HATE EACH OTHER NOW! MAYBE ARTUR DIED IN SOME SORT OF HIDEOUS ACCIDENT!
7/15
© 2008 by NEA, Inc.
IN OTHER WORDS, ASSUME THE BEST.
RIGHT! I'M A "GLASS-HALF-FULL" KIND OF GUY.
Peirce

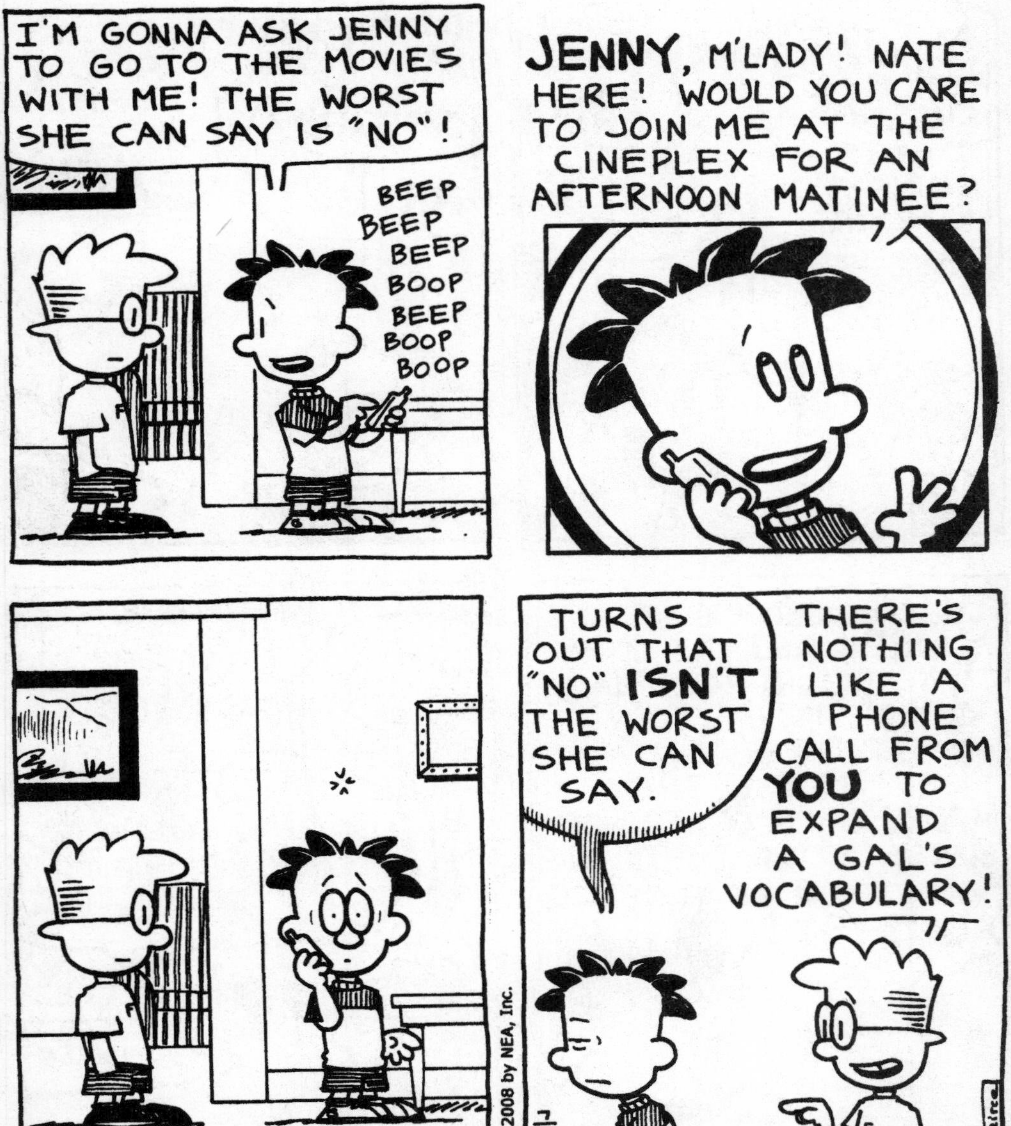
I'M GONNA ASK JENNY TO GO TO THE MOVIES WITH ME! THE WORST SHE CAN SAY IS "NO"!
BEEP BEEP BEEP BOOP BEEP BOOP BOOP
JENNY, M'LADY! NATE HERE! WOULD YOU CARE TO JOIN ME AT THE CINEPLEX FOR AN AFTERNOON MATINEE?
© 2008 by NEA, Inc.
TURNS OUT THAT "NO" ISN'T THE WORST SHE CAN SAY.
THERE'S NOTHING LIKE A PHONE CALL FROM YOU TO EXPAND A GAL'S VOCABULARY!
7/16
Peirce

SPECIAL DELIVERY

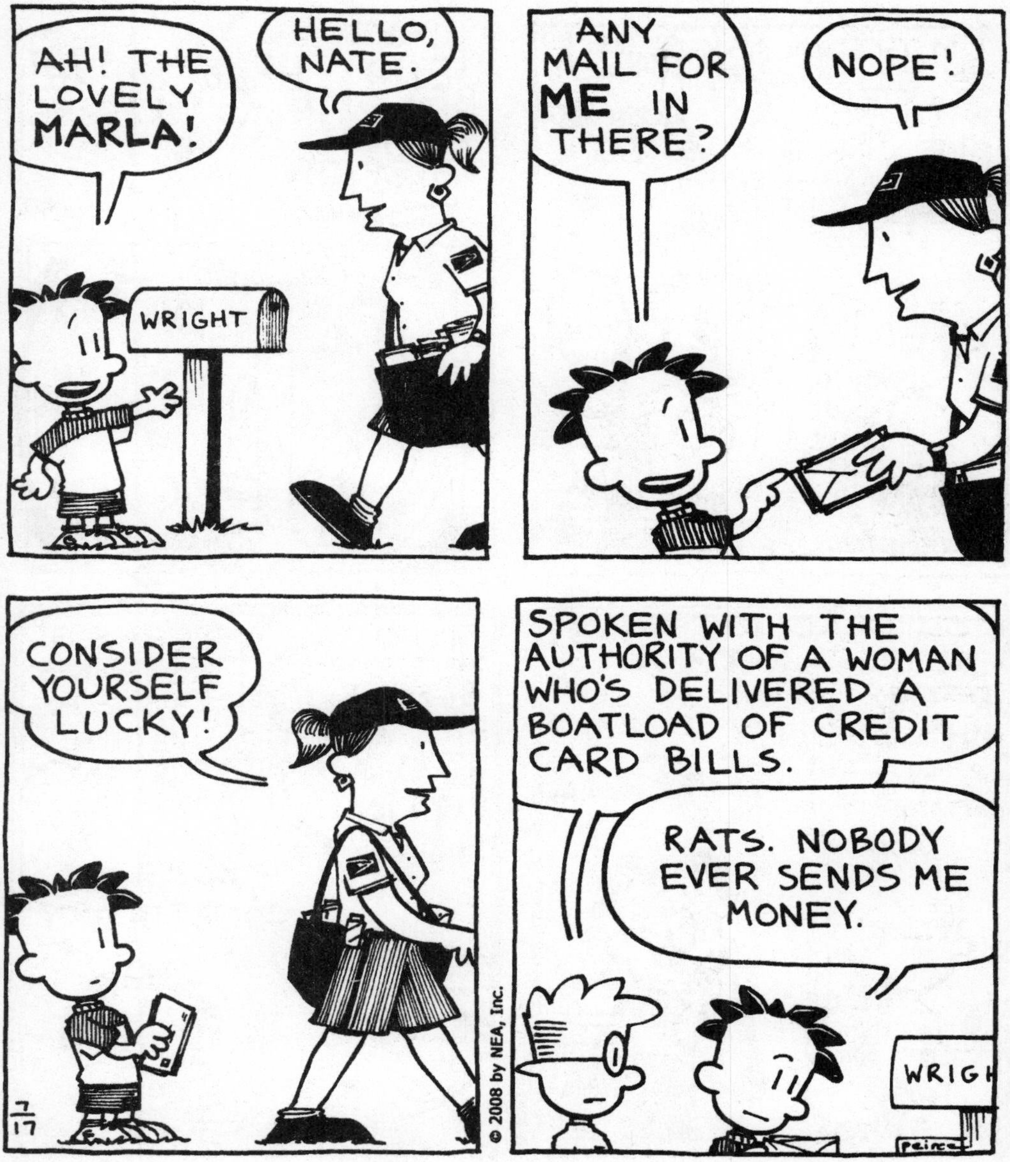
AH! THE LOVELY MARLA!
HELLO, NATE.
WRIGHT
ANY MAIL FOR ME IN THERE?
NOPE!
CONSIDER YOURSELF LUCKY!
7/17
© 2008 by NEA, Inc.
SPOKEN WITH THE AUTHORITY OF A WOMAN WHO'S DELIVERED A BOATLOAD OF CREDIT CARD BILLS.
RATS. NOBODY EVER SENDS ME MONEY.
WRIGH
peirce

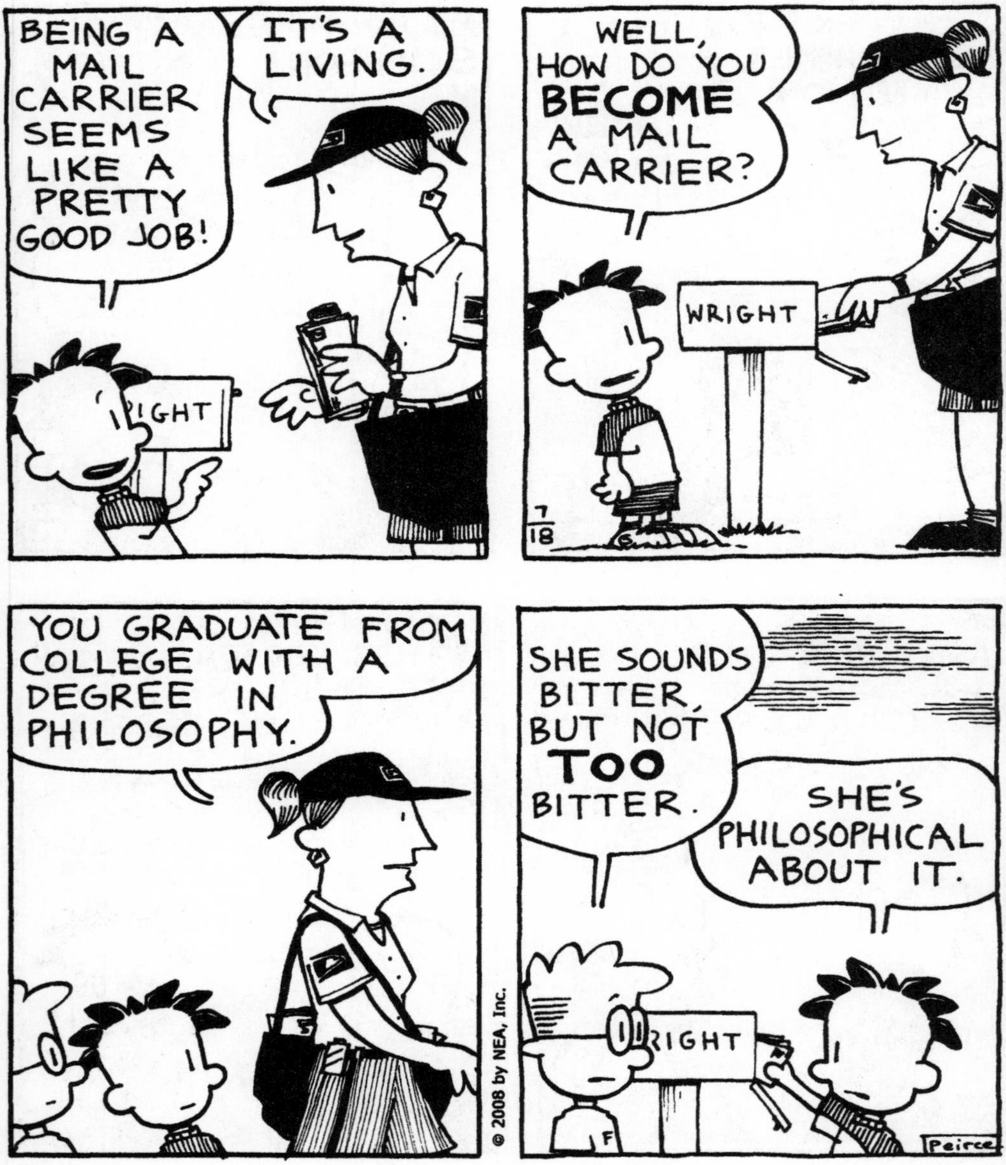
BEING A MAIL CARRIER SEEMS LIKE A PRETTY GOOD JOB!
IT'S A LIVING.
WELL, HOW DO YOU BECOME A MAIL CARRIER?
WRIGHT
7/18
YOU GRADUATE FROM COLLEGE WITH A DEGREE IN PHILOSOPHY.
SHE SOUNDS BITTER, BUT NOT TOO BITTER.
SHE'S PHILOSOPHICAL ABOUT IT.
Peirce

DESTINATION VACATION

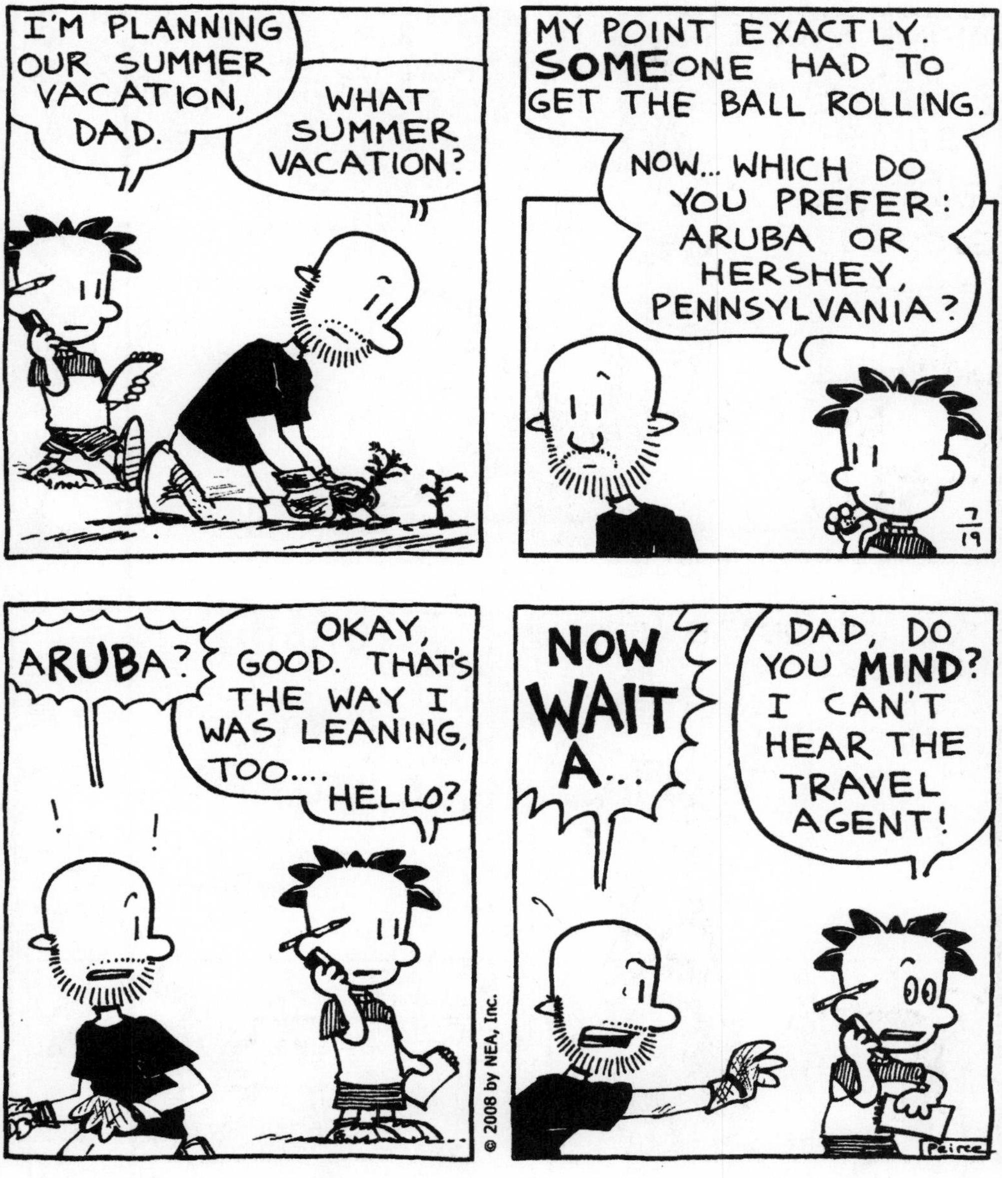
I'M PLANNING OUR SUMMER VACATION, DAD.
WHAT SUMMER VACATION?
MY POINT EXACTLY. SOMEONE HAD TO GET THE BALL ROLLING.
NOW... WHICH DO YOU PREFER: ARUBA OR HERSHEY, PENNSYLVANIA?
7/19
ARUBA?
OKAY, GOOD. THAT'S THE WAY I WAS LEANING, TOO.... HELLO?
!
!
© 2008 by NEA, Inc.
NOW WAIT A...
DAD, DO YOU MIND? I CAN'T HEAR THE TRAVEL AGENT!
Peirce

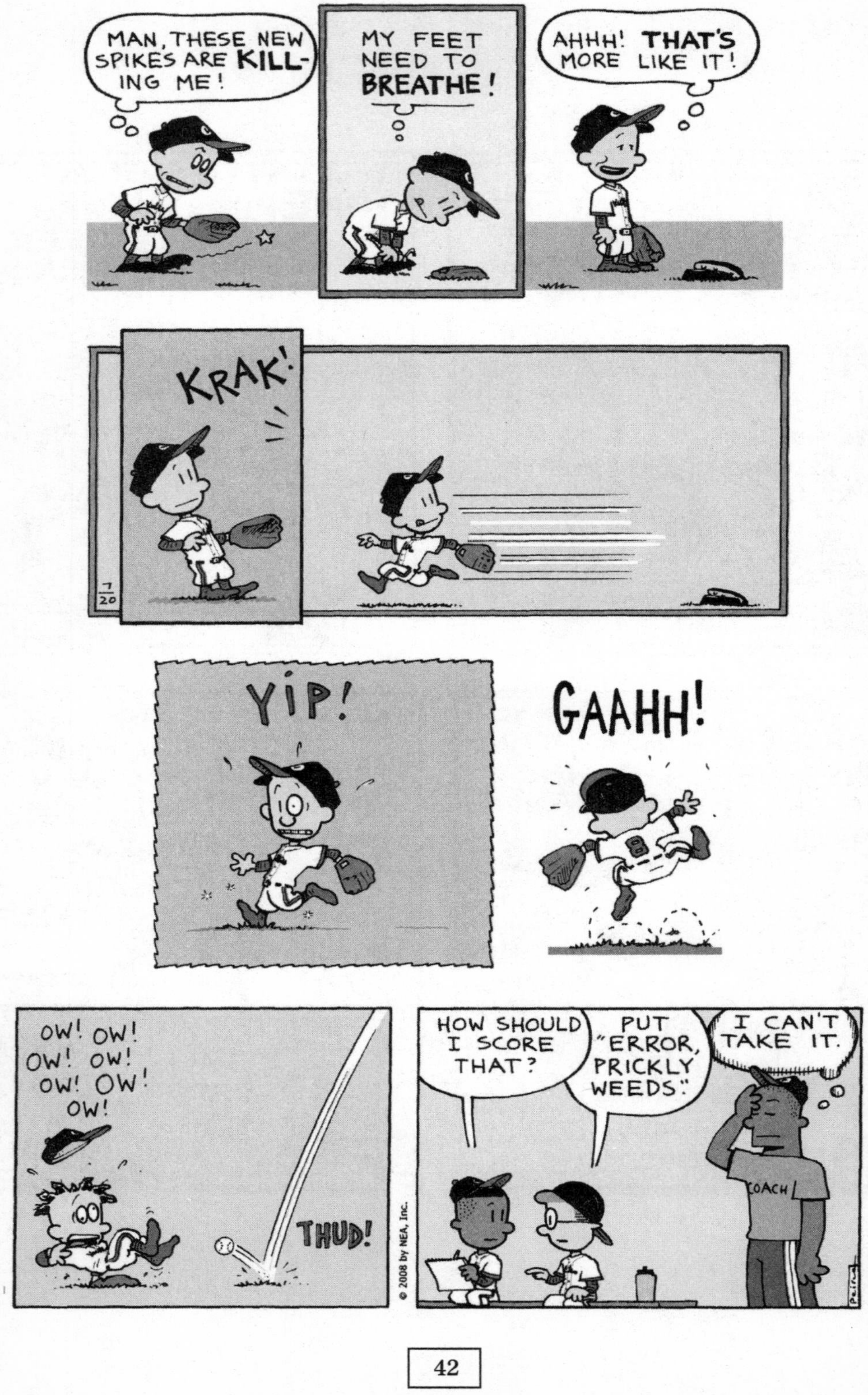

MAN, THESE NEW SPIKES ARE KILL-ING ME!
MY FEET NEED TO BREATHE!
AHHH! THAT'S MORE LIKE IT!
KRAK!
7/20
YIP!
GAAHH!
OW! OW! OW! OW! OW! OW! OW!
THUD!
© 2008 by NEA, Inc.
HOW SHOULD I SCORE THAT?
PUT "ERROR, PRICKLY WEEDS."
I CAN'T TAKE IT.
COACH

FAMILY (DYS)FUNCTION

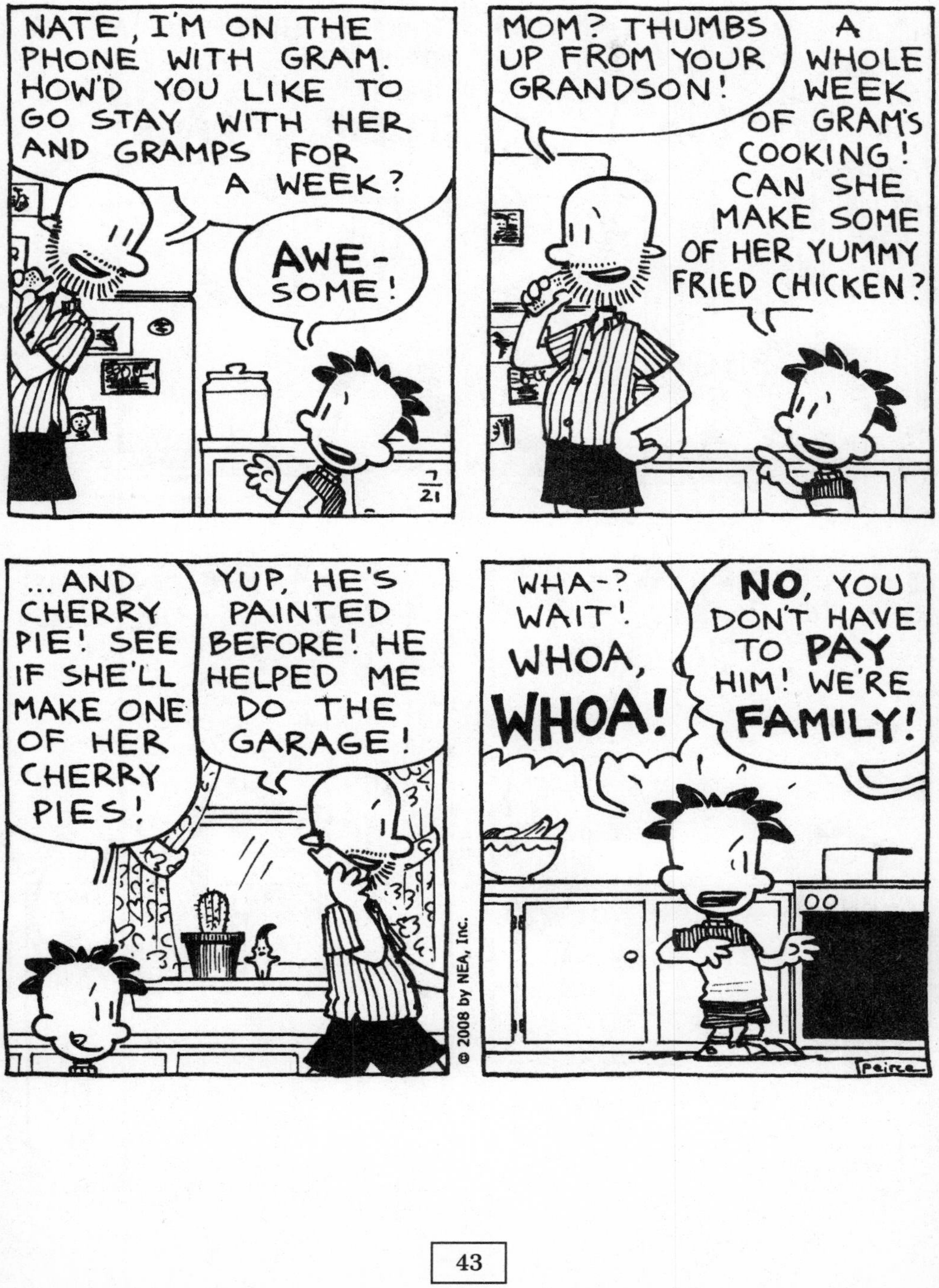
NATE, I'M ON THE PHONE WITH GRAM. HOW'D YOU LIKE TO GO STAY WITH HER AND GRAMPS FOR A WEEK?
AWE-SOME!
7/21
MOM? THUMBS UP FROM YOUR GRANDSON!
A WHOLE WEEK OF GRAM'S COOKING! CAN SHE MAKE SOME OF HER YUMMY FRIED CHICKEN?
...AND CHERRY PIE! SEE IF SHE'LL MAKE ONE OF HER CHERRY PIES!
YUP, HE'S PAINTED BEFORE! HE HELPED ME DO THE GARAGE!
© 2008 by NEA, Inc.
WHA-? WAIT! WHOA, WHOA!
NO, YOU DON'T HAVE TO PAY HIM! WE'RE FAMILY!
Peirce

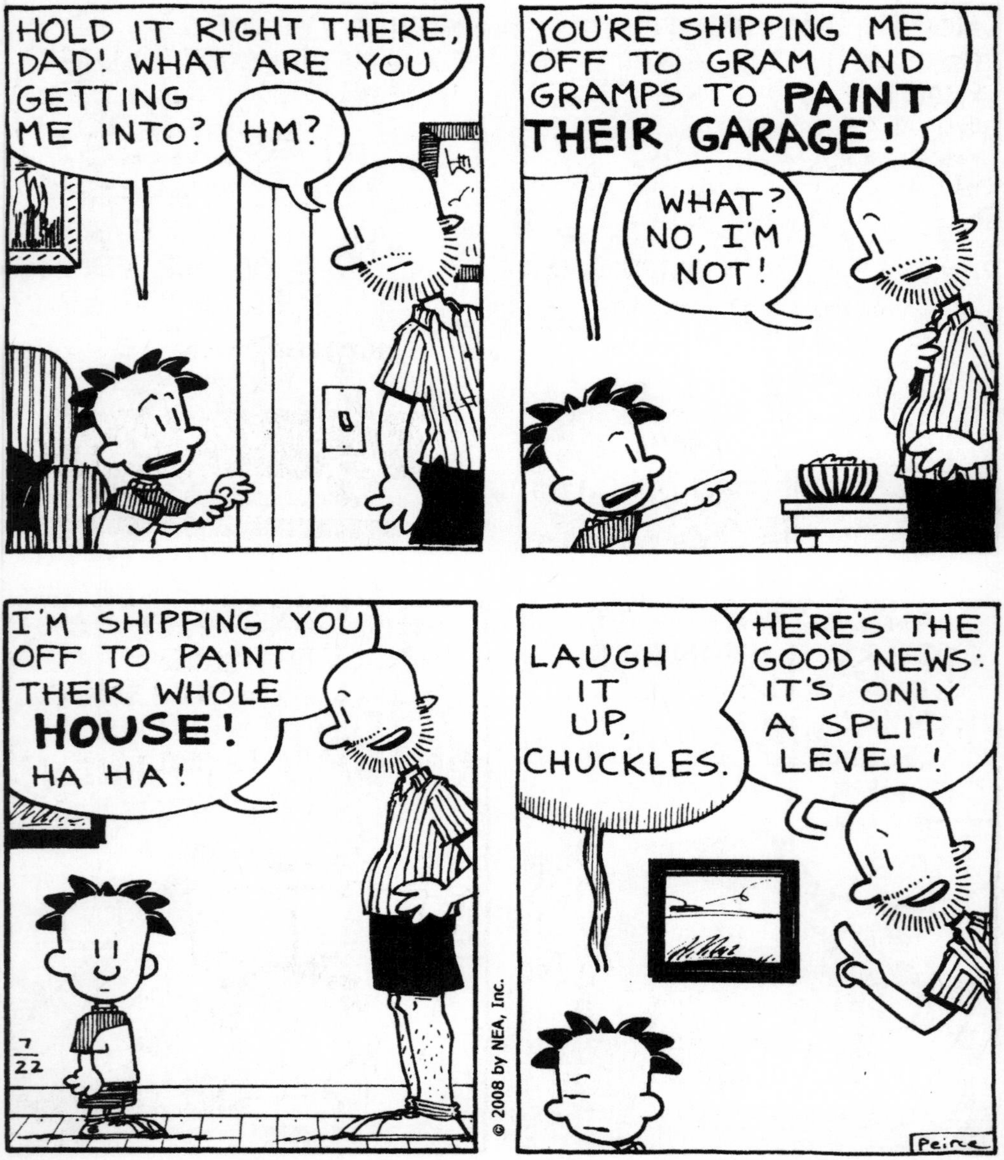
HOLD IT RIGHT THERE, DAD! WHAT ARE YOU GETTING ME INTO?
HM?
YOU'RE SHIPPING ME OFF TO GRAM AND GRAMPS TO **PAINT THEIR GARAGE!**
WHAT? NO, I'M NOT!
I'M SHIPPING YOU OFF TO PAINT THEIR WHOLE **HOUSE!** HA HA!
7/22
© 2008 by NEA, Inc.
HERE'S THE GOOD NEWS: IT'S ONLY A SPLIT LEVEL!
LAUGH IT UP, CHUCKLES.
Peirce

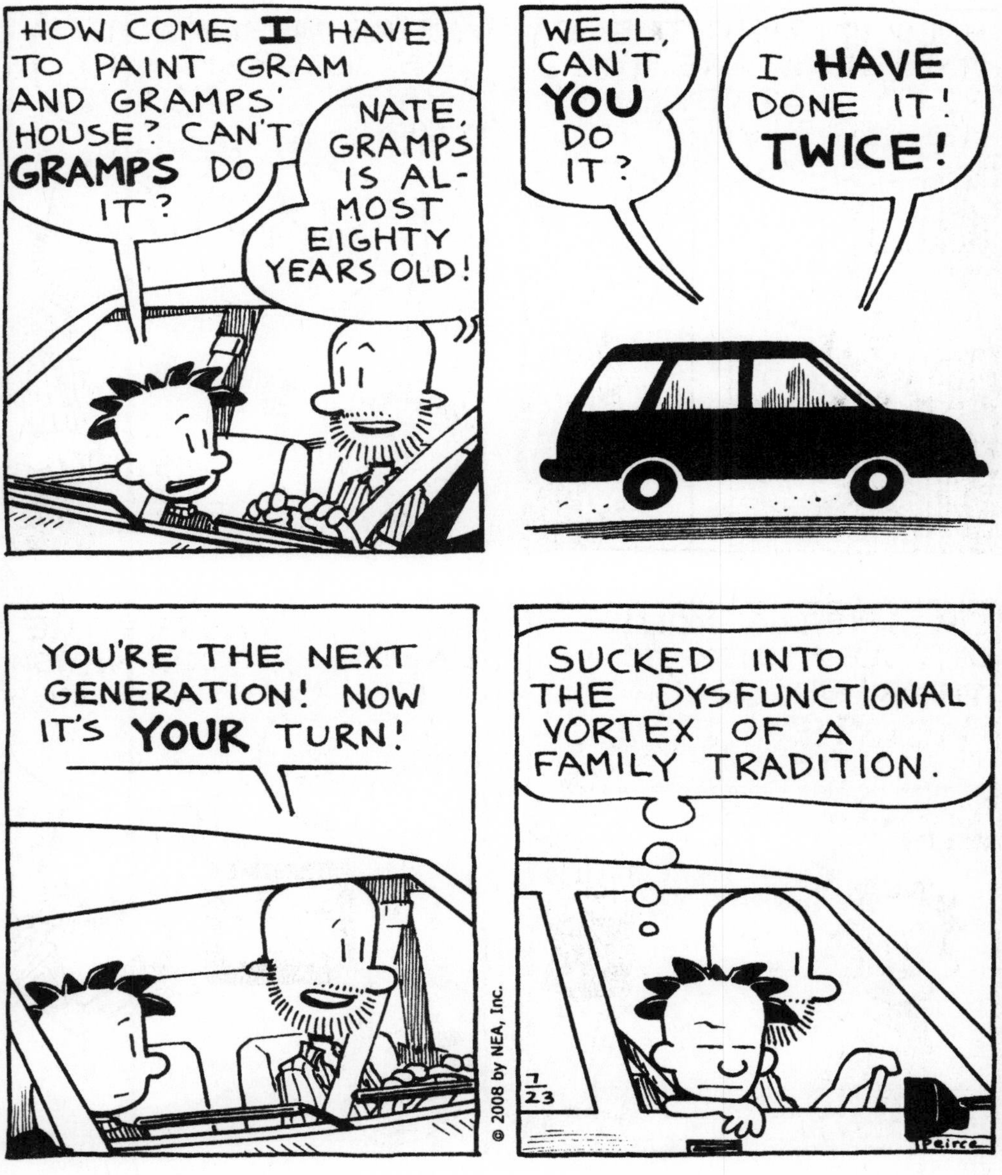
HOW COME I HAVE TO PAINT GRAM AND GRAMPS' HOUSE? CAN'T GRAMPS DO IT?
NATE, GRAMPS IS AL- MOST EIGHTY YEARS OLD!
WELL, CAN'T YOU DO IT?
I HAVE DONE IT! TWICE!
YOU'RE THE NEXT GENERATION! NOW IT'S YOUR TURN!
SUCKED INTO THE DYSFUNCTIONAL VORTEX OF A FAMILY TRADITION.
© 2008 by NEA, Inc.
7/23
Peirce

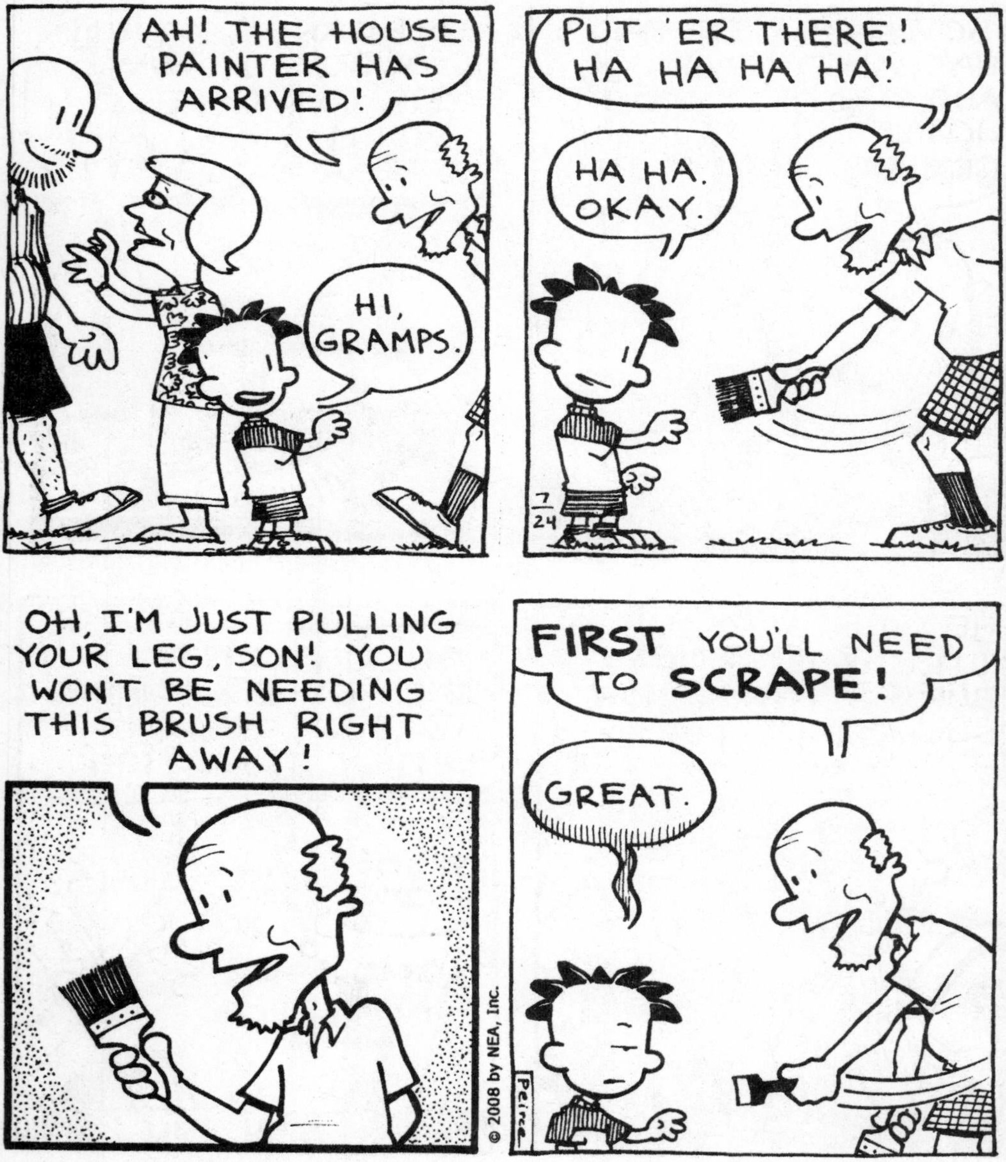
AH! THE HOUSE PAINTER HAS ARRIVED!
HI, GRAMPS.
PUT 'ER THERE! HA HA HA HA!
HA HA. OKAY.
7/24
OH, I'M JUST PULLING YOUR LEG, SON! YOU WON'T BE NEEDING THIS BRUSH RIGHT AWAY!
© 2008 by NEA, Inc.
PEIRCE
FIRST YOU'LL NEED TO SCRAPE!
GREAT.

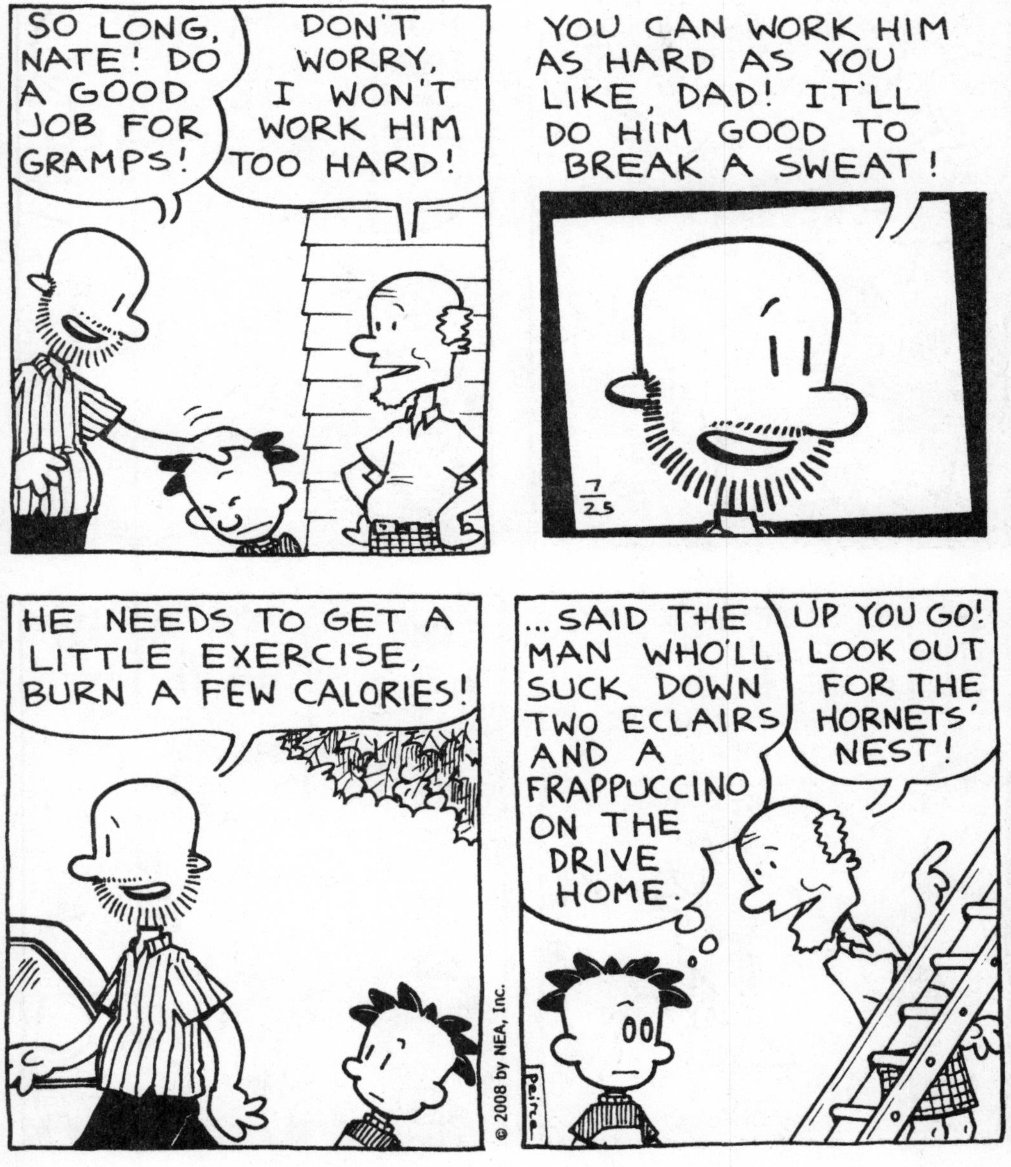
SO LONG, NATE! DO A GOOD JOB FOR GRAMPS!
DON'T WORRY, I WON'T WORK HIM TOO HARD!
YOU CAN WORK HIM AS HARD AS YOU LIKE, DAD! IT'LL DO HIM GOOD TO BREAK A SWEAT!
7/25
HE NEEDS TO GET A LITTLE EXERCISE, BURN A FEW CALORIES!
...SAID THE MAN WHO'LL SUCK DOWN TWO ECLAIRS AND A FRAPPUCCINO ON THE DRIVE HOME.
UP YOU GO! LOOK OUT FOR THE HORNETS' NEST!
Peirce

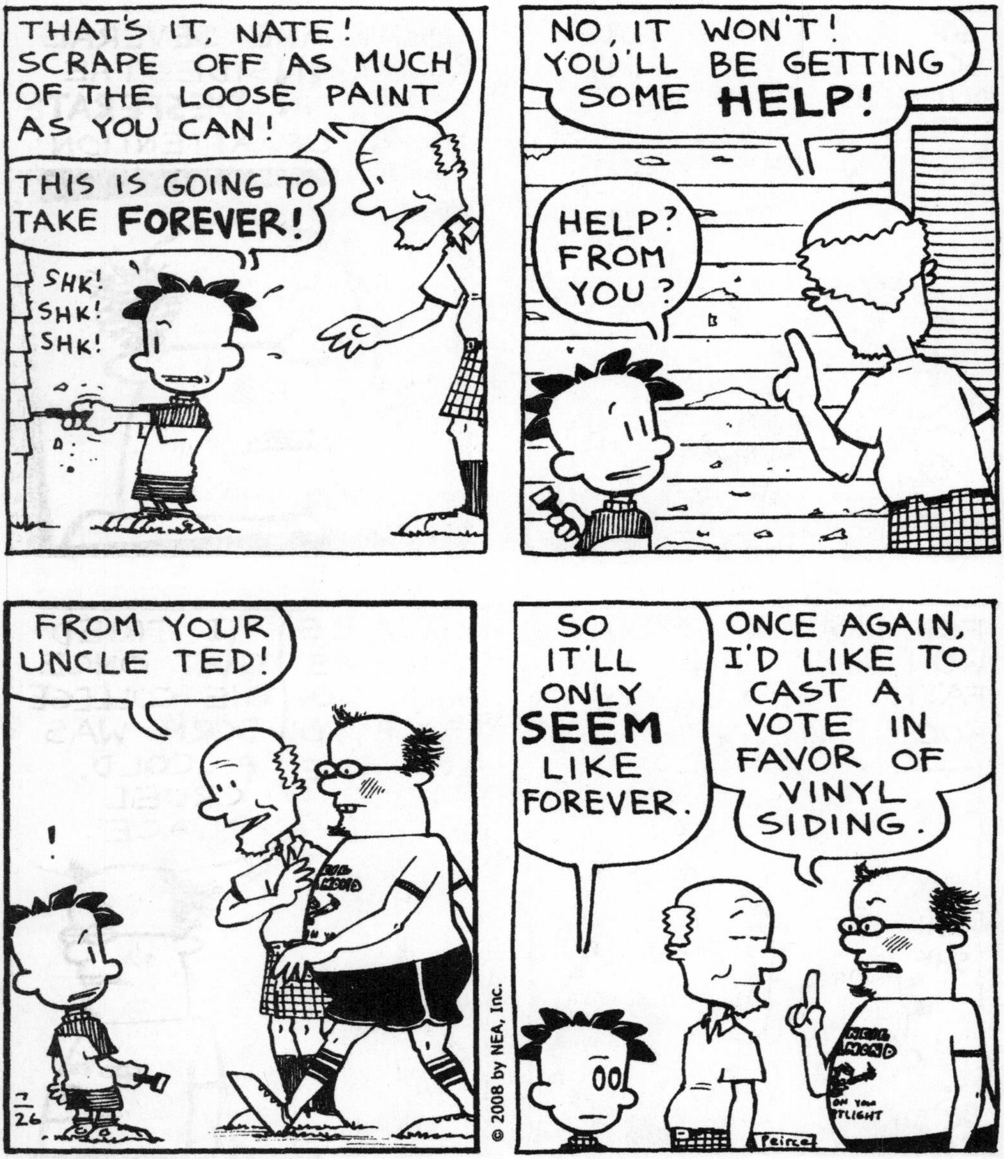
THAT'S IT, NATE! SCRAPE OFF AS MUCH OF THE LOOSE PAINT AS YOU CAN!
THIS IS GOING TO TAKE **FOREVER!**
SHK! SHK! SHK!
NO, IT WON'T! YOU'LL BE GETTING SOME **HELP!**
HELP? FROM YOU?
FROM YOUR UNCLE TED!
!
7/26
© 2008 by NEA, Inc.
SO IT'LL ONLY **SEEM** LIKE FOREVER.
ONCE AGAIN, I'D LIKE TO CAST A VOTE IN FAVOR OF VINYL SIDING.
Peirce

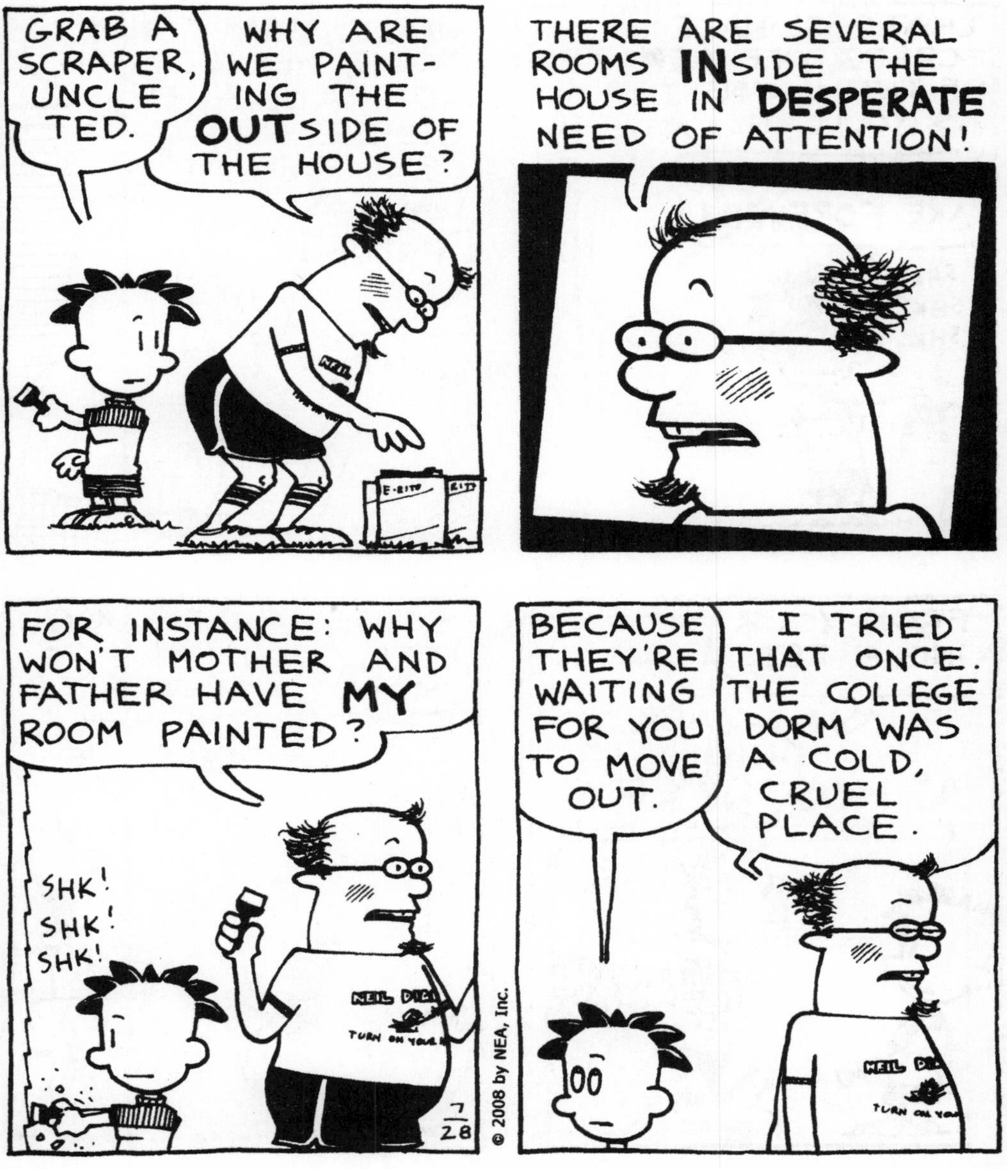
GRAB A SCRAPER, UNCLE TED.
WHY ARE WE PAINTING THE OUTSIDE OF THE HOUSE?
THERE ARE SEVERAL ROOMS INSIDE THE HOUSE IN DESPERATE NEED OF ATTENTION!
FOR INSTANCE: WHY WON'T MOTHER AND FATHER HAVE MY ROOM PAINTED?
SHK! SHK! SHK!
7/28
© 2008 by NEA, Inc.
BECAUSE THEY'RE WAITING FOR YOU TO MOVE OUT.
I TRIED THAT ONCE. THE COLLEGE DORM WAS A COLD, CRUEL PLACE.

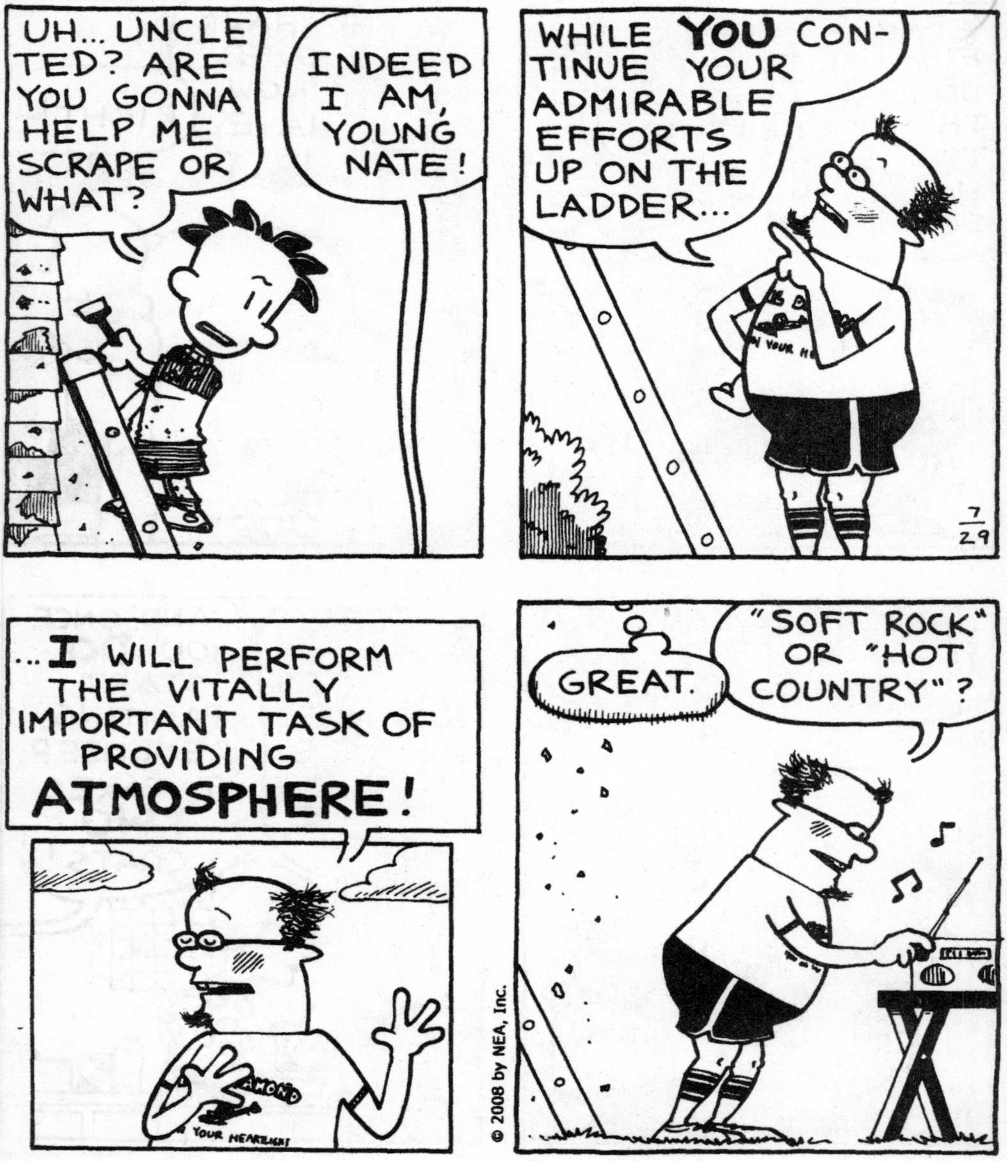
UH... UNCLE TED? ARE YOU GONNA HELP ME SCRAPE OR WHAT?
INDEED I AM, YOUNG NATE!
WHILE YOU CONTINUE YOUR ADMIRABLE EFFORTS UP ON THE LADDER...
7
29
...I WILL PERFORM THE VITALLY IMPORTANT TASK OF PROVIDING ATMOSPHERE!
GREAT.
"SOFT ROCK" OR "HOT COUNTRY"?
© 2008 by NEA, Inc.

GRAMPS! I'M FINALLY ALL DONE WITH THE SCRAPING! THE WHOLE HOUSE IS SCRAPED!
WONDERFUL!
SO THE HARD PART'S OVER, RIGHT? NOW ALL I HAVE TO DO IS PAINT IT!
RIGHT!...
...AFTER YOU SAND IT, POWER-WASH IT AND PRIME IT.
7/31
IF YOU HEAR A THUD, IT'S JUST ME THROWING MYSELF OFF THE LADDER.
...AND ONCE YOU **DO** START PAINTING, REMEMBER IT TAKES **TWO** COATS!

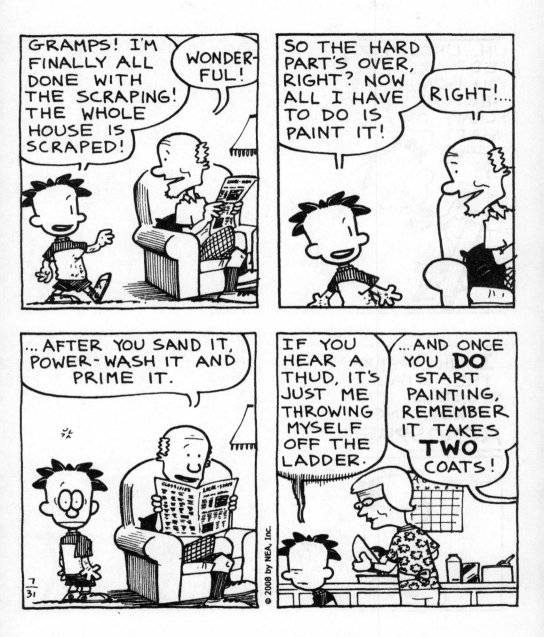

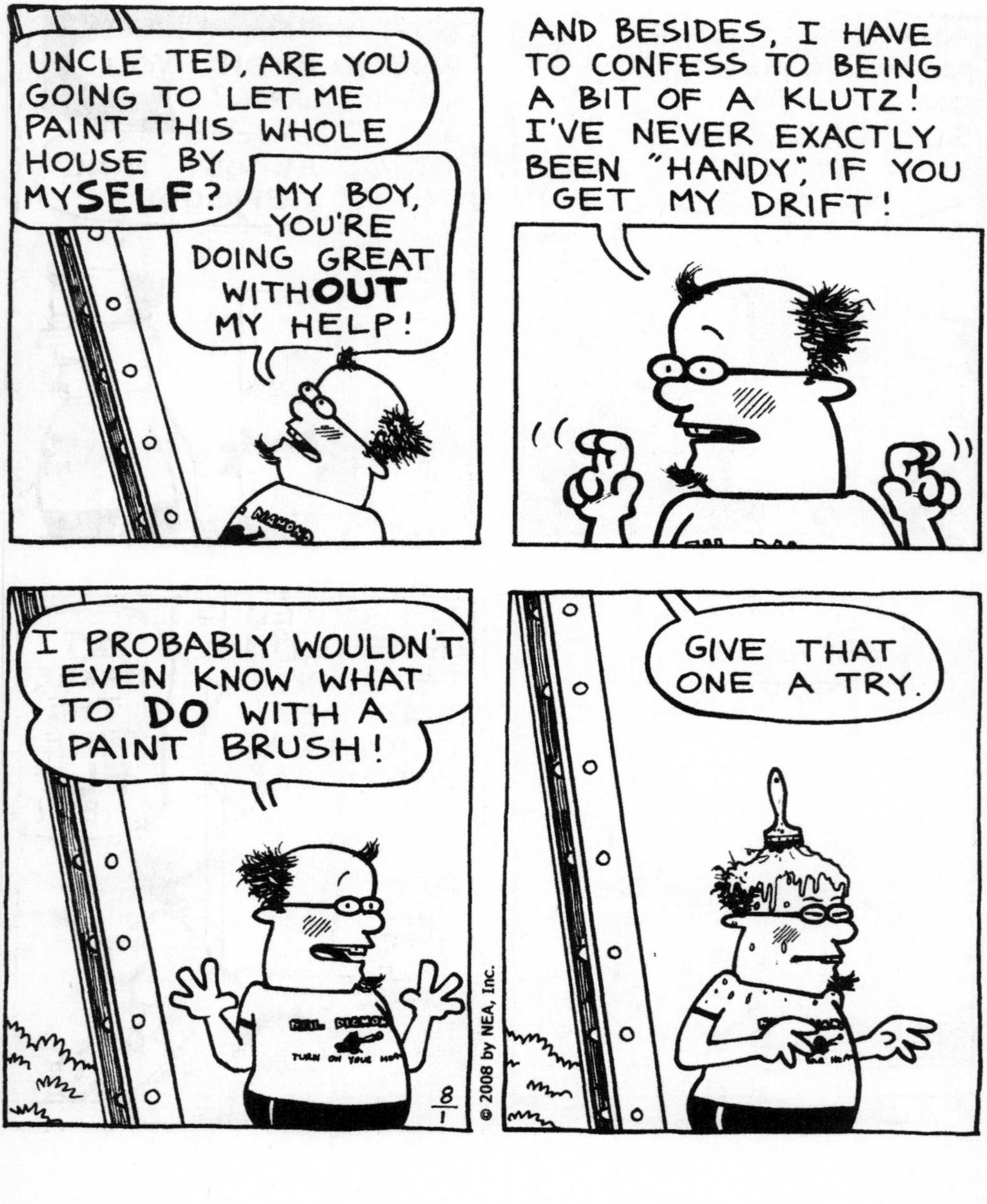
UNCLE TED, ARE YOU GOING TO LET ME PAINT THIS WHOLE HOUSE BY MYSELF?
MY BOY, YOU'RE DOING GREAT WITHOUT MY HELP!
AND BESIDES, I HAVE TO CONFESS TO BEING A BIT OF A KLUTZ! I'VE NEVER EXACTLY BEEN "HANDY," IF YOU GET MY DRIFT!
I PROBABLY WOULDN'T EVEN KNOW WHAT TO DO WITH A PAINT BRUSH!
8/1
© 2008 by NEA, Inc.
GIVE THAT ONE A TRY.

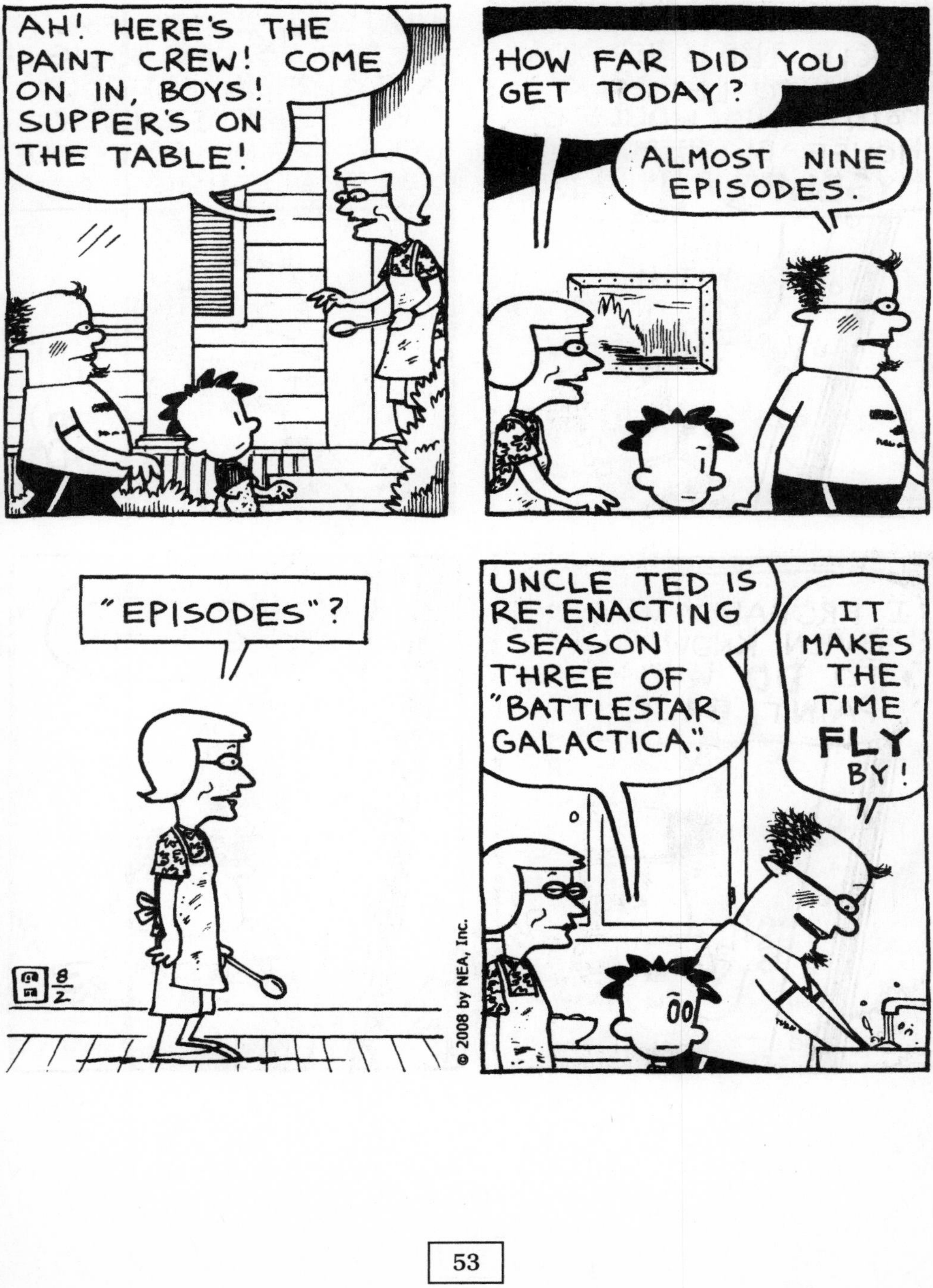
AH! HERE'S THE PAINT CREW! COME ON IN, BOYS! SUPPER'S ON THE TABLE!
HOW FAR DID YOU GET TODAY?
ALMOST NINE EPISODES.
"EPISODES"?
UNCLE TED IS RE-ENACTING SEASON THREE OF "BATTLESTAR GALACTICA".
IT MAKES THE TIME FLY BY!
8/2
© 2008 by NEA, Inc.

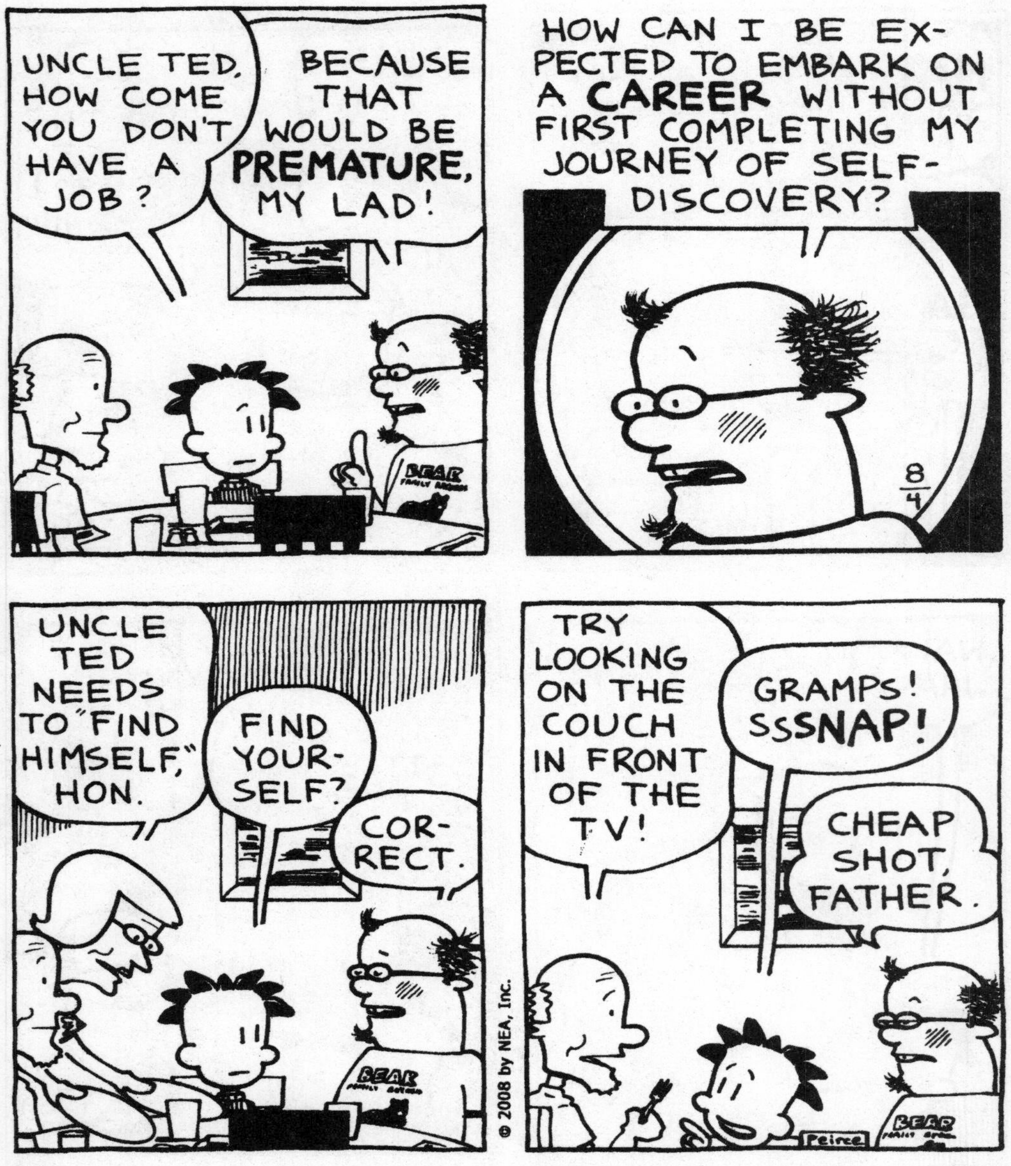
UNCLE TED, HOW COME YOU DON'T HAVE A JOB?
BECAUSE THAT WOULD BE **PREMATURE,** MY LAD!
BEAR FAMILY BREWERY
HOW CAN I BE EXPECTED TO EMBARK ON A **CAREER** WITHOUT FIRST COMPLETING MY JOURNEY OF SELF-DISCOVERY?
8/4
UNCLE TED NEEDS TO "FIND HIMSELF," HON.
FIND YOURSELF?
CORRECT.
BEAR
© 2008 by NEA, Inc.
TRY LOOKING ON THE COUCH IN FRONT OF THE TV!
GRAMPS! SSSNAP!
CHEAP SHOT, FATHER.
Peirce
BEAR

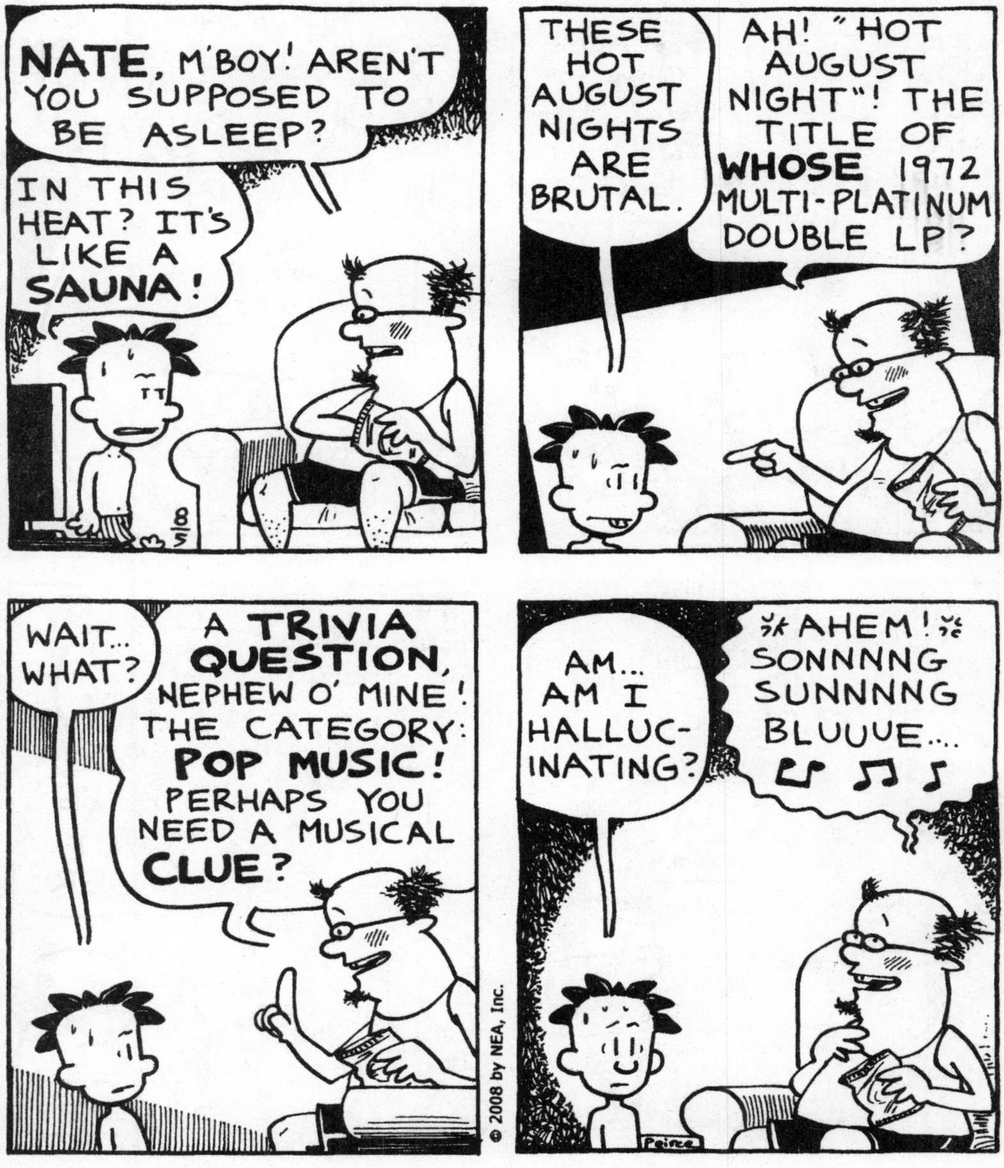
NATE, M'BOY! AREN'T YOU SUPPOSED TO BE ASLEEP?
IN THIS HEAT? IT'S LIKE A SAUNA!
8/5
THESE HOT AUGUST NIGHTS ARE BRUTAL.
AH! "HOT AUGUST NIGHT"! THE TITLE OF WHOSE 1972 MULTI-PLATINUM DOUBLE LP?
WAIT... WHAT?
A TRIVIA QUESTION, NEPHEW O' MINE! THE CATEGORY: POP MUSIC! PERHAPS YOU NEED A MUSICAL CLUE?
© 2008 by NEA, Inc.
AM... AM I HALLUC-INATING?
AHEM! SONNNNG SUNNNNG BLUUUE....
Peirce

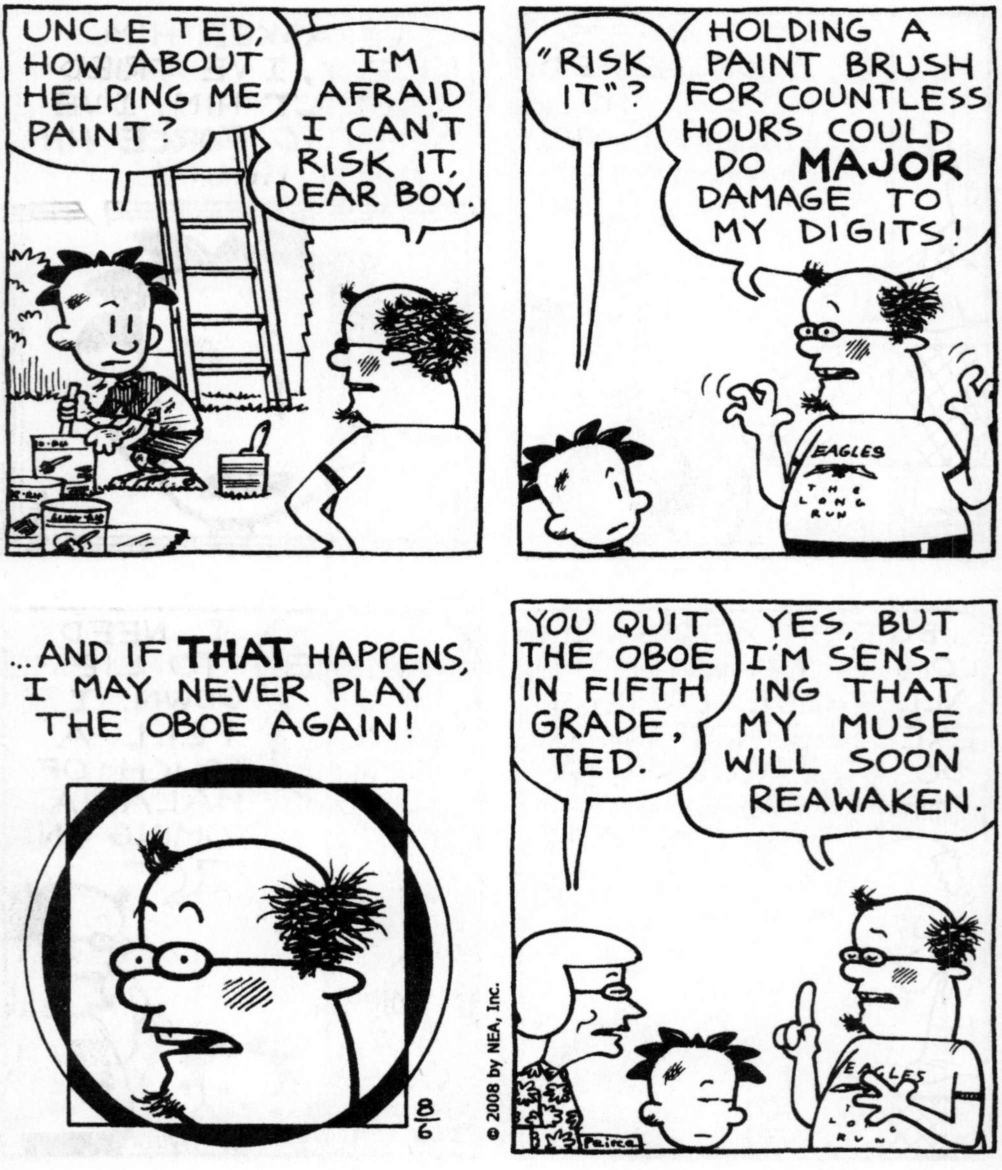
UNCLE TED, HOW ABOUT HELPING ME PAINT?
I'M AFRAID I CAN'T RISK IT, DEAR BOY.
"RISK IT"?
HOLDING A PAINT BRUSH FOR COUNTLESS HOURS COULD DO **MAJOR** DAMAGE TO MY DIGITS!
EAGLES THE LONG RUN
...AND IF **THAT** HAPPENS, I MAY NEVER PLAY THE OBOE AGAIN!
8/6
© 2008 by NEA, Inc.
YOU QUIT THE OBOE IN FIFTH GRADE, TED.
YES, BUT I'M SENSING THAT MY MUSE WILL SOON REAWAKEN.
EAGLES
Peirce

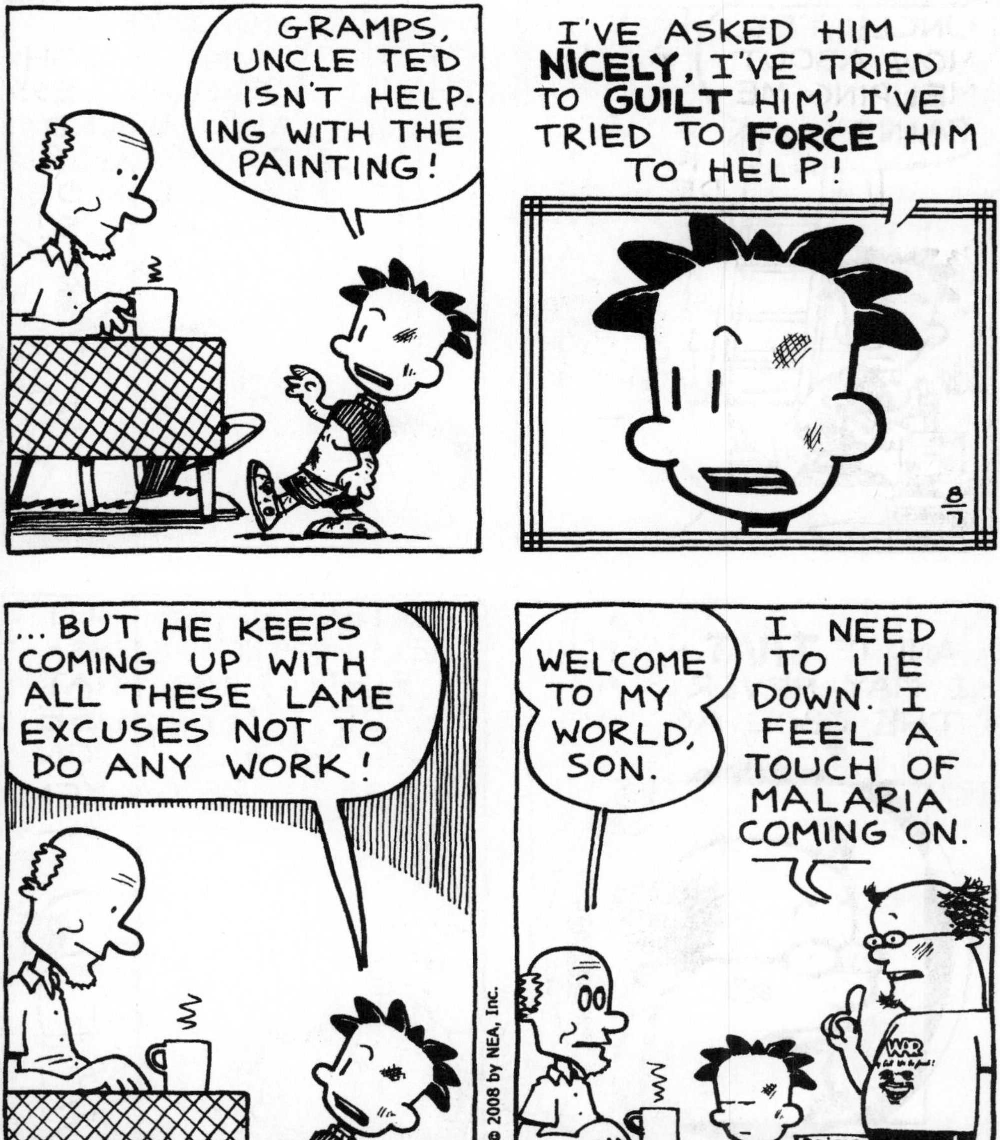
GRAMPS, UNCLE TED ISN'T HELPING WITH THE PAINTING!
I'VE ASKED HIM **NICELY**, I'VE TRIED TO **GUILT** HIM, I'VE TRIED TO **FORCE** HIM TO HELP!
8/7
... BUT HE KEEPS COMING UP WITH ALL THESE LAME EXCUSES NOT TO DO ANY WORK!
WELCOME TO MY WORLD, SON.
I NEED TO LIE DOWN. I FEEL A TOUCH OF MALARIA COMING ON.
Peirce

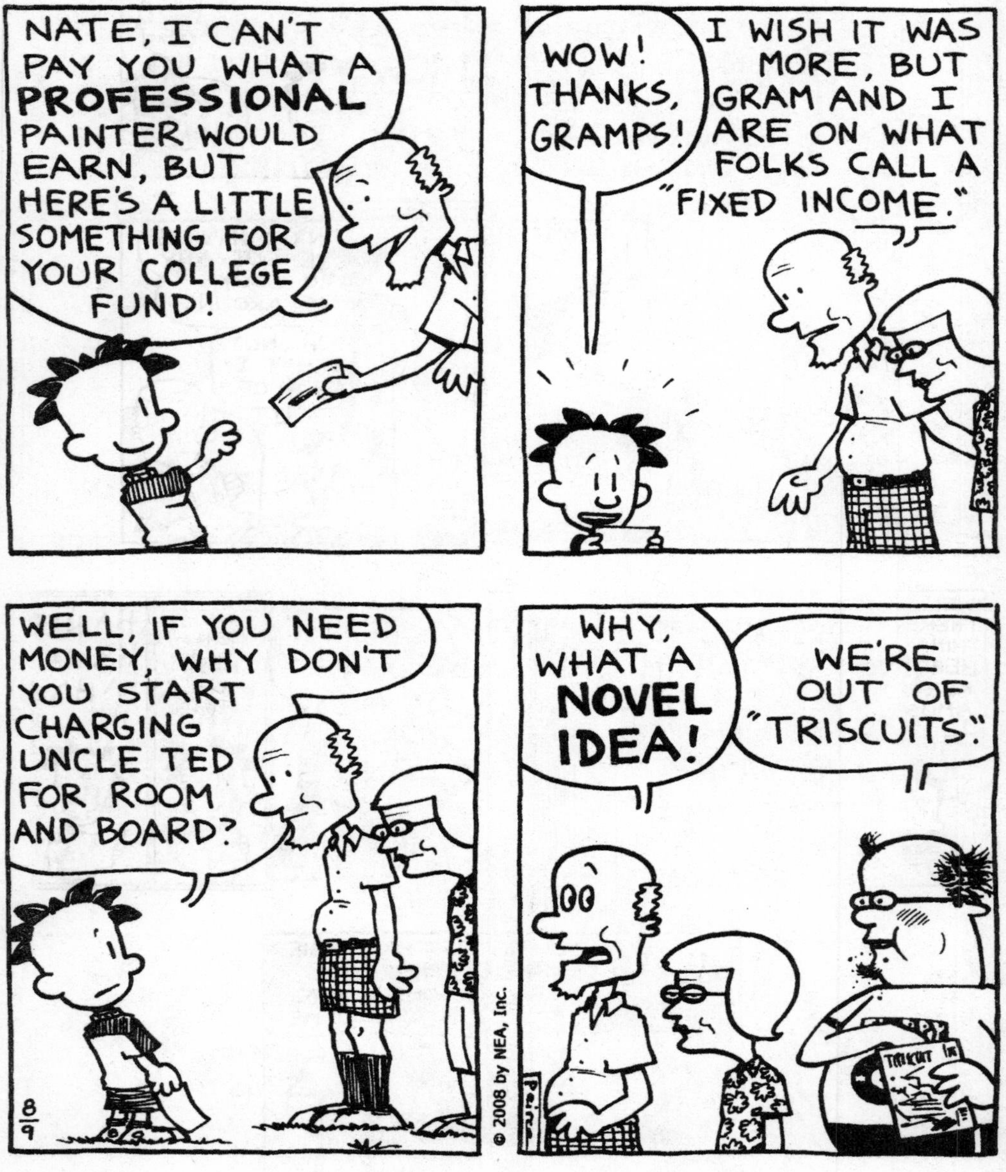
NATE, I CAN'T PAY YOU WHAT A **PROFESSIONAL** PAINTER WOULD EARN, BUT HERE'S A LITTLE SOMETHING FOR YOUR COLLEGE FUND!
WOW! THANKS, GRAMPS!
I WISH IT WAS MORE, BUT GRAM AND I ARE ON WHAT FOLKS CALL A "FIXED INCOME."
WELL, IF YOU NEED MONEY, WHY DON'T YOU START CHARGING UNCLE TED FOR ROOM AND BOARD?
8/9
WHY, WHAT A **NOVEL IDEA!**
WE'RE OUT OF "TRISCUITS."

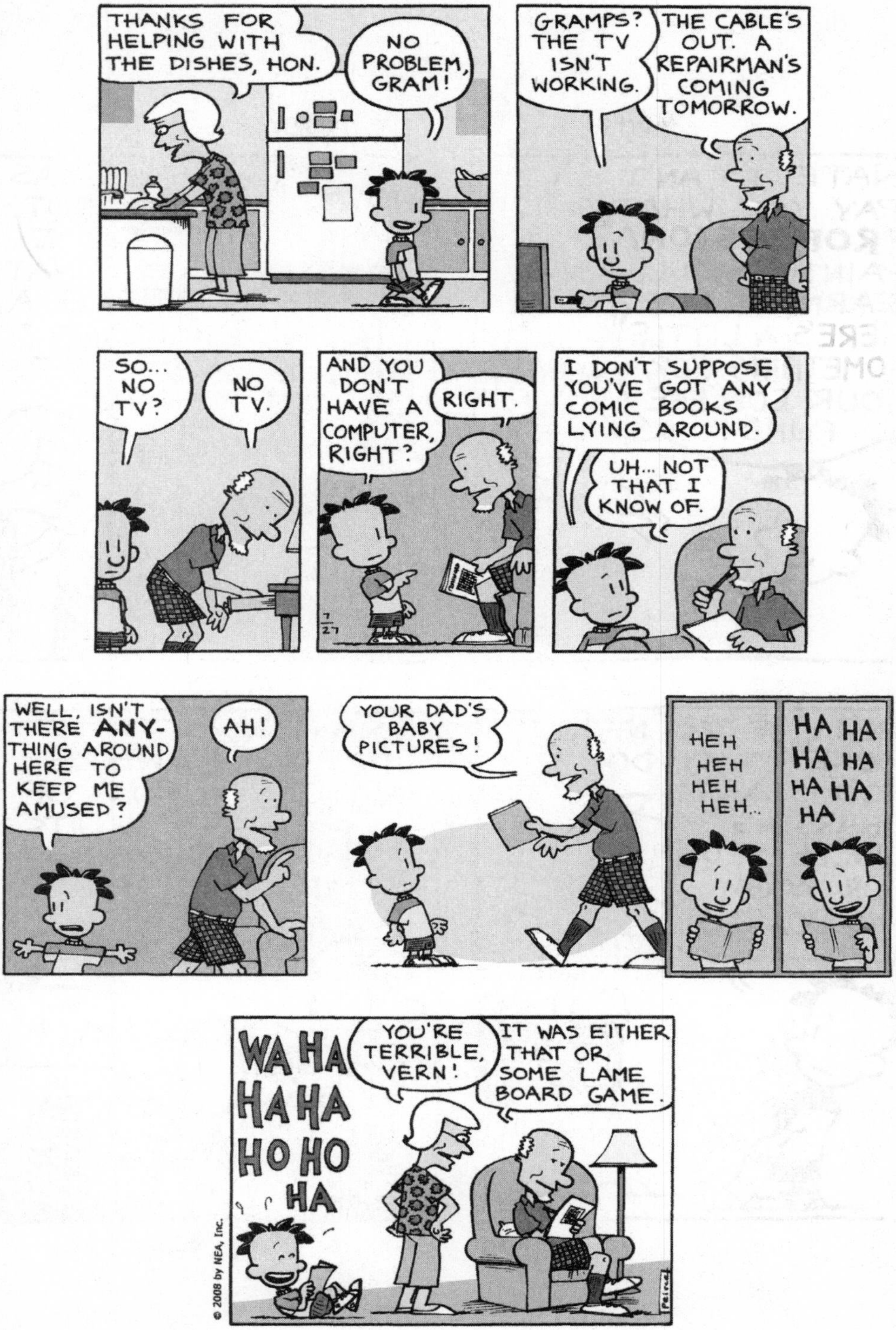
THANKS FOR HELPING WITH THE DISHES, HON.
NO PROBLEM, GRAM!
GRAMPS? THE TV ISN'T WORKING.
THE CABLE'S OUT. A REPAIRMAN'S COMING TOMORROW.
SO... NO TV?
NO TV.
AND YOU DON'T HAVE A COMPUTER, RIGHT?
RIGHT.
I DON'T SUPPOSE YOU'VE GOT ANY COMIC BOOKS LYING AROUND.
UH... NOT THAT I KNOW OF.
WELL, ISN'T THERE ANYTHING AROUND HERE TO KEEP ME AMUSED?
AH!
YOUR DAD'S BABY PICTURES!
HEH HEH HEH HEH...
HA HA HA HA HA HA HA
WA HA HA HA HO HO HA
YOU'RE TERRIBLE, VERN!
IT WAS EITHER THAT OR SOME LAME BOARD GAME.
© 2008 by NEA, Inc.
Peirce

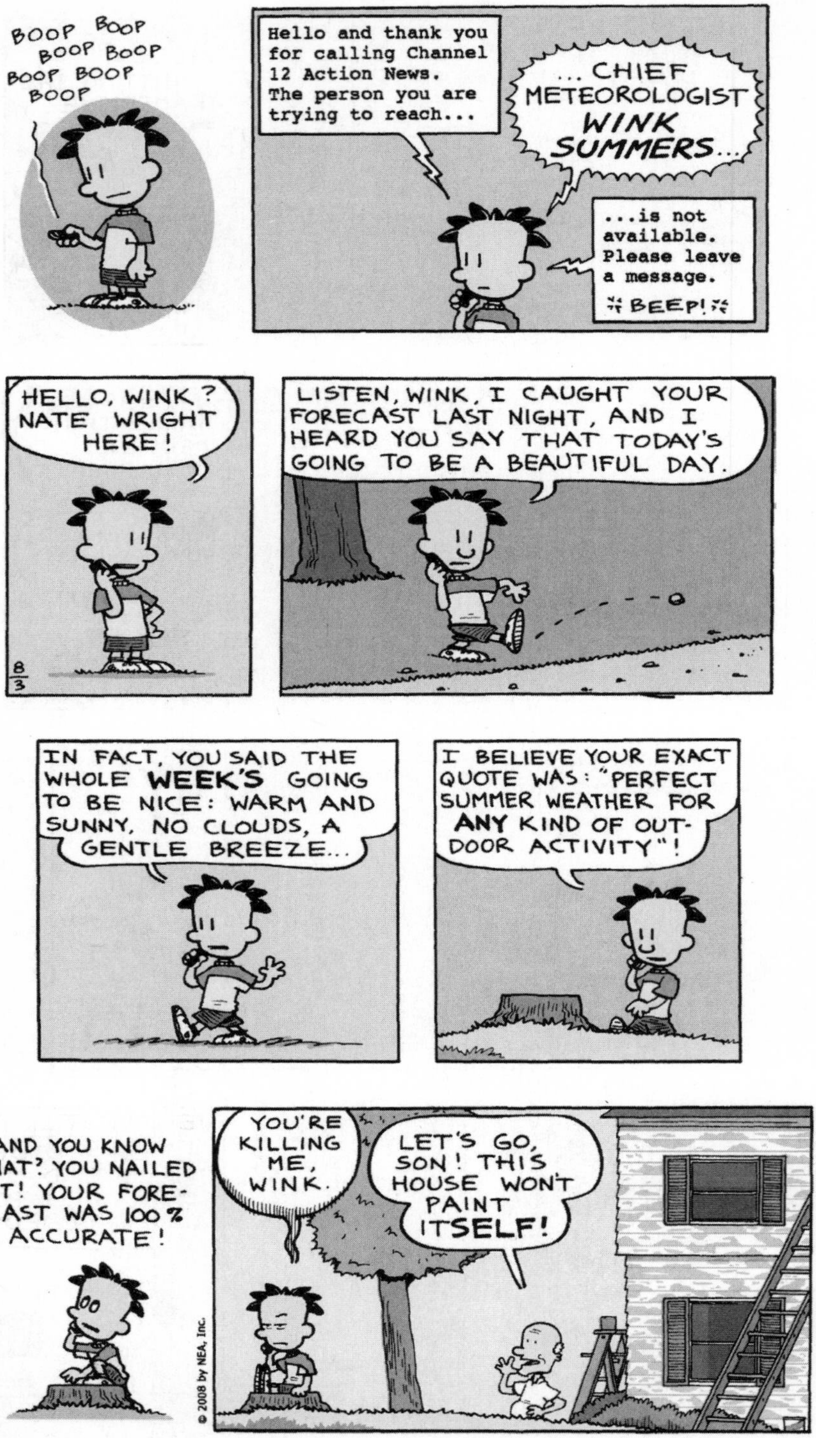
BOOP BOOP BOOP BOOP BOOP BOOP BOOP
Hello and thank you for calling Channel 12 Action News. The person you are trying to reach...
... CHIEF METEOROLOGIST WINK SUMMERS...
...is not available. Please leave a message.
BEEP!
HELLO, WINK? NATE WRIGHT HERE!
8/3
LISTEN, WINK, I CAUGHT YOUR FORECAST LAST NIGHT, AND I HEARD YOU SAY THAT TODAY'S GOING TO BE A BEAUTIFUL DAY.
IN FACT, YOU SAID THE WHOLE WEEK'S GOING TO BE NICE: WARM AND SUNNY, NO CLOUDS, A GENTLE BREEZE...
I BELIEVE YOUR EXACT QUOTE WAS: "PERFECT SUMMER WEATHER FOR ANY KIND OF OUT-DOOR ACTIVITY"!
AND YOU KNOW WHAT? YOU NAILED IT! YOUR FORE-CAST WAS 100% ACCURATE!
YOU'RE KILLING ME, WINK.
LET'S GO, SON! THIS HOUSE WON'T PAINT ITSELF!
© 2008 by NEA, Inc.

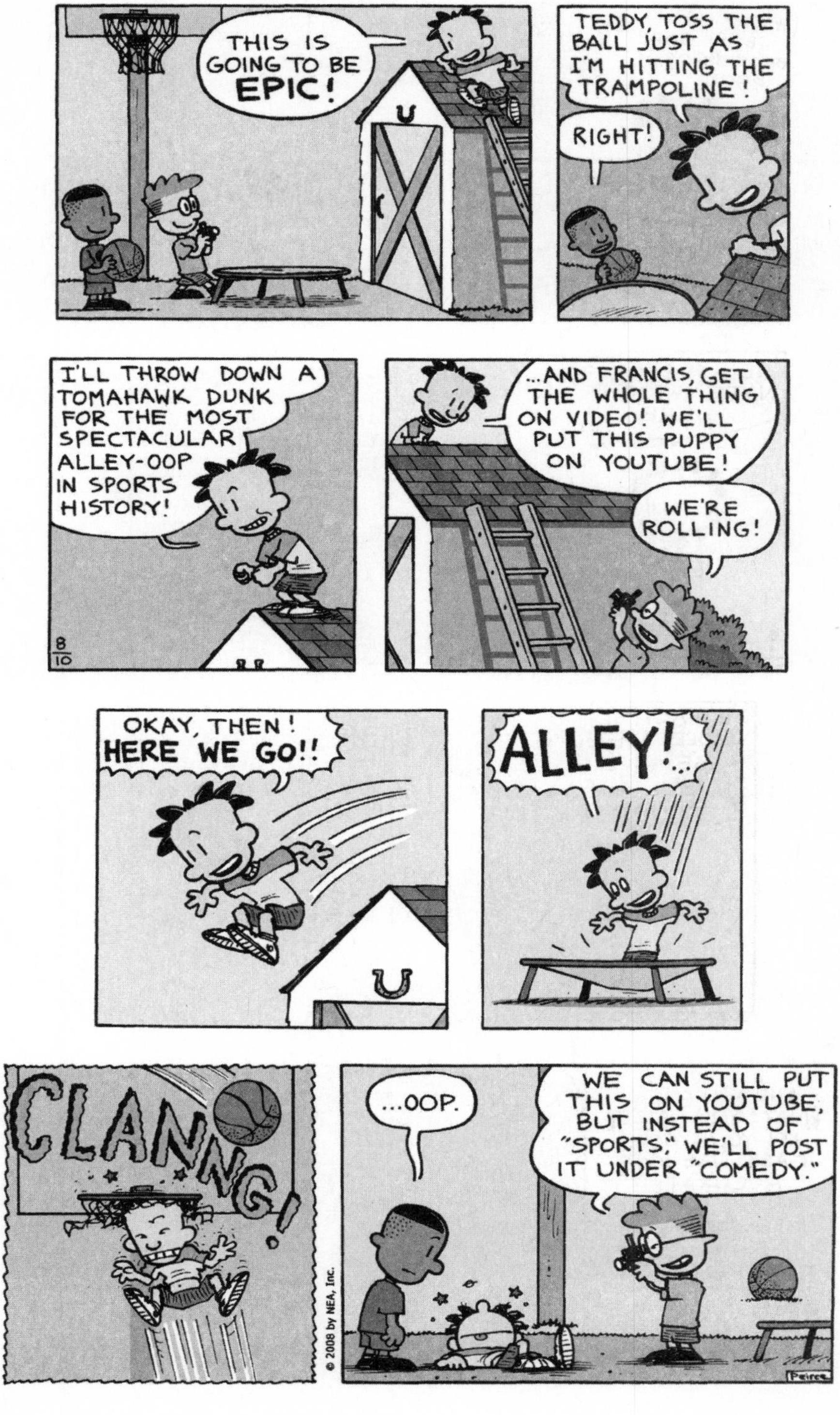
THIS IS GOING TO BE EPIC!
TEDDY, TOSS THE BALL JUST AS I'M HITTING THE TRAMPOLINE!
RIGHT!
I'LL THROW DOWN A TOMAHAWK DUNK FOR THE MOST SPECTACULAR ALLEY-OOP IN SPORTS HISTORY!
8/10
...AND FRANCIS, GET THE WHOLE THING ON VIDEO! WE'LL PUT THIS PUPPY ON YOUTUBE!
WE'RE ROLLING!
OKAY, THEN! HERE WE GO!!
ALLEY!...
CLANNG!
© 2008 by NEA, Inc.
...OOP.
WE CAN STILL PUT THIS ON YOUTUBE, BUT INSTEAD OF "SPORTS," WE'LL POST IT UNDER "COMEDY."
Peirce

WELCOME TO THE REAL WORLD

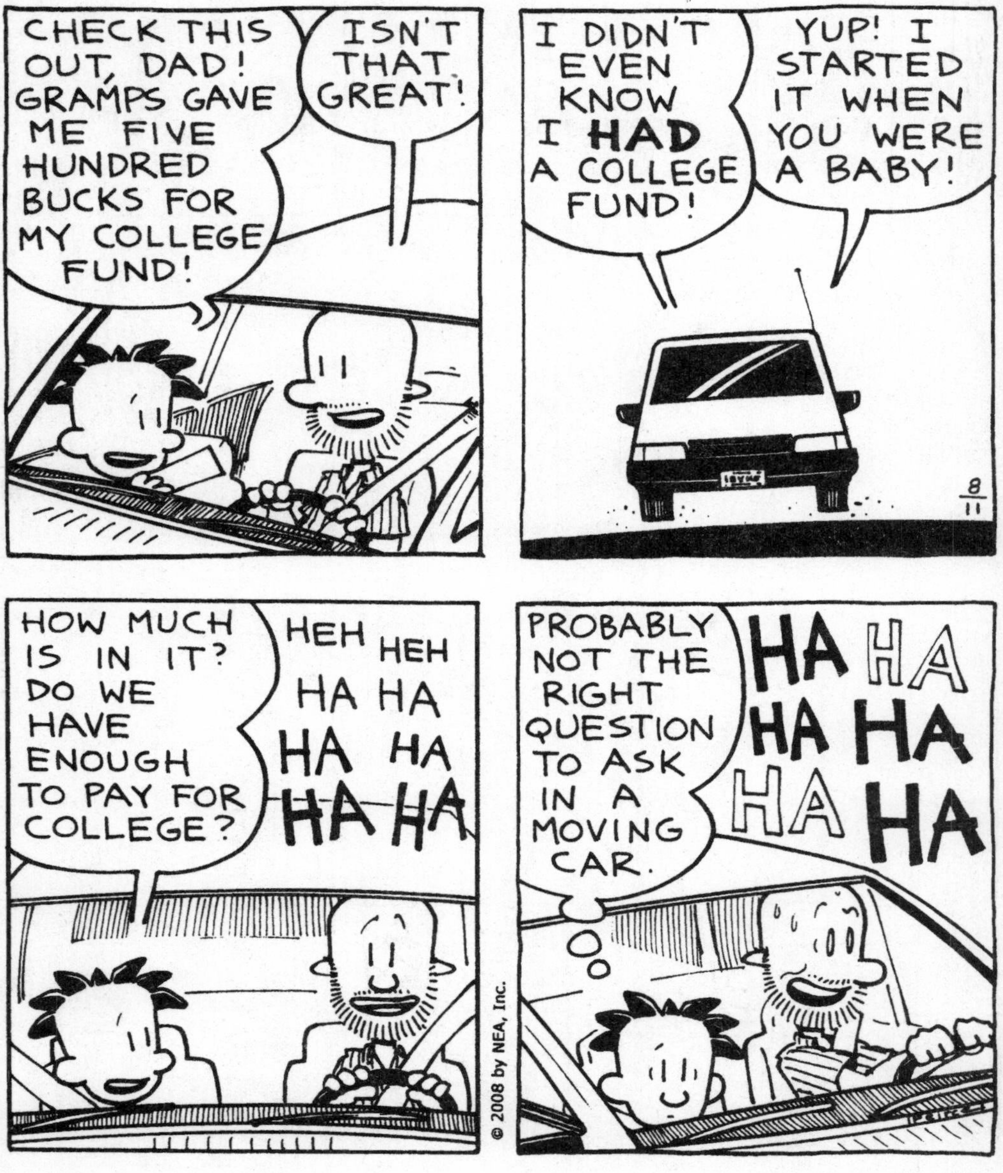
CHECK THIS OUT, DAD! GRAMPS GAVE ME FIVE HUNDRED BUCKS FOR MY COLLEGE FUND!
ISN'T THAT GREAT!
I DIDN'T EVEN KNOW I **HAD** A COLLEGE FUND!
YUP! I STARTED IT WHEN YOU WERE A BABY!
HOW MUCH IS IN IT? DO WE HAVE ENOUGH TO PAY FOR COLLEGE?
HEH HEH HA HA HA HA HA HA
PROBABLY NOT THE RIGHT QUESTION TO ASK IN A MOVING CAR.
HA HA HA HA HA HA
© 2008 by NEA, Inc.

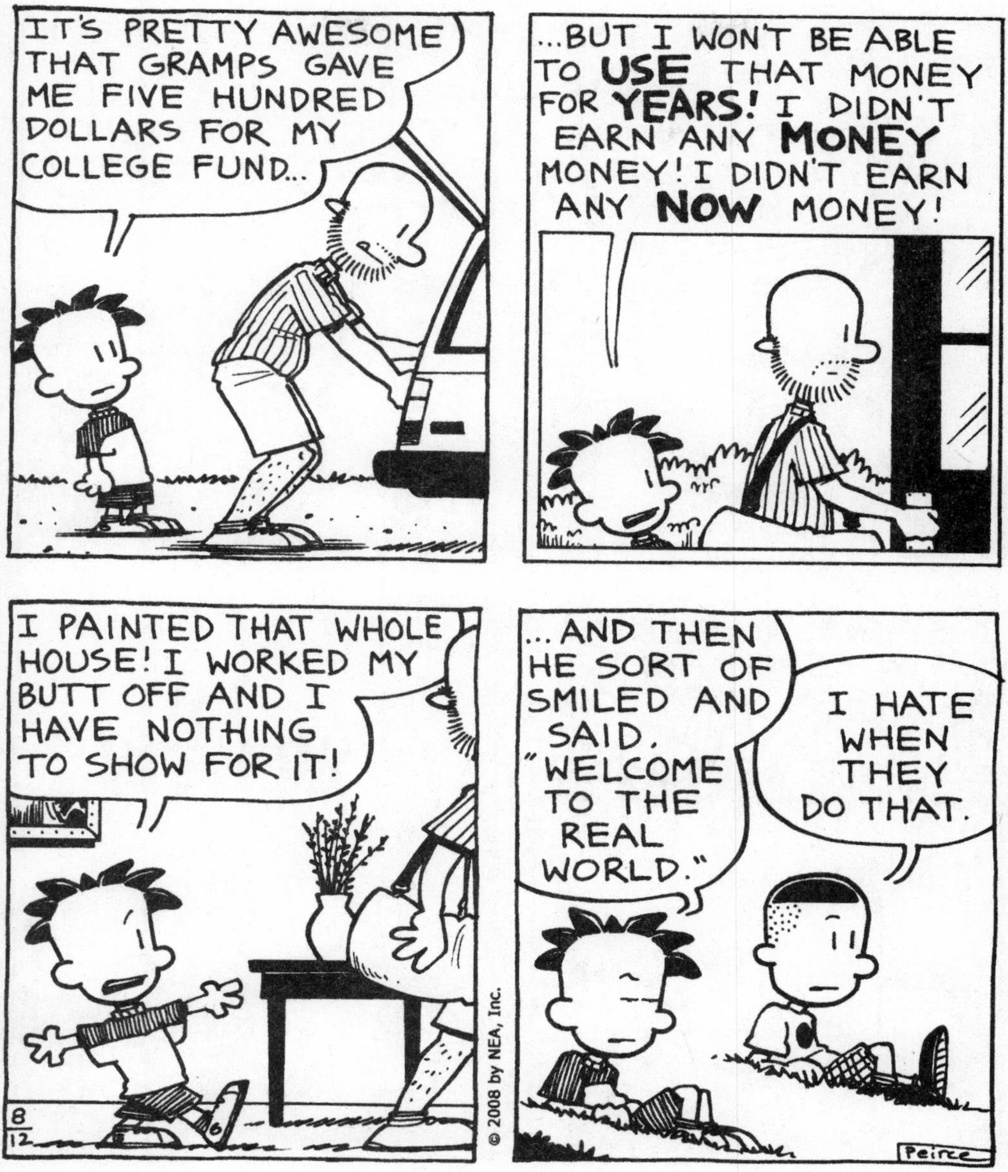
IT'S PRETTY AWESOME THAT GRAMPS GAVE ME FIVE HUNDRED DOLLARS FOR MY COLLEGE FUND...
...BUT I WON'T BE ABLE TO USE THAT MONEY FOR YEARS! I DIDN'T EARN ANY MONEY MONEY! I DIDN'T EARN ANY NOW MONEY!
I PAINTED THAT WHOLE HOUSE! I WORKED MY BUTT OFF AND I HAVE NOTHING TO SHOW FOR IT!
...AND THEN HE SORT OF SMILED AND SAID, "WELCOME TO THE REAL WORLD."
I HATE WHEN THEY DO THAT.
8 12
© 2008 by NEA, Inc.
Peirce

NOTHING TO DO

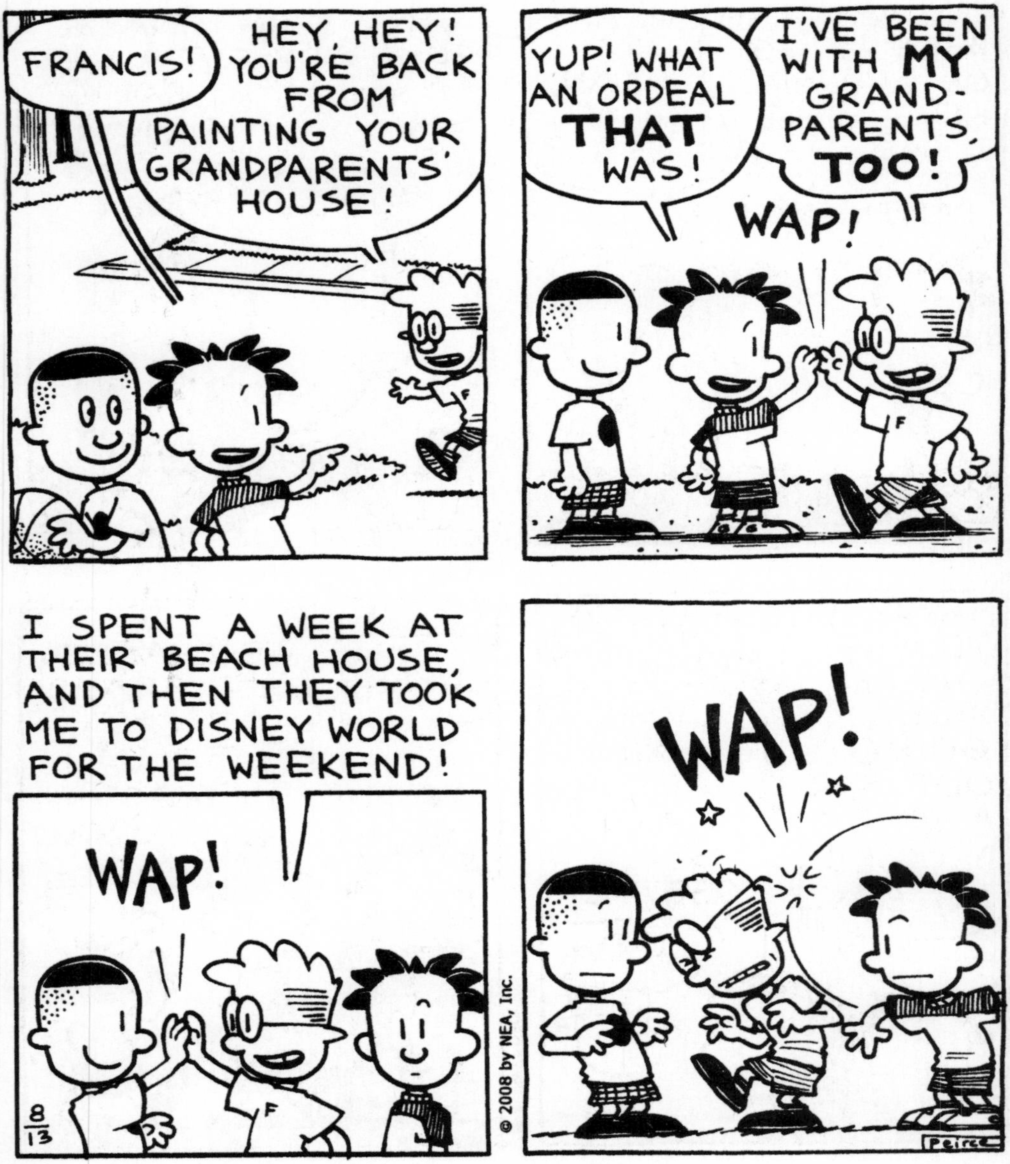
FRANCIS!
HEY, HEY! YOU'RE BACK FROM PAINTING YOUR GRANDPARENTS' HOUSE!
YUP! WHAT AN ORDEAL **THAT** WAS!
I'VE BEEN WITH **MY** GRAND-PARENTS, **TOO**!
WAP!
I SPENT A WEEK AT THEIR BEACH HOUSE, AND THEN THEY TOOK ME TO DISNEY WORLD FOR THE WEEKEND!
WAP!
8/13
© 2008 by NEA, Inc.
WAP!
Peirce

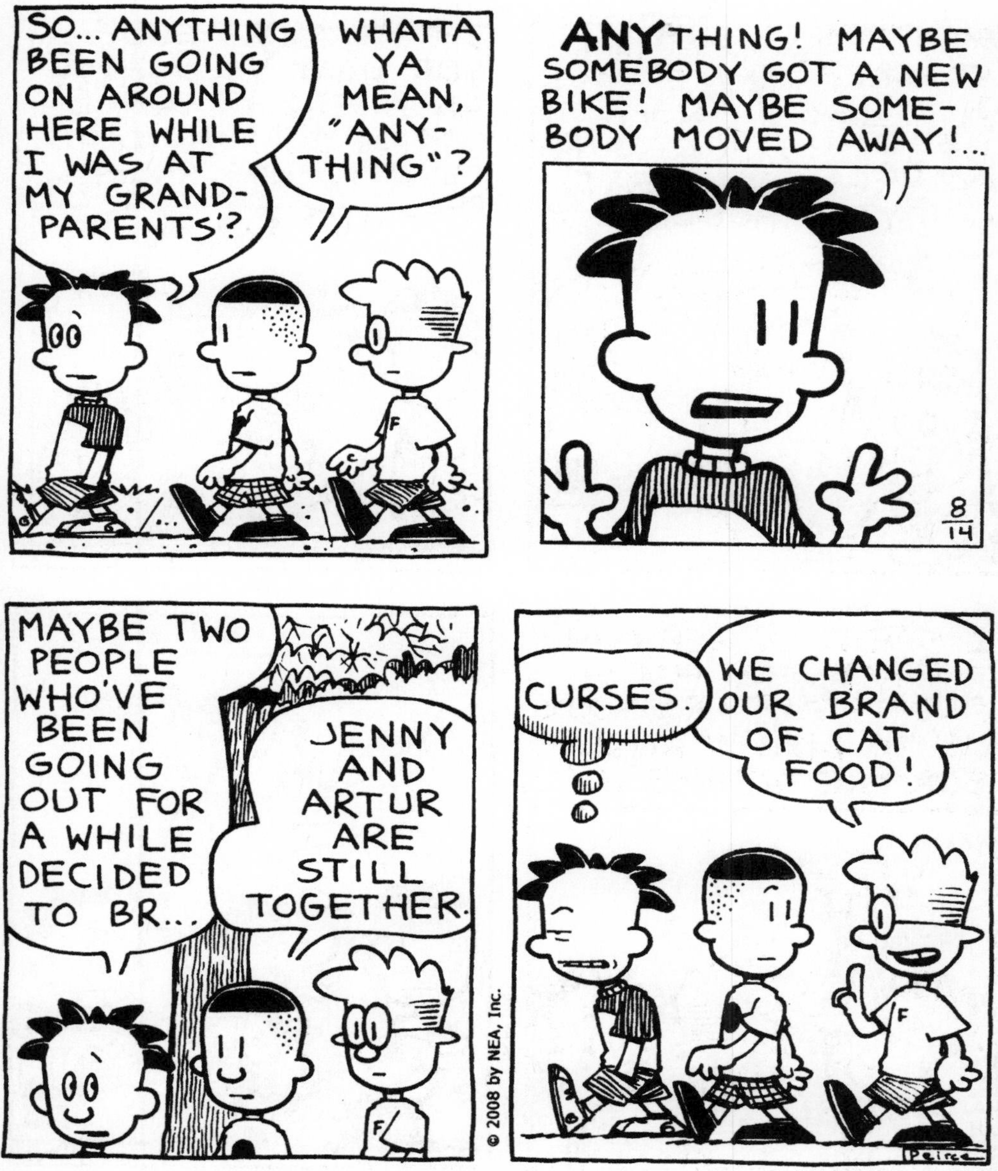
SO... ANYTHING BEEN GOING ON AROUND HERE WHILE I WAS AT MY GRAND-PARENTS'?
WHATTA YA MEAN, "ANY-THING"?
ANYTHING! MAYBE SOMEBODY GOT A NEW BIKE! MAYBE SOME-BODY MOVED AWAY!...
8
14
MAYBE TWO PEOPLE WHO'VE BEEN GOING OUT FOR A WHILE DECIDED TO BR...
JENNY AND ARTUR ARE STILL TOGETHER.
© 2008 by NEA, Inc.
CURSES.
WE CHANGED OUR BRAND OF CAT FOOD!
Peirce

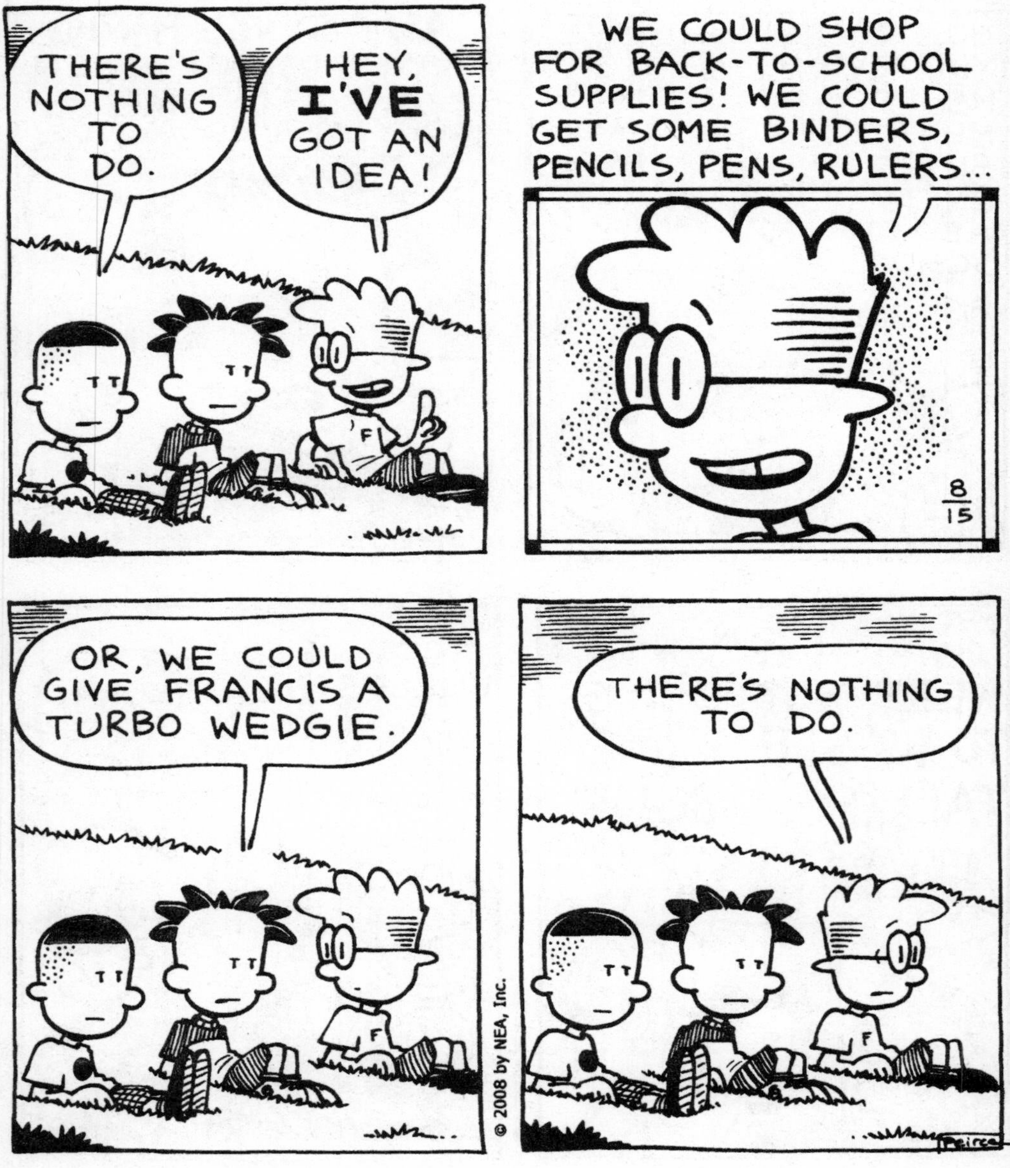
THERE'S NOTHING TO DO.
HEY, I'VE GOT AN IDEA!
WE COULD SHOP FOR BACK-TO-SCHOOL SUPPLIES! WE COULD GET SOME BINDERS, PENCILS, PENS, RULERS...
8/15
OR, WE COULD GIVE FRANCIS A TURBO WEDGIE.
THERE'S NOTHING TO DO.
© 2008 by NEA, Inc.
Peirce

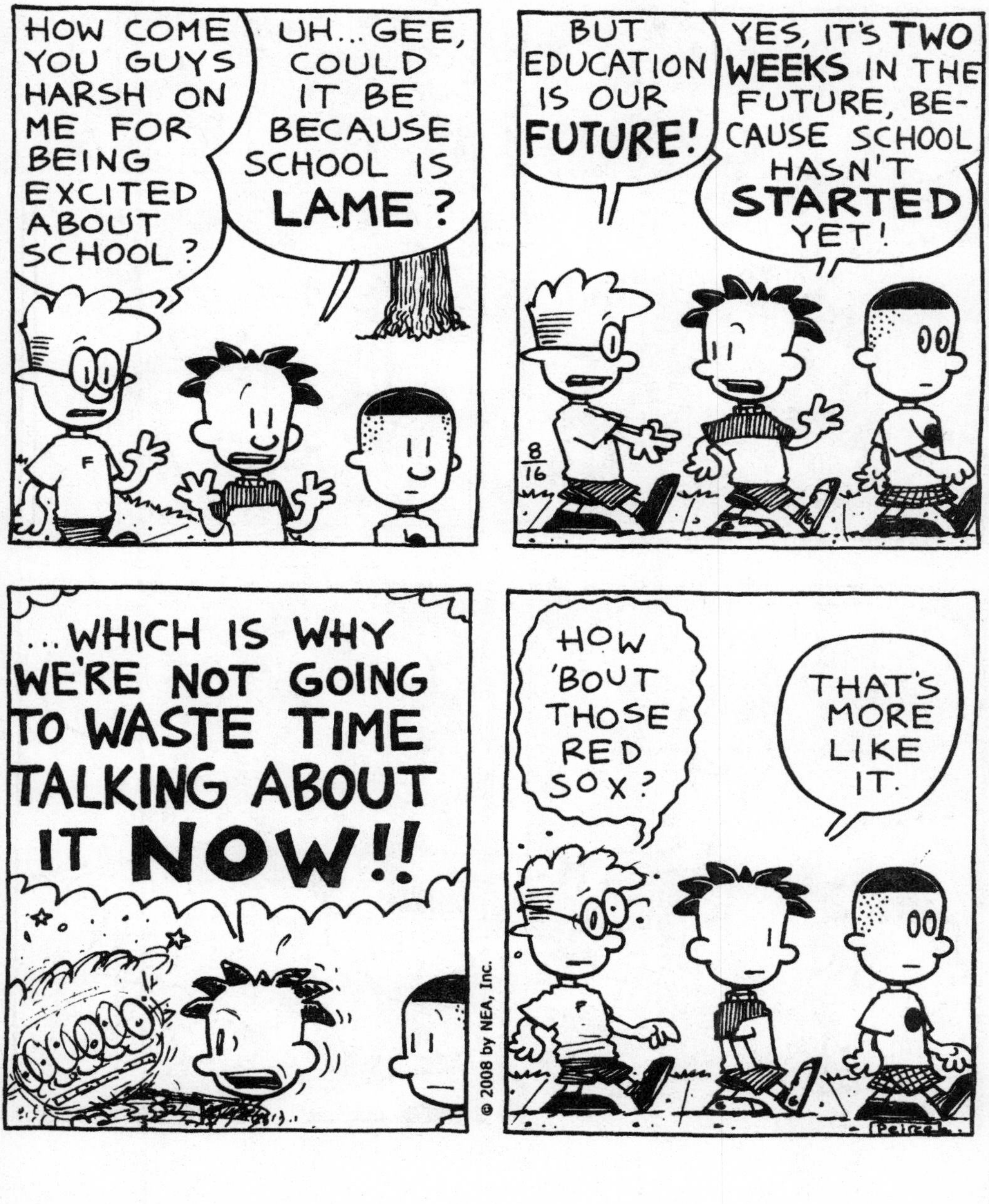
HOW COME YOU GUYS HARSH ON ME FOR BEING EXCITED ABOUT SCHOOL?
UH...GEE, COULD IT BE BECAUSE SCHOOL IS LAME?
BUT EDUCATION IS OUR FUTURE!
YES, IT'S TWO WEEKS IN THE FUTURE, BECAUSE SCHOOL HASN'T STARTED YET!
8/16
...WHICH IS WHY WE'RE NOT GOING TO WASTE TIME TALKING ABOUT IT NOW!!
© 2008 by NEA, Inc.
HOW 'BOUT THOSE RED SOX?
THAT'S MORE LIKE IT.
Peirce

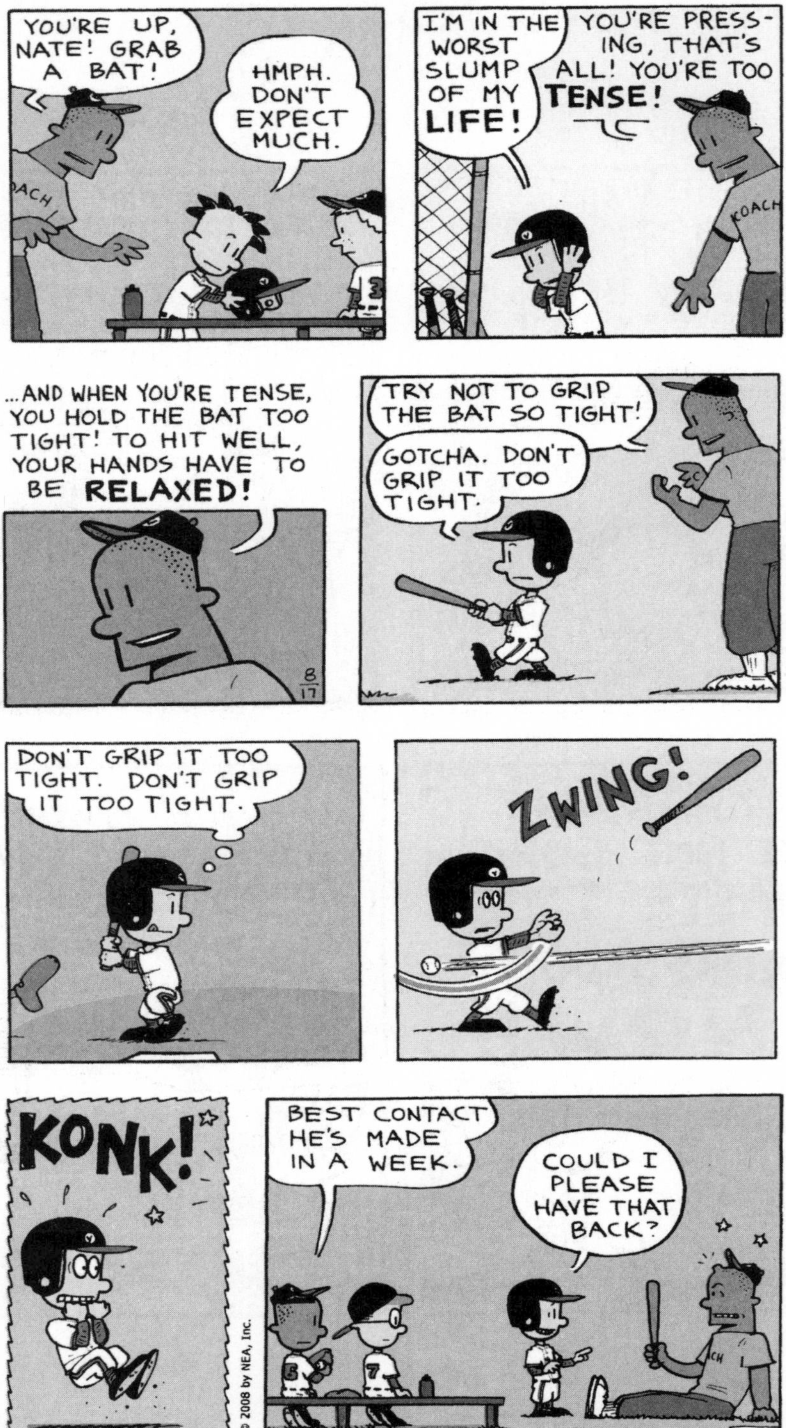
YOU'RE UP, NATE! GRAB A BAT!
HMPH. DON'T EXPECT MUCH.
I'M IN THE WORST SLUMP OF MY LIFE!
YOU'RE PRESS-ING, THAT'S ALL! YOU'RE TOO TENSE!
...AND WHEN YOU'RE TENSE, YOU HOLD THE BAT TOO TIGHT! TO HIT WELL, YOUR HANDS HAVE TO BE RELAXED!
8/17
TRY NOT TO GRIP THE BAT SO TIGHT!
GOTCHA. DON'T GRIP IT TOO TIGHT.
DON'T GRIP IT TOO TIGHT. DON'T GRIP IT TOO TIGHT.
ZWING!
KONK!
© 2008 by NEA, Inc.
BEST CONTACT HE'S MADE IN A WEEK.
COULD I PLEASE HAVE THAT BACK?
Peirce

MASTER OF DISASTER

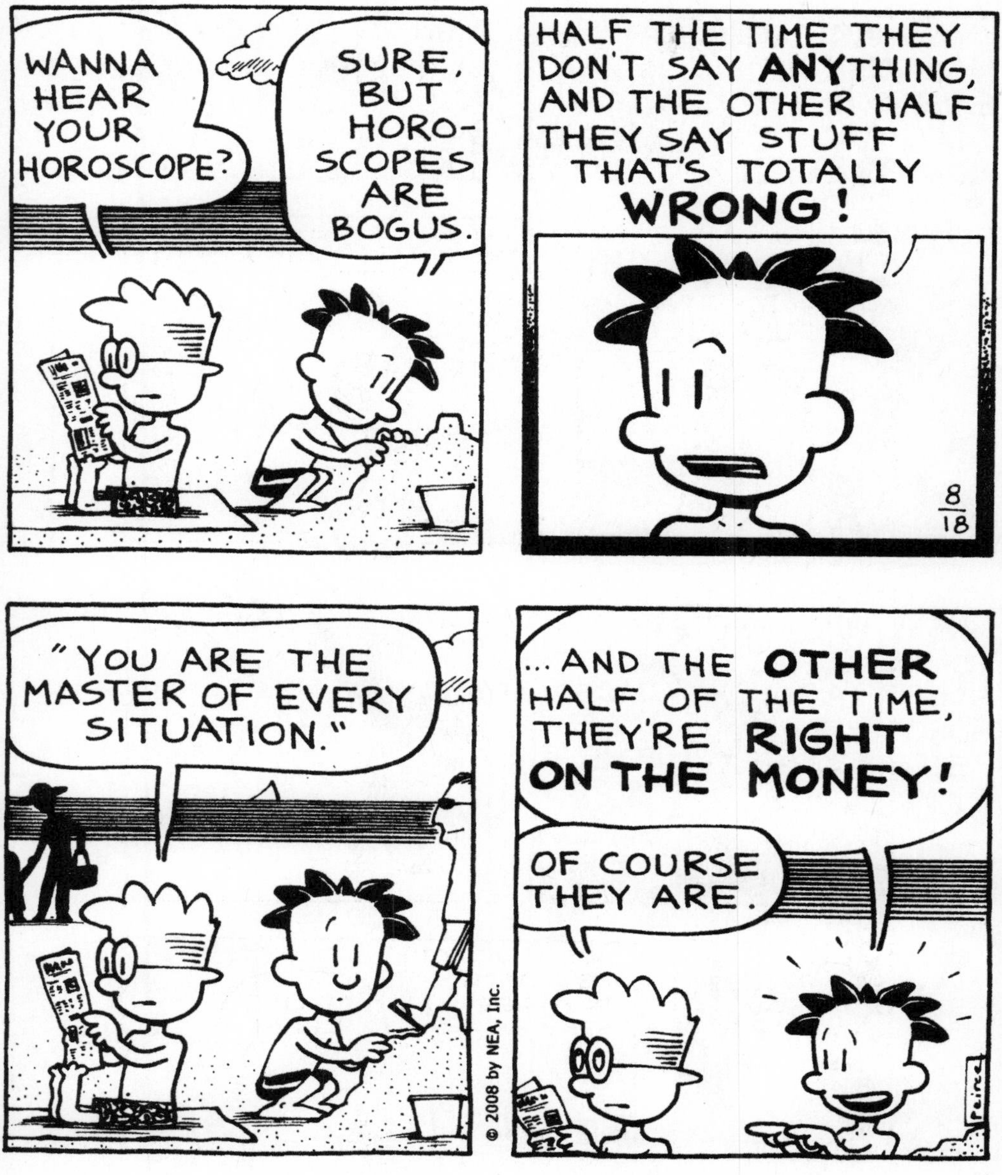
WANNA HEAR YOUR HOROSCOPE?
SURE, BUT HORO-SCOPES ARE BOGUS.
HALF THE TIME THEY DON'T SAY **ANY**THING, AND THE OTHER HALF THEY SAY STUFF THAT'S TOTALLY **WRONG**!
8/18
"YOU ARE THE MASTER OF EVERY SITUATION."
...AND THE **OTHER** HALF OF THE TIME, THEY'RE **RIGHT ON THE MONEY**!
OF COURSE THEY ARE.
Peirce

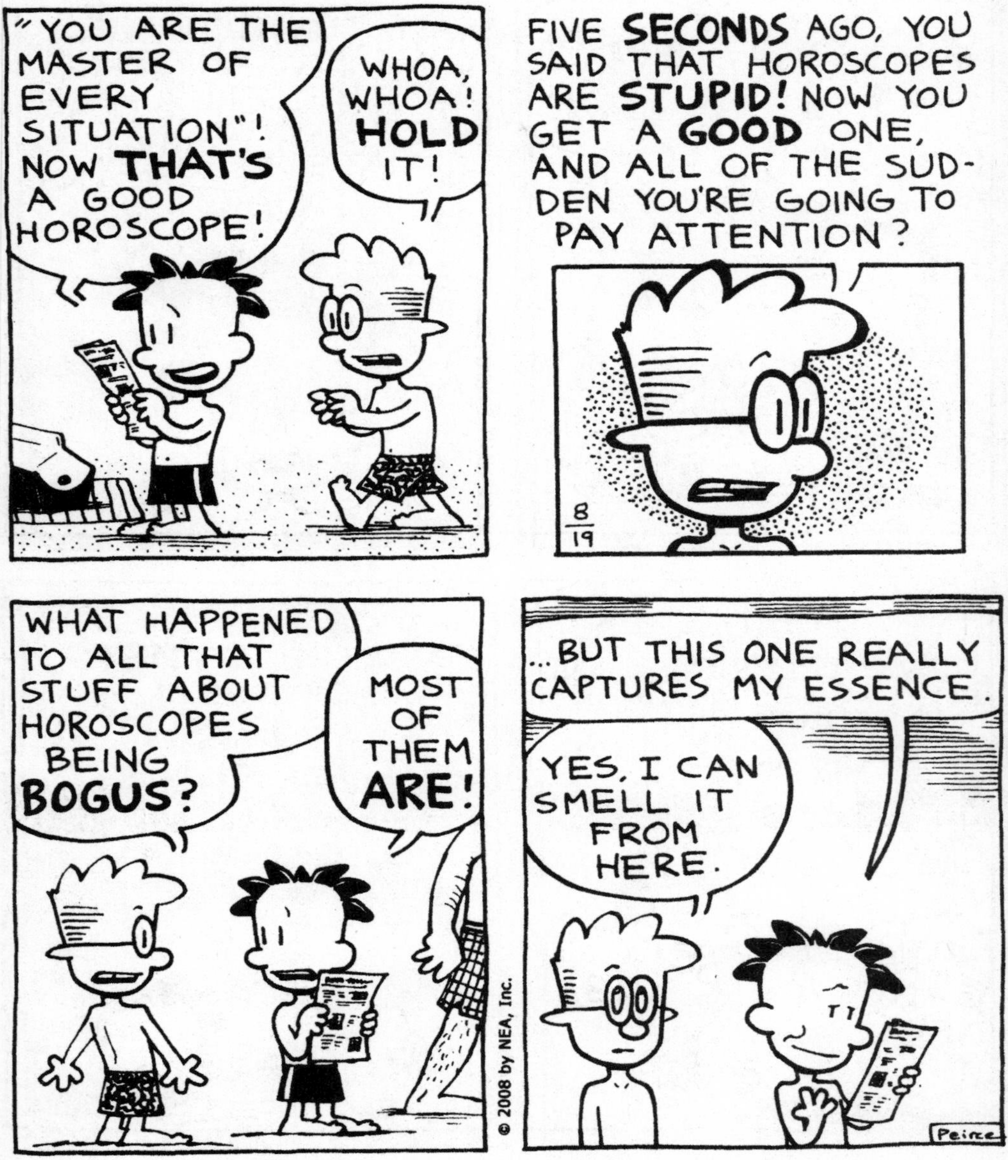
"YOU ARE THE MASTER OF EVERY SITUATION"! NOW THAT'S A GOOD HOROSCOPE!
WHOA, WHOA! HOLD IT!
FIVE SECONDS AGO, YOU SAID THAT HOROSCOPES ARE STUPID! NOW YOU GET A GOOD ONE, AND ALL OF THE SUDDEN YOU'RE GOING TO PAY ATTENTION?
8/19
WHAT HAPPENED TO ALL THAT STUFF ABOUT HOROSCOPES BEING BOGUS?
MOST OF THEM ARE!
...BUT THIS ONE REALLY CAPTURES MY ESSENCE.
YES, I CAN SMELL IT FROM HERE.
Peirce
© 2008 by NEA, Inc.

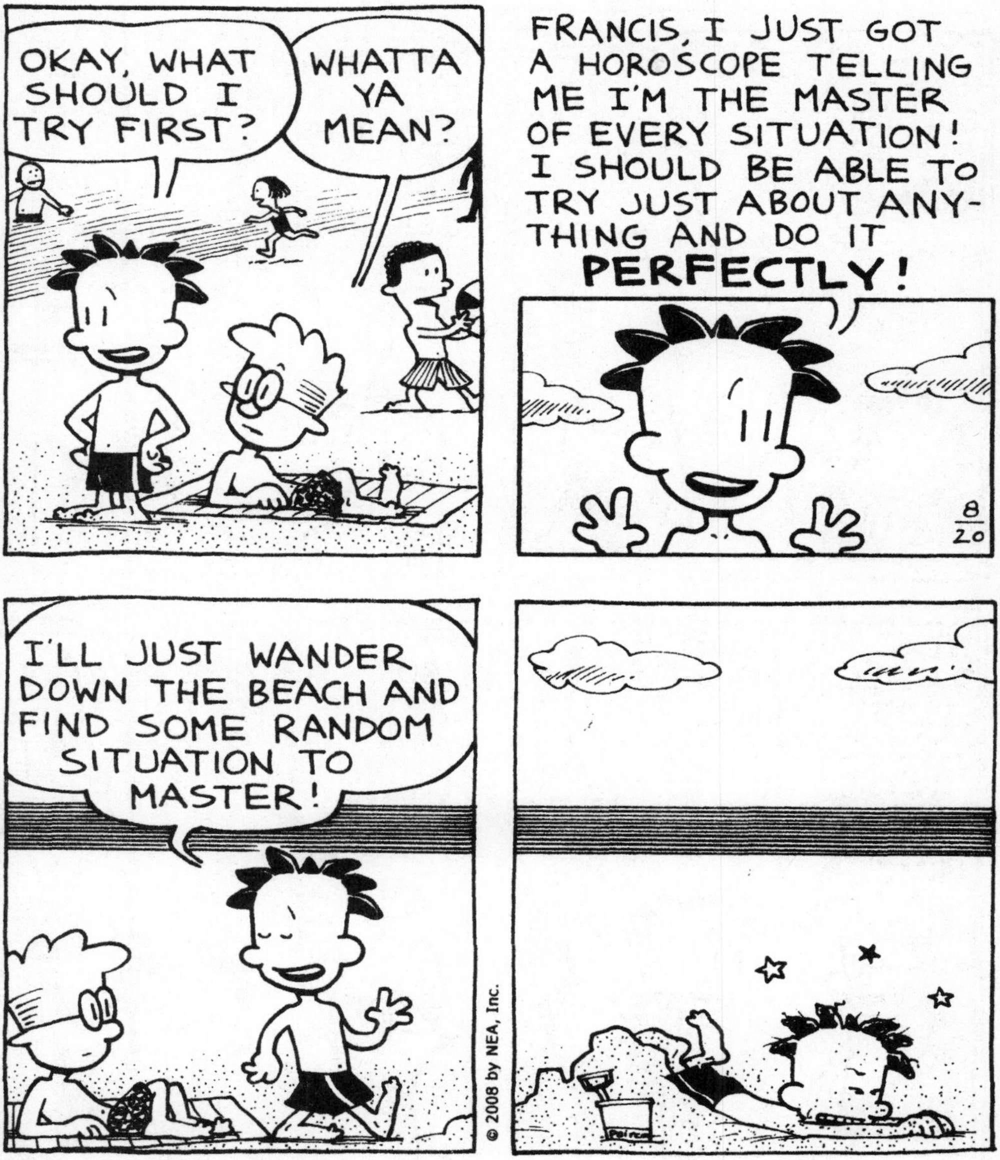
OKAY, WHAT SHOULD I TRY FIRST?
WHATTA YA MEAN?
FRANCIS, I JUST GOT A HOROSCOPE TELLING ME I'M THE MASTER OF EVERY SITUATION! I SHOULD BE ABLE TO TRY JUST ABOUT ANY-THING AND DO IT **PERFECTLY**!
8/20
I'LL JUST WANDER DOWN THE BEACH AND FIND SOME RANDOM SITUATION TO MASTER!
© 2008 by NEA, Inc.

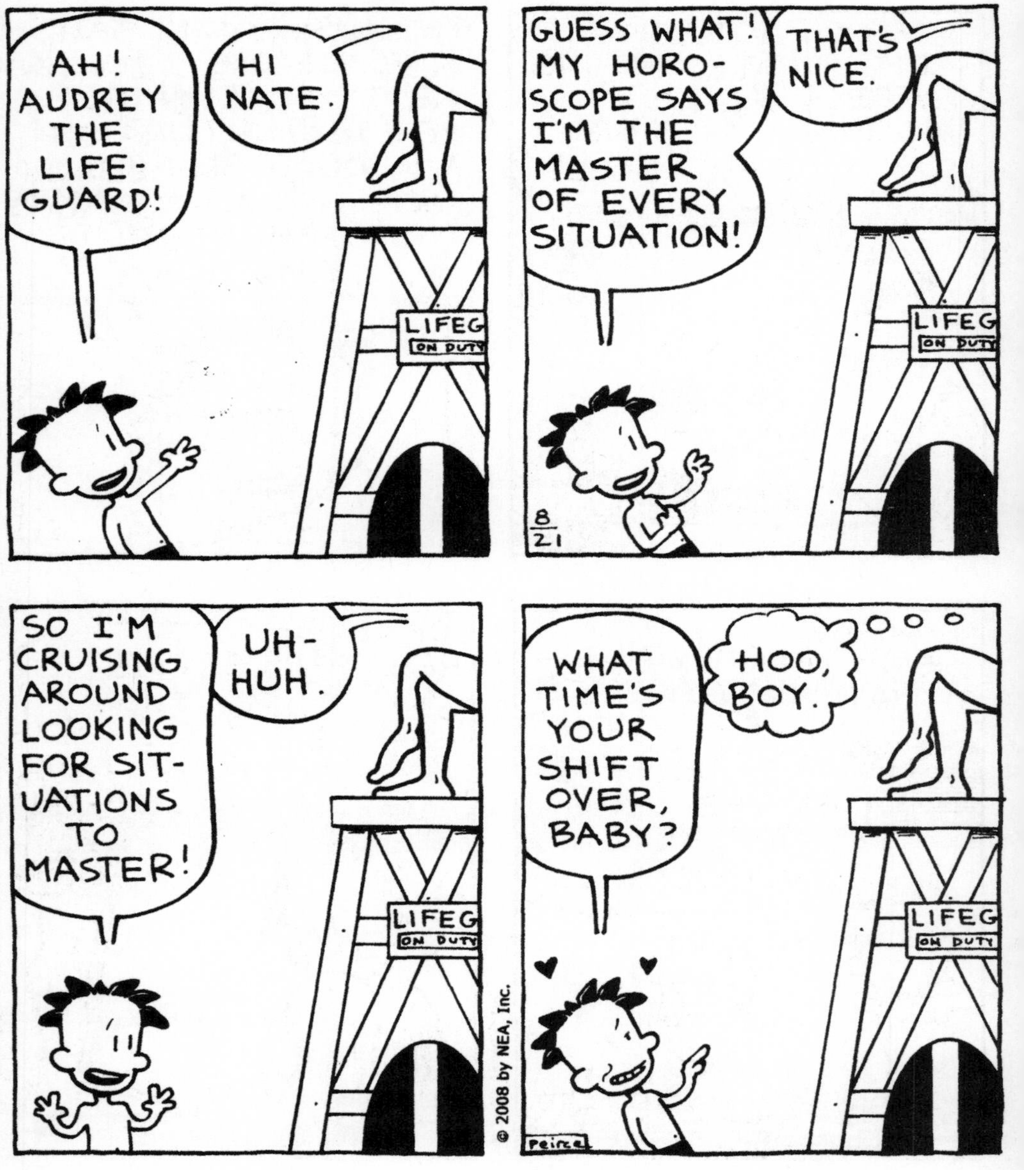
AH! AUDREY THE LIFE-GUARD!
HI NATE.
LIFEG
ON DUTY
GUESS WHAT! MY HORO-SCOPE SAYS I'M THE MASTER OF EVERY SITUATION!
THAT'S NICE.
8/21
SO I'M CRUISING AROUND LOOKING FOR SIT-UATIONS TO MASTER!
UH-HUH.
WHAT TIME'S YOUR SHIFT OVER, BABY?
HOO, BOY.
Peirce

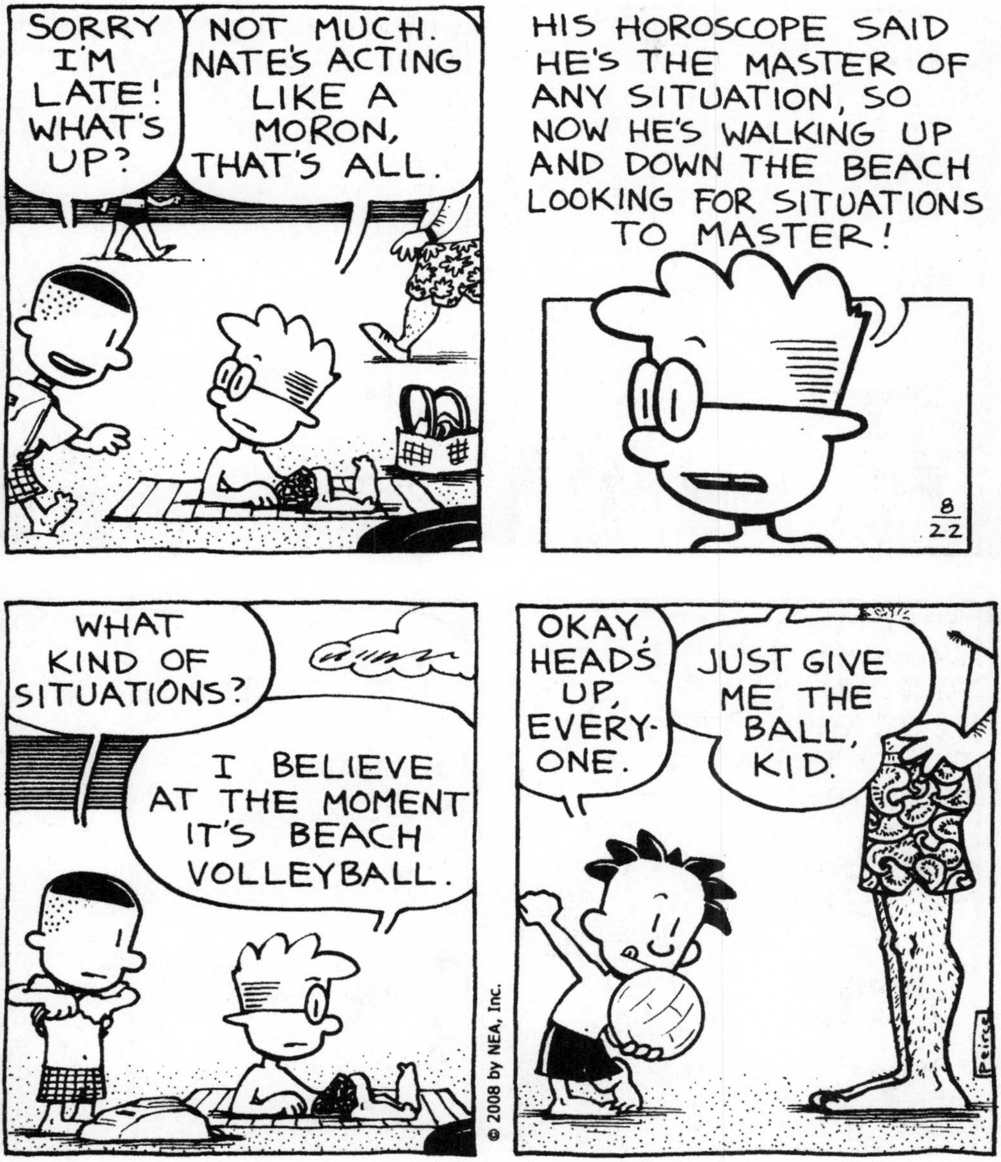
SORRY I'M LATE! WHAT'S UP?
NOT MUCH. NATE'S ACTING LIKE A MORON, THAT'S ALL.
HIS HOROSCOPE SAID HE'S THE MASTER OF ANY SITUATION, SO NOW HE'S WALKING UP AND DOWN THE BEACH LOOKING FOR SITUATIONS TO MASTER!
8/22
WHAT KIND OF SITUATIONS?
I BELIEVE AT THE MOMENT IT'S BEACH VOLLEYBALL.
© 2008 by NEA, Inc.
OKAY, HEADS UP, EVERY-ONE.
JUST GIVE ME THE BALL, KID.
PEIRCE

WHAT HAPPENED TO YOU?
I GOT HIT IN THE FACE WITH A FRISBEE.
I DON'T GET IT! MY STUPID HOROSCOPE SAID I'D BE THE MASTER OF EVERY SITUATION!
OOP! HOLD IT!
I GAVE YOU YESTERDAY'S HOROSCOPE BY MISTAKE! THIS IS TODAY'S!
8/23
© 2008 by NEA, Inc.
DOES IT MENTION FRISBEES?
"YOU HAVE A SASSY, FUN-LOVING SPIRIT."
Peirce

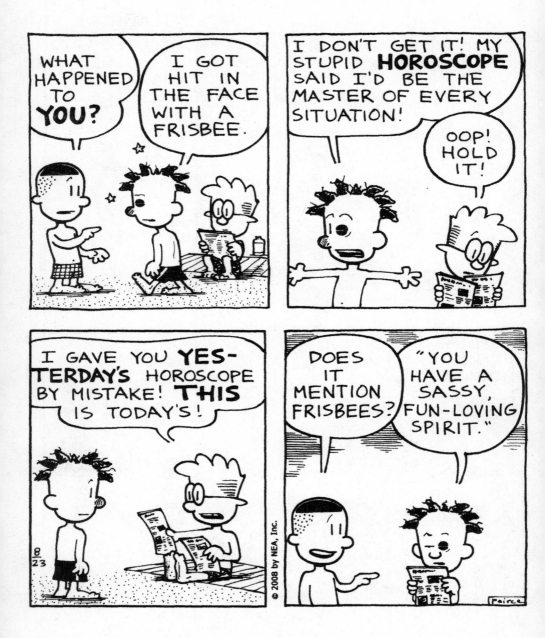

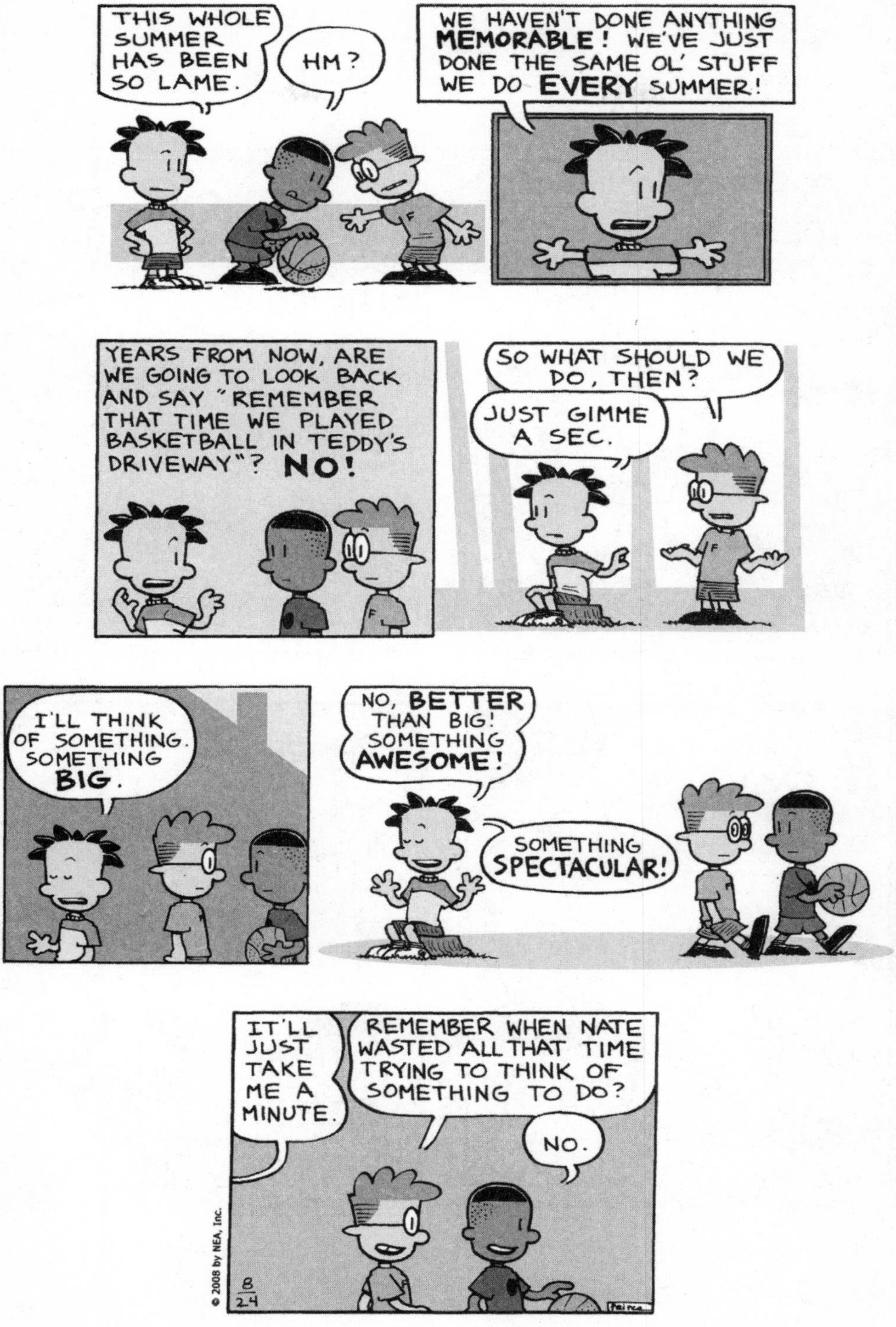
THIS WHOLE SUMMER HAS BEEN SO LAME.
HM?
WE HAVEN'T DONE ANYTHING MEMORABLE! WE'VE JUST DONE THE SAME OL' STUFF WE DO EVERY SUMMER!
YEARS FROM NOW, ARE WE GOING TO LOOK BACK AND SAY "REMEMBER THAT TIME WE PLAYED BASKETBALL IN TEDDY'S DRIVEWAY"? NO!
SO WHAT SHOULD WE DO, THEN?
JUST GIMME A SEC.
I'LL THINK OF SOMETHING. SOMETHING BIG.
NO, BETTER THAN BIG! SOMETHING AWESOME!
SOMETHING SPECTACULAR!
IT'LL JUST TAKE ME A MINUTE.
REMEMBER WHEN NATE WASTED ALL THAT TIME TRYING TO THINK OF SOMETHING TO DO?
NO.
8/24
Peirce

BUY BYE

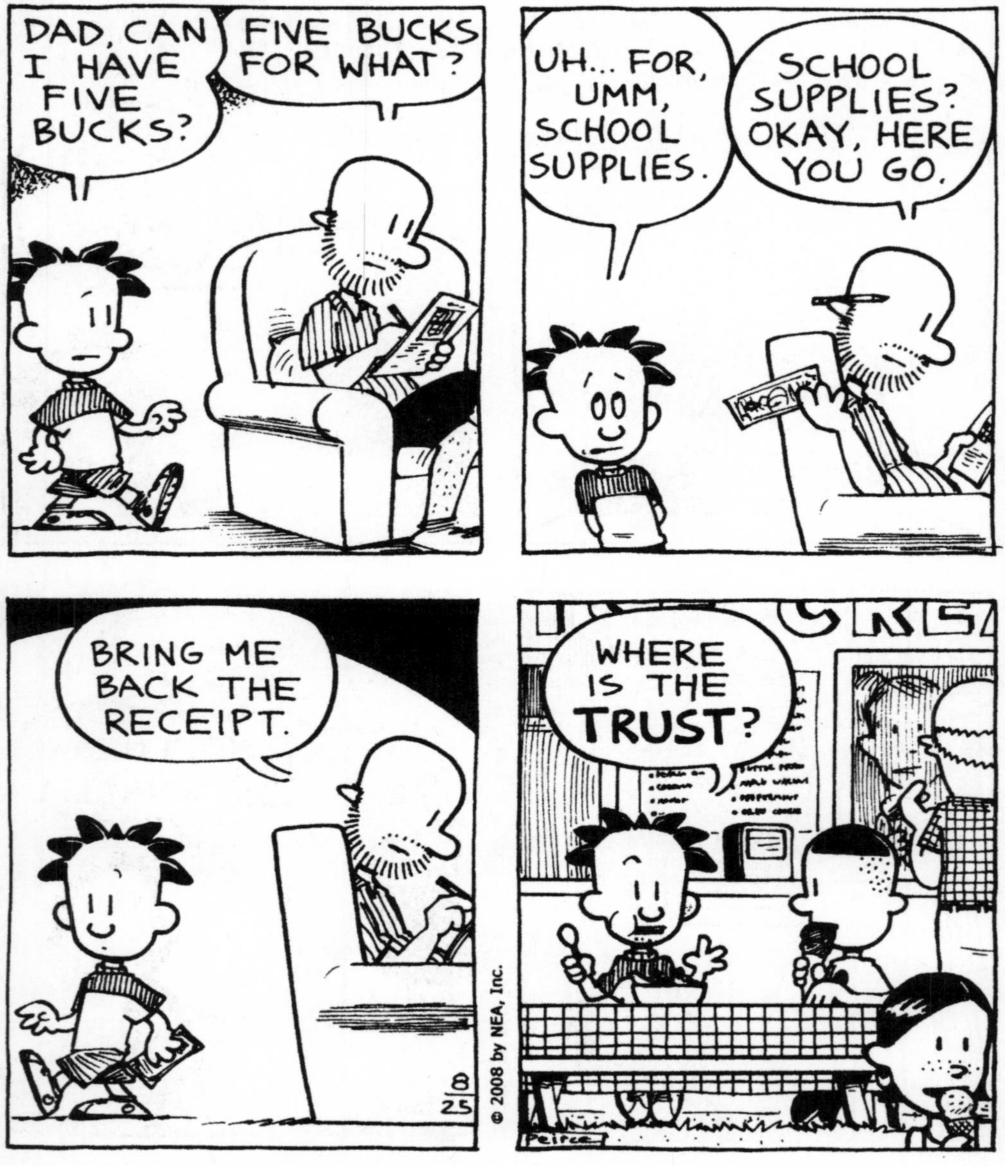
DAD, CAN I HAVE FIVE BUCKS?
FIVE BUCKS FOR WHAT?
UH... FOR, UMM, SCHOOL SUPPLIES.
SCHOOL SUPPLIES? OKAY, HERE YOU GO.
BRING ME BACK THE RECEIPT.
8/25
© 2008 by NEA, Inc.
WHERE IS THE **TRUST**?

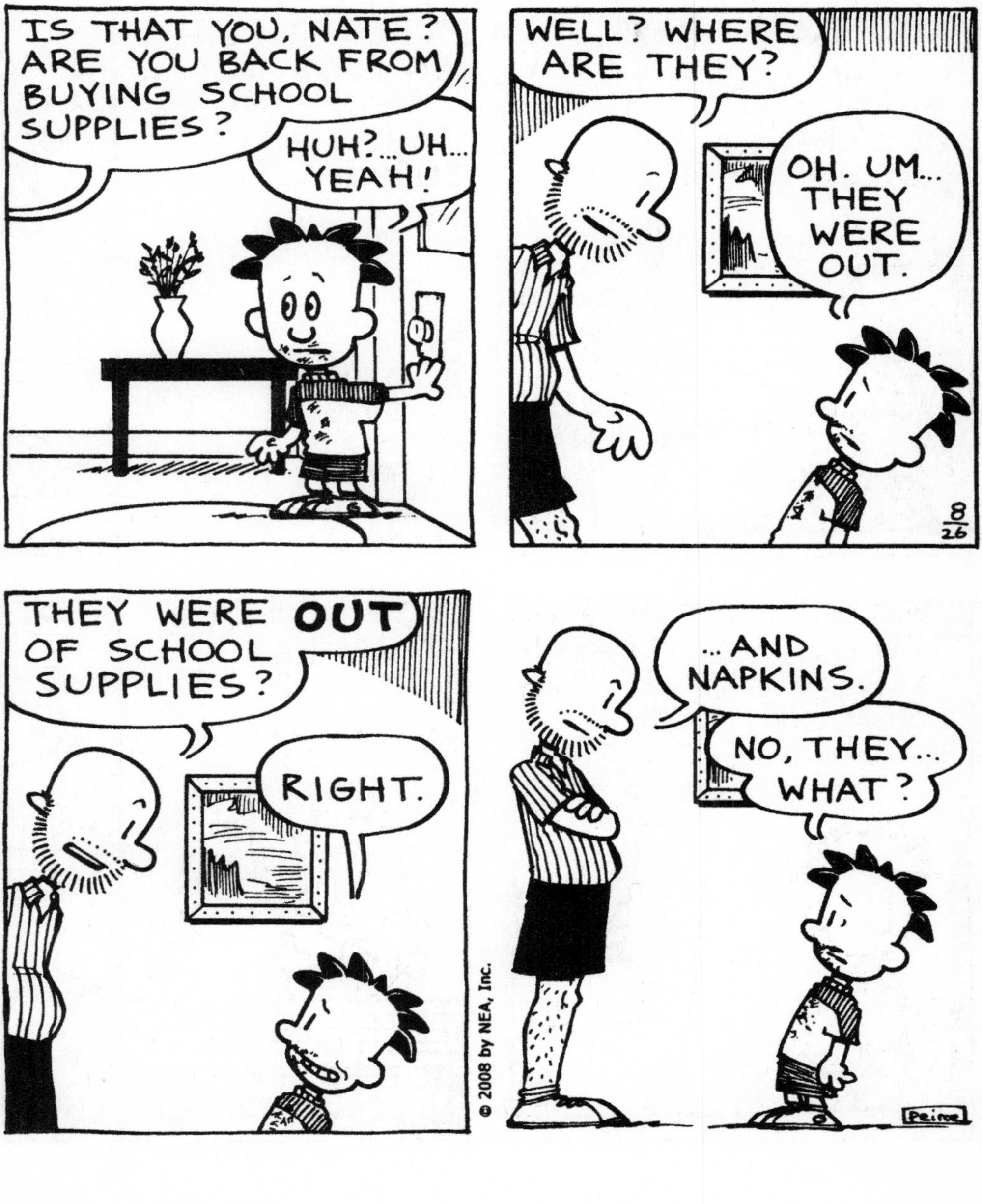
IS THAT YOU, NATE? ARE YOU BACK FROM BUYING SCHOOL SUPPLIES?
HUH?...UH... YEAH!
WELL? WHERE ARE THEY?
OH. UM... THEY WERE OUT.
8/26
THEY WERE OUT OF SCHOOL SUPPLIES?
RIGHT.
© 2008 by NEA, Inc.
...AND NAPKINS.
NO, THEY... WHAT?
Peirce

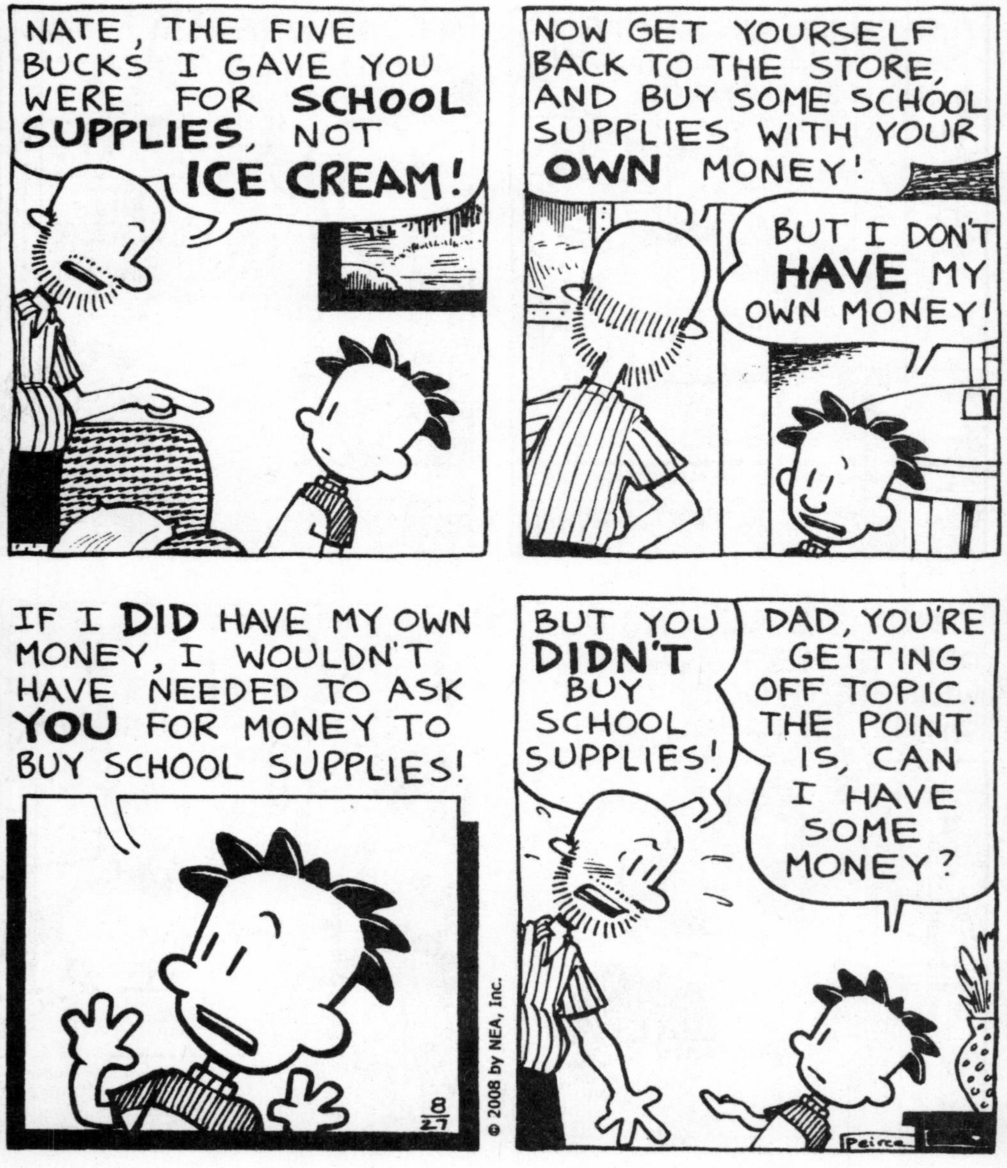
NATE, THE FIVE BUCKS I GAVE YOU WERE FOR SCHOOL SUPPLIES, NOT ICE CREAM!
NOW GET YOURSELF BACK TO THE STORE, AND BUY SOME SCHOOL SUPPLIES WITH YOUR OWN MONEY!
BUT I DON'T HAVE MY OWN MONEY!
IF I DID HAVE MY OWN MONEY, I WOULDN'T HAVE NEEDED TO ASK YOU FOR MONEY TO BUY SCHOOL SUPPLIES!
8/27
© 2008 by NEA, Inc.
BUT YOU DIDN'T BUY SCHOOL SUPPLIES!
DAD, YOU'RE GETTING OFF TOPIC. THE POINT IS, CAN I HAVE SOME MONEY?
Peirce

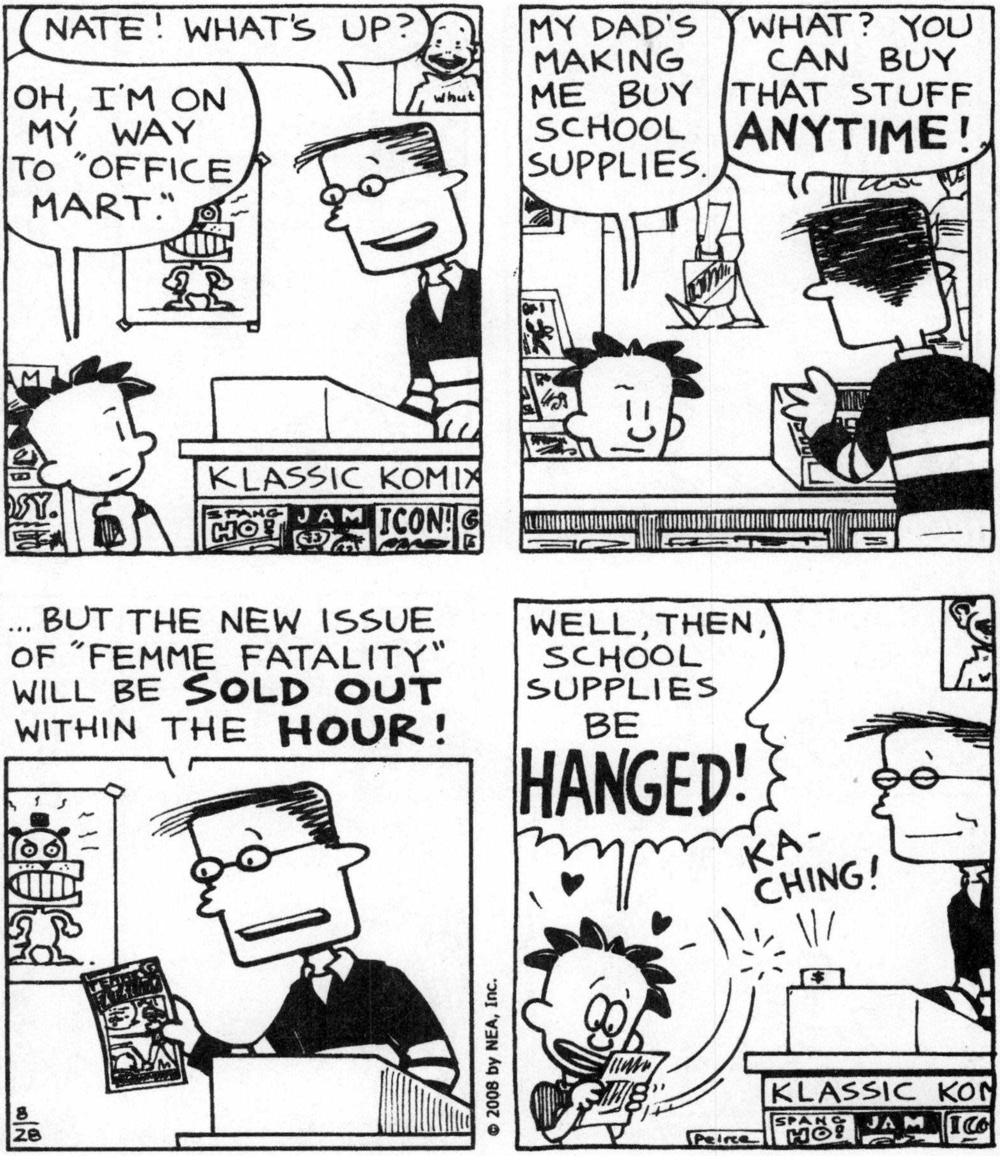
NATE! WHAT'S UP?
OH, I'M ON MY WAY TO "OFFICE MART."
KLASSIC KOMIX
MY DAD'S MAKING ME BUY SCHOOL SUPPLIES.
WHAT? YOU CAN BUY THAT STUFF ANYTIME!
... BUT THE NEW ISSUE OF "FEMME FATALITY" WILL BE SOLD OUT WITHIN THE HOUR!
WELL, THEN, SCHOOL SUPPLIES BE HANGED!
KA-CHING!
KLASSIC KO
8/28
Peirce

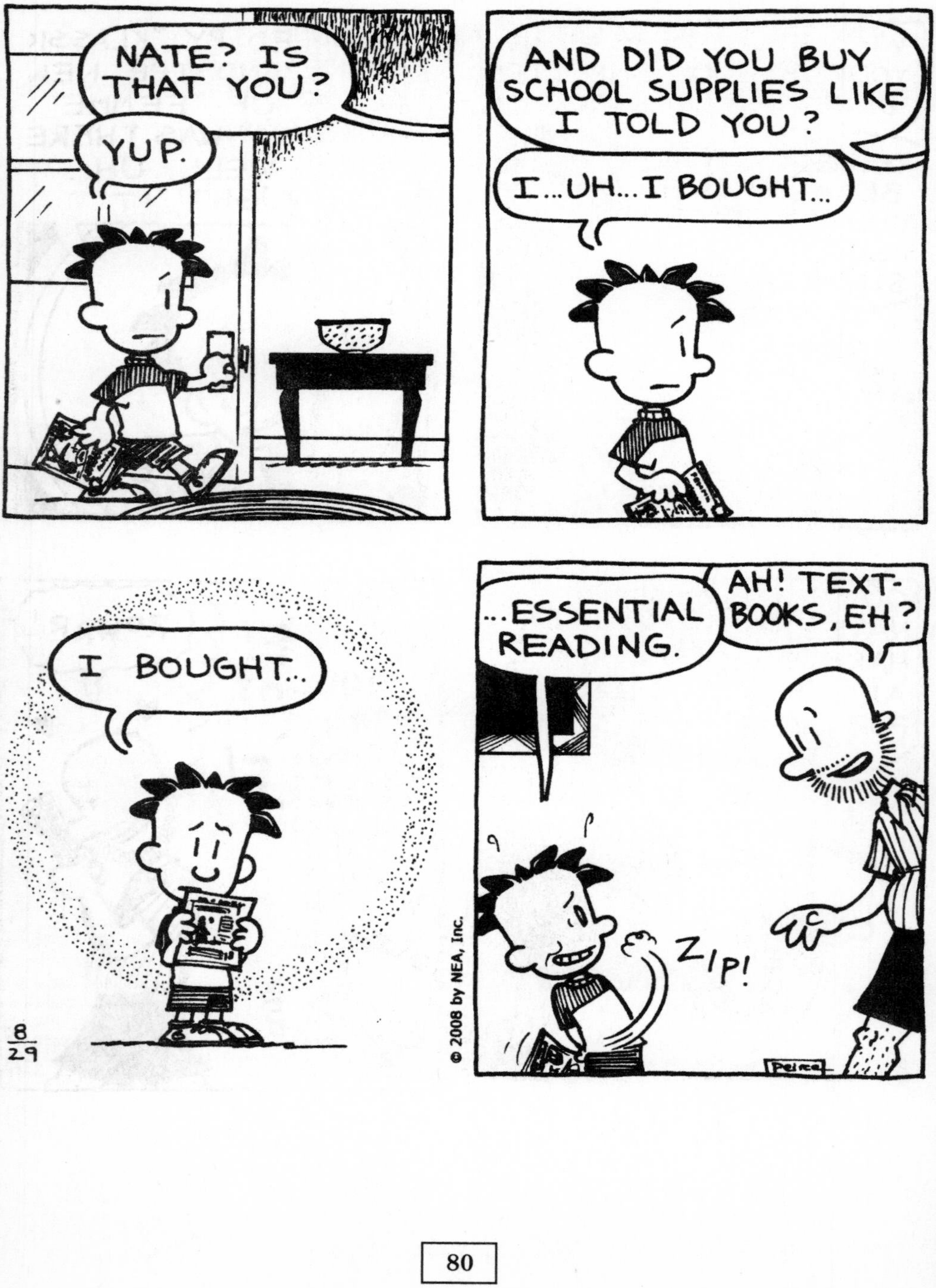
NATE? IS THAT YOU?
YUP.
AND DID YOU BUY SCHOOL SUPPLIES LIKE I TOLD YOU?
I...UH...I BOUGHT...
I BOUGHT..
8/29
AH! TEXT-BOOKS, EH?
...ESSENTIAL READING.
ZIP!
PEIRCE
© 2008 by NEA, Inc.

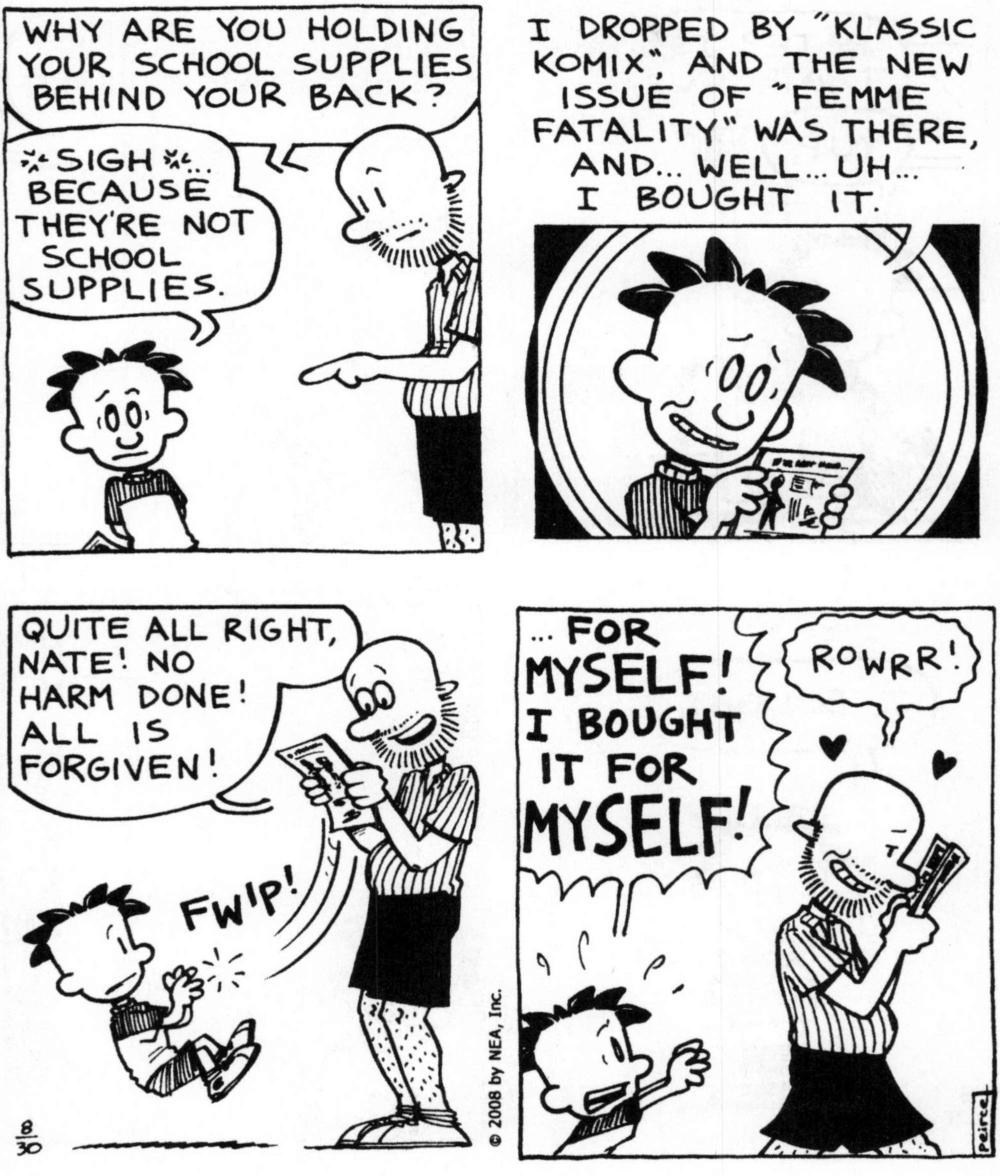
WHY ARE YOU HOLDING YOUR SCHOOL SUPPLIES BEHIND YOUR BACK?
SIGH... BECAUSE THEY'RE NOT SCHOOL SUPPLIES.
I DROPPED BY "KLASSIC KOMIX", AND THE NEW ISSUE OF "FEMME FATALITY" WAS THERE, AND... WELL... UH... I BOUGHT IT.
QUITE ALL RIGHT, NATE! NO HARM DONE! ALL IS FORGIVEN!
FWIP!
8/30
© 2008 by NEA, Inc.
... FOR MYSELF! I BOUGHT IT FOR MYSELF!
ROWRR!
peirce

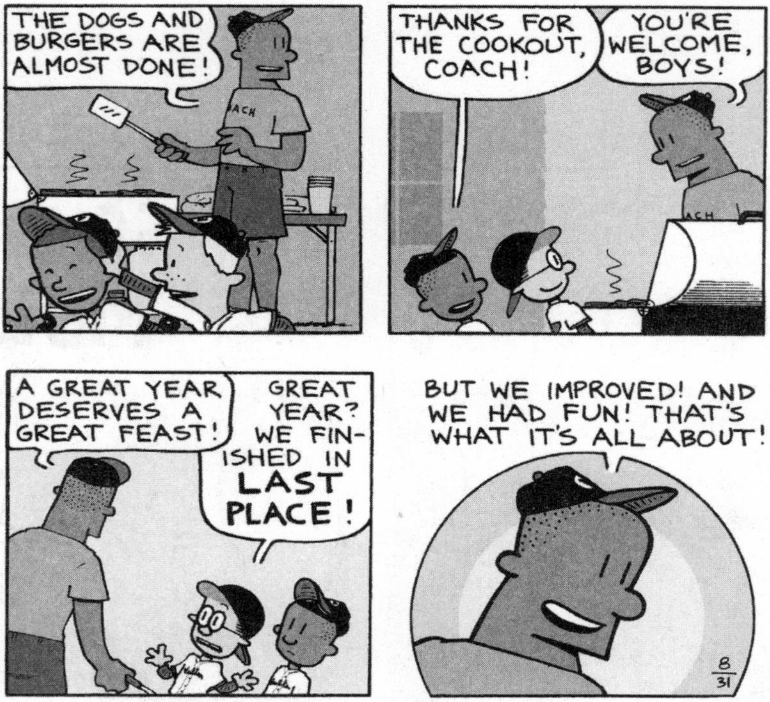
THE DOGS AND BURGERS ARE ALMOST DONE!
COACH
THANKS FOR THE COOKOUT, COACH!
YOU'RE WELCOME, BOYS!
A GREAT YEAR DESERVES A GREAT FEAST!
GREAT YEAR? WE FINISHED IN LAST PLACE!
BUT WE IMPROVED! AND WE HAD FUN! THAT'S WHAT IT'S ALL ABOUT!
8/31

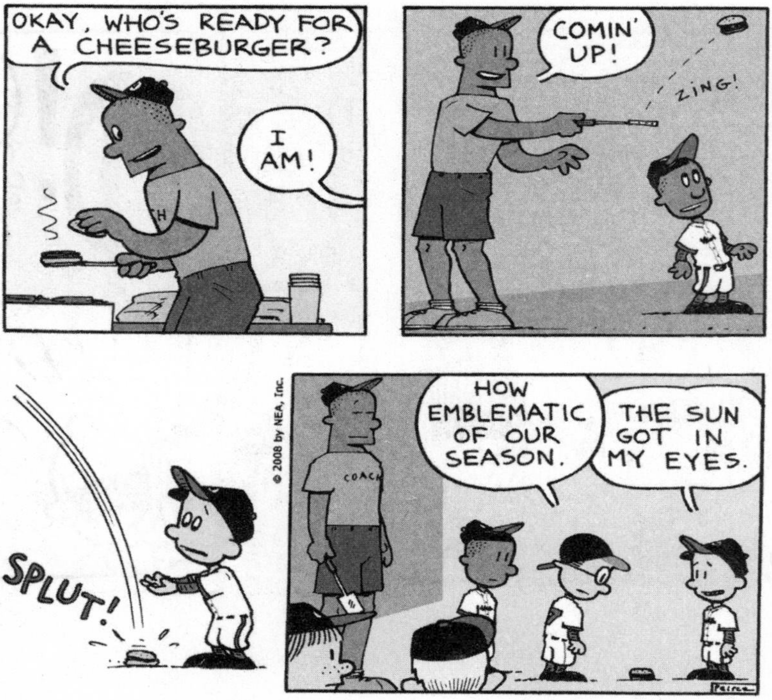
OKAY, WHO'S READY FOR A CHEESEBURGER?
I AM!
COMIN' UP!
ZING!
SPLUT!
© 2008 by NEA, Inc.
COACH
HOW EMBLEMATIC OF OUR SEASON.
THE SUN GOT IN MY EYES.

MOLD!

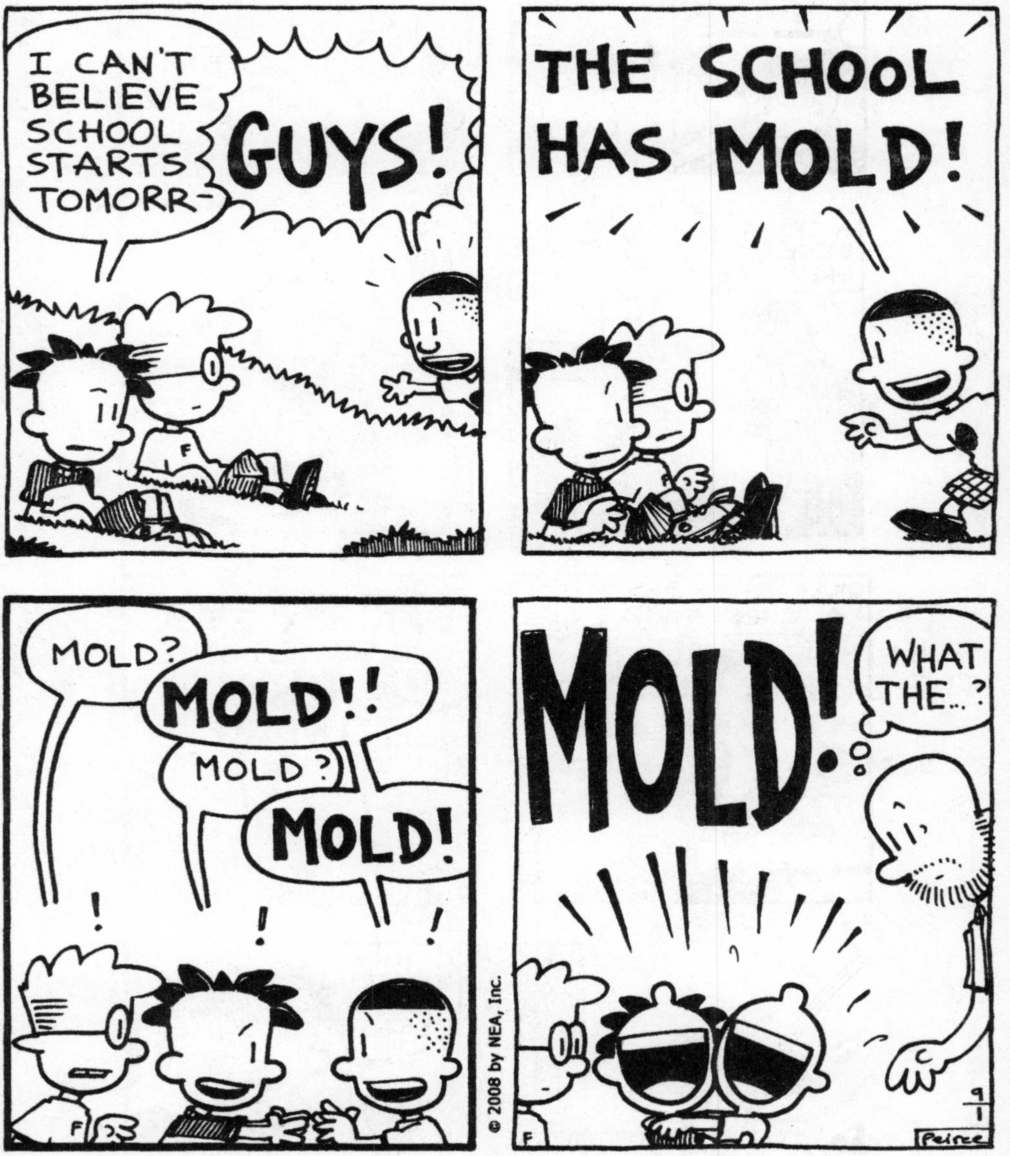

I CAN'T BELIEVE SCHOOL STARTS TOMORR-
GUYS!
THE SCHOOL HAS MOLD!
MOLD?
MOLD!!
MOLD?
MOLD!
!
!
!
© 2008 by NEA, Inc.
MOLD!
WHAT THE...?
9/1
Peirce

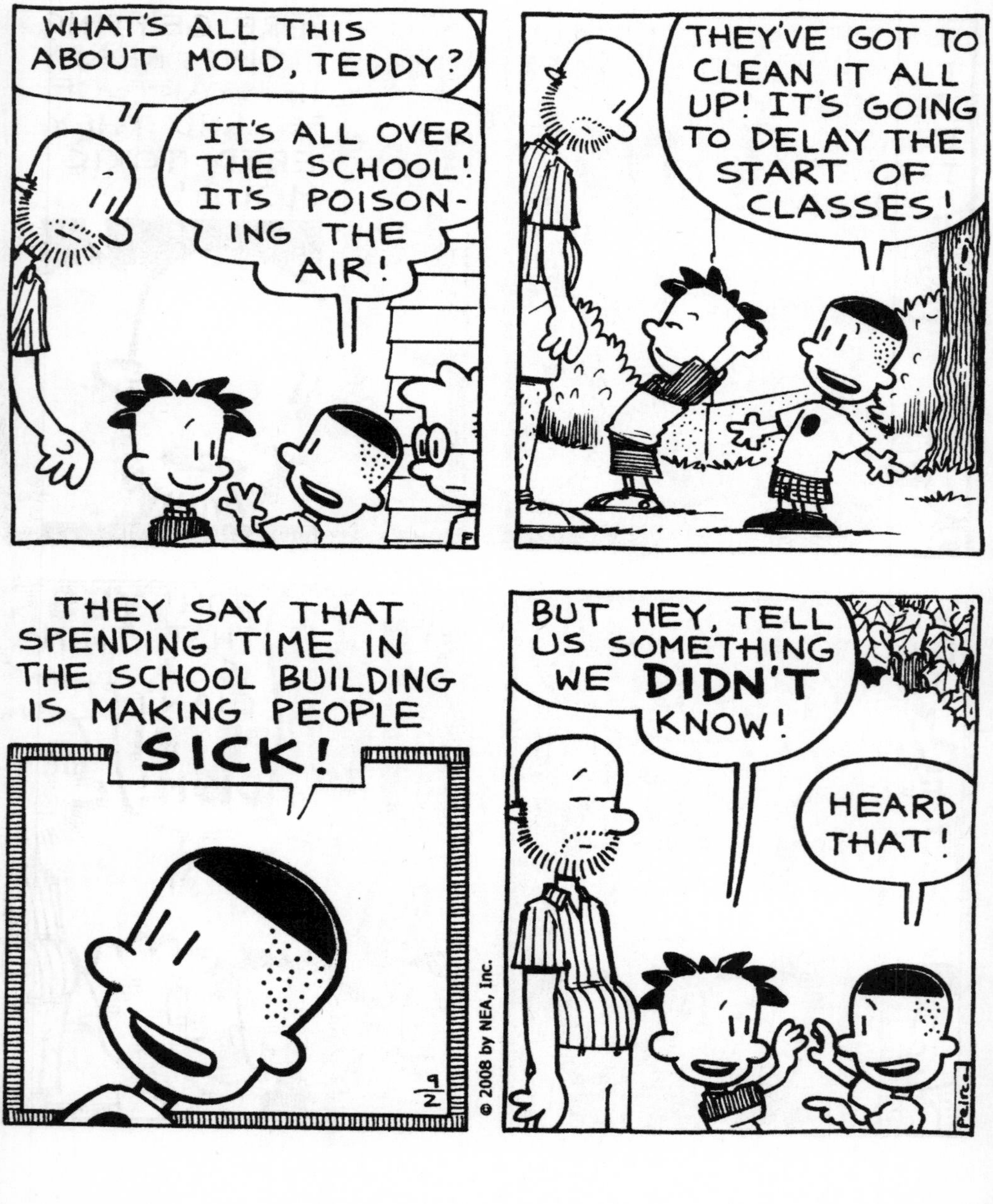
WHAT'S ALL THIS ABOUT MOLD, TEDDY?
IT'S ALL OVER THE SCHOOL! IT'S POISONING THE AIR!
THEY'VE GOT TO CLEAN IT ALL UP! IT'S GOING TO DELAY THE START OF CLASSES!
THEY SAY THAT SPENDING TIME IN THE SCHOOL BUILDING IS MAKING PEOPLE SICK!
BUT HEY, TELL US SOMETHING WE DIDN'T KNOW!
HEARD THAT!
9/2
© 2008 by NEA, Inc.
Peirce

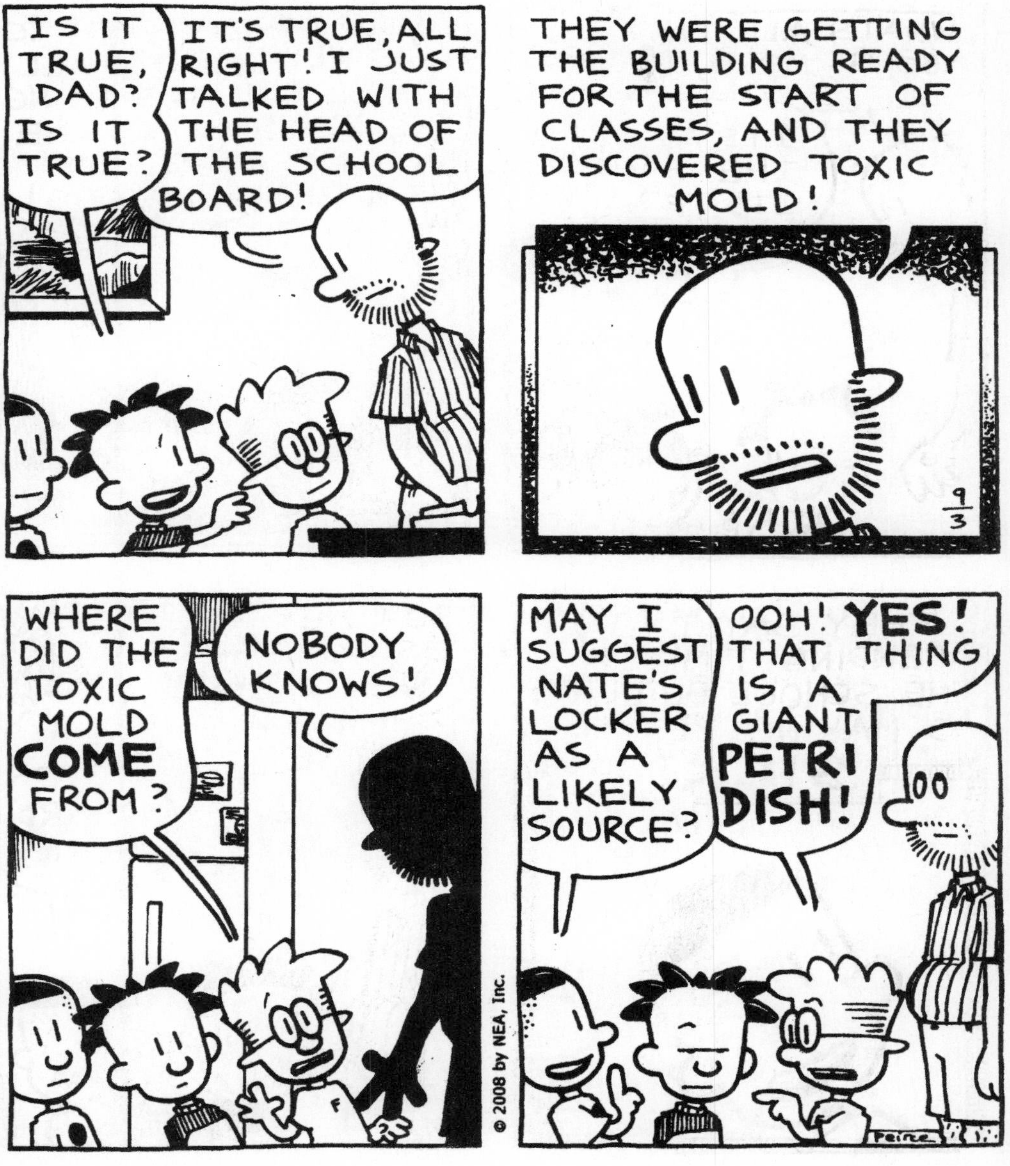
IS IT TRUE, DAD? IS IT TRUE?
IT'S TRUE, ALL RIGHT! I JUST TALKED WITH THE HEAD OF THE SCHOOL BOARD!
THEY WERE GETTING THE BUILDING READY FOR THE START OF CLASSES, AND THEY DISCOVERED TOXIC MOLD!
9/3
WHERE DID THE TOXIC MOLD **COME** FROM?
NOBODY KNOWS!
© 2008 by NEA, Inc.
MAY I SUGGEST NATE'S LOCKER AS A LIKELY SOURCE?
OOH! **YES!** THAT THING IS A GIANT **PETRI DISH!**

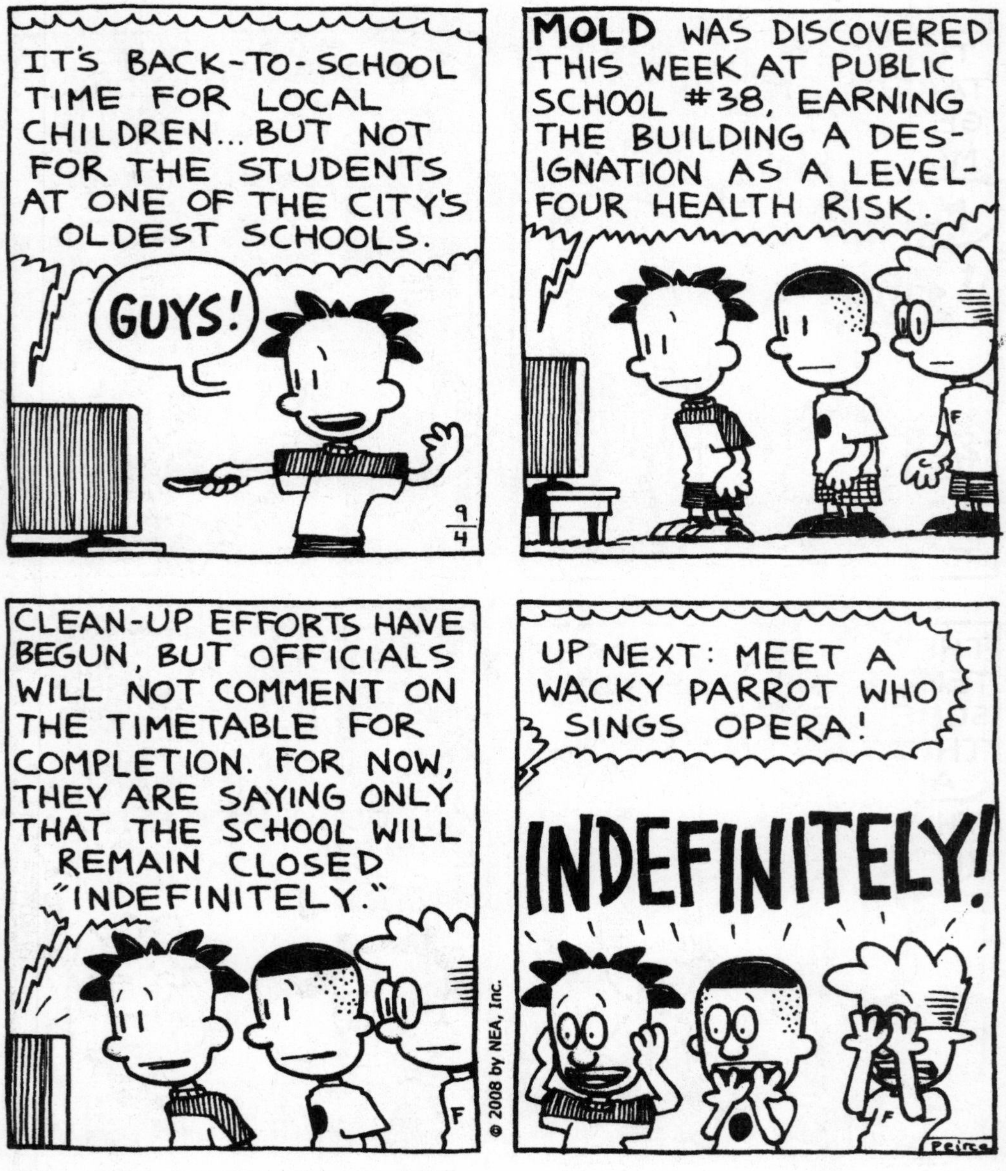
IT'S BACK-TO-SCHOOL TIME FOR LOCAL CHILDREN... BUT NOT FOR THE STUDENTS AT ONE OF THE CITY'S OLDEST SCHOOLS.
GUYS!
9
4
MOLD WAS DISCOVERED THIS WEEK AT PUBLIC SCHOOL #38, EARNING THE BUILDING A DESIGNATION AS A LEVEL-FOUR HEALTH RISK.
CLEAN-UP EFFORTS HAVE BEGUN, BUT OFFICIALS WILL NOT COMMENT ON THE TIMETABLE FOR COMPLETION. FOR NOW, THEY ARE SAYING ONLY THAT THE SCHOOL WILL REMAIN CLOSED "INDEFINITELY."
© 2008 by NEA, Inc.
UP NEXT: MEET A WACKY PARROT WHO SINGS OPERA!
INDEFINITELY!
Peirce

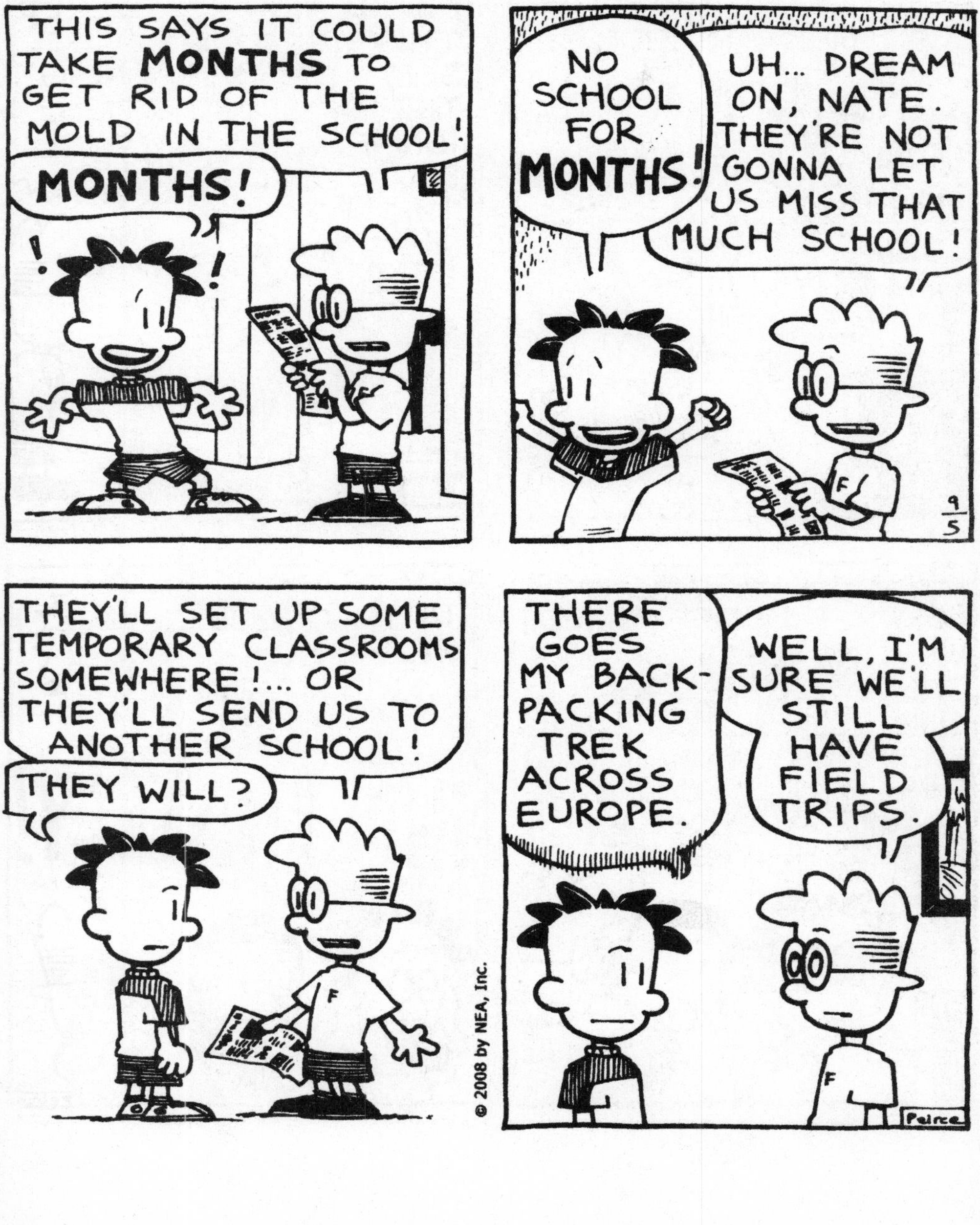
THIS SAYS IT COULD TAKE **MONTHS** TO GET RID OF THE MOLD IN THE SCHOOL!
MONTHS!
! !
NO SCHOOL FOR **MONTHS!**
UH... DREAM ON, NATE. THEY'RE NOT GONNA LET US MISS THAT MUCH SCHOOL!
9/5
THEY'LL SET UP SOME TEMPORARY CLASSROOMS SOMEWHERE!... OR THEY'LL SEND US TO ANOTHER SCHOOL!
THEY WILL?
THERE GOES MY BACK-PACKING TREK ACROSS EUROPE.
WELL, I'M SURE WE'LL STILL HAVE FIELD TRIPS.
Peirce

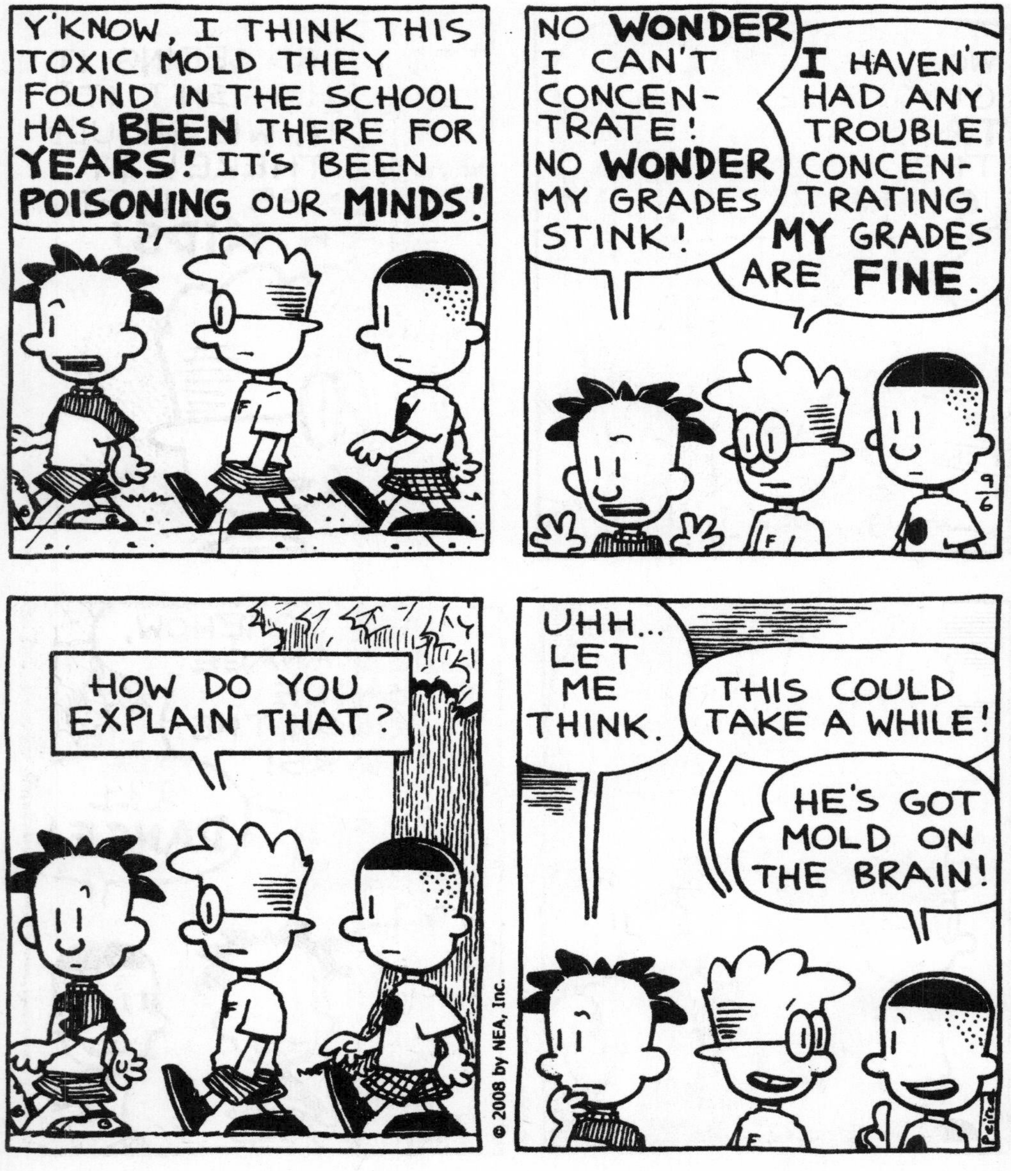

Y'KNOW, I THINK THIS TOXIC MOLD THEY FOUND IN THE SCHOOL HAS BEEN THERE FOR YEARS! IT'S BEEN POISONING OUR MINDS!
NO WONDER I CAN'T CONCENTRATE! NO WONDER MY GRADES STINK!
I HAVEN'T HAD ANY TROUBLE CONCENTRATING. MY GRADES ARE FINE.
9/6
HOW DO YOU EXPLAIN THAT?
© 2008 by NEA, Inc.
UHH... LET ME THINK.
THIS COULD TAKE A WHILE!
HE'S GOT MOLD ON THE BRAIN!
Peirce

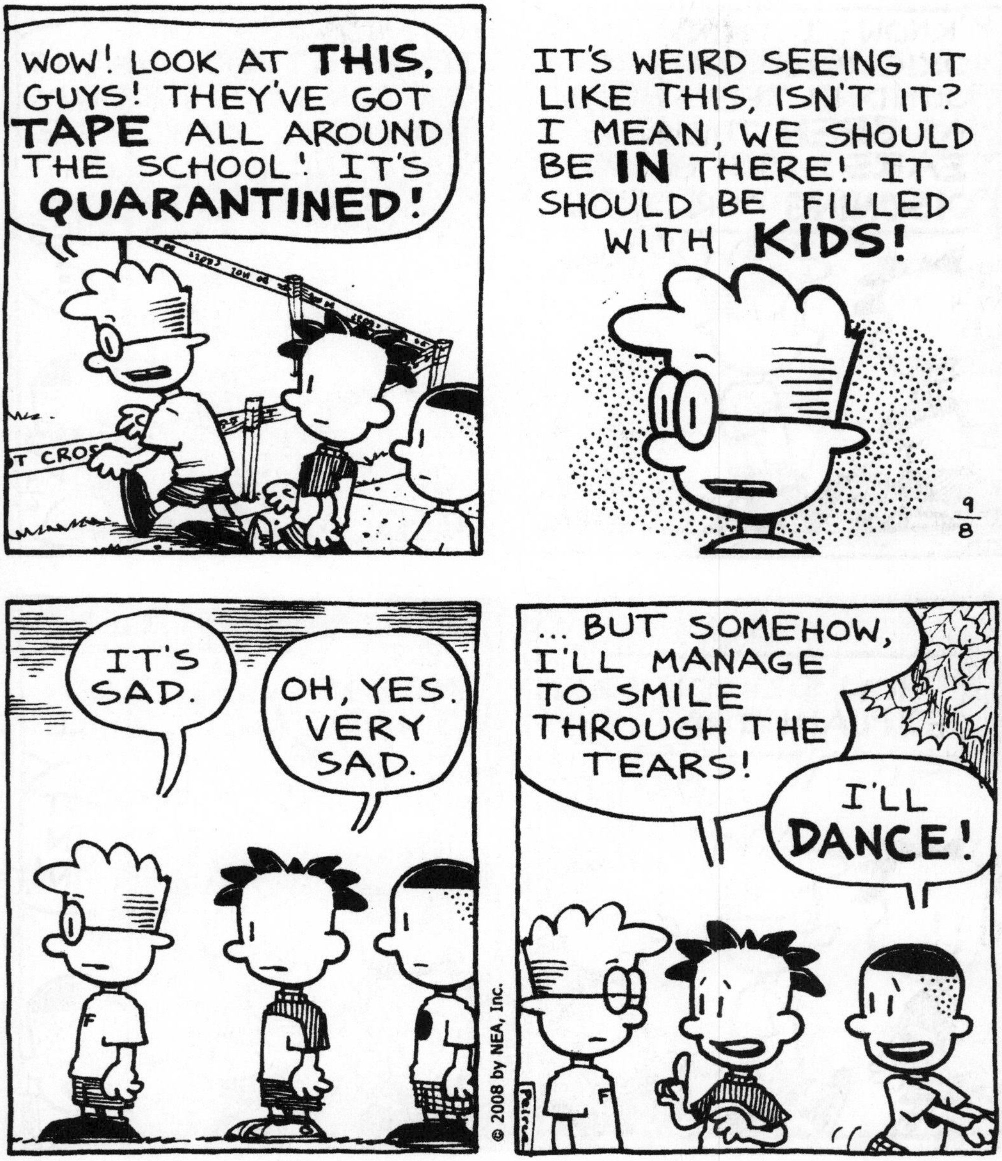
WOW! LOOK AT **THIS**, GUYS! THEY'VE GOT **TAPE** ALL AROUND THE SCHOOL! IT'S **QUARANTINED!**
IT'S WEIRD SEEING IT LIKE THIS, ISN'T IT? I MEAN, WE SHOULD BE **IN** THERE! IT SHOULD BE FILLED WITH **KIDS!**
9/8
IT'S SAD.
OH, YES. VERY SAD.
© 2008 by NEA, Inc.
... BUT SOMEHOW, I'LL MANAGE TO SMILE THROUGH THE TEARS!
I'LL **DANCE!**

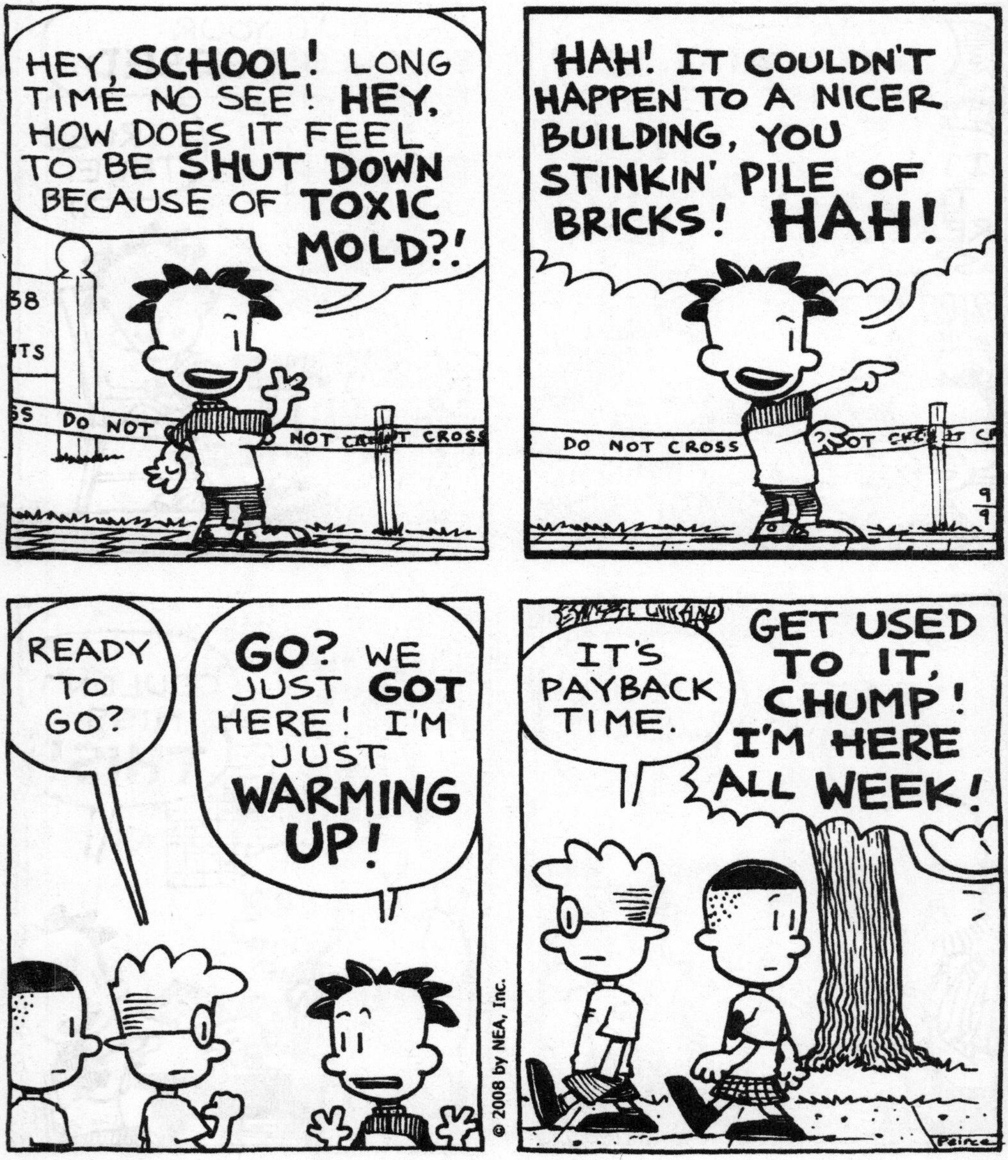
HEY, SCHOOL! LONG TIME NO SEE! HEY, HOW DOES IT FEEL TO BE SHUT DOWN BECAUSE OF TOXIC MOLD?!
DO NOT CROSS
HAH! IT COULDN'T HAPPEN TO A NICER BUILDING, YOU STINKIN' PILE OF BRICKS! HAH!
DO NOT CROSS
9/9
READY TO GO?
GO? WE JUST GOT HERE! I'M JUST WARMING UP!
© 2008 by NEA, Inc.
IT'S PAYBACK TIME.
GET USED TO IT, CHUMP! I'M HERE ALL WEEK!
Peirce

WHAT ARE YOU DOING UP?
IT'S TIME TO GET READY FOR SCHOOL!
UH... BUT YOUR SCHOOL'S **CLOSED**.
TRUE. TRUE...
... BUT **ELLEN'S** ISN'T!
GRUB.. SNX...
...MMMPH...
ZZZZZZ
COULDN'T MISS **THIS!**
© 2008 by NEA, Inc.

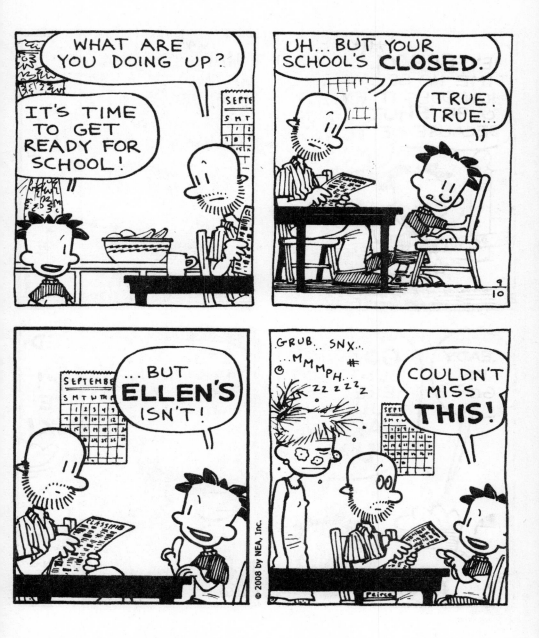

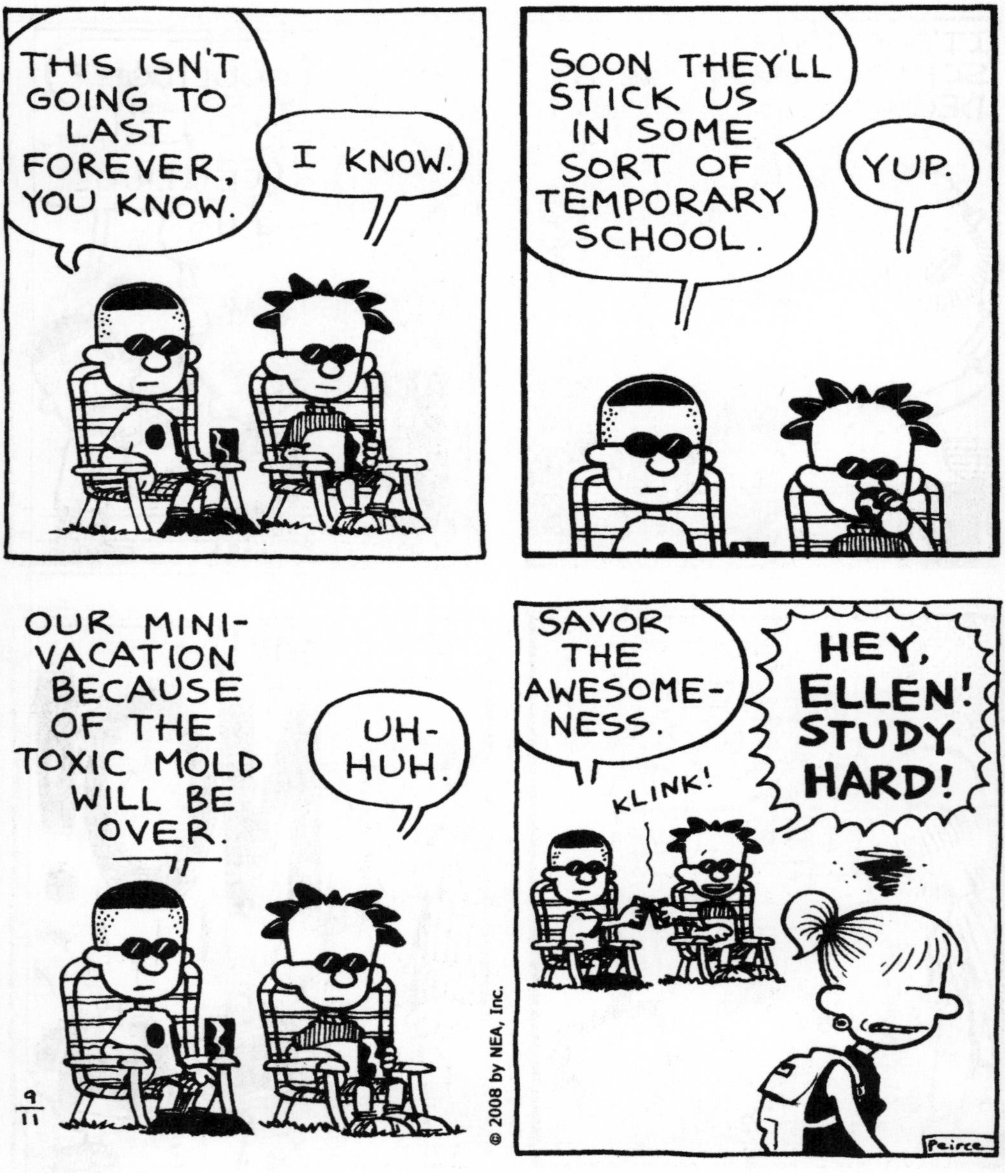
THIS ISN'T GOING TO LAST FOREVER, YOU KNOW.
I KNOW.
SOON THEY'LL STICK US IN SOME SORT OF TEMPORARY SCHOOL.
YUP.
OUR MINI-VACATION BECAUSE OF THE TOXIC MOLD WILL BE OVER.
UH-HUH.
SAVOR THE AWESOME-NESS.
KLINK!
HEY, ELLEN! STUDY HARD!
9/11
© 2008 by NEA, Inc.
Peirce

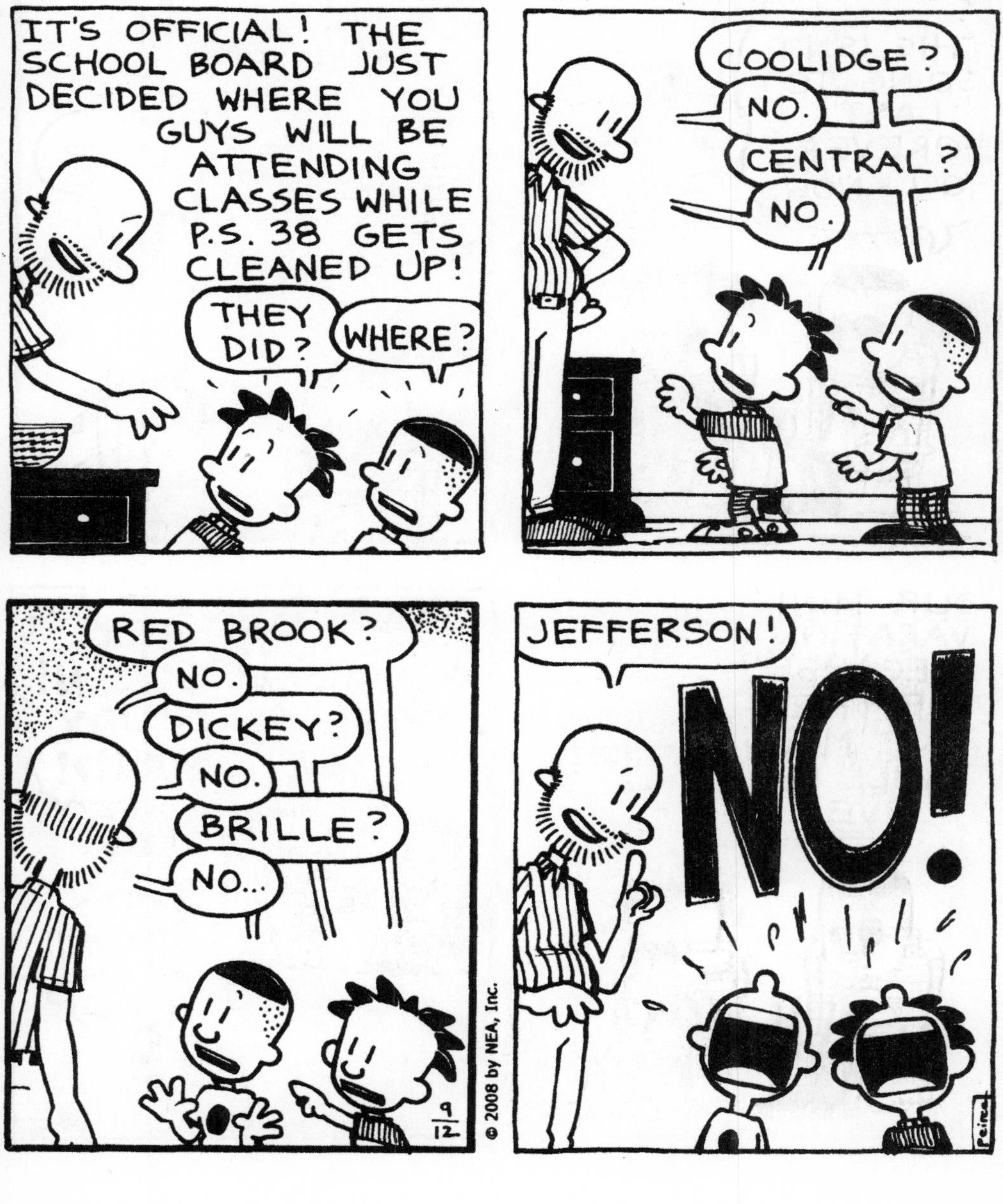
IT'S OFFICIAL! THE SCHOOL BOARD JUST DECIDED WHERE YOU GUYS WILL BE ATTENDING CLASSES WHILE P.S. 38 GETS CLEANED UP!
THEY DID?
WHERE?
COOLIDGE?
NO.
CENTRAL?
NO.
RED BROOK?
NO.
DICKEY?
NO.
BRILLE?
NO...
JEFFERSON!
NO!
9/12
© 2008 by NEA, Inc.
Peirce

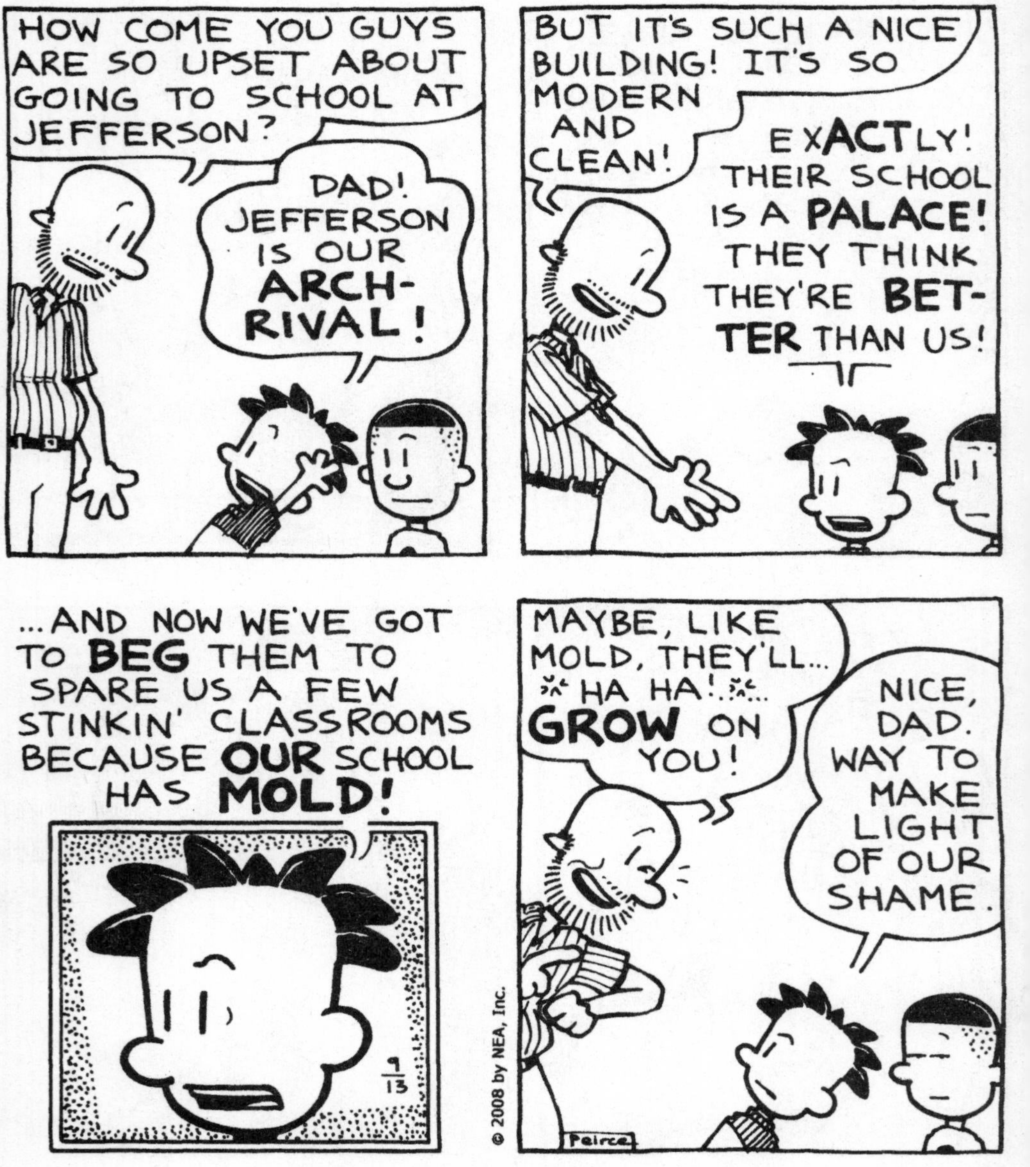
HOW COME YOU GUYS ARE SO UPSET ABOUT GOING TO SCHOOL AT JEFFERSON?
DAD! JEFFERSON IS OUR ARCH-RIVAL!
BUT IT'S SUCH A NICE BUILDING! IT'S SO MODERN AND CLEAN!
EXACTLY! THEIR SCHOOL IS A PALACE! THEY THINK THEY'RE BETTER THAN US!
...AND NOW WE'VE GOT TO BEG THEM TO SPARE US A FEW STINKIN' CLASSROOMS BECAUSE OUR SCHOOL HAS MOLD!
9/13
© 2008 by NEA, Inc.
MAYBE, LIKE MOLD, THEY'LL... HA HA! GROW ON YOU!
NICE, DAD. WAY TO MAKE LIGHT OF OUR SHAME.
Peirce

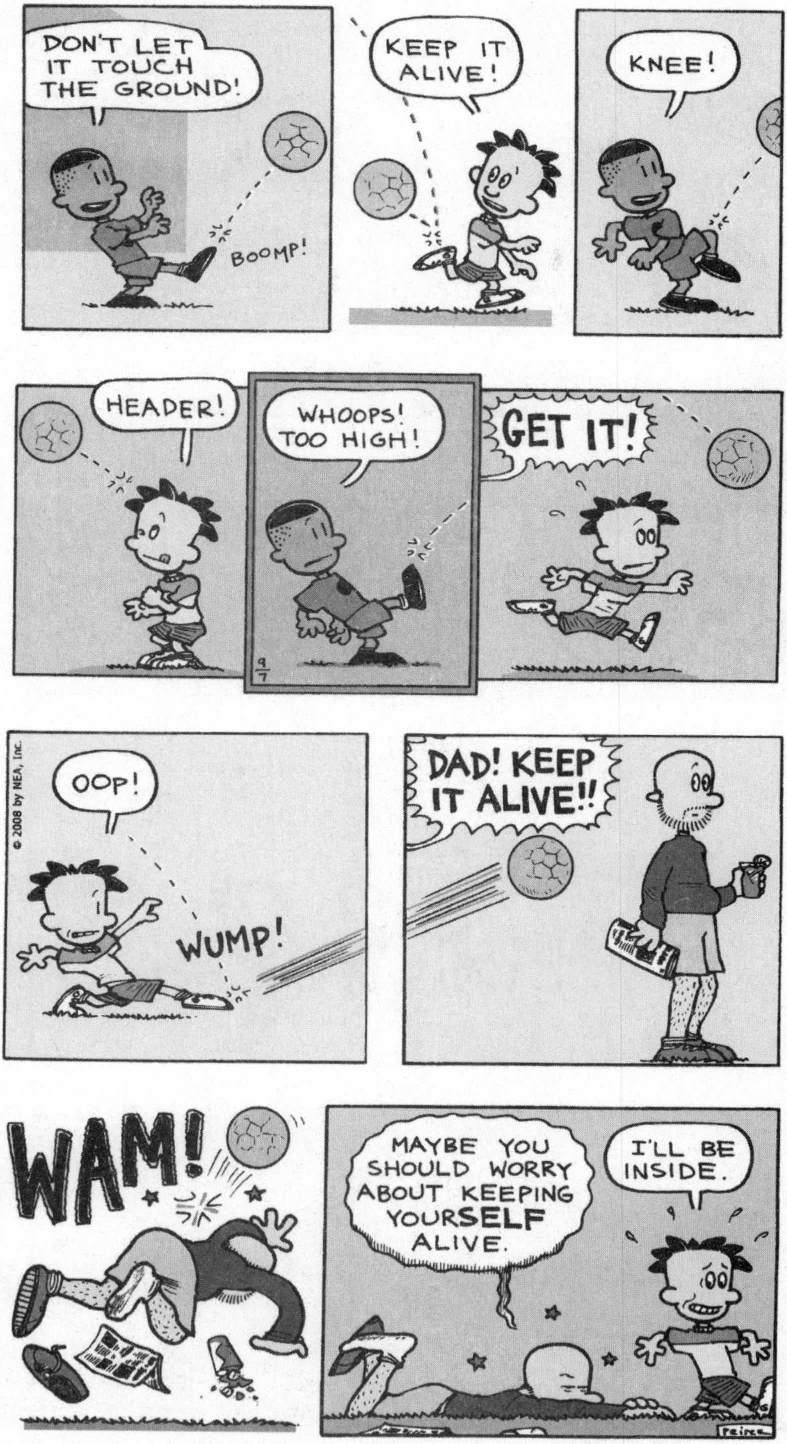
DON'T LET IT TOUCH THE GROUND!
BOOMP!
KEEP IT ALIVE!
KNEE!
HEADER!
WHOOPS! TOO HIGH!
9/7
GET IT!
© 2008 by NEA, Inc.
OOP!
WUMP!
DAD! KEEP IT ALIVE!!
WAM!
MAYBE YOU SHOULD WORRY ABOUT KEEPING YOURSELF ALIVE.
I'LL BE INSIDE.
peirce

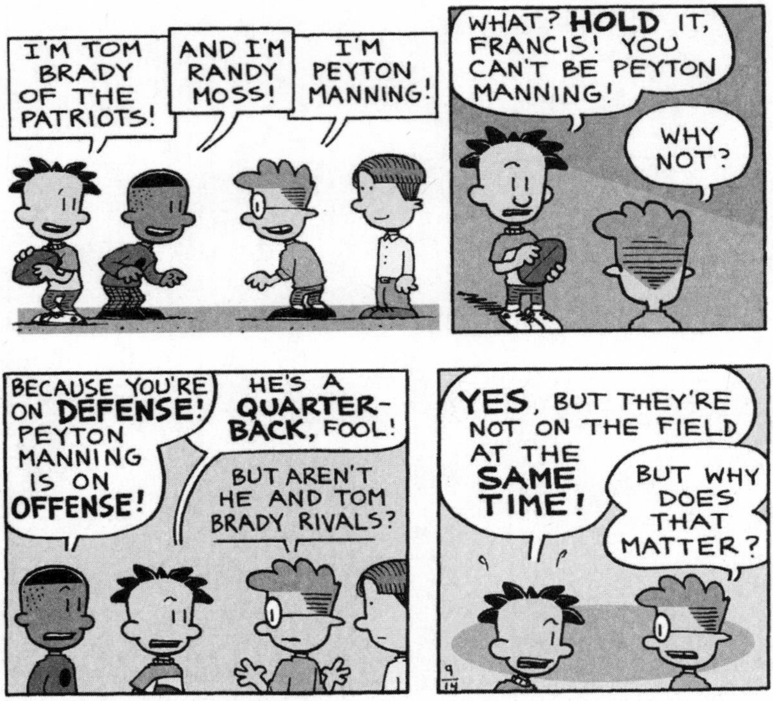
I'M TOM BRADY OF THE PATRIOTS!
AND I'M RANDY MOSS!
I'M PEYTON MANNING!
WHAT? HOLD IT, FRANCIS! YOU CAN'T BE PEYTON MANNING!
WHY NOT?
BECAUSE YOU'RE ON DEFENSE! PEYTON MANNING IS ON OFFENSE!
HE'S A QUARTER-BACK, FOOL!
BUT AREN'T HE AND TOM BRADY RIVALS?
YES, BUT THEY'RE NOT ON THE FIELD AT THE SAME TIME!
BUT WHY DOES THAT MATTER?

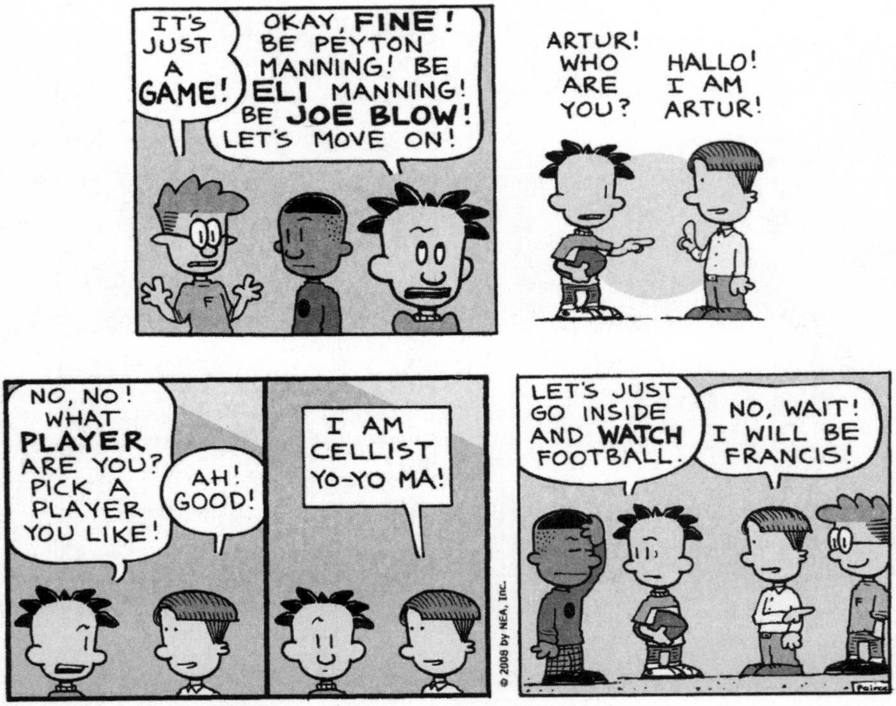
IT'S JUST A GAME!
OKAY, FINE! BE PEYTON MANNING! BE ELI MANNING! BE JOE BLOW! LET'S MOVE ON!
ARTUR! WHO ARE YOU?
HALLO! I AM ARTUR!
NO, NO! WHAT PLAYER ARE YOU? PICK A PLAYER YOU LIKE!
AH! GOOD!
I AM CELLIST YO-YO MA!
© 2008 by NEA, Inc.
LET'S JUST GO INSIDE AND WATCH FOOTBALL.
NO, WAIT! I WILL BE FRANCIS!

WHAT A DUMP

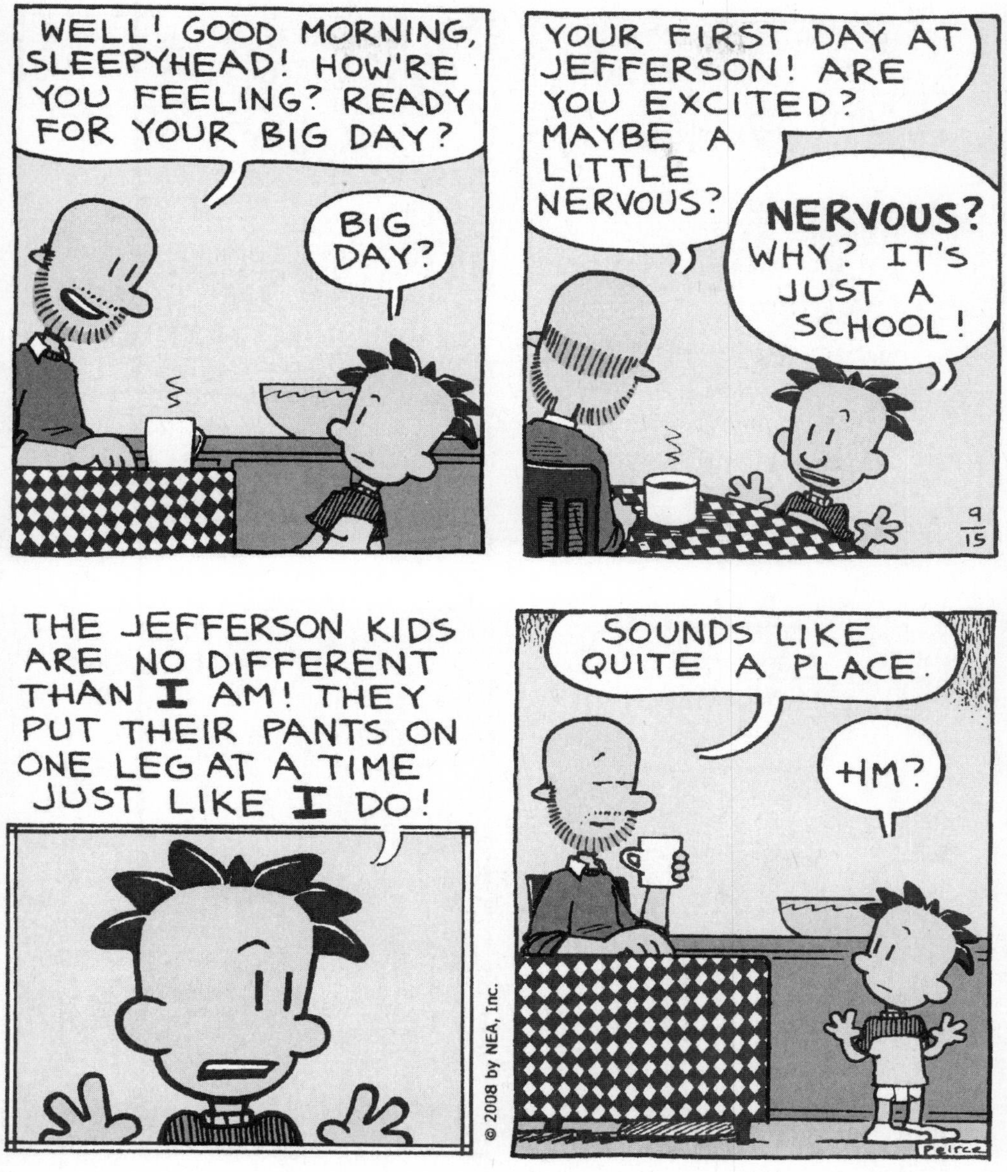

WELL! GOOD MORNING, SLEEPYHEAD! HOW'RE YOU FEELING? READY FOR YOUR BIG DAY?
BIG DAY?
YOUR FIRST DAY AT JEFFERSON! ARE YOU EXCITED? MAYBE A LITTLE NERVOUS?
NERVOUS? WHY? IT'S JUST A SCHOOL!
9/15
THE JEFFERSON KIDS ARE NO DIFFERENT THAN **I** AM! THEY PUT THEIR PANTS ON ONE LEG AT A TIME JUST LIKE **I** DO!
SOUNDS LIKE QUITE A PLACE.
HM?
Peirce

HOOL
BUS
I CAN'T BELIEVE WE'RE GOING TO SCHOOL AT **JEFFERSON!** I **HATE** JEFFERSON!
SAME HERE. THEY'RE SO OB**NOX**IOUS!
LET'S MAKE SURE THEY KNOW WE'RE DOING THIS BECAUSE WE **HAVE** TO, NOT BECAUSE WE **WANT** TO GO TO THEIR STINKIN' SCHOOL!
RIGHT! WE'LL BE **IN** JEFFERSON, NOT **OF** JEFFERSON!
9/16

GOOOOOD MORNING, LADS!
J
J
Peirce
HOOL
BUS
SCHOOL SPIRIT!
YOU LOOK LIKE A REJECT FROM AN "ALVIN & THE CHIPMUNKS" AUDITION.
J

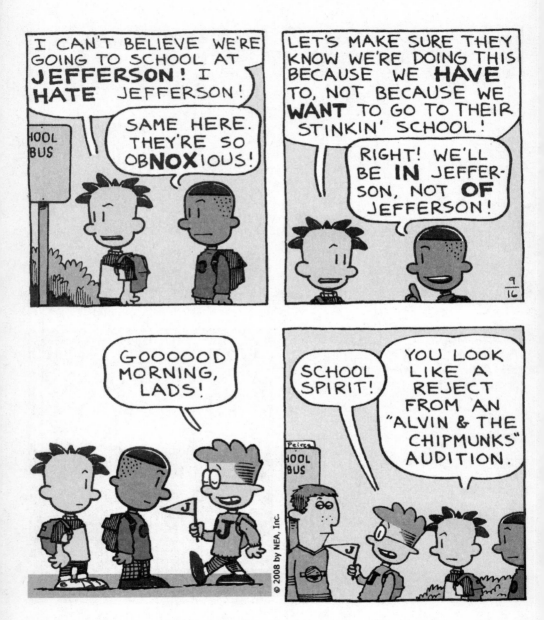

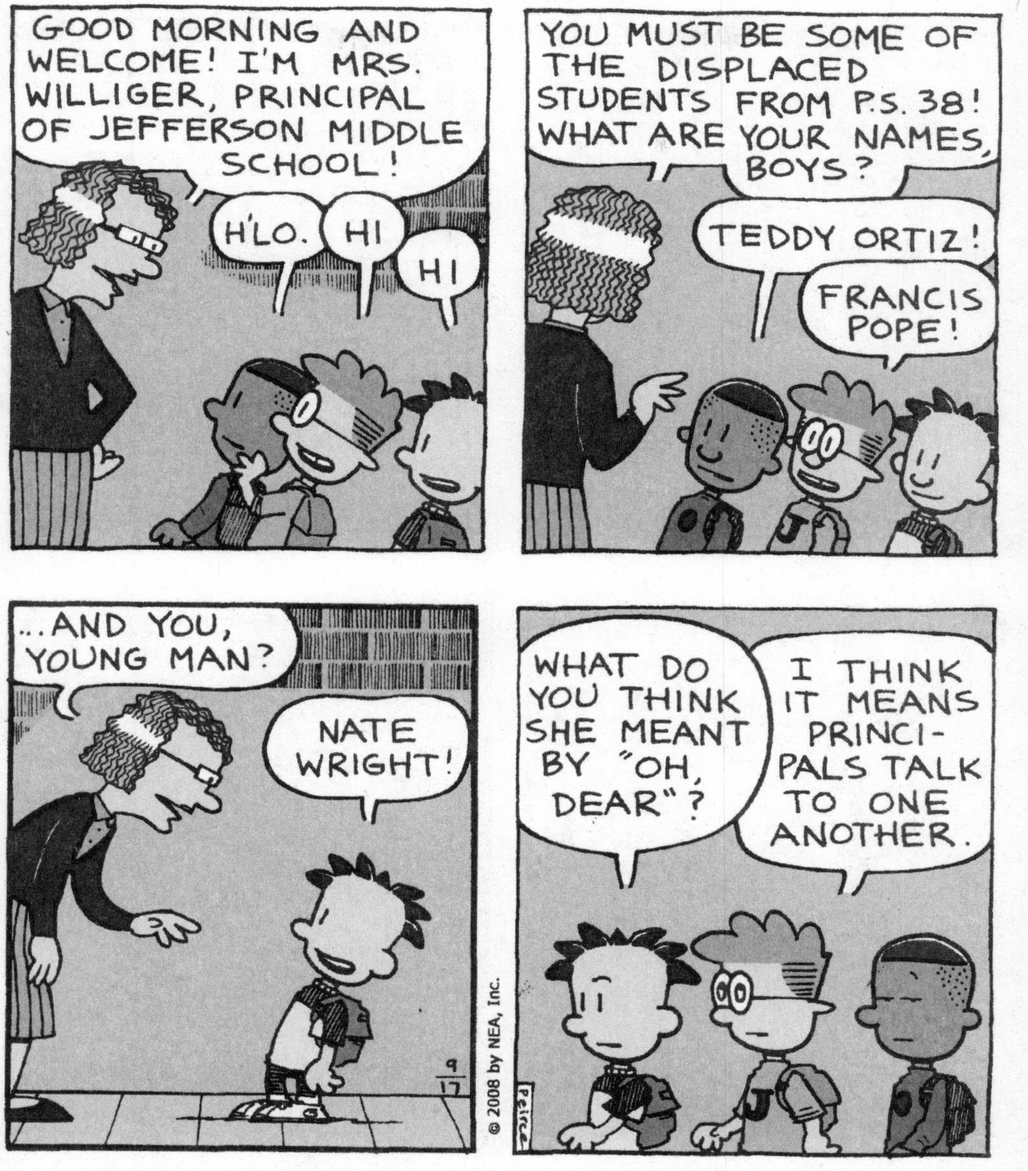
GOOD MORNING AND WELCOME! I'M MRS. WILLIGER, PRINCIPAL OF JEFFERSON MIDDLE SCHOOL!
H'LO.
HI
HI
YOU MUST BE SOME OF THE DISPLACED STUDENTS FROM P.S. 38! WHAT ARE YOUR NAMES, BOYS?
TEDDY ORTIZ!
FRANCIS POPE!
...AND YOU, YOUNG MAN?
NATE WRIGHT!
9/17
© 2008 by NEA, Inc.
WHAT DO YOU THINK SHE MEANT BY "OH, DEAR"?
I THINK IT MEANS PRINCI-PALS TALK TO ONE ANOTHER.
Peirce

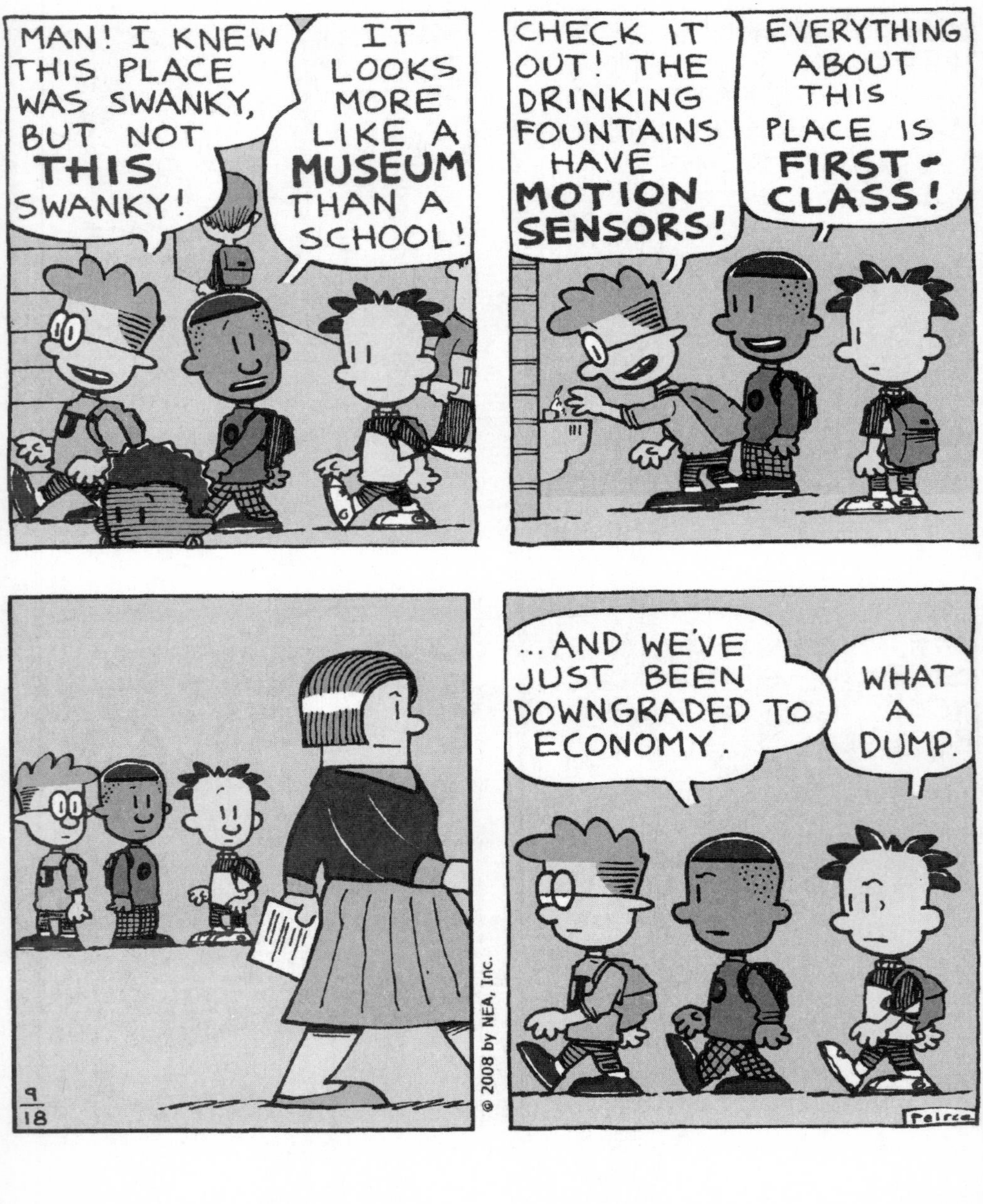
MAN! I KNEW THIS PLACE WAS SWANKY, BUT NOT **THIS** SWANKY!
IT LOOKS MORE LIKE A **MUSEUM** THAN A SCHOOL!
CHECK IT OUT! THE DRINKING FOUNTAINS HAVE **MOTION SENSORS!**
EVERYTHING ABOUT THIS PLACE IS **FIRST-CLASS!**
9/18
© 2008 by NEA, Inc.
...AND WE'VE JUST BEEN DOWNGRADED TO ECONOMY.
WHAT A DUMP.
Peirce

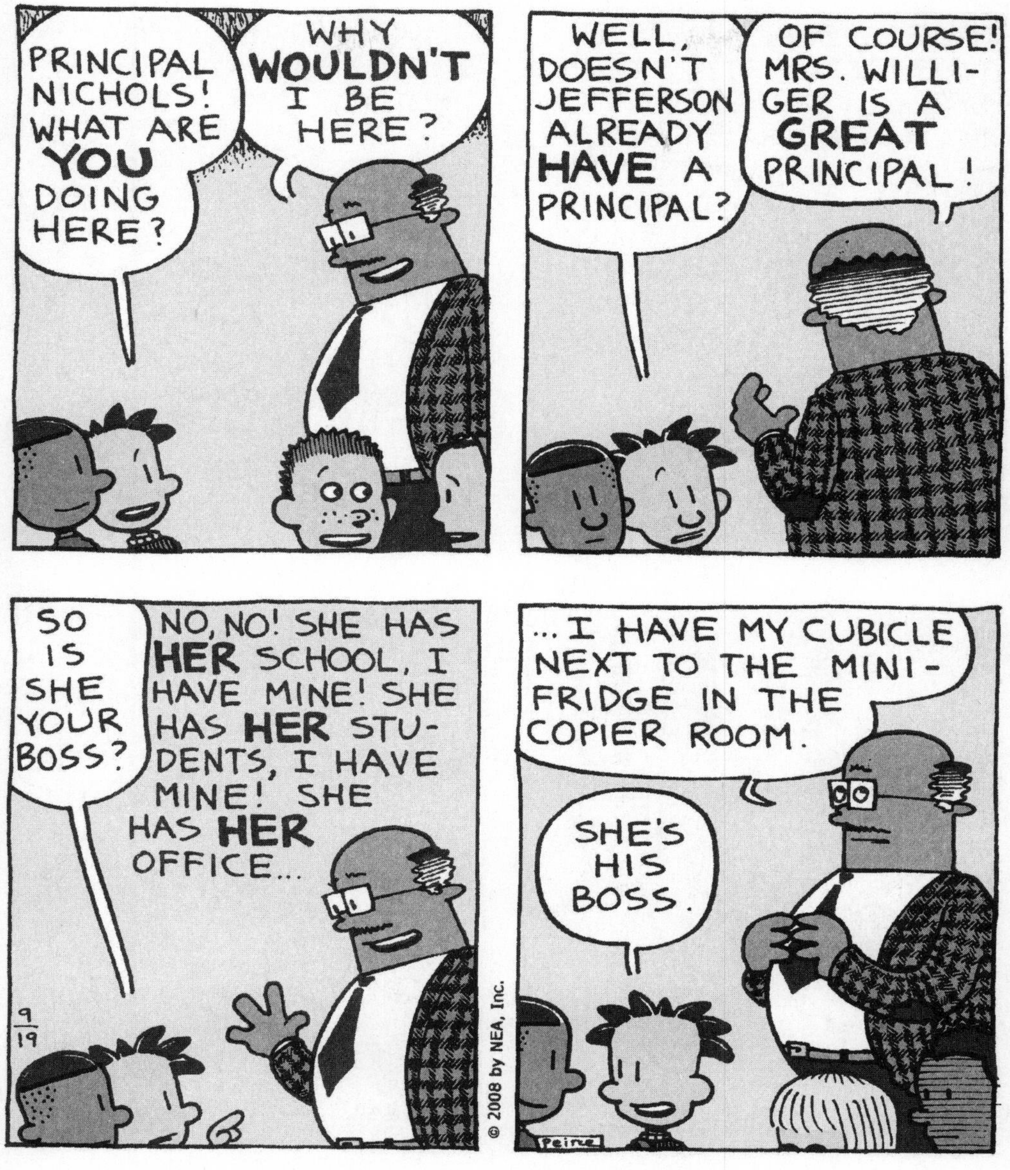
PRINCIPAL NICHOLS! WHAT ARE YOU DOING HERE?
WHY WOULDN'T I BE HERE?
WELL, DOESN'T JEFFERSON ALREADY HAVE A PRINCIPAL?
OF COURSE! MRS. WILLIGER IS A GREAT PRINCIPAL!
SO IS SHE YOUR BOSS?
NO, NO! SHE HAS HER SCHOOL, I HAVE MINE! SHE HAS HER STUDENTS, I HAVE MINE! SHE HAS HER OFFICE...
9/19
© 2008 by NEA, Inc.
...I HAVE MY CUBICLE NEXT TO THE MINI-FRIDGE IN THE COPIER ROOM.
SHE'S HIS BOSS.
Peirce

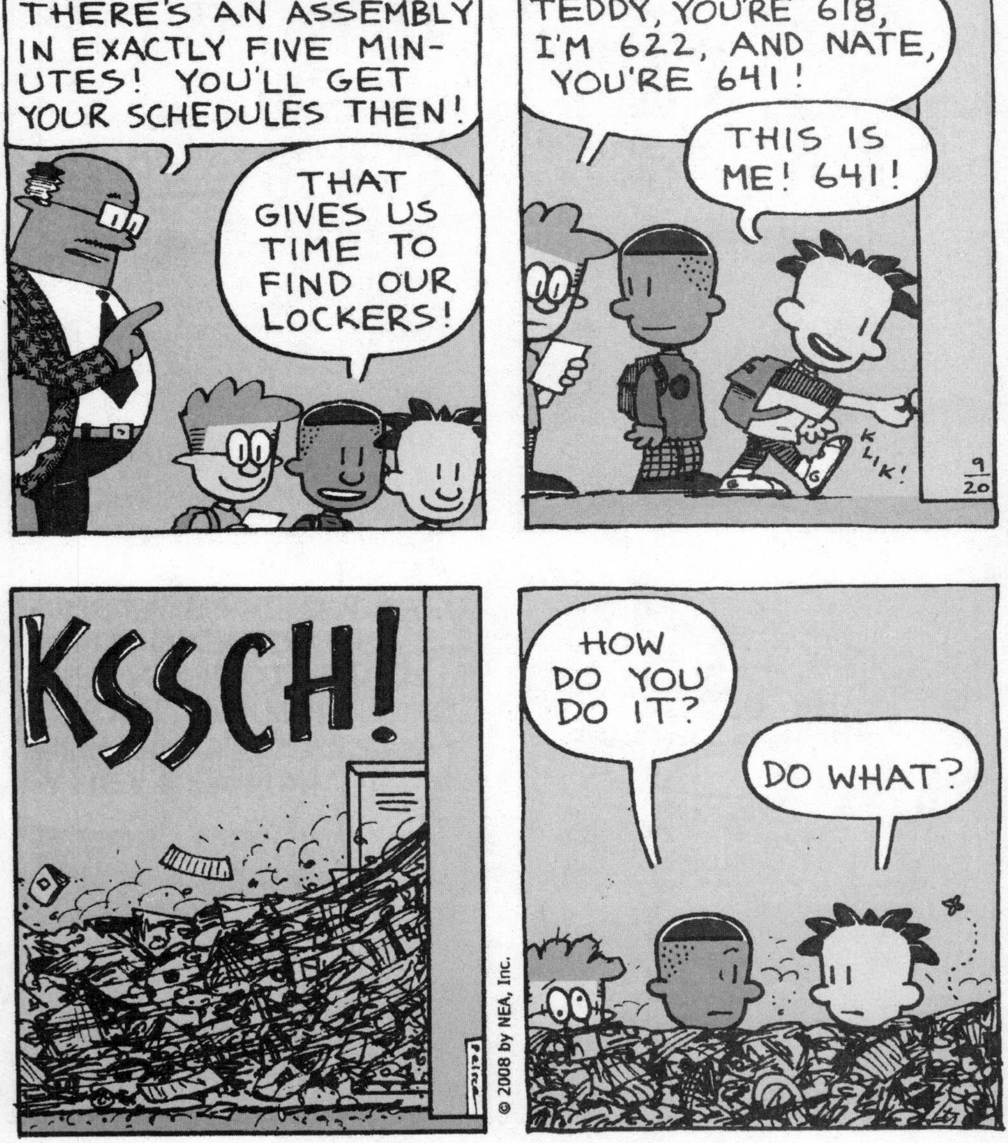
THERE'S AN ASSEMBLY IN EXACTLY FIVE MIN-UTES! YOU'LL GET YOUR SCHEDULES THEN!
THAT GIVES US TIME TO FIND OUR LOCKERS!
TEDDY, YOU'RE 618, I'M 622, AND NATE, YOU'RE 641!
THIS IS ME! 641!
KLIK!
9/20
KSSCH!
HOW DO YOU DO IT?
DO WHAT?

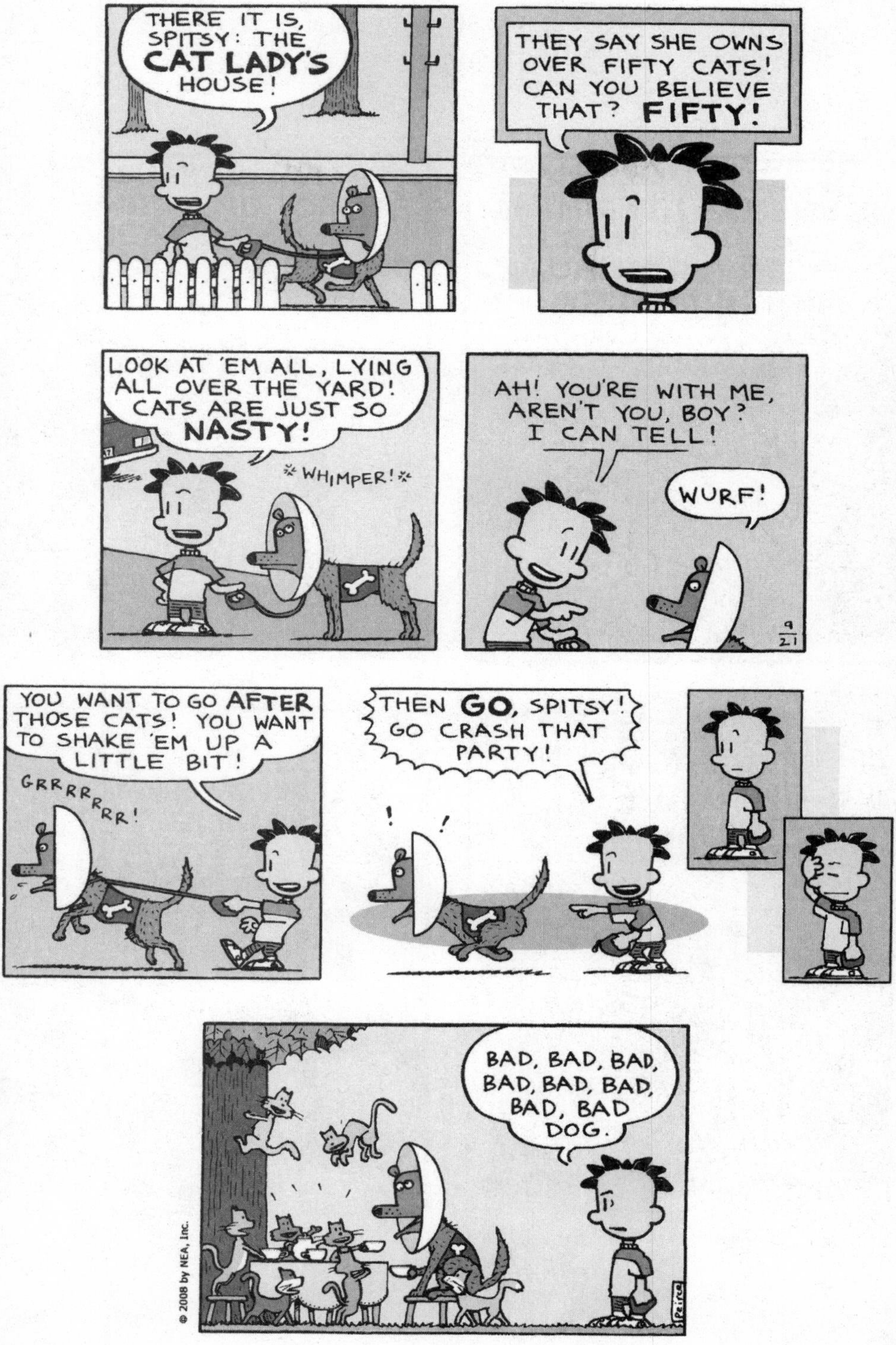
THERE IT IS, SPITSY: THE CAT LADY'S HOUSE!
THEY SAY SHE OWNS OVER FIFTY CATS! CAN YOU BELIEVE THAT? FIFTY!
LOOK AT 'EM ALL, LYING ALL OVER THE YARD! CATS ARE JUST SO NASTY!
WHIMPER!
AH! YOU'RE WITH ME, AREN'T YOU, BOY? I CAN TELL!
WURF!
9/21
YOU WANT TO GO AFTER THOSE CATS! YOU WANT TO SHAKE 'EM UP A LITTLE BIT!
GRRRRRRRR!
THEN GO, SPITSY! GO CRASH THAT PARTY!
! !
BAD, BAD, BAD, BAD, BAD, BAD, BAD, BAD DOG.
© 2008 by NEA, Inc.
Peirce

LUCKY, LUCKIER, LUCKIEST

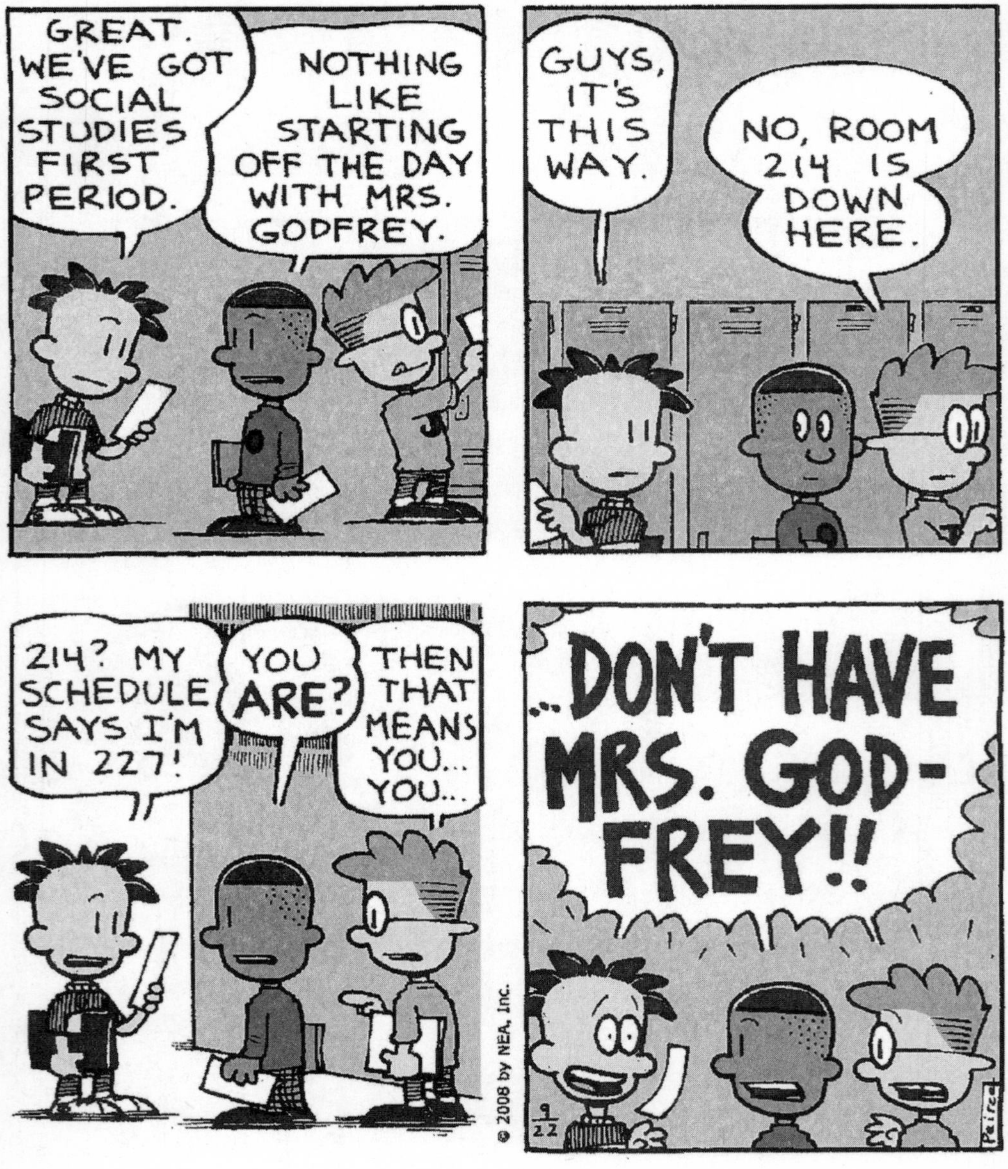
GREAT. WE'VE GOT SOCIAL STUDIES FIRST PERIOD.
NOTHING LIKE STARTING OFF THE DAY WITH MRS. GODFREY.
GUYS, IT'S THIS WAY.
NO, ROOM 214 IS DOWN HERE.
214? MY SCHEDULE SAYS I'M IN 227!
YOU ARE?
THEN THAT MEANS YOU... YOU...
...DON'T HAVE MRS. GOD-FREY!!
© 2008 by NEA, Inc.
9/22
Peirce

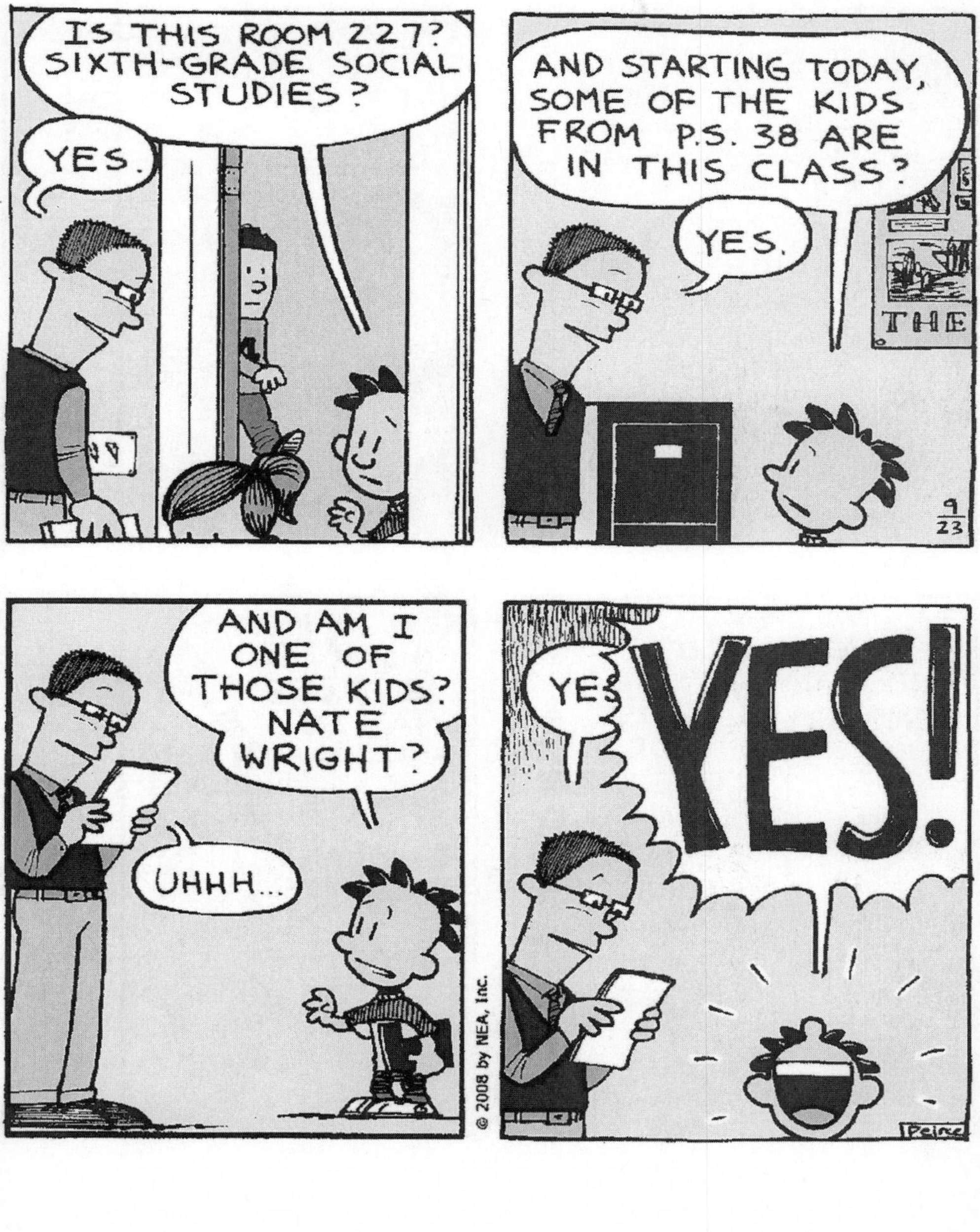
IS THIS ROOM 227? SIXTH-GRADE SOCIAL STUDIES?
YES.
AND STARTING TODAY, SOME OF THE KIDS FROM P.S. 38 ARE IN THIS CLASS?
YES.
THE
9/23
AND AM I ONE OF THOSE KIDS? NATE WRIGHT?
UHHH...
YES
YES!
© 2008 by NEA, Inc.
Peirce

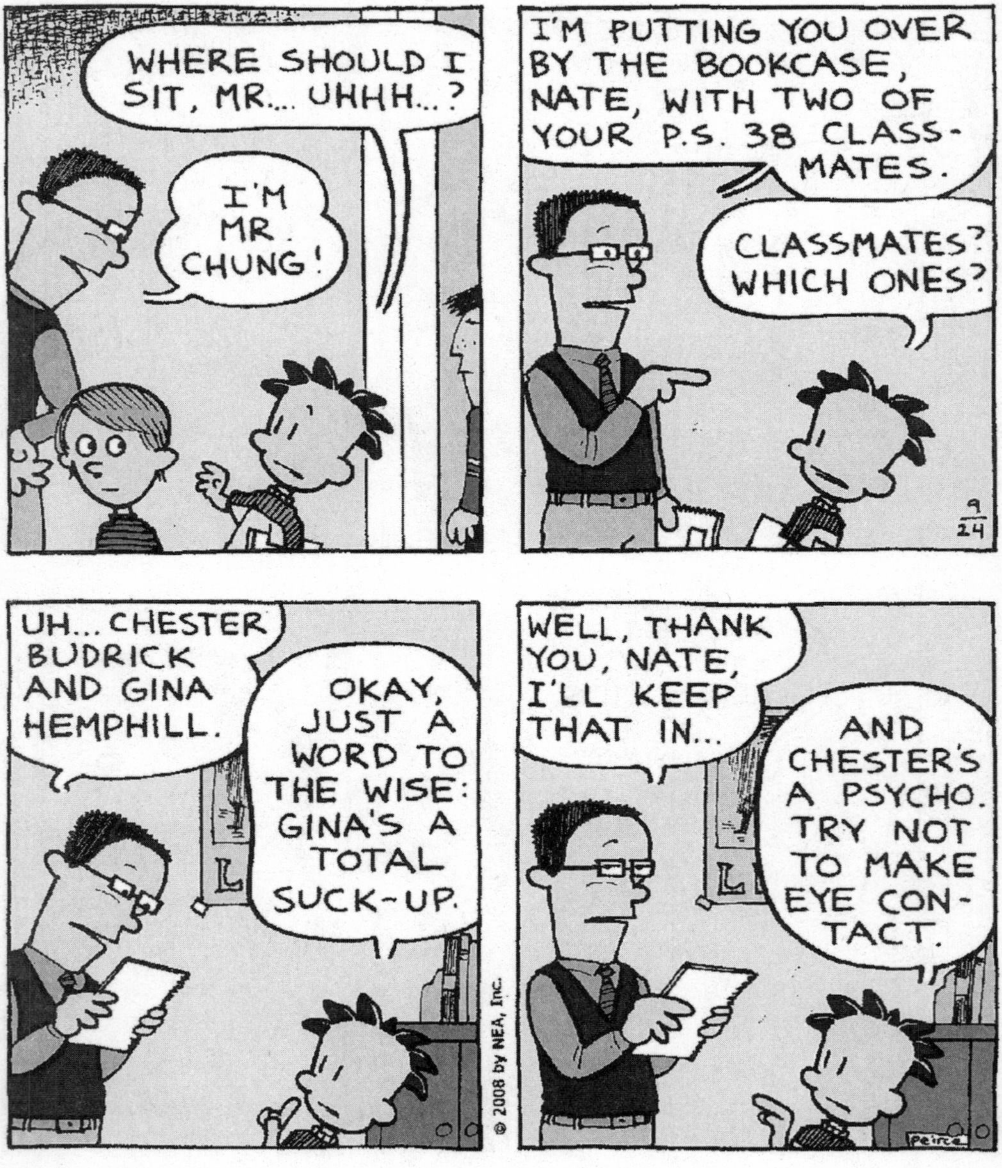
WHERE SHOULD I SIT, MR.... UHHH...?
I'M MR. CHUNG!
I'M PUTTING YOU OVER BY THE BOOKCASE, NATE, WITH TWO OF YOUR P.S. 38 CLASS-MATES.
CLASSMATES? WHICH ONES?
9/24
UH... CHESTER BUDRICK AND GINA HEMPHILL.
OKAY, JUST A WORD TO THE WISE: GINA'S A TOTAL SUCK-UP.
© 2008 by NEA, Inc.
WELL, THANK YOU, NATE, I'LL KEEP THAT IN...
AND CHESTER'S A PSYCHO. TRY NOT TO MAKE EYE CON-TACT.
peirce

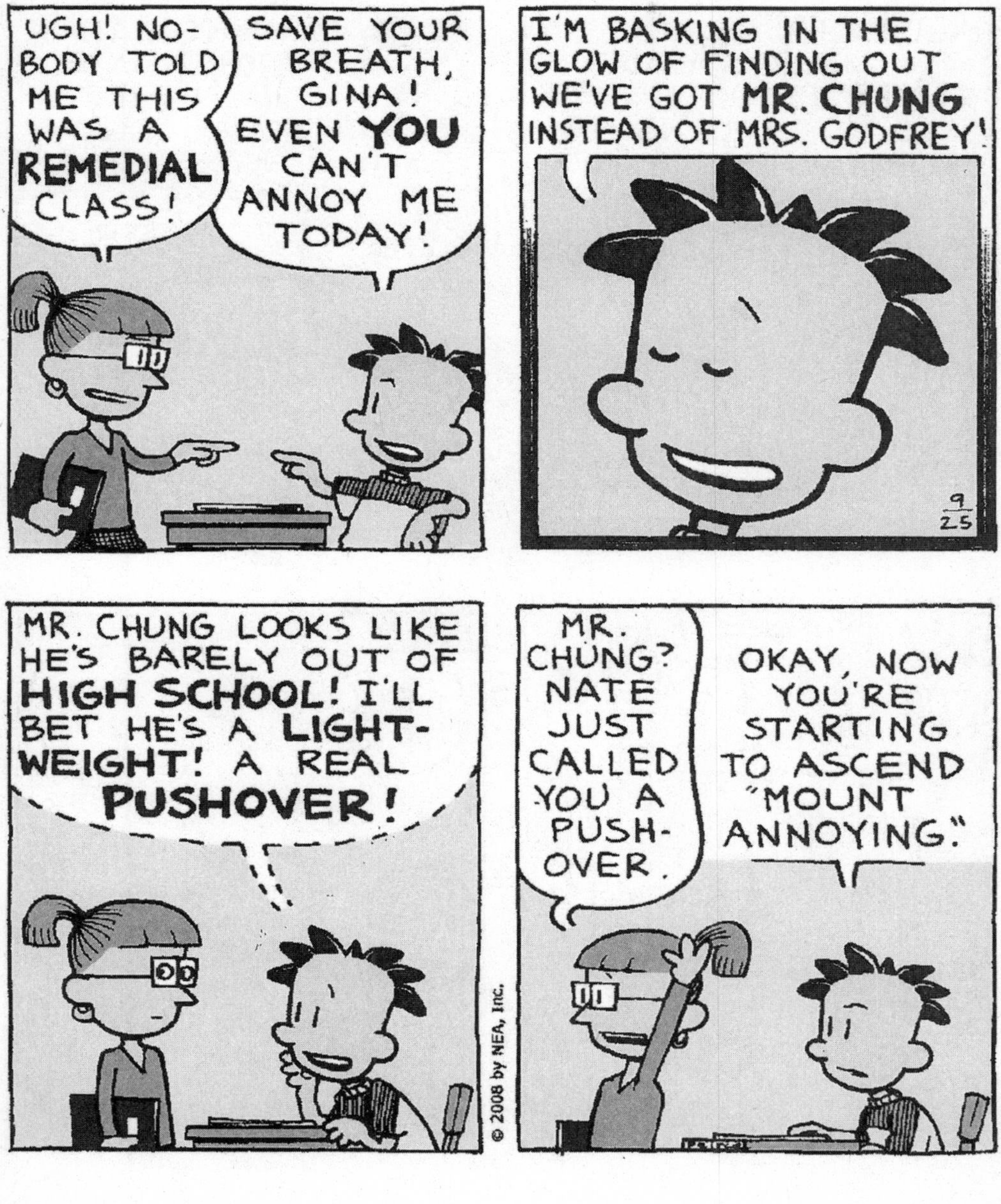
UGH! NOBODY TOLD ME THIS WAS A **REMEDIAL** CLASS!
SAVE YOUR BREATH, GINA! EVEN **YOU** CAN'T ANNOY ME TODAY!
I'M BASKING IN THE GLOW OF FINDING OUT WE'VE GOT **MR. CHUNG** INSTEAD OF MRS. GODFREY!
9/25
MR. CHUNG LOOKS LIKE HE'S BARELY OUT OF **HIGH SCHOOL!** I'LL BET HE'S A **LIGHTWEIGHT!** A REAL **PUSHOVER!**
© 2008 by NEA, Inc.
MR. CHUNG? NATE JUST CALLED YOU A PUSHOVER.
OKAY, NOW YOU'RE STARTING TO ASCEND "MOUNT ANNOYING."

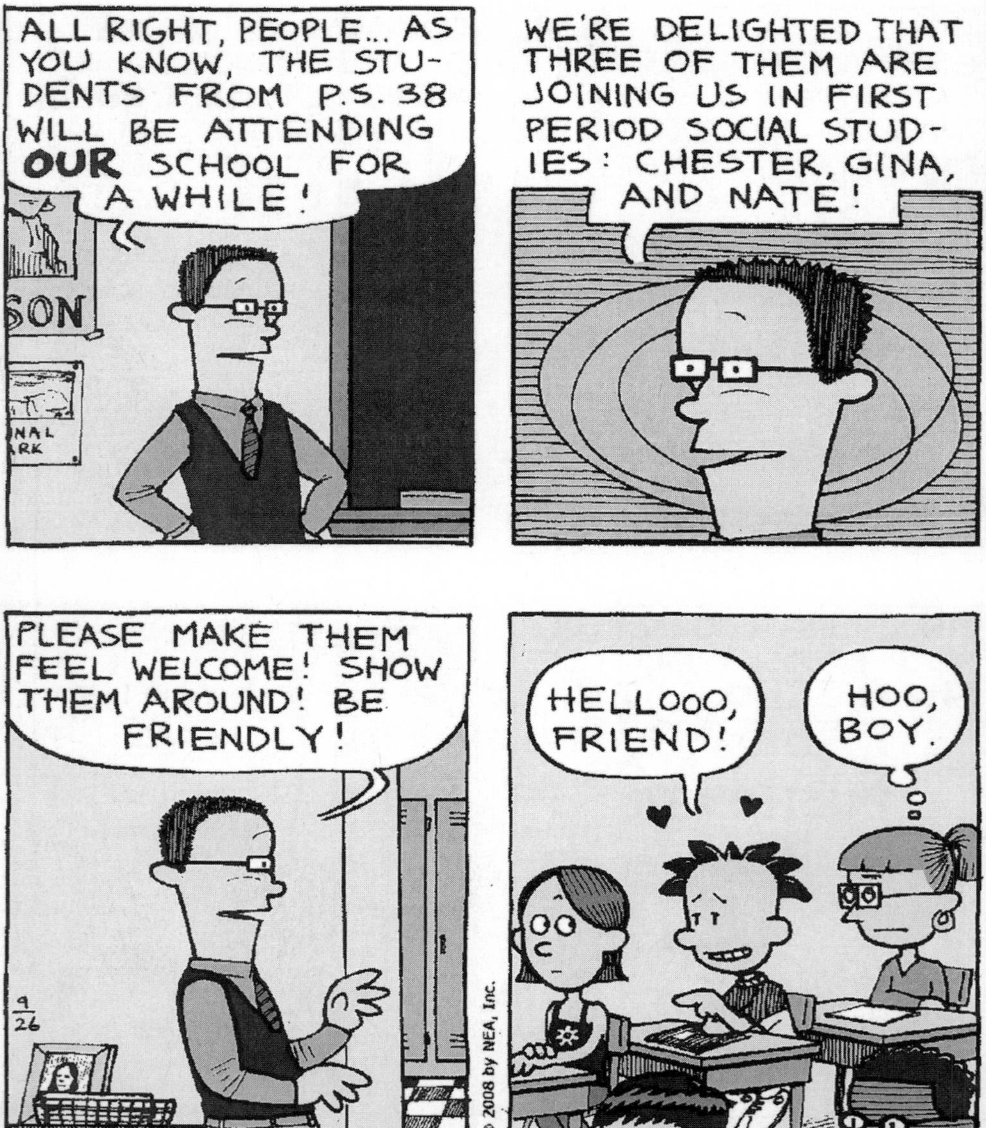
ALL RIGHT, PEOPLE... AS YOU KNOW, THE STUDENTS FROM P.S. 38 WILL BE ATTENDING **OUR** SCHOOL FOR A WHILE!
SON
NAL
ARK
WE'RE DELIGHTED THAT THREE OF THEM ARE JOINING US IN FIRST PERIOD SOCIAL STUDIES: CHESTER, GINA, AND NATE!
PLEASE MAKE THEM FEEL WELCOME! SHOW THEM AROUND! BE FRIENDLY!
9/26
Peirce
© 2008 by NEA, Inc.
HELLOOO, FRIEND!
HOO, BOY.

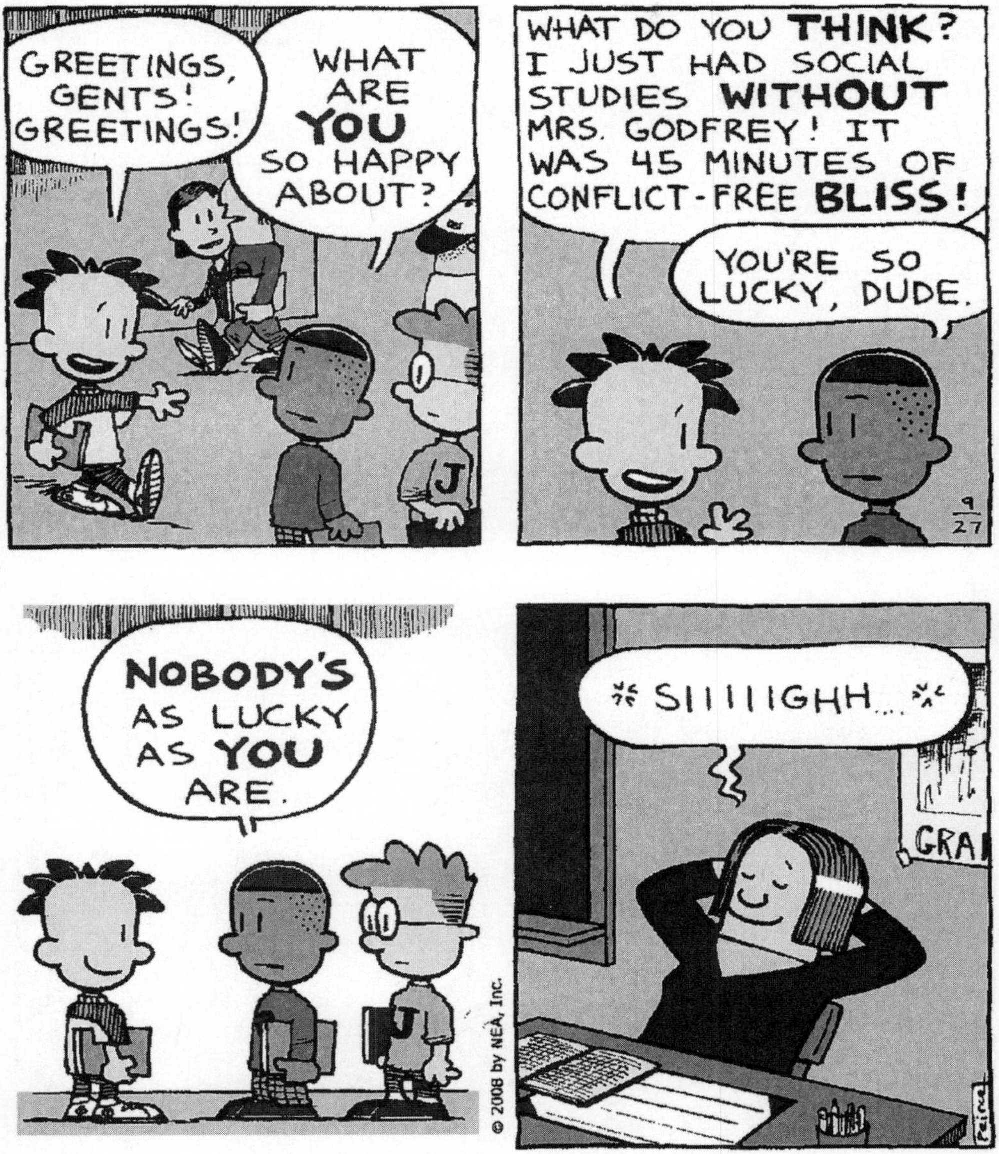
GREETINGS, GENTS! GREETINGS!
WHAT ARE YOU SO HAPPY ABOUT?
WHAT DO YOU THINK? I JUST HAD SOCIAL STUDIES WITHOUT MRS. GODFREY! IT WAS 45 MINUTES OF CONFLICT-FREE BLISS!
YOU'RE SO LUCKY, DUDE.
9/27
NOBODY'S AS LUCKY AS YOU ARE.
© 2008 by NEA, Inc.
SIIIIIGHH...
GRA
Peirce

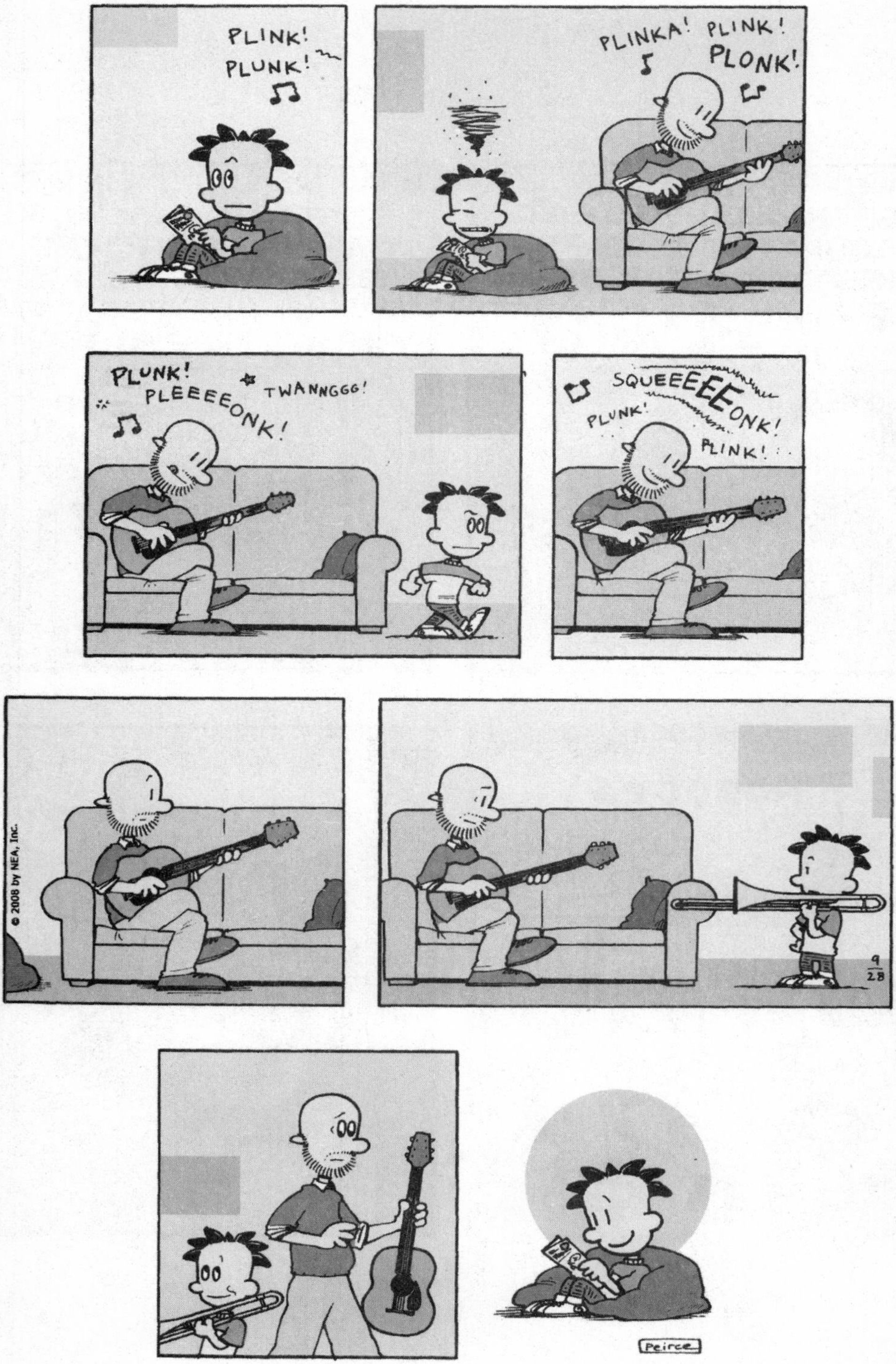
PLINK! PLUNK!
PLINKA! PLINK! PLONK!
PLUNK! PLEEEEEONK!
TWANNGGG!
SQUEEEEEEONK!
PLUNK!
PLINK!
© 2008 by NEA, Inc.
9/28
Peirce

GET REAL

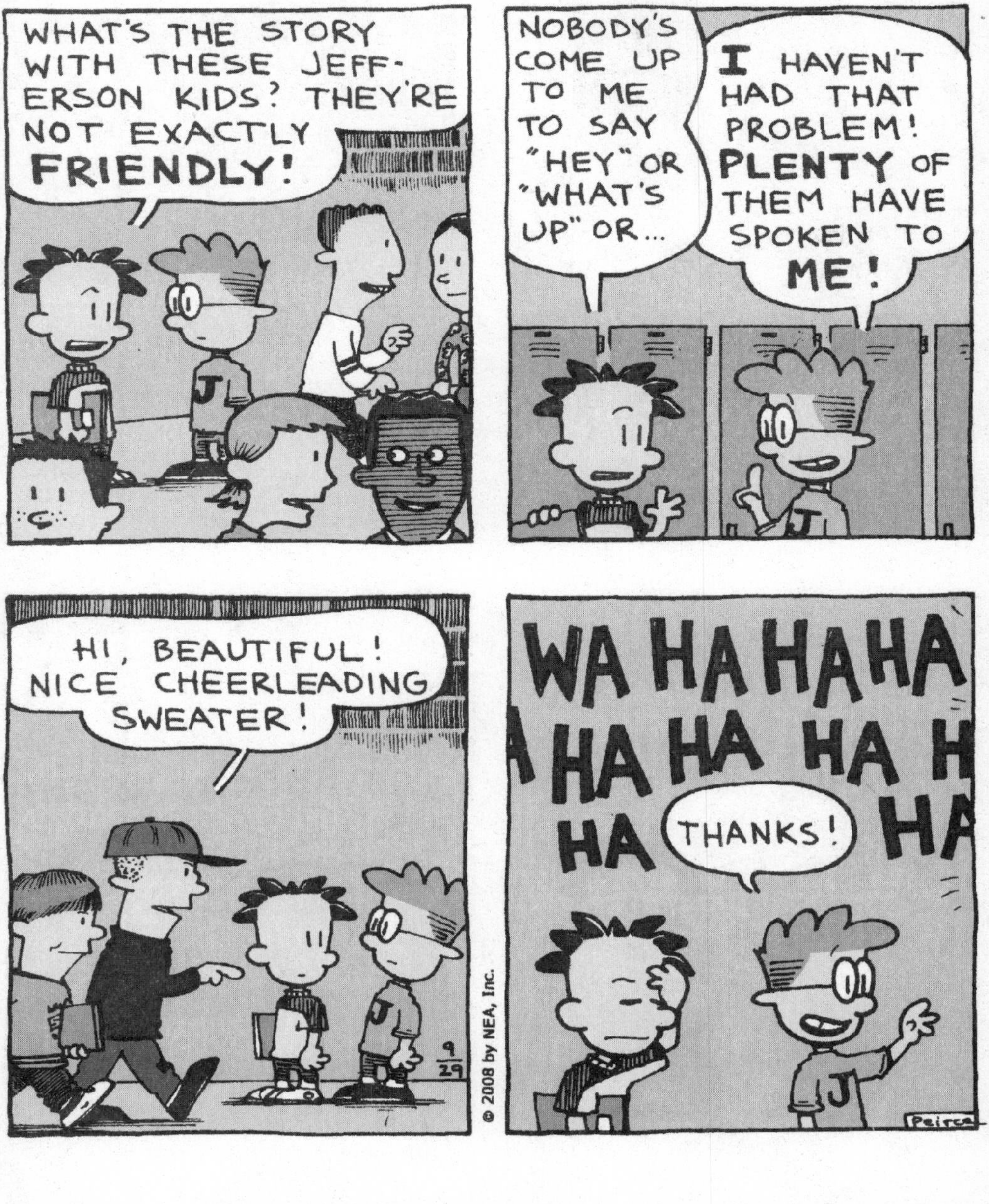
WHAT'S THE STORY WITH THESE JEFF-ERSON KIDS? THEY'RE NOT EXACTLY **FRIENDLY!**
NOBODY'S COME UP TO ME TO SAY "HEY" OR "WHAT'S UP" OR...
I HAVEN'T HAD THAT PROBLEM! **PLENTY** OF THEM HAVE SPOKEN TO **ME!**
HI, BEAUTIFUL! NICE CHEERLEADING SWEATER!
9/29
© 2008 by NEA, Inc.
WA HA HA HA HA
HA HA HA HA H
HA HA
THANKS!
Peirce

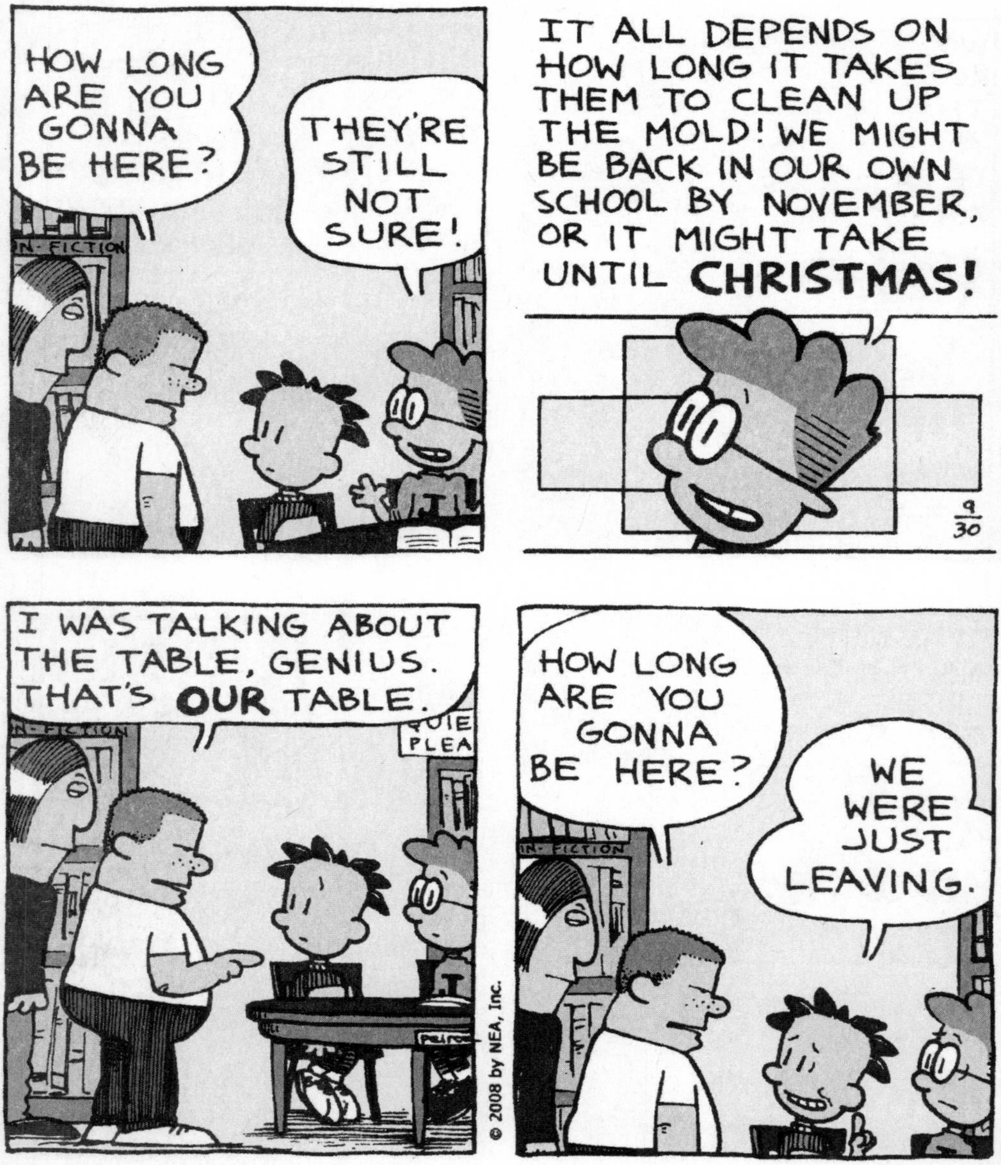
HOW LONG ARE YOU GONNA BE HERE?
THEY'RE STILL NOT SURE!
N-FICTION
IT ALL DEPENDS ON HOW LONG IT TAKES THEM TO CLEAN UP THE MOLD! WE MIGHT BE BACK IN OUR OWN SCHOOL BY NOVEMBER, OR IT MIGHT TAKE UNTIL **CHRISTMAS!**
9/30
I WAS TALKING ABOUT THE TABLE, GENIUS. THAT'S **OUR** TABLE.
QUIE PLEA
© 2008 by NEA, Inc.
HOW LONG ARE YOU GONNA BE HERE?
WE WERE JUST LEAVING.
N-FICTION

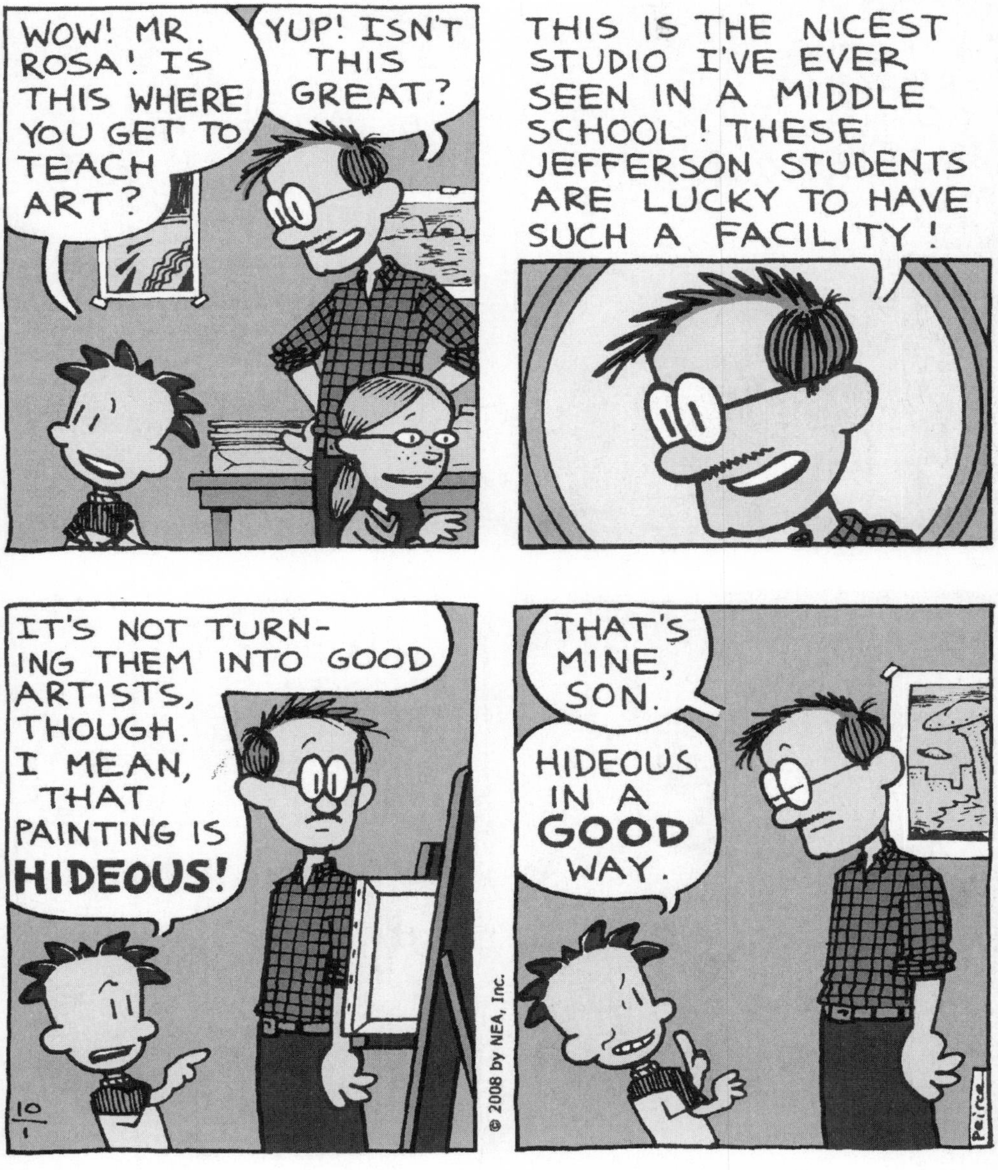
WOW! MR. ROSA! IS THIS WHERE YOU GET TO TEACH ART?
YUP! ISN'T THIS GREAT?
THIS IS THE NICEST STUDIO I'VE EVER SEEN IN A MIDDLE SCHOOL! THESE JEFFERSON STUDENTS ARE LUCKY TO HAVE SUCH A FACILITY!
IT'S NOT TURNING THEM INTO GOOD ARTISTS, THOUGH. I MEAN, THAT PAINTING IS HIDEOUS!
THAT'S MINE, SON.
HIDEOUS IN A GOOD WAY.
10/1
© 2008 by NEA, Inc.
Peirce

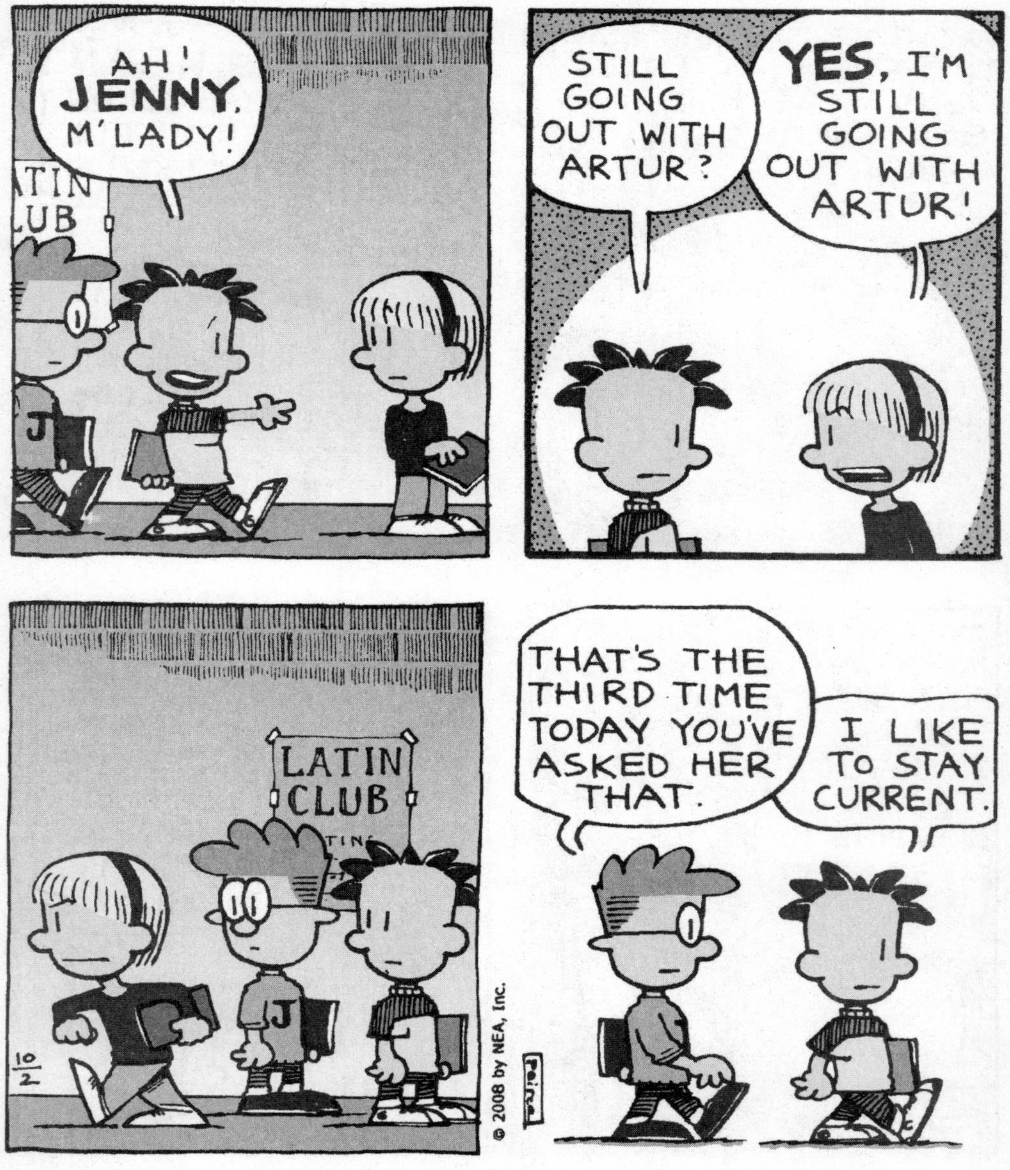
AH! JENNY, M'LADY!
LATIN CLUB
STILL GOING OUT WITH ARTUR?
YES, I'M STILL GOING OUT WITH ARTUR!
LATIN CLUB
© 2008 by NEA, Inc.
THAT'S THE THIRD TIME TODAY YOU'VE ASKED HER THAT.
I LIKE TO STAY CURRENT.

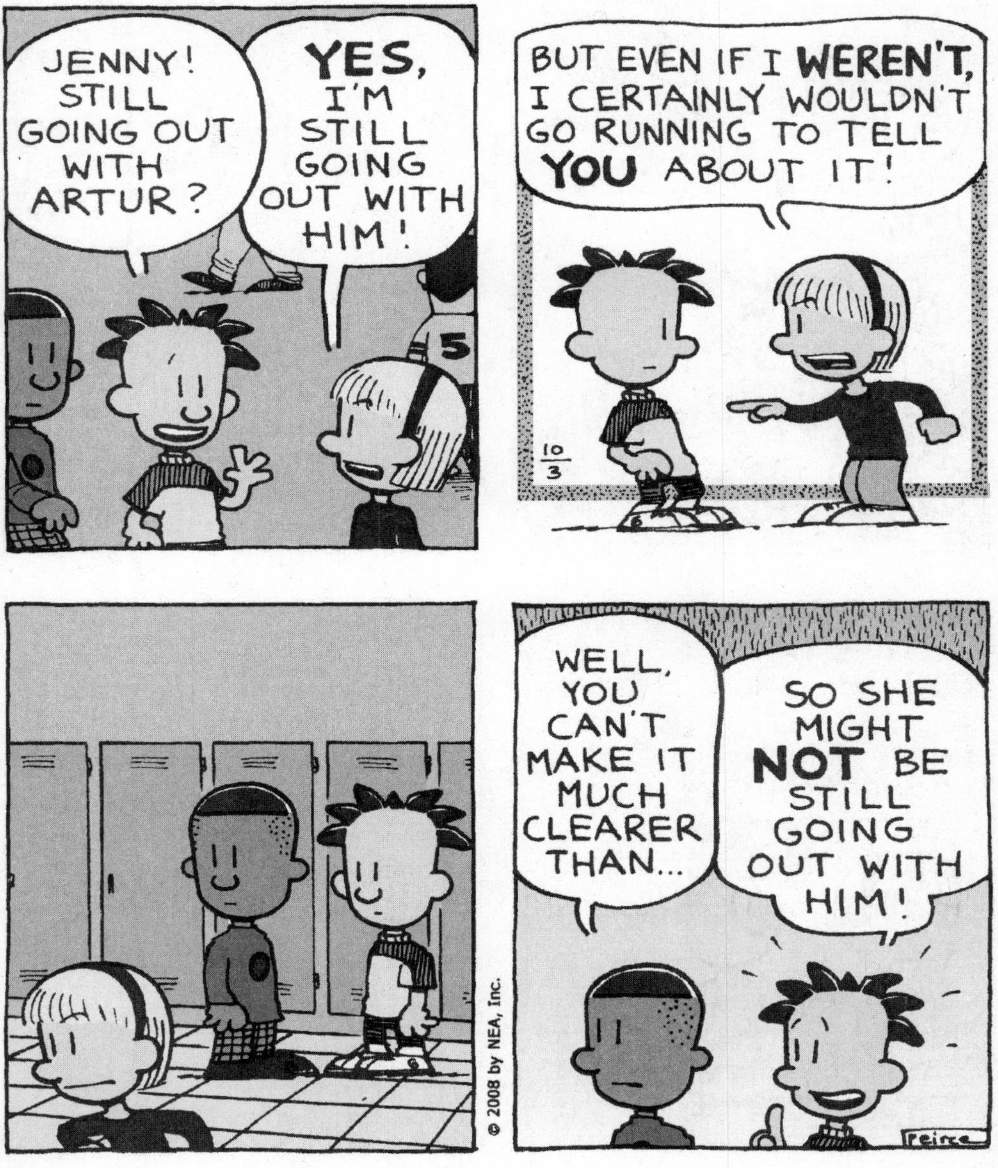
JENNY! STILL GOING OUT WITH ARTUR?
YES, I'M STILL GOING OUT WITH HIM!
BUT EVEN IF I **WEREN'T,** I CERTAINLY WOULDN'T GO RUNNING TO TELL **YOU** ABOUT IT!
10/3
WELL, YOU CAN'T MAKE IT MUCH CLEARER THAN...
SO SHE MIGHT **NOT** BE STILL GOING OUT WITH HIM!
Peirce

HEY, YOU'RE FROM P.S. 38, RIGHT? DO YOU KNOW THAT GIRL?

YEAH, THAT'S JENNY.

IS SHE... YOU KNOW... "TAKEN"?

SHE'S GOING OUT WITH ARTUR... FOR NOW.

BUT IT'S ONLY A MATTER OF TIME BEFORE SHE REALIZES SHE'S MADLY IN LOVE WITH **ME**. SO THERE'S ABSOLUTELY NO **WAY** SHE'LL END UP WITH **YOU**.

SOME PEOPLE JUST HAVE NO CONCEPT OF REALITY.

© 2008 by NEA, Inc.

116

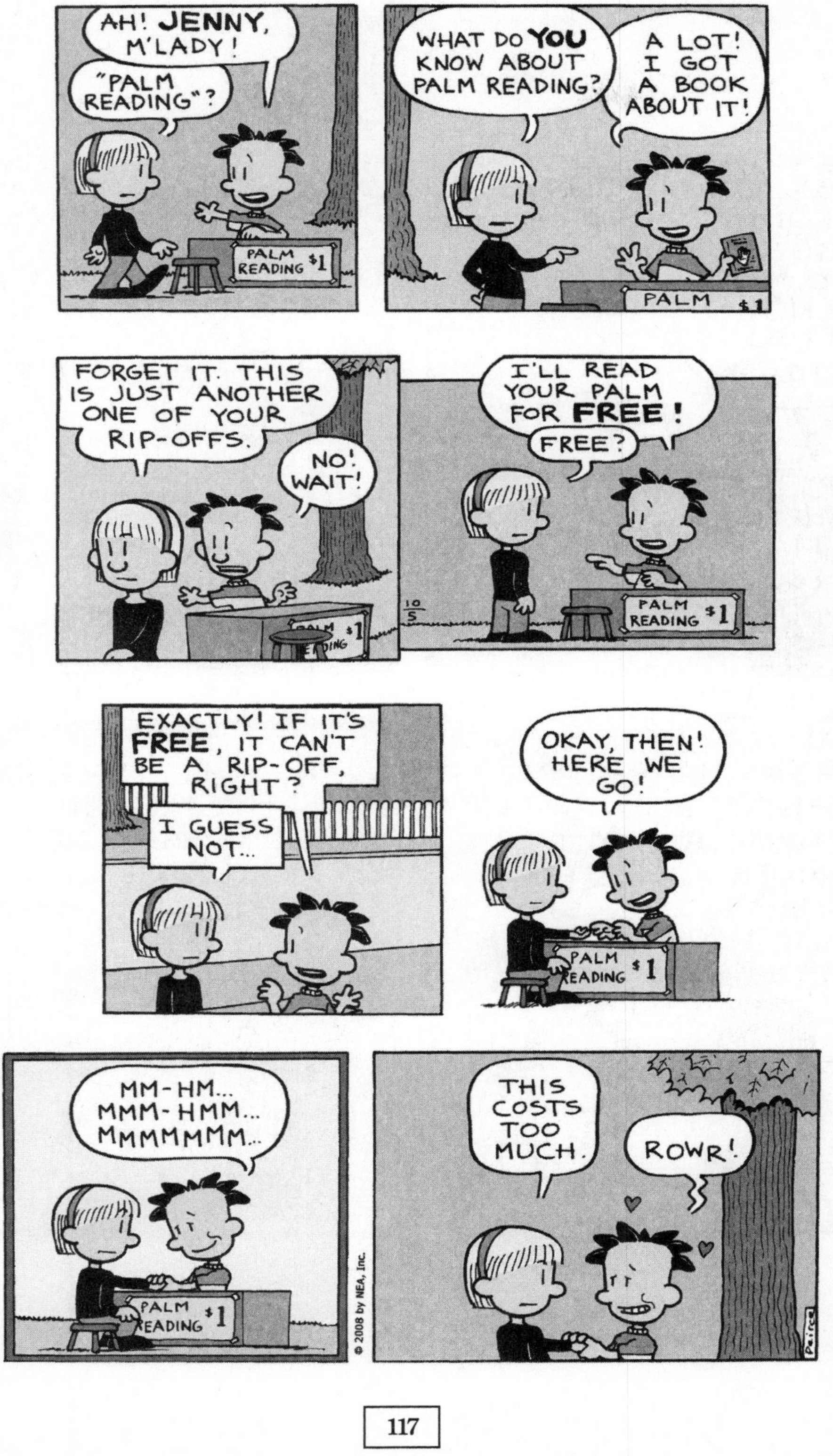
AH! JENNY, M'LADY!
"PALM READING"?
PALM READING $1
WHAT DO YOU KNOW ABOUT PALM READING?
A LOT! I GOT A BOOK ABOUT IT!
PALM $1
FORGET IT. THIS IS JUST ANOTHER ONE OF YOUR RIP-OFFS.
NO! WAIT!
I'LL READ YOUR PALM FOR FREE!
FREE?
10/5
PALM READING $1
EXACTLY! IF IT'S FREE, IT CAN'T BE A RIP-OFF, RIGHT?
I GUESS NOT...
OKAY, THEN! HERE WE GO!
PALM READING $1
MM-HM... MMM-HMM... MMMMMMM...
PALM READING $1
© 2008 by NEA, Inc.
THIS COSTS TOO MUCH.
ROWR!
Peirce

HERE GOES NOTHING

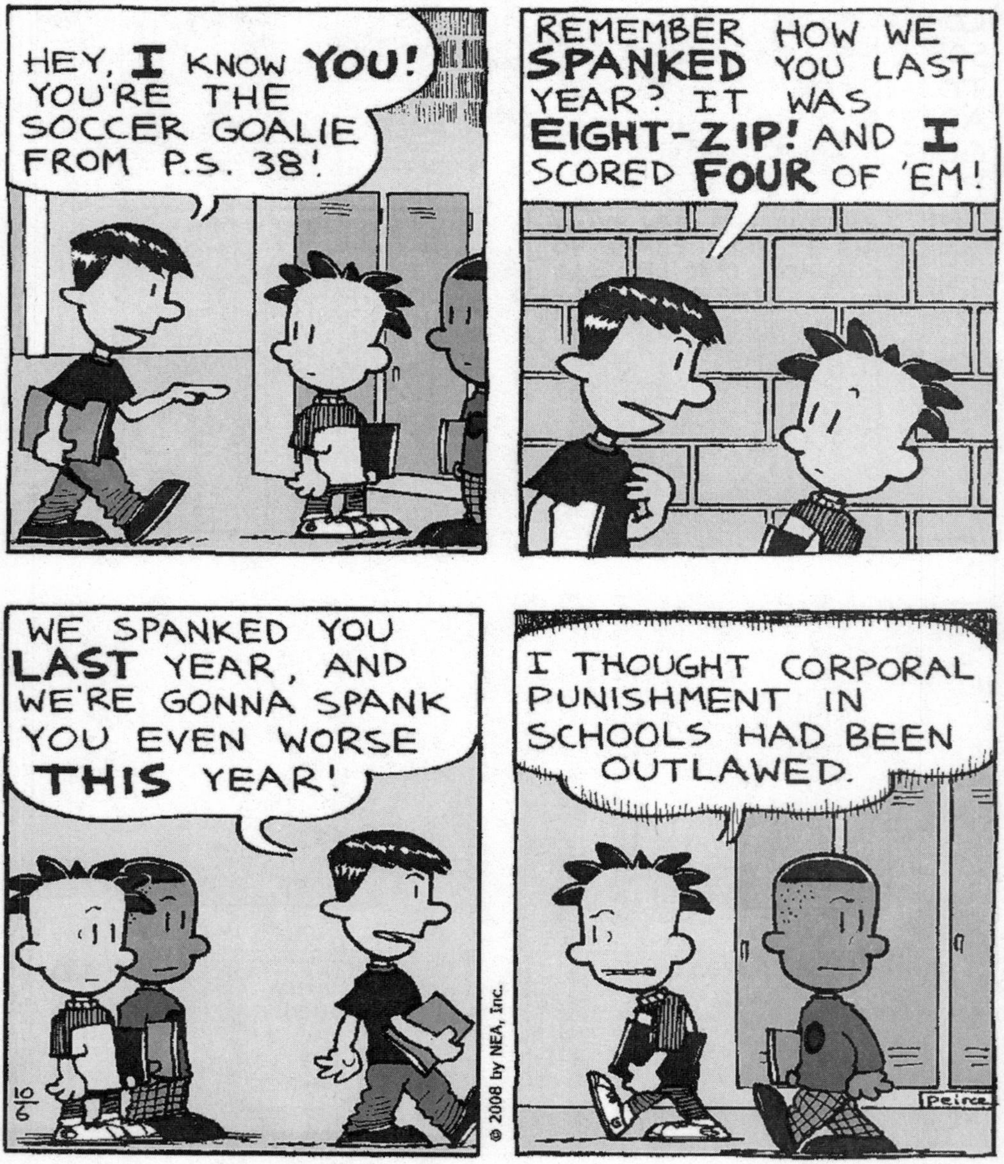
HEY, I KNOW YOU! YOU'RE THE SOCCER GOALIE FROM P.S. 38!
REMEMBER HOW WE SPANKED YOU LAST YEAR? IT WAS EIGHT-ZIP! AND I SCORED FOUR OF 'EM!
WE SPANKED YOU LAST YEAR, AND WE'RE GONNA SPANK YOU EVEN WORSE THIS YEAR!
10/6
© 2008 by NEA, Inc.
I THOUGHT CORPORAL PUNISHMENT IN SCHOOLS HAD BEEN OUTLAWED.
peirce

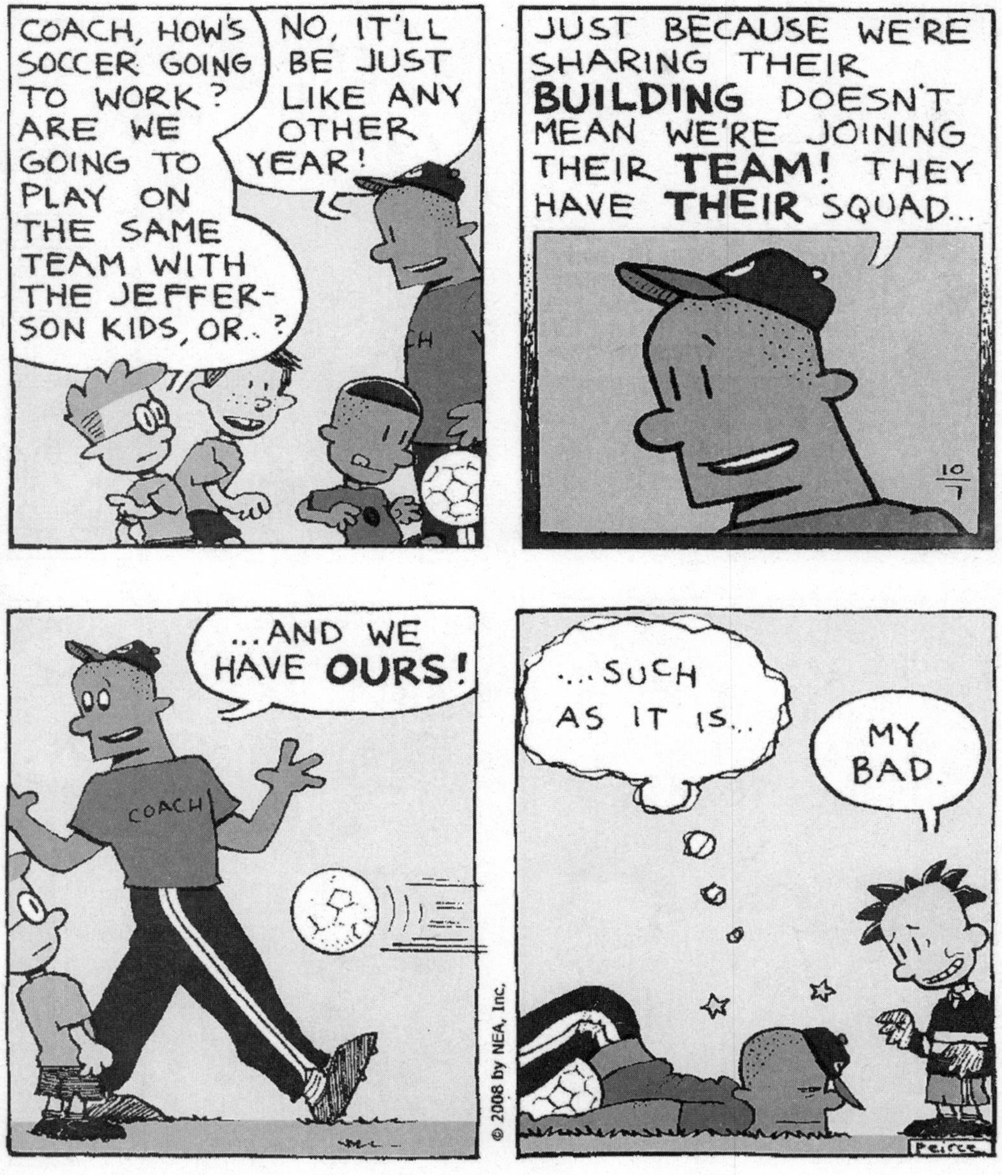
COACH, HOW'S SOCCER GOING TO WORK? ARE WE GOING TO PLAY ON THE SAME TEAM WITH THE JEFFERSON KIDS, OR..?
NO, IT'LL BE JUST LIKE ANY OTHER YEAR!
JUST BECAUSE WE'RE SHARING THEIR BUILDING DOESN'T MEAN WE'RE JOINING THEIR TEAM! THEY HAVE THEIR SQUAD...
10/7
...AND WE HAVE OURS!
COACH
...SUCH AS IT IS...
MY BAD.
PEIRCE

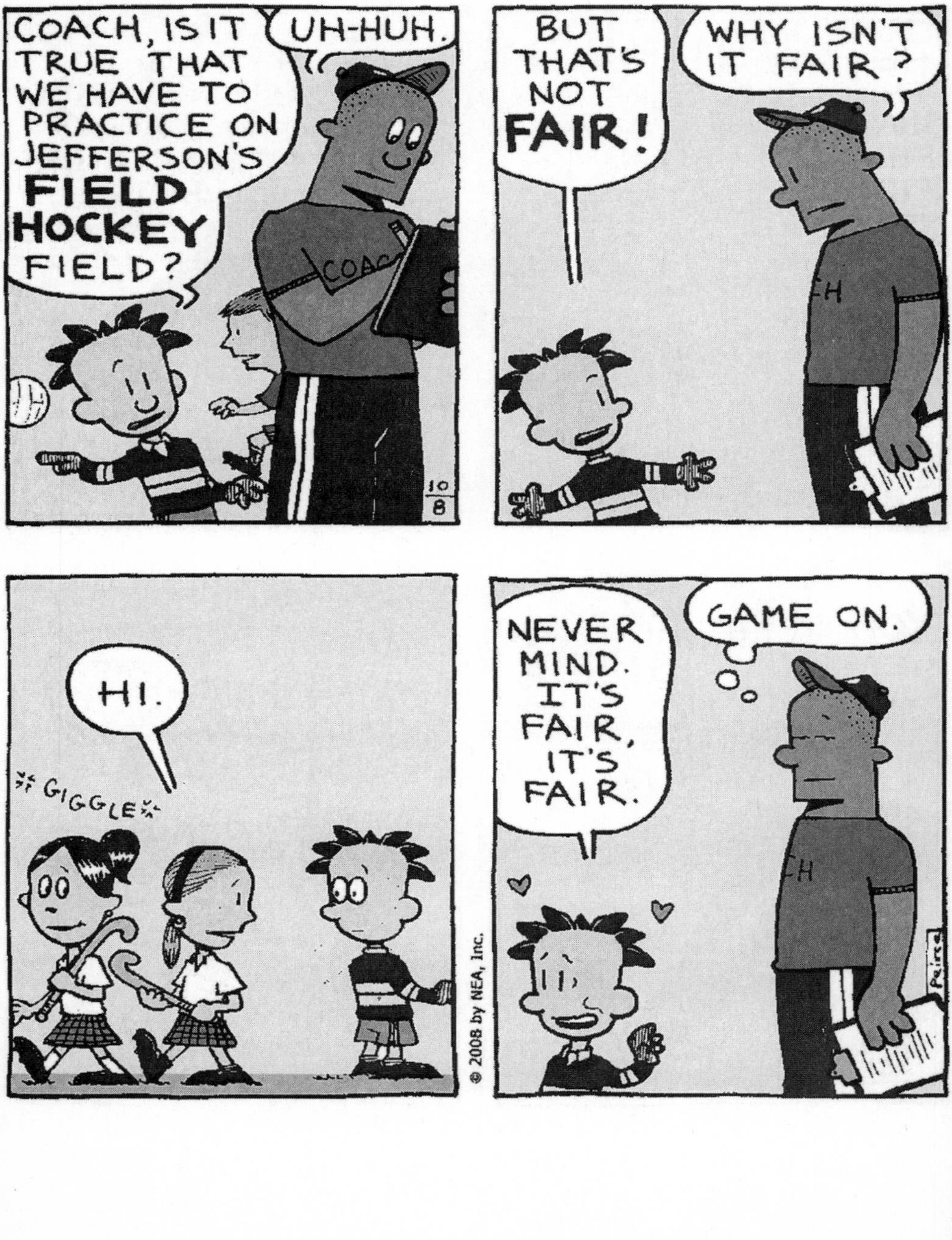
COACH, IS IT TRUE THAT WE HAVE TO PRACTICE ON JEFFERSON'S FIELD HOCKEY FIELD?
UH-HUH.
COACH
BUT THAT'S NOT FAIR!
WHY ISN'T IT FAIR?
HI.
GIGGLE
NEVER MIND. IT'S FAIR, IT'S FAIR.
GAME ON.
© 2008 by NEA, Inc.
Peirce

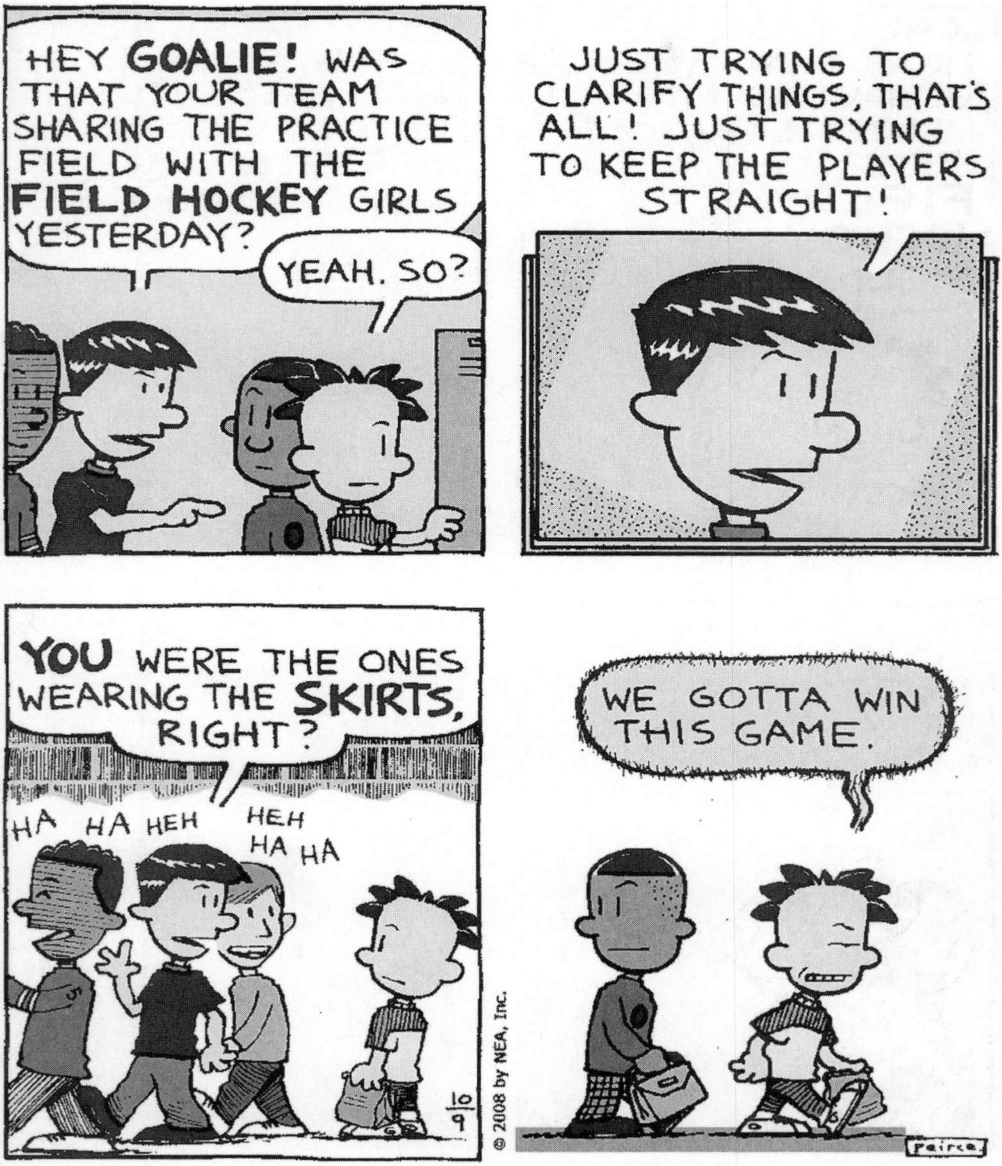
HEY GOALIE! WAS THAT YOUR TEAM SHARING THE PRACTICE FIELD WITH THE FIELD HOCKEY GIRLS YESTERDAY?
YEAH. SO?
JUST TRYING TO CLARIFY THINGS, THAT'S ALL! JUST TRYING TO KEEP THE PLAYERS STRAIGHT!
YOU WERE THE ONES WEARING THE SKIRTS, RIGHT?
HA HA HEH
HEH HA HA
10/9
© 2008 by NEA, Inc.
WE GOTTA WIN THIS GAME.
peirce

AH! GOALIE! I HAVE A PICTURE TO SHOW YOU FROM OUR YEARBOOK!
7TH G
SEE? THAT'S ME, SCORING A GOAL! AND THAT'S YOU, FLOPPING AROUND ON YOUR STOMACH!
10/10
THERE'LL BE A LOT MORE OF THAT WHEN WE PLAY YOU LADIES NEXT WEEK!
HEH HEH!
HA!
HA
HA HA!
WE GOTTA WIN THIS GAME.
Peirce

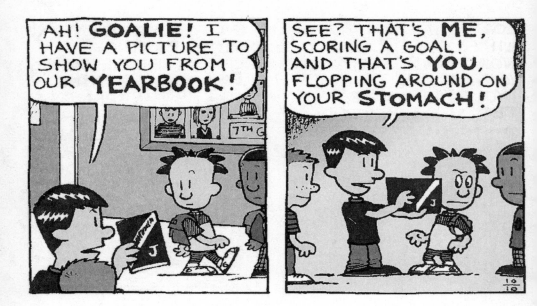

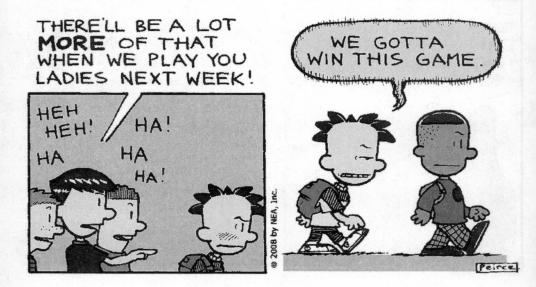

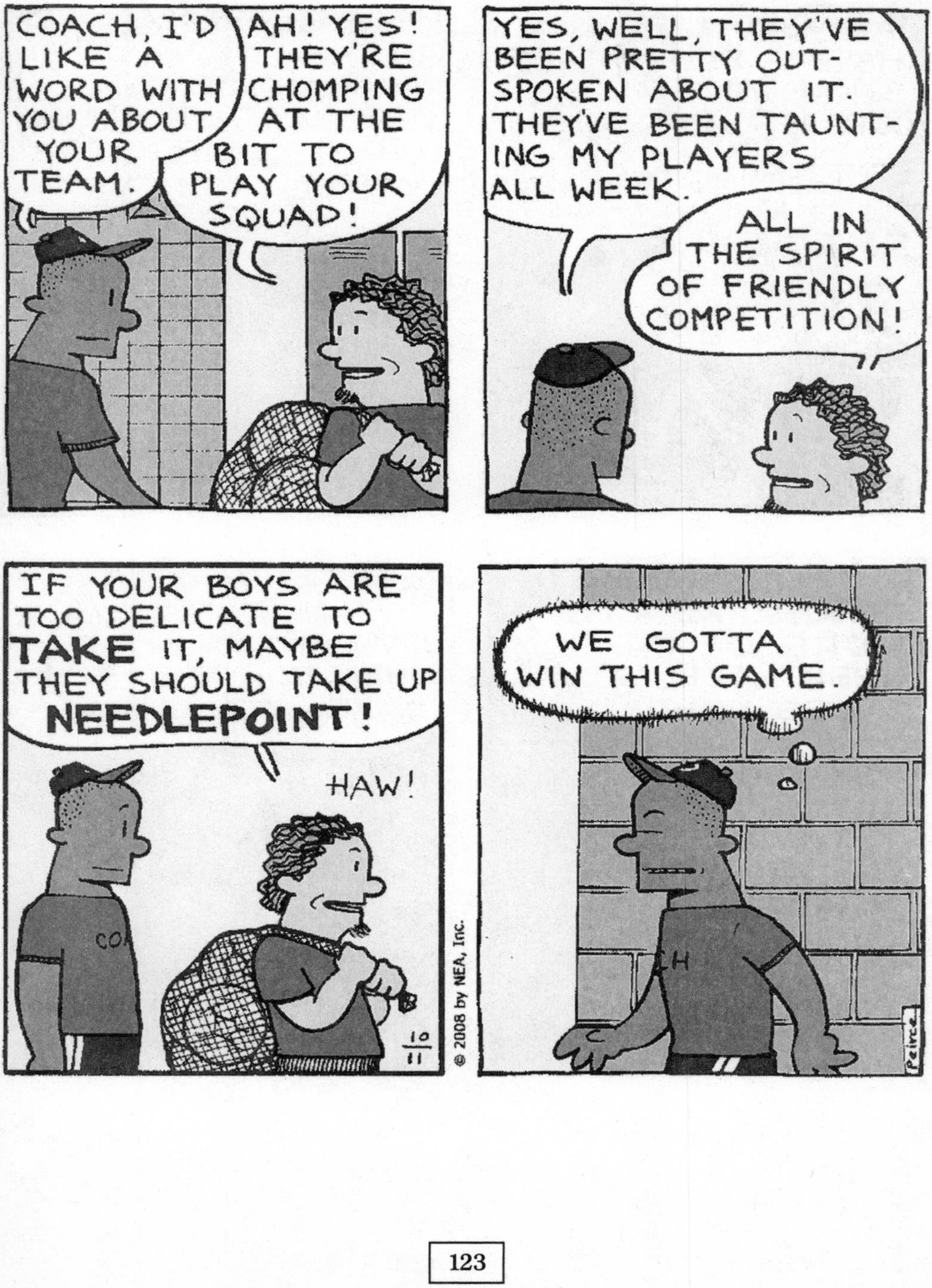
COACH, I'D LIKE A WORD WITH YOU ABOUT YOUR TEAM.
AH! YES! THEY'RE CHOMPING AT THE BIT TO PLAY YOUR SQUAD!
YES, WELL, THEY'VE BEEN PRETTY OUT-SPOKEN ABOUT IT. THEY'VE BEEN TAUNT-ING MY PLAYERS ALL WEEK.
ALL IN THE SPIRIT OF FRIENDLY COMPETITION!
IF YOUR BOYS ARE TOO DELICATE TO **TAKE** IT, MAYBE THEY SHOULD TAKE UP **NEEDLEPOINT**!
HAW!
10/11
© 2008 by NEA, Inc.
WE GOTTA WIN THIS GAME.
Peirce

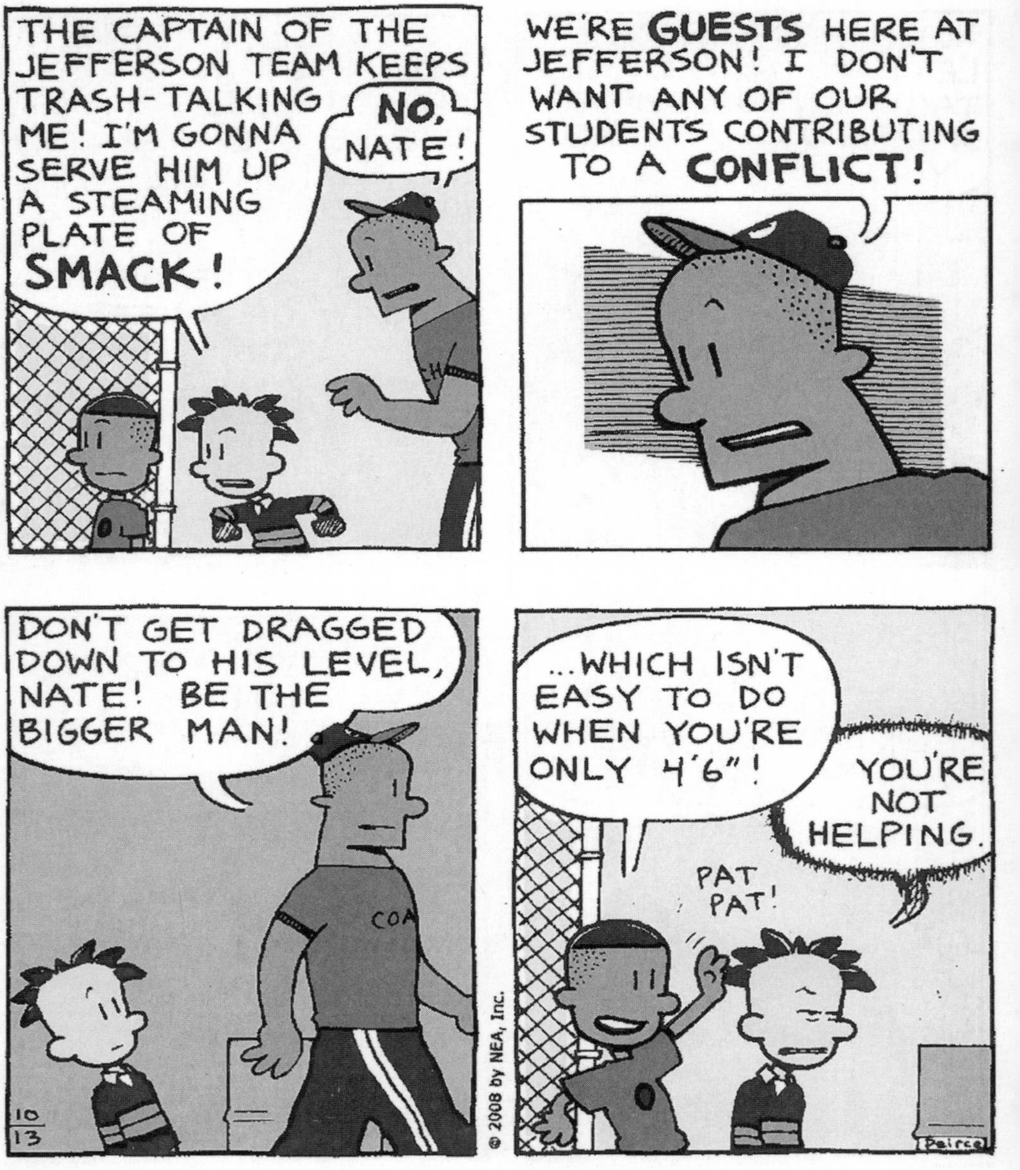
THE CAPTAIN OF THE JEFFERSON TEAM KEEPS TRASH-TALKING ME! I'M GONNA SERVE HIM UP A STEAMING PLATE OF SMACK!
NO, NATE!
WE'RE GUESTS HERE AT JEFFERSON! I DON'T WANT ANY OF OUR STUDENTS CONTRIBUTING TO A CONFLICT!
DON'T GET DRAGGED DOWN TO HIS LEVEL, NATE! BE THE BIGGER MAN!
...WHICH ISN'T EASY TO DO WHEN YOU'RE ONLY 4'6"!
PAT PAT!
YOU'RE NOT HELPING.
10/13
© 2008 by NEA, Inc.
Peirce

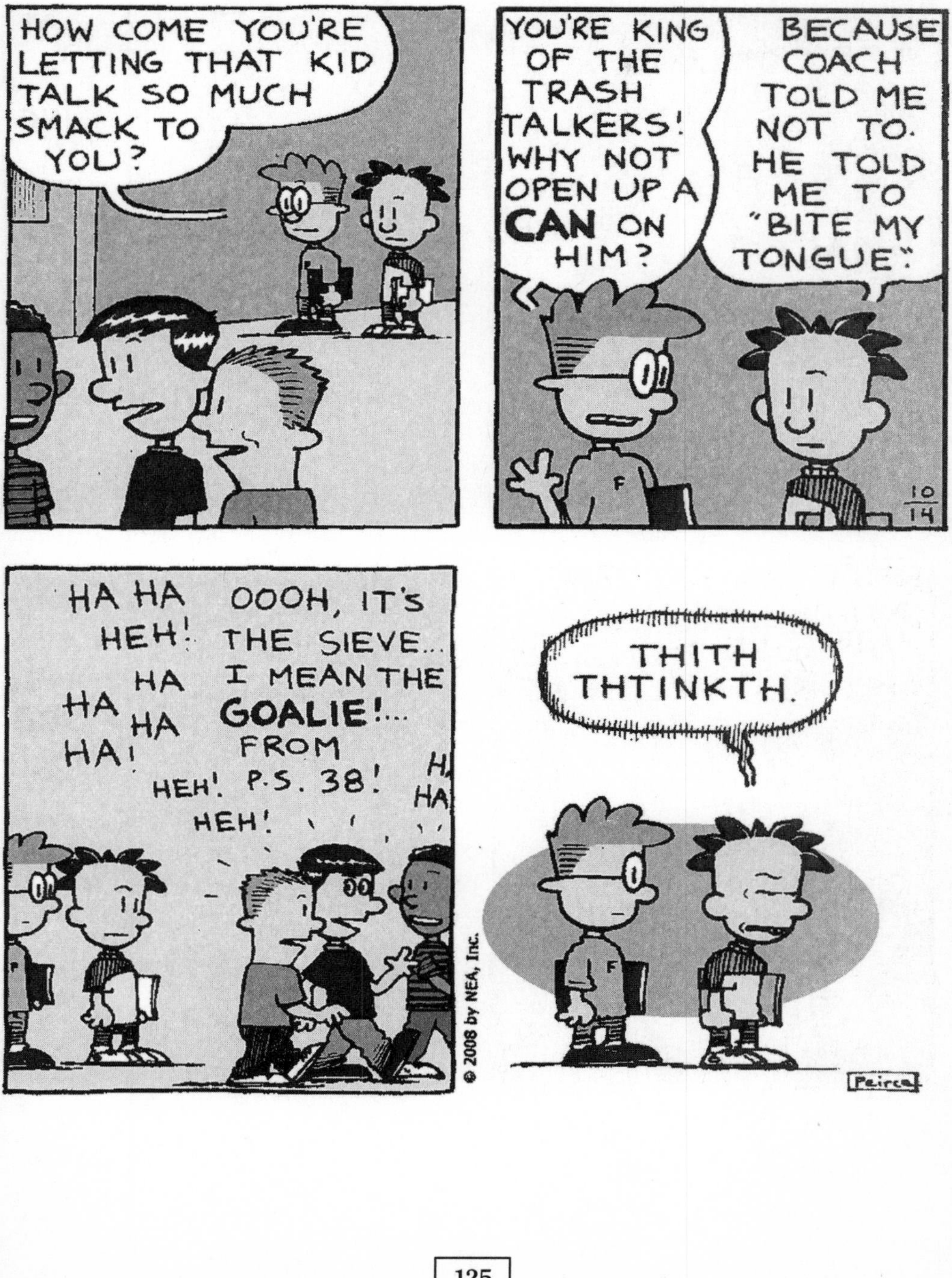
HOW COME YOU'RE LETTING THAT KID TALK SO MUCH SMACK TO YOU?
YOU'RE KING OF THE TRASH TALKERS! WHY NOT OPEN UP A **CAN** ON HIM?
BECAUSE COACH TOLD ME NOT TO. HE TOLD ME TO "BITE MY TONGUE."
10/14
HA HA HEH! HA HA HA HA!
OOOH, IT'S THE SIEVE... I MEAN THE **GOALIE**!... FROM P.S. 38!
HEH! HEH!
HA HA
© 2008 by NEA, Inc.
THITH THTINKTH.
Peirce

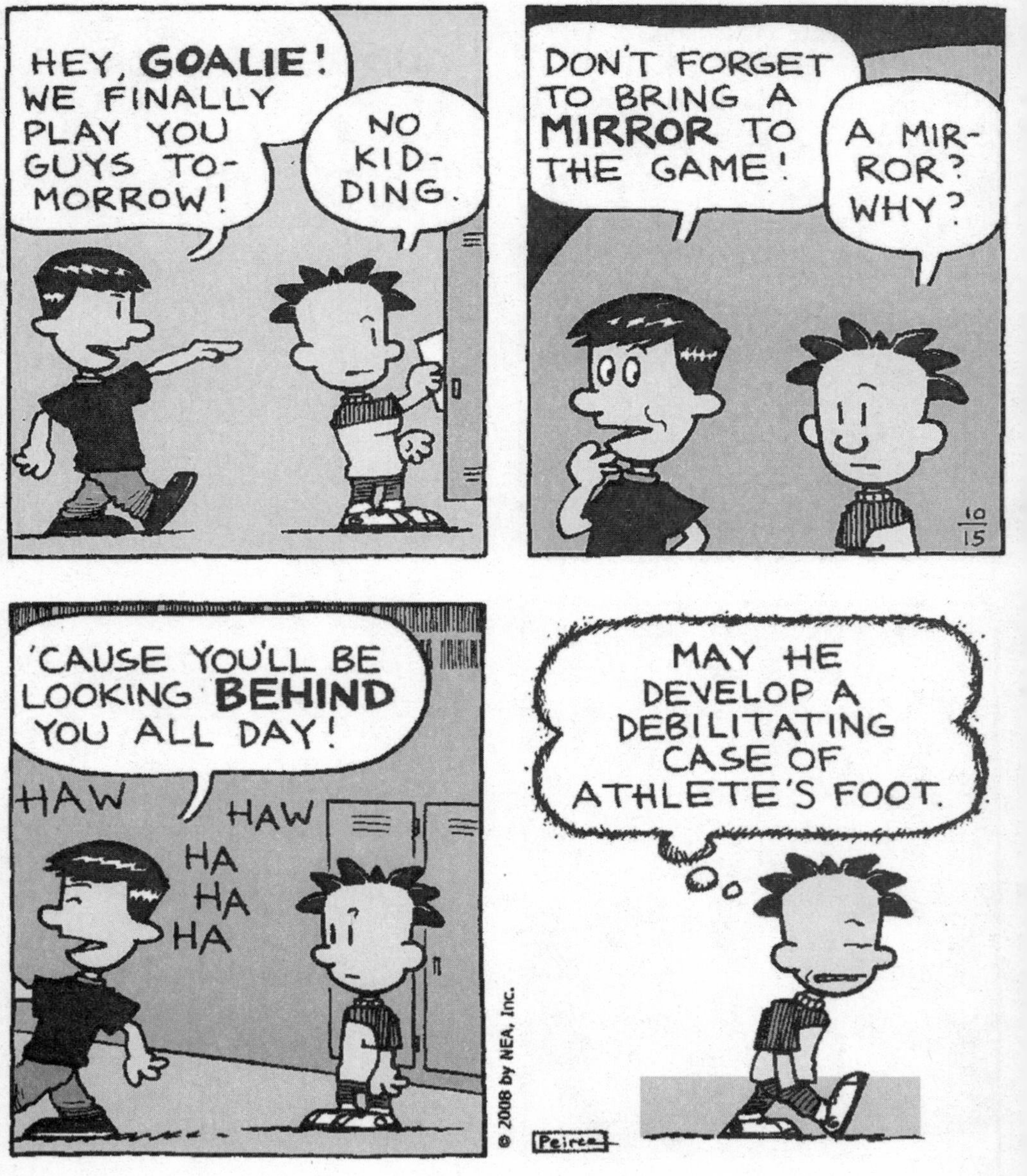
HEY, **GOALIE**! WE FINALLY PLAY YOU GUYS TO-MORROW!
NO KID-DING.
DON'T FORGET TO BRING A **MIRROR** TO THE GAME!
A MIR-ROR? WHY?
10
15
'CAUSE YOU'LL BE LOOKING **BEHIND** YOU ALL DAY!
HAW
HAW
HA HA HA
© 2008 by NEA, Inc.
MAY HE DEVELOP A DEBILITATING CASE OF ATHLETE'S FOOT.
Peirce

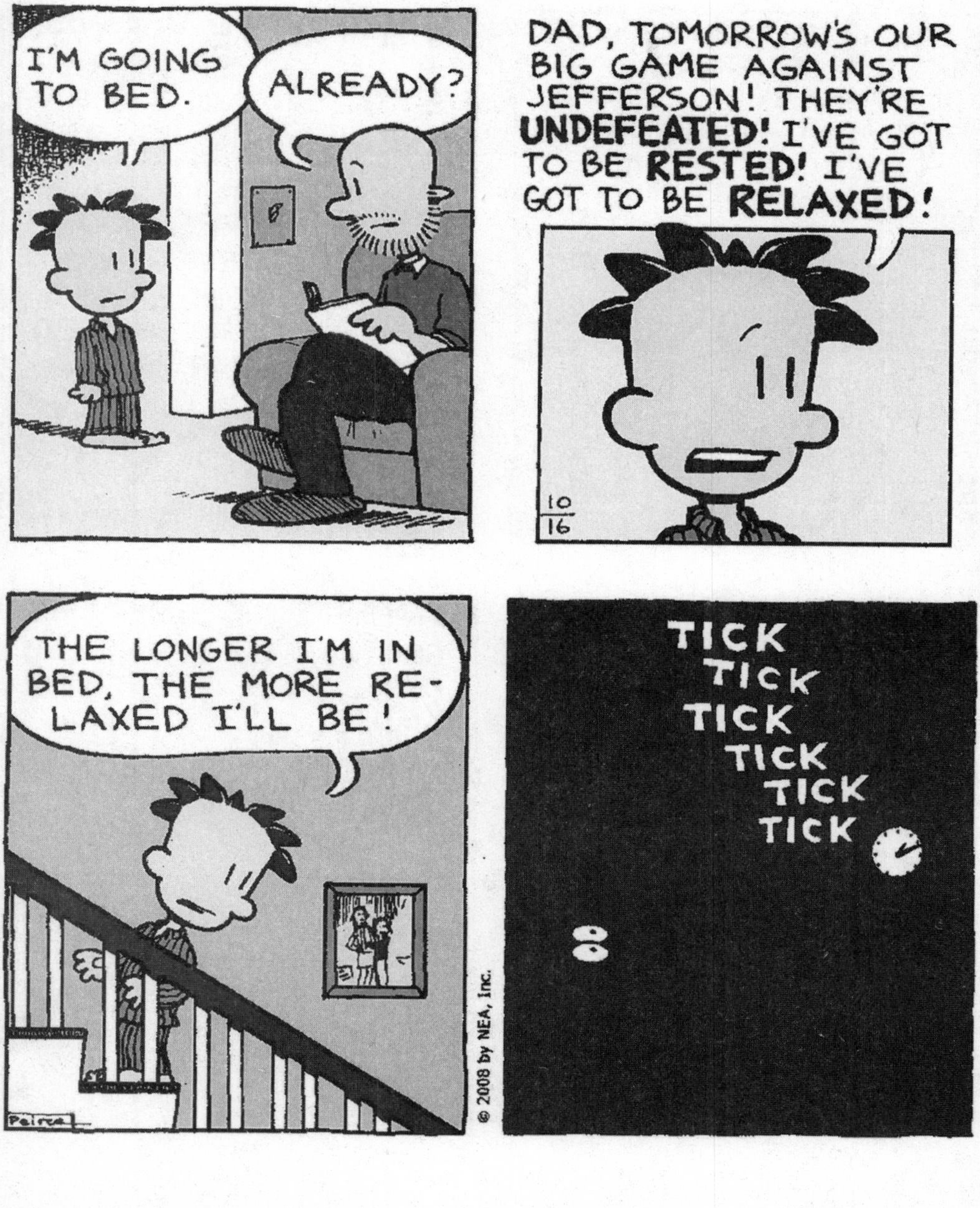
I'M GOING TO BED.
ALREADY?
DAD, TOMORROW'S OUR BIG GAME AGAINST JEFFERSON! THEY'RE **UNDEFEATED!** I'VE GOT TO BE **RESTED!** I'VE GOT TO BE **RELAXED!**
10/16
THE LONGER I'M IN BED, THE MORE RE-LAXED I'LL BE!
Peirce
TICK
TICK
TICK
TICK
TICK
TICK

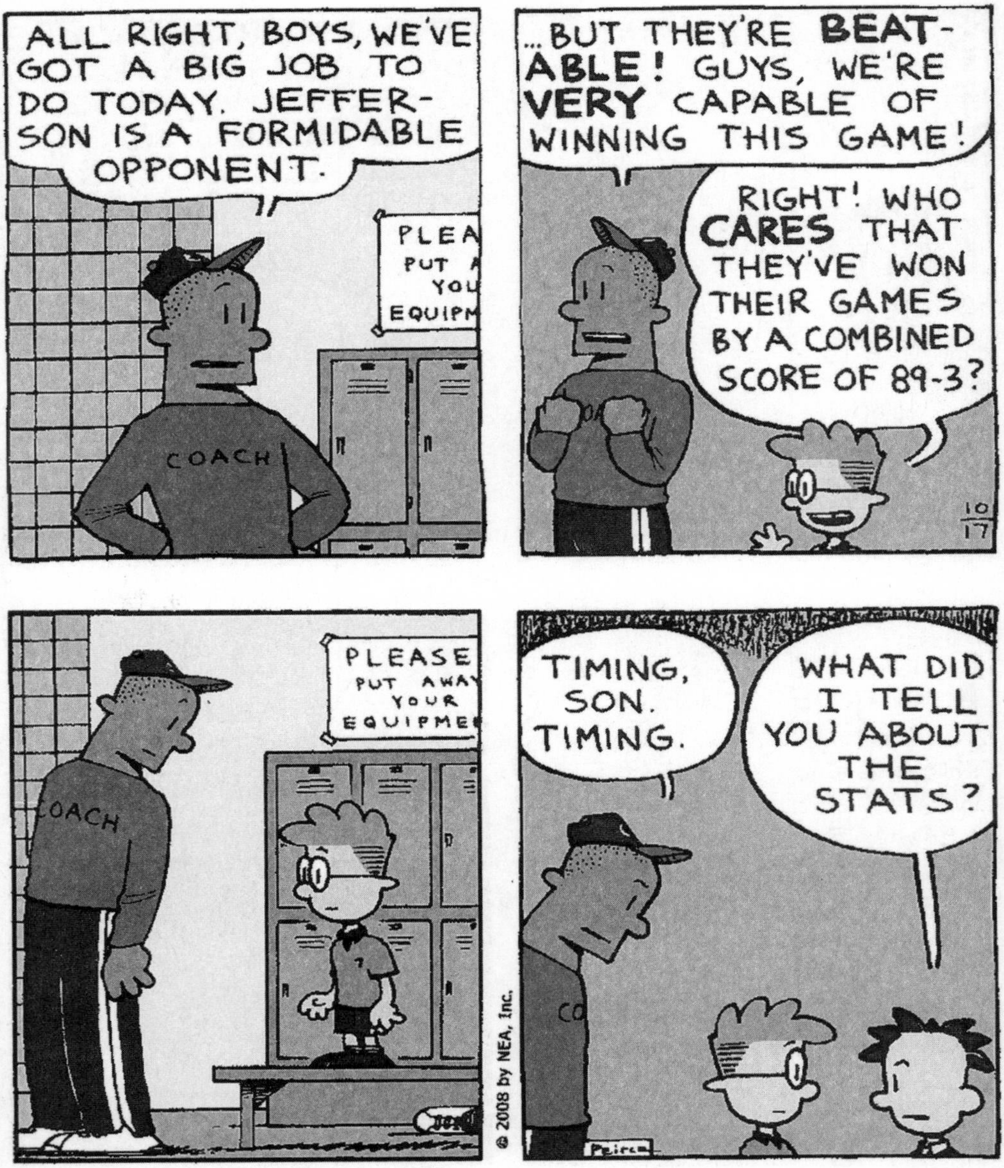
ALL RIGHT, BOYS, WE'VE GOT A BIG JOB TO DO TODAY. JEFFERSON IS A FORMIDABLE OPPONENT.
COACH
...BUT THEY'RE **BEATABLE!** GUYS, WE'RE **VERY** CAPABLE OF WINNING THIS GAME!
RIGHT! WHO **CARES** THAT THEY'VE WON THEIR GAMES BY A COMBINED SCORE OF 89-3?
10/17
PLEASE
COACH
© 2008 by NEA, Inc.
TIMING, SON. TIMING.
WHAT DID I TELL YOU ABOUT THE STATS?
Peirce

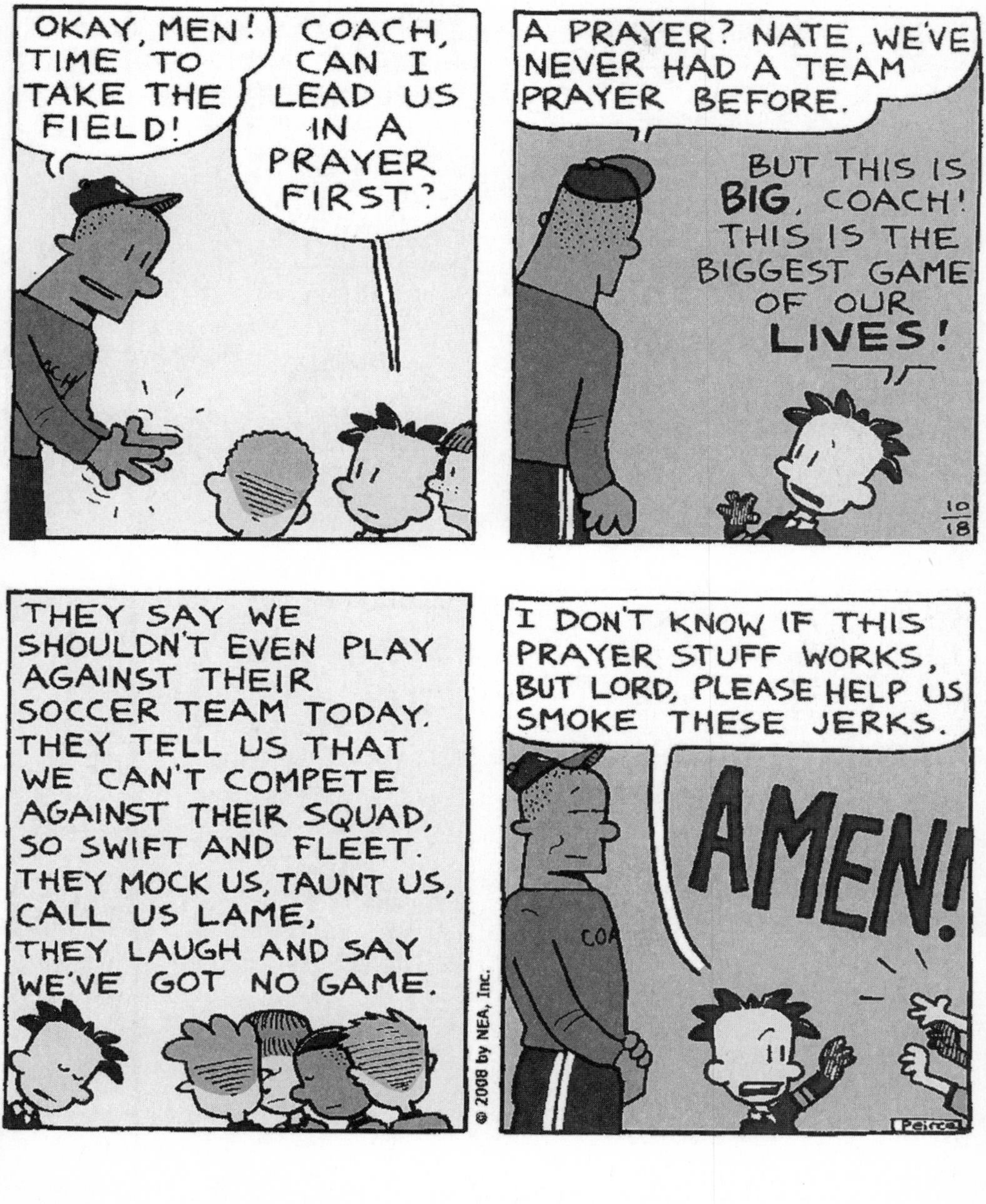
OKAY, MEN! TIME TO TAKE THE FIELD!
COACH, CAN I LEAD US IN A PRAYER FIRST?
A PRAYER? NATE, WE'VE NEVER HAD A TEAM PRAYER BEFORE.
BUT THIS IS BIG, COACH! THIS IS THE BIGGEST GAME OF OUR LIVES!
10/18
THEY SAY WE SHOULDN'T EVEN PLAY AGAINST THEIR SOCCER TEAM TODAY. THEY TELL US THAT WE CAN'T COMPETE AGAINST THEIR SQUAD, SO SWIFT AND FLEET. THEY MOCK US, TAUNT US, CALL US LAME, THEY LAUGH AND SAY WE'VE GOT NO GAME.
I DON'T KNOW IF THIS PRAYER STUFF WORKS, BUT LORD, PLEASE HELP US SMOKE THESE JERKS.
AMEN!
Peirce

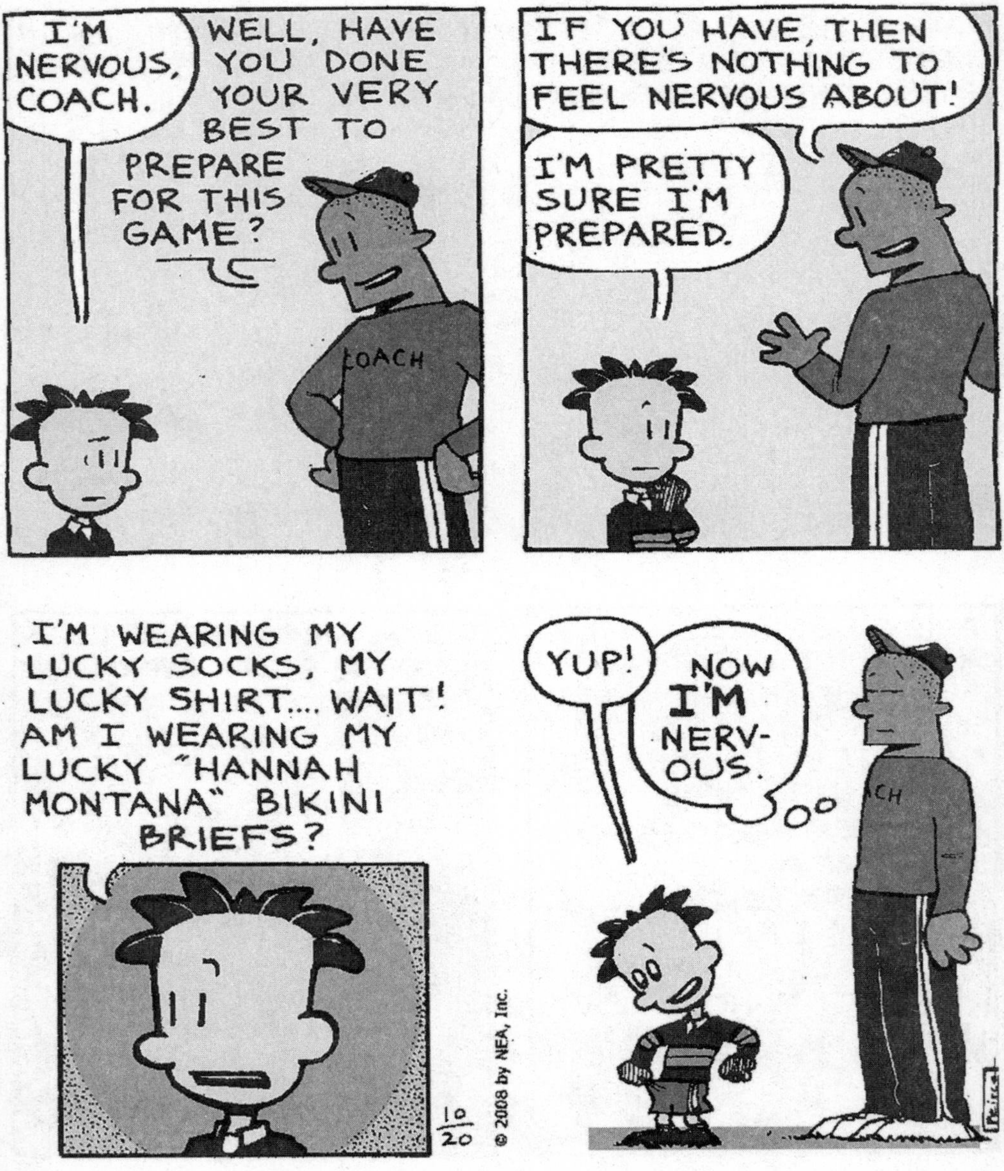
I'M NERVOUS, COACH.
WELL, HAVE YOU DONE YOUR VERY BEST TO PREPARE FOR THIS GAME?
COACH
IF YOU HAVE, THEN THERE'S NOTHING TO FEEL NERVOUS ABOUT!
I'M PRETTY SURE I'M PREPARED.
I'M WEARING MY LUCKY SOCKS, MY LUCKY SHIRT.... WAIT! AM I WEARING MY LUCKY "HANNAH MONTANA" BIKINI BRIEFS?
YUP!
NOW I'M NERVOUS.
10/20
© 2008 by NEA, Inc.
Peirce

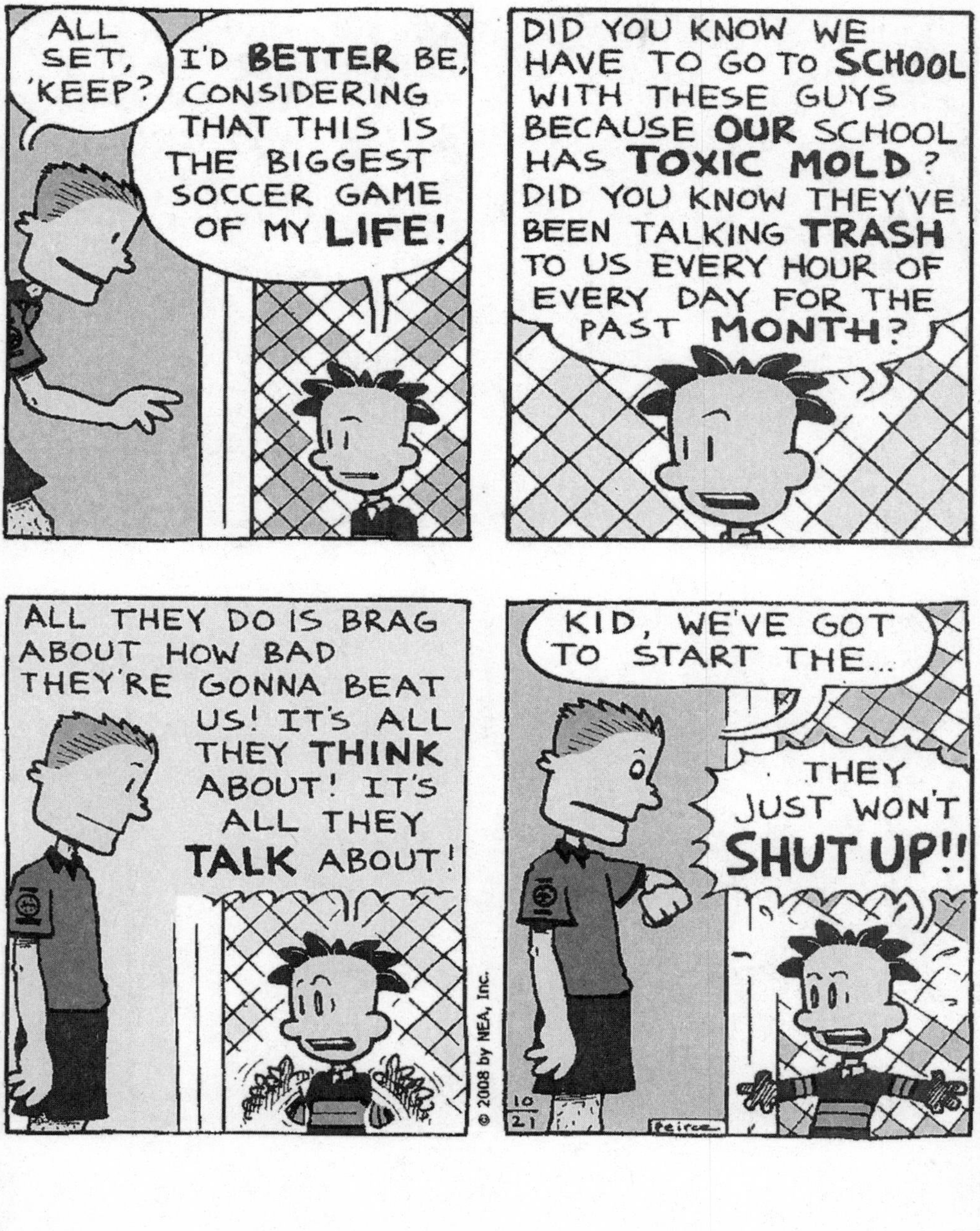
ALL SET, 'KEEP?
I'D BETTER BE, CONSIDERING THAT THIS IS THE BIGGEST SOCCER GAME OF MY LIFE!
DID YOU KNOW WE HAVE TO GO TO SCHOOL WITH THESE GUYS BECAUSE OUR SCHOOL HAS TOXIC MOLD? DID YOU KNOW THEY'VE BEEN TALKING TRASH TO US EVERY HOUR OF EVERY DAY FOR THE PAST MONTH?
ALL THEY DO IS BRAG ABOUT HOW BAD THEY'RE GONNA BEAT US! IT'S ALL THEY THINK ABOUT! IT'S ALL THEY TALK ABOUT!
KID, WE'VE GOT TO START THE...
THEY JUST WON'T SHUT UP!!
10 21
Peirce

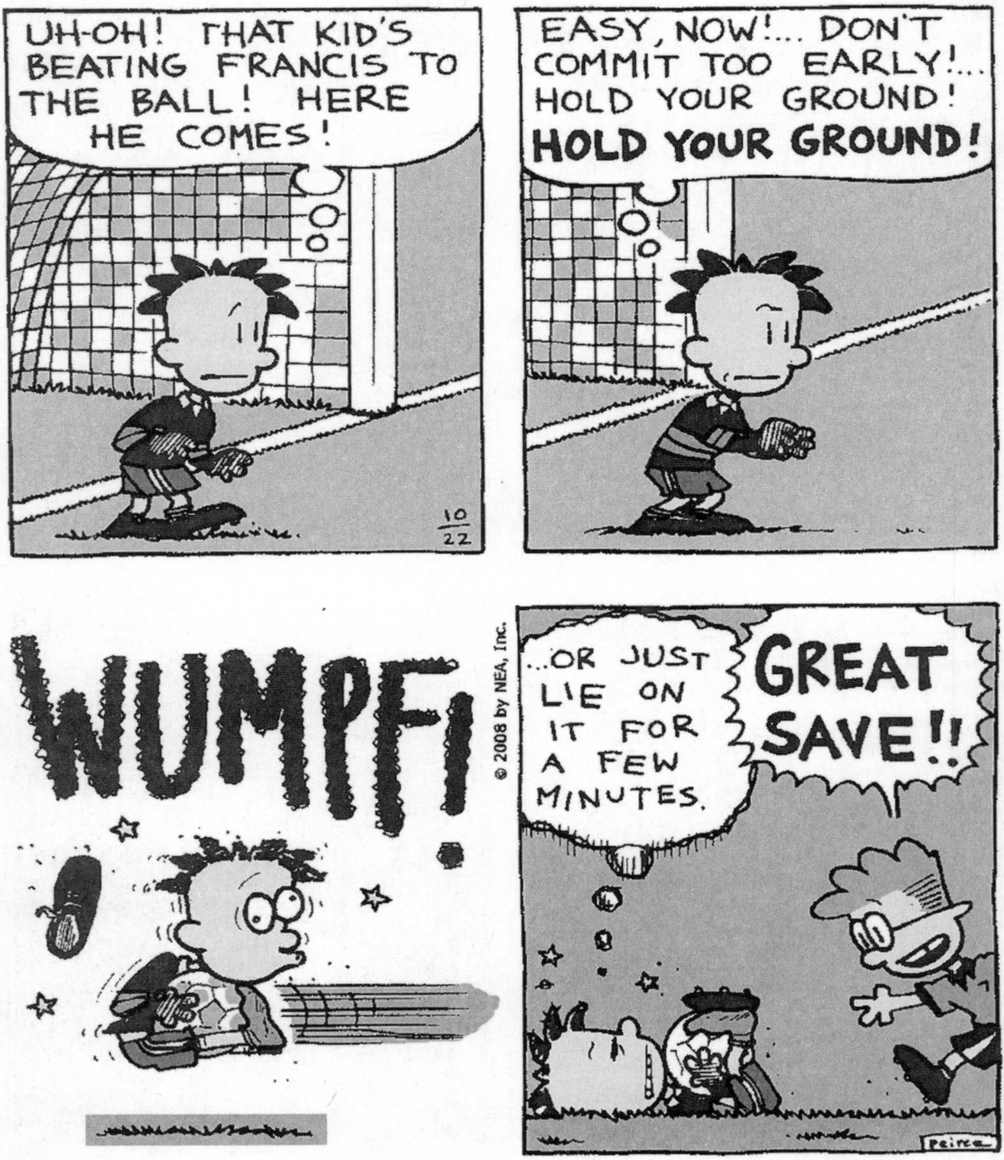
UH-OH! THAT KID'S BEATING FRANCIS TO THE BALL! HERE HE COMES!
10/22
EASY, NOW!... DON'T COMMIT TOO EARLY!... HOLD YOUR GROUND! HOLD YOUR GROUND!
WUMPF!
© 2008 by NEA, Inc.
...OR JUST LIE ON IT FOR A FEW MINUTES.
GREAT SAVE!!
peirce

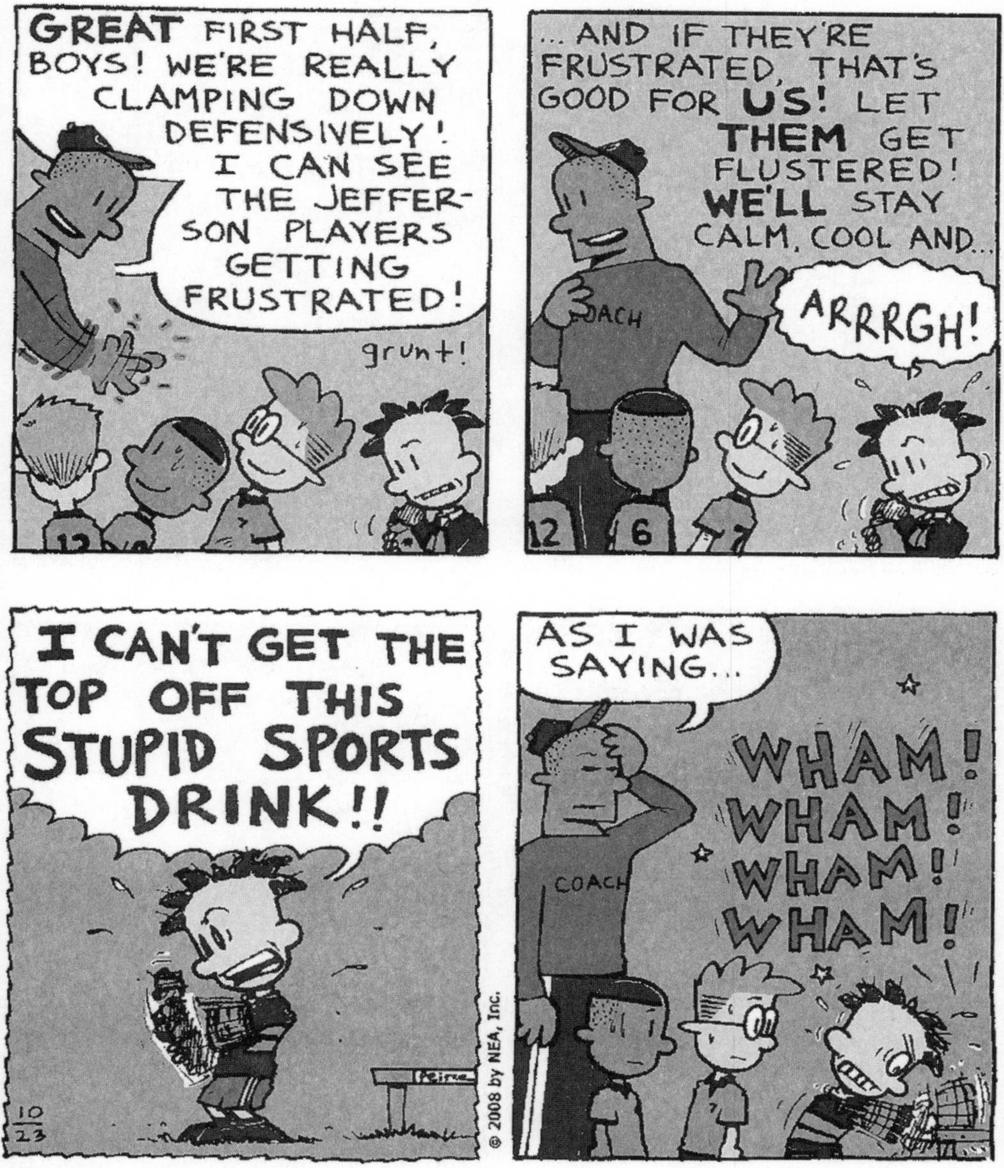
GREAT FIRST HALF, BOYS! WE'RE REALLY CLAMPING DOWN DEFENSIVELY! I CAN SEE THE JEFFERSON PLAYERS GETTING FRUSTRATED!
grunt!
... AND IF THEY'RE FRUSTRATED, THAT'S GOOD FOR US! LET THEM GET FLUSTERED! WE'LL STAY CALM, COOL AND...
ARRRGH!
I CAN'T GET THE TOP OFF THIS STUPID SPORTS DRINK!!
AS I WAS SAYING...
WHAM! WHAM! WHAM! WHAM!
© 2008 by NEA, Inc.

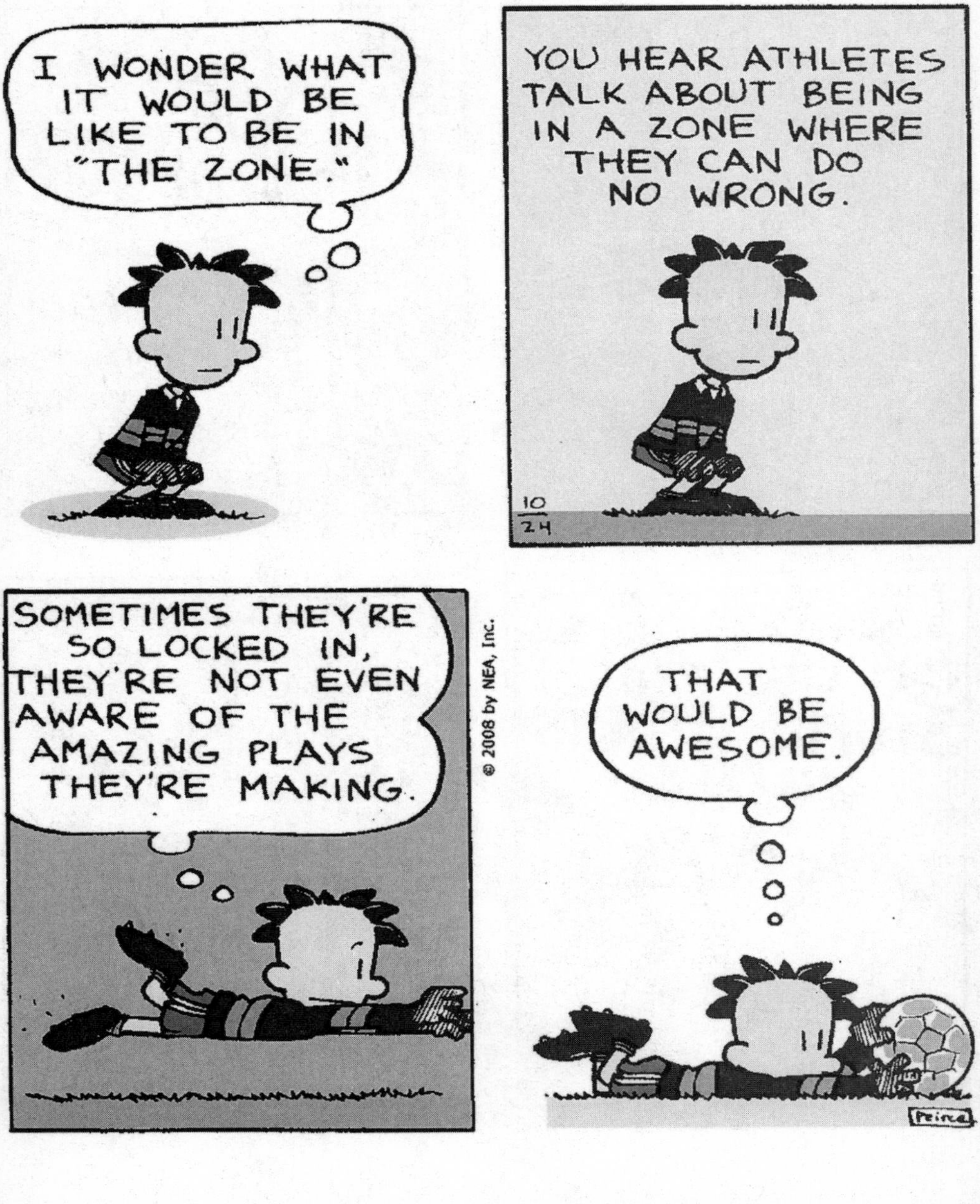
I WONDER WHAT IT WOULD BE LIKE TO BE IN "THE ZONE."
YOU HEAR ATHLETES TALK ABOUT BEING IN A ZONE WHERE THEY CAN DO NO WRONG.
10/24
SOMETIMES THEY'RE SO LOCKED IN, THEY'RE NOT EVEN AWARE OF THE AMAZING PLAYS THEY'RE MAKING.
© 2008 by NEA, Inc.
THAT WOULD BE AWESOME.
Peirce

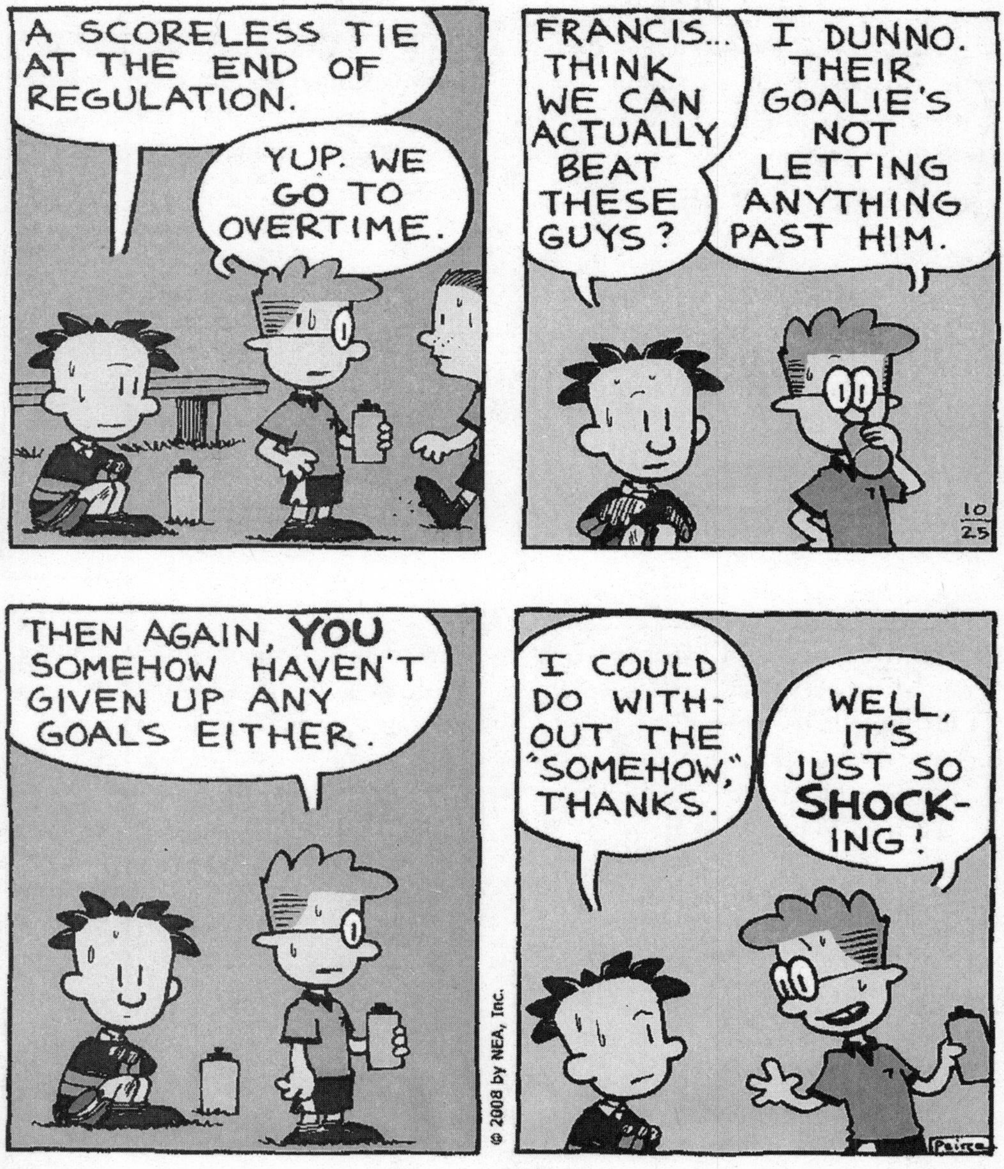
A SCORELESS TIE AT THE END OF REGULATION.
YUP. WE GO TO OVERTIME.
FRANCIS... THINK WE CAN ACTUALLY BEAT THESE GUYS?
I DUNNO. THEIR GOALIE'S NOT LETTING ANYTHING PAST HIM.
10 25
THEN AGAIN, **YOU** SOMEHOW HAVEN'T GIVEN UP ANY GOALS EITHER.
© 2008 by NEA, Inc.
I COULD DO WITH-OUT THE "SOMEHOW," THANKS.
WELL, IT'S JUST SO **SHOCK**-ING!
Peirce

RULE 7.2 If the score is tied at the conclusion of a 70-minute match, a ten-minute overtime period is played.

RULE 7.3 If at the conclusion of the overtime period no winner has been determined, the outcome of the match is decided by a series of penalty kicks.

FORMAT Five players from each side are selected by their respective coaches to take penalty kicks in alternating order.

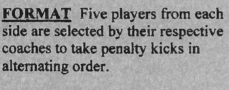

The team that successfully converts more penalty kicks than its opponent is declared the winner.

GULP!

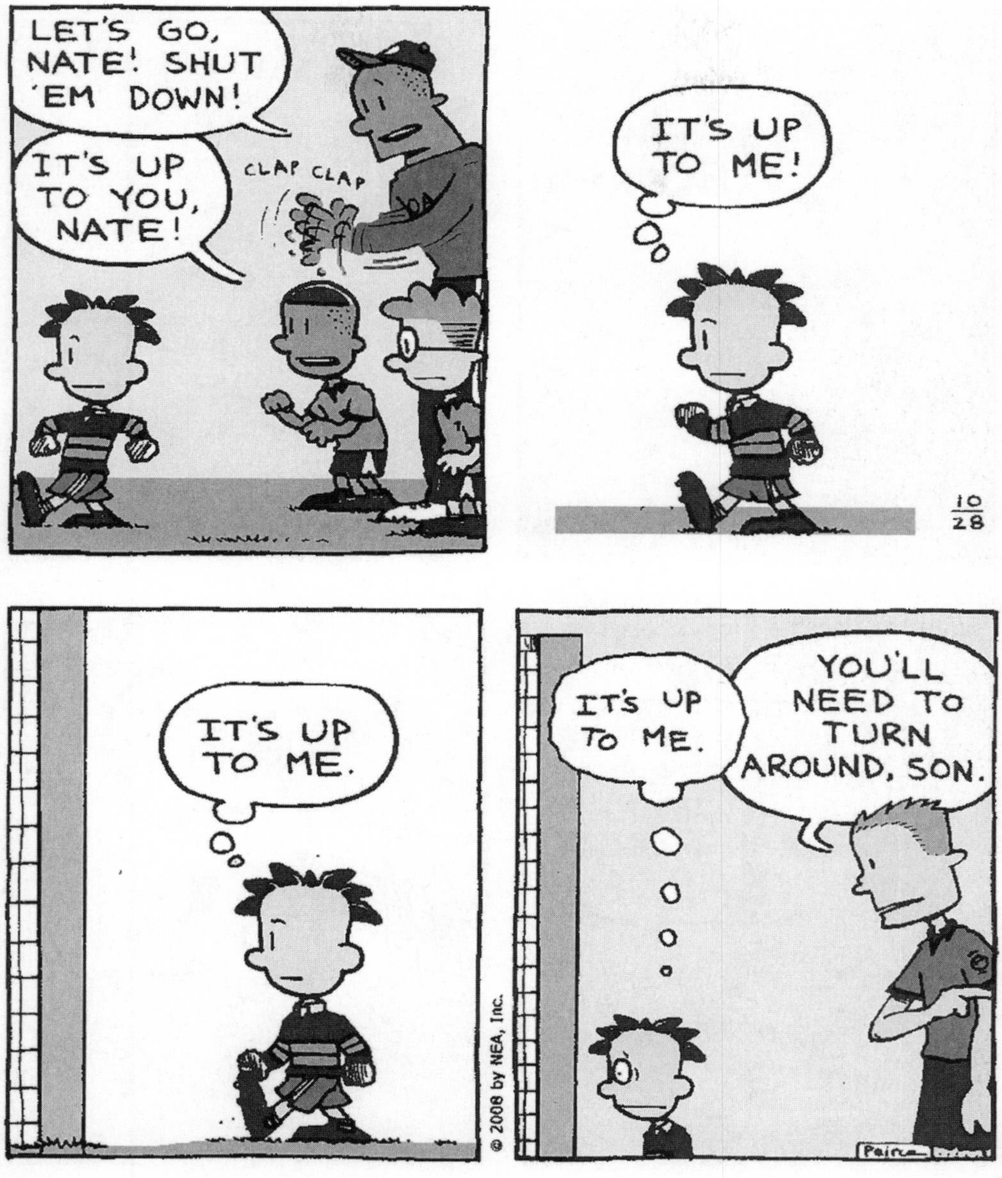
LET'S GO, NATE! SHUT 'EM DOWN!
IT'S UP TO YOU, NATE!
CLAP CLAP
IT'S UP TO ME!
10/28
IT'S UP TO ME.
IT'S UP TO ME.
YOU'LL NEED TO TURN AROUND, SON.
© 2008 by NEA, Inc.

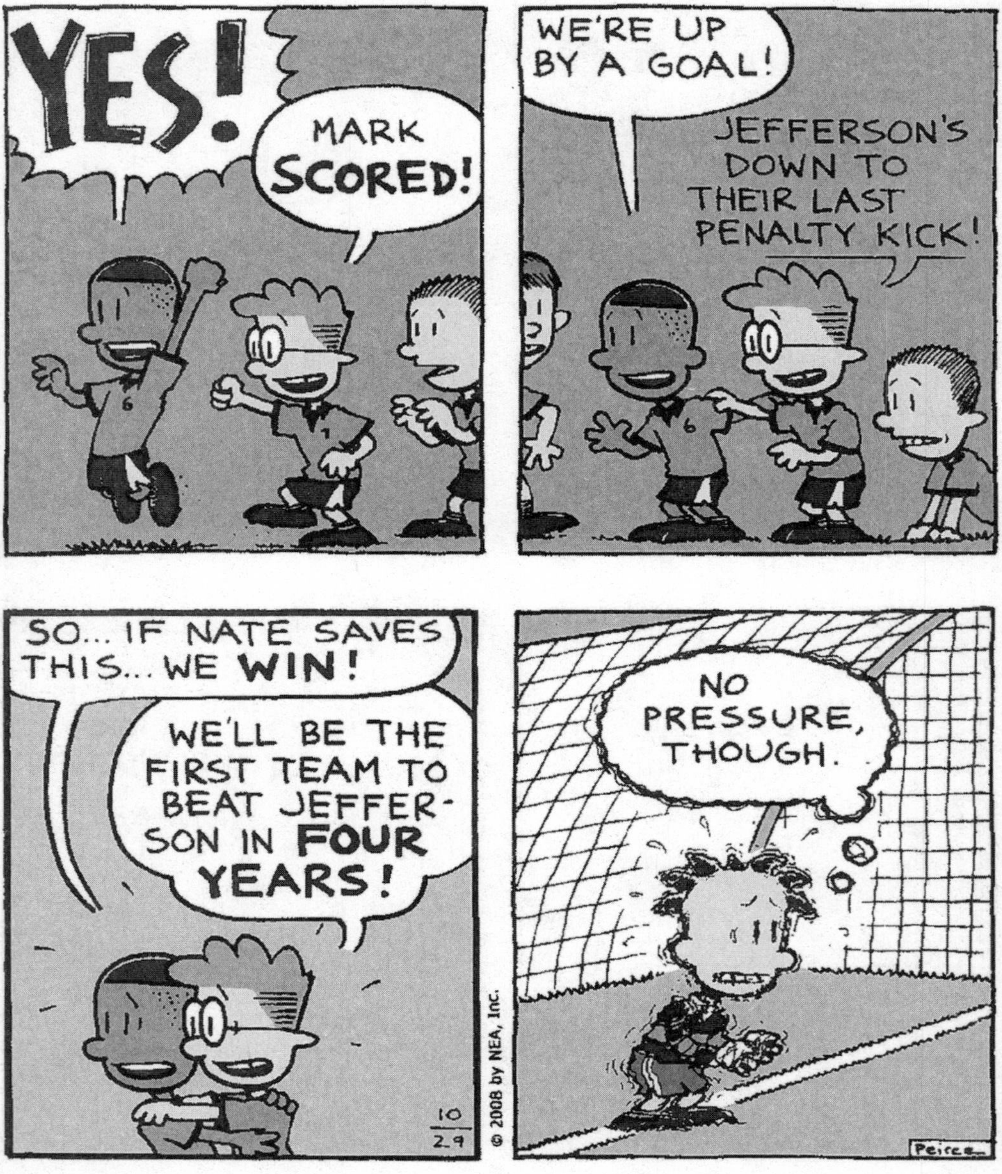
YES!
MARK SCORED!
WE'RE UP BY A GOAL!
JEFFERSON'S DOWN TO THEIR LAST PENALTY KICK!
SO... IF NATE SAVES THIS... WE WIN!
WE'LL BE THE FIRST TEAM TO BEAT JEFFER-SON IN FOUR YEARS!
© 2008 by NEA, Inc.
NO PRESSURE, THOUGH.
Peirce

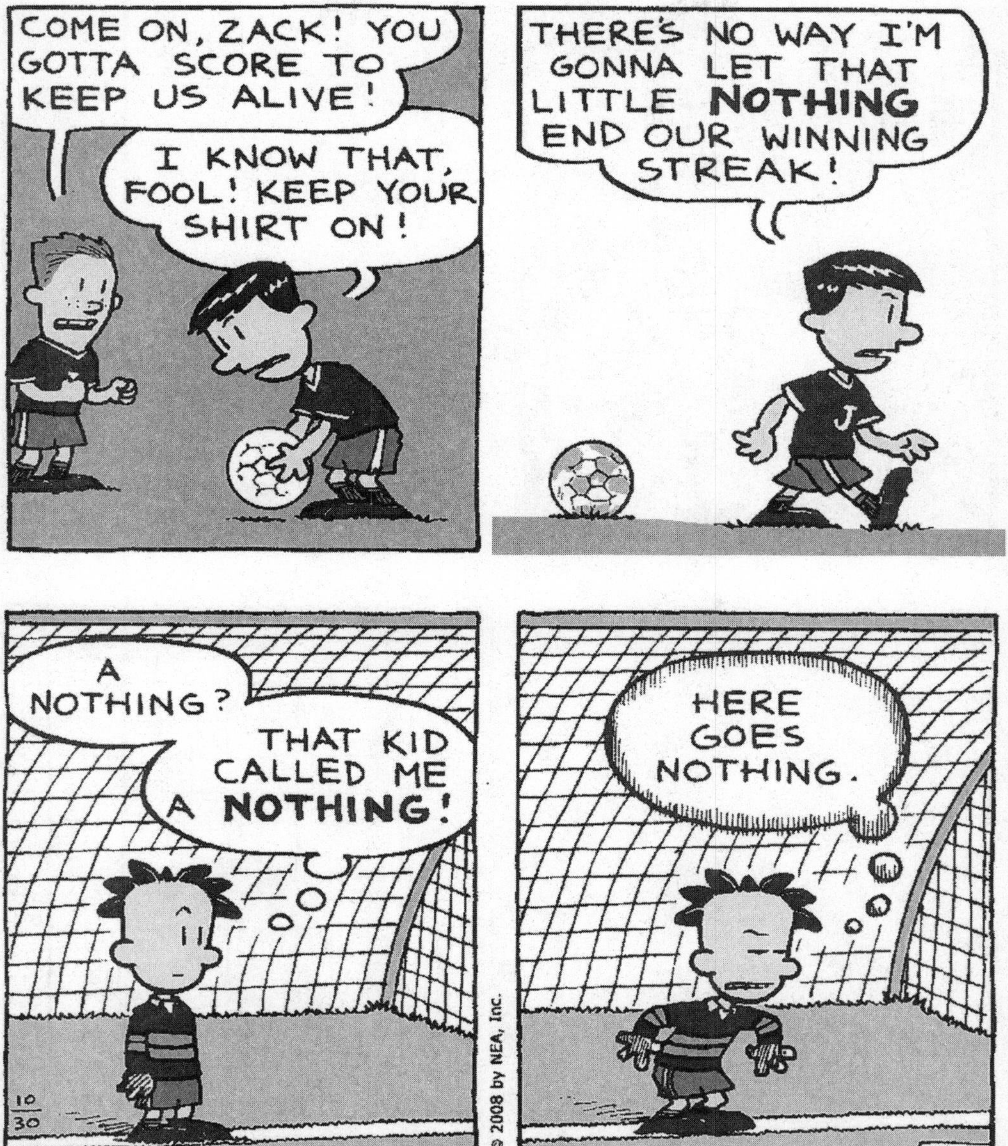
COME ON, ZACK! YOU GOTTA SCORE TO KEEP US ALIVE!
I KNOW THAT, FOOL! KEEP YOUR SHIRT ON!
THERE'S NO WAY I'M GONNA LET THAT LITTLE **NOTHING** END OUR WINNING STREAK!
A NOTHING?
THAT KID CALLED ME A **NOTHING**!
HERE GOES NOTHING.
10/30
© 2008 by NEA, Inc.
PEIRCE

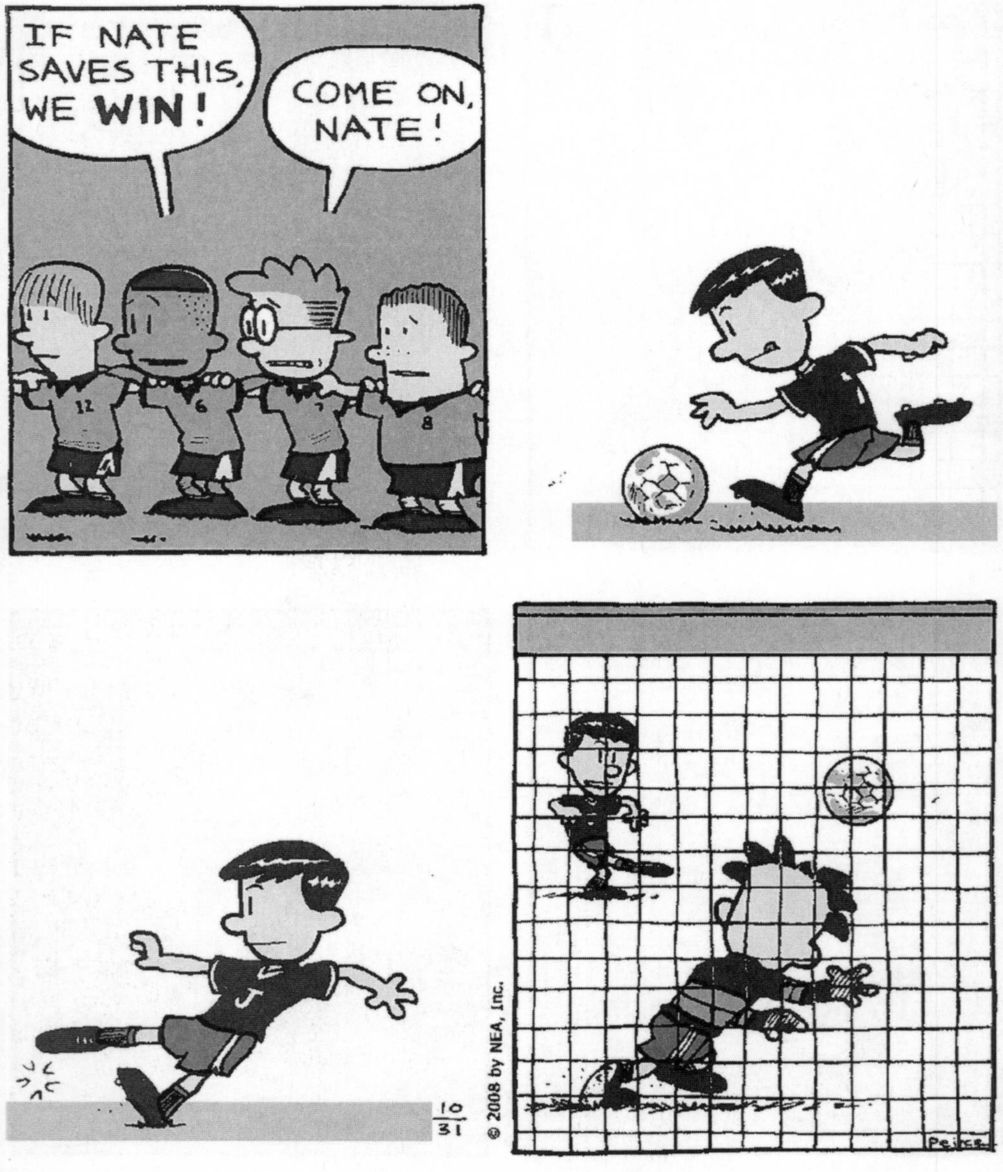
IF NATE SAVES THIS, WE **WIN**!
COME ON, NATE!
10/31
Peirce

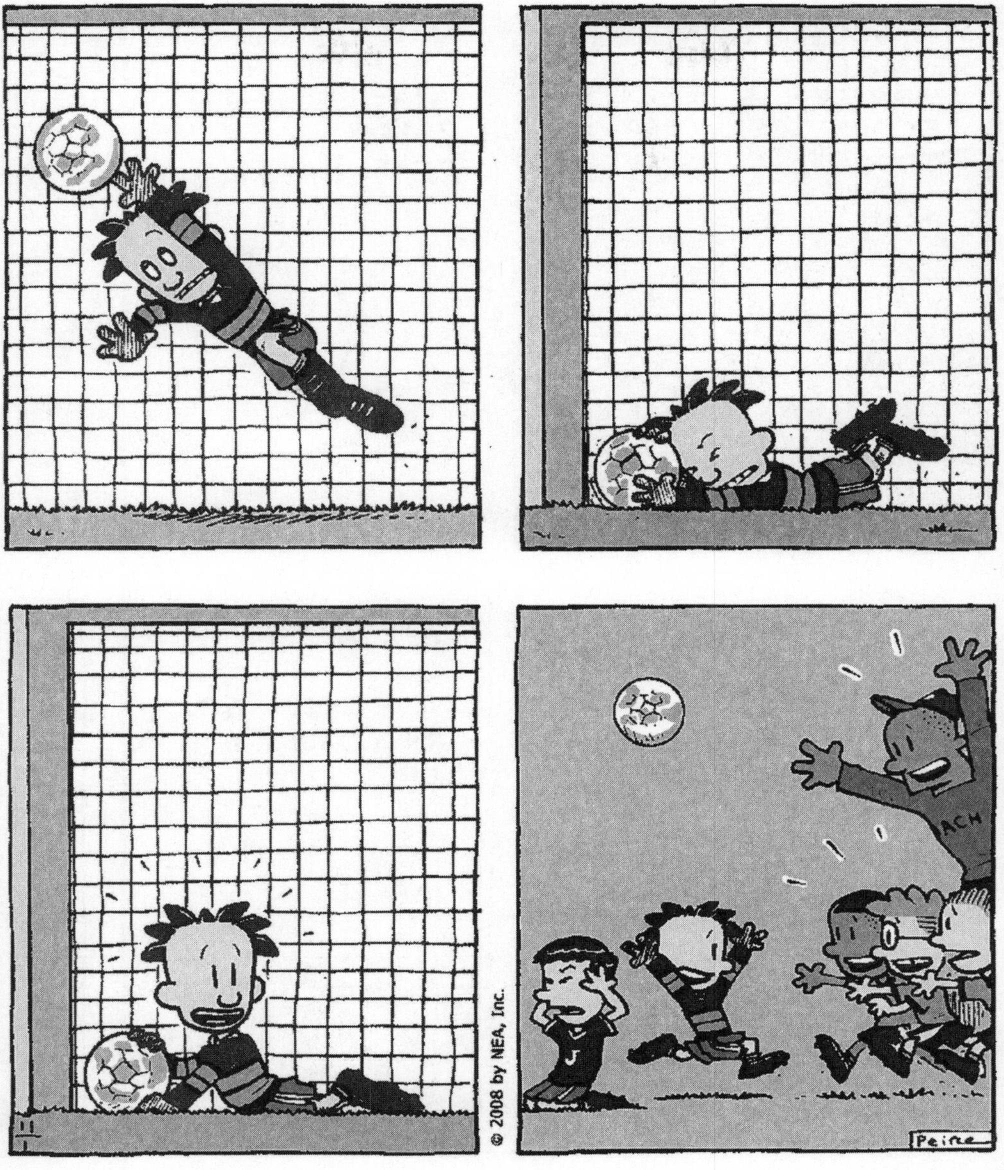
ACH
© 2008 by NEA, Inc.
Peirce

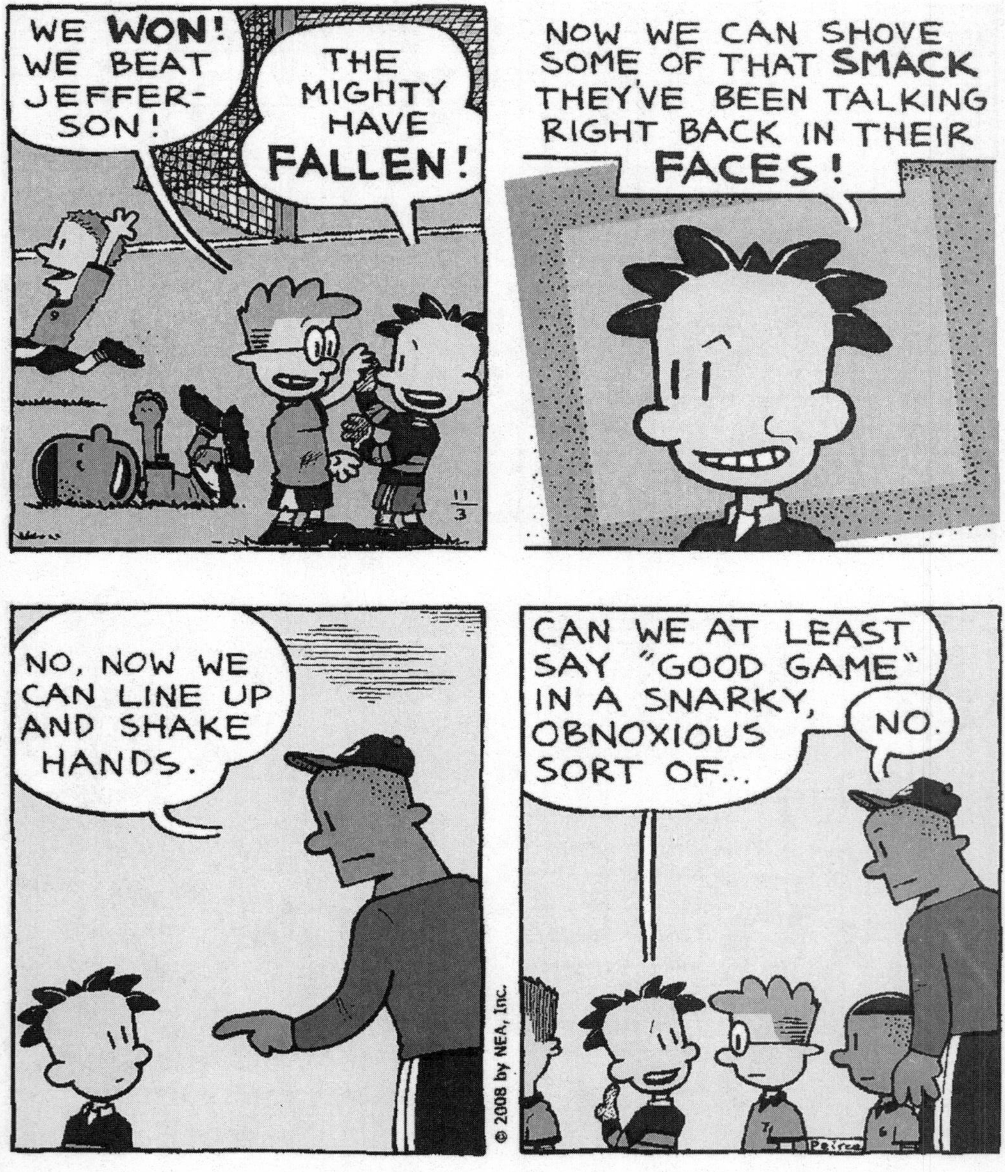
WE WON! WE BEAT JEFFERSON!
THE MIGHTY HAVE FALLEN!
11
3
NOW WE CAN SHOVE SOME OF THAT SMACK THEY'VE BEEN TALKING RIGHT BACK IN THEIR FACES!
NO, NOW WE CAN LINE UP AND SHAKE HANDS.
© 2008 by NEA, Inc.
CAN WE AT LEAST SAY "GOOD GAME" IN A SNARKY, OBNOXIOUS SORT OF...
NO.
Peirce

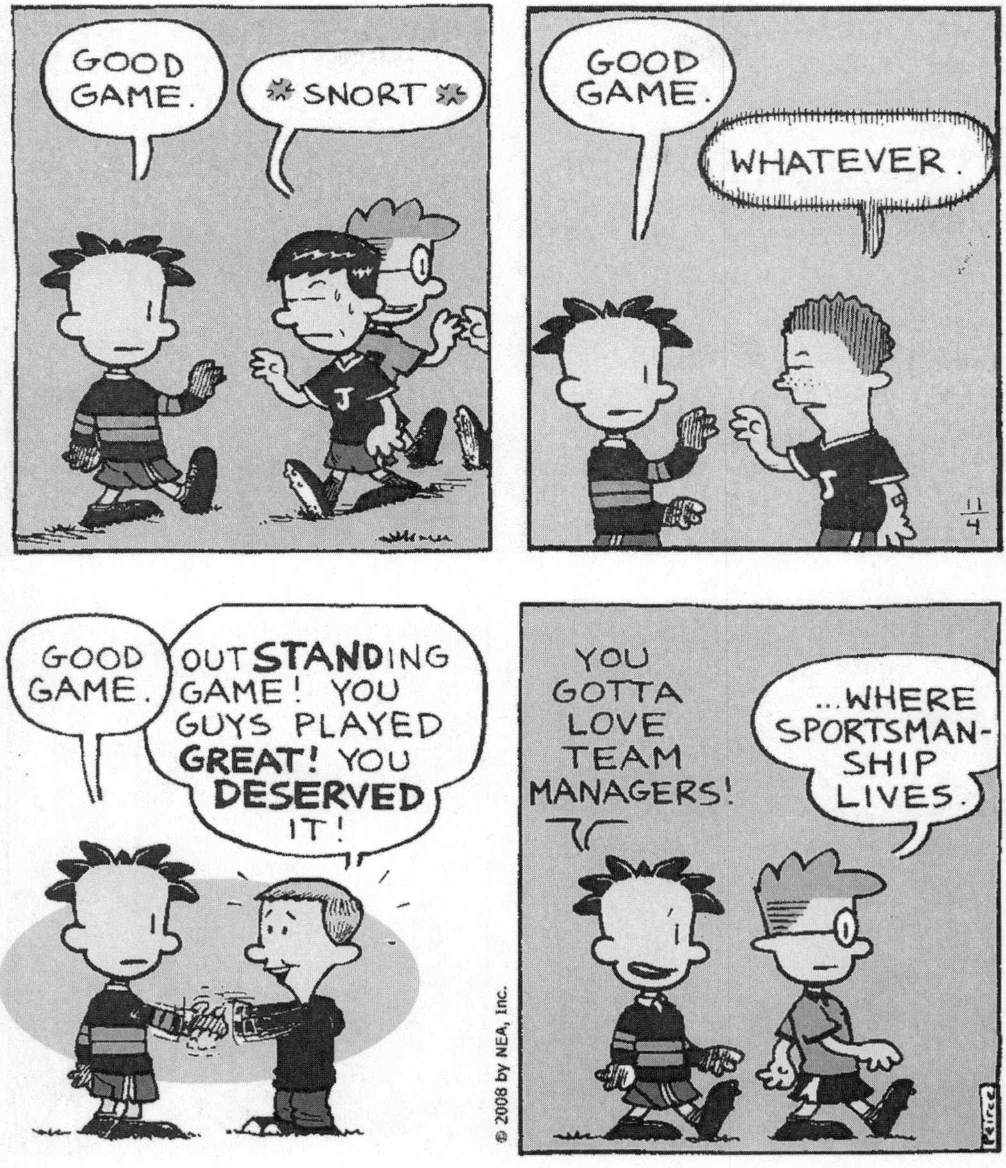
GOOD GAME.
SNORT
GOOD GAME.
WHATEVER.
11/4
GOOD GAME.
OUTSTANDING GAME! YOU GUYS PLAYED GREAT! YOU DESERVED IT!
YOU GOTTA LOVE TEAM MANAGERS!
...WHERE SPORTSMANSHIP LIVES.
Peirce

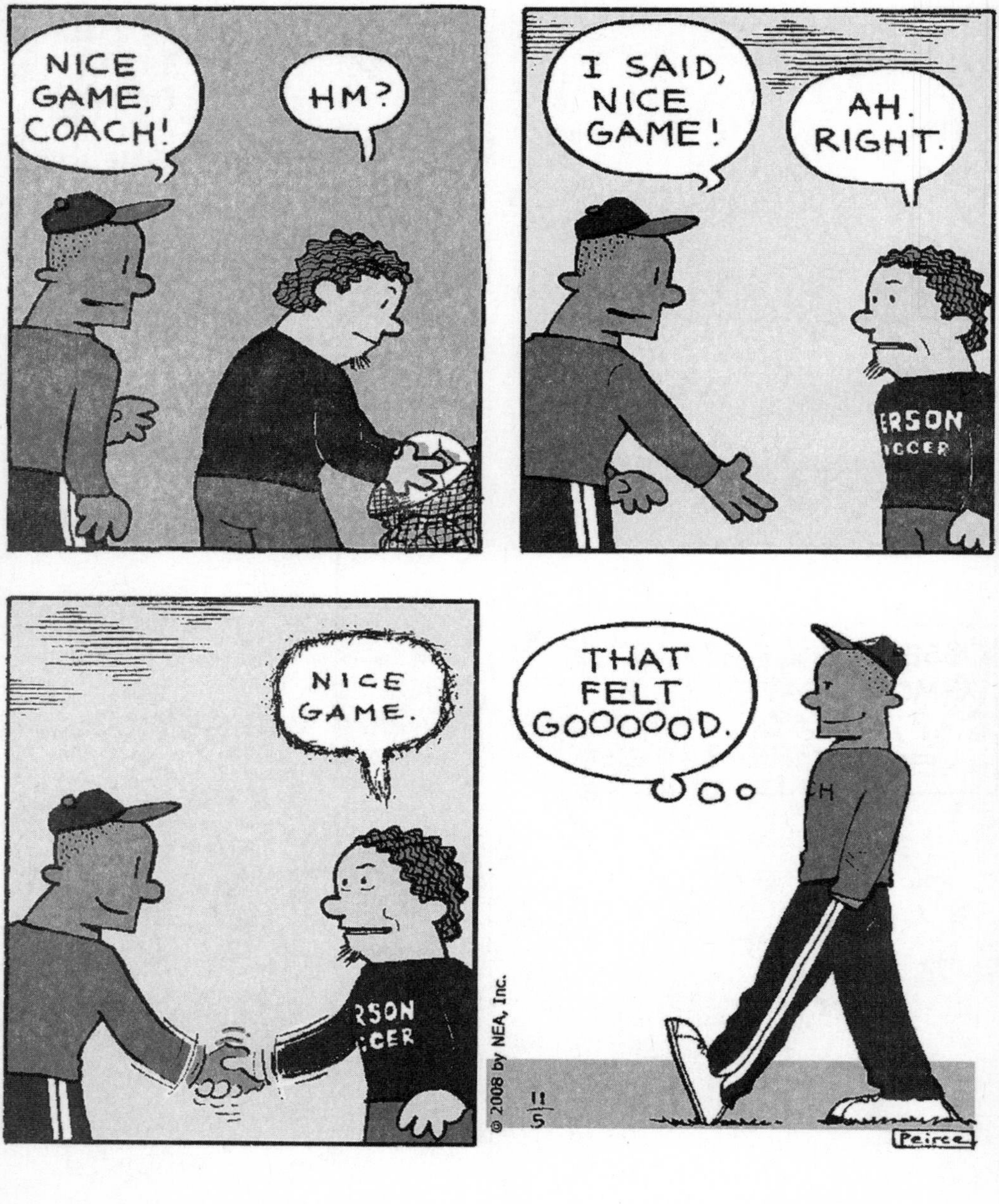
NICE GAME, COACH!
HM?
I SAID, NICE GAME!
AH. RIGHT.
ERSON
OCCER
NICE GAME.
RSON
CER
© 2008 by NEA, Inc.
11/5
THAT FELT GOOOOOD.
Peirce

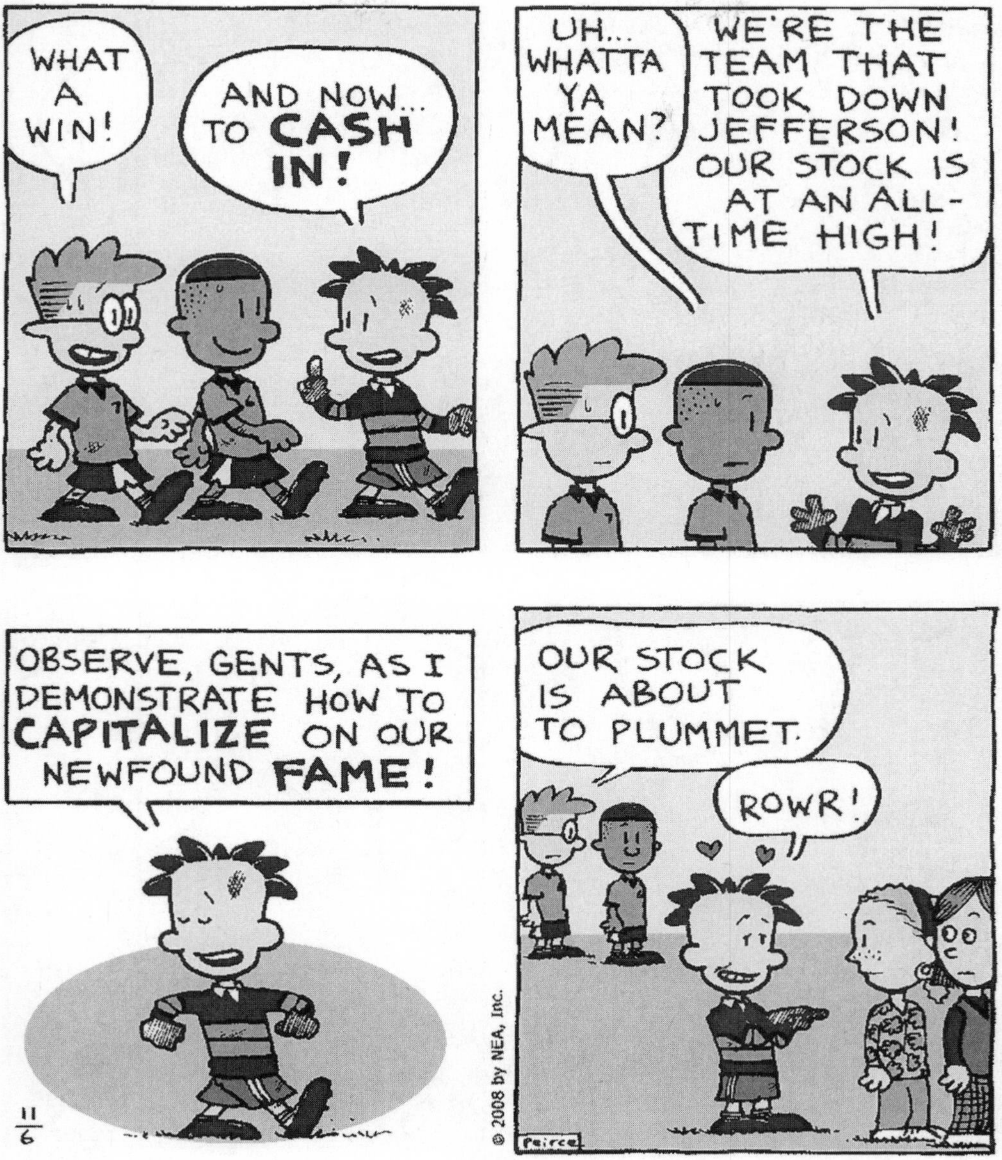
WHAT A WIN!
AND NOW... TO CASH IN!
UH... WHATTA YA MEAN?
WE'RE THE TEAM THAT TOOK DOWN JEFFERSON! OUR STOCK IS AT AN ALL-TIME HIGH!
OBSERVE, GENTS, AS I DEMONSTRATE HOW TO CAPITALIZE ON OUR NEWFOUND FAME!
OUR STOCK IS ABOUT TO PLUMMET.
ROWR!
11/6
PEIRCE

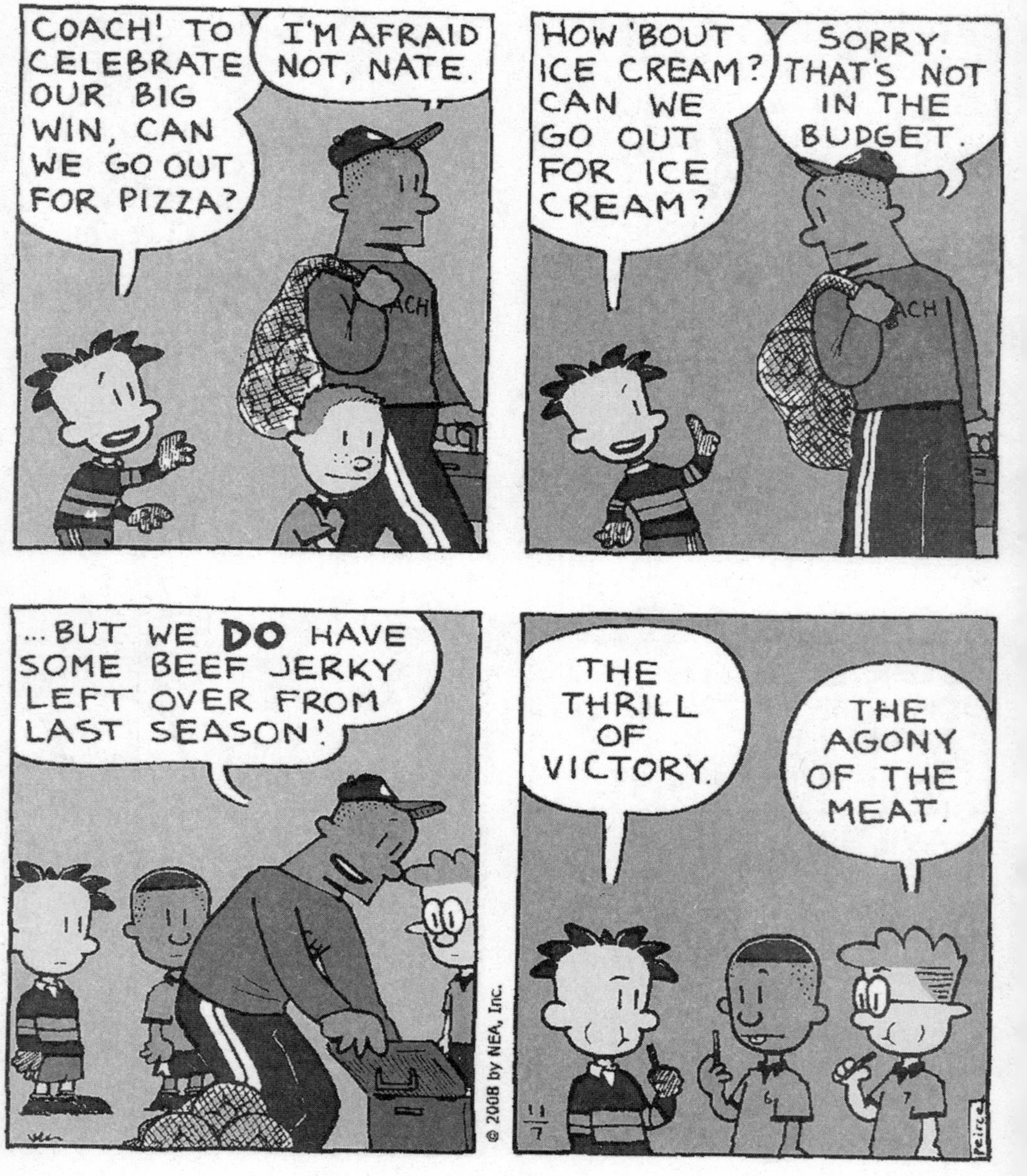
COACH! TO CELEBRATE OUR BIG WIN, CAN WE GO OUT FOR PIZZA?
I'M AFRAID NOT, NATE.
ACH
HOW 'BOUT ICE CREAM? CAN WE GO OUT FOR ICE CREAM?
SORRY. THAT'S NOT IN THE BUDGET.
ACH
...BUT WE DO HAVE SOME BEEF JERKY LEFT OVER FROM LAST SEASON!
© 2008 by NEA, Inc.
THE THRILL OF VICTORY.
THE AGONY OF THE MEAT.
11/7
6
7
Peirce

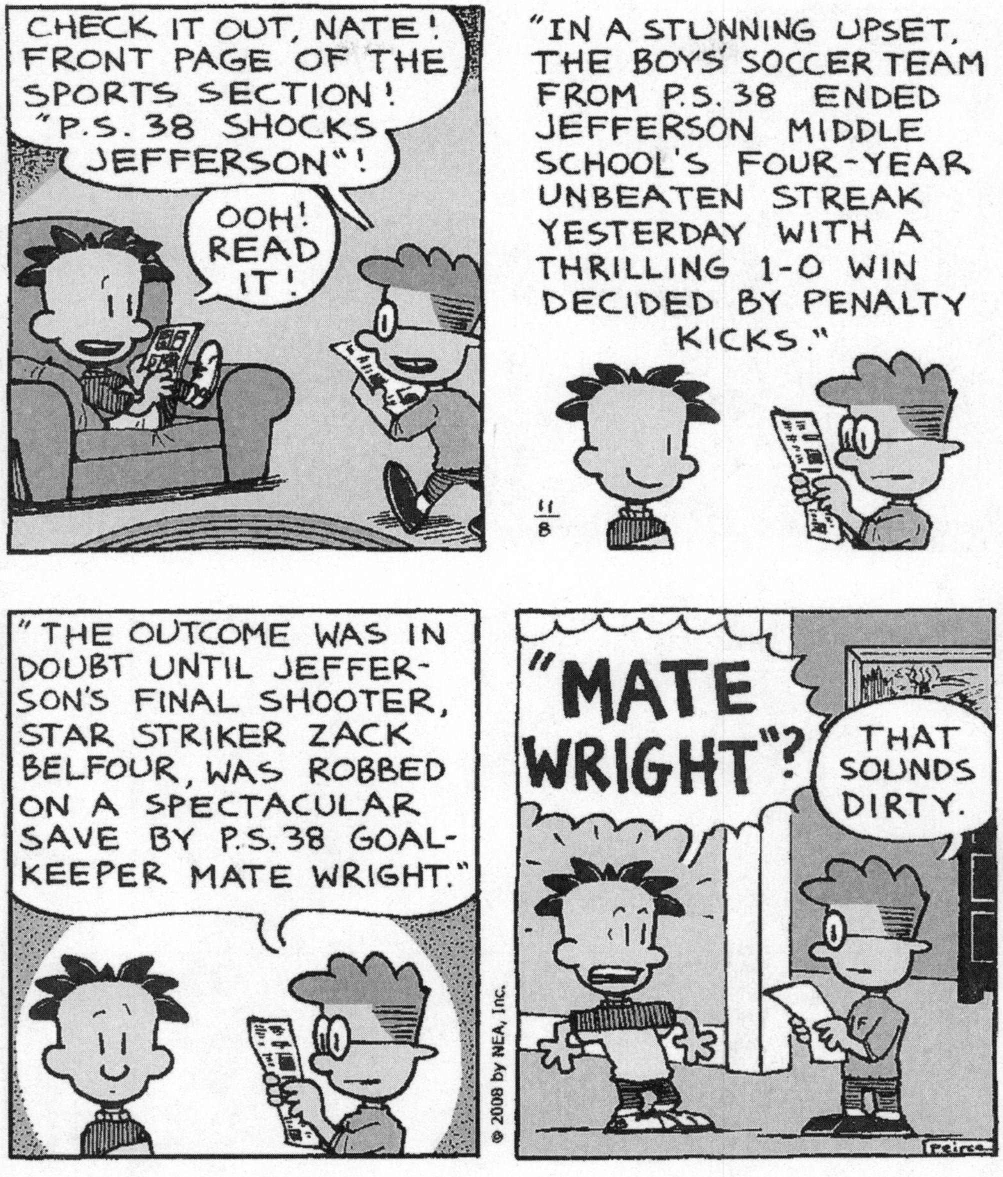
CHECK IT OUT, NATE! FRONT PAGE OF THE SPORTS SECTION! "P.S. 38 SHOCKS JEFFERSON"!
OOH! READ IT!
"IN A STUNNING UPSET, THE BOYS' SOCCER TEAM FROM P.S. 38 ENDED JEFFERSON MIDDLE SCHOOL'S FOUR-YEAR UNBEATEN STREAK YESTERDAY WITH A THRILLING 1-0 WIN DECIDED BY PENALTY KICKS."
11
8
"THE OUTCOME WAS IN DOUBT UNTIL JEFFERSON'S FINAL SHOOTER, STAR STRIKER ZACK BELFOUR, WAS ROBBED ON A SPECTACULAR SAVE BY P.S. 38 GOALKEEPER MATE WRIGHT."
© 2008 by NEA, Inc.
"MATE WRIGHT"?
THAT SOUNDS DIRTY.
Peirce

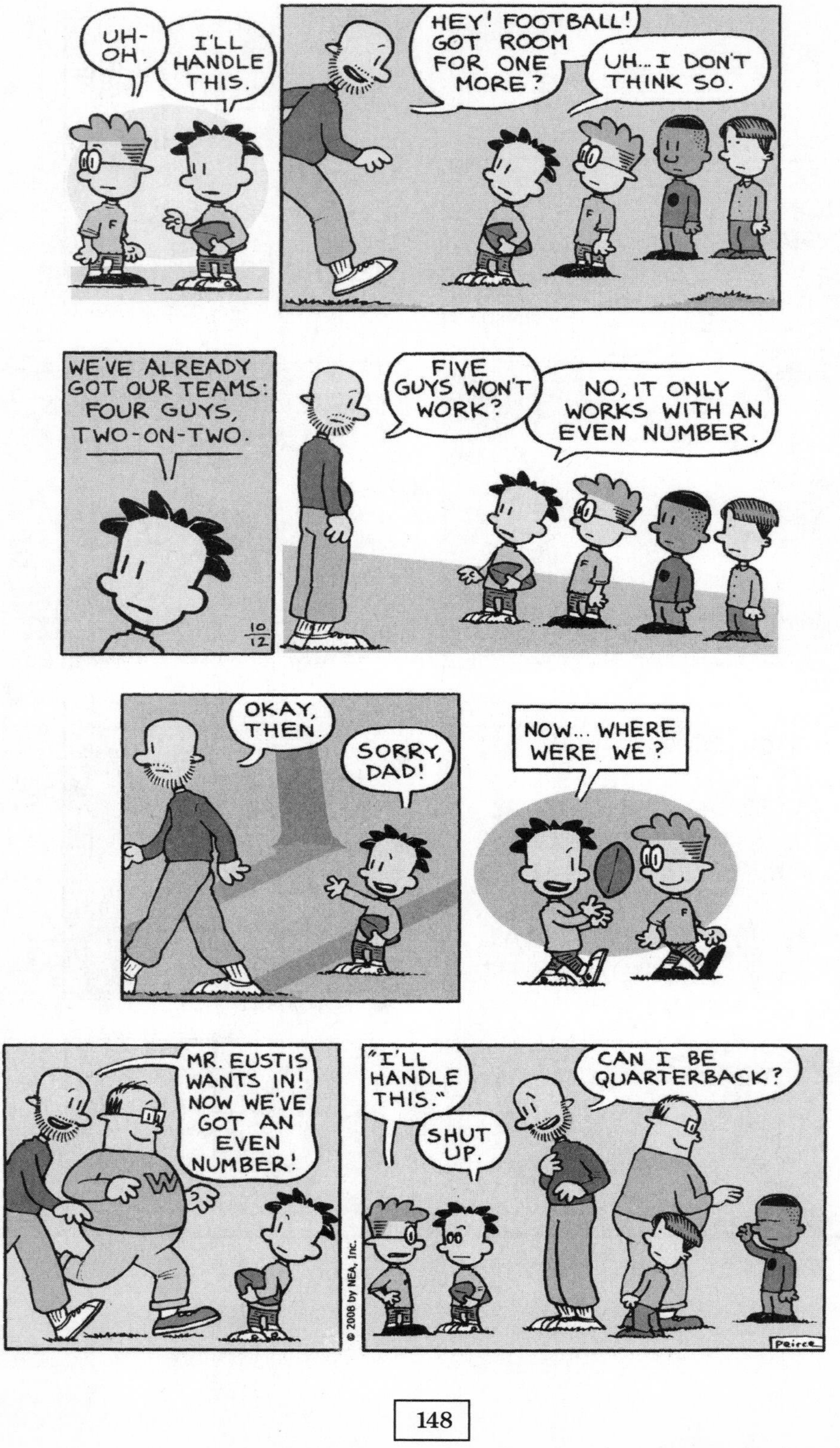
UH-OH.
I'LL HANDLE THIS.
HEY! FOOTBALL! GOT ROOM FOR ONE MORE?
UH... I DON'T THINK SO.
WE'VE ALREADY GOT OUR TEAMS: FOUR GUYS, TWO-ON-TWO.
10/12
FIVE GUYS WON'T WORK?
NO, IT ONLY WORKS WITH AN EVEN NUMBER.
OKAY, THEN.
SORRY, DAD!
NOW... WHERE WERE WE?
MR. EUSTIS WANTS IN! NOW WE'VE GOT AN EVEN NUMBER!
© 2008 by NEA, Inc.
"I'LL HANDLE THIS."
SHUT UP.
CAN I BE QUARTERBACK?
Peirce

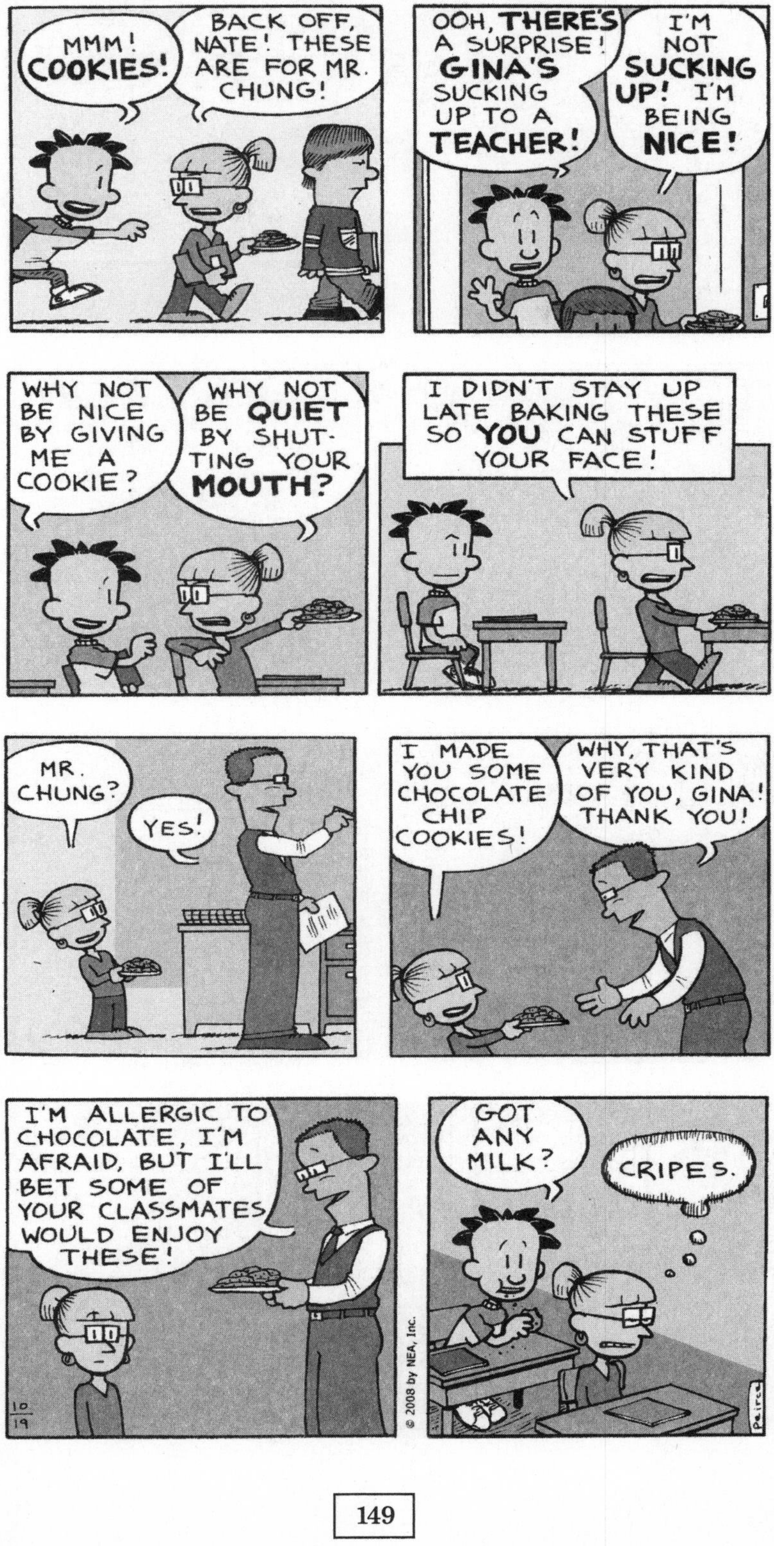
MMM! COOKIES!
BACK OFF, NATE! THESE ARE FOR MR. CHUNG!
OOH, THERE'S A SURPRISE! GINA'S SUCKING UP TO A TEACHER!
I'M NOT SUCKING UP! I'M BEING NICE!
WHY NOT BE NICE BY GIVING ME A COOKIE?
WHY NOT BE QUIET BY SHUTTING YOUR MOUTH?
I DIDN'T STAY UP LATE BAKING THESE SO YOU CAN STUFF YOUR FACE!
MR. CHUNG?
YES!
I MADE YOU SOME CHOCOLATE CHIP COOKIES!
WHY, THAT'S VERY KIND OF YOU, GINA! THANK YOU!
I'M ALLERGIC TO CHOCOLATE, I'M AFRAID, BUT I'LL BET SOME OF YOUR CLASSMATES WOULD ENJOY THESE!
10-19
© 2008 by NEA, Inc.
GOT ANY MILK?
CRIPES.
Peirce

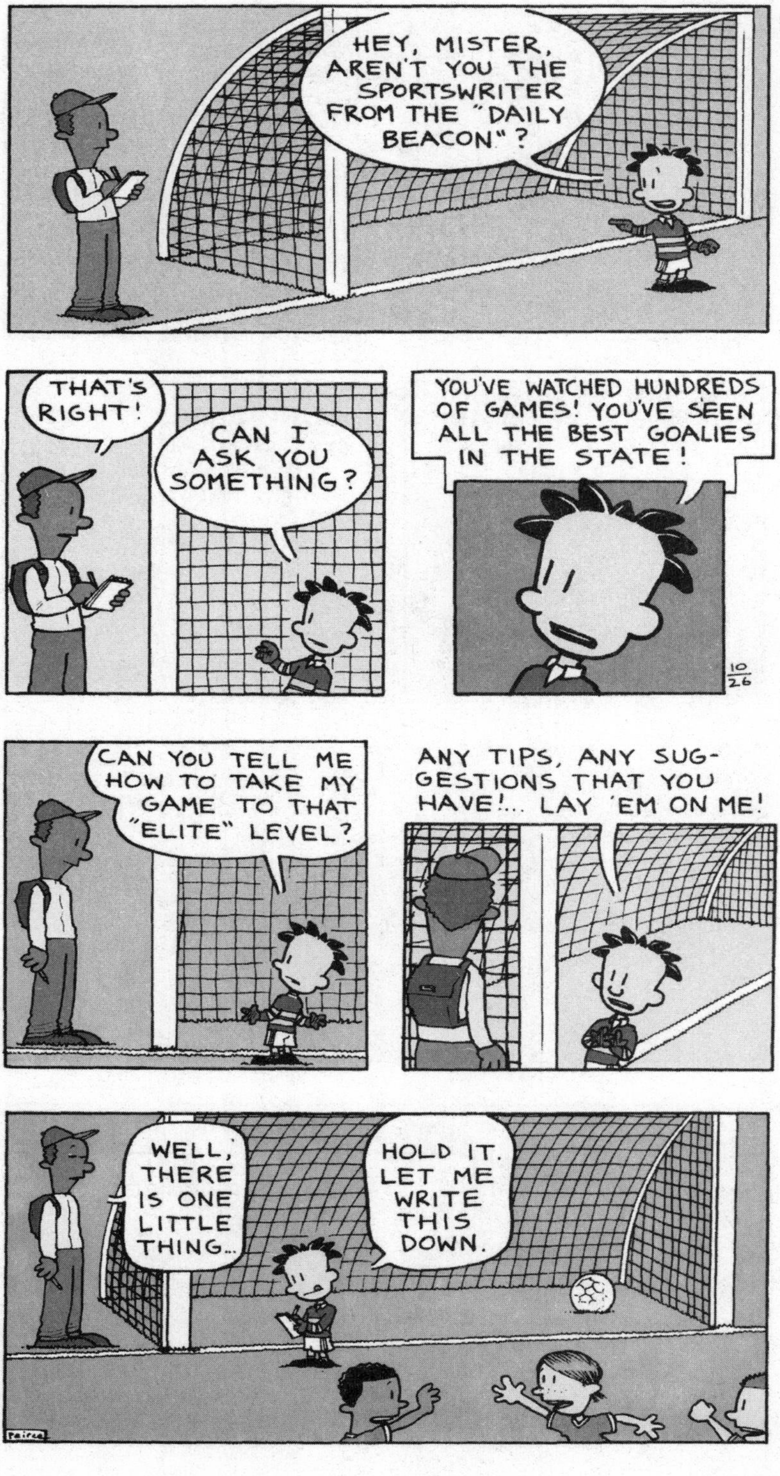
HEY, MISTER, AREN'T YOU THE SPORTSWRITER FROM THE "DAILY BEACON"?
THAT'S RIGHT!
CAN I ASK YOU SOMETHING?
YOU'VE WATCHED HUNDREDS OF GAMES! YOU'VE SEEN ALL THE BEST GOALIES IN THE STATE!
10/26
CAN YOU TELL ME HOW TO TAKE MY GAME TO THAT "ELITE" LEVEL?
ANY TIPS, ANY SUGGESTIONS THAT YOU HAVE!... LAY 'EM ON ME!
WELL, THERE IS ONE LITTLE THING...
HOLD IT. LET ME WRITE THIS DOWN.
Peirce

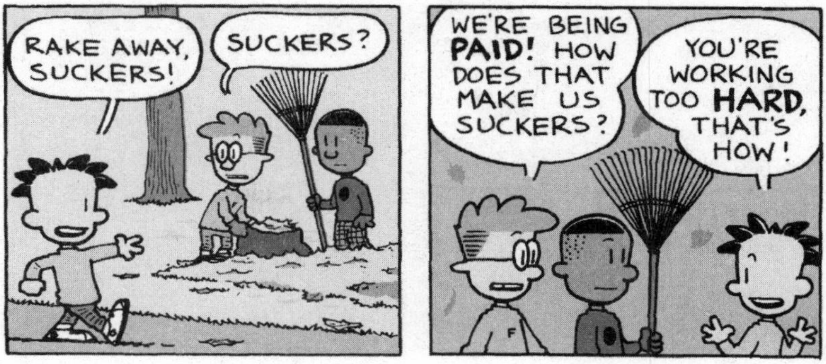
RAKE AWAY, SUCKERS!
SUCKERS?
WE'RE BEING **PAID!** HOW DOES THAT MAKE US SUCKERS?
YOU'RE WORKING TOO **HARD,** THAT'S HOW!

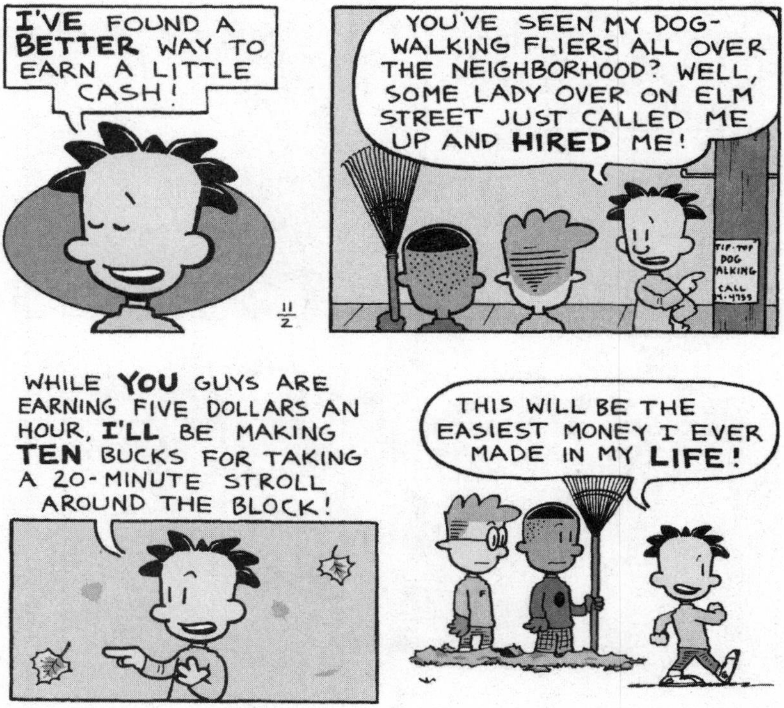
I'VE FOUND A **BETTER** WAY TO EARN A LITTLE CASH!
11/2
YOU'VE SEEN MY DOG-WALKING FLIERS ALL OVER THE NEIGHBORHOOD? WELL, SOME LADY OVER ON ELM STREET JUST CALLED ME UP AND **HIRED** ME!
WHILE **YOU** GUYS ARE EARNING FIVE DOLLARS AN HOUR, **I'LL** BE MAKING **TEN** BUCKS FOR TAKING A 20-MINUTE STROLL AROUND THE BLOCK!
THIS WILL BE THE EASIEST MONEY I EVER MADE IN MY **LIFE!**

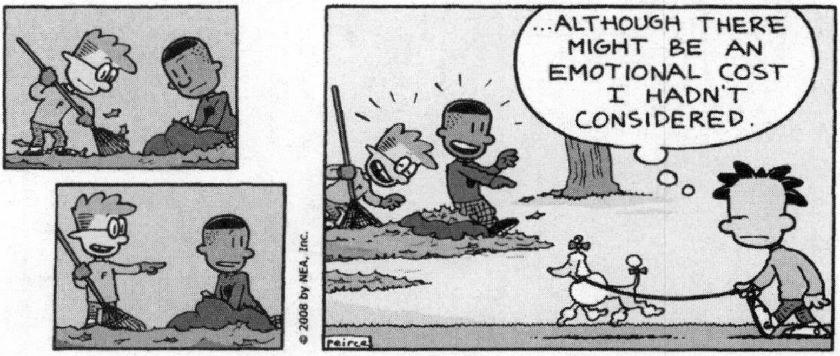
...ALTHOUGH THERE MIGHT BE AN EMOTIONAL COST I HADN'T CONSIDERED.
© 2008 by NEA, Inc.
peirce

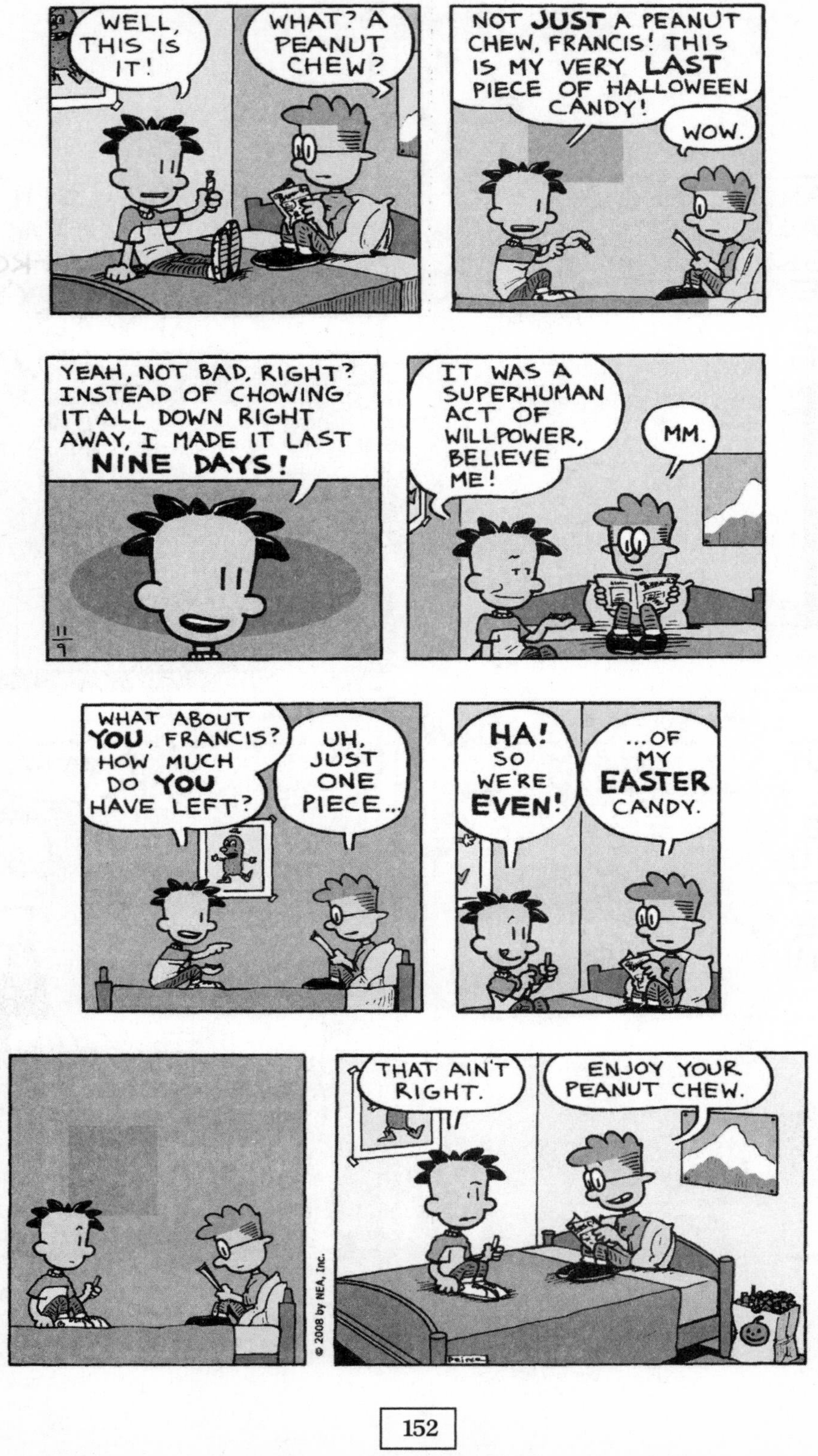
WELL, THIS IS IT!
WHAT? A PEANUT CHEW?
NOT JUST A PEANUT CHEW, FRANCIS! THIS IS MY VERY LAST PIECE OF HALLOWEEN CANDY!
WOW.
YEAH, NOT BAD, RIGHT? INSTEAD OF CHOWING IT ALL DOWN RIGHT AWAY, I MADE IT LAST NINE DAYS!
11/9
IT WAS A SUPERHUMAN ACT OF WILLPOWER, BELIEVE ME!
MM.
WHAT ABOUT YOU, FRANCIS? HOW MUCH DO YOU HAVE LEFT?
UH, JUST ONE PIECE...
HA! SO WE'RE EVEN!
...OF MY EASTER CANDY.
THAT AIN'T RIGHT.
ENJOY YOUR PEANUT CHEW.

CATFIGHT!

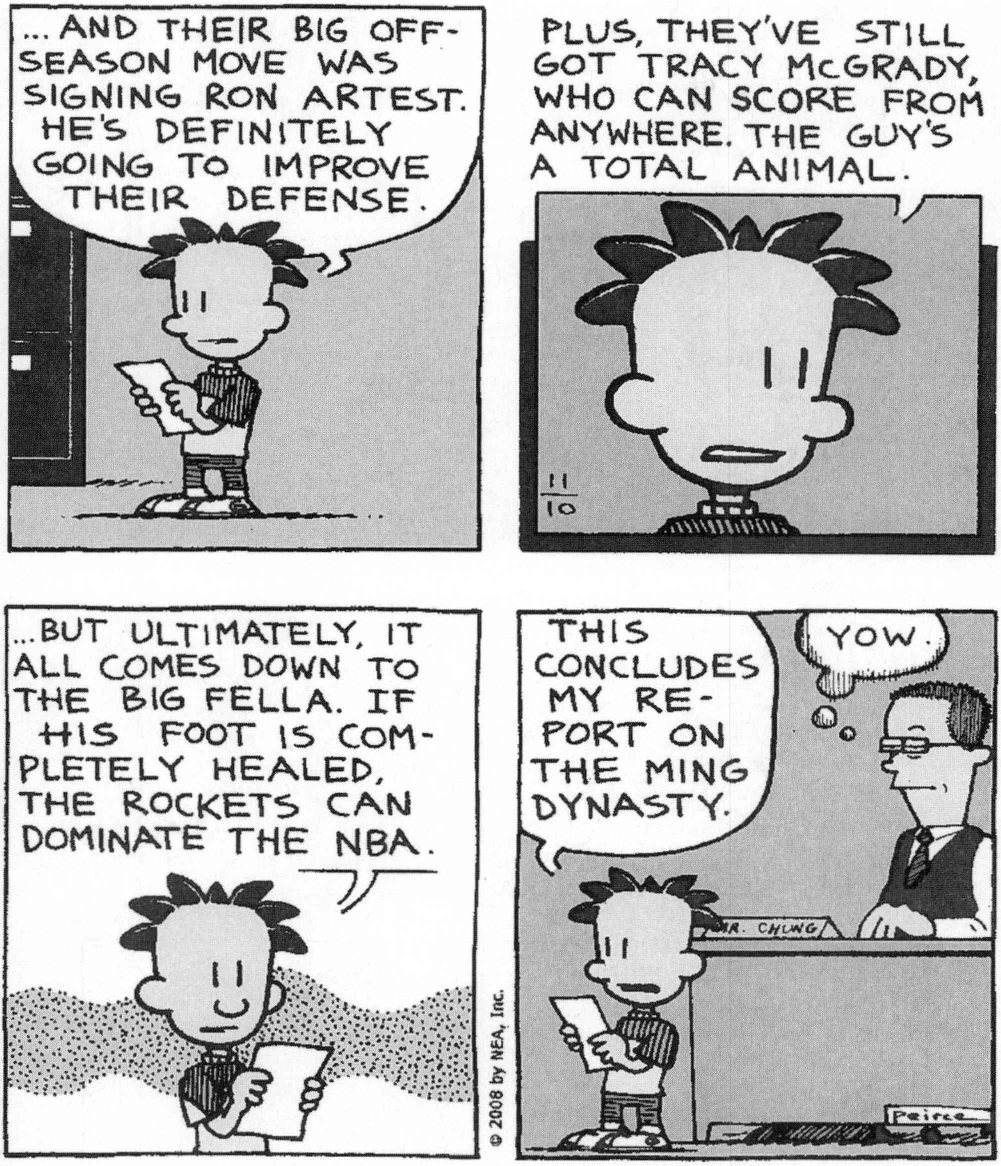

...AND THEIR BIG OFF-SEASON MOVE WAS SIGNING RON ARTEST. HE'S DEFINITELY GOING TO IMPROVE THEIR DEFENSE.
PLUS, THEY'VE STILL GOT TRACY McGRADY, WHO CAN SCORE FROM ANYWHERE. THE GUY'S A TOTAL ANIMAL.
11/10
...BUT ULTIMATELY, IT ALL COMES DOWN TO THE BIG FELLA. IF HIS FOOT IS COMPLETELY HEALED, THE ROCKETS CAN DOMINATE THE NBA.
© 2008 by NEA, Inc.
THIS CONCLUDES MY REPORT ON THE MING DYNASTY.
YOW.
MR. CHUNG
Peirce

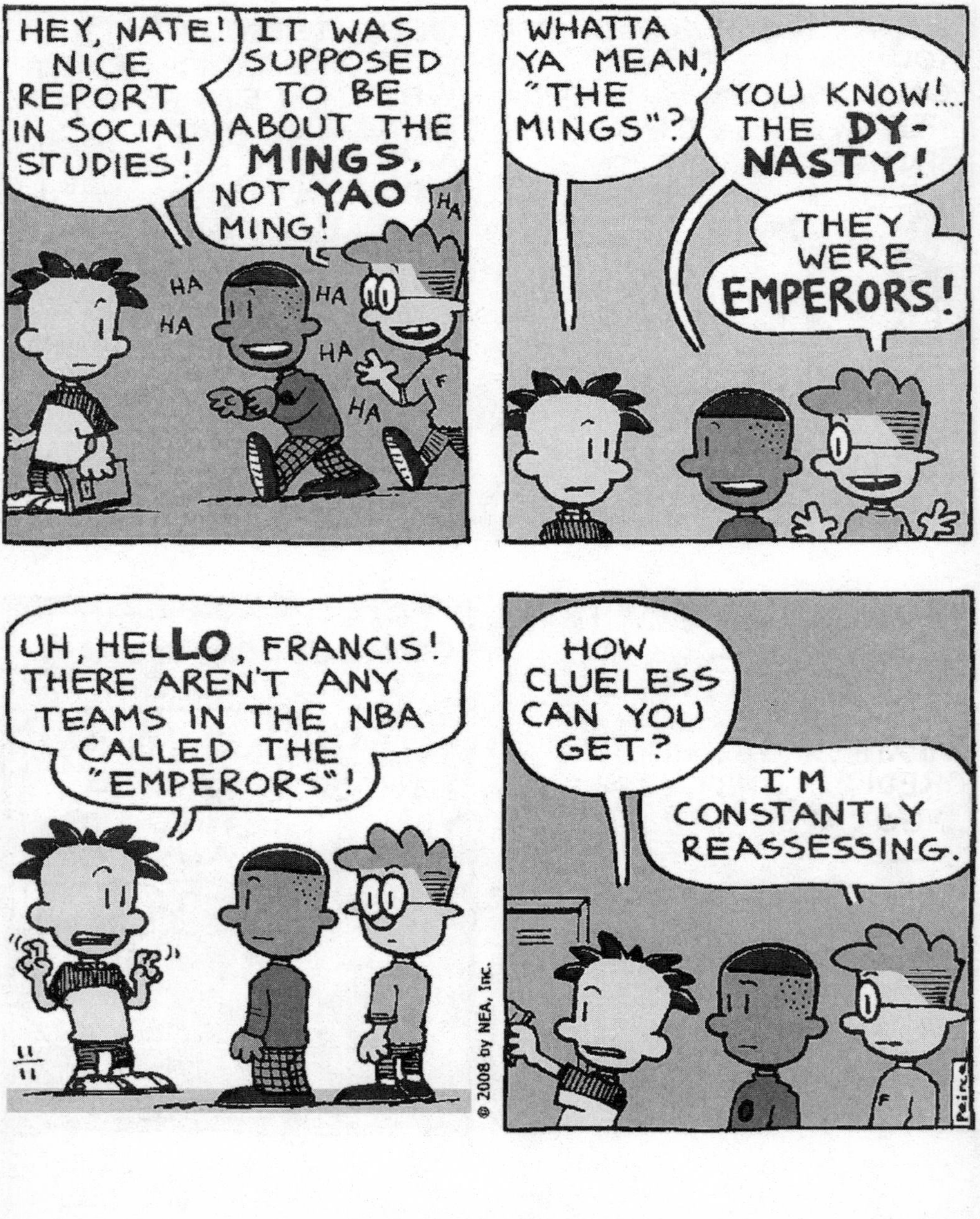
HEY, NATE! NICE REPORT IN SOCIAL STUDIES!
IT WAS SUPPOSED TO BE ABOUT THE MINGS, NOT YAO MING!
HA HA HA HA HA HA
WHATTA YA MEAN, "THE MINGS"?
YOU KNOW!... THE DY-NASTY!
THEY WERE EMPERORS!
UH, HELLO, FRANCIS! THERE AREN'T ANY TEAMS IN THE NBA CALLED THE "EMPERORS"!
HOW CLUELESS CAN YOU GET?
I'M CONSTANTLY REASSESSING.
© 2008 by NEA, Inc.
Peirce

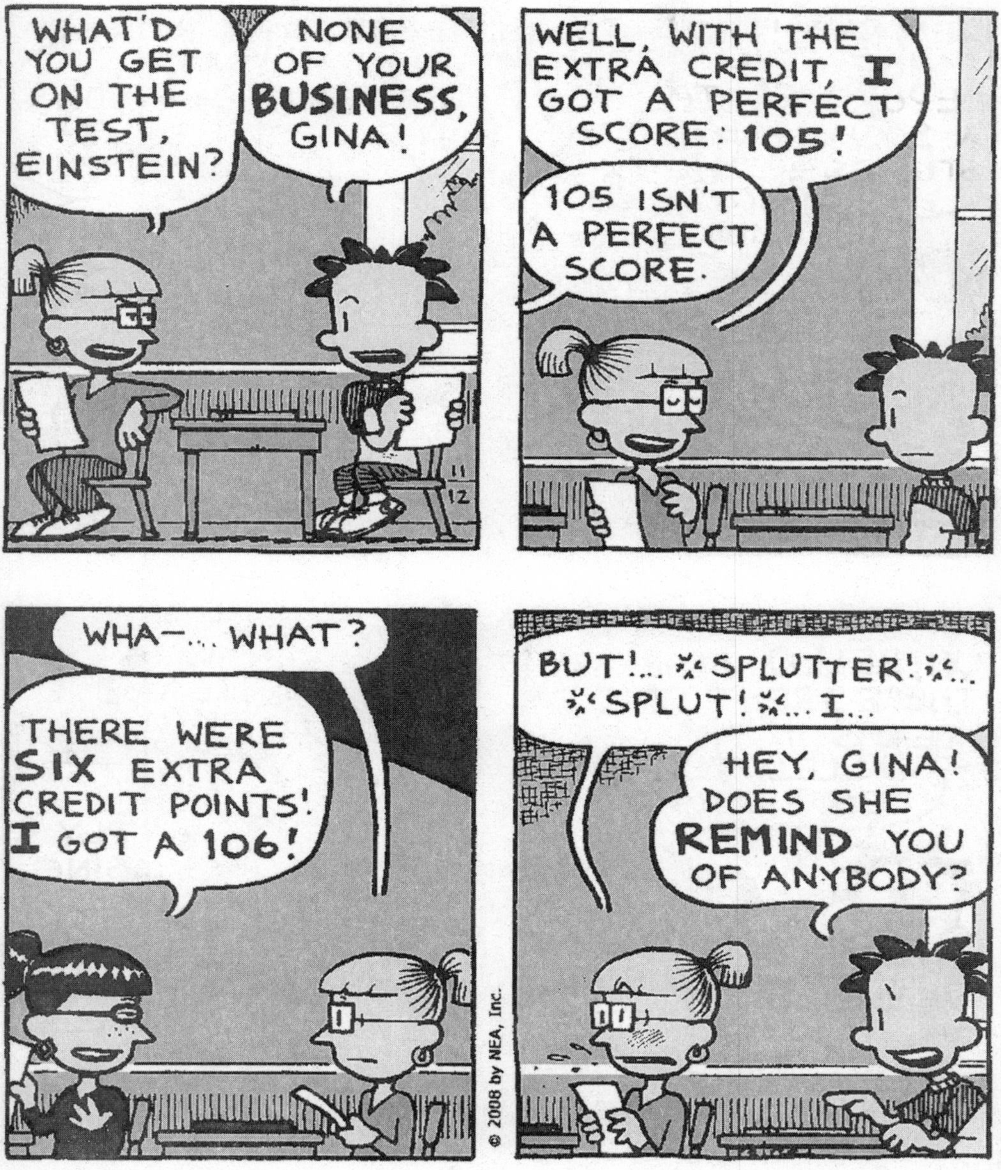
WHAT'D YOU GET ON THE TEST, EINSTEIN?
NONE OF YOUR **BUSINESS**, GINA!
WELL, WITH THE EXTRA CREDIT, **I** GOT A PERFECT SCORE: **105**!
105 ISN'T A PERFECT SCORE.
WHA-... WHAT?
THERE WERE **SIX** EXTRA CREDIT POINTS! **I** GOT A **106**!
BUT!... SPLUTTER!... SPLUT!... I...
HEY, GINA! DOES SHE **REMIND** YOU OF ANYBODY?
© 2008 by NEA, Inc.

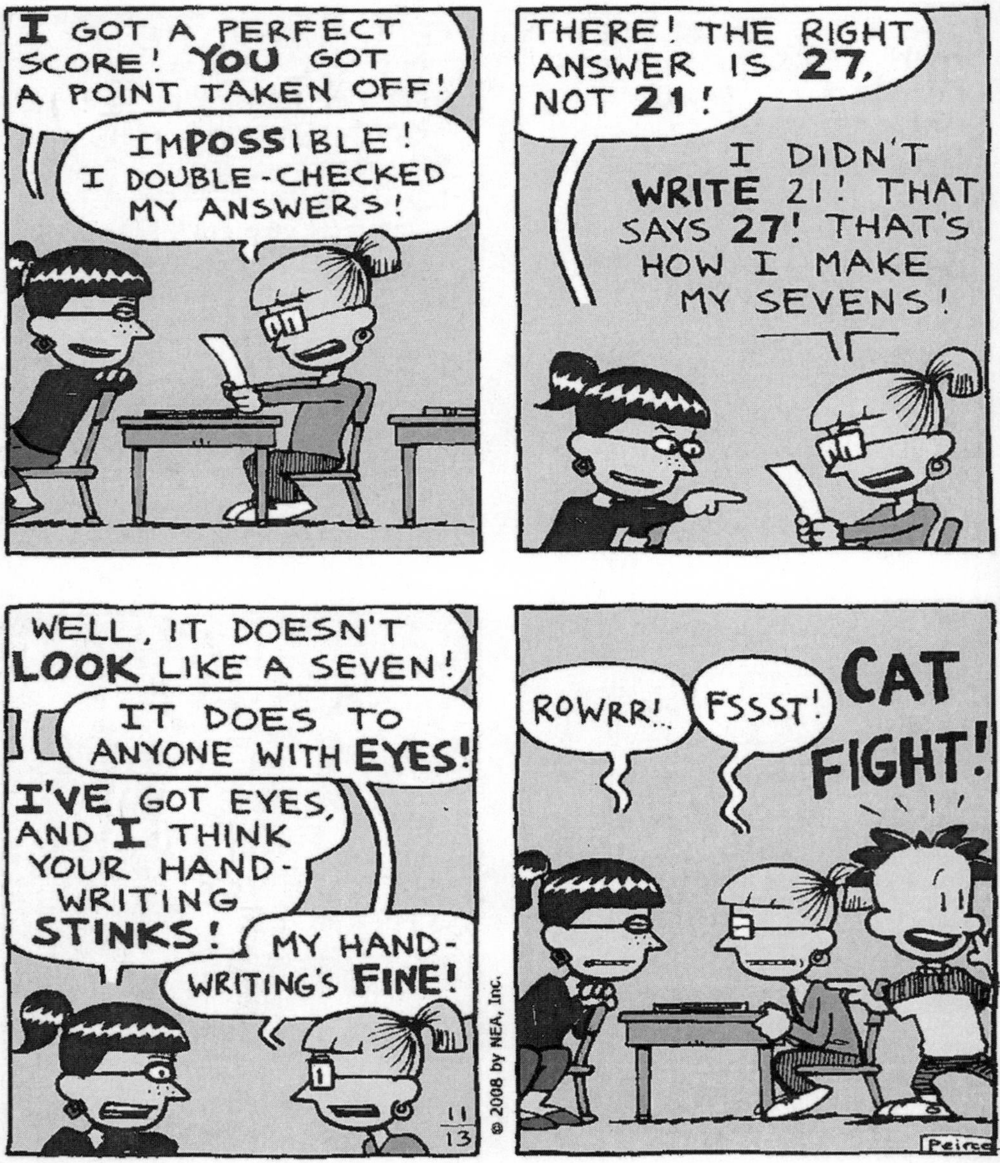

I GOT A PERFECT SCORE! YOU GOT A POINT TAKEN OFF!
IMPOSSIBLE! I DOUBLE-CHECKED MY ANSWERS!
THERE! THE RIGHT ANSWER IS 27, NOT 21!
I DIDN'T WRITE 21! THAT SAYS 27! THAT'S HOW I MAKE MY SEVENS!
WELL, IT DOESN'T LOOK LIKE A SEVEN!
IT DOES TO ANYONE WITH EYES!
I'VE GOT EYES, AND I THINK YOUR HAND-WRITING STINKS!
MY HAND-WRITING'S FINE!
11/13
© 2008 by NEA, Inc.
ROWRR!..
FSSST!
CAT FIGHT!
Peirce

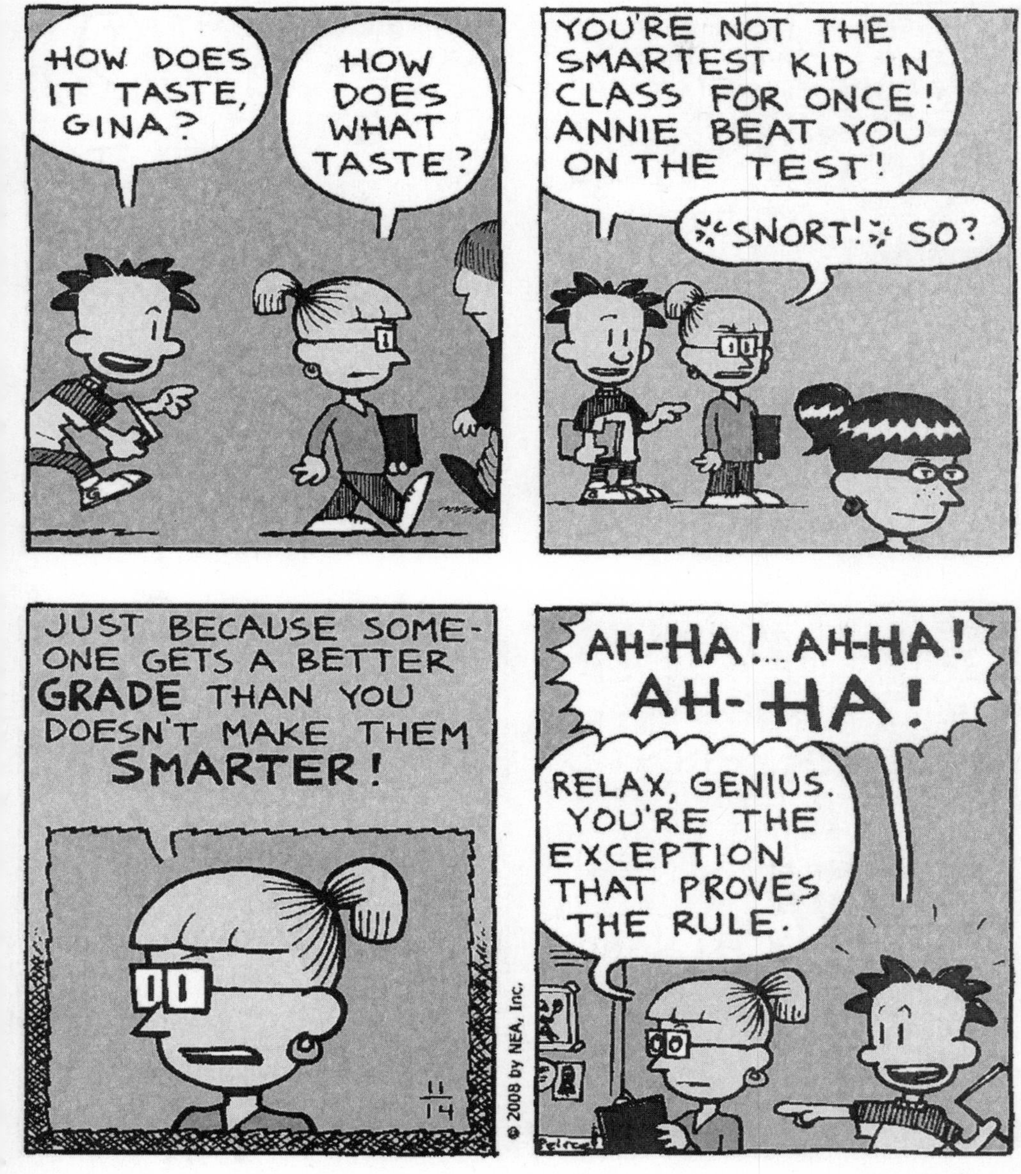
HOW DOES IT TASTE, GINA?
HOW DOES WHAT TASTE?
YOU'RE NOT THE SMARTEST KID IN CLASS FOR ONCE! ANNIE BEAT YOU ON THE TEST!
SNORT! SO?
JUST BECAUSE SOME-ONE GETS A BETTER GRADE THAN YOU DOESN'T MAKE THEM SMARTER!
11/14
AH-HA!... AH-HA! AH-HA!
RELAX, GENIUS. YOU'RE THE EXCEPTION THAT PROVES THE RULE.

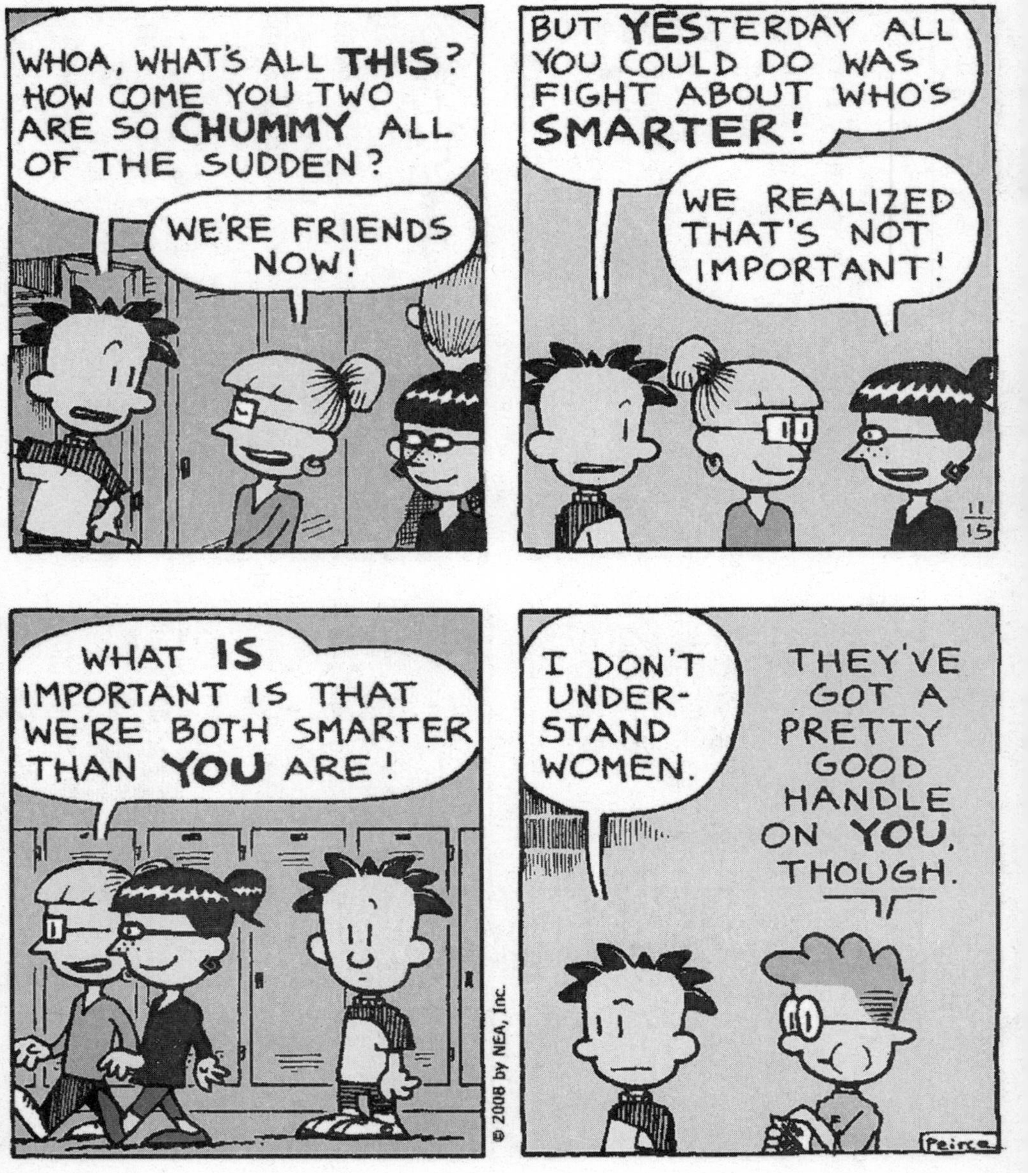
WHOA, WHAT'S ALL THIS? HOW COME YOU TWO ARE SO CHUMMY ALL OF THE SUDDEN?
WE'RE FRIENDS NOW!
BUT YESTERDAY ALL YOU COULD DO WAS FIGHT ABOUT WHO'S SMARTER!
WE REALIZED THAT'S NOT IMPORTANT!
11/15
WHAT IS IMPORTANT IS THAT WE'RE BOTH SMARTER THAN YOU ARE!
© 2008 by NEA, Inc.
I DON'T UNDER-STAND WOMEN.
THEY'VE GOT A PRETTY GOOD HANDLE ON YOU, THOUGH.
Peirce

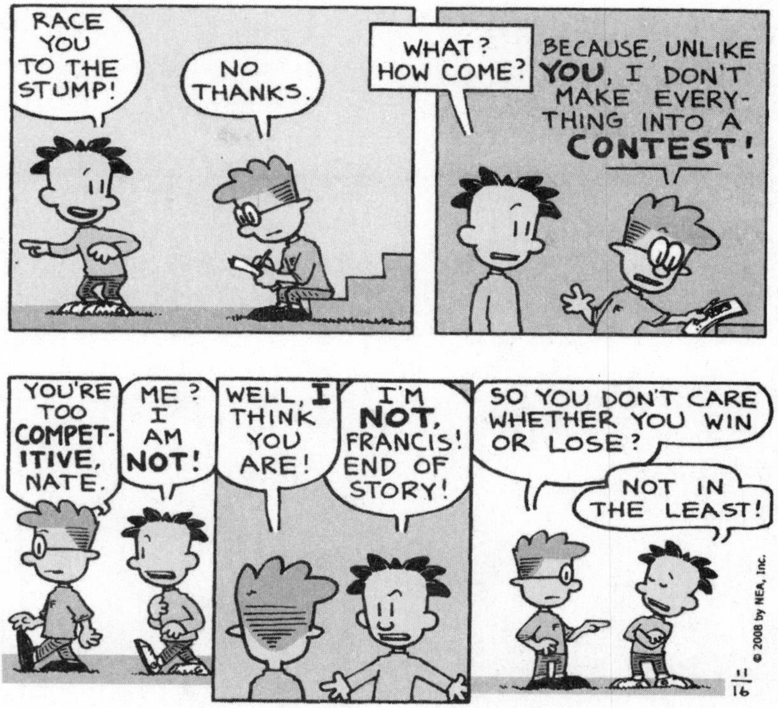
RACE YOU TO THE STUMP!
NO THANKS.
WHAT? HOW COME?
BECAUSE, UNLIKE **YOU**, I DON'T MAKE EVERYTHING INTO A **CONTEST**!
YOU'RE TOO **COMPETITIVE**, NATE.
ME? I AM **NOT**!
WELL, **I** THINK YOU ARE!
I'M **NOT**, FRANCIS! END OF STORY!
SO YOU DON'T CARE WHETHER YOU WIN OR LOSE?
NOT IN THE LEAST!
© 2008 by NEA, Inc.
11/16

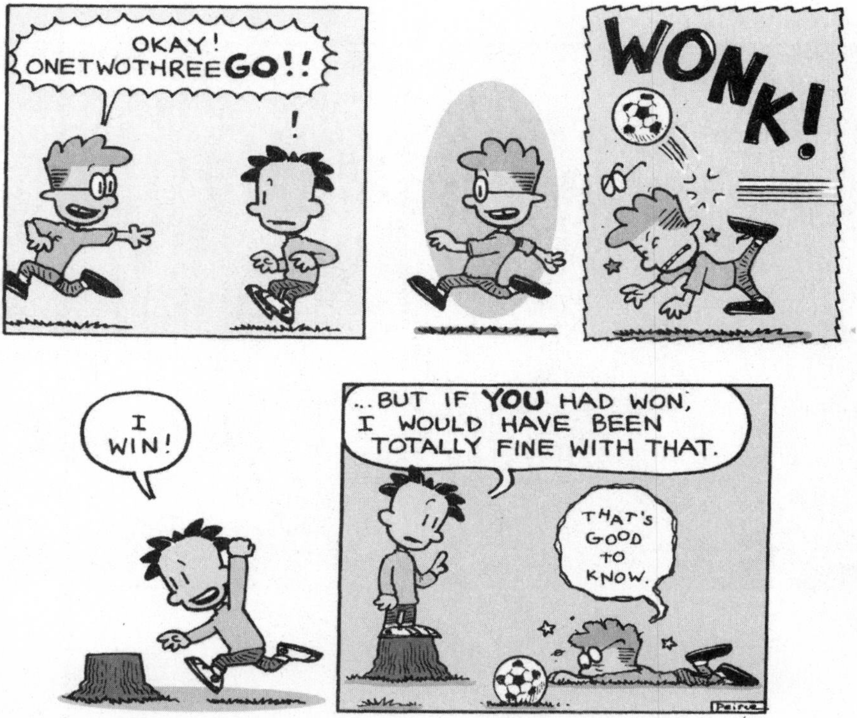
OKAY! ONETWOTHREE**GO**!!
!
WONK!
I WIN!
...BUT IF **YOU** HAD WON, I WOULD HAVE BEEN TOTALLY FINE WITH THAT.
THAT'S GOOD TO KNOW.
Peirce

NATE WRIGHT, SUPERBLOGGER

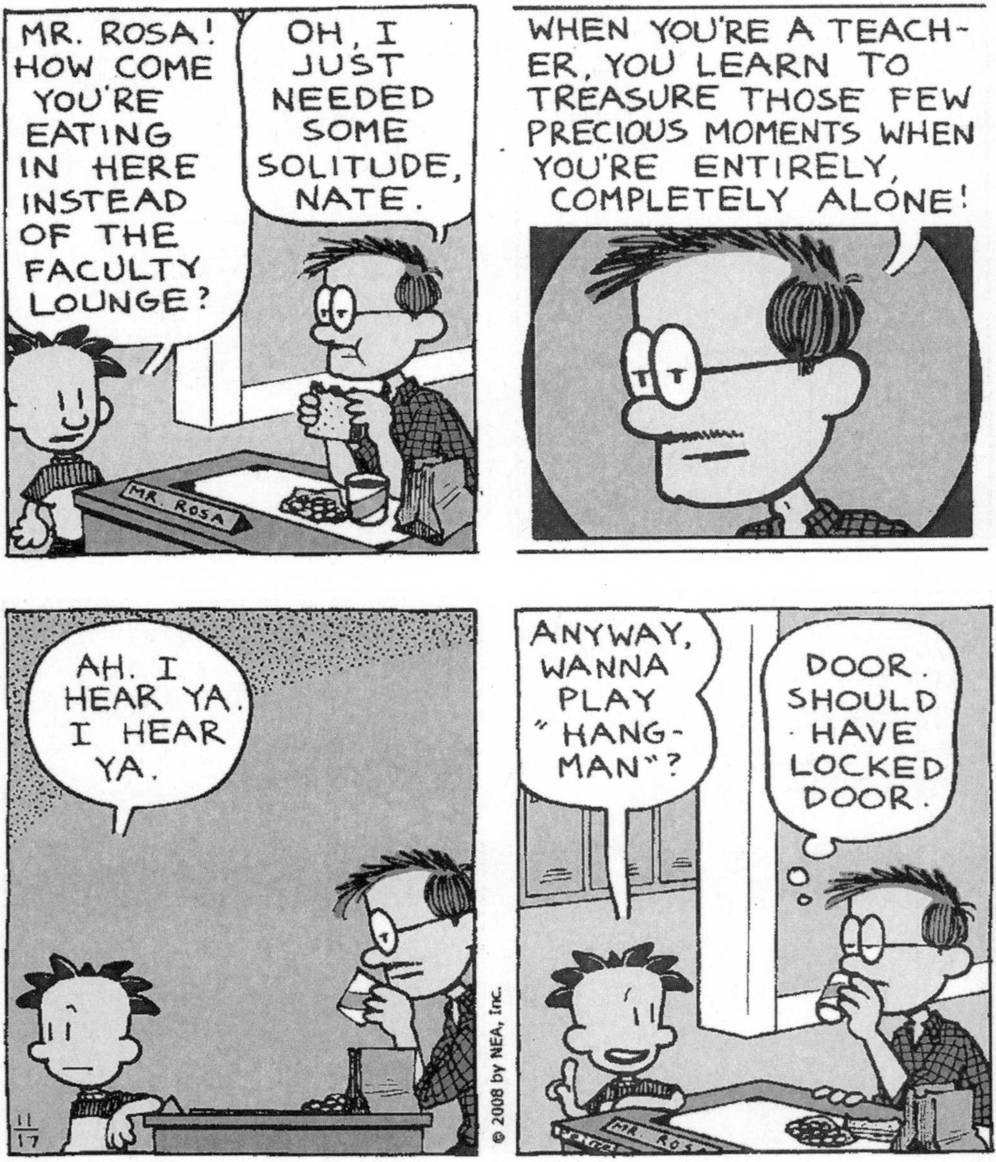
MR. ROSA! HOW COME YOU'RE EATING IN HERE INSTEAD OF THE FACULTY LOUNGE?
OH, I JUST NEEDED SOME SOLITUDE, NATE.
MR. ROSA
WHEN YOU'RE A TEACHER, YOU LEARN TO TREASURE THOSE FEW PRECIOUS MOMENTS WHEN YOU'RE ENTIRELY, COMPLETELY ALONE!
AH. I HEAR YA. I HEAR YA.
11/17
© 2008 by NEA, Inc.
ANYWAY, WANNA PLAY "HANGMAN"?
DOOR. SHOULD HAVE LOCKED DOOR.
MR. ROSA

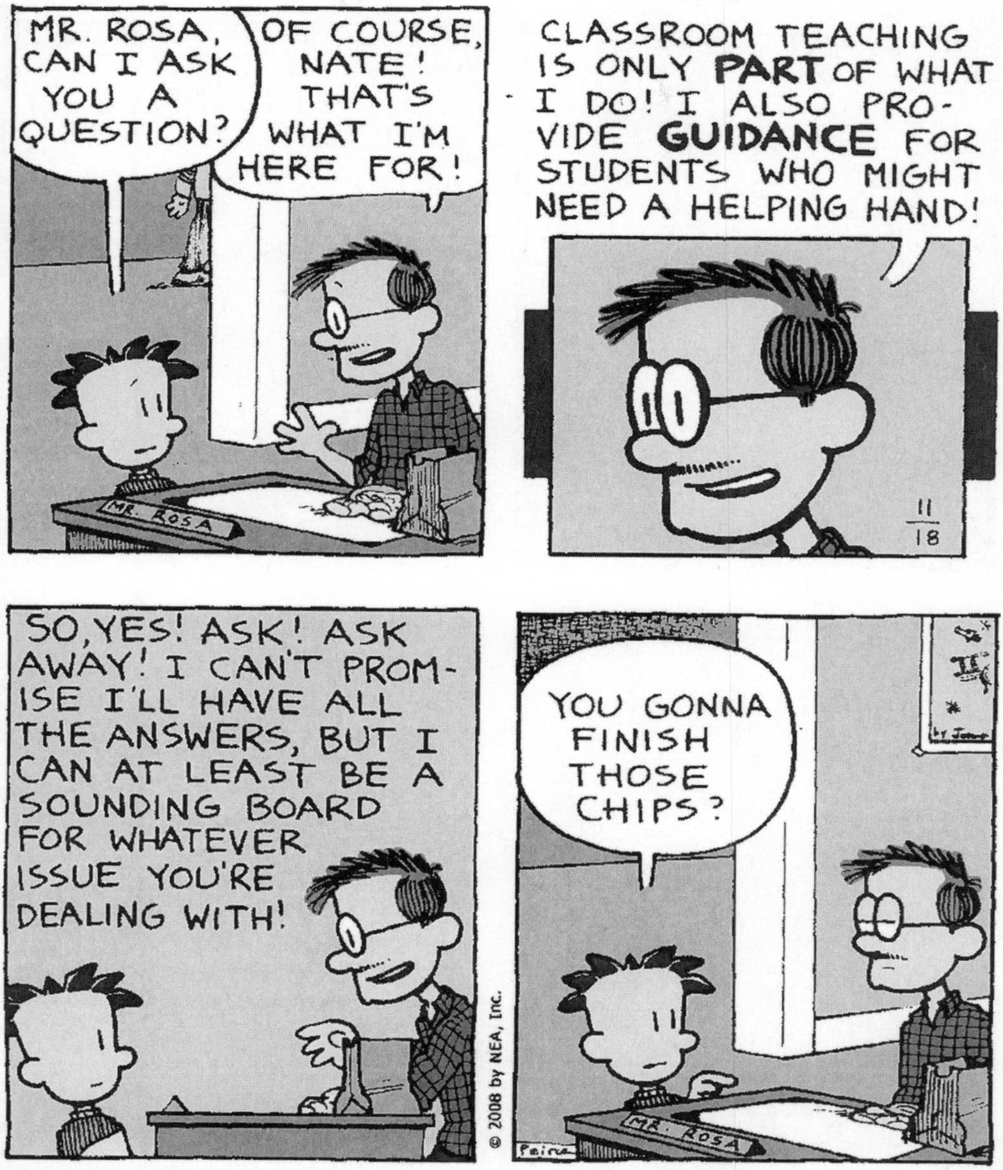
MR. ROSA, CAN I ASK YOU A QUESTION?
OF COURSE, NATE! THAT'S WHAT I'M HERE FOR!
MR. ROSA
CLASSROOM TEACHING IS ONLY PART OF WHAT I DO! I ALSO PROVIDE GUIDANCE FOR STUDENTS WHO MIGHT NEED A HELPING HAND!
11/18
SO, YES! ASK! ASK AWAY! I CAN'T PROMISE I'LL HAVE ALL THE ANSWERS, BUT I CAN AT LEAST BE A SOUNDING BOARD FOR WHATEVER ISSUE YOU'RE DEALING WITH!
© 2008 by NEA, Inc.
YOU GONNA FINISH THOSE CHIPS?
MR. ROSA

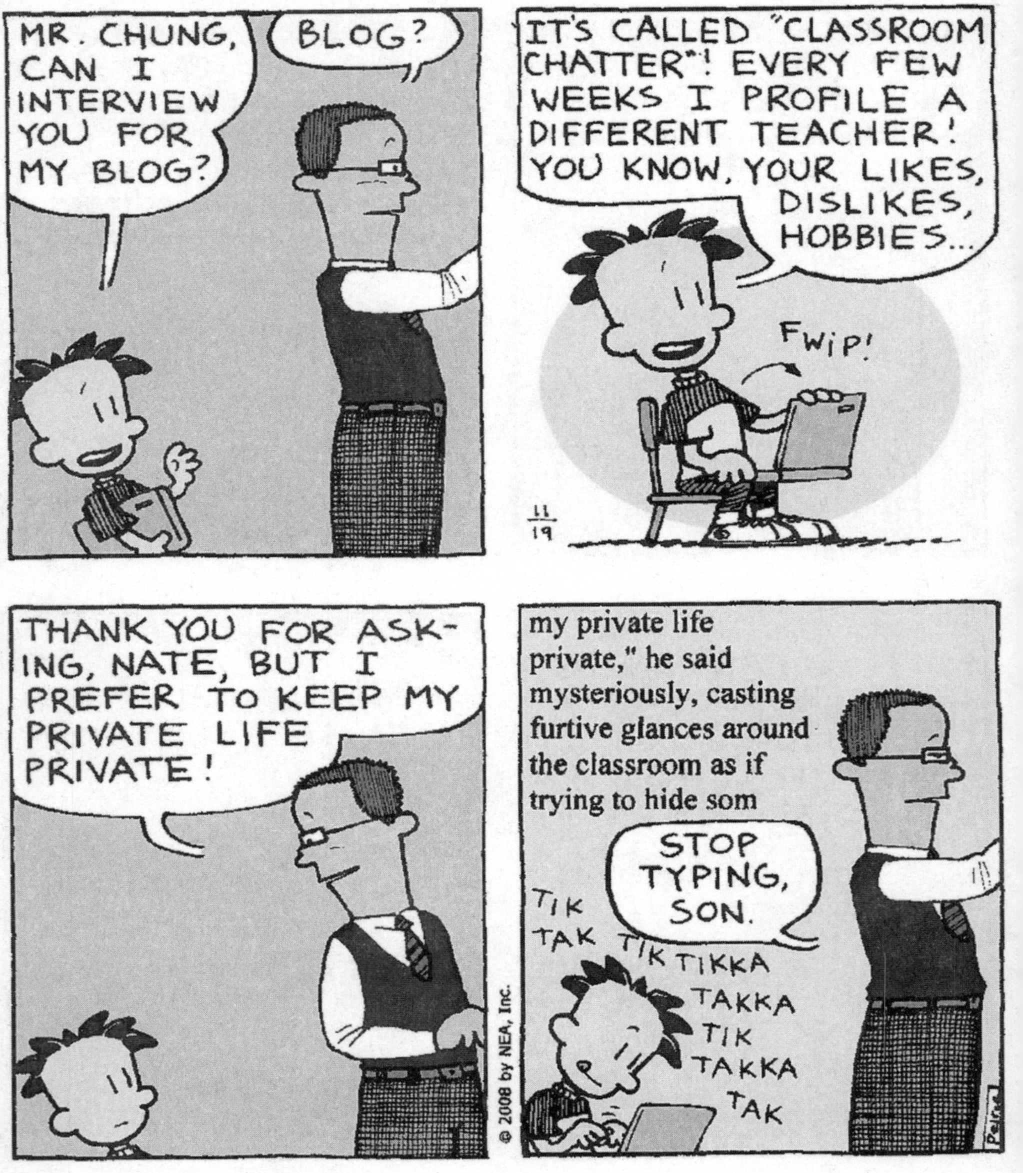
MR. CHUNG, CAN I INTERVIEW YOU FOR MY BLOG?
BLOG?
IT'S CALLED "CLASSROOM CHATTER"! EVERY FEW WEEKS I PROFILE A DIFFERENT TEACHER! YOU KNOW, YOUR LIKES, DISLIKES, HOBBIES...
FWIP!
11
19
THANK YOU FOR ASK-ING, NATE, BUT I PREFER TO KEEP MY PRIVATE LIFE PRIVATE!
my private life
private," he said
mysteriously, casting
furtive glances around
the classroom as if
trying to hide som
STOP TYPING, SON.
TIK TAK TIK TIKKA TAKKA TIK TAKKA TAK
Peirce

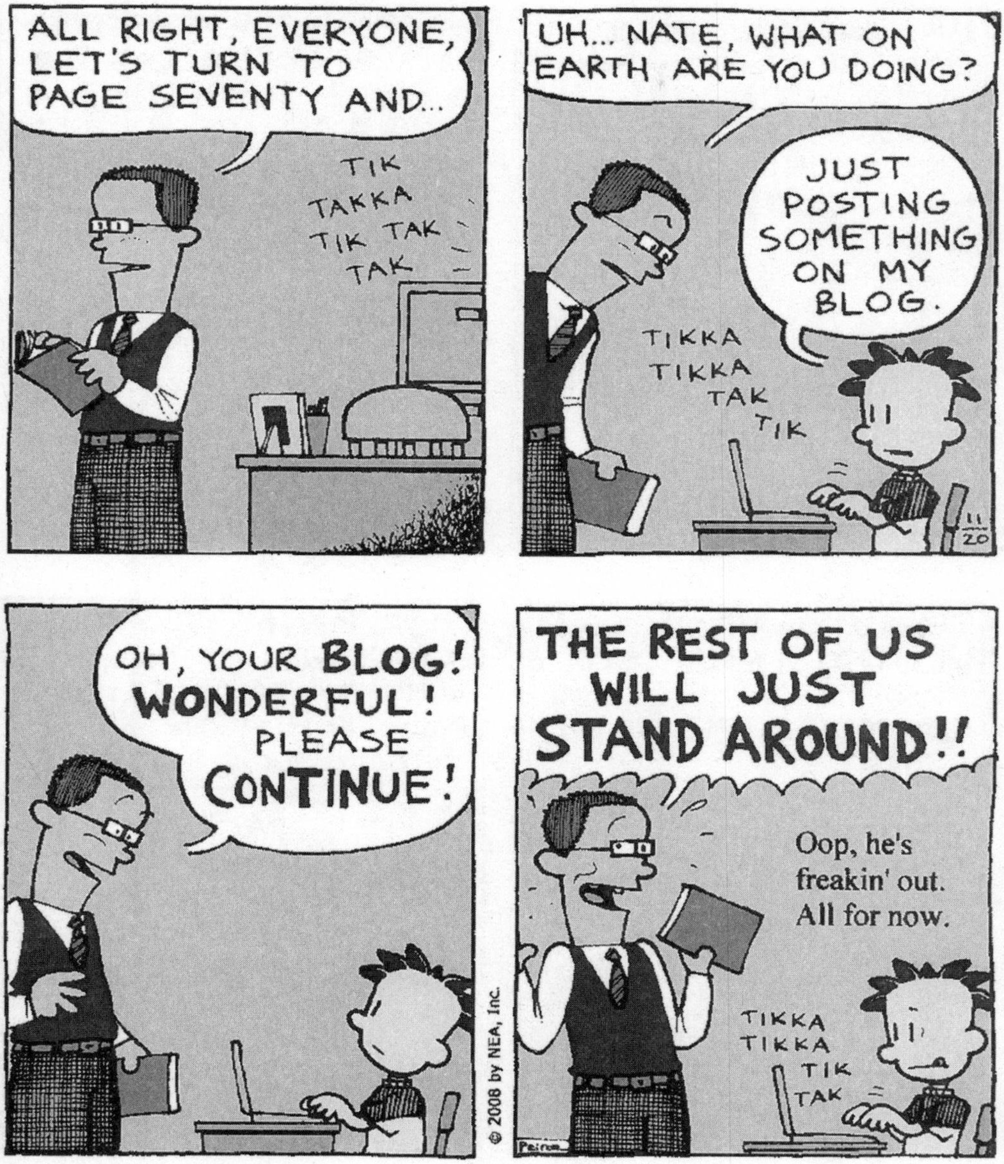
ALL RIGHT, EVERYONE, LET'S TURN TO PAGE SEVENTY AND...
TIK TAKKA TIK TAK TAK
UH... NATE, WHAT ON EARTH ARE YOU DOING?
JUST POSTING SOMETHING ON MY BLOG.
TIKKA TIKKA TAK TIK
11 20
OH, YOUR BLOG! WONDERFUL! PLEASE CONTINUE!
THE REST OF US WILL JUST STAND AROUND!!
Oop, he's freakin' out. All for now.
TIKKA TIKKA TIK TAK
Peirce
© 2008 by NEA, Inc.

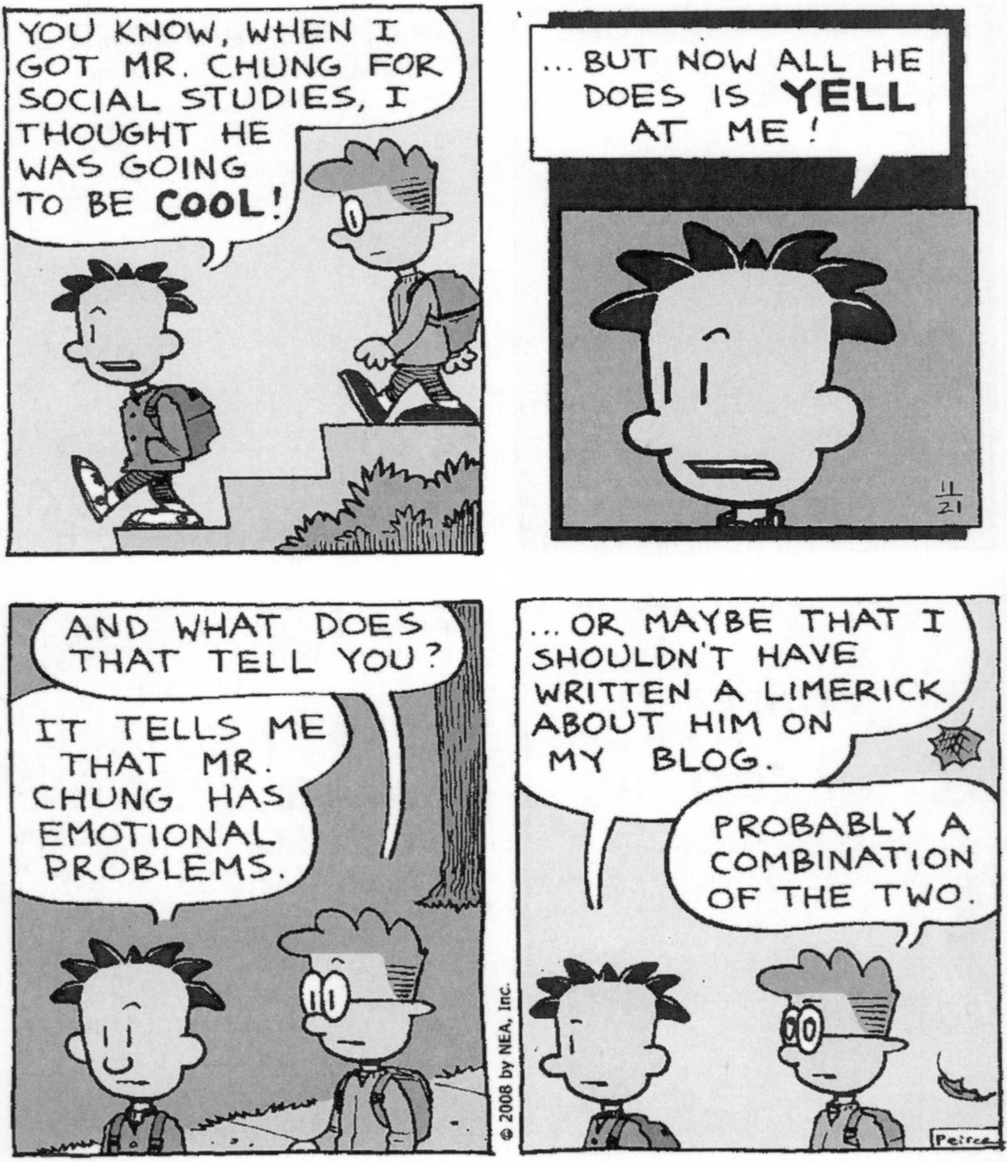

YOU KNOW, WHEN I GOT MR. CHUNG FOR SOCIAL STUDIES, I THOUGHT HE WAS GOING TO BE COOL!
...BUT NOW ALL HE DOES IS YELL AT ME!
11/21
AND WHAT DOES THAT TELL YOU?
IT TELLS ME THAT MR. CHUNG HAS EMOTIONAL PROBLEMS.
© 2008 by NEA, Inc.
...OR MAYBE THAT I SHOULDN'T HAVE WRITTEN A LIMERICK ABOUT HIM ON MY BLOG.
PROBABLY A COMBINATION OF THE TWO.
Peirce

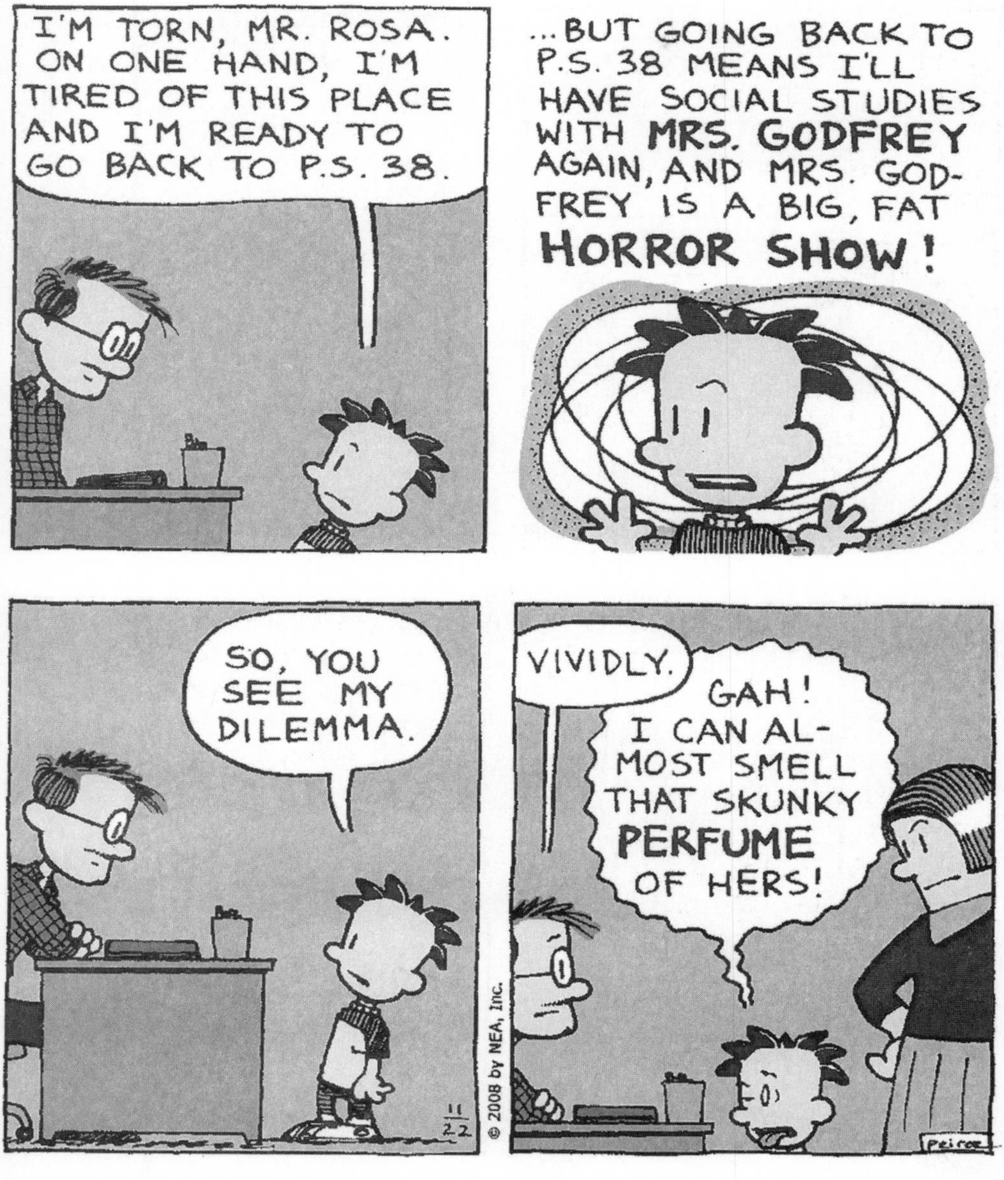
I'M TORN, MR. ROSA. ON ONE HAND, I'M TIRED OF THIS PLACE AND I'M READY TO GO BACK TO P.S. 38.
...BUT GOING BACK TO P.S. 38 MEANS I'LL HAVE SOCIAL STUDIES WITH MRS. GODFREY AGAIN, AND MRS. GODFREY IS A BIG, FAT HORROR SHOW!
SO, YOU SEE MY DILEMMA.
VIVIDLY.
GAH! I CAN ALMOST SMELL THAT SKUNKY PERFUME OF HERS!
© 2008 by NEA, Inc.

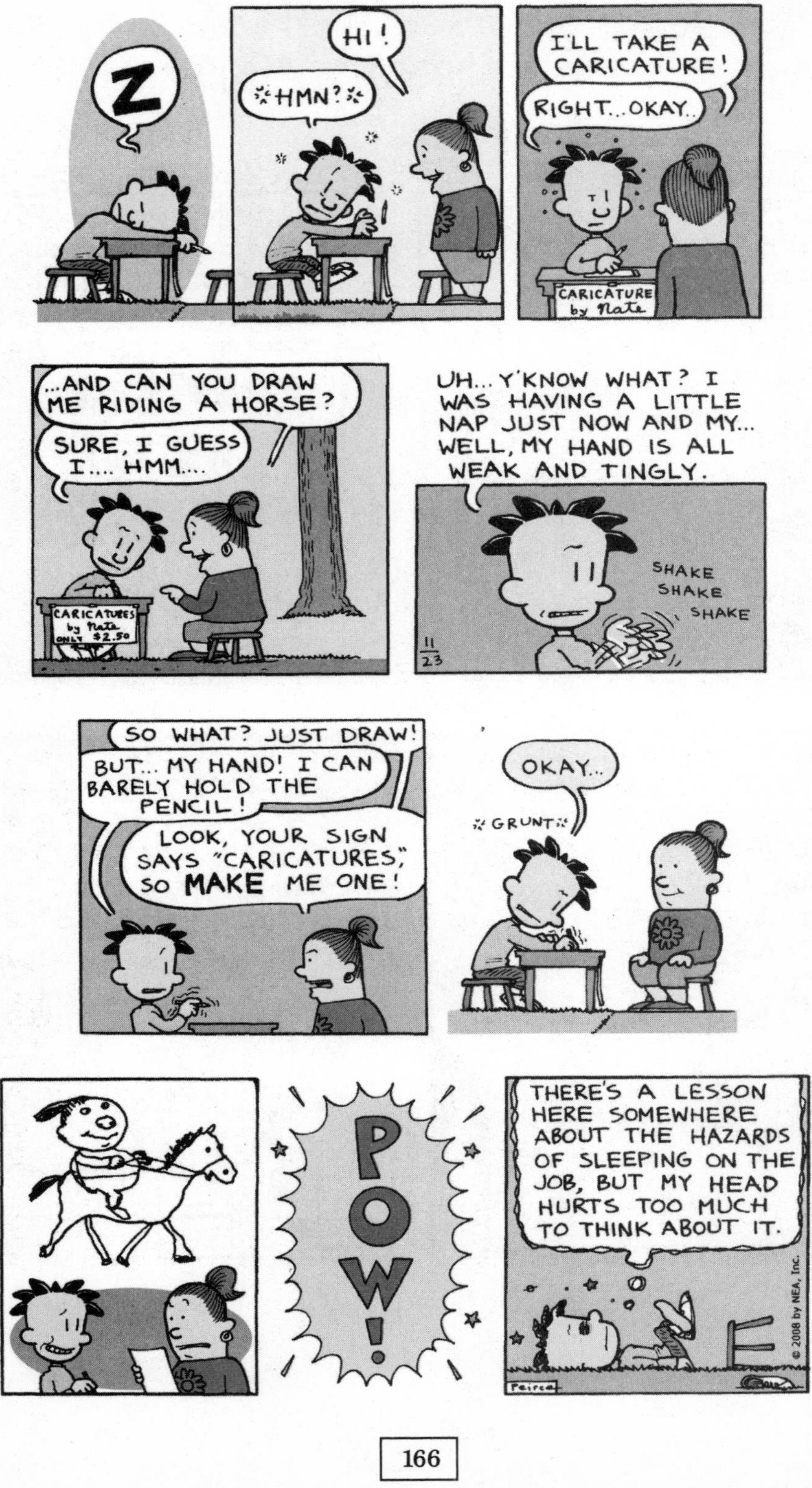
Z
HI!
HMN?
I'LL TAKE A CARICATURE!
RIGHT... OKAY..
CARICATURE by Nate
...AND CAN YOU DRAW ME RIDING A HORSE?
SURE, I GUESS I.... HMM....
CARICATURES by Nate ONLY $2.50
UH... Y'KNOW WHAT? I WAS HAVING A LITTLE NAP JUST NOW AND MY... WELL, MY HAND IS ALL WEAK AND TINGLY.
SHAKE SHAKE SHAKE
11 23
SO WHAT? JUST DRAW!
BUT... MY HAND! I CAN BARELY HOLD THE PENCIL!
LOOK, YOUR SIGN SAYS "CARICATURES," SO MAKE ME ONE!
OKAY...
GRUNT
POW!
THERE'S A LESSON HERE SOMEWHERE ABOUT THE HAZARDS OF SLEEPING ON THE JOB, BUT MY HEAD HURTS TOO MUCH TO THINK ABOUT IT.
© 2008 by NEA, Inc.
Peirce

NATE'S "FIRST" THANKSGIVING

MR. CHUNG, INSTEAD OF **WRITING** MY REPORT ON THE FIRST THANKSGIVING, CAN I DO IT IN COMIC BOOK FORMAT?

HM. I DON'T KNOW, NATE.

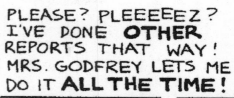

PLEASE? PLEEEEEZ? I'VE DONE **OTHER** REPORTS THAT WAY! MRS. GODFREY LETS ME DO IT **ALL THE TIME!**

WHOA. HOLD IT. I JUST... ✂KOFF!✂... I JUST USED **MRS. GODFREY** AS AN EXAMPLE OF THE WAY A TEACHER SHOULD DO THINGS!

11/24

© 2008 by NEA, Inc.

FEELING QUEASY... CALL THE SCHOOL NURSE...

...OR PERHAPS THE DRAMA TEACHER.

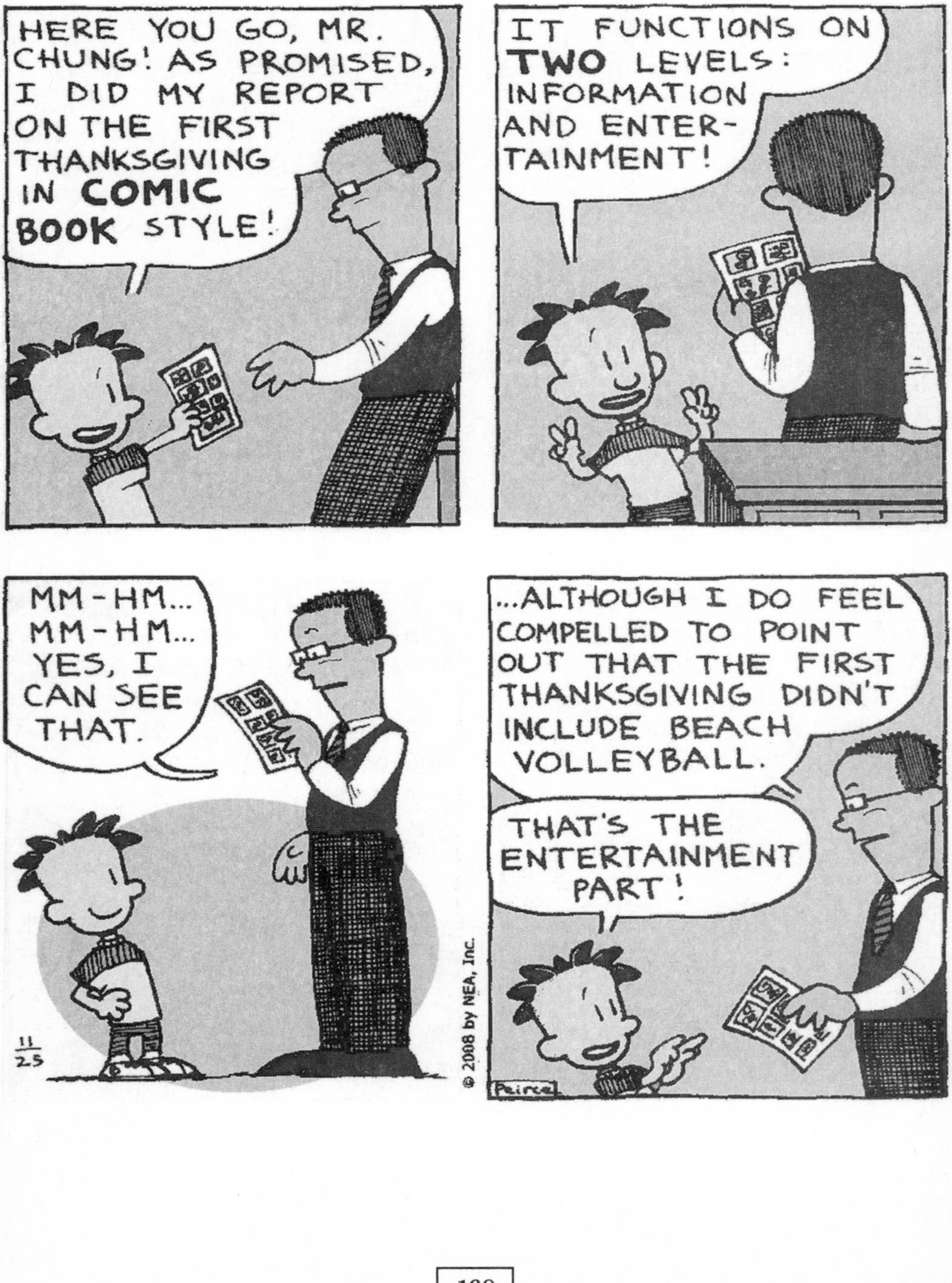
HERE YOU GO, MR. CHUNG! AS PROMISED, I DID MY REPORT ON THE FIRST THANKSGIVING IN **COMIC BOOK** STYLE!
IT FUNCTIONS ON **TWO** LEVELS: INFORMATION AND ENTER-TAINMENT!
MM-HM... MM-HM... YES, I CAN SEE THAT.
11
25
© 2008 by NEA, Inc.
...ALTHOUGH I DO FEEL COMPELLED TO POINT OUT THAT THE FIRST THANKSGIVING DIDN'T INCLUDE BEACH VOLLEYBALL.
THAT'S THE ENTERTAINMENT PART!
Peirce

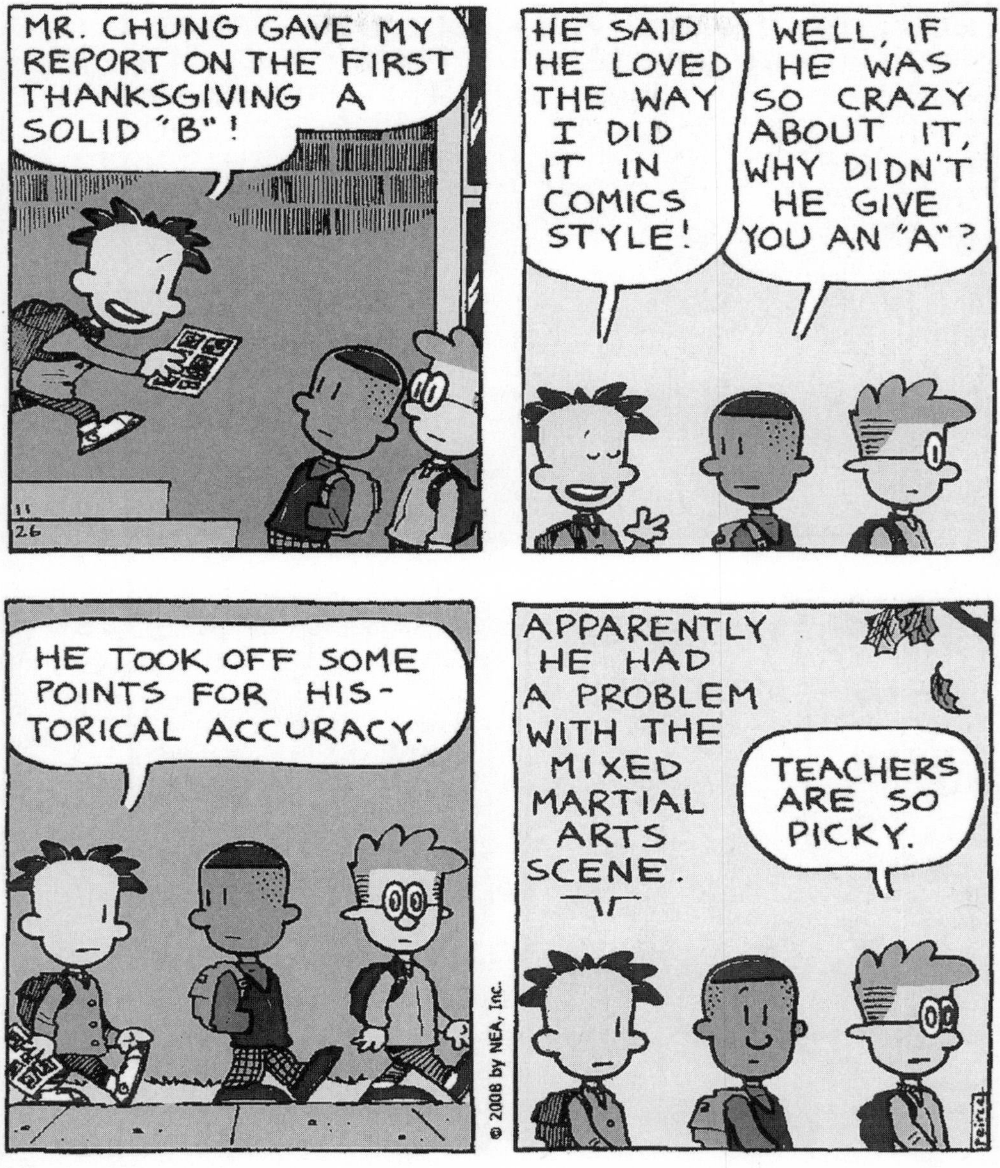
MR. CHUNG GAVE MY REPORT ON THE FIRST THANKSGIVING A SOLID "B"!
11 26
HE SAID HE LOVED THE WAY I DID IT IN COMICS STYLE!
WELL, IF HE WAS SO CRAZY ABOUT IT, WHY DIDN'T HE GIVE YOU AN "A"?
HE TOOK OFF SOME POINTS FOR HIS-TORICAL ACCURACY.
© 2008 by NEA, Inc.
APPARENTLY HE HAD A PROBLEM WITH THE MIXED MARTIAL ARTS SCENE.
TEACHERS ARE SO PICKY.
Peirce

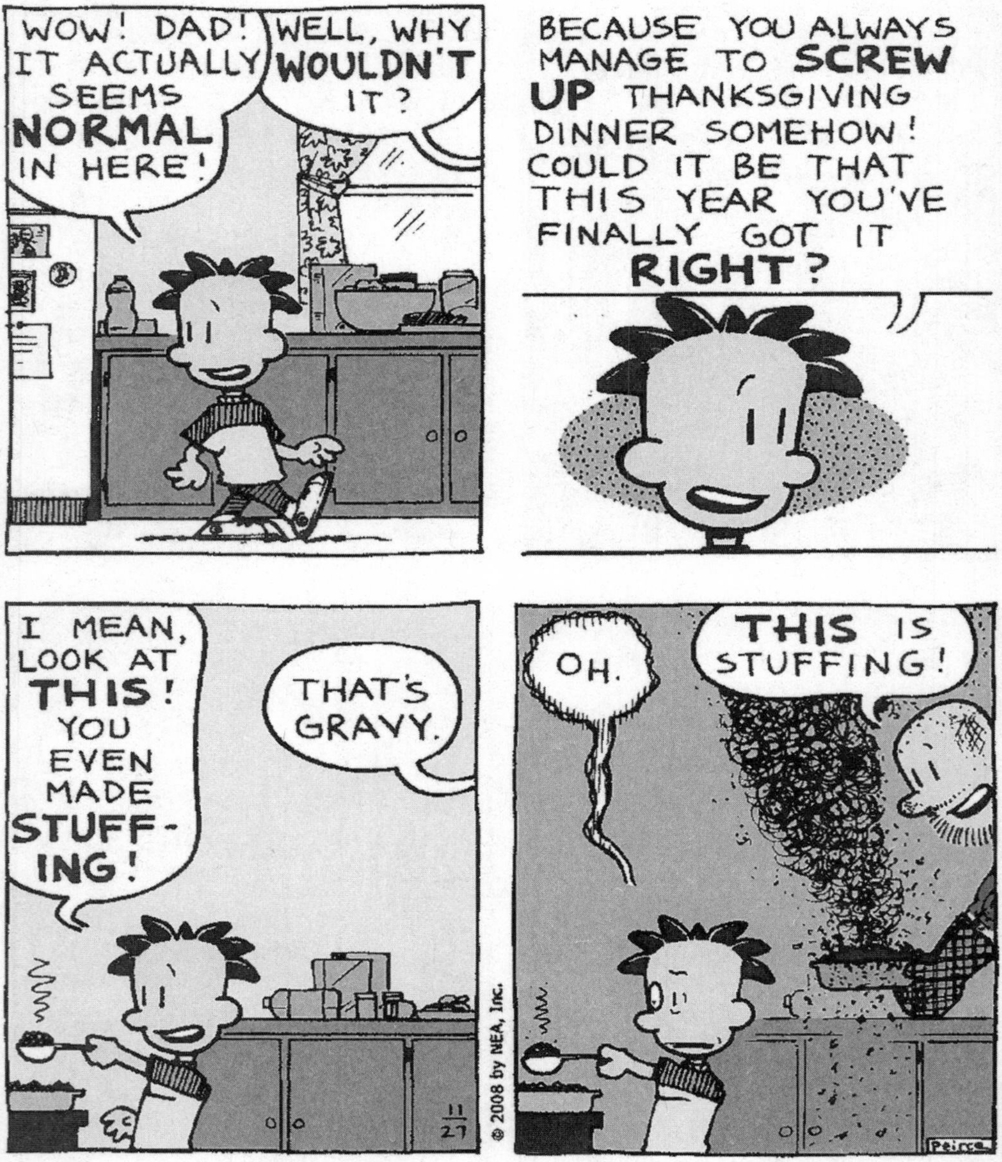
WOW! DAD! IT ACTUALLY SEEMS NORMAL IN HERE!
WELL, WHY WOULDN'T IT?
BECAUSE YOU ALWAYS MANAGE TO SCREW UP THANKSGIVING DINNER SOMEHOW! COULD IT BE THAT THIS YEAR YOU'VE FINALLY GOT IT RIGHT?
I MEAN, LOOK AT THIS! YOU EVEN MADE STUFF-ING!
THAT'S GRAVY.
11 27
© 2008 by NEA, Inc.
OH.
THIS IS STUFFING!
Peirce

OH, THE PAIN!

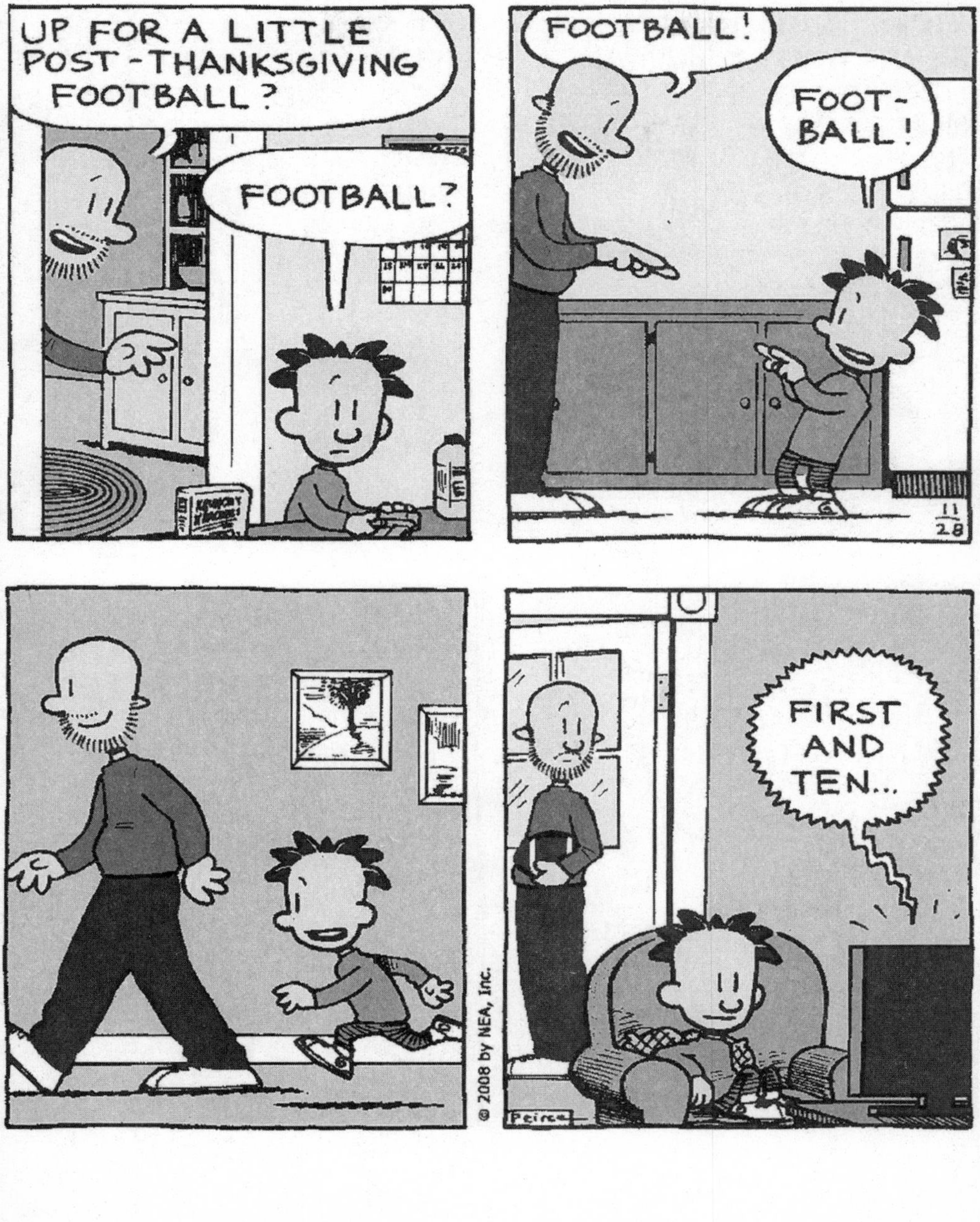
UP FOR A LITTLE POST-THANKSGIVING FOOTBALL?
FOOTBALL?
FOOTBALL!
FOOT-BALL!
11 28
© 2008 by NEA, Inc.
FIRST AND TEN...
Peirce

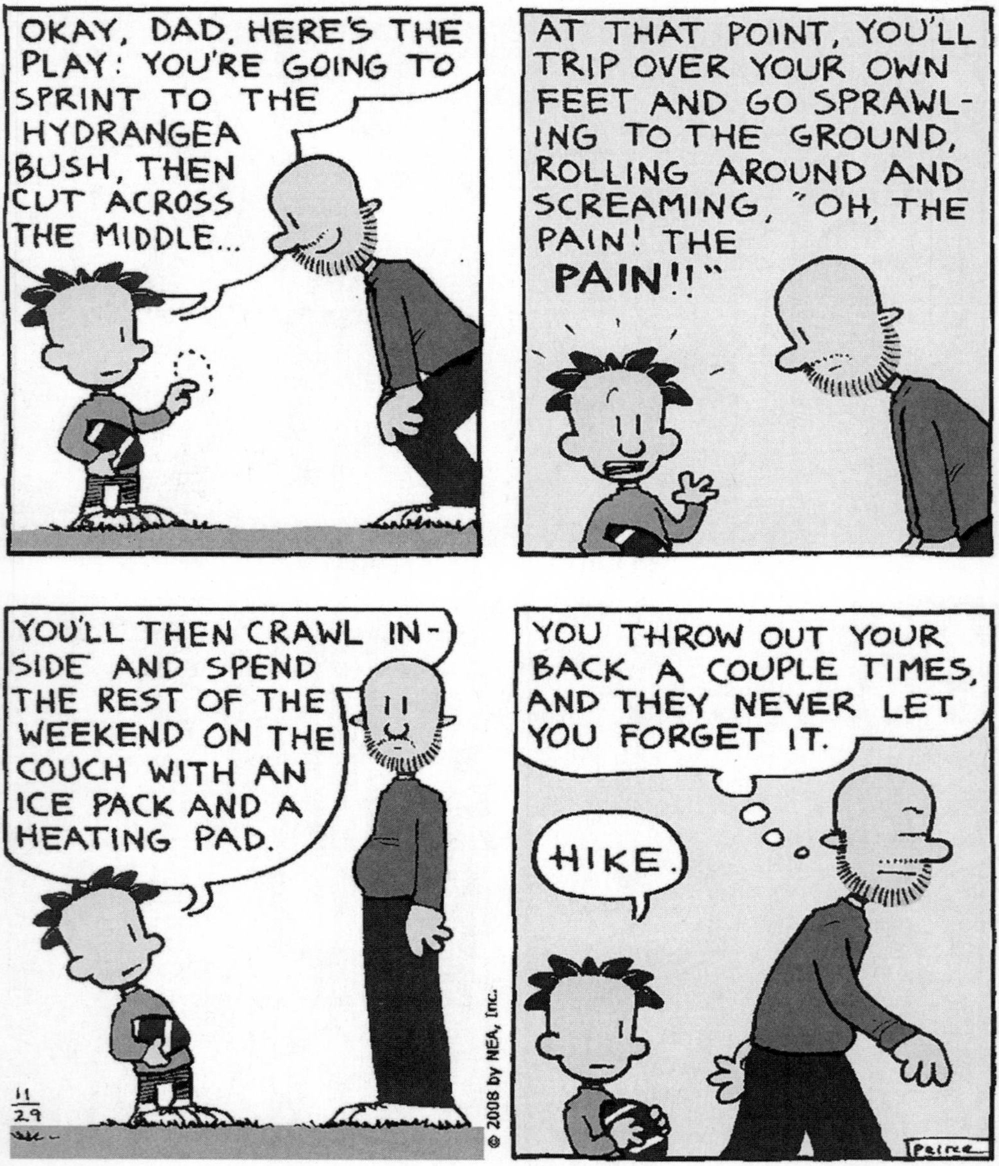
OKAY, DAD. HERE'S THE PLAY: YOU'RE GOING TO SPRINT TO THE HYDRANGEA BUSH, THEN CUT ACROSS THE MIDDLE...
AT THAT POINT, YOU'LL TRIP OVER YOUR OWN FEET AND GO SPRAWLING TO THE GROUND, ROLLING AROUND AND SCREAMING, "OH, THE PAIN! THE PAIN!!"
YOU'LL THEN CRAWL INSIDE AND SPEND THE REST OF THE WEEKEND ON THE COUCH WITH AN ICE PACK AND A HEATING PAD.
11/29
© 2008 by NEA, Inc.
YOU THROW OUT YOUR BACK A COUPLE TIMES, AND THEY NEVER LET YOU FORGET IT.
HIKE.
PEIRCE

THE MEANING OF WOOF

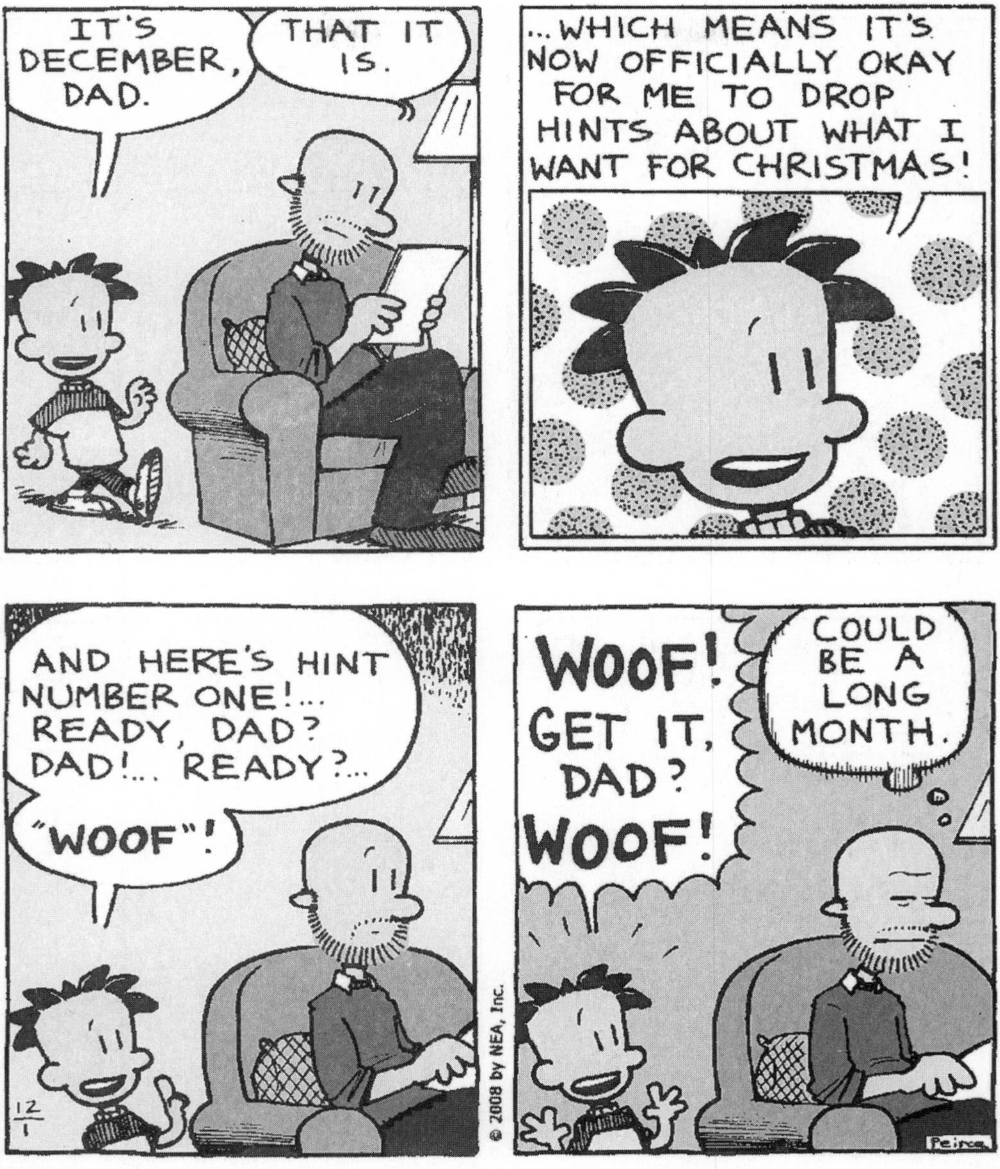
IT'S DECEMBER, DAD.
THAT IT IS.
...WHICH MEANS IT'S NOW OFFICIALLY OKAY FOR ME TO DROP HINTS ABOUT WHAT I WANT FOR CHRISTMAS!
AND HERE'S HINT NUMBER ONE!... READY, DAD? DAD!... READY?... "WOOF"!
12/1
© 2008 by NEA, Inc.
WOOF! GET IT, DAD? WOOF!
COULD BE A LONG MONTH.
Peirce

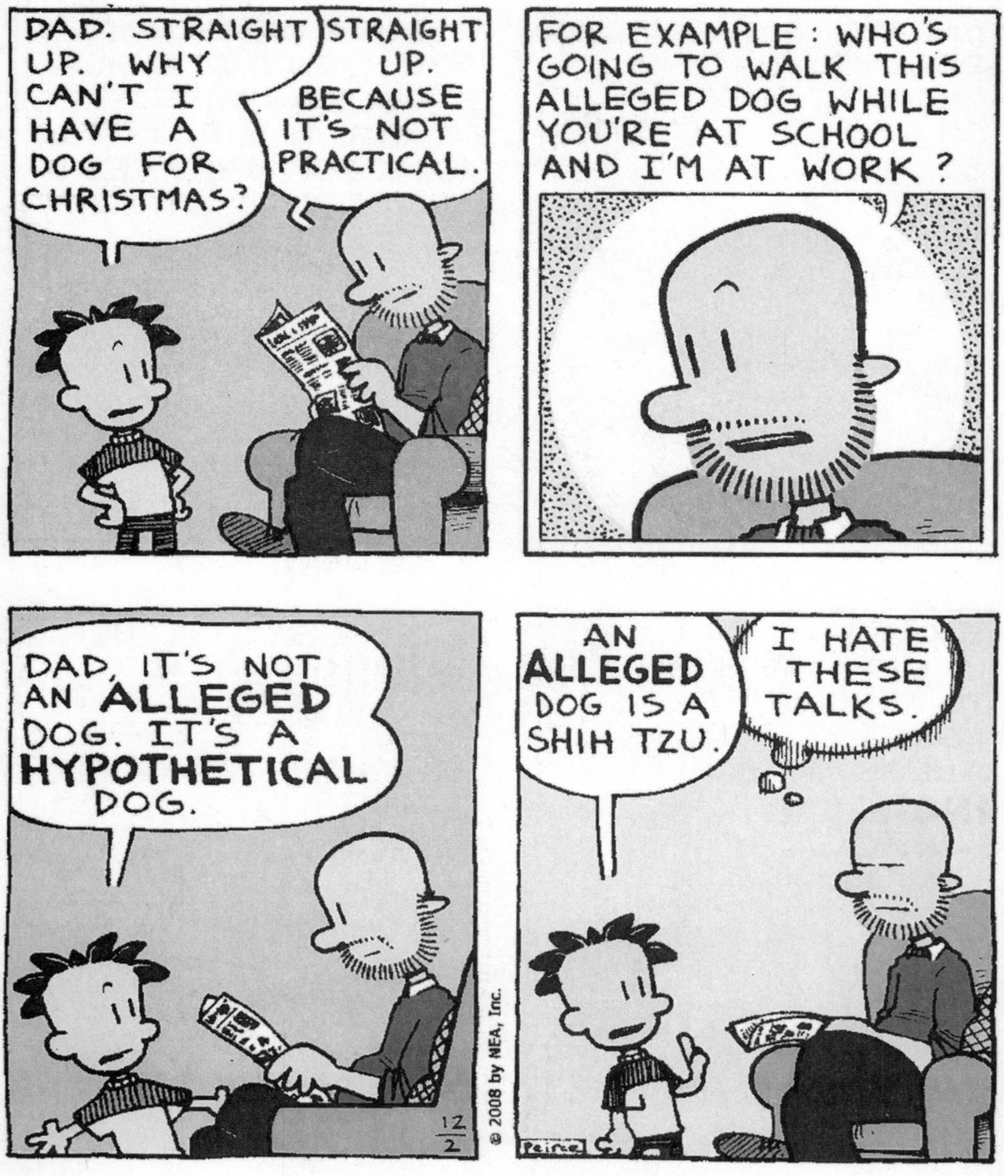
DAD. STRAIGHT UP. WHY CAN'T I HAVE A DOG FOR CHRISTMAS?
STRAIGHT UP. BECAUSE IT'S NOT PRACTICAL.
FOR EXAMPLE: WHO'S GOING TO WALK THIS ALLEGED DOG WHILE YOU'RE AT SCHOOL AND I'M AT WORK?
DAD, IT'S NOT AN **ALLEGED** DOG. IT'S A **HYPOTHETICAL** DOG.
12/2
© 2008 by NEA, Inc.
AN **ALLEGED** DOG IS A SHIH TZU.
I HATE THESE TALKS.
Peirce

DAD! INSTEAD OF ASKING FOR A DOG AS A CHRISTMAS GIFT, HOW 'BOUT I JUST BUY A DOG WITH MY ALLOWANCE MONEY?
NATE...
YOUR ALLOWANCE ISN'T SUFFICIENT TO BUY A DOG, LET ALONE FEED IT AND PAY FOR ITS MEDICAL EXPENSES!
EXACTLY! WHICH IS WHY IT'S TIME TO DISCUSS A LONG-OVERDUE ALLOWANCE INCREASE!
LET US TURN OUR ATTENTION TO CHART NUMBER ONE...
SIGH.
12-3
© 2008 by NEA, Inc.
Peirce

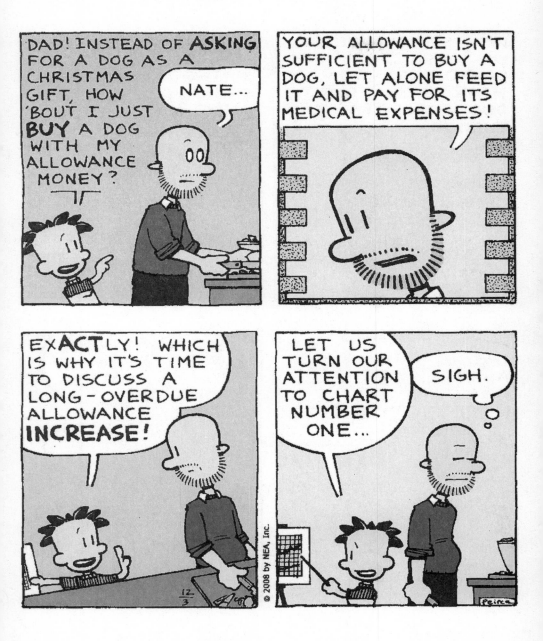

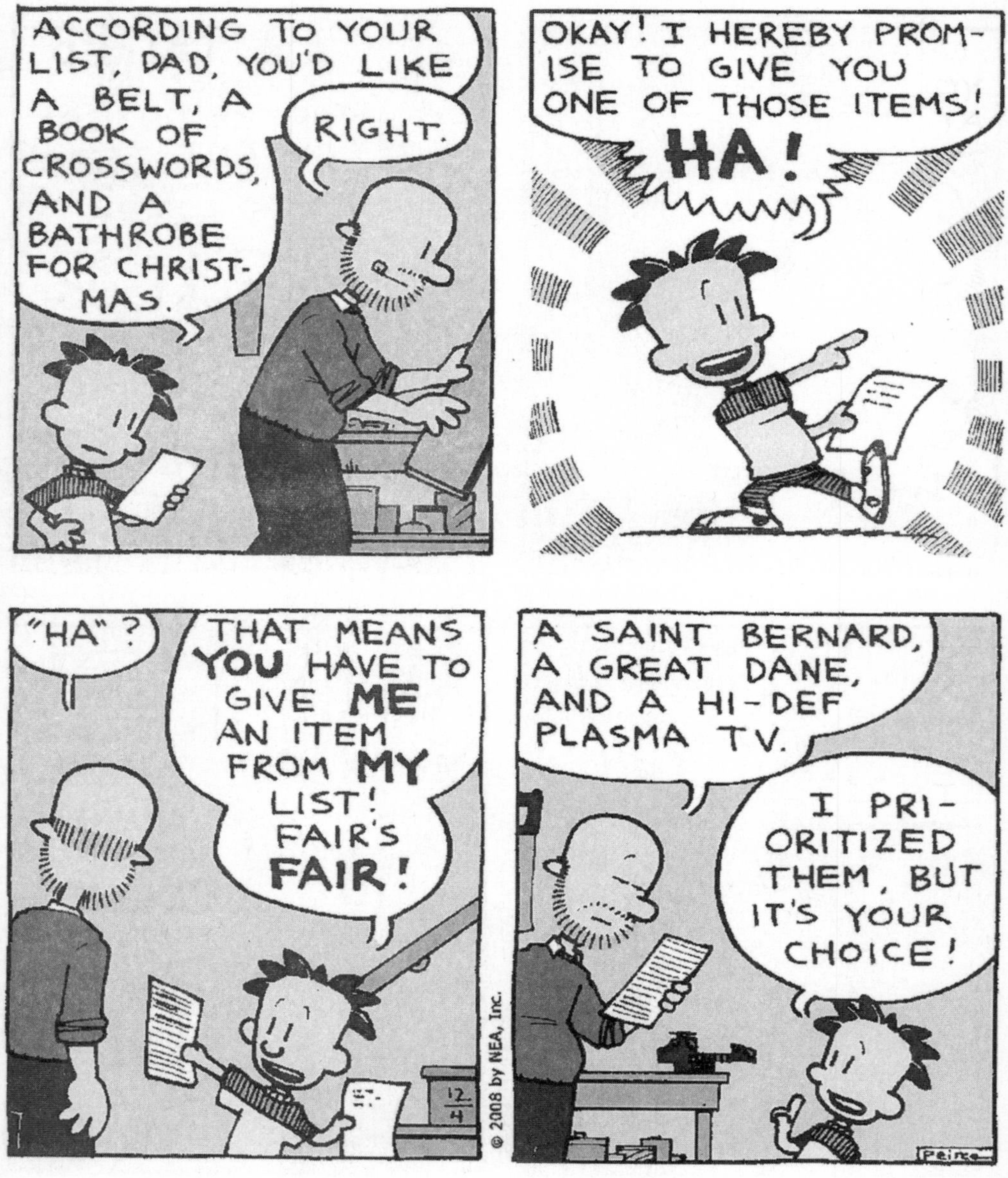
ACCORDING TO YOUR LIST, DAD, YOU'D LIKE A BELT, A BOOK OF CROSSWORDS, AND A BATHROBE FOR CHRISTMAS.
RIGHT.
OKAY! I HEREBY PROMISE TO GIVE YOU ONE OF THOSE ITEMS!
HA!
"HA"?
THAT MEANS YOU HAVE TO GIVE ME AN ITEM FROM MY LIST! FAIR'S FAIR!
12/4
© 2008 by NEA, Inc.
A SAINT BERNARD, A GREAT DANE, AND A HI-DEF PLASMA TV.
I PRIORITIZED THEM, BUT IT'S YOUR CHOICE!
Peirce

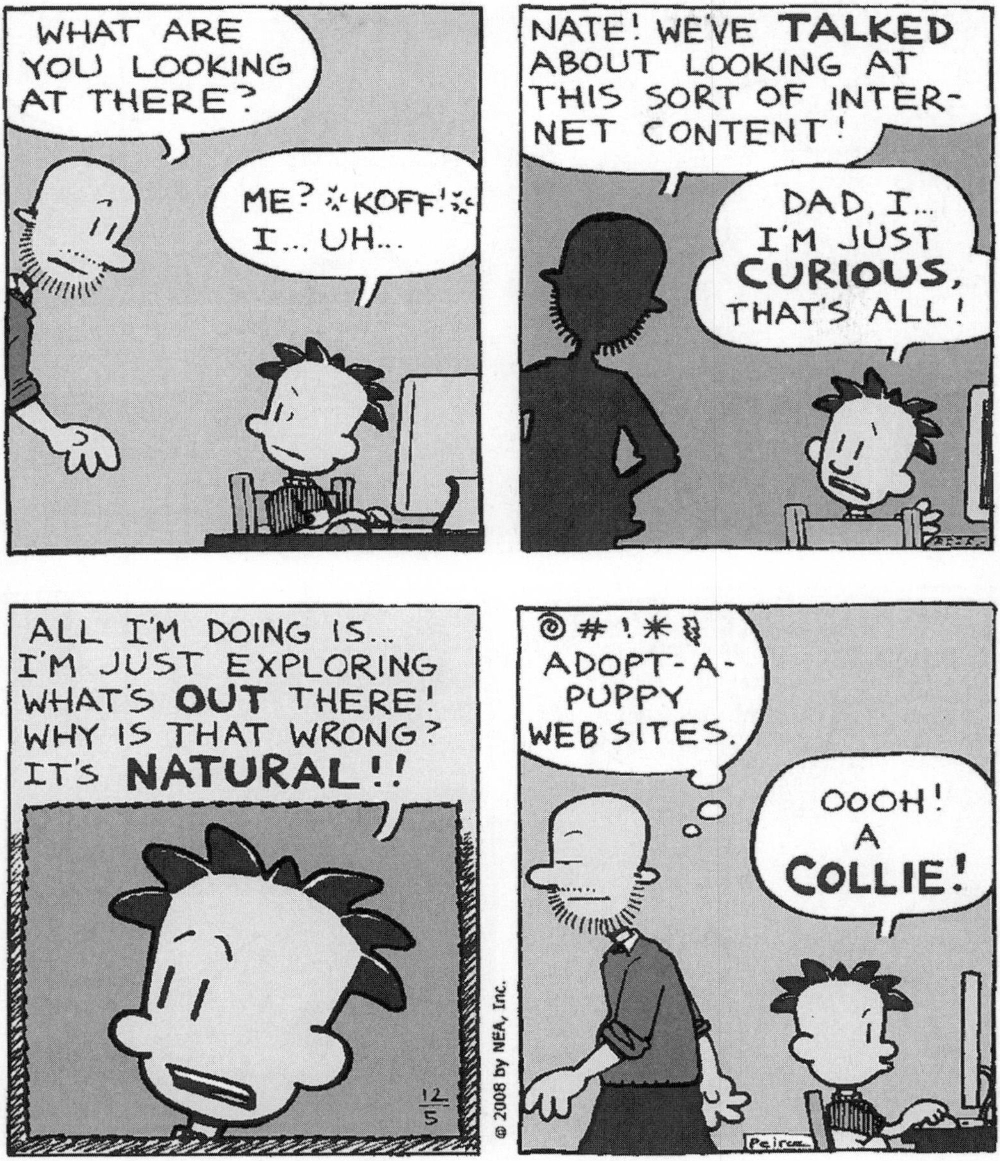
WHAT ARE YOU LOOKING AT THERE?
ME? *KOFF!* I... UH...
NATE! WE'VE **TALKED** ABOUT LOOKING AT THIS SORT OF INTER-NET CONTENT!
DAD, I... I'M JUST **CURIOUS**, THAT'S ALL!
ALL I'M DOING IS... I'M JUST EXPLORING WHAT'S **OUT** THERE! WHY IS THAT WRONG? IT'S **NATURAL**!!
12/5
© 2008 by NEA, Inc.
@#!*
ADOPT-A-PUPPY WEB SITES.
OOOH! A **COLLIE**!
Peirce

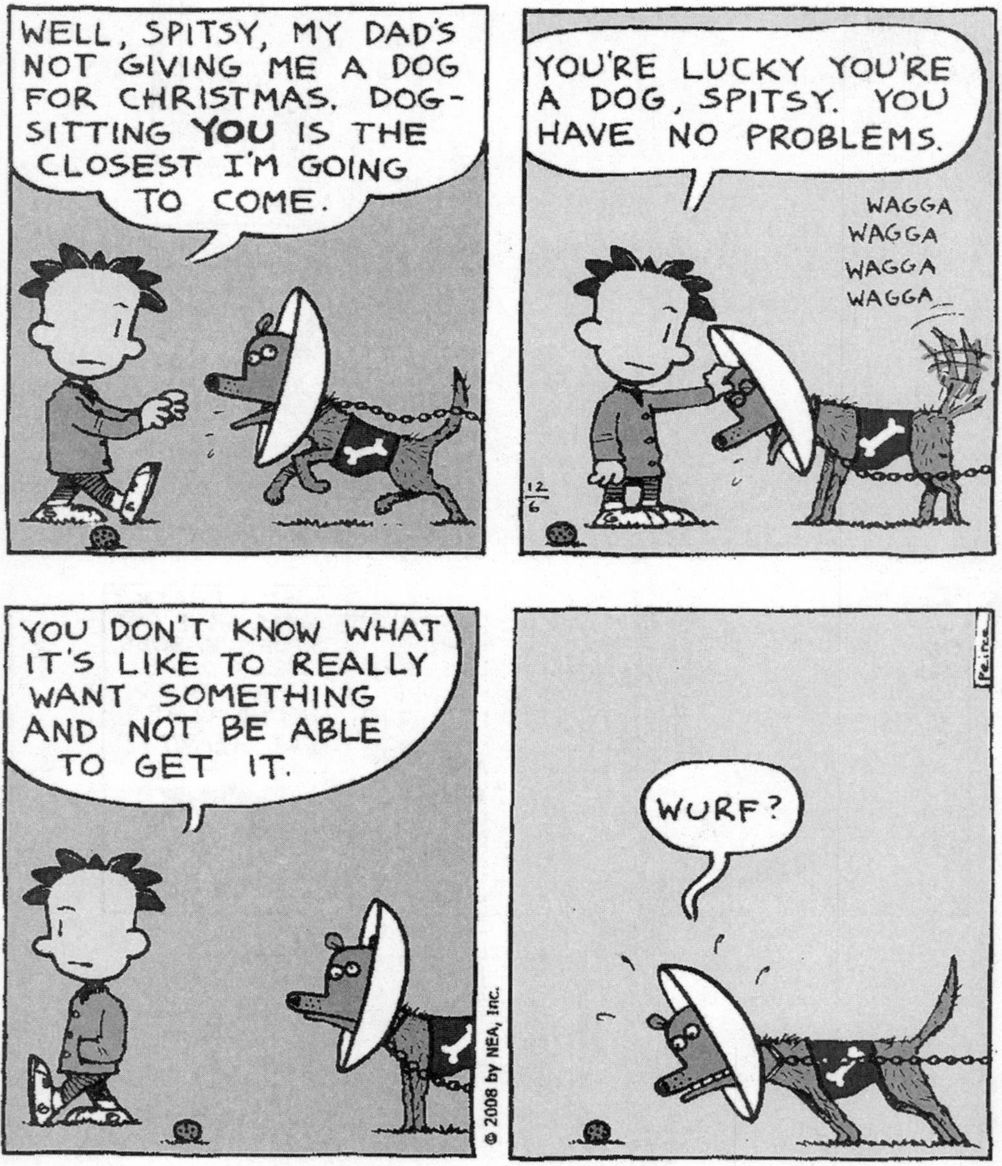
WELL, SPITSY, MY DAD'S NOT GIVING ME A DOG FOR CHRISTMAS. DOG-SITTING **YOU** IS THE CLOSEST I'M GOING TO COME.
YOU'RE LUCKY YOU'RE A DOG, SPITSY. YOU HAVE NO PROBLEMS.
WAGGA WAGGA WAGGA WAGGA
12/6
YOU DON'T KNOW WHAT IT'S LIKE TO REALLY WANT SOMETHING AND NOT BE ABLE TO GET IT.
© 2008 by NEA, Inc.
Peirce
WURF?

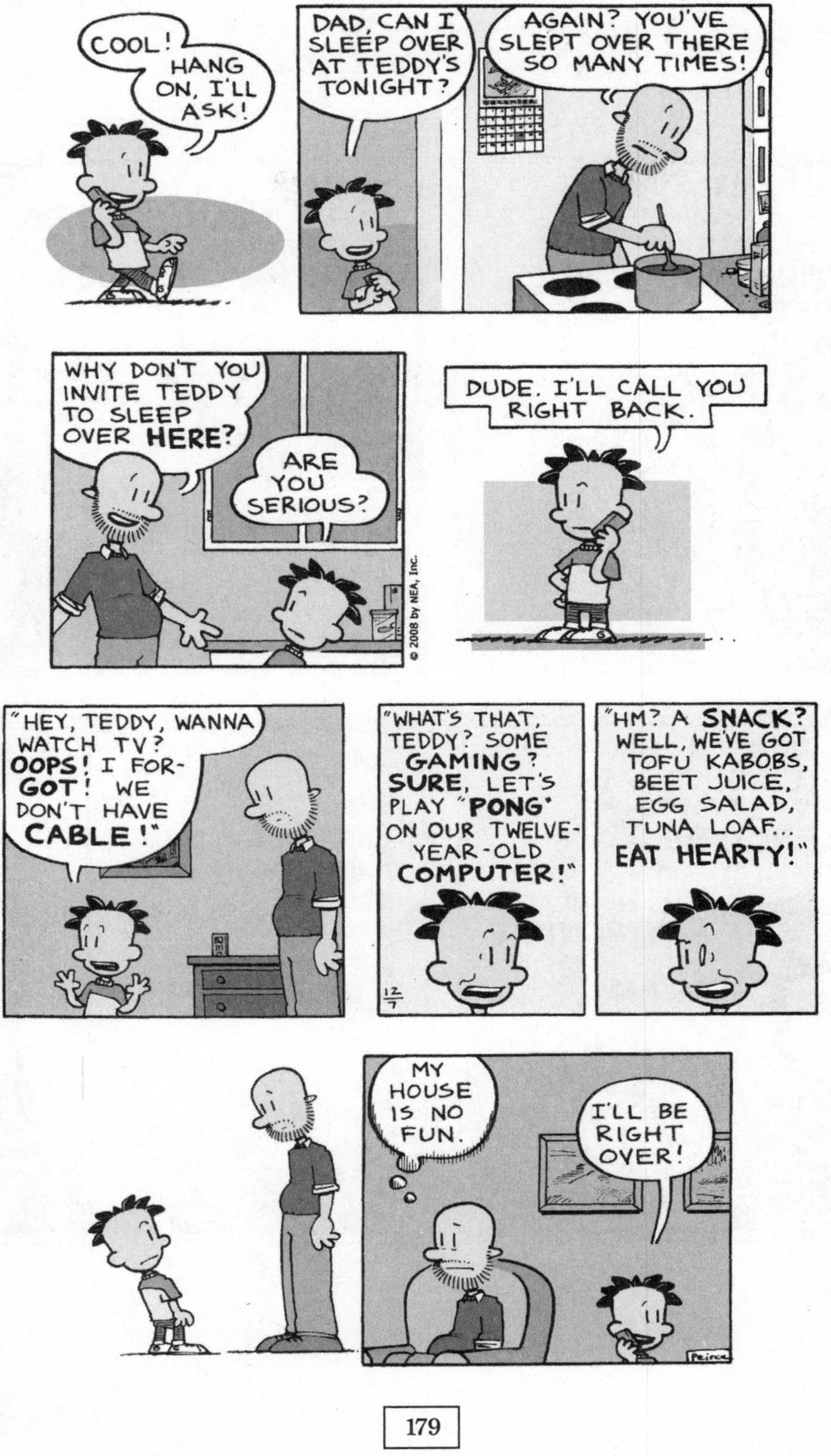
COOL! HANG ON, I'LL ASK!
DAD, CAN I SLEEP OVER AT TEDDY'S TONIGHT?
AGAIN? YOU'VE SLEPT OVER THERE SO MANY TIMES!
WHY DON'T YOU INVITE TEDDY TO SLEEP OVER HERE?
ARE YOU SERIOUS?
© 2008 by NEA, Inc.
DUDE. I'LL CALL YOU RIGHT BACK.
"HEY, TEDDY, WANNA WATCH TV? OOPS! I FORGOT! WE DON'T HAVE CABLE!"
"WHAT'S THAT, TEDDY? SOME GAMING? SURE, LET'S PLAY "PONG" ON OUR TWELVE-YEAR-OLD COMPUTER!"
12/7
"HM? A SNACK? WELL, WE'VE GOT TOFU KABOBS, BEET JUICE, EGG SALAD, TUNA LOAF... EAT HEARTY!"
MY HOUSE IS NO FUN.
I'LL BE RIGHT OVER!
Peirce

KISS THIS JOINT GOOD-BYE!

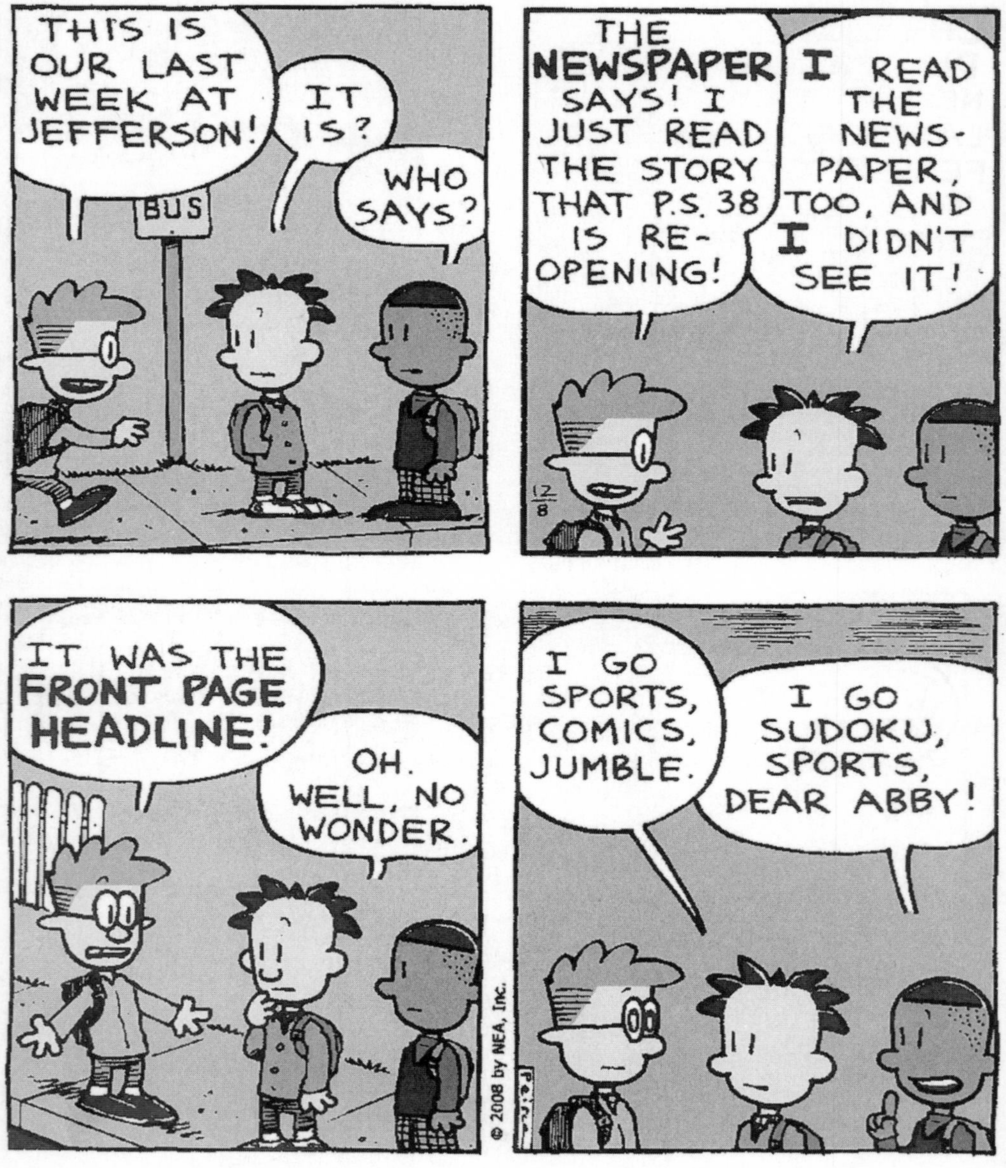

THIS IS OUR LAST WEEK AT JEFFERSON!
IT IS?
WHO SAYS?
BUS
THE NEWSPAPER SAYS! I JUST READ THE STORY THAT P.S. 38 IS RE-OPENING!
I READ THE NEWS-PAPER, TOO, AND I DIDN'T SEE IT!
12/8
IT WAS THE FRONT PAGE HEADLINE!
OH. WELL, NO WONDER.
I GO SPORTS, COMICS, JUMBLE.
I GO SUDOKU, SPORTS, DEAR ABBY!
© 2008 by NEA, Inc.

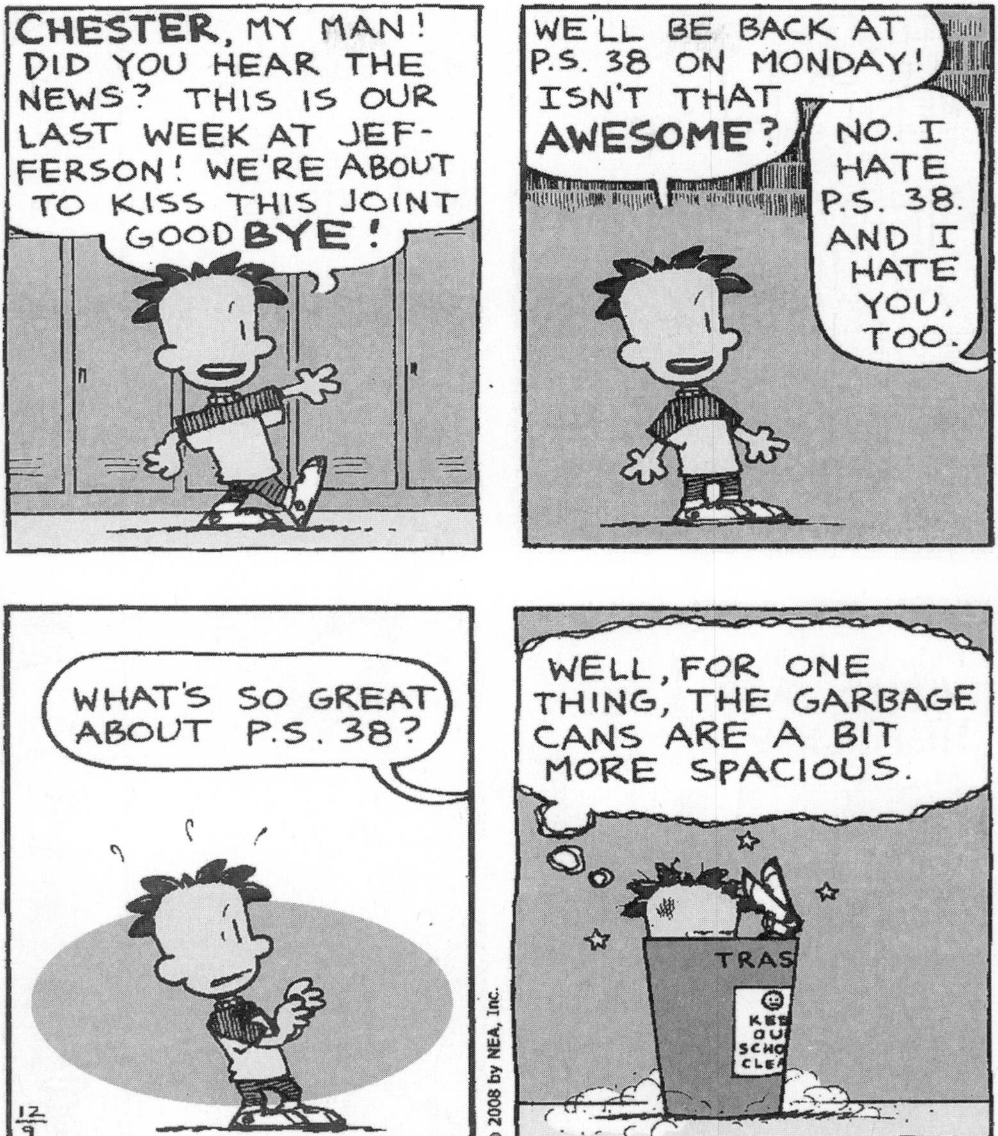
CHESTER, MY MAN! DID YOU HEAR THE NEWS? THIS IS OUR LAST WEEK AT JEFFERSON! WE'RE ABOUT TO KISS THIS JOINT GOODBYE!
WE'LL BE BACK AT P.S. 38 ON MONDAY! ISN'T THAT AWESOME?
NO. I HATE P.S. 38. AND I HATE YOU, TOO.
WHAT'S SO GREAT ABOUT P.S. 38?
WELL, FOR ONE THING, THE GARBAGE CANS ARE A BIT MORE SPACIOUS.
TRAS
12
9
© 2008 by NEA, Inc.
Peirce

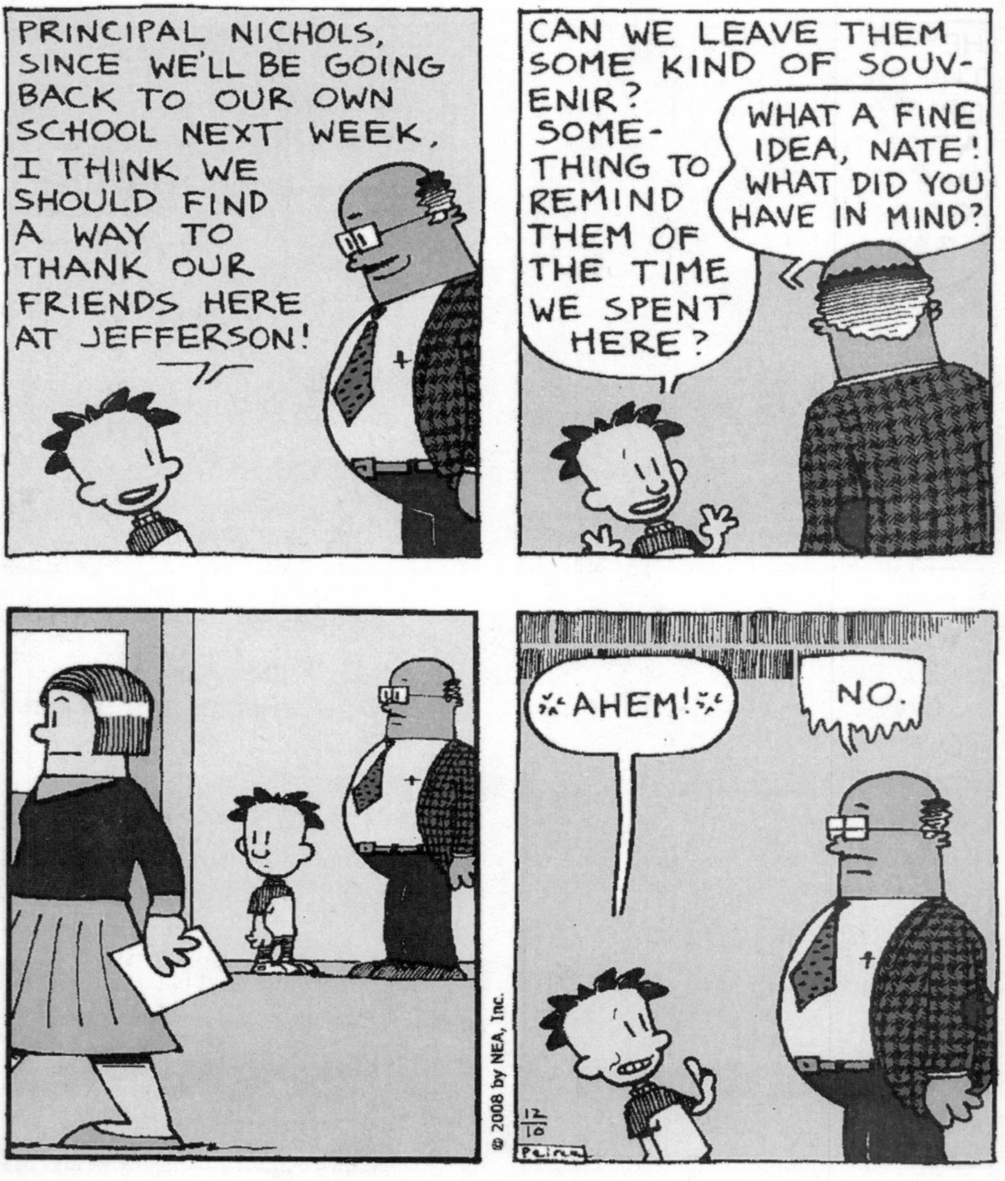
PRINCIPAL NICHOLS, SINCE WE'LL BE GOING BACK TO OUR OWN SCHOOL NEXT WEEK, I THINK WE SHOULD FIND A WAY TO THANK OUR FRIENDS HERE AT JEFFERSON!
CAN WE LEAVE THEM SOME KIND OF SOUV-ENIR? SOME-THING TO REMIND THEM OF THE TIME WE SPENT HERE?
WHAT A FINE IDEA, NATE! WHAT DID YOU HAVE IN MIND?
AHEM!
NO.
© 2008 by NEA, Inc.
12/10
Peirce

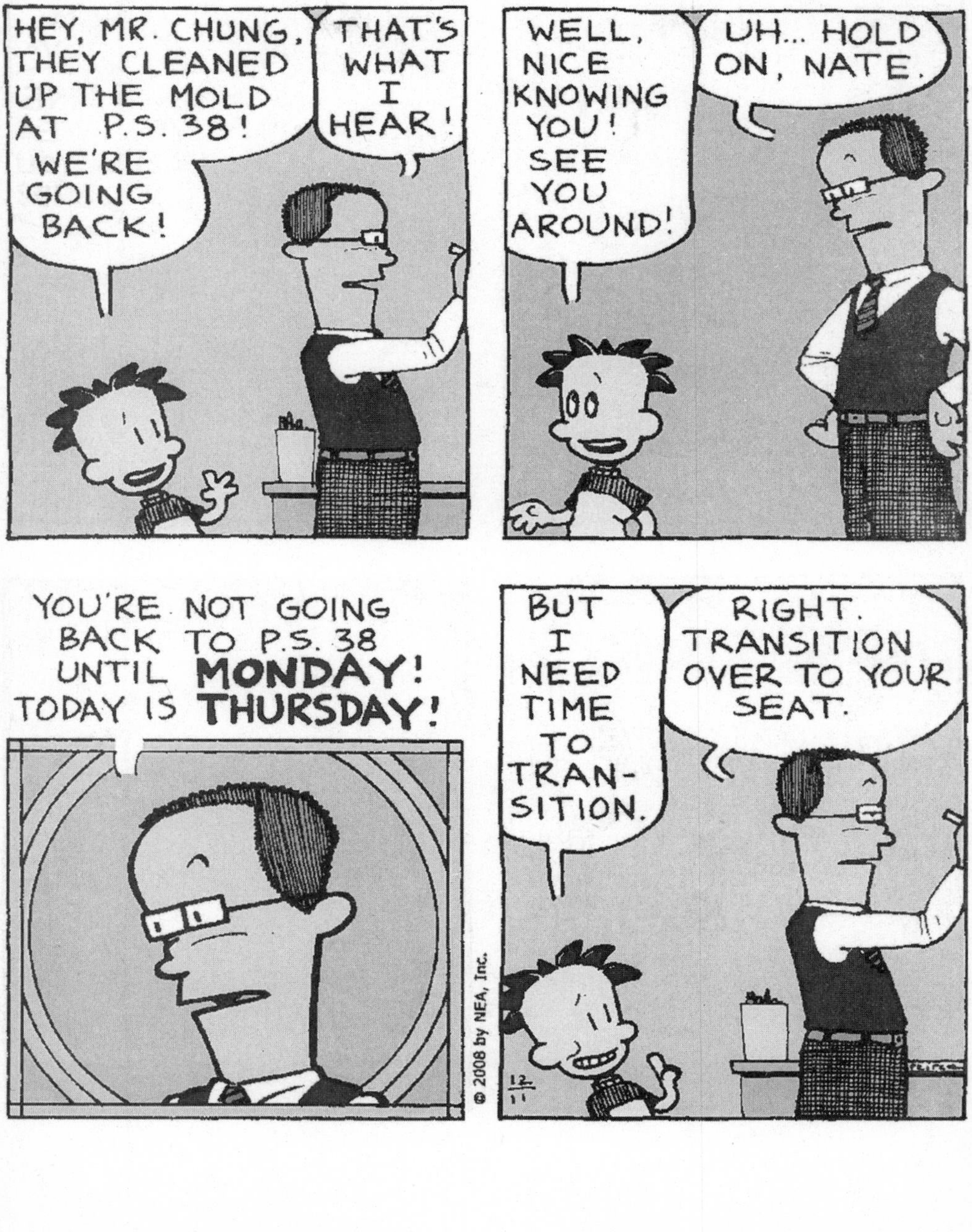
HEY, MR. CHUNG, THEY CLEANED UP THE MOLD AT P.S. 38! WE'RE GOING BACK!
THAT'S WHAT I HEAR!
WELL, NICE KNOWING YOU! SEE YOU AROUND!
UH... HOLD ON, NATE.
YOU'RE NOT GOING BACK TO P.S. 38 UNTIL **MONDAY**! TODAY IS **THURSDAY**!
BUT I NEED TIME TO TRAN-SITION.
RIGHT. TRANSITION OVER TO YOUR SEAT.
© 2008 by NEA, Inc.
12. 11

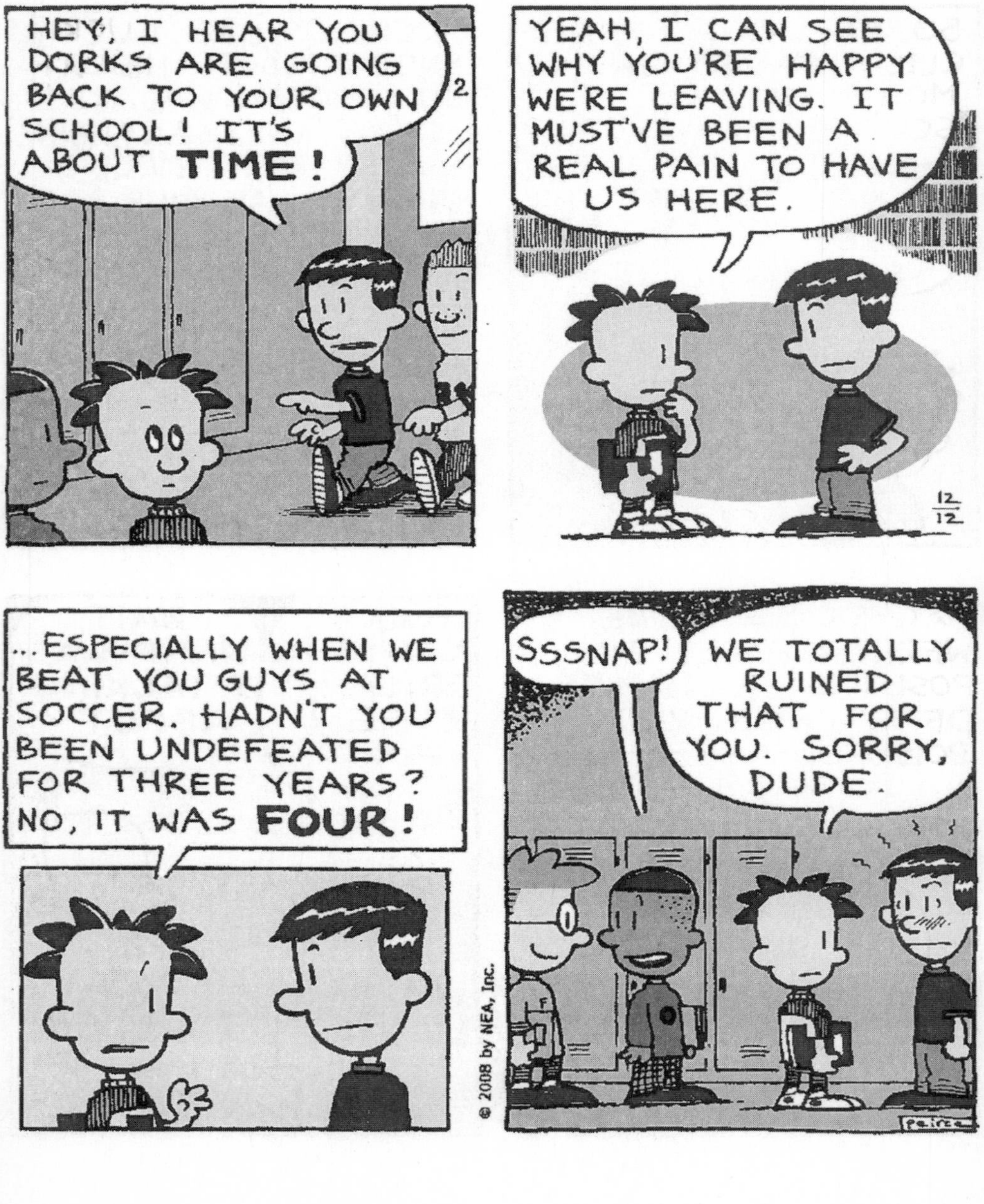
HEY, I HEAR YOU DORKS ARE GOING BACK TO YOUR OWN SCHOOL! IT'S ABOUT **TIME**!
YEAH, I CAN SEE WHY YOU'RE HAPPY WE'RE LEAVING. IT MUST'VE BEEN A REAL PAIN TO HAVE US HERE.
...ESPECIALLY WHEN WE BEAT YOU GUYS AT SOCCER. HADN'T YOU BEEN UNDEFEATED FOR THREE YEARS? NO, IT WAS **FOUR**!
SSSNAP!
WE TOTALLY RUINED THAT FOR YOU. SORRY, DUDE.
© 2008 by NEA, Inc.

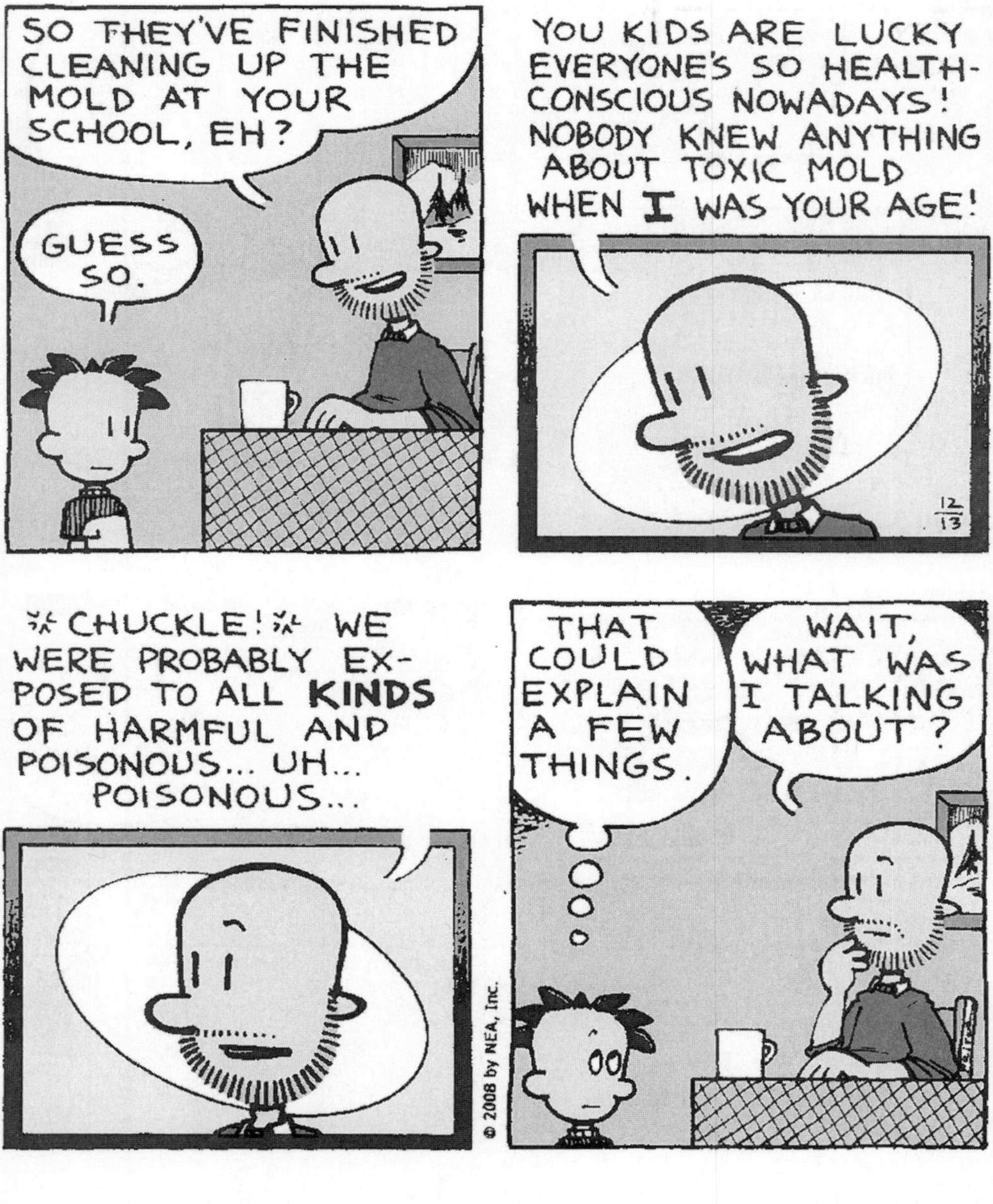
SO THEY'VE FINISHED CLEANING UP THE MOLD AT YOUR SCHOOL, EH?
GUESS SO.
YOU KIDS ARE LUCKY EVERYONE'S SO HEALTH-CONSCIOUS NOWADAYS! NOBODY KNEW ANYTHING ABOUT TOXIC MOLD WHEN I WAS YOUR AGE!
12/13
CHUCKLE! WE WERE PROBABLY EX-POSED TO ALL KINDS OF HARMFUL AND POISONOUS... UH... POISONOUS...
© 2008 by NEA, Inc.
THAT COULD EXPLAIN A FEW THINGS.
WAIT, WHAT WAS I TALKING ABOUT?

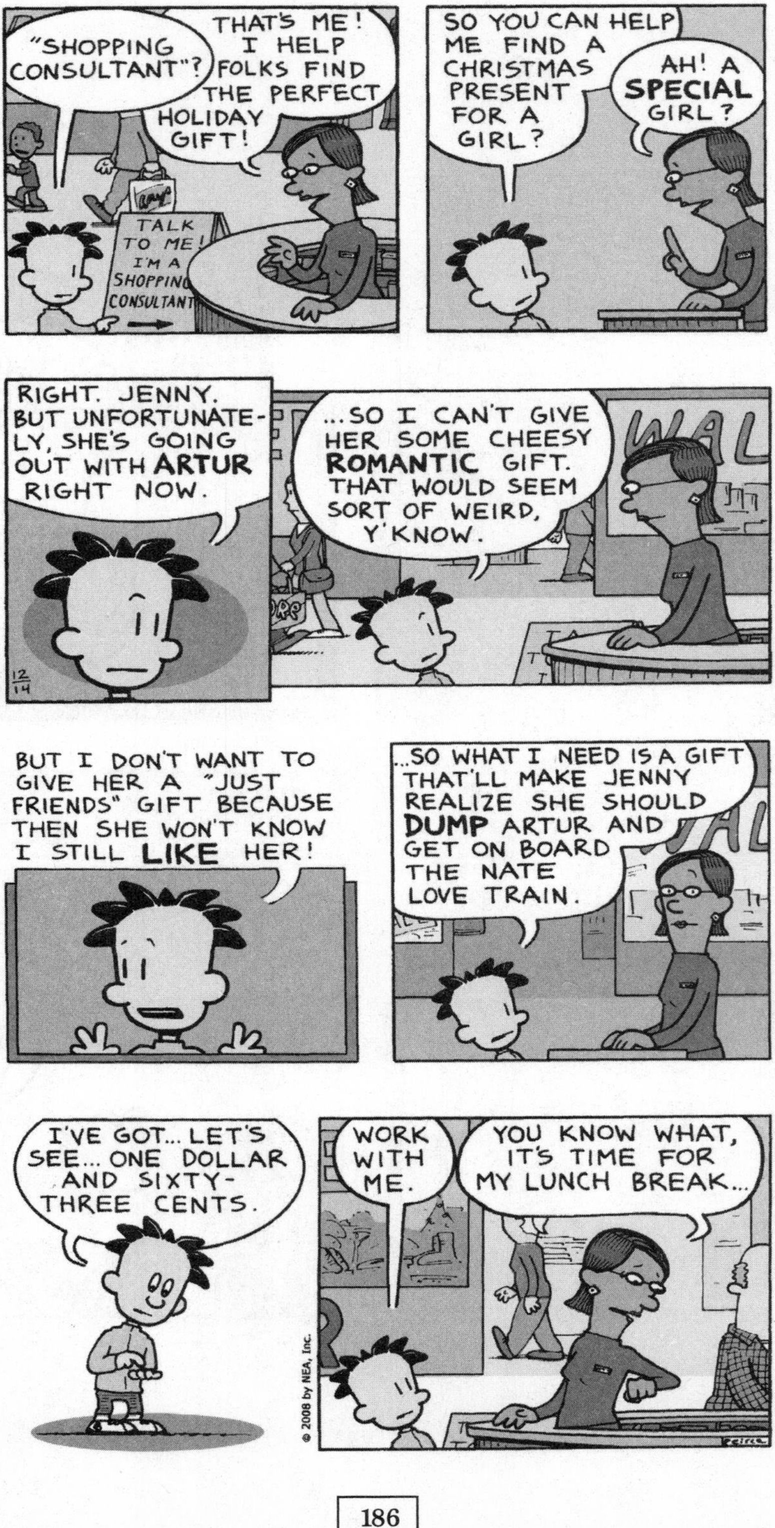
"SHOPPING CONSULTANT"?
THAT'S ME! I HELP FOLKS FIND THE PERFECT HOLIDAY GIFT!
TALK TO ME! I'M A SHOPPING CONSULTANT
SO YOU CAN HELP ME FIND A CHRISTMAS PRESENT FOR A GIRL?
AH! A **SPECIAL** GIRL?
RIGHT. JENNY. BUT UNFORTUNATE-LY, SHE'S GOING OUT WITH **ARTUR** RIGHT NOW.
...SO I CAN'T GIVE HER SOME CHEESY **ROMANTIC** GIFT. THAT WOULD SEEM SORT OF WEIRD, Y'KNOW.
BUT I DON'T WANT TO GIVE HER A "JUST FRIENDS" GIFT BECAUSE THEN SHE WON'T KNOW I STILL **LIKE** HER!
...SO WHAT I NEED IS A GIFT THAT'LL MAKE JENNY REALIZE SHE SHOULD **DUMP** ARTUR AND GET ON BOARD THE NATE LOVE TRAIN.
I'VE GOT... LET'S SEE... ONE DOLLAR AND SIXTY-THREE CENTS.
© 2008 by NEA, Inc.
WORK WITH ME.
YOU KNOW WHAT, IT'S TIME FOR MY LUNCH BREAK...

HOW BAD CAN IT BE?

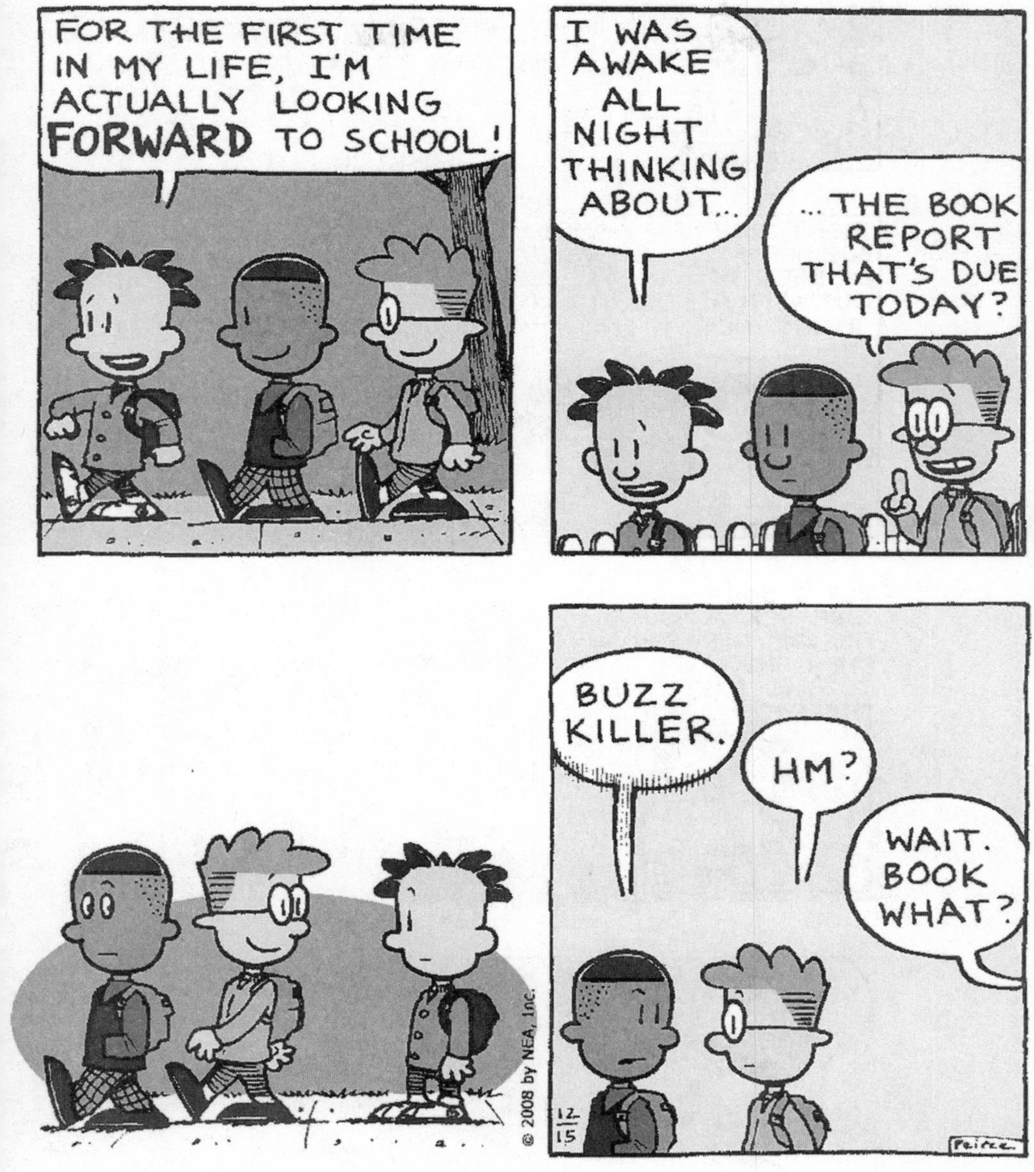

FOR THE FIRST TIME IN MY LIFE, I'M ACTUALLY LOOKING **FORWARD** TO SCHOOL!
I WAS AWAKE ALL NIGHT THINKING ABOUT...
...THE BOOK REPORT THAT'S DUE TODAY?
BUZZ KILLER.
HM?
WAIT. BOOK WHAT?
© 2008 by NEA, Inc.
12-15
Peirce

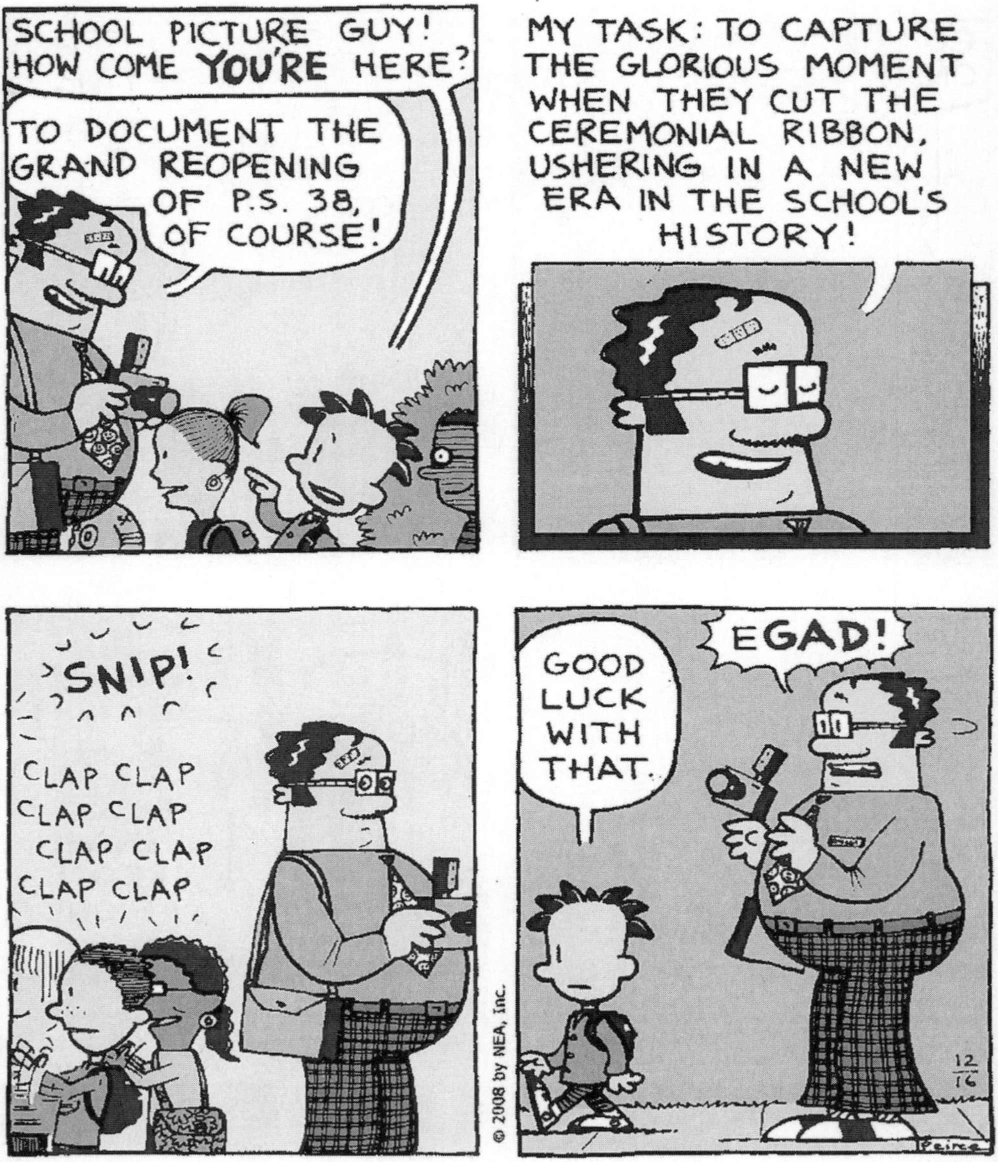
SCHOOL PICTURE GUY! HOW COME YOU'RE HERE?
TO DOCUMENT THE GRAND REOPENING OF P.S. 38, OF COURSE!
MY TASK: TO CAPTURE THE GLORIOUS MOMENT WHEN THEY CUT THE CEREMONIAL RIBBON, USHERING IN A NEW ERA IN THE SCHOOL'S HISTORY!
SNIP!
CLAP CLAP
CLAP CLAP
CLAP CLAP
CLAP CLAP
GOOD LUCK WITH THAT.
EGAD!
12/16
Peirce

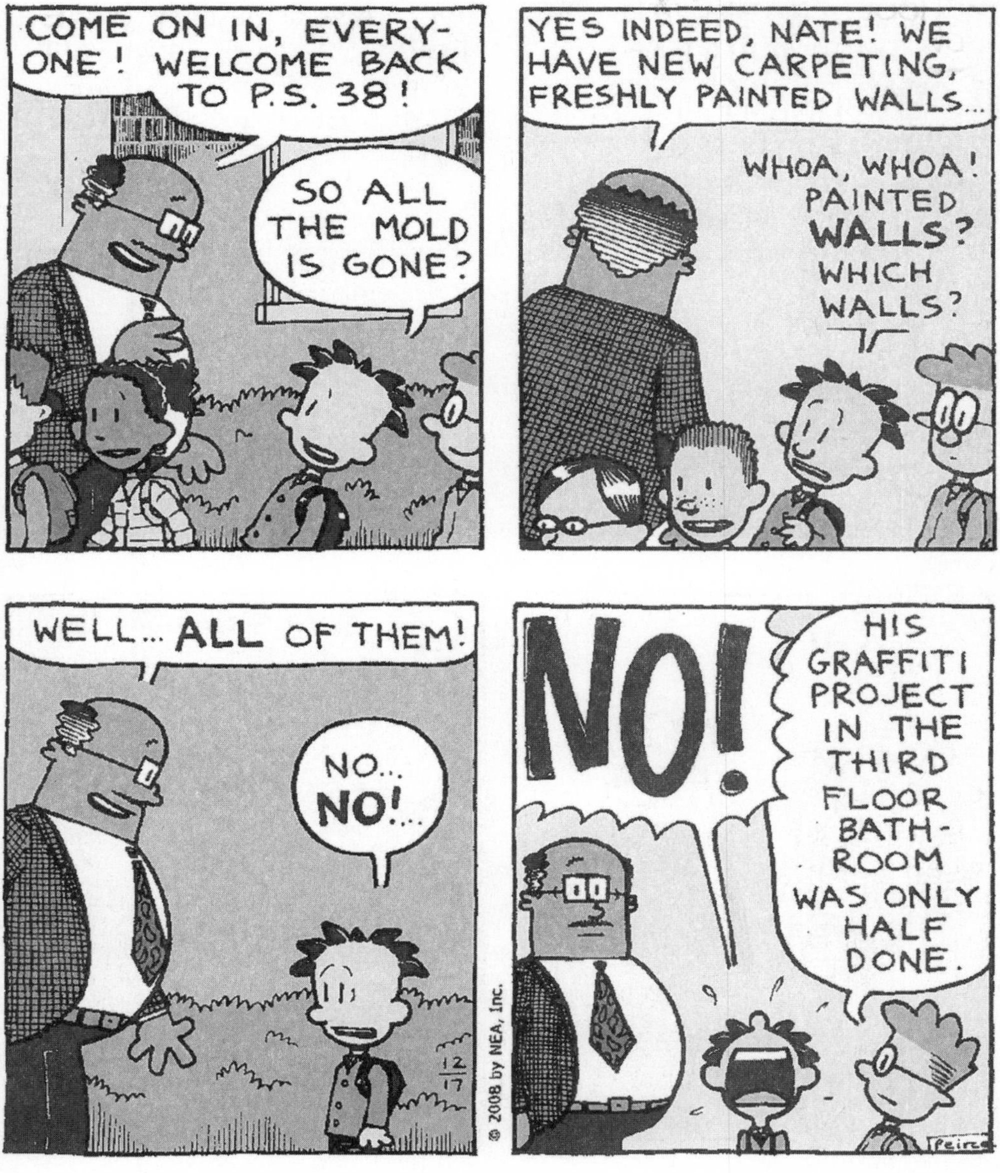

COME ON IN, EVERY-ONE! WELCOME BACK TO P.S. 38!
SO ALL THE MOLD IS GONE?
YES INDEED, NATE! WE HAVE NEW CARPETING, FRESHLY PAINTED WALLS...
WHOA, WHOA! PAINTED WALLS? WHICH WALLS?
WELL... ALL OF THEM!
NO... NO!...
12/17
© 2008 by NEA, Inc.
NO!
HIS GRAFFITI PROJECT IN THE THIRD FLOOR BATH-ROOM WAS ONLY HALF DONE.
Peirce

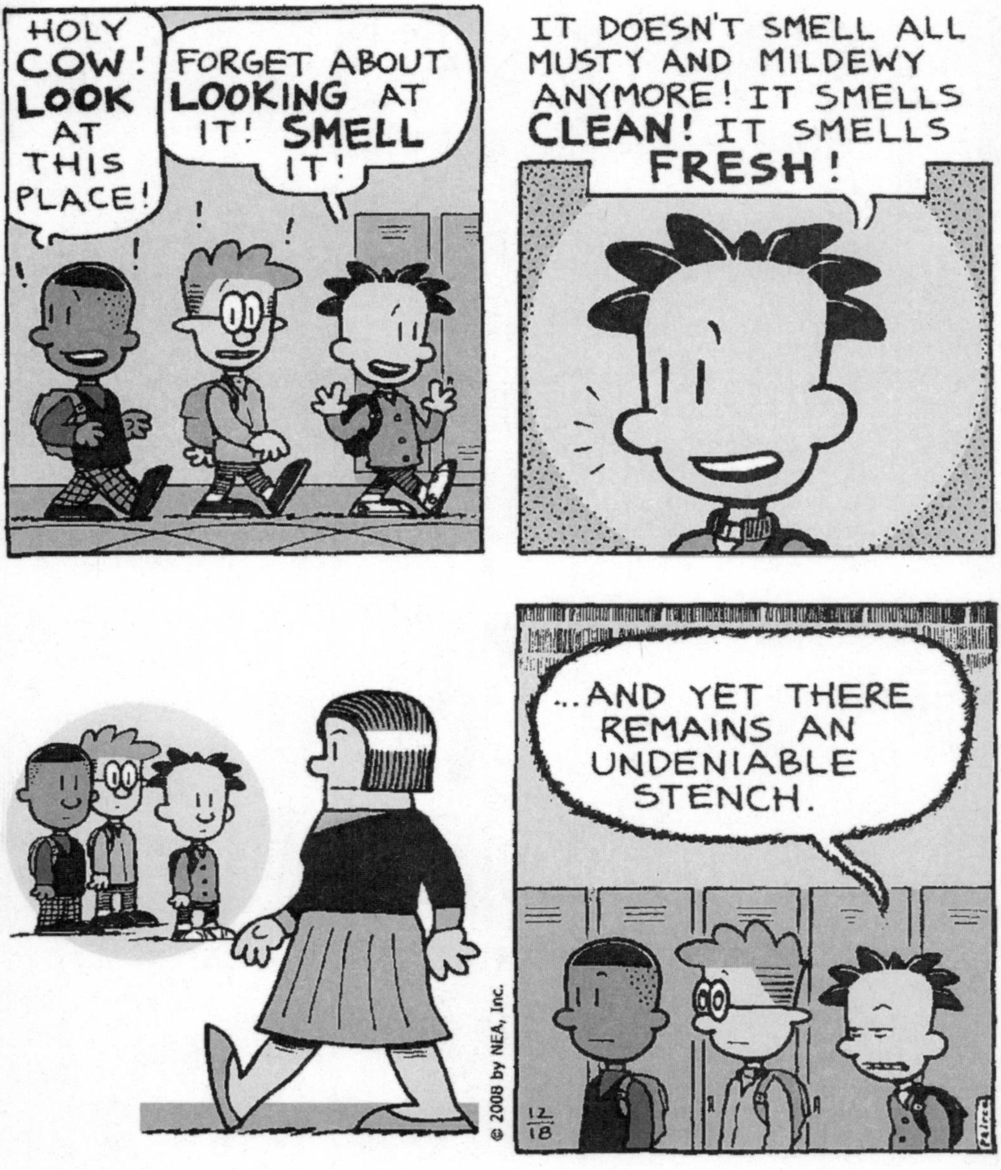
HOLY COW! LOOK AT THIS PLACE!
FORGET ABOUT LOOKING AT IT! SMELL IT!
IT DOESN'T SMELL ALL MUSTY AND MILDEWY ANYMORE! IT SMELLS CLEAN! IT SMELLS FRESH!
...AND YET THERE REMAINS AN UNDENIABLE STENCH.
© 2008 by NEA, Inc.
12/18

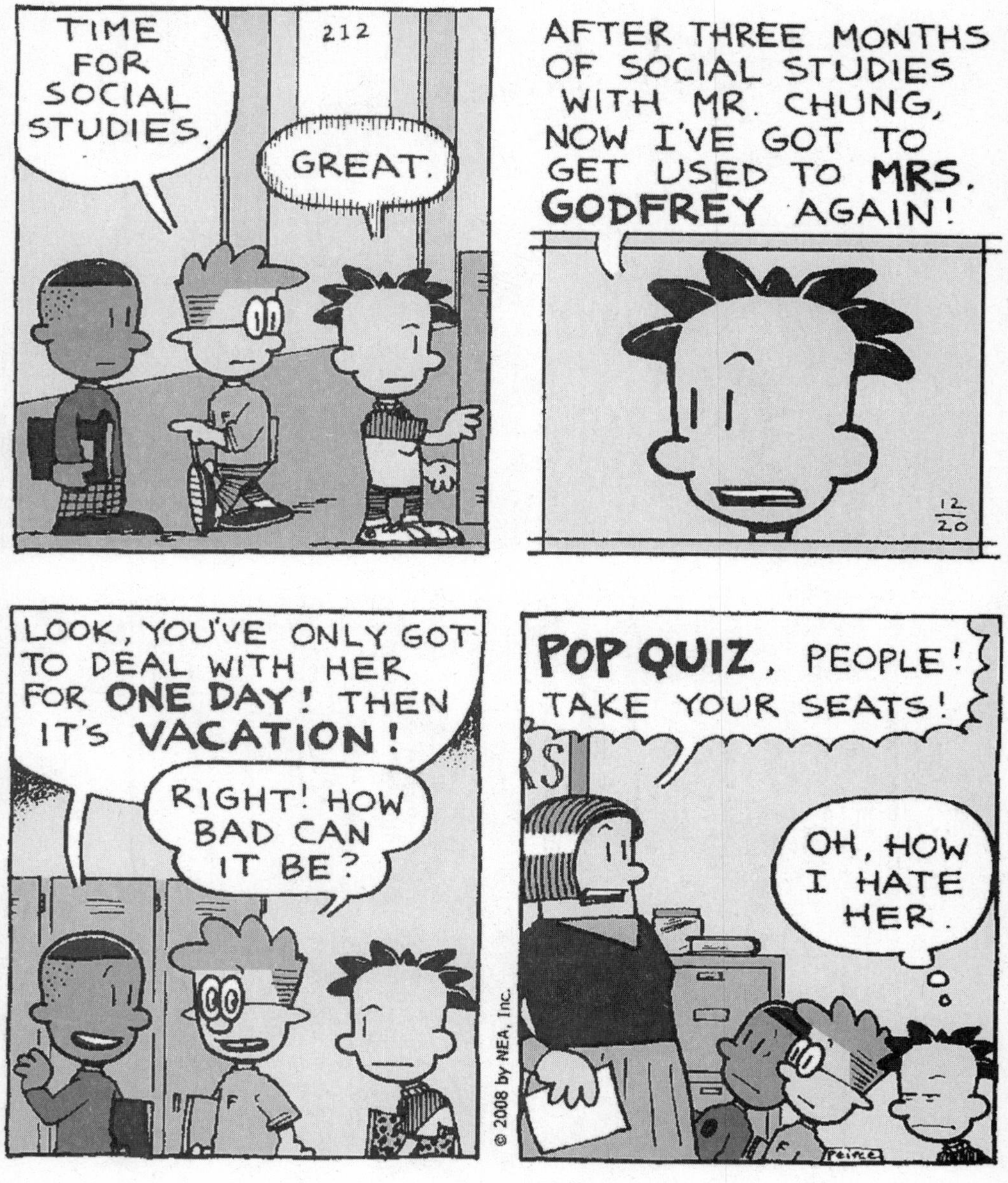
TIME FOR SOCIAL STUDIES.
GREAT.
212
AFTER THREE MONTHS OF SOCIAL STUDIES WITH MR. CHUNG, NOW I'VE GOT TO GET USED TO **MRS. GODFREY** AGAIN!
LOOK, YOU'VE ONLY GOT TO DEAL WITH HER FOR **ONE DAY**! THEN IT'S **VACATION**!
RIGHT! HOW BAD CAN IT BE?
POP QUIZ, PEOPLE! TAKE YOUR SEATS!
OH, HOW I HATE HER.
© 2008 by NEA, Inc.

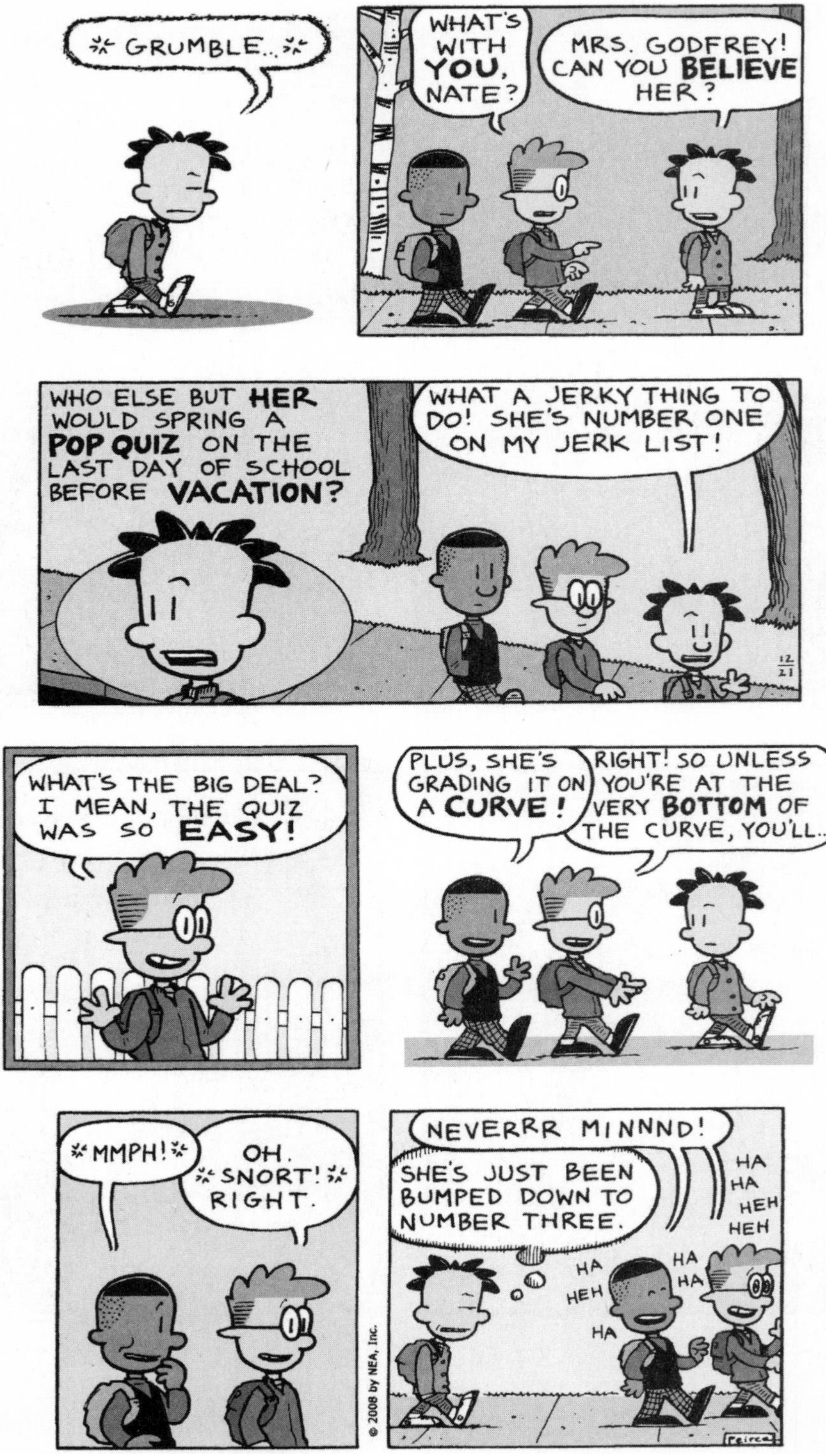

GRUMBLE...
WHAT'S WITH YOU, NATE?
MRS. GODFREY! CAN YOU BELIEVE HER?
WHO ELSE BUT HER WOULD SPRING A POP QUIZ ON THE LAST DAY OF SCHOOL BEFORE VACATION?
WHAT A JERKY THING TO DO! SHE'S NUMBER ONE ON MY JERK LIST!
12/21
WHAT'S THE BIG DEAL? I MEAN, THE QUIZ WAS SO EASY!
PLUS, SHE'S GRADING IT ON A CURVE!
RIGHT! SO UNLESS YOU'RE AT THE VERY BOTTOM OF THE CURVE, YOU'LL...
MMPH!
OH. SNORT! RIGHT.
© 2008 by NEA, Inc.
NEVERRR MINNND!
SHE'S JUST BEEN BUMPED DOWN TO NUMBER THREE.
HA HA HEH HEH
HA HEH HA
HA HA
Peirce

HOUSE GUEST PEST

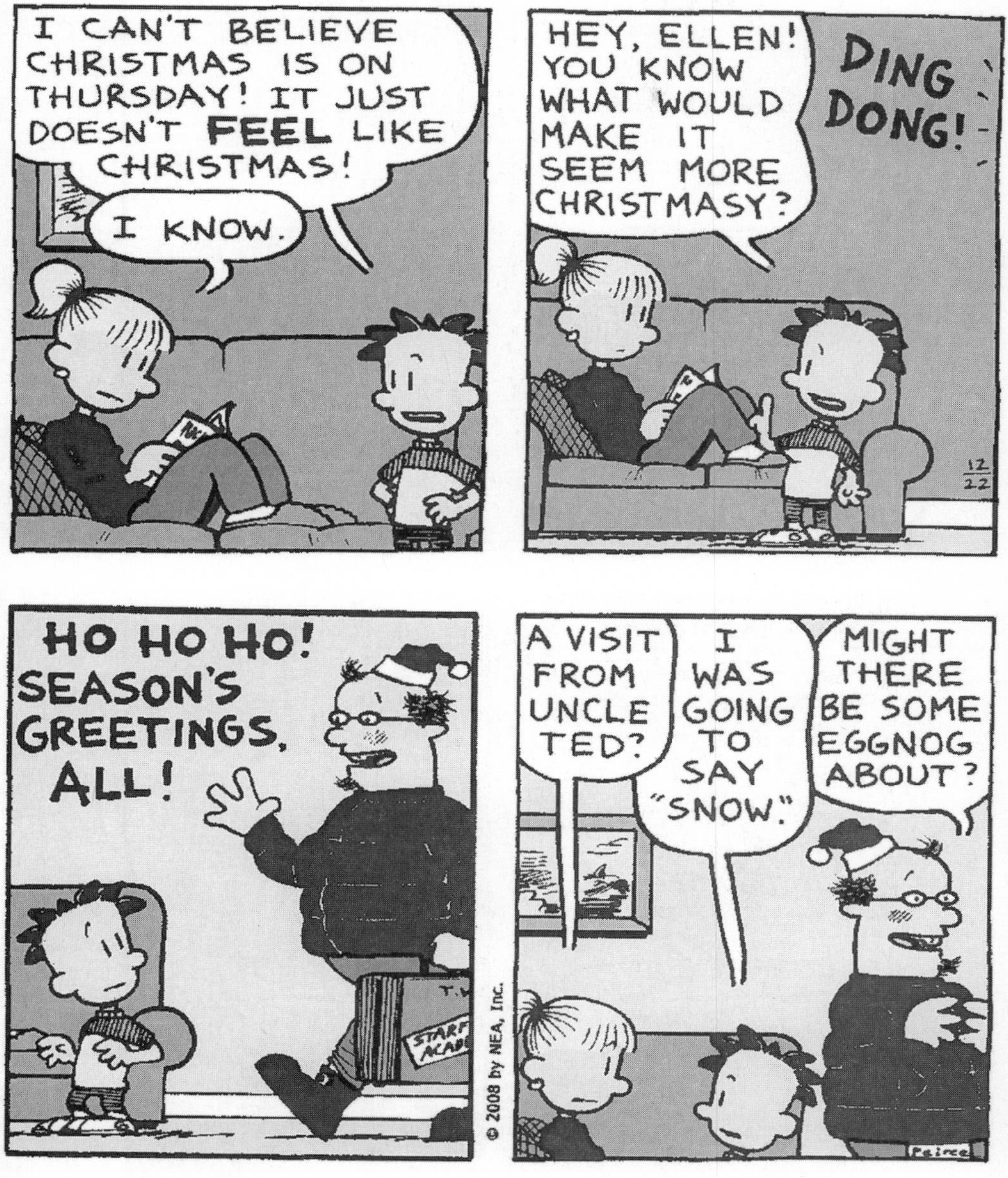

I CAN'T BELIEVE CHRISTMAS IS ON THURSDAY! IT JUST DOESN'T **FEEL** LIKE CHRISTMAS!
I KNOW.
HEY, ELLEN! YOU KNOW WHAT WOULD MAKE IT SEEM MORE CHRISTMASY?
DING DONG!
12/22
HO HO HO! SEASON'S GREETINGS, ALL!
© 2008 by NEA, Inc.
A VISIT FROM UNCLE TED?
I WAS GOING TO SAY "SNOW."
MIGHT THERE BE SOME EGGNOG ABOUT?
Peirce

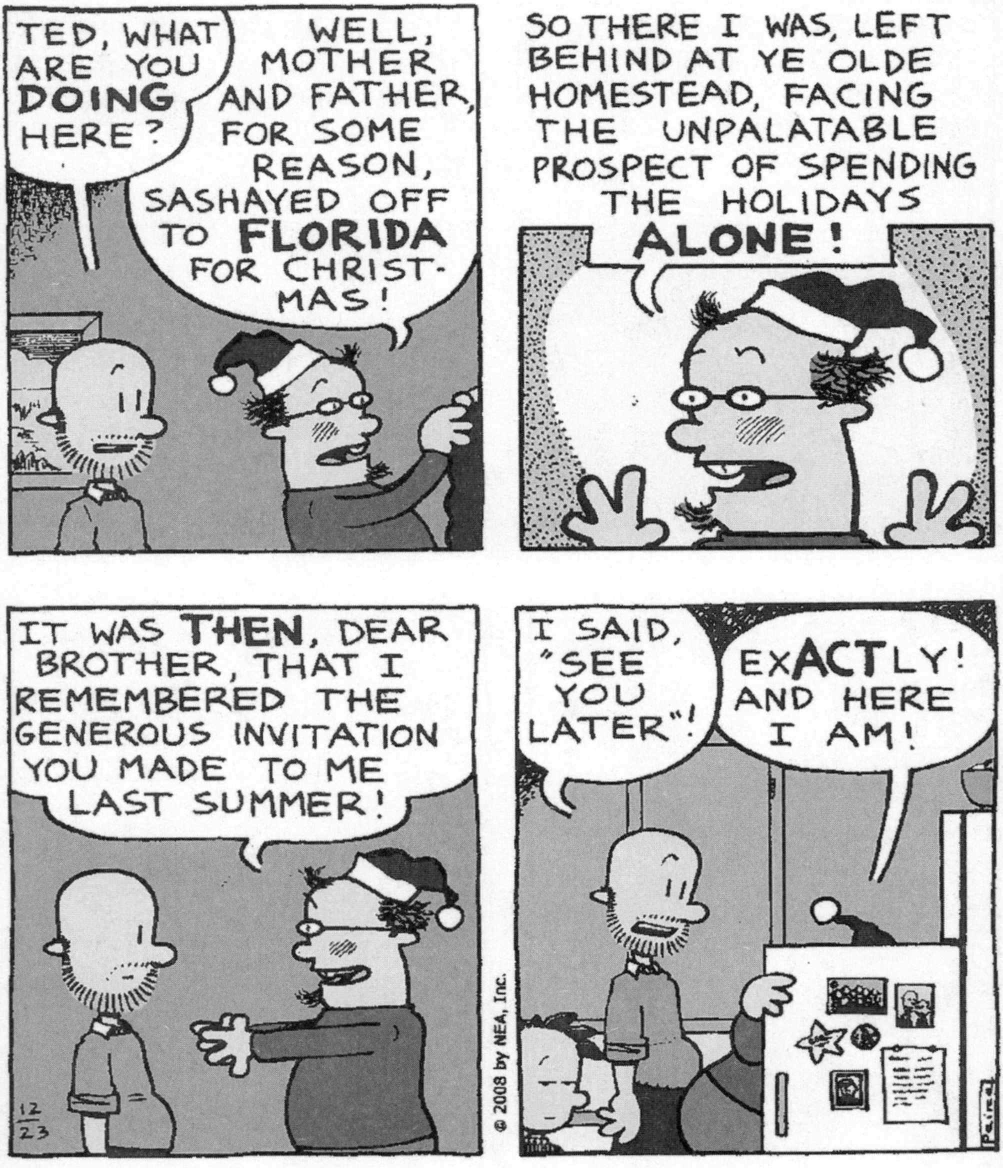
TED, WHAT ARE YOU DOING HERE?
WELL, MOTHER AND FATHER, FOR SOME REASON, SASHAYED OFF TO FLORIDA FOR CHRISTMAS!
SO THERE I WAS, LEFT BEHIND AT YE OLDE HOMESTEAD, FACING THE UNPALATABLE PROSPECT OF SPENDING THE HOLIDAYS ALONE!
IT WAS THEN, DEAR BROTHER, THAT I REMEMBERED THE GENEROUS INVITATION YOU MADE TO ME LAST SUMMER!
12/23
© 2008 by NEA, Inc.
I SAID, "SEE YOU LATER"!
EXACTLY! AND HERE I AM!
Peirce

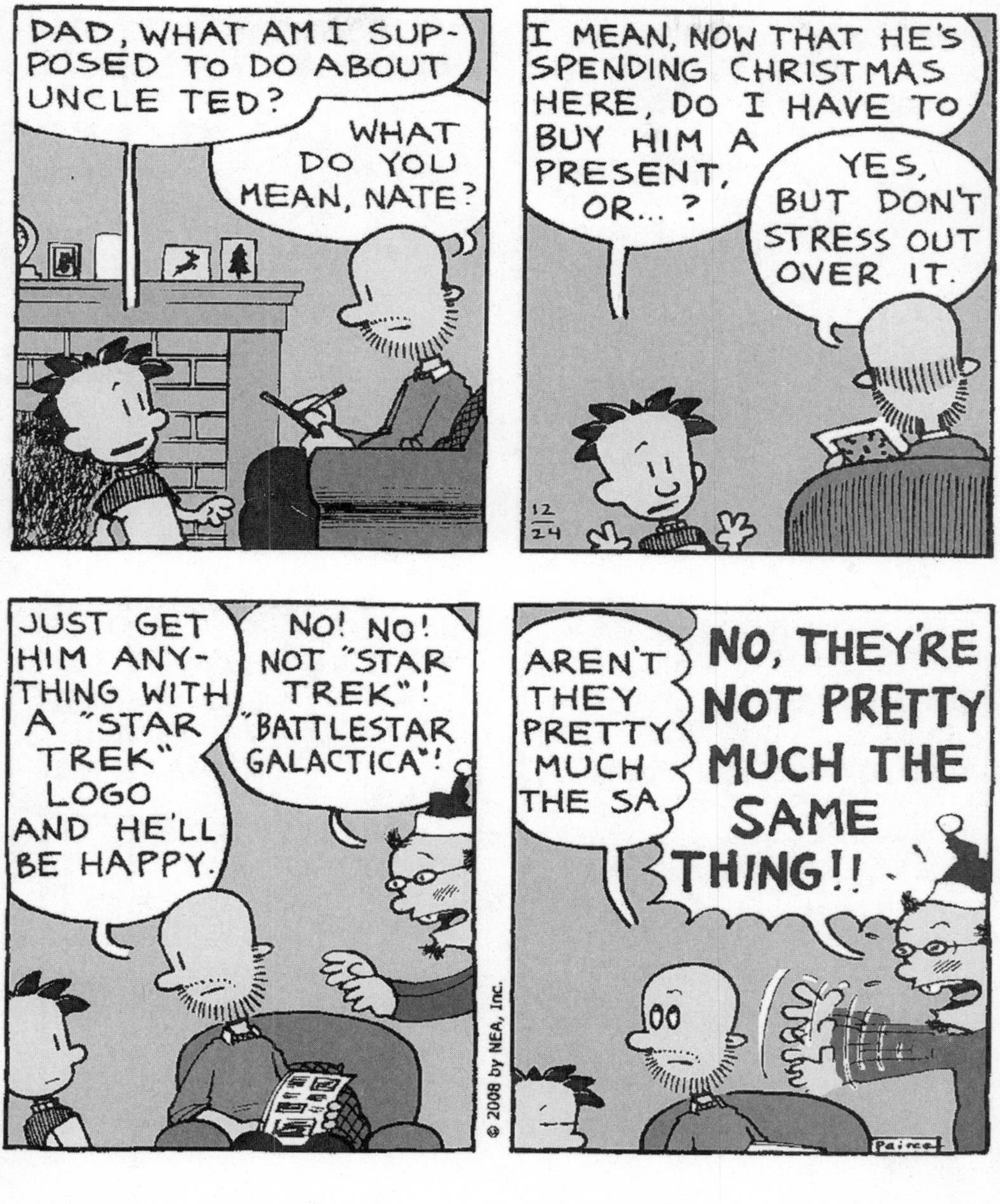
DAD, WHAT AM I SUPPOSED TO DO ABOUT UNCLE TED?
WHAT DO YOU MEAN, NATE?
I MEAN, NOW THAT HE'S SPENDING CHRISTMAS HERE, DO I HAVE TO BUY HIM A PRESENT, OR... ?
YES, BUT DON'T STRESS OUT OVER IT.
12/24
JUST GET HIM ANYTHING WITH A "STAR TREK" LOGO AND HE'LL BE HAPPY.
NO! NO! NOT "STAR TREK"! "BATTLESTAR GALACTICA"!
AREN'T THEY PRETTY MUCH THE SA
NO, THEY'RE NOT PRETTY MUCH THE SAME THING!!
Peirce

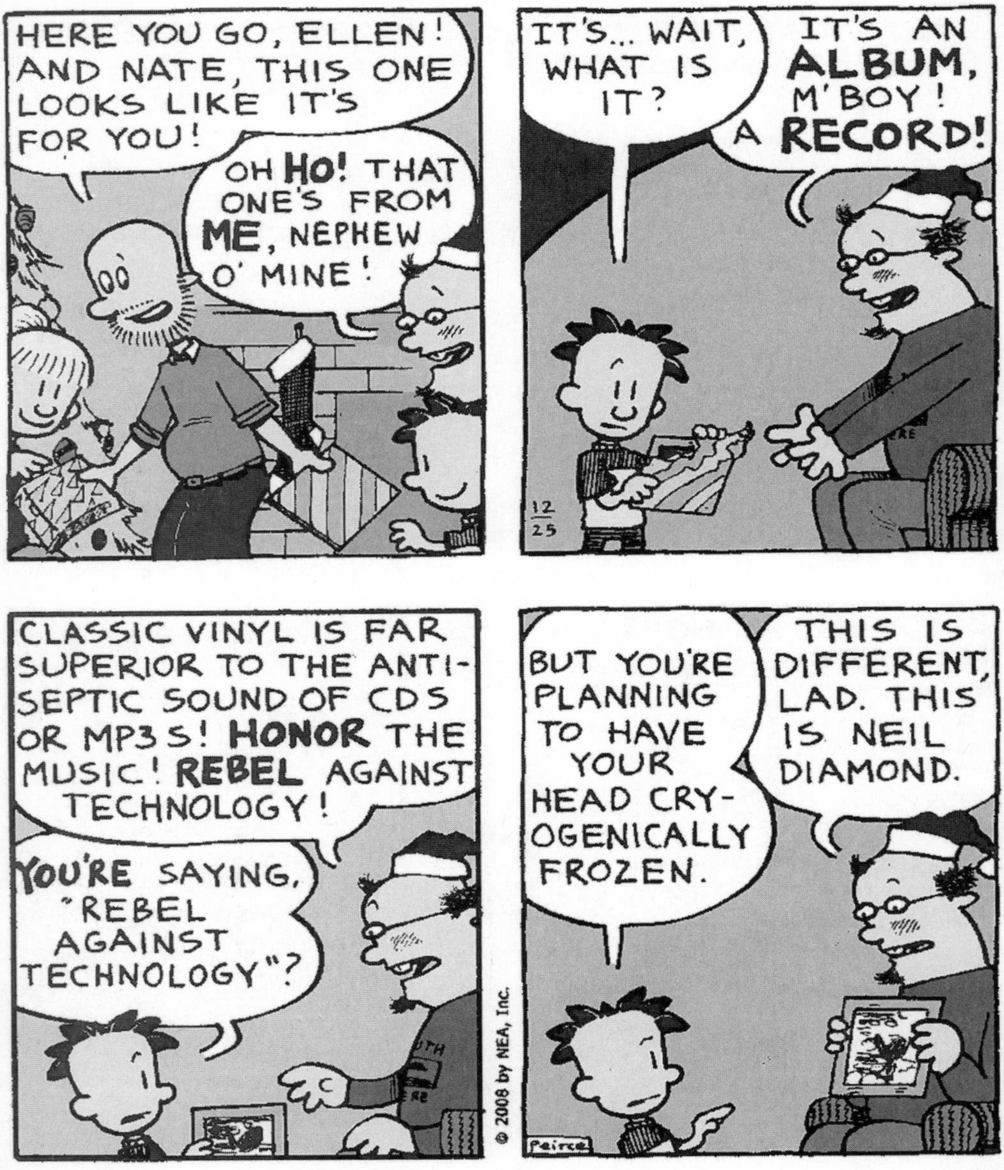
HERE YOU GO, ELLEN! AND NATE, THIS ONE LOOKS LIKE IT'S FOR YOU!
OH HO! THAT ONE'S FROM ME, NEPHEW O' MINE!
IT'S... WAIT, WHAT IS IT?
IT'S AN ALBUM, M'BOY! A RECORD!
12 25
CLASSIC VINYL IS FAR SUPERIOR TO THE ANTI-SEPTIC SOUND OF CDS OR MP3S! HONOR THE MUSIC! REBEL AGAINST TECHNOLOGY!
YOU'RE SAYING, "REBEL AGAINST TECHNOLOGY"?
BUT YOU'RE PLANNING TO HAVE YOUR HEAD CRY-OGENICALLY FROZEN.
THIS IS DIFFERENT, LAD. THIS IS NEIL DIAMOND.
Peirce

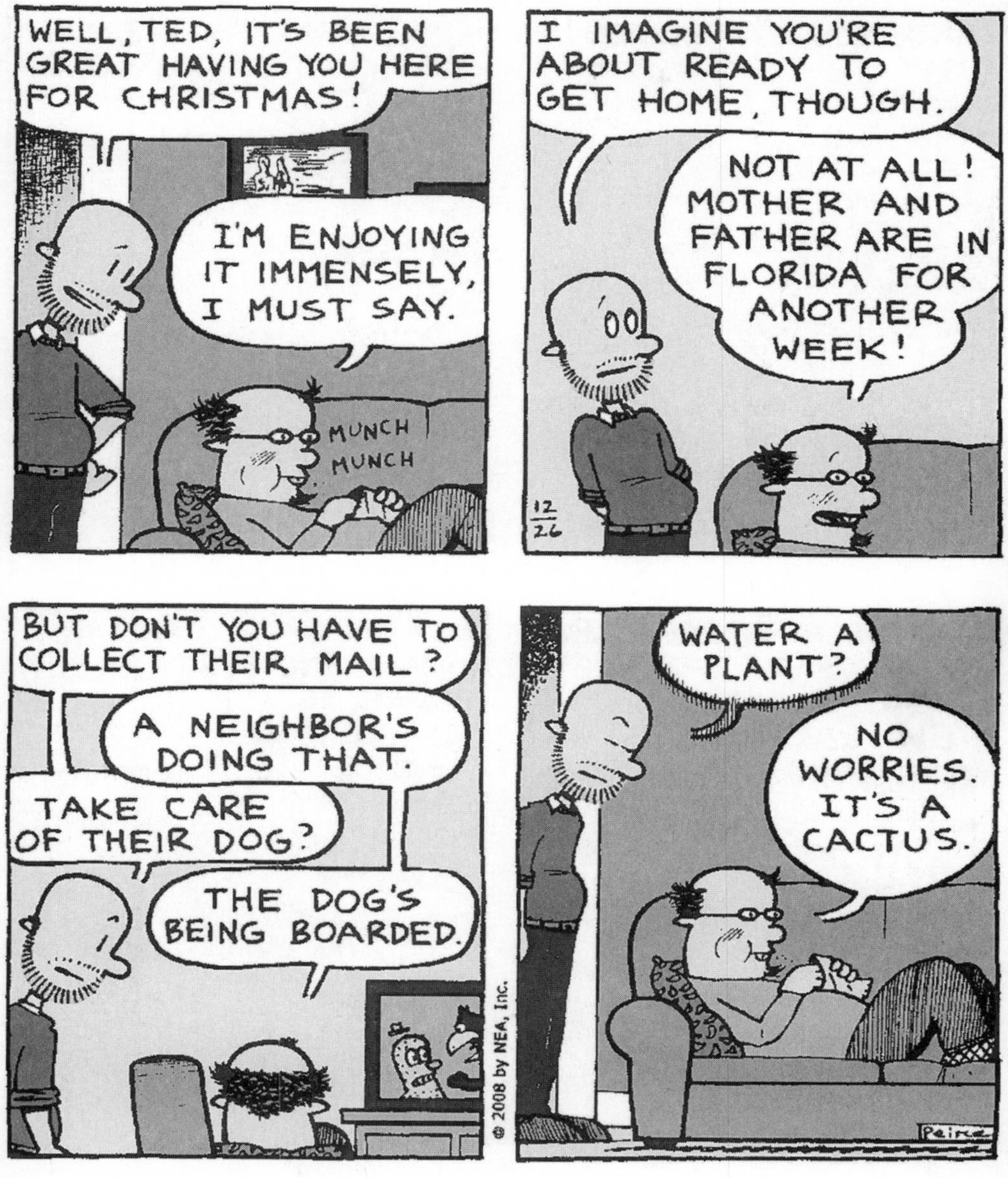
WELL, TED, IT'S BEEN GREAT HAVING YOU HERE FOR CHRISTMAS!
I'M ENJOYING IT IMMENSELY, I MUST SAY.
MUNCH MUNCH
I IMAGINE YOU'RE ABOUT READY TO GET HOME, THOUGH.
NOT AT ALL! MOTHER AND FATHER ARE IN FLORIDA FOR ANOTHER WEEK!
12/26
BUT DON'T YOU HAVE TO COLLECT THEIR MAIL?
A NEIGHBOR'S DOING THAT.
TAKE CARE OF THEIR DOG?
THE DOG'S BEING BOARDED.
© 2008 by NEA, Inc.
WATER A PLANT?
NO WORRIES. IT'S A CACTUS.
Peirce

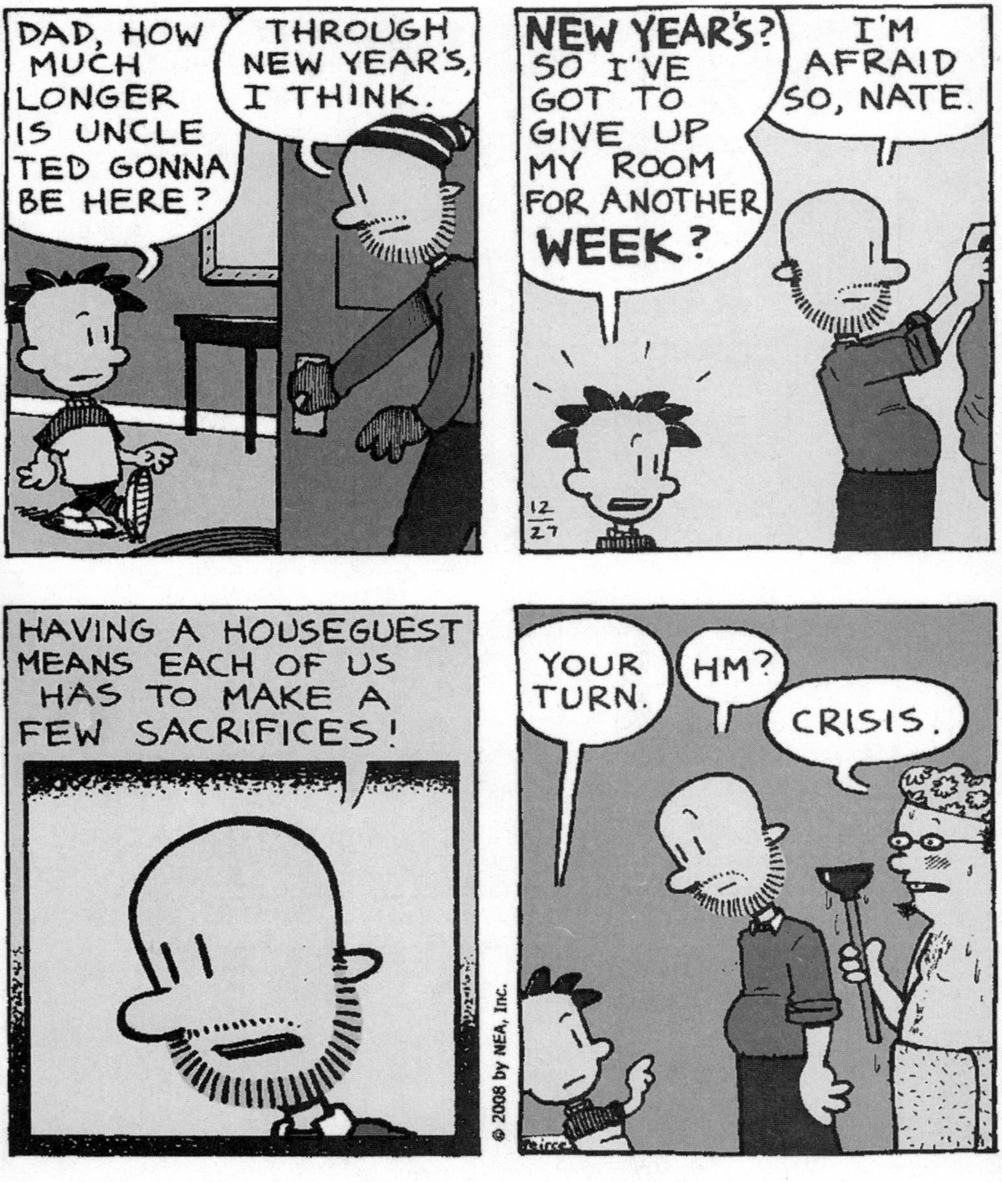
DAD, HOW MUCH LONGER IS UNCLE TED GONNA BE HERE?
THROUGH NEW YEAR'S, I THINK.
NEW YEAR'S? SO I'VE GOT TO GIVE UP MY ROOM FOR ANOTHER WEEK?
I'M AFRAID SO, NATE.
12/27
HAVING A HOUSEGUEST MEANS EACH OF US HAS TO MAKE A FEW SACRIFICES!
YOUR TURN.
HM?
CRISIS.
© 2008 by NEA, Inc.

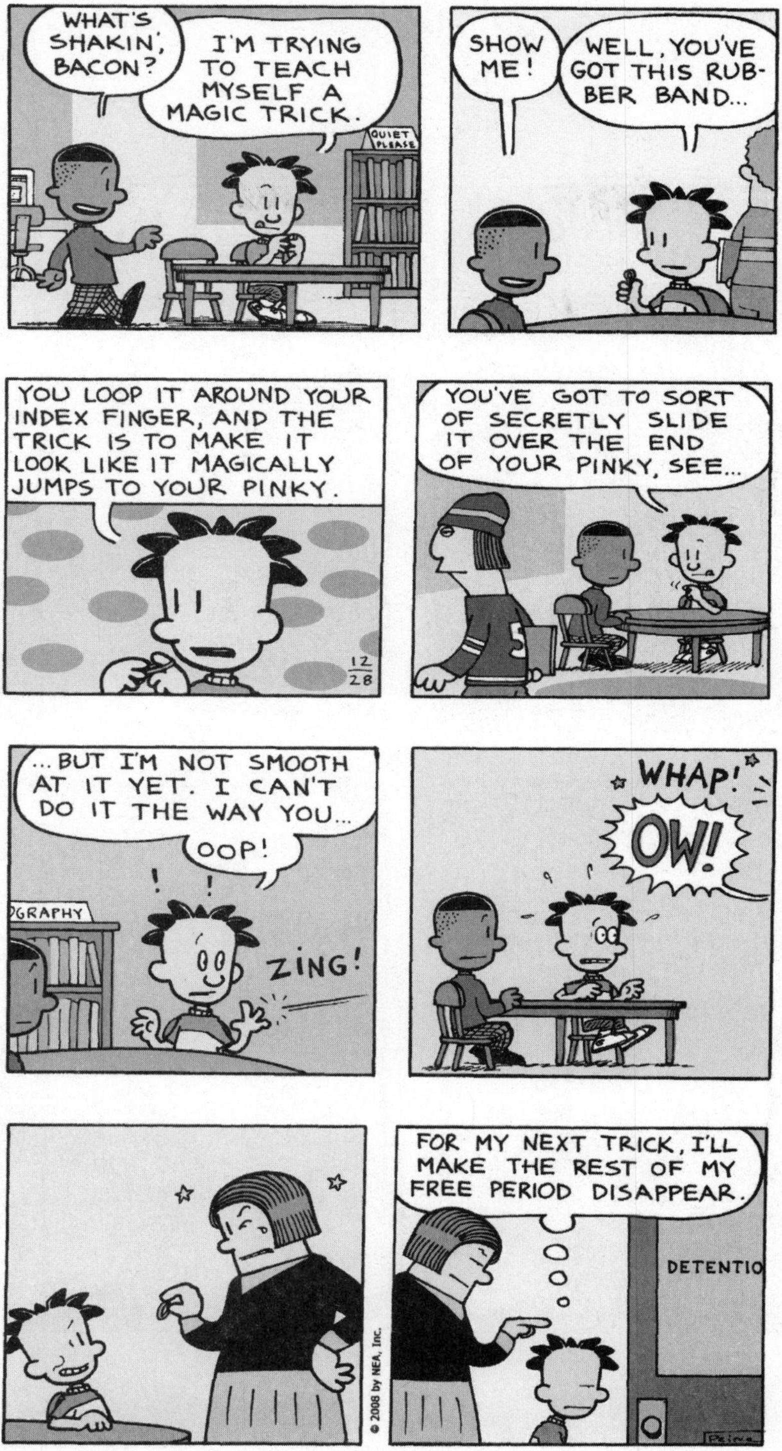
WHAT'S SHAKIN', BACON?
I'M TRYING TO TEACH MYSELF A MAGIC TRICK.
QUIET PLEASE
SHOW ME!
WELL, YOU'VE GOT THIS RUB-BER BAND...
YOU LOOP IT AROUND YOUR INDEX FINGER, AND THE TRICK IS TO MAKE IT LOOK LIKE IT MAGICALLY JUMPS TO YOUR PINKY.
12 28
YOU'VE GOT TO SORT OF SECRETLY SLIDE IT OVER THE END OF YOUR PINKY, SEE...
...BUT I'M NOT SMOOTH AT IT YET. I CAN'T DO IT THE WAY YOU...
OOP!
! !
OGRAPHY
ZING!
WHAP!
OW!
© 2008 by NEA, Inc.
FOR MY NEXT TRICK, I'LL MAKE THE REST OF MY FREE PERIOD DISAPPEAR.
DETENTIO

NO MORE MONOPOLY

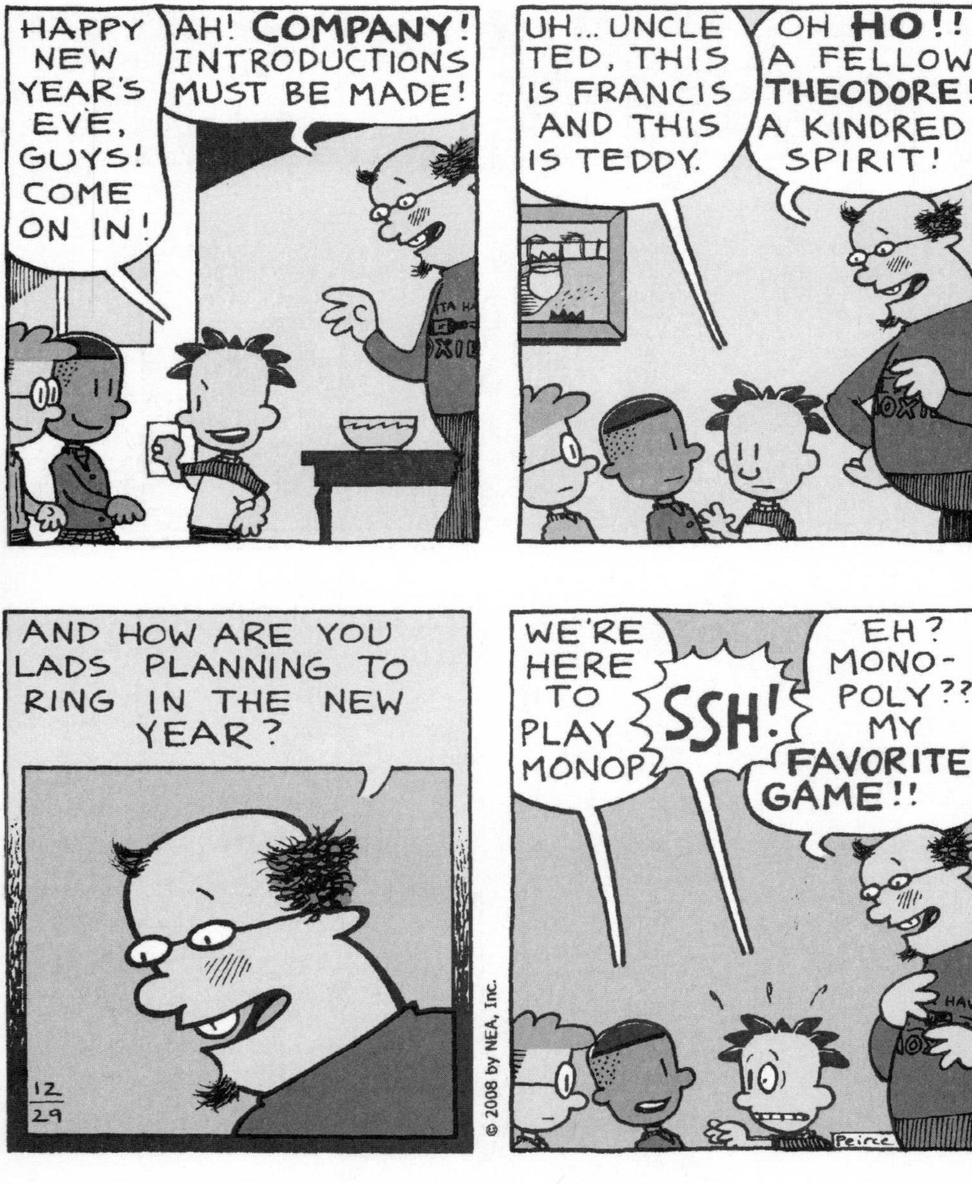

HAPPY NEW YEAR'S EVE, GUYS! COME ON IN!
AH! COMPANY! INTRODUCTIONS MUST BE MADE!
UH... UNCLE TED, THIS IS FRANCIS AND THIS IS TEDDY.
OH HO!! A FELLOW THEODORE! A KINDRED SPIRIT!
AND HOW ARE YOU LADS PLANNING TO RING IN THE NEW YEAR?
12/29
WE'RE HERE TO PLAY MONOP
SSH!
EH? MONO-POLY?? MY FAVORITE GAME!!
Peirce

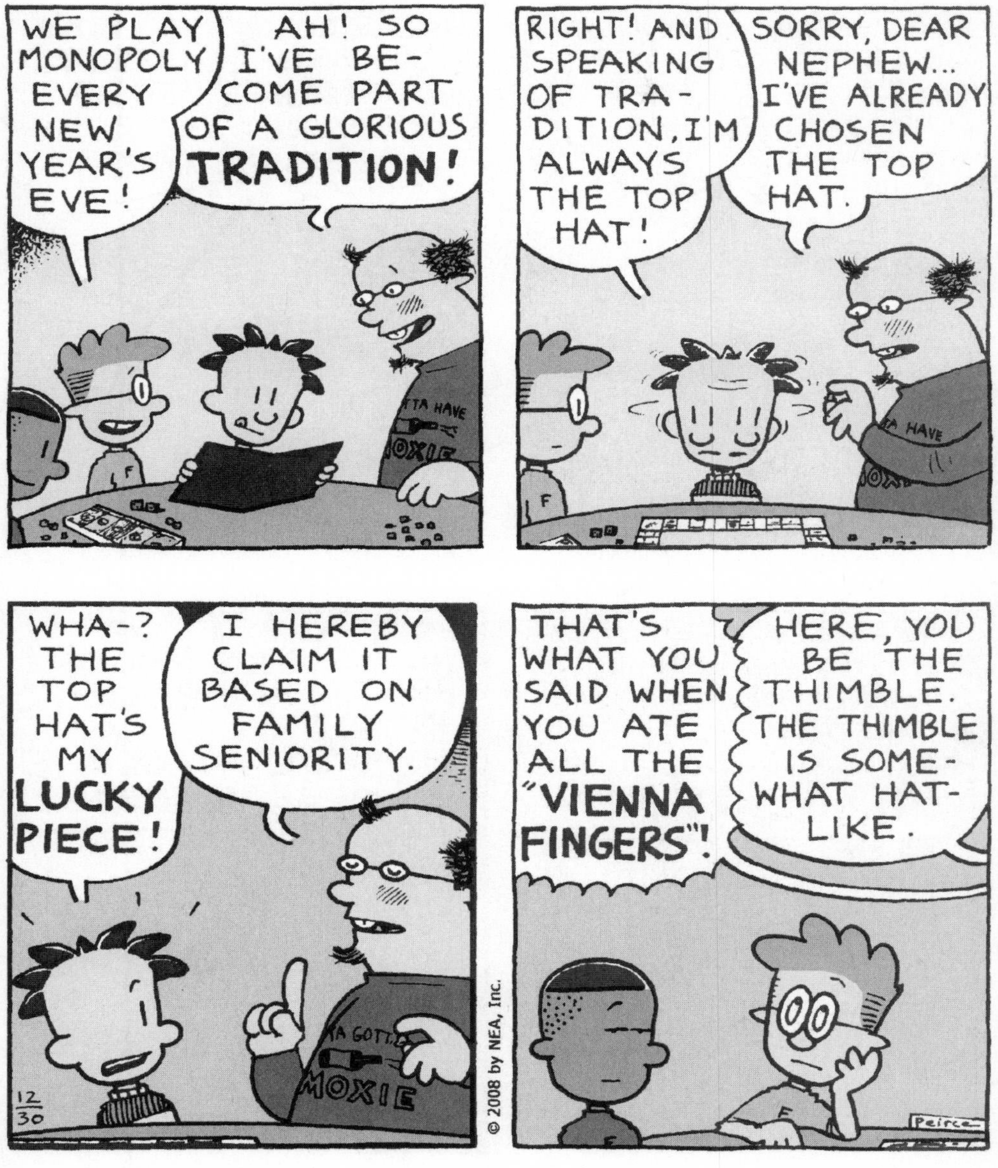
WE PLAY MONOPOLY EVERY NEW YEAR'S EVE!
AH! SO I'VE BE-COME PART OF A GLORIOUS **TRADITION!**
RIGHT! AND SPEAKING OF TRA-DITION, I'M ALWAYS THE TOP HAT!
SORRY, DEAR NEPHEW... I'VE ALREADY CHOSEN THE TOP HAT.
WHA-? THE TOP HAT'S MY **LUCKY PIECE!**
I HEREBY CLAIM IT BASED ON FAMILY SENIORITY.
THAT'S WHAT YOU SAID WHEN YOU ATE ALL THE "**VIENNA FINGERS**"!
HERE, YOU BE THE THIMBLE. THE THIMBLE IS SOME-WHAT HAT-LIKE.
12/30
Peirce

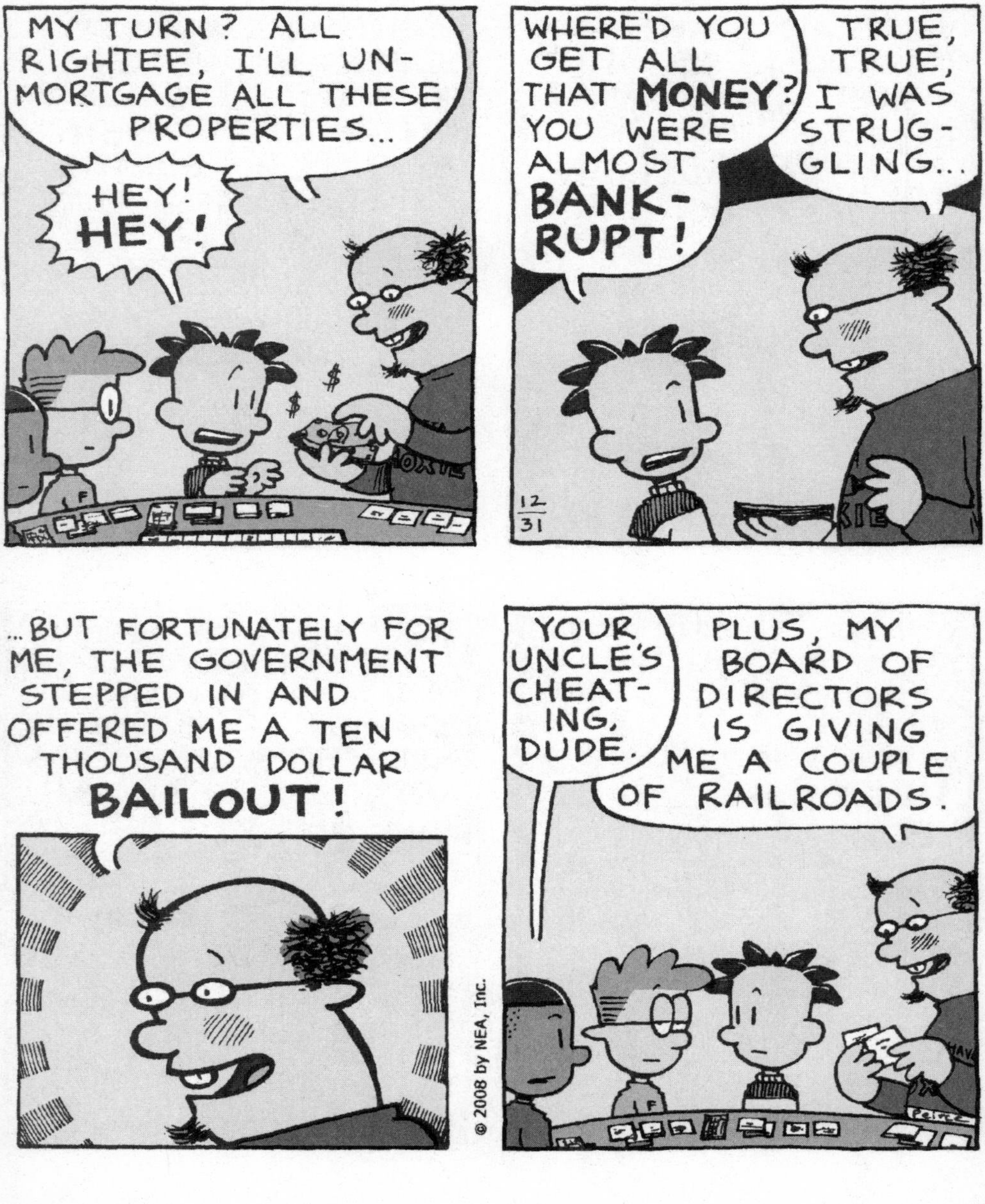
MY TURN? ALL RIGHTEE, I'LL UN-MORTGAGE ALL THESE PROPERTIES...
HEY! HEY!
WHERE'D YOU GET ALL THAT MONEY? YOU WERE ALMOST BANK-RUPT!
TRUE, TRUE, I WAS STRUG-GLING...
12/31
...BUT FORTUNATELY FOR ME, THE GOVERNMENT STEPPED IN AND OFFERED ME A TEN THOUSAND DOLLAR BAILOUT!
YOUR UNCLE'S CHEAT-ING, DUDE.
PLUS, MY BOARD OF DIRECTORS IS GIVING ME A COUPLE OF RAILROADS.

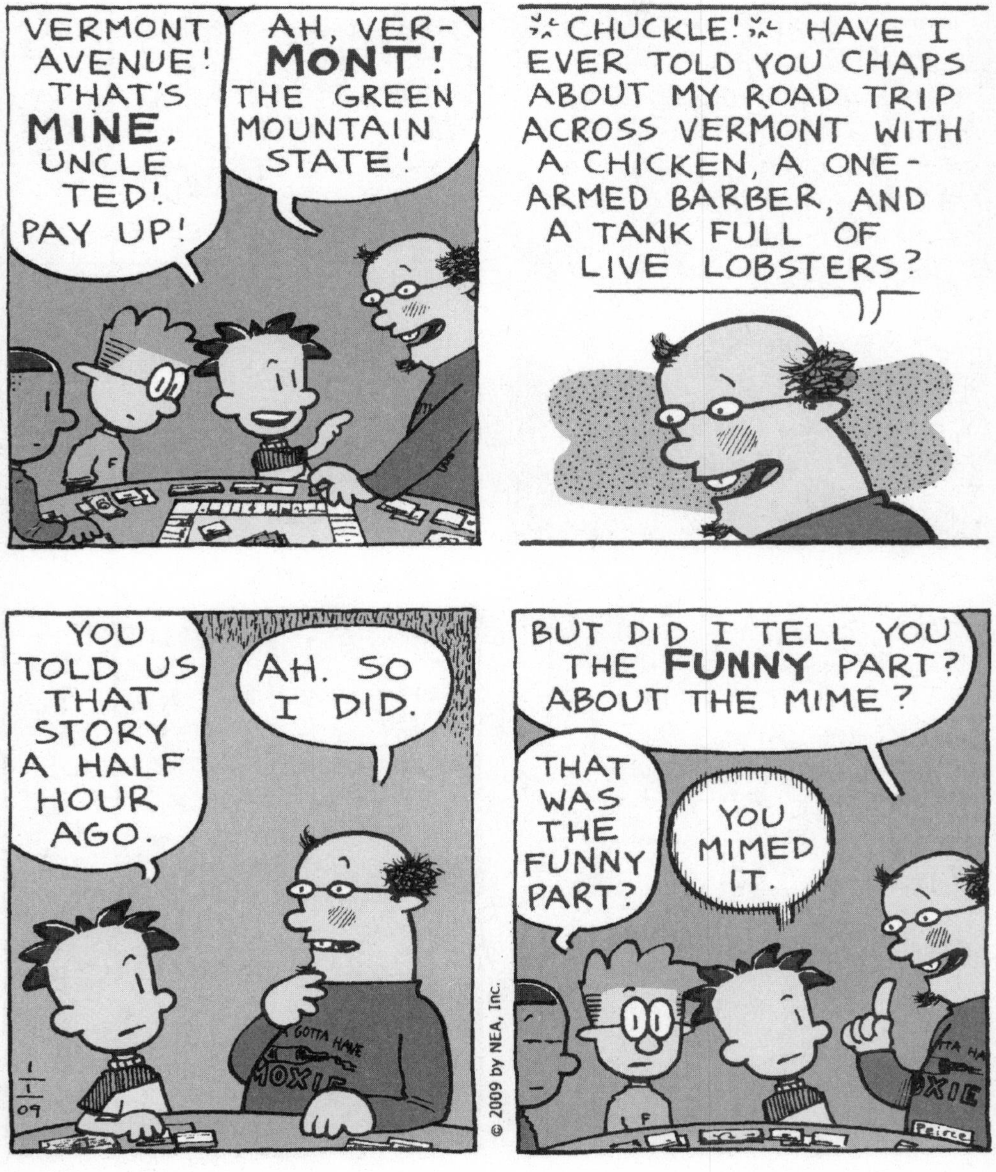
VERMONT AVENUE! THAT'S MINE, UNCLE TED! PAY UP!
AH, VER-MONT! THE GREEN MOUNTAIN STATE!
CHUCKLE! HAVE I EVER TOLD YOU CHAPS ABOUT MY ROAD TRIP ACROSS VERMONT WITH A CHICKEN, A ONE-ARMED BARBER, AND A TANK FULL OF LIVE LOBSTERS?
YOU TOLD US THAT STORY A HALF HOUR AGO.
AH. SO I DID.
GOTTA HAVE MOXIE
1 1 09
© 2009 by NEA, Inc.
BUT DID I TELL YOU THE FUNNY PART? ABOUT THE MIME?
THAT WAS THE FUNNY PART?
YOU MIMED IT.
Peirce

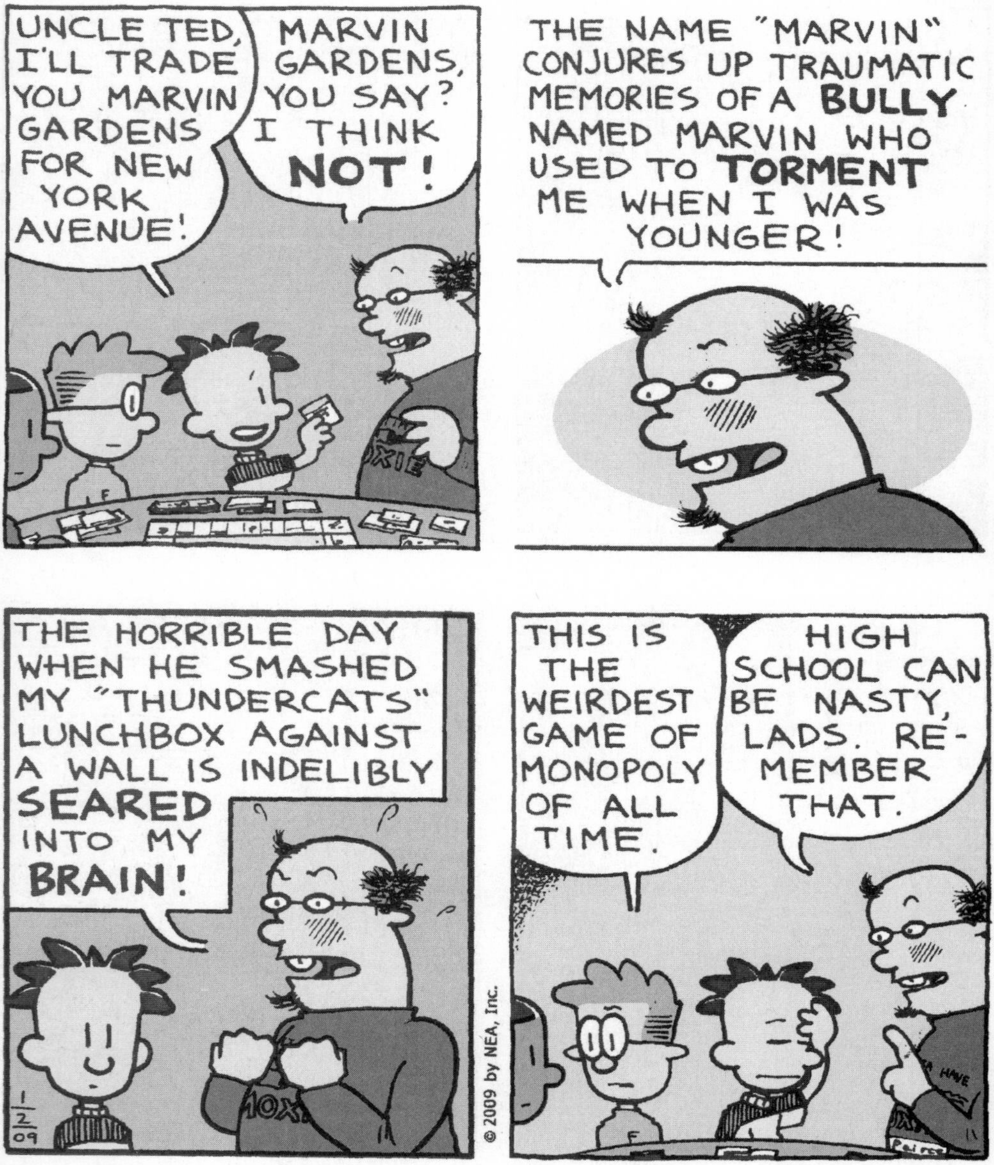
UNCLE TED, I'LL TRADE YOU MARVIN GARDENS FOR NEW YORK AVENUE!
MARVIN GARDENS, YOU SAY? I THINK NOT!
THE NAME "MARVIN" CONJURES UP TRAUMATIC MEMORIES OF A BULLY NAMED MARVIN WHO USED TO TORMENT ME WHEN I WAS YOUNGER!
THE HORRIBLE DAY WHEN HE SMASHED MY "THUNDERCATS" LUNCHBOX AGAINST A WALL IS INDELIBLY SEARED INTO MY BRAIN!
THIS IS THE WEIRDEST GAME OF MONOPOLY OF ALL TIME.
HIGH SCHOOL CAN BE NASTY, LADS. REMEMBER THAT.
1/2/09
© 2009 by NEA, Inc.
Peirce

...AND THAT CONCLUDES OUR DISCUSSION OF WHY THE ORANGE PROPERTIES ARE THE BEST ECONOMIC VALUE ON THE ENTIRE BOARD!
Z...
GREAT SCOTT! I COMPLETELY LOST TRACK OF THE TIME! IT'S ALMOST MIDNIGHT! THE NEW YEAR IS NIGH!
1/3/09
YA GOTTA H
IS EVERYONE READY FOR THE BIG MOMENT? DOES EVERYONE HAVE A NEW YEAR'S RESOLUTION READY TO ANNOUNCE?
I RESOLVE TO NEVER PLAY MONOPOLY WITH YOUR UNCLE AGAIN.
LET'S ALL SING "AULD LANG SYNE"! I'LL GET MY ACCORDION!
© 2009 by NEA, Inc.
Peirce

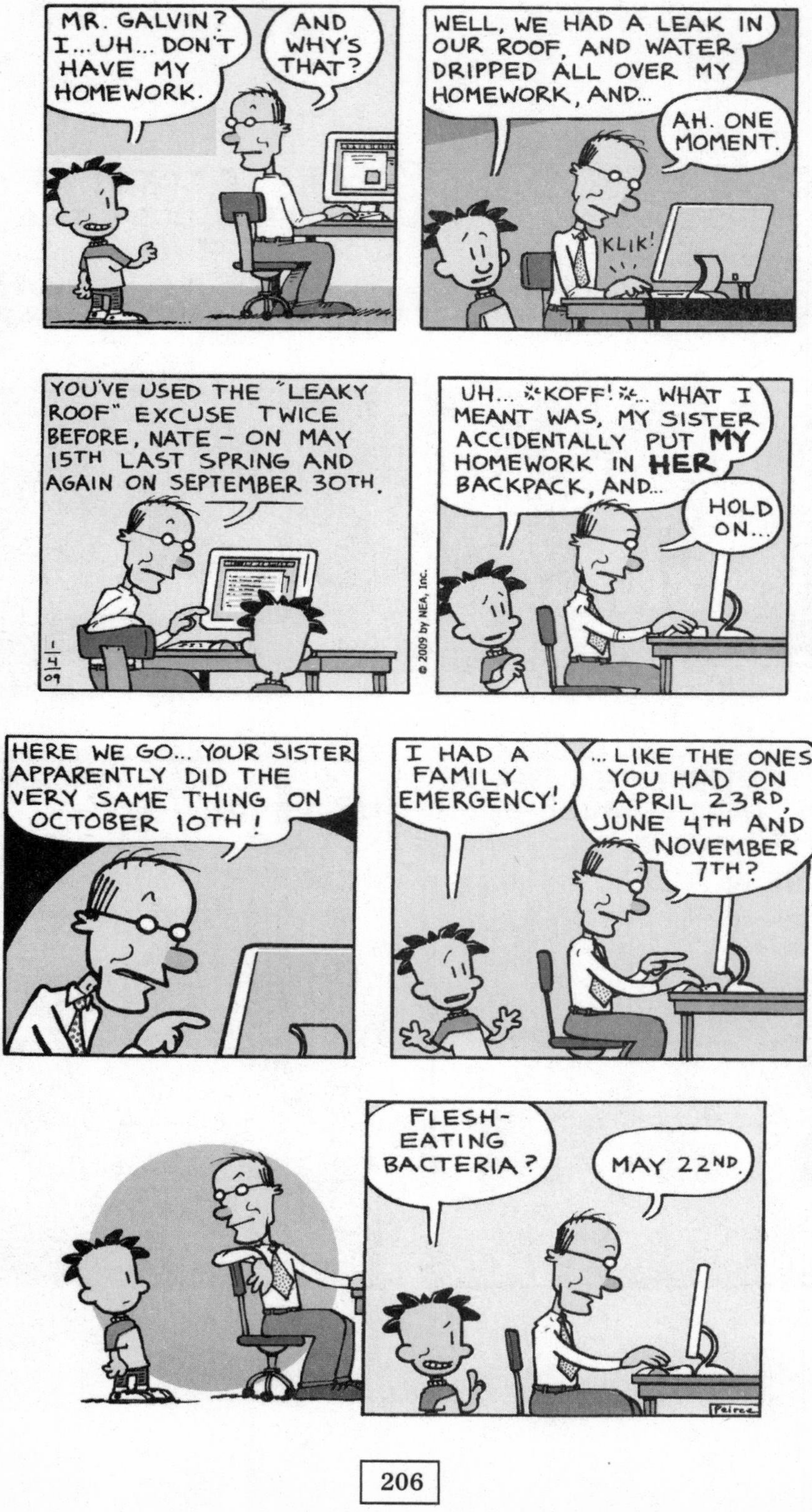
MR. GALVIN? I... UH... DON'T HAVE MY HOMEWORK.
AND WHY'S THAT?
WELL, WE HAD A LEAK IN OUR ROOF, AND WATER DRIPPED ALL OVER MY HOMEWORK, AND...
AH. ONE MOMENT.
KLIK!
YOU'VE USED THE "LEAKY ROOF" EXCUSE TWICE BEFORE, NATE – ON MAY 15TH LAST SPRING AND AGAIN ON SEPTEMBER 30TH.
1/4/09
© 2009 by NEA, Inc.
UH... *KOFF!*... WHAT I MEANT WAS, MY SISTER ACCIDENTALLY PUT MY HOMEWORK IN HER BACKPACK, AND...
HOLD ON...
HERE WE GO... YOUR SISTER APPARENTLY DID THE VERY SAME THING ON OCTOBER 10TH!
I HAD A FAMILY EMERGENCY!
... LIKE THE ONES YOU HAD ON APRIL 23RD, JUNE 4TH AND NOVEMBER 7TH?
FLESH-EATING BACTERIA?
MAY 22ND.
Peirce

MAKE IT OR BREAK IT

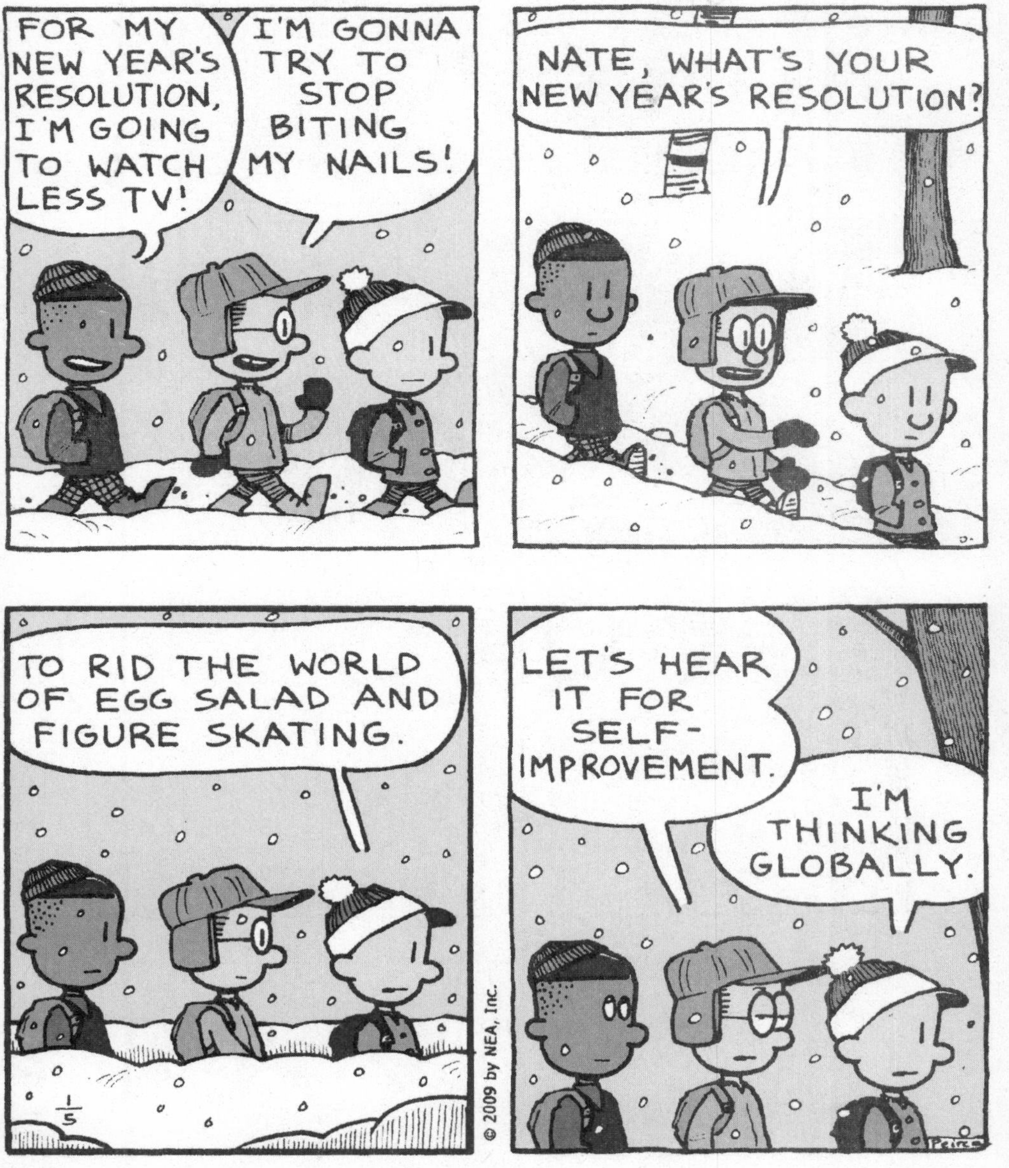

FOR MY NEW YEAR'S RESOLUTION, I'M GOING TO WATCH LESS TV!
I'M GONNA TRY TO STOP BITING MY NAILS!
NATE, WHAT'S YOUR NEW YEAR'S RESOLUTION?
TO RID THE WORLD OF EGG SALAD AND FIGURE SKATING.
1/5
© 2009 by NEA, Inc.
LET'S HEAR IT FOR SELF-IMPROVEMENT.
I'M THINKING GLOBALLY.
Peirce

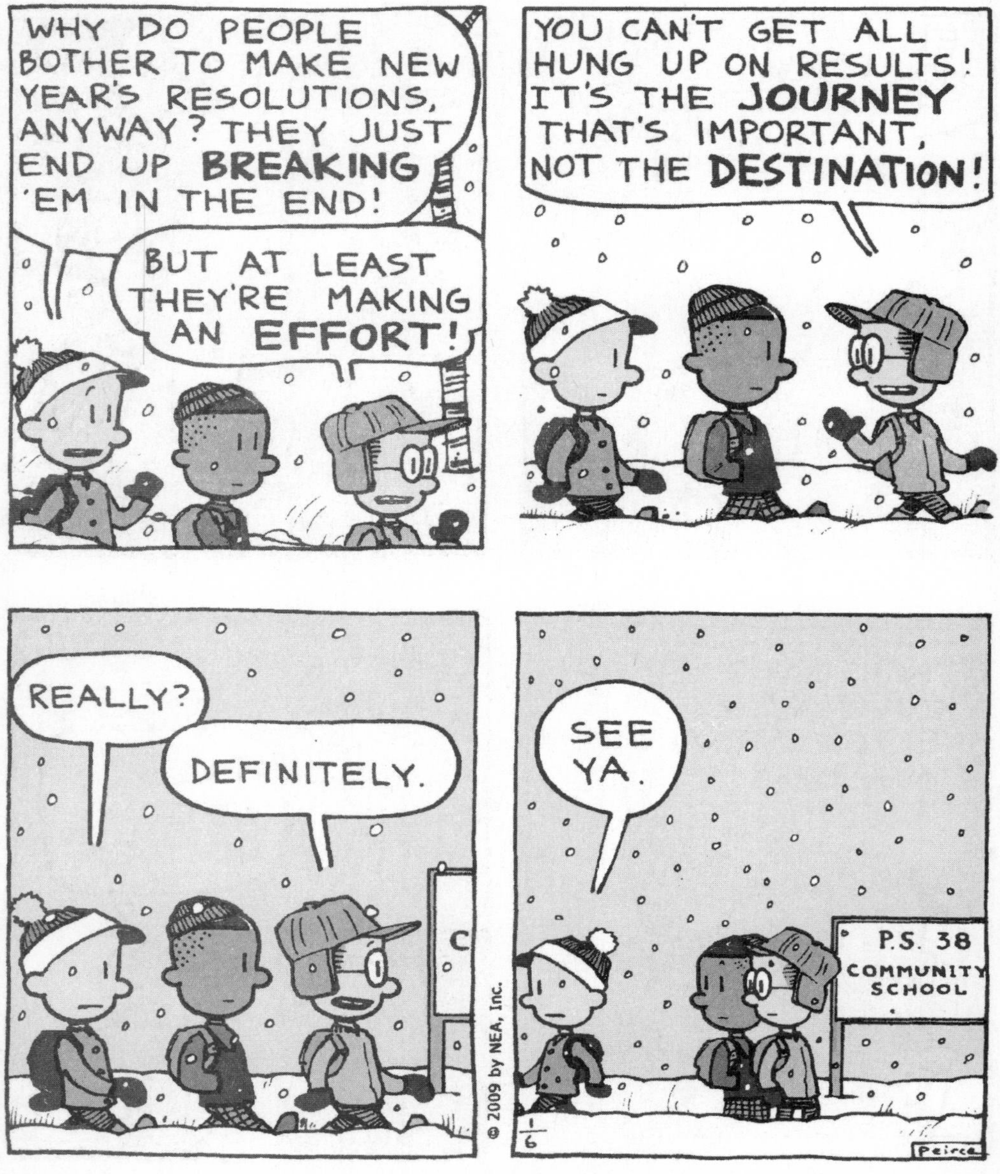
WHY DO PEOPLE BOTHER TO MAKE NEW YEAR'S RESOLUTIONS, ANYWAY? THEY JUST END UP BREAKING 'EM IN THE END!
BUT AT LEAST THEY'RE MAKING AN EFFORT!
YOU CAN'T GET ALL HUNG UP ON RESULTS! IT'S THE JOURNEY THAT'S IMPORTANT, NOT THE DESTINATION!
REALLY?
DEFINITELY.
SEE YA.
P.S. 38
COMMUNITY
SCHOOL
© 2009 by NEA, Inc.
1/6
Peirce

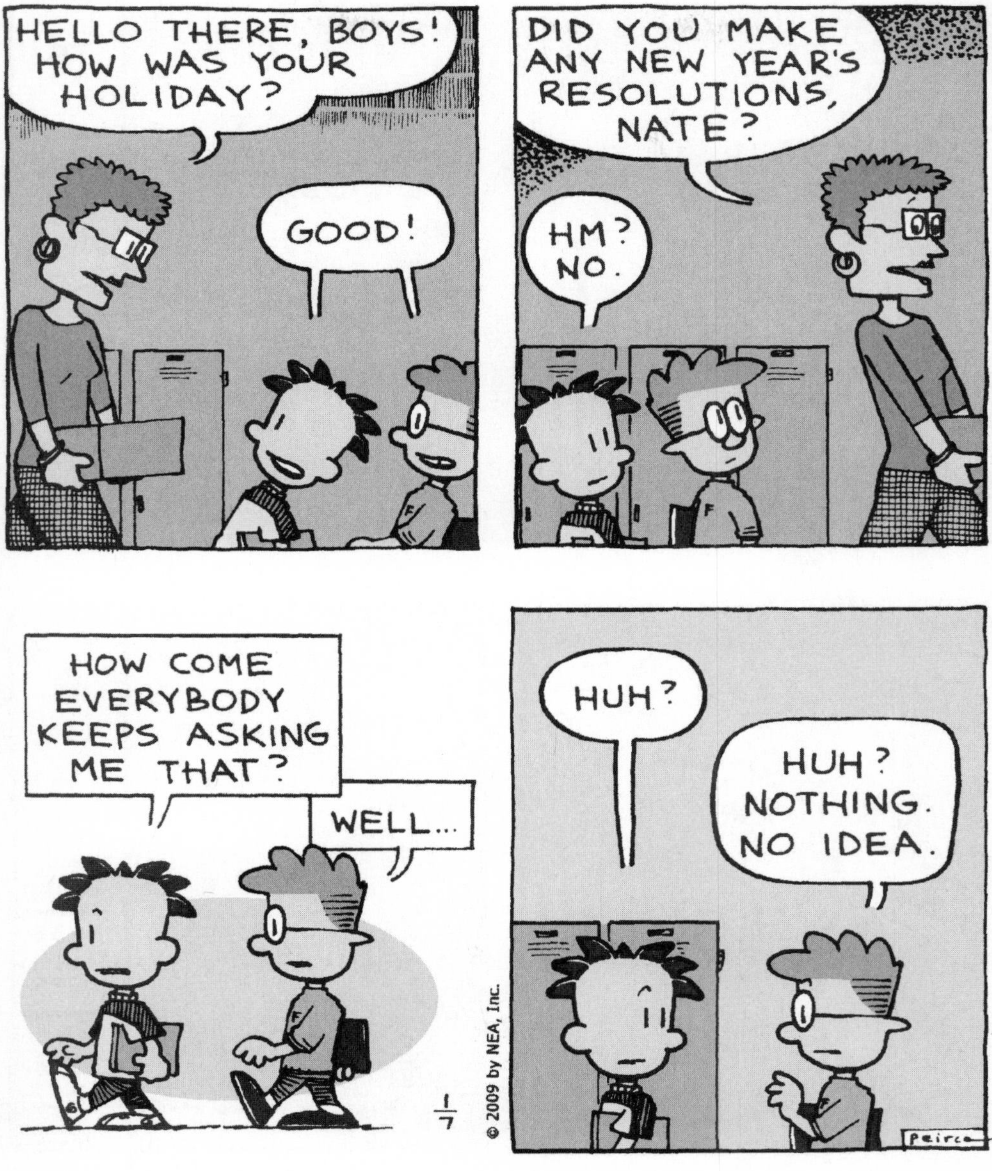
HELLO THERE, BOYS! HOW WAS YOUR HOLIDAY?
GOOD!
DID YOU MAKE ANY NEW YEAR'S RESOLUTIONS, NATE?
HM? NO.
HOW COME EVERYBODY KEEPS ASKING ME THAT?
WELL...
1/7
HUH?
HUH? NOTHING. NO IDEA.
Peirce

PET NAMES

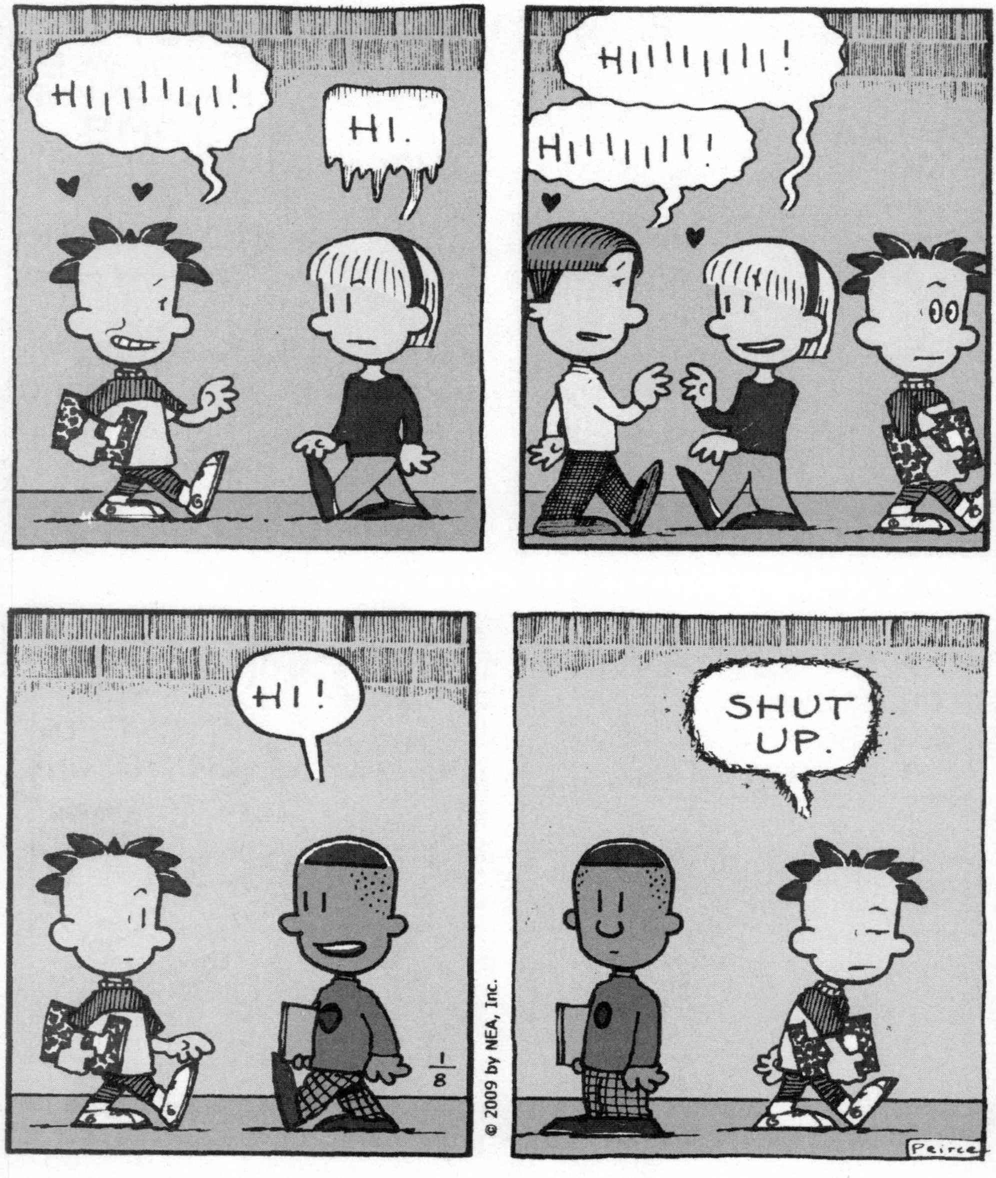
HIIIIIII!
HI.
HIIIIIIII!
HIIIIIII!
HI!
SHUT UP.
1/8
© 2009 by NEA, Inc.
Peirce

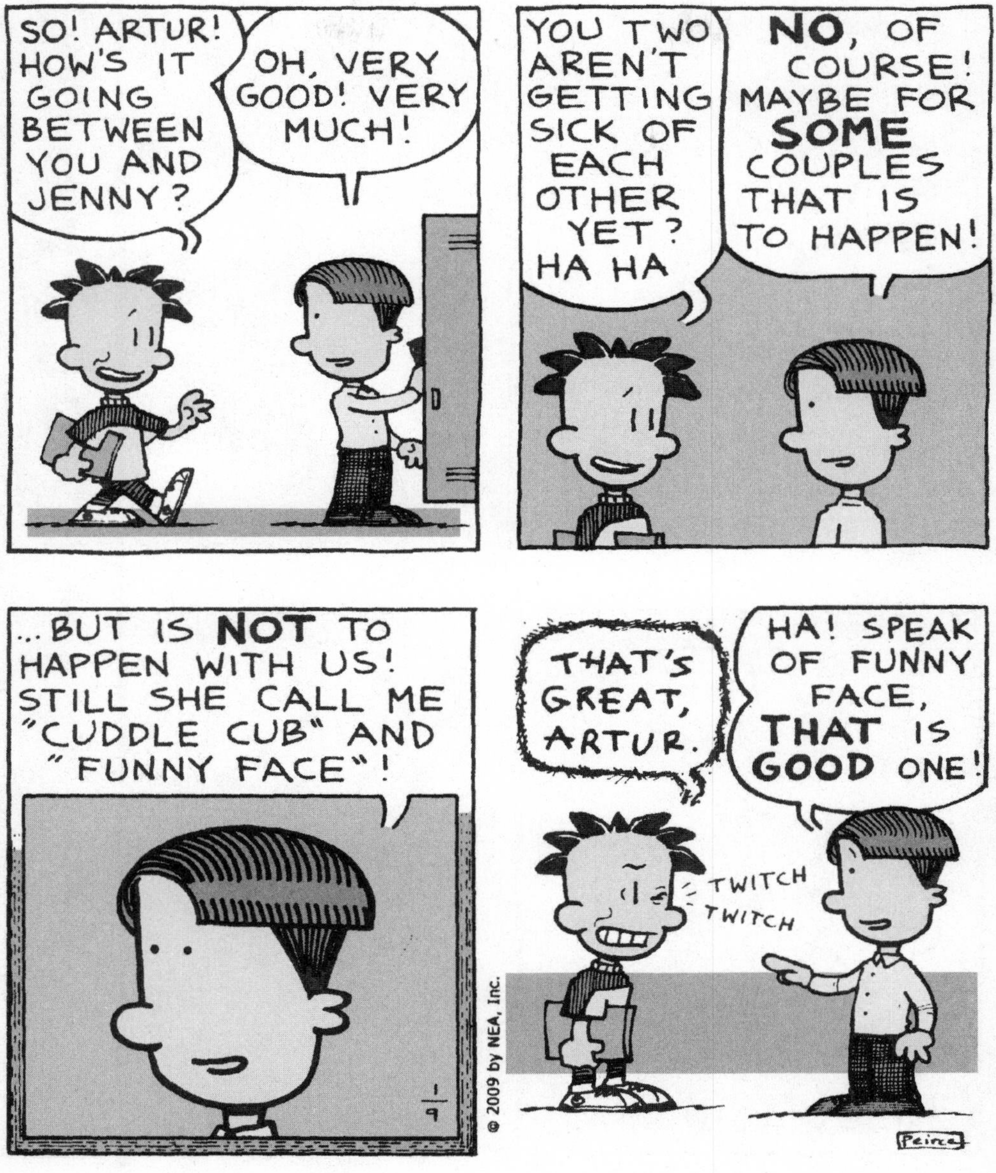
SO! ARTUR! HOW'S IT GOING BETWEEN YOU AND JENNY?
OH, VERY GOOD! VERY MUCH!
YOU TWO AREN'T GETTING SICK OF EACH OTHER YET? HA HA
NO, OF COURSE! MAYBE FOR SOME COUPLES THAT IS TO HAPPEN!
...BUT IS NOT TO HAPPEN WITH US! STILL SHE CALL ME "CUDDLE CUB" AND "FUNNY FACE"!
1/9
© 2009 by NEA, Inc.
THAT'S GREAT, ARTUR.
HA! SPEAK OF FUNNY FACE, THAT IS GOOD ONE!
TWITCH
TWITCH
Peirce

STUCK ON NATE

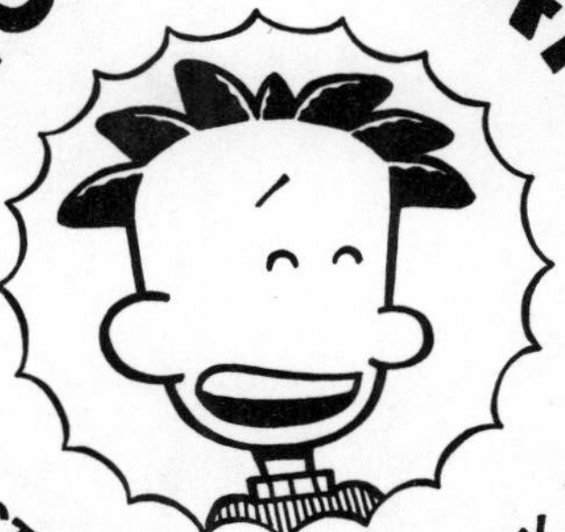

BONUS ACTIVITIES TO CRACK YOU UP!

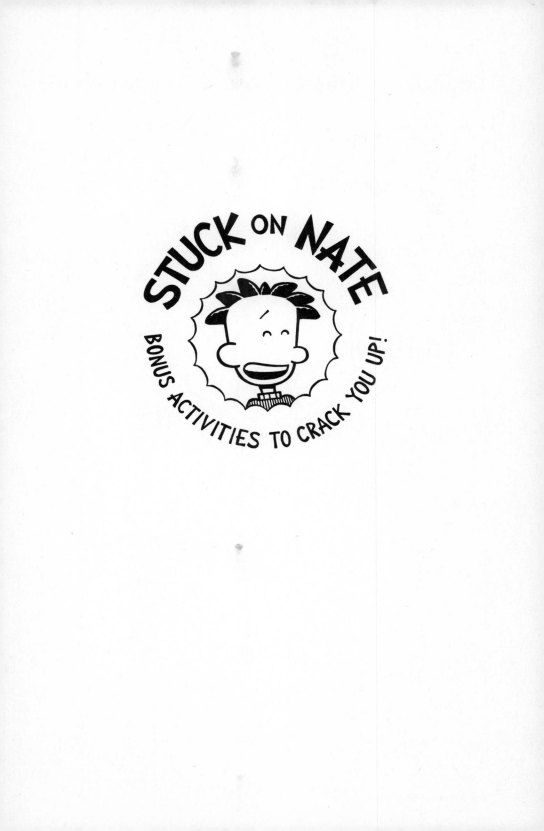

ALL MIXED UP

Can you match each of Nate's sketches to the correct strip?

1
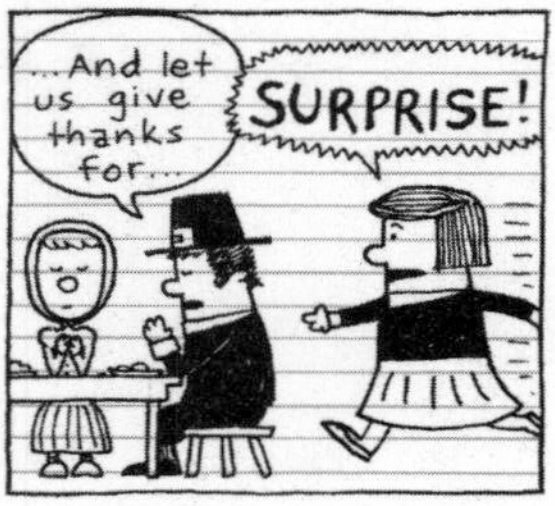
...And let us give thanks for...
SURPRISE!

2
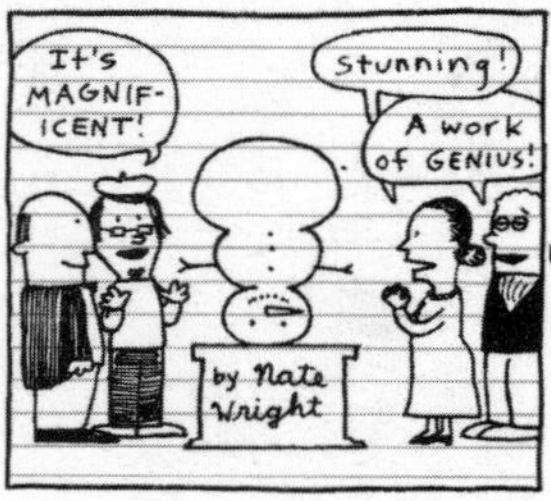
It's MAGNIF-ICENT!
Stunning!
A work of GENIUS!
by Nate Wright

3
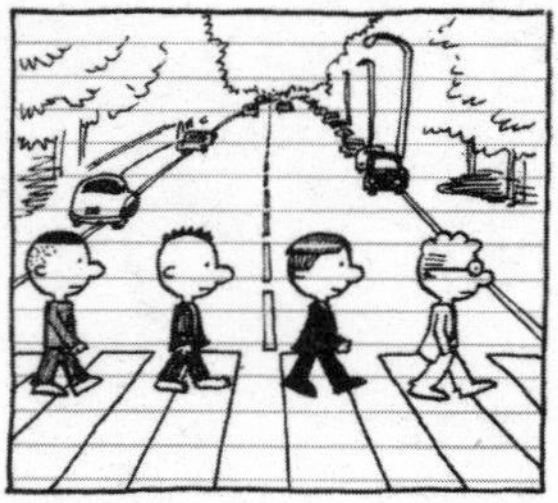

4
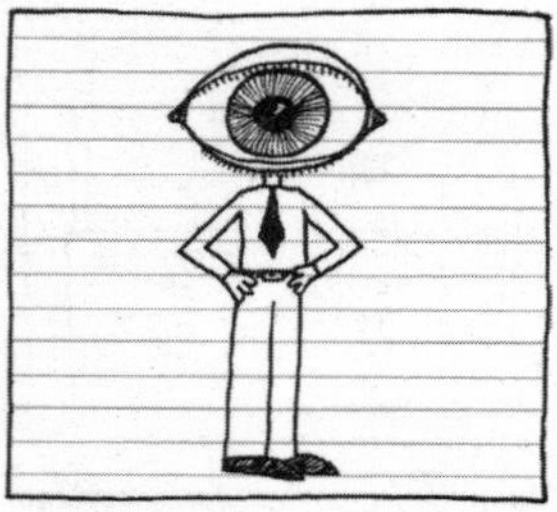

5
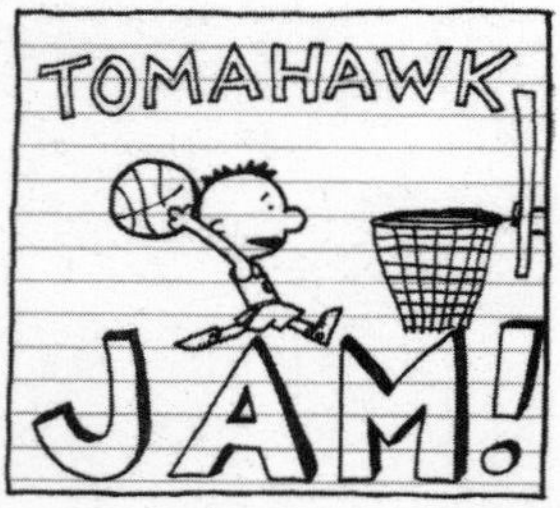
TOMAHAWK
JAM!

A
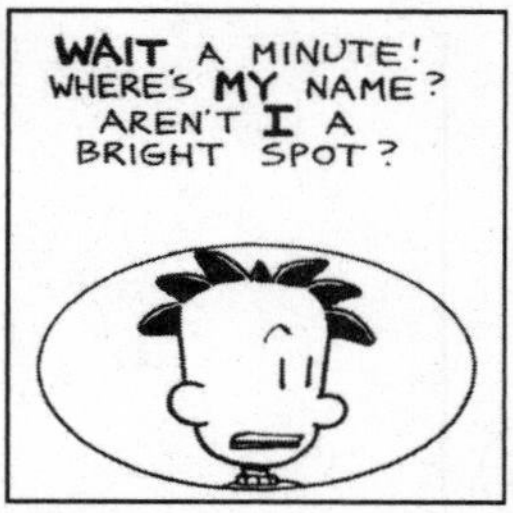
WAIT A MINUTE! WHERE'S MY NAME? AREN'T I A BRIGHT SPOT?

B
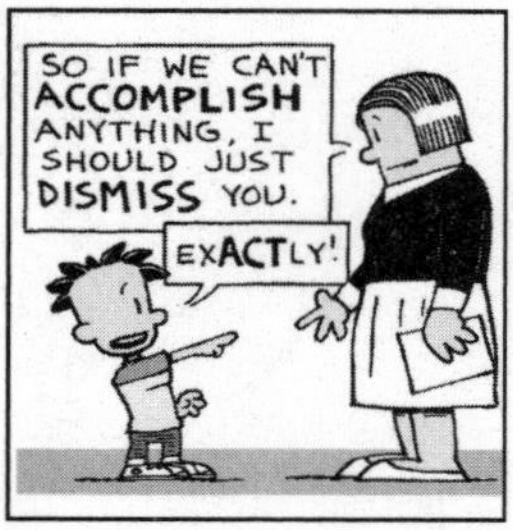
SO IF WE CAN'T ACCOMPLISH ANYTHING, I SHOULD JUST DISMISS YOU.
EXACTLY!

C
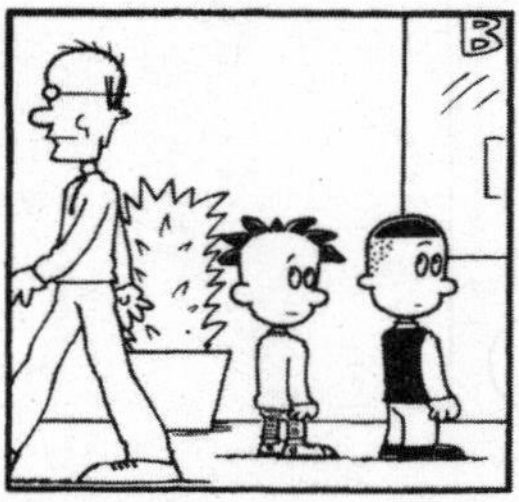

D
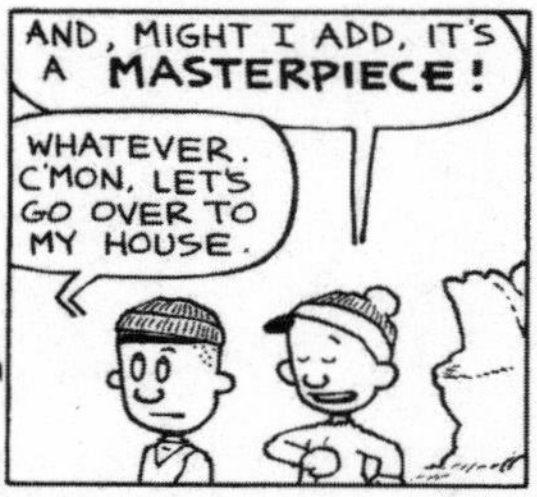
AND, MIGHT I ADD, IT'S A MASTERPIECE!
WHATEVER. C'MON, LET'S GO OVER TO MY HOUSE.

E
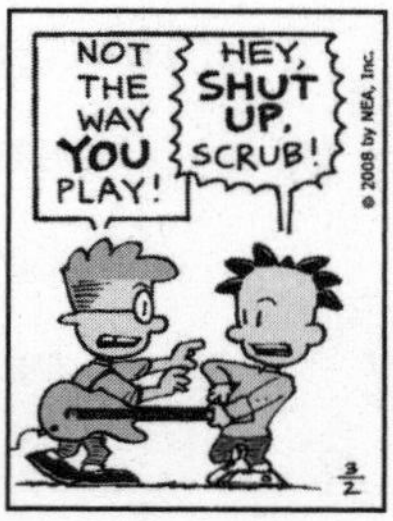
NOT THE WAY YOU PLAY!
HEY, SHUT UP, SCRUB!
© 2008 by NEA, Inc.

Answers: 1B, 2D, 3E, 4C, 5A

SUPERCOOL CAPTIONS

Can you come up with captions for Nate's sketches?

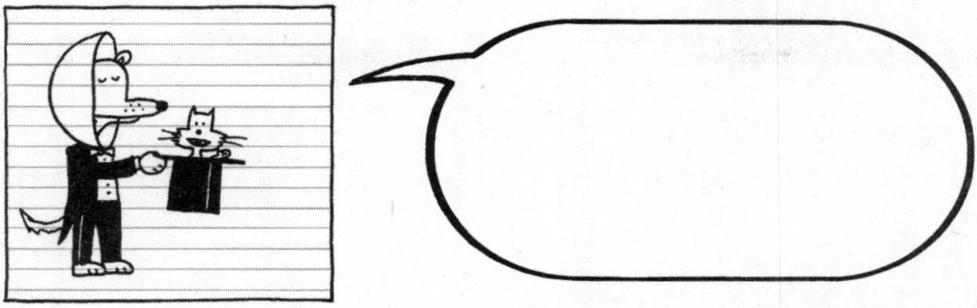

A

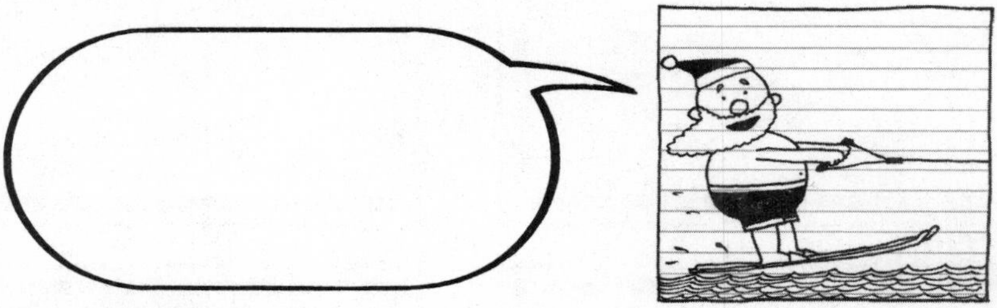

B

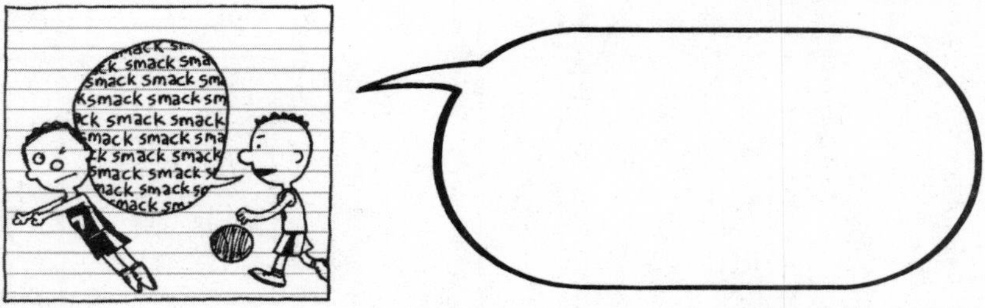

C

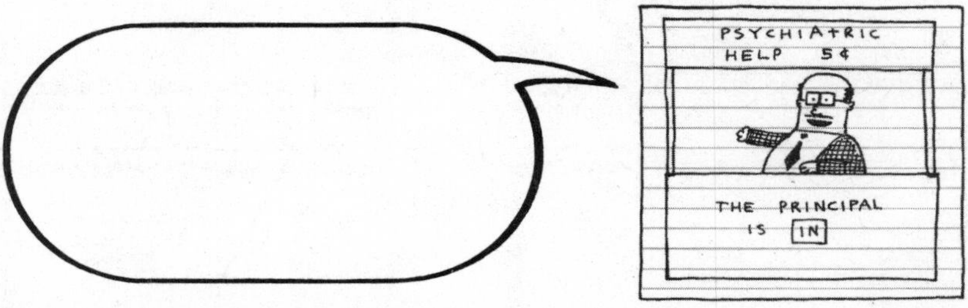
PSYCHIATRIC
HELP 5¢
THE PRINCIPAL
IS IN

D

SUPER CHALLENGE: Guess which sketch goes with the Sunday comic strips on pages 49, 59, 112, 151:

Comic A goes on page ____________.

Comic B goes on page ____________.

Comic C goes on page ____________.

Comic D goes on page ____________.

Answers: A: 151; B: 49; C: 59; D: 112

WHAT A PRETTY FACE!

Nate's dad has framed some of Nate's self-portraits. Draw yourself doing the same things as Nate!

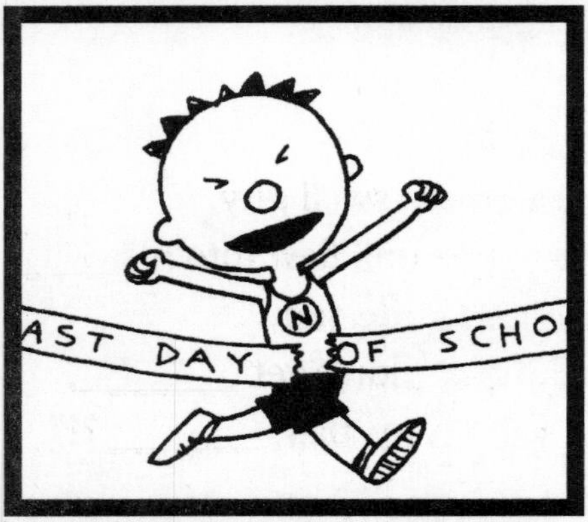
AST DAY OF SCHO

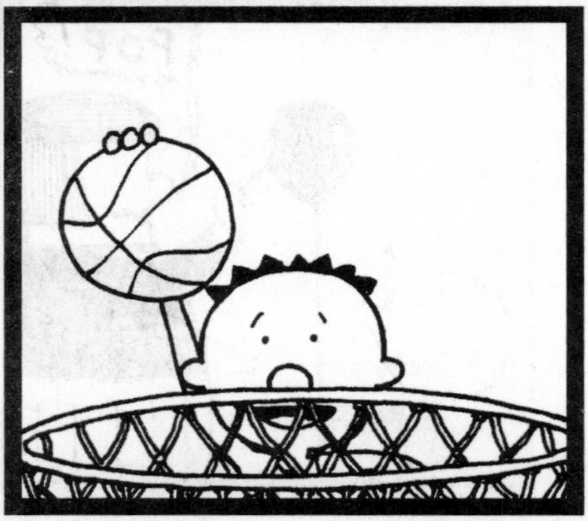

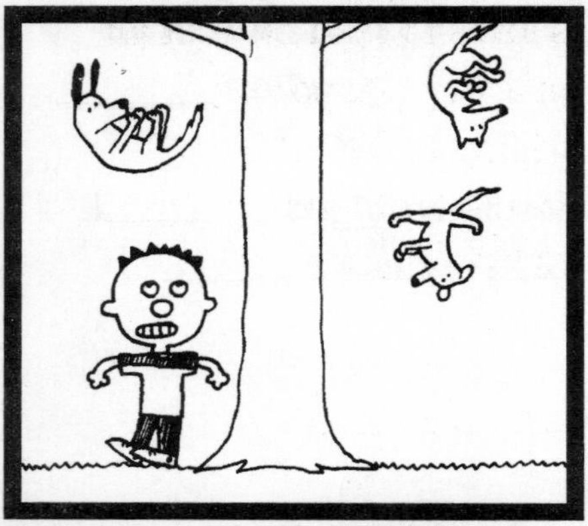

RHYTHM & RHYME

A picture is worth a thousand words. Fill in these limerick poems and create your own, all inspired by Nate's Sunday strip art!

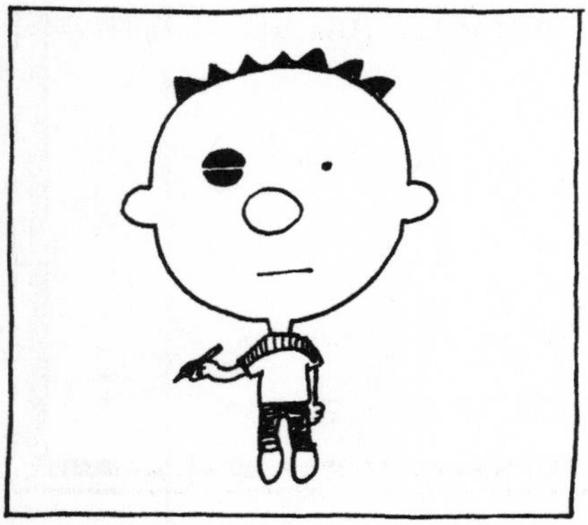

Nate is a pretty swell guy
But one day a ball flew into his ______.
It made him quite sad,
Though he couldn't get ________,
He did yell "Why, ball, ________?!"

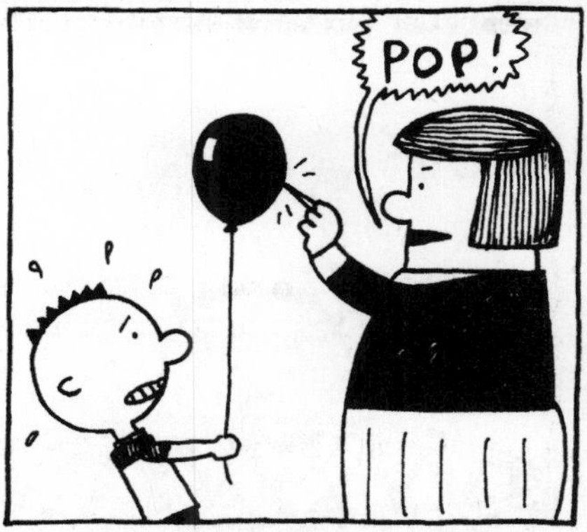
POP!

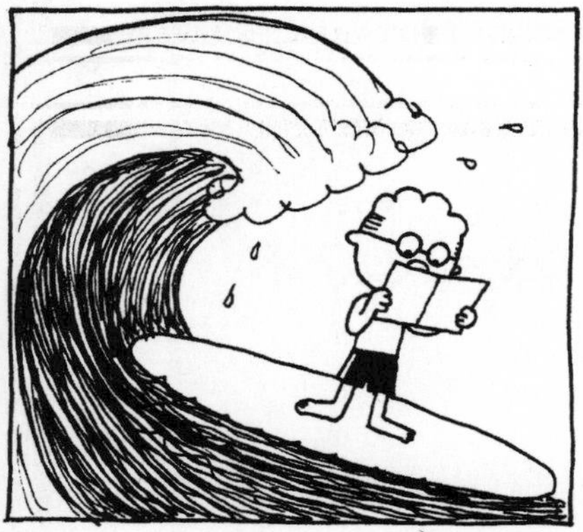

Francis loves to read most of all
Even on a wave standing ________.
I'd be willing to bet
(If the book didn't get ________)
He wouldn't notice a ________!

AWESOME ANNOUNCEMENTS

Have you suffered through those BOOORING announcements at school? What would you say if you had the microphone? Change it up and shout out something FUN!

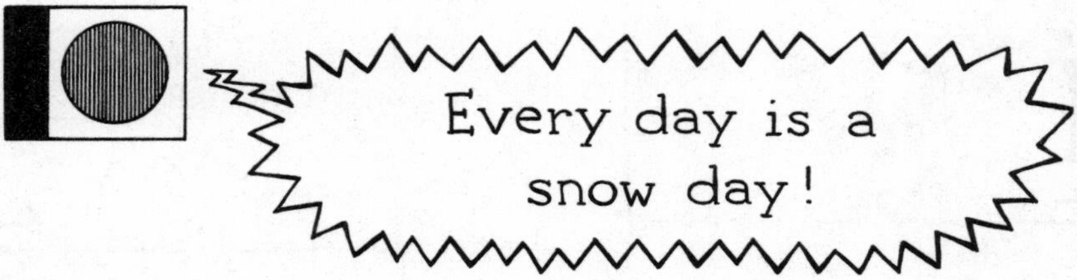
Every day is a snow day!

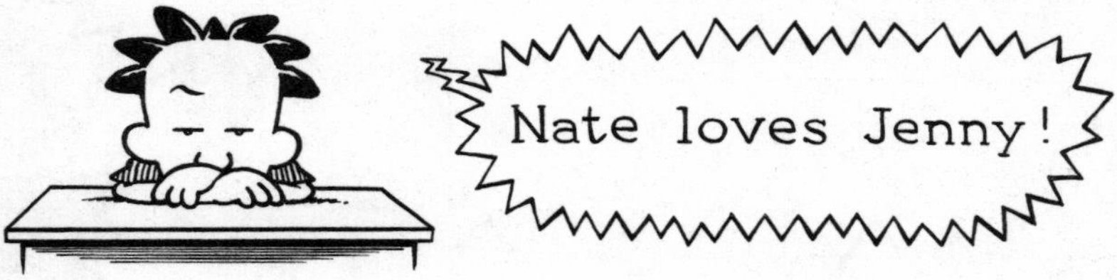
Nate loves Jenny!

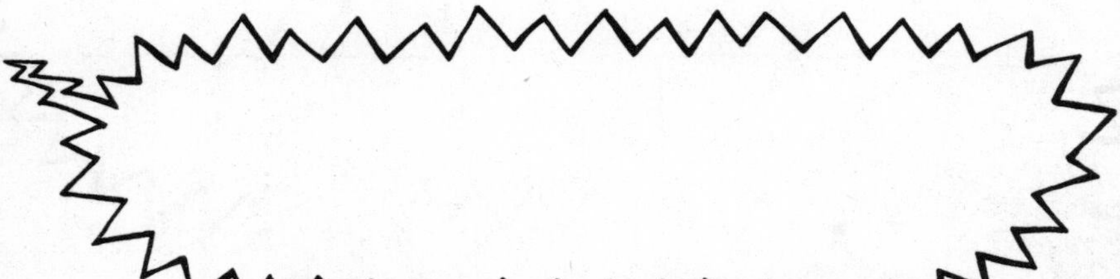

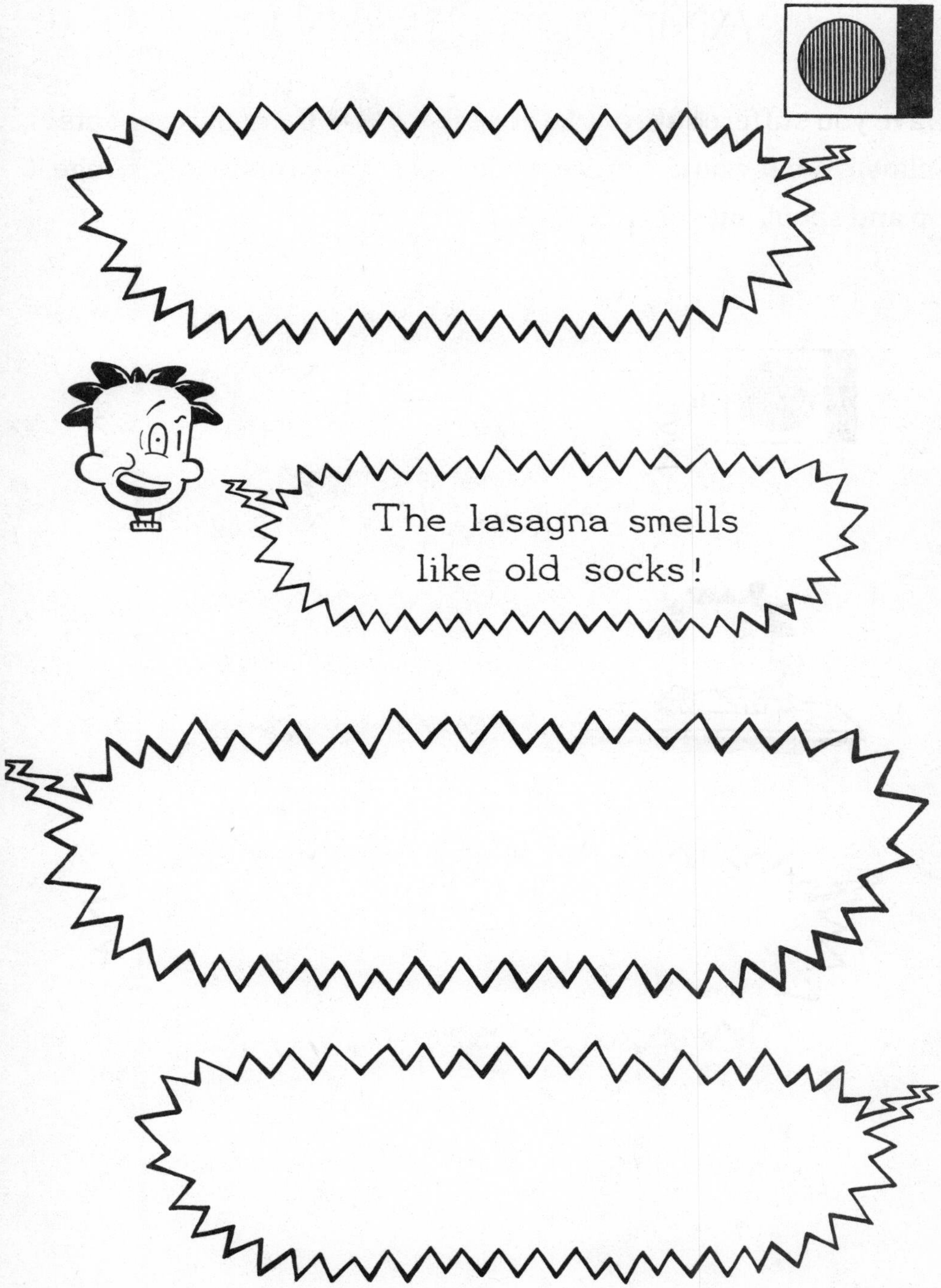
The lasagna smells like old socks!

READ ALL THE BIG NATE BOOKS TODAY!

NOVELS